W9-BVA-961

By John Jakes

CHARLESTON
ON SECRET SERVICE
CALIFORNIA GOLD
THE BOLD FRONTIER

The Crown Family Saga

AMERICAN DREAMS
HOMELAND

The North and South Trilogy

NORTH AND SOUTH
LOVE AND WAR
HEAVEN AND HELL

The Kent Family Chronicles

THE BASTARD
THE REBELS
THE SEEKERS
THE FURIES
THE TITANS
THE WARRIORS
THE LAWLESS
THE AMERICANS

Praise for John Jakes

"The godfather of historical novelists." —*Los Angeles Times*

"Jakes's bent for historical accuracy is unmatched in commercial fiction." —*San Francisco Chronicle*

Charleston

"Sure to lure readers . . . [a] masterly tale . . . [an] extraordinary family . . . during the most violent era of Charleston's history."
—*The Washington Post*

"A great read . . . fascinating historical anecdotes."
—*The Charleston Post and Courier*

"An entertaining saga with plenty of action."
—*The Orlando Sentinel*

On Secret Service

"Draws you back into the Civil War and the wrenching days preceding Abraham Lincoln's assassination. The factual details are simply astonishing: You walk the muddy streets, smell the acrid smoke of battlefields, and experience firsthand the inner workings of a vast conspiracy." —Patricia Cornwell

"[Jakes] gets the big story right, while writing in a clear style, keeping the narrative moving briskly from cliff-hanger to cliff-hanger, serving up portions of steamy sex in between, and offering us plenty of heroes and heroines to admire and several villains to hate. Even a deep-dyed Civil War buff . . . will find himself turning the pages to see what happens next."
—*Civil War Book Review*

continued . . .

The Crown Family Saga

Homeland

"First-rate . . . chock-full of fascinating period detail . . . brings to life the sounds, smells, and tastes of turn-of-the-century America in a manner comparable to Michener's *Hawaii* and Doctorow's *Ragtime*. An absolute must." *—Publishers Weekly*

"This intelligently written novel, full of colorful characters, moves swiftly along, vividly resurrecting the America of the 1890s. Quite simply, *Homeland* is John Jakes's best work."

—The Philadelphia Inquirer

"A powerful tour de force, a rich, sweeping story of America as only Jakes can tell it . . . *Homeland*, interspersed with real characters such as Teddy Roosevelt, Black Jack Pershing, and Jane Addams, is a marvelous blend of fact and fiction, the stuff of great historical novels. Another winner from an old pro."

—Nelson DeMille

American Dreams

"Jakes has a grand old time spinning his yarns. . . . He mixes his fictional offspring with the likes of Charlie Chaplin and Mary Pickford, making us feel as if we too have brushed our shoulders with celebrity." *—Toledo Blade*

"Realistic detail and period color galore keep this swift-moving story grounded . . . as the automobile and WWI arrive to shake the republic out of its golden idyll." *—Kirkus Reviews*

"A worthy successor to *Homeland*."

—The Columbia State (SC)

The North and South Trilo

North and South

"In the history of U.S. book publishing, there's success story quite like that of John Jakes."

—The New

"A panoramic, populous . . . lusty trek through th American history . . . thick as a brick with period de from extensive research." *—San Francisco*

Love and War

"A feisty assortment of fictional heroes and heroines."

—

"Massive, lusty, highly readable. . . . In delicious detail are wicked and tawdry doings of a memorable cast of characters a graphic, fast-paced amalgam of good, evil, love, lust, w violence, and Americana."

—The Washington Post Book Wor

Heaven and Hell

"Remarkably vivid." *—Los Angeles T*

"He shows you George Armstrong Custer, Andrew Jo Buffalo Bill Cody, and a vast array of historical figures contending ambitions control the events . . . but he als you what people wore, what they read, and what th and ate. . . . What you get is the feeling that this is li art." *—Chicago*

★ THE ★
WARRIORS

The Kent Family Chronicles

VOLUME VI

JOHN JAKES

With a New Introduction by the Author

A SIGNET BOOK

SIGNET
Published by New American Library, a division of
Penguin Group (USA) Inc., 375 Hudson Street,
New York, New York 10014, USA
Penguin Group (Canada), 90 Eglinton Avenue East, Suite 700, Toronto,
Ontario M4P 2Y3, Canada (a division of Pearson Penguin Canada Inc.)
Penguin Books Ltd., 80 Strand, London WC2R 0RL, England
Penguin Ireland, 25 St. Stephen's Green, Dublin 2,
Ireland (a division of Penguin Books Ltd.)
Penguin Group (Australia), 250 Camberwell Road, Camberwell, Victoria 3124,
Australia (a division of Pearson Australia Group Pty. Ltd.)
Penguin Books India Pvt. Ltd., 11 Community Centre, Panchsheel Park,
New Delhi - 110 017, India
Penguin Group (NZ), 67 Apollo Drive, Rosedale, North Shore 0632,
New Zealand (a division of Pearson New Zealand Ltd.)
Penguin Books (South Africa) (Pty.) Ltd., 24 Sturdee Avenue,
Rosebank, Johannesburg 2196, South Africa

Penguin Books Ltd., Registered Offices:
80 Strand, London WC2R 0RL, England

Published by Signet, an imprint of New American Library, a division of Penguin Group (USA) Inc. Published by arrangement with the author. Previously published in a Jove paperback edition.

First Signet Printing, January 2005
10 9 8 7 6 5 4

Copyright © John Jakes, 1977
Introduction copyright © John Jakes, 2005
All rights reserved

REGISTERED TRADEMARK—MARCA REGISTRADA

Printed in the United States of America

Without limiting the rights under copyright reserved above, no part of this publication may be reproduced, stored in or introduced into a retrieval system, or transmitted, in any form, or by any means (electronic, mechanical, photocopying, recording, or otherwise), without the prior written permission of both the copyright owner and the above publisher of this book.

PUBLISHER'S NOTE
This is a work of fiction. Names, characters, places, and incidents either are the product of the author's imagination or are used fictitiously, and any resemblance to actual persons, living or dead, business establishments, events, or locales is entirely coincidental.

The publisher does not have any control over and does not assume any responsibility for author or third-party Web sites or their content.

If you purchased this book without a cover you should be aware that this book is stolen property. It was reported as "unsold and destroyed" to the publisher and neither the author nor the publisher has received any payment for this "stripped book."

The scanning, uploading, and distribution of this book via the Internet or via any other means without the permission of the publisher is illegal and punishable by law. Please purchase only authorized electronic editions, and do not participate in or encourage electronic piracy of copyrighted materials. Your support of the author's rights is appreciated.

For my mother

CONTENTS

Introduction: Enjoying the Sweep of History

It can be tedious to hear an author cite his reasons for liking this or that book he produced, yet in the case of *The Warriors,* I find it hard to keep from it. The sixth novel of *The Kent Family Chronicles* covers a short span of years, yet encompasses some of the most significant, exciting, not to say epic events of our history.

In my introduction to the preceding volume, *The Titans,* I noted that the Civil War is a subject continually eliciting worldwide interest. Professor James M. McPherson in his prizewinning one-volume history of the war, *Battle Cry of Freedom,* says that the Civil War has produced more books by a factor of ten or more than any other era in America's past. Further, the war brought about the greatest redirection of national life, in the shortest time, that we've ever experienced.

Lagging not far behind the Civil War in terms of universal appeal, however, is the opening of the American West. I expect that's why I favor *The Warriors:* it rolls up a lot of our most dramatic moments in a single volume.

Consider that the book opens with the harrowing battle of Chancellorsville in Virginia as the war grinds to its agonizing close. It cuts away for a glimpse of the ravaging of Southern plantations by Union troops, especially their less-than-attractive foragers, commonly called bummers.

Then we travel West, to watch the building of the transcontinental railroad. The conclusion draws us into the era of the robber barons, a subject more fully explored in the next volume, appropriately titled *The Lawless.* Any wonder that I enjoyed writing the book despite the frantic pressures to get it out faster, ever faster?

When I lecture or speak to writers' groups, during the Q&A, someone inevitably asks, "Do you do all of your own research?" The answer is yes.

And, yes, it's a formidable workload, nearly doubling the time required to produce a novel, yet I've never been willing to surrender the responsibility. Preparing to write a new book is like enrolling in a new graduate program—digging into a new era, mining it for everything I didn't know before (which is always "plenty"). In the case of *The Warriors*, I was able to delve into three broad subjects at once. I wouldn't give up the pleasure.

Now that my friends at New American Library have returned *The Warriors* to readers in this handsome new edition, I hope that you, too, will find not only entertainment in the story, but the sweep of our history during a few short years that were long on events of major importance.

—John Jakes
Hilton Head Island
South Carolina

And I saw askant the armies,
I saw as in noiseless dreams hundreds of battle-flags,
Borne through the smoke of the battles and pierc'd with missiles I saw them . . .

I saw battle-corpses, myriads of them,
And the white skeletons of young men, I saw them,
I saw the debris and debris of all the slain soldiers of the war,
But I saw they were not as was thought,
They themselves were fully at rest, they suffer'd not,
The living remain'd and suffer'd, the mother suffer'd,
And the wife and the child and the musing comrade suffer'd,
And the armies that remain'd suffer'd.

1865:
Walt Whitman,
in the
Sequel to "Drum-Taps,"
written in the summer
and published in the autumn
following Lincoln's death.

THE KENT FAMILY

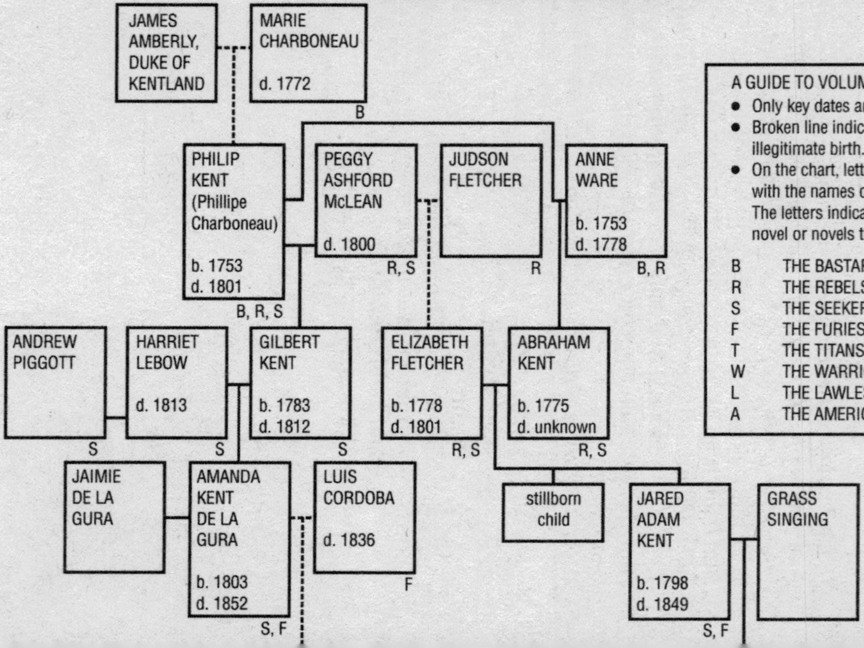

A GUIDE TO VOLUMES I–VIII

- Only key dates are shown.
- Broken line indicates an illegitimate birth.
- On the chart, letters appear with the names of characters. The letters indicate in which novel or novels the character appears:

B	THE BASTARD	(1770–1775)
R	THE REBELS.	(1775–1781)
S	THE SEEKERS	(1794–1814)
F	THE FURIES	(1836–1852)
T	THE TITANS	(1860–1862)
W	THE WARRIORS	(1864–1868)
L	THE LAWLESS	(1869–1877)
A	THE AMERICANS	(1883–1890)

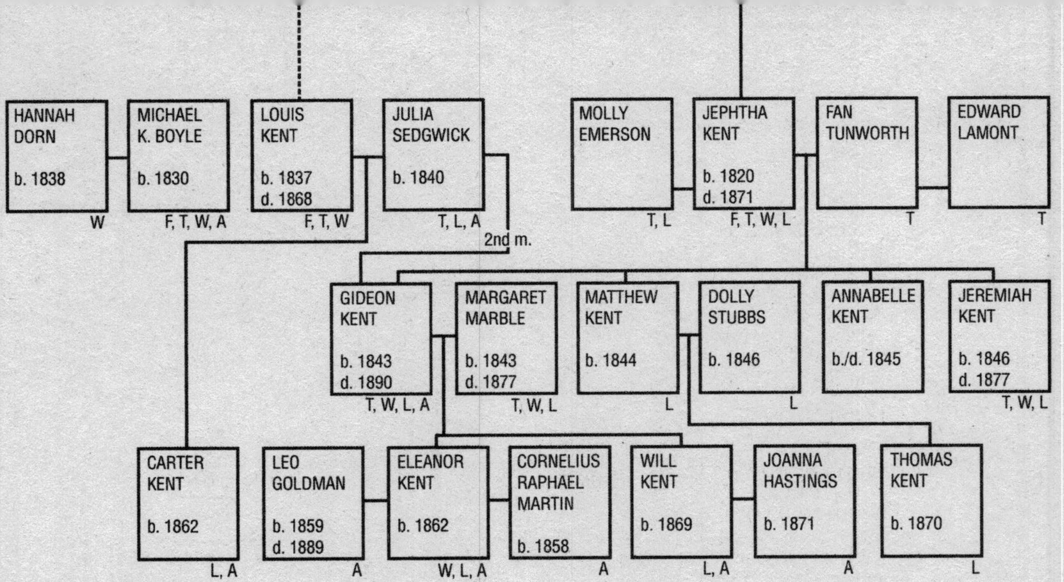

HANNAH DORN b. 1838 W
MICHAEL K. BOYLE b. 1830 F, T, W, A
LOUIS KENT b. 1837 d. 1868 F, T, W
JULIA SEDGWICK b. 1840 T, L, A
2nd m.
MOLLY EMERSON T, L
JEPHTHA KENT b. 1820 d. 1871 F, T, W, L
FAN TUNWORTH T
EDWARD LAMONT T
GIDEON KENT b. 1843 d. 1890 T, W, L, A
MARGARET MARBLE b. 1843 d. 1877 T, W, L
MATTHEW KENT b. 1844 L
DOLLY STUBBS b. 1846 L
ANNABELLE KENT b./d. 1845
JEREMIAH KENT b. 1846 d. 1877 T, W, L
CARTER KENT b. 1862 L, A
LEO GOLDMAN b. 1859 d. 1889 A
ELEANOR KENT b. 1862 W, L, A
CORNELIUS RAPHAEL MARTIN b. 1858 A
WILL KENT b. 1869 L, A
JOANNA HASTINGS b. 1871 A
THOMAS KENT b. 1870 L

Prologue at Chancellorsville

The Fallen Sword

i

Major Gideon Kent was worn-out. Worn-out and plagued by a familiar edginess he only permitted himself to call fear in the silence of his mind. The feeling always came on him during a battle.

About six o'clock that afternoon, he'd witnessed more than the beginning of a battle. He'd seen the start of a slaughter. Thousands upon thousands of his Confederate comrades had gone charging out of the second-growth timber called the Wilderness, bugles blaring, bayonets shining.

Noisy blizzards of wild turkeys fled before the howling men and their streaming battle flags. The surprise attack had caught the Dutchmen—the German regiments in Von Gilsa's brigade—taking their evening meal in Dowdall's Clearing, most of their arms stacked.

The Germans were manning the end of General Howard's exposed flank. The Southerners tore into them. Stabbing. Screaming. Blowing heads and limbs away at point-blank range. On horseback, the commander of the II Corps, Army of Northern Virginia, had closely followed his charging lines, his eyes blazing with an almost religious light. Now and then the commander's hands rose to the thickening smoke in the gold sky as though thanking his God for the carnage.

The general's outrageously risky attack had succeeded. That much had been evident while Gideon observed the first few minutes of the engagement. Then he was summoned away. His own commander, the restless Beauty Stuart, saw that the terrain and the element of surprise made cavalry not only unnecessary but useless. So he requested permission to take a regiment and a battery up to Ely's Ford on the Rapidan River, where some worthwhile damage might be done to a Union wagon park. Gideon, assigned to General Stuart's staff, had gone along.

Around eight o'clock Stuart had sent him back to deliver a report to the general commanding II Corps. Some Union horses had been discovered—part of Stoneman's elusive force. Stuart's message said he was preparing to attack, though he stood ready to swing about if the commander of II Corps needed him.

That the commander needed no one had become clear to Gideon as he'd maneuvered his way south again through almost impenetrable woodland to reach the Fredericksburg Turnpike, where he was now riding, armed with saber and revolver.

The surprise attack had rolled the enemy back for a good two or three miles. Gideon could dimly see the evidence: hundreds and hundreds of blue-uniformed dead sprawled in the lowering dark. To the east, the battle was still raging. Artillery had joined the combat, and shot and shell had ignited stands of timber along the fringes of the Wilderness.

By now the sun had set—it was Saturday, the second day of May 1863—and Gideon was moving toward the center of the fighting. He had begun to wonder if he'd been given the right directions by some officers he'd met a ways back. Was II Corps' commander really somewhere ahead? Impossible to tell on this increasingly black road flanked by stunted trees and thick underbrush.

His little stallion, Sport, had trouble keeping his footing on the rock-studded highway. The wiry long-tailed Canadian horse—Canucks, the Yank cavalrymen called them—had fallen into Gideon's hands after Fredericksburg. It was a short-legged shaggy prize, coveted and cared for almost as attentively as Gideon looked after himself.

But the damp, hard winter at Camp No-Camp—the name was another of Jeb Stuart's whimsies—had taken its toll. A week ago, despite Gideon's best efforts to keep the captured horse on firm, dry footing whenever possible, he'd discovered the telltale signs of greased heel. Sport's front hoofs had suffered too much mud. They were rotting.

Still, the animal was game, moving steadily if not rapidly through the tunnel of trees. Somewhere not far ahead lay that white-columned farmer's manse at the crossroads dignified with the name Chancellorsville.

The road had grown dark as the devil. But above, there was an eerie light compounded of the glow of the rising full moon, the pulsing glare of the Federal cannon to the east, and the sullen red of burning woodlands around the horizon.

Gideon speculated about whether the fighting might go on throughout the night. Perhaps not. For some reason unknown to him—but evidently clear to the generals—the Yanks commanded by Fighting Joe Hooker had failed to commit their admittedly superior numbers to the battle. Old Marse Robert's mad double gamble seemed to be on the point of succeeding.

Gideon started. On his left—to the north, where smoke drifted through the gargoyle tangle of tree trunks—he thought he heard infantrymen moving.

He reined Sport to a walk. Whose troops were those?

He immediately decided he'd go only another quarter mile or so in his search for the leader of II Corps. The lines were obviously still shifting. And he couldn't be positive the information given earlier was correct—that the general and a small party of officers, couriers, and Signal Corps sergeants had ridden east on this same turnpike to scout ahead of the re-forming lines. If he didn't soon locate the man his father had known in Lexington before the war, he'd turn about and seek better guidance. Beauty Stuart didn't like officers on his staff to be tardy delivering reports on the cavalry's position.

He started and gasped as an artillery barrage exploded a half mile to his right. He heard the crash of falling branches. That patch of sky was now something out of an artist's conception of hell. It flickered and shifted through every shade of red. It seemed the whole Virginia countryside below the Rappahannock was afire.

Again he heard screams—distant but unnerving. In the dark to his right, beyond the road's south shoulder, he sensed more men moving.

Were they Yanks caught behind the forward sweep of the Confederate ranks? Or were they friendly reinforcements being brought up, responding to the general's favorite command—*"Press on! Press on!"* The general drove his men so hard and fast they were sometimes called the foot cavalry.

Gideon didn't like not knowing who was out there. His hand dropped to the butt of the Le Mat revolver tucked in his sash as he nudged Sport forward with his knees. He began to be quite concerned that the general might have advanced well beyond the point of safety.

All day an unconfirmed story had circulated among Stuart's staff members. The story ran that the commander of II Corps had risen after a bad sleep and sipped some cold coffee before starting his men on the audacious flank march that culminated in the charge at Dowdall's Clearing. While the general drank the coffee in the cold dawn air, his scabbarded sword had been standing against a nearby tree. And then, with no one touching it—no one even near it—the sword had suddenly clattered to the ground.

Gideon didn't count himself especially superstitious. Yet that story bothered him more than he liked.

And there *was* reason for worry. He'd ridden quite a way down the Fredericksburg Turnpike.

Why hadn't he found General Stonewall Jackson?

ii

He tried to push the worry out of his mind. In a moment it became easy. Another shell arched overhead. Gideon ducked as it blew up trees about half a mile behind.

He wished to God he could see more clearly. Even if there were men on the road ahead it would be almost impossible to detect them from a distance. Pressing his threadbare gray trousers against Sport to urge him on, he strained to see through shadows and drifting smoke now tinged red by the fire glare, now yellow by the full moon.

To counter his weariness and fear, he again reminded himself that the battle seemed to be going favorably. By all logic it shouldn't have been going that way at all.

Estimates said Hooker had brought down between a hundred and thirty and a hundred and fifty thousand men—including Stoneman's cavalry, which had disappeared somewhere further south. The Union commander was desperate to give Lincoln a decisive victory after the debacles of McClellan, the political general who'd dawdled and ultimately failed on the Peninsula, and Burnside, of the formidable side whiskers, who'd been routed at Fredericksburg.

Fighting Joe's gigantic Union force was faced by less than half as many Confederates. And few of those were in good shape after a winter of privation in the camps around Fredericksburg. Gideon remembered all too well the pathetic sights of the cold season: young boys, most of them barely fifteen, their uniforms in tatters, their mouths scurvy-rotted, grubbing in the forests for wild onions—

Feet wrapped in scraps of blanket leaving scarlet tracks in the mud as men filed out of the religious services held to keep their spirits up—

The round, alarmed eyes that first glimpsed the curious bulblike bags carrying men in big baskets and bobbing on anchor ropes in the blowing mists north of the river—

Gideon himself had been one of those startled and worried watchers. He had never before laid eyes on an observation balloon, but he'd heard about them. The balloons were a disheartening sight. They were more evidence of the superior resources and ingenuity of the industrial North. Against it the South could only muster dogged courage and the spirit epitomized by Jeb Stuart's baritone voice bellowing "Jine the Cavalry" as he led his brigades into a firefight.

Finally Hooker's onslaught had come. He'd hurled his columns over the Rappahannock on pontoon bridges. General Lee had then done the unthinkable—split the outnumbered Army of Northern Virginia into even smaller components. First he'd left ten thousand under Early at Fredericksburg. Then he'd sent twenty-six thousand with

Jackson. That left fourteen thousand Confederates to confront the Union center, which consisted of three entire corps, something like seventy thousand men.

Lee's division of his strength was deliberate. By taking a supreme risk, he hoped for a supreme triumph. Stuart's riders had spotted a weakness in the Union plan. Hooker's right wing straggled out southward, unprotected.

Only last night, Major Hotchkiss, an engineer, and Reverend Lacy, both of whom knew the countryside well, had located a route through the tangled woods along which Jackson might march down, around, and behind the exposed Union right. And so, after his sword had fallen, Stonewall had buckled it on, and with Lee's approval, started at seven this very morning, urging his twenty-six thousand men to *"Press on!"*

Toward the close of the day, the stern, curious soldier who resembled some Old Testament prophet, had ripped into Howard's encamped Germans, the surprise march a complete success.

Gideon, a tall, strong-shouldered young man who would be twenty next month, took a fierce pride in that kind of daring. He found it in Jackson, in Marse Robert, and in his immediate superior, General Stuart, to whose staff he'd been assigned just after the Fredericksburg triumph. Again outnumbered at Chancellorsville, the Southern commanders had had to strike more boldly, gamble everything. Only a general whose military skills approached genius would have agreed to dividing inferior manpower not once but twice, in the faint hope of turning what appeared to be almost certain defeat into possible victory. Only other generals of equally incredible vision and audacity could have executed such a plan.

Moonlight through a break in the trees lit Gideon's tawny hair for an instant. He'd lost his campaign hat around six o'clock when a Yank ball had blown it off. As he thought of brave, imaginative Lee and the hard-driving Jackson, he barely heard another rattle of brush on his left.

Vaguely he realized the turnpike was dipping downward. The soft *chock* of Sport's rotting hoofs changed to a mushy sound. There was swampy ground at the foot of the little hill. But Gideon paid only marginal attention to the terrain. He was happily bemused by the real possibility of a victory.

With a few more decisive routs of Lincoln's procession of inept or hesitant generals, the Confederacy might be able to negotiate a peace. Then he could go back to Richmond. Back to his wife and their infant daughter. It was time. Of late he'd been bothered by a feeling that his luck was playing out.

A year earlier, when he had been chosen as one of the twelve hundred men to ride with Stuart to scout McClellan's Peninsular army, he'd nearly lost his life at Tunstall's Station. He'd been leading a detachment burning the rolling stock on the York River Railroad. Some of his men had started firing revolvers to celebrate. Some corporal's careless shot had blown Gideon's beloved roan Will-O'-the-Wisp out from under him.

Stunned, he'd lain unnoticed while the freight cars crumbled around him like fiery waterfalls, setting his uniform afire. Somehow he'd found enough strength to crawl to a ditch and roll frantically until he'd put out the flames. He'd spent the night in that ditch, half conscious and hurting. At dawn he'd discovered that Stuart's horsemen had all ridden on and the district was swarming with Yanks.

He'd crawled out of the ditch, limped into some trees, and hidden out all day, delirious with pain. After dark he'd managed to rouse himself and move on, finally blundering into the dooryard of a small tobacco farm. The farmer had put him to bed, and the farmer's wife had dressed the worst of his burns with poultices.

The family tended him for over five weeks. At last the itching tissue had sloughed off his arms and chest, leaving only faint scars.

Then Gideon had disguised himself in country clothing and slipped back into Richmond to find his wife—who had feared him lost forever.

That sort of brush with death—his first had come at Manassas in '61—had relieved him of all conviction that this war was glorious. Stuart still fought with zest, and Gideon still joined the cavalry's singing as they rode. But his emulation of his commander's spirit was forced. He now found the war a necessary but filthy business. He wanted it over, settled with as much advantage to the South as could be gained.

Perhaps that was why he felt so strangely euphoric just

now. If a victory could be wrenched out of the night's confusion it might lead at long last to the European recognition Jeff Davis sought for the government. It might lead also to a negotiated peace, with the South once again prospering as a separate nation on the American continent. But most importantly, it might lead him home to Margaret and little Eleanor.

Gideon's head jerked up. Musketry rattled ahead. He reined Sport to a dead stop. The fire-reddened moon hung above the trees but did little to relieve the gloom on the turnpike.

The firing died away. Gideon scratched his nose. The air stank of powder—and worse. Hoof thrush wasn't his mount's only affliction. Too many hours of a saddle on Sport's back had opened one of the familiar and nauseous sores that plagued cavalry horses. Gideon could smell the fetid ooze beneath him; the sore ran constantly. It pained him to think he was only worsening it by riding his spunky mount so hard.

But he only had one horse. And he also had a very important dispatch in the pouch thrust into his frayed, dirty sash.

Now that the muskets were silent, he could hear a party of horsemen approaching. He quickly swung the stallion to the north side of the road. The moon glinted cold and hard in Gideon's blue eyes as he scanned the turnpike.

The small arms fire from the direction of Chancellorsville started again, then gradually died away beneath the rhythmic plopping of hoofs. The horses were coming up the slight incline from the low place.

Next he heard voices. Did they belong to friends, or to enemies?

iii

Gideon drew his Le Mat. He thought briefly of heading Sport into the brush beyond the flinty shoulder. But then he heard more sounds of movement and decided against it.

Dry-mouthed he waited. Should he hail?

No, better wait and see whether the broken moonlight revealed gray uniforms—or blue ones.

A horseman materialized, followed by several others. The leading rider, thin to the point of emaciation, turned his head at the sound of another shell bursting south of the road. Gideon saw the rider was wearing gray. The man had a straggling beard, eyes that glittered like polished stones, and an unmistakable profile.

Relieved, Gideon holstered the revolver. He'd found Jackson.

He touched Sport gently with his spurs. The stallion started forward. Behind the general, Gideon thought he saw six or eight mounted men in a double column. There could have been several more; it was impossible to be sure in the bad light. He headed the stallion back across the turnpike, moving toward the general at an angle.

As he opened his mouth to hail, someone hidden in the woods to Jackson's left let out a shout. From the same spot a horizontal line of flame flashed. Rifled muskets roared, volleying at the road.

iv

The general's horse reared. Gideon crouched over Sport's mane just as a ball whizzed past his ear. To Jackson's rear, men yelled out as he fought to control his alarmed mount.

"Who's there?"

"Damn Yanks!"

"No, those have to be our men, Morrison."

"No firing! *Cease firing!*"

In answer to the last cry from the road, the unseen riflemen volleyed again.

Sport shied, neighing frantically. Over the roar of the guns, Gideon heard a fierce, familiar wail from the dark trees—

The Rebel yell.

The men in the woods weren't the enemy. Perhaps they were from A. P. Hill's division. The officers Gideon had met earlier had told him the division was supposed to be advancing somewhere in this area. With visibility so poor, Jackson and his party had been foolish to push out so far ahead of the Confederate lines.

Gideon kicked Sport forward, realizing from the rising clamor of voices that soldiers were crashing through the trees on his side of the road as well. He'd evidently escaped an attack because he was a single rider, proceeding in relative quiet.

The voices on the turnpike grew louder, creating confusion as horses screamed and reared: *"Who are you men out there?"*

"Hold your fire! You're firing at your own officers!"

"Damned lie!" a Southern voice howled from the blackness. "It's the Yank cavalry we was warned about, boys. *Pour it to them!*"

"General!" Gideon shouted, riding toward Jackson, who in turn was spurring his horse toward the side of the road Gideon had just left. Gideon let go of the reins in a desperate attempt to reach for Jackson's shoulders and drag him out of the saddle. He touched the fabric of Jackson's uniform. Then his hands were pulled away as Sport's right foreleg went into a hole.

The stallion careened sideways, almost fell. Gideon tumbled from the saddle, landing hard as a new volley boomed from the thickets toward which Jackson was riding.

Sport clambered up, apparently unhurt. On hands and knees Gideon blinked and gasped for breath. He saw Jackson's tall figure stiffen, heard him cry out.

Jackson's right hand flew upward as though jerked by an invisible rope. Then his left arm flailed out. Gideon scrambled to his feet, realizing from the way the general was swaying that he'd been hit. And not just once.

Another howl of pain from the tangle of men and horses told him someone else had taken a ball. "Boswell's shot!" a man cried, just as another volley roared from the road's north side.

The turnpike was bedlam. Wounded men slid from their saddles. Terrified horses bolted.

Gideon staggered toward Jackson. The general was still in the saddle. With both arms dangling at his sides, Jackson had managed to turn his horse's head away from the direction of the last volley. Gideon still hoped to reach the commander and pull him down before the concealed soldiers fired again.

A riderless horse crashed into him from behind, spilling

Gideon on his face. A rock raked his cheek. He yelped as a hoof grazed his temple. Instinct made him cover his head with both forearms.

Just as he did, he had a distorted view of the bearded general being carried forward by his plunging mount. A low-hanging branch bashed Jackson's forehead, knocking him to the ground.

Still more shouting.

"Sergeant Cunliffe?"

"He's down too. Dead, I think."

From somewhere in the trees, a strident voice: "Who's there? *Who are you?*"

An officer bent low and running toward the fallen general screamed, "Stonewall Jackson's staff, you goddamn fools!"

Gideon heard Jackson's name shouted out in the dark on both sides of the road. Then he heard cursing, accusations. Finally a voice identified the unseen marksmen as part of the Thirty-third North Carolina—General Hill's division.

On his feet again, Gideon lurched toward the half-dozen shadowy figures clustering around the fallen commander. A sudden memory gave him a sick feeling.

The sword fell.

No one touched it.

A hand seized his shoulder. Whirled him. A revolver gouged his chin. "Who the hell are—?"

"Major Kent, General Stuart's staff," he panted. Shock became rage. He slammed a fist against the revolver muzzle and knocked it aside without thinking that a jerk of the soldier's finger could have blown his head off. "I've dispatches from—"

The man paid no attention, spun back toward the general.

"How is he?"

"A ball through his right palm."

"He took another in the left arm. No, looks like two."

"Don't move him!"

The voices sounded childish in their hysteria. In the woods on both sides of the turnpike, men began to hurry toward the road, heedless of the noise. An officer in gray confronted one of the first infantrymen to emerge from the trees. With a slash of his revolver muzzle, the officer laid the soldier's cheek open. Moonlight shone on running blood as the rifleman reeled back. The officer brandished his revolver at the other ragged figures beginning to creep into sight.

"Fucking careless butchers! *You shot Stonewall!*"

Somewhere a boyish voice repeated the name. Someone else began crying.

How many Confederates had been hit in those volleys? Gideon had no idea. He counted three sprawled bodies on the turnpike—perhaps a fourth partway down the slope of the little hill. A party of riders clattered up from the west, was challenged, then told the news. The new arrivals joined the men already kneeling around Jackson. One bearded fellow with a heavily braided sleeve thrust his way through the group. With a start, Gideon recognized A. P. Hill, three staff officers right behind him.

The stunned Hill dropped to his knees, gently lifted, and cradled Jackson's head in his arms. One of Jackson's aides pulled a knife and began to slit the general's left sleeve from shoulder to cuff. Blood leaked out of both of the general's gauntlets.

Like most of the rest, Gideon stood staring, overwhelmed by the tragic accident. He caught an occasional glimpse of Jackson's stern face. The eyes were open, shining in the moonlight. The branch that had struck the general's forehead had opened a cut. Trickles of blood ran in his eyebrows.

Beyond the southern shoulder of the turnpike a tumultuous shouting had started. Men relayed word of the shooting. Even further out, Gideon caught the sound of horsemen cantering. More Confederates moving up? Or the enemy cavalry for which Jackson and his party had been mistaken?

A man who identified himself as Morrison, the general's brother-in-law, crawled to Hill's side.

"For God's sake, sir, let's get him into the shelter of a tree."

General Hill raised an anguished face. "Send a courier for the corps surgeon."

No one moved.

"Do you hear me? Fetch McGuire at once!"

"And an ambulance!" a second voice bawled.

"We've got to move him," Morrison insisted. "Captain Wilbourn?"

"Here."

Another man pressed through the group around the fallen general. Laboriously, Wilbourn and Morrison lifted Jackson and dragged him toward the shoulder, ignoring the protests of several others about possibly worsening the injuries. In the forest the shouting and the drum of hoofs intensified.

Gideon wrenched his head around and called, "They're making so damn much noise, the Yank outposts will hear!"

No one heard him. Everyone was shouting at once. Wilbourn and Morrison seemed the only men sufficiently self-possessed to do what had to be done; the others kept yelling warnings, orders, questions.

Someone ran up to report that at least two men were dead for certain. A courier snagged the reins of a horse—Sport, Gideon saw with consternation—mounted, and galloped off before he could protest.

He turned back, tense and still shaken. Wilbourn propped Jackson against a roadside tree, gently pulled off the blood-soaked gauntlets, then carefully unfastened the general's coat. Jackson was still conscious. He groaned when Wilbourn found it difficult to free his right arm from the sleeve.

"Kerchief!" Wilbourn demanded.

A. P. Hill produced one. Wilbourn knotted it around Jackson's upper left arm, then asked for another. He used it to tie a crude sling. Gideon thought he saw bone protruding through the mangled flesh of the general's arm.

Breathing hard, Wilbourn leaned back on his haunches. "General? We must see to your right hand."

Jackson's lids fluttered. His voice—so often stern—was a mild whisper. "No. A mere trifle—"

General Hill stamped a boot down, hard. "It's too dangerous to wait for an ambulance here. Rig a litter. Use my overcoat. Branches."

Trying to banish the persistent image of the fallen sword, Gideon darted toward the brush on the north side of the road. A private, a starved-looking boy whose ragged gray uniform was powder stained, leaned on his rifled musket, staring at the wounded man. In the smoky moonlight the boy saw Gideon's enraged face. He seemed compelled to plead with him.

"Don't blame us, Major. Jesus, please don't blame us. We heard the Yankee horse was movin' this way. We thought it was them—"

"You didn't think at all!" Gideon cried, raising a fist. The boy cringed away. It was all Gideon could do to keep from hitting him.

Finally, muttering a disgusted obscenity, he shoved past the boy, dragged out his saber, and began cutting a low branch. More of the damn fool North Carolina troops were drifting out of the woods. They stood like silent, shabby wraiths, gazing at Jackson. Gideon hacked at the branch with savage strokes, as though it were a human adversary.

When the branch dropped, he started to chop off a second one. He grew conscious of a faint whistling, coming from the east and growing louder. He glanced up, his palms cold all at once. Whether it was coincidence or the result of all the noise in the wood, the Federal gunners had chosen that moment to open a new bombardment.

He flung himself forward against the trunk as the Tarheel soldiers scattered. The shot burst at treetop level, almost directly above him. The shock wave slammed his cheek against the bark.

Bits of metal and wood rained down. None struck hard enough to hurt him. But the explosion and fall of debris touched something raw in him—something abraded by the months of separation from his wife, by the wretched conditions of the winter camp where the brave songs had begun to sound hollow and infantile. He was suddenly gripped by a paralyzing panic.

He broke it with an enraged yell. He snatched up the first branch, yanked the second off the trunk by sheer force, jammed his saber under his arm, and stumbled back toward Jackson.

A shell exploded close by. The road lit up momentarily. Crouched over with the branches in his hands and the saber jutting from his armpit, Gideon dodged a shower of burning twigs while his mind reproduced the dreadful image again: *the untouched sword scabbard slowly, slowly toppling—*

At First Manassas, Jackson had stood like that stone wall

and earned his famous nickname. He was more than a master tactician. He had become a legend to thousands of Confederate soldiers who'd never even seen him, a name in newspapers that gave hope to those at home when hope seemed futile. He was the supreme example of the South's one matchless weapon—raw courage in the face of superior numbers and industrial strength.

Gideon's panic became almost overwhelming. The Confederacy couldn't afford to lose Stonewall Jackson. General Lee couldn't afford to lose him. The survivors on the road *had* to save him!

Even if they died doing it.

V

The Yank bombardment became almost continuous. Shells were being lobbed in every few seconds. Exploding shot spattered the turnpike like metal rain. Gideon reached the group of men around Jackson and began to jab the two branches into the sleeves of Hill's gray overcoat. He worked with desperate haste, driven by the conviction that Jackson was the only man who could execute Lee's most daring strategies and win victories that textbooks said were impossible.

"He's not that badly hurt," Morrison breathed. Whether it was true or only a prayer, Gideon didn't know. But he tended to believe Morrison was right. The greatest danger to Jackson at the moment was the shelling.

An eighth of a mile east, another charge blew a huge pit in the turnpike, raising a cloud of dirt that sifted down on the men a moment later.

Captain Wilbourn leaned over Jackson's head to shield him from the falling earth. As the upper limbs of a nearby tree caught fire, he jumped to his feet. "Get that litter up and carry it out of here!"

Gideon and three other men grabbed the cut limbs with the coat stretched between. The men at the bottom end had the hardest job—holding the branches and the skirt of the coat to keep it taut. Jackson was lifted onto the litter, then cautiously raised.

Gideon tried to walk steadily—ignoring the detonations,

the glaring lights, the flaming trees, the hissing grapeshot. Through the woods on both sides of the highway, bugles pealed, officers bellowed orders, men crashed through the thickets. Occasionally a piercing scream signaled the killing or wounding of one of those men by artillery fire. Gideon breathed hard, the dispatch from Stuart entirely forgotten as he concentrated on one simple but immensely important task.

Getting Jackson to the rear. Out of the shell zone. Getting him to a place where he could be treated. Saved.

He's only wounded in the forearm, Gideon thought. *If he doesn't bleed to death—if we can reach the surgeon in time without all of us getting blown up—he'll be all right.*

He ducked his head as another shell burst. A flaming limb just missed his left side, the heat scorching for a moment. He tried not to think about how desperately the Army of Northern Virginia needed this peculiar, unkempt man who had once taught at the Military Institute in Lexington, where Gideon had been raised. He just kept walking, lifting one foot carefully after the other, trying not to jostle the litter.

Steadily, they bore Jackson westward. The cannonading never stopped. One litter bearer went down, hit by a piece of shot. A major from Hill's staff reached out to catch the branch as the wounded man let go.

But the major wasn't quick enough. The litter tilted. Jackson rolled off. When he struck the ground, he uttered no sound.

The general's brother-in-law, Morrison, knelt beside him, tears in his eyes. "Oh, Lord, General, I'm sorry."

Smoke drifted away. The moon appeared again, lighting the bearded face. Jackson's tongue probed his lips, as if he were thirsty. His eyes looked bright, fierce.

"We'll be on our way again within a minute—" Morrison began.

"Never mind," Jackson whispered. "Never mind about me."

"Come on!" Morrison exclaimed. "Lift him!"

They carried the general for another eight or ten minutes, until they reached the ambulance that had been summoned. Once Jackson had been laid inside and the vehicle turned around, Gideon trotted along behind—it moved slowly to avoid sudden jolts—and presently the ambulance and the men accompanying it reached a hospital tent in a dark field out of range of the Union artillery.

Without his horse—God only knew what the messenger had done with Sport—Gideon had little choice but to remain outside the tent for an hour. And then another. Finally Dr. Black, the surgeon, came out wiping his hands on a bloody apron.

Lantern light shone on the faces of the dozen or so men who'd been waiting for word. The surgeon glanced from face to face while the cannon continued to rumble beyond the burning trees on the eastern horizon.

"I have successfully amputated the general's left arm," Dr. Black said. "The bone was beyond repair. If there are no complications, he'll soon be back to lead his men again."

Gideon shouted like a boy. So did the others. Hats sailed into the air as the weary doctor turned, gave a faint smile of satisfaction, and stumbled back into the tent.

Gideon sank down on the ground, incredibly tired. While a few of the men continued to whoop and dance around him, he leaned his forehead on his knee and thought: *At least I've helped do one thing in this war that I can be proud of.*

After two years of fighting in which he had changed from a cheerful, contentious young man eager to see battle to a weary professional who now knew the dreadful cost of the South's principles, it was good to be able to single out even one such accomplishment.

He yawned. Closed his eyes. It was good.

Though he knew he should get up and hunt for Stuart, he didn't. He was too tired. He sat upright in the glow of the lantern outside the medical tent, struggling to keep his eyes open.

It would soon be Sunday, he realized. Maybe it was Sunday already.

Would Margaret be going to church in Richmond? *Must write her,* he reminded himself. *Write to tell her how we saved old Stonewall—*

Eight days later, before Gideon found the spare moments to put his thoughts to paper, Thomas Jonathan Jackson lay abed in a small house at Guiney's Station—

Dying.

vi

—It was pneumonia, they say. Jackson was making a good recovery. Then, quite abruptly, Wednesday I believe it was, he began to sink.

I've been told it was a relatively peaceful death, though the general suffered periods of delirium near the end. His wife Mary Anna was among those at the bedside. They sang a hymn he requested.

According to what we've been told, the general spoke twice, once to issue an order for A. P. Hill to "come up" with his infantry, the second time to utter a most peculiar remark—"Let us cross over the river, and rest under the shade of the trees." Some claim the word was "pass," not "cross." But no one knows what he meant.

I didn't realize he was so young; he had observed his thirty-ninth birthday only in January.

I've considered trying to write my father in New York where he is once again preaching. I wanted to tell him Stonewall has died. But I am sure no letter of mine would reach the North, and he will doubtless read of the passing, since Jackson's exploits were so widely discussed.

In Lexington, the general was a friend to my father when he had no others. He will mourn the cruel accident, I am sure, even though he believed his friend had given his loyalty to the wrong side.

It is hard for me to express my feelings just now, Margaret. We won a sound victory at Chancellorsville—though at a high cost. I've heard there were as many as 13,000 of our boys killed, maimed, or lost. We would have made the success an even better one if Fighting Joe had not lost his taste for fighting—something it appears he never had to begin with!—and got away across the Rappahannock pontoons before we could catch him. And the loss of Jackson has robbed the victory of all sweetness.

Even General Stuart, with whose command I was reunited before the fighting ended, seems in poor spirits. He is being praised in some quarters, and d——d in others, as a result of his handling of Jackson's infantry. He took command when A. P. Hill fell wounded the same night Stonewall was shot.

You may say I place too much importance on Jackson, but I do not believe so. It's the common feeling that, between them, Lee and Jackson would one day have pounded the Lincoln crowd into submission to our point of view. Lee was like an anvil and Jackson a hammer, and whenever the Federals were caught between them, they were lost. Now Lee's hammer is gone. He is reportedly grieved almost beyond consolation, though outwardly maintaining a show of courage. Men claim—rightly, I think—that when we lost Jackson, we lost the irreplaceable.

I even sense a new attitude among those on our side. I can't quite put it into the proper words, but there is not much talk of winning now, only of a long hard fight with a truce the most we can hope for, and defeat being more likely. The feeling did not seem present a few months ago, and certainly not a year ago. I hope the mood will pass, but I wonder. Something has *changed.*

In truth, I have changed too. I am ashamed to put unmanly thoughts on paper, but I cannot help them. I was never before afraid that we would lose, but I am afraid now. I am even more afraid of what will happen to us—you and Eleanor and myself—if the worst comes to pass. The last time I saw father, he quoted Scripture and stated that the Kent family need not forever be harmed by the war. But what of we three?

I never felt strongly that the nigras should remain perpetually enslaved—the plain truth is, I never thought much about their condition at all; a mistake, I am beginning to believe.

But my doubts about certain aspects of the war do not alter the fact that I have taken part in what the North calls the rebellion. Will I or any other soldier on this side be easily forgiven for that? I doubt it. Of more importance is this question. Even if I am forgiven, how will we make a life for ourselves when peace comes again?

You know the many, many hours I have spent during the winter studying the books you have sent, trying to teach myself to put words down in a proper order, and with some intelligence, because a good officer—especially a staff officer—must have that skill. But I am a grown man, and I still lack a decent education. War is the only trade I know.

You must forgive much of what I have written. I am

caught up in the sad spirit of these days, and should not pass my gloom along to you. I love you with all my heart and pray for your safety and that of our dear child there in the capital which the enemy wants to destroy so very much.

Will write again the moment I can. Let us hope God and the circumstances of the war enable me to do so in a more cheerful spirit.

Give the baby hugs and kisses for me.

Your husband, G. K.

★ Book One ★

In Destruction's Path

Chapter I

Soldier Alone

i

Slowly, so he wouldn't make a sound, the kneeling Confederate corporal stretched his right hand between the slats of the corn crib on the small Georgia farm.

The interior was black. He couldn't see what he was after, but he was determined to find food. His belly hurt, though he didn't know whether it hurt from hunger or from the onset of another attack of dysentery.

Better get hold of something to tide you over, he thought. All he'd had to drink for the past two days had been creek water, his only nourishment a few berries. If he starved he'd never reach Jefferson County. And he had to reach it. That was why he'd risked sneaking the quarter of a mile from a clump of pine woods to the back of this crib on a small farm in Washington County. While he'd crossed the open ground, he'd kept the crib between himself and the rundown house, which appeared to be deserted. From the safety of the trees, he'd watched house and crib for a quarter hour before venturing out.

He couldn't find any corn in the crib. He pressed his right shoulder harder against the slats, stretching and wiggling his fingers, groping. He was a lean young man of eighteen. His face, which always tended to a gauntness inherited from his father, looked even more bony than usual. He had his mother's fair hair, but accumulated dirt had given it a dingy brown cast. Large dark eyes and a straight, well-formed nose were spoiled just a bit by a mouth that took on an almost cruel thinness when he was determined.

The Georgia twilight had a curious, cold quality despite the huge red ball of the sun dropping over a patch of woodland where leaves were changing to yellow and vermillion. Or perhaps he only thought the oncoming dusk seemed cold because he was alone. It was Sunday, the twentieth of November 1864, the eve of winter.

Grunting softly, his hand searched to the right, to the left.

Nothing.

He jammed his eye up next to an opening between two higher slats but saw only darkness. *Lord, was the crib empty?*

He looked disreputable, kneeling there. His cadet-gray tunic, designed to cover his trousers to a point halfway between hip and knee, was torn in five places. From the two rows of seven buttons, just four remained. His point-down chevrons had come half unsewn, and the light blue trim that edged the tunic and identified him as an infantryman had almost raveled away. Dust and weather had soiled the light blue collar and cuffs as well as the matching sides and crown of his kepi-style forage cap that hid the white streak in his hair. A duck havelock hanging down from the back of the cap to protect his neck from the weather had turned from white to gray. A canvas shoulder sling held his imported .577-caliber Enfield rifled musket upright against his back.

Like any good soldier, he had strong personal feelings about his weapon. It was his companion, his means of survival. And he was good with it. That was a surprising thing he'd discovered during his first weeks of service. Perhaps it was his upbringing—his grandfather had taught him how to shoot. But whatever the reason, he'd quickly become a proficient marksman. He was fast at reloading, with an instinctive feel for the intricacies of handling firearms—such things as wind velocity and tricks of sun and shadow that could affect accuracy. He'd been complimented more than once on being a fine shot. The compliments helped develop a conviction that, without a weapon, he was not complete. His gun had become an extension of himself.

Straining to find something inside the crib, he failed to hear the footsteps. The farmer must have slipped out of the house in a stealthy way, somehow spotting him on his passage across the field. His first warning was a shadow that fell over the side of the crib.

"Y'all get up from there, you damn thief."

He jerked his head around, saw the man: paunchy, gray-bearded; old, weather-worn clothing; filthy toes showing at the tip of one worn-out boot.

Thick-fingered hands clasped the handle of a pitchfork. The tines caught the sundown light and glittered like thin swords.

"I said get up!" the man yelled, lunging from the corner of the crib.

The soldier reared back. The tines of the pitchfork stabbed into the slat where his cheek had been pressed a moment before.

The man yanked the pitchfork loose. The corporal steadied himself, feet spread wide, hands held up in front of him. "Look, I only wanted a little food—"

The pitchfork flashed red. The corporal eyed the points. Would they stab at him again, without any warning?

The man's slurry voice showed his fury. "What corn I got belongs to me and the missus and my two little girls. You ain't gonna touch it."

"All right." The corporal backed up a step. "Just be careful with that fork. I still have a ways to travel."

The man squinted at him. "Where you bound?"

"Home," the corporal said, resorting to an evasion he'd used before. He was thankful he'd ripped the Virginia regimental emblem from his cap, in case the man could identify the insignia of state units.

"Where's home?"

"What's it to you?" the corporal shot back, resenting the man's hostility to someone in Confederate gray.

The farmer came forward again, the fork held horizontally, the tines a foot from the younger man's belly.

"Goddamn it, boy, *you answer*!"

"That's a hell of a way to talk to a soldier from your own army!" He tried a bluff, lowered his left hand to touch the brown-spotted bandage knotted around his thigh. "I got mustered out. I was hit."

A grumble of doubt. "That a fact. Listen, I know they're sending boys back to service shot up a lot worse 'n you. You ain't tellin' me the truth."

The corporal was angry. This ignorant clod couldn't begin to understand his concept of devotion to duty, could never understand why he was traveling alone across central Georgia, hiding out during the daylight hours, stealing and getting shot up for trying to pilfer a chicken to eat.

"You say you're goin' home—"

"That's right."

"What's your name?"

"Kent. Corporal Jeremiah Kent."

"Well, now, Corporal Jeremiah Kent, you just tell me where your home's at."

"Mister, I don't mean you any harm. You wouldn't miss an ear or two."

The pitchfork stabbed out, the tines indenting the fabric of his tunic just above the belt. "Boy, answer the question. *Where's home?*"

Alarmed, he risked a little of the truth. "I'm headed for Jefferson County."

The farmer's face twisted in an ugly sneer. Very softly, he said, "Then you're tellin' me lies. You ain't no Georgia boy. I know by the way you talk. You come from someplace up north. Carolina, mebbe. Virginny. But not Georgia. You run away?"

The tines poked deeper. Jeremiah felt one pierce his tunic, prick his skin.

"You're a goddamn deserter."

Furious, Jeremiah didn't know how to answer the accusation. In a way it was true, yet he'd traveled for miles with no sense of dishonor. Traveled with pride and purpose, in fact.

"I sent two sons to Mississippi and lost both. *Both!* I ain't feedin' or shelterin' no damn runaway coward!"

The last word exploded in a rush of breath. At the same instant, the farmer's hands jerked back at his right side. Then with full force he rammed the pitchfork forward. Jeremiah jumped sideways. A tine slashed another hole in his tunic. The points hit a crib slat so hard they hummed.

Jeremiah's mouth looked thin and white as he laced his fingers together. Color rushed into his cheeks. While the farmer struggled to wrench the tines loose, Jeremiah slammed the back of the farmer's neck, using his interlocked hands like a hammerhead.

The farmer staggered. Jeremiah struck again, ruthlessly hard. *Time to quit fooling with this old man.*

The man dropped to his knees, his palms pressed against the slats of the crib as he gasped for air. A little of the harshness went out of Jeremiah's eyes as he whirled and dashed toward the pines, hoping the farmer had no firearm within quick reach.

Short of breath and dizzy—the sickness seemed to be coming on again—he slowed at a point halfway across the field and turned his head around.

Lord God! The damned lunatic was chasing him! The raised pitchfork shimmered in the red light. Despite his age, the man ran with powerful strides.

Jeremiah bolted for the trees. How could you explain anything to a father who'd seen two sons killed in a war that was ending in failure? How could you make such a man comprehend that you were out here alone because you believed, above all else, in honoring promises and obeying orders? Especially orders from someone who'd saved your life?

Eyes slitted, head back, mouth gulping air, he drove himself. Reached the sanctuary of the sweet-smelling pines and kept going, brambles slashing at his legs, needles on low branches raking his cheeks.

Finally, deep in the woods, he leaned over to catch his breath, near fainting from the aches in his chest and midsection. Somewhere behind he heard the farmer thrashing in the brush.

"Yellabelly! They gonna catch you! They gonna *hang* you! You an' every other goddamn deserter!"

The thrashing sounds diminished. Presently the woods fell silent except for the shrieking of a jay. He'd eluded the man. But he couldn't elude the accusation. It enraged him.

He started on, mentally minimizing the failure of his raid on the crib. He probably couldn't have kept corn kernels in his stomach anyway. He was undoubtedly getting sick all over again. He'd just keep moving.

His fury toward the farmer abated slowly. A man like that wouldn't understand what he was doing; no one could understand except a dead Confederate officer, and two women Jeremiah had never seen.

As he limped from the woods and angled toward a dirt highway in the deepening darkness, his heartbeat slowed. He climbed the shoulder of the road and turned in the right direction after a backward glance to assure himself the farmer hadn't taken to horseback after him.

No, he hadn't. The road stretched silent, winding into the black and scarlet autumn sunset.

He swallowed, concerned about being sick again. Sickness would only delay him further. Was there anyone left in the whole damn world who'd understand what he was doing? What if those women called obeying an order desertion? If they did, his flight and all its perils would count for nothing.

Just like the war itself.

ii

A mile or so down the road Jeremiah began pondering a question he'd asked himself many times, without finding an answer. What really had become of the war he'd gone to fight? That brave, honorable war for the St. Andrew's cross of the Confederacy and all it represented?

He thought he knew part of the answer. The bravery had been rendered worthless by military routs, and a widespread sense of impending defeat. The honor had been turned into a mockery by behavior he'd witnessed among the men on his own side.

Gradually, the shock of his encounter with the farmer passed. He honestly couldn't blame or hate the man now that he'd escaped him. The beautiful night soothed the anger and brought understanding.

A high-riding white moon blazed, then darkened as thin clouds sailed past. The color of the countryside changed from moment to moment: silver to sable to silver again. A breeze rustled the branches of a plum orchard to his left, out there past a little brook that ran beside the road. He heard the sound of rabbits hopping in the orchard. Somewhere, late-blooming wild roses fumed their sweetness into the air.

His belly began to growl again. His intestines seemed to be clutched by a strong hand, then released.

The sickness had left him helplessly weak for half a dozen days at Lovejoy's Station where he'd rested in early September, recovering from a light wound. At Jonesboro a Yank ball had sliced the flesh of his left upper arm. The ball would have killed him if it hadn't been for Lieutenant Colonel Rose.

Rose had been trying to rally the troops under his command during the Jonesboro action. He'd seen the Union sharpshooter take aim at Jeremiah, who was kneeling and loading with frantic speed. Rose had lunged and knocked Jeremiah over—again demonstrating that he was the kind of man Jeremiah wanted to be himself—

An honorable soldier.

Scarcely eight hours later, Rose lay beneath the lantern of a field hospital, mortally wounded.

That night he revealed a side to his personality Jeremiah had never seen before—deeply hidden bitterness and pessimism. Pain destroyed his pretense when he gave Jeremiah a letter to his loved ones. Rose had written the letter a few days earlier, using the only material available—brown butcher's paper.

Jeremiah could still vividly recall how Lieutenant Colonel Rose had looked in those moments before his death. The field hospital lantern lit the sweat in his beard like little jewels. He grimaced, summoned strength as best he could, whispered to his orderly, "Take the letter home for me, Jeremiah. My wife and daughter—they'll need you more than this pitiful army needs you. My God, you know we're done for. Have you counted—"

A violent, prolonged fit of coughing interrupted him. Jeremiah stayed rigid, not wanting to turn and see why a man on another of the plank tables was shrieking. The rasp of a saw told him why.

"—counted the numbers we're losing every day? Some will go back where they came from, but some will turn into scavengers."

Jeremiah had seen it already. Enlisted men disobeyed their officers, slipped out of camp after an engagement and prowled among the Union dead, stripping them of personal effects, prying loose gold teeth, even stealing uniform buttons.

"They'll be roaming all over Georgia soon. I don't care what others tell you, war—war ruins some men. It ruins land but worse, it—ruins people. You've seen what's happening. Desertions. Profiteering. Brutality to prisoners. Andersonville—"

Another spasm of coughing. Rose went on, more faintly. "Andersonville! Right here in Georgia—an affront to God and everything that's decent. It's no different on the other side. And now there's Sherman to fret about. I fear for my wife's safety. Go to her. Don't let anything stop you—or turn you into what some men in this army have become. You're better than that. Any man"—he grimaced—"would be proud to call you his son. I would. I've never had a son."

Jeremiah's eyes filled with tears, but he felt no shame.

"I did you a service," Rose whispered. "So you must do one for me. As soon as you can—promise?"

The sight of the officer's pain nearly broke his heart. But he had to answer truthfully. "Sir, I—I couldn't. That'd mean deserting."

Rose's eyes opened wider, resentful. He clenched his teeth, raised himself on one elbow. "Then I—I order you to go. You understand, Corporal Kent? I'm your commanding officer and I'm *ordering you.*"

Ordering him? That tangled the whole request so fearfully, he didn't know how to deal with it. He stood mute while Rose glared.

"You will carry out the order?"

"I—"

"You will." It was no longer a question. "Promise me." The harshness became pleading. "Please promise me—"

He whispered: "Promise, sir."

Rose fell back, his chest heaving as he labored to breathe. Almost before Jeremiah realized it, a surgeon was covering Rose's face. Then men wrapped his corpse in a bloodied canvas and carried it outside to dump it beside three dozen others. Hardly aware of the throb of his bandaged arm, Jeremiah wept.

The order he'd promised to carry out lingered in his mind. He'd promised. There was no question of *when* he'd leave, only of how. He had to get away without being caught.

It took a while. The combination of his none-too-serious wound and the chronic intestinal ailment of the army put him out of action for six days, forcing him to stay at Lovejoy's Station while General Hood moved most of the troops further west, to Palmetto—hopefully out of Sherman's range.

Eventually Jeremiah was ordered on to Palmetto with a dozen other men who'd recovered from injuries. He remained at Palmetto during most of September, waiting for orders. He saw Jefferson Davis from afar when the President slipped in to confer with Hood over problems plaguing the disintegrating command structure.

Jeremiah's promise to Rose became an obsession. Quite often he was tempted to read the letter he guarded so carefully. But he felt that would be a dishonorable violation of Rose's confidence. Even though the concept of an honorable war had become almost a joke, he clung steadfastly to the belief that he must continue to behave in an honorable way at all times.

Yet watching desertion-ridden companies at Palmetto shrink to half a dozen men made it hard. So did the loss of all the little amenities he'd taken for granted when he was younger. The way your hands felt clean after scrubbing with harsh yellow soap. There was no longer any soap.

How your mouth tasted better in the morning after using salted water and a toothbrush. He'd lost his toothbrush through a hole in his tunic pocket. The whole Confederacy was short of salt. He had resorted to a twig and his own stale spit.

Food had grown progressively poorer and scarcer. There was usually soup, if you could dignify it with that name. Water thickened with some corn meal. Occasionally he'd get potatoes, which he'd mash up and cook with a precious bit of meat. He'd learned to save the chunk of meat, wrap it in a scrap of cloth and reuse it the next day. He'd cooked one such chunk of pork over and over until it was black and smelled like garbage.

It was no wonder the dysentery felled him again, this time for neatly three weeks.

When he recovered, it was already mid-October. He was

glad he hadn't tried to get away yet. Some of the deserters had been caught, brought back, and sent to prison. But he was growing fretful, impatient.

I am *ordering* you—

Promise me—

"Promise, sir."

General Hood had taken the army and disappeared into the northwest, hoping to cut Billy Sherman's supply lines from Tennessee. Since Jeremiah's unit was gone, he was ordered out with a contingent of Georgia Militia to find and join Hood. He was still physically weak. Couldn't keep up—or at least had an excuse for pretending he couldn't. One dawn, the militiamen left him behind.

He was free.

He rested three days in a glade above Atlanta, then headed southeast to deliver the letter. Technically, he supposed he *was* a deserter. But not in his own mind.

He circled wide around besieged Atlanta and crossed the shell-blackened, trench-scarred fields with caution. With one expert shot he bagged a wild turkey, then gutted and roasted it. He had no salt to add as a preservative, but the meat would still last him a while.

Careful as he was to avoid being stopped or questioned, he was defenseless against one threat: the disease in his system. He lost four more days in another patch of forest, lying on the ground hour after hour, wracked by fever, and bowel trouble. It was from those woods, a week ago, that he'd seen more evidence of how ruthless the conflict had become.

He'd seen a sky blackened by fire-shot smoke. Heard thunderous reverberations from dynamite charges. The South's transportation center and major rail junction was being systematically destroyed by men who didn't give a damn about fighting honorably, only about winning their war to free the nigra and crush the rebels. He remembered wondering, hatefully, how many noncombatants had been blown up along with the rolling stock and roundhouses in Atlanta.

Now, a good two miles from where he'd encountered the farmer, he was forced to stop. Out of breath. Light-headed.

The darkness of the countryside oppressed him. The

moon was temporarily hidden. Perhaps it was the lonely dark that made him think of his mother, Fan Lamont.

She'd sent him off to this failing war with a curious and contradictory set of admonitions.

She'd hated to see him go. Expressed grave concern about his safety. Warned him to be as careful as he could.

Yet she was proud of his enthusiasm. Didn't refuse when he begged to enlist. And, at the last moment, urged him to fight well and—most importantly—*honorably*.

He suspected that the fervency that had finally overcome her fear had had something to do with his stepfather's mysterious death in Richmond in 1861. It seemed that Edward Lamont, the actor, had tumbled down a flight of stairs in the building where he and Fan had been living. Jeremiah had been in Lexington at the time, staying with Fan's father, Virgil Tunworth. The boy had heard the account of Lamont's death from his grandfather.

When Fan returned to the little town in the Shenandoah Valley after the funeral, Jeremiah began to have a feeling the accidental fall wasn't the whole story. Based on the somewhat nervous way Fan answered his questions, he had decided there must have been something disgraceful about Edward's death. Something Fan was desperate to counterbalance by giving reluctant permission for the last of her three sons to risk his life for the cause.

Fight well and honorably.

Jeremiah soon became thankful he had never told the entire truth about the war in the few letters he had sent home. He'd said nothing about the spoiled meat dishonest suppliers sold to the army, nothing about the wretched living conditions, nothing about the men who fled under fire at Chickamauga, and the wholesale desertions later. He hadn't wanted his mother to know how bad conditions were. She had enough to fret about with her home threatened and the well-being of Jeremiah's two older brothers constantly in doubt. Everyone in the Confederacy knew the risks taken by General Stuart's regiments. And Matthew—who was too easygoing to bother with more than one or two letters a year—was somewhere on the Atlantic between Liverpool, the Bermudas, and the Carolina coast, serving as supercargo on a blockade runner.

In Jeremiah's opinion, that was both honorable and dashing. Typical of Matt, too. Jeremiah had always admired and envied Matt, even though their times together had been few. Fan's second son had been away at sea since Jeremiah was a small boy.

If it had been possible, he'd gladly have exchanged places with Matt. His brother had a naturally happy disposition. Loved games, particularly baseball, a game he and thousands of other boys and young men had created in parks and fields and dusty lots, adapting it from an old English game Matt called rounders.

How vividly Jeremiah remembered the sweaty excitement on Matt's face one autumn afternoon years ago—he could recall the color and texture of the sunshine, though not the date—the ebullience with which Matt whooped and pranced when he came home, celebrating the way he'd pounded out three aces with his bat, and singlehandedly carried his ball team of five black boys and four white ones to a victory.

Matt possessed a talent for drawing that he'd somehow discovered in himself when he was young. In his imagination, Jeremiah could still see some of the charcoal sketches Matt had sent home occasionally after taking his first berth on a Charleston cotton packet. The style of the drawings was bold, personal, and unforgettable. Though Jeremiah had seen less of Matt than he had of Gideon, he felt a closer bond with Matt, and prayed he was safe.

The cloud drifted away from the moon. He drew deep breaths. The Enfield on his shoulder actually weighed only eight pounds fourteen and a half ounces, but it seemed ten times heavier tonight.

He pulled the canvas sling off and laid the piece in the dirt, shutting his eyes until the attack of dizziness passed.

While he stood swaying in the center of the road, his right hand strayed to his belt, closed unconsciously, protectively over the piece of oilskin containing the precious letter he'd promised to deliver.

He opened his eyes. The small animal noises had stopped in the plum orchard. Or perhaps he didn't hear them because of the ringing in his ears.

He licked the dry inside of his cheek, sniffed his own abominable, unwashed smell. He wanted to stop awhile but felt he shouldn't. What if the farmer was hunting a horse, still intending to chase him?

Well, if that happened, let it. He'd just take to the fields, where he could easily elude one pursuer. He'd make faster progress if he had a short rest.

He sank down on the shoulder, the Enfield near his feet. For a brief moment a shameful despondency swept over him. Everything was failing. The war was lost, or would be soon, now that Lincoln had been returned to the Presidency of the North just a couple of weeks ago.

Lincoln hadn't run as a Republican, but under some new label—the National Union party, Jeremiah thought it was. As his running mate, Abe the Ape had chosen a damned, ignorant Tennessee politician named Johnson who'd betrayed his own kind and sided with the North, claiming the Constitution forbade any other decision. The bottle forbade any other decision, Rose had commented a day or two before his death. Johnson, he said, was a drunkard.

Johnson would have no hand in carrying the war forward, though. Just as Jefferson Davis did, Lincoln personally picked and supervised his generals.

At first he'd chosen poor ones. The pompous Democrat, Little Mac McClellan. Old Burnside. Hooker, who had inexplicably lost his nerve at Chancellorsville and squandered a chance for a stunning victory.

But Jackson had been accidentally shot by men on his own side at Chancellorsville, and that battle had turned out to be less of a Southern triumph than it might have been, even though J.E.B. Stuart had led the infantry from horseback, flourishing his saber, jumping his stallion into enemy cannon emplacements, and creating on the spot, to the tune of "Old Dan Tucker," a derisive song urging Old Joe Hooker to come out of the Wilderness and fight.

But then Jackson had perished of pneumonia. His presence had been missed when Lee made his bold foray into Pennsylvania a month later. Even Meade, who'd defeated Lee in the North, wasn't merciless enough to satisfy Lincoln. The Yankee President wanted, and ultimately found, a supreme commander who fought like a madman: Unconditional Surrender Grant. Another drunkard!

But he'd been sober enough to crush Vicksburg in the west. Sober enough to take charge of the Army of the

Potomac in March of this year, and begin to spend his soldiers by the thousands, the tens of thousands, as though they weren't human beings but manufactured parts in a grinding, unstoppable war engine lubricated by blood and more blood.

The zest, the zeal that had led the South to stunning successes early in the war had all but vanished.

Jeremiah could recall one or another officer speaking with sad pride of Pickett's rush up a gentle hillside toward a clump of trees on the final day at Gettysburg, where Lee had ultimately failed in his attempt to reprovision his army with Yankee grain and Yankee meat, win a daring victory on enemy ground, prove the folly of Davis' policy of only fighting a defensive war on Southern soil, and perhaps frighten the enemy into suing for peace—all at one time!

The heroes such as Pickett were still praised, but few of the living pretended their heroism had made much difference. If the Confederacy hadn't surrendered in fact, it had surrendered in spirit. Even the most ardent patriot now had trouble believing otherwise.

That the South was indeed facing defeat had been borne out by Fan's last letter, written late in June and weeks in transit. The fury of the war had found Fan at last. But that hadn't been the only sad news.

The letter contained tragic tidings about Gideon.

iii

Having escaped death on the Peninsula in '62, Jeremiah's oldest brother had ridden unscathed through action after action—until chance took him to a place called Yellow Tavern on the eleventh of May. There, he and General Stuart had met Union horse soldiers of a kind they'd never encountered before.

Even a year earlier, under Pleasonton, the Yank cavalry couldn't match the South's. But it had been growing steadily—dangerously—better. Now, led by Sheridan, it had turned into a scythe sweeping across Virginia. At Yellow Tavern the blade had struck and killed Jeb Stuart.

Stuart's men had run into fierce, competent opposition. The most dangerous Yanks turned out to be Michigan men, riders who sported red neckerchiefs, and whose regimental band played them into the charge with "Yankee Doodle." They were commanded by an officer almost as flamboyant as Stuart himself—twenty-four-year-old George Armstrong Custer, the "boy general," who led them, screaming, *"Come on, you Wolverines!"*

Custer wore gold spurs, slept with a pet raccoon, and dressed his long curls with cinnamon oil. Jeremiah had read occasional newspaper accounts describing him as a man who expressed no great personal animosity toward Southerners; he was just out to whip them.

Like Stuart, he thrived on being called a daredevil. The personal motto he'd brought with him from West Point was "promotion or death"—though from the way he often defied caution in battle, the motto apparently meant *his* promotion would be earned by the deaths of others. A Democrat, he still managed to remain the darling of the Washington Republicans, the public, and a press that eulogized him as Napoleon's successor.

At Yellow Tavern one of Custer's Wolverines had shot Stuart out of the saddle. Another had engaged Gideon—or so his immediate superior wrote Fan the following week. During the combat, horseman against horseman, Gideon had reared back in his saddle to dodge a saber stroke, lost his balance, and tumbled to the ground. In a matter of seconds enemy troopers had swarmed around him, taking him prisoner.

So now Gideon was either dead, or alive and rotting in one of the prison pits of the North. Fort Delaware, or possibly Elmira in New York.

And as if that loss hadn't been grievous enough, Fan's letter also reported that Hunter's cavalry had swept through the Valley to Lexington. In the surrounding countryside, the Yankee horsemen had burned mills, granaries, farm implements—then buildings in the town, including the Military Institute, Governor Letcher's residence, and other private homes. Only old Washington College had been spared at the last moment because some of Hunter's men refused to torch an institution honoring the nation's first President.

Fan tried to conceal her sadness when she wrote her youngest son. But it came through clearly in the final paragraphs which spoke of the privation sweeping the Confederacy as the enemy blockade bottled up port after port.

Profiteers had driven prices out of the reach of ordinary people. Fan commented that she had no good cotton stockings left, but would make do with old ones since she couldn't afford eight dollars for a new pair.

She'd forgotten what coffee tasted like, she said. Southerners who had cornered the existing supply demanded up to forty dollars a pound.

And when her doctor had prescribed a dose of calomel, it was unaffordable at twenty dollars the ounce.

Even the physical look of the letter was testimony that the end was coming. There was no more writing paper to be had in Lexington, Fan noted. So an enterprising merchant had devised some from an old roll of wall paper. Inside the envelope, and on the back of each sheet, was a crudely printed floral pattern.

It was almost over.

Rose had been right. His wife and daughter undoubtedly needed Jeremiah's help more than the army did. With the Rose women, he'd find a place where his presence would make a difference again.

But if he was going to find them, he couldn't sit in the moonlight. Weary as he was, he had to keep moving.

With effort, he stood up. Reached down for the Enfield. When his fingers were an inch from the weapon, he heard a sound on the road behind him.

He straightened, searching the shifting silver shadows of the landscape.

He couldn't see them; they were too far away. But he heard them.

Mounted men. Coming fast.

That farmer. *That damned, vengeful old man!*

He hadn't been satisfied to locate one horse and ride after Jeremiah alone—he'd had to roust out his neighbors and lead them in pursuit.

Jeremiah shivered, remembering the farmer's warning.

As punishment for his desertion, he'd hang.

Chapter II

"Sixty Thousand Strong"

i

Almost as soon as the appalling thought struck him, Jeremiah began to question whether it made sense. How the devil could an old man muster a party of neighbors in a rural area? There were damn few males left on homesteads anywhere in the South, unless you counted boys and old men. Horses were equally scarce, that much Jeremiah knew for certain.

Still, those *were* horsemen hammering toward him. Who could they be?

Georgia Home Guards? No, he'd heard they couldn't find mounts either.

Enemy cavalry, then? Some of the ruffians who rode with the blond-bearded Yank Judson Kilpatrick?

He didn't know. But he didn't intend to linger in the middle of the road and find out. The riders were coming faster than he'd anticipated. The moon's whiteness lit a rolling, phosphorescent cloud of dust at the crest of a hill he judged to be no more than half a mile away. Figures that seemed part man, part horse, appeared and vanished in the swirling dust.

Jeremiah grabbed the Enfield and sprinted for the ditch

to the left of the road, where the brook ran. A small boulder hidden in the long grass tripped him. With a curse, he went tumbling down the incline. He splashed into the shallow water, remembering at the last moment to twist his body to keep the oilskin pouch and his cartridge box dry.

The dust cloud rolled toward him, the hammer of hooves growing steadily louder. As he lay with his right side in water that felt incredibly cold, he realized he'd dropped the Enfield when he fell.

He raised himself a little—the movement seemed to create a noise loud as a waterfall—just as the first of the horsemen thundered by. Once more a cloud cleared the edge of the moon. There, plainly visible on the shoulder, his piece shone bright.

Someone saw it. Yelled. The horsemen reined in, the leading riders turning back. As he sank down and lay still, Jeremiah tried to count the looming figures. A dozen, maybe more.

A man dismounted, cocking a pistol. He reached for the Enfield. He wore a forage cap much like Jeremiah's.

"Enfield, Captain." The man raised the piece to his chest. "I can feel stamping—C.S.A."

Another man pointed. "Weeds are matted down right there. Whoever dropped it may be hidin'."

Two more pistols were cocked. The horses fretted and stamped. A tall man rode through the group to the side of the road nearest the brook. He leaned over his horse's neck, as if studying the ground. Then he called out, "You down there. You better come out."

Jeremiah thought the voice had a soft, relaxed sound. A Southern sound.

The tall man drew a carbine from a saddle scabbard. *"I said, come out."*

Soaked, Jeremiah staggered to his feet and clambered through the grass to the road, his hands raised above his head.

ii

The barrel of the tall man's carbine glowed in a spill of moonlight. Water dripped from Jeremiah's fingers, from the bandage on his thigh, the torn hem of his tunic, the havelock attached to his cap.

"Captain?" one of the men exclaimed. "He looks like one of ours!"

They *were* Southerners. The moon showed him dusty cadet gray sleeves and trouser legs that matched his own, except for the yellow trim. This wasn't as bad as being caught by Yanks—unless the men were as ferocious about desertion as that old farmer.

The captain waggled his carbine. Jeremiah glimpsed a double line of gold braid on his cap as he asked, "Who are you?"

Jeremiah pivoted slightly so the moonlight would show the chevrons on his sleeve. "Corporal Kent, sir."

"Turn. I can't see the badge on your cap."

"I lost it, sir." He'd learned a lesson from the farmer. He tried to sound calm, as if he had nothing to hide. "I'm from the Sixty-third Virginia, last with Reynolds's brigade, Stevenson's division—"

A horseman further back growled, "Didn't know they was any Virginny boys with the Army of Tennessee, Cap'n."

"Two or three regiments, I think." The captain was a heavy man, with jowls. Moonlight on one cheek showed a scattering of pox scars like miniature black craters. "Corporal, give me the name of your corps commander."

Cautiously, Jeremiah said, "You know we were Hood's Corps, sir. But General Hood was leading the whole army, so our actual commander was General Lee. General Stephen D. Lee," he added for authenticity.

The mutter of a couple of the men said they recognized that he was telling the truth. The captain raised the carbine to quiet them. Then he sharply added, "Were you with Bob Lee in Pennsylvania?"

"No, sir, I mustered in a month afterward."

Another voice, suspicious: "Didn't your regiment lose a flag at Gettysburg?"

"Not to my recollection." He'd heard enough of the history of both Virginia units that had been transferred to the west to recognize the trap. "I think it was the other bunch in the Army of Tennessee. The Fifty-fourth. When I joined up, my regiment belonged to the Second Brigade, Department of Western Virginia. But we were put on the cars along with the Fifty-fourth and—"

"You detached from service?" the captain interrupted.

Jeremiah's hands grew colder. He struggled to keep his voice level. "Yes, sir. I was invalided out at Palmetto, after General Hood left for Tennessee."

He lifted his leg to show the bloodied bandage, even though the pain grew ferocious when he bent his knee. But maybe they'd be less suspicious than the farmer. Blood was blood. They couldn't tell he'd gotten the wound from another of those damned old country boys who didn't want soldiers, *any* soldiers, prowling around their property.

The last of the turkey meat had run out when he was near Milledgeville. On the outskirts of Atlanta he'd slipped into a chicken house after dark. In spite of his efforts to keep quiet, he'd roused the flock. Wakened by the squawking, the poultryman had come charging from his house. He hadn't even issued a challenge or asked a question, just blasted away with a shotgun as Jeremiah dashed off. Once out of danger, he'd cut four buckshot out of his leg with a sheath knife he kept in his right boot. Then he'd cleaned the wound as best he could and bandaged it with his torn-up underdrawers.

The captain wanted to know more about the wound. "In what action were you hit?"

"Jonesboro," Jeremiah said promptly. "Afternoon of the last day of August."

The dismounted man holding the Enfield said, "Well, I know Steve Lee was there, all right."

The captain: "Last day of August, you say. Sure as hell taking a long time for that to heal, isn't it?"

"Infection set in. For a while the doctors thought I might lose the leg altogether. Got knocked down with dysentery at the same time. Actually I had two wounds. The one in my shoulder's come along just fine. This one, though—doesn't seem to want to mend right."

While the captain digested the information, Jeremiah decided he'd better tell as much as he dared. These men sounded more persuadable than the farmer. He might be able to outwit them. But not if he seemed reluctant to talk.

"My commanding officer, Lieutenant Colonel Rose, he came out of the Thirty-sixth Georgia in Cummings' brigade. After Chickamauga he was assigned to division staff for a while. I was picked to be his orderly and courier. He got shot at Jonesboro too. Died the same night. Before he passed on, he ordered me to go to his plantation if I got out. He said only his wife and daughter were left to run it." He added an invention he thought sounded logical, and might divert their suspicion even more.

"The colonel told me his nigras were getting fractious because of Old Abe's proclamation—"

"Yep, that's sure as hell happening," someone agreed. "All over."

"Where's this plantation?" the captain asked him.

Jeremiah began to feel a little less tense; maybe the issue of desertion wouldn't come up at all if he kept trying to convince them he was doing what he thought to be his duty.

"Near Louisville, across the Ogeechee River in Jefferson County. Seems like I've been walking for days to get to it."

"Well, you have thirty or forty miles still to go," the captain informed him. "More or less due east." A hand scratched at the pox scars. "I gather you felt this personal business more important than returning to your unit?"

Jeremiah scowled. To help them see his anger, he yanked off his forage cap. The sudden movement shied a couple of the horses.

The moon struck his dark eyes and matted hair as he straightened to his full height. In the light, the white streak showed plainly, starting at the hairline above his left brow and tapering to a point at the back of his head.

Honesty had failed him with the farmer; he didn't intend to repeat the mistake. "Sir, I told you—I was invalided out! It was either head home for Virginia—too blasted far away—or stay in Georgia and do what the colonel asked of me while he was dying. My unit had already moved out north again. I felt I owed the colonel's womenfolk some protection—'specially since the colonel saved my life at Jonesboro."

"Oh?" The captain cocked his head. "How'd he do that?"

Jeremiah told him the story.

"You have any proof to support what you're saying?" the captain asked.

Jeremiah almost reached for the oilskin pouch. He held

back; the contents of the letter were still unknown to him. What if Rose had written his wife saying he intended to urge his orderly to desert?

"No, sir, I'm sorry. I have nothing."

"What's the name of this here plantation?" the dismounted man with the Enfield said.

"It's called Rosewood. After the colonel's people."

"I've heard of it," the captain told him. "I come from near Savannah. My papa was a cotton broker before he died. I believe he did business with the Rose family at one time—" All at once he sounded more tolerant. "If your unit's gone to Tennessee and you were pronounced unfit to serve, I suppose you made the best choice."

Jeremiah breathed a bit easier. The captain went on. "And those women you mentioned—they're liable to need all the protection they can get. All of Georgia's liable to need it, matter of fact."

"What do you mean, sir?"

Hunching forward, the captain said, "Corporal, do you have any notion as to who we are?"

Jeremiah tried to smile. "I know you're on the right side. And those yellow facings say you're cavalry."

"My name's Dilsey. Captain Robert Dilsey. We're with General Joe Wheeler. Scouting Sherman."

"*Sherman!* But he's back near Atlanta!"

Dilsey shook his head. "Not anymore. Fact is, we're about all that stands between that son of a bitch and the seacoast. Excepting of course, the Home Guard that Governor Brown's trying to turn out." One of Dilsey's troopers snickered contemptuously. "But old men carrying rakes and hoes aren't going to be worth a hoot against Billy Sherman."

Thunderstruck, Jeremiah gasped, "You mean he's on the move?"

Dilsey sighed and nodded. "Started last Wednesday. Marched out in two columns, sixty thousand strong. Slocum has two infantry corps on the left wing, Howard two more on the right. And that Kilpatrick's riding along with them."

"Where's Sherman going?"

A shrug. "Appears he's headed straight across the state to the ocean. Looks like he's just said to hell with maintaining supply lines and is poling off in this direction to do any damage he can."

Another caustic voice: "Mebbe he's tired of fightin' men. Mebbe he wants to fight females and young'uns for a change."

The captain didn't take it as a joke. "Certainly possible. He's got a reputation for being half crazy sometimes. A move in this direction violates every sound principle of strategy. But he's coming—along with that blasted butcher, Kilpatrick. You know what they call Little Kil's riders, Corporal? The Kill-cavalry. We're moving southeast to stay ahead of them. Trying to find out for certain where they're actually going. Harass them, if we can."

The announcement of the sudden advance by the general who'd captured and burned Atlanta still sounded unbelievable. Jeremiah groped for words. "But—but I don't think there are any troops left to fight in this part of the state!"

The man with the Enfield said, "Well, there's you."

He puzzled over the laughter the remark produced as Dilsey said, "There *is* plenty of food in Georgia for a change. Finest crop in years, I'm told. And Bob Lee's army still depends on what comes out of this breadbasket. So if you look at Sherman's move in that light, if makes more sense. I'd guess he's after the food, though he may be after Savannah as well."

"That's crazy!" Jeremiah cried.

"Any man who burns damn near a whole city doesn't fight like a gentleman, Corporal—or by the book. You'd better keep on toward Jefferson County and tell the Rose ladies Old Billy's probably coming their way."

The man with the Enfield spat. "Goddamn soon."

iii

Despite the stunning news, Jeremiah felt oddly elated. He'd convinced Dilsey of the authenticity of his story, done it just right, too. The word desertion hadn't even been uttered.

One of the cavalrymen spoke. "Captain, we ought to be movin'."

"Agree," Dilsey said. "Kent, we'd fill your canteen if you had one. We've fetched along some goobers to eat. Hand him some, Mullins."

Jeremiah raised his arm to accept the handful just as Dilsey uttered a hard, peculiar chuckle that chilled him. Again Dilsey scratched his face.

"You're lucky to be alive, Corporal, you know that? We stopped at a farm a few miles back. Watered our horses from the well. We heard about you."

Jeremiah closed his fist on the goobers, almost dropped them slipping them into his pocket. What a fool he'd been. What a damn fool. He hadn't tricked Dilsey for one minute.

The captain pointed at Jeremiah's leg.

"That injury may hurt. But as the old farmer said, lots of boys shot up worse than you are still with their regiments. So I don't expect you were invalided out. I expect you up and left. As for the rest—I'm willing to accept it. Strikes me it has too many warts to be an outright lie. I don't know what persuaded you to tell me the truth—or ninety percent of it, anyway. You didn't tell the farmer. But as I say—you're lucky you changed your mind. If you'd just handed me that tale about going home—"

Dilsey rammed his carbine in the scabbard. He reached down and snatched the Enfield from the dismounted trooper, then aimed it at Jeremiah's chest, his smile humorless. "I'd have used your own weapon on you. Killed you where you stand."

He flung the Enfield. Jeremiah barely managed to catch it. Dilsey laughed at him, a hollow, unfriendly laugh.

"As things worked out, however, you're going to find yourself smack back in the war. Why, you may turn out to be the only young man within forty miles of that plantation. Commander of the whole resistance! Hope you can handle that. After running away, seems fitting you should be required to try."

Seething, Jeremiah watched Captain Dilsey and his men reorder themselves into a column of twos. Moonlight spilled across the officer's back; his face was hidden. When he spoke, he sounded cheerful and cruel at the same time.

"Good luck to you, Corporal. I hereby promote you to general in command of Jefferson County."

He wheeled his mount with a ferocious yank of the rein and galloped off along the country road, his men right behind. Their passing left another phosphorescent dust cloud that soon hid them from sight.

iv

Sixty thousand, Jeremiah thought, the barrel of the rifled musket shaking in his hand. *Sixty thousand led by the wickedest soldiers in the whole damn Union army!*

By letting him go on to Rosewood alone, Dilsey had punished him. He too had failed to understand Jeremiah's sense of duty and loyalty—

How that soft-spoken man must have been laughing to himself all during Jeremiah's babble about Colonel Rose. For a moment the humiliating anger was almost beyond bearing.

It began to pass when he reminded himself that he *was* still alive. And Sherman's coming would indeed give him a chance to fight again. All in all, despite thinking he'd fooled Dilsey and the shock of Dilsey's announcement that he hadn't, he concluded that things could have been a devil of a lot worse. The hand clasping the Enfield grew steadier.

Jeremiah laid the weapon down, shelled and swallowed four of the goobers given him by the cavalrymen. They settled hard in his stomach, producing almost instantaneous pain. He was forced to sit down on the shoulder of the road, clutching his middle, praying for the pain to ease.

It didn't.

A bird shrilled in the plum orchard. But miserable as he felt, he still believed his luck had taken a better turn. One Enfield would make no difference in Tennessee. It could make a lot of difference in Georgia.

Under the black and silver sky, he jammed the butt of the Enfield into the grass and literally climbed hand over hand to get to his feet. He still felt shaky and frightened. Tortured by spasms of pain, he stepped onto the road, hurrying—

He went only a quarter of a mile before he began to stagger. The goobers came up in a retching heave. He was forced to unfasten and drop his trousers and crouch dizzily awhile.

Covered with cold sweat and aching from his breastbone to his groin, he eventually managed to start walking again. He passed another ramshackle farmhouse. A cow lowed in the vast dark. Pushing himself with every bit of his remaining strength, he kept trudging on.

Toward Jefferson County.

Toward two women he'd never met.

Toward a chance to fight honorably again—

Sixty thousand strong, he kept thinking. *Jesus Almighty!*

Yet in spite of the terrifying numbers and his physical agony, his spirit wouldn't break. Mentally, he felt stronger and more determined than he had in weeks.

I'll get there.

I'll get there before Billy Sherman—if I have to crawl every foot of the way.

Chapter III
The Slave

i

The first sensation was heat: stifling heat, too intense for November.

An insect whined at the back of his neck. With his eyes still closed, he tried to raise his right hand to swat it. He couldn't seem to summon enough strength to draw his hand from what felt like mud.

The insect landed on his havelock, then on exposed skin. He clawed his hand out of the mud as the insect bit—a faint, nearly painless sting. The whine diminished.

Panicky, he tried to recall where he was. That is, where he'd been when he sprawled on the ground at twilight on—

Tuesday. Yesterday had been Tuesday.

Late in the day he'd forded the Ogeechee River, bypassed the little town of Louisville, and tried to follow directions given him by a farmer's boy. Somehow he'd taken a wrong turn at a crossroad. The road he was walking had petered out in brambles at the edge of a bare cotton field near the river.

Still sick, he'd blundered ahead—straight into a maze of little tributaries of the river, a place of rank water and steaming gloom produced by huge cypresses and live oaks.

He'd slopped across one shallow backwater and up the far bank, intending to lie down and rest only a few moments. That was all he remembered until now.

He grew alarmed by a weightlessness in two places where there should have been weight. The precious Enfield no longer pressed against his shoulder; his cartridge box was missing from his belt.

His face felt scorching, oily. He knew he had the fever again.

He dragged his left hand back. Fumbled at his waist.

The oilskin pouch was still there, thank God.

He heard a foot squish down in mud. Heard a man breathing. His teeth started to chatter as he opened his eyes.

Ten inches from his nose a small turtle lay upside down on the curve of its shell. The turtle had withdrawn its head and legs. He couldn't tell whether it was alive or dead. A short distance beyond the turtle he saw a man's feet, calves, and the bottoms of tattered trousers. His panic worsened.

Thick, horny toenails were half hidden in rust-colored mud. But Jeremiah could see the skin well enough—

Black skin.

ii

He heard a heavy, mellow voice, neither friendly nor hostile. "You 'wake, mister soldier?"

Jeremiah's head jerked up. His temples throbbed from the sudden move. His lips compressed, he jammed his fists into the red clay bank where he'd slept. Doubled his knees. Eventually staggered to his feet, his uniform filthy, his face and hair caked with mud.

"Who are you? Where am I?"

The black man was superbly built, with a slender waist and a broad chest. A ragged shirt cut off at the shoulders exposed thick arms. He was about thirty, Jeremiah guessed. His skin was so dark it had a blue cast.

The man's eyes were almost perfectly oval, with huge brown pupils. He stood in a placid, relaxed pose. Yet Jeremiah couldn't escape an irrational feeling that the Negro was simmering with hostility.

"Which question you want me to answer first?"

Jeremiah saw a double image of the black's curly head. He squeezed his eyelids shut and spread his feet, hoping to keep his balance.

"Tell me where I am."

"This here's a swamp down by the acreage we call the bottom."

"Who calls it that?" The black's lackadaisical air angered him. "Don't you know how to be civil to a white man?"

"Why, 'course I do." But Jeremiah thought he saw a corner of the man's mouth twitch. "The bottom land belongs to Rosewood."

"Rosewood," he repeated. "Colonel Henry Rose's place?"

The black licked his lips. Staring into those round brown pupils, Jeremiah thought, *My Lord, he hates me. Or he hates the uniform I'm wearing, anyway.* He was increasingly aware that he lacked any weapon except the sheathed knife in his boot. Without the Enfield he felt naked.

"Reckon there ain't another Rosewood in the county."

"It's the place I've been hunting." Fingers plucked at the pouch on his belt. "I'm carrying a message for the colonel's wife."

The black stared, as if he didn't comprehend.

"Is this Wednesday?"

It took a while for the black man to decide to reply. "That's right, Wednesday. Every Wednesday Miz Rose gives me an hour in the mornin' to come catch coolers." His glance flicked to the turtle. "Can't abide 'em myself. But I sell 'em to Miz Rose for soup. She's real kind, lettin' us niggers make a little money of our own." The last words carried a faintly caustic edge.

"Then you're from the plantation. One of the slaves—"

A quick, adamant shake of the head. "No more."

"Oh?"

The man smiled. "Year ago January, Linkum said I wasn't property. Jubilee's come, mister soldier."

Yet he spoke the words joylessly, sounded angry. Jeremiah was growing increasingly angry with the man's quiet arrogance. "If you think you're free—"

"I *know* I'm free."

"Then what the hell are you doing around here?"

A shrug. "Waitin'."

"For what?"

"To see who wins. If you boys lose, I can go off anyplace I choose. But if you win, an' I leave ahead of time, I could be in a peck of trouble. Don't appear likely that you're goin' to win, though. Still—can't be too careful. Isn't that right?"

Smart bastard, Jeremiah thought. *Smart, wily bastard. Getting out of this swamp alive may take some doing.*

He scanned the area, saw nothing but narrow watercourses winding between mud banks and the great trees. Sunlit insects flitted over green-scummed water like flakes of living gold.

"What's your name?"

"Price."

"Which way's the house?"

"Yonder," Price told him, with such a faint inclination of his head that he might have meant any point on a whole quarter of the horizon.

"Your overseer anyplace close by?"

Price smiled. "Don't think so. He went off to fight jus' like the colonel. Ain't come back. Any overseein' to be done, Miz Catherine does it."

"That's the colonel's wife—"

" 'Pears you know a lot about the Rose family, mister soldier."

"My name is Kent. *Corporal* Kent. You call me that, hear?"

Silence. The black's eyes wandered down to the turtle, which appeared to be dead.

Even more sharply, Jeremiah said, "And lead me up to the house. I told you I have an important paper for your mistress. The colonel gave it to me before—"

Abruptly, he held back from breaking the news of Rose's death. The colonel's wife and daughter deserved to hear it first.

Price looked indifferent. God, what were those wicked Yanks in Washington City thinking about, granting freedom to men like this?

Of course Jeremiah knew very well what they were thinking about: the possibility that the blacks might rise up against their masters and aid the Northern war effort. Lincoln's detested proclamation in the first month of 1863 hadn't been so generous as to free every black man in the land, not by a damn sight. The President and that vicious pack of Republicans he served had only declared blacks were free in the rebelling states.

Lieutenant Colonel Rose had commented caustically on that limitation one time. "Old Abe has enough trouble on his hands without antagonizing the border states. Besides, I've read some of his speeches. He doesn't believe nigras are the white man's equal. He'd just as soon ship them all to Liberia and be shed of them. He's freeing *our* nigras to make it hotter for us, that's all. He's no humanitarian, he's a cheap politician who'll use any available trick to beat us down."

Jeremiah had accepted that as gospel; it jibed with all the anti-Northern talk he'd heard as a boy. Lincoln's proclamation was merely one more example of how dishonorably the enemy was conducting the war. Let the North—and nigras like this one—praise Abe Lincoln as a high-minded emancipator; Jeremiah knew that wasn't the truth at all.

With a move that rippled the muscles of his right forearm, Price reached up to flick sweat from his shiny blue cheek. He grinned, his eyes still mocking. "You don' finish a lot of your sentences, mister soldier."

Sentences? That was a mighty fancy word for an ordinary field hand. The realization confirmed his feeling that this was a dangerous man. Price probably knew how to read and write—had no doubt learned in secret, in defiance of the law.

"That's my business."

The smile remained fixed. "Guess it is. You say you got a paper from the colonel 'fore somethin' happened to him?"

"Before I left him. Also none of your affair. You take me to the house—right after you tell me something." He swallowed hard, trying to stand steady. Price cocked his head, waiting.

"You tell me what happened to my musket."

Price blinked twice, his expression deliberately blank. Jeremiah wanted to hit him.

"Musket?" Price turned his head right, then left. "Don't see no musket anyplace round here—"

"I had my Enfield and my cartridge box with me when I passed out! They're gone."

"Can't help that. I didn't spy any such 'quipment when I come onto you lyin' there. Guess somebody must have stole it during the night."

"Who the hell would wander through a place like this during the night?"

"Oh, mebbe some of the other niggers from the neighborhood, mister—ah, Corporal," Price corrected himself with an obviously forced politeness. "No, I surely can't tell you what happened to that gun and that box. You didn't have 'em when I found you, and since I was the only one awake right about then, guess you'll just have to take my word for it."

Jeremiah took a step forward, almost falling. "You stole them. You hid them someplace. *Didn't you?*"

Price's gaze admitted it. But his face grew pious. "Now that's a frightful thing to 'cuse a man of, Corporal. Me, a field buck, steal a white man's weapon an' hide it? Why, I could be whipped half to death for such a thing, if Miz Catherine was the kind who whipped her niggers. No, sir, I jus' don't know what become of those things you're talkin' 'bout. You'll just have to take my word."

Price's dazzling grin scorned him as a fool. Jeremiah concluded he might have been wrong about the cause of Price's insolence. The man's pigmentation might have nothing to do with it—

I wouldn't trust this son of a bitch if he were as white as me.

Price leaned down to scoop up the dead cooter. He sounded almost obsequious. "Care to hang onto my arm, Corporal?"

"No, thank you."

"You sure lookin' poorly. It's 'bout a mile to the house—"

"I'll manage!"

The black watched him, the smile gone. Jeremiah felt increasingly threatened. *He's taken the Enfield and hidden it where he can go back and find it. Use it.*

"This way, then."

Jeremiah staggered after him, wondering whether Lieutenant Colonel Rose's widow knew exactly what sort of treacherous rascal she was harboring. As if things weren't bad enough with those sixty thousand bluebellies somewhere to the northwest and no male overseer on the place, the two women he was going to meet were threatened by a mean, devious nigra who now had a gun.

Jeremiah's head pounded. He was shivering uncontrollably. The path out of the swamp seemed an endless maze.

He forced himself to keep up. Price might be older, but Jeremiah realized he couldn't let the black man think he was stronger or smarter—even though Price had already outfoxed him by purloining the musket and ammunition.

Price cast a quick glance backward. Jeremiah looked him straight in the eye. The black pretended to study a wild turkey roosting in a live oak, but Jeremiah thought he heard the man snicker.

Got to watch out for that one, he thought.

Walk behind him all the time.

Behind *him. Never ahead.*

Chapter IV
Rosewood

i

PRICE AND JEREMIAH approached Rosewood from a gently sloping cotton field that had been harvested earlier in the autumn. Though he was dizzy and hot—particularly now that he and the black man were into the full glare of the sunlight—he felt a peculiar sense of happiness at the sight of the plantation. To him it was very nearly a second home, so often and so lovingly had the slender, courtly Henry Rose described it.

Rosewood's land, accumulated by the colonel's father and grandfather, totaled about a thousand acres. Something like sixty-five slaves had worked the property, three-quarters of which the colonel had put into cotton, the remainder going into corn.

Originally Rosewood had been a rice plantation. But in the past two decades cotton had proved a far superior cash crop, even though the product of Rose's fields never commanded the premium prices of the cotton grown in Alabama, Mississippi, and Louisiana.

The plantation had a prosperous if oddly deserted look this Wednesday morning. Directly ahead stood two large, immaculate barns. Beyond them Jeremiah glimpsed the end of the white-painted three-story manse that faced a dirt highway on his left. A half-mile road led from the highway to the house between rows of live oaks Rose's grandfather had planted. Festoons of tillandsia hung from the branches, providing extra shade all the way to the white-painted fencing, the gate, and the bell with a rope pull.

As he and Price approached, more of the house came into view. He saw the front piazza, shaded by lattices twined with cypress vines. Square pillars reached up to a second-floor gallery running the entire length of the house. Starting near a well at the back of the building and running away from it at a right angle stood two long rows of slave cottages. The paint on the cottages had peeled in a few places, but otherwise they looked well kept. Directly behind the last two was a small picket-fenced burial ground.

Black men, women, and children idled in the dirt lane dividing the rows of tiny houses. An elderly slave tending a garden patch turned to stare at the gray-clad stranger and Price as they rounded the barn and passed three large hog pens. Magnolias had been planted near the perimeter of the pens. Rose had told Jeremiah he'd done that so the smell of the blooming trees would partially mask the stench of pig manure. This morning the stench was overpowering.

Past the manse Jeremiah saw the large gin house and two equally big corn cribs. Several blacks hailed Price from the cabin street. He acknowledged the greetings with little more than a curt nod. His arrogance told Jeremiah the man was someone special among his own kind.

A crowd had gathered near the stone well at the head of the lane, plainly curious about Price's companion. But Price's erect posture and steady stride seemed to preclude interference.

"Reckon we might find Miz Catherine in the office," the big man remarked as they walked onto the rear piazza. The cooling shade made Jeremiah feel better. But not much.

Price tossed the dead turtle onto the ground beyond the piazza. A naked tot darted toward it from the well. One swift glance from Price sent a young woman dashing out to pick up her child before he could touch the prize. She had a frightened look on her face.

Jeremiah leaned a sweaty palm against the side of the house, struggling to catch his breath. He felt close to passing out again. "Give me a minute—"

Price folded his arms, waiting. The black's silence seemed a condemnation of Jeremiah's weakness.

Voice rasping, Jeremiah said, "Pretty quiet for a weekday."

"That's true. Cotton's all baled. Corn's in. We're waitin' to see what's goin' to happen."

"What do you mean?"

"Judge Claypool's nigger, Floyd, he come rammin' over in the judge's buggy yesterday. He said there was Yanks on the march from Atlanta. A whole lot of Yanks."

The unblinking eyes fixed on Jeremiah. "You see any Yanks while you was comin' this way?"

Jeremiah shook his head. "But I met some cavalrymen. They said General Sherman's left the vicinity of the city with sixty—with some men."

"Well, now!" All at once Price seemed quite interested.

"Don't get your hopes too high. The cavalry boys didn't know which route the troops were taking."

"Judge Claypool's Floyd, he said Mr. Doremus of Louisville rode back from Milledgeville, an' when he left, the Yanks was almost there. That was Monday. Could be a mighty interesting Thanksgiving."

Thick-tongued, Jeremiah repeated, "Thanksgiving?"

"That's right." The corner of Price's mouth quirked up again. Damn the black thief for treating him like a slave instead of a master! "Didn't you 'member Thanksgiving's only two days away? We usually have a mighty big dinner for Thanksgiving. Maybe this year, the Yanks'll roast us instead. What d'you think?"

"I think you better shut up with jokes like that."

Price chuckled. "Yes, sir."

Jeremiah had completely forgotten the holiday. The amused gaze of the slave irritated him. He was willing to bet Price would love exactly the sort of Thanksgiving he'd described. Price would probably help the damn Yanks overrun Rosewood—using the Enfield he'd stolen.

The brief happiness he'd felt at finally reaching his destination was fading, driven from his mind by the black's silent contempt and the knowledge that he still had to inform the colonel's wife about her widowhood. He assumed she didn't know, and he didn't look forward to telling her. It would require tact; the proper words, a clear head. And his head was anything but clear. His ears buzzed; his eyes watered; his legs felt boneless. He wondered how much longer he could stay on his feet.

"My," Price murmured, evidently still thinking of Sherman. "We could sure have a real jubilee of a Thanksgiving round here—" Then, with a touch of impatience: "We can go inside whenever you feelin' up to it."

He wasn't, but he said, "I'm feeling up to it."

Price bobbed his head, leading him to the rear entrance.

As they stepped across the threshold, Price underwent an abrupt and noticeable transformation. He seemed to lose two or three inches in height. He bent his head forward slightly. His step became slower. The buck was trickier than old Billy Sherman himself!

They walked down a cool, dim hall smelling of furniture oil and more faintly of roasting sweet potatoes. Price's posture gave him an almost servile look. He knocked at an open doorway on the left. Immediately, Jeremiah heard a firm feminine voice.

"Come."

Dreading the encounter with Mrs. Rose, Jeremiah walked unsteadily toward the door as Price disappeared, scraping his bare feet in what was almost a shuffle.

ii

The light in the small, cluttered office had a hazy quality. The polished oak floor seemed to tilt. Price stood between Jeremiah and the woman at the desk. He couldn't see much of her except for a skirt, but he did glimpse objects on the desk. Open ledgers. A pen laid aside. A large ring with a dozen or more keys on it. A cut glass goblet half full of something that looked like fruit wine. Blackberry, he decided.

"Yes, Price, what is it?"

The slave deliberately thickened his speech. "Miz Catherine, I found this yere officer lyin' sick down in the swamp beyond the bottom. He come to find you—"

Blinking to clear his vision, Jeremiah quickly took in the details of the office. Two walls were entirely covered with shelves crowded with books. On the spine of one he recognized a design his mother had shown him once: a gold stamping of a partially filled and stoppered bottle—the mark of the publishing house of Kent and Son, owned by the despised Northern branch of the family.

Near the ledgers on the desk stood a small oil painting depicting a sad-eyed, sandy-bearded man. Rose. Beside it was an even smaller frame with a curling lock of bright red hair sealed under glass above a small square card. On the card in ink that had long ago faded, someone had written:

Serena, 1846

Serena was Rose's daughter by his first marriage. The colonel had alluded to the marriage several times, but never discussed it in any detail—nor his former wife. Jeremiah had gotten the impression that Serena's mother must have been the wrong sort. Rose was close-mouthed about her, in contrast to his constant praise of Catherine.

He'd said Catherine was a woman of warm, loving temperament—the closest a gentleman ever came to admitting his wife had a passionate streak. He described her as intelligent and trusting of her fellow human beings, willing to believe only the best about them—including the slaves—but not lacking the strength to take action if her original opinion proved wrong. Jeremiah was going to have to warn this paragon of womanhood about Price.

Dimly, he realized Price was still speaking with a slurry politeness quite different from his earlier rude mockery.

"—poor officer, he lost his gun during the night. Those trash niggers of Judge Claypool's who fish round here probably picked it off him. I think we ought to report it to the judge right quick. We sure don't want no niggers with muskets runnin' loose—'specially with them Yanks on the way like this officer says."

Damned liar, Jeremiah thought. But his throat was too dry to utter the accusation. Besides, the most important matter at the moment was the news about Rose and the letter.

Price stepped back politely as the woman stood up.

"Good morning, young man." Catherine Rose extended her hand, unconcerned about the mud on Jeremiah's fingers.

The colonel's widow was a handsome woman in her forties, with broad hips, a slim waist, and full breasts tightly bound by a faded gingham dress. She had a generous mouth set in an oval face, and intelligent, direct gray eyes. On her cheek just to the right of her lips was a tiny mole, like a punctuation mark. Her light brown hair was beginning to whiten.

The hand grasping Jeremiah's was neither soft nor smooth. "Price says you want to see me?"

"Yes, Mrs. Rose. My name's Corporal Kent—"

Recognition widened her eyes. "Henry's orderly! He wrote about you once. And in a highly complimentary fashion. You don't look well," she added with a quick frown.

"I'm fine, ma'am."

"But Price said he found you unconscious."

"Just sleeping, that's all."

Skeptically, she surveyed him. The odor of fruit wine was unmistakable. "You're pale as death. Skinny, too."

"I was hurt in action near Atlanta."

"Good heavens, you've come all the way from *Atlanta?*"

"Yes." His hand groped for the oilskin pouch. "Before I left, your husband gave me a letter to deliver. My home's Virginia, but I promised him I'd bring this to you."

He handed her the pouch. Tears filled her eyes.

Then Catherine Rose seemed angry at her own weakness. She dashed a hand against her cheek. She began to examine the pouch as if it were some kind of holy article. A wistful, affectionate smile softened her face. Jeremiah could understand why Rose had spoken highly of her.

Come to think of it, Rose had been lavish in complimenting both his women. While Mrs. Rose opened the pouch, Jeremiah recalled a rare moment of comradeship when Rose had rambled for a while about his daughter's relationship with her stepmother.

Rose had said his wife lavished every attention on the child of that first marriage. Yet the colonel believed his daughter somehow considered herself Catherine's rival for his affection. She was a good child, Rose said. High-spirited, but with a certain reserve that made it extremely difficult for him to ever know what she was thinking. The rivalry between mother and stepdaughter was only suspected, never overt or disruptive. Catherine's affection and forbearance prevented that.

One other detail about Mrs. Rose slipped into his mind—the woman was a transplanted Yankee. It was apparent after she glanced briefly at the letter without reading it. He detected a faint nasal quality in her voice that was distinctly un-Southern.

"You were very kind to bring me this, Corporal Kent. You've seen my husband recently?"

Jeremiah's forehead burned.

"Yes, ma'am. Fairly recently. He gave me the letter at Jonesboro, before General Sherman took Atlanta."

"Jonesboro?" She whispered it. "Jonesboro was in late August."

"Ma'am, haven't—haven't you received any word about him yourself?"

"Not for weeks. And we've had only scattered reports of the disasters the armies encountered." A tolerant smile. "Henry was never too faithful about writing letters home. Sometimes, before he left, I practically had to force him to pick up a pen to write someone on business. Or when a special occasion absolutely demanded a letter. A birth in the family of one of his relatives. A death—"

Her hand closed on the pouch and letter. She looked at Jeremiah. "Oh, dear Lord in heaven. He's dead. That's why you're here—"

"I—" Somehow he couldn't get the words out.

"That's why you've traveled so far."

Overcome, Jeremiah could only swallow and nod.

Catherine Rose dropped the letter and pouch. She walked around him, unsteadily, but without hurrying. At the door she called, "Serena?"

"He wrote the letter a night or two before he took a ball in the Jonesboro action—" Jeremiah began.

Clutching the doorframe, Catherine Rose raised her voice slightly. "Serena? Come down!"

"—he saved my life. After the"—Jeremiah realized he was rambling, but he couldn't help himself—"after the surgeons said they couldn't do anything for him, he begged me to bring that letter to you. I swore I would."

"Serena!"

She struck one frustrated blow on the jamb of the door. Then she clenched her fist and lowered it to her side as if it were a separate living organism she had to fight. The ringing in Jeremiah's ears turned to a high, windy whine. Without warning, his legs gave out.

He started to tumble forward. With quick action, Price could have caught him. The black didn't move.

Arms folded across his huge chest, Price watched the young soldier fall. Jeremiah had a swift impression of Price's eyes. Malicious. Amused. But the slave's "Oh, my!" had had an appropriately alarmed sound.

Jeremiad's jaw slammed on the polished oak floor. He heard an exclamation from Mrs. Rose. Running footsteps—Serena hurrying to the office?

The footfalls grew softer instead of louder. The roar in his ears drowned them out. Gasping, he flopped over on his back, his mind a jumble of frantic thoughts.

Sherman's on the way.

That black bastard's got my Enfield.

She'll be too upset to pay any mind.

But I've got to warn—

Darkness cut off the rest.

CHAPTER V
THE WOMEN

i

HE WOKE AT TWILIGHT, in a bedroom at the second floor front.

He lay awhile in the high bed, reflecting that perhaps he was beginning to mend. His belly didn't ache quite so badly. The ear trouble and dizziness had left him. Best of all, he felt clean.

His filthy uniform had disappeared. He wore a man's flannel nightshirt which because of his height reached only to his knees. A flush burned his cheeks when he realized someone had undressed and washed him and re-bandaged his leg wound with new, spotless linen. He hoped it had been one of the nigra women he'd seen around the place.

Downstairs, voices murmured. He swung his legs off the edge of the bed, stretching luxuriously. He was stiff. Still a mite feverish, too. But he was astonished to discover he was hungry.

When he stood up, barefoot on the smooth, pegged floor, he felt a familiar pressure. He located the chamber pot in a corner. The china surface was decorated with a hand-painted scroll bearing the words *A Salute to Old Spoons.*

Spoons? He studied the pot, then recalled the man to whom the word referred. He laughed for the first time in longer than he could remember.

He picked up the pot, lifted the lid and looked inside. On the bottom, the artist had enameled a man's portrait. Jeremiah recognized the puffy cheeks, drooping mustache, and cocked eye of the infamous Beast Butler, the military governor of conquered New Orleans. Butler had earned the South's hatred with a regulation specifying that any New Orleans gentlewoman caught showing disrespect to the occupying troops would be dealt with as if she were a prostitute. Sometimes the Beast was called Old Cockeye. He'd also been called Spoons because he'd reportedly plundered silverware from the city's finer houses. Jeremiah replaced the pot on the floor, pulled up his nightshirt, and cheerfully pissed on old Spoons.

He was just replacing the lid when he heard steps in the hall. Hastily he clambered back into bed. A knock was followed by a respectful, "Sir?"

"I'm awake. Come in."

A small, fragile black woman appeared. She was barely five feet tall, with wrists no thicker than both his thumbs put together. She must have been seventy, but the eyes in the dark, lined face sparkled. She glanced at the white streak in his hair as she set a mug containing a steaming drink on the table beside the bed.

"You feeling any better, sir?"

"Much, thank you. By the way, my name's Jeremiah, Jeremiah Kent."

A nod. "Miz Catherine told me. I'm Maum Isabella." She touched the mug. "I brought you this to see if you could keep something down."

"Smells first-rate. What is it?"

"One of my toddies. Peach brandy laced with white sugar. If it sets well, I've got ham in the kitchen. Ham and hominy."

Jeremiah sipped the sweet beverage and found the first taste not only bearable but delicious. He wiped his lips with his wrist and smiled at the diminutive black woman who stood with her hands folded at the waist of her patched skirt. There was nothing servile about *her* speech or demeanor, no pretense of the kind he'd seen Price indulge in. The woman obviously occupied a position of importance in the house and knew it.

"That's damn—that's very good, Maum—"

"Isabella, sir."

He gestured at his nightshirt. "Who fixed me up this way?"

"Miz Catherine did. Soon after you passed out downstairs."

Blushing, he said, "You mean she didn't go to pieces when she learned about the colonel?"

The old woman shook her head. "Miz Catherine knew the risks when he went off to serve. She's mighty grieved, of course. So's everybody on the place—excepting two or three bad niggers."

He presumed Price was included in that last group.

"Miz Catherine's a mighty strong lady—for a Yankee woman," Maum Isabella added, allowing herself a small, wry smile. "Also, we have a house to run. Chores to do. She allowed herself 'bout a half hour of crying, that's all. She'll be up to see you soon, I imagine. Serena too."

The mention of the younger woman seemed to carry less enthusiasm than the reference to Mrs. Rose. Then, sympathetically, she said, "You must have seen some hard fighting."

He didn't understand the reason for her words, so he only nodded.

"What I mean—" A frail hand pointed. "You're mighty young to be turning gray."

"Oh, this—" He ran his fingers through the white streak. "That's from Chickamauga. A Minié ball knocked my cap off—grazed the top of my head. The ball was almost spent, so all I got was a good thump. Guess it did something to the hair, though. A surgeon said it would grow back the right color, but it hasn't."

"I see." Her curiosity satisfied, she started for the door. "Well, you want anything, just stomp on the floor and someone will come up right quick. Oh, I nearly forgot. Tomorrow morning—"

"Thanksgiving."

"We don't have a lot to say thanks for this year," the little black woman declared. "The colonel's gone. Those Yanks are coming out from Atlanta."

"So the word's gotten around?"

"Yes, sir. I heard about what you told Price. By now most everyone on the place knows."

"Maum Isabella, may I ask you a question that might not be any of my business?"

"You can surely ask, Mr. Jeremiah. I'll decide about a reply when I hear the question."

"Where'd that buck come from? Price, I mean. Has he always been on the plantation?"

"No. The colonel bought him five years ago in a batch of half a dozen niggers Mr. Samples owned. Mr. Samples had the next farm over from this one. He went to his reward very suddenly. Had no kin to take over the property, so the colonel picked up part of the acreage and some of his people too. All good people except that Price. He came from Louisiana when he was young. He was raised by a man who treated him bad. Maybe that explains why he acts mean. But it doesn't excuse it. I've always had a queer feeling about Price."

"What sort of feeling?"

"He could have been raised in a pig lot or a palace and he'd still have come out mean." She smiled. "The Yanks don't have a corner on meanness, you know. Fact is, there ain't a single group in all God's creation dares claim their baskets are free of bad peaches."

"Price sure strikes me as one."

Maum Isabella didn't disagree. "Most of the niggers on the place can't abide him. There *are* a few who encourage him on the sly. They like to see him get away with being uppity. Miz Catherine should have sold him off long ago. Well, I got things to do. I expect the mistress will be here soon. We'll have dinner tomorrow afternoon, late. In the morning there's to be a memorial service in the parlor. For the colonel. Most everybody'll be there."

The sentence implied a question about his presence. Jeremiah nodded, his dark eyes shining in the candle glow. The toddy had warmed and relaxed him. The scent of roses and dahlias drifting in from the bluish dark was like a balm after the stenches of war: pus, dirt, offal, powder, blood—

"So will I. The colonel was a good man. He saved my life."

At last Maum Isabella looked as if she approved of him.

"I'm happy to hear you'll be able to pay your respects," she said as she opened the door. She marched out as Jeremiah reached for the toddy.

He was incredibly content. He savored not only the drink but the comforting feeling of being halfway well again. Well, clean, and in a safe haven.

A *temporarily* safe haven, he reminded himself. Out there in the Georgia dark, Sherman's soldiers were marching relentlessly. Rosewood might lie directly in their path.

He finished the toddy. He couldn't pretend he wasn't frightened by the possibility of Sherman's approach. But the idea brought a touch of pleasure as well. After too long a time, he might again be called to do something worthwhile in this war.

ii

Catherine Rose looked in about twenty minutes later.

She was dressed more formally than when he'd first met her. She'd changed from her faded gingham to a full-skirted black gown with rustling underlayers that bulked the skirt into the fashionable hooped shape.

Her bodice looked different than before. Her breasts were pushed up higher, more pointed and prominent. He assumed she was wearing one of those steel-boned corsets. The kind he'd seen in his mother's empty room in Lexington one time, and stolen in to touch with a feeling of experimentation and acute embarrassment.

Even though Jeremiah was eighteen, his knowledge of the intimate details of a woman's life were limited. In the army he'd often bragged about visiting a lady of easy virtue when he was only fifteen. It was the typical young soldier's lie. He was totally innocent—and ashamed of it. Now the sight of Mrs. Rose's figure generated a lewd excitement all the more thrilling because it was shameful.

Clad in black as she was, the widow's only concession to her duties as mistress of a household was a lace-edged apron of white lawn. Even the heavy crocheted net holding the large chignon at the back of her head was black. She'd dressed her hair since he'd last seen her.

"Corporal Kent." She greeted him with a small, strained smile.

"Evening, ma'am."

"Maum Isabella reports you're feeling somewhat better." She stood at the foot of the bed, composed but pale.

"Thank you, I am. Please call me Jeremiah."

"Of course. I'm truly sorry you had to suffer so much to bring that letter to Rosewood."

"Why, that's all forgotten, ma'am," he fibbed. "You're the one who—" Caught in an awkward trap, he didn't want to finish.

The mole beside her mouth lifted as she tried to smile with greater warmth. Her eyes were puffy. Otherwise she was in perfect control. He admired her courage.

She finished the sentence for him. "Who has suffered? I'll admit I did let down for a little while. But the truth is, even before you arrived, I was beginning to think something had happened to Henry. He usually forced himself to write a letter every three or four weeks. A few lines. But I hadn't received one in two and a half months."

She drew a cane chair to the bed and sat down. He smelled the fruit wine again, strongly.

"Besides, there's no time for excessive indulgence in grief. With all those stories of Yanks loose around Milledgeville, we must get busy. I need to make a list of what we should hide—food, furnishings, valuables—in case Sherman does come this way."

"I want to help any way I can," he said, suddenly self-conscious about being alone with a woman in this flower-scented bedroom. It hardly mattered that the woman was at least twice his age. "I'll be out of bed before you know it."

"Very kind of you, Jeremiah. I appreciate your willingness. I'll feel free to call on you. Some of the bucks on the place may not stay."

"Not stay? Why?"

"Judge Claypool's boy, Floyd—he came over yesterday—he told me a great many nigras are running away from their masters to travel with Sherman's army."

An awkward pause. Jeremiah felt compelled to say something more about her husband. He struggled—not at ease with sentiments appropriate to such a moment.

"Whatever happens, you must let me help. I wouldn't be

drawing a breath if it wasn't for the colonel. I'm truly sorry he—"

A red-knuckled hand lifted. "Not necessary, Jeremiah. Your feelings for him are evident. And your loyalty. You got here."

Her eyes focused on the gallery, and the dark. "Henry was an excellent husband. I liked him from the first time he came to tea at Christ College. That's where I was teaching when we met. I was an instructor in the classics. I'm originally from Connecticut."

"Yes, he told me."

"I came down to Georgia to accept a position at the female institute at Montpelier when I was twenty-two. Henry had recently—had lost his first wife—" Her voice trailed off. "His aunt was also on the faculty at the institute. She introduced us. She was an Episcopalian, but Henry was a Congregationalist as I am. I never regretted my decision to marry him. Or to bring up his child."

Another pause. Then she asked how Henry Rose had died.

He described the circumstances in a guarded way, emphasizing the colonel's heroism and omitting the more gruesome details. He made no mention of the blood, the filth, the brutality of the field hospital—nor of Rose's despair about the course of the war. Catherine nodded from time to time. Once he thought he saw tears in her eyes.

She asked about her husband's body. Again he resorted to partial honesty. He cited the confusion that always followed a battle and took the blame for not keeping track of Rose's remains. He avoided any reference to the heap onto which those canvas-covered bodies were dumped one after another. He tried to finish with something positive.

"He was thinking of you right to the end, ma'am. Never a word about himself. Just about you. How you'd need assistance—"

A small sigh. "It appears we will. It pains me to say it, but over the last few months I've noticed a change in the attitude of a few of the nigras. They still do their duties, but they've become"—she searched for the proper term—"impudent."

He saw no reason to skirt the issue any longer. "Is Price one of them?"

"The worst, I'm afraid."

"Well, then, I should tell you what I really think happened to my musket."

Before he could begin, the door opened. A girl walked in.

Her dress was as black as her stepmother's. But her bright red hair framing pale cheeks shone a fire, so that like she hardly seemed in mourning.

The girl was taller than Catherine, with pale blue eyes and a splendid figure. There was an astonishing perfection about her features. Together with her delicately white skin, it gave her an almost angelic air. But the liveliness of her eyes flawed the effect.

She came quickly to the bedside, her skirts gathered up in her hands. The older woman turned. "I thought perhaps you'd forgotten us, Serena."

"No, not at all," the girl answered, ignoring the hint of criticism in Catherine's remark.

Serena Rose studied Jeremiah. She was a lovely creature, but plainly not the older woman's child.

"I do hope you're comfortable, Mr. Kent," she remarked with a smile that struck him as sweetly polite rather than sincere.

"Fine, thank you."

He knew the girl was two years older than he was: twenty. The difference seemed an abyss. And even before he'd spoken his three-word answer, she glided to a wall mirror to study her hair. Somehow that angered him.

iii

"You could be a bit more cordial to our guest, my dear."

Serena spun around, her smile still ingenuous. "Was I being otherwise, Catherine? I'm so sorry."

She was hard to read: reserved, every move studied. While Catherine's politeness masked feelings she felt it might be unseemly to reveal, Serena's behavior apparently concealed a lack of any feeling whatever. Or, if she did have feelings, she kept them deeply hidden. He began to suspect she'd come up to the bedroom solely because it was an obligation.

"I apologize if I was rude to you, Mr. Kent," she said. "The news about Papa, and all this talk about the Yankees—it's quite upsetting."

"I can certainly understand—"

"But now we have a trustworthy man to help us," Catherine said.

"That's reassuring," Serena replied, though a flicker of her eyes suggested she doubted *man* was an appropriate term for Jeremiah. He was both repelled by the girl's cool manner and attracted by her physical beauty—of which she was quite conscious. She stood so that he had a clear view of her figure—her bosom—in profile. In a perfunctory way, she asked, "Where do you come from, Mr. Kent?"

"I was serving with the Sixty-third Virginia until I was reassigned as your father's orderly on the division staff."

"Virginia," Serena repeated. "That's a mighty long way from Georgia."

He decided he might as well get some of the details out of the way. He told them a little about his family. First his mother, still in the endangered Shenandoah. Then his brother Gideon, captured in the firefight that slew Jeb Stuart at Yellow Tavern.

No, he replied in response to a question from Catherine, there was absolutely no word of Gideon's whereabouts, and he was worried. Men were known to be dying by the hundreds in the Northern prisons, now that Grant had put a stop to the exchange of prisoners in order to further deplete the South's manpower.

The account of his middle brother was only slightly less grim. For a few moments he spoke glowingly of Matt's sunny nature, his fondness for games, the memorable quality of his drawings. Then he told them Matt had been—and presumably still was—on a blockade runner, a fast, Liverpool-built steam vessel slipping back and forth between the Bermudas and Wilmington on the Cape Fear River. But Matt's last, badly spelled letter had been delivered to Lexington over eight months ago. There'd been no news since. Either Matt hadn't written again, or a letter from Fan with news of him had failed to reach Jeremiah. Whatever the circumstances, there was a question mark after Matt's name nearly as ominous as the one after Gideon's.

Jeremiah concluded with a brief mention of the other branch of the family: his father, Jephtha, from whom his mother was divorced, and who was now a Methodist pastor again—this time in the Northern wing of the divided church up in New York. Jephtha had originally been an itinerant parson in Virginia before the Methodists split over the slave issue. Then he'd been a newspaperman on the New York *Union*.

"There's at least one more in the family up north, but I know even less about him. His name's Louis. He has a wife and a small boy, and he's a rich man. Owns that newspaper Jephtha worked for, plus part of a steelworks, some kind of cotton factory, and a publishing company in Boston called Kent and Son. I saw a book from the company in your office, Mrs. Rose."

Serena's blue eyes showed greater interest. "So the Northern relatives are the ones with money, Mr. Kent?"

"Yes, Miss Serena. I'm afraid that's true for the present. Eventually, though, my brothers and I—"

Before he could finish, and tell them he and Matt and Gideon might one day be wealthy in their own right, Catherine interrupted. "I think we've taxed Jeremiah quite long enough."

Serena pouted. He'd piqued her curiosity. She was gazing at him as if trying to guess the ending of his unfinished sentence.

"He was kind enough to describe how your father died," Catherine said.

There was no response. If the girl felt any emotion she never showed it. Jeremiah was fascinated by her good looks, but he began to think he didn't like her much as a person.

"And we were discussing the attitude of some of the nigras when you came in." Catherine swung back to Jeremiah. "I hate to tire you further. But you mentioned something about a musket?"

"The same one Price talked about in the office," Jeremiah said, nodding. "I slept all last night on the creek bank where he found me. When I woke up, the musket was gone. My cartridge box, too. Your nigra claimed someone else must have come along and taken it. But I'm pretty certain he took it."

Catherine frowned.

"I think he *hid* it," Jeremiah went on more firmly. "I don't believe it's safe to have a nigra you call impudent hiding a gun when the Yanks are on the way."

The discussion sparked a combative look in Serena's eyes. "Now let me get this clear. Price claimed he *didn't* take the musket?"

"That's correct, Miss Serena. He said some nigras who fish down there must have pilfered it."

"And you have no evidence one way or the other?"

He admitted that was true.

Catherine Rose chewed her lip. "I hesitate to make an issue without proof. If the Yanks arrive we'll need the support of every nigra on the place. Price has a mean streak in him. But it's usually directed at the other slaves."

"He's been saucy to you lately, Catherine," Serena flared.

"I know. But I still don't think he'd do us any harm."

"Mrs. Rose, I beg to disagree." Jeremiah struggled to sit up straighter in bed, ignoring the way his nightshirt hiked over his knees, much to Serena's amusement. "I think that buck should be questioned until he admits the theft."

"So do I!" Serena exclaimed, the candles putting little reflections in her pupils.

Again Catherine negated the idea with a shake of her head. "We have always conducted the affairs of Rosewood in a humane and Christian way. Right or wrong, we'll continue to do so. At this difficult time, I won't have the nigras losing their trust in me because of Price."

"I heard most of them hate him," Jeremiah responded.

Catherine sighed. "Maum Isabella's been talking again. She's right. But there are delicate balances on a plantation such as this one. If I accuse Price, he'll never admit the theft because there's no evidence against him. To force a confession, I'd have to punish him. Then the nigras might switch their loyalties—even if only briefly. I'd become their enemy. I don't want to be their enemy with Sherman on the loose."

"But, Catherine—" Serena protested.

"Child," the older woman broke in, her voice soft but strong, "I have the final say in this. Even granted Price is lying, I don't intend to provoke more turmoil. We'll give him the benefit of the doubt and stay alert. That's enough for the time being."

Serena stamped her foot. "Stay alert till he breaks in one night and shoots us!"

"Serena, don't argue."

Red-cheeked, the girl blazed back, "Yes, I will! You're too easy on the niggers! Mr. Kent's warned us, but you won't pay any attention. You're always so blasted anxious to have everyone think you're a saint!"

The color draining from her face, Catherine whispered, "I try to behave in a Christian way."

"When the neighbors are here! They never see that blackberry wine you're always—"

"Be quiet!"

Catherine stared at Serena until the younger woman looked away.

Jeremiah was embarrassed yet morbidly fascinated by the sudden display of hostility between the mother and stepdaughter. Sensing his discomfort, Catherine stood up.

"It's no disrespect to Jeremiah if we don't press the issue with Price. We'll be careful."

Careful isn't enough, he thought. *I saw that buck's eyes down by the river—you didn't.*

Serena refused to surrender. "We should do more than that. We should force Price to admit he's lying. *Whip* him!"

"I will hear absolutely nothing more on the subject."

Catherine said it with such vehemence that Serena looked as if she'd been struck. She opened her mouth to retort, then noted the fierceness of Catherine's gaze and whirled away. Jeremiah thought the older woman's prudence was ill-advised. But it wasn't his place to enter into a family feud whose nature and origins he didn't understand.

Trying to take the sting out of the confrontation, Catherine walked over and reached for her stepdaughter's arm. Serena turned again, drawing back. For a moment the women faced one another.

Finally Serena stepped aside, her cheeks pink, her face far from angelic.

Catherine walked toward the door. Serena hesitated, then followed.

"Good night, Jeremiah," Catherine said in a strained voice. "Maum Isabella will look in presently to see whether you need anything."

"I am feeling a wee bit hungry—"

"Then I'll send her up immediately."

Opening the door, she reached for Serena's arm a second time. The girl gasped as the older woman literally dragged her out.

Jeremiah sank back in bed, disturbed. In his opinion, Catherine Rose's ideas about handling the situation with Price were all wrong. He'd need to be watchful. Very watchful.

And those two women—they were certainly a puzzlement. They might be related by marriage, but they clearly weren't related by temperament.

Settling himself against the pillows, he inhaled the sweet scent of the blossoms outside the house. Just what kind of hornet's nest had he blundered into on this plantation?

Chapter VI

Shadow of the Enemy

i

"Mr. Kent?"

The whisper brought him bolt upright in bed, surprised and terrified. Then the terror varnished as he realized who had spoken. But bewilderment lingered.

The candles had gone out. From the angle of the November moonlight falling across the gallery, he judged the hour to be very late. Serena Rose was kneeling beside the bed, her face no more than a blur in the silver-blue gloom.

She repeated his name. He mumbled, "I'm awake," although he was still drowsy. Turning on his side, he could feel the warmth of her breath on the back of his hand.

"Catherine doesn't know I'm in here. You won't say anything?"

"Won't say—?" He fought a yawn, knuckled his eyes. Answered more coherently: "No, 'course not."

"I wanted to tell you I went down to the cabins." Her voice was low, the words rushed. "I asked Leon to help me. Leon's a buck who was born at Rosewood, he's trustworthy. We talked to Price." Her tone hardened. "I ordered half a dozen laid on him out by the burial ground."

"Laid—?" His lethargy left him. "You mean the whip?"

She nodded. "We don't use it often, but we have one."

"You did the right thing," he said with conviction. His mouth had that bloodless, cruel look for a moment. "Did Price confess?"

"Not on your life! He just took the whipping without a word. But you should have seen the way he looked at me!"

She clutched his wrist. He felt something wet on her fingers when they brushed the cuff of his nightshirt.

"He stole the musket, Mr. Kent. I know he did!"

"What if your stepmother discovers that you—"

"She won't. Leon won't say anything to Catherine. I forced him to promise. I doubt Price will say anything either. He's scared of me," she hurried on. "He understands I'm not soft the way Catherine is. And tattling, that's not his style. He'll wait for a chance to get back at me."

"Then you took a risk you shouldn't have taken. I'd have been on my feet soon. I could have—"

"I didn't want to wait a minute longer. I had to find out whether he was up to something. Now I'm sure he is. Catherine's wrong and you're right. But now there are two of us to keep a sharp eye on him. Catherine's too trusting, Mr. Kent. She still believes some of those pretty words they taught her in church when she was a girl. She doesn't realize how that nigger hates us!"

Her fingers closed tighter on his wrist. The tips still had that curious wet feel.

"I just wanted to say you're right—and I'm glad you're here to look after us."

He didn't quite realize what had happened until it was over. She came off her knees and leaned near, planting a quick kiss on his cheek. For a moment her breast brushed his forearm. Under the coverlet his body responded quickly and automatically.

He could see very little of her face in that moment when it was close to his—half of it was in darkness, half a pale blur. In the moonight her red hair glowed almost white.

With a rustle of gathered skirts, she scrambled to her feet. Why the devil was she so interested in him all of a sudden? he wondered. The first time she'd come into his room she'd hardly paid any attention to him. Why had she reversed herself? Was it because she and her stepmother were at odds? Because she wanted to win him to her side?

Serena squeezed his hand. "I'd better scat out of here. I think Catherine's asleep, but I'm not sure. Her room's down the hall just beyond mine. I know some of the house niggers are still up. If one of them sees me, by this time tomorrow people all over the county will be calling me a scarlet woman." She uttered a low laugh, sounding more amused than worried.

He had no time to say anything as she hurried away. The door clicked shut before he knew it.

He was still mightily confused—downright stunned, in fact—by the swift secret visit. Of course he was gratified that the girl had swung over to his side of the argument about Price. But she'd indeed taken a scandalous chance—risked compromising her reputation by slipping into his room. Apparently she wasn't afraid of such gambles.

Serena's eagerness to punish the black bothered him, too.

Not that Price didn't deserve punishment. He did—if only as a warning. What troubled Jeremiah was her tone of voice during parts of the conversation. She'd sounded as if she'd actually *enjoyed* ordering the man lashed. Puzzling over her curious nature, he drifted into sleep.

When he woke in the morning, he happened to glance at the sleeve of his nightshirt. He caught his breath.

He gazed at the brown stain on the cuff and realized why Serena's hand had felt wet. Leon hadn't been the only one who had touched the whip.

He spent ten minutes naked in front of the washstand, scrubbing at the stain. He couldn't get it all out because the blood had dried. A telltale blotch remained. Not too noticeable, he hoped.

He poured the discolored water into the chamber pot and hastily put the lid in place with a hand that shook just a little. He'd have whipped Price dispassionately, for the sake of prudence. She'd apparently whipped him for pleasure.

Lord! An angel face like that—what was behind it? Part of him was drawn toward discovering the answer. Another part warned he'd be into dangerous depths if he did.

ii

"O God, our help in ages past,
Our hope for years to come—"

Jeremiah moved his lips, unfamiliar with the words of the hymn sung with such lusty confidence by the people in the sitting room of Rosewood just after eleven o'clock that same Thanksgiving morning.

Outside, a brilliant sun shone. During the past hour, some twenty white neighbors had arrived. The men were all elderly, the women of varying ages. Dressed in Sunday clothes, the visitors stood unself-consciously among the plantation's blacks who filled the rest of the room. More of the slaves packed the entrance hall and part of the front piazza near the main door.

Even Price had come to pay tribute to the departed colonel. Jeremiah could see him just outside the sitting room arch, bellowing the hymn as if what Serena had described last night had never happened.

"Our shelter from the stormy blast,
And our eternal home."

Noting Price's erect posture and cheerful expression, Jeremiah wondered if he'd dreamed the nocturnal visit.

Serena had again dressed like her stepmother—in black crepe. As the group sang, she played the London-made pianoforte. For a number of reasons Jeremiah was decidedly uncomfortable in the midst of the gathering.

Just after he'd washed out the blood, Maum Isabella had delivered a pair of the colonel's linen trousers and a luxurious white silk shirt, as well as underclothing. Everything was too small. He looked and felt like a bumpkin in the ill-fitting garments. Neither did he like wearing a dead man's clothes.

And before the service, he'd been required to meet all the guests and repeat an involved series of falsehoods about his wounds and fictitious discharge. Grave-faced people, among them a couple named Jesperson, had bobbed their heads sympathetically in response to his romanticized description of Henry Rose's death.

"Under the shadow of Thy throne,
Still may we dwell secure—"

Pretending to sing, he found his mind returning to the crosscurrents that seemed to be aswirl in the house. There was a curious, secretive quality about them. For instance, while standing at Catherine's elbow and speaking with two of the visitors, he'd picked up the unmistakable tang of blackberry wine again. If she'd drink before company came, she was under greater tension than she permitted others to see.

The right hand of the Congregational pastor, the Reverend Emory Pettus, arced back and forth as he led the hymn to its loud climax. Pettus was an immense, paunchy man in a warm-looking black alpaca coat with a secession rosette in the lapel. He kept his eyes on the ceiling and sang in a bellowing baritone.

"Sufficient is Thine arm alone,
And our defense is—"

Abruptly Serena lifted her fingers from the keyboard and turned toward the open front windows nearby. Her net-bound chignon glowed even with the morning sun muted by the gently stirring lace curtains.

The various singers straggled on to a weak finish. Pettus frowned as Catherine took her hand from the hymnal she'd been sharing with the minister.

"Serena, why did you stop?"

The girl pointed outdoors. "I heard the bell ring. Twice."

"Nonsense." Catherine smiled frostily. "No one would ring the bell and disturb—"

She was interrupted by a commotion on the piazza. A white-haired old fellow with palsy tottered to a window, mumbling complaints. Outside, a black shouted, "Miz Catherine? Buggy comin' up the lane!"

"I told you someone rang the bell!" Serena was vindicated.

Catherine ignored her, looking concerned. A slave boy

of fourteen or fifteen slipped through the crowd in the sitting room, an apologetic expression on his face.

"Who is it, Zeph?" Catherine asked.

"Marse Claypool, ma'am."

The one referred to as the judge? Jeremiah wondered. Catherine had already commented on the surprising absence of the Claypools.

Jeremiah heard a rattle of wheels and the sound of hoofs scattering small stones. The nigras outdoors shouted questions as the vehicle halted. The horses of the other rigs pulled up in front began to neigh and stamp. Catherine hurried to one of the open windows, thrust the curtains aside, and stuck her head out, not a little annoyed.

"Theodore, we're right in the middle of the service!"

"My profound apologies." The man had a wheezy voice, sounded out of breath. "I'd have been here sooner, but I was waiting for Floyd to come back from another trip to Milledgeville. Those folks indoors—all of you—better pay attention! The Yanks are in the capital!"

The guests all began talking at once. The slaves murmured among themselves. Over the noise, Catherine called, "Are you sure?"

"Positive. The first of them arrived day before yesterday. Two whole corps of Union infantry, the Fourteenth and the Twentieth. Sherman's with their commander, General Slocum."

Absolute pandemonium then. A portly woman near Jeremiah gasped, closed her eyes, and started to faint. Her male companion tried to catch her, failed, and knelt beside her, chafing her wrists and whispering, "God preserve us. God preserve us."

Jeremiah shoved his way to the windows to hear the rest.

"—wouldn't believe what's happening in Milledgeville, Catherine. The Yanks are tearing up the railroad tracks! Heating the ties and bending 'em around trees. Sherman's hairpins, that's their clever little name for 'em. Floyd said he saw soldiers destroying books from the state library. And Secretary of State Burnett's wife"—the unseen man paused to suck in another breath as the guests and the blacks fell silent—"she had to bury the state seal under her house and hide documents from the legislature in her pigsty."

Catherine leaned halfway out the window. "In heaven's name why?"

"Because that infernal Sherman has issued orders that his men can forage liberally on the country. Those were his exact words—*'forage liberally!'* Of course the sanctimonious devil's also announcing that he hasn't authorized his men to enter homes or molest citizens unless there's guerrilla resistance."

"But the Home Guards are mobilized!" someone exclaimed.

The judge snorted. "Precisely. That qualifies as resistance. So Sherman looks the other way while his scalawags rob private dwellings and burn farms and plantations where the owners have tried to hide some of their crops. Evidently *that's* guerrilla resistance, too! Believe me, Floyd saw barns and gins being put to the torch—houses being gutted in Milledgeville—he talked to one family whose whole place was torn down! They had to take refuge in an overturned boxcar in the rail yards."

Jeremiah pressed up beside Catherine and lifted the curtain. In the drive he saw a bony, perspiring old man seated in a two-wheeled hooded chaise. Red dust covered the man's frock coat and trousers.

"Can't the militia stop them?" Jeremiah asked.

"Old codgers like me? Boys? A few cavalrymen?" Claypool harumphed. "I doubt it."

"Are they headed this way?"

"Well, they seem to be after rail junctions and the larger towns, so I expect they are. They'll probably come right past here on the way to Millen."

Consternation again.

The man whose wife had fainted helped her to her feet, muttering apologies to Catherine. She didn't hear, standing with one hand shielding her half-closed eyes. The man and his wife edged through the crowd toward the hall. Reverend Pettus announced that they'd better end the service and return to their homes at once.

The words were superfluous. A small stampede had already started, guests jabbering and pushing the blacks aside to get to the buggies and phaetons outside. Jeremiah was suddenly thankful he still had the sheathed knife tucked in his boot. Sherman's shadow was growing longer. Touching Rosewood now.

Still, he had a hard time believing the Yanks would destroy undefended private property on any large scale. Surely they couldn't be that dishonorable. The outbreak in Milledgeville must be an isolated case. Even the razing of Atlanta had had some strategic purpose. But the incidents the dusty old man in the chaise described had none at all, unless you counted the kind of thing Jeremiah was witnessing at this moment: the creation of utter panic among defenseless civilians.

One phaeton was already gone, clattering down the lane in a cloud of sunlit dust. The driver lashed his team as though Satan were three feet behind.

"Catherine? What are we going to do?"

Jeremiah and the older woman both turned at the sound of Serena's voice. The girl didn't appear worried, merely curious.

Judge Claypool came struggling in against the tide of the exodus, talking first to one person, then another. "—swear to Jesus—oh! Excuse my language, Reverend—it's all true! They've got a flock of runaway niggers dogging 'em wherever they go. Disloyal, disreputable niggers, every one!"

The judge's announcement in the hall caused another, somewhat more restrained stir, this time among the blacks. Claypool fanned back his dusty coat to display a holstered horse pistol. "Thank God we have none of that kind around here. If we did they'd be candidates for shooting. And I don't mean by Yanks."

Serena prodded her stepmother. "Well, Catherine?"

"If they come," Jeremiah said abruptly, "we'll stand up to them."

"Really?" Serena inquired. "How?"

"War or no war, they have no right to ruin private property. We'll make them understand that."

Serena's blue eyes grew amused. "My, you certainly have faith in the decency of Yankees."

The sarcasm rankled. He *had* to believe the cruelty of the battlefield couldn't spread into civilian territory. He had nothing else to believe in any longer. It was his last article of faith. He tried to justify it.

"I just don't think any army would go on burning and

looting that way. Sherman's men have probably done it around Milledgeville because that's the capital."

Catherine took encouragement from the words. "I'm sure he's right, Serena. Provisioning an army off enemy land's one thing. Ruining civilian property is another. They certainly won't continue—"

"Don't be too damn sure, Catherine," Judge Claypool warned.

"By God, we won't stand for it," Jeremiah blurted. "It's against all the laws of decency!"

Someone laughed.

He spun, his eyes locking with those of Price.

The slave's face was blank again. But Jeremiah was positive Price was the culprit. A young woman with her hair covered by a bandana was backing away from him. And Maum Isabella was staring at him too, lips pinched tight together.

Jeremiah glared at the slave but drew no response. Price's pupils might have been brown stones.

A few remaining guests clustered around Catherine, offering apologies and empty condolences before they departed. Jeremiah drew Serena aside.

"We'd better get your stepmother working on her list."

"What list?"

"The one she mentioned last night. Covering anything on the place that ought to be hidden. Are there firearms in the house?"

"No, none. Papa took everything." With her back to Price, who hadn't changed his position in the hall, she whispered, "There's a musket somewhere—" She seemed to be goading him.

"We'll do the best we can without it," Jeremiah declared, even though the lack of the Enfield left him feeling less than whole.

The vehicles belonging to the guests rattled down to the highway one after another. Maum Isabella had put grief behind her and was shooing some of the nigras through the house toward their cabins. At last Price turned and strolled off in the same direction.

Dust boiled through the open windows of the sitting room, billowing the curtains and settling on the polished wood of the pianoforte. A last visitor tipped a table and spilled back issues of the *Southern Literary Messenger* in his haste to depart. As the copies plopped on the carpet, Jeremiah heard faint laughter again, then Maum Isabella's voice, loud and scolding.

"Jeremiah?"

He turned to Catherine.

"Serena asked a very pertinent question. We must plan what we're going to do if the enemy comes."

Remembering the laughter, Jeremiah thought, *He's already here.*

Chapter VII
Warnings

i

Thanksgiving dinner was a tense, joyless affair.

Jeremiah suspected it might turn out that way the moment Catherine appeared, bringing her cut glass decanter of blackberry wine out in the open—right to the table. As she set it down she murmured an excuse about needing a "medicinal tonic" after the strain of the service and Judge Claypool's arrival with the bad news from Milledgeville.

Maum Isabella hadn't stinted on preparing a good meal. But Jeremiah and the two women barely touched their food. Unpleasant questions seemed to come up almost at once. Would Sherman actually reach the Louisville district? Would his troops behave as badly as they had in the capital? Jeremiah gave encouraging answers, as much to reassure himself as to reassure them.

Catherine inquired about his initiation into the war. The words he used in reply automatically carried his thoughts to a place he preferred to forget:

To a hillside in the northwest part of the state. In September twilight a year ago, he'd gone up that hillside with his bayonet fixed and his palms sweating, ducking and starting at his first exposure to the whine of Minié balls.

The Confederates had been trying to take a position held by the Yank general, Pap Thomas. After the battle, Thomas came to be called The Rock because his lines held and blew back charge after Rebel charge while, behind them, routed Rosecrans fled for Chattanooga. Jeremiah narrated an account of the engagement, but said nothing about how terrified he'd been at first.

He described the ball that had grazed his scalp and produced the streak of white hair. He told them how he'd shot his first Yank—the first one he was certain he'd killed, that is. But he didn't mention the disturbing feelings he'd experienced watching the young man fall.

He'd shot as he was supposed to shoot—obeying orders—yet his reaction to the hit had been a kind of cold joy. He tried not to remember the joy. It didn't fit with his concept of war honorably conducted.

He hated to admit there was an aspect of his nature, slowly strengthened as he gained proficiency with firearms, that could be termed ruthless. At times he even denied the trait's existence. But it was there, and he guarded against giving in to it.

Once in a while he did succumb. Before escaping from the farmer with the pitchfork, he'd struck the back of the man's neck and felt absolutely no pity. Nor had he experienced any qualms about the whipping of Price.

While Jeremiah talked, he noticed Serena picking at her cloved ham and glancing around the room in a restless way. She was certainly a creature of moods. Last night, she'd declared she was his ally. This morning he seemed to bore her. He concluded that her night visit must have been solely an act of defiance directed against her stepmother. His account of his experiences in battle didn't interest her. This afternoon he was merely a guest to be tolerated. A boy.

It was infuriating.

Yet he couldn't help being fascinated. The late afternoon sun haloed her red hair and profile, making her look like some beautiful image from a church window.

Catherine drank two goblets of blackberry wine during the meal. She didn't touch the quill pen, the inkstand, or the foolscap sheet in front of her place. One line was written at the top of the sheet in a delicate, slanting hand:

To be done

Somehow she seemed unable to get down to working on the list, or even to discussing it, permitting the conversation to veer off in other directions.

"Jeremiah." She refilled her goblet a third time. "How was the colonel's state of mind when—when he—"

She couldn't complete the sentence.

A black woman cleared the unfinished dish of dessert plums from his place as he answered, "Well, apart from fretting about you two, he seemed to be in good spirits the night before we fought at Jonesboro."

A lie. He balanced it with a truth. "He was annoyed, though."

"Why?"

"There was something special he wanted to read. The next part of a serial story in a New York weekly. Someone had given him two old copies that contained the first two chapters, or whatever you call them."

"Installments," Serena said.

He felt humiliated again. "Anyway, it was some sort of spooky story by a writer named Wilkie—" Memory faltered a second time.

"Wilkie Collins?" Catherine asked.

"Yes, I think that's it. He said the two things he wanted most were to see you"—the remark was intended to include Serena, but she paid no attention—"and to finish *The Woman in White.*"

Catherine sighed and dabbed her napkin against the corner of her mouth. "He had a fine mind. He was a literate, Christian man. We had good times just talking, or going over the ledgers. Small things."

"Small things were all he cared about," Serena complained.

Voice thicker, Catherine retorted, "You mustn't speak disrespectfully of your father."

"I'm not being disrespectful. I'm telling the truth!" At last she faced Jeremiah, who occupied a place at one side of the long table, between the women seated at the ends. "I don't know how many times I begged Papa to take us to Savannah so we could have dinner at the Pulaski House. Best food in the whole state, everyone says. Best in the whole South! But he wouldn't, he was always content around here. Do you know I've never been out of Jefferson County except for part of a year at Christ College where Catherine taught? I wanted to see New Orleans, Savannah—even Washington. And all I ever saw were silly books and silly women in a stuffy old lyceum!"

Catherine bristled, waggling her goblet. "You also saw a few disreputable young men who took you buggy riding after hours. Who compromised you by bringing along spiritous liquors."

Serena glanced at her stepmother's glass. "You're a fine one to talk!"

Catherine scowled. "Serena—"

The warning went unfinished because the girl spoke immediately. "Well, you are!" She turned to Jeremiah. "Catherine's always been a pillar of the county temperance society. Of course none of those nice ladies has any idea there's always a jug of blackberry wine handy around—"

"*Enough, Serena!* When there's a war, things—things change. Your father's been gone a long time. Sometimes a person needs help to keep going."

Serena's laugh had a vicious sound. "And everything's fine as long as it's taken on the sly!"

Catherine set the goblet on the table and stared at it, sadly. Jeremiah wanted to run. Only politeness kept him there, caught in the hostility boiling between the two women.

Although Catherine's unhappy concentration on the goblet was an admission of guilt, Serena didn't find that satisfying enough. "I tell you, sometimes I just get sick to death of the way you look down on me! You act like Moses on the mount! One of these days—"

Flushed, she held back the rest. Catherine looked at her, half stunned, half furious. "What, Serena?"

"Nothing."

"No, I insist. Finish the sentence. Did you mean to threaten me?"

"No, I—really, I didn't. I apologize." Her voice was flat, insincere.

Jeremiah grimaced. She obviously *had* meant the uncompleted sentence as a warning. But prudence—or a second thought that represented more deviousness than caution—had convinced her to keep it to herself.

Still, she wasn't through baiting the older woman, though she did it indirectly, speaking to him again.

"Catherine's always been just heartbroken that I didn't last the year at the institute. I was supposed to study for a degree in the arts, but one of the proctors smelled spirits when I came in ten minutes late one night. A whole ten minutes! That was the end of my grand education. Not that I cared! I was glad to leave that stupid place."

The colonel's widow picked up the quill and tapped the nib against the inkstand. "I don't believe we need subject Jeremiah to an account of your unfortunate record at Montpelier."

He tried to ease the tension with a smile and a shrug. "I was never much for studying either. My mother couldn't get me to do lessons when we traveled."

With that, he finally succeeded in attracting Serena's full attention.

"Did you travel many places?"

"All over the South. My stepfather—he's dead now—he was an actor."

Serena seemed genuinely interested. "Oh, you must have seen such wonderful sights!"

He made a face. "Hotel rooms. Dirty theaters. Sooty railroad cars. Depots in the middle of the night."

"You're not being honest. I can't imagine anything more exciting than visiting different cities and towns. I want to travel one of these days. Travel—stay in fine hotels—"

She searched his face a moment. Did he? she seemed to ask silently. Catherine's quill went *tap* against the inkstand, then, quickly, *tap* again.

"What about that relative of yours in New York?" Serena wanted to know. "Did you ever visit him?"

"My second cousin once removed? No, I've never set eyes on Louis Kent."

"He's a wealthy man, though—didn't you tell us he's a wealthy man?"

"Very wealthy." He nodded. He'd been unable to gain her attention for so long and he wanted to keep it. The boast came easily: " 'Course our side of the family—the

Virginia side—has money too. My brothers and I will come into a lot of it when our father dies."

"You will?" She folded her hands under her chin, "You're not making that up?"

"Absolutely not." To convince her, he related how his father, the Reverend Jephtha Kent, had inherited a California gold claim and a subsequently formed mining corporation from Jeremiah's grandfather, a mountain man and prospector in the 1849 rush. Serena still acted dubious as he went on.

"Gideon, Matt, and I will come into equal shares when father passes away—although thanks to the war, I don't know what's happened to either one of them lately. Matt was always footloose—I expect he's taking care of himself, wherever he is. But I really worry about Gid. We're not sure if he's dead or in prison up north. If he's dead, I suppose his wife in Richmond inherits his share. But however it turns out, even a third of the earnings of that California company will be mighty handsome."

Teasing, Serena said, "If there *is* a California company."

Catherine exhaled, an abrupt, exasperated sound. "Serena, I don't know what to do with you. I've never heard you speak more rudely to anyone—with possibly one exception."

Jeremiah fought back another wave of anger.

"That's all right, Mrs. Rose. I'm used to doubters. Boys in the army called me a liar every day of the week. The truth is"—he grinned in a disarming way—"I'm not bright enough to make up a story like that."

Catherine's eyes were warm as she responded, "Or malicious enough to try to deceive people. I believe you."

Serena studied her mother. Perhaps Catherine's conviction had persuaded her. She was more polite when she said, "Why, I do too! I was only having a little fun."

"You have peculiar notions as to what constitutes fun, Serena. You have peculiar notions about a good many—"

Serena didn't let her finish. "What are you going to do with all that money when you get it?"

Less angry now—though Catherine wasn't—he shrugged again, and replied honestly, "Hadn't given it much thought. It'll be a long time before I see any of it. My father's in fine health, and I wouldn't wish him anything less—even if he is a damn Yankee."

That admission represented a change in his attitude that had taken place gradually over the past couple of years. He could still recall a vivid, ugly scene in a hotel room in Washington when Fan and his father had screamed at one another. Lamont had tried to intercede, and Gideon had wound up caning Jephtha unmercifully. Jeremiah had been terrified, understanding none of it.

Later, after Lamont's funeral, Fan had spoken to him and said Gideon and Jephtha were reconciled now—and that it had been Lamont, not Jephtha, who'd been responsible for the violent quarrel. She'd refused to explain further, and he'd never been able to learn more of the details. But her statements were an additional bit of proof of something suspicious about Lamont's death.

He sat up a little straighter, conscious of Serena watching him closely. He had her now! Even if she still wasn't wholly convinced about the California gold, she was at least treating him as if he were something more than a worthless boy.

Surrendering to an ugly impulse, he decided he'd fix her for all her previous slights. He shifted the position of his chair so he faced Catherine. "I think we've talked enough about money. Maybe we should get to work on your list."

The older woman smiled, but in a tired way. "I suppose you're right. I've been avoiding it. I hate to think of why we must make a list at all."

The wine had definitely affected her speech. Slowed and slurred it. Lent it a despairing note. She inked the quill. Thought a moment.

"We must put some salt away. What little we have left."

She made a notation, then pondered again.

"Two barrels of flour."

She marked it down.

"I have two bolts of kersey in the sewing room. I wouldn't want to lose those."

"Heavens, no!" Serena exclaimed.

What a wretched excuse for a Thanksgiving dinner this had turned out to be! Of course, he admitted to himself a moment later, he hadn't exactly eased the situation by giving in to his impulse and turning his back on Serena. But he felt too embarrassed to shift the chair again.

While he watched Catherine Rose working on her list, he missed seeing the speculative look in Serena's blue eyes. She was no longer interested in her stepmother.

She was watching him.

ii

Late that night, unable to sleep, he lay with his hands clasped beneath his head, pondering the peculiar and venomous conversation between the Rose women.

All he could settle on as possible causes for their barely controlled animosity were two things. The first was Catherine's evident need for strong drink, coupled with the fact that she concealed the need from her neighbors and the members of the temperance society. The second was Serena's undisciplined behavior, which had apparently gotten her expelled from the young women's institute. Still, both reasons seemed too trivial to generate the kind of hostility that had crisscrossed the dining table.

He recalled certain other words of Catherine's. Serena had *"peculiar notions."* Could that possibly be a polite term for crazy? The girl's nature plainly included a violent, reckless streak. The blood he'd washed from the cuff of his nightshirt said as much.

Yet the underlying reason for the animosity between the two continued to elude him. Not that he much cared to probe for it.

Trouble was, the longer he stayed at Rosewood, the more likely he was to uncover it. The women were revealing more and more of themselves as each day passed. Perhaps the stress of living with the threat of Sherman's army made such a situation inevitable. He didn't like being in the middle of it. But he was.

Well, at least he'd scored a point or two against Catherine's bitchy stepdaughter. He was no longer quite so much of a child in her eyes.

His feelings about her were complex and upsetting. There was something damned dangerous about her. Yet the memory of her blue eyes and red hair kept him awake and aroused for almost an hour.

iii

During the next two days, Catherine put Jeremiah in charge of the heavier work called for by the Thanksgiving Day list. He was helped by a husky, companionable nigra named Leon—the one Serena had called on when she tried to whip a confession out of Price.

Jeremiah and the black man dug a pit behind the slaves' burial ground. There they buried the casks of salt and flour.

Next they loaded the plantation wagon with bales of cotton, the two bolts of kersey, and two more of denim cloth carried from the sewing room. Leon hitched mules to the wagon and showed Jeremiah a straggling track that led off into pine woods a quarter mile behind the little cemetery.

In a clearing far back in the woods they erected a lean-to of limbs and brush to protect the cache of cotton and cloth, to which they presently added two small barrels of molasses and a large chiming clock Henry Rose had presented to Catherine as a wedding present. Catherine had confessed she felt a mite ridiculous hiding an item of sentimental value such as the clock. But she had no basis for making decisions about what the Yanks might want other than reports received once or twice a day from the citizens of Louisville. They sent their nigras around the neighborhood to say that Sherman's army was indeed coming, and the general's order giving permission for his soldiers to *forage liberally* was being interpreted as permission to steal anything the invaders pleased.

Leon and Jeremiah tried to operate circumspectly on their trips into the pines. The big, innocent-eyed slave reported that Price seemed in extremely high spirits. When Jeremiah questioned him about any references Price might have made to a stolen Enfield, Leon allowed as how Price hadn't said anything directly about the musket. But he *had* been bragging that he'd be "fixed mighty good" if the enemy showed up at the gate by the highway. Jeremiah wished there were at least one weapon in the house besides kitchen implements and his knife.

He and Leon kept an eye out for Price whenever they drove the loaded wagon back into the trees. They never once saw the buck watching. But since the other nigras had observed the wagon's comings and goings, Jeremiah was sure Price was well aware of their activity.

Leon reported that something like a quarter of the blacks on the place were whispering about being free soon. A few more questions on Jeremiah's part revealed that a fierce split was developing at Rosewood. The more loyal nigras were being lectured by Maum Isabella until they promised they wouldn't assist the invaders in any way. And although the malcontents went about their duties as usual, they did so with a changed attitude. Leon summed it up.

"They didn't use to say nasty things about Miz Catherine, but they sayin' plenty of 'em now. And every other word, almos'—it's jubilee. Jubilee comin'—"

Did that mean only a celebration of new freedom? Jeremiah wondered. Or was it a code word that included reprisals?

Wherever he went on the plantation, he kept his sheathed knife in his boot.

iv

After the final trip back from the cache about midday on Saturday, Jeremiah was in the barn unhitching the mules when a long shadow fell across the matted straw on the floor. He turned, caught his breath—

Price was leaning in the entrance, arms folded.

"You and Leon sure been busy, mister soldier."

"Listen, Price! You know my name."

"Reckon I don't have to use it, though. Reckon I don't have to do anything you say with those Yanks so close. What you and Leon hidin' back in the pines 'sides cotton?"

"Go ask Mrs. Rose!"

The anger didn't ruffle the black.

"Oh, I doubt she'd tell me. Whatever you're puttin' away, I bet the Yanks find it. They goin' to find you too. 'Less of course you plan to hide out."

"Price, one more goddamn word out of you—"

A chuckle. "An' what? You get after me? You tear into

me? Any time, mister soldier. Any time you want, you welcome to try." He unfolded his arms, started away, then paused. "Yanks gonna get you. Oh, yes, you bet they are." The brown pupils seemed to grow larger. "If they don't, I will."

"Price, how come you despise me so much?"

The forced calm in Jeremiah's voice brought a smirk to the other man's face. "Why, that's easy. You one of the soldiers been fightin' to keep me property 'stead of a free man."

"Bullshit."

Startled, Price raised an eyebrow. "How's that?"

"You heard. Here's the way I figure it. For you, being property's only an excuse. The day you brought me here, I saw how you scowled at the mama of that little girl who ran to see your turtle. I think you like people to be scared of you. Nigra, white—I don't think it makes a particle of difference so long as you keep 'em scared. I bet there's not one damn person in creation you do like—or would ever treat kindly. I met a couple of officers in the army just like you."

"Mister soldier, you think whatever you want. That won't change the way things come out 'tween us."

"Just how do you propose to fix me, Price? With my musket?"

The black put on a pious expression whose exaggeration was almost ludicrous. "*Musket?* You still got a notion I stole *that?*" A soft, clucking sound indicated how pathetic he found the idea. "I don't need no musket, mister soldier." He held up both hands, sunlight behind him shining between his fingers. "Just need these."

He sauntered out of sight, his shrinking, distorted shadow lying at an angle across the straw at the barn entrance for what seemed like half a minute after he himself had disappeared.

Chapter VIII
With Serena

i

Catherine Rose had more than a thousand dollars in Confederate bills in her office. On Saturday, Jeremiah locked the bills in a trunk in the steaming attic, along with pouches of valuable papers: deeds, ledgers, the colonel's will. Downstairs, he returned the key to Catherine, who put it back on the ring with the others.

New padlocks had been hastily obtained from Louisville the day before. Jeremiah and Leon installed them on the doors of the gin house, corn cribs, and barns. As though locks could stop Sherman's men!

But doing something was better than doing nothing, especially when the highway had begun to show increased activity.

Poor farm families, slaveless, passed in rickety wagons, fleeing the county. A Home Guards unit consisting of twelve elderly men and four boys marched by. Eight horsemen wearing yellow-faced gray arrived—a contingent of General Wheeler's cavalry. As they watered their horses at the trough near the well they reported the situation was worse than anyone had imagined.

Sherman's sixty thousand were sweeping across the state

on a broad front. In its wake the army left burned buildings, ruined fields, slaughtered livestock, and occasionally—one of the troopers whispered to Jeremiah—raped women.

The leader of the cavalrymen warned Catherine Rose to leave the plantation. She thanked him for his concern, said no, and sent the riders on their way.

ii

Late Sunday afternoon Jeremiah was on his knees in the sitting room, using his knife to cut a slit in the back of an expensive horsehair sofa.

Once the cut was made, Catherine started to hand him the family silver. He slid each piece through the slit and worked it down into the sofa's stuffing. Perhaps eighty or ninety pieces were jammed in before he pushed the sofa back against the wall.

He walked around in front and sat, deliberately letting his weight come down hard. The sofa clinked and jingled like some peculiar musical instrument.

"God a'mighty!" he sighed. "Any Yank sits here, he'll discover the silver right off."

"I'm hoping they'll be decent enough not to intrude into the house—" Catherine began, interrupted abruptly by a distant crackling.

Jeremiah dashed to one of the open windows, jerked the curtains aside, stuck his head out into the sunlight. He heard the crackling again.

"That's musketry!"

Catherine turned pale. She and Jeremiah rushed outside, joined a moment later by Serena, who appeared around a corner of the house. They stared at the lane, the highway, the fields beyond. The crackling was repeated a third tune, but more faintly.

Jeremiah wiped sweat from his forehead and turned to Rose's widow. "Wherever they are, they're close. I'd better take the wagon and mules into the pines. Where's Leon?"

"I sent him down to the bottom to hide three crates of chickens."

"All right, I'll go alone."

"Let me help," Serena volunteered, startling him.

Although it was the Sabbath, the girl wore an everyday cotton dress. Catherine had decided not to waste time attending church services in Louisville.

The day was warm, with a languid, summery feel unusual for the end of November. A haze hung in the air and a sultry breeze blew. As Jeremiah scanned the blurred contours of the land to the north and west, he suddenly spied something that made his belly hurt.

He pointed. Serena strained on tiptoe. Finally Catherine saw it too. A thin, almost invisible streak of black smoke rising beyond the trees along the Ogeechee, an oblique mark across the reddening afternoon sky.

Catherine pressed a fisted hand to her chin. "Something's on fire."

"We'd better go right now," Jeremiah said. "I'll hitch the mules."

"You'll need help with that too," Serena said, surprising him again. She didn't seem the sort for physical labor. Her duties during the last couple of days had been limited to light tasks, including the gathering of pieces of jewelry, which Catherine had put into a small leather bag she wore beneath her skirt. The bag was fastened around her waist by a length of rope. Naturally Jeremiah hadn't seen the bag. Serena had described it.

He couldn't get over the change warm weather and tension had produced in the girl. Dirt smudged one cheek. Sweat rings showed at the armpits of her dress. Somehow, though, her untidy state didn't detract from her prettiness, actually seemed to enhance it by lending her a more human, less remote quality.

She dashed for the house. "I'll fetch a shawl. It'll be cool by the time we walk back."

Staring after her, Jeremiah again chided himself for his interest in the girl. The interest was even more foolish and harder to explain in the light of what he already knew about her temperament.

Maybe the attraction had nothing to do with Serena personally. Maybe it was just a normal combination of curiosity and inexperience with the opposite sex. Yet he doubted that. He found himself wondering how Serena's body looked, naked, beneath all those clothes.

Not just any woman's body. *Hers.*

He had difficulty dealing with his feelings about her. Turning his back on her at Thanksgiving dinner had compensated for earlier slights, and he'd tried to start off the next day fresh—as though nothing unpleasant had happened earlier. She too had behaved differently, had actually been cordial a few times. And when a mood was on her—a mood that prohibited cordiality—at least she didn't act contemptuous of him. He suspected one possible reason for her change, but preferred not to think about it.

He didn't exactly *like* Serena. Not in the way you liked a friend, a camp comrade. Yet he was attracted to her, even though caution suggested it was unwise. Caution, however, came from the head. His interest lay in another direction entirely. He felt an embarrassing stir in his groin when he thought of riding alone with her into the pines.

Catherine seemed to have no objection to their going off together. She was preoccupied, watching the smoke rise in the west. "Damn them if they're burning private property! *Damn* them for making war on homes and farms!"

Surprised by her use of profanity, he offered another of his reassurances. "We won't let them do it here, Mrs. Rose." But it was becoming more a hope than a certainty.

For a moment he forgot Serena, imprisoned again by the kind of despairing mood that had gripped him when Rose spoke to him just before he died. There was no honor in this scurrying around to hide family possessions. Hell, it was downright disgraceful!

He stared at the column of smoke and tried to convince himself it didn't mean what it seemed to mean. And he silently repeated his vow to stand up to the Yanks if they came, and demand they deal honorably with the residents of Rosewood.

iii

Bess and Fred, the mules, were balky. Jeremiah was glad to have Serena's assistance in hitching them.

She'd combed her hair, pinned her shawl to her bodice with a brooch, and put on cologne. He caught her scent as he maneuvered the wagon out of the barn. Serena closed the door, padlocked it, and climbed up beside him, sitting so close on the splintered seat he could practically feel her leg beneath her skirt.

He drove straight down the dirt track between the slave cabins. Beside one of them, Price rested in the shade. He surveyed the wagon without a flicker of expression. Jeremiah shook the reins to speed the mules.

"Damn it, why's he lying around as if he doesn't have a care?"

"He doesn't," Serena said. "The Yanks are almost here. Besides, what else is there to do except wait?"

"He would have to see us drive off! He'll know where we've hidden the wagon. He's probably found the cache already."

"Leon wouldn't tell him."

That relieved him a little. "You're right. And Leon's the only other one who knows."

"Leon's trustworthy. He's behaving himself too. Some of the rest are getting more and more sassy. In the kitchen just this morning, Maum Isabella had to slap Francy. She sauced me when I gave an order. I slapped her once myself for good measure."

She sounded pleased about it.

Serena began to hum. It took Jeremiah a few moments to recognize the melody. The way she speeded it, the hymn sung at her father's memorial service sounded more like a minstrel tune. Lord, what an odd one she was!

He reached down to his boot to make sure the sheathed knife was secure. The wagon rolled by the slaves' burial ground and back toward the dark privacy of the pines.

Once into the relatively cool shade of the trees, he began to feel increasingly nervous. The mules plodded. A fly deviled his cheek. He brushed at it several times, then tried a slap. The fly disappeared. All at once Serena stopped humming and leaned against him.

"Jeremiah."

"Yes?"

Softly: "I'm mighty glad you came from Atlanta."

The touch of her shoulder started his loins quivering in that embarrassing way. He squinted down the weed-grown track. "Is that right? I had a notion it didn't make a bit of difference to you."

"You were wrong. It does."

"Well, Miss Serena, you'll forgive me, but for a day or two, you surely didn't act like it."

"I was all upset! Because of Papa. I loved Papa more than anybody on this earth."

It might be true, he thought, but it didn't change the fact that she'd undergone an almost complete reversal.

"Besides—"

She slipped her hand between his elbow and his ribs, linking her arm with his. In the silence of the woods—silence interrupted by another far-off stutter of gunfire—he felt nervous and hot. Her cologne even masked the scent of the pines. The pointed firmness of her left breast pressed his arm.

"—we need a man on the place. Women just can't control a bunch of unruly niggers."

"Price is the one to worry about. When he wouldn't confess to stealing my Enfield, we should have locked him up."

"Or shot him," Serena said in a matter-of-fact way. He was stunned; he'd had the identical thought, but he wouldn't have spoken it to anyone.

"Too bad we didn't have another gun," she added.

Recovering, he said, "I'll keep watching him."

He had doubts about his ability to cope with the black on a man-to-man basis, though. He was rapidly regaining his strength. The bandaged wound on his leg troubled him less and less often. But he had no illusions about Price being a weakling. And he recalled the threat in the barn: *"Yanks gonna get you. If they don't, I will."*

To impress her and reinforce his own determination, he added, "If any of those Yanks show up, we'll just have to talk to 'em straight and tell 'em we expect decent treatment."

Serena giggled.

"What's so blasted funny?"

"Sometimes you *are* priceless! You think Yankees'll act polite just because we ask?"

I have to believe that. It's one of the reasons I'm here. Where I came from, there was no honor left. Not after your father died.

"Yes, I do. They damn well better respect civilian territory. They will, Serena. I'll bet that every place there's been trouble, people have provoked them."

"Now you sound exactly like Catherine," she sighed as the wagon rounded a bend.

The mules flicked their ears to drive off the huge blue flies. The slow, lazy rhythm of the hoofs, the fragrance of her cologne, the isolation, and the feel of her breast touching his sleeve drove him into a state of almost uncontrollable excitement.

At the same time he felt uneasy, endangered, somehow. But it was a sharp, sweet danger, tinged with the lure of the unknown. Tense as he was, he wouldn't have stopped the wagon for a minute.

Yet he did stop it all at once, his tongue stuck in his cheek and his head cocked.

Serena frowned. "What's the trouble?"

He put a finger to his lips. Cold-eyed, he pointed off to the right, whispered, "Thought I heard something."

"Jackrabbits."

"No. Louder. Heavier."

They listened. He was sure he hadn't been wrong. But the telltale rustling of pine needles and the rattle of disturbed underbrush wasn't repeated. He hawed softly to the mules and set the wagon rolling again.

iv

Serena gazed at dusty bars of sunlight slanting between the trees. "Getting late. It'll be dark before we're finished."

"Maybe not," he muttered. The notion of being alone with her after nightfall had become almost too nerve-racking to bear.

"Know something, Jeremiah? For a long time Catherine thought Price was the best buck on the place."

"She made a mistake."

A curt laugh. "Not her first. She always thinks the best of everybody. There was only one person she never thought well of."

"Who?"

"My real mama."

The words had an unforgiving sound. He let her go on. "I heard Catherine arguing about it with Papa once. He said my mama was a lady, a private music teacher, and

Catherine wasn't to forget it. But she said he was a liar. Said the kind of lessons my mama gave didn't take place on any old piano stool."

He nearly laughed, but was thankful he hadn't when Serena turned to look at him. Her blue eyes were smoldering. "She called my mama a filthy name."

"What was it?"

"I won't repeat it. Why, you know a lady isn't even supposed to say she has legs. She has *limbs.* Once Catherine and I had a real fuss over that, too. But she did call my mama a filthy name."

He risked the question. "Did she call your mother that name without any cause?"

"Makes no difference! She was my *mama!*"

Silence for a while. He'd overstepped. But Serena's anger was evidently directed at Catherine for the moment. Sounding melancholy, she continued.

"I've never even seen a picture of her. There was a picture in the house at one time, but it was burned. Papa said Catherine burned it. Believe me, Catherine isn't as pure and forgiving as she lets on!"

"I've never met a perfect person yet, Serena. You should be able to understand why your stepmother isn't wild about your father's first wife. When my mother remarried, my father felt the same way about her new husband."

"*But Catherine didn't have to use a filthy word!* I can't forgive her for that. Ever!"

She drew a deep breath.

"One of these days I'm going to pay her back."

The soft, quiet statement sent another shiver chasing down his spine. He recognized the cruelty in the words because he was tainted with a cruel streak himself.

Serena stared straight ahead. "Guess it must have been true about Mama. But Catherine didn't have to say it. That's the point—she *said* it."

"Did she ever say it to you?"

"Yes indeed. After I overheard the conversation with Papa, I marched right in to see her—she'd been helping herself to that wine she takes on the sly—and we went at it for the best part of half an hour. She called Mama that filthy name right to my face!"

"Well, I'm beginning to understand why you and Mrs.

Rose don't get along too well," he said with a humorless smile.

Her teasing had a wicked undertone. "Why, Jeremiah Kent, you're quicker than I thought!"

Stung, he retorted, "Thanks for such a kind compliment."

"Oh, I didn't mean to anger you."

She raised her head, pecked his cheek. Her lips felt warm and moist.

"Truly I didn't."

To cover his awkwardness, he batted at another fly buzzing near his ear. The pines were growing darker, suffused by the sun's deep red. It seemed too early in the day for sunset, he thought, though it *was* almost December. Back home in Virginia, there might have been a light frost by now.

Serena perked up a little. "I won't have to fret about Catherine forever, though. She'll go to her grave eventually and I'll be free of her. I'll have a good husband—"

He was relieved to have an opportunity to drop the subject of Serena's stepmother. In a lighter tone, he responded, "Got one picked already?"

She shook her head. "But I know what I want. A man with some money. Money he's willing to use to make more money. Papa's father and grandfather had the knack. They knew how to buy up land. Increase the crop yields. Papa bought a little more acreage for Rosewood, but he was happiest just standing still. He kept the place almost the same as it was when he inherited it. I want a man with bigger ideas. One who won't be content sitting in an office going over books—or reading ghost stories for excitement in the evening. I want a man who can run Rosewood right!"

Jeremiah grinned. "You're talking as if it's already yours."

"It will be when Catherine dies—same as with that California gold mine you spoke about. With Rosewood and my husband's money, we'll be able to build a really big place. Travel, too. Into Savannah to the Pulaski House. Maybe to Europe. I'll find a man like that. I know I will. I know because I can offer a man a lot—"

She gave him an almost brazen smile.

"Rosewood and some other nice things. Provided he treats me right."

"I"—he was almost afraid to speak—"I think it'd be grand to treat you right. Take you places—I mean it'd be grand for that husband you're talking about."

Disappointment: "Oh."

"Now what'd I do?"

"Nothing. Guess I had the wrong idea."

"What idea?"

"For a minute I had a notion you might be talking about yourself."

He couldn't help blushing. "Oh, no. You're older than I am."

"But you've been to war! That ages a boy pretty fast, I'm told."

He was at a loss to explain her sudden warmth except for one reason he'd been trying to forget: the Thanksgiving Day conversation about how he and his brothers would be wealthy men when Jephtha Kent passed on.

He'd always been aware in a vague way that his father would leave him a considerable amount of money. But he'd hardly ever dwelled on the consequences of the inheritance: what he'd do with it, or how it could make him important to others. Now, for almost the first time, he began to understand.

With the realization there came questions. How much money *would* be his? Thousands of dollars? Millions? He couldn't comprehend *millions,* except that it must be a devil of a lot.

It would be good money, too. Gold, not cheapened Confederate paper.

Millions!

He was a bit overcome by the thought—then disgusted by the realization that he'd been right about the reason for Serena's changed behavior. He wanted to let her know he was aware of the reason. Something held him back—perhaps the way she squeezed his arm again as the wagon creaked deeper into the hazy shadow of the pines.

Tell her you know!

He faced her but still couldn't say it, overcome by the bold, almost inviting way she was gazing at him. Smiling—

Lord above, she was a beautiful girl! That was the problem.

Leaning near again, she whispered, "I imagine a boy becomes pretty experienced in a war, doesn't he, Jeremiah?"

"Y-yes," he said, not knowing how to respond to the obvious meaning of the question. "In only one day at Chickamauga, I learned how to stay alive."

She made a moue. "I meant experienced in other ways."

His tongue felt stiff. "Women—things like that?"

" 'Course."

"Well, I suppose—yes, it's true," he lied. Aware of the immorality of speaking to a female about the unspeakable, he still blurted, "How about you?"

"Jeremiah, that's not a proper thing to ask a girl!"

But she was pleased.

Blushing again. "I—I was just curious."

"Decent young ladies don't do such things—and if they do, they don't discuss them!" Tormenting him with her sly smile, she peered down the track and thrust out a finger. "Isn't that your cache?"

Jeremiah squeezed his legs together to hide the stiffness, furious at her for leading him on, yet thankful at the same time that she hadn't permitted things to go further. Something in his mind kept warning him:

Leave her alone. She's too deep. Too devious.

And she's not innocent—

A part of him longed to believe she was. He was frightened anew by the intensity of that yearning.

"I said, isn't that your cache?"

He nodded, dry-lipped. He just didn't know how to handle a girl like Serena Rose.

The mules meandered into the little clearing, all but dark now. Awkwardly, he separated his arm from hers, guided the mules to a stop.

"We'll unhitch 'em and tie 'em, and I'll fork out some of the fodder Leon and I brought in. Then you can give me a hand pushing the wagon out of sight."

He spoke very quickly to cover his flustered feeling. He looped the reins around the brake handle and climbed down.

Serena slid to the side of the wagon where he stood. She bent over, her bosom touched by dull red light seeping through the pines. She looked down at him, her tongue licking slowly over her upper lip.

She extended her arms. "You'll have to help me."

He reached up, too eagerly. She stood, suddenly appeared to stumble or lose her balance—no accident, he was sure.

Crying out, she tumbled on top of him.

Chapter IX
Red Sky

i

They sprawled on the ground. He started to roll away, his neck prickled by a burr, only to feel her hand on his chin.

She pulled him close, so close they were lying side by side, thighs touching. Her hand slipped to his cheek.

"Jeremiah, you listen to me. The day you showed up, I thought you were just a boy. I was wrong. You're a grown man."

Her mouth came nearer.

"If you want, you can kiss me."

He did—tentatively. All at once she pressed both palms against his face. With tantalizing slowness, she caressed his lips with her tongue.

Then she moved her body tighter against his, giggling again, this time because of the feel of his bigness.

"Here, *here!*"

She guided his hand, closed it on her breast. His fingers were clamped so tightly, he thought he could detect lace beneath her faded dress.

"Maybe I could give you lessons like the ones my mama gave. But you were in the army. I 'spose you don't need them—"

Another kiss, harder, deeper.

"You've probably had lots of girls."

And another. Her wet mouth slid up over his cheek. The tip of her tongue teased his skin.

"You probably don't even like me much because of the foolish way I treated you the first couple of days."

They lay in almost total darkness. Over her shoulder, he glimpsed the mules' ears twitching away flies.

Get away! he thought. *She's all tangled up inside. About her real mother, and her stepmother—and she doesn't give a hang for you. It's that money she found out about—*

"Jeremiah, Jeremiah," she murmured, beginning to move her left leg beneath her skirt. The leg rubbed slowly, languorously against his. "Do you like me any at all?"

"A lot, Serena—a lot." The feel of her leg turned him so rigid he hurt.

"You're not fibbing to me?"

"No. No."

All at once he knew they wouldn't stop. Knew it as surely as he knew his name.

She'd had other lovers before, or at least there was reason for suspicion. The way she talked. The practiced touch of her hands. And he didn't want his first experience to happen with a soiled woman. Despite the way soldiers bragged, no decent man wanted that.

Yet something perverse in him refused to call a halt to the kissing and fondling. He wanted to discover how experienced she was. And answering that question would answer a larger one: How did a man behave with a woman? Any woman?

Her lashes were soft on his cheek as she clasped his wrist and tugged. Somehow her skirt had hiked up.

"You can feel me if you want."

He did, pressing hard against the cotton underclothes until she moaned. He almost yelled when she put her hand on him in a way he'd never imagined any woman would be so bold as to do. She kissed his ear, murmuring. "You'd be a good husband, I'll bet. A fine husband."

He tried to comprehend all the implications of that astonishing word. They were too many and complex. And now wasn't the time. He flung a leg over her hip—

Instantly, she rolled her head to the side. He saw red light reflected in her pupils.

"What's wrong, Serena?"

"Just wait a minute."

"But I thought—"

"*Wait* a minute!"

Fury then: "Damn it, I thought you wanted—"

" 'Course I do! I want it as badly as you! Just calm down a little! I noticed the sky all at once—" She struggled to sit up. "What time is it?"

Still frustrated, he growled, "How should I know? I don't own a watch."

"Look over there. The sun's down but the sky's all red."

He jumped up, realizing what it might mean.

He ran to the west edge of the clearing. He could see little through the pines except the seepage of scarlet light that encompassed almost half of the hidden horizon.

Jolted back to his senses, he swallowed. "Serena—" He wiped his face. "That's not sun—that's fire."

"Dear God!"

She scrambled to her feet, knocking bits of weed from her skirt and raking two burrs from her red hair.

"Is it the soldiers?"

"I don't know. We'd better hurry back."

He was angry about the interruption. She sensed it, and raised her head to give him an almost chaste kiss on the lips.

"Yes, we'd better. I'm sorry. There'll be times later—"

"Will there?"

"If you want it."

No, I don't! There's something tangled and wrong about—

The loveliness of her face overwhelmed him. "I do."

He slipped his arms around her waist for one more fierce kiss. Then they set to unhitching Bess and Fred, hurriedly tying them on long tethers and forking out fodder. Finally, shoving and straining, they rolled the wagon tongue-first into the brush.

They couldn't conceal all of it. The back still jutted into the clearing. Jeremiah pulled out his knife and whacked off pine boughs to cover most of it. He smelled smoke now, drifting out of the west.

He checked the lean-to where the household items had been stored, then caught Serena's hand and raced toward the track. They ran through the dark of the pines, stumbling in weedy patches, their faces lashed by branches not seen soon enough.

The smell of smoke grew stronger. The red glare in the night sky brightened.

ii

As they hurried up the lane between the slave cottages, he breathed hard, pain stabbing his chest because of the long run. His bandaged leg ached. Serena clung to his arm, barely keeping pace.

He grew aware of a stir and buzz on the porches of the cottages. An infant bawled. He heard a palm strike. The baby shrieked louder. He groped for Serena's hand and practically dragged her toward the house.

Probably not one buck, woman, or youngster was sleeping tonight. He sensed rather than saw them sitting or standing in small groups in the darkness—whispering and pointing at the glow in the west.

Twice he heard laughter. Some of the nigras weren't frightened at all. The red sky was a signal. *Jubilee!*

When he and Serena started across the rear piazza, a figure bolted from the shadows and ran at them. Serena screamed.

iii

Jeremiah whirled her behind him—then breathed easier, recognizing Leon's hulking shoulders.

"Marse Jeremiah?"

"Not now, Leon."

"Yes, you got to listen! Price—he's gone."

"What?"

"That's right. Nobody seen him since just after you drove off in the wagon. He must of run away when he heard the Yanks was so close."

"We're better off rid of him." Serena declared.

Jeremiah gestured her silent. "Did you tell Mrs. Rose?"

Leon shook his head. "Didn't want to upset her. Things bad enough already."

He grimaced. "If we're lucky, Price is on his way to the blessed freedom of Linkum land."

"Marse Jeremiah, we ain't that lucky. I bet he's hidin' out in the pines, plottin' mischief."

A shudder rippled across Jeremiah's back. He tried to sound unworried. "Thank you for warning us, Leon. Come on, Serena. Hurry!"

iv

They ran straight through the house and out to the drive, where he'd heard voices and glimpsed a spill of lamplight.

Holding the light, Maum Isabella looked surprisingly composed. So did Catherine. The same couldn't be said for the wispy woman in faded bombazine who was seated in the hooded chaise.

The women swayed from side to side, sweaty faced and fanning herself with a kerchief. Jeremiah would have chuckled at the woman's expression, except that he knew she was fearfully frightened.

Next to her sat a haggard Judge Claypool. Two scruffy nigras, each lugging an old portmanteau, stood immediately behind the chaise. As Jeremiah and Serena approached, Claypool exclaimed, "—not staying a moment longer!"

"Where are you going?" Catherine asked.

"Savannah. Nell has a sister there. If you have any brains, you'll get out too."

For a moment Catherine Rose didn't reply. She turned slightly, acknowledging the presence of Jeremiah and her stepdaughter. Her gray, fatigue-shadowed eyes remained calm until she noticed Serena's mussed shawl, dusty skirt, and tangled hair.

Catherine said nothing. But she gave Serena a steady, knowing look. Her face seemed to sadden, then firm again as she returned her attention to the judge. "No, Theodore. We'll stay."

"I swear to God, Catherine"—the old man snatched his wife's kerchief and swabbed the perspiration glistening in the white stubble on his chin; the abrupt movement shifted his coat, revealing the holstered horse pistol—"you have no idea of how many there are. Hundreds. Thousands! All around Louisville. On foot. On horseback. In wagons—the damn wagons are loaded with stolen furniture! Why the hell does an army need furniture? I saw soldiers carrying chicken coops, others leading livestock. They're taking everything! And some of the stragglers—why, you've never laid eyes on such scum!"

"Theodore," she broke in, "this is my home, I'd rather try to defend it than leave."

"Same thing that witless Clive Jesperson said ten minutes ago!"

"Clive Jesperson is right. If we leave, everything will be gone for certain."

"Well, it's your decision. But you'd better get rid of any wines and spiritous liquors because I hear the Yanks want alcohol almost as much as they want food."

"I'll take your advice, thank you."

"Ought to take all of it and *get out!*"

Claypool noticed Jeremiah watching him with disapproval. He blurted, "Nell's heart isn't strong. I'd stay, but I don't feel it's fair to risk—"

"We understand perfectly," Catherine put in, saving him from humiliation. She turned to the ragged blacks. "Floyd—Andrew—you look after Judge Claypool and his wife. Go on now, Theodore. We'll be fine."

Finally, Mrs. Claypool spoke. "You're foolish, Catherine. Foolish! God be merciful over your mistake."

Claypool was almost incoherent with frustration. "Isn't the Almighty she needs to beg for mercy—it's General Sherman! *Giddap!*"

He lashed the reins over the back of his horse, nearly tumbling his panicked wife into the drive as the chaise lurched forward and took the curve with its right wheels lifting off the fine-crushed stone. A moment later the chaise was rattling down the lane toward the highway, the two blacks with the portmanteaus running and puffing behind.

Jeremiah heard the gate open. Someone disturbed the bell rope. The bell tolled once. The mournful echo was a long time dying.

Slowly, the carriage noise faded in the broad band of darkness lying on the land. At the upper edge—treetop level—the darkness shaded from maroon to vivid scarlet. The light shifted constantly, glimmering feebly in one quarter of the sky, intensifying in another. Smoke blew, blurring the distant trees. The wind carried the stench. It came most strongly from the left, from heavy woodlands through which the highway curved torturously before breaking into the open in front of Rosewood.

"It's the Jesperson place," Catherine whispered. "That's where the smoke is. Oh, poor Mr. Jesperson! He's worked all his life to build that little patch into a decent farm."

Jeremiah hardly heard. He was most concerned about the darkness. Unseen, the Yanks were approaching through it. Unseen, Price might be lurking in it.

With that damn gun! he thought, feeling for one ghastly moment just as terrified as he had when he'd first climbed toward Union marksmen at Chickamauga.

Chapter X

The Prisoner

i

On the Monday morning following Thanksgiving, hundreds of miles to the north, Gideon Kent sat cross-legged among the all but silent Confederate officers who formed a ring around the single small stove in the barracks.

During the night the weather had changed. Severe winds out of the northwest had brought snowflakes whirling down on the island the local residents called Pea Patch. The wind speared through dozens of ill-fitting joints in the boards of the shedlike structure.

The barracks had been Gideon's home for six months. The sergeant in charge of this particular pen had lit the stove about half an hour earlier—nine thirty—after tossing in a handful of wood chips. One handful. And he'd done it smiling that unctuous smile Gideon had come to loathe.

"There, boys. Don't say Father Abraham doesn't care about your welfare. You'll be cozy all day and all night too."

A couple of officers had muttered obscene replies. But not loudly. By now, most of the inmates were well acquainted with the temperamental idiosyncrasies of Sergeant Oliver Tillotson. Staying safe in the state that passed for living was just slightly preferable to risking Tillotson's wrath.

The sergeant was always cheerful when he dispensed items necessary for mere survival. A few stove chips or the morning's ration of three hardtacks were presented as though he expected the prisoners to be grateful for his generosity, and by extension, that of the commandant, Brigadier General Schoepf.

Tillotson dealt harshly with complaints. Some said he patterned his behavior after the officer who controlled the island. This Gideon couldn't verify. He'd only seen Schoepf once, from a distance, as the commandant was entering the little Gothic chapel built, ironically enough, by the so-called chain gang: murderers, thieves, and deserters from the Union army who were kept at Fort Delaware along with the Confederate prisoners. Unfortunately he saw Tillotson every day except the Sabbath.

The stove's iron door stood wide open. Yet the heat did almost nothing to dispel the chill in the shed. Gideon's teeth started to chatter. He clenched them. It helped a little.

He'd wakened well before daylight, vainly struggling to find warmth by readjusting his one small, worn blanket. The blanket was folded so half of it cushioned his feet and calves and the other half covered them. But the blanket, now draped over his shoulders, and the grimy overcoat and the filthy clothing beneath, couldn't begin to restore heat to his emaciated body; not even with Tillotson's largesse blazing inside the stove.

The thin paperbound book he was attempting to read slipped from his stiffening hands. Around him he heard the Confederate officers speaking in quiet, resigned voices. Discussing what they always discussed.

How long the war would last.

How they were unlucky enough to be captured and sent to the most feared prison in all the North.

Their loved ones.

And escape. That was a truly laughable subject.

Ridiculous rumors circulated on the island at least once a week. Most sprang from the occasional issues of *The Palmetto Flag*, a pro-Southern newspaper published up the river in Philadelphia. *The Flag* was not permissible reading for the prisoners. But they heard from certain guards that it hinted more than once that the twelve thousand Confederate inmates might break out and seize the whole river corridor.

Which twelve thousand? Gideon usually asked himself when he heard the latest story. *Last month's? Or this month's?* The population of the island in the Delaware River was constantly changing. New prisoners arrived; former ones who hadn't survived the dirt and foul food and sporadic physical abuse were flung into pits in Salem County, over on the Jersey shore. When the air was clear, a man allowed up on the dikes could look out and see gravediggers preparing new pits. The work never stopped.

In Gideon's opinion, if the sponsors and writers of *The Palmetto Flag* wanted an insurrection, they'd have to plan and conduct it themselves. The prison population contained few men strong enough to fight anyone for longer than fifteen or twenty seconds; it required all of a man's depleted strength and mental stability just to endure from day to day.

Growing colder, Gideon gave up trying to read. He let his eyes drift around the circle. Did the other men feel as dispirited and miserable as he?

Most looked as if they did, though there were exceptions. Two officers on the opposite side of the ring, for example. Hughes and Chatsworth. They were disliked by the rest of the inmates of the pen because both had come to Fort Delaware with an ample, and unexplained, supply of Yankee currency. No doubt they had wealthy and influential relatives in the North. In any case, the two had quickly formed an alliance.

With their money Hughes and Chatsworth could solicit extra favors from Tillotson. They bought slivers of soap they refused to share. At the moment they were playing checkers with pebbles. Their board was a section of siding marked off with charcoal. They'd paid Tillotson fifteen dollars for the piece of lumber, and made no secret of it.

The two officers sometimes rented the board to others. But the price was high. Part of the day's rations of each man who wanted an hour's game. There weren't many takers—nor much cordiality toward the profiteers. Hughes and Chatsworth took turns sleeping with the board so it wouldn't be stolen.

Near Gideon were four men much better liked. John Hunt Morgan's brothers, one a captain and one a colonel, were playing euchre with Cicero Coleman, late of the Eighth Kentucky Cavalry, and Hart Gibson, who'd been assistant adjutant general on John Morgan's staff.

John Hunt Morgan was dead now; they'd heard that in October. The audacious cavalryman had raided into the North, been captured, then escaped from a prison in Columbus, Ohio, only to be shot down in a minor skirmish near Greeneville, Tennessee. Another loss of an able man that was creating a disastrous pattern for the South.

Morgan might have been luckier than the rest of us, Gideon said to himself, his closed eyes watering. The book slid out of his lap. For a moment he was too listless to retrieve it from the rank-smelling straw littered on the floor. His mind was drawn along a steadily darkening current of thought: *Might have been better to go quickly, like Stuart, instead of this way, one miserable hour at a time.*

He stretched, hoping the movement would stir him out of his depressed state. He knew he shouldn't permit himself to think such morbid thoughts. He'd worked hard to survive on this damned island by remembering his wife and his small daughter—and his consuming desire to start a new life once he was free.

He'd made an effort to use the time in prison constructively. Use it to continue to make up for the abysmal lack of knowledge that was his constant burden:

If I don't know how to read well, and write well—how to think *well when I walk out of this place—I won't be able to support Margaret and the baby with anything except menial work.*

For them, he wanted to be able to do more than that. So whenever he could, he read. Old issues of *Leslie's Illustrated Weekly,* or pro-Union newspapers from Wilmington and Philadelphia. Sergeant Tillotson passed them out now and then, but always as if he were some blasted millionaire bent on good works and wanting everyone to appreciate it. Tillotson inevitably made it a point to indicate the columns and the engravings dealing with Union successes in the field.

Gideon wished for one of the papers or a *Leslie's* right now. He couldn't concentrate on the peculiar unrhymed lines in the cheaply printed volume Tillotson had grudgingly delivered to him the day before Thanksgiving. The book had been oddly wrapped in a triple layer of brown paper bound with an inordinately long piece of twine.

Except for short topical verses contributed to Virginia papers, Gideon had read practically no poetry during his boyhood and adolescence. He'd found the first few pages of the work called *Leaves of Grass* beyond him.

And he'd been brutally disappointed when *Leaves of Grass* was all Tillotson had handed him; just one slim volume with a short message from his father folded and inserted next to the title page. He'd been hoping for a good-sized shipment of books, hoping for it ever since early November, when he'd received an already opened letter written from the parsonage of the small Methodist church on Orange Street in New York City, where Jephtha Kent had again taken up his original calling.

In the letter, Jephtha had described how difficult it had been to locate his son.

He'd begun his search after a note from Lexington reached him via a route he preferred not to describe. Gideon supposed the route was across the warring lines. He'd heard there was still a good deal of illegal trading and smuggling going on. At any rate, Fan had informed Jephtha their eldest son was a prisoner. She didn't know where.

Former newspaper contacts in Washington made inquiries. They reported to Jephtha that Major Gideon Kent was incarcerated along with other officers, enlisted men, civilian political prisoners, and Yankee felons on the island located where the Delaware River took a sharp, almost ninety-degree turn toward the southeast, below Wilmington.

Gideon hadn't wanted his reply to be read. His request might be snipped out by the censor. So he'd answered Jephtha with the help of an overworked, prickly tempered physician from the prison infirmary. The doctor voluntarily visited the barracks every few days, checking on the health of the inmates. He was one of the few Yanks at Fort Delaware who seemed to give a damn about the captives—and he usually went away in bad spirits, grumbling and cursing over what he'd seen.

Gideon had persuaded the doctor to smuggle a sealed letter off the island in his satchel and post it. The letter asked Jephtha for books.

Presently a second communication from Jephtha arrived. It said he'd attempted to gain permission to visit his son. The permission had been denied. Still, Jephtha's Washington contacts might at least make it possible for Gideon to receive reading material. He'd gotten his son's letter. But he'd wisely phrased the statement about books as if the idea were his own.

Thus, on the day before Thanksgiving, Tillotson had brought Gideon the volume of poetry. "A gift from that Copperhead father of yours, sir." Tillotson mockingly addressed all the officers in the shed as *"sir."*

The note the censor had allowed to remain in the book promised that Jephtha would pass along any information he might unearth concerning Gideon's two younger brothers. Their welfare was part of Gideon's constant burden of fear.

He feared for Margaret and little Eleanor as Grant's war machine maneuvered toward Richmond.

But he feared for Matthew, too, vanished on a blockade runner.

And for Jeremiah, who'd mustered in and had been shipped on the cars to the Army of Tennessee.

God, he said to himself, blue-lipped and shivering, *how long can a man last, not knowing what's happening to his loved ones?*

How long can a man last that way—in a place like this?

The pessimistic thought was again counteracted by shame. When they'd shipped him north in a fetid boxcar, he'd vowed he'd live through the worst the Yanks could offer. But he'd had no notion of how bad the worst could be.

His normal weight was a hundred and sixty pounds. He guessed he'd lost at least thirty of those pounds by now. Flesh had been steadily stripped from his tall frame by the inadequate rations: three hardtacks at nine a.m., and three more in midafternoon, plus an occasional piece of moldy bacon or a gill of watery slop Tillotson, with a straight face, called rice soup.

And water. God above, what water!

During the baking summer, the prison tanks had nearly gone dry due to a lack of rain. A water boat had run up nearby creeks to resupply them. But the unspeakable stuff that came gushing out of the boat's hoses was tainted with brine; the boat hadn't gone upstream far enough to escape the salty tidewater.

And whenever the hoses refilled the tanks, the influx stirred a hideous sediment in their bottoms. Once Gideon had tried a cup from a new supply and vomited when he saw bits of leaves in it, along with the eye of a fish and several white wormlike creatures writhing in the murky fluid.

Now he drank water only when absolutely necessary. He also avoided the stomach-turning delicacies to which some of the other officers had resorted in desperation.

This morning all the circumstances of life in the prison seemed to come down on him with a ferocious pressure.

The shed was so frigid he could barely move. His hunger, his physical weakness, the roughness of his unwashed skin—and the bitterness he felt because his father had only been able to send him one book of incomprehensible poetry—stirred a rage in him that was almost overpowering.

He yearned to strike out. But at what? At whom?

His captors? Old Tillotson?

Futile.

But trying to survive in this pestilential place was proving futile too. All through August he'd watched men sicken and die as the sun broiled the alluvial mud of the Pea Patch. Overloaded boats had carried corpses stacked like cordwood to the Jersey pits.

He'd seen hysterical men turn on their guards, only to be beaten half to death, then carried away, to the infirmary. Those men disappeared too. The infirmary was said to be run on a reasonably humane basis. But the injuries dealt out to those who rebelled were usually too severe for repair; punishment for guards who defended themselves was nonexistent.

Margaret, he thought, the water in his half-closed eyes

turning to tears. *Margaret, I've been trying to pull through this. Believe me I have. But you don't know how hard it is.*

His right hand fumbled beneath his filthy coat. Pressed the pocket of his uniform blouse almost unconsciously. His fingers probed until he found the reassuring contours of the scrap of cloth in which he carried the little memento of his daughter. A lock of her hair; it had been with him since a few days after she was born. Some prisoners kept Bibles or Testaments. The precious curl from Eleanor's head was his religious token.

Touching it through the dirty cloth of his uniform, he wished for the impossible—a less hostile war. One in which the hatreds hadn't built so steadily, until they affected every phase of the struggle.

Mounting hostility between the warring sides was responsible for so many men being imprisoned in this wretched condition. When the North had begun organizing army units of runaway blacks, Jefferson Davis had decreed that any such soldiers captured, as well as their white officers, were not to be treated as prisoners of war, entitled to exchange. They were to be returned to the states from which the slaves had escaped, there to be punished under local laws. In May of '63, General Halleck had responded by ordering exchanges halted altogether. When Grant had assumed command, he'd made certain Halleck's policy was strictly enforced.

And after the war—what then? Tillotson bragged that he was a "hard peace" Republican, as opposed to the re-elected Lincoln, who favored more compassionate terms as soon as the conflict ended, as it surely would, with the South defeated. When that happened, wouldn't the hostilities linger?

Hell, what did he care? He just wanted to *get through it,* survive this time and this place by reading, learning, filling his head with words and ideas that might help him start again when—*if*—he were ever shipped home to Richmond.

If there was still a Richmond

The Yankees wanted that city worst of all, wanted it captured, even destroyed.

And Margaret was there.

The shed and all it represented had become unbearable to Gideon. Painfully conscious of his lack of strength, he staggered to his feet, then apologized to another cavalryman, Colonel Basil Duke, for bumping into him. Red, exhausted eyes turned his way when he broke through the ring of men huddled around the stove and lurched away. No one spoke.

He stumbled down the dark aisle between the pine bunks, pausing beside his own to slip the book of poems under the folded blanket. Then he moved on toward the end of the building, to an open doorway, Tillotson's lamplit cubicle.

With a hand that felt like granite, he gripped the jamb of the door, gulping less poisonous air, and savoring the heat from Tillotson's stove. Because it was enclosed by thin walls, the stove concentrated a fair degree of heat in the tiny room. Oilcloth had been tacked over two drafty windows.

Oliver Tillotson glanced up from a copy of *Leslie's*. He was about sixty, overweight, but no weakling even though he was far too old for combat. He wore a holstered Colt on his hip. In front of him on the desk sat a small, cheaply framed photograph of a dour woman and five adolescent boys in stiff paper collars and ill-fitting suits. Next to the group portrait lay the symbol of authority Tillotson affected—a stick cut from a walnut limb; a stick darkened and worn smooth by the pressure of Tillotson's pudgy fingers.

The stick was two feet long, perhaps three inches in diameter. Gideon had seen it used on two officers in the barracks. One had complained to Tillotson about his arrogance and refused to be quiet when Tillotson ordered it. The other had found maggots in a piece of bacon and turned on the guard, screaming, berserk. Both men had been beaten, sent to the infirmary, and never seen again.

As Gideon leaned in the doorway soaking up the soothing heat, Tillotson frowned. The sergeant had a red Saint Nicholas face, the effect enhanced by a neatly trimmed white goatee, white brows, and white hair. There was a deceptively benign look about him even when he was annoyed, as he was now.

"You wanted something, Captain?"

Tillotson played games. He knew most of his charges by name and rank. But he pretended they were indistinguishable one from another. As, indeed, they usually were: unwashed, like Gideon; emaciated, like Gideon; their beards down to midchest, like Gideon's; their eyes half wild and half cowed, like Gideon's.

"I'd like permission to take a turn outside," Gideon said in a voice hoarse from the cold.

Tillotson appeared bemused. "Outside, sir? But it's wintry—"

"It's no better in the barracks."

"You Rebs," Tillotson sighed. He laid *Leslie's* aside. Picked up the walnut stick. Pointed at the family portrait. "When I go home weekends, I tell Ethel how you complain. You never seem happy you're alive rather than dead. My, it's puzzling."

"Is it, now?" Gideon breathed. "I'm certainly sorry you're puzzled. Would it help if I asked whether you eat a decent meal now and then? Or go to bed under enough blankets so you can sleep eight hours without waking?"

With his left hand, Tillotson stroked the end of the stick. "Careful, please, Captain," he said with a broad smile.

"Major. *Major* Kent, and you know it."

"No, you all look alike to me." Tillotson shrugged, his blue eyes maliciously merry. "Just like the niggers you people have penned up and maltreated for over two hundred years. Kent. Kent—oh, yes. Now I remember. Our dedicated reader. Preparing himself for better things when the war's over. You received a book from your Copperhead papa in New York."

Gideon almost swore, fought the oath back. Tillotson clucked his tongue, shook his head.

"I glanced at that material before I delivered it. Nonsensical stuff. Filthy! Ethel and her circle of women at church have discussed that poet. He should be prohibited. He should be arrested. You'll never qualify yourself for anything, reading such swill."

Tillotson was leaning forward, as if offering advice to a nephew of whom he was fond. All at once, sarcasm crept in. "I suppose such material is all right for Rebs, though. Appropriate to your humbled station. Sweets to the sweet, but dregs to the dregs, mightn't we say?"

A vein beat in Gideon's temple. "I asked for permission to go out, not for a lecture."

"Oh, but you Rebs *need* lecturing." Tillotson smiled.

"You must be taught not to complain so much. I can't fathom why you don't like it here."

"Well, it isn't exactly a vacation resort, is it?"

A hostile look on the Christmas face. "And I suppose you fancy our Northern boys are enjoying a holiday in those sinkholes down South? Libby? Andersonville? I suppose you think they're resorts compared to this? You don't know when you're well off, Captain!"

Gideon was seething. *"Major."*

Tillotson slashed the stick in a swift arc and struck the desk, *thwack.*

"Captain, you're vexing me with your disrespect. I have a position of authority to maintain."

"The only one you've ever had, I expect."

Three rapid blinks and Tillotson's mouth shaped into a surprised *O* told Gideon he'd scored an accidental hit. The prison was full of incompetents; men worthless elsewhere. He'd seen a fair number of the same kind in the Confederate army. In all ranks.

But even incompetents would strike out if someone wounded them.

"Hold your tongue! Remember you're speaking to the Government! In this barracks, sir, I am just as important as Mr. Lincoln. More! You'll never set your traitorous eyes on our President. You deal with him through me."

Another whack of the stick emphasized the last word. Then a smile crept back on Tillotson's jowly face. But there was spleen in it. The spleen of a man thrust into a position in which a whim, a change of mind, a word or two could preserve or ruin other men's lives.

"Am I clear to you, sir?" Tillotson asked. "When you walk in here, you are dealing with the *only legal government of this nation.*"

Gideon's forehead slicked with sudden sweat. The fat, arrogant turd! He'd like to take him by the throat and—

No! Remember Margaret. Remember the baby. You've got to come through this whole. If you love them it's your duty to survive.

He blessed the memory of his wife and child. Without its sustaining power in that moment when he looked at Oliver Tillotson basking in the warmth of his private stove, he might have tried to kill the man.

"I say, *sir,* am I clear?"

Gideon answered very softly, "Clear."

"Then ask again. Briefly and respectfully."

A deep breath. "I am requesting permission to take a turn outside."

Tillotson waved the walnut stick. "Much better, sir. *Much* better. Go freeze if you wish. But please close the door. I neglected to do it, and I wouldn't want too much heat escaping into the shed. Brisk temperatures are healthy for you and your comrades."

"Certainly," Gideon answered. "Everyone out there is reveling in the healthful cold."

Another venomous glance. "I'm delighted." A jab of the stick. *"Close the door."*

With a hand tingling one moment and going numb the next, Gideon obeyed. Tillotson had already returned to his reading.

ii

He walked out of the shed, passing between two boys in blue capes. Each sentry's rifle was equipped with a bayonet.

The clouds blowing by seemed only a few hundred feet overhead. Snowflakes swirled down from them. The bite of the wind made Gideon feel even worse than before. Almost immediately, his teeth started to chatter again. He regretted his decision to venture into the open. The sights outside the barracks were even more depressing than those within.

Fort Delaware had been built on a treeless slab of ground several feet below water level. Stone dikes blocked out the river, obstructing the view of the Jersey and Delaware shores. The frozen mud was crisscrossed with ditches that oozed subterranean water on warm days. And the other sheds and fenced enclosures stretching around him were packed with gray men. Gray-garbed, gray-faced, gray-spirited.

Ghosts.

He saw the pale oval of a motionless and sorrowing face framed in the window of one of the barracks. Several young boys were tramping up and down in front of the privates' pen, hugging themselves, stamping their bare feet. When shoes wore out, no replacements were issued.

Over near the Delaware side, the chain gang labored. Sullen, murderous-looking men. The men hauled large carts full of stones used to repair the dikes. Teams of two men were roped to each cart like human beasts of burden. The work of each team was directed by a guard who sat atop the stones piled in the cart, unconcerned about adding his extra weight. Most of the guards were alternately swearing at their charges and shouting at them to pull harder.

Gideon weaved toward a group of officers crouched beside a breathing hole dug out of the mud. There were similar holes everywhere; he threaded his way between.

One of the officers turned to acknowledge his arrival. "Hallo, Kent. Care to join the hunting party?"

Gideon's stomach flip-flopped. "Thank you, no."

"Fresh meat and rat soup if we're lucky."

"Jesus, stop," Gideon said, covering his mouth. He was feeling more nauseated by the moment.

There was a sudden flurry of activity around the hole. Exclamations of glee. Men hunching forward. The crunch of rocks on bone, then pulping sounds. One of the officers laughed, the snow-flecked wind whipping the sound away quickly.

Another officer, no older than Gideon but with a beard already pure white, held up the bloody and still-twitching prize—a plump, hairy water rat. One of the hundreds that infested the island and dug their runs under the hard surface.

"Shouldn't be so persnickety, Gideon," said the officer who'd spoken first. "Doesn't taste half bad once you're accustomed to it."

The white-bearded officer agreed. "Like young squirrel, in fact."

But he'd seen cooked rat meat. White, sickeningly white. He turned away. "Thanks kindly for the invitation. Another time."

"You'll get hungry enough one of these days."

The devil! Gideon thought, staggering on. Tillotson had been right. It was too blasted cold out here.

He noticed a subtle change in the air. Stuck out his tongue. Caught a droplet of water.

The wind had shifted. A mist was blowing upriver from the Atlantic. The snowflakes were turning to freezing rain.

Gideon wiggled his toes inside his cracked boots. Little sensation. None in one big toe. He was better off inside.

He hurried, but all it amounted to was an awkward limp not much faster than his normal walk. As he approached the shed, a man came shooting around the corner, leaning into the wind and holding his flat-crowned black hat on his head.

The man's long gray beard danced on his shoulder, whipped like the ends of the green and black plaid scarf wound round and round his throat and the collar of his shabby, loose-sleeved raglan.

Gideon stepped aside, but tardily. The leather medical bag in the man's right hand gave his leg a sound whack.

The man jerked to a halt, squinted.

"Kent! Very sorry. Can't see too well without my spectacles."

"Morning, Dr. Lemon," Gideon replied, without annoyance. Dr. Cincinnatus Lemon of Delaware City was the man who'd listened to his plea for books, circumvented General Schoepf's strict regulations about the frequency of outgoing and incoming prisoner mail, and posted the letter to Jephtha.

"Been meaning to come by and look in on you," Dr. Lemon said in a voice louder than normal. He was past sixty. His hearing was failing along with his sight. "Something I wanted to ask."

A sharp look at the barracks sentries. "But not here." He risked letting go of his hat to seize Gideon's arm. "Come along to my office."

Relieved to have an excuse to stay out of the barracks a while longer, Gideon nodded. When the two started away, one of the sentries called, "Just a minute, Reb."

Dr. Lemon spun. "Just a minute, nothing! I'll take this prisoner anywhere I please!"

"But, Doctor, he's not allowed out of sight of—"

"He is if I say so. Shut your mouth and go dry your ears."

The sentry reddened. "Where are you taking him?"

"Why, I plan to spirit him into my office, squeeze him

into an empty chloroform bottle, and float him down to the ocean and home to Dixie. Come along, Kent!"

While they crossed the yard, Lemon complained, "Damned cheeky farm boys. Farm boys and doddering old farts, that's all we have on this island. Sorry to say those categories include me. Kent, will you hurry up? I'm freezing what freely translates from the Latin as my arse."

iii

A crowded little room in one wing of the infirmary building served as a communal office for several full- and spare-time physicians attached to the fort. The office was nearly as untidy as Dr. Lemon himself. But it had a stove with plenty of fuel. Gideon sank onto a stool two feet from the open door and raised his hands to the blessed warmth.

Lemon flung off his hat, scarf, and raglan and dumped his satchel on top of them in a corner. While he fished for his glasses in his patched frock coat, someone screamed in one of the wards. Lemon winced.

"Your commander—Stuart—he used to sing a lot, didn't he?"

"Yes, he did. Why?"

Lemon's spectacles sparkled with the flames from the stove as he seated himself at a desk strewn with supply requisitions and patient reports. "I doubt he'd have been so cheerful about this cursed war if he'd heard the music I listen to all day."

Gideon massaged his hands. Some of the numbness was leaving. "I'm afraid I sang right along with him."

"Damn fools, both of you. Americans killing Americans. It hardly calls for a cheery serenade."

"You're right. I decided the same thing after First Manassas—with a little prodding from the young woman I married. We should have stopped the war long before it began. I guess no one knew how."

"They knew. Old men like me—they knew. Some of 'em, anyway. But *they* didn't have to march off to war and die. All they had to do was stay home, pound podiums, and spew slogans. No matter which side you're on, that's inevitably more popular than trying to stop the waste of human life. The filthy, immoral waste of God's gift—"

Veined hands brushed aimlessly over the accumulated papers, as though Lemon couldn't bear to pick them up. The doctor's shoulders were permanently stooped, his face weather-darkened and creased by deep folds and shallow wrinkles. "I'll tell you what I wanted—"

He stopped in midsentence, studying Gideon. The younger man thought there was rheum in the doctor's eyes. Lemon whispered, "Uncanny."

"Pardon?"

Lemon jabbed an index finger between his glasses and his nose, ridding his right eye of the glistening water.

"I said uncanny. I can never get accustomed to your appearance."

Gideon tried to smile. "Pretty disreputable, I admit."

"Not what I meant. Mrs. Lemon and myself, we have seven daughters and one son. *Had* one son. You could be his younger brother. We lost him at Antietam."

"I'm sorry to hear it."

"You'd be even sorrier if you knew who shot him."

"Who?"

"One of the men in his own damn company. Mistook him for a Reb."

"Just about what happened to Stonewall Jackson."

"Just about," Lemon agreed glumly. "My boy took a wound in the chest from a round ball. It damaged too large an area of lung tissue. A round ball always does. A conical ball from a rifled piece would have given him a chance. Cleaner wound. Less tissue destroyed. Conical balls are worse in the abdomen, though. Usually perforate the bowel. The round ball travels more slowly. Often pushes the bowel aside without harming it. It *had* to be a round ball in the lung—from one of his own!"

He closed his right hand into a fist and stared at the desk. In a few moments he composed himself sufficiently to eye Gideon again. "I must say you do look hideous. Not surprised, though. Here—"

He shot out of the chair, opened one of the glass doors of a cabinet cluttered with bottles of pills and tinctures, fished behind them and brought out an amber flask filled with a dark fluid.

"This'll warm you up. Take a fast swig in case someone comes in."

Gideon unstoppered the bottle. Inhaled the almost-forgotten aroma of whiskey. He tilted the bottle and swallowed, twice.

"Thank you, Dr. Lemon." He handed it back.

"Hippocrates is no doubt applauding me from the beyond," Lemon said, ramming the bottle into its hiding place and slamming the cabinet door. The glass vibrated.

"I seldom get his congratulations any more. I'm a disgrace to the profession—because this place is a disgrace. Oafs like your Sergeant Tillotson keep sending me patients I don't want, lack the room to care for, and can seldom save after they're ministered to by our tender staff of keepers. I've protested to that damn Hungarian who runs the island. Think he pays any attention? *Pfaugh!*"

Lemon hurled himself back into his chair, the anger darkening his leathery cheeks. "Mad, this whole business. *Mad!* There had to be a more sensible way to set the nigras free!"

Gideon licked the inside of his upper lip, still tasting the whiskey. His stomach felt warmer. "I wish we'd found it," he told the doctor.

"At least some men such as yourself have a chance of pulling through. You're determined to get out of this infernal place with your bones and your sanity intact, and start over."

Gideon smiled wanly. Lemon had no idea how close he'd come to losing that determination.

"Which brings me to what I wanted to ask. Did Tillotson—"

A knock. Annoyed, Lemon snapped, "Yes?"

An orderly in a blood-spotted smock looked in.

"Oh—Dr. Lemon. I didn't know whether you were here." He cast a suspicious eye at Gideon.

"What do you want?" Lemon demanded.

"It's about Dunning. In the privates' pen—?"

Lemon sat very still. "The question in your voice is a damned insult. I remember every one of my patients. What about Dunning?"

The orderly fidgeted because Lemon's stare was so intimidating. "I—I found him this morning. Still huddled in his usual corner. But—"

"Gone?"

White-faced, the orderly nodded.

"God*damn* it!" Lemon roared, hurling the whole pile of papers from the desk with one sweep of his hand. The orderly backed toward the doorway.

"Get out. Get out! I'll sign the certificate!" Lemon shouted. The door closed quickly.

Lemon slumped. Presently he faced Gideon again. "And do you know what I'll be forced to write down for cause of death? Nostalgia."

When Gideon frowned, puzzled, Lemon burst out, "Homesickness. Nostalgia! The boy was seventeen years old. For the past five weeks he's spent every waking hour sitting in a corner. No speech. Hardly any movement. When I speak—when I *spoke* to him, he behaved as if he didn't hear me, or even knew I was present. I paid one of those greedy incompetents in charge of his pen—paid him from my own pocket!—to force food down him. Wasted effort. *Wasted!*"

For a moment, Gideon thought Lemon might burst into tears—or destroy every paper and piece of furniture in the office.

He did neither, managing to calm himself again. He removed his glasses to polish them on a clean, worn pocket kerchief.

"You have your own problems. No need to share mine. But God Almighty! If only there'd been enough men of sense to shout down the fire-eaters *and* the worst of the abolitionist crowd. Well, what's the use of speculating? There weren't."

He resettled his spectacles on his nose. "It's the reading material I wanted to inquire about. I delivered the parcel to Tillotson. I've been derelict in asking whether that exquisite specimen of humanity gave you the books."

Gideon's ears were buzzing slightly from the warmth of the office and the sudden effect of liquor on his nearly empty belly. The last word brought his head jerking up. With difficulty, he focused his eyes on the hunched, shabby man at the desk.

"Books? I got one—"

"One only?"

"That's right. Poems by some fellow named Whitman."

"Damn!"

"My father sent *you* the package?"

"Why not? You said you mentioned my name and position in the letter I smuggled out for you."

"True, I did, but—"

"I expect he wanted to be certain the books reached you. I knew I should have brought 'em into the pen personally. Didn't take the time because I had to do three amputations that morning. But I guarantee there were more books than one. There were half a dozen. Books with meat in them. The sort of thing you said you needed to help educate yourself."

"How do you know there were so many?"

"The parcel had been opened and inspected before it was delivered to this office. The contents were listed on a form I had to sign. Let's see—"

An index finger *tap-tapped* a pile of papers.

"There was a second edition of John Bartlett's *Familiar Quotations*. A volume of essays and poems by Oliver Holmes. Reade's *Cloister and the Hearth*—that's a romance. Historical stuff, but not bad. There was Waldo Emerson's *Conduct of Life*. And your father even included *Parson Brownlow's Book* published two years ago. Brownlow's a hard peace maniac from Tennessee, but I expect your father thought you were man enough to hear what the shrillest anti-Southern voices are still saying. The Whitman was the final item in the package—you got none of the others?"

"None."

"That thief!" Lemon seethed. "That miserable shit of a thief. Kent, wait! Let me report it to Schoepf. Don't brace Tillotson yourself, you'll only damage your chances of getting out of—"

The slam of the door cut off the rest of the warning.

Gideon was barely conscious of the cold as he reeled into the open, his ears still buzzing and his stomach aching from the liquor. He crossed the yard in a limping run, understanding now why so much twine and paper had been wrapped around a single book.

One of the barracks sentries made a snide remark about Gideon's kissing the doctor's behind to obtain favors. He paid no attention. A larger anger occupied him as he lurched past the armed men. His blue eyes took on a glazed, almost demented look as he kicked open the barracks door and, a moment later, Tillotson's.

iv

"See here, sir!"

The sergeant leaped up, *Leslie's Weekly* drifting to the desk in disordered sheets.

"Who gave you leave to crash in that way? When the door's closed, the order is *knock*."

"You're a thief, Tillotson," Gideon rasped. "You're a thieving Yankee son of a bitch."

Tillotson's pink face paled. His eyes darted, worried. Gideon swayed on his feet, dizzy from the cold and the alcohol, yet buoyed by his rage.

"I'll not stand for such profane, insolent talk from a prisoner," Tillotson warned, raising the walnut stick hastily plucked from beside the family photograph.

"You gave me *one* book! My father sent more. Where are the rest?"

Tillotson blinked. "The rest? I don't understand, sir!"

"The rest of the books in the package Dr. Lemon delivered to you!"

"Dr. Lemon?" The way the sergeant pronounced the name gave it an unclean sound.

"I just saw him."

Tillotson sniffed. "Evidently. Serving spiritous liquors to prisoners is against the rules of—"

"Shall I fetch him over here to repeat his story?"

Oliver Tillotson eyed the unsteady figure in front of his desk, calculating Gideon's physical strength—or lack of it. Then, surprisingly, he smiled. "Not necessary. I expected this matter to come up eventually."

"So you admit it!"

"Why not, sir? You have no voice in what you receive and what you don't. The other books—decent literature, I might add—are safe in my house in Salem. Christmas is coming. The wages here—well, they're hardly adequate for a man with a large family. Every bit helps. I let you have one book, so let's not make an issue of the rest."

"I'm surprised you didn't steal them all!"

"Why, I wouldn't have anything by that Whitman in my home. He's notorious. A pervert, they say. We're God-fearing people. But my boys, now—they'll be delighted to find Reade and the Holmes book under the tree. 'The Chambered Nautilus' is a first-rate poem. First-rate!"

"You had no damn right—" Gideon began.

"I wouldn't make an issue of it, Major Kent," Tillotson purred, stroking the stick. "Leave this office immediately."

The order, and the insulting tone, shattered Gideon's control. Even as he circled the desk, he knew he was inviting reprisal. But he couldn't help himself—and hardly cared.

Before Tillotson could react, Gideon caught the sergeant's throat in both hands.

The obese man's eyes opened wide a moment, terrified. Then he lunged upward from his chair, pushing Gideon. He sidestepped, a wrenching movement—

"Assistance! Assistance here!"

Bellowing, Tillotson tore loose from Gideon's strangling grip. In the shed proper, Gideon heard raised voices—the other prisoners, wondering about the outcry.

Gideon groped for the sergeant's throat again, feeling perilously weak. Tillotson brought the walnut stick arcing toward the side of his head.

A moment after the impact, Gideon's legs buckled. His cheek raked the corner of the desk. He fell to his knees, clung to the desktop with both hands.

"Assistance!" Tillotson screamed, beating the stick on Gideon's knuckles.

Damn fool, Gideon thought as pain tore along his forearms. *Damn fool to lose your head when you don't have any strength left.*

The door burst open. The guards appeared, bayonetted rifles at the ready. Tillotson hit Gideon's knuckles again. Gideon let go of the desk, sliding sideways.

Tillotson darted around the desk and booted him in the ribs, twice. Gideon flopped over. Heard men running.

The sergeant's white hair was disarrayed. "Waldo, come in! Prentice, stay outside and close the door. If anyone tries to push by, use the bayonet. No matter what you hear."

The door shut. Gideon couldn't focus his eyes. He saw two Saint Nicholas faces, one lapped over another.

Tillotson crouched down, the stick in one hand. With his other he seized Gideon's beard and yanked.

Gideon's head jerked up, wrenching a neck muscle. Tillotson hung on, wet-lipped, panting. Gideon lifted his right hand. He could barely bend his fingers, let alone form a fist. Tillotson beat his hand down to the floor with two blows.

"Waldo, kneel on his belly. That's the way. Major Kent assaulted me. *Assaulted* me. Can you fancy that? It's necessary for us to discipline him. Oh, yes. Severely!"

The sergeant's figure loomed, distorted, as he rose and lurched to the open stove. He thrust the tip of the walnut stick into the flames. Almost instantly, Gideon smelled burning wood.

"Did you know Major Kent is a student, Waldo? A reader?" Tillotson's chest heaved; he was still out of breath from the surprise attack. "He hopes to improve himself. Wants to be ready to be welcomed back into the populace when the war's done. But he's also rebellious. Dangerously so. I've been too lenient."

The smell of charring wood grew stronger. Gideon saw a wisp of smoke curling past Tillotson's sweaty face.

"Too lenient," the big man repeated, smoothing his small goatee. Outside, Gideon heard a clamor of questions from the other officers, then the guard warning them he'd fire if they came any closer.

Tillotson was at last able to chuckle. "I believe we should make it somewhat more difficult for Major Kent to practice his rituals of self-improvement."

Terrified by a sudden suspicion, Gideon tried to struggle up. "You sadistic, fat old—"

Tillotson drew back his right boot, then drove it forward, kicking Gideon's temple.

His head snapped over—violently. What little strength he had left drained away. He began to float in a kind of haze. Tillotson sounded far off.

"One more such remark, Major, and we'll make it impossible for you to study. Impossible. I trust that sort of lesson won't be required. Clamp your hand on his head, Waldo. Hold him still!"

Then Gideon saw it. The walnut stick. Its smoothly rounded end glowing red. An inch down, the wood smoked.

Tillotson dropped to both knees, adding his restraining

hand to the guard's. Gideon tried to wrench his head away. Failed.

He felt the heat. He watched the red tip of the stick grow and grow, like the August sun doubling, tripling in size. Behind it, Tillotson's avuncular face glistened with sweat.

Gideon's hand moved unconsciously toward the wrapped lock of hair in the pocket of his blouse. He lacked the energy to reach it.

"You were very rash to assault me, sir," Tillotson scolded, slipping the heated stick between his wrist and the guard's.

The second after Gideon's left eyelid closed reflexively, the stick touched it.

Tillotson put weight on the stick. Gideon arched his back, the pain nearly unbearable—

The pressure lifted. His spine struck the floor. He gasped for one good breath, couldn't seem to fill his lungs. He was too weak to resist any longer.

Tillotson released his chin and used his free hand to carefully lift Gideon's left eyelid. The flesh of the lid was burned, stinking.

"Yes, indeed, you made a mistake, Major. As that fellow Poe wrote in one of his queer tales—no one attacks me with impunity. No one, sir!"

Panting, he jammed the stick against the exposed eye.

Gideon screamed.

★ *Book Two* ★

War like a Thunderbolt

CHAPTER I

ENEMY AT THE GATE

i

AS THE SOUND of Judge Claypool's chaise faded away, Catherine confronted Serena and Jeremiah in Rosewood's drive. "It certainly took you long enough to hide the wagon."

"Got dark, ma'am," Jeremiah said quickly, to prevent an outburst from the girl. "Made the work of maneuvering the wagon a mite harder."

Catherine looked pointedly at her stepdaughter's bedraggled dress. "If that's *all* you did. Work."

Before Serena could retort, the older woman turned to Maum Isabella. "I expect we'd better heed the judge's advice. You and the house girls empty the sour mash jugs in the larder. Pour out every drop. The wines and cordials in the sideboard—get rid of those too."

At last Serena had a chance to retaliate. "Even your favorite blackberry?"

"Everything."

"You mean to say you can get along without it for more than twenty-four hours?"

Catherine stayed calm. "I can. Go help the girls."

Serena's eyes mirrored the fire smearing the horizon. "That's nigger's work!"

"It's *our* work now. You *do* it."

"Blast it, I won't!"

Catherine stepped forward, digging her fingers into her stepdaughter's shoulder. Serena wrenched away. For a moment Jeremiah saw pure enmity in the eyes of both women.

But Catherine wouldn't be denied. She grabbed her stepdaughter again. Serena winced. Her right hand fisted. Jeremiah thought she might strike out.

Catherine stared her down. Maum Isabella stepped up to Serena's side and touched her gently. "Come on, Miz Serena. The work won't take long."

"I'll be glad to lend a hand—" Jeremiah began.

But Catherine shook her head. "I want you out here with me. We've got to keep watch."

Serena's height gave her a certain advantage over her stepmother. But Catherine's will offset any physical difference between them. Catherine's will—and Catherine's eyes. With a disgusted exclamation, Serena flounced into the house. Maum Isabella followed, carrying the lamp.

Catherine walked a short way down the piazza. The distant firelight falling through the cypresses made a lattice of light and shadow on her cheeks. In a polite voice, she asked, "Would you fetch a couple of chairs out here, Jeremiah? We might as well be comfortable while we wait."

He went into the house, hearing muttered complaints above the clink of glassware in the dining room. Serena rebelling—even as she did what she'd been ordered to do. As a kind of soothing counterpoint, Maum Isabella kept up a running patter of talk.

Jeremiah carried the chairs out one at a time, arranging them a yard to the right of the dark open windows of the sitting room. Catherine settled herself gracefully.

He took a place beside her, checking to make sure the sheathed knife was secure in his boot, and the hilt tugged up enough to be easily grasped in a hurry. Noticing Catherine's quizzical look, he explained, "Just seeing to my knife. We may need it soon."

"You've been saying we wouldn't."

"I know. But the stories keep getting worse. Now there's that fire—I thought the burnings would surely stop."

Catherine's nod was slow, grave. In contrast to her firmness with her stepdaughter, she looked almost beaten now.

Her shoulders slumped. She stared down the lane of live oaks toward the highway. Finally, grasping the arms of the chair as if to draw strength from them, she said, "For the moment let's try to forget General Sherman. I sent Serena inside because I wanted to speak privately about another matter. One that's very important. To you."

Her faint intonation of warning set him on edge. Guardedly, he replied, "What is it?"

He already suspected the subject and wished he were somewhere else.

Her first sentence proved his suspicion was correct. "It shouldn't have required so much time to hide the wagon."

"Mrs. Rose, I told you—the darkness was a handicap. We—"

"Spare me your fibs, Jeremiah," she broke in softly. "I'm not angry. You're too young to know what you're doing. Or, rather, what's being done *to* you."

He bristled. His tiredness, and the tumultuous emotions Serena had aroused, pushed him close to anger again. Catherine kept gazing at the red-tinged oaks while she continued.

"I dislike raising indelicate subjects. But I feel I must. I've noticed a change in Serena's attitude toward you. A very rapid and abrupt change. You don't lack intelligence. Surely you've noticed it as well?"

A nod admitted it.

"Do you know the reason for it?"

"I have an idea."

"Tell me."

"No, ma'am. You tell me."

"Isn't it obvious? She's discovered you're not a poor boy. In fact I expect you've more wealth and—if we survive this war—better prospects for the future than the half-dozen beaux Serena's had since she was dismissed from Christ College. No, please don't interrupt. I must say this while there's time. Young men in the neighborhood know Serena's character. Oh, she's charming to the eye. But those same young men—before they all went off to the army—Jeremiah, there wasn't one among them who called more than three or four times. Her behavior shocked them. I feel un-Christian saying this about my late husband's child. But—"

A shrug. He knew she wasn't telling the truth. She loathed Serena as much as Serena loathed her.

"—but it's for your own benefit. I was a teacher, you know. I've worked with young people. You think you're grown, but you're not, Jeremiah. You're still—unshaped. Malleable. You must understand one fact above all." A long sigh. "Serena is—not possessed of a stable temperament."

Catherine turned in her chair and gazed directly into his eyes. "Do you understand what I'm attempting to say?"

He wanted to swear, wanted to curse her for speaking against the girl who'd roused such intense feelings within him. He restrained the impulse and settled for a deprecating laugh.

"Think so. But my own mother used to say as much about me."

Catherine shook her head. "I can't believe that."

"Oh, yes, ma'am. She did. She claimed my brothers and I all inherited what she called a cussed streak. We got it from our great-grandmother, a Virginia lady named Fletcher."

"Well, you don't strike me as cussed, as you call it. Just very young. Very susceptible to—"

Another pause. Somewhere inside, perhaps in the hall, he thought he heard a footstep.

"—to feminine ways."

Catherine leaned toward him.

"I'm deeply appreciative of what you've done for us, Jeremiah. Just your presence—a male presence—has been a great comfort. And the loyalty to my late husband that brought you here is commendable. But the moment the trouble's over—the moment the Yanks are gone and it's safe for you to travel—you must leave. I won't repay you by allowing you to become—entangled with Serena. You're a decent young man. But still"—a gesture—*"malleable."*

Suddenly there was a raw sound to her voice. "I tried to raise her well! But Henry favored her too much. Overruled my discipline constantly!"

Because you despised her real mother, and he tried to make up for it?

He didn't utter the question aloud. But he was becoming

convinced Catherine Rose was striking back at a dead woman through her child.

"I hope you do understand what I'm trying to say, Jeremiah. I'm worried that you'll allow Serena to"—again she searched for words—"to exert an influence you're too inexperienced to resist."

His resentment had become overwhelming. "Ma'am, I'm fully old enough to look out for—"

She refused to let him finish. "I won't be so rude as to subject you to questions about why you took such an unusual amount of time hiding the wagon. Or why Serena came back so disarrayed. Frankly, I don't need to ask. I simply want to beg you to leave as soon as you can. I've seen the way you look at her. She's a handsome girl. I don't deny that. But there are—depths to her that you can't begin to perceive after such a short acquaintance. She has traits in common with her mother. She's greedy. Lewd. She"—the momentary compression of Catherine's lips pronounced final judgment even before she finished the sentence—"she is not moral." A whisper then: "*Not a moral person.* All the young gentlemen who called soon realized it."

Jeremiah exploded, "Mrs. Rose, I can't believe you care so little about your own stepdaughter!"

Catherine didn't take offense. "I told you I tried. For years! Finally I saw the truth I'd been attempting to avoid. That's why I wouldn't want Serena—associated permanently with a person I liked or respected. And I like and respect you."

One hand reached out, clasping his fingers. The pressure was intense.

"Leave her alone, Jeremiah. For your own sake."

The almost frantic clutch of Catherine's fingers repelled him. Without realizing it, he'd become Serena's partisan. It had happened, he supposed, during the frenzied kissing and fumbling an hour ago.

"Jeremiah?"

"What?"

"Give me your promise you'll leave when you can."

"No, ma'am, I can't do that."

"Why not?"

How could he confront her with the fact that she'd become suspect on several counts? There was her talk of Christianity and kindness coupled with her hypocrisy about taking wine. There was the old animosity toward Rose's first wife he'd learned about from Serena. And most of all, there was this quiet, venomous attack.

He couldn't explain those reasons. Much as he resented all she'd said, and knowing full well that Serena's new interest was most likely caused by the money, he still couldn't turn on Mrs. Rose. She'd treated him well. Perhaps she'd convinced herself she was still doing so.

"Jeremiah—*why not?*"

He was rescued when Catherine jerked around in her chair, to face the highway. Almost at once he caught the sound too. A lowing and bleating—out there in the darkness.

Then, muffled but unmistakable, the ragged rhythm of marching.

Catherine leaped up. "There's livestock on the road!"

"And men," he said, as she gathered up her skirts and ran along the piazza.

"If it's the Yanks, they aren't going to set foot on this property!"

All at once she was gone, dashing wildly down the lane between the live oaks whose trunks showed faint redness on their western sides.

ii

Jeremiah didn't follow her. He was too stunned and upset by her attack on Serena.

The lowing and bleating and out-of-cadence tramp of boots grew steadily louder. Finally he drove himself into motion, left the piazza, took three strides across the drive.

"God*damn* her vile tongue!"

He whirled.

Serena stood in the main doorway.

iii

He might not have existed; the girl paid no attention to him. She gazed down the lane where Catherine had vanished. She was trembling.

Suddenly she riveted her eyes on his. He almost cringed at the hate he saw.

"I went into the sitting room to hunt for one last decanter."

She needed to say nothing more. He remembered the open windows not far from the chairs and the sound of a furtive footstep.

Serena's knuckles were white as she gripped the jamb. "You're not going to listen to her, are you? I'm not half so wicked as she wants you to think!" She beat a fist against the wood. "Sometimes I wish one of those Yanks would come around here and *kill* her!"

Jolted, he exclaimed, "My God, you don't mean that!"

She covered her eyes. "No. No. But—she makes me so blasted *mad*!"

She rushed forward. "Jeremiah, she's detested me since the day she married Papa. You know why? Because she detested my mama's reputation. She felt that having me around all the time soiled her—even though I never did anything to make her feel that way!"

The girl seized his shoulders. "If you listen to her—to those vicious stories she makes up—it'll ruin everything!"

Excited by her touch, he started to ask her to explain exactly what would be ruined.

Laughter—raucous male laughter—burst out down by the gate. For a moment he'd forgotten the strangers on the road. The laughter reminded him.

He spun, his heart hammering, just as Catherine's faint cry of protest rang out.

"I think the Yanks are here. I have to go."

"No. You wait!"

"Serena—"

"You *wait!* This is too important." Her urgency, and her hand, held him at her side.

"Jeremiah, you have to trust me. It's important to me that you do. I don't want you to think I'm the sort of person she says. 'Course I've flirted with boys. I admit it.

Maybe I've even done more than flirt. But never anything truly wrong. Never! The rest—anything you thought I meant back in the woods—that was teasing. I'm not experienced." Tears glistened in her eyes. "That was all teasing. Dumb, idiotic teasing!"

"Can I believe you?"

"Yes—and I want you to—I do!" She pressed against him.

But he asked what needed asking, "What's the reason, Serena? The money?"

"I'd be a ninny to say no. Any girl's anxious for a good catch. But that isn't the only reason. If you were eighty years old and rich as Midas, I wouldn't look at you. Not for a minute."

Relief flooded through him. She'd caught him off guard by being so candid about the inheritance. What lingered to bother him was her claim of inexperience. The implication of chastity. Did he dare believe that—much as he wanted to—after what had happened in the pines?

Catherine's faint cry sounded again. Someone had hold of the bell rope. *Clang!*

"Serena, I can't wait any longer!"

Clang! Clang! The bell raised echoes across the smoky countryside. He gave the girl a last anguished look and ran for the road. Ran toward the woman who needed his help. Ran from the girl he wanted against all doubt and reason—

She is not moral.

That was a damning accusation. But where did the guilt, the immorality really lie? Who had been honest about her change of heart?

Serena.

Who had belittled—condemned—the very child she'd raised. And done it secretively?

Catherine.

The balance tipped, heavily and finally, in favor of the girl who'd stirred fierce new longings with her mouth, her hands, her body.

His long tawny hair streamed behind him as he raced down the lane beneath the festoons of tillandsia. Ahead, he saw a lantern bobbing like an immense firefly. He glimpsed men and livestock. Heard an altercation growing louder and more acrimonious.

SHE IS NOT MORAL.

For an instant, he was unsure of his decision. Then, equally swiftly, he was ashamed of the doubt. Above all, he *wanted* to believe Serena.

And he couldn't flee—not later, and certainly not now. Directly ahead, where the lantern's yellow light paled in a sudden drift of smoke, he saw the boisterous Yanks.

iv

By the time he reached the closed white gate, Catherine had taken possession of the rope dangling from the bell post just inside. Two companies of scruffy, bearded men in Union blue had halted on the highway. The column of uneven ranks had come along the straight stretch leading out of the dense forest separating Rosewood from the Jesperson farm, which had evidently been torched. Thick, pungent smoke drifted from that direction.

In the cornfield on the highway's far side, a herd of about two dozen cattle and as many sheep milled. By the lantern's light, Jeremiah could just discern ragged drovers prodding the cattle into a steadily shrinking circle. The drovers' shouts and profanity were loud in the night air.

The soldiers outside the fence jabbered at one another in a guttural foreign language. Jeremiah supposed they must be some of the Dutchmen serving with the Northern army. Among the miscellany of arms they carried he spied several of the new Spencer rifles. The deadly repeaters held seven balls and could be fired every three or four seconds by a practiced hand. He'd seen one of the pieces, captured after Chickamauga. Lieutenant Colonel Rose had once remarked that the Spencer's rapid-fire capability would give the Yanks a final, decisive advantage in the war.

Some of the Union men had other, more unusual equipment with them: spades and axes, slung over shoulders or trailing in the dust. The lantern held by a burly sergeant with a bad complexion revealed the team and driver of a white-topped wagon stopped in the dark to the left. Some nigras clustered around the front of the wagon, clapping and joking. Jeremiah counted five—and was relieved that Price was not among them.

One of the nigras wore a top hat and an emerald-colored frock coat. The young woman with the group was gowned in shimmering orange silk. Undoubtedly the clothing had been stolen from a former master and mistress.

Beside the sergeant with the lantern stood two officers. One, the senior, was a square-faced, middle-aged man with mild brown eyes and a ragged uniform blouse. Hovering close to him, a younger lieutenant with a pointed chin eyed Jeremiah and wiped the heel of his right palm with the tips of his fingers. The nervous hand hovered beside the butt of his holstered revolver.

The older man addressed Catherine in heavily accented English. "Captain Franz Poppel, madam. This advance party of engineers is widening and corduroying roads for General Sherman's army."

"You mean you're going to tear up the highway?"

"No, this road is adequate. However—"

"Roadwork isn't all you're doing!" Catherine exclaimed, pointing to the cornfield. "You're stealing livestock from civilians too!"

Poppel acknowledged guilt with a blush and bob of his head. The sharp-chinned lieutenant turned to her, eyes flinty. "What we do is our business."

Poppel held up a hand. "Lieutenant Stock means we are under orders to forage according to our requirements."

The lieutenant refused to be silenced. "This your property, woman?"

"Would I be down here if it weren't?"

"Show a little more respect, if you please," the lieutenant snapped, taking two swift strides to the fence. He reached across, caught Catherine's upraised arm—her hand was still on the bell rope—and jerked it down against the top rail of the fence.

The rope danced. The bell pealed. The lieutenant levered Catherine's arm down harder. "Else we'll teach you how."

"Stock!" Poppel exclaimed as Catherine's body twisted. She was in pain, but she didn't cry out.

Captain Poppel moved too slowly to get between his lieutenant and Catherine. *So this is what we're going to be up against?* Jeremiah thought bitterly, bending down fast to reach the top of his boot. He hadn't forgiven Catherine for her remarks about Serena. But she was still a woman.

"Secesh there—he's got a knife!" the sergeant cried.

The lantern began to swing wildly as the man retreated. Jeremiah's hand streaked up, the knife flashing light from pitted steel. Two long steps and he was at the fence.

His left hand shot out like a hook to catch the startled lieutenant by the back of the neck. The lieutenant's grip broke. Catherine scrambled away.

Jeremiah jerked the lieutenant forward. Off balance, the man fell, the side of his head slamming the rail. Jeremiah held the man's head against the rail with one hand, and with the other slid the edge of the knife against Stock's throat.

"You've mauled Mrs. Rose the first and last time." His voice was soft, but his mouth had set in that thin, cruel line.

Bent at the waist, the lieutenant tried to free his revolver with his right hand.

"Go on, get the gun!" Jeremiah whispered. He dug the knife-edge deeper. *"What's holding you?"*

A thread of blood began to trickle toward Lieutenant Stock's collar. There were alarmed exclamations from the ranks. Jeremiah was aware of a blue barrel aimed at his head. Then a dozen more.

"They fire," he warned Poppel, "your man's done."

Stock and the captain realized he meant it. Stock's hand dropped away from his holster. His eyes watered.

"Madam," Poppel exclaimed to Catherine, "beg your son not to provoke this kind of trouble!"

"He's not my son—" she began.

"Shoot the fucking Secesh!" a soldier shouted. Other men yelled agreement.

Sweating, Jeremiah held the knife steady against Stock's quivering throat. "Yes, feel free," he told Poppel. "I guarantee you'll lose one engineer. It's up to you."

Chapter II
Invasion

i

"No firing!" Poppel exclaimed, facing the road. "That is an order!" He spun to Jeremiah. "Let him go."

"So your boys can pick me off? No, thank you."

Poppel swabbed his face with his sleeve. "What do you want?"

"Your promise," Jeremiah answered. "Not to touch this woman again. Not to harm this property or anyone on it."

"We intend to camp on your land tonight—" Poppel began.

"Inside the gate," Jeremiah said with a jerk of his head. "Under the trees. Nowhere else."

"Captain," Stock panted, "don't take orders from a goddamn *boy*!"

"This is my responsibility—not yours," Poppel replied. A nervous flick of his eyes toward Jeremiah. His tongue crept over his perspiring upper lip. Then he nodded.

"All right. Stock should not have mistreated her. I agree to the terms. We will camp on your land but will not intrude on your privacy. In the morning we will move on. We'll require provisions, however. Corn. Pigs."

"We're supposed to surrender our food just because you say so?" Catherine blazed.

Captain Poppel pointed at the ranks of men. Jeremiah

saw the blue muzzles still poised. Saw hostile faces behind them. A nervous finger could blow him away—

"These are hungry men. We take nothing our orders prohibit us from taking. I will make certain no property is harmed. But I insist on provisions. And," he added to Jeremiah, "that knife."

Suddenly the strain wrenched his face. "Trust me! Else one of those men is liable to shoot you down."

"Can I rely on your word?" Jeremiah asked, searching the captain's face.

"On my word, and on this."

Poppel drew his own revolver. To his soldiers, he said, "After the young man gives me the knife, the first one who moves against him or the woman, I shoot. Now put the rifles down."

Grumbles, low cursing.

"Put them down!"

Slowly, the blue muzzles lowered. Jeremiah studied Poppel again, trying to assess the man's honesty. He thought he could trust him. It was a risk, but the alternative was far less attractive. Wounded or killed, he'd be no use to Catherine and Serena.

"Now let him go," Poppel said.

Jeremiah released the lieutenant's head and pulled the edge of the knife away from his bleeding throat.

The lieutenant's eyes were murderous. But before his fingers reached the butt of his revolver, Poppel cocked his.

"Hands down, Stock. We struck a bargain."

Stock fumed. Poppel extended his other hand.

"The knife now, young man."

He wanted to believe Poppel was decent, not lying. Catherine's expression seemed to urge him to cooperate. "I promise you will not be harmed!" Poppel cried.

"We"—Catherine's voice sounded unsteady—"we'll rely on this officer's word, Jeremiah. Give him the knife."

He dropped the blade into Poppel's palm and stepped back. The captain exhaled loudly, relieved. His gun remained centered on a button on Lieutenant Stock's blouse.

"Very good. Form up the men, Stock." When the lieutenant hesitated, Poppel roared, *"Go!"*

Stock swabbed his neck with a bandana, pivoted, and stalked toward the grumbling soldiers.

"You wait till we leave!" a soldier shouted at Jeremiah and Catherine. "You'll be rooting around in ashes!"

Red-faced, Poppel whirled. "Be quiet! We do not burn private property."

"Then"—Catherine pointed shakily toward the heavy forest to the left—"who fired the Jesperson farm?"

"Not my soldiers," Poppel replied. "With one or two exceptions, these are decent men. They have wives. Families. Homes of their own. I personally guarantee their good conduct. Unfortunately I cannot guarantee the manner in which this entire campaign is being waged. There *are* some units that act without restraint. However, mine is not one. Now may we come onto your land?"

Catherine sighed. "All right."

Poppel bobbed his head again, crisply. "We will camp under those trees. No one will enter the house except myself and my sergeant. I am required to search the premises for concealed arms and ammunition."

Out by the men, Stock shouted, "If that Secesh boy says different, we'll blow his damned head off."

The statement was meant more for the troops than Jeremiah. Shouts of agreement in German greeted it. Poppel whirled again, angry. The noise faded while Jeremiah stood with his hands clenched, hoping he hadn't gambled wrongly.

Catherine's eyes begged him for restraint. He decided threats couldn't really hurt him. What mattered was the captain's ability to exert his authority and enforce his pledge; there seemed no lack of such ability. The Dutchmen were all avoiding Poppel's fierce eyes.

Catherine stood back from the gate.

"Open it for them, Jeremiah."

Some of Jeremiah's tension drained away. In reply to Catherine's instruction, the captain murmured, "Thank you, madam."

Jeremiah reached for the pin. Despite Judge Claypool's reports of devastation and Poppel's remarks about disorderly troops, perhaps a little hope was justified after all. If men like Poppel proved to be in the majority, maybe the Yank march across Georgia might not be so savage and disgraceful as rumor said it was.

ii

He and Catherine stood back while a still-fuming Lieutenant Stock led the first soldiers into the lane.

Others followed quickly, spreading out beneath the oaks on either side. Poppel still had his revolver drawn as he waited beside Catherine and Jeremiah, alert to any signs of disobedience. There were sullen looks, angry remarks in German. But no attempted violence. Poppel's assertiveness and decency had taken the heat out of the situation. Under the trees, some of the soldiers were actually laughing.

The last of the men in blue passed. The noisy blacks started to follow. Catherine whirled to the officer.

"I insist you keep the nigras off the property!"

Poppel shook his head. "I can't do that, madam. They are free to go with us wherever they choose. However, I'll order them not to approach the house."

Flushed, Catherine watched the blacks going by. All at once her eyes opened wide. She recognized the yellow-skinned girl in the orange gown.

"Nanny? Nanny, why aren't you with Mrs. Hodding in town?"

" 'Cause I don't belong to Miz Hodding no more," the girl spat. "I belong to *me*! Linkum and Uncle Billy both say so!"

"You ran away?"

"*Walked* away! I'm free now."

"But Mrs. Hodding has no one to care for her. No one except you."

A shrug. "Too bad."

"Is she all right?"

The girl grinned. "Mighty fine. Last I seen her, she was sittin' in a chair in her parlor with a nice little round hole in her forehead."

Catherine swayed. "Oh, my God. Why?"

"She got bumptious with some of the sojers in town. Somebody took a gun an' fixed her. Wasn't me, but I wish it had been. Miz Hodding laid a rod on me plenty of times. She sold off my little baby boy when he only five! Wouldn't even let me name him Franciscus like I wanted. Made me call him Robert Rhett, same as some old Secesh up in Carolina she admired. She had it comin' to her." The grin reappeared. "You better be careful too."

Linking her arm with that of a laughing young buck, Nanny hurried on up the lane. Captain Poppel looked embarrassed. "There *have* been regrettable incidents."

"Do you really regret them?" Jeremiah shot back.

"Believe it or not, young man, I do. Admittedly, some on our side don't. Sometimes war becomes a handy excuse for behavior that otherwise would never be tolerated. Stock's a prime example. But I doubt every man in Confederate gray is above reproach either. However, I have given my word that no such incidents will take place here. Of course, you must continue to cooperate—"

"What choice do we have?" Catherine responded in a bitter voice as the wagon creaked into the lane and the soldiers flung themselves down among the trees, yawning and chattering in their foreign tongue.

iii

By midnight the grass under the live oaks glimmered with dozens of small lights. The Union soldiers had speared their bayonets into the ground and stuck stubs of candles in the rings.

Catherine had permitted three of Poppel's men to take a pair of hogs from the pen, shoot them, and haul them down the lane. The dead animals had been hacked up by two of the Germans who knew something about butchering. The hogs were roasting now, on spits improvised from bayonets and branches.

The smell of roasting pork drifted up to the piazza. A couple of dozen of the plantation blacks had gathered in the driveway, awed by the sight of some of their own kind mingling freely with the Yanks. But Maum Isabella's presence kept the watchers in line. Several times, a stern warning prevented one or two from running down to join the visitors.

Catherine had returned to her chair. Jeremiah stood nearby, tense and tired. Just as he was wondering where Serena had disappeared to, Captain Poppel and his burly sergeant approached. The sergeant waited in the drive, eyeing a couple of the black women, while Poppel moved down through the shadows cast by the lattices.

"Madam?"

"My name is Mrs. Rose. You can at least be civil enough to use it."

"Of course. My apologies. I must trouble you for your keys."

"Keys?"

"Yes, I'm instructed to open any locked rooms, chests, cupboards, and the like. To conduct a search for those arms I mentioned."

"You took my knife," Jeremiah said. "We didn't have anything else."

Fatigue edged Poppel's voice with irritation. "You will permit me to make that determination."

Catherine stood up. "I'll get the keys for you." She vanished inside the house.

Captain Poppel tried to be cordial to Jeremiah. "What's your last name, young man?"

"Kent."

"A Georgian, are you?"

"Virginian."

"Then how is it that you're on this plantation?"

"Mrs. Rose's husband was my commanding officer. He was killed. When I was invalided out, I came to Rosewood to look after things."

"Praiseworthy," Poppel murmured. "Most men would have fled to wherever they could find safety. Where were you when you were hit?"

"Jonesboro."

"Come now, it's not necessary to be so curt. This is a dirty business, and I don't like it any better than you. I did not leave my own farm to wage war on civilians. Are you the only man on the place?"

"The only white man," Jeremiah responded, less testily.

"Well, it's good you are here. Some of the units following us—I did not care to be explicit in front of Mrs. Rose—they are totally out of control. Men are constantly breaking ranks. Running off to loot and—and other things. Stock would do so if I permitted it. May I ask whether there are any white women besides Mrs. Rose present?"

"Her stepdaughter."

"Is she attractive?"

"What the hell difference does that make?"

"Answer me, if you please!" Poppel erupted. "I am worn-out and not in good humor. You caused me a considerable amount of trouble down at the gate—" He drew a deep breath. "I was merely asking the question to be of help. If the young woman is good looking, and other units stop here, there could be—difficulties."

Jeremiah let out a long breath. "Well, I'm sorry I blew off a minute ago. You seem to be sticking by your bargain."

An offended tone: "Did you think I would not?"

"I hoped you would." Fervently: "More than you can appreciate." Jeremiah rolled his shoulders forward. Twisted his head from side to side. Suppressed a yawn. "Lord, I'm tired."

"Quite understandable." Poppel nodded.

"Captain, considering what you said about more soldiers coming, maybe you could return my knife. It's all I have to defend this place."

"There's no *defending* possible, Mister Secesh," another voice interrupted in a laconic way. The heavyset sergeant had strolled onto the piazza and was leaning against one of the lattices. Jeremiah heard wood crack. The sergeant didn't move, adding, "Uncle Billy's going all the way to the ocean. We got this whole fucking state by the tail."

"That's quite enough, Meister," Poppel said. "Stay where I put you—in the drive!"

Scowling, the sergeant stalked off. When he was out of earshot, Poppel leaned close. "I gave your knife to Stock. A souvenir to promote his cooperation. Have you ever led men?"

"No."

"Well, it is not entirely a matter of force and bluster. Sometimes you must drive them, but sometimes you must also appease them. I have learned that with difficulty. Now concerning your question—"

Catherine reappeared, key ring jingling. She'd evidently retired to remove the ring from the bag tied under her skirts. She handed the keys to Poppel and returned to her chair.

"Search all you want. Just don't touch personal things."

"I'll go with him," Jeremiah offered.

He'd spoken loudly enough for the sergeant to hear. The man exclaimed, "Hell, no. You got no say in this!"

Again Poppel's upraised hand stopped him. "Meister, shut your mouth. He may come."

iv

For an hour the three ranged the house and surrounding area, Jeremiah holding a lamp while the sergeant guarded him with a drawn revolver and Poppel unlocked drawers in the office, trunks in the attic, and the new padlocks on the outbuildings. Presently Jeremiah grew less uneasy. Poppel was acting with great restraint.

In the attic, for example, he discovered the thousand dollars' worth of Confederate bills and the legal papers in the trunk. He examined everything, but replaced all the items carefully and saw that the trunk was once again locked. Again Jeremiah began to feel a touch of optimism. If Poppel proved to be the harshest officer with whom they had to deal, honorable treatment of the women of Rosewood might not be such a far-fetched idea after all.

Sometime after one in the morning, Poppel completed his search and dismissed the sergeant. The captain confessed to a thirst for coffee. He and Jeremiah headed for the house while the sergeant trudged back toward the campsite, where the little candles still flickered in bayonet rings, and loud voices sang a marching song:

"Hurrah, boys, hurrah!
Down with the traitor, up with the star!"

In the kitchen, Jeremiah was surprised to discover Serena seated at the table, a cup of tea in front of her. The Union captain swept off his dusty campaign hat, even bowed.

"Madam. Franz Poppel."

"Miss Serena Rose, Captain," Jeremiah said.

"Delighted!" the captain said. Serena didn't reply.

"Where've you been?" Jeremiah asked her.

"In my room." A glance at Poppel. "Couldn't stand to watch any damn Yankees pawing through everything."

"Captain Poppel's been very decent," Jeremiah countered, moving around Maum Isabella, who was tending the huge iron stove. A spicy smell rose from the oven. "You baking gingerbread?"

"That's right," the tiny black woman answered. "I figured that if we give the soldiers a little something extra, they might go away and leave us be."

"We'll go away in any case." Poppel nodded. "But I'm grateful for the kindness." His eyes rested briefly on Serena's profile. "There are many more men coming, however."

The girl looked at Jeremiah. But he was too weary to interpret whatever she meant to ask or imply. Poppel continued to shoot covert looks at her while Maum Isabella brought the coffee to a boil, poured a mug, and set it down on the table with a faintly insolent thud. Abruptly, Serena excused herself and left.

"I wonder if Mr. Kent and I might have a word in private?" Poppel asked the black woman.

Expressionless, Maum Isabella walked out. Poppel sat down. No one had offered him a seat before.

"That red-haired girl—she's quite handsome."

Jeremiah managed a smile. "I don't need a Yank to tell me that."

Poppel craned around, looking through the doorway leading to the front of the house. He took another sip of coffee, then leaned forward.

"Permit me to make you an offer, Mr. Kent."

"What kind of offer?"

"Kindly keep your voice down! Mrs. Rose—she is handsome but not young. However, that redhead—" Tired as he was, the captain could still sigh appreciatively. "Lovely. Now listen carefully. I was quite serious when I said there are undisciplined men with the army. And I cannot return your knife. However, in the morning, I will go up to the attic again. For one more search."

"You already searched it top to bottom!"

"Young man, are you witless?"

"I'm worn-out. I don't know what the hell you're saying."

Another swift look toward the door. "Up in the attic, I can hand you a spare revolver I happen to have in my kit. You should keep it hidden. Because of that girl."

"I see. I'm sorry I was so thick."

"No matter." Poppel waved. "We have reached an understanding. I would not want anything on my conscience. Such as leaving you wholly unprotected, should other units pass this way."

He drained the mug. "I have two daughters of my own back in Missouri, you see. Sixteen and eighteen. If our positions were reversed, yours and mine, I hope you would do as I am doing."

"Yes, sir, I'd try."

"The attic, then. Tomorrow morning. But if you reveal a word of my offer to anyone, I withdraw it."

He stood, picked up his dusty hat, and clumped out of the kitchen. Belatedly, Jeremiah called after him, "Captain? Thank you."

A slight hesitation in the captain's step showed the words had been heard.

V

At dawn, Captain Franz Poppel's woodcutters and road builders assembled on the highway while the drovers prodded the confiscated livestock to their feet in the field where they'd bedded for the night.

A portion of the white fence separating the plantation from the road had been smashed by the soldiers, but there was no other visible damage. Two more hogs were hauled from the pens, shot, and their carcasses trussed and flung into the white-topped cook wagon. Corn from one of the cribs was loaded next. Then Poppel staged his little show, announced a search of a corner of the attic he claimed to have overlooked. No help needed—he would see to it personally.

Alone with Jeremiah, Poppel slipped his hand beneath his blouse. He drew out a stained rag wrapped around something with the unmistakeable contours of a revolver. He pulled the rag away, revealing the dirt-speckled gun.

"Take it, Kent. It's a rebel piece anyhow."

The attic was dark and warm; Jeremiah was sweating. Gingerly, he lifted the revolver from Poppel's palm.

The gun measured about thirteen inches, muzzle to butt, and had seen hard use. The feel of the metal sent a shiver up his back. For the first time since he'd awakened to find Price standing over him, he felt whole again.

"Where'd you get this, Captain?"

"I confiscated it at Resaca. From a dead man."

"Never seen one like it."

"Imported model. A Kerr piece, .44-caliber. We do not use them."

Squinting, Jeremiah examined the cylinder. "Five-shot. Four shots left.

"None in the chamber, of course. It's double-action, by the way. I am sorry I have no spare ammunition."

"Four shots are better than none."

"I advise you to hide it well," Poppel said.

Jeremiah pondered a moment, then began to roam through the attic's clutter. At every step he tested the planking by putting his weight on his right leg. At last, back in a corner, he discovered a loose board.

He knelt, tugged at one edge. The pegs had rotted. The end of the board lifted easily. He slipped the Kerr .44 down between the joists, then replaced the plank. As a further precaution, he moved a sheet-draped dress form from another corner to a point just in front of the hiding place.

"Excellent spot," Poppel observed. "I doubt any looter would trouble to rip up an attic floor." He started out.

"Captain?"

"Yes, Mr. Kent?"

"I'm honestly sorry for a couple of the things I said to you."

The captain smiled without humor. "Contrary to what you may have been led to believe, Mr. Kent, not all Northern men are ravening beasts. I only hope you have no reason to need that weapon."

vi

For two hours after Poppel's engineers had tramped on, Rosewood was relatively quiet. Jeremiah hoped the worst was over.

Catherine had retired to her room for a nap, complaining of being unable to sleep during the night. Serena had also vanished again. But he was too tense to rest.

He sat in the kitchen drinking coffee with Maum Isabella, who told him tartly, "Those bad-mannered Yanks ate every last bite of gingerbread without so much as a thank you. No, I take that back. One said it. One of the very first. He also asked for a plate and laid a coin in it. Nobody else paid, though. And a man at the end of the line picked up the coin, slipped it in his pocket, and walked out grinning big as you please."

"Well, we're still fortunate to have gotten off so light—"

Down at the gate, the bell began clanging.

vii

By the time Jeremiah reached the piazza, Catherine was at the foot of the staircase, rubbing sleep from her eyes. She joined him outside as horsemen came thundering up the lane. Blue-coated horsemen. Some of the coats were no better than rags.

Dust billowed behind the riders, making it difficult for Jeremiah to determine how many there were. Across the fields toward the river, he could see infantrymen moving. Hundreds of them, trampling the furrows. A long line of wagons stretched from the woods down the highway. The countryside was covered by men moving on foot and in the white tops, covered—like a land suffering a biblical plague.

The cavalrymen reining up in front of Rosewood looked more like riffraff than soldiers. New riders arrived every few seconds, barely visible in the dust.

Their commander was a man in his late thirties, with sallow skin, thin arms and legs, and the beginnings of a paunch. His eyes were the color of dried mud.

Head on, his face resembled a pear, bulging below the ears. A half-moon of fat hung beneath his stubbled chin. He greeted Jeremiah and Catherine with a mocking touch of his hat brim, then addressed them in a nasal voice unpleasant to ears accustomed to mellower Southern speech.

"Your servant. Major Ambrose Grace of the Eighth Indiana, General Kilpatrick's Third Cavalry Division."

"The Kill-cavalry," Jeremiah said.

A purse-lipped smile twitched the major's mouth. "Sometimes we're complimented with that term, yes."

Suddenly, laughing men shied their mounts aside. Jeremiah groped for the support of one of the white pillars when he saw a black on a mule jogging out of the dust cloud. Catherine drew a breath, loud and sharp.

Price tugged the mule to a stop beside the commanding officer.

"This here's the place I was tellin' you about when I met up with you last night, sir," Price said. "Plenty of good things on this place—an' I know where every one of 'em is hid. I'll help you get 'em all," he added, reaching down to grasp the Enfield musket lying across his thighs.

A bit of red clay clung to the stock. The cartridge box hung from the black's rope belt.

"Damn you," Jeremiah said. "You had it after all."

Price's blue-black face wrenched into a chilling smile.

"Did you really think I didn't, mister soldier? Or that I wouldn't come back an' use it?"

CHAPTER III
THE BUMMERS

i

JEREMIAH TOOK A STEP toward Price. With his attention centered on the black man, he only heard the slither of metal on metal as Major Grace pulled his saber and extended his arm.

"Hold on!"

Jeremiah found himself blocked by the blade. The point touched his shirt. The major twisted the sword slightly. The point pierced cloth, pricking Jeremiah's chest.

With mock seriousness, the major added, "I can't have you threatening one of our most valuable informants."

Furious, Jeremiah yearned to reach up and knock the saber aside. But if he did, he'd probably be gutted on the spot.

Some of the cavalrymen snickered as he stood motionless. The laughter as much as called him a coward. Humiliated, he promised himself he'd get back at them—every one.

Catherine appeared more shaken than he'd ever seen her. Her voice was barely audible as she spoke to the slave with the Enfield. "How could you do this? My husband always treated you decently. So did I."

Price's brown eyes brimmed with animosity. "I don' call bein' kept as property decent treatment."

"But we always tried to take good care of our—"

"Your little bitch stepdaughter took care of me, all right," he broke in. "She took care of me with the whip, her an' Leon. They tried to make me tell about this here gun."

"They did no such thing!"

Price shrugged. "She never told you, that's all. Miz Serena, she ain't just mean, she's a sneak."

"You foul-mouthed bastard!" Jeremiah cried. Only Ambrose Grace's blade pressing into his breastbone kept him from lunging.

"That's enough," Grace said to him. To Price: "You mean to say there's another white female on these premises?"

"Yes, sir. Mighty fetching little piece, too. She might strike your fancy," the black added with a quick smile.

"Have to look into that," Grace murmured. Catherine fisted her hands. Jeremiah's belly hurt.

Grace gigged him again. "Would you kindly step back so I can dismount? I'd like to conduct our business as politely as possible."

Jeremiah didn't budge. Grace frowned.

"Now see here, Reb. If you don't obey I'll have to split you wide open. That's a poor beginning for a friendly visit to this fine home."

"You aren't setting foot inside my—" Catherine began.

"We certainly are," Grace interrupted. "Else this young man's dead on the spot."

ii

Catherine drew a deep breath.

"You'd best do as he says, Jeremiah."

It was the surrender of Stock all over again—only this time the roles were degradingly reversed.

For a moment he was unable to think clearly. He wanted to snatch the saber and turn it on the snide, smiling officer whose unclipped hair straggled from beneath his hat to his frayed blue collar.

"Jeremiah!"

"No, Mrs. Rose. I'm not moving till we get a promise from this—*gentleman* that we'll receive honorable treatment. You especially."

The Indiana cavalryman looked thunderstruck. "*Honorable treatment?* My God, you Rebs have brass! Fair treatment's what you'll get, boy. Fair treatment appropriate to your treason. You and your kind want to keep the niggers penned up 'till the trump of judgment blows. You tried to tear this nation apart to do it! You expect sweet forgiveness? Hasn't it occurred to you that you'll have to pay a penalty for your little adventure in rebellion?"

"We paid the price in the field. We're still paying it."

"Won't come close to settling the debt. And I'll dictate what happens around here, not you."

Grace exerted more pressure on the saber. "Now either stand back or we'll dig you a nice grave."

"Jeremiah, *please*!" Catherine cried. "We'll report this man to his commanding officer."

Another burst of laughter from the lounging riders. Grace shared it, then said, "Go right ahead. Lieutenant Colonel Fielder A. Jones. We haven't met up with him for three days." The major's eyes pinned Jeremiah. "What's it to be? I'll give you about five more seconds."

White-lipped and feeling the worst sort of idiot for thinking he could reason with such a man, Jeremiah retreated.

"Much better!" Major Grace slid his saber back in the scabbard and dismounted, asking Price, "Who is this pup? The woman's son?"

"No, sir. Some Reb who showed up a few days ago."

"Too yellow to stay and fight, were you? One skirmish and your hair turned white—typical of your side, I'd say."

Jeremiah's cheeks darkened.

"Price?"

"Yessir, Major?"

"You come indoors with us. We need your guidance to forage efficiently." He addressed a mounted corporal: "Burks, locate General Skimmerhorn—immediately."

Jeremiah didn't understand why some of the cavalrymen nudged one another until Grace explained to Catherine, "General Skimmerhorn is our forager-in-chief. I believe he came from one of General Howard's infantry regiments. Quite a number of men have been wandering away from their units. Skimmerhorn and some others—ah—attached themselves to us. Up near Gordon, the local folk referred to them as bummers. I prefer to call 'em foragers. Skimmerhorn's turned out to be so excellent at supervising them, I gave him an unofficial promotion. Private to general."

Grace talked as though he were making light conversation at a social gathering. He reached for Catherine's arm to escort her inside. She pulled away, the mole beside her mouth stark black against her white skin.

Grace chuckled in a tolerant way, continuing, "Have you heard what we did between Sparta and Gordon? The rebel plantations over there put up so much resistance, General Kilpatrick had us burn out every one of them. I trust the same thing won't be required here. Of course we can't display too much leniency. I'm not positive about Uncle Billy's whereabouts, but if he and his headquarters guard were to come jaunting along that road tomorrow or the next day, I'd surely want them to see signs of a job properly done."

The threat was stated in a good-natured way. Grace concluded, "I sincerely hope you appreciate what you're involved in, ma'am. A military masterpiece. That's truly the only word for it—masterpiece. I predict people will marvel over it for generations."

Evidently Grace expected Catherine to agree. She was so dumbfounded, she couldn't even speak.

"Uncle Billy's a genius. No other general would have the nerve to cross enemy country."

"I'm delighted to be informed that what you're doing is a masterpiece," Catherine replied with a withering look. "Otherwise I might have reached a mistaken conclusion that it was something much less grand. Vile, in fact. Disgusting and vile."

"Oh, I can appreciate how it looks from your side. But try to keep my view in mind. That way, we'll have fewer problems. We surely don't want problems of the sort we encountered around Gordon, do we?"

Speechless again in the face of the smiling threats, Catherine turned and walked across the piazza. The major followed. He was distinctly bowlegged.

Price went next, giving Jeremiah a sideways glance of

amusement as he walked by. The black's bare feet were caked with dried mud.

The other troopers began to dismount. Down by the highway, half a dozen men were using hatchets to destroy a section of the fence, ignoring the gate and creating a wider entrance for the canvas-topped supply wagons.

The dust raised by the cavalry horses was settling. Jeremiah was able to see the fields directly across the road. Men were still moving through them in ragged columns of fours. The lines stretched all the way to the woodlands on his left. Somewhere a regimental band blared the old South Carolina hymn tune that had been transformed to "John Brown's Body," and then, with new lyrics by some Northern woman, into the hated "Battle Hymn of the Republic."

On the fringes of the marching companies smaller groups of men drifted, keeping to no particular formation. Some of these men were breaking away and heading toward Rosewood, whose fence was now being systematically smashed a length at a time.

Jeremiah thought of the Kerr revolver in the attic. Much as he wished he had it right now, he didn't intend to go after it with Yanks in the house.

I must save it, he said to himself. *Save it until I can make every one of those four balls count.*

iii

In the sitting room, Price was plumping himself down in a wing chair as Jeremiah entered. The black drew up an ottoman and put his right foot on it. Tiny bits of mud fell on the embroidered fabric.

Price stared at Catherine to see whether she'd react. Though she was still furious, she didn't.

"Now, ma'am," Major Grace said, "we'll be requisitioning supplies and equipment from you."

Nodding in a weary way, Catherine said, "I've heard that speech before. Within the last twenty-four hours, in fact."

Grace's eyebrows raised. "Another unit stopped here?"

"Much better looking and considerably more polite than yours?"

The major's voice lowered. "The less of that sort of talk, the safer you'll be. Evidently I wasn't sufficiently clear when I made the point outside."

"You were. Go on. Just have the decency to avoid words like requisitioning. Say what you mean. Stealing."

"Call it whatever you damn please, we plan to take most of your foodstuffs. We'll leave a few kitchen implements, but we want all your cooking utensils. The War Department's so tightfisted, we aren't issued any. We'll require every oven you have. Every skillet. Every coffee mill and coffeepot."

"That's Sherman's idea of a military masterpiece?" Jeremiah fumed. "Robbing homes of *coffeepots?*"

Grace's eyes flickered angrily. "Don't feel sorry for yourself, Reb. You have no idea what war's really like. Georgia has no idea! You think the people of this state are faring badly? Wait till we reach the state that first fired on the Federal flag. We have orders to reduce everything to ashes. *Everything.* Believe me, South Carolina will be made to feel the sin of secession much more than Georgia—unless a lack of cooperation here forces me to provide a sample of what's in store for Charleston."

Alarmed, Jeremiah watched him stroll toward the horsehair sofa, still speaking harshly. "I suggest you limit your antagonistic remarks and consider yourselves fortunate."

"Fortunate?" Catherine exclaimed. "Your gall is absolutely—"

Before the confrontation could grow any hotter, there was a diversion—Serena's sudden appearance in the hall, yawning.

"I was trying to nap but I heard a fearful— Oh, my God!"

A single glance took in Price's foot on the ottoman, and Grace's uniform as he pivoted toward her. The major greeted her with an insincere grin.

"Good day, ma'am. I haven't had the pleasure."

He swept off his hat. His long, dirty hair began as a fringe midway down the sides and back of his head. Above, he was bald.

"Ambrose Grace. Major, United States Cavalry."

"My—my stepdaughter Serena," Catherine said with effort.

Grace licked his lips. His eyes slid to the bodice of Serena's dress. Jeremiah was barely able to stand still.

"Charming child. Lovely. We don't raise them one bit handsomer in Indiana. However"—a falsely rueful expression—"we're here on business, not to be social."

Slapping dust from his hat, he sprawled on the horsehair sofa, which gave off a series of jingling sounds.

Grace sat upright, blinking. "What's this? A musical sofa?"

" 'Spect they hid stuff in there," Price remarked. "Like I said, they been hidin' it all over."

"Let's find out, shall we?"

Grace rose and drew his saber. With two crisscrossing strokes he slashed the sofa's back. Catherine pressed her hand to her mouth as he reached into the opening and began flinging handfuls of stuffing and silver on the carpet.

Boots thudded in the hall. Serena darted aside as a man stomped in—the most appallingly unclean human being Jeremiah Kent had ever seen, or smelled.

"General Skimmerhorn reportin' for duty, Major."

"Just in time! Here's a trove for you."

Six more pieces of silver clattered on the rug.

Jeremiah couldn't take his eyes off the odd, hulking creature Grace had characterized as his forager-in-chief. If the bearded, broad-shouldered Skimmerhorn had ever belonged to a military unit, it was impossible to tell. He wore a bizarre collection of stolen and improvised apparel. A black stovepipe hat. A coat stitched together from four contrasting sections of Oriental carpeting. Gray trousers with one knee torn out, and each leg decorated with the red stripe of the Confederate artillery. Cracked work shoes with the tips gone and grimy toes showing. In his right hand he held a gunny sack.

Under Skimmerhorn's coat Jeremiah saw a Navy Colt, and tied to his belt by thongs, two souvenirs of his work: a small skillet and a dead chicken with its neck wrung.

General Skimmerhorn gave Serena an appraising look, then turned his attention to his superior. Grace gestured.

"You may have all this silver as your reward for supervising the foraging."

"Yes, sir—thankee!" Skimmerhorn crouched and began to grab knives and spoons and shove them into the sack.

Catherine rushed forward at the sound of boisterous men

in the hallway. There were half a dozen, two in uniform, four in civilian clothing. They pushed and shoved to be first up the stairs.

"Where are they going?" Catherine demanded of the major.

"Why, to forage."

"They have no authority."

"Indeed, they do." The major slapped the hilt of his saber. "This."

The men vanished. Serena looked nearly as distraught as her stepmother. A few seconds later, there was a crash from the second floor.

At the back of the house, Maum Isabella cried out as a door splintered. The cry was followed by a horrendous clatter of crockery breaking.

"Now," Grace said to Price, "what else should we be searching for?"

"They's a clearing back in the pines where they put a lot of things. Mules. A wagon—"

"You followed us!" Jeremiah whispered. "It was you I heard in the brush!"

"That's right, mister soldier." Price grinned. But the smile didn't reach his eyes.

He hates me and he's going to kill me, Jeremiah thought. *He's liable to kill us all before this is over.*

Price described the contents of the cache in the clearing. When he finished, Grace asked, "Catch that, Skimmerhorn?"

"Most of it," the forager replied in a phlegmy voice.

He shoved the last pieces of silver in his sack, hawked, and blew a gob of spit on the carpet.

"We'll confiscate the cotton, kersey, and denim cloth," Grace advised him. "If the clock's fancy like the nigger says, I'll keep it for myself." Price didn't seem annoyed at being referred to as a nigger by the Union officer. "Could use a good clock in the feed store back in Vincennes. Turn the wagon and mules over to the wagon master. Mix some kerosene with the molasses. Oh, and don't forget kerosene in the well when we're ready to go."

"Jesus!"

Grace glanced at Jeremiah. "What's wrong, Reb? Did you expect us to leave you amply provisioned? You still don't understand Uncle Billy's style of fighting. He makes war for a double purpose—I've heard him say so. First he fights to gain physical results and second, to inspire *respect.* Respect for—"

Price snapped his fingers. "Major?"

"What?"

"Jus' remembered. They put salt an' flour in the ground out behind the slaves' graveyard. Two barrels of each. I can show you where."

"Excellent. Dig them up, General. Kerosene in those too."

"And mebbe a little piss to spice it?" Skimmerhorn asked, scratching his gray-streaked auburn beard with a hand on which an open sore glistened.

Grace shrugged. "You're in charge."

"I'll see to it." Skimmerhorn tipped his stovepipe and ambled out with the sack over one shoulder.

A man came clattering down the stairs and burst into the room wearing a lacy, ivory-colored gown over his uniform.

"Lordy, Major, lookit! First time I ever been a bride!"

"Absolutely stunning," Grace chuckled.

Catherine lunged.

"That's my wedding dress!"

Grace shoved her back. "Union property now." He held her wrist until she realized she wasn't strong enough to break loose. When she ceased struggling, he let her go with another warning.

"Your outbursts are going to make this genuinely unpleasant, ma'am."

"It couldn't be any more unpleasant than it already is. You're *filth*!"

Grace turned scarlet. Lifted his hand to hit her, but managed to restrain himself. His voice shook.

"I personally am going to conduct the search for arms and ammunition. Give me your keys."

Catherine stared at him, her lips moving without sound. Grace raked a palm across his hairless skull. "Goddamn it, I'm losing patience! *Your keys*!"

"I—I have them put away in a private place. I'll have to retire to get them."

"What private place?"

Now it was her turn to redden.

"I said, *what private place?*"

"On"—Jeremiah could barely hear her—"on my person."

"Oh." Grace brightened again. "Well, this is wartime. We're forced to overlook the niceties. Get them out."

"Not in front of—not while everyone's—?"

There was sick disbelief in her eyes. Price giggled.

Catherine regained a measure of control. "If I do, will you promise me there'll be no further damage to the house?"

"I can't offer any assurances. We'll definitely torch your barns, your gin house, and corn cribs. As to this building—" Another shrug. "No assurances."

"Catherine, you'd better give him the keys," said Serena, a warning note in her voice.

Grace sat down on the gutted sofa, crossing one leg over another, and studying the line of Serena's hip before he lifted his gaze to her face.

"You're not only a pretty child—you're intelligent." His glance slashed back to Catherine. "Ma'am, I'm waiting."

"Will you—will you at least allow me to turn my back?"

Grace sighed. "If you must."

Jeremiah couldn't stand this much longer. Hooting laughter, the crack of furniture, heavy running and jumping racketed from overhead. Each whoop, each crash, pierced him like an invisible bayonet. What a fool he'd been to think all the Yanks would be as decent as Poppel. He *deserved* the contempt of Grace and the rest.

At least he'd deserved it until this moment. Now all his illusions about humane treatment—decency—the rules of war were vanishing, replaced by a consuming, almost uncontrollable anger stronger than any he'd ever felt before.

His mouth took on that slitted white look. Through one of the piazza windows he could see tents being erected down by the lane, and cook fires blazing. In the drive, another band of blacks in confiscated finery clapped while three young women danced in a circle.

Catherine turned away from the men. She pulled up her outer skirt, then the underskirts of crinoline, corded calico and pleated horsehair. Finally, after much rustling and maneuvering, she dropped the skirts and turned back, tears on her cheeks.

She passed the key bag to Grace just as General Skimmerhorn appeared in the doorway.

"Got most of the foraging started, sir." He'd exchanged his gunny sack for a wicker-covered jug. He raised the jug and took a long drink. "Anything else we overlooked?"

Grace relayed the question to Price with a lifted brow and a word: "Nigger?"

"A big buck named Leon—he carried three crates of chickens down to the bottom land near the river."

"Did he now! Well, we certainly wouldn't want any chicken dinners left on the table. General, another assignment for you."

Skimmerhorn drank again, scratched his crotch. His eyes slid to Catherine.

"All by myself?"

Grace laughed. "Need a guide, do you? Take her along. See that she's not mistreated, though. You know Uncle Billy's instructions—we're not to harm civilians."

He winked.

"Yessir," Skimmerhorn replied with feigned seriousness. "I'll be right nice to her."

They all understood: Serena, Jeremiah, and Catherine—who screamed and bolted for the hallway.

Skimmerhorn darted in front of her. Caught her around the waist. "Here, woman, there's no call for that. I mean to treat you just fine—*Christ!*" he yelped as Catherine's nails raked his face.

The forager reeled back, three paralled scratches oozing blood on his cheek.

Half crouched, Catherine resembled a trapped animal. Skimmerhorn's eyes narrowed as she tried to dart past him. The forager hopped to the right, then the left, blocking her. Finally, with a sharp outburst of breath—"Hah!"—he caught her arm and bent it back so she was forced to her knees.

"We're gonna have a fine time huntin' them hens, woman. You're right lively."

Jeremiah's control broke.

"You sons of bitches!" he yelled, charging straight at Skimmerhorn.

CHAPTER IV

SERENA'S PLAN

i

PRICE KICKED THE OTTOMAN aside and stuck out his leg. Jeremiah failed to see it. He tripped, windmilling his arms as Serena lunged at Skimmerhorn.

The forager backhanded her across the face, sending her sprawling. Jeremiah had a distorted glimpse of the fall just as he recovered his balance. At least she stood up for Catherine when it counted.

He lowered his head and lunged at Major Grace, who had jumped between him and Skimmerhorn. Before Grace could draw his saber, Jeremiah struck him with his shoulder. The impact knocked Grace onto the gutted sofa. The momentum carried Jeremiah forward on top of him. He worked a knee over to the major's belly and bore down, pounding at the man's face with wild, hard blows.

"Get him off!" Grace howled, jerking his head from side to side to dodge the punches. Jeremiah lifted his knee, drove it into the officer's groin.

Grace grunted. Grimaced. Absorbed a glancing blow on his chin, then shoved. The two spilled off the sofa.

Jeremiah fell awkwardly, whacking his head against the

sofa's corner. Dazed, he flopped on his back. He tried to turn over.

Price loomed, planting his muddy feet on either side of Jeremiah's legs. He raised the Enfield with the muzzle toward the ceiling, then smashed the butt into Jeremiah's middle.

With a choking cry, Jeremiah tried to twist out of the way and avoid a second blow. Too late. The stock slammed his belly again.

Again—

Price's face remained expressionless. But not his eyes. He put even more effort into the fourth blow.

Jeremiah rolled all the way over onto his stomach, retching. Grace careened to his feet and booted Jeremiah's temple, spitting obscenities.

Jeremiah's forehead dug into the carpet. His back heaved. He heard Catherine's cries as Skimmerhorn manhandled her out of sight. A moment later he had another impression of movement—Price, gliding out after the forager.

He struggled to raise his belly. Clutched it with his palms. That didn't ease the pain.

Growling one filthy word after another, Grace stamped on the small of his back.

Jeremiah yelled, his body driven flat. His vision grew more distorted. Fragmented thoughts went screaming through his head.

God, it's no better here than with the army.

No decency left in this war.

Nothing but meanness.

Meanness and hate—

In spite of his pain, his own hate was fierce and powerful. But it wasn't powerful enough to keep him from sinking into darkness.

ii

"Jeremiah?"

Barely conscious, he fought to speak: "Mama? Mama, is that—?"

"Come to your senses! It's me."

He realized his mistake. Not Fan's voice. Younger. He'd

been watching misty images of Lexington while consciousness returned.

He shifted his position slightly. He was still lying on a floor. Something pricked the underside of his left shoulder.

"Wake up, Jeremiah. You've been stretched out there almost two whole hours!"

Wetness on his shirt. At the spot where he'd felt the pricking. He reached for it with his right hand. Bits of glass fell from his sleeve, tinkling on the wood. When he attempted to sit up—an agony—something sharp jabbed his buttocks. His eyes snapped open.

"God! There's glass all over!"

Serena's face came into focus. Beyond her, outside the latched window of the first-floor office, a Union soldier stood guard.

With her help, he staggered to his feet, gaping at the carnage. The shelves were bare. Books were strewn everywhere. Some had been ripped in half.

The desk showed eight or ten fresh knife or sword scars. All the drawers had been pulled out and stamped to pieces. The chair had been reduced to kindling.

On the floor near the spot where he'd been lying, he noticed the small oil painting of Lieutenant Colonel Rose, out of its frame, and torn in half. In a corner lay the remnants of another frame, and nearby, the lock of Serena's bright red baby hair and the card, crumpled.

He stared, disbelieving, while the girl uttered a sad laugh.

"Aren't they kind? They started their search for arms and ammunition in here."

"What"—he licked the inside of his mouth, massaged his bruised belly; his dizziness was passing—"what time is it?"

"Two or three o'clock. I'm not sure."

The office was stifling. He started for the hall entrance.

"Won't do any good. We're locked in."

He leaned his back against the door, picked a long splinter of glass from his trousers, and surveyed the wrecked office again. He was disgusted—sickened—not so much by the damage as by his own failure to prevent it. He'd been unable to exert even the slightest moderating influence on the Yanks.

And after Poppel, he'd been encouraged. He'd really believed the Union soldiers might not be as bad as they'd been painted.

All at once the infuriating sense of failure was replaced by a sharp fear: What if they'd found the Kerr .44 in the attic? What if they'd decided to parade the dress form, as Catherine's wedding gown had been paraded? What if someone had accidentally discovered the loose plank?

He prayed they hadn't. Prayed he could get his hands on the Kerr piece before Grace's cavalry moved on. How pathetic to have thought even briefly that there was any other way to deal with the enemy.

Another memory jolted him. "What's happened to your stepmother?"

"I don't know." Her voice was curiously flat. "That—what was the word? Bummer? He dragged her out. I tried to stop him. Grace caught me and put me in here."

"Then by now she's been—"

He couldn't say the rest.

"I expect she'll live through it."

Jeremiah's mouth dropped open. He couldn't believe the matter-of-fact way in which she'd spoken. Or the emotionless expression on her haggard face. Her dress was disarrayed, her hair too. But she seemed icily composed.

"My God, Serena, is that all you can say—*she'll live through it*?"

"Well, she will! May hurt her Christian conscience some, but it could be a lot worse. They could shoot her—they aren't going to do that."

He supposed Serena's fatalistic view was logical. But he also suspected there was another reason she wasn't particularly anxious about her stepmother's plight. Maybe she was even a little pleased.

Some of his shock must have showed. She cried suddenly, "Jeremiah, they've *got* her! We can't do anything about what's already happened. Let's worry about what *might* happen. We've got to see the Yanks don't burn this house, or poison the well. They're going to fire the cribs and gin house, Grace left no doubt about that. But this building—"

Bitter, he broke in, "What the devil can we do about it?"

"I can talk to Major Grace."

"Talk?" He was thunderstruck.

"You heard me. Talk. I called the guard in the hall just before you woke up. Told him to fetch that no-good Yankee son of a bitch right away."

She tossed her head to rid her brow of a stray lock of scarlet hair. Somehow there was defiance as well as strength in the movement. Her smile grew sweetly vicious.

" 'Course, I didn't use those words. I was polite—well, polite as I *could* be, considering what they've done." She seized his arm as he swayed. "You all right?"

"Yes." But he was having difficulty standing.

"You look awful."

"Another five or ten minutes, I'll be fine."

"That's all the time I expect to spend with Grace."

"Serena, what the devil are you fooling with him for?"

"Why, I'm going to beg him to leave the house alone."

He was startled, yet impressed by the calculating expression in her blue eyes. She went on.

"He put on a fierce show in the sitting room. Men have to do that—bluster some—in front of other men they boss around. But if I can get him alone—"

The thrust of her idea erased his appreciation of her calm. "You've lost your damn mind! Before you came downstairs, *I* tried to reason with him and couldn't."

"Reason with him? I'll bet you sassed him and practically bit his head off. Right in front of his men, too."

A guilty look said she was right.

"I hate him as much as you do, Jeremiah. But I think he fancies me a little. He sure enough stared at me as if he did. Your tactics didn't work. Let me try mine."

Sarcasm in his voice: "You believe nice friendly words and smiles will have an effect on a man like that?"

"Might." She nodded. Then, piqued: "You have any better suggestions?"

"I suggest you forget the whole idea right now."

She stamped her foot. "What's the matter with you? Don't you understand Rosewood may be all we'll have left after these men move on? We won't even have Rosewood—or water fit to drink—if one of us doesn't do *something!*"

Her anger blunted his. He let another, deeper concern surface. "But, Serena, that man—he's a bad sort. The worst."

"I know what you're saying."

"Do you? He could take advantage—"

"You think I don't appreciate that?"

She rushed to him. One hand touched his sweaty cheek.

"Doesn't it scare you?"

" 'Course it does. But I want to save this house. And I don't want them to hurt you again. Considering the way you behaved, they might take a notion to do it."

Part of him responded to her sympathetic tone, but another part resented having someone else fight his battles. He stalked away three steps, crunching glass under his boot.

"I still say you're a damn fool."

"Now don't get all pettish just because you failed and I might not."

Stung by the truth, he swung around and glared.

"Jeremiah, it's not a case of man or woman, one better than the other. You tried—there's no shame in trying and being tromped on, two against one. This is our trouble, *ours*—together. While you get your strength back, I'll do what has to be done. At least make an effort—"

"What the hell happens if he starts to—to mistreat you?"

"Like the man who took Catherine?"

He nodded.

A small, sly smile curved her mouth. "I think I can handle him. I think I can make him do what I want and still keep myself out of a scrape."

There it was again: the maddening implication of experience.

"You're pretty sure of yourself."

The smile disappeared. She was upset by his reaction.

"I'm not! I'm scared to death. But I'm still going to try."

She glided close, letting him feel the contours of her body against his leg and aching chest. Her hand stroked his face again.

"I don't want to spend two seconds with that man. But I will if there's a chance to keep this house standing. It's all we have."

Softly he said, "You and Catherine—"

Arms around his neck. A light kiss on his mouth. "You and I. Don't you see? I want something left for *us.*"

"It's her house too."

Quick anger in her eyes was just as quickly hidden. "Oh, yes, I know it is! But I can't help thinking of you."

Another kiss, longer. Then she leaned her cheek against his shoulder. "I'm fond of you, Jeremiah. Fonder than you realize. We're going to be together when this is over. This house is going to belong to us." She pulled back, her eyes disarmingly wide. "Even if it takes some put-on sweet talk, with my knees banging together while I try to convince the major I believe he's a wonderful, kind man who surely wouldn't burn Rosewood to the ground."

"You—you won't do anything more than talk?"

"He lays one hand on me, I'll scream till they hear clear over in Louisville!"

Another change of mood, the sly look returned. "Truly, I think I can handle that Indiana roughneck."

"And find out what's happened to your stepmother?"

"Yes, that too." She sounded less than enthusiastic.

For a moment he almost believed she possessed the feminine wiles to pull it off. But the plan still struck him as unacceptably dangerous.

The protest he started to make was silenced by the feel of her body tight against his. Sore and anxious as he was, she could still reach him. Convince him with a brush of her lips. With words that carried promises—

We.

Us.

"Actually," she said at last, "there's no guarantee the major will even answer my message. So you're worrying for nothing until—"

A hand rapped on the other side of the door.

"Until right now," he said with a grim smile.

Serena stepped to the door. Smoothed her hair.

"Yes?"

"Major Grace, ma'am." He sounded quite friendly. "I was informed you wished to speak to me?"

"I do. Will you please unlock the door?"

"If that Reb's awake, tell him to stand well back."

"Do it, Jeremiah."

When he hesitated, still tormented by fear for her safety, she clenched her teeth. *"Do it!"*

He retreated to a corner, stumbling over ruined books.

"All right, Major."

The key rattled. From his vantage point, Jeremiah

couldn't see the officer. Serena stepped out of sight behind the open door.

"Thank you for coming, Major. I'm anxious to speak to you because of the terrible things happening on this place. I want to plead with you to control your men. Not take such harsh measures. But I'd prefer to discuss it somewhere else, if we might. Privately?"

Jeremiah leaned his head against the wall and shut his eyes. How smooth and assured she sounded, in perfect control. He found himself admiring her nerve, and the ruthless way she went about manipulating Grace. There'd been an almost seductive lilt in her voice.

"Why, yes, Miss Serena. I believe I can spare a few minutes to listen to what you have to say. I must warn you, though. I'm not a man easily persuaded."

"We'll see. Shall we go to the sitting room?"

"By all means."

iii

The major took time to lock the door. His footsteps, and Serena's lighter ones, faded slowly. Then someone's weight made the door creak. The hall sentry, back on duty.

The guard outside the window remained motionless. Over the man's shoulder Jeremiah saw an ecstatic celebration in progress down among the slave cabins.

Young women danced in Catherine's dresses. One buck strutted with a torn Confederate battle flag draped over his head and shoulders like a shawl. Three of the foragers pursued a pair of girls across a ramshackle porch. The bummer in the lead had his hand up one girl's skirt, from behind, as they disappeared inside.

Crouching, Jeremiah rubbed at his chest where it hurt the worst. He gazed at Henry Rose's torn portrait.

The painted sections of the genteel, bearded face lay at right angles to one another. Broken apart—just the way everything at Rosewood was being broken by the actions of unprincipled men. Again he felt contempt for the pathetic soldier who'd tramped midnight roads, obeying an order, fulfilling a promise; believing he could fight honorably, meaningfully again on the plantation.

He did admire Serena's determination. But he was positive her scheme would come to nothing. Ambrose Grace would no more listen to her than he'd jump to obey an order from Robert Lee. North and South, dishonorable men had seized any excuse—nigra freedom, defense of their homeland, punishment of the enemy—as a justification for indulging their worst impulses. The Franz Poppels of the world were rarities. Even Poppel himself had admitted as much by secretly giving him the Kerr.

He brushed glass aside. Knelt. Touched one of the ripped halves of Rose's image. His fingertip rested on the rough-textured paint that created a melancholy eye.

I've failed you so far. But it isn't over yet.

The yearning to race up to the attic became almost unbearable.

He drew deep breaths. His chance would come. Serena was bound to fail. The question was—how badly?

If she got through her interview without a physical assault by Grace, Jeremiah decided he'd bide his time. No more outbursts. No more foolish assaults when more than one man was present to beat him to the ground.

But if he heard the slightest alarm—a cry from her—then somehow he'd batter the damn door to pieces. He'd do as much as he could—go as far as he could toward the attic—before the sentry or one of the other Yanks shot him down.

Either way, the answer was his, not Serena's. The answer was the hidden gun.

He licked his lips, increasingly sure. He'd only stopped arguing with her because she was so adamant, and because she'd linked her plan with other plans for their future together.

He *wanted* the future at which she'd hinted. He realized that despite everything—including Catherine's spiteful warnings—he was falling in love with Serena.

Yes, there was a certain cruel edge to her personality. But there was a similar edge to his—sharpening moment by moment. To have denied her a chance to test herself—even though he felt she was foolhardy—well, it might have wrecked everything between them. She didn't want any protection—*or* any suggestion that she was a simpering female incapable of independent action. Maybe that's what had rankled poor Catherine so; she'd raised a child who didn't conform to the acceptable standards of feminine behavior. Jeremiah was glad she didn't conform. It made her a woman worth having.

He'd let her flirt and wheedle, and remain ready to act if Grace molested her. Even if Grace didn't, he was sure to reject her appeals. Then Jeremiah could step in. He knew how, finally. The only thing that would make an impression on the Union officer was the Kerr revolver.

Impression—

He laughed over the inadvertent aptness of the thought. He'd make an impression, all right.

Three inches deep in the center of Grace's forehead.

CHAPTER V

NIGHT OF RUIN

i

FIFTEEN MINUTES PASSED.

Twenty.

Jeremiah lingered close to the door, listening for an outcry from the front of the house. Once in a while he caught the soft sounds of the hall sentry shifting position. But that was all.

Growing more and more worried, he paced the office. He didn't hear anyone approach outside. He started violently at the quick, hard rapping.

He rushed to the door. Pressed his ear against it.

"Serena? Are you all right?"

She sounded shaky when she answered. "Yes. He—he agreed."

"What?"

"I talked my fool head off. Flattered him—practically crawled for him. But he agreed to leave the house standing."

He couldn't believe it. She was more persuasive than he'd ever imagined.

"Did he try to—?"

"No. Seems there are a few rules General Sherman's

pretty fierce about. His officers not harming women is one of them. Any man who's caught— Well, I just got the feeling Grace wouldn't chance it."

"Serena, is anyone listening to this?"

"The guard's a ways down the hall. The major told him to stay there while I talked to you."

"But you're sure the house is safe?"

"I don't know how safe. There are men rampaging all over the place. But it won't be burned. Jeremiah, the major ordered me locked in my room for the night."

"Why not back in here?"

"Guess he's worried we might cook up some kind of trouble for him." A low laugh. "He doesn't know we've already gotten what we wanted. Now you stay calm in there. I'll be fine."

"I don't trust—"

"I tell you he's scared white about *any* of his troopers injuring women!"

"Doesn't make sense! He let Skimmerhorn—"

"Skimmerhorn's not one of his men. He can always claim he had no control over him."

"He's a liar."

" 'Course he is. But he's protecting himself."

"What did you learn about Catherine?"

"Nothing yet. Skimmerhorn isn't back. Maum Isabella promised to keep watch."

"Damn it, Serena, we've got to find out about her!"

"I can't!" She sounded close to tears. "I've done all I could. Now you—you rest. Don't fret about me. Just remember"—she was moving away—"we're going to be together soon. I love you, Jeremiah."

The unbelievable words left him openmouthed. He banged a fist against the door in sheer surprise and happiness, overwhelmed by her unexpected success—and the whispered admission of her feelings.

A brief period of euphoria tempered his hateful feelings about Ambrose Grace, and distracted him from what was taking place outside. But before the night was over, he had spent a great deal of time at the window—

There, his hatred of Grace renewed itself, and grew stronger and stronger as the hours passed with no news of Catherine.

ii

All that Monday night he watched the systematic ruin of Rosewood.

The part of the property visible to him swarmed with the enemy, coming and going on foot and on horseback. Once darkness fell, cook fires were started wherever the Union soldiers and foragers pleased. With the fires lit, the activity outside took on the aspects of a nightmare.

Figures of horses and men became specters of flame and shadow. It seemed to him there were more stragglers in castoff clothing than blue-clad cavalrymen. Foot by square foot, the bummers devastated the expanses of lawn between the main house and the head of the lane leading to the slave cabins. They used sabers and ramrods to jab the earth and tear out slabs of turf as they hunted for buried possessions.

By torchlight, eight or ten bummers worked the slaves' burial ground in the same way, knocking over hand-hewn wooden markers and crosses of sticks and unearthing bodies—or parts of them. At one point Maum Isabella rushed at three of the men ripping up the cemetery. A spade glinted, swung by a pair of grimy white hands. The old black woman fell and crawled off into the dark before she could be hit again.

When digging up the grass and the burial ground yielded no treasures, forty or fifty of the enemy divided into two groups and staged a sort of sham battle with buckets of pine knots fetched from the woods. The knots were lighted and hurled at those on the other side. For a while the night sky was crisscrossed with arching traceries of fire and sparks.

Other men invaded the slave cabins, carrying out blankets, pans, or any other useful item. The few blacks who tried to stop them were knocked down, and if they resisted further, beaten.

A foul smoke from campfire garbage began to blur the scene, heightening Jeremiah's feeling that he was gazing through a window at hell.

His thoughts kept returning to Catherine. Then to Serena.

To what she'd said.

"I love you."

Those words foretold almost unimaginable happiness if he and Serena survived the night and the next few days.

Shortly after midnight, half a dozen cavalrymen converged on the three hog pens.

Two dismounted soldiers tore the first gate off its hinges. The horsemen milled just outside, revolver and rifle barrels catching the glare of the firelight. One pistol exploded. The hogs stampeded into the open, terrified by the snorting horses and whooping men. The office window shook from volleys of gunfire.

The sight of the dumb beasts falling, blood pouring from their snouts, bellies, brainpans made him turn away, nauseated. He listened to the shooting and the squealing for about twenty minutes, crouching in a corner with his hands clenched and his mouth a slit.

Is this what Grace calls sparing Rosewood?

iii

He must have dozed. Daylight hazed by garbage smoke brightened the window as he roused to hear another urgent tapping from the hall.

The office smelled sour. In the night he'd been forced to urinate. Now his stomach hurt. He was starved.

The knocking came again. Louder. He stumbled to the door.

"Who is it?"

"Serena." Her voice sounded unnaturally faint and husky.

"What's wrong?"

"When I got up an hour ago, Grace let me out. Catherine still wasn't back. I got permission to go down to the bottoms. Had to sneak past three Yank camps to get there. I spent half an hour searching. I—I found her."

The last words were so hoarse and full of anguish, he had a premonition about the rest. "How is she?"

Serena's voice broke. "Half her clothes were torn off. She'd been dragged two or three hundred yards. She was all filthy with red clay. She—she's dead, Jeremiah."

He shut his eyes. "Jesus Christ in Heaven."

Somehow she managed to tell him the rest. "About half the slaves have run away. But Leon's still here. I sent him to—carry her back. She was lying facedown in the water. Drowned."

Suddenly the girl began sobbing. "She wasn't my mama—I never pretended to like her. But I didn't want anything like—like this—"

The words grew incoherent. His belly felt heavy as a stone. He pressed both palms against the wood.

"Serena? Serena, listen to me!"

The sobbing lessened a little.

"Did you tell the major?"

"Right—right away." Bitterness: "He's scared out of his wits. He kept saying he's only responsible for men directly under his command."

"It was that son of a bitch Skimmerhorn, wasn't it?"

"Can't be anyone else, can it? Grace questioned him. But he denied he killed her. Denied it over and over. The major's letting it go at that."

He closed his eyes a second time, but opened them almost immediately. There was no longer any doubt about what he had to do.

"Serena, get me out of here. Get Major Grace to unlock the door. Tell him I won't cause any trouble."

"I don't know whether he'll believe—"

"*Make* him believe it! You persuaded him last night—do it again!"

No response except faint crying.

"Serena?"

"I hear you."

"Get me out. *Any way you can.*"

"Y-yes. All right. I'll try."

Ten minutes later, the bald cavalry officer came personally to turn the door key.

iv

"Kent—" Grace looked pale, far less assured than he'd been yesterday. "I assume Miss Serena told you."

"About Mrs. Rose? Yes."

"I deeply regret—"

"Shit."

"I do!"

"Because you may be in trouble with Uncle Billy Sherman? What a pity."

"Kent, listen to me! Skimmerhorn's given me his word he wasn't the one. He—took her, yes—"

"Against her will."

"But he didn't do anything more! She was alive when he left her. Someone else must have found her." The man seemed genuinely terrified. "Look, Kent. Understand. In wartime, things happen that can't be helped."

"You could have helped. You gave him permission."

"I'll deny it. I'll deny it to heaven!" Desperate, he tried bluster. "General Sherman said it right, just before Atlanta. War's like the thunderbolt, he said. It follows its own laws. It doesn't turn aside even if the virtuous and charitable stand in its path."

Sanctimonious bastard! How anxious, now, to ease his own conscience and avoid disciplinary action.

"I doubt Sherman was referring to rape, Major. I doubt he was referring to murder either."

Yet who besides Sherman had turned these monsters loose?

All at once Grace's muddy eyes took on the look of a helpless boy. "I realize Mrs. Rose didn't stand in the way by choice. But the woman's *dead*. What's the use of arguing about blame?"

"None. So long as *you* aren't blamed."

"Kent, for Christ's sake!"

"All right." Jeremiah sighed, masking his feelings. "It's done. No more argument. I can't stand this damn room one minute longer. Just let me out of here and—"

He was interrupted by hysterical wailing from another part of the house. Maum Isabella.

Grace sniffed the rank odor of urine. "Under the circumstances—considering what's happened—the excesses—if you give me your pledge to cause no trouble for the next few hours I'll release you. We'll be gone by late afternoon."

Jeremiah's mouth soured. "How can I possibly cause trouble? What can I do against all the men you've got?"

He held up both hands. "I'm not exactly heavily armed. Just let me out. I need to eat something and use the privy."

He thought the plea might work. Grace was sufficiently

upset—no longer the controlled, arrogant officer of yesterday. Blinking rapidly, the major studied him.

"If you pledge not to—"

"Yes," Jeremiah said, careful to sound beaten. "I give you my word. No trouble."

The major hesitated a moment longer. "Just remember—the guilt isn't mine. If you try to tell anyone it is, you'll never prove it."

"That I know," Jeremiah said, no longer lying.

Grace pivoted and moved unsteadily down the corridor, leaning a hand against the wall to support himself.

Jeremiah stood rigid in the open doorway. *You don't care that Mrs. Rose is dead. You only want to save your stinking Yankee skin.*

He clenched his fists but didn't move until Grace was out of sight.

V

Rosewood was a shambles. He discovered broken furniture everywhere. Feather pillows from the bedrooms had been ripped open, and their contents strewn like snow throughout the downstairs. Near the front entrance, someone had defecated. The stench was vile.

By the time he approached the door to the kitchen, he noticed his boot soles were sticky. Molasses had been spread all over the dining room carpet. Then corn meal had been spilled and ground in. The feathers were the finishing touch.

In the kitchen, Maum Isabella and the four house girls wailed like demented creatures. They stood or knelt around the body of Catherine Rose laid out on the long butchering block. The body had been covered with a tattered blanket. Except for the face.

Jeremiah forced himself to approach the body, stare at the livid bruises on Catherine's cheeks and forehead, the dried red clay in her hair. He didn't want to forget that face. Not until he'd done what must be done.

On her knees at the end of the improvised bier, Maum Isabella wrung her hands and rocked back and forth, tears running in the seams in her dark face. As he started to turn away, one of the other women screamed at him, "Cry for her, Marse Kent. *Cry for the poor woman*!"

He shook his head. "It's too late."

His eyes looked feverish as he crossed the dining room with its sweet reek of syrup. Feathers stirring brought on a violent sneeze. His boots crunched the meal.

He checked the hallway.

Clear.

He stole up the staircase toward the attic. He found the wire dress form toppled over and bent beyond repair.

But the loose plank hadn't been disturbed.

vi

General Skimmerhorn was dippering a drink from the well on the rear piazza.

Two laughing, frock-coated bummers went trotting past on stolen horses. The neck of one of the animals was decorated with a shawl Jeremiah recognized as Serena's. Out of sight beyond the house, wagons rambled. A blare of brass and riffle of snare drams kept cadence for the men beginning to march.

General Skimmerhorn noticed him half hidden by a lattice. The forager dropped the dipper back into the well. Droplets of water spattered his carpet coat when the dipper rope snapped taut.

Using his left hand—it was concealed behind the lattice—Jeremiah touched the front of his dirty linen shirt, making sure it bloused out sufficiently around his waist. Then he started toward the well.

Skimmerhorn brushed back the lapels of his coat so he could grab for his Navy Colt quickly.

"What you want, boy?"

"A word with you, General." He tried to sound appropriately cowed.

Skimmerhorn broke wind noisily, edging around to the well's far side. He was obviously wary of the lank-haired young man standing stoop-shouldered and motionless. Behind the forager lay one of the shot hogs, its entrails spilling from its belly and aswarm with crawling white things. The morning air was dark gray, heavy with humidity, and fouled by the fumes of smoldering garbage.

"If you come to talk about the woman, I'll tell you what I told the major. I didn't have nothin' to do with killin' her." Skimmerhorn scratched his beard. "I took her to the bottoms, right enough. Had my pleasure with her. Even got so het up, I clean forgot we was after three crates of chickens. Never did find 'em. She passed out 'fore I could ask her where they was. But I left her *alive!* And a long way from that water where I hear the girl found her."

"Facedown." Jeremiah's attempted laugh came out as a snort. "She just crawled right on down to the water and drowned herself, did she?"

"What do you want me to say? Some women do queer things if they get mauled a little."

"Get raped, you mean."

"I didn't kill her! I ain't gonna stand and jaw about it!" He started away.

"Wait!" Jeremiah exclaimed, then added an appeasing word, "Please."

Skimmerhorn swung around, suspicious.

"I didn't mean to quarrel. Nothing's going to bring Mrs. Rose back."

"An' *I* didn't drown her—just you keep that in mind!"

Oddly, Jeremiah felt the forager was telling the truth. There was a desperate quality in Skimmerhorn's speech—an anxiety to absolve himself—that seemed genuine.

"Shit, boy, you seen the fields. There's hundreds of men movin' between here and the river. Any one of 'em could of done it."

"I know. If you say you didn't, I believe you."

"Well, that's a heap better." Skimmerhorn acted relieved. He settled his stovepipe hat on his greasy hair, a touch of his cockiness creeping back. "You're bein' sensible. Now is that all you wanted?"

"No, sir." Carefully he began the plea he'd rehearsed in silence. "After you go, we'll need some corn." He pointed to one of the cribs. "I'd like to ask you to bring some out. A sack or two—"

Skimmerhorn started to snicker.

"I can make it worth your while."

Skimmerhorn's greed overcame his caution. "How? You got nothin' we ain't took already."

"You're wrong. There's something valuable back in the pines. One thing Price didn't see me bury."

A quick glance down the street between the slave cabins. Most of the blacks remaining on the plantation had disappeared indoors. Just one small boy was visible, seated on a slanting stoop in a forlorn posture and staring into space as if he'd been abandoned.

"Where is Price?"

"I dunno," Skimmerhorn answered. "He's been all over the place since yesterday. I 'spect he's struttin' around somewhere with that musket of yours. Listen, get on with it. What'd you bury?"

"A small sack. Mrs. Rose's jewelry."

"Jewelry! That a fact!"

"Look, General"—he tried to sound whiny, pleading—"we've got to have at least a little corn to tide us over. You could take some out of one of the cribs before they set fire to them. I don't suppose they'll let me near the cribs." He eyed the soldiers guarding the doors of the buildings. Skimmerhorn's nod said his guess was correct. "But you can get in. If you hide two bags I'll show you the buried jewelry. Mrs. Rose doesn't need it any longer."

Skimmerhorn pondered the proposition. "How far we got to go to find it?"

"Only about half a mile into the pines."

The forager closed his hand on the butt of the Navy Colt. "Wouldn't be smart for you to play tricks on me, Reb."

"No tricks. We have to eat."

Another speculative glance at Jeremiah, and the forager made his decision. "Find us a shovel and let's go. I'll take a peek in the sack. If it's good jewelry, mebbe I will fetch that corn. But I don't promise nothin' till I see the goods."

"That's fair." Jeremiah nodded. "All right if I come around the well?"

Skimmerhorn drew his Colt.

"Slow. Good an' slow."

Jeremiah nearly smiled. So far it had worked perfectly. He kept his voice appropriately apologetic. "It'll take me a minute to turn up a shovel. Ought to be one down by the cabins. Then we'll be on our way."

General Skimmerhorn chuckled. "Goin' on a little treasure hunt. Right pleasing idea. Yes, sir, right pleasing. You finally come to your senses."

I did, General. Finally.

"I know when we're whipped," he lied.

Chapter VI

Day of Death

i

Jeremiah and Skimmerhorn walked toward the lane, the bummer two paces behind. Pretending to scratch his chest, Jeremiah loosened his shirt a little more.

A soldier standing guard by one of the cribs hailed the forager, wanting to know where he was bound. Skimmerhorn waved the Navy Colt.

"Little private errand. Be right back."

They went from cabin to cabin in search of a shovel. Each of the small houses had been stripped. Finally Jeremiah spotted the tool they needed lying near the edge of the burying ground. By now he was breathing so rapidly he was sure Skimmerhorn would notice the change.

But he didn't. The general was in good spirits, strutting and whistling "The Battle Cry of Freedom."

They followed the rutted track into the pines. The gray daylight barely penetrated here. The earth smelled dank. For a while the silence was broken only by the forager's whistling. Then he struck up a conversation.

"You know, boy, now that you've calmed down some, I can say I truly feel it's a pity about that woman. I wanted to enjoy her, an' I did. But I don't wish no female dead on account of me. Sure is a shame. Nobody'll ever catch the man who did it, I 'spose."

Jeremiah's shrug pretended weary agreement. *But someone will be punished for it.*

"Still," Skimmerhorn went on, "you an' that little red-headed gal ought to consider yourselves lucky. You'll be alive when we move on. The major says he don't plan to burn the main house."

"Miss Serena persuaded him to be lenient." Jeremiah nodded.

Skimmerhorn laughed. Jeremiah puzzled at the salacious sound of it.

"I'd love to have a morsel o' her persuasion." He nudged Jeremiah's elbow with the Colt. "She given you any?"

"I don't know what you mean."

"Persuasion!" A wink. "The sort a lively female dishes out when she's flat on her back."

"Flat on her—what the hell are you talking about?"

"You mean you don't know? Well, don't get testy about it. I figgered it'd be all over the house by now. She an' the major, they was locked up in her room most of the night."

Jeremiah nearly stumbled.

"I was hangin' around shortly before the men started killin' the hogs at midnight. The major come down in his trousers and undershirt to check on things. He got to braggin' some. Said that little girl went at it like an animal. A wild animal. They'd done it three times already—that is, if he wasn't lyin'—and he claimed she was ready for more. Starved for lovin'!"

Jeremiah's cheeks ran with sweat. His voice was barely audible. "You're the one who's lying."

Skimmerhorn chuckled again, less friendly. "I ought to clout you for sass, boy. I'm givin' you gospel." He raised the Colt, barrel straight up, and planted his other palm over his heart. "Swear it! The major said he meant to try somethin' with her from the very first. But she got him alone in the sitting room and damned if she didn't beat him to it. 'Magine a girl that sweet-looking raising such a subject? Kind of shockin' even to an old rascal like me. It's the old saw about a book an' its cover, I reckon."

Jeremiah wanted to turn on the forager right then. Finish him. Stop the filth coming out of his mouth. But he didn't;

he was suddenly haunted by the memory of Catherine's warning.

She is not moral.

He recalled his astonishment when Serena claimed to have persuaded Grace with words alone. He tried to deny that Skimmerhorn's story could be true. The harder he tried, the less he succeeded.

"Yessir, she practically begged him for it, the major said. She wouldn't of had to beg me! I'd have been up her skirts first time she flounced 'em at me!"

It was true. It had to be true. Why would the forager invent such a tale?

And she'd said, "I love you."

His faith in her suddenly seemed even more pathetic and contemptible than his misguided belief that Yanks could act decently. His head swam. Everything was crumbling away. Crumbling into corruption, lies, dishonor—

And he hated Skimmerhorn all the more for having spoken.

The bummer halted, considerably less good-humored. "Boy, you told me half a mile. We've gone that an' more."

"I must have judged it wrong. We're close."

Panicked, he searched the terrain ahead. Saw a break in the underbrush.

"There. Turn off to the right."

"I got fish to fry back at the house. More valuables to pack up before we move on. Let's step lively."

"Yes, sir." Jeremiah quickened the pace.

He led Skimmerhorn to the spot where he'd glimpsed an overgrown path. He had no idea where the path went. And he was worried about the sound. They weren't sufficiently far from the plantation. But Skimmerhorn was impatient.

His head was hurting. Rage was mounting in him. Rage at the war. At Serena. And particularly at this man who'd destroyed an illusion with a few crude sentences.

He had meant to go a good distance along the overgrown path. But the pressure of his wrath grew too great. He stopped after a dozen steps. Here the path widened slightly. He pointed into the tangle of weeds and brush.

"Back in there."

Skimmerhorn bent forward, peering past him. While the man's attention was diverted, Jeremiah raised his hand from his belt buckle and undid two buttons on his shirt, covering the movement by swinging the shovel slowly up to his shoulder with his other hand.

"Lord, it's hot as an oven in here!" Skimmerhorn complained. He crouched. Pushed weeds aside with the muzzle of the Colt. "Don't look like a clump of sod's been turned in there for ninety-nine years." He started to rise and twist his head toward Jeremiah. "If you're shittin' with me, boy—"

Jeremiah's sweaty palm was already under his shirt. With his other hand he let the shovel fall. He drew the hidden Kerr before Skimmerhorn realized what was happening.

Skimmerhorn was fast, though. He pivoted on the toes of his boots, jerked the Navy Colt up with one hand, and punched Jeremiah's groin with the other.

Jeremiah reeled back, stumbling on the shovel. He lost his balance. Skimmerhorn fired from a crouch.

The underbrush rustled behind Jeremiah, a kind of reptilian hiss, as the bullet spent itself. Only the fall had saved him. Before Skimmerhorn could aim and shoot again, Jeremiah fired.

The bullet from the Kerr blew away part of Skimmerhorn's right temple. He sat down hard on his rump. A spasm of his finger discharged the Colt a second time. The bullet buzzed away harmlessly.

Skimmerhorn swayed. His head lolled slowly to the right while a dark stain appeared between his legs. Blood poured down the side of his face, soaking his carpet coat, and reddening the needles on the branch his dead weight finally bypassed. The branch sprang back into place, flecking Jeremiah's shirt with scarlet.

The fingers holding the Colt clenched, then relaxed. Jeremiah wiped his mouth. Twisted toward the dirt track. Surely they'd heard the shots up by the house.

He thrust the Kerr in his belt and forced himself to approach the corpse. Insects were already clouding around Skimmerhorn's shattered skull. Sourness climbed in Jeremiah's throat as he pulled the Colt from the dead man's grip.

He straightened up and turned away, his face a study in confusion and pain.

I love you. She'd said that right after she'd whored all night!

He started to walk. In a moment he was running. Not

toward the dirt track and Rosewood, as he'd originally planned. Not back to Serena, to protect her. Let her look after herself. She was quite accomplished at that!

He fled deep into the pines, where it was rank and dark. He thought he could escape her there. Escape the shattering memory of Skimmerhorn's words.

But he found he couldn't escape them—or the fury that shook him between spells of grief-stricken confusion.

ii

No one came hunting for him.

Or if they did, he failed to detect the sounds of a search. By nightfall he'd lost even a minimal concern about Serena's safety. He was pondering whether to leave—strike out for some back road and never see Rosewood again—when he noticed a red shimmer through the trees.

A light wind had sprung up, scouring some of the rankness from the air. Fire. Reluctantly, he left the little dell where he'd spent the day alternately gripped by a sense of total betrayal and an overwhelming hatred embracing the Yanks, the war, and *her.*

He didn't want to go back. The only thing that held him was the memory of Henry Rose.

Rosewood was the dead colonel's only monument. Jeremiah couldn't stand by and permit the house to burn. He felt it might, despite Grace's promises. He didn't trust the cavalry major. He had to go back. He had to discharge this last obligation to the man who'd saved his life.

When he reached the perimeter of the woods, he broke open the Colt, swore, and flung it away. General Skimmerhorn had fired his last two rounds defending himself.

He felt the Kerr under his shirt. Three bullets left.

He crept out of the trees and stole forward through the high weeds. When he reached the slaves' burial ground, he bellied down between overturned slabs and broken crosses, peering up the lane. The sky was bright red, the sound of the conflagration a roar.

Both barns had already burned. Little more than the glowing beams and rafters remained. As he watched, they crumbled and crashed inward.

The corn cribs were alight, but the flames were only beginning to eat through the walls. The smoky air had a strange tang. Roasting corn.

The gin house was on fire as well. It stood nearest the main building. The wind was blowing from behind it.

At the head of the lane between the cottages he glimpsed perhaps two dozen men and women silhouetted against the blaze. The nigras who hadn't run away. Then he caught his breath as he recognized a familiar figure beyond the slaves, standing at full height on the rim of the stone wall.

He climbed to his knees, then began angling to his right, toward the cover afforded by the cottages on that side of the road. He saw no Yanks up by the house. Perhaps Grace had fired the buildings, assembled his men, and ridden on. But he thought he understood the confrontation near the house.

He crept to the porch of the last cottage. From that vantage point he could make out something metal-bright in the hands of the man standing guard over the well.

His own Enfield.

He crawled off the porch, hurried past the end of the cottage, and cut back to the left, running like someone possessed. As he ran, he moved further and further away from the cottages, so he could dash behind the first of the fired cribs standing at the extreme right at the head of the lane.

The crib's whole roof was burning. The wind was driving smoke and clouds of sparks ahead of it. Once the gin house was fully afire, the combined heat from it and the burning cribs would carry the blaze to Rosewood. For the moment he didn't give a damn about that. It was Price he wanted.

He kept running. His chest hurt. He tripped once, landing on his belly and cursing loudly. But the crackle of the fire covered the sound.

As he sped behind the second crib, the one nearest the highway, its burning side crumbled outward. He leaped wide. A splitting beam came down, nearly braining him. He slapped at sparks in his hair and kept running straight ahead into the dark. When he was opposite the front drive, he skidded to slow himself, and turned toward the piazza.

He searched the lane and the highway.

No tents.

No soldiers.

There was more fire in the sky, now in the direction of Millen. But the army had gone.

He lunged across the piazza, calculating his best point of attack. The larder—next to the kitchen. It led directly onto the rear piazza.

He opened the front door cautiously.

Darkness. Silence.

He dashed through the ruined dining room, and the kitchen where the lamps had been extinguished. Firelight through the smoke-stained windows outlined Catherine Rose's corpse. Candle wax had melted and rehardened at her head and feet.

He slipped into the larder. Even indoors, the heat was intense.

He pulled the Kerr from under his shirt. Outside he heard a voice he recognized. Serena's.

"Price, you've got to let us at the water!"

The man laughed. "No."

"But if we don't wet down the siding, it'll catch!"

"Let it!"

Three or four men yelled agreement. There was one fervent "Amen!" Price had the Enfield. The blacks were either frightened of it, or siding with him.

Price's voice boomed. "Let it burn, you white slut. You ain't giving orders to niggers no more. We're free people!"

Someone clapped. Another *"Amen!"* Then came a sound of scuffling. Maum Isabella's cry rang out.

"We're free to water the house down if we please!"

"No!" Price boomed back. "I ain't the only one who wants to see it burn."

"Yes, you are, you damned scalawag nigger. The rest of these so-called friends of yours are too scared—or too stupid—to know how mean you feel about Miss Serena and her poor dead stepmother. You stand up there with that gun, thinking you're some almighty angel—"

That amused Price. "Ol' angel of death, Maum. Ready to shoot the first buck who comes close. *Or* the first woman."

"You're just as mean as the worst white soul-driver!" Maum Isabella shrilled. "Just as mean. *Twice as mean!*"

"Old woman," Price warned above the cries of protest and agreement, "you stay away. Else I'll drop you with this here."

Jeremiah hit the larder door with his shoulder and took two long strides across the piazza, the Kerr coming up in his right hand while his left steadied it.

Beyond the well, where Price stood with his legs wide-spread on the rim, menacing the half circle of slaves, Maum Isabella halted all at once. Her eyes popped at the sight of Jeremiah. Several of the other blacks saw him too. On his right he glimpsed Serena, her red hair limp, her face sooty.

He smelled the unmistakable aroma of wood catching fire. The wind was spreading a huge flag of flame from the gin house and the collapsing cribs, blowing banners of sparks against the end of the main building.

Jeremiah had a clear target: Price's massive body. The big buck saw the reaction on the black faces. He started to turn, just as a yellow-skinned slave pointed and yelled, "Behin' you, Price!"

The yellow-skinned man hurled himself forward, perhaps in the hope of knocking Price off the well rim, out of danger. Both hands locked on the Kerr, Jeremiah aimed carefully, fought an impulse to let his rage drive him to a fast, inaccurate shot.

Price spun, sought his target, whipped the Enfield to his shoulder. Jeremiah fired.

The bullet took Price in the left arm. Drove him up on tiptoe as it sprayed blood and fragments of splintered bone like red needles in the firelight.

Price started to topple forward. The buck bowled into him, knocking him sideways off the well.

The slaves scattered, shrieking, as Price disappeared. Running toward the well, Jeremiah shouted, "Maum Isabella, grab the Enfield!"

The yellow buck got it first.

Jeremiah was about six feet from the well when the buck's distorted face popped up on the far side. The man was trying to help Price to his feet. Maum Isabella darted toward them.

A bloodied right hand grasped the well's rim. Like some kind of dead creature rising from its grave, Price appeared, pulling himself up. Now he was using both his right hand, and astonishingly, his left, even though his left sleeve was soaked red and pierced by jutting pieces of bone.

Price's hate-filled eyes found Jeremiah. His face and neck glowed with sweat. A vein in his throat throbbed.

Jeremiah still had both hands on the Kerr. His forearms were trembling as he extended the gun. He nearly couldn't bring himself to look into those fiery eyes. Maum Isabella was darting and feinting at the yellow buck who jabbed with the Enfield's muzzle to fend her off.

Why doesn't Price fall? No man is that strong.

"Maum Isabella?" Jeremiah's voice had a cracked sound. *"Stand back!"*

Price's red hands gripped the well rim a moment longer. His eyes glowed bright as the blazing gin house. Then will and rage seemed to drain from him. He searched for Jeremiah again, found him. This time, his eyes seemed duller.

"Mr. Jeremiah? You hit me bad. Leave me be now."

Jeremiah laughed. "Finally remembered my name, did you?"

"Please." Price lifted his gory right hand. *"Leave me be now!"*

A memory of Major Grace's remark about the thunderbolt darted into Jeremiah's mind. He glanced at Serena. Price uttered an almost plaintive cry as he watched Jeremiah's face change.

The yellow buck was still sweeping the Enfield in an arc to drive back three slaves—Leon and two others. But Maum Isabella had retreated. All at once Jeremiah seemed to see Serena in place of Price. He wasn't frightened any longer. He felt quite different from when he'd defended himself against Skimmerhorn. He and the Kerr were welded into one—and there was joy in the thin curve of his mouth. He fired.

Price shrieked. The bullet blew a black-and-red hole in his tattered shirt just below the breastbone. The nigras screamed. Price fell.

The yellow buck was obviously unfamiliar with the operation of the Enfield. Jeremiah twisted at the waist, still holding the Kerr double-handed. The muzzle pointed at the buck's ear. The buck dropped the rifled musket and ran toward the dark at the front of the house. Maum Isabella flung a stone after him.

Screaming, milling, the remaining nigras didn't know what to do until Serena wheeled on them.

"Buckets from the kitchen! Hurry, damn you—Leon! Willis! Get a move on!"

Jeremiah stuck the Kerr back under his shirt, comforted somehow by the heat of the metal against his bare skin. He swabbed sweat from his eyes.

Serena quickly organized the nigras into a fire-fighting line. The stony smile remained fixed on Jeremiah's face as he walked around the well. Leon and some of the others began frantically passing buckets down a hastily formed human chain as two women—one of them Maum Isabella—worked the well's crank arm. To reach it, she had to stand on Price's body.

Jeremiah glanced down at the openmouthed corpse. He felt no remorse. He could halfway admire Price now. The man had been vicious but, in his own way, brave. A worthy adversary.

Jeremiah was proud of having killed him.

Serena rushed to him, pushing hair off her forehead. There was an odd, almost frightened light in her blue eyes as she gazed at his curiously amused expression. He ignored her for a moment, glancing toward the house. Some of the bucks were piling onto each other's shoulders to empty buckets and wet down the end of the building. Even though the barns, the cribs, and the gin house with its baled cotton and packing screw were gone, the heart of Rosewood would survive. It was the only memorial he could leave to the colonel.

But Henry Rose had been right there in the field hospital. War—Sherman's thunderbolt—was a destroyer. It destroyed hope. He'd learned the lesson; and it had transformed him.

Serena flung herself into his arms. "Oh, Jeremiah, I thought they'd carried you off, or something worse—"

He shoved her away. Seized her wrist, his fingers biting so hard she winced. He dragged her toward the piazza.

"Jeremiah, let go! What's wrong with you?"

He paid no attention.

He pulled her through the larder to the kitchen, then flung her away. She caught herself on the iron stove, her eyes huge and terror-stricken as he stepped behind the block bearing Catherine's body. His mouth remained a bloodless line.

iii

"Jeremiah, I don't understand why you're treating—"

"You whored for him."

"What?"

"Whored!"

"What are you saying?"

"Grace. *You whored for him.* Skimmerhorn said so. Before I shot him."

"You shot—?" Disbelief in her eyes.

"That's right. Back in the pines, this morning. Grace spared this house because you whored for him."

"Sweetheart—"

As she said it and started around the block, he called her the foulest name he knew.

She stopped, stunned. "Jeremiah, I—I had to!"

"You said you cared about me. You don't. I was taken in for a while, but now I know it's just the money you want, not me. You wanted the house too. And there's not a thing you won't do to get what you want, is there? Lie. Whore—"

"Don't keep saying that!" Serena lunged at the still body. "She called my mama that name. 'Whore,' she said. 'Whore, *whore*!" She struck Catherine's waxy cheek. The pale head flopped over on the boneless neck.

Recovering, she pleaded, "Jeremiah, I *had* to do what Grace asked!"

"He didn't ask. *You* begged. Skimmerhorn told me."

Caught, she started to say something else. But he saw the truth on her face. All at once her eyes looked crazed.

"Admit you begged him, Serena."

"Yes." She spat it again. "*Yes!* He was good, too. Almost as good as a lot of the others. Better'n you'd ever be! You're just a boy!"

"A dumb boy with money you wanted. Christ, you're as dishonorable as the rest. Catherine tried to warn me. But I was too stupid to listen. Well, I'm not going to stay here. You've got the house now. I wish your father or Catherine had it instead of you, but"—a tired shrug—"nothing I can do about that." Then, louder: "You should have died instead of your stepmother."

"I'm *glad* she's dead. I'm glad some soldier whose name

I'll never know caught her and drowned her. Maybe he raped her again before he pushed her in the water. I hope he raped her till it hurt. *Till it drove her crazy!*"

He shuddered. "You pretended to be very sorry when you thought you still had me fooled. You're good at saying one thing and doing another. Almost as good as the Yanks and Billy Sherman."

"She called my mama a whore!"

"I expect she was right," he said, and turned away. "Good-bye, Serena."

iv

He started toward the dining room, heard her breathing quicken; then a sound he didn't recognize until she came rushing at him. The sound had been a drawer sliding.

He spun, his back against the wall. He saw demented eyes reflecting the outside fire, a butcher knife raised in her grimy fist.

She stabbed downward.

Weary as he was, the fear pumping in him gave him just enough quickness. He jerked his head to the side. The blade raked his cheek and snapped in half when it struck the door beside his head.

He caught her wrist with his left hand as she tried to cut him with the broken blade. Unaccountably, tears misted his eyes.

"She said you weren't moral. She never told me you were insane."

"Take your damn money! I don't care. I'll find someone else!" She was hysterical. "Someone who's rich and—and—" She was spitting at him; he felt the spray wetting his already damp cheeks. Her right arm shook. He had to push hard to keep the shattered but still lethal knife from his throat.

"And a man. Not a boy! Not a child! Not a baby. *Baby, baby, baby!*"

As she screamed he pulled the Kerr with his right hand and fired the last bullet into her stomach.

V

Dark woods arching over a dark road. Faint fire in the sky, in the direction of Millen.

He was running again.

He didn't dare do anything else. Maum Isabella had heard the shot and rushed in to find him standing over Serena's lifeless body. She'd cried one word, *"Murderer!"*

Where would he go? He didn't know. But he had to get away.

Westward, that was the best direction. Out of the path of Sherman's army. As he limped along, it began to dawn on him that he could never go back to Virginia. The war would end; people like the Claypools would return to Jefferson County and ask how Catherine and Serena Rose had died. Maum Isabella would tell them, and one day, someone might come riding to Lexington to find him.

He had to flee a long way, long way. Never tell Fan what he'd done. Never give her the slightest hint. To keep from hurting her. And to keep from being found.

He'd tried to be honorable, and this was how it had ended. There was no place for honor in war. Or in the world.

God, how Serena had gulled him! And he'd been so willing! Not merely willing. Eager. He'd had warnings about her, hints of her deception. He'd ignored them, permitting himself to succumb to her charms—and her lies: *I love you.*

The experience had changed him, he knew that. He'd killed three people since sunup and hardly felt any guilt.

That didn't alter his desperate situation—a situation he faced with relative calm until he reached a ford in a creek near the Ogeechee. He halted on the bank, overcome.

He sat down and wept for twenty minutes.

At the end, he glanced up, wiped his face, blinked at the stars, and thought: *I'm sorry I failed you, Colonel. You told me war ruined people, and you were right. It ruins them because they don't understand how to fight and win. I understand now.*

He splashed into the ford, less emotional. He'd definitely head west. That was safest. Perhaps he'd go far west. Hundreds of miles away, he might be safe from the wrath of the unforgiving Yanks who'd keep the war going in their own way even after the South surrendered.

He paused in the middle of the ford, gazing down at his fragmented image in the water. He felt naked and incomplete without a weapon.

Should have gone back for the Enfield. It had been too dangerous with Maum Isabella screaming at him.

He'd find another. Steal one. Kill for one, if need be. The war had taught him a good many fine, valuable skills.

He kept gazing into the water. *There lies Jeremiah Kent. Served dishonorably in the conflict between the states, died, and rose again—*

Rose as a new man who understood the world and how it functioned.

Without honor.

Without honesty.

Without pity.

Jeremiah Kent. He probably didn't dare use that name any longer. What would he call himself?

He shifted his left leg. The water image rippled apart, no longer recognizable.

Straightening his shoulders, he stumbled up the other side of the ford, a last spill of starlight scattering on the white streak in his hair and his emotionless face before he disappeared into the wooded dark.

Chapter VII

"Let 'Em Up Easy"

i

The boxcar trucks clattered. But not so loudly Gideon couldn't hear the pale artillery captain reading from the paper.

" '*After four years of arduous service marked by unsurpassed courage and fortitude, the Army of Northern Virginia has been compelled to yield to overwhelming numbers and resources.*' "

The artilleryman was seated with his back to the opposite wall of the car, about four feet to Gideon's left. Directly across the way, another Confederate—a Virginian, flanked by two more paroled prisoners—puffed one of the cigars he'd bought in the B & O depot. His face grew more and more disgusted as the artilleryman kept reading for the benefit of those nearby.

" '*I need not tell the brave survivors of so many hard-fought battles, who have remained steadfast to the last, that I have consented to this result from no distrust of them.*

" '*But feeling that valor and devotion could accomplish nothing that would compensate for the loss that must have attended the continuance of the contest. I determined to avoid the useless sacrifice of those whose past services have endeared them to their countrymen.'* "

"Shit," the Virginian said, and stuck the cigar back in his mouth.

The artilleryman twisted his head to the left, frowned at the source of the interruption and went on. " *'By the terms of the agreement officers and men can return to their homes, and remain until exchanged. You will take with you—'* "

"Stop reading that!" the Virginian demanded, the cigar nearly bitten in half between his teeth. "It's over a month old—and every line says *coward.*"

The artilleryman gave him a cool stare. "I wouldn't refer to anything written by our former commander as cowardly, sir. This is the first reprinting I've seen of his general order disbanding the army."

"Well, I don't want to hear it."

"Then don't listen."

"Some of us want to hear it," Gideon said. "Continue, sir."

The Virginian's look was hostile, the artilleryman's appreciative. The latter resumed.

" *'—take with you the satisfaction that proceeds from the consciousness of duty faithfully performed, and I earnestly pray that a Merciful God will extend to you His blessing and protection.'* "

The pale man faltered. He cleared his throat.

" *'With an unceasing admiration of your constancy and devotion to your country, and grateful remembrance of your kind and generous consideration for myself, I bid you all an—affectionate farewell.'* "

Slowly, the artilleryman folded the paper, murmured, "It's signed 'R. E. Lee. General'."

He let the hand with the paper fall between his knees. Because of the bad light in the car, Gideon couldn't be sure whether there were tears in the man's eyes.

None in the Virginian's, though. He shook his head. Growled another obscenity. He was in his early thirties, lank and sallow. He wore a torn linen duster over a farmer's shirt and trousers.

"Yella," he said emphatically. The soldiers on either side of him nodded tentative agreement. The artilleryman's head jerked up; Gideon almost expected a challenge. But the Virginian was too busy focusing attention on himself.

"One of Lee's own officers had the right idea. Said all troops still in the field should head for the hills. Keep the war going!"

The artilleryman shook his head, as if unable to comprehend such stupidity. He leaned back against the boxcar wall and shut his eyes.

"But, no! The gray fox wouldn't have it. Claimed the country'd take years to recover if the boys were in the hills, bushwhacking. I say what's wrong with that? Strikes me old Marse Robert was just plain tired of fighting. So he put on his sword, sashayed up to that farmhouse, and rolled over for Grant like a tame dog. Then he wrote *that* piece of sentimental swill!"

A stab of the cigar toward the artilleryman. There was no response. The pale soldier was dozing, or pretending to doze. He wouldn't waste energy on the Virginian.

Beneath the leather patch covering his left eye socket, Gideon felt an annoying itch. He fought the impulse to lift the patch and push at his upper lid. Instead he smoothed his long, tawny beard. He didn't know which was worse, the itch or the Virginian's ranting.

To watch the man, Gideon kept his head turned a bit to the left. For about a month after Dr. Lemon had rushed him to the prison surgery, administered ether, and removed his burned eye, he'd been unable to focus his good eye properly. Gradually, though, he'd trained himself to keep his head turned slightly at all times, so one eye took in almost as much as two had before. By now the habit was becoming unconscious.

Some of the forty Confederates in the car were still listening to the lanky man's remarks. But not all. Down at the other end, one boy in butternut rested his head on his forearms, his forearms on his knees, and wept without sound, imprisoned in some secret grief. Most of the other men either seemed indifferent to the Virginian, or like Gideon, resentful.

"Why, even my old chief, Colonel Mosby—" The man plucked the cigar from his mouth and cut a smoky arc with the stub held between his index and middle finger. The smoke whipped away toward a hole chopped in the side of the car above him. The hole let in flickering shafts of sunlight and fresh air. But not enough air to cleanse the car of the stench of dirt and sweat and wounds still oozing pus.

"He disbanded the rangers last month. Voluntarily! I read about it right after I was let out. Couldn't believe it—John Mosby truckling to the Yanks for a parole! Said he was a soldier, not a highwayman."

The man spat into the straw between his knees.

"Wanted to get his shingle back up so he could practice law again. I'll tell you, I about puked. There weren't any tougher fighters than John Mosby's Partisan Rangers. We had less than two hundred men most of the time, and a lot of the boys tended their fields by day and rode by night. Even so, with Yanks all over the place, we had most of Loudoun and Fauquier counties under control. People took to calling the territory Mosby's Confederacy. Before I got trapped by some of Custer's men, Mosby was a regular fighting cock. Now, all of a sudden, he up and quits just like Lee!"

"I wish you'd quit, too," Gideon said in a weary voice. "The war's over."

Slowly the Virginian drew the cigar from his teeth.

"You speakin' to me?"

"That's right. What the hell good does it do to keep talking that way?"

"I'll talk any way I blasted please. They haven't whipped all of us yet. They haven't whipped Captain Leonidas Worthing!"

"Well," Gideon replied with a sour smile, "you just go right on fighting, then. But be good enough to do it silently."

The man in the duster surveyed Gideon's filthy overcoat, saw no emblems of rank. "Where'd you get on this train, soldier?"

"Major," Gideon snapped. "Major Kent of Stuart's cavalry. I got on at Baltimore, just like you."

Worthing absorbed the information. Gideon ranked him—though it really made no difference since Worthing had belonged to what was essentially a guerrilla group. It made no difference now that the meeting had taken place at Appomattox Courthouse; now that the Army of Northern Virginia had surrendered and received General Order Number Nine; now that Fort Delaware had become a memory, though one Gideon would carry all his life.

There, Dr. Cincinnatus Lemon had summoned other guards, succeeded in breaking into Tillotson's office, and ordered Gideon rushed to his surgery table where he discovered the heated stick had penetrated Gideon's cornea.

For the sake of speed, Lemon had chosen to do an evisceration, rather than a relatively slower enucleation which took the whole eyeball and its connective muscle. "Damned medical professors can't make up their minds which is best anyway," Lemon informed him later. "We've been doing enucleations since '41, but the pedants still quibble, quibble, quibble!"

Lemon had widened the corneal opening with a scalpel, scooped out the contents of the sclera with an evisceration spoon, then repaired the cornea with silk sutures. Afterward, regular applications of mercuric chloride ointment prepared to his specifications kept the site of the operation clean.

Gideon had become despondent when he discovered he'd lost part of his vision. But Dr. Lemon waved every complaint aside, growling that it was an insult to his skill. It was Lemon himself who brought a hand glass and forced Gideon to look at his own face for the first time.

He was startled. The eyelids overlapped neatly; just a slight bulge suggested the empty sclera beneath. The eyeball itself, gristly white and lacking a pupil, was far from pretty. But the closed lids hid it well, and in a way not at all disfiguring.

As if he were discussing a choice of menu items, Lemon held a bedside debate with himself on the merits of a prosthesis versus a patch. He didn't care for the quality of available artificial eyes, and thus made Gideon's decision for him. It had to be a patch. Lent a man a certain air of dash and mystery, didn't Gideon agree?

Lemon's bristly good cheer was infectious. Gideon soon stopped thinking how unfortunate he was, and became thankful he'd pulled through. His spirits improved even more when Lemon arrived with word that he'd succeeded in getting Tillotson transferred to the most squalid and dangerous shed in the prison—the one housing the criminals from the Union army. All in all, Gideon would be eternally grateful to the skillful, kindly doctor.

But now he was impatient to get home to Margaret and Eleanor, and to begin piecing his life back together—though he had no idea how he'd do it.

That was what frightened so many of the silent men in the car, he supposed. How would they start again? Unless they hailed from family farms, what could they do to earn a living? The cities would be flooded with returning veterans as well as hundreds of thousands of freed nigras. Gideon was eager to start over, but fearful there'd be no place.

For the present, he drove that particular worry from his mind.

"So," Worthing said to him, mockingly, "you're another one who thinks we should have quit like we did?"

"We were beaten. What else could we do?"

Worthing leaned forward. *"Keep fighting."*

Gideon shook his head. "You heard Lee's order. They say he was sick of watching men die for nothing. When he lost the Petersburg line, he knew it was the end. He did the right thing."

"Not for me. You sound like Old Abe! Go home. Forgive. Forget. Those Republicans won't forgive *anything!* That Johnny Booth should have shot the whole damn pack of 'em, not just Lincoln."

If Worthing hoped for a response from the scathingly delivered remark about the dead President, he was disappointed. Gideon admired the way Lincoln had behaved during the last few days of his life. According to the papers, he'd gone to Richmond on a James River steamer less than forty-eight hours after Davis had abandoned the city and Lee had given up the Petersburg lines. Richmond's new military governor had asked Lincoln how to treat the people of the city and he'd replied, "If I were in your place I'd let 'em up easy."

Gideon would be eternally grateful for those words. Before he'd embarked on the trip back to Virginia, Dr. Lemon had voluntarily telegraphed Richmond for him, telegraphed Margaret and received a four-word reply:

All well. Hurry home.

She didn't know about his eye. But at least she'd survived the devastation of the city that Sunday in April when Davis and his cabinet had fled by railroad for Danville, the three trestles over the James burned and blown behind them. After supply and ammunition warehouses had been torched so they wouldn't fall into enemy hands, a large area of the city had been gutted by the spreading fire. That same night Admiral Semmes had blown up his pathetically small James River Squadron; shells in the magazines had erupted for hours, like an aerial display on the Fourth of July.

Presumably Margaret might have seen the first of the Federals coming into Richmond shortly after seven the next morning. They'd come from the east. Cavalrymen.

Black cavalrymen.

Maybe she'd even seen Lincoln himself walk all the way up from Rockett's Landing to the center of the city, accompanied by his son Tad and a small military guard. Nigras had poured into the streets to watch him pass. Clapped. Sung hymns. Even knelt in front of him. During that visit, he'd told the military governor to *"let 'em up easy."* On his way home, near City Point, a band on the presidential steamer had serenaded him. He'd called for "Dixie," saying with a smile that the melody was now Federal property. The whole nation's property.

And then he'd been shot in his box at Ford's Theatre.

Trying to keep frustration out of his voice, Gideon asked Worthing, "You plan to keep on fighting, do you?"

Worthing peered at the end of his cigar. "I expect I got to live just like anybody else. Before the war, I left Loudoun County to work on railroads all over the South. Surveying, grading, laying track—I'll get me another railroad job if I can. But I don't aim to forget what happened."

"And fight about it?"

"Should the occasion arise—" Worthing let the sentence hang, a smug smile on his face.

"You're a damn fool," Gideon said, turning away.

Worthing flung the cigar down and jumped to his feet. "Don't talk to me like that, you son of a bitch!" The butt smoldered in the straw, ignored as Worthing lurched across the car.

Men stirred in the gloom. Sleepers woke at the sound of

an altercation—and at the slowing of the rhythm of the trucks. The B & O special was grinding to a halt.

Gideon shoved up from the floor, disgusted that he still had to keep on battling—and with one of his own kind. Other men, including the artilleryman, tried to step between them.

"No call for this, boys."

"We're all tired."

"It's been a damn long trip for all of us."

Worthing pushed and batted at the intervening arms. "I'm not gonna take any mouth from a coward!"

Gideon refused to be stared down. "All right," he sighed. "If you want to keep your war going, I'll accommodate you."

Someone stamped on the cigar and smoking straw as Worthing reached across the arms of the men trying to keep him separated from Gideon. The boxcar rocked to a stop. Worthing swayed, off balance.

The door rolled back, flooding the smoky interior with the sunlight of a May day in 1865. Gideon's right eye slitted against the golden glare. A gray-haired, heavyset brakeman in a ragged blue Union overcoat leaned into the boxcar.

"Lads?" he shouted. "Time for a stretch!"

Or a fight, Gideon thought.

ii

The weeping boy never raised his head. Worthing glanced around to the brakeman. "Why the devil are we stopping?"

"This here's Relay House. Switch point. 'Fore we go on to Washington, we got to wait for a train comin' from Annapolis with some more of you uncaged birds."

Gideon's eye adjusted to the brilliant light. He saw rusty tracks, and beyond, spring green hills.

Switching his gaze back to Worthing, he said, "We can discuss our differences outside. More room." His tone unmistakably said he was prepared to do something besides carry on a discussion.

Worthing's unpleasant eyes scrutinized him, measuring

his size and probable strength. Despite the patch on his eye, Gideon looked formidable.

The brakeman scratched a graying eyebrow. "What the hell's goin' on in there, boys? Don't none of you want a breath of air?"

A man with the right leg of his gray trousers pinned up at the knee maneuvered his padded crutch under his armpit. Steadying himself by pushing his left palm against the wall of the car, he hopped toward the door. "I do. This place stinks to hell."

Gideon continued to stare at Worthing with one sun-touched blue eye. "Well, friend?"

Worthing finally smiled in a contemptuous way. "Hell, I'm not gonna quarrel with a wounded man. Even a yella one."

"Don't worry about my sight."

"No, I don't fight cripples." Worthing pulled a fresh cigar from his duster, lit it as he stalked toward the rectangle of light. Gideon suspected Worthing had said one thing while meaning quite another. Even though one of Gideon's eyes was useless, Worthing had decided it might be an even contest. He probably didn't care for even contests.

Worthing shoved the man on the crutch out of the way. Someone snickered. Worthing's neck reddened. As he poised to jump down, he was blocked by the blue-coated brakeman standing close to the door. He booted the brakeman under the chin.

Several of the Confederates yelled in surprise and disgust. The gray-haired man sprawled on the gravel between the tracks. Worthing jumped down. Gideon knew he should stay out of it, but he was so sick of men like this—the Tillotsons for whom the war had become an end instead of a means—that his bad temper got the better of him. He shouldered past the artilleryman and the others who'd been attempting to prevent a fight. He hurled himself through the open door onto Worthing's back, driving him to the ground.

iii

Grimy Confederates began to pour out of the long line of boxcars and stream toward Gideon and Worthing from both directions. But Gideon didn't intend to give them a prolonged show. He had the advantage, and he used it.

He dragged Worthing to his feet from behind, pulled Worthing around. The Virginian's stubbled face twisted in alarm. Evidently Gideon's strength surprised him. He tried to stab his freshly lit cigar against Gideon's cheek.

Gideon ducked, punched Worthing in the stomach to double him. Then, with his other fist, he delivered a hard chopping uppercut to Worthing's mouth. Worthing reeled back, blood running from a cut in his lip.

Some soldiers behind Worthing cushioned his fall. The Virginian tried to struggle free. Before he could, Gideon shouted, "Put him in another car or I'll kill him."

The soldiers saw the intensity of Gideon's expression and dragged Worthing away.

"Come along, now."

"Come on this way, Cap'n."

"Ain't right that two who fought on the same side should go at each other."

Worthing protested, screaming curses from his bloodied mouth. But Gideon noticed the Virginian didn't make more than a token effort to escape those restraining him.

Panting, Gideon dropped his fists. His heartbeat slowed. He was quietly thankful the fight had been so brief, thankful Worthing had turned out to be largely bluster—at least against an adversary who could hold his own.

He walked over to the gray-haired brakeman, who was still seated on the ground, looking baffled. "What the hell did I do to that Reb?"

"He was mad at me, not you."

"Could have fooled me."

Gideon grasped the man's arm and helped him to his feet. "He hurt you?"

"Not much." The man worked his jaw back and forth. Smiled. "Thank you, soldier. Miller's the name. Daphnis O. Miller."

"Beg pardon? Your first name is—?"

"Daphnis." The man pulled a face. "Don't know what it means and never have. Sounds like it belongs to a woman. I think my mother made a mistake."

Gideon smiled. "Oh, I doubt it."

"You can, but I don't. It's been the curse of my life."

"Where are you from, Mr. Miller?"

"Jersey City. Got temporarily promoted from switchman to brakeman by the grand and glorious United States army. What's your name, young fellow?"

"Gideon Kent."

"Pleasure to meet you." Miller extended his hand.

They shook. In the simple greeting, flesh against flesh, Gideon suddenly found a small hope. The issue of an independent and sovereign South had been settled. If a Union trainman and a former Confederate officer could impulsively clasp hands, maybe the country could make a start at burying the animosities of three generations and healing the wounds of four years of carnage and bitterness. He felt a little more certain of it when several of the hundred or so Confederates taking the air outside the long train paused to apologize to Miller for Worthing's attack.

The paroled Confederates began to wander across the switch tracks and sprawl on a grassy bank. A balmy breeze warmed Gideon's unwashed face.

"Jersey City, you said. You're a fair distance from home, Mr. Miller."

"That's so." The brakeman nodded. "But they need us to run these prisoner trains—beg your pardon. Guess you ain't a prisoner anymore."

"Take it you're a railroad man?"

"That's right. Where were you locked up?"

"Fort Delaware."

Miller grimaced. "Heard that was a hellhole."

"Compared to the fort, I expect hell would be a spa."

"A what?"

"Resort. Vacation place."

Gideon restrained a smile; the reading had helped. Dr. Lemon had somehow cajoled and threatened until Tillotson had returned the stolen books, which Gideon had devoured while he was recuperating in the prison infirmary. Now and again he tried a new, unfamiliar word, always with a bit of awkwardness, and always feeling he might be thought to be acting superior by the person to whom he uttered the word. But he didn't mean to sound superior. He simply needed to practice.

"What branch of service you from?" Miller inquired.

"Cavalry. Jeb Stuart's. I was captured at Yellow Tavern."

"Mighty fine outfit, the papers said."

Quietly: "That's understating it."

"Where's your home, Kent?"

"Lexington, Virginia, originally. Presently Richmond."

"Did you have a trade before the war?"

Gideon's stomach quivered. "No, none. I was too thickheaded to learn one. I'll pay for it now. I have a wife and baby to support. I'll have to find work."

In spite of the difficulties he faced in doing that, he'd made one firm decision in prison. Even if his father offered, he wouldn't accept so much as one dollar of help. The California inheritance would be his someday. But until it was, he meant to make his way on his own, hardship or no. If he didn't, he'd have no pride of accomplishment.

"Jobs are gonna be mighty scarce," Daphnis Miller observed as they started strolling beside the train.

"And not too many available for a man who's half blind, I suspect."

It was said with a smile, and no trace of self-pity. Yet the truth of his situation haunted him. What *could* a man do who was less than whole?

"Well," Miller chuckled, "you ever get desperate enough to work in a rail yard, come to Jersey City an' look me up."

"Railroading a rough business, is it?"

"Let's put it this way. A fellow who couples cars for a living and has both hands, all his fingers, an' two good legs is one of three things: Mighty quick, mighty lucky—or new on the job."

Gideon laughed. A whistle sounded eastward, the source hidden by the boxcars. The chug of a second train approaching grew steadily louder. Miller answered a hail from another brakeman up near the engine.

"Keep your pants on, Feeny, I'll be there. Kent, I truly 'preciated what you done. That Reb looked as if he wanted to tear me apart."

"He wanted to tear somebody apart. I don't think it mattered who it was."

"Damn job's gettin' as bad as workin' in the Erie yards. Well, so long. Thanks again."

"Mr. Miller?"

The trainman turned.

"Do me one small favor in return."

Miller's white eyebrow lifted, inquiringly.

"Don't say Reb anymore. We're all Americans again."

Miller smiled in a sheepish way. "Guess you're right. Didn't mean anything nasty by it. But it's gonna take a while to get out of the habit."

He waved and hurried off.

Gideon leaned against the boxcar, fighting to keep his hand down. The blind eye itched again. The brakeman was right. Men on both sides would be a long time breaking the habit of using certain words.

Reb.

Traitor.

Damn Yank.

Enemy.

Men would be a long time forgetting.

iv

Presently, more boxcars were switched and coupled to the end of the first train. The whistle blew three times and the Confederates began to clamber back aboard the cars. Spirits had improved. There was a good deal of laughing and joking.

Gideon sank down in the place he'd occupied before. Miller appeared outside, spied him, and waved as he slid the door shut, leaving only the chopped hole to ventilate the boxcar as the train resumed its journey to Washington.

So much to do, Gideon thought. *See if my little girl even recognizes me. Doubt if she will.*

Find a way to support Margaret.

Try to discover what's become of Matt and Jeremiah.

Visit my mother down in Lexington—

For a moment the odds against successfully beginning a new life seemed overwhelming. Especially when he remembered Worthing and Tillotson. There were haters on both sides. They'd make Lincoln's idea—*"Let 'em up easy"*—difficult to turn into a reality. And with the Illinois President gone and his policies already being disavowed by many Northerners, the auspices were poor.

Indeed, they hadn't been too promising while Lincoln was still alive. Gideon had studied an account of the hysterical celebration in Washington two nights after Davis' abandonment of Richmond. Lee had not yet surrendered and even then, on a platform in front of the Patent Office, Vice President Andrew Johnson had roared to a howling mob that he would hang Jefferson Davis "twenty times." As for others who'd participated in the rebellion—Gideon could recall Johnson's chilling words almost exactly: *"I would arrest them, I would try them, I would convict them, and I would hang them. Treason must be made odious! Traitors must be punished and impoverished!"*

So cried the obscure Tennessee Democrat, under fixtures specially arranged to blaze the word *UNION* from the top of the pillars of the Patent Office on the night all Washington shone with candle and gas illuminations to celebrate the fall of the enemy capital. Now Johnson was serving in the office Lincoln had still held on that evening when Johnson had shouted, *"Hang, hang!"*

Fortunately no one had expressed an interest in hanging Gideon. He was alive, and there was a wonderful, warm girl waiting for him in Richmond. He intended to devote himself to her and to their daughter, to giving them a comfortable, secure existence. He was done with war. Never again would he actively seek a fight, for whatever lofty principles. To that he'd made up his mind.

His thoughts kept returning to Margaret. They'd spent very little time together during the past three years, so each memory was just that much more vivid.

The sight of her. The feel of her lying close in the cool hours of the night. Her ardor as a wife—it sent a pleasurable thrill of anticipation chasing through him.

Somehow, no matter how formidable the obstacles, they'd overcome them together. Rebuild the life—the marriage—begun when he'd returned to Richmond after First Manassas. He felt more optimistic when he recalled the innate decency of Northerners such as Dr. Lemon and the trainman, Miller, with his words about looking him up in Jersey City. Miller obviously hadn't meant what he said; he'd merely been trying to express his gratitude in familiar terms. But at least he'd said *something.* It was encouraging.

Down at the end of the car, the boy in gray was still crying. His back heaved, but Gideon could hear no sound above the rattle of the wheels.

He smoothed his beard again, clambered up, and stepped over outstretched legs. Maybe there was something he could do to alleviate the boy's misery.

He knelt beside him. Laid an arm across the shuddering, butternut-clad shoulders.

"Son?"

Not even twenty-two years old himself, Gideon was calling this stripling son. But he saw nothing incongruous. He'd lived through enough struggle, enough perils, for three adult lifetimes.

"Son?" he repeated.

No answer.

"Any way I can help?"

Still silence. The boy didn't raise his head.

Gently, Gideon patted his back. After a moment the violent spasms began to subside.

Gideon remained where he was, neither speaking nor being spoken to, just moving his hand up and down, up and down, softly, an almost fatherly touch. Somehow it helped the boy.

The whistle on the Baltimore and Ohio engine shrieked. The boxcars clattered faster, carrying those wounded in body and those wounded in spirit on toward home.

★ *Book Three* ★

THE FIRE ROAD

CHAPTER I

ESCAPE TO THE WEST

i

HE FIRED. RELOADED. Fired again. Every round seemed to miss.

The gray-faced men were cleverly hiding in the tangled second-growth timber fifty yards out in front of the log and brush breastwork. With startling abruptness, one or two would dart from cover, shoot, and jump back out of sight. He fired at one such marksman and an instant later, blinked. Where there'd been a target, there was nothing but the smoke.

Beside him, a boy no more than seventeen took a ball in the side of his face. The boy's shriek of pain turned to a whimper as he fell. The crackle of gunfire up and down the Union defense line quickly muffled the sound.

He squinted over the breastwork then, wondering whether the Irish Brigade of Hancock's II Corps had been sent into the tangled woodland known as the Wilderness, or into the nether regions.

Smoke billowed everywhere. Artillery rumbled like a storm in a sky he couldn't see. Not far overhead, tree branches formed a thick web that shut out most of the late afternoon light above, and intensified the light below: the spurting flash from rifle muzzles, the flickering light of large limbs and small twigs blazing and raining sparks.

Directly over him, a branch crumbled apart. A hot piece of charred wood dropped onto his neck. He yelped, jerked the trigger, saw a slab of bark fly from one of the gargoyle trees behind which the enemy lurked.

Even this deep in the forest, he could feel a fairly stiff breeze blowing. Somehow it failed to dispel the smoke, though it fanned the scattered fires. The Rebs kept sniping.

On his right, young replacements who'd joined the Brigade only weeks ago scrambled back as balls chunked into the crazily piled, hastily cut logs. One of the boys cried out, "Mother of Mary! *She's catchin'!*"

The brush atop the logs a yard to his right burst into flame. Snapping, roaring, the fire raced both ways along the improvised fortification. More men of the Brigade leaped away. Out in the shifting red smoke, the Rebs howled in pain or in defiance and kept volleying.

The fire swept past him, not a foot in front of his nose. The intense heat drove him back. In moments, the entire breastwork was burning.

He heard a bugle call. The blare was suddenly aborted by a scream. Someone shouted, "Fall back! *Fall back!*"

Beyond the barrier of fire, the gray soldiers seemed to be on the move. He tried to find a target, then wiped sweat from his eyes with the back of a hand. He couldn't believe what he was witnessing.

Among the stunted trees, boys in butternut were advancing. Some had no weapons. In silence, they pleaded for mercy with outstretched hands. Minié balls smashed into their soiled blouses, piercing the fabric. No blood ran from the wounds.

He fought back a desire to scream and flee from this impossible battle taking place below the Rapidan. He clutched his rifle with both hands, as if gripping it would help keep his duty uppermost in his mind, keep him from running away.

The wall of fire rose higher.

Four feet.

Six.

From the other side, a woman called his name:

"Michael?"

He rose on tiptoe, risking death from the Confederate balls that had begun to whiz past again. A gust of wind tore holes in the flames. He saw her wandering among the gray men, saw her small, well-proportioned body with exquisite clarity in spite of the smoke. Her glossy dark hair had a scarlet nimbus. Her bright blue eyes reflected the glare of burning trees. Repeatedly, the advancing soldiers jostled her. They seemed unaware of her presence.

"Michael?"

A few Union soldiers were returning the Confederate volleys. Any second she'd be hit.

"Julia, go back!"

She didn't hear. Her head kept turning, her eyes searching for him.

He flung down his rifle, crouched, and ran at the burning breastwork. His left boot slipped on the body of a dead comrade. His leap was bad. He crashed chest-first into the sagging timber.

Fire scorched his ragged blouse. The last two metal buttons dropped off, their threads burned away. The pain on his exposed skin was hideous, but he bore it, scrambling up and over the collapsing fortification. By the time he cleared it, both his sleeves were afire.

He could still see her out there, helpless and unable to locate him. The gray men, pleading with their hands, continued to brush by.

"Julia? Here I am!" He waved his arms. The blue sleeves trailed fire. She'd come all this way to find him. He couldn't abandon her.

"Here, Julia. *Here!*"

A Confederate rifleman stepped from a turbulent cloud of smoke. Shot. Michael felt the ball slam into his belly.

Fire curled up his legs, filling his nostrils with the stench of burned leather. Another ball struck his left shoulder. She turned away in the red musk, shaking her head sadly. She started back to the gargoyle trees where the Rebel wounded flailed and bayed.

"Julia? *Julia!*"

Afire and hit, he began to topple forward. A third Rebel ball thumped into his body. Despairing, he continued to fall slowly, so slowly. At the impact of a fourth ball, he heard a deep, sonorous tolling.

He took another bullet in his left thigh. The bell tolled.

He took one in his right arm. The bell tolled.

Soon it was pealing without pause. It was the only sound he heard. It mocked his failure to reach the woman he wanted against all reason. It knelled his death in the Wilderness as he drifted face-first into a pit of dark where ground had been only a moment before.

ii

Someone jabbed his hip.

Terrified, he heard men grumbling. Sounds of motion above the bell's strident clang.

Michael Boyle's eyes popped open. He gasped loudly the instant he realized he'd been dreaming again.

He lay on his side in the cramped top bunk. In tiers of three, the bunks lined the walls of the eighty-five-foot railroad car lit at each end by a hanging lamp.

Moment by moment, the nightmare was fading. He searched for another familiar detail, found it in the pale rectangle of the charcoal drawing he'd tacked to the wall beside his head. Once he saw the drawing, he knew, finally and positively, that he was alive and whole.

Dry-mouthed, he scratched his crotch, wondering whether the cooties had gotten him at last. The bell beside the door at the car's end was being rung to wake the workers. Again he felt a jab on his hip.

He rolled over to face the aisle. The man who occupied the bunk below, Sean Murphy, stood on his own bed, his head on a level with Michael's eyes. Murphy was fifty or thereabouts, robust, pie-faced, genial. He had surprisingly little gray in his curly, copper-colored hair and huge fan of a beard. He poked Michael a third time.

"Sleep all mornin', lad, and our boss'll be on your ass worse than he is already. Rise an' shine!"

"I'm coming," Michael growled. He sat up without thinking, banged his head on the wooden roof, and swore.

He swung his legs out of the bunk and jumped down among the other Paddies tumbling from their bunks with varying degrees of speed and ill humor. Murphy's bright blue-green eyes raked Michael's six-foot frame; noted the sweat rings under the arms of his long underwear. Murphy clucked his tongue.

"You must have had some night, Michael me boy."

"What makes you say that?"

"For the last hour 'twas all I could do to catch a few winks. You been tossin' and babblin' something awful. What was goin' through your head?"

Michael stepped on the edge of the empty bottom bunk, reached to the lower end of his own, and dragged out his faded flannel shirt, trousers, and boots. He dumped the clothing in the aisle, where he proceeded to dress amidst the buffeting of earlier risers already stumbling toward the end of the car.

He disliked having to answer Murphy's question. How could he admit he'd been dreaming of a woman who didn't belong to him and never would? A woman he'd come all the way out here to escape and couldn't? Guardedly, he said, "I was back in the Wilderness. The last afternoon, when I got hit." Michael still bore a scar on his left hip. A Confederate ball buzzing in over the barricades had slammed him out of action—and out of the war.

"You dream of that every other night," Murphy sighed, helping Michael pull his galluses over his shirt. "That was two years ago, lad. Seems like you'd be forgettin' it by now."

He recalled the fire, the smoke, the feeling of forever being cut off from safety and sanity.

"If you'd been there, Sean, I doubt you'd forget it."

"But the war's over. I keep remindin' you of that."

Michael knotted a red bandana around his neck and finally managed a smile. He was a tall Irishman of thirty-six with fair hair already showing gray, a horizontal white scar across his forehead, and steady golden-brown eyes close to the color of the handlebar mustache he'd grown since coming west. Like his hair, the mustache was gray streaked.

There was no flab left on him, either. He was spare and hard after eleven weeks as a rust eater on what he and the other Paddies referred to as the U-Pay.

"Out of the way, I'm hungry," a man named Flannagan complained, giving Michael a shove. Michael stiffened. Double-chinned Sean Murphy laid a hand on his arm:

"Easy—*easy!* You're edgy as the devil this morning."

Michael let himself be restrained and took no offense. Murphy had become a good friend. Murphy was the man who'd persuaded him to leave the Chicago saloon where he'd been sweeping floors and tending bar. Together they'd ridden the cars west to the end of the existing rail lines, then traveled on to Omaha.

And Murphy's remark was embarrassingly accurate. Of late, Michael had found Louis Kent's wife slipping into his dreams with increasing frequency. No matter how far a man fled, apparently certain things could never be outrun.

He'd tried running once before, when he'd finally admitted how he felt about the spoiled and lovely spouse of Amanda Kent's only son. In a rage, he'd taken her at the family's country seat up the Hudson River from New York. The way he'd taken her amounted to rape. Almost immediately he'd realized it was more an act of lust than anger; he'd wanted her secretly for a long time. He'd enlisted in the 69th New York to escape the cause of his feelings, but found he couldn't.

After the Wilderness, the desire to flee had still been with him. But it was complemented by another drive, just as strong. He was sick at heart after seeing so much death. Weary of watching life and property being destroyed. He'd wanted an antidote—a feeling of accomplishing something, building something. So Julia had been one reason but not the only reason he'd left the Washington hospital as soon as he could, accepted his discharge, and headed for new country.

He'd spent a season in Ohio, planting and harvesting corn while Lee gave up to Grant at Appomattox, the bloodletting ended, and the Northern punishment of the beaten enemy commenced. Late in '65 he'd moved on to Chicago and held unsatisfying menial jobs in a packing house, a tannery, the saloon. During those months, the nation watched in astonishment as Andrew Johnson—"His Accidency, the President"—swung away from his pronouncements about hanging Southerners and began carrying out the conciliatory Reconstruction policies foreshadowed in Lincoln's 1864 inaugural.

In Ohio and Illinois, too, the memory of Julia stayed with him.

Then crusty widower, Sean Murphy, approached him in

the Chicago saloon, and they became drinking companions and eventually friends. Michael listened with interest when Murphy spoke of leaving his poor-paying drayman's job for higher wages and cleaner work in the open air beyond the Missouri. There, the long-delayed transcontinental railroad was going forward at last. Michael decided to pack his few belongings and join Murphy and a number of other Paddies heading for the prairie.

The men went west in a spirit of hope, enthusiasm and pride, declaring that the Irish had built the Erie Canal, a marvel in its day, and by God they'd build the century's newest and greatest marvel too—

"No denials, Michael?"

He forced himself from his reverie. "What's that?"

"I remarked—several hours ago, it seems—that you woke up nervous as an Orangeman in County Cork. Again."

Michael smiled. "Why, Sean, you should know moodiness is typical of an Irish fellow. Especially when he's throwing down a mile of rail a day, and working for a bastard to boot."

Murphy looked unconvinced. He headed up the aisle between the tiered bunks in the eight-foot-high car. He and Michael were now the laggards. Most of the other laborers had piled out the door at the end, where a rack of repeating Spencer rifles gleamed under the hanging lantern.

"I agree it ain't quite the soft duty I thought it'd be," Murphy said. "But thirty-five greenback dollars a month is a sight better than what I was earnin' haulin' kegs up and down Lake Street. Wait a damned minute, will you? Got to lace up my blasted boot again."

Murphy knelt. Michael scratched his groin and gazed at the rifles in the racks. Would they be needed against the Sioux or Cheyenne?

So far there'd been only four raids, each one over before Michael even heard about it. The pattern was always the same. He and the other men would be wakened late in the night by yells and the bang of Spencers. They'd tumble outside, rifles in hand, only to find the drovers who guarded the railroad's cattle firing futile shots into the darkness from which some Indians had come slipping silently to run off half a dozen head.

After the first theft, Michael and Sean Murphy had learned that information about the Plains tribes given them gratuitously in an Omaha saloon was false. They'd been told the hostiles never struck after the sun went down, fearing that if they were slain at night, their spirits couldn't find the way to the Indian equivalent of heaven. A drover guarding the herd explained the real reason Plains braves generally avoided nocturnal attacks: the gut strings on war bows grew damp and lost their tautness in the night air. Night thievery of cattle was commonplace, however, since it seldom required the discharge of even a single arrow. There'd been no casualties to the railroad men on any of the raids thus far.

But couriers galloping in from further west, where the grade was being prepared, had recently brought disturbing news about the Indians.

Early in the spring, peace commissioners had been dispatched by the Federal Government to attempt to arrange a treaty with the Sioux and Cheyenne. The tribes stood in the way of miners heading north toward the Big Horn Mountains—the Powder River country—where there'd been a gold strike.

The dispatch of the commission sprang from a shift in Congressional policy. Washington now thought it easier to buy peace on the High Plains than to fight for it. According to what Michael had heard, important chiefs of the Oglala and Brulé Sioux had journeyed to Fort Laramie to listen to the offer of one Mr. Taylor of the Indian Office.

The tribes would be given an annuity of seventy-five thousand dollars a year, plus firearms for hunting, if they'd guarantee the safety of whites traveling the Bozeman Trail to the new diggings. The negotiations had proceeded smoothly at first, then they were abruptly ruined by the arrival of a Brulé chief, Standing Elk, who had encountered a column of white soldiers commanded by a Colonel Carrington. The soldiers were on their way to the Powder River country to build stockades.

Red Cloud, the most influential of the Sioux at the Fort Laramie parley, listened to the report of the army column with shock and anger. Offers of peace were being made even as soldiers tramped northwest to seize the disputed territory! Red Cloud and a great many other braves stormed out of the fort, promising war as repayment for the deception. So even though the U-Pay had experienced no serious trouble as yet, every man at the railhead knew circumstances were ripe for it.

"Broke the damn thing!" Murphy exploded. Part of a thong dangled from his hand. He stood up and stuffed the thong in his pocket. Michael turned away from the rifles and the gloomy thoughts they generated. Murphy returned to the subject of a few moments ago.

"I wanted to speak to you about the boss. I agree it's a damn shame we drew him as head of our gang—"

"I can't figure out how a Reb got such a good job, Sean."

"Corkle told me the fellow ran railroad construction crews in the South, before the war."

"I heard that too. But he's still a Reb, and this is mostly a Union outfit."

"All I can guess is, the Casements believe the only war they should fret about is a war with the calendar. They put experienced men where they can get the best use from 'em."

"Suppose so." Michael nodded. "All that's past is forgiven—or so you're always saying," he added with a wry smile.

"Well, we both understand I've been known to prevaricate on occasion." Murphy grinned. He remained in the door, intentionally blocking Michael's passage. "There ain't a hotter Southron at the railhead than the wretch we're workin' for—nor one who likes more to keep fightin' the late, unlamented war. Friend to friend, Michael, you're a mite too willing to butt heads with him on that subject—not to mention others."

"I have a reason. No, make it three."

"Such as?"

"He's a bully. He's a loudmouth. And he's a liar about the war. He won't admit fighting for the principle of states' rights was so much blarney. He and his kind may have fought well, but they were fighting for an immoral cause."

Here Murphy looked dubious; Michael's remark didn't reflect the conventional thinking of most Irishmen, who viewed blacks as an economic threat.

"Nigger slavery, y'mean?"

Another nod. "I also get sick of him claiming it's only

the Northern factories that beat the South. He's partly right, but I'll tell you this. At the Round Tops, I saw no factories perishing, I saw Irishmen and Dutchmen. In the Wilderness I didn't see factories perishing, just Yankee boys."

"Well, have a care, Michael. He's no sort to fool with—and I've been wanting to remind you of it."

"I don't need reminders. I work with him every day. Thanks for your good thoughts, however. I'll behave. I'm through with fighting. I'm here to work."

" 'An' they shall beat their swords into plowshares, an' their spears into pruning hooks—' " Murphy recited the passage with a merry smile. " 'Neither shall they learn war any more'?"

"That's the general idea," Michael replied soberly.

"Book of Micah," the older man announced proudly. "Fourth chapter, third verse. See? I ain't the godless lout you boys are always accusin' me of bein'."

"But it's from the second chapter, fourth verse, of Isaiah as well as from Micah."

"What? It is?"

"Yes. And you left out the part about nation not lifting up sword against nation."

Murphy blinked. "My stars, I never took you for a Bible student!"

"It's the only book my mother owned when I was a boy in the slums. She died when I was seven, but she'd already taught me to read a few passages, and persuaded me to study it to learn moral behavior. When she passed away, and I went on the streets and worked on the docks, I kept a Bible with me. For every moral lesson I took out of the pages, I saw two of the opposite kind happening in New York. But it was my principal teacher of decent English."

"And you're way ahead of me on the subject of the boss. Relieved to hear it." Murphy winked. "Certainly 'twasn't him you were thinkin' of last night. Along with the war, you had a gal on your mind, didn't you?"

Curtly: "No."

"Why, you did! You kept yellin' her name in your sleep."

Michael's face went blank. "You must have heard wrong."

"I'm positive I did not. Who is she, lad? Some Chicago

colleen you never mentioned to me? Or one of them farm lasses you met down in Ohio?"

"Sean," Michael said, his smile affable but not his eyes, "we may be friends, good friends. But certain things are none of your affair. Quit swinging your clapper and let's go eat."

The younger man's expression had grown so grim, Murphy acquiesced without a murmur.

CHAPTER II
THE RAILHEAD

i

THUS, AT DAWN on a Saturday morning near the end of August 1866, Michael Boyle and Sean Murphy climbed down from one of the four cars standing with a locomotive coupled at the rear. Steam was already up on the 4-4-0 Danforth and Cooke wood burner named *Osceola*. The engine's cowcatcher pointed east along the single track.

Osceola and a quartet of double-sized boxcars constituted the railhead work train—the "perpetual train" as it was called by the Paddies who were pushing the line westward in an effort to silence doubters, lure more investors, and turn the foundering U-Pay into a success.

Dr. Thomas Durant, the vice president and general manager of the Union Pacific, had in fact made a public commitment to finish two hundred and forty-seven miles of roadbed across the Nebraska Territory as soon as possible. Milepost 247 would be erected on the hundredth meridian. Until the meridian was reached, the line's charter to build and operate the eastern portion of the transcontinental railroad would not become official. So a growing number of ex-soldiers and day laborers from the cities were driving toward the meridian at a pace even the hardiest newcomers had trouble keeping up with at first. Michael well recalled the agony he'd suffered during his first two weeks at the railhead. Every night, he'd dragged himself up to his bunk, his whole body in pain.

Already there was noise and movement around the perpetual train. The sun had barely risen. But the light was bright enough to reveal a barren yet strangely beautiful ocean of grass, gently rolling, and treeless for as far as a man could see. The light burnished the greenish-gray buffalo grass and here and there illuminated radiant patches of purple pasqueflower, crimson wild geranium, and yellow prairie smoke.

West of the four huge freight cars lay the grade, prepared by gangs following the location stakes as far as a hundred miles in advance of the moving railhead. To the rear stretched the shimmering parallel rails, running a good two hundred miles to the Missouri River. Back past Fort Kearney at milepost 191—the last real outpost of civilization, if a ramshackle infantry stockade and a collection of shanties could be called civilization. Back past the division point at Grand Island. Back past Fremont, only forty miles out of Omaha—or Bilksville as it was called by those who still considered the railroad a foolish venture destined to fail.

Fremont was as far as the rails had gotten by January of '66, even though Dr. Durant and other officials of the line had broken ground at Omaha almost a year earlier. There'd been poor progress until two men, the Casement brothers, had submitted a bid as subcontractors for track laying. Now the line was advancing at the rate of two rails every minute, four hundred rails every mile—and a mile of new track between sunup and sunset, six days a week. Michael found the speed astonishing—just as he found the sights of the prairie fresh and astonishing almost every morning. Today was no exception.

He stretched, beginning to throw off the lethargy of sleep and the memory of the nightmare. He drew in deep breaths of the cool, sweet air tanged with the smell of burning wood and the reek of valve oil from the funnel-stack locomotive. Men were hurrying from the two bunk cars to the dining car, second from the head end. The first car served as a combination office and kitchen.

A few late risers were rolling out of hammocks slung

beneath the car where Michael and Murphy slept. Others were climbing down from tents erected on top. General Jack Casement's army of rust eaters was growing week by week. Over four hundred men worked at the railhead now.

Smoke drifted across the paling stars, breeze-borne from vents in the roof of the kitchen. Michael thought he smelled fresh bread. He certainly smelled cow dung. To his left, five hundred head were rousing and milling, prodded by the drovers. The herd were the railhead's traveling meat supply; the four Indian raids had not cut into it substantially.

The lowing cows raised dust. But the Platte River, shallow, twisting and beginning to glow with sunlight, was still visible through the cloud. On the far side of the river characterized as "a mile wide and an inch deep," Michael could discern the ruts of the Overland Trail leading on to Fort Laramie and Oregon. Sometimes the road was noisy with freight wagons, or a stagecoach, or parties of buffalo hunters. This morning it was deserted.

But it had seen traffic during the night. He smiled at the sight of a couple of the transcontinental telegraph poles planted beside the trail. The poles had been pushed until they tilted to a forty-five-degree angle. Buffalo had passed, pausing to scratch off some of their shedding hump manes.

Michael and Sean Murphy trudged on toward the nearest line of men waiting their turn in the dining car. A similar line had formed at the car's other end. The morning bell rang at five thirty. In less than an hour, the first of the iron trains carrying a carefully calculated quantity of rails and ties, spikes and chairs would come chugging in from the supply base at Kearney. Then the workday—twelve hours or more—would begin.

The activity and numbers of men around the work train hardly suggested the difficulties the transcontinental line had encountered since the passage of the Pacific Railroad Acts. Michael knew a great deal about the Union Pacific's history. The supply trains brought newspapers as well as mail, and he'd become an avid student of the project.

The concept of a rail link between the oceans had been under discussion for years. Proposed routes had been debated in Congress and at the cabinet level for a decade. In the fifties, while he was Franklin Pierce's Secretary of War, Jefferson Davis had obtained surveys of several possible routes. But the start of the four-year rebellion had interrupted the decision process, even though Lincoln by then had enough data on which to act.

In California a young engineer named Theodore Judah had located and mapped a feasible route through the Sierras. Other surveys, including those by the Union Pacific's new chief engineer, former U.S. Army general Grenville Dodge, had shown that the most practical route from the Missouri began at Omaha and ran toward the point where the Overland Trail joined the Platte.

Finally Lincoln had moved. He saw the railroad as a means of symbolically unifying the Atlantic and Pacific states and of solidifying the Union's hold on all the land between. Congress and the President had put the first Pacific Railroad Act into law in July of 1862, chartering two corporations: the Union Pacific, which was to build the line from the Missouri River, and the Central Pacific, which would begin eastbound construction at Sacramento.

The terms of the Railroad Act seemed ideal for attracting risk capital. The government had granted both corporations ten miles of land in alternating sections on either side of a four-hundred-foot right of way, ten miles in return for every mile of track laid. Resale of this land to settlers, it was presumed, would help finance the project. In addition, the Act had authorized Federal subsidies in the form of thirty-year bonds. The amount of the subsidy per mile of completed track depended on the terrain. On the plains, the rate was sixteen thousand dollars a mile. It jumped to forty-eight thousand a mile in the Rocky Mountains and the Sierras.

Control of the Central Pacific was in the hands of a group called The Big Four. The first of the quartet was California's governor, Leland Stanford. His partners were three merchants from the Sacramento Valley—a grocer and vegetarian named Mark Hopkins, and a pair of hardware merchants, Collis Huntington and Charles Crocker. Their eastern counterparts were a group of businessmen led by Dr. Durant, a canny man who'd abandoned medicine for a career as a railway promoter.

Despite the government's generosity, the sale of each corporation's stocks and bonds had lagged because of the financial community's disinterest. No shrewd investor wanted to dump money into a railroad across a wilderness when so much more could be made supplying war material to the Federal Government. So a second Railroad Act had become necessary in '64. Among its other provisions, it doubled the land granted per mile; the two companies would eventually control over twenty-one million acres.

But even this failed to attract capital. By mid-1864, the Central Pacific had laid exactly thirty-one miles of track. The Union Pacific's rails didn't extend beyond the Omaha city limits.

Once more Lincoln had stepped in, this time primarily on behalf of the Union Pacific. He'd sought the services of "the King of Spades"—Massachusetts congressman Oakes Ames, who'd made a fortune from the manufacture and sale of Ames Old Colony Mining Shovels. Lincoln wanted Ames to put not only his money but his personal prestige behind the line. Oakes Ames and his brother Oliver poured in a million of their own funds, and attracted another million and a half—but it was still not enough. War profiteering and skepticism continued to deter investors.

Michael had read a good deal about the directors of both railroads. He'd also heard his share of gossip. Durant's crowd and The Big Four might be greedy, but they were neither lazy nor stupid. They wanted the line built not only because it might yield unprecedented profits, but also for the sheer thrill of accomplishing an engineering feat of incredible magnitude.

There was mounting evidence, however, that the directors of the lines were beginning to indulge in freebooting on a grand scale. Big Four director Huntington, for example, had scored a major coup with the subsidies. It had been President Lincoln's responsibility to fix the place at which the sixteen-thousand-dollar Sacramento Valley subsidy was replaced by the forty-eight-thousand-dollar one for construction in the Sierra foothills. Huntington had enlisted a friendly geologist who reported that the Sierras actually "began" at Arcade Creek, twenty-four miles west of the point designated in Theodore Judah's original survey. At Arcade, reddish mountain soil could be found mingled with the blacker dirt of the Valley. The fact that the soil had washed down there was glossed over.

Armed with the "dramatic new findings," Huntington

had launched a campaign in Washington. Prompted by a cooperative Congressman, Lincoln restudied his maps and accepted the Central Pacific claim—thus giving the line an additional two dozen miles at the considerably higher rate. "Pertinacity and Abraham's faith," ran a wry report of the maneuvering, "removed mountains."

Dr. Durant recognized a major problem confronting the Union Pacific. A record of accomplishment was needed to attract capital and reverse unfavorable public opinion. *Accomplishment! Track laid!* The line wouldn't even be in business permanently unless the hundredth meridian was reached.

But slogans and rallying cries weren't enough to overcome the obstacles facing the U.P. First, every bit of equipment, food, water, and rolling stock had to be brought to Omaha by freight wagon or by steam packet from St. Joseph or St. Louis. The two nearest railroads east of the Missouri, the Rock Island and the Cedar Rapids & Missouri, both stopped a good hundred and fifty miles short of the river—as Michael had discovered when he'd journeyed west from Chicago. He, Murphy, and the other Paddies had completed the last stage of their trip by coach and on foot.

No bridge existed between Council Bluffs and Omaha. Anything arriving by wagon had to be ferried around the Missouri's dangerous sandbars. The line's very first Danforth and Cooke locomotive, the *Major General Sherman,* had been shipped in sections on a riverboat and laboriously reassembled at its destination.

The Central Pacific had been luckier on a couple of important counts. The forested slopes of the Sierras provided all the hardwood the line needed to fuel its engines—and for ties. The Nebraska plains, by contrast, had no trees except the porous and unsatisfactory cottonwood.

The C.P. also faced no immediate threats of Indian trouble along its first miles of roadbed. But the line had to traverse mountains—blasting and tunneling through, or creating torturous switchback cuts that wound around the peaks. Charles Crocker, the line's construction boss, had found a solution to the unwillingness of some men to risk themselves in such hazardous work. Crocker had begun to hire Chinese. The so-called Celestials proved to be first-class powder monkeys, expert at working with the explosives used to blast a path through solid granite.

Michael had read that not a few of the white men working on the Central Pacific hated the Chinese. But Crocker was delighted with them. They worked diligently, and had one appealing moral virtue their white brethren lacked: they drank nothing stronger than tea. Crocker's inspiration had been lauded in a toast that amused Michael: "To the Pacific Railroad—the only piece of crockery ware made out of China."

In spite of minor successes, such as Crocker's discovery of a workforce that could plow through the Sierras without fear and without delay, Michael knew skepticism about the concept of a transcontinental line remained widespread. Even four short years before, the Union hero of the Georgia and Carolina march—the very man for whom the Union Pacific's Engine Number 1 had been named—had greeted the first Railroad Act with the comment that he wouldn't care to spend money on a coast-to-coast ticket to be used by his grandchildren.

Both railroads were drawing their share of press criticism, though for some reason roving correspondents treated the Central Pacific less harshly than they did the eastern line. Headquarters was reportedly still grumbling about articles by the editor of the influential Springfield, Massachusetts, *Republican.* He'd written that the job of laying track across the relatively level plains was "baby work." He and other Eastern pundits couldn't fathom why the Union Pacific was progressing so slowly—unless, as many said, it had been destined to fail from the beginning.

But now 1866 looked to be a watershed, thanks to the arrival of the Casement brothers, John S. and Daniel T.

Jack Casement had been brevetted to brigadier in the Union army. He was almost constantly at the railhead. Daniel remained in Omaha, calculating how many five-hundred-pound rails or chemically treated cottonwood ties were needed each day, or journeying out to the supply bases at Fremont and Kearney to coordinate the schedules of the iron trams.

To be accurate, the Casements didn't work directly for the Union Pacific. Nor did Michael or Murphy and/or any of the other rust eaters. The actual work of building the road was contracted by a company called the Crédit Mobilier. In French the name meant movable loan. The Crédit Mobilier sold its services directly to the U.P. Some said its prices were never questioned.

That rumor tended to validate another Michael had heard about Dr. Durant and some of his fellow U.P. directors. It was said they also served secretly as directors of the subcontracting firm. If that were true, Michael saw no reason why a mile of track couldn't be billed at twice or triple its actual cost. One pocket, in effect, would pay another. In a cynical way he almost admired the suspected scheme. It would make thievery on a stupendous scale not only possible but easy.

In fact he'd reflected that such an arrangement might one day attract the interest, and money, of Mr. Louis Kent. Louis was at home among men willing to take not altogether legal risks for immense gain. One such venture—a trading company formed to do business secretly with the South during the early days of the war—had been exposed by Michael, Jephtha Kent, and the Boston banker, Joshua Rothman.

Jephtha had published a series of newspaper articles on Louis' company, Federal Suppliers. In those days Jephtha had been Washington correspondent for the Kent paper, *The New York Union.* But Jephtha had rashly warned Louis about the series prior to publication, hoping the matter could be settled quietly. Michael had told Jephtha that Louis would never dismantle a profitable business solely because of a threat, and he'd been right. Jephtha had been discharged from the *Union,* and Rothman had been forced to arrange for the articles to appear in Greeley's *Tribune.*

Michael's role had been that of a corroborative witness. Along with Rothman, he'd been present when Louis made his original proposal about setting up the company. Thus he was able to verify Rothman's statements in Jephtha's copy.

The company had vanished almost as quickly as it had arrived. Louis had suffered severe public embarrassment, though no actual prosecution had been launched by the government since the company was not in existence long enough to engage in a provably illegal act. If there had been a desire in Washington to prefer charges against Louis, Michael had never heard of it. After disconnecting himself from the Kent's longtime law firm, Benbow and

Benbow—like the Rothman Bank, too scrupulous an institution for his taste—Louis had hired other lawyers. Michael suspected he'd sent one or two of them hustling to the capital to distribute cash and make sure any contemplated government action was quashed.

Louis had also avoided substantial monetary loss simply because he'd planned to set up Federal Suppliers with funds that were not actually his. He meant to use the California gold money Amanda Kent had pyramided and left to Jephtha, her cousin Jared's son. That money would one day pass to Jephtha's three boys.

Rothman had balked at the proposal. He was chief steward of Amanda's California holdings, and refused to permit Louis to manipulate the accrued profits. Out of the conflict came Rothman's conviction that for the sake of the family's honor, Louis must be stopped—no matter where he finally secured his capital. He *had* been stopped.

Even though Louis had experienced no depletion of his personal fortune, the scandal was enough to earn Michael, Jephtha, and the banker the undying enmity of the young financier. That was another reason Michael had been glad to leave the East. He wasn't so much afraid of Louis as sick of him and all he represented. Rather, all he failed to represent after the Kent family had built its fortune and reputation through a combination of idealism and honest, unashamed enterprise.

Michael seldom thought about Louis anymore—or any of the eastern Kents, for that matter.

Except Julia.

A vivid image of her face troubled him again as the line edged forward to the dining car. The image vanished when he became aware of someone watching him from a similar line at the car's far end.

It was the crew boss he and Murphy had discussed earlier. The Virginian, Captain Leonidas Worthing.

ii

Worthing wore a straw hat and faded gray duster. A stump of cigar jutted from his teeth. He claimed to have served with Mosby's Partisan Rangers. There were a great many veterans in Jack Casement's little army, but few Confederates. And those few were generally rust eaters like Michael himself. Worthing was the exception.

The light spreading over the Prairie lit Worthing's unfriendly face as men began to leave the dining car, their turn at the tables over. Worthing tossed away his cigar and elbowed his way to the head of the line. A workman objected. Worthing said a few words that made the worker flush and back away.

The Southerner turned his back on the man he'd intimidated. He stared at Michael again, tapping a leather riding crop against his faded trouser leg.

Lord, how Michael detested that swaggering oaf! Twice he'd protested when Worthing badgered some member of Michael's gang, which was only one of several gangs the Virginian supervised. One argument had nearly reached the point of violence. Then General Jack Casement had stepped in. Casement stressed cooperation. The work was arduous enough without personal feuds being added to the burden. But Leonidas Worthing didn't share Casement's philosophy.

Half a dozen Paddies came clattering down the steps. The car was emptying quickly. As Michael and Murphy moved forward again, they saw one of their crew walking toward them from the head end. Evidently he'd already eaten; he was picking at his upper gum with the point of a Bowie knife.

"Hallo, Christian," Murphy called, waving.

"Morning, lads." The young man nodded, wiping his knife on the sleeve of his old wool shirt.

Christian was lean and dark, with high cheekbones and straight black hair that reminded Michael of Jephtha. Christian admitted to being a Delaware Indian and hailing from Ohio, but that was all anyone knew about him. Startling blue eyes suggested at least one white parent or grandparent. Whether he'd been given his name as a symbol of a hoped-for religious conversion, or merely because it had a pleasing sound, was a mystery. But he was soft-spoken, well-mannered and mule-strong. He amused Michael because he liked to sprinkle his conversation with words and phrases picked up from the Paddies.

"How's the beef?" Murphy asked him.

"Tougher than usual. Beans about the same. Potatoes overcooked. Boiled to mush, practically."

"Ah, that's plenty good enough for you, Chief," another man in line laughed. Christian took it in good humor:

"Don't sauce me, spud-grubber, or I'll utter my celebrated bloodcurdling whoop and summon the tribe to relieve you of your none too attractive hair." Less cheerfully, he leaned close to Michael. "I had the misfortune to run into himself as I was coming out."

"The captain?"

Christian nodded. "Keep clear. He's in a nasty mood."

Murphy sighed. "When is he not?"

"Nastier than usual, I mean. See you presently, lads." The Indian drifted away.

Murphy shook his head. "He talks prettier English than men born to it. Bet his old man was a missionary who went wild in one of them Ohio villages where the savages beat the drums an' dance nekkid all night."

"Sean, don't ever visit Ohio."

"I passed through Cleveland on my way to Chicago. Never seen the natives, though."

"The natives, as you call them, would sorely disappoint you. They don't beat drums, nor do their dusky daughters dance under the moon. In fact they don't have dusky daughters. They're just a lot of proper second-generation farmers and mechanics who hop after the coin six days a week and pray on Sunday."

"Just good Americans, huh?" Murphy said, grinning. Then he yelled at some Paddies who'd stopped to chat in the car entrance, "Will you kindly get your fannies down here so those of us still waitin' can have a chance at the elegant fare?"

"Oh, don't be in no hurry, Sean Murphy," one of the group called back. "You've no surprises waiting."

There were seldom surprises at mealtime. Though wholesome enough, the morning, noon, and evening menus were the same seven days a week, except when an occasional band of independent buffalo hunters rode in to sell a fresh kill. But the Union Pacific bread was always newly baked and warm, the coffee strong—and at the moment Michael was ravenous, perhaps because of the crispness of the air. It smelled of autumn.

He wondered if they really would reach the meridian before the first heavy snow. If not, the line would probably go under. Winter on the plains was reported to be brutal; he already knew construction would be halted during the worst months.

Finally the car entrance cleared, and the line moved faster. Michael followed his friend inside. A long table ran from end to end, with benches on either side. A little sunlight leaked through grimy windows, but hanging lamps were still needed.

Two Paddies on the far side finished their meals. To leave, they climbed on the bench and walked across the table, incurring the wrath of a cook's helper bringing in a fresh platter of beef and a wooden bucket of steaming coffee.

Other helpers with long-handled rag swabs darted in and out among the men who were scrambling to find places. Each tin plate was nailed down, only the coffee cups standing free. The helpers used the swabs to wipe each plate quickly.

Michael and his companion wedged in among the workers spreading out along the benches. Experience had taught Michael not to hesitate. He planted himself in front of a plate, grabbed a fork, and stabbed a slab of beef. Another fork from the other side narrowly missed his wrist.

He jerked the beef to his plate, then shoved his cup through a thicket of hands around the coffee bucket. He managed to dip out a full cup without spilling any. He lifted a leg over to the bench, ready to sit down, and felt a tap on his shoulder.

Across the table, three men grabbing handfuls of potatoes quieted suddenly. Sean Murphy, already seated, glanced behind Michael, then directly at him, with a look of warning. Michael's scalp prickled.

With deliberate slowness, Michael laid his fork beside his heaped plate. Then he put the coffee cup down. He turned to find Captain Leonidas Worthing pushing up the brim of his straw hat with his riding crop.

"Boyle, you've taken my spot. Move somewhere else."

It wasn't a request. It was a demand.

Chapter III
The Captain

i

"Boyle, I'm waiting."

Leonidas Worthing said it with an insincere smile that revealed brown teeth. At the right corner of his mouth, a sore glistened. A little souvenir from one of the soiled doves of Omaha, perhaps?

Michael held his temper. "I see no place cards, Captain."

"True, but I decided to sit here so I can speak to Murphy about speeding up the work of your gang. Of all the ones I'm in charge of, it's by far the worst. Too many weak sisters." He left no doubt that he included Michael. "Fellows who'd rather bellyache than earn a day's wages honestly."

Michael knew what the Virginian meant by bellyaching: remarks he'd made over a pipe after working hours. They'd evidently reached the captain through someone who toadied to him. But the remarks were truthful.

Still getting no response, Worthing grew impatient. "If you intend to dispute my right to this seat, Boyle, kindly tell me."

On the other side of the table, one man nudged another expectantly. Michael refused to be forced into a quarrel.

"Captain," he said quietly, "why is it you're always hunting excuses to fight?"

Worthing surprised him with a laugh.

"Because I believe in doing a good job!"

"And because you're not partial to Yanks?"

"If you expect me to be partial to your kind, you're a fool. I rode with Colonel Mosby, you know."

"Aye, so we've heard," Murphy sighed. "A score of times."

"But I never told you the circumstances of my capture, did I? I had the misfortune to lose my mount and get caught by some of General Custer's glory hunters. You know what those kindly fellows did before they loaded me on a prisoner train? They gave me a dose of their favorite punishment. Tied me to a wagon wheel. Arms over my head—" The crop shot up as he pantomimed it. "Legs stretched out. Then they gave the wheel a quarter turn. They left me hanging with the hub goddamn near breaking my spine. For fourteen hours! When I woke up on the train, I found I'd pissed and shitted myself like a baby."

"Jaysus, Captain," Murphy gulped. "I *was* attemptin' to enjoy my breakfast."

The Virginian paid no attention. "One of my fellow prisoners on the train said that when I was put aboard, I had spit—foam—all over my chin. I couldn't remember my own name for the best part of a day. Handsome treatment for an officer, wouldn't you say?"

Michael shrugged again. "I can't excuse it. But I wasn't there. I'm not to blame."

"Oh, yes." Worthing jabbed the crop into his chest. "You wore the blue."

"You're going to harass every Union man in this outfit just because you were treated badly?"

"*Harass!* Mighty fine word for a slum Irishman." Another jab with the crop. "Mighty fine!"

Michael's temper was heating. He seized the crop and pushed it down. "Of course I forget one fact. You don't limit yourself to harassing men. Last week you practically whipped that lorry-car boy to death with this thing. And merely because he was a little clumsy handling the horse. You surely didn't learn much from John Mosby, Captain. You didn't learn men work better when they're led, not driven. I suspect you're too stupid to learn anything so simple."

Livid, Worthing swung the crop. "You damned high-assed mick!"

Michael's right hand shot across to catch Worthing's forearm. The dining car was completely silent.

There was a test of strength as Michael struggled to hold Worthing's arm steady. His face reddened. Veins rose thick on the back of his hand.

Worthing tried to wrench away. Michael held him. But his anger had subsided a little; he thought it best to bring the confrontation back into saner limits.

"Captain, if we keep this up"—a quick gasp for breath—"we won't be ready to work at six thirty. What do you say we both try to forget the war's over?"

"Hell if I will!"

Michael's shoulder began to throb. He felt tension in Worthing's arm. The man was readying for another attempt to pull free. Already Michael had humiliated him, and he realized that he'd probably have to fight. God knew what trouble he'd land in with Casement for that.

Boots thudded on the steps at the west end of the car. The door banged open.

"General Jack wants all the crew bosses. Right away!"

Several diners grumbled and left their places. Michael weighed the risk, accepted it, and released Worthing's arm.

"That includes you, I believe."

He watched the crop, waiting for it to come slashing at his cheek. Worthing's hand whitened. Michael mentally gauged how far back he could jump and still throw a punch. The man at the door bellowed again.

"Worthing, shake a leg! The telegraph says the iron train's forty minutes late out of Kearney."

Eye to eye with Leonidas Worthing, Michael waited. Finally the ex-Confederate ran the tip of his tongue over his upper lip. The hand holding the crop relaxed and regained its color. The other crew bosses trooped out as the man who'd summoned them stormed forward.

"Damn it, Worthing. Casement said *now,* not Christmas!"

Worthing waved the crop. "Shut up. I'm coming." He

inclined his head toward Michael's. "Wasn't good luck for you when they put you on one of my gangs, boy."

"Surprise me with something else, Captain. And don't call me boy again or I'll knock you down so you won't get up for a while. I answer to the name of Boyle."

Worthing reddened. Michael could see grins on the faces along the table. Sean Murphy's was broadest of all.

"Ah, who gives a shit what your name is?" The crop wigwagged; Worthing was trying to make light of his humiliation. "A mick's a mick, except you—you're special. You've been headed for trouble since the day you climbed off the cars."

"I could give you a few reasons why." There was anger in Michael's eyes again; he'd had enough. "But I'd be wasting my breath."

"Reasons—" Worthing nodded, licking the brown stump of an upper tooth. "Lies you've been spreading around free and easy among your pals. That nigger. The half-breed I got stuck with—well, you remember one thing. There's a good forty miles or more until we hit the meridian. That's forty days. And you'll be working for me every damn one of 'em. I guarantee you won't feel like celebrating when we put down milepost two forty-seven."

He touched the crop to Michael's jaw.

"Before we get there, *boy,* I'm going to break your back."

ii

Worthing spun and stalked to the door, shoving two workers out of his way. Michael barely heard the compliments directed at him. He was experiencing one of those shameful moments in which he wished he'd never met Mrs. Amanda Kent de la Gura. A good deal of her style—her refusal to be intimidated by those she considered in the wrong—had rubbed off on him while he'd worked for her.

But he'd joined Jack Casement's rust eaters to find peace, not endless quarreling.

He sank down on the bench beside Murphy, staring with lusterless eyes at his plate of beef and cup of cooling coffee.

He had always been teased about his appetite. His belly seemed to have a limitless capacity—no doubt because he'd gotten so little to eat as a child. He never tired of cramming himself, and the enormous amounts of food he ate never added so much as one extra pound. But his earlier anticipation of breakfast was altogether gone.

I'm going to break your back.

"Lord, Fergus, did you hear that feller from the office?" a Paddy on the opposite side asked his companion. "First iron train forty minutes late. 'Spose it's Injuns?"

"Eat up!" Murphy urged Michael, who shook his head.

The man named Fergus shrugged. "The further we go beyond Kearney, the more likely it is. The Injuns don't like this railway cuttin' into their buffla grounds."

"But I thought General Dodge pacified the savages before he signed on with the U-Pay."

"It don't take 'em long to get *un*pacified these days," Fergus replied. "You heard what happened at Fort Laramie. Out this far, the only Injuns we got for friends are the one or two workin' on the line, and a few hang-around-the-forts. The buckos with the devil in 'em—ones like that Red Cloud—they don't pay any attention to what the tame Injuns say, do—or sign. Touch the pen, I mean. They can't write English so they just touch a pen to a treaty an' some clerk fills in their names."

Fergus' companion looked puzzled. "I dunno what you mean, hang-around-the-forts."

"That's because you ain't been out here long enough," Fergus announced in a smug tone. "Hang-arounds are Injuns who pitch their tipis near a post to trade an' beg for handouts. Liquor. Hot coffee with lots of sugar in it. Everybody back East thinks the Injuns are crazy for the alcohol, but a buffla hunter told me it's coffee with sugar they fancy most. Why, for years on the Holy Road—"

"What the devil is *that?*"

"You look at it every day! Holy Road's what they call the old emigrant trail across the river—just like this here's the Fire Road. The Injuns used to make a game of stoppin' wagons and askin' for sugared coffee as the price of lettin' white folks pass through."

"I don't know why we're gabbling about the red heathens," Sean Murphy put in, his words muffled by a mouth stuffed with beans. His cuff served as a napkin to catch the juice. "We've rails to worry about. Train'll more likely be an hour late, but we still have a mile to lay, regardless."

"We'll get it done," Michael said, more confident than he felt.

"Mebbe," Fergus said. "But I have a funny feeling it's to be one of those days that bust a man's privates."

Or break his back?

Michael drank a little of the tepid coffee. Tried to forget Worthing's threat. He forced a smile.

"Cheer up, Patrick Fergus. We do get paid this evening, you know. And with a start such as we've just had, the day can become no worse, only better."

But he was wrong.

Chapter IV

"A March as Glorious as Sherman's"

i

Sean Murphy's prediction proved accurate. The iron train pulled by the engine *Vice-Admiral Farragut* arrived an hour late. Not an auspicious beginning for a Saturday, the one workday Casement's men eagerly anticipated.

As soon as the day's work was over, gold or greenbacks would be handed out from the office car, and a man could spend the rest of the evening drinking, rattling dice on a blanket, playing euchre—whatever he fancied—with no fear that too little sleep or an aching head would hamper him next morning. Sunday was for sleeping, reading, writing letters, laundering and mending clothes, or taking a lazy dip in the Platte.

This Saturday, the men knew the evening's fun would be cut short. Late train or no, a mile of track had to be laid. Michael and Murphy drifted through the crowd watching the *Farragut* chug in from the east. They saw sour faces everywhere.

Michael also noted some longing glances directed toward an attraction that had been with the moving railhead ever since it passed Grand Island, a dusty little settlement populated mostly by German families hoping to build a future out of small farms or, as soon as the railroad lured more settlers, business establishments.

The attraction was an ordinary wagon. Drawn by two mules, it creaked along beside the advancing rails six days a week and stopped where they stopped each night. This morning the mules had not yet been hitched, were still tethered to the tailboard. What made the wagon of interest were two large barrels lashed to the side. A dipper on a chain hung from each. One barrel bore the name *DORN* in crudely painted white letters. The other said *WHISKEY.* There were two more barrels tied to the wagon's far side, and others stored under the patched canvas top. Beyond the wagon Michael glimpsed the large partitioned duck tent erected every evening.

He couldn't personally swear the interior of the tent was partitioned. But certain venturesome rust eaters declared it was. On several occasions, these men—usually tipsy—had tried without success to get a midnight peek at a member of the family of the liquor merchant who'd lit out from Grand Island in an attempt to make money satisfying one of the vices tolerated by the U-Pay management—thirst.

Gustav Dorn, the bearded Dutchman who owned the rig and sold the whiskey, had a fondness for his own product. Michael had occasionally bought a half-dipper of forty rod from him. Dorn was always unsteady on his feet. He spoke broken English rendered nearly unintelligible by sips of his own stock.

At the moment Dorn was nowhere to be seen. His son, a plump blond boy of about fourteen, sat on the wagon seat, guarding the liquor and the nearby tent with an old but powerful Hawken percussion rifle. Casement's orders prohibited any liquor being sold until the day's quota of track had been laid.

As Michael watched, the tent flap lifted. The third member of the family appeared, carrying a coffeepot to a cook fire of buffalo chips. Why in God's name the German had brought his daughter to the all-male railhead was beyond Michael's comprehension. The only explanation he'd heard had come from the boy, via Murphy. According to Sean, Gustav Dorn believed his daughter was safer traveling with him than she would have been if she'd remained behind, alone, in Grand Island.

Dorn's daughter was seldom on display at the railhead. She only came outdoors to prepare meals for her father and brother. She spent the rest of her time in the tent, or in the wagon when it was en route between stops. Michael had also heard the girl was a religious sort and read the Bible a good deal.

He studied her while she hung the pot over the coals and poked them with a stick. As usual, she wore a man's outfit: trousers, a too-large woolen coat, a soft-brimmed old hat. Her hair was pushed up under the hat. That and the shapeless clothing virtually disguised her sex.

He'd never seen the girl up close. Some others had; she'd voluntarily doctored a few minor cuts or sprains, there being no physician in the workforce. Her patients reported she was young and pretty, though not much given to friendliness. An understandable defense, he figured. One smile of encouragement and half the men in Jack Casement's crew would have stormed her tent with their pants at half-mast.

But the real deterrents to social intercourse—and attempts at another kind—were the Hawkens the family had brought along. On one occasion Michael had glimpsed the girl carrying one of the hunting rifles. He assumed she wouldn't have fooled with it if she were a novice at using it.

Without having met the girl, Michael admired her pluck. It took nerve to come to the railhead, even with protection. But he suspected Dorn's daughter couldn't be as pretty as described. Being the only female for a hundred miles could elevate plainness to stunning beauty in the eye of the lustful beholder. An objective analysis would probably reveal her to be a thin-lipped sort, cold-blooded, and disapproving of human weakness. No doubt she hoped to save her father's soul from eternal damnation, since he was engaged in a trade at odds with the precepts of the book she supposedly read for hours on end.

She was out of sight now—back inside the tent—and Michael's musings were cut short by a rising noise level that signaled the start of work.

With billows of steam and the squeal of drivers, the train of flatcars from Kearney pulled in behind *Osceola.* Foremen started shouting. From the disorganized crowd loitering on either side of the track, five-man gangs coalesced with surprising speed.

The gangs climbed aboard the flatcars and began unloading the day's supplies, starting with eight-foot ties of two kinds: stronger ones of oak or cedar, and softer, less durable ones of cottonwood impregnated with a zinc chloride solution to toughen and preserve them; the process was called burnettizing. Four treated ties would be laid for every harder one.

Wrought-iron chairs were manhandled off and piled beside the track, along with rails, fish plates for joining the rail sections, and casks of spikes and bolts. Then the *Vice-Admiral Farragut* began to back down the track, followed by *Osceola* hauling the four gigantic boxcars. Clanking and puffing smoke, the two trains withdrew beyond the stacked materials, leaving the western end of the track free.

Michael and Murphy started, searching for the other members of their five-man gang as two lorry cars—lightweight four-wheeled carts—were lifted onto the track and loaded with the required number of ties, rails, chairs, fish plates, spikes, and bolts. The pair of Irishmen soon located a third—sour, sallow Liam O'Dey.

O'Dey was in his late twenties, but looked twice that. Unable to find work in his native Philadelphia, he'd left a wife and seven children ages six to fourteen. Somehow he'd hoodwinked his employers into thinking he was in good health. A consumptive cough said otherwise.

He dragged a news clipping from his pocket and showed it to Michael.

"Ye'll have a fine laugh out o' this. It's from one of the papers at home. Me old lady sent it."

Michael scanned the type. Evidently the piece was an editorial, one of the few favorable ones he'd seen. O'Dey coughed, then pointed. "See there? It says we're engaged in a 'second grand march to the sea!' "

Michael read the next lines:

> Sherman, with his victorious legions sweeping from Atlanta to Savannah, must have been a spectacle no more glorious than this army of men a-march from Omaha to Sacramento, subduing unknown wildernesses, surmounting

untried obstacles, and binding across the broad breast of America the iron emblem of modern progress and civilization. All honor, not only to the brains that have conceived, but to the indomitable wills, the brave hearts, and the brawny muscles that are actually achieving the great work!

"My," Michael said, smiling. " 'Indomitable wills.' 'Brave hearts.' 'A march as glorious as Sherman's!' We've come into our own, lads. We're heroes just like the general."

O'Dey coughed again, spat on the ground. "At least we are to some pup of a scrivener who ain't been out here to see the filthy hard work for himself."

Murphy put in, "No doubt the writer's opinion will be sharply revised if we fail to reach the meridian before the heavy snows."

O'Dey crumpled the clipping and thrust it back in his pocket. "Bunch of twaddle," he said with his usual petulance. "Having Worthing in command, I feel more like one of the victims of Savannah than a conquerin' general."

"Ssst!" Murphy gestured. "Here he comes."

Worthing strode up to them, an angry glint in his eye. He waved his crop at the trio.

"Out where you belong—and snappy! Where's the nigger and the half-breed?"

A stoop-shouldered but powerful black man in his twenties slipped up to the rear of the group and waved the blue bandana he'd been using to swab his cheeks. The sun promised intense heat before the day was done.

"Right here's one, Captain," the black man said, winking at Michael to show that his toothy, truckling grin wasn't meant to be taken seriously.

"Find that scummy Indian. Get a move on!" Worthing pivoted away, heading for another of the gangs he supervised.

"Mornin', all," the black said as the four men began to trot toward the last pair of rails spiked down the preceding night.

"Morning, Greenup," Michael said. Greenup Williams was a freedman from Kentucky, one of about a dozen blacks in the workforce.

"Captain sure does look thunderous today," Greenup observed.

"He and Mr. Boyle exchanged a few intemperate words in the dinin' saloon," Murphy informed him.

"That so? Well, let's hope everybody stays peaceable the rest of the day. I got a hankering to visit the whiskey wagon quick as I can."

O'Dey managed to sound gloomy even though gasping for breath. "Captain Worthing will—no doubt have us—whistled out and too—weak to raise a dipper by the time we see sunset." He came to a halt as the others trotted on, cupped his hand over his mouth, and bent forward, coughing hard.

The three reached the last pair of rails. O'Dey straggled along a moment later. Down the line, Christian appeared, rushing to join them.

"Hey, Chief, you late." Greenup grinned as the new arrival dragged his galluses up over his shoulders.

Christian feigned annoyance. "Doesn't the Union Pacific permit a man to perform his natural functions in the morning?"

Michael spied Worthing striding along behind the Indian. He tried to warn Christian with a glance but failed.

Half a mile back, a cart boy led a workhorse to the first lorry car. The boy was a towhead named Tom Ruffin. He'd run away from an Indiana orphanage to join the great enterprise. The boy tied the horse to the cart, then climbed on the animal's back.

Christian stretched a suspender and rolled his tongue in his cheek.

"No, on reflection, I guess it doesn't. The only function that interests himself is the breaking of a man's spine. Or spirit."

"Christian—!" Michael began. By then Worthing had reached the Delaware. He jabbed the nape of Christian's neck with his crop.

Christian spun, one hand dropping toward the sheath of his Bowie knife. Worthing grinned.

"You're right about that, Injun. And I just put you on my list. Now shut up and get ready to lay some track."

Shoving Christian aside, he stalked by.

The Delaware fumed. Sean Murphy pressed a palm against his belly and bowed to the Virginian's back. "Yes, sir, yer majesty, yer eminence."

Michael smiled. Greenup Williams laughed aloud. Worthing's head jerked. The back of his neck grew pink. But he didn't turn or break stride. He kept walking east, ready to signal the cart boy to bring the lorry car.

O'Dey looked unhappy. He seldom fraternized with the others and resented the bickering that frequently interrupted the flow of work.

Despite Worthing's threat in the dining car, Michael felt surprisingly devilish all at once. Sarcasm and laughter were weapons Worthing didn't understand, and against which he had no defense. *Your majesty. Your eminence.* He'd have to remember those.

By now Worthing had assembled all of his gangs. They were gathered along both sides of the last section of track. Worthing shouted and waved his crop. A half mile away, Tom Ruffin kicked the horse with his bare feet. The rope snapped taut. The cart was jerked forward.

Sparks shooting from beneath its iron wheels, the cart came rolling toward the waiting workers, the mounted boy hallooing and thumping the animal with his heels. As the cart neared the end of the track, men sprang forward, seized it, and dragged it to a halt. Two of the men shoved wooden chocks under the wheels while Tom Ruffin leaped down, quickly unfastened the rope and led the snorting horse off the roadbed.

Each of the waiting gangs knew its specific job. The moment the horse was clear, a second large group surrounded the cart. Pairs of men lifted ties, ran them out ahead of the last rails and lowered them to the hard-packed grade. Back where the supplies had been dumped, another cart boy was restraining his fretful horse and awaiting his signal. The rails went down at the rate of two every sixty seconds—no interruptions.

Worthing shouted a command. Other men beside the cart grabbed chairs, positioned them on the ties. Then, on Worthing's next order, Michael's five-man gang on the south side of the grade and another gang on the north converged on the cart.

Michael and Christian grabbed a twenty-eight-foot rail and began to haul it forward. The rail slid easily because the cart bed was equipped with greased rollers. As soon as the rail was halfway out, O'Dey and Greenup Williams took hold. Sean Murphy caught the tail end. Simultaneously, a second rail had been unloaded by the gang working from the other side.

At a fast walk, the five-man gangs carried the heavy lengths of iron over the new ties. Michael could already feel the first strain in his shoulders. By day's end, it would turn to pain.

Murphy shouted, *"Down!"* His opposite number on the other gang was only a moment behind with a similar command. Both gangs lowered their rails into the chairs waiting on the interspersed hardwood and cottonwood ties.

Men with notched wooden gauges jumped in, jamming the gauges down while Michael and the others in the two rail gangs kicked and shoved. Finally the rails were fitted tightly in the notches.

Meanwhile, the cart had been dragged off the tracks. Tom Ruffin rehitched his horse and started back for more supplies.

Other men positioned the fish-plate joints and began bolting the new sections of iron to the old. Next, the spike gangs moved in with their mauls.

Workers crawled ahead of them, dropping spikes into holes, and scuttling on as the mauls came down. Michael continually marveled at the intricate timing of the operation. A careless spikeman could brain a spike handler if he swung too soon. But in all the time he'd worked at the railhead he'd never seen it happen.

The tie, chair, and rail gangs left the spikers behind and ran forward. In a moment the second lorry car arrived on the newly laid track. A new section of ties went down—and the process of removing the rails from the cart was repeated.

A familiar rhythm established itself while Captain Worthing stalked up and down, shouting, cursing and demanding that the various crews under his command go faster, to make up for time already lost.

ii

The morning advanced, the sun climbed, and Michael began to sweat. The labor was monotonous, mindless. But the five men on his gang had learned to work well together and took pride in their efficiency. Every man was important to the total effort. Behind the perpetual train, and interrupted only by the arrival of supplies, other crews would be finishing yesterday's track by shoveling and leveling fill between the ties.

South of the Platte an emigrant wagon packed with household goods rolled by in a haze of dust, the driver wigwagging his rifle. A woman and a small girl in sunbonnets waved.

No one broke the rhythm of work, but there were some shouts, inviting the older woman to pause for the night, and earn a pile of extra money. Michael was thankful the family couldn't hear the cheerfully filthy remarks.

Such raillery was common enough whenever the rust eaters sighted a wagon with a woman in it. But the bawdiness upset Worthing. He considered any deviation from routine a violation of his authority. After the wagon passed from sight, Greenup Williams didn't help matters by starting to whistle "Marching Through Georgia."

"Better"—breathing hard, Michael was lowering a rail on Murphy's signal—"better pick a less partisan tune, Greenup."

"Oh, shoo," Greenup said, grinning. "I ain't no chained slave on the captain's little old plantation."

"True," Christian observed as the gauge men moved in. "But if himself would get it through his dumb skull that his side lost, we'd be a lot better off. But no, he—"

Suddenly Michael saw a long shadow behind the Delaware, then Worthing himself. The captain's gray duster was wet with sweat. Droplets glistened in the stubble on his cheeks.

"No singing, nigger," Worthing said. "And no remarks from you, either."

Flick. The crop stung the side of Christian's cheek. A spot of blood shone in the sun.

Christian nearly lost his grip on the rail. Michael felt a tearing strain in his shoulders as he absorbed an extra share of the five-hundred-pound weight. He braced the rail on his knee and got it to the ground without mishap.

Bent nearly double and trying to help, Christian said through clenched teeth, "Yes, *sir.*"

"Your eminence," Michael added, realizing too late that he'd let his temper slip.

With the rail down, the five men darted back to help those with the notched gauges. Worthing extended the crop, touched the bloody place on Christian's cheek, affected a sympathetic smile.

"Tickled you a mite harder than I intended."

Christian glowered, one hand perilously near the hilt of his Bowie. Worthing glanced at Michael, then back to the Delaware.

"Tell you what. You rest ten minutes. Yonder's the water bucket. Wash off that cut, and we'll let Boyle handle the head end of the next few rails."

Christian started to protest. Worthing fanned himself with his straw hat.

"Go on, Christian," he said. "Take care of yourself. Paddy Boyle's strong enough for a bit of double duty."

"Hold on, Captain!" Murphy exclaimed. "One man can't haul the front of a rail all by—"

"Be quiet," Worthing snapped. "Paddy Boyle can. Can't you?"

Suddenly Worthing's face twisted. His smile grew fixed and ugly. He jabbed the end of the crop into Michael's throat.

"Answer me, *boy*."

It was all Michael could do to keep from tearing the detestable crop out of the Virginian's hand and using it on him. But he swallowed, backed up a step.

O'Dey yelped. Michael ducked, nearly brained by the backswing of a spiker's maul.

Alarmed, Sean Murphy and Greenup Williams pulled him down the slanting side of the roadbed, out of danger. Worthing kept watching as he put his wide-brimmed straw back on his head.

"You can do it—can't you, *boy?*" he asked. Every syllable carried insult.

"You're damn right I can," Michael growled, and turned his back, awaiting the next lorry car.

He saw Christian by the water bucket, slopping the contents of a dipper over his cheek. The Delaware's glance was sympathetic. Michael tried to ignore it—as well as the ache in his shoulder blades and the mumbled lamentations of O'Dey, who hated trouble.

"You drop any rails," Worthing called, "I'll see you're docked a week's wages. You hear me, *boy?*"

iii

When the cart arrived and the gangs moved in, Michael seized the rail with both hands and yanked. The other three men tried to give him as much help as possible. But the moment the length of iron was lifted free of the rollers, an excruciating pain shot through his shoulders and down his arms.

He staggered on the hard-packed bed, nearly stumbled over a tie. The noises of men shouting, horses neighing, mauls thudding, metal clanging became a torturous din.

"Down!"

Michael groaned as he bent, dropping more than lowering the rail onto the ties. He staggered back, his chest heaving and sticky with perspiration. He snickered in a humorless way at the thought of the Philadelphia clipping. He seriously doubted old Billy Sherman had ever enjoyed such a glorious drenching of sweat while conducting his glorious march. And the editorial writer probably kept himself comfortable in a saloon bar while composing his rhapsodic sentences about brave hearts and indomitable wills. The only accurate statement in the account was the reference to brawny muscles. A man needed those and, to deal with a Worthing, iron balls besides.

As soon as the rails were gauged and the spike men began hammering, he dragged off his shirt and flung it away. He unbuttoned his underwear, shucked out of the sleeve and pushed the top half of the garment down over his belt. Behind him he heard Worthing chuckle.

Michael reddened. He'd show Worthing he could handle two men's work—and do it without a murmur or a mistake. He'd take all the bastard could give—and more. By God he would!

Murphy sidled up, whispered, "I can slip a word to Tommy Ruffin. Have him fetch Casement. You know—so's his arrival looks accidental."

Michael rubbed his palms over his sweat-slippery forearms. "Casement's in Kearney. Left yesterday."

"Then I'll get someone else."

"No."

"But—"

"No, Sean! Not on your sainted mother's life."

CHAPTER V

RAGE

i

TIME BEGAN TO DISTORT as badly as his vision. He seemed to have been alone on his end of the rails for a century, though the reality of it was undoubtedly more on the order of a half hour.

Intense pain had spread down the center of his back and outward, toward his ribs. His palms had blistered quickly. Despite several protests from Christian that he was feeling fine, Leonidas Worthing refused to put him back on the job.

"You rest a spell longer. Before he died, Old Abe said we're supposed to treat coloreds like white people. I assume that includes you right along with Williams." His tone was mocking as he continued, "You're due the same courtesy, the same—*watch it, boy*!"

Michael's hands had slipped. The front end of the rail thudded down. Only a clumsy stagger to the side kept his right boot from being crushed. He stood next to the rail, wiping his eyes and fighting dizziness.

"Ready to quit, Paddy Boyle?"

Michael drew a long breath and thought of Mrs. A, as he'd called Amanda Kent when she was alive. She wouldn't have truckled to anyone like Worthing. Or admitted she couldn't handle the work.

"No."

Another ten minutes passed. Ten more rails, each heavier than the last. Still Worthing refused to send Christian back to help.

The five-man gang on the opposite side of the roadbed kept working without comment, though Michael occasionally caught a commiserating glance directed his way. It didn't do a thing to help him regain his failing strength. But it hardened his resolve to suffer Worthing's punishment until he dropped.

Dimly, Michael saw towheaded Tom Ruffin kicking his horse along the line with a fresh load of supplies. He rubbed his bare, sweating shoulders. Deep in the muscles, fires seemed to be burning.

He gulped more of the hot morning air, readying himself for the next effort.

The cart arrived, lather dripping from the horse's flanks. By the time the ties were removed, Ruffin hadn't yet unhitched the animal. He was having trouble with the knotted rope. Worthing waved to his men.

"Keep going! Pull the rails off and the devil with the horse!"

Michael and his three companions moved in. This time the head end of the rail felt as heavy as the whole earth. Before it was three yards out from the rollers, the rough iron popped a huge blister on Michael's left hand. Draining water slicked his palm.

The rail slipped, banging down on the front edge of the cart. O'Dey and Greenup lost control. The rail slid forward, the end nudging the horse's rump.

The animal neighed and shied, tangling its hoofs between the ties. All at once the horse was tumbling sideways.

The other gang had lifted its rail clear of the cart. When the horse started to fall, they jumped back, and let the rail drop. The horse went down on top of it.

Michael's gang struggled to regain a hold on their rail, finally moved it out past the front end of the cart. But somehow, at that moment, O'Dey stumbled. The rail tore out of Michael's hands. The forward end struck the horse's thrashing hind legs.

The horse bellowed, pinned. Michael bowed his head, shaking with rage over the blunder.

Worthing stormed toward him.

"Now you've done it, you lout!"

The horse screamed again. Men came running from up and down the roadbed. Ruffin knelt by the frantic animal, then jumped away from its flailing front hoofs. "Leg's broke, I think."

"You've cost us time, Paddy Boyle. Invaluable time." Worthing sounded pleased.

"Listen here!" Murphy exclaimed. "You were the one hollering for us to go ahead before the boy got the horse untied!"

"Nevertheless, that'll be two weeks' pay docked for Boyle. Maybe he'll even be rousted back to Omaha."

Michael wanted to plant a fist right in the middle of the Virginian's face. But he didn't. He was furious over the way he'd let Worthing maneuver him into responsibility for an accident—though he was convinced the man had planned to keep him working alone until a mishap occurred.

Tense, perspiring faces ringed him. Work had come to a stop. One man was running pell-mell toward the office car to report the incident.

Before Michael could say a word, Christian shouldered past him. With his back to Michael, the Delaware said, "You're the one who deserves firing."

Worthing's crop whipped upward. Christian snatched it from his hand and sent it sailing over the frantic horse and the men beyond.

Worthing's cheeks reddened. Michael touched the Indian's arm.

"Christian, you don't need to take my part in—"

The Indian paid no attention. "No one caused the accident but you, Captain. And that's what we'll tell General Jack when he's back from Kearney."

Murphy and Greenup agreed loudly. O'Dey remained silent. So did most of the other workers, not wanting to risk losing pay.

From the office car, a party of men approached on the run. Worthing tried to laugh away Christian's threat.

"You think Casement'll believe a mission-English Injun over a white man? I seriously doubt it."

"So do I." Christian smiled, startling the Virginian. "However, you don't qualify as a white man or any other kind of man. The most appropriate word for you is animal."

Worthing's right hand shot under his sweaty duster, reappearing with a hideout weapon—a four-barrel derringer Michael had never seen before.

"Jesus and Mary!" O'Dey squealed. Men scattered.

Christian reached for the hilt of his Bowie—but a moment too late. Exhausted and dizzy as he was, Michael managed to lunge forward and knock the Delaware aside just as the derringer exploded.

Worthing's ball hit Christian's right calf. The Delaware did a kind of jig step to the side, regained his balance, then collapsed on his right knee, clutching his leg, and wincing.

Michael's restraint collapsed, too. Head down and fists up, he went for Leonidas Worthing.

ii

He felt no need for niceties. He yanked Worthing's wrist to his mouth and sank his teeth in until he tasted blood.

That disposed of the derringer. He saw it wink and flash, falling, as he rammed his knee in Worthing's groin.

The Virginian doubled. Michael lifted his other knee. It caught Worthing under the chin, smashing him back onto the fallen horse. The animal's head jerked up, and it trumpeted its pain again.

Michael barely heard the shouts of encouragement from Murphy and Greenup as he dropped on Worthing's gut with both knees. He laced his hands together and began to pummel Worthing's head—chopping, brutal blows he seemed powerless to stop, even though he was incoherently ashamed of his anger.

This is what I did in the war. This is what I came out here to balance with something better.

Yet he kept striking harder. *Harder—*

Worthing's grabs at his forearms were ineffectual. Blood

and mucus dribbled from the Virginian's nose. Michael's head hummed as his locked fists rose and fell, turning the Virginian's face to a smear of red.

Finally hands dragged him back. His legs crumpled and he fell over in a faint.

iii

"That all?" The very brevity of the question indicated how furious Casement was.

The cluttered cubicle in the front car of the work train was heavy with afternoon heat. Michael had wakened about three-quarters of an hour after the brawl. He still felt its effects in the aching sides of his hands, now purpling with bruises.

He'd cleaned himself up, pulled his underwear and shirt back on, swallowed some coffee, and been hustled under guard to Casement's office, there to be locked in until the construction boss arrived. Shortly before noon the preceding day, Casement had ridden alone to Kearney to straighten out some supply problems.

John Stevens Casement was no more than a year older than Michael: thirty-seven. He stood a scant five feet four inches with boots on. The boots didn't even touch the plank floor as he perched in his chair in front of a rolltop desk littered with survey maps, work rosters, and sheets of cost figures.

Plainly dressed in a wool shirt and old trousers, Casement had a tough, imposing aura despite his slight build—an aura enhanced by the brilliant red of his full beard and the piercing quality of his pale eyes. He didn't blink as he gazed up at Michael, who stood in front of him with his feet wide apart. Spells of dizziness and nausea were still making him wobbly.

"Yes," Michael answered, "that's how it happened." After a moment he added, "I do feel compelled to offer an apology. I had enough fighting in the army to last me a lifetime, and when I came out here, I vowed I'd done my last. I'm ashamed of the way I went after Worthing. I had to prevent him from shooting Christian, but I'm sorry about the rest. No, let's say disappointed. In myself."

Casement tented his fingers. Thought a while.

"I don't like it," he announced in his customary blunt way. "I don't like it one blasted bit, Boyle—even though I know you're telling the truth."

Michael blinked. "You do? How?"

"Did you think I'd fail to ask questions before I came in here? Murphy, Tom Ruffin, that freedman, Williams—even O'Dey—they all told it pretty much the way you did. How Worthing ordered the Indian off the job. Demanded your gang go ahead while the horse was still hitched. Everything."

His mind sluggish, Michael finally thought to ask, "How is Christian?"

Casement shrugged. "Flesh wound. Worthing's ball went right through his calf. No bone damage. He'll mend quickly."

"Where is he?"

"I asked the liquor peddler's daughter to clean him up and tend him for a few days. She arranged a pallet in her tent." Casement's mouth quirked "Old Dorn may be a sot, but he's never too addled to ask for money. The daughter's a decent young woman. She'd have tended the Indian for nothing. But the old man stepped in with his hand out, and I had no time to haggle."

"Did you talk to Christian?"

"I did. He was coherent enough to support your story."

Michael said nothing. But he was relieved.

"I was doubtful about hiring Captain Worthing," Casement continued. "I made my decision on the mistaken assumption the war was over for all concerned. The trouble is, I can hardly afford to discharge even one man short of his committing murder. I've moved Worthing back to supervising the unloading of the iron trains. I don't suppose he'll be any more cooperative there, but at least you two will be somewhat removed from one another. You marked him up pretty fierce, you know," Casement finished. It didn't sound like a reprimand.

"Where's Worthing now, General?"

"Confined to his bunk. Raving like the very devil, I suppose. From now on you stay out of his way. Clean out of his way, understand? If he comes after you, I'll deal with him."

"I can't let other people be responsible for my quarrels."

Casement slapped a palm on the desk. A rolled map slid to the floor.

"You'll do what I say, Boyle, or you won't work on this line! The horse had to be shot. You and that fool Reb have cost me half a day. Half a mile of track!"

His chair squeaked as he swung around and pointed to a calendar nailed above the desk.

"Time—*time*! That's what you cost me. No one on this line seems to fully understand that we must operate like an army. We have an assigned objective—one that I fully intend to reach on schedule. But doing it requires discipline. The moment we lose discipline, we're courting failure. I made promises to Dr. Durant and the directors. I won't let a lot of damn squabbling disrupt this army, ruin my timetable, and turn me into a liar!"

He subsided, drawing a long breath.

"Any fighting will be done with those Spencers we carry. Do you know what I saw at sunup, riding back from Kearney? Braves on the horizon. Sioux, Cheyenne—I couldn't tell which. But there were two or three dozen. This railroad's just another invasion of their territory like the one that drove Red Cloud out of Fort Laramie in a fury. The Plains tribes are afraid of us. They're afraid of the locomotives, and they're afraid of the telegraph wires—you can't blame them for fighting back. Especially after what's been done to some of them. Idiots like that Colonel Chivington massacring babies at Sand Creek two years ago—we even have to contend with things for which we weren't responsible! So if there's any fighting to be done, I want it confined to Indian raids. God knows no one will do that fighting for us. The army's still spread too thin out here. How long has it been since you saw any troopers gallop by?"

"Not since we passed Fort Kearney," Michael admitted.

And both men knew the Kearney fort was of little use in defending the railroad. It was an infantry, not a cavalry post. What few men the army had available were miles to the west, protecting the grading and bridging crews.

"Exactly. So I repeat, Boyle—any fighting will be done out of necessity, *not* to settle private feuds. I won't have a single man compounding our problems."

Quietly, Michael asked, "Does that mean you want me to quit?"

"No, damn it! Didn't you hear me say I need every hand? Why do you think I still tolerate Worthing's presence?"

"May I inquire as to how much pay I'm losing?"

"None—this time. But if you get into it with him once more I'll have your pay *and* your job."

"If he starts it—" Michael began.

"You walk away!"

Michael pondered, reluctantly shook his head.

"I appreciate your side of it, General. I want to see this line go through. So do most of the men. They'll say little about it—they'd be scorned as sentimental—but they're as anxious to reach the meridian as you. It's become a point of pride."

He looked Casement in the eye. "But I'm not sure I can pay the price you've set. As I told you, I had a bellyful of fighting in the Irish Brigade. On the other hand, I will not be trampled on."

He thought Casement was about to smile. He didn't. Instead, he said crisply, "Entirely up to you. We understand each other."

"Yes, sir," Michael started to leave.

"Boyle."

Michael turned back.

"You tell another man I said this and I'll deny it to the gates of paradise. I wish you'd broken the back of that son of a bitch."

At last Michael grinned.

"I almost wish I had too, sir."

"Mind now"—another stabbling finger—"it has nothing to do with his former service—except that being on the losing side affected his attitude. If any man could have taken care of him, it would be one of Colonel Meagher's own."

Michael's grin widened. "That's always how we felt in the Irish Brigade. We could do the job when others couldn't."

Casement sobered. "But you lost your chance. Don't seek another."

Michael offered no assurances. He couldn't.

"Do you have any objections if I look in on Christian this evening, General?"

"I don't care if you look in on Satan himself so long as you avoid Worthing and help me lay a mile of track a day, six days a week. Now get out of here, find yourself a replacement, and take charge of Worthing's gangs."

A stunned look. "Take charge?"

Exasperated, Casement waved. "Someone's got to fill the man's spot! You're diligent. You know the routine. You're promoted. Until and unless you promote yourself back to Omaha."

Casement sat down, whirled his chair toward the desk, and immediately began to sort through the accumulated papers, the astonished Irishman already forgotten.

CHAPTER VI
JEPHTHA'S DECISION

i

STARTING SHORTLY BEFORE three in the afternoon, General Jack Casement personally took charge at the end of the track.

From the supply handlers, Michael had already dragooned a fifth member for his gang—a plump, bow-legged acquaintance of Murphy's named Artemus Corkle. And to the surprise of Murphy and the rest, Michael insisted on being a working supervisor. He handled the fifth position on the gang and kept an eye on the various other crews when he wasn't carrying rails.

He felt miserable, childishly weak after the brawl. But he drove himself, unwilling to surrender to the aches and dizziness. If he were to establish his authority, it had to be done at once, while the other gangs were still grateful Worthing had been removed.

The strategy worked. Casement watched with approval as Michael prodded and cajoled some spike men who'd gotten sloppy, never showing his fear that he'd pass out at any moment.

But Michael's performance was all that Casement approved. Although the noon meal had been shortened from one hour to twenty minutes, by the time the sun began to slant low over the prairie, setting the Platte alight with red ripples, not quite three-quarters of a mile of track had been put down. Casement grumpily called a halt. He murmured a word of congratulations to Michael, then announced there'd be no Sunday labor. But the lost quarter of a mile would be made up Monday.

Casement retired to his quarters, a scowl on his face. He wasn't the only one scowling. As the men straggled back toward the perpetual train, the Saturday night conversation was short on laughter and long on complaints. Business at Dorn's whiskey wagon commenced almost at once.

Normally, Michael Boyle loved the calm of the prairie evenings. The stark lines of the horizon were softened by the dusk. Lanterns on the work train shone like large yellow stars below the smaller, bluer ones glimmering in the purple arch of the darkening east.

The beauty of the Nebraska sunset held little attraction for him tonight. He was worn throughout from his effort to stay alert and on his feet during the seemingly interminable afternoon. He was tormented by pain in his hands, shoulders, and back. He was increasingly ashamed of having lost control and turned on Worthing. And he couldn't forget the captain was still at the railhead, his face pulped, and his authority destroyed. Sean Murphy had reported the Virginian was still lying in his bunk in one of the sleeping cars—not Michael's, fortunately. No doubt Worthing would soon be plotting retaliation—if he wasn't already.

Casement's charge not to indulge in further fighting rankled too. Michael wanted to do a good job of handling his new responsibilities. That was the sole reason he'd driven himself so cruelly all afternoon.

But if it came to a test of loyalty to General Jack—loyalty meaning turning the other cheek to the Virginian—Michael knew which way his decision would go.

At the evening meal he said little to his companions, Murphy and Greenup Williams. After a while they ceased their jokes about earning promotions with bare knuckles and let him eat in silence.

When their plates and cups were empty, the men walked to the office car and waited their turn at the paymaster's cubicle. Some of the rust eaters took all of their wages in greenbacks or gold. Others had part or all of their pay posted to their accounts. Michael chose the last alternative; he didn't plan to buy any whiskey tonight. He intended to sit with Christian—if Dorn's daughter would permit him inside the tent.

During the final hour of the workday, a combination payroll and commissary train had chugged in: two cars, a tender, and a locomotive whose engineer had decorated the top of his headlight box with spreading stag antlers. The train also brought mail. After having his wages marked down, Michael walked back to see whether there might be a letter from Jephtha.

To his surprise, he discovered two.

ii

In his bunk, Michael poured a little of his carefully hoarded tobacco into the bowl of his clay churchwarden, lit the pipe, and wriggled into a comfortable position for reading.

One of the two letters addressed in Jephtha Kent's familiar, boldly slanted hand was extremely thick. He opened the other, slimmer one first. It took him about a minute and a half to scan the message Jephtha had penned in mid-July.

Jephtha's first wife Fan had been prostrated by a heat seizure and had died two days later. Jephtha and his current spouse, the likable former proprietress of a Washington boardinghouse, were leaving next morning for the burial services in Lexington. Gideon, his wife, Margaret, and their four-year-old daughter, Eleanor, were going too. Gideon was again searching for work, Jephtha noted.

That last disturbed Michael. Gideon and his family weren't having an easy time of it in New York.

Michael had never met Jephtha's three sons. Yet he felt a curious kinship with them due to his closeness to their father. In spirit, he might have been their cousin or half brother.

Of the three, he knew most about Gideon—because Jephtha had had more to tell. Previous letters written from Jephtha's small Methodist parsonage had contained a good deal of information about Gideon Kent's activities and attitudes since the end of the war.

Michael knew Gideon had been glad to see the conflict end. And he'd been fortunate that his rank of major excluded him from those classes of military men to whom Andrew Johnson's General Amnesty Proclamation of May '65 did not apply. Southern army colonels, navy lieutenants, and any officer trained at West Point or Annapolis who'd returned to the South to fight were still considered guilty of treason until personally pardoned. Had Gideon been a colonel at the time of his parole, he'd have been forced to seek the services of a new breed of legal specialists operating in Washington. The pardon attorneys or "brokers" could speed an individual application to the President's desk for a fee of $100 or $200. Even in making peace there was profit for scoundrels and opportunists, it seemed.

Michael knew Gideon had been dismayed at the South's defeat. But he'd accepted it—and considered that chapter of his life closed. He'd told his father he was ready to get on with the business of making a life for himself, his wife, and daughter. He'd even shown Jephtha a document he'd written out as a reminder. It was a verbatim copy of the widely publicized loyalty oath required of those who received individual clemency from Johnson.

Whoever took the oath vowed before God to support and defend the Constitution of the United States and to abide by the laws of the Union, including all proclamations dealing with Negro freedom. Various groups of noncombatant Southerners exempted from Johnson's general amnesty—postmasters, judges, tax collectors, even former Confederate government printers—had to swear the oath before they could again buy or sell real estate, apply for patents or try to recover their own land if it had been confiscated as enemy property.

Gideon hadn't been required to take the oath. He'd written it out as a private, personal declaration. Jephtha was delighted his son had returned to civilian life in a positive frame of mind, determined not to let the past, or his prison injury, ruin his future.

Despite the loss of his left eye, Gideon—at least according to Jephtha—looked handsomer than ever, even rakish with the black patch.

More important, he seemed to possess a new drive. Before the war he'd been easygoing, an indifferent student. The time in prison had made him realize he knew nothing except cavalry tactics. He'd decided he'd better settle down and try to learn a skill—or at least find gainful employment in some place where the economy was still thriving.

Considering the question of secession settled, and the country whole again, the place Gideon had chosen in preference to burned-out Richmond was New York.

Jephtha had used his connections in newspaper circles to get his eldest son a position as an apprentice in the pressroom of Gordon Bennett's highly successful *New York Herald.* Working for the *Union* owned by Louis Kent was out of the question.

Gideon's supervisors had reportedly praised his diligence and quick wits. But he'd quit quietly at the end of six months, unable to tolerate the confining indoor work. Reading the news in a letter, Michael had recalled hearing Jephtha once say his son was happiest outdoors, no matter what the weather. Gideon had taken a second job driving a wagon for a construction company.

The man who hired him evidently hadn't been concerned about his obviously Southern speech. That wasn't the case with the manager of the firm's wagon fleet. Gideon lasted exactly two days—discharged and replaced by a former Union soldier. The manager refused to pay wages to a "Southron traitor." And according to this current letter, Gideon had been unable to find another position. Michael wasn't surprised. The labor market was being flooded by returning veterans and newly freed blacks migrating from the South.

In previous correspondence Jephtha had confessed that he'd tried to offer financial assistance to his son. But Gideon had a stubborn pride and a determination to succeed by virtue of his own hard work. Provided anyone would let him work.

Margaret had evidently made a fine adjustment to New York, though. She liked the city, and had helped tide the little family through lean times by doing piecework for some of the better emporiums specializing in individually designed gowns for wealthy women. Gideon's wife was experienced in that area because of the time she'd spent in her aunt's Richmond apparel shop.

Jephtha had also remarked that Margaret had done a marvelous job of creating a comfortable home in a small rented house in lower Manhattan. And she helped and supported Gideon in his effort to make up for his lack of education through constant reading.

Naturally Jephtha regretted Gideon hadn't cared to stick with the printing trade. As a printer, he could have carried on the family tradition begun with Philip Kent's founding of the firm of Kent and Son in Boston—another business unfortunately still under Louis Kent's ownership.

But Jephtha was clearly resigned to Gideon's going his own way—if he could ever find that way in a city glutted with Northerners and blacks eager to take any job.

Jephtha and his son never saw Louis Kent socially. Louis despised the elder Kent for his role in exposing the illegal wartime trading venture. And Gideon was a kind of living accusation that Louis had been a shirker. Undoubtedly Louis had paid the maximum fee—a trifling three hundred dollars out of his millions—to exempt himself from the 1863 Conscription Act that had sent mobs of poor New Yorkers into the streets for four days to riot, burn, and hang blacks from lampposts as a protest against the war and a draft lottery that only the wealthy could escape.

Actually, Michael was thankful for the rift separating Louis from his relatives. Julia Kent was in his thoughts often enough as it was. It would have been too painful if Jephtha's letters described personal encounters with her.

The shorter letter closed with Jephtha saying that fifteen months after the conclusion of hostilities, he still knew nothing of the whereabouts of his two younger sons.

Always a poor correspondent, Matthew had last written his father early in 1865, from Havana. Matt's skipper, McGill, had been preparing to take his schooner *Fair Amanda* to one of the last ports still open to the Confederacy—neutral Matamoros, across the Rio Grande from Brownsville, Texas.

That same, final letter from Matt had contained several of the charcoal sketches he'd started making on his own, without formal training, when he was much younger. Jephtha had mailed a drawing to Michael. It was tacked up in the bunk.

He glanced at the sketch now. A sinuous black man, youthful but totally bald, dominated the foreground. He was wearing only a pair of ragged trousers and balancing a metal can on one shoulder.

The black's other hand was extended, as if he were pleading with someone. His grin was infectious, his eyes merrily sly; the whole figure was bent forward to suggest a subservience that was affected and hence not degrading.

The lines of the figure were echoed in a few strokes suggesting a palm in the extreme background. Between the tree and the black was a smaller figure, a lighter-skinned gentleman in a white suit and wide-brimmed hat. He had a cheroot in his mouth and a small girl in his arms. In contrast to the controlled rigidity of the watcher, the black was all motion and suppleness.

Matt had signed the drawing *M. Kent,* and lettered a caption:

MILK VENDIR & SUGAR PLANTER, HABANA-'65

Jephtha had often mentioned his second son's total inability to spell.

There'd been no further word of Matt since that final letter. Saddening, Michael thought with another glance at the picture. Not only had Jephtha perhaps lost a son, but possibly the world had lost a young man whose talent might someday have developed to an important level. Michael was no student of art. But he liked the composition of the drawing, the artful balance of line against white space. Matt's style had a crude vibrancy that, once seen, wasn't easily forgotten, or confused with another's work.

The final paragraph of the shorter letter was the saddest of all.

Of Jeremiah I know even less, and fear him dead. Many military records were either destroyed or lost when Davis and his crowd fled Richmond and carried their government into its brief exile. I am sure Jeremiah's regiment was in the Atlanta theater, and that he was present in the ranks in the autumn of 1864. Beyond that point I have been unable to trace him. I suspect I will never know his fate—nor where he fell in the midst of the chaos attending Sherman's triumph in Georgia. To go to Fan's burial with that knowledge weighing on my mind is grievous, indeed. Thankfully, God's hand is ever present to lighten the burden.

Hoping you are well, I remain

Faithfully, Jephtha

iii

Michael turned his attention to the second, thicker envelope. The pages—ten or more, inscribed on both sides—had been written in early August, following Jephtha's return from Lexington.

There was pain in the very first paragraph. Lexington had reminded Jephtha not only of the rift which had destroyed his family and deprived him of his itinerancy, but of the death of his good friend, General Thomas Jackson, at Chancellorsville. Michael already knew Gideon had been present when Stonewall had been accidentally shot down by men from his own side.

But there was elation in the letter as well.

We were back from Lexington scarcely twenty-four hours when, with the abruptness of a thunderbolt, we received a communication from Matthew—execrable spelling and all!

In almost the final week of the war, his skipper did indeed run his schooner to the mouth of the Rio Grande, forty miles below Matamoros. Munitions from the schooner were put aboard the customary lighters for transport up the river. A ferocious squall struck without warning and destroyed every one of the small craft, and drowned McGill and several crewmen. Matthew survived with severe injuries, recovery from which literally required months. We had hardly absorbed the joyous news when, concluding an arduous trip overland from Texas, Matthew himself appeared on our doorstep!

Here Michael was so startled, he inadvertently sucked too hard on the churchwarden and drew smoke into his lungs. He coughed for almost a minute before he was able to resume reading.

My son greeted us as if he had not been away for more than an overnight holiday. He then announced he was sailing for Liverpool, where he is to marry a young woman with whom he fell in love during his initial visit to the British Isles! For the first time since my return to the pulpit, I confess I availed myself of the medicinal bourbon Molly hides in the pantry.

Matt's surprising liaison came about this way:

While McGill was still skippering a steam blockade runner into Wilmington, the vessel was badly hulled by Federal cruisers, and sank. All hands gained the Carolina shore. Eventually McGill and Matt returned to Bermuda, then traveled to Liverpool to arrange for construction of a second steamer, which McGill financed from profits. The vessel was built at the Birkenhead Ironworks, across the Mersey from the city proper; the very same yard which launched Semmes' Alabama *and several other Confederate raiders.*

The young woman to whom Matthew lost his heart is the daughter of a steam fitter employed by the Lairds, proprietors of the Birkenhead Yard. Matthew first saw the girl there. He struck up a conversation with her at a mass meeting held in the city to express support for Lincoln's emancipation decree. Matthew had gone to the meeting to—as he put it—hear what the other side was saying.

The young woman, I might note, was an ardent foe of the slave system; and Matthew told me in a strangely disarming way that he soon concluded the "other side" was right. I do not think romance alone was responsible for his change of heart. He finally thought the matter through. He still kept on with his seagoing duties out of loyalty to his captain and the cause, however.

The name of the young woman is Miss Dolly Stubbs. If Molly and I may believe the photograph Matt showed us, she is a lovely, lissome girl with blond hair and a face that speaks of good humor, pertness, and determination.

Once Molly and I had recovered from the detonation of Matthew's "bombshell," I commented upon my son's long silences during the war. He looked bewildered and scratched his head in a rather absent fashion. He ignores clocks; he totally lacks a sense of the passage of time.

When I asked what exactly he had done while away for so long, his reply was characteristically vague and breezy. "Why," he said, "McGill and I ran guns in and we ran cotton out until a boiler explosion sent the second steamer to the bottom off Bermuda.

"Then we went to Cuba and McGill used his last money to purchase a sailing schooner to operate in the Gulf. In between all that I taught the Bermuda nigras and the Cubans and the Liverpool shipyard boys to play our version of baseball, when I wasn't sketching or falling in love. It was all damn lively. I had very few spare moments in which to write letters."

No spare moments in almost five years? The most sanguinary struggle in our nation's history "damn lively?" I must say Matthew is a unique boy!

Gideon and Matthew got along well during the five-day visit. It was altogether a happy reunion; they seem to like one another even after long separation.

But beyond a prompt marriage, I have no notion of what Matt's future plans may be. Nor does he. Hardy and outgoing, he is apparently content to travel wherever the winds of chance and his romantic alliance may blow. He will never be industrious like Gideon—who, by the way, is still unable to find work. But for the moment, Matt has no need to be industrious. His share of the profits from his various voyages was no small sum. He was handsomely attired in the latest gentleman's fashions when Gideon's family, Molly, and I saw him onto the Liverpool steamer.

Once recovered from the excitement of Matt's visit, I returned to prayerful consideration of a matter much on my mind of late. I have not mentioned it to you before, and it is time I did.

I am no longer a young man, Michael. I have been giving considerable thought to the disposition of the California money. I would like to use a portion of it to repurchase the Boston publishing house before I die.

Of course I know next to nothing about the book trade, only a little something about newspapering. But I would like to have Kent and Son back in the family, since the company is of small importance to Louis in comparison to the Union, *his textile and steel interests.*

Louis—need I tell you—has no grasp of the worthy purpose of publishing, nor any interest in it. Kent and Son today is in even worse straits than it was when it was the property of that blackguard Stovall. The firm has, in fact, ceased publication of conventional books altogether. Shifting with the tides of popularity and opportunism, it now issues nothing but cheaply printed fiction weeklies, which may be had for one of those new copper and nickel five-cent pieces the Congress authorized in May.

Even Rose Ludwig's novels have been stripped of boards and republished in gaudy paper covers. I am thankful Amanda's dear friend is no longer alive to suffer the degradation of her work by a man solely interested in profit.

Louis obviously hopes to duplicate the success of the Beadle firm by imitating their "nickel novelettes." To this end, he has discharged poor Dana Hughes, and replaced him with a staff of hacks. Do you wonder I would like to buy out such a pack of rascals?

The decision, of course, belongs to Louis—and I suspect he will turn his back on any overture I might make. I know his hatred of me. Still, imitators usually fail—and should this prove true with Kent and Son, greed might get the better of emotion. One never knows with men such as my esteemed cousin.

So I will watch the situation. I want the firm fully as much as I want my great-grandfather Philip's sword, his portrait, and the other family artifacts Louis keeps at Kentland with no regard for the tradition or the ideals they symbolize.

I honestly cannot say what I would do with the publishing company if I had it—beyond rehiring Dana Hughes at once. But I still dream of restoring it, along with the aforementioned heirlooms, to—how shall I put it? Clean hands. Honorable hands.

In the event such a purchase is ever possible, I propose to divide the ownership of Kent and Son equally between Gideon, Matthew, and you.

The last word struck Michael like a blow. He started, spilling burning flakes of tobacco on his shirt. One left a hole in the fabric before he batted them out.

Don't be astonished, Michael. You are more a Kent than Amanda's own son. Should acquisition of the firm ever become a reality, you would enjoy an additional security you well deserve. I say "additional" for good reason. Jeremiah is clearly gone for all time. Thus I can, in good conscience, transfer his share of the California wealth to you. I have so stipulated in a new will.

iv

"God above!" Michael breathed. His hand shook so badly, he dropped the sheets.

He collected them hastily, then fumbled more time away putting them back in proper order.

Still stunned, he read the last paragraph again. He wasn't dreaming.

Do not think this a rash act on my part. You were of inestimable value to Amanda. I know she loved you. After her death, it was you who raised Louis, and helped restore me to life when I fled Lexington, turned out of my own house. I owe you a great debt. The family owes you a debt. And you are as much a Kent as I.

Indeed, my vanity even makes me wish your last name could be ours, but that would be an affront to your parents. So you shall be a Kent in all respects except the name.

Michael leaned back and closed his eyes. He tried to assess all Jephtha's decision could mean to him. How it would change his existence—for it certainly would.

But believing, *really* believing what he'd just read was still too difficult. He forced his attention back to the letter.

v

The rest was less personal, more philosophical—but no less charged with emotion.

Jephtha turned to the war's aftermath, mentioned the gratification he'd derived from the Constitution's thirteenth amendment, ratified only the preceding December. The amendment had forever abolished the institution of black slavery. He'd also been heartened by the passage of certain other pieces of national legislation.

It was a milepost on the march for human liberties when the Congress overturned Johnson's veto in February, thereby extending the life and enlarging the scope of the Freedman's Bureau, which can be of continuing service to the Southern Negro. The Radicals say Johnson used the veto to pander to the South's Democratic aristocracy. But any man who reads Johnson's record correctly will know the class he despises most, North or South, is the privileged class. He idolizes men who work their own land, his beloved "mudsills." The President's greatest fault, if it can be termed that, is perhaps a too-strict adherence to the Constitution. He felt the Freedman's Act could not be legal since the eleven Confederate states were not represented in the national legislature and had no voice in the act's passage.

As you may know, Johnson likewise vetoed Lyman Trumbull's civil rights bill, which declared that all persons born in the country are automatically citizens, entitled to equal rights and protection under the law. Trumbull introduced the bill to negate the Supreme Court's Dred Scott decision. Here, too, the President hewed closely to his interpretation of the Constitution, maintaining that the matters covered by Trumbull's bill are solely the province of the individual states. He still insists the bill as finally enacted over his veto is another step—in his words, "a long stride"—to centralization and concentration of legislative power in Washington.

To be doubly sure Johnson's view would not one day be declared Constitutionally correct by the High Court, many of the same provisions of Trumbull's bill were introduced into the fourteenth amendment passed in June and now being submitted to the states for ratification.

The struggle between Johnson and the Congress has become a sorry, stained business—carried forward on both sides with mounting acrimony. As Mr. Voorhees, the Democrat, so aptly put it, the actions of Thad Stevens and his Radical Republicans serve notice that the war to restore the

Union was an utter failure; the war is over, and yet the Union is rent in twain.

Michael knew what Jephtha meant. The Omaha and St. Louis papers had told him a war of quite a different sort had been under way in the capital almost since the hour the bells tolled Lincoln's death. Some of the more extreme Republicans had supposedly hailed the assassination as a godsend, assuming the new President would throw Lincoln's Reconstruction plans into the dustbin and take a harder line.

They'd gotten a shock when Johnson began to implement policies dating all the way back to an 1863 formula for establishing new Southern governments after the war. At that time Lincoln had been willing to grant executive recognition to rebel states in which ten percent of the eligible voters of 1860 took an oath of loyalty and agreed to support emancipation.

No such easy terms would satisfy the Republican extremists any longer. As a result they were at war not only with the President and the Democrats but with the more conservative members of their own party; a fierce and bitter war rooted in a fundamental dispute over the nature of the four-year military struggle.

In the papers, old Thad Stevens, the cynical and vituperative leader of the House's radical wing, constantly referred to the seceded states as "conquered provinces" whose future condition depended on "the will of the conqueror."

Johnson's position, and that of the more moderate Republicans, was simply that the Southern states had never seceded because it was impossible for them to do so under the Constitution. They were still states, to be dealt with accordingly. Jephtha mentioned Stevens.

Though in his seventies, he possesses the unrelenting energy—and savagery—of a man half his age. He busies about Washington with his queer black wig askew and his club foot dragging, never bothering to deny press accounts of his liaison up in Lancaster with his mulatto housekeeper, Lydia Smith. He is aligning his forces for the coming battle to determine whether the President or the Congress shall dictate Reconstruction policy.

And a battle it will surely be. I am kept informed about it by occasional letters from colleagues. Twice in the past year I have been down to Washington in person. And Theo Payne, that good and downtrodden man who continues to edit the Union *under Louis' direction, brings his brood to supper every fourth week or so—the only evening of the month on which he is forced to remain sober!—so I am not unfamiliar with the conflict that may yet prove more harmful to the country than the war itself.*

Payne told me the Washington war has even reached into the spirit realm! You do know there is quite a craze back here for nontheological séances purporting to put relatives in touch with deceased loved ones?

According to Payne, a Mrs. Cora Daniels of Four and a Half Street, Washington, recently spoke using the voice of a "Mr. Parker," one of the departed. "Parker" predicted Johnson would soon arrest many of the radicals, convene a "congress of Southerners and Copperheads" and "force patriots," such as Stevens, to retreat to another location—Ohio was mentioned—there to set up a rival Congress! The bizarre business ended with "Parker" stating we would soon be engaged in a second Civil War—this time largely fought on Northern soil. I trust I convey how tragic I find all of this. No one has hoped and prayed longer than I for an end to bloodletting. Now it appears we must have more, albeit brought about with different weapons.

Neither has anyone hoped and prayed longer than I for an end to the foul business of slavery. Yet now that it is accomplished, I wonder how smoothly the freedmen can be brought into the main stream of American society.

Even such a staunch Unionist as General Sherman has said that universal suffrage—the issue by means of which Stevens and his crowd mean to force their control of Reconstruction on the President—may lead to "new convulsions" in the country.

Although I sometimes speculate as to how much of Thad Stevens' venom springs from the destruction of his Pennsylvania iron foundry by Lee's troops on their way to Gettysburg, I feel Stevens cannot be entirely faulted.

The new Southern legislatures established under the Lincoln formula showed an old face with their so-called Black Codes intended to control the behavior of the liberated slaves. Some of the Codes prohibit blacks from riding in rail cars set aside for whites. No intermarriage is possible without penalty of imprisonment. Parentless Negro children apprenticed under court guidance are subject to recapture, exactly like slaves, if they flee from cruel masters.

In these and similar laws I heard again the rattle of the chains. The rights of new citizens must be guaranteed—and chief among these rights is suffrage. But I have begun to smell a taint in the Radicals' espousal of it. I first caught a whiff last December, when I sat in the House gallery and listened to Stevens challenge the administration.

He would keep the Southern states from any active role in government until the Constitution has been "amended so as to secure perpetual ascendancy to the party of the Union"—meaning, of course, the Republicans.

With cynical candor, he predicted that unless the Negroes were given the vote, the balance of power would swing to the Southerners and the Democrats. But if suffrage could be made universal, he said, there would "always be Union men enough in the South, aided by the blacks, to divide the representation, and continue Republican ascendancy." So, you see, it is not an honorable war, but one with a secret purpose. The "secret" becomes more blatant day by day.

You might also be interested—or dismayed—to know that many a Northern businessman has smelled the opportunity inherent in this immoral plan. One such is Louis. He has long been a notorious trimmer, pretending to favor first one side, then another, as seemed expedient. Now, however, he has declared himself not only a Republican like you and me, but a Thad Stevens Republican!

Michael's mouth quirked in distaste as he drew smoke from the pipe, exhaled, and let the fragrance of the tobacco mask some of the fetid smell of the deserted car. Outside he heard a whoop from the direction of Dorn's wagon. He reminded himself that he owed Christian a visit as soon as he finished reading.

I do not believe Louis has joined the Stevens' wing from humanitarian motives. He would be the last to welcome freed blacks at his dining table, no matter how much he prates about the wisdom of universal suffrage. I imagine he only sees the potential for power—the deliberate and pitiless manipulation of human beings that could assure Republican supremacy for years to come. No doubt he has allied himself with the cause in order to be on the winning side. The taint has crept even into our family.

Thus the war goes on. Different from the last, but no less furious. You would be appalled by the actions of politicians in both camps as they seek to influence public opinion by enlisting the support of popular war heroes. How ardently both sides court Grant!—though Johnson appears to have him in his pocket for the moment.

Second only to the supreme commander is Custer, the "boy general." His chief military talent seems to have been the ability to commit huge numbers of men to slaughter in order to secure commendations for himself and advance his career.

Yet he remains overwhelmingly popular. He was here late in March, attending lavish dinners at the Manhattan Club, and was constantly in the company of Democrats. He himself belonged to the McClellan clique whose political views divided and nearly destroyed the Army of the Potomac for a time, just as surely as did McClellan's own vacillations and presidential ambitions.

The Republicans, it is said, would like Custer in their camp—and never mind his views about the fitness of blacks for citizenship. On the subject of permitting Negros to vote, Custer is fond of stating he'd "as soon think of elevating an Indian Chief to the Popedom of Rome." Can you doubt that the aim of some Republicans is not justice throughout the land, but absolute rule by their party?

Everywhere, in fact, there is much to dismay men of conscience. Davis is still in prison at Fort Monroe, facing indictment for treason. Lee—honorable, misguided Lee whom I also saw in Lexington at the time of Fan's funeral—is eking out a living as president of Washington College. Good neighbors who know his straits send bags of walnuts, potatoes, and pickles to his household table while Northern newspapers vilify him as a "sinister conspirator"—this proud, torn, Christian man who refused a plea at Appomattox that he give his soldiers leave to take to the hills and woods and continue to fight as partisans. He told them to go home, admit defeat, build new lives. Yet he is labeled "sinister." Is this the "malice toward none" of which Lincoln spoke, and which Johnson is struggling to implement?

Still, I am not totally without hope. While the political war rages here in the East, there is a counterbalancing dynamism—a sense of our nation being only moments away from the dawn of a mighty age of expansion, if we can but keep the Union whole. Never, they say, has there been a period of such enormous industrial growth—or such visions of a prosperous, thriving land from sea to sea.

You are part of one of the remarkable enterprises that can bring those visions to reality. The transcontinental railroad will open the West to commerce and settlement in a manner undreamed of even a decade ago. Public land is there for the taking, a hundred and sixty acres of it available to any man, thanks to the Homestead Act.

Though we live in a troubled time, it is also a time of promise. I try to believe a spirit of healing, not hatred, will prevail. I try to have faith that even the schemes of a rapacious new class of moguls who care nothing for the human lives they exploit to see their factories prosper—yes, and their railroads built—will, in the end, yield blessings we cannot imagine.

Michael, forgive this long discourse written late at night. Poor Molly despairs of my nocturnal ponderings and scribblings. But there are not many others with whom I can share my deepest thoughts.

I wish you good health and success in your courageous venture in a part of the country foreign to you. From such willingness to strike out in bold new directions was this country born—and, as I recall, the Kent family founded!

Slowly, Michael laid the churchwarden on his belly. He stared at the last sheet in his blistered hand. The paper seemed to fade, replaced by Julia Kent's blue eyes.

Courage?

Bold new directions?

Jephtha, I'm glad you don't know all the truth.

With effort, he returned to the brief conclusion.

I look forward to any descriptions you can send of the exciting enterprise in which you are involved. May God bless and protect you. Remember that from this hour, my revised will makes you a bona fide *member of the family to which, by word and deed, you have belonged for many years.*

Your kinsman, Jephtha

Michael was still touched and overwhelmed by Jephtha's act of generosity. All at once an idea came to mind. An important idea.

He gathered up the pages, folded them, and slipped both letters beneath his blanket. He jumped down from the bunk and quickly left the car.

vi

Two stragglers were all that remained at the paymaster's cubicle. Michael fretted impatiently while one received his greenbacks, and the balding clerk noted the wages of the second in a thick ledger. The clerk yawned as Michael stepped to the counter.

"Give me the book containing the B's, Charlie. And your pen."

"What is this, Boyle? You've already received—"

"I know. But my name isn't listed properly."

"What?"

"Just ink your pen and give it to me."

Annoyed, the clerk handed him the pen, together with another ledger. Michael thumbed the pages. Located the correct line. He slashed a stroke through three words, hoping his dead parents would forgive him for abandoning Aloysius, which they had bestowed. His eyes looked wet as he wrote carefully.

He returned the pen and rotated the ledger so the clerk could read it.

"There. That's the correct version."

The clerk peered. "That's all you wanted? What the hell does it matter if we've got your middle name right or wrong? You're paid the same either way."

"It matters more than you'll ever appreciate," Michael replied softly. "Much more."

He turned and left while the puzzled clerk studied the drying ink that spelled out *Michael Kent Boyle.*

CHAPTER VII

DORN'S DAUGHTER

i

MICHAEL STEPPED DOWN from the office car and breathed deeply. The air had turned cool and invigorating. His assortment of aches and bruises seemed less troublesome now.

The dark near the train was relieved by two torches stabbed into the ground at the corners of Gustav Dorn's whiskey wagon. Dorn himself was dispensing liquor from one of the barrels. He was a short untidy man with a gray-shot beard. His huge belly hung over his belt. He seldom smiled.

At the moment he had at least thirty customers lined up. Each drinker took the dipper from Dorn and swallowed whatever amount he'd bought while those waiting shouted for him to hurry. When the customer had finished, he went to the merchant's son a few steps away.

The phlegmatic-looking boy was perched on a small box behind a crate. His Hawken lay across his knees. The customer deposited his money on a tin plate lying on the crate. Occasionally the boy had to change a greenback or a coin. The rest of the time he paid no attention to the drinkers, staring out past the nearest torch in a joyless, vacant way.

As Michael walked closer to the wagon, one man who'd evidently passed through the line more than once spilled the contents of his dipper. Those waiting laughed and hooted. Dorn demanded payment. The worker refused.

Beyond the train, a cow lowed. Michael paused by one of the torches to watch the outcome of the dispute. Dorn spoke English badly but got his point across.

"You buy—you pay. Not my fault you sloppy."

"I'll be damned if I'll give ye a cent for somethin' I never tasted, Dutchie." There was humor in the customer's eyes, but testiness in his slurred voice. He wobbled around to get a judgment from those in line. "What d'ye say, lads? Am I fair or not fair?"

"Fair, fair!" a couple of his friends yelled.

Dorn snapped his fingers and barked German at his son. The stolid fat boy raised the Hawken. With a start, Michael saw the hammer was back, ready to fire.

Dorn looked smug as he tapped the customer's shoulder. The man batted his hand away. Excitedly, the workers in line pointed to the rifle. The drinker saw it and turned pale.

Torchlight shimmered on the Hawken's thirty-four-inch barrel. The St. Louis–made gun might be a good twenty years old, but at short range it could ruin a man with its .50-caliber ball. Dorn made clear that he intended nothing else.

"Shit with fair, Paddy. You pay. Now. Or my boy, he take the price out of your hide."

Grumbling, the man dug a hand into his pocket. He clenched his fist around the coin, then raised his hand as if he meant to hit the merchant.

Dorn retreated a step. "Klaus!"

The Hawken jutted forward across the top of the crate.

After another glance at the rifle, the drinker lowered his hand. He gave Dorn the coin.

The little act of extortion finally produced a smile from the merchant. He waved the man aside and brandished the dipper at the line. "Next fellow! Step lively, hah? Got a business to run here."

The boy returned the Hawken to his knees, uncocked. Michael shook his head. The East had no monopoly on greed. And if the little scene he had witnessed was typical of the way Dorn conducted his trade, serious trouble was bound to erupt eventually.

He walked by the rear of the line, waving to acquaintances. Out in the dark near the end of the track, a fire of buffalo chips blazed. A group of Paddies sat around it. One started a song on an old concertina.

Michael recognized it instantly: "Corcoran to His Regiment," sometimes known as "I Would Not Take Parole." Corcoran had commanded the New York 69th at First Manassas, been captured and imprisoned in Richmond. Paddies by the fire—men who'd never come anywhere near the Irish Brigade but were still proud of its record—bellowed the words.

"Raise the green flag proudly,
Let it wave on high—"

The song conjured memories for Michael—memories of smoke, thundering shells, wounded comrades begging for help as the ranks plunged past them. Bits of terrain he'd seen in Pennsylvania and Virginia—woodlands, hillsides—blended in his imagination like a mural by a deranged artist.

"Liberty and Union
Be your battle cry!"

Sean Murphy lurched to his feet. Fists on his hips, he began to jig while the singers applauded in rhythm.

"Faugh-a-ballagh shout
From your center to your flanks—
And carry death and terror wild
Into the foeman's ranks!"

"Faugh-a-ballagh." How stirring that Gaelic cry to clear the way had been during the early days, and how sadly futile in the weeks and months after Gettysburg, when the ranks were so disastrously thin.

Michael returned a hail from one of the revelers, declined an invitation to join them, and strode on. He wanted no more fighting—not even in memory.

Yet he'd gotten more of the real thing this very day. The railroaders' music reminded him of the peace that seemed to elude him. The thrill of Jephtha's news was all at once blunted by a recollection of Leonidas Worthing.

Quickly, Michael looked behind him. His gaze encompassed torches at the whiskey wagon, the smudged yellow of the train's windows, the starry dark above. For a moment he'd been certain he was being observed. He saw no indication of it.

An uncontrollable gloom settled over him. He'd traveled thousands of miles to escape war, but as long as Worthing remained at the railhead, he was smack back in the middle of one. A lone man or a regiment—either could kill you.

Despite his gloom and nervousness, he forced himself to stand still while he relit his churchwarden. Then he hurried on to the Dorn tent.

ii

The tent stood a good twenty yards behind the wagon. A lamp inside made the front section glow. The rear was dark. He stepped to the flap and called softly.

"Hallo?"

"Who's there?"

"Beg pardon, Miss Dorn—is that you?"

The unseen girl laughed. "I've seen no other women in this godless place. I expect so."

A feminine silhouette appeared suddenly on the front of the tent. Unlike her father, she spoke without an accent.

"Who might you be?"

"The name's Michael K. Boyle."

"Oh, yes, Papa mentioned you." It was crisply said, with a faint edge of reproof. "The one who caused the trouble."

"The one who was on the receiving end of the trouble, if you don't mind! I had no hand in causing it." Not quite true. But the unseen girl had irked him.

"Well, it makes no difference," she replied in an airy way. "It was still ungodly quarreling."

That was two references to godlessness in a space of seconds. Disgusted, he blew out a puff of smoke. She must be a proper prude, all right.

He tried to control his annoyance. "Whatever the cause,

the result was the shooting of my friend Christian. I understand you're tending him?"

"That's correct. He'll recover splendidly."

"I came to visit him—which is pretty blasted difficult with this tent between us. Would you be so kind as to let me in?"

She ignored his sarcasm. "Are you alone?"

He had a good notion to inform her that a dozen wild-eyed rapists were hovering behind him.

"I am."

"All right, then. But your friend's asleep."

A hand lifted the flap. Michael ducked, starting inside, then stopped short. His mouth opened. The churchwarden fell from his lips. He caught it in time, letting out a loud *"Oww!"* as his thumb accidentally jabbed into the hot bowl.

Licking his thumb and wincing, he didn't move. He was still thunderstuck.

A single lamp hung from the ridgepole. An open Bible lay on a stool beside an untidy cot along the left wall. To judge from the garments strewn on it, the cot belonged to her father or brother. The twin of the boy's Hawken was propped against an equally messy cot on the right—another male domain; a pair of patched trousers lay beneath.

Directly in front of him—no longer disguised by distance or a shapeless coat and hat—was the real cause of his surprise.

In one way, the workers whose hurts she'd tended had exaggerated. But perhaps to men of forty, a woman in her late twenties could properly be called young. Their other claim had been understated. She was more than just pretty. Without benefit of paint or furbelows, she was lovely.

iii

"For heaven's sake come in or go out, one or the other, Mr. Boyle," she said in a sharp tone. She wore trousers of denim cloth tucked into heavy boots, and a man's work shirt that fit tightly over large well-shaped breasts. She had her father's square jaw but a more generous mouth and clear, blue-gray eyes. Hair the color of summer wheat was drawn into a bun at the back of her head.

Her skin had a sunburned coarseness—more noticeable on the backs of her hands. The knuckles were red. Yet he found the weather-beaten look curiously attractive. She had fine wide hips and smelled not unpleasantly of strong soap.

"I'm afraid I'm not familiar with your first name—" he began.

"Is there any reason why you should be? It's Hannah. Now do you wish to see your friend?"

She turned sideways, inadvertently drawing his eye to the curve of her breast. When she noticed, her cheeks pinked. "Mr. Boyle!"

He jerked to attention. "Yes?"

"He's behind the canvas partition. I don't think it would be advisable for you to wake him up. Just glance in."

He didn't know what to make of the woman. She seemed to have more than a touch of her father's stern temperament, and some of her remarks would have been downright disagreeable had they not been tempered by her smile and a pleasant voice. Her gaze was uncomfortably direct.

Michael shifted the pipe from one hand to the other. She gestured. "You burned your thumb."

"Nothing serious."

"A burn is always serious for a man who works with his hands. You've blisters, too, I see. I have some salve that would help. I'll apply it before you leave."

"Truly, it's not necessary."

"Yes, it is. Women know more about such things than men. However, I'd appreciate it if you'd extinguish your pipe." She smiled. "Smoking is a wasteful, unhealthy habit."

"Oh, I see! Whatever you say, Miss Dorn." His tone was as tart as hers of a few moments ago.

He stuck his arm outside, turned the pipe over, and shook the remaining embers and tobacco to the ground. When he faced her again, he surrendered to an ungentlemanly impulse and said, "Do you consider smoking worse than drinking whiskey? Or selling it?"

Immediately he regretted the clumsy sarcasm. Instead of anger, it produced a look of hurt. She hid it by turning away.

"Though it's no affair of yours, I don't condone my father's trade, nor"—softly—"nor his own dependence on the product he sells."

She looked at him again. "But he is my father. My brother Klaus is very young. Someone must look after them."

"I didn't mean to imply—"

"That my father's a drunkard? He is. Don't the roughnecks in this camp know that by now?"

He was too embarrassed to answer.

"You see, Mr. Boyle, my father owns a small store in Grand Island. General merchandise. The store is failing because Papa's too fond of his whiskey to attend to its management or care about his customers. And he'll let no one help him, except in the most menial way. When he chose to try to make some extra money by temporarily closing the store, fixing up the wagon, and driving all the way out here to this hideous place, I had a choice. Let him take Klaus and bring harm to himself or both of them by provoking others with his brusqueness—railroad men are not so placid as farmer's wives, they say—or come with them. I'm afraid Papa's only the first of many who'll be following the tracks to take advantage of men's vices. Now if that satisfies your curiosity about my motives—?"

She spoke well, he was thinking. She was uncommonly well educated, or more likely self-taught.

"Miss Dorn, I didn't mean to pry—or annoy you with my tactless remark about the whiskey."

"That's all right. I just wanted you to know I was here for the sake of people, not profits."

The words carried an odd undertone. Pain?

He was at a loss to understand why she'd revealed so much in a few sentences—unless she'd contained a deep hurt for too long, and had no one but a stranger with whom to share it.

That gave him a little better insight into her character. She might be strong, but she wasn't marble. Not marble at all, he thought with another covert glance at her bosom.

He walked to the canvas partition and raised it at the divided center. Christian lay on a cot by the rear wall, snoring lightly. His dark skin tended to blend with the shadows in the unlit back section. But the neat white bandage on his right calf was bright in the lamplight falling over Michael's shoulder.

He was conscious of time ticking by. He couldn't prolong

the visit much more, though for some unfathomable reason, to prolong it was exactly what he wanted. He was conscious of Hannah Dorn's fragrance—the clean, bracing odor of soap.

Finally he dropped the canvas and turned. She'd returned to the stool. The open Bible rested on her knees.

"Thank you," he said. "He looks fine."

A bob of her head. The wheat-colored hair glinted. "I fixed him soup. He took every drop. I also gave him half a dipper of Papa's whiskey to help him sleep."

"Oh, then you're not averse to drinking?"

"Mr. Boyle, don't bait me. Alcohol does have its purposes. Everything on earth has God's purpose concealed somewhere within it if you search hard enough." It was a quiet, rational-sounding declaration. He tried to detect a touch of the sanctimonious in it and failed.

He indicated the open book. "Are you searching now?"

"I do so whenever I can." She touched the page. "I was reading Second Chronicles."

He tried another smile. "I'm afraid my knowledge of scripture has shrunk to some memorized verses."

"Boyle's an Irish name. Are you Catholic?"

Damn, how direct she was! He'd never met such a woman. "Are you?"

She smiled, enjoying the sparring. "Lutheran."

"Well, I am a Catholic—or I used to be. I've not been inside a church for a long time. Is my specific religion of importance?"

"Why, yes, it is."

"You dislike Catholics? You're not alone."

"I do not dislike Catholics. I asked for another reason entirely. We're isolated out here, among rough men. Those who profess any faith at all belong together. For mutual protection, wouldn't you say?"

She was still smiling. He did too. "I honestly couldn't offer a worthwhile opinion. My religion's like—like an object you carry out of habit but seldom use."

She met his gaze, then averted her eyes. He detected a tinge of color above the collar of her shirt. A point scored! Hannah Dorn wasn't quite so holy as she pretended. She was self-conscious with a man in her quarters.

"Well," she said, "at least you're honest. That's a virtue."

He touched the pipestem to his forehead. "Thank you kindly for the compliment. I'll be going along—"

He was totally unprepared for her next remark. "If you're thirsty, I could warm some coffee."

The pink colored her throat again. He knew his earlier guess had been right. She had her religion, but it wasn't quite enough to counterbalance a certain loneliness. He wasn't sure he wanted any further involvement with such a curiously complex creature.

Torn, he hedged. "That would be very hospitable. But it's growing late."

"Not that late. I'd like some coffee myself. And I do want to attend to your hands. But outside. It's less compromising." The half smile was at her own expense. "I suspect I know what the men in camp are saying about me. Any woman who travels to a place like this—"

"You're wrong," he interrupted. He pointed to the Bible. "They say you're devout." His hand moved to indicate the Hawken. "And definitely not to be interfered with. You wouldn't believe how much that combination disappoints them."

She laughed; she had beautiful, regular teeth. The effect was dazzling.

"I do know how to use the rifle. Both of the Hawkens are loaded with the extra charges of powder hunters use to stop buffalo. I don't hold with killing, but I'm willing to wound the first man who tries anything improper. It's a matter of principle."

"Oh, of course," he murmured, straight-faced.

"Mr. Boyle, you're laughing at me."

"No, ma'am! You're just not—not what I expected."

"Please don't tell me what you did expect," she teased, "or our acquaintance will probably come to an abrupt end. I must admit I'm glad you stopped by. I don't often get to talk to anyone with some degree of education. It's a pleasure." Her eyes sparkled in the lamplight. "Even though you clearly have vices."

"Now you're the one who's laughing."

"So I am. Forgive me. Let's go out, shall we?"

Again she smiled, as if eager to establish at least a tentative friendship. He raised the canvas to allow her to precede him.

She left the Hawken where it stood, carrying a coffeepot in one hand and her Bible in the other. The two objects struck him as representing a contradiction. Warmth and reserve. But it was just that contradiction that made her intriguing—and, somewhat to his surprise, made him interested in knowing her better.

His eye fastened on the swaying curve of her buttocks. Delightful sight!

Or it was until caution intruded:

Have a care, Boyle. Don't broaden your interest to include wanting to know her in the biblical sense or she's liable to blow your head off.

Wait. Not your head. She doesn't condone killing. No doubt she'd aim for a functional member more closely allied with your vices.

Bet she'd hit it dead on, too.

The mere thought made him wince as he followed her from the tent.

Chapter VIII

The Bible and the Knife

i

Hannah Dorn asked him to rekindle the fire with fresh buffalo chips stored behind the tent. As he went to fetch them, he recalled with amusement the first evening he'd been sent to collect them on the prairie.

He'd been at the railhead no more than two days. Sean Murphy had soberly instructed him to go to a nearby wallow and bring back any chips he found. "Wallow chips are the very finest," Murphy had assured him.

He'd returned with a huge load, carefully piled half a dozen together, and touched a match to them. He'd already been informed the chips ignited easily and produced a virtually smokeless fire.

By the time he'd struck ten matches, Murphy was laughing so hard tears came. Then he explained the joke played on greenhorns. Bison rolled in wallows to find relief from biting flies and mosquitoes. The mud that dripped from their bodies when they emerged formed unburnable but otherwise perfect counterfeits of real chips containing partly digested grass. Since that night, Michael had sent several newcomers to similar wallows; it was a sort of ritual of initiation.

He gathered the chips and walked back toward the fire, asking himself why he was interested in the company of Hannah Dorn when Julia was the only woman he really cared about.

Perhaps I'm making it too complicated, he thought as he rounded the corner of the tent. Hannah was placing a stool near the ashes. *I've been away from any sort of female companionship a long time. There's no sin in enjoying a bit of it—even though, for all of this lady's good looks, she's a strong, spiky sort.*

He didn't quite believe that assessment, though. Once or twice, Dorn's daughter had inadvertently revealed a softness—a vulnerability—beneath the shell of her religious conviction. He saw evidence of it again now—a noticeable uneasiness as she fidgeted with the lid of the galvanized tin coffeepot, peered down inside, replaced the lid, then lifted it again for another doubtful glance.

"It's the last of the morning coffee, Mr. Boyle. Very strong, I'm afraid."

"Couldn't be stronger than the poison they pour in the dining car," he laughed, dumping the chips.

Hannah used a thong to tie the pot's wire bail to a tripod improvised from three rusty iron rods. She dug matches from her pocket. Michael extended his hand.

She passed him two matches. Their hands touched. She inhaled softly at the unexpected contact.

He pulled his fingers back quickly. *Damned if I'm not as nervous as she!*

The chips caught almost instantly. Soon scraps of flame were tossing in the night breeze. He sat down cross-legged near her stool. Out of sight beyond Dorn's wagon, the workers had begun to sing again, this time "The Vacant Chair," a slow, mournful war ballad about a family's loss of a son. He turned his head to listen as a soprano voice soared above the rest. That would be Tom Ruffin, the lad from Indiana. One by one the older men stopped singing. Only the boy's voice was left—pure and almost painfully sweet under the Nebraska stars.

"You were in it, then?"

Startled, he swung around. "What brought that to mind?"

"The look on your face when you heard the song from the war."

He tried to shrug as if the music raised no memories.

"Yes, I was in it. The New York 69th of the Irish Brigade. I was in it up until the Wilderness, where I took a wound." A bitter smile. "It was a struggle all the way. The fighting was enough to scare twenty years off your life every time you went in. And practically from the beginning, we never had enough men. After Gettysburg—we were only in sharp action on the second day—we had just about three hundred muskets left. We carried five regimental flags, every one supposed to represent something like a thousand soldiers. We tried to fight ten times as hard, as if we were a true brigade; but it was futile because so many had been lost along the way."

Studying him, she asked, "Were you proud of fighting?"

"Proud of killing other Americans?"

Michael's hand strayed to his mustache. An index finger smoothed the gold and gray hair as his eyes fixed on the fire.

"No. I came to hate it."

She was pleased. "As all men should who keep the commandments God gave Moses."

He grimaced. "I'm afraid my hatred of the war only appeared *after* I broke that commandment a number of times."

"How many?"

"Four that I saw for certain. Possibly more. I preferred never to be too sure."

His head lifted.

"On the other hand, Miss Dorn, I'd like to believe that when we *were* required to kill, we did it for a just cause."

"The Southern side thought the same."

"Admittedly."

"There should have been another way to settle the differences."

He sighed. "A great many men more clever than I tried to find one. For thirty years they tried. The differences were too strong. Too fundamental—ah, well. It's over."

But the memories weren't. Helpless, he was pulled back to a July afternoon of billowing smoke and blaring bugles. He heard again the incredible, earth-shaking bombardment from Seminary Ridge that had preceded the slaughter of Pickett's infantrymen as they advanced gallantly toward the clump of trees, only to be shot down, blown down, stabbed down—the highest cresting of the Southern tide, men called it. Michael's brigade had watched it from afar. His inner eye saw the gray-clad bodies tumbling, singly and in great masses, as other Irishmen—the Pennsylvania 69th of the Philadelphia Brigade—blunted the assault at Pickett's center.

He wrenched himself from the reverie.

"I do confess I took pride in our unit. The Union commanders put special faith in the Irish Brigade. Before an action, they'd ask, 'Are the green flags ready?' The flags were decorated with bright golden harps and sunbursts. A man could usually see the gold even in the thickest smoke. But by the end, there were too few marching behind the flags."

"Too few on both sides," Hannah agreed. "I've read that altogether four hundred thousand were lost."

"I've heard more than half a million, and perhaps the same number injured. No one will ever know for certain. Both sides kept shamelessly poor records. An officer I met in the hospital told me some Confederate units were still listed on the rolls when only six or eight from the original complement were left."

She sensed his distaste for the subject and shifted to a slightly different one. "You said you belonged to a New York regiment. Did you mean the state or the city?"

"The city."

"It's your home?"

"Was." He nodded. He pointed at the dark bulk of the train. "That's my home now."

"Why did you come out here?"

He pondered the question. Should he be honest? Yes. But not entirely.

"Several reasons. To find work. Earn money—"

"Was there no work in New York City?"

"I could have returned to the docks, I suppose. I started there, as a longshoreman, when I was young."

She smiled. "Come, now. You're far from old."

"But getting there." His own smile faded. "When I left the hospital, I wanted a particular sort of work. No, better to say I needed it. Everywhere in the East, there are crippled men. Stumbling along the streets having left part of themselves in some damn—some bloody field or forest. It's too depressing a reminder of the price we paid to hold the Union together.

"I've read they're recruiting cavalry regiments for service against the Indians out here, and because so few able-bodied men are left, the Army's waiving many of its restrictions. The Plains Army will accept one-armed fellows, or men who've lost an eye. Men with a limp are welcome in the cavalry since a limp won't impair their riding. We'll be a nation of invalids for a generation. I hoped to see less of that on the railroad.

"But there's a more important reason I came to the U-Pay. I decided I'd done my share of destroying things. Property. Lives. I wanted work to balance that. I wanted to build, not tear down. The railroad's a worthy enterprise, even though many say it's controlled by schemers who aren't above bribing Congressmen to get it finished. But the heart of it's good, and important. Unfortunately"—a rueful smile—"I haven't been entirely successful in my effort to get away from fighting. I allowed myself to be drawn into the scrape with Worthing. He deserved what he got, but I'm ashamed I was the one to dish it out."

She continued to study him without speaking. He'd experienced a strange release in describing his past. Unexpectedly, he found himself telling her most of the rest.

"I also left the East because of personal problems. Before the war, I was employed by a wealthy family. The Kents."

The name produced no response.

"I was discharged—rather, I did a thing or two which made it impossible for me ever to work for them again."

Such as telling Louis I would not cooperate in his scheme to trade with the enemy.

Such as nearly raping his wife that very same night at Kentland, then finding myself smitten with her—

He sat up straighter in an effort to clear his mind. For a moment Julia's blue eyes seemed to glow near Hannah Dorn's face. He blinked. The vision vanished.

"No need for you to listen to any more, Miss Dorn. It's a tedious story, full of mistakes and regrettable lapses into many of those vices you abhor."

"Why, Mr. Boyle, that almost sounds like an insult." But she wasn't angry.

"Please, I don't mean to mock your faith. I expect these times require more of it, not less. But as I suggested inside, I—just don't have any of my own."

"I don't believe you. Every man has something he wants to achieve."

"Yes. To lay a mile of track a day."

"I mean some goal he wants to reach."

"To get the job done. To reach the hundredth meridian, then see the Atlantic and the Pacific joined by the rails."

"And that's all?"

He nodded.

"What will you do when the railroad's completed?"

"I've no idea."

"That's a sad and aimless way to go through life, Mr. Boyle."

"In truth, it is. But it's better than making war."

His brows knit together. He was unsettled at the way this woman was drawing out confessions he'd never intended to make.

She lifted the Bible from her lap, stood up, and touched an index finger to the pot. She withdrew it quickly; the coffee was hot enough.

"At least you're better off than Papa," she said. "You have a goal to last you a while. Papa never thinks beyond the next dipper from the barrel. We had very high hopes when we came to America in 1850. I recall it well—I was twelve when we made the passage in steerage. I can still hear Mama talking before we left Hamburg about how grand the future would be. Better by far than what we were leaving."

She untied the thong with one hand and held the pot bail with the other. "There are two china mugs on the washstand, Mr. Boyle."

He walked into the tent, returned with the cups, and let her pour. She held the pot by the bail and the bottom, as if it weren't even warm.

Steam drifted from the mugs as she finished pouring and bedded the pot in the ash of the disintegrating chips. She accepted one of the mugs. Her eyelids dropped briefly as their fingers accidentally touched a second time.

He sat down again. "You came from Germany, you said."

She took her seat on the stool, stared into the mug, spoke softly. "Papa was the last of fourteen brothers. Fourteen men and not a girl among them to marry off. The family brewery couldn't support him as well as a wife. Eight of his brothers also had to make their way in other kinds of work. It was Mama's savings and Mama's insistence that brought us here from Hamburg. We got as far as Cincinnati. Papa tried the butcher trade. First working for a shop owner to learn it, then opening a place of his own. But as a young man, he'd gotten too fond of beer and spiritous liquors. The habit was fixed. In Cincinnati he abused his customers. Word soon got around. The business failed. Papa managed to make a little on the sale of the building, but it was nothing more than luck."

"And your mother?"

"Mama wore herself out raising my brother Klaus. He was born in '52. She also worked with the Cincinnati Negro railroad, helping blacks who'd escaped from Kentucky on their way to Canada. One night six years ago, she and two other women and I were giving food bundles to three runaway boys on the Cincinnati waterfront. We were set on by a farmer who'd rowed across the river to recapture the boys. There was no violence, just a good deal of rough talk. The farmer did brandish a gun, however. And Mama's heart was bad. She suffered a seizure and died that night."

"I'm sorry."

"It took Papa a year to recover, realize the butcher shop had failed, and sell it. We came from Cincinnati to Nebraska because Germans had settled here too. Papa set up the store in Grand Island, and within two or three months it was Cincinnati all over again. He drove customers away with his foul temper and his discourtesy."

"Yet you've stayed with him."

"I said it before—he's my father. And there's Klaus to look after. The strong man doesn't pass by the weak merely because the weak man's flawed. We're all flawed."

Her free hand came to rest on the dark pebbled cover of the Bible on her knees.

"Christ taught that."

With her head bowed, she drank, then resumed. "Whatever happens to Papa, I'll stay in the territory. Mama's belief in America was justified, that much I've learned since

I've grown up. And perhaps it's not Papa's fault that he isn't strong enough to take advantage of the opportunity this country affords. Nebraska is a good land. All it needs are good people who believe in God and hard work. In a few years Grand Island will have schools, and churches, and be as fine a town as any other. I'll stay—even after Papa's gone."

"You do have a strong faith," Michael said, hoping she understood it as a compliment.

She bobbed her head, self-effacement. He was conscious again of how lovely she looked with her face patterned by the firelight. But he still didn't quite know what to make of her odd combination of piety and vulnerability.

All at once Hannah set her mug between her boots and opened the Bible.

"Mama taught me to believe in three things, Mr. Boyle. Work. Cleanliness. And this book. I know some people would laugh at me for saying that."

He raised a hand. "Not I. Truly, I do wish I had things to believe in other than this infernal railroad. The family I worked for had such things. But they turned away from—never mind. Go on."

"There's little more to say—except one thing. I do believe what's in these pages. And I believe this country offers greater hope than any other land on earth. America will always be a blessed place if we abide by its purpose, and this book."

He looked dubious. "At the moment, I wouldn't classify the East as a blessed place. It's poisoned with hatred."

"No more so than here. That fellow you fought—how is he different from all those politicians tearing at one another? Or the businessmen the papers rail about? There's always wickedness in the world, Mr. Boyle. But we can turn away from it and enjoy the blessings of life here. We have guidance."

She patted the book. "I was reading something along those very lines when you arrived. Second Chronicles, chapter seven, verse fourteen—"

He was envious of the peace he saw on her face as she quoted without looking up the passage.

" 'If my people, which are called by my name, shall humble themselves, and pray, and seek my face, and turn from their wicked ways, then will I hear from heaven, and will forgive their sin, and will heal their land—' "

He wished he could believe her answer was the right one—and easily implemented. Their eyes met for a long moment. Then she succumbed to embarrassment. Resting her palms on the book, she gazed down at them. He was gripped by an impulse to stand, circle the fire, and touch her.

He didn't. If she knew that a certain tension below his belly was in part responsible for his feeling, no doubt she'd run inside the tent for the Hawken—

What in the devil's happening to you, Michael Boyle?

The answer was the same as before: a normal reaction to a long period spent without speaking to a woman more than casually.

But he tended to reject it. *This* woman was the one who fascinated him.

He tried not to deprecate her obvious faith in the words she'd quoted. But he couldn't help a touch of cynicism. "That's a laudable message. Perhaps I should copy it and have it delivered to Captain Worthing."

"The man with whom you had the trouble?"

"Yes, have you met him?"

Distastefully: "No, but Klaus keeps me informed. Worthing is one of Papa's better customers. I hope you'll have no more to do with him."

Something prickled Michael's backbone.

It isn't up to me.

"I'd better not," he laughed. "General Casement warned me. Any more brouhahas and I'll probably be discharged."

"Let me say something, Mr. Boyle—and I beg you not to be offended by it."

He was on guard. "Go ahead."

"I believe a man finds what he seeks, whether it's trouble or peace."

"I fear it's not quite so simple."

"Not always. But in a general sense, yes."

"Well, it certainly hasn't worked in my case. I look for peace but don't find it."

"Perhaps you haven't looked in the proper spot."

"If you mean the Bible, you're correct."

"You might try it sometime."

"I wish I could—believing in what I was doing, I mean."

"That comes eventually. First there must be the intent."

He couldn't help feeling irked, and would have expressed the feeling if she weren't so sincere. He did make one admission.

"To a certain extent you're correct about finding what you seek. I could have knuckled under to Worthing. I refused."

"This is a difficult place. Among rough men, you'll always face such choices."

"And you don't face them in Grand Island?"

"Not as many." She smiled. "That's one of the few benefits of what people call the advance of civilization. In any case, before I go to bed, I'll pray Mr. Worthing won't force you into a situation in which you'll be tempted to fight again. If you do it will only make your unhappy feelings that much stronger."

His mingled amusement and anger faded when he realized she was utterly serious. Serious and concerned. He didn't know what to say.

The singing was over. The cooling air carried a winy tang. For no reason he could fully explain, sitting quietly beside Hannah produced a sense of calm he hadn't known in months.

The silence lengthened. He was acutely conscious of the woman's femininity. His body kept responding in a way she'd certainly find objectionable. He decided he'd better leave.

He drained his coffee—cold now—and contrived to stand up with a kind of twisting motion, so she wouldn't catch a glimpse of his trousers.

"Miss Dorn, I thank you for the company, the coffee, and the conversation."

"I enjoyed it, Mr. Boyle," she said with a little nod. "You're a sensitive and literate man."

"No, only a rust eater," he laughed. "Your speech is finer. I'm wondering how you learned English so well."

"Mama. She believed that since this was to be our country, we should study the language, and its finest usage. Papa wouldn't but I did. I had no formal schooling here, mind, but I had great men for teachers. Shakespeare. John Milton. Wadsworth—"

She lifted the Bible. "And the translators who worked for good King James."

She laid the book, on the stool as she rose, mercifully keeping her eyes on his face.

Boyle, you're behaving like the worst adolescent!

So he was. He couldn't help it.

Hannah Dorn walked around the dying fire. Her stride was long, determined.

"Wait here one moment. I still have a bit of doctoring to do."

Shortly she emerged from the tent with a small milk-glass pot. The salve it contained had a foul color and a tarry smell. But it proved marvelously cooling as she spread it on his blistered palms and burned thumb. She rubbed vigorously until the salve was absorbed into the skin.

"Feels much better," he muttered, amazed anew at the reaction the feel of her fingers produced.

"I'm glad." She extended her hand.

After a moment's hesitancy—his palm was still slick—he clasped it. He squeezed a bit harder than necessary. She didn't seem to mind.

"I thank you again, Miss Dorn."

"The pleasure's been mine."

"Perhaps when Christian's awake tomorrow, I might look in a second time?"

The gray-blue eyes held his. "I wish you would." Then, with more animation, she added, "A second visit might even result in a halfway peaceful Sunday with Papa. He's given up all hope of gentlemen spending more than a moment speaking to me. The Hawken and the Bible seem to get in the way. But I"—she was forcing herself, wanting to say something and not quite able; at last she managed it—"I am not a shrew, I hope."

"On the contrary. Grand company! Sometime tomorrow, then—perhaps late in the day?"

She teased again, "But there are no worship services to keep you occupied in the morning, Mr. Boyle."

"There's the Platte for taking a bath. If you were downwind of me you'd understand why I'll be occupied for a while."

She laughed. "Fair enough."

He waved as he left, unconsciously beginning to whistle

"Corcoran to His Regiment" without a single thought of the song's significance.

ii

He walked by the whiskey wagon. The customers had departed. Klaus Dorn was slumped over the crate with his plump cheek squashed against his forearms and the Hawken on the ground. The whiskey merchant lay against a wheel of his wagon, the backs of his hands in the dirt, his mouth opening and closing. Spittle trickled from the corner of his lips as he snored. The dipper on its chain swayed slowly back and forth in the wind, inches from his lolling head.

A sorry sight, Michael thought, wrinkling his nose. Even at a distance he could smell the liquor on Dorn. No wonder the girl retreated to her Bible.

As he entered the darkened sleeping car and approached his bunk, Sean Murphy whispered from the bed below his.

"That you, Michael Boyle?"

"No, it's Worthing come to lie in wait."

"Don't jest," Murphy grumbled. "Greenup ran into him earlier. He's staggering about with a face dark as a rotten pudding. He's promising things."

Michael laid his churchwarden up on the bunk and started to unbutton his shirt. "What things?"

"Very ugly. You be on watch."

"I am."

Murphy sniffed. "Jaysus, you smell like a pill shop!"

"Miss Dorn gave me some salve for my blisters."

"Ah, yes, one of the lads did notice you callin' on her."

"Merely to ask about Christian."

"Took you an hour or more to ask, did it?"

In the lowest bunk of the three, Liam O'Dey stirred, then whined, "Will you both shut your claps so a man can catch a wink?"

"Up your arse, O'Dey," Murphy replied. "Tomorrow's Sunday."

"I'm tuckered from Saturday!"

"Fiddledeedee. You've an entire day to relax and pursue your favorite activity, which is complaining."

The thought of Sunday pleased Michael as he dragged off his shirt and tossed it up beside his pipe. What an odd, flinty woman was Hannah Dorn! A rifle, a Bible, a tosspot father, a witless brother—and loneliness. Yet he was anticipating the day—anticipating seeing her again—as he hadn't anticipated anything in a long while. He'd have a bath, slick his hair, and drop by early in the afternoon.

The prospect made him chuckle.

"Ah, that's a dirty laugh if ever I heard one!" Murphy said. "What did the dear girl do after she doctored you? Admit you to the privacy of her quarters and give you a peek at her rosary?" The last word was juicily lewd.

"She has no rosary. She's one of the Luther crowd."

"Oh, God, don't mix with them!"

"Jesus and Mary, must we get filth an' theology blabbered all night?" O'Dey grumbled, thumping his mattress with his fist.

"Screw yourself if you're not too feeble, you sour old man," Murphy said, then let go with a loud, rasping fart to heighten the insult. O'Dey exclaimed, *"Agh!"* and thumped the mattress a few more times.

Again Murphy whispered, "I share but one thing with O'Dey downstairs. Exhaustion. Good night to you, Michael."

Michael's hands ached as he braced one against the bunks and used the other to pull off his boots. Undressing standing up was easier than doing it flat on his back. All at once it struck him that no thought of Julia Kent had crept into his mind for quite a while.

"I said good night, Michael Boyle."

"Good night, Sean."

Hannah's eyes glimmered in his mind. Part of the scriptural quote lingered too.

If my people seek my face—turn from their wicked ways—I will heal their land.

The second boot came off. He pushed his trousers down and pulled one leg free. A strained muscle in his thigh shot pain to his hip and calf. Too bad he couldn't get Miss Dorn's biblical message to the Virginian. Worthing's land, the South, still wanted a deal of healing. Instead, it was receiving punishment. That was a big part of the man's trouble, Michael was sure. On the other hand, he might be letting his imagination run too free. Perhaps Worthing had been sufficiently chastened by the beating.

As he tossed boots and trousers to the bunk and started to climb up, he decided it was ridiculous to worry over the captain when he wasn't at all sure the man would take action. Though Murphy had mentioned threats, there was a vast gulf between words and deeds.

At that exact moment he pulled himself so his head was level with his blanket.

"Christ Jesus!" he breathed.

iii

"D'you say something?" Murphy asked drowsily from below.

Stricken speechless, it took Michael a moment to answer. "Just blathering to myself."

His eyes remained riveted on the knife. A carving knife pilfered from the kitchen, by the look of it. He'd been unable to see it from the aisle below.

Someone must have come into the car earlier, while it was empty. His blanket had been hacked to pieces, left in tatters, with sections of Jephtha's letter scattered about. The knife had been driven into the mattress where Michael usually rested his head.

With a sweaty hand he pulled the knife loose and laid it on his clothes at the foot of the bed. He was shaking as he climbed up into the jumble of slashed wool and cut paper, calling himself the worst of fools for believing, even briefly, that Captain Worthing's enmity would confine itself to threats.

He hoped Hannah Dorn wasn't praying too hard. It was wasted effort. He would be forced to fight again.

Chapter IX
At Lance Point

i

Sleep came hard that night. Michael lay with his hands clasped beneath his head, struggling to disconnect his thoughts from the significance of the tangle of hacked blanket and ripped paper on which he was trying to rest. Trying and failing.

Worthing was determined to finish it with him—and to torment him with the realization that the reckoning would come unexpectedly, at a time of his own choosing.

Michael's eye wandered to the pale rectangle of Matthew Kent's drawing of the Havana milk vendor. For some reason the drawing had been spared, further proof, if he needed it, that Worthing wasn't entirely rational. A man whose violence was controlled would have destroyed everything in the bunk. Worthing had cut and slashed with such fury that he'd missed the picture. That worsened Michael's depression.

As did further introspection about his own behavior with Hannah Dorn.

He'd come whistling back to the car like some moonstruck swain, delighted by the possibility of a friendship. Now he had doubts about his breezy mood. Had it been a trick of his mind? Perhaps he'd unconsciously deceived himself about the whiskey merchant's daughter. Perhaps he was using her as an antidote for the altogether foolish longing for Louis' wife.

Images of Julia's nude body slipped in and out of his mind as he tossed and wriggled in the ruins of the bed. Images of a woman he could never have.

The uncontrollable desire humiliated him. It also cheapened and insulted Hannah Dorn. She'd treated with him in good faith, not knowing he wanted to be with her to attempt to submerge his feelings for another woman.

Ah, what a nasty, tangled mess it had all become!

He must have lain awake three or four hours before he dozed off, exhausted. Dreams of Worthing's face haunted him through the night. When he drifted out of sleep again shortly after ten on Sunday morning, he felt no better.

Men were leaving their bunks one at a time, moving at a leisurely pace, and keeping their voices pitched low so as not to wake those still in bed. As Michael stirred, Sean Murphy whispered his name from below. He remained motionless and silent. He didn't reply to Murphy's second whisper. Or his third. Finally Murphy rose, pulled on his clothes, and left the car.

As soon as Michael was sure he wouldn't be disturbed, he unrolled an extra blanket tucked at the foot of the bunk, stood on Murphy's bed and spread the blanket carefully to conceal the havoc of Worthing's knife. He'd dispose of the cut cloth and shredded paper after dark. The knife itself he wedged between the bunk frame and the car wall; he'd get rid of it after dark, too. He never even considered showing it to Murphy—or reporting the incident to Casement.

Murphy hailed him as he entered the dining car. Michael couldn't refuse to sit with his friend. Greenup Williams arrived a moment later. It registered on Michael that both men had dressed with unusual care. Murphy wore his one white shirt and an old satin cravat. Greenup had donned his best work clothes and an ancient emerald-colored velvet jacket, somewhat too elegant to be owned by any rust eater, white or black. Michael assumed the jacket had been given Greenup by someone for whom he'd once worked.

"I heard you tossin' most of the night again," Murphy said between swallows of coffee. He nudged Michael. "Thoughts of Miss Dorn keep you roused, did they?"

Michael shook his head.

Greenup laughed. "My, he's full of chatter today."

"Merely in awe of the splendid plumage of you fellows," Michael murmured.

"One of the boys who was shaving when I woke told me Mr. Stackpole and his wagon arrived in the middle of the night."

In response to Michael's blank look, Murphy amplified, "Mr. Stackpole is one of the lads in the U-Pay Photographic Corpse."

"Corps," Michael corrected.

Murphy didn't take umbrage. "I needn't know how to say it, just enjoy it. Greenup an' me, we're going to have our pictures took. Spruce up and join us."

Michael knew the railroad had a small number of roving photographers whose wagons—traveling darkrooms—followed the tracks to create a pictorial record of the line's progress. Though the bulky cameras were in fairly wide use, Michael was still in awe of them. He found the science of photography one of the miracles of the century.

"I'd have too sour a mug and spoil the picture," he said with a shake of his head. When they repeated their entreaties, he continued to say no.

Finally Murphy shrugged and gave up. Greenup frowned—his first overt acknowledgment that he recognized something was awry with Michael. By then Michael was on his feet. He bid the two goodbye, picked up a week-old Omaha paper someone had left behind, and hurried back to the bunk car to razor his face and trim his mustache before going down to the river for a bath.

Much of the joy had been drained from the anticipated excursion. He was fleeing again. Fleeing his confusion over Julia and Hannah Dorn—and his worry about Worthing.

Outside the sleeping car, he did stop a few moments to observe Murphy, Greenup—and O'Dey, who had evidently incorporated himself into the portrait group without permission—fidgeting and posing near the short boxy wagon shrouded with black drapes. Inside, Mr. Stackpole could be heard grumbling and swearing as he coated his glass plates with whatever mysterious chemical mixture caused an image to form on them. In the dirt behind the wagon Michael noticed two padlocked wooden boxes of a sort he'd seen once before. Finished plates were kept in there after being chemically treated to fix their images.

Finally, Mr. Stackpole emerged to deposit his tripod on the ground. He returned for his large camera with brass lens ring. Stackpole was middle-aged and impatient, fussing loudly as he fastened the camera to the tripod. A small crowd was collecting. Quite a few men had dressed for portraits.

"All right," Stackpole announced finally, "let's have the first group."

He adjusted the black drape spread over the camera, then waved at Murphy and his two companions. "No, no, not there! Away from the shadow of the car!"

"Join us, Michael," Murphy urged again.

"No, thank you. I—" All at once he spied someone lounging up by the tender. Arms folded, the man was facing the crowd and the photographer. Cigar smoke trailed away from his mouth. He paid no attention to the workers swarming past him; Sundays, the engine and tender were uncoupled and turned over to those among the crew who fancied themselves marksmen. But all Michael saw was the distant dark blotch of one man's face.

Worthing's.

Watching him.

"No," he repeated, "I've need of a bath."

And I've need to get away because I've come over a thousand miles and I haven't outrun Julia, or the fighting. I wonder if I ever will.

"Come on," Greenup said to him. "It'll only take a min—"

"A bath, and that's that!"

The severity of Michael's tone brought a frown to Murphy's face. "Lad, what on earth's wrong with you this morning?"

"In place, in place!" Stackpole interrupted, manhandling O'Dey and Greenup to the spot he'd chosen. "I have a great many exposures to make while the light's good."

"Michael?" Murphy repeated.

"No!" Michael shouted so loudly Murphy looked hurt. Michael spun away.

With the newspaper tucked under his arm, he walked rapidly toward the end of the track. But in his mind he was running. There was no escape. None, anywhere.

That truth rode his shoulder like an invisible hobgoblin as he cut across the tracks and quickened his step, fleeing toward the bank of the Platte.

ii

He walked almost a mile through knee-high buffalo grass on the north bank of the river. *Osceola*'s whistle shrilled twice—a final summons to those who meant to go chugging east along the line, clinging to the tender, pilot, and running boards while they pinked at any buffalo in sight.

The sky was a muted blue, lightly hazed by thin clouds. A moderate wind blew out of the northwest, setting the long grass and patches of bright red wildflowers to rippling. Michael was conscious of the morning's surpassing loveliness. It eased his tension a little. He plucked one of the wildflowers and stuck it in the pocket of his shirt. The poppy bobbed in a jaunty way as he tramped along the bank.

The prospect of visiting Dorn's tent again was palling on more than one count. If he went to call on Christian and the woman, he'd be forced to speak politely to the thick-witted German. And he was in no mood to be polite. The memory of Julia had spoiled his happy feelings of the preceding evening.

What compounded his confusion was a new admission that, in spite of Julia, he *did* have a certain persistent desire to see Hannah Dorn again. She was attractive, intriguing in an odd way. A deep sort, that was the term for it.

Then he admitted another reason for his interest—one which surprised him. Though he didn't consider himself a religious man, he'd been stirred by some of her remarks last night.

He actually wished she were right. Wished solutions to problems were as simple as she made them out to be. What a blessing it would be if something so direct as a return to the kind of Christian behavior described in her Bible could indeed heal the country, tame the violence that erupted even at the reasonably well-ordered railhead, and overcome the widespread hate and corruption Jephtha's long letter had described. Although Amanda Kent had never been a practitioner of formal religion, her faith in certain principles reminded him of Hannah Dorn—and of his own woeful lack of convictions.

I am a Kent now, he reminded himself. *I had better get to work and find something to believe in. Something to work for again—*

The railroad was no longer quite enough. Especially not since he'd realized he had fled to it because it promised escape.

Which he hadn't found—

That brought him straight back to Worthing.

Caught up in his thoughts, he found himself at the edge of a grassless patch where half a dozen small cones of earth had been clawed out of the ground to form a village of what more experienced men on the U-Pay called prairie dogs. One of the curious, popeyed little creatures was sitting bolt upright in its hole, foreclaws raised, and quivering. It saw or at least sensed his presence and plummeted out of sight.

Michael carefully skirted the burrows so as not to disturb them. He returned the wave of a group of naked men splashing and wringing out laundry in the shallows to his left. He kept walking. He wanted privacy, wanted to be a good distance from fellow workers who might be anxious for conversation.

A rich, loamy smell rose from the sun-drenched earth. Clouds of huge grasshoppers buzzed near him. The land here was slightly more rolling. Ahead, a line of low hills made it impossible to see the far western horizon.

He stopped short of the hills and glanced back. The nearest bathers were a good half mile distant. He tossed the newspaper down and pulled a lump of yellow soap from his pocket. After tugging off his boots, he peeled away every scrap of clothing.

He flung the garments among the reeds at the river's edge, enjoying the feel of the sun on his bare spine and buttocks. He crouched in the shallow water and began to soap the pieces of clothing.

One by one he rinsed them and laid them on the bank to dry. He flipped the soap after them and returned to the muddy river with the paper.

He got to his knees, then stretched prone in the tepid water. It barely covered the lower half of his body. With his head up and his elbows in the mud, he studied a moving blur—bison—far in the south beyond two tilted, hair-covered telegraph poles. The wind blew puffs of dust from the ruts of the emigrant trail.

He turned to the paper to focus his mind on something other than personal problems. The leading story was a report on one of the featured speeches at the National Union convention in Philadelphia in the middle of the current month.

In '64, Lincoln and Johnson had run under the National Union banner. The President was again attempting to use it to form a coalition of Democrats and moderate Republicans opposed to the radicals. Republican Congressman Henry Raymond, founder and editor of *The New York Times,* had delivered the speech quoted—and done so at some risk to his career, the paper observed. As soon as the cheers of the audience faded and Raymond's remarks were reported to Washington, the capital began to stir with rumors that the traitorous Raymond would be removed from national chairmanship of the Republican party.

But evidently he'd been willing to accept that risk. In Philadelphia, Raymond had unequivocally supported the views of President Johnson. He'd declared that, constitutionally, only the individual states could establish qualifications for the franchise; that the Southern states had never seceded and therefore had to be represented in Congress; and that the fourteenth amendment, worthy though it was, couldn't be ratified except by two-thirds of all the states—which included those formerly in rebellion.

According to the account, Raymond's speech had been no anti-Negro diatribe, not even a disguised one. The *Times* editor had declared slavery dead for all time and called for equal protection of the rights and property of every person, regardless of race.

But if Jephtha's letter was accurate, Michael mused, not even Raymond's sentiments about human rights would appease the radicals. Whether right or wrong about the Constitution, Johnson was flying in the face of important segments of public opinion. It had not gone down well early in the year when the President had confronted the noted black abolitionist, Douglass, at the White House, and calmly advised him that, in addition to violating the Constitution, immediate Negro suffrage would unleash a race war.

Michael was still unable to decide whether Johnson was courageously stating the truth, then and now, or revealing a prejudice against blacks. The article, however, only reinforced his disheartening feeling that Jephtha was correct about the ferocity of the new political war being waged by men not the least interested in the counsel of Miss Hannah Dorn's Bible.

Somewhat more enjoyable was a reprint of a piece by an eastern journalist named Bell. He had visited the railhead a few weeks earlier, and written a description of the track-laying operation. Its accuracy was pleasantly surprising, and its conclusion rhapsodic:

> *It is a grand "anvil chorus" that those sturdy sledges are playing across the plains. It is in a triple time, three strokes to the spike. There are ten spikes to a rail, 400 rails to a mile, 1,800 miles to San Francisco—21,000,000 times are those sledges to be swung; 21,000,000 times are they to come down with their sharp punctuation before the great work of modern America is complete.*

"Twenty-one million times—is that a fact?" Michael murmured. Impressive—though he couldn't swallow the notion that the "anvil chorus" was grand. Its performance was grueling, prosaic, noisy—and full of sour notes such as the outburst of a Leonidas Worthing. But at least reporters were beginning to write a few favorable items about the U-Pay.

A hail startled him. He rolled over. Saw towheaded Tom Ruffin approaching briskly along the bank, a look of concentration on his face and a thick piece of cottonwood in his right hand.

"Good morning, Tom," Michael called back. "Heard you singing last night. Splendid!"

The boy stopped. "Thank you, Mr. Boyle."

Michael waved a wet hand at the grass Ruffin was studying. "Lose something?"

"No, sir. Hunting a fool hen—or whatever you call it."

"I think the correct name is grouse, or maybe partridge. Not sure. But I haven't seen any."

"General Jack told me they were mighty delicious roasted. And so dumb you could walk up and brain 'em with a stick."

"So I've heard. Guess they deserve to be called fool hens."

The boy shielded his eyes and peered at the low hills ahead. "Might be some up that way." He waved and hurried on.

Michael rolled back onto his belly, forgetting Ruffin for ten minutes. Then, abruptly, a yelp—almost like an animal's bark—drifted from behind the hills where the boy had vanished.

He paid little attention until he heard the cry a second time. It was high-pitched and quickly muffled.

Michael raised his head. Not an animal at all, he realized. It sounded like Ruffin—in some kind of difficulty. Perhaps the boy had stumbled into a burrow and wrenched his leg.

He strode up the bank, wiped water from his legs and tugged on his trousers. Barefoot and bare-chested, he went running to the crest of the first hill.

And stopped, openmouthed. In an instant, his heart was beating with frantic speed.

iii

Evidently they'd come from the west. They must have ridden their large-headed, thin-legged calicos—the small but sturdy brown, bay, and white ponies Irishmen called piebalds—all but silently to the low place behind the screen of hills. He had an impression of considerable numbers of riders—thirty at least, every one of them armed with bows and decorated hide shields. Every one of them was watching him.

Most of them appeared quite large in relation to their mounts. That meant Cheyenne, didn't it? He'd been told the Cheyenne were, on the average, taller than the Sioux.

Out in front of the rest, a paunchy yet powerful-looking warrior of about forty held Tom Ruffin under his left arm as if the boy were an empty meal sack.

The boy's heels hung down, kicking and making the warrior's calico skittish. The boy was prevented from crying out by the brown left hand clamped like a claw over his face. The Indian's right hand held a fierce-looking bow horizontally. The godawful weapon was eight feet long, at least—

And it was more than a bow, Michael saw suddenly. It had a pointed iron head. The head pressed the side of young Ruffin's neck. Wind fluttered the feathers decorating the bow lance.

Michael stood silent and stunned in the blowing buffalo grass, his frightened gaze taking in the dark cheeks, the nut-colored eyes, the hands gripping bows and shields, the animal-skin shirts with long twisted strands of hair knotted in the fringing. Scalp locks taken from their enemies—?

As he glanced from face to expressionless face, he found no friendliness. He shivered, all but certain several of the motionless horsemen were ready to reach for arrows in quivers slung over their backs. He knew that if he bolted to sound an alarm he'd be killed before he ran six steps.

And the nearest workers were half a mile away. Very faintly, he heard their shouts and splashing.

So, he thought with a mixture of terror and sadness, *it seems I've found another enemy.*

And another war.

Chapter X
Hunter's Blood

i

Some thirty miles southeast of the railhead on a simmering afternoon in the same month, a handsome, twenty-six-year-old Oglala Sioux and his white companion found what they had been seeking for the better part of a week.

The Sioux, whom the white man called Kola, knew the search was over when his friend came scrambling down the side of the ravine to the dry wash where Kola had been told to wait with the rickety wagon. Two mules were hitched to the wagon. The wiry buffalo pony that was their common property was tied to the tailgate.

From the expression on his friend's face, Kola suspected the find was a good one. The young white man's dark eyes sparkled when the sun touched them beneath the brim of his low-crowned plainsman's hat. Like nearly everything else the partners owned, the hat had been stolen.

As always, the sight of the white man stirred a profound, almost religious feeling of affection within the Sioux. Only a few of the white's quirks bothered Kola. One was altogether minor, and by now almost amusing.

Six months earlier, the white man had found the Sioux brave half dead, beaten in most uncharacteristic fashion by the husband of a woman named Sweet Summer. In his pain, the young Sioux had tried to thank his benefactor. Again and again he'd pointed alternately to the white man and then to himself while repeating the word *kola* to indicate each was now a special friend to the other. The Sioux had had a regular *kola* during his boyhood years—Lively Cub, who'd taken the name Brave Horse after counting his first coups.

Although the white man soon came to understand what *kola* meant in a general sense, he took a fancy to the word. He preferred it to the Sioux's adult name, Clever Hunter.

"Kola, we hit some luck. There's a small herd lying down with their cuds, right up yonder." One of the white man's grease-stained buckskin gauntlets lifted toward the rim of the wash.

"How many, Joseph?" Kola asked in the badly accented English he'd learned hanging around the fort.

"Eighteen, twenty—" Joseph brushed a pestiferous fly from the long fair hair hanging over the back of his collarless flannel shirt. Suspenders held up his threadbare trousers. But his boots were sturdy.

"Couple of calves, too," Joseph added. "We'll let them go."

Kola shared his friend's happiness with a smile. Joseph was five or six years Kola's junior, but seemed older. He was lean, strong and, most importantly, trustworthy. At least he had never proved himself otherwise during their half-year association.

If Joseph tended to be somewhat more reckless than a Sioux, that was a peculiarity of his white temperament. Kola did not question it too deeply. The saving of his life by Joseph had been a sending of the gods. *Wakan.* Holy. Therefore an event of great meaning for the future. Shortly after their meeting, a night vision had confirmed it.

Occasionally Kola was disturbed by the pitiless set of Joseph's mouth when he fired one of their weapons. The Sioux killed to eat, and slew their enemies only when absolutely necessary. For honor, pleasure—and the preservation of tribal manpower—they preferred counting coup instead.

But Joseph was his *kola.* For that reason, and another even more compelling, the Sioux brave never spoke about disturbing aspects of his friend's behavior. The reason was

Kola's certainty that Joseph was guided by his own inner voice.

Every Sioux heeded this most sacred and mysterious of all instructors. It told him where he must go, and how he must behave. It sometimes spoke when a man was awake, but more often it spoke through dreams.

Even the *winkte,* the target of so many warrior jests, did no more than follow the promptings of his inner voice when, as a boy, he chose to don women's clothing and face paint for the rest of his life. Thus every *winkte*—and they were numerous—was revered as well as scorned. A *winkte* was often asked to name a newborn so the child would never suffer sickness, for instance. Almost without exception, the inner voice of a human being was *wakan.*

So Kola believed that in all things, Joseph was only obeying the inner voice Kola would never hear, just as Joseph would never hear his. The belief made Kola forgiving of behavior he might otherwise have questioned.

The Sioux, a dark, supple young man wearing only a buffalo skin breechclout and moccasins with bull rawhide soles, glanced at the scorching sun which appeared to be sitting on the rim of the gully. The sun's glare threw the outline of his large sharp nose across one side of his face and created tiny shadows beside the two puckered scars in the hard flesh above his nipples. At eighteen he had committed himself to the religious frenzy of the gazing-at-the-sun dance, stamping and reeling for hours around the sacred pole until his zeal gave him strength to mortify his own flesh. The wooden skewers inserted under his skin by the shaman had torn free and fallen, bloody at the ends of the braided ropes attached to the pole. The twin scars were testimony to his courage.

The sun was a fearful and sacred thing to the Indian: another tangible sign of the presence of *Wakan Tanka*—the Great Mystery, the driving force and spirit of life which was in every place, every person, and every occurrence, though in ways not always discernible. This afternoon, however, the sun had a more practical significance.

"The time is late, Joseph. The buffalo will move soon to the night bedding place."

"Or find a larger herd." Joseph nodded. Kola had taught him that, in August, when the rutting season began and the bulls and cows grew impatient to breed, the animals tended to gather and migrate together in huge numbers—a thousand, two thousand—which made hunting more difficult. "We'll get them before they do," the white man continued. "I've already picked out the cow leading them."

Kola murmured a syllable to show the pleasure he took from his friend's confidence. In the spring when they'd first traveled together, Joseph had been unable to distinguish a leader in a herd of massive bulls, smaller cows, and their calves. Out of gratitude, Kola had taught him much. Kola did not hate white men with the ferocity of some of his race. He'd been around forts too long as a youth. And he'd been cast out from his own tribal group because of the wrath and influence of Sweet Summer's husband.

Joseph reached down to scratch his right leg just above the boot where he hid his skinning knife. "There are half a dozen bulls, the rest cows. Been through a grass fire not too long ago. Hides look burned on the hindquarters where they've shed. Two of the bulls and two of the cows must have had their eyes ruined when they stampeded through the fire."

A scowl ridged Kola's brow. "Four of them do not see?"

"Practically sure of it."

The Sioux digested that. It made what they were about to do more difficult. The bison lacked good vision even when they hadn't been injured. But they possessed sharp senses of smell and hearing to offset the lack. Blind buffalo—common on the prairie—were even more alert to alien scents and sounds.

"Is there a hiding place where the wind is right?"

"Some brush. I have it all laid out."

Joseph spoke in a quiet, pleasant voice, slurring, and softening some of his words. Kola had encountered a few whites who talked the same way. Driving small herds of longhorn cattle, they had ridden up from the southern part of the land mass Joseph had frequently tried to describe for him, but whose immensity defied Kola's imagination. He was also unable to form more than a rudimentary mental picture of the fantastic collections of structures Joseph called cities, that the white man assured Kola were plentiful beyond eastern rivers Kola had never seen.

A happy curve relieved the severity of Joseph's mouth as he gestured to his companion. "Let's unpack the guns."

A strong *kola,* this stranger who had fed and cared for him until he could walk and function again. A *kola* who handled white men's weapons well, although with a strange, almost possessive fondness.

Kola tied the reins of the mules and clambered into the rear of the wagon. He unwrapped the blanket and removed the three loaded rifles, along with a hide cartridge pouch. Kola noticed how perspiration appeared on Joseph's upper lip and a smile brightened his eyes at the sight of the trio of powerful buffalo killers.

ii

Conscious of the lateness of the hour, the two men still exercised caution in climbing from the ravine and working their way in a large semicircle to the brush from which Joseph would attempt to force the small herd into a stand. In fifteen minutes they were in place, both kneeling, the buffalo guns laid out side by side within easy reach of Joseph's right hand.

The equipment for the hunt consisted of three single-shot pieces: a rather battered Laidley-Whitney .50 caliber, and two fine Ballard .45s, all three capable of accepting the 70-grain powder charge required to bring down a rampaging bull. Kola didn't know where Joseph had gotten any of the buffalo killers. The white man was not talkative on the subject, except to say—usually with one of those mirthless smiles—that he wasn't the original owner of any of the rifles. Kola, however, had shown him how to use them on their proper targets.

The small herd rested about sixty yards away. The immense bodies were half concealed by the windblown grass. Great jaws moved slowly as the animals chewed the regurgitated grasses they'd cropped during their morning graze. Kola noted the tawny hides of the two calves nestling next to their mothers.

Joseph wiped a gauntlet across his wet brow and pointed. With a nod, Kola acknowledged and endorsed Joseph's selection of the presumed leader. Both the bulls and the cows had angry red hindquarters. Their winter protection—long, shaggy hair and thick, woollike undercoats—had been shed or rubbed away. On the flanks of the resting animals Kola could easily discern scorch marks and large sores. At close range he would have seen many more sores; the bare hides attracted swarms of biting insects during the summer months.

Joseph held out his right hand. Kola passed him the first of the Ballards, then laid out extra cartridges from the pouch. The success of a stand depended not only on the witlessness of the buffalo but upon the speed and accuracy with which the hunter singled out the successive leaders.

Slowly, Joseph raised the Ballard to his shoulder. There was no sound except the faint murmur of the wind blowing from the direction of the herd. Joseph's hands lost color as he took a firmer grip and laid his cheek into sighting position.

All at once, in the ravine behind them, one of the mules brayed.

Not loudly. But the sound was enough to bring the cow leader to her feet.

The rest of the herd lumbered up. Kola watched Joseph's mouth go white and his eyes flick angrily toward the disastrous noise. Then Kola heard another sound from the same direction. The tinkle of bit metal—? He was almost positive.

He had no time to think of who it might be. The herd was starting to move. Joseph fired.

The lead cow bellowed, struck exactly where Kola had taught Joseph to hit. Behind the last rib, the point at which a bullet or an arrow would pierce and destroy the air sacs white men called lungs. Kola had not needed to teach Joseph how to shoot. He was an unerring marksman.

The herd grew frantic as the cow teetered and collapsed on her forefeet, shoulders heaving. A blind bull swung toward the source of the shot, then went plunging past the dying leader. Even nineteen bison with two calves trailing set up a formidable rumble in the ground.

Joseph never took his eyes from the running herd. His tension was betrayed only by the sweat rivering down his cheeks and neck. He thrust the Ballard to the ground. Kola slapped the second one into his palm. In seconds, Joseph was ready to fire.

But he held his shot while Kola swiftly and expertly reloaded the first rifle. Joseph was watching the fleeing herd. Letting them go far enough. Fifty yards. Seventy-five—

Suddenly a lumbering cow separated from the rest, veering north. The others followed. With the new leader identified, Joseph fired. A cry of pain, and she went down.

The buffalo kept running, widening the distance between themselves and the hunters. Soon the animals would be out of range of the Laidley-Whitney Joseph held ready. But the pattern repeated itself. A new cow charged to the front. Joseph dropped her with a thunderous roar of the gun.

They waited. The critical moment—

A blind bull slowed and lowered his shaggy head.

A calf straggled to a stop.

A cow dashed on, then turned back.

After another few seconds, the entire herd, baffled by the loss of three leaders in quick succession, came to a halt. It was the classic stand every hunter hoped for if his timing and his luck were good.

A smile curled Joseph's mouth. He swabbed the filthy cuff of his shirt across his forehead. Then, with barely a sound, he climbed to his feet.

"It was well done, Joseph," Kola whispered as he finished loading the Laidley-Whitney. There was genuine admiration in his voice.

"Because I had a fine teacher. Now we can take our time. You'll have a nice feast tonight."

Kola could practically taste the savory brain and small intestine that would be left after the work of slaughtering. His mouth watered, and he thanked the holy spirits for bringing him into the presence of this white man. With a merry glint in his eye, he fell into the routine of loading and passing the buffalo guns to Joseph, who simply stood in place and shot the stupefied buffalo one by one.

Shadows lengthened on the baking prairie. The wind soon stank of blood and the contents of emptied intestines—to Kola the sweetest aroma on earth. As the last cow dropped and the forlorn calves wandered around the corpses searching for their mothers, the Sioux reminded himself that before he and Joseph moved north to the fire road, he must cut out and scatter the hearts of the dead animals so the herd would regenerate itself.

The echoes of the last shot went rolling away into the

sullen red haze along the western horizon. Joseph relaxed, squatted down, and exhaled loudly. He laid the second Ballard on the ground.

"Well, my friend, there's the stake that'll keep us alive come winter."

Kola glanced at the dead buffalo. He was aware of the increasing slaughter of the herds upon which his people depended for food, clothing, shelter, horse gear, weaponry, religious objects—even the hair-stuffed calfskin balls and netted hoops the children used in their games. No useful portion of the animal was ignored. Yet for a dozen summers and more, white hunters had been slaying buffalo in enormous numbers, and wasting most of the precious parts. Now here he was, doing the same. He wouldn't have done so except for the promptings of his inner voice which had told him he was destined to ride with Joseph. But as he eyed the dead animals, he couldn't keep a touch a disapproval from his voice.

"We will sell all of them?"

"Yes. All."

"Keep nothing for ourselves?"

"Kola, we can buy shirts cheaper than we can skin and sew them. We'll sell off the hindquarters to the Union Pacific at a dime a pound, just the way that fellow Cody's doing down south on the line's other branch. Further east, we should net a dollar and a quarter for every hide, two bits for every tongue. The people back east want fine quality lap robes and delicacies for dinner. If we don't supply them, others will. We'll have a stake and some profit left over—wait."

Kola saw Joseph's eyes dart past his shoulder. Back toward the rim of the ravine. He knew it must have been a horse he'd heard, because Joseph's eyes were wide as he grabbed for the Laidley-Whitney.

"No!" someone shouted in a loud, rough voice. "You're covered."

Joseph's fingertips hovered an inch from the buffalo gun. Slowly he withdrew his hand. His lips barely moved. "Three of them. Where in the hell did they come from?"

"Nothing personal, y'know," the harsh voice called. "We just want those buffalo. Touch the guns and we'll blow you down."

iii

Joseph surrendered to the thieves without protest. Their leader announced his terms. They would relieve Joseph and Kola of the wagon, the dead buffalo, and the pony, leaving only the mules. Joseph accepted the statements with a resigned shrug. He even agreed to enjoy the hospitality of a cook fire laid at the rim of the ravine by the trio of tattered, foul-smelling white men. When Kola started to protest, Joseph laid a hand on his arm.

"Got to eat, don't we? Might as well be their food as ours."

Kola felt betrayed. He had never seen his friend so resigned—or so uncaring. By the time darkness fell, Joseph and the three other whites were seated around a chip fire in the cooling air—exactly as if they were longtime acquaintances.

To show his pique, Kola squatted several yards away. He was still astonished at the way Joseph had given up their guns and the animals whose sale would have kept them sheltered and fed when the snows drifted on the plains.

Sullen, Kola watched Joseph amiably accept a cup of coffee and a tin plate of beans from the leader of the thieves, a revolver-toting fellow with a cocked eye, a long, untrimmed gray beard, a gray military overcoat that reached below his knees, and a leaf-crowned hat with a five-pointed star cut out of the felt just above the greasy band.

"Thank you," Joseph said as he took the plate. Down in the ravine, the horses belonging to the thieves stamped and fretted. "I'll need something with which to eat."

"Use your hands." The leader smiled from directly across the fire. "I don't think it would be prudent to lend you a knife."

Kola frowned, trying to grasp an elusive thought hovering in his mind. He couldn't.

Joseph's eyes lingered on the leader's weather-beaten face. The leader was the only one of the trio who exhibited any sign of strength or character. The thief seated on Joseph's left was a shivering boy of seventeen or eighteen. He wore a forage cap, a sweat-stained shirt, a blue neck bandana, and a holstered revolver that looked much too large for his frail, nervous hands.

The thief guarding Joseph's right was a stubby man in a ripped blue coat. A gold ring shone in the pierced lobe of his left ear. Quietly, he began singing to himself:

"Oh bury me not in the deep, deep sea,
Where the dark blue waves
Will roll over me—"

"No chanteys, Darlington," the leader said. "If you're going to sing that song, use the prairie words. You keep forgetting you're a landsman now."

"Not by choice, mate." Darlington concentrated on his beans.

The leader shook his head. "Sorry excuses for hands, aren't they?"

Joseph didn't reply. The man with the earring seemed irritated. He limited his protest to a glance. The leader added, "A man takes what he must."

"Including another man's kill," Joseph remarked with a frosty smile. "I'm sorry to say I don't consider than an honorable action, mister—?"

"Major," the older man broke in. "Major T. T. Cutright."

"Southern, aren't you?"

"Yes. I judge the same from your voice. Were you in the war?"

Joseph's lids screened his eyes a moment. Kola thought he saw something secretive glimmer there. But he immediately lost interest. He was still outraged by Joseph's cowardly acquiescence to the demands of the thieves who had ridden up behind them at precisely the wrong moment. As soon as the men were gone, he would separate from his companion. He thought he'd gotten to know him since the spring grass greened. Now he was discovering he hadn't. And Joseph's inner voice had abruptly turned him in a new, unacceptable direction.

"Last with General Hood." Joseph nodded in reply. "You?"

Cutright wiped bean juice from his beard with the sleeve

of his gray overcoat. "I saw service, but I'd prefer not to say where. There was an unfortunate incident."

"What happened?"

"My commander was yellow. When he ordered a retreat, he took a ball in the back of his head. I was accused."

Joseph said nothing. Cutright laid his plate aside, reached for his coffee. "You haven't told me your name, sir."

"Kingston. Joseph Kingston."

Cutright sat up straight. "Kingston?"

"That's right. Something wrong?"

"Not exactly wrong, but—" Cutright looked a bit more wary. "I come from near Fort Worth. I heard of a Joseph Kingston who shot a crooked monte dealer there last winter, then murdered a peace officer who came to arrest him. That Mr. Kingston fled before he could be apprehended. There's a bounty on his head. Two hundred dollars."

Joseph's face took on a curious, stony quality. "I've never been in Fort Worth. Coincidence, undoubtedly."

Cutright uttered a short, wry laugh. "Undoubtedly."

Kola stared at his companion, suddenly struck by something he'd forgotten. It had been stirring in his mind ever since Cutright's reference to a knife. The thieves had taken the three buffalo rifles to add to their own stock of two. But they'd only subjected Joseph to a cursory visual search. They'd completely overlooked the hidden skinning knife.

All at once Kola grew warm. Could the undiscovered knife be the reason for Joseph's apparent cooperation? He fervently hoped so. Despite his bare flesh—he hadn't been permitted to go to the wagon for his shirt and leggings—his entire body felt hot.

Let Joseph be tricking them, he prayed. The meeting when he found me was *wakan,* and the dream afterward told me I would be his *kola,* and he mine, till the end of our lives.

"The wagon down in the wash belongs to you?" Cutright inquired.

"I'm the present owner, yes."

Cutright's cocked eye glowed as he inclined his head in a skeptical way. "Not quite the same thing."

Once more Joseph didn't answer.

"Your friend there. The Indian—"

"Call him what he is, please," Joseph asked quietly. "An Oglala Sioux. His name is Kola. It means special friend."

"Peculiar traveling companion for a white man."

Joseph shrugged again. "I found him on the prairie up north of the Platte. He'd fancied the wife of one of the leaders of an *akicita* society in his tribe. I've learned Sioux don't normally take offense when their wives crawl into the blankets with another man. They just throw the woman out of the tipi and cut off her braids—oh, and once in a while her nose—and that's the divorce. To do much more would give the woman more importance than she deserves. Apparently women don't count for much among the Sioux. Did you know they're even sent to live in special lodges when they bleed once a month? According to Kola, the men believe a woman in her cycle poisons a man's medicine and weapons."

Joseph drank a little coffee. "But as I say, most times a husband takes small notice of infidelity. To do otherwise would be like making a fuss over a dog pissing on the tipi. But there are exceptions to everything. Sweet Summer's husband was an exception. He not only divorced her—he waylaid Kola and thrashed him half to death. I came across him and nursed him back to good health. A dream told him we should ride and hunt together. Kola says the Sioux put great stock in dreams."

"Well," the man with the earring growled, "hope he ain't had too many dreams about sellin' off the buffla to the railroad. Those dreams are at five fathoms now, and don't you forget it."

Cutright frowned. "You needn't act so sour, Darlington. Mr. Kingston's being sensible about his state of affairs." To Joseph: "He ran the engine room on a Federal cruiser during the war. He's accustomed to bossing men around. But he isn't accustomed to the courtesies of the plains. Nor is Timmy there. Timmy's my wife's nephew. These days a man running cattle only gets the kind of help he can afford."

Joseph perked up. "Cattle?" He reached down to scratch his right calf. The bearded Cutright shifted his hand toward his bolstered revolver, but Joseph's smile reassured him. "Just a louse."

He kept on scratching the right side of his calf. "Damn, they're pesky! You were running cattle?"

"Fifty head." Cutright nodded, relaxing again. "The most I could lay my hands on. Seems everyone in Texas is scrambling for longhorns to drive north. The restaurants and butcher shops back east want all the beef they can get."

"I don't see any sign of a herd—"

"No, you don't." Cutright looked glum. "I lost them about fifty miles south. They'd gone too long without drinking, and we came across some damn alkali water. I got my leader, an expensive steer named Crump, started exactly right. If my luck had held, he'd have stampeded them all right past the stuff. But he broke a leg and they went for the water before we could stop them."

"The alkali water poisoned them?"

"Yes, sir, Mr. Kingston, all but one. We've butchered and eaten it since. I should have brought more men with me, but times are hard. Rather than go home empty-handed, I'll now be able to make a little money selling the buffalo to the railroad. It's better than nothing."

"But it's also stealing."

Both Darlington and Cutright scowled. "You're not going to get contentious, are you, Mr. Kingston?" the latter asked. "I've a wife and brood of six back home. They're depending on me. A moment ago, you seemed sensible about the realities of the situation."

"I recognize the realities," Joseph agreed. "I'm just disappointed in a former Confederate officer's doing such a thing."

"Told you." The indifferent blinking of Cutright's good eye put a furrow on Joseph's forehead. "Hard times."

Joseph finally appeared to agree. One more weary shrug only heightened Kola's confusion. Had he been wrong about the skinning knife? If so, he was more determined than ever to abandon his cowardly companion the moment the gray-coated fellow and the others moved on.

Just then—unexpectedly—Joseph turned to glance at him. In the guttering light of the fire his dark eyes were oddly intense.

Kola pursed his lips, frowned, trying to signify he didn't understand whatever Joseph wanted to communicate. Joseph gave up. He turned to Cutright again. "Wonder if I might have leave to stand?"

Cutright chuckled. "Lice still troubling you?"

"Too much coffee's troubling me." He poked a finger into his trousers above his groin. "I'll just step over there." He bobbed his head toward Kola and the starry dark behind him.

"All right," Cutright said "Slowly, though."

He edged back the overcoat so he could reach the butt of his revolver. Six inches to the right of his knee lay the confiscated Laidley-Whitney. Loaded, as Kola recalled.

Smiling, Joseph rose, faced left, took a step, winced, and stopped directly behind the shivering boy wearing the bandana. "Damn!" Joseph cried again, crouching, and slapping his right calf as if another louse had attacked.

Cutright reached for his revolver but checked his hand when he heard the whack of Joseph's palm. He understood why Joseph had moved suddenly.

Seated directly between Joseph and Cutright, the boy started to turn. Joseph didn't straighten. His right hand dropped to his boot.

Cutright shouted, "Damn you, what—? Timmy, your gun!"

The Texas boy juggled the coffee cup from which he'd been sipping and made an ineffectual grab at his holster. Joseph moved with astonishing speed, slipping the skinning knife out of his boot and slashing a six-inch gash in the boy's gun arm with a single continuous stroke.

The boy shrieked and flopped forward, eyes glazing. The contents of the cup splattered the fire and started it hissing and smoking.

"Goddamn deceiving son of a bitch!" Cutright screamed, the same instant Joseph yelled Kola's name.

The cry and the jerk of Joseph's head was signal enough. Overjoyed, Kola ran, leaped, and landed on the white named Darlington. He grappled for Darlington's drawn revolver. Joseph had already launched himself straight across the smoking fire, falling on Cutright with no concern for his feet being in the scorching coals.

The impact jarred Cutright. The revolver in his right hand thundered. Joseph jerked his head aside, just in time to keep from being killed.

Darlington's revolver exploded. Kola felt a rush of air near his shoulder as the bullet spent itself in the dark. Darlington was no match for Kola's strength and renewed faith. Kola clawed Darlington's face with one hand, dug the nails of his other into Darlington's wrist, and the revolver was loose.

Kola threw it away and jumped up. He stomped on Darlington's stomach. The man retched and grabbed his belly, rolling from side to side. Panting, Kola swung around.

Joseph had gotten Cutright's revolver out of his hand. He was standing with his left boot on the Texan's chest.

Cutright's hands were raised. The palms shone with sweat. Grimy fingers quivered. His good eye focused on the revolver Joseph was aiming down at him.

"Lord, Kingston, please don't—"

"Don't do what you planned to do to us?" Joseph's mouth was so thin, it appeared to be no more than a slit. "You don't think I believed your story about letting us go? You said you have a family near Fort Worth. And you'll want to do business up this way again, I presume. You wouldn't want Kola and me turning up to cite you for theft. You were going to kill us before you left."

Cutright's popeyed silence was confession enough. Kola crouched quickly beside the writhing Darlington. But there was no danger. The man was in pain, talking incoherently, and starting to weep.

Joseph remained with one boot on Cutright's chest.

"You're not going to shoot me—?" Cutright breathed. Kola burst out laughing. The Texan sounded like a man beseeching the holy spirits. "You gave up too quickly! You—you don't have the sand."

Joseph's smile was chilly. "I led you on, Major. You thought I didn't have the sand. That was your error and my advantage."

"You *are* the one from Fort Worth," Cutright wheezed. "Got to be."

"The two-hundred-dollar bounty would have been a nice extra profit for you."

"I swear, I didn't plan—"

"Shit. You murdered your commanding officer. Why should I expect better treatment?"

Joseph steadied the revolver and blew a hole between Cutright's eyes.

iv

Before Cutright's body had stopped its violent jerking, Joseph flung the revolver away. He picked up the Laidley-Whitney and motioned Kola back. From across the cook fire, he aimed at the screaming Darlington, who flopped over on his stomach and frantically started to crawl.

The buffalo gun boomed. Darlington skidded three feet forward, an immense hole torn through the clothing covering his backbone. Even Kola, who was accustomed to blood, averted his head.

Joseph laid the buffalo rifle beside Cutright's revolver. He sighed.

"Dishonorable men deserve to be treated in kind. Kola?"

The Sioux turned, momentarily frightened at the sight of his companion standing on the other side of the fire. Joseph resembled some demon risen from swirling smoke and tiny, licking flames.

Truly, Kola thought, this is a warrior to be feared more than any Sioux chieftain. He is so feared, his own kind offer money for his body. This is a great warrior indeed.

Kola couldn't tell whether his companion was saddened by what had occurred, or took pleasure from it. One moment Joseph's expression led Kola to believe the young white man had enjoyed killing the thieves. Then Kola thought he detected regret, or at least uncertainty, as Joseph looked at the moaning boy lying on his side with his head close to the embers. The boy's hair was smoldering.

"Pull the boy out before he burns to death. That hair stinks to hell."

Kola hurried to obey.

"Sit him up," Joseph instructed. "Slap him some."

Joseph watched impassively as Kola propped the boy up and smacked his face several times. Groggy with pain, the boy finally opened his eyes. He recognized Joseph and Kola, then saw the bodies of his uncle and Darlington.

"Oh, my Lord!" He sounded sick as he seized his blood-soaked arm.

"No complaints," Joseph said. "You took your chances when you threw in with those two. You'd have stood by while they shot us. Probably even pulled a trigger yourself. Stand up."

Aghast, the boy exclaimed, "I'm bleeding to death!"

"Maybe. Maybe not. You'll find out after you've walked twenty or thirty miles."

"I can't walk!"

Joseph shrugged. "Your choice. Pitch me the knife, Kola."

"No, no, I'll go." The boy weaved to his feet.

"South," Joseph instructed. "If I ever see you north of the Republican River, you'll be dead for sure."

Red seeped between the fingers with which the boy clutched his arm. He glanced at Cutright again, then blazed, "You damn murderer! You could have left him alive!"

"Impossible."

"How can you kill like that?"

"I had excellent training, directed by Mr. Jefferson Davis. After you kill one or two, the others come easy. Now you better get out of here before I change my mind."

"I'll remember your name, Kingston. Swear to God. I'll remember it to the hour I die."

Joseph laughed. "Save yourself the trouble. By the time you're planted, I'll have had a peck of names."

"Someone'll find you."

"Someone will find *you,* stone-cold stiff, if you don't start walking."

"I need food and water."

"No."

"At least a bandage!"

"All you get from me is a chance to save your conniving hide. That's more than you deserve. Now *walk!*"

The boy started off, wincing with every laborious step.

"Wrong way!" Joseph barked. "*That's* south."

Like a sleepwalker, the boy stumbled in an erratic half-circle and lurched in the right direction. Joseph watched until he was lost on the dark prairie.

Joseph jerked off his low-crowned hat and busily fanned himself, drying sweat that shone like grease on his forehead. The white man's next remark was intended to be conversational but had a strained quality.

"Now we can go ahead and take the buffalo up to the railroad. We're also three horses to the good. I'd call it a passable day's work."

Saying that, he turned away. But not before he astonished Kola with a sad, almost grief-stricken glance. With his back toward the Sioux, he added, "A man should know better than to do a dishonorable thing like stealing another man's kill. *He should know better!*"

There was no regret in the last few words. Only anger.

Kola overcame the piercing fright produced by Joseph's unexpected ferocity. He realized again that he would never understand the man's unfathomable nature. But outwardly—ah, outwardly, Joseph was a *kola* of whom he could be eternally proud.

He let his awe and pride drive a yell of joy out of his throat. He circled the fire, stood over Cutright's body, and raised his clout, exposing his genitals to the dead man's staring eyes—his people's ultimate insult to a vanquished and contemptible enemy.

Joseph walked back to his coffee cup and picked it up. Before drinking he said in a casual way, "We don't need to waste time disposing of them. The turkey buzzards will do it in a day or two. Besides, they don't deserve decent burial."

He tossed his head back and drank. A spurt of fire in the thinning smoke reddened the streak of white hair that began at his hairline over his left brow and tapered to a point at the back of his head.

★ Book Four ★

Hell-on-Wheels

Chapter I

The Cheyenne

i

Michael Boyle had seldom experienced the kind of consuming fright he felt during those first moments when he stood rooted on the summit of the low hill, trying to decide whether to run and attempt to warn the railhead. It was worse than the fear he'd suffered charging enemy lines with the Irish Brigade. At least with the Brigade, there had been others around him sharing the peril.

He was most conscious of the weapons arrayed against him. The short hunting bows. The quivers bristling with arrows. The knives. The war hatchets with shafts wrapped in bright red cloth and metal heads, not stone.

The knife blades and hatchet heads meant the weapons were trade goods, factory made. The Cheyenne—if that was indeed what they were—had either bargained for them at forts or stolen them in raids.

He saw no revolvers or rifles. But he understood Plains Indians owned few of those. Firearms which the Indians did manage to acquire were carefully guarded and used only on hunts or important forays against enemy tribes. It was a small, hopeful sign.

He licked at sweat on his upper lip. The warriors remained motionless, watching. The feathers in their sunlit black hair bobbed in the breeze.

The Indian holding Ruffin—the one with the immense bare belly—kept staring too. A hint of a smile appeared on the man's thick-lipped mouth. But the eight-foot bow lance was rock steady. If Michael responded wrongly, or acted precipitously, the iron head would pierce Ruffin's throat in an instant.

One by one, other details registered. On all the calico ponies, plaited horsehair was looped and knotted around the lower jaws to create both bit and bridle from a single long strand. Quirts held by muscular hands rested against naked thighs. The quirts resembled miniature whips—three thongs of rawhide attached to a carved round of wood heavy enough to deal a man a crippling blow.

About two-thirds of the Indians rode bareback. The rest, including Fatbelly, had hide saddles, little more than beaded pads. The leader's gear also included a blanket under the saddle, beaded bright yellow and red. Fringes hung from each corner of the square.

The big-bellied Indian bore scars on his shoulders and had pendulous breasts. The scars were in pairs. Michael recalled hearing a Paddy describe rituals in which Plains Indians pledged their lives to the protection of their people—and the annihilation of their foes—and shed blood in self-mortification as proof of their intent. The scars as well as the leader's air of authority said he was the one with whom Michael had to deal.

Weary of Michael's hesitation, Fatbelly gigged the lance head deeper into Tom Ruffin's neck. A line of blood trickled. Ruffin's legs thrashed. Above the clasping hand, the boy's eyes pleaded with Michael.

Fatbelly raised his eyebrows. His forehead creased like a wrinkled hide. The lift of the brows asked an unmistakable question: *What will you do?*

ii

Michael had no idea—except that he'd decided not to run and abandon Ruffin. In a voice as steady as he could manage, he asked, "Do you talk English?"

Half a dozen of the braves—all in their twenties—snickered and whispered among themselves. One let out a low but frightening whoop, then spat over the ears of his pony. The fat-bellied Indian whipped the lance to the right, then thrust it over his head. The young men laughing at Michael fell silent. The smirks disappeared.

Fatbelly grinned in a disarmingly friendly way. Michael wasn't deceived. It would be foolish to trust the Indian—or regard him as a weakling because of his age, or his flabby breasts and stomach. The rest of him looked hard. The act of raising the lance had tightened huge muscles in his upper arm.

The Indian's smile grew wider, revealing brown gums studded with broken teeth. He nodded in a vigorous way.

"English," he said, garbling it so that it came out *Anglish.* The thumb of the hand holding the lance straightened, pointing at the Indian's chest. "English!" There was an almost childlike quality about the declaration.

When the Indian continued, he mauled the pronunciation of nearly every word. "I have traded at white forts. But we are not Laramie Loafers—"

Some of the others understood and growled agreement.

"We do not come to bring war. We like black coffee that is sweet. We want to see the fire road you are making. No war, only see."

He widened his eyes, blinking several times. The illustration almost made Michael laugh, not in derision but genuine amusement. The fat-bellied man almost resembled a small boy—except for that bow lance he'd quietly shifted back to Ruffin's throat.

"We friends." It came out *frans.* "No war. Just coffee." More blinking. "Just look."

Amusing as the Indian's enthusiastic declaration was, Michael remained wary. He'd heard tales of braves who had ridden up to a government fort to trade with perfect cordiality one day, only to return the next and launch a vicious attack. They were unpredictable as the plains weather, Casement claimed. So he didn't put much stock in Fatbelly's assertions. Though his heart was beating less rapidly, Michael kept a frown on his face.

"Very well. If you're friendly—"

Fatbelly's nod was again impatient. "Friends. *Friends!*"

"Then put the boy down."

The Indian cocked his head, acting baffled. Michael suspected the man understood more than he let on.

Michael resorted to gestures. A finger at the boy, ther at the buffalo grass.

"*Down.* Let him go. Don't hurt him."

The Indian pondered. Shook his head. "You are many We are few. We keep him till we see the fire road and ge coffee. Then we let go. Is not wise to believe all you white say. You say friends, then you turn many guns against us."

Something ugly flickered in the man's eyes. His smil disappeared.

"Two summers ago it was so when Black Kettle campe at Sand Creek."

Michael winced; he knew the infamous reference.

In the autumn of '64, Indian raids in the Colorado territory had resulted in the organization of a Denver-base military unit of six hundred white men. The men—mostl riffraff—had been commanded by a fanatic Army office named Chivington, who also happened to be an ordaine Methodist minister. Chivington led his men to a nearb Cheyenne encampment.

Though not responsible for the raids, the inhabitants o the camp—Black Kettle's people—had feared reprisal an sought sanctuary from rising anti-Indian sentiment. Th Army had proposed Sand Creek as safe territory. Blac Kettle had moved there, even raising the Stars and Stripe on a pole—and then he'd watched Chivington's regimen of ruffians ride in. For three or four hours, the whites ha galloped back and forth, smashing tipis and butcherin close to fifty braves, women, and children.

"I had a sister there," Fatbelly said. "Sister?"

Michael nodded to signify comprehension.

"She never stole cows, never cut talking wires"—a sta of the lance toward the telegraph poles across the Platte— "but her hair was taken. This hair"—the lance lifted t touch his head—"this hair too." He lowered the lance t his groin. "It was held up in a large place for whites wh laughed."

Michael had no answer to satisfy the Indian's anger. H knew scalps of Cheyenne children and the pubic hair o

Cheyenne women had indeed been paraded on the stage of at least one Denver theater following Chivington's raid.

Michael was no expert on the confused policies and operations of the Army in the West. But he did know officers assigned to the troubled territory during the war had generally been incompetents. The best men had been assigned to the Union forces pitted against the Confederacy.

With men of poor quality in charge on the plains, it was no wonder decisions were poor as well. Such men didn't believe it necessary to locate and punish the Indians actually responsible for a given act of murder or arson. For effective control of what was termed the Indian problem, punishment of any Indian would do. Fatbelly's sister had evidently been one of the innocents who suffered from such witless retaliation.

"No," the Indian grumbled, tightening his hand over Ruffin's purpling face. The boy's eyes bulged. He looked ready to expire for lack of breath. "We let this one go if we find no war. We let go after we drink coffee!"

The finality of it convinced Michael he'd better postpone further argument. He'd shaped a strategy for handling the situation, but before he had a chance to implement it, Fatbelly barked at him again.

"Are you the fire-road boss?"

Michael shook his head. "I only lay track."

The Indian didn't understand.

"I work. *Work.*" Michael flexed his hands. Pantomimed lifting something. The Indian grunted.

"My name—" Was that an unfamiliar word? Dry-lipped, he began again. "I"—a finger to his chest—"I am called Boyle." He repeated it.

"Bile." Fatbelly nodded. "I am—"

A rush of gibberish. Michael kept shaking his head. Finally the Indian went back to English.

"Guns Taken."

"Ah. Guns Taken." Michael's bobbing head indicated his comprehension.

The Cheyenne's grin returned. "Took three guns when I was ten summers. Three! From a white fort. I rode away fleet as the wind before they could close the gates and catch my pony. I was honored and became Guns Taken instead of Dog Barks, the name I was given at the hour my mother bore me."

There was enormous pride in the statements and the broad smile accompanying them. The innocence of the declaration relieved Michael's anxiety a bit. Almost made him like the fellow, in fact.

But it was dangerous to be lulled. Casement insisted the Plains Indians were not the primitive simpletons too many whites made them out to be. The Sioux and Cheyenne could be cunning. And volatile.

"Three *big* guns!" the Indian bellowed.

Michael nodded hastily. "Yes, yes, I understand." Evidently he hadn't acted sufficiently impressed. His failure wiped the smile from the Indian's face. Guns Taken thrust his lance at Michael.

"We go to the fire road. Now."

Knees pressing against his pony, the warrior started forward. Michael held up his hands.

"Wait."

He pushed his palms toward the Indian. Guns Taken's scowl deepened. Michael swallowed, wondering whether the man would fling his lance.

"Let me go first," Michael told him, mixing improvised pantomime with the words. "You stay here while I go ahead—ahead—so there will be no angry men. Let me speak to the boss of the fire road. It may take me a little while, so don't be alarmed. I promise to tell him you are not here for war. Then he will make you welcome."

Guns Taken shook his head hard. Michael's meaning was either unclear or the Cheyenne was again pretending. Tense, Michael went through it twice more, finally making the Indian understand he would precede the party and take whatever time was required to assure there was no trouble. He was not only concerned about Tom Ruffin's safety, but anxious for Jack Casement to get the men at the railhead firmly under control before the Indians appeared. He hoped he was doing the right thing.

Turning his pony, Guns Taken addressed the young men in his band. The Cheyenne spoke a swift flow of words Michael couldn't fathom. But gestures and expressions left no doubt about some of the reactions:

Complaints. Angry protests. Guns Taken silenced his braves with repeated shouts.

A couple of the Indians let Michael take the brunt of their displeasure. The ferocity of their glances made him shiver.

But Guns Taken was in command. Michael was again encouraged when the big Indian walked his pony forward three steps and gave a final nod.

"You go. The boy stays till the fire-road boss says come in."

"No. I want the boy." With both hands he motioned to Ruffin, then the grass. "Let him down."

"You *go!* Boy stays." The dark eyes shone with a sad cynicism. "Then there will be no guns fired to greet us. If there are guns fired, Bile"—the smile reappeared, but it had a terrifying lack of humor; the Cheyenne pricked Tom Ruffin's neck a second time—"the boy is yours. Dead."

The bargain was clear. *Jesus,* Michael thought, *why me in the middle of this?*

All the Cheyenne began to jabber, waving at him, impatient for him to leave. Guns Taken thrust the bow lance at him a second time.

"Too much talk already! We thirst for coffee. *You find boss!*"

Michael started off, then paused. "Tom?"

Guns Taken uncovered Ruffin's mouth. In a surprisingly calm voice, the boy replied, "What, sir?"

"Keep still and they won't hurt you. I'll be back soon."

Even with Guns Taken's hand clasping his face again, Ruffin managed a nod. The Irishman turned his back, crossed the summit of the low hill and broke into a run going down the slope. Despite Tom Ruffin's grit, Michael wondered if he'd see the boy alive again.

CHAPTER II

ARMED CAMP

i

MICHAEL RAN with all his strength, plunging through the thick buffalo grass along the river. Sweat began to flick off his forehead.

He sped by the spot where he'd dropped his clothing and drew abreast of the first group of naked bathers laughing and enjoying a water fight. Wigwagging his arms, he yelled, "Back to the train! There are Indians yonder. They have Tom Ruffin."

Up to his knobby knees in the water, Liam O'Dey scratched his testicles. "Ah, Michael Boyle, let's have none of your feeble jokes this morning."

Michael shook a fist. "It's no damn joke! I talked to them. If you stay here, the boy's liable to be murdered. Get moving!"

He spun and dashed on while O'Dey and his companions clambered up the bank for their clothes.

He stopped to warn three more groups, and sent a man from the last one running on down the river to summon in the others—a good hundred or so, strung out in the shallows for at least a mile to the east. Michael himself angled toward the perpetual train, waving his arms frantically again.

Osceola was pulling out. Armed men clinging to the sides of the locomotive and tender saw him coming. One poked his head into the cab. The engine stopped with a squeal and spurting of steam.

Michael went pounding around the edge of the beef herd. The disturbed animals began to low. Michael's shouts and arm waving brought two of the drovers charging at him. One brandished a long stick.

"Quit yer damn yellin' or ye'll stampede 'em."

"Indians!" Michael yelled, pointing west. The drover turned pale and crossed himself.

As Michael rushed on, noisy, half-naked men started streaming toward the train from points all along the bank. He reached the office car, vaulted up the steps two at a time, and ran along the narrow corridor. The door of Casement's cubicle stood ajar. Michael heard a voice he recognized.

"Either I get my job back from that mick, or I won't be responsible for what happens to—"

A bull-voiced Casement broke in. "You *will* be responsible or I'll ship you back to Omaha under guard, Worthing!"

Michael kicked the door open and grabbed the jamb with both hands, too upset to worry about the presence of the Virginian. Worthing pivoted toward him. His face was puffy and discolored. His left eye had swollen shut.

"Well!" he said in a nasty way. "The very mick under discussion."

ii

Casement ignored him, eyes on Michael's sweaty face. Michael gulped air. He couldn't seem to get enough.

"What the hell's wrong, Boyle?"

"We have visitors, General. About a mile west. Thirty Indians. Cheyenne, I think."

"Merciful God!" Casement breathed. "That's all we need."

"Pity they didn't lift your fucking hair," Worthing said,

touching a knuckle to the bloated yellow-blue mass of his left cheek.

"Let him talk!" Casement said. "You saw the Indians yourself?"

"I did. I had conversation with them. The head man speaks passable English. They captured Tom Ruffin. The boy had gone off to catch a grouse—"

In a few sentences he explained what had happened. At the end, Worthing gaped. "You mean to say you let a pack of filthy savages hang on to the boy while you turned tail?"

Red-faced, Michael snarled, "The leader had a lance this long"—he flung his arms wide—"square in Ruffin's neck. The head man said they don't want a fight, General Jack. Just sugared coffee and a look at the equipment. I said I'd come on ahead and guarantee there'd be no trouble. We won't get Ruffin back safely any other way."

"Ah, God," Worthing sighed. "I'd have *taken* him back."

Casement stamped over in front of the Virginian. Though the top of the construction chief's head only reached Worthing's chin, his anger was sufficient to intimidate the Virginian.

"One more word and I'll have you locked up."

The ex-Confederate's open eye glared. Michael heard men piling into the corridor, asking questions and calling for Spencers from the sleeping cars. Casement gestured.

"Shut the door."

Michael did.

"Now tell me. Do you think the hostiles were lying? Do they want their blasted coffee—or a scrap?"

Weary, Michael leaned against the wall and rubbed at the sweat on his belly.

"Hell, General, I'm no student of red men. One minute, the leader—his name's Guns Taken—struck me as a straight-out sort. Then I'd get a feeling he was saying one thing and thinking another. I can't honestly tell you whether they've come like children to a candy store, or are just pretending."

"A little of both, maybe," Casement said. "The fools in the Indian Bureau always make the mistake of thinking we're up against savages out here. That was your word, wasn't it, Worthing? Savages?"

Worthing seethed in silence as Casement went on.

"But they aren't savages. They've a society hundreds of years older than ours—and most are smarter than many an Army officer I've met. You won't see a Sioux or Cheyenne risking twenty men to rustle half a dozen cows, but some Army lieutenants would commit three companies to save one government heifer." Agitated, he tugged at his beard. "How are they armed? Any muskets or rifles?"

"None that I saw. They're carrying knives, hatchets, bows—and the head man has that devilish lance. It's all tricked up with feathers and a string for firing arrows."

Casement muttered a despairing obscenity. "Then he's a Bowstring. If so, they *are* Cheyenne." Noticing Michael's puzzled look, Casement explained, "The bow lance is a characteristic of the Bowstrings, one of the Cheyenne warrior societies. It means the leader's no boy on a lark, but a man to be reckoned with. Did he harm Ruffin?"

"Gigged his neck and drew a little blood. More for my benefit than anything else, I think. But he said he'd kill the boy if there were any traps when he came in."

Casement turned away and pondered, palms resting on his cluttered desk. Finally his head snapped up.

"All right. The boy counts most. We'll pull every man off the engine, and issue a limited number of rifles. You go to the cooks, Boyle. Have them start brewing coffee. Gallons of the stuff. Pour on the sugar."

Worthing couldn't believe it. "You'll *permit* them to ride in here?"

"Exactly. I'll not truckle to them, nor let them think we're weaklings. That's why I want some Spencers in sight. But neither will I incite them."

"Jesus." Worthing still looked thunderstruck. "Our herd's been hit how many times? Three? Four?"

"We have lost animals, not men."

"But we should show 'em they can't get away with it!"

Casement shook his head. "We don't know whether these Indians are the same ones who stole our stock. To punish them as if they were is not only wrong—it's foolhardy. I'm not even considering Ruffin when I say that. Punishing the wrong Indians is the mistake Chivington made at Sand Creek. It's the same mistake the goddamn Army makes every day of the week. It's one big reason the trouble never stops!"

"This Guns Taken," Michael put in, "he claims he lost a sister at Sand Creek."

Casement groaned. "Then we've double the worry. They're not only Cheyenne, but Cheyenne with a grudge."

"What fucking difference does it make if they're not the ones who drove off the stock?" Worthing fumed. "They'll see the beeves and be back to help themselves. I say stop 'em ahead of time!"

"Oh," Casement murmured, "you subscribe to the theory that all of their kind should be wiped out, do you?"

"As long as a single one causes trouble, yes!"

"Worthing, you're an ignoramus. *We're* the intruders. We're deep into the tribal buffalo grounds—the Republican herd's one of the largest in the West. They see the buffalo being shot by white men; they see their land being cut up by these tracks; they see innocent members of their race being punished for the depredations of guilty ones—I'll not compound the problems already created and risk losing men and time!"

Worthing stormed toward the door. "This is the goddamnedest outfit of yellowbellies I've ever seen. I'm going to get a Spencer and wait for—"

Michael was bowled aside as Casement lunged and fastened his hands on Worthing's gray duster. Before the taller man could react, Casement hurled him against the cubicle's outer wall. The planking vibrated.

Casement rose on tiptoe, cheeks red as his quivering beard.

"Captain Worthing, you have taxed my patience to the limit." A shake of the man's lapels. "*To the limit!* You lost the damned war, and I am sick to death of your trying to win it all over again by besting every man who strays across your path!"

Worthing's hands clenched. For a moment Michael was certain there'd be a fight. Then he recalled that the Southerner liked odds favorable to himself. But Worthing did fire a verbal salvo.

"I'll settle with you for this, Casement. You and the mick both. Count on it."

"I already received that message," Michael said. "In my bunk."

Releasing the Virginian, Casement missed the glance of

venomous understanding between the other two. The construction boss wiped his hands on his thighs, as if he'd touched something unclean. He jerked the door open and confronted a press of men who bombarded him with questions.

"What's this about Injuns, Gen'ral?"

"Heard they got the Ruffin boy."

"A hundred of the heathen, someone said."

"Lads are breakin' out the Spencers—"

"You"—Casement grabbed the nearest man—"go through the sleeping cars and issue a direct order from me. Twenty rifles out—no more! Have the gang bosses distribute them to men they can trust to keep their heads. The Indians may mean no harm."

Michael saw doubtful expressions as well as frightened ones. He was conscious of Worthing staring at him but didn't turn his head.

"At least they say they don't. They merely want coffee and a chance to examine our equipment. We'll take them at their word until they prove we shouldn't. You, and you"—Casement singled out three more men—"you boys escort Captain Worthing to his car and keep him there."

Worthing began to swear. Casement paid no attention.

"Sit on him. Tie him. Bash his head in—I don't care. But he's not to be allowed outside or permitted to place his hands on a weapon. I'll not let one hothead bloody this whole camp."

"Come on, Reb," one of the appointed men said as the others closed in. "You just been to Appomattox all over again."

The cursing Virginian was manhandled out of sight. Michael wished Worthing's guards weren't so eager to show how much they disliked him—or so free with taunts about the South's defeat. They might only make the Virginian angrier and more reckless.

Casement began dispatching other men to round up the workers and have them assemble on the north side of the last sleeping car, where they would be hidden from any watchers Guns Taken might have sent to the hilltop. Michael worked his way along the packed corridor to the kitchen and called for fresh coffee from the startled cooks.

Within five minutes he was outside, and Jack Casement

was preparing to address the growing throng around the steps of the bunk car.

iii

Michael stood toward the rear of the crowd. Above the clamor of voices, he heard someone call his name.

He turned. Hannah Dorn was hurrying toward him, bundled in her shapeless coat. The floppy hat concealed her bright hair.

Her brother Klaus was with her, carrying his rifle. Then Dorn appeared from behind the wagon, buttoning his fly and belching. He looked unsteady on his feet. He too had his Hawken.

"Mr. Boyle—" Hannah touched Michael's arm. In the band of shadow cast by the hat brim, her eyes widened in surprise and embarrassment.

It took her a moment to recover and ask, "What's the difficulty?"

"Surprise guests. Thirty Cheyenne—down there behind those hills. They've captured one of the lorry car boys, and—hold on." As he said the last words, he unconsciously reached across with his right hand and squeezed her forearm.

Then he too was struck by a realization that he was being overly familiar. He jerked his hand away.

Their eyes met again. He felt just as chagrined as she'd been a moment ago. Very nearly stammering, he added, "Casement—Casement will explain."

The construction boss spoke in a loud voice. At the announcement of the presence of Indians—the rumor verified—there were exclamations of astonishment and alarm. At scattered spots in the crowd, a Paddy demanded the intruders be met with volleys from the stored rifles. Casement shouted them down.

"Absolutely not! There'll be no shooting unless I give the command. They have Ruffin, and they may honestly mean us no harm."

"But, General, we outnumber 'em!"

"That would be no consolation to any man killed or maimed in an unnecessary fight. Of course we outnumber them. We could storm out there and drive them off. But I doubt we'd see Ruffin with his scalp again."

Nervously, Michael glanced toward the blowing buffalo grass on the line of hills. Perhaps the Cheyenne were gone and Tom Ruffin was already dead. Contradictory images of Guns Taken flitted in his mind. He saw a guileless child, then a sly trickster. Which was the true picture?

He forced his attention back to Casement.

"We'll remain calm, keep all but twenty rifles out of sight, see exactly what they want, and hope they'll depart peaceably when they get it."

"You know what they want!" a voice burst out behind Michael. Hannah Dorn closed her eyes before she swung to look at Gustav Dorn.

Hannah started working her way toward him. "Papa, please. Let General Casement run things."

Even from eight feet away, Michael smelled the whiskey on the unkempt merchant. Dorn weaved on his feet as he flourished his rifle.

"You got shit in your head, Casement! It's more than coffee the red devils are after. It's guns! It's liquor—" He brought the Hawken up to his chest. "Sons of bitches touch my whiskey, I blow their heads off. You touch this gun, I do the same for you."

iv

"Papa, that won't help," Hannah pleaded. She took hold of the Hawken. "Put it down."

"Damn woman—*let go!*" Spit flecked Dorn's lips as he wrenched the rifle out of Hannah's grip. Michael felt a spurt of anger, started for Dorn.

Casement yelled, "Take that rifle away from him!"

Dorn began to back up, putting the Hawken on cock. A sharp intake of breath came from Michael's left—from Sean Murphy. Several Paddies scuttled aside, out of range of the weaving muzzle.

Licking at the corner of his mouth, Dorn dropped into a crouch.

"Nobody takes it. First who tries, I shoot."

"Dorn?"

The merchant swung toward Michael. The Hawken's barrel steadied, aimed at the younger man's belly.

"What's your two cents, Paddy?"

Michael extended his hand. "Give it up before you're hurt. The boy's life is more important than your liquor."

"Paddy, you stay away from me. I got a big ball ready for you if you don't—"

Michael took three more steps—a yard closer to the German—before he halted. He wiped his mouth. "Be reasonable, Dorn."

"You come on," Dorn interrupted, wiggling the Hawken. "You come right on, Mr. Mick. As soon as you walk one step more, I shoot your goddamn thick head to pieces—*ahh!*"

He squealed as Hannah's fingers shot in from behind and clamped on his neck. She'd gone creeping around his flank while his attention was fixed on Michael.

Dorn lunged to the side, seized the Hawken's muzzle, and swung blindly. The stock slammed Hannah's jaw. *Jesus, it could go off!* Michael thought as the girl stumbled, her hat tumbling from her head. Bent low, he ran at the German.

He ripped the Hawken from Dorn's fingers and tossed it to a man who juggled it as if it were a poisonous snake. Dorn aimed a clumsy punch at Michael's midriff. Michael jerked his belly back out of the way and used his longer reach to seize Dorn's ears. He yanked, hard.

Dorn staggered, shrieking obscenities. Men encircled him. Michael retrieved the Hawken and uncocked it. He noticed Sean Murphy had slipped up to the bewildered Klaus and relieved him of his rifle. He reached down to help Hannah to her feet.

"I'm sorry I provoked him. I'm sorry he hurt you."

"Oh—" Tears filled her eyes. Ashamed, she spun so he couldn't see. She snatched up her hat and whispered, "What does one more time matter?"

Her grief hurt him too, somehow. He wanted to reach out to her, comfort her.

Dorn thrashed and yelped as more men surrounded him. Michael wondered how Hannah Dorn's faith could withstand her father's behavior. All she believed seemed negated and made a mockery by the merchant's pathetic yet potentially lethal rage.

Almost ready to walk to her and risk humiliating her further by making her look at him, Michael was prevented by Casement calling for attention.

V

"Now that we seem to have things in hand, let's try to get through the remainder of the day without any casualties. It's up to you men—each and every one. I want no Indian Bureau commissioners descending on us to ask why we harmed innocent visitors."

If indeed they're innocent, Michael thought.

"I want to write no reports to General Dodge and the directors of the line, and more important, no letters to wives or sweethearts explaining how a good worker was needlessly slain."

There were still a few grumbles about Casement's lack of nerve. But most of the rust eaters agreed with Michael's silent assessment: It took more courage for Casement to exercise restraint than it did to indulge the kind of hostility that made Dorn and Worthing such threats. General Jack's forceful voice overrode the last muttered objections.

"Our job is to save Ruffin, then lay track and reach the hundredth meridian as fast as we can. Remember that!"

Except for Dorn cursing among his captors, the crowd was still.

"Boyle?"

"Here, sir."

"Go tell the Indians to come in."

"Right away, General."

"And, Boyle—"

Michael turned back. Three gang bosses had appeared behind Casement. All three had a pair of Spencers in each hand, and several of the tubular butt magazines in their belts. Casement indicated the weapons.

"Do you want one?"

Michael almost answered yes. He would have felt far safer. But he thought of Tom Ruffin. The sight of a rifle might provoke an impulsive stab of that bow lance. One thrust was all it would take to kill the boy.

"No, I'd better go without."

Casement nodded, a thin smile relieving the severity of his mouth for a moment.

Heart hammering, Michael set off along a lane that opened in the crowd. The men had fallen so silent he could hear the whine of the prairie wind and the hiss of steam from *Osceola.*

Chapter III
The Race

i

Twenty minutes later, Michael returned to the railhead, a pale but unhurt Tom Ruffin by his side. Behind them, riding single file with Guns Taken leading the procession, came the Cheyenne.

Virtually every worker had turned out to watch. Hundreds of Paddies stood or sat in small groups. A few looked openly hostile, others anxious. But the majority were merely curious.

Approaching the finished track west of the perpetual train, Michael searched for the seven-shot repeating rifles distributed while he was gone. He spied the first two with the stock drovers. A wise precaution, he decided when he heard a burst of Indian talk. He turned to see a young brave point to the cattle and make a smirking comment to the rider behind. On the faces of several of the Cheyenne he saw undisguised envy.

His eyes moved back to the train. Most of the workers had gathered along the north side. He noticed one man still relaxing in a hammock slung beneath a sleeping car. No, not precisely relaxing—the barrel of a Spencer was visible.

Two men lounged beside their tent on the car's roof. The

mellow sunlight of the mare's-tail sky set the barrel of another Spencer flashing.

The man holding the repeater shifted position. The flare of light vanished. But not before Guns Taken and his braves took note.

Closer scrutiny showed Michael the location of other rifles. Casement had arranged things well. The Spencers were inconspicuous but not invisible. The unarmed workers were aware of the guns. In front of a Paddy with a rifle in the crook of his arm, Liam O'Dey sweated and fiddled with his holy beads.

Casement came striding around the end of the nearest boxcar. He too carried a rifle, and had buckled on a holstered Colt. He stopped on the track, his red beard snapping in the breeze.

Along the north side of the train, Michael heard swearing. He craned to see the source—two cooks hurriedly setting planks on a couple of barrels. A third man came scrambling down from the kitchen, rag-wrapped hands gripping the bail of a huge enamel pot trailing steam from its spout.

Casement's eyes darted to the boy at Michael's side. "He's fine, sir," Michael said quickly. "Guns Taken kept his word."

The track boss nodded and gazed past him as the procession halted. Guns Taken dismounted and walked forward with bow lance in hand. His bare stomach quivered. Though the Indian was more than a little bowlegged and his huge melon of a belly looked soft, Jack Casement didn't relax.

Guns Taken stopped a foot from the construction boss. The Cheyenne's six-foot height and Casement's shortness presented a curiously comic picture. Guns Taken peered down at the smaller man with a guarded smile Casement didn't return.

Casement made the peace sign with his free hand. Guns Taken replied using the identical gesture. Casement's hand began to dart, point, describe fluid curves.

After a minute of the sign talk Michael didn't understand, Casement dropped his hand to his side. Guns Taken grunted in a way that seemed to signify satisfaction. Michael scanned the crowd again, finally located Hannah

Dorn, her father and brother among a half-dozen men near the whiskey wagon.

Dorn appeared as truculent as ever. Three of those close to him carried Spencers. No accident, that grouping. Michael hoped the men guarding Leonidas Worthing were equally alert and well armed.

Again Casement spoke with his hand. Guns Taken answered, "Yes, English. Talk English if you want. We are friends. Come only to watch how you build the fire road. Watch and drink sweet coffee."

Casement hoisted a thumb over his shoulder. "It's ready. Our present to you. We welcome a peaceful visit."

"First"—Guns Taken cocked his bow lance toward a rail—"show how these are put in the earth."

"No." Casement shook his head. "No, we are not working today."

Guns Taken didn't like that. He chattered to his warriors. Several scowled and grumbled. Michael saw hands tighten on quirts or reach toward knives. Casement saw it too. He spoke firmly to recapture the attention of the leader.

"This is a holy day for my men. A day of rest. They pray to God"—his swift-moving hand amplified the explanation—"drink coffee. Sleep. Tend their clothing. Some ride the fire horse up and down the track—"

Guns Taken failed to understand the last word until Casement's finger indicated the same rail to which the Indian had pointed.

"Track."

"Uh. Track!"

"But there is no work on it today."

Guns Taken accepted the fact grudgingly. "All right. Give us the coffee. Show us the fire horse."

Casement turned slightly. "Come this way."

The big Cheyenne didn't move. Back along the train, Michael noticed the photographer, Stackpole, readying his camera and black cloth with slow, cautious movements. Guns Taken glanced at the motionless workers. The small clusters looked almost posed. The Indian couldn't miss the rifles.

Michael thought the tall Indian's eyes lingered a moment on the whiskey wagon. *Lord, he can't read what's painted on the barrels, can he?*

Abruptly, the Indian stabbed the head of his bow lance into the fill between two ties. "Too many guns here."

"Not to harm you," Casement assured him. "Out here we must carry guns for our own safety. We have been raided at night. Cattle have been stolen—"

"We steal no cattle!"

"I am not saying you do." Casement's jaw thrust out. A touch of pugnacity sharpened his tone. "I have no way of knowing, however."

That displeased the big man. "Others. *Others!*"

"Very well, I believe you speak the truth," Casement replied, emphasizing it with more gestures. His hand kept moving as he started for the train. "Let there be peace while you examine—uh, see—the fire road. Come. Drink and see."

Guns Taken spent a few more seconds weighing the advisability of accompanying Casement to the side of the train where so many men were gathered. Some were still half undressed from their swim.

The Indian drew a deep breath, appearing to stretch himself an inch or two in the process. He looked not only taller but regal. His bearing was a declaration that he felt no fear among so many whites.

Moving with impressive grace, he returned to his pony and leaped onto its back in a surprisingly agile fashion. He raised the lance above his head. Still in single file, the Cheyenne began to walk their calicos toward the train.

Casement stood aside and beckoned Michael. The construction boss slipped the Colt from his holster, pressed it into Michael's hand and said in a low voice, "Stay with me. You're one of the few I can trust to keep a level head. I assume you know how to use one of these?"

Guns Taken rode by. His shadow flitted across Casement's face. The Cheyenne gazed straight ahead, not bothering to acknowledge the two white men.

"Yes, I've gone out on the engine pinking at rabbits once or twice."

"Let's hope there'll be no need for you to pink at anything else."

ii

At the improvised coffee station, the cooks were busy filling tin cups. Stackpole approached with his tripod over his shoulder. He asked permission to take a photograph. The Cheyenne jabbered excitedly and shook their fists at the black-shrouded box.

"You've seen a camera?" Casement asked.

"At forts." Guns Taken nodded. "It is the box-which-steals-the-spirit. A part of a man is drawn into it and held captive there forever."

Casement controlled a smile. "Very well, no photographs." He ordered the camera removed by the crestfallen Mr. Stackpole.

Then he called on three workers to come forward and help him distribute coffee to the still-mounted guests. The Indians gulped the contents of the cups with lip-smacking pleasure. Michael eyed the group beside the whiskey wagon. Dorn was talking and gesturing, obviously resentful the Cheyenne were being so royally treated.

Guns Taken drained his cup. His bow lance rested across his thighs. He thrust the cup down at Casement in an arrogant way.

Obviously irked, the construction boss nevertheless took the cup, had it refilled, and brought it back. Guns Taken drank every drop, then flung the cup on the ground.

"The fire horse!"

A bit testily, Casement said, "Right there it is. The engine is a regular 4-4-0 type. That is"—he pointed—"four wheels on the front truck, four drivers, but no wheels beneath the cab. It weighs just under thirty tons, burns wood, and was named for a famous chief of the Seminoles, Osce—"

Bored, Guns Taken interrupted with a sharp shake of his head. "No talk. Talk makes no sense."

"Then ride up and see the damned thing for yourself!"

Guns Taken was amused by the other man's losing his temper. This time his head shaking was unbearably slow. He enjoyed making Casement uncomfortable.

"Show us the fire horse *running*."

Casement started to refuse, then thought a moment.

"All right. Boyle?"

Michael moved to his side.

"We'll take her a few miles down the track. You climb on the pilot board so they stay off. I'll ride in the cab. If they demand a demonstration, by God I'll give them one to remember."

Michael trotted to the head of the engine, scrambled up on the platform of the cowcatcher, and squatted down while the Cheyenne walked their ponies closer to the locomotive. Their eyes grew huge at the sight of the hissing contraption with a smoke plume drifting from its funnel stack.

Casement mounted to the cab and barked orders to the engineer and fireman. Suddenly the whistle blasted. A calico reared, nearly upsetting its rider.

Another Cheyenne grabbed for his hatchet, yelped something that must have been a curse and flung the weapon.

Michael ducked. The hatchet clanged off the front of the engine not far from his head. He tightened his trigger finger just a little. Casement leaned out of the cab.

"Guns Taken, keep your braves quiet! That's the sound the fire horse makes when it's ready to run."

The whistle screamed again, joined by the clanging bell. The Indian ponies shied. Guns Taken clapped his free hand over his mouth, his eyes round as a child's again. The bell kept ringing as the engine lurched forward.

The Indians scattered to both sides of the track. Michael felt wind against his face as he squinted at the braves trotting along beside him, awed by the slow *whump* of the drive rods and the grind of the wheels. The ringing bell was interrupted by a third howl of the whistle that brought alarmed looks to several dark faces.

That fear wasn't good, Michael thought. Fear could lead to anger.

In a moment he was proved right. One of the braves kicked his pony and raced up beside the cowcatcher, shaking his bow and screeching at the iron monster starting to spew sparks along with the smoke.

Osceola was gathering speed, its rods moving back and forth with a steadily accelerating beat. The front truck rattled. The huge driving wheels squealed on the rails. The brush of the wind against Michael's face became a push.

Twenty yards ahead, Guns Taken flourished his bow lance, kicked his pony, and went charging east beside the track.

His braves howled and followed, racing on either side of the right of way. The ponies raised dust that blew in Michael's face and started him coughing.

The Indians rode hard, waving hatchets, quirts, and bows and uttering cries of scorn. The engine fell behind. The yelps and barks grew jubilant as the braves increased the distance between themselves and the fire horse.

Abruptly, Michael felt the engine lurch. The rhythm of the rods began to quicken.

He shot out a hand to grip one of the vertical bars by which a man could hold his place on the cowcatcher. The locomotive swayed around a slight curve, gaining speed again. Plainly Casement meant what he'd said about a demonstration. Politeness was one thing, defeat that suggested weakness quite another.

Clanking and rumbling, *Osceola* moved steadily faster. Spark-filled smoke streamed from the stack. Swaying from side to side as he clung to the bar, Michael thought he heard the engineer call for more wood. He definitely heard the wood crash into the firebox. Within seconds, the locomotive began to close the gap.

The Cheyenne looked over their shoulders and started flogging their ponies with bare heels. Their cries of pleasure became cries of outrage.

Michael's bones throbbed as he knelt on the pilot board. He was all but blinded by billowing dust. Chuffing and thundering, the locomotive drew up opposite the slowest rider.

Osceola passed the Indian and, moments later, another. He shook his bow at Michael.

The engine caught up with four more Cheyenne on the other side. Their mounts were already lathered. They fell behind.

A cacophony of rattling, clanking metal beat against Michael's ears. The engine swayed more and more violently. The whistle screamed, and the bell never stopped ringing. Michael's hand was white on the bar.

Soon, half the Cheyenne had been outdistanced. After another half mile, only Guns Taken remained unbeaten.

He rode bent forward over his pony's neck. He kicked the game animal without mercy and kept glancing back at the puffing monster. The Cheyenne's spine and shoulders glowed with sweat.

The engine noise was like a cataclysm shaking the earth. The point of the cowcatcher drew up even with Guns Taken. The warrior's mouth worked, but the roar drowned his cries as he urged his mount to greater and greater effort.

To no purpose. Inexorably, *Osceola* began to pass him.

Through the dust, Michael had a last glimpse of the Cheyenne's face turned toward his adversary. Tears or sweat shone beneath his enraged eyes.

Bell jangling, whistle bellowing, the locomotive left him behind in a cloud of smoke, sparks, and drifting ash.

iii

With a yowl of iron, the engine began to slow down. The bell stopped ringing. Michael exhaled and slackened his hold on the bar.

Over the next half mile, *Osceola* ground to a halt, jerked into reverse, and began to chug backward toward the railhead. Without any warning, Guns Taken was there beside the track, his bow lance clutched in his right hand.

He sat absolutely still as he watched the locomotive go by. Wind blew smoke from the stack and gusted it down into his face.

Sparks made his pony sidestep, start to rear. Guns Taken jerked on the plaited hair and gave the animal half a dozen vicious kicks until it stood quietly again. Then he jerked the bridle and began to follow the engine back toward the work train.

One by one the other Cheyenne appeared on either side of the cowcatcher and fell in behind their leader. On each sunlit face Michael saw mingled fear and fury.

The Indian procession trailed *Osceola* at a distance of about a quarter mile. Not one brave spoke. Michael wondered at Casement's wisdom in demonstrating the engine's speed. It was never good to humiliate an enemy. He'd learned that from Louis Kent and Worthing, among others.

The Cheyenne jogged slowly after the locomotive, their

eyes brimming with the hatred men reserved for a conqueror whose power they had come to feel at a cost of great pain and lost pride.

iv

When the engine braked, Michael jumped down. He thrust the Colt into the waist of his trousers and ran back to join the sooty-faced Casement climbing from the cab.

"I don't believe our visitors took kindly to losing, General."

Casement ignored the Irishman's rueful smile and shrugged in what amounted to a callous dismissal.

"I didn't intend that they should. Maybe if they're sufficiently impressed before they depart—"

"You mean frightened."

"Call it what you please. I hope I've persuaded them to leave us alone."

Michael inclined his head. "Look at the head man."

Guns Taken was riding past the engine, scanning it as if it were a thing of filth.

"He doesn't enjoy being whipped."

"But he has been. That was my purpose. To whip him. Peaceably but positively. Don't forget, Boyle"—Casement's glance said he wasn't overjoyed to have Michael question his actions—"our objective is still to get the line through with a minimum of trouble. If their pride has to take a licking before they realize they can't stop us, so be it. I didn't order Charlie to open her to full throttle just on a whim."

Michael let the matter drop, though he still had doubts as to whether intimidating the visitors had been wise. Guns Taken gave the locomotive a last withering look. There was no longer any pretense of friendliness on his face as he jabbed the bow lance at the boxcars.

"Show us those, white man."

The Cheyenne didn't miss Casement's faint smile. "Certainly."

The sullen Indians dismounted. Casement ushered the first of them into the second bunk car, Michael's. The construction boss hadn't lost all sensitivity to the perils of the situation. Captain Worthing was in the other car.

Michael waited at the steps, letting the Cheyenne climb up and enter one at a time. None of the Indians uttered a sound. An almost eerie silence had descended on the camp. In Worthing's car, someone yelled.

Christ, keep a tight hand on that fool!

The last brave passed him, intentionally stumbling, and driving an elbow into his ribs. Michael's hand jerked toward the Colt but he kept his temper. He met the Cheyenne's defiant gaze calmly and motioned for the Indian to precede him.

When he had, Michael grasped the handrail and went up the steps, fervently hoping Casement could conclude the visit and get the Indians away from the railhead before their anger exploded.

CHAPTER IV
SLAUGHTER

i

IN THE BUNK CAR it very nearly did.

Guns Taken hovered at Casement's elbow, leading the line of braves down the aisle. The Indians stared but remained silent.

At the end of the car, Guns Taken paused beside the partially empty rifle racks. From his position at the rear, Michael heard the Cheyenne leader say something in a quarrelsome tone. The exact words were lost because the others blocking the aisle started growling agreement.

Gradually the hubbub diminished. Michael caught Casement's firm, "No."

"White man—"

"*No.* Absolutely not."

The line moved again. The Cheyenne shuffled out of the car. Michael drew abreast of Casement, who was still stationed beside the racks. The red-bearded construction boss whispered, "The big one's really hot now."

"Why?"

"He wanted some of these rifles, gratis."

Outside, Guns Taken stood beside the roadbed, both hands on his bow lance. His braves had gathered behind him. The track boss went down the steps. Michael started to follow, then snapped his head around at the sound of ferocious thumping in the adjoining car.

Several of the Cheyenne heard the noise. Hands dropped to the hilts of knives and hatchets. But there was no further disturbance.

Guns Taken shook his lance at the car just vacated. "You show us something else."

"What?"

"Show that the men of the fire road are truly friends. Give us"—he held up his left hand, the fingers spread—"this many guns."

Casement said quietly, "I've already told you the guns belong to the railroad."

Guns Taken thrust his fingers close to Casement's nose. The smaller man didn't blink.

"This many!" Guns Taken insisted.

"No, and that's final."

Michael eased the Colt into his hand. The mood of the confrontation was growing ugly. All along the train, watching workers were stirring, anticipating trouble—

More temperately, Casement went on. "We have welcomed you peacefully. We have shown you the strength of the fire horse. We have poured sweet coffee."

Guns Taken spat on the ground to show what value he placed on everything Casement had mentioned. The moment produced an unexpected ambivalence in Michael. He admired the audacity of the Cheyenne leader. It took courage to make demands in the face of vastly superior numbers. At the same time, he felt sorry for Guns Taken and his braves. In the masses of white men—and the humiliating speed of the locomotive—the warriors had glimpsed their coming defeat. Perhaps even their extermination.

Once more the construction boss resorted to sign language along with words. "I am deeply sorry Guns Taken is angered. We wish only friendship. But we cannot give away rifles which might be turned against us."

Guns Taken thrust his bow lance into the shoulder of the roadbed, raking a long gouge in the gravel. He whirled and addressed his braves. Muttering, they followed him back to the ponies. While the Indians mounted, more cursing and thumping erupted in the other sleeping car.

Re-forming his braves into single file, Guns Taken began to ride out the way he had come in. He maneuvered his pony close to the front ranks of the workers, forcing them to fall back. A few didn't want to, but the more prudent prevailed. The potential troublemakers were virtually dragged out of the way.

Michael and Casement followed the procession on foot. Michael observed the heightened tension—the scowls, the whispers—among the men, and despite good intentions, fell victim to it himself.

The hoofs of the ponies plopped in the silence. Puffs of dust blew away in the breeze. Guns Taken gazed down contemptuously at the Paddies he passed.

All at once he reined his pony to a stop opposite the whiskey wagon.

Dorn's half dozen guards stepped closer. The merchant was still fuming. Behind him, Hannah stood white-lipped, her hat in her right hand and her wheat-colored hair glinting in the sun. Her eyes remained fixed on her father.

Guns Taken pointed the bow lance at one of the barrels.

"We drink water before we go." He rubbed his palm across his throat. "We have a great thirst."

Casement strode forward. "That's not water. You can't—"

Guns Taken paid no attention. He climbed off his pony and started toward the wagon. Casement caught up, snagged his arm.

"Guns Taken, the answer is no."

The last word ignited the Cheyenne's temper. "No, no! I have heard *enough* no!"

He shoved Casement away. Dorn cursed and took a step. Three of his guards caught and held him as Hannah pleaded for him to restrain himself. Then, without warning, Guns Taken lunged and rammed the iron head of the bow lance into a whiskey barrel.

ii

Wood cracked and split. The Cheyenne jerked the lance head free, wonderment on his face. The odor of the pale brown liquid spurting to the ground was unmistakable.

The other Cheyenne identified it too. They began to murmur and gesticulate. One laughed.

"Goddamn you, let go!" Dorn puffed, trying to free himself. "If that red bastard steals—"

"Papa, be still!" Hannah cried.

Guns Taken drove his bow lance into the barrel again, increasing the size of the hole.

Chortling, the fat-bellied Indian squatted and put his mouth to the spouting stream of forty-rod. Dorn broke loose.

Casement called a warning. Men tried to catch the merchant, failed. He was halfway to the crouching Indian when one of the younger Cheyenne flung himself from his horse. Michael saw metal flash.

The young warrior ran with astonishing speed. Over by the train, a Spencer came up—too slowly. Dorn fastened his hands on Guns Taken's neck. The younger Indian uttered a piercing yell and drove the blade of his trade hatchet at Dorn's forehead.

Bone cracked. Dorn shrieked and staggered, the hatchet buried in the front of his skull. Blood trickled down both sides of the blade and into his eyesockets.

iii

"Papa!" Hannah screamed, running to help him.

Dorn fell against the wagon, dying on his feet. The blood poured down the folds beside his nose to his white-streaked beard. The young brave turned on Hannah, ready to fight barehanded. Michael jerked his Colt level but the girl was in the way.

He dropped the revolver and flung himself between the Indian and Dorn's daughter. Casement shouted something he couldn't hear. A Spencer blasted from the roof of the office car.

Had Michael not caught Hannah's waist and dragged her down, the rifle ball would have hit her. It thwacked the wagon bed a second after Dorn's guards scattered.

Michael sprawled on top of Hannah as Guns Taken

scrambled to his feet and dashed for his pony. Hannah screamed again, hysterical now.

Lying on top of her thrashing body, he heard the hammer of boots, confused yells and curses, then a second explosion. The ball plowed a furrow a foot from where he had pinned Hannah to the ground.

He twisted his head to look. Through a tangle of mounted Cheyenne, Michael glimpsed Leonidas Worthing on the sleeping car steps. The Virginian levered a spent cartridge out of the breech of his rifle. His gray duster was torn, his face marked by cuts. Behind him, two of his three guards staggered into view. Both were badly bloodied.

The guards tried to jump Worthing. He eluded their hands, leaped down from the platform, and aimed at the Indians milling around Guns Taken to protect him while he vaulted to the back of his pony.

Casement was directly in the line of fire. He flung himself to the ground. The ex-Confederate blew a Cheyenne off his horse. Blood pattered on the ground next to Michael and Hannah. The shot unleashed pandemonium.

Two rifles roared. Another Indian shrieked. Michael jumped up, retrieved his Colt. A Cheyenne was aiming an arrow at Casement, who was climbing to his feet. Michael fired.

The Cheyenne toppled sideways off his pony. Michael winced at the sight of the gaping wound in the Indian's belly.

Guns Taken kicked his pony and went racing away toward the end of the track. Here and there a Spencer banged. But Casement's judicious placement of the guns now had an unexpected consequence. Those with the weapons were so spread out, and so many men were milling everywhere, the rifles couldn't be used effectively. Drifting smoke from *Osceola* and dust raised by the Indian ponies only compounded the problem.

Virtually unmolested, the rest of the Cheyenne swung westward and galloped after their leader, who obviously knew they stood no chance, and refused to squander more lives in a futile fight.

Casement was on his feet now, wigwagging his rifle. "Let them go. *Let them go!* Someone see to the Dutchman."

"Stand aside, you damn coward," Worthing yelled, appearing behind Casement and clubbing at him with the stock of the Spencer.

Casement dodged. Worthing bellowed, "I'll get one or two more before—"

Casement beat Worthing's arm with the muzzle of his Spencer. The bloodied, demoralized men who'd permitted Worthing to escape goggled from the bunk car steps.

Casement avoided a second blow from Worthing's rifle. The dust thickened. The last two Cheyenne leaned down from horseback with amazing suppleness, snatched up their two dead, and went racing away toward the trackless grade.

Michael and other men were rushing to help Casement. But not quickly enough. The Virginian's third blow glanced off Casement's temple and knocked him down.

Michael ran faster. Worthing saw him coming. Something uncontrollable had taken possession of Worthing. The Cheyenne were out of range, but he still wanted a target. The Spencer muzzle shifted through a quarter of a circle, aimed at Michael.

Worthing's eyes glowed with perverse joy. Michael flung himself face forward in the dirt as the rifle thundered. The ball hit Dorn's wagon and sent splinters flying.

"Pack of cowards!" Worthing bawled. "Wouldn't have happened if you'd listened to me. You, Boyle." He peered through the dust. "You're the one responsible."

He aimed for Michael again but couldn't get a clear shot. Too many men were hurrying to Casement's aid. They pulled up short as the muzzle of Worthing's rifle menaced them. On his knees, Casement groped for Worthing's leg.

Worthing had to concentrate on the closer adversary. Again he seized the rifle by the barrel. Started to bring it down stock first on Casement's head.

Lying prone with his gun hand extended and his view all at once unimpeded, Michael yelled Worthing's name. The man in the duster didn't hear. Or if he did, he was too angry to care. He bashed Casement on the top of the head.

Casement cried out. Once again Worthing found Michael and leveled the rifle at him. *God forgive me,* Michael thought, and pulled the trigger.

The Colt boomed and bucked. Two men who had almost succeeded in reaching Casement took headers in the dirt.

Michael's shot caught Worthing squarely in the chest, bulging his eyes and hurtling him backward.

Sick, Michael leaned his cheek on his forearm.

It's the war again. In another place, another time, but it's the war all the same.

I was a fool to think I could ever escape.

iv

The railhead was in total confusion. Men were running, shouting. The one on the roof of the westernmost car fired vainly after the retreating Indians. It was too late. The last riders disappeared beyond the low hills near the river.

The sunlit air smelled of blood, powder, the excrement of dead men. Michael wobbled to his feet as a black face emerged from the drifting dust.

"Greenup? Look after General Jack."

The black and Sean Murphy reached the construction boss just as he struggled to a sitting position, blinking and coughing. A patch of lacerated scalp gleamed redder than Casement's hair.

"I—I'll be up in a moment." Casement gasped. He pushed with his hands, finally managed to stand. "How many are—hurt?"

"Catch him!" Greenup cried as Casement collapsed.

Sean Murphy and the black started to lift the fallen man. "Don't!" Michael warned. "Not till you see how badly he's injured."

He spun to a couple of Paddies who had crept forward to examine Worthing's corpse. One wore a torn shirt. Michael had seen him behind the Virginian on the bunk car steps. He shook the Colt in the man's face.

"How the hell did that lunatic get loose?"

"Jumped us," the man panted, wiping his nose with the torn shirt's tail. "Fought like a catamount."

"Thanks to you, he did almost as much harm as the Cheyenne."

"But we couldn't help—"

"Shut your goddamn mouth!" Michael pivoted away.

He was growing sick at his stomach. He tasted sourness

in his throat. Quiet began to settle all at once. A final rifle shot crashed and echoed.

In the silence, Hannah cried out. It wasn't a scream. It was lower, a hurt, guttural sound. Michael flung the revolver away, turned and saw her crouching beside her father's body.

She was trying to touch him. She rocked back and forth on her heels, her fingers an inch from the clothbound shaft of the hatchet. Young Klaus leaned against a wagon wheel, crying.

Michael forced himself to walk.

"Miss Dorn?"

No response.

"Miss Dorn, come away. We'll take care of him."

She raised her head and looked straight at him. He might have been transparent.

Suddenly her hand closed on the red-wrapped shaft. She wrenched the weapon out of Dorn's skull. "Jaysus, she's gone daft!" a man yelped.

Stunned workers watched Hannah clamber to her feet, a strange moaning sound coming from her clenched teeth. The hatchet dripped red onto the worn toes of her boots.

She seemed like some tortured animal, staring around the ring of astounded faces. Michael stretched out his hand.

"For God's sake, Miss Dorn, give me—"

With a wailing cry, she turned and dashed to the wagon, to the one liquor barrel left unbroken.

Both hands on the hatchet handle, she swung the weapon in a lateral arc, smashing the wood.

She struck a second time.

A third.

The staves cracked. Liquor gushed over her trousers. Still she kept swinging, trying to find something to destroy—something to blame for the corpse on the ground behind her.

Michael edged closer. "Careful, lad!" Sean Murphy called. "She may turn on you."

"We can't let her do herself harm."

He shot his hands out, seizing her wrist.

She wrenched, trying to tear free. The hatchet head grazed his left thumb, drawing blood.

God, she was strong. Strong and wild with grief.

Desperate to avoid the slashing head, he pressed her wrist with the nails of his right hand. While she shrieked at him to let go, the hatchet slipped, plopping into the slime of mud created by the spilled liquor.

He wrapped one arm around her waist and dragged her against his chest. She struggled, but he held fast.

She kept crying. The reaction to the killings struck him then. He began to shake, almost as badly as she was shaking. He fought to shut out sounds. Klaus hiccuping as he attempted to control his crying; Casement protesting feebly that he was fine.

Gradually Michael's trembling passed. He stood with both arms protectively closed around Hannah Dorn, asking himself whether the price of anything valuable—the price of Union, the price of freedom for the blacks, the price of a mile of track a day—always had to be *this.* Had to be war. A big war or a little one, with identical, inevitable endings—

Savagery. Blood. Loss. Suffering.

She came so far, he thought as he wrapped his arms tighter around her shuddering body. *I came far too. Neither of us found a whit of peace.*

His heart broke for her. Again this morning, the faith she professed had been made to seem worthless. He lifted a hand to stroke her hair.

It failed to calm her very much. She kept sobbing and shuddering. An anonymous voice clamored out of his memory: *"Jaysus, she's gone daft."*

He didn't doubt that for a short time she had. What frightened him now was something far more important. After what she'd seen, would she ever be rational again?

Without realizing how it had come to pass, he discovered the answer mattered.

Mattered desperately.

CHAPTER V

"TO EVERY PURPOSE UNDER HEAVEN"

i

A GRIM-FACED JACK CASEMENT sat propped in his bunk in a tiny cubicle adjoining his office. It was shortly past seven that same evening. Michael had been summoned.

Casement looked uncomfortable in his bulky nightshirt. Lengths of bandage were wrapped around his head. He directed his visitor to a stool with a quick, almost irritable gesture.

Michael sat down, waited. A ceiling lamp illuminated half of Casement's face. He gnawed his lower lip, changed position, grimaced.

"Boyle, you were right."

"Concerning what, sir?"

"Humiliating the Indians. Letting the engine beat them. It was my decision, and it was a bad one. If I hadn't mishandled the situation we might have gotten them out of the camp with no casualties."

Michael shrugged in a tired way. "Why worry now, General? It's done."

"It certainly is not! I'm obliged to tell General Dodge. More important, I'll have to write a report for the directors. Frankly, I'm thinking of falsifying it. If I put the truth on paper, I'll be trumpeting to the world that the line's run into more difficulty—exactly the sort Dodge predicted. In Omaha, he told me privately we'd be lucky not to lose a man for every mile of track laid west of Kearney."

Michael said nothing. He liked the hard-driving little man too much to encourage such questionable behavior.

He wondered exactly what Casement wanted of him, then decided the construction boss would let him know when he was ready. He kept silent while Casement yanked his nightshirt over his pale knees and shoved at the bedding to raise himself.

"Don't you see, Boyle—if anything gets into print concerning what took place this afternoon, Dr. Durant, Dix, and the rest of the officers will have an even harder time attracting capital. God knows the job's difficult enough already. Now personally"—he covered his mouth, coughed—"I don't give a damn what people say about me. My brother and I are merely contractors. We can push the line through whether we're pilloried in the press or not—"

A pause. Then a sardonic smile quirked Casement's mouth.

"No, I'm lying to you. I do care about my reputation. I've always despised being a small man. That's why I want to build part of the biggest damn construction project of this century. But it *is* the truth when I say I'm not thinking solely of myself. The more trouble reported to Wall Street and Washington, the more the line's in danger of collapsing altogether."

His eyes pinned Michael. "The next two months are crucial."

Michael felt compelled to be honest. "I don't see how it's possible to suppress what happened today."

"It's possible for six or eight weeks. That's all I need. All the line needs—nothing in print until we pass the hundredth meridian. Of course the men will talk. They'll talk to the supply train crews. But rumors in Omaha are one thing, newspaper stories quite another. I've already taken one step to forestall problems. I've telegraphed headquarters saying I'll permit no more journalists at the railhead till we reach the meridian."

"I realize the meridian's an important goal. But what difference does it make whether the story's spread before we get there?"

"Because"—Casement hesitated; when he resumed, he sounded almost conspiratorial—"because Dr. Durant has informed me he's planning a mammoth rail excursion."

"A what?"

"A trip out here on a special train, to celebrate the line passing the meridian. Keep that to yourself. Otherwise I'll get a second-best effort out of the lads. All they'll be thinking of is a celebration—and they'll crucify me if they learn they won't be taking part."

"Can you tell me any more about this excursion?"

Casement's sour look suggested the whole scheme was an irritant.

"Yes. Durant telegraphed the details last week. Even though the Federal acts don't require us to reach the meridian until next year, we *have* to reach it before winter. As you know, the line's charter is unofficial until we do. But that's not half so important as the cash problem. If we go one more year without a big infusion of capital, the line may wash right down the drainpipe. So the good doctor has come up with this"—an annoyed wave—"this publicity party! The purpose is to impress invited guests from New York and Chicago. A hundred of them, perhaps more. Reporters. Potential investors. Foreign nabobs. The military. Members of Congress—maybe even Andy Johnson himself. It's the same sort of holiday that Central Pacific arranged last year for Schuyler the Smiler."

"Who?"

"Schuyler Colfax, that Republican trimmer from Indiana. Speaker of the House."

"Oh, yes."

"It's evident Durant means to stage something ten times as lavish as the Central Pacific excursion. He's already purchased the Lincoln car—the armored one built for Abe in sixty-four. Only time the poor devil traveled in it was when he went home to Springfield. Dead. Anyway, Durant's cleaning out the till to make the trip a success. My God, the man's a gambler!"

"I've heard railroad promotion requires that kind of temperament." Michael smiled.

"He has it. He's putting thousands into four new coaches being built in the Omaha shops right now. When the excursion train arrives, there'll be every kind of lawful diversion you can think of—and no doubt some unlawful ones to boot. There'll be fireworks. Lectures on phrenology. Demonstrations of horsemanship and Indian tactics by Frank North's tame Pawnee scouts. Picture takers all over the place—food catered by that high-priced Kinsley outfit in Chicago—and Rosenblatt's Band of St. Joseph and the Western Light Guard providing the music."

"Sounds like quite an investment."

"Quite a risk, you mean. I've wired Durant I won't permit the festivities to interfere with work. But I know he needs the excursion to attract cash. A press account right now, describing an Indian attack, will practically guarantee its failure."

He scrutinized Michael. "Do you understand why I'm considering a falsified report?"

"Now I do."

"I suppose I'm also fishing for advice."

"And for someone to ease your conscience by endorsing a fake story?"

"Mr. Boyle, some men would boot your ass for that remark." But he was smiling.

Michael wasn't. "I'm just trying to establish what you want of me. Is it advice on whether to lie?"

"Don't be presumptuous. Besides, there's no way to lie about two dead men. I'm talking about a—" He tilted his hand back and forth, a gesture of equivocation. "Call it a coloration of the facts. It can be done. I won't have to account to Worthing's kin. I had the employee records brought in a while ago. The departed captain listed no relatives except a distant cousin in Mississippi. The Dorn girl, though—with her father murdered, she could make trouble for us."

He scratched his nose. "Suppose I put nothing really damaging on paper. Suppose we just had a camp altercation—reported as such."

Casement studied the other man, awaiting a response. When he got none, he prodded, "The difficulty is still the young woman. Have you seen her?"

"Yes. About half an hour ago, I called at the tent to offer my sympathies."

"Does she intend to stay here?"

"No."

"I didn't think so. When she goes home, she's liable to talk. Word could reach Omaha—"

"That's true."

"Goddamn it, Boyle, give me some facts! How *is* Miss Dorn? How's her state of mind?"

"About what you'd expect it to be. It's obvious Dorn wasn't the most admirable parent in the world. But he *was* her father."

"Is she calm?"

"Under the circumstances, I'd say she's quite calm."

"Resentful? Does she blame the railroad?"

"Not that I'm aware. She's humiliated because she fell to pieces. And of course she's hurting."

Nor is she the only one.

He bent forward. "General, I'd like to ask a question. May I have leave to quit the gang?"

"*Quit?* You may not! I need every man."

"I meant only for a few days. I expect the Dorns will be leaving for Grand Island as soon as possible. The boy's doing all he can to look after his sister, but he's hardly old enough to provide adequate protection on the trip. Someone should go with them. Armed."

"Someone who could urge her cooperation along the way?"

Casement's flinty stare told Michael the terms of the bargain had been proposed.

"Yes. Considering what you've said about the importance of the next six or eight weeks, it wouldn't bother my conscience to do that."

Casement scratched his beard. "How far do you propose to travel with her?"

"As far as Kearney. East of there, she and her brother should be relatively safe. Cooperation aside, General, I believe we owe Miss Dorn that protection. She's tended men who were injured."

"You don't have to remind me. She's a fine person." He pondered. "All right, you can go."

"I'll need guns. A Spencer. Several magazines of ammunition. A revolver."

"I'll sign the order tonight. Now. What does Miss Dorn propose to do with her father's remains?"

"Why, remove them to Grand Island, I suppose."

"I don't want that body seen by anyone in Grand Island. Any half-witted mortician who's been out here more than thirty days could guess what sort of weapon killed Dorn." Casement's voice grew sterner, more businesslike. "Talk to her again this evening. Tell her the corpse will putrefy before she gets it to Grand Island. Tell her a burial here will be much easier on her than riding home with a decomposing body. Since"—again he hitched himself higher in the bunk—"since I don't intend to be lying here much longer, I recommend we bury Dorn and Worthing at dawn. I'll read the service."

"All right, let me see what I can do. I wonder, though—"

"Wonder what?"

"Do you think you should be up quite so soon?"

"Tomorrow is a workday. We have Monday's track to lay—and the balance of Friday's. I'll be up."

Michael rose. "Very well. I'll speak to Miss Dorn immediately."

"And tactfully. Tactfully!"

"Of course."

"On your way out, fetch me a pen and some paper from the desk. I'll write your gun requisition—and begin drafting my report. A friendly visit by a few Cheyenne"—his mouth twisted; Michael detected guilt in Casement's eyes—"following which, a quarrel developed amongst the men. Worthing and Dorn were the casualties. It's the Eastern money I'm thinking about. The meridian. The excursion—" His eyes almost pleaded for understanding.

"Yes, sir," Michael answered, feeling weary as he stepped out of the lamplight to the adjoining office. He rummaged on Casement's littered desk.

It's the Eastern money I'm thinking about.

It's winning the war I'm thinking about.

Always, the object was to win, no matter what the cost in lies, or human lives, or human misery. For him, the price was growing too high.

Perhaps great enterprises automatically meant conflict. The saving of the Union, the binding together of the oceans with iron cords—perhaps each required a warlike attitude for success.

And clearly Casement wasn't entirely happy with what he had to do, even though he wanted to see the line go through.

Michael understood human motives and human progress were seldom pure. Amanda Kent, whose ruthlessness had sometimes tarnished her idealism, had taught him that. So he didn't scorn Casement too much as he delivered the paper and pen before saying good night. He too believed the line should go through.

But he didn't know how much longer he could fight this different but still sanguinary war. He didn't know how much longer he could pay the personal price of constant struggle and no peace.

ii

The canvas-wrapped bodies of Gustav Dorn and Leonidas Worthing lay side by side between two shallow trenches dug near the right of way. Despite the unpopularity of both men, death demanded respect; almost the entire camp had turned out to stand silently under the vast, cloudless sky sprinkled with paling stars. A clean, sweet wind blew out of the northwest. To the east the treeless prairie was reddening.

Michael stood across the circle from Hannah Dorn. She'd proved cooperative—more accurately, indifferent—about Casement's scheme, and agreed to be evasive about her father's death when she returned to Grand Island.

She looked tired but composed. She'd put on her shapeless coat again. Her hat hung from her right hand. Her left rested on her brother's shoulder. He was trying not to cry. Hannah's eyes, a little shinier than usual, betrayed her own grief.

Casement read from Hannah's Bible. She had selected the passages.

" 'To every thing there is a season, and a time to every purpose under the heaven.' "

Michael's head was bowed just far enough to permit him to watch her. His red bandana snapped in the wind. Away in the east he heard the hoot of the iron train, rolling in early. To his left, Sean Murphy scratched his armpit, then blushed when Greenup Williams and Christian, propped on a handmade crutch, both noticed.

" 'A time to be born, and a time to die; a time to plant, and a time to pluck up that which is planted!' "

He believed he knew why Hannah had asked Casement to read from Ecclesiastes. After Sunday's almost senseless violence, she needed reassurance that there was a divine reason for one of those lumpy canvas sacks—a reason why a man who had tried to find a place in a new land had failed and perished.

As far as Michael was concerned, drunkenness and a vile temper were the causes of Dorn's death. He sought no other explanation, and certainly found no hidden purpose in the event, not even while listening to words from the holiest of books.

" 'A time to kill, and a time to heal; a time to break down, and a time to build up.' "

Casement sounded uncomfortable with the sonorous language. Michael lost track of the next few verses, pondering earlier ones.

A time to kill. A time to heal.

A time to break down. A time to build up—

From First Manassas to the Wilderness, he'd seen the killing and the breaking down. He'd come out here not only to escape the memory of Julia but also to have a hand in building something worthwhile. Now he was utterly disillusioned. The price of helping to build the U-Pay was confronting a Leonidas Worthing. The price was more killing. The price was another war.

Maybe that was the way of the world. The only way.

Dear Lord, what a hateful idea! He yearned to believe it wasn't true. But every scrap of evidence accumulated during the past few years said it was.

His earlier enthusiasm about his unofficial adoption into the Kent family was gone. He had no idea as to how he'd use the money he would someday inherit. In fact he had no interest in it, because there was no longer any hope of discovering personal peace, or a way to conduct his life that didn't involve brutal struggle.

Still, he had to do something. This battleground was

surely no worse than another he might stumble into if he were stupid enough to repeat his earlier mistake and again flee in the hope of finding a calm haven.

There was none.

" '*—A time to love, and a time to hate; a time of war, and a time of peace.*' "

A lie, he thought. God have mercy on me, but that last is a lie.

iii

Casement's pause was a signal to the men he'd chosen earlier. Michael, Artemus Corkle, Sean Murphy, and five others stepped forward. Four of them handled each of the canvas bags. They lowered the bodies into the trenches with great care.

Michael picked up a shovel from a pile brought to the grave site late in the night. The whistle wailed in the east. A pillar of smoke rose on the brilliant red horizon.

While Casement turned to the New Testament, moistening his thumb nervously on his tongue several times, Michael and the others began shoveling dirt into Dorn's trench. Casement sounded hoarse as he resumed, reading this time from one of the Gospels. St. John, Michael thought it was.

" '*Jesus saith unto her, Thy brother shall rise again. Martha saith unto him, I know that he shall rise again in the resurrection at the last day.*' "

Chunk, a shovel of dirt landed on the sack. Michael heard a soft outburst of sobbing from Klaus Dorn and glanced up as Casement continued to read. Hannah was watching Michael with a curious expression whose meaning he couldn't interpret well.

For a few moments he didn't hear Casement's words. Hannah's look had captured him. There was pain in it. But there was doubt too.

Did she believe what Casement was quoting? Her faith was strong. Or had been. Was it still? Somehow he hated to see her tested so severely. Her faith was her whole way of life.

" '*Jesus said unto her, I am the resurrection, and the life;*

he that believeth in me, though he were dead, yet shall he live. And whosoever—' "

The whistle screamed. Hannah's head turned, her eyes furious at the intrusion.

But the supply train wouldn't stop. The work wouldn't stop. Otherwise men—and women—would grieve too long. Accomplish nothing. Permit a bitter sense of futility to drain them of hope, as Michael was drained. He inverted his shovel, *chunk,* full of impotent anger all at once.

" '*—whosoever liveth,'* " Casement repeated, louder because of the whistle, " '*and believeth in me shall never die.'* "

Slowly he closed the book.

"Amen."

Michael flung one more load of dirt into the trench. The canvas was nearly hidden. Sean Murphy leaned on his shovel handle and crossed himself. Michael found his own hand rising, making the holy sign he'd traced so infrequently since his childhood. In his heart and mind, a strange, unexpected prayer stirred.

He prayed that Hannah Dorn, a decent woman, would not grieve too long, or have her faith destroyed as his had been.

iv

When the trenches were covered, men set crude wooden crosses in place. Michael walked to Hannah and Klaus.

He waited until a small group of workers had offered their shy, clumsy condolences and melted away into the larger crowd Casement was leading toward the train. Finally the last man, Christian, hobbled off. Michael stood awkwardly silent, his shovel canted over his shoulder and his neckerchief fluttering in the breeze.

"What is it, Mr. Boyle?"

To his relief, she was dry-eyed; her pain was contained.

"Whenever you're ready to go—tonight, tomorrow—"

The whistle of the iron train interrupted him. Hannah spun again, sunrise reddening her eyes. She crammed the floppy brimmed hat on her head and gazed with loathing at the smoke plume.

At last her features smoothed. "The sooner I'm away from this despicable place, the better I'll feel."

"I can't say I blame you."

"You don't like it either?"

"After yesterday? Not much. I think I told you I came out here because I was sick of fighting, and all I've done is fight."

"Leave."

He sounded as he felt—despondent. "And go where? Where will it be any different?"

She looked at him sympathetically. He was ashamed of revealing his weakness, his nakedness of soul. He turned away and laid the shovel on the earth.

Thankfully, she forgot his inadvertent admission when the whistle bellowed again. Over its noise, her voice turned hard. "I'll have the tent packed and the mules hitched in half an hour."

Chapter VI

The Coming of the Godless

i

At twelve-mile intervals, special crews following the railhead had erected pine-jacketed water tanks beside the track. The sun was setting that evening when Michael, Hannah, and Klaus made camp in the shade of one such tank. It resembled a primitive wash tub on thick timber legs, and looked incongruous on the rolling prairie—an ugly intrusion of civilization.

While Michael and Klaus unfolded and raised the tent, Hannah laid a fire to heat coffee and broke out jerked beef and biscuits. Michael was using a stone to hammer a peg when he heard a creak of wheels south of the right of way. He dropped the stone and shot out his hand.

"Klaus. The rifle."

Hannah hurried to his side. "What's wrong?"

Still crouched, Michael put the Spencer beside his boot. "As yet, nothing."

A wagon drawn by mules rolled through purple shadows on the east side of a round hill. A tarpaulin had come unhitched on the rear of the wagon's bed. As the wagon creaked into the glare of sunset light, the breeze flapped the tarp and revealed slabs of black-speckled meat.

An Indian clad in a hide shirt and leggings drove the mule team. Beside the lead wheel closest to the track rode a lean white man on a wiry pony. He was in his early twenties, wearing a threadbare flannel shirt without a collar and trousers held up by suspenders. Long hair visible under his plainsman's hat shone fair in the sunset.

Michael breathed faster. The two men took note of the campers but made no sign of greeting. The white man's saddle was equipped with what looked like a handmade leather scabbard divided into two sections. The stocks of a pair of buffalo guns jutted from it. The Indian had a third rifle on the seat.

Wagon and rider soon passed close enough for Michael to note the white man's gaunt, high-cheekboned face. It was curiously familiar. He was sure he'd seen it before, but didn't know where. Maybe the man looked like a Union soldier he'd met briefly and forgotten.

The black specks proved to be flies swarming on the raw slabs of meat.

"I thought they were hunters." Michael nodded.

"Is that buffalo in the wagon?" Klaus wanted to know.

"Appears to be. Notice the bundle of hides there at the back?"

"Are they going to the railhead, Michael?" Hannah asked.

"I assume so. Probably to sell the meat."

Klaus looked disappointed. "They're not going to stop."

"Just as well," Hannah told him. "They're carrying too many guns for honest men."

Michael scratched his mustache. "Odd combination, a white and a Sioux. At least the other one's chunky enough to be a Sioux."

"Sure don't look friendly," Klaus murmured, just as the white man jerked two fingers to his hat brim to acknowledge their presence. Then he booted his mount and sped west raising dust.

The Indian whipped the mules with the reins. The wagon rapidly grew smaller. Michael still felt he'd seen the white hunter before. But he couldn't pinpoint a time or place. He relaxed and forgot about it when the travelers disappeared, leaving only a haze to mark their passage.

Presently the three sat down to eat. Michael kept the

Spencer within easy reach. He'd also fetched a borrowed Colt from the wagon and buckled the holster belt around his hips.

Klaus munched a biscuit, drank some coffee, yawned, and said good night. A moment later the lantern Hannah had hung inside the tent went out.

Twilight was rapidly deepening into darkness. Hannah clasped her hands around her knees and gazed at Michael through the tatters of flame. Her strained expression finally compelled a response.

"Are you feeling any better, Miss Dorn?"

"Better than I was this morning. By the way, you're perfectly entitled to call me Hannah."

"Thank you. I've been concerned about you. You've said so little all day. I know your father's death wasn't easy to bear."

"I'll bear it. I believe the words General Casement read from St. John."

"I admire your conviction—as I think I noted when we first talked."

"Then you've no faith in life after death?"

"Let's say my view on that is more a question than an opinion."

"But you aren't without a belief in something. You *will* be going back to the line?"

"Yes. For want of anything better to do."

Hannah swept off her hat and laid it on the parched grass near the fire. "Do you know what I was thinking about while we drove?" He shook his head. "The passage from Ecclesiastes. I believe those words too. I believe there must have been a reason for Papa's death."

Although the theological waters were growing a bit deep, Michael said, "You mean some purpose to it?"

"Exactly."

He was dubious. "What is it, then?"

"Why, I—I don't know." She glanced away. He had the feeling she knew the answer but was unwilling to reveal it. Spots of color in her cheeks reinforced the suspicion.

"Tell me, Mr. Boyle—"

"Fair's fair. If I'm to call you Hannah, you must call me Michael."

An appreciative smile. "All right, Michael." The sound

of it was pleasing. "I'd like to know a bit more about you. Did you leave a family to come west?"

"Only my adopted family. The Kents. I believe I mentioned them."

"Yes. They were people you admired—"

"Some of them."

"Have you ever been married?"

The question was so matter-of-fact, he was stunned. Why the devil would a woman who'd just lost her father be interested in such a subject?

"No, never," he answered. "There is—was—a woman, but she—ah—best we forget it. May I have more coffee?"

She poured with a steady hand. He was conscious of the intimacy of the fire, and of the handsome curve of her full bosom beneath the shabby coat that grew taut when she leaned forward.

He heard a rustle and a series of rapid thumps south of the track. Possibly one of the huge plains jackrabbits bounding by. All the red light had leached from the west. A thousand stars shone, but none quite so bright as the blue-gray eyes of the woman close to him.

How lovely she is by firelight.

"You seemed upset a moment ago," Hannah said as she returned the pot to the coals. "I didn't mean to intrude in a delicate area."

He waved. "No intrusion. I just prefer not to discuss the woman."

"Why?"

A sadly cynical smile. "If I told you the tedious truth, it wouldn't enhance my already low standing in your eyes."

This time her smile was disarming. "Your standing is not low at all, Michael. What is the truth?"

Lord, she had a way of digging into a man!

"I joined Meagher's Irish Brigade to escape an altogether sordid situation. If you must know, I coveted another man's wife—which I believe is definitely frowned upon by the Bible."

The coffee tasted as bitter as his mood had become. He shouldn't be revealing his past to a virtual stranger, yet he was. Perhaps he was like Casement discussing his report. Perhaps he secretly wanted a judgment about the degree of his guilt. Against all good sense, he kept on.

"The relationship was, in fact, adulterous. Which makes me a violator of more than one commandment, does it not?"

Asking for scorn, he got none. "Christ says all men can be forgiven. Did the woman love you?"

"No."

"But you loved her."

"I wanted her. I don't know if it was the same thing as love."

"Do you think of her a great deal?"

He started to lie, changed his mind.

"All the time."

"Does she write you?"

"Never. She doesn't know where I am. Or care."

A long silence.

"When you've finished your work out here, are you going east to look for her?"

"She's still married."

"That isn't quite an answer."

Sometimes I want to go, but—

"The answer is no."

"So the truth is, you didn't come out here just to compensate for what you did in the war. You were running away."

"Hannah Dorn," he exclaimed with a sharpness leavened by a smile, "you can't be interested in my personal life at a time like this!"

"Oh, yes." She nodded, smiling too. One of those dazzling smiles that softened her sternness and made her look so beautiful. "Every man, every human being, has something of interest to tell. But I'm sorry if my questions offended you."

He stretched out, leaning on his elbow. "Not at all. It's just that my story's—well—it's entirely in the past."

"What about your future?"

"Beyond the railroad, I have none. Time we changed the subject. Will you and Klaus be staying in Grand Island?"

"Yes. I'll take over the store and run it as best I can. The store is part of the reason I was thinking so hard on Ecclesiastes all afternoon. Perhaps God meant Papa to die so I could do something about the chaos he made of the business."

He would have laughed, except that you didn't laugh at someone bereaved and groping for answers. Softly, she continued.

"Perhaps I can turn it into a profitable enterprise, then do something for Klaus. Papa never permitted Klaus to think about attending a college. Papa didn't consider education worthwhile. I do. If the store succeeds, I might be able to send Klaus East for a year or two—"

Another smile. "You've maneuvered me into talking about myself."

"I'm interested in your plans," he said, meaning it. "Maybe the terrible business yesterday will mean the start of better times for you and your brother."

"In certain circumstances, that's entirely possible."

She was staring at him again. He couldn't understand why she acted embarrassed.

Abruptly she scrambled up, snatched her hat, and walked toward the tent. Her cheeks were pink again. But her voice held no trace of emotion. "I'd like to rest now. Will you be comfortable out here?"

"Quite comfortable."

"Good night, then."

"Good night, Hannah."

The tent flap fell. He was unexpectedly depressed not to have her still with him, sharing the fire's warmth, sharing deep feelings it was a relief to speak aloud at last.

ii

Quickly, though, puzzling questions intruded. Why in the world did she want to know about his past and his future? And why had she suddenly grown so nervous about the drift of the conversation?

He had no idea. But he was positive she'd been probing his background for a reason.

He left the Spencer near the fire and walked to the wagon a few yards from the tank. Starlight glinted on the rails. Somewhere a wild bird warbled. The tethered mules twitched their ears and snorted as he approached.

The liquor barrels, two sound and two broken, had been stripped from the wagon and left behind. He reached over the tailboard and found the small canvas bag in which he'd packed a fresh shirt, his razor, his churchwarden, and tobacco. He lit the pipe and strolled in a wide circle so Hannah wouldn't catch a whiff of the immoral smoke. As he puffed, a frown deepened on his forehead.

Blast it! That woman wants something of me. What is it? And why the devil do I care all at once?

He could find no adequate answer for either question, even though he asked them endlessly as he sat on guard beside the fire all night long.

iii

They started east at sunup. Michael tied his red bandana around his forehead because it promised to be a hot day. About eight, they spied a peculiar caravan coming toward them. Two open phaetons, dilapidated but serviceable, following the track.

The first carriage was piled high with portmanteaus, crates, and what appeared to be folded canvas. The driver, a bearded, vacant-eyed young man, had a buck-and-ball shotgun resting across his lap.

In charge of the second phaeton was a man of quite a different sort, about forty, heavyset, red-faced. Points of a scraggly mustache hung below his jaw. He wore one of the short untapered sack coats that had been introduced about ten years earlier but were still considered cheap and ostentatious in some circles. The color of the one-button coat matched that of the thin brown lines forming large checks on the man's gray trousers.

A black silk cravat spilled over the top of his red velvet waistcoat. His hat, cocked at a jaunty angle, was hard brown felt with a red band and a crown shaped like half a melon. An English hat. Michael didn't know the correct name. It was sometimes called a bowler, after the hatter who'd designed it, or a derby, after the earl who'd adopted it and given it social approval. He'd seen many of the hats back east.

While the first phaeton continued on, the flashy gentleman reined in his plodding team. Beside him, a pale, coarsely attractive girl fanned herself with a lace handkerchief.

The girl was barely Klaus' age, but she was dressed as if she were twice that. Her wrinkled bloomer frock was orange-dyed organdy. Matching Turkish pantaloons showed beneath the short skirt. A black velveteen bodice, tight on her large breasts, had been repaired several times. The ribbons dangling from her wide-brimmed straw hat were frayed at the ends.

In the second seat, also facing forward, sat two other women, thirty or thirty-five. One had a faint mustache and a heavy scattering of pockmarks on her cheeks. All three females looked uncomfortable in their heavy, gaudy clothing.

The fellow in the melon hat smiled. But his dark eyes had the warmth of lumps of unlit coal. Again Michael had encountered someone he thought he'd seen before, and again he couldn't recall where.

"Good morning, friends," the man said. "Brown's the name."

The man swept off his hat and tipped it. Before he set it back on his hairless head, Michael saw a bruise and a diagonal white scar on the sunburnt scalp. Recognition came instantly.

"Could I trouble you to tell us whether it's far to the railhead?" Brown asked.

"No, it isn't." Michael was conscious of Hannah sitting stiffly beside him. Brown's three traveling companions surveyed her clothing and unpainted face with amused looks. Back in the bed of the wagon, Klaus was goggling.

"You'll make it before dark," Michael added.

"Thanks kindly. We're anxious to get there and set up."

"And get these goddamn hot clothes off," the young girl said. Brown's glance made her cringe.

The pockmarked woman laughed. "Nancy's always eager to go to work."

Hannah clenched her hands in her lap. Brown turned, his smile fixed but his eyes furious.

"Alice, be so kind as to keep your language decent."

The woman looked as terrified as the girl. She swallowed and lowered her eyes as Brown said to Hannah, "Very sorry for the impropriety, ma'am." To Michael, he said, "I'm positive we've run into each other before."

"We have."

"Where?"

"A card palace in Omaha. You won a big pot and were in a generous mood. You bought everyone at the bar a stein of lager."

Brown snapped his fingers. "That's it. You were standing right next to me. Going out to work on the line."

"Correct."

Brown's smile changed again, growing unctuous. "Still there?"

"I'll be returning in a day or two."

"Then perhaps we'll have the pleasure of renewing acquaintances. When we do, I'd appreciate a favor."

"Such as?"

"Such as your confining your remarks about our first meeting to what we just discussed. My winning that pot. Buying a round. Forget the rest."

He spoke in a casual tone. No one would have construed his remarks as a threat—unless they'd seen his eyes.

Michael shrugged in a noncommittal way. Brown looked less than pleased.

By now the young girl was paying attention to the Irishman. He was mortified when she smiled and let her gaze range up his legs to his groin. Then she looked him in the eye and slowly licked her painted lower lip. He could feel Hannah's shoulder tremble with tension.

"Safe journey to you," Brown said. *"Hah!"* He flicked the reins to start the team.

iv

Turning, Hannah watched the phaetons bounce along westward. When she spoke, her voice seethed. "I knew Papa would only be the first."

Michael shrugged again. "With a project as big as the railroad, you must expect enterprise of all sorts."

"*Enterprise!* Godless people, that's what they are. That Brown looks absolutely vicious."

"He is."

"He hinted about something that happened in Omaha—"

"He has quite a reputation there. The night we met, he proved he deserves it."

"Is he a sharp?"

"What's a sharp, Hannah?" Klaus asked.

"A gambler."

"Among other things." Michael nodded. "He was referring to an incident that took place shortly after he stood everyone to drinks. He was caught cheating at stud poker."

"Who caught him?"

"A poor fat fellow from the U-Pay roundhouse. Brown had bilked him before. He was watching for hidden cards; he claimed he saw them. With some friends urging him on, he swung a punch. Brown charged around the table bellowing about his honor. He half killed the U-Pay lad with his head."

"His *head?*"

"Didn't you see the scar and the bruise when he took off his hat? The barkeep called him Butt Brown. Butt, two t's. Apparently he can well nigh destroy a man with his fists and his skull. The U-Pay chap lasted half a minute. Brown would have left him dead or crippled if others hadn't intervened. Before I left Omaha, I heard Brown has killed at least four men."

Hannah shuddered. "Filth. And Papa wanted to mix with them. Do business just as they do—" Klaus was tugging at her arm. "What is it?"

"Who were those women? Do they work for the railroad?"

Michael wanted to laugh but felt it wiser to refrain. "My boy, they certainly do. At least that's their intention. In polite company, Mr. Brown's damsels are known as soiled doves."

"If you please, Mr. Boyle! He's not old enough."

"Not *old* enough? I disagree! If he goes East to school, or even if he remains in Grand Island, I'm sure he'll see more and more of such women. You'll have to explain eventually."

"Explain what?" Klaus insisted.

"He said eventually!" Hannah snapped.

"Mr. Boyle?"

"No, Klaus. I bow to your sister."

"Thank you." She was still simmering. Klaus sighed and crawled to the rear of the wagon.

Michael picked up the reins and set the wagon in motion. "For weeks we've been hearing there would be sharps and whor—uh, persons of questionable moral character coming out to set up tents and travel with us."

"And you'll soon be back among that kind!"

The rancor in her voice made him caustic. "I take it you disapprove of card playing along with tobacco?"

"I do."

Irked, Michael craned his head to make certain Klaus was occupied. The boy was glumly staring at the dust cloud left by the phaetons.

"Tell me, Miss Dorn. Do you also disapprove of what's discreetly referred to as congress between men and women?"

She whirled on him. "Are you trying to make me out a prude, Mr. Boyle?"

"Inquiring! Merely inquiring!"

"Evidently you think I'm a prude because I believe in the Bible?"

"Some say the two go hand in hand."

She stared straight ahead again. "I admit I despise women of the kind that aroused such curiosity on your part."

"*Curiosity?* Damn it, I was only being polite!"

"That young slu—young woman had something on her mind besides social intercourse."

"What the hell is this? Why do I have to answer to you?"

"You don't. But you're too fine a man to squander your life among—" She bit her lip. "I've said too much. I'm sorry."

He let out a long breath. "The fault's mine. I had no right to mock your beliefs."

"I shouldn't have expressed them so tactlessly. I know the Lord said to forgive women like that. I try—but I hate the way they cheapen one of God's finest gifts! Sell it, like a measure of flour—"

He was still sufficiently piqued to say, "This fine gift you mention—you speak of it only in the abstract, I suppose."

A quick look over her shoulder—Klaus was paying no attention.

"If you mean have I slept with a man, I have not. But I talked at length with Mama on the subject. Crude as Papa was, she said he still brought her a great deal of—Boyle, you're blushing! Who's the prude?"

A smile softened the retort and broke the tension. He laughed, then raised a hand.

"Guilty. You took me by surprise. You take me by surprise quite often."

"That," she declared, "is because people are not books containing just a single page to be understood in one quick reading."

He chuckled. "No, I'm certainly discovering that's true of you."

"You might think me uninterested in—the topic you brought up. On the contrary, I'm not. At the proper time, in the proper place, my husband won't find me wanting. He'll find me inexperienced. But—not without ardor. Not without—oh, *fiddle!*" she cried, utterly flustered.

The exclamation caught Klaus' attention. "Hannah, I never heard you cuss before."

"I was not cursing!"

"But you came close." He was grinning.

"You be still!" A whisper. "We mustn't discuss it any further."

"All right," he agreed, even though he thought turnabout only fair play. Last evening she'd asked a good many personal questions, for a reason he was just beginning to guess—with considerable discomfort.

Or am I a conceited oaf? Flattering myself?

He thought it wise to try to lighten the conversation. He rolled the tip of his tongue in his cheek. "Actually, you need have no fear about my virtue when I go back to work. I don't patronize women such as Mr. Brown employs. Nor am I particularly fond of gambling. In fact I have no intention of honoring Brown's request. I'll warn my friends about him. No sense in them squandering their wages and betting against a man who wins nine times out of ten. I watched him that night. He lost on an average of once every twenty minutes. For the sake of effect, I don't doubt."

"You see? That only proves the railhead's an ungodly

place and will obviously grow worse. There are better and safer places a man could spend his time."

"What places?"

She didn't answer.

"What places, Hannah?"

"If it isn't clear to you by now—"

Her lips pressed together. "Never mind."

Angry at herself, or him—or both—she pointed east. "Drive faster."

He did. His wild suspicions hadn't been so wild after all.

At first he was astonished. Then he was touched. But that mood quickly vanished. He knew how a forest animal must feel coming across a hunter's iron trap directly in its path.

He'd have gotten angry all over again if what she wanted hadn't been so upsetting.

Chapter VII
The Vow

i

Next morning Hannah left Klaus asleep and came down from the campsite on the edge of Kearney to see him aboard the westbound supply train.

Full daylight was still a good half hour away. Only two lamps glowed in the improvised huts and unpainted plank buildings that straggled along the north side of the river opposite the old infantry stockade.

The air was chilly. Pungent wood smoke drifted back from the locomotive as Michael approached a stake-sided flatcar loaded with rails tied down with heavy rope. There were four such cars between the tender and two boxcars at the end of the train.

He'd spent the night outside the tent again, wrestling with cold blankets and sleeplessness. He felt edgy and tired as he laid the Spencer and canvas pouch on the stacked rails. When he turned back, Hannah took him by surprise. She leaned forward and gave his cheek a quick, chaste kiss.

He was speechless for several moments. Then all he could do was blurt, "Why—thank you, Hannah Dorn."

She ignored the forced levity in his voice. "You've been very kind, Michael. Despite all you say about being irreligious, you're a good and compassionate man. I apologize for my temper when we met that Mr. Brown. You're not like him. It was shameful of me to imply that you are."

"I appreciate the compliment, but it isn't necessary."

"It is. I don't want you believing I'm nothing but a prude."

He caught her nervous hands between his palms. "Believe me, Hannah. No one faults you for your principles, least of all me. God—uh, heaven—knows I could use some of my own."

She glanced toward the locomotive. Sparks rose and vanished above the stack. "I hardly slept last night." She covered her eyes. "Oh, I'm such a clumsy, graceless person. I don't know how to do this."

"Do what?"

"Tell you—" He felt her hands tighten within his. "You'll laugh."

"No."

Her eyes caught starlight. "Last night, I—I prayed for hours. There *is* a purpose for everything. Even for Papa being struck down as he was—Michael," she interrupted herself, "where will you go when construction's shut down?"

"I suppose I'll stay at the winter camp, wherever that may be."

"Stay with all those sinful people?"

"What else should I do?"

In a quick burst of breath, she said, "Come back to Grand Island. I can make the store succeed if I have a man to help me. I told you I prayed. I repeated the words from Ecclesiastes over and over."

Her speech grew less breathy, became soft and direct. "I know now Papa's death came so there'd be room for another man. You were meant to take his place."

Once again he couldn't speak. He was shaken to the center of his being. He'd already concluded this might be the reason behind yesterday's questioning—not to mention her flirtation with the subject of sex.

He tried to pierce her air of certainty with another little laugh.

"Miss Dorn, permit me to say with all politeness, you're touched in the head."

"No, I'm not. You're a man looking for a place, Michael Boyle. God has revealed it."

Hostile all at once because he felt threatened by her confidence, he exclaimed, "Not to me! My place is up the line, pushing those rails to the meridian. Do you realize I'm thirty-six years old? Before I'm too blasted feeble to do anything but sit in a chair and look back at all my mistakes—all the years I spent taking human life—I want once—*once!*—to know I've done something worthwhile. *Something!*"

"Do it, then. But start back before the snows are too deep for travel."

"You're the damnedest woman I ever met!"

"I would appreciate your not cursing. This is too serious."

The whistle tooted. One of the train's two brakemen waved his lantern from beside the last car.

"Come back and help me build a good store. Then another. Those godless people will keep moving west, chasing the easy money. The territory will soon be ready for civilized things. Where we live, we'll help build a town. A fine, decent one."

An impulse to say yes swept over him. He fought it.

"No, Hannah."

"Why not?"

"I can't, that's all."

"*Why not?* Am I unattractive?"

"You're very attractive. But—"

He was unable to finish. Honesty would only hurt her.

But she'd been hurt already. A tear sparkled on her face. Angrily, she wiped it away.

"You don't think you could ever love me? I don't expect you to love me now, Michael."

"Hannah, stop!"

"You love that other woman."

"No," he lied. "But I like you too much to pretend I feel anything more."

"Love will come. Give it a chance. Give *me* a chance."

She flung an arm around his neck and kissed him on the mouth with unmistakable passion. He felt the sweet curve of her breasts against his body, then her tears on his face.

With her mouth still close to his, she whispered, "I've love enough for both of us. Come back."

"And if it didn't work, and I left again? I'd hurt you worse than I'm doing right now."

"I'll accept the risk."

He shook his head. "I would never subject you to that kind of uncertainty, that kind of—"

The whistle howled.

He seized two of the stakes and hauled himself up to the rails. The train lurched forward.

The trucks began to click slowly. Spark-filled smoke gusted around him. Through it, he heard her call, "Before the snow!"

The smoke cleared. As the last car passed she stepped to the center of the track and waved.

Damn! He didn't love her. Better to hurt her again, this moment, than subject her to prolonged pain. He shook his head in an exaggerated way. She couldn't mistake the finality of it. Yet her head remained unbowed and she blew him a kiss, as if she were supremely confident.

ii

He sat down on the stacked rails and watched her figure shrink in the starry dawn. Soon she was a speck against the widening band of red-gold on the eastern horizon. Then she was gone.

He tried to excuse himself for hurting her by summoning anger.

"I'll be damned and double-damned. That queer, Bible-reading girl did *bait a trap as if I were some woods animal!"*

The anger didn't help. He almost wished he could have jumped right between the trap's jaws. She was a fine, handsome woman. But he didn't love her enough.

Love?

To the best of his recollection, it was the very first time he'd thought the word in connection with his unexpected fondness for her. He *had* lost his heart just a little, without realizing it. But what he felt for her wasn't enough to make him change his mind about returning to the railhead.

The iron train gathered speed on the Nebraska plain. Far to his right, a herd of shaggy buffalo swept down from a ridge, trampling the earth loudly enough to be heard above the train's roar. Flickering light from the firebox reddened his cheeks as he stood up and faced west, one hand on a stake, his feet braced wide apart. The change of position didn't help clear his mind of the confusion.

That woman is mad!

No, in her own way, that woman is as strong as Amanda Kent.

Handsome, too.

And not nearly so pious as she pretends. He well remembered the fervent feel of her mouth.

He tried contempt.

Outrageous, the way she picked a husband! "God's made a place!" Fancy such nerve!

She wouldn't say it's nerve, she'd say it's faith.

And would it be so bad a place?

I cannot *go there under false colors!* About that, he was adamant.

Yet he was beginning to loathe himself for having hurt her so badly.

The buffalo veered off and vanished in the north. The train swayed. He gripped the stake tightly to keep from being hurled off.

The points of his mustache and the ends of his bandana flicked against his face. He peered through the smoke and specks of soot but never saw the vast prairie rushing by.

That's all I do, hurt or kill others.

That is all I ever do.

iii

Some eight miles further down the track, with the sun clear of the horizon, he was startled from his bleak reverie by a series of piercing blasts from the whistle. He recognized the signal; the train was stopping.

On the roof of the last boxcar, the brakeman who'd been sitting with his legs dangling over the side struggled to turn the horizontal wheel. Its vertical rod applied pressure to the primitive brakes.

Iron squealed back there, then up front, where the other brakie worked the wheel on the first flatcar. He leaped to the second car as the couplers crashed and the cars began to shunt against one another, slowing down with the kind of erratic jerking that frequently caused a break-in-two on a downgrade.

The front brakie pointed to the south. Michael clambered to the top of the rails as the train came to a standstill. Near the river turkey buzzards wheeled and darted at the ground.

A queasy feeling fluttered his stomach. Where the carrion birds swooped, patches of buffalo grass shone bright red.

iv

He jumped down from the flatcar, his Spencer cocked. The fireman had another, the engineer a third. The two brakies—boys working their way up from yard switchman to engineer—were unarmed. They followed the older men, looking as bilious as Michael felt. Suddenly he smelled the blood stench.

"Appears to be a body lyin' out there," the fireman said, swallowing. The men started running. The noise sent the buzzards flapping away.

Michael's mouth was dry as he began to glimpse white and red lumps strewn along the bank. "More than one body."

"No horses—" the engineer muttered.

"And they'd have been on the other side of the river if they was travelin' in a settler's wagon," the engineer put in. "Buffla hunters, mebbe? Chasing that herd we seen?"

They were a quarter mile south of the track now. Michael nearly stumbled on a foot-wide rock all but concealed in the waving grass. He glanced down.

"Oh, Mother of God."

On the rock lay an ear cut from a human head. Blood was drying brown in the breeze. Beside the ear rested an eyeball, a crushed white globe with a dark spot—the pupil—turned up to the light.

One of the brakies turned around and staggered back

toward the tracks, coughing up vomit and slopping his trousers.

They found the remains of what they calculated to be four men. At first Michael thought two of the victims might be the pair he'd seen at the water tank the preceding evening. Then he knew he was wrong. None of the flesh was brown. And he spied no wagon tracks.

There was little doubt the men were hunters, though. Scraps of deerskin shirts and pants were scattered everywhere. Not one body was whole.

A mutilated head rested against another stone. The ears were gone, and the nose. The point of the chin had been worked off with a knife or hatchet. The hair had been lifted, and a pit opened in the top of the skull so the brain—or part of it, slimy gray and fly covered now—could be removed and placed beside it. Michael could barely stand to look.

"Injuns?" the fireman asked.

"Yeah," the engineer said. "It's the way they work when their tempers are up. I seen something similar once before."

Wherever Michael stepped, he found more evidence of the massacre. Amputated feet. Arms chopped at the shoulders. Entrails twining through the grass like lifeless red snakes. Mutilated genitals had been placed on what remained of a torso. One head covered with gashes still had part of an arrow jutting from the mouth. The arrowhead had been driven up behind the upper teeth and the shaft broken at midpoint.

Tears in his eyes, Michael finally lurched away from the carnage. He was trembling.

Who had done it? Guns Taken and his Cheyenne? It made little difference. The remains were mute proof of the savage level to which the coming of the railroad had raised the war between the whites and the Plains tribes.

A conference was held, well away from the site of the massacre. The engineer would report to Casement, and ask for a work crew to come back, pick up the remains, and search for identification. "We stay here any longer, we'll be late to the railhead," the engineer said. It was an excuse, but Michael was thankful for it.

Soon the train was headed west again. The memory of

what he'd seen beat at Michael's mind. The trembling returned. He was almost pitched off the flatcar before he closed both hands on one of the stakes. Jumbled images spun past his inner eye.

The trees of the Wilderness bursting afire.

A splendid green banner tumbling toward summer grass, its wounded bearer trying to hold it aloft, failing, and weeping as he stained the silken sunburst with his blood.

Pickett's line, human wheat scythed down slowly in the powder haze of a steamy July afternoon.

Worthing's face when Michael's bullet hit him.

The dismembered bodies of men who must have known fear, love, hope, laughter, and who had found death by following the twin tracks of what purported to be civilization—

Clutching at the stake, Michael cried, "Enough!" Cannon thundered in his brain. All the hurt men of the endless wars seemed to wail in chorus.

"Enough!"

The rear brakeman shouted something he didn't hear. Slowly, he gained control of himself. He wiped his tear-tracked face with the back of a hand.

It wasn't sufficient for a man to cry out against the struggles that rent the land. A man had to do something more than curse bloodletting when he too was responsible for it—

A man had to do something to defy and defeat what he detested. Amanda Kent had taught him that long ago. He remembered the family motto. Take a stand. Make a mark.

Seated again, he gazed at the sky.

If you're there, listen to me.

Never again will I knowingly hurt another person the way I hurt Hannah Dorn.

Never again while I breathe will I lift my hand against another human being, no matter what the provocation.

Never.

V

At the railhead, Adolphus Brown was supervising the raising of a large tent. The girls were already inside, setting up cots, hanging canvas partitions, and uncrating whiskey bottles. Brown's half-witted young helper, Toby Harkness, swung a sledge to peg the last guy rope.

Although it was barely daylight, the feisty little construction boss, Casement, had already called on Brown to inform him his presence would be tolerated because Casement realized the men required certain diversions. But Brown was under orders not to open for business until the end of the workday. Something else was on Brown's mind at the moment, though.

Toby leaned on the sledge, grinning. "All done. Butt? I said all done."

"Oh. Good. Now hang up the sign the way I showed you."

"Boss, what's chewing on you this morning?"

Brown fanned himself with his hard felt hat. *Going to be a sonofabitching hot day.*

"Boss?"

"That Paddy we encountered driving out here."

Toby scratched his beard. "Hell, he seemed pretty harmless."

"Depends. He knows me from Omaha. Some of the others here might also. They could talk. Discourage trade."

"We got the place to ourselves!"

"Not for long. I know of three gents who'll be arriving with their outfits inside of a week. In a month, there'll be a small city of tents following the line. We could end up sucking the hind tit."

"I promise you, Butt. Those micks get in our way, I'll talk to 'em. They don't listen"—Toby caressed the handle of the sledge—"I'll talk a little louder."

Adolphus Brown felt a burden lift. He clapped his derby on his scarred head and laid an arm across the younger man's shoulder. "Toby my boy, you know what I'm thinking almost before I think it. That's why I admire you."

Toby smiled in a way Brown found hilarious. The lout had all the brains of a sparrow. Brown managed to keep a straight face as Toby declared, "Nobody ever admired me before I met up with you."

"That was their mistake."

"Because if some mick shoots off his mouth, I'll fix 'em."

"And do a splendid job, too." Brown grinned as they

strolled toward the tent entrance. Inside, Nancy and Alice were bickering like ruffled hens. He must keep his patience. By sundown he'd have them on their backs, with their attention focused on the only spot where a woman's attention belonged.

"Yes, sir, a splendid job. I can count on that as surely as I can count on a winner when I need one."

He jutted his hand toward Toby's face. The sleeve garter and attached elastic worked perfectly, popping the spade ace into his fingers as if it had materialized from the air.

Toby giggled like a child, grimy fingers over his mouth. "Lordy, Butt." He giggled again. "Not out here where everybody can see."

Brown pointed toward the dining car. "Everybody's in there, stuffing. Getting ready to bust their asses and lay a mile of track quick, so they can pay us a visit. You get busy with that sign."

"Yes, sir," Toby said in an almost worshipful way.

Brown hid the card in a slit in his red velvet waistcoat and entered the tent whistling. Toby was a crackerjack. Stupid but a crackerjack. Any Irishman who flapped his mouth about Omaha would regret it.

CHAPTER VIII
MERIDIAN 100

i

"DOWN!"

On Michael's signal, the five men lowered the rail. About two and a half feet of it projected beyond a splintered board stuck in the earth beside the right of way. Faded white numerals were painted on the board:

247

The moment the rail touched the ground, Sean Murphy whirled to the crew on the other side of the grade. "Beat you!" Disgruntled, they placed their rail as Murphy wig-wagged his arms and bellowed in the direction of the perpetual train; "It's done! We're past!"

Voice after voice took up the shout. Mass insanity seemed to seize the hundreds of men strung out at the railhead this crisp afternoon, the fifth of October.

Christian, fully recovered, put his hands on his waist, bent backwards, shut his eyes, and wailed, "Whooo-*aaaah!*" Artemus Corkle—permanently on the crew now; Michael had replaced the complaining O'Dey—ran down from the right of way, performed two quick somersaults, then raised himself on his palms and proceeded to walk with his legs in the air, bleating like a calf.

"WHOOO-AAAAAAAH!" Christian howled again. Jostled by screaming men, Michael accepted a maul from one of them.

"Take a lick, Boyle. Someday you'll want to show this place to your grandchildren."

With a melancholy smile, Michael hammered the spike twice. He passed the maul to Murphy, who was laughing and crying at the same time.

The shouting intensified, spreading eastward, picked up by hundreds of throats. The engineer of the locomotive behind the perpetual train doubled the noise by blowing the whistle and ringing the bell.

In five minutes, all work had come to a stop. Greenup Williams snagged Michael's waist and hand, danced him around in a circle, then cupped his mouth and yelled at the western horizon, "We done it, Charlie Crocker! You listenin'? Meridian one hundred! We'll be all the way across the plains while you're still sitting on your behind in those mountains!"

Guards atop the cars of the work train fired their Spencers at the sky. North of the train, men and a few women poured from a disorderly collection of tents, the ever-growing movable town that packed itself into wagons and buggies every day or so, following the railhead. Someone had christened the tent village Hell-on-Wheels. It was appropriate, Michael thought. All sorts of riffraff had been attracted to it, exactly as Hannah had prophesied. Sean Murphy was fond of telling the more recent additions to the workforce, "The place is fast becoming civilized, several men having been killed here already."

Michael had already had a run-in with one of the tent town's citizens—Harkness, the dull-witted young man, who worked for Butt Brown.

Harkness had caught Michael alone one September evening when he was returning from a chat with the drovers. He demanded Michael stop talking to new workers about Brown's curious habit of winning against all opponents.

Patiently Michael explained that he never sought opportunities to discuss Mr. Brown. Though he didn't admit it, the fact was he'd only volunteered information to a few close friends. The rest of the time he merely answered newcomers' questions honestly. He put Harkness on notice that he'd continue to do so.

Evidently trade at Brown's Paradise was already suffering because Harkness replied with threatening language. He emphasized his warning by repeatedly jabbing a finger into Michael's chest.

Michael's temper flared. But he suffered the rest of the tirade, and a few more jabs, without resorting to his fists. He meant to keep the pledge he'd made on the car from Kearney.

Toby Harkness departed with a smirk on his face, apparently convinced he'd been dealing with a coward. Michael had already accepted the fact that such opinions would be the price of fulfilling his vow—

Now Michael watched Butt Brown slip a pepperbox derringer from his waistcoat and begin shooting over his head. Further up the dirt street between the tents and the train, he suddenly spied the white buffalo hunter and his Sioux companion.

In August, the two had already been gone by the time he returned to the railhead. Now they were back, strolling and enjoying the celebration. The white man waved his plainsman's hat once or twice, and tipped it to a soiled dove in front of Brown's Paradise. Even at a distance, a white streak in the hunter's fair hair stood out clearly.

Michael assumed the pair had brought in another load of buffalo meat. He was still convinced he'd met the white man during the war. He made up his mind to inquire.

A troop of the cavalry now guarding the workers on a full-time basis galloped by, the men no more than blurs in their dark blue blouses and light blue, yellow-striped trousers. Sabers swinging in crazy arcs, they went pounding west, screaming as enthusiastically as the Paddies. Their bugler blew the charge.

Meridian one hundred.

It was a goal every man had concentrated on for months. With the goal reached, Michael had to confront the reality of the next phase of his life: more grueling, lonely work of the same kind. He didn't like the prospect very much.

He did feel a sense of pride in having helped push the line this far. As of today, the Union Pacific's charter was official. The eastern skeptics would be silenced, and perhaps the line would begin to attract the investors it needed. Within ten days to two weeks, Dr. Durant's much publicized Great Pacific Railway Excursion train would be chugging out of Omaha bearing its select group of government dignitaries, military officers, and potential stockholders. Jack Casement was undoubtedly already sending a telegraph message to Durant, informing him of the day's accomplishment.

Meridian one hundred. He was proud of having been part of the effort.

Yet something was lacking. He felt disconnected from the revelry, and unenthusiastic about the work ahead. The unease wasn't new. It had been with him ever since the trip to Kearney. He'd grown moody and uncommunicative. Sean Murphy had commented on it several times.

A man came charging from the office car, repeating his news as he ran, "No more work! General Jack says we can take the rest of the day an' have a good time!"

More cheering. Michael started for his quarters, his face composed but not his spirit.

Men waved and screamed with renewed fervor when Casement appeared on the steps of the office car, a jubilant smile on his face. The rifle fire grew almost continuous, the roar of the Spencers proclaiming the victory and challenging anyone within earshot—God Himself, up in the hazy autumn sky—to accomplish something more wondrous.

It was a triumph, and Michael knew it. Why, then, did he feel so remote from it?

Because he constantly remembered the price paid in blood to achieve it? Remembered the dead men, including the four butchered hunters who had never been identified?

Or was it because, of late, he found Julia Kent's face frequently and disturbingly replaced in his thoughts by that of Hannah Dorn?

ii

After supper he walked from the dining car to the row of lamplit tents where rowdy men were already plumping down their wages for overpriced whiskey, a chance to beat a professional at three-card monte, or a quarter hour with one of the fourteen or fifteen soiled doves inhabiting the portable town.

He passed Brown's Paradise. A reveler staggered out. Before the tent flap fell, Michael was gratified to see no other patrons inside. He had nothing personal against Brown. But he figured the new men arriving every day or so should understand the risks of visiting the establishment.

At the rear of the narrow lane between Levi's Bird Cage Saloon and Tidwell's, his destination, he spied a wagon parked in the semidarkness. A tarp-covered wagon, with a black-haired man rolled in a blanket on the hard ground beneath.

He recognized the white hunter's Sioux partner. The Indian cradled a rifle close to his chest while he dozed.

Inside Tidwell's, the only railhead establishment selling general merchandise, a cheerful, overweight man slapped his hands on the plank counter.

"How do you do, sir? Bucyrus Tidwell's the name." He rolled a gold-plated toothpick from one side of his mouth to the other. "Help you find something?"

Michael surveyed the hand-labeled jars, bottles, and boxes on makeshift shelves. Everything from calomel to cartridges. He tugged his churchwarden out of his hip pocket.

"I need some tobacco."

Tidwell hefted an amber jar and carried it toward the balances. "Got some choice Virginia. Six bits." His smile widened. "Per ounce."

"Per *ounce*? You're joking."

Less cordially, Tidwell said, "I know my own prices."

Michael was observing the sums chalked on the jars and boxes. He'd never been in Tidwell's before. Disgusted, he said, "And you haven't set a fair one on anything. Your profit looks to be three or four hundred percent."

Tidwell shrugged. "Costs a lot to have freight forwarded here."

"Not that much."

"There also ain't no comparable store between here and Kearney." Tidwell's smile returned, an arrogant half-moon. "You want to walk there for tobacco, feel free."

"Damn gouger," Michael growled, pivoting away. "I'll go without."

"Do that, you cheapskate papist!"

Michael broke stride, fought his anger, then walked on. He batted the tent flap aside with a savage slap.

iii

Jeremiah Kent lay on a blanket-covered cot located in a second, smaller tent directly behind Brown's Paradise. He'd discarded his clothes on the dirt floor, anxious to satisfy himself with Nancy. Now that they'd finished a romp, he was content to relax a bit, taking pleasure in his own nakedness—he'd bought a bath at The Tonsorial—and in hers as she lay straddling him. He barely felt her weight.

A lamp, trimmed low, rested on a crate in the corner. Hanging canvas separated the crowded nook from two similar ones in the tent. Beyond the canvas to his left, one of the other whores was puffing and moaning while her customer growled a continuous stream of profanity. Peculiar way to enjoy a woman, Jeremiah thought.

Nancy tightened her spread legs against his. Where the roughness of her hair brushed him, he felt himself stir. Languorously, he fondled the globular breasts bobbling above his chest. His thumbs worked slowly on the brown tips. She had her palms braced on the cot so he could touch her that way.

"Honestly didn't think you'd come back, Joe—"

"I like my full name better, hon. Joseph."

"All right, Mr. Joseph," she laughed, moving one hand to stroke his cooling forehead and the white-streaked hair above.

"First time I called on you in August, I told you I'd be back."

"Is it me you like, or just any ol' gal?"

He lifted his head to buss her lips. "You."

A shudder rippled down her back. She squeezed him harder with her thighs. Then she rested her head on his shoulder.

"I'm glad that friend of yours didn't come in with you.

Butt won't let us take none of his kind. Nor niggers, neither."

"Kola knows that. He goes to see Miss Gold Tooth, down the line."

"Us girls up here won't even speak to that disgusting old whore. She'll take anybody—" Suddenly she kissed his throat. "Oh, Joseph, you're so damn nice!"

He chuckled. "You don't have to deliver the speech your boss taught you."

"He didn't tell me to say it," she breathed. "It's good with you. With all the others—'specially those blasted Irishmen—it's just work."

"I'm flattered. But I'd say 'all the others' is overstating it. This place appears to be crying for trade."

"It is. Butt's mighty upset."

"Since there's no line waiting, he won't care if we have another go—"

"Yes, he will! He's mighty strict about the clock. You only paid for one time. Fifteen minutes. We used that already."

The anxious words faded into a murmur of pleasure as he reached behind her and started to rub her bare buttocks.

"Joseph, Joseph—you're a sweet boy. But we don't dare. Butt would have my hide."

"I've got your hide, Nancy. Gonna keep it a while, too."

There was a more pronounced stir in his groin. Quickly she shifted her pubis, lowered herself, and moaned as she felt the rigidity.

"God, you just melt me," she whispered, kissing his ear, his eyelid, his cheek while his thumbs pressed harder against her breasts. "You got a mean look sometimes, but you're sweet and easy on a girl—must be the Southron in you. Were you in the war?"

"Yes."

"D'you ever meet up with that old Reb Davis?"

"In a manner of speaking. You might say Mr. Jefferson Davis was responsible for teaching me some of life's most valuable skills."

"What'n the fire's that mean?"

"Never mind," he laughed, pulling her head down.

She wriggled. "Sweet, we *got* to think of the time. If you don't pay—"

"Be quiet," he said, affably but firmly, and kissed her.

She gave up without protesting and kissed him back, her mouth open, and her tongue darting. Now she was moving her hips, raising them and lowering them faster each time. A faint sound—not next door, outside—distracted him. He opened his eyes.

Over her shoulder he saw a distorted shadow cast on the canvas by an outdoor lantern.

"Hey in there, Kingston."

"Shut up!" Roused now, he clutched Nancy's perspiring back.

"Your time's up."

"Oh, it's that damn pea-headed Toby—" Nancy panted. Jeremiah thrust. "Oh. *Oh.*"

The shadow stirred. "You don't put your pants on, Kingston, I'm comin' in."

Jeremiah stopped the movement of his body, raging because he'd just slipped comfortably into the girl. The silhouetted arm of the proprietor's assistant moved toward the opening in the canvas. Jeremiah dropped his right hand beside the cot. Seized the Ballard that laid atop his clothes.

"Boy, if you set foot in here, I'll blow you all the way to the river."

The silhouetted arm dropped. "But you got to pay again."

"After."

"No, before. It's Mr. Brown's rules."

"Hell with his rules. I'll settle up later—" Jeremiah's voice acquired a harder edge. "You better skedaddle because I see your shadow just perfect against the lantern. Leave us alone or I'll put one through you with this buffalo gun. Not even your own mother'll recognize you."

Quickly, the shadow shrank and disappeared. In the next cubicle, clothing rustled and the whore said in a monotone, "Oh, that was sure sweet. Thanks a lot."

Jeremiah relaxed, shifted his right hand back to Nancy's hips and returned to more pleasurable pursuits.

iv

Adolphus Brown was in a vile temper. He leaned his elbows on the board resting on two barrels and surveyed his clientele. One miserable Paddy, passed out on the floor.

For the first time this evening, two of the girls were occupied in the annex, but the third was still alone. He'd already taken a turn up and down the street. He knew his competitors had more customers than they could handle.

Brown pulled a tarnished pocket watch from his waistcoat, snapped it open, and checked the time. Toby came rushing in.

"Butt—"

"Those two finished with Alice and Nancy?"

"Yes, sir—that is, Alice got done on the dot. But that buffla hunter told me to leave. He'n Nancy, they're goin' at it again."

Brown's eyes clouded. "I assume he paid you—"

"No, Butt. He—he said he'd shoot me if I went in to collect."

Brown slapped his palm on a worn deck lying on the board. "I'll have that bitch for breakfast!"

Toby fingered his beard. "Ain't her fault. That Kingston's an ornery sort."

Brown's glance was scathing. "You mean he has enough sand to scare you off? I thought better of you, my boy."

Humiliated, Toby stood speechless. Brown started to say something else, but then Liam O'Dey slipped inside the tent. With a jerky swipe of his hand across his mouth, he hurried to the counter.

"This one on the house, Mr. Brown?"

"Why in shit should it be?"

"Well, sir, because"—nervously, O'Dey glanced at the entrance—"that time before, you asked me to keep my ears cocked. I'm still doin' it."

"You said it'd be a pleasure, seeing as how Boyle tossed you off his gang."

"That's right. Not ten minutes ago, I overheard that bastard speakin' with four of the greenhorns who arrived yesterday. He was next door to Tidwell's, outside, and I was inside—he didn't see me slip in behind him. He wasn't bothering to keep his voice down, either. He told the greenhorns he couldn't advise them about any of the places except this one, where"—O'Dey touched the deck—"where he said the railroad bibles are not straight."

Brown cursed, grabbed the deck, and flung it. Cards fluttered down. Toby was wide-eyed.

Gaining control, Brown jerked his hat off, mopped his scarred pate, and settled the hat back on his head. "Toby, you'd better go see that loudmouth again. Guess your first call made no impression. This time you must talk louder—unless, of course, the customer we were discussing watered your guts too badly."

"No, Butt! I just didn't want to go into the dark against a man lugging a hunting rifle—"

"I'll handle him." Brown nodded, grabbing a bottle of Overholtz cut with Platte River water. He shoved the bottle into O'Dey's white hand.

"Two swallows."

O'Dey drank greedily.

"Now get out."

When he was gone, Brown motioned Toby to his side. There was a pathetic eagerness in the young man's eyes.

"We can't fool with the mick any longer, Toby. Waited too damn long already."

He frankly feared reprisals from Casement if one of the workers was seriously injured. But as things stood at the moment, his choices were to take a risk or pack up and leave.

"Watch the Irishman till he's alone," he cautioned. "Be sure no one sees you."

"It'll be easy, Butt," Toby said, bobbing his head. "First time I braced him, he wouldn't raise a hand. He's yella."

"Well, you talk to him in your most persuasive way."

"Loud, Butt?"

With a steady gaze, Brown said, "As loud as you know how."

"Yes, *sir!*"

Toby scuttled from the tent. Brown jerked out his watch again, noted the hour and minute, and thrust it back in his pocket. He stalked to the entrance, muttering and kicking strewn cards. By God, he was through letting pious micks ruin his trade, and randy itinerants take advantage of him!

Before stepping into the street, he paused to consider his strategy. He pulled out the four-barrel derringer, removed the shells and returned the pepperbox and the shells to separate pockets. He left the tent smiling.

V

In the dark behind the annex tent, Toby frantically rummaged among empty crates in one of the unhitched phaetons. He was ashamed of the way he'd disappointed Butt. Ashamed and anxious to make amends.

He hadn't told Butt the real reason he'd balked at entering the annex, though Butt had guessed it. Toby had seen the young, soft-spoken hunter once in August, then again this evening. Both experiences had left him inexplicably frightened.

He didn't frighten easy, either. But there was something vicious about Kingston's eyes. They were worse than his employer's eyes, even when Butt was boiling mad.

He found what he sought. A handle broken from a spike maul. Thick enough and stout enough to beat a man to death in three blows.

With the maul handle clutched to his side, he slipped deeper into the darkness as Butt Brown stormed out of the main tent and headed for the entrance to the annex. Nancy's wordless voice came through the canvas, uttering cry after strident cry.

CHAPTER IX
KINGSTON

i

"MR. KINGSTON?"

The voice pushed at the edge of his mind, barely audible because of Nancy's outcries and the roar of his own breath. Her nails dug, then scraped his back. Bodies shuddering, they reached the end together.

"Mr. Kingston, this is Brown."

"Oh, God," Nancy panted, limp on top of him all at once. Jeremiah whispered for her to be quiet, then shifted his head away from hers. Clearly delineated on the front canvas, he saw the motionless silhouette of the stocky man in the melon-shaped hat.

"I hear you," he said as his breathing became more regular. He slid his hand down to the Ballard.

"Believe there's been a slight misunderstanding—"

Jeremiah blinked. Brown sounded friendly.

"Might we discuss it a moment?"

"Go ahead."

"No, I mean out here."

Jeremiah ran his tongue to the corner of his dry mouth. Despite Brown's puzzling cordiality, something smelled of danger. Far in the distance, drunken men sang a sad Irish ballad. A revolver banged. A woman laughed, shrill as a crow's caw.

"Toby should have known better than to interrupt," Brown resumed. "The lad's not too heavy upstairs. You're welcome to Nancy's company for as long as you want to enjoy it, provided you pay in advance. Trade's light this evening—I'll even set you a special all-night price." A pause. "Mr. Kingston?"

"Still listening."

"Oh, good. Gentlemen can always reach an accommodation. If you'll step out, it'll only take a moment. I'm not armed."

Nancy's mouth was tight against Jeremiah's ear. "Joseph, I think he's fooling you. He always carries a hideout gun. And he doesn't do favors—"

"Kingston?" the voice prodded. The shadow jerked toward the adjoining cubicle. "Alice, stay there!"

The woman next door complied without a murmur. Jeremiah heard her return to her customer and quietly urge him to remain where he was.

"Pardon me for doubting you, Mr. Brown," Jeremiah called, "but during the celebration this afternoon, I distinctly recall you shot off a pocket gun. I wouldn't care to hold a conversation with that gun somewhere about."

A chuckle. "You're quick, Mr. Kingston. I do have the gun. It's empty. Check it."

The shadow bent. The canvas stirred. An object slid in the dirt beneath.

"There. Proof of my good faith."

"I tell you something's funny," Nancy breathed. "Isn't like Butt to surrender his weapon."

There was a smile in Jeremiah's voice. "Maybe he *is* anxious to have me stay the night. As he said, business isn't all that grand."

Naked, he stole to the front partition. He located the pepperbox and examined it against the glow from the outside lantern.

"Empty, all right," he called.

"Then if you're satisfied, come out. As soon as we agree on the price, I'll leave you alone."

Jeremiah debated. What if Brown had a second gun? A hidden knife? Nancy suspected it.

Still, she might be inordinately cowed by the man. And he *would* enjoy a whole night at a bargain rate.

"Mr. Brown?"

"Here, sir."

"Be right with you soon as I put my pants on."

"Excellent!"

He struggled into his trousers, shushed Nancy's next warning, then patted her hair.

"Gonna be all right, hon. We'll have a fancy time right till the cock crows."

He left the Ballard beside his hat and returned to the front. "Stand back two or three paces, if you please, Mr. Brown."

The shadow shrank. Jeremiah raised the flap. Brown stood at the far edge of a pool of butter-colored light between the main and secondary tents. Quickly Jeremiah eyed the other man. Smiled.

"You don't mind if I'm cautious? Show me the linings of your coat. Spread 'em wide."

Brown looked annoyed, but did as Jeremiah asked. No bulges or unexplained slits were visible. He gave a satisfied nod and left the tent.

"Didn't mean to talk so sharp to your boy—" He dug in the pocket holding the bills from the sale of the latest kill. "How much will that be for all night?"

Brown had his hat in his right hand and was mopping his pate with the other. He dropped the hat, shot his arms forward, and caught Jeremiah's ears. "Damn cheating Reb!" he cried.

Brown jerked Jeremiah's head forward and simultaneously lowered his own. The top of his skull hit Jeremiah's face like a log ram.

Angry and dazed, Jeremiah backstepped. Brown released him. The impact of Brown's blow multiplied the images he saw. Blood began to trickle from his nose.

He'd never come up against a man who fought in such unorthodox fashion. He didn't know what to expect. He staggered to the side, hands hunting a support. Brown sidled forward, lunged for his shoulder.

Jeremiah managed to elude the grasping hands. He put his left foot behind him. His bare sole came down hard on a sharp stone embedded in the ground. He teetered, off balance. Brown lowered his head and charged.

He butted Jeremiah just above the belly. With a grunt, Jeremiah reeled over and slammed on his spine, conscious of Nancy outside the tent, her soiled wrapper clutched to her breasts.

Butt Brown landed on top of him, both knees in Jeremiah's midsection. Jeremiah's vision cleared just enough to give him a sharp look at the saloon keeper's face. At the very least, the man meant to maim him.

"Nancy, the rifle!" As he called to her, the edge of Brown's hand chopped his throat. He gagged.

A second, even less clearly defined figure appeared behind the young prostitute, then scampered away. Alice's customer.

Brown had Jeremiah's ears again. He lifted Jeremiah's head and pounded it against the ground.

Then again, *slam.*

Jeremiah threw a punch. It grazed Brown's jaw but did no damage. Brown's lips peeled back. His nose shone with sweat. Blood smeared Jeremiah's mouth and chin. He nearly fainted when Brown rammed his head down a third time.

"Think you can come in here"—Brown bashed his forehead with a heavy fist—"high-assed and snotty and break my rules? *No, sir*!"

A knee bore into Jeremiah's crotch, the pressure excruciating. Brown had taken him by surprise. The advantage had belonged to the stocky gambler ever since. Brown's face was dark as a beet, his eyes pitiless.

"Rifle—" Jeremiah croaked as Brown chopped his throat again.

Nancy hesitated. Brown's knee jerked, digging. Jeremiah almost screamed from the pain in his groin.

Once more Brown resorted to ear pulling. He tugged Jeremiah's head up and snapped his own head forward. The scarred skull loomed, shooting straight at Jeremiah's eyes.

He managed to wrench onto his side. Brown had meant to knock him out with a butt to the forehead. He absorbed the blow on his ear. His head rang.

He wedged his hand between his body and Brown's. Found the man's belt buckle. Hoisted with all his strength and succeeded in hurling Brown off.

When Jeremiah reached his feet, he wobbled. Blood and mucus continued to drain from his nose. His head and his testicles hurt unbearably. Where was Brown?

He found him, indistinct in the lantern's glow. The saloon keeper was disheveled but steady. He lowered his head. Ran at Jeremiah.

Something hard jabbed Jeremiah's side. He saw a flash of metal, caught hold and yanked the Ballard away from Nancy. He dodged clumsily, twisted, and booted Brown's behind. The kick and the momentum of Brown's charge hurled him to the ground. His jaw snapped hard against the dirt. Jeremiah's first advantage.

He pressed it. Using the Ballard as a club, he swung down from straight overhead. He broke the stock on Brown's skull.

Brown yelled. Jeremiah hurt too much to stop or be merciful. The Ballard barrel seemed to fuse with his hands as he kicked Brown's ribs.

The stocky man retched, flopped onto his back. A hand brushed Jeremiah's forearm.

"Leave him be, Joseph! He's whipped."

Nancy's words made no impression. Both pride and body had been injured too badly. He knelt on Brown's waistcoat, the positions of a few moments ago reversed. Gripping the Ballard at muzzle and breech, he shoved it down like a bar across Brown's throat.

The man's eyes popped. Fingers groped for Jeremiah's face. He straightened his arms. Pushing. *Pushing—*

Brown couldn't reach him.

He laughed at the sudden and pathetic fright in the saloon keeper's eyes. It took only a few moments more to cut off the man's air supply. Brown's discolored tongue shot between his clenching teeth. His body arched three times, each spasm less violent than the one before. Then he collapsed. Jeremiah didn't lift the rifle for another thirty seconds.

When he staggered to his feet, he was still shaking with rage directed mostly at himself. The saloon keeper's treachery and wild fighting style had nearly cost him his life.

Alice lifted the tent flap, took one peek at his red smeared face, and darted back inside. He realized Nancy was weeping.

"Joseph?"

"What?"

"Is he—?"

"Yes."

"I gave you the gun just so you could scare him off!"

He barely heard. His rage subsided, replaced by a forced calm. This unexpected turn changed the situation completely. He had to flee—without delay.

"Hand me my clothes, Nancy. Appears I won't be seeing you for a while."

Nancy stood with the wrapper fallen away from one reddened nipple. His eyes fixed on her wet face. For a moment weary despair swept over him. She was actually sorry the crazy bastard was dead! And terrified of him because he'd done the deed.

"I said I want my clothes, goddamn it!"

Nancy rushed inside. His heartbeat was slowing. He stepped to the edge of the annex, glanced toward the main street. Against the smoky glare of lamps and the bulk of the train, men passed back and forth, making so much racket the scuffling had gone unheard.

That gave him a margin of time. He'd wake Kola, hitch the mules, and be rolling across the prairie in fifteen minutes. Kola would have to drive. He felt too groggy.

Nancy brought his hat, boots, shirt, and long underwear. He held out the Ballard.

She wouldn't touch it.

His fondness for her was swept away by disgust. Were all whores like this? Miserable with their pimps, and just as miserable without them?

He laid the rifle on the ground. Used his shirtsleeve to swab some of the mucus and blood from his mouth and chin. Then he climbed into his drawers, donned his shirt, and pulled up his suspenders.

"Joseph, you didn't need to kill—"

He pointed the Ballard at her exposed breast. "Don't go soft on me, hon. What do you think he meant to do to me? Now listen. You stay in that tent half an hour before you fetch anyone to look after the body."

His dark eyes held pinpoint reflections of the lantern. His lips thinned to little more than a slit.

"If anybody comes chasing me sooner than half an hour,

Nancy, I promise I'll see you again. Someplace. I won't be coming for your services, either."

"God." A shiver. "You aren't the kind of man I thought you were."

"I can say the same about you. Brown was a no-good, reckless—"

"He took care of me!"

"You expect me to stand still and let some dishonorable son of a bitch jump me and put out the lights? No, ma'am! Get inside!"

He jerked the Ballard at her. She reacted like a startled rabbit, hurrying to the sanctuary of the tent.

"Half an hour—no sooner!" he called. Unsteadily, he walked toward the rear of the annex.

For a moment he felt sick at his stomach. Why did it always end the same way?

Because you enjoy doing a man to death. Don't deny it. You started to enjoy it the moment you pulled the trigger on Serena Rose.

All right, he *had* taken pleasure from watching Brown's last moments. But the gratification had been costly. It created a whole host of new problems.

He'd have to change his name again. He probably should have changed it before he reached the railhead. That Texas boy he'd foolishly spared was no doubt raising a halloo down south. Searchers might come this far north. They'd discover Joseph Kingston had come this far as well.

Fuzzy-headed and still in pain, he staggered on. He passed three more gambling establishments and pulled up short. In the leak of light from the street, he spied Kola's empty blanket beneath the wagon.

And two men, one unfamiliar, squared off against each other.

They saw him. It was too late to run.

ii

A few minutes earlier, Michael had decided to satisfy his curiosity about the stranger before returning to the bunk car to turn in.

He cut between Tidwell's and the packed, noisy Bird

Cage. At the rear of the tents he stopped, disappointed. The blanket beneath the wagon had been abandoned. The Indian had evidently gone off to search for his friend.

As he turned to retrace his steps, the corner of his eye caught movement at the far edge of the saloon tent. A shambling figure appeared around the corner.

Michael's stomach spasmed. He recognized Butt Brown's bearded helper. The young man carried some kind of club.

Toby slouched through the shadow cast by the Bird Cage. "Hullo there, mick."

Michael drew a deep breath. Had Brown's helper been following him while he strolled? There could be no other explanation for the young man's abrupt appearance.

"Butt sent me to see you."

"A few weeks ago, you and I said all that was necessary."

"Thought we did," Toby agreed. "But we hear you're still spoutin' off about Butt."

"The way I answer questions about your boss is my affair." Michael tried to act relaxed as he swung to the left, in the direction of the main street. "Good night—"

He heard the hiss of air as the maul handle came down. He sidestepped, but not soon enough. The handle slammed his right shoulder.

He lurched, dropped to one knee. Toby jumped in front of him, grinning.

"Plan to give you a few more like that. Then maybe you'll plug your mouth. Don't you make it too easy on me, though. Robs it of all the sport."

Quietly, Michael said, "I'm not going to fight you."

"Yes, you are."

"No."

"Damn coward, that's what you are! I knowed it the first time we met up."

Toby Harkness had shifted to a position directly between the mercantile and gambling tents. Michael's path was blocked.

He climbed to his feet and forced his hands open; they'd fisted almost without his being aware of it.

"Stand out of the way."

Toby hawked and blew spit on his trousers.

"All right," Michael said, his anger bubbling so fiercely

he could barely contain it. He pivoted a hundred and eighty degrees. "I'll take another route."

He wrenched his head as the maul handle whistled in from behind. Despite his quick move, the wood clipped him alongside the ear. His hand shot up to cover the side of his head. Toby giggled.

Anger shone in Michael's eyes. "Back off! I'm not going to fight."

"I told Butt you was yella." Toby poked Michael's cheek with the smoothed end of the handle. "Yella from tip to toe."

Michael jerked his head out of the way, narrowly avoiding the next thrust. He refused to shout for help. But neither would he answer Brown's thug in kind.

Just stay calm. You knew one day it would come to something like this.

"Yella dog, yella dog!" Toby chanted. The handle gigged Michael beneath the eye.

Toby gave the wood a twist, then stabbed it into his midsection. "Ain't you gonna howl for me, Mr. Yella Dog?"

"You witless bastard!"

"Hey, the dog can bark! Bark some more—" He took a shuffling step. "Come on, let's hear a yelp."

Toby smacked the handle lightly against the ear he'd already hit.

"I said yelp!"

The handle struck Michael's temple.

"Yelp!"

He brought the handle down on Michael's right shoulder.

A pitiless inner voice spoke the truth of it. *There is no way out of this unless you go after him.*

He wanted to do it. The desire was like a dizzying drunkenness.

Growing incoherent, Toby rammed the handle into Michael's belly. "You yella mick fucker! *Act like a man!*" When Toby spit this time, the moist gob landed beside Michael's nose.

He cursed and surprised Toby by fastening both hands on the maul handle.

Don't!

He was too enraged to heed the cautioning voice, or care about the vow. He tore the handle out of Toby's fingers. The younger man was startled, slow to react. Michael raised the handle over his head, his clenched hand white.

Eyes on the length of wood, Toby began to retreat.

DON'T!

With a slashing outward motion, Michael flung the handle. It turned end over end, clattering against the wagon. He turned his back on Toby—perhaps the hardest thing he'd ever done—and started to walk.

He felt neither victorious nor proud of himself, only ashamed.

He heard Toby run for him, heavy boots scuffing the ground. He turned. Toby dug in his heels a couple of feet away. A smile crept back on his oafish face.

Slowly Toby flexed his fingers.

"What the hell's going on?"

The white man with the streaked hair lurched out of the dark, a rifle in one hand, hat and boots in the other. The white man's sleeve was marked with blood. So was his face.

Toby recognized the stranger, who paused behind Levi's Bird Cage.

"Where's Kola? Where's the Indian?"

"I don't know—" Michael began.

"You"—Toby sounded less confident, started edging toward the fallen length of wood—"you fold your hand, mister. My confab with this here mick is private."

The hunter glanced at the maul handle. "And one-sided, from the look of it. I'd suggest you light out of here, boy. If the Irishman takes you, no one will shed a tear. You've lost your number one backer."

"What—what d'you mean?"

"You'll find out presently. Just break this up and get going."

Toby seemed to see the blood on the hunter for the first time. "Did you do somethin' to Butt?"

"Shut up and *move!*"

The hunter walked away from the hard-breathing young man. He tossed his hat and boots onto the wagon seat. Toby dashed for the maul handle. He got hold of it just as Michael called, "Look out for yourself, mister!" The hunter pivoted at the waist.

Swung with Toby's full strength, the handle landed athwart his temple and knocked him backward. He floundered against the wagon wheel, stabbing the split stock of his rifle into the dirt to prop himself up. Toby kicked the stock. Reflected light from the tent street shone in the hunter's eyes as he crashed to his knees, hurt but refusing to quit.

Toby reached for the hunter's hair. "What'd you do to Butt?" With an almost regretful expression, the hunter fired the rifle from his hip.

The spurt of light blinded Michael a moment. The reverberating roar silenced the clamor in the Bird Cage. When he opened his eyes, he no longer saw the slightest remorse on the hunter's face.

Bucyrus Tidwell popped into sight between the tents. "Who's out there?"

Toby uttered a series of whimpers. Dropped the maul handle. Leaned his forehead against the wagon and clawed the side with both hands. Then, with a lazy slowness, he slid down until there was no more wood to lean against.

He fell face first on the rumpled blanket. Where his chest had rubbed the wagon, a wide swathe of red glistened like new paint.

Almost instantly, men were shouting and clamoring around Michael. He barely saw the hunter collapse on his side, not unconscious but laboring to breathe. Blood had begun leaking from the man's nose. His eyes closed.

"What the hell's the row?" Tidwell boomed, just as the Sioux, rifle in hand, came slipping into sight at the far side of the Bird Cage. He saw his fallen friend, ran to him, knelt, then glanced up with furious eyes.

"Who did this?"

Michael shoved through the growing crowd, ignoring shouted questions. He pointed to Toby.

"He did part of it. The youngster was after me. Your friend came along, the boy went for him, and your friend took him out. I don't know who bloodied him."

As if there weren't pandemonium enough, a woman began to scream. Down in the direction of Brown's Paradise, Michael thought. The direction from which the hunter had come.

The Sioux cradled the white man's head in his lap.

"Joseph? Joseph, do you hear? I woke and could not find you. I went searching—"

"That's all we need, more goddamn Injun trouble," someone complained.

"There won't be any," Michael said. "He's the white man's partner. The white man helped me."

The keening scream was joined by a second one. Michael walked over to the Sioux, who watched him with suspicion.

"Your friend's hurt. He needs attention. You want to pick him up or shall I?"

The Indian saw half a dozen drawn revolvers in the mob spilling from the lane between Tidwell's and the saloon. Out in the street, a man yelled, "Fetch General Jack!"

"We stay here—" the Sioux began.

"No," Michael said. "I think he'd better rest on the train until this is cleared up."

The Indian stayed motionless. A revolver cocked, loudly.

"You'll be safer somewhere else!" Michael insisted. "Some at this railhead don't like any Indians but dead ones. Did you say your partner's name is Joseph?"

"Yes, Joseph Kingston. He is my *kola.* My sworn friend."

The name meant nothing. Undoubtedly he'd been wrong about having seen the white man before.

"Well, now he's mine too," Michael replied. "You can trust me. Let me have your rifle so some drunken idiot doesn't take a potshot at you. Come on, give it to me."

Doubtful, the Indian searched Michael's strained face. Then he complied.

"Pick him up and bring him along to the train. We'll put him in my bunk."

CHAPTER X

A MATTER OF TRUTH

i

STRANGERS MURMURED in a half-lit dark. They spoke English, but the accents were not his own. Some of the voices carried a Yankee harshness. Others had a certain lilt he'd first heard at the railhead. Irish talk.

Jeremiah came fully awake. His groin, his nose, and his forehead throbbed. When he grew conscious of his surroundings, fright dried his throat.

He was boxed in a bunk—prisoned below, above, and on the right. Only when he floundered over on his side facing the amber light did he see no wall.

His eyes focused on the man who'd almost taken a beating at the wagon. A slender Paddy with a weathered face and brown eyes flecked the color of the lamps in the—

Bunk car, that's where he was. The place was rank with the odor of unclean bodies, abuzz with conversation. About him, he presumed.

He was resting at the top of a tier of three beds. The Irishman with the graying hair and mustache stood on the lowest one, trying to pull up the blanket while Jeremiah pushed it away.

"Easy, lad," the Irishman said. His voice had an echo. Or was that only in Jeremiah's head?

His upper lip felt tender when he explored it with his tongue. Someone had washed his face. The sense of confinement—of threat—intensified.

"Easy, now. You're safe. You've been looked at. Jack Casement knows a bit of field medicine. Nothing's wrong with you except you've got a bashed nose and a bushel of bruises."

"Where's my rifle?"

"The Indian has it."

"Where is he?"

"Sitting down here." The Irishman motioned to the lowest bunk. Jeremiah couldn't see Kola. "No harm will come to him. By the way, my name is Boyle. I've learned yours is Kingston. You needn't speak if it hurts too much. But I want to thank you for what you did."

The golden brown eyes picked up lamplight. A sadness touched the stranger's face as he went on. "The boy's being wrapped for burial. I hate to see him dead, but under the circumstances I've no call to quarrel. Do you want some broth? One of the cooks is willing to—"

"I want out of here."

"Afraid that isn't possible as yet. Casement plans to speak with you. Meantime, you should rest."

"I want out of here!" Jeremiah sat up too quickly, knocking his head on the plank ceiling. Despite his determination, his bones seemed to lose their stiffness. He lay down again, breathing hard.

The light of the car lanterns shimmered, then began to compress, squeezed between layers of darkness. The Irishman touched him.

"Would a drink of whiskey help?"

The panic of enforced confinement still gripped him as he lost consciousness.

ii

—*sorrysorrysorrysorry*—

"What? What did you say?"

"I said—"

It was the Irishman again, barely perceived as Jeremiah's

sleep-clotted eyes came open. The man was still standing on the lower bunk. Evidently time had passed. Some lamps in the car had been extinguished. His aches weren't quite so painful.

Outside, cannon fire rumbled. Then he realized it was a distant prairie storm.

"I said, I'm sorry to wake you. Jack Casement insists on seeing you right now. I tried to persuade him to wait until morning. But he's exercised about all the trouble tonight."

"No objection," Jeremiah said. He was grateful. He didn't want to stay penned in this smelly prison any longer than necessary. Out in the stormy dark there were dead men crying his name. He needed to be away before the living heard.

He clenched his teeth. Started to swing his legs toward the edge of the bunk. The pain wrenched his face.

"Take my hand," Boyle offered.

"No. Stand back."

He hadn't realized how difficult it would be. He struggled until he was on his belly with his legs hanging over the aisle. When the Irishman steadied his elbow, he jerked his arm away resentfully.

He muttered an apology. He wasn't himself because of the confinement, the sense of being entrapped by unfamiliar faces, dim ovals in the equally dim wash of yellow light. Wriggling into position to drop to the floor, he glimpsed Kola with the Ballard. A reassuring sight.

He saw a rectangle of paper tacked to the wall near the head of the bunk. Some drawing of a nigra carrying a—

His eyes opened wide. A guttural sound rose in his throat. He was unable to control the tears of astonishment.

"Joseph?" That was Kola.

"Kingston, what's the trouble?" The Irishman.

"Nothing!" he said, louder than he intended. "Brown almost kicked my balls off, you know. Hurts a bit."

He blinked, clearing his eyes. But it wasn't so easy to rid himself of the surprise and anguish that had torn him like a bullet when he saw two words below the drawing's caption.

M. Kent.

iii

Who was the Irishman? Where had he gotten the picture that was unmistakably Matt's? He wanted to ask, but wouldn't until he was in better control of himself.

Fortunately there were distractions: the effort to walk, Kola supporting him, the Irishman hovering.

They reached the platform between cars. Wind battered his face. Northwestward, a white light flared and spread on the horizon, soon followed by a prolonged roll of thunder. A cloud of dirt carrying bits of grass and other debris went sailing by. Beyond it he glimpsed men laboring to keep one of the tents from falling.

"What time is it?" he asked Boyle.

"Something after three in the morning."

"Bad blow coming."

"Fast," Boyle replied, holding the next door. "This way."

Jeremiah had seen but never spoken to Jack Casement. He was no man for trifling, that much Jeremiah knew the moment he was ushered into the office. Casement was fully dressed, fully awake, and unfriendly.

"Boyle here is pleading you're too banged up to be on your feet, Kingston—that is your name?"

Jeremiah confined his answer to a nod.

"I overruled him. I want tonight's business settled. I have already talked with an Alice Peaslee—do you know a woman called Alice Peaslee?"

"One of Brown's whores."

"Yes. Nancy Dell, the female who caused one of the incidents, is apparently too distraught to speak to anyone."

Casement tipped back and forth in his chair. It squeaked. Even when he sat all the way forward, his legs didn't touch the floor. His glance was nearly as fiery as his beard.

"Alice Peaslee satisfied me that her employer, Adolphus Brown, attacked first."

Relieved, Jeremiah said, "That's correct."

"Two men are dead, however. Brown and his boy of all work."

"Toby came at me with the handle of a sledge. He"—Jeremiah located Michael leaning in a shadowy corner; thunder pealed—"he was all over this gentleman. When I suggested he stop, he turned on me."

"You found it necessary to shoot him?"

"At that moment"—Jeremiah shrugged—"yes."

"Well, you were apparently provoked on both occasions, and Boyle supports the second part of your story. The prostitute confirmed the other part. So I have no cause to detain you. Butt Brown was one of the worst influences in this camp, if there can be any degree of difference between men of his stripe. But I don't want your kind at the railhead either, Mr. Kingston. I don't want murderers here."

"I defended myself!"

"In the first case, apparently you did. The boy is another matter. I want you to take your wagon and your Indian friend and get out. Immediately, and for good."

"Sir," Boyle protested, "you should at least let him rest a bit mor—"

"Immediately," Casement repeated, and swung his squeaking chair to face the desk. He reached for a pile of papers and within seconds was immersed in them. There was no appeal.

iv

Michael helped Kingston and the Sioux hitch the mules. The storm was coming rapidly. Swollen clouds were visible overhead whenever the lightning flashed.

As soon as the wagon was ready, Kingston ordered the Indian to drive to the end of the track and wait. A few moments later, still moving with a lack of steadiness, he led his buffalo pony in the same direction.

"Walk with me a moment, Mr. Boyle."

Michael was puzzled by the hoarseness of Kingston's voice. He didn't know what to make of the hunter. The man was neither illiterate nor constantly rough-spoken. But there was a remote, unfeeling air about him that made Michael thankful Kingston wasn't his adversary. The man seemed able to keep his head while bearing a great deal of pain.

They struggled against the wind, passing behind the tent town. Half a dozen of the canvas structures had been struck in anticipation of the thunderstorm. The rest flapped and tilted toward the east, their poles creaking, their guy ropes whining. Only the Bird Cage showed a lamp.

"Devil of a shame you're turned out so soon, Kingston. Casement has not quite forgotten he's no longer commanding or disciplining Union soldiers."

Kingston laughed in a curt way. "Was he an officer? I suspected."

The buffalo pony shied as they passed the last tent and took the wind's full force. Kingston held his plainsman's hat on his head as they labored toward the grade. Another lightning burst revealed the buffalo guns bobbing in the handmade saddle scabbard.

"I have a question for you," Kingston said.

"What is it?"

Kingston opened his mouth, then hesitated. The question Michael heard was not the one Kingston meant to ask, he thought.

"Why did you permit that boy to maul you?"

"I don't know whether I can explain. I was in the war—"

"Yank side, of course."

Michael nodded. "From your speech, I'd guess you were on the other one."

"Yes, I was. Go on."

"I grew sick of the fighting. I journeyed out here to get away from it and didn't. I had to kill again. I won't bore you with the story, but I promised myself I'd never fight again."

"Think you can stick by such a decision?"

"I can try."

Kingston grunted, then dabbed his sleeve against a thread of blood below his purpled nose. When he spoke again, it was with a wry sadness.

"I admire your determination. I didn't find the war a pleasant or uplifting experience either. But when I came out of it, whole in body if not exactly whole of mind, I made a different choice. I decided I'd never let any human being best me in a fight for my life. Nor would I suffer the behavior of dishonorable men. Your position has its merits, though. I'd urge you to stick by it—"

What the devil was this? Michael wondered. Something close to sadness had crept into Kingston's voice.

Or was he merely imagining that, deceived by the noise of the raging wind?

No, it wasn't imagination. He saw that when the lightning illuminated the prairie again. The rails shone like streaks of iridescent fire, leading beyond the meridian marker to the wagon, the restive mules, the motionless Indian. Kingston's eyes were wet.

"—because if you do, you stand a chance of being a happy man. Don't let any bastard chivvy you into changing your mind."

"Toby nearly did. He kept calling me a coward."

"Not surprised. But I've had a taste of each kind of life. In many ways, yours demands more courage—"

Kingston's voice broke. He pivoted away. Michael squeezed his eyes shut against the blowing grit. He couldn't fathom why this young man who killed so easily seemed eager to counsel him. He was taken by surprise when Kingston seized his arm.

"Where did you get the picture?"

"What?"

"The drawing in your bunk. Where did you get it?"

"Why, from the artist's father."

"Do you know him?"

Michael was alarmed by the intensity of the question. Kingston's fingers dug into his sleeve. Puzzled and annoyed, Michael pulled away. "See here. I hardly consider this an occasion for discussing—"

"Goddamn it, answer me! Do you know the artist's father?"

"Yes, I know him."

Lightning lit heaven. Thunder shook the earth.

"He's my father too," Kingston said.

"Jesus Christ, that's it," Michael breathed. No wonder he'd missed the obvious. He'd been looking in the wrong direction.

"What are you talking about?" Kingston said.

"Your face. It's like Jephtha's."

V

Kingston—or Jeremiah Kent, as he announced himself to be—repeatedly refused to answer Michael's questions about his past. He wouldn't explain how he'd gotten from

Georgia to the railhead, or why he was traveling with a Sioux and calling himself by another name.

Hoping to break through the stubborn barrier of refusals, Michael told him Jephtha Kent believed his youngest son to be dead.

"In a sense that's true, Mr. Boyle. Now what do you know about my brothers?"

Still shaken, Michael described Matthew's survival of the blockade and his marriage, then Gideon's unsuccessful struggle to find a place for himself in New York City, where Jephtha was preaching.

"So both of them came out alive. I'm glad. Is my mother well?"

"She—she died this past summer."

A glare of lightning showed Michael the other man's bent head. Jeremiah made no sound.

"King—Jeremiah—blast! I can't get used to calling you Jeremiah—"

"Don't. It isn't my name any longer, just as Kingston won't be after tonight."

"You've got to tell me where you've been! How you got here—"

"No, Boyle. I refuse. But what about you? I don't recall hearing anyone speak of you. What's your connection with my father?"

Hoping cooperation would engender more of the same, Michael explained. Jeremiah nodded from time to time, and said when Michael finished, "Well, if my mother ever mentioned you before I left Lexington, I've forgotten. I'm happy to hear my father's alive."

"He'll be happy to learn you are, too."

"You're not going to tell him."

"Of course I am! As soon as pos—"

Jeremiah interrupted with a shake of his head. "You won't tell him a thing unless you want to hurt him."

"Good God, it wouldn't be fair to keep this news from—" Michael stopped. There was a measure of truth in what the younger man said. Which truth had priority? He thought of one way he might answer that. "There's a circumstance which could change your mind. You surely recall the California money—"

"Amanda Kent's money? Yes."

"When Jephtha concluded you'd been killed, he decided to will me your share. He adopted me unofficially into the family—in my bunk I have his letter explaining why."

"What you've just said proves he did the right thing. You could have kept the information to yourself. You're a proper Kent, all right."

"Well, I'd never surrender that part. But the inheritance is yours. It doesn't belong to me any longer."

"It certainly does. Consider it your reward for never informing my father, my brothers—anyone—that we've met."

"You *can't* ask—"

"Not ask. Demand."

"You expect me to keep it from Jephtha forever?"

"Unless you don't give a damn about him, yes."

Michael's composure was shattered. Too many shocks had piled one onto another. His eyes started to fill with angry tears. "I can't do it!"

"You can and will. I saved you. For that, and for the money—you owe me. Use the money to give yourself a decent life. Buy a home when you're done working out here. Marry a good woman. Raise a family—" Mockingly, he asked, "You *can* find use for the money, can't you?"

"Why"—suddenly Michael saw a possibility, and felt guilt—"of course. But it would be wrong to—"

"The decision isn't yours."

Up where Kola waited with the wagon, one of the mules brayed. Jeremiah gripped Michael's arm again, gently this time.

"To convince you my father mustn't know, I'll say this much. I was in Texas for a while. I got into a difficulty. Unfortunately, it's become hard for other men to bring me down. And hard for me to let them."

Michael asked himself whether he'd lost his senses. There was a crusty, almost arrogant pride in Jeremiah's voice.

"By the time I left Fort Worth, they had a bounty on my head. By now I expect there's a second one."

"Why?"

"Not important. But I think you'll read about Joseph Kingston in some paper, and fairly soon. When you do, Kingston will be long gone. I'll have another name. Now do you understand why I don't want my father or my brothers to know how I'm living?"

He reached for the double scabbard. Touched one of the buffalo rifles. "I plan to keep living the same way for a good many years."

Michael shuddered. Jeremiah's eyes softened again.

"So you're welcome to the inheritance. I could never put it to use."

"You could travel. Europe, the Orient—you could live well."

"Hell, I haven't even begun to see this country. Besides, I've no head for managing money. The war left me with somewhat limited talents."

"The money could funnel through me. Jephtha need never find out."

Jeremiah pondered. Cocked his head, smiling a little. "Tempting"—the smile disappeared—"but there might be a slip."

"It's unfair to ask me to keep silent. It's damned unfair, and it's wrong!"

"Perhaps. But you'll do it. Your opinion doesn't matter. My father and brothers are the only ones who count in this."

Michael uttered a sigh of frustration. Swiped his forehead with his palm as if his head hurt. "Oh, I suppose"—his voice strengthened—"I suppose sparing them is the honorable thing, but—"

"Honorable?" Jeremiah broke in. "I hadn't thought of it that way." He touched his hat. "I'm grateful you put it in such a light."

Michael felt a splash of rain on his cheeks. Lightning showed him great tumbling clouds directly above, the storm's leading edge sweeping over the railhead.

Jeremiah lifted his foot to his stirrup. He grunted as he hauled himself into the saddle. The rain intensified, blurring, then hiding the wagon waiting out beyond the unfinished track.

"Do I have your promise you'll keep silent, Mr. Boyle?"

Drenched and confused, Michael hesitated. Suddenly Jeremiah's pony reared. He lashed it with the rein until all four hoofs were on the ground. He jerked one of the buffalo guns from the scabbard. He pointed the rifle at Michael's head.

"This piece may misfire because of the downpour"—he

was shouting to be heard—"but if that's the case, I'll deal with you another way. Since you've abandoned fighting, I should have no trouble. I want your promise or I'll see you dead right here."

The rain roared in the silence.

"Boyle?"

Michael lifted his head. "All right. For his sake."

The thin-lipped face jerked in what might have been a smile. Jeremiah slid the rifle back to its place.

"Now say it again. I want to hear the promise given freely."

Not knowing whether he was right or wrong, Michael said, "I promise."

"I'm obliged. I urge you to get out of this damn place while you're still in one piece. Use the money. Amount to something. Find a home and stay there. I'll tell you something about being able to go home. It seldom seems important until you can't do it."

He turned the pony's head. "Goodbye, Mr. Boyle."

"Jeremiah!"

The younger man fought to control the fretful animal.

"Would you have shot me if I hadn't given my word?"

"Yes."

He kicked the pony and galloped west beside the right of way, quickly lost in the rainstorm.

Chapter XI

A Matter of Faith

i

By the time Michael reached the sleeping car, he was soaked and exhausted. But Jeremiah's words denied him rest.

Get out of this damn place while you're still in one piece.

Amount to something.

Find a home and stay there.

The line was past the meridian. He'd helped accomplish that much. But the cost was high.

Killing Worthing.

Watching Dorn and two Cheyenne braves perish when it might have been prevented.

Finding the remains of the massacred hunters.

Being instrumental in Toby's death.

Important as the railroad was to the country, he could never again separate it from violence and suffering.

Jeremiah's face kept intruding as he changed to dry clothes. He barely heard O'Dey's whined complaints about his noise.

He grieved for Jeremiah, by turns callous and considerate.

He grieved for Jephtha too. And Matt, and Gideon. Still,

a painful lie about an unknown grave would be less hurtful to them than the truth—

All at once he rebelled against the burden he'd accepted when he gave his word. But the rebellion lasted only a short time. Amanda Kent had never insisted a man or woman should feel no sorrow or anger. She had insisted sorrow and anger must never keep a man or woman from the right course. He'd keep his promise.

He took down the drawing of the milk vendor and studied it by the feeble light of the one lamp still lit at the end of the car. Instead of the figures on the paper, he saw Jeremiah's eyes. An old man's eyes, aged by distrust and deceits and acts of rage. He and Jeremiah were different, yet in one way they were alike. In the flawed mirror of Jephtha's youngest son he at last confronted an image of what he was—and might become.

He hoped to God he possessed the will to keep his vow. He prayed he'd never reach the point where he would be capable of emulating Jeremiah's curious pride in killing another human being. He didn't think so.

Yet between himself and the hunter there remained a fearful bond. They were both rootless. Both running. Jeremiah had little choice. He did. And he'd come to understand the folly of flight. It was time to seek a hope of peace, however tenuous, some other way.

He laid the drawing up at the head of his bunk and walked forward through the dark train. The only sound was the pelt of rain.

Fortunately Jack Casement was still awake.

ii

Before the first supply train arrived, he went out to the end of the track. It had occurred to him the Kents were collectors of mementos of their common past. He had become a Kent. He wanted a souvenir of his work on the transcontinental line.

The storm had obliterated footprints and wagon tracks. He crouched in the driving rain and scooped a handful of mud and crushed stone from between two ties. He used his soggy bandana to wrap it, tying a secure knot.

When the bandana's contents dried out, he'd hunt up a box for keeping them. Someday, years from now, he might be able to open the box and discover time had erased recollections of decidedly unromantic sweat, tortured muscle, and dead men, leaving only a single fine memory of having lent his hand to building the greatest marvel of the age.

iii

The boy's alarmed voice brought Michael up short at the rear corner of the unpainted building. The front of the building had shown no light—not surprising since the hour was close to midnight. With the exception of two pine-board saloons down near the right of way, Grand Island's business establishments and small homes were dark.

The empty supply train whistled twice as it chugged onto a siding. The whistle had a forlorn sound in the drizzle. The rain had lasted nearly sixteen hours.

On the dark, roofed back porch, Michael thought he saw the unmistakable outline of a Hawken. Aimed his way.

"Only me, Klaus."

The boy scooted to the edge of the porch. "Mr. Boyle?"

"Yes. May I come forward?"

"Sure." The Hawken's butt plate thumped on wood. "You're back from the railhead?"

"So it appears." Michael flexed the cold, stiff fingers curled around the staff to which he'd tied his bundle of personal belongings and an oilskin tube with the drawing carefully rolled inside. "Up a mite late, aren't you?"

"We stay on watch till the saloon crowd settles down. We've had three break-ins lately."

"Ah."

Michael glanced at the slit of light beneath the back door. "Your sister's awake, then?"

"Yes, sir." The boy thumped the door, then pushed it open.

"Hannah? Guess who's here."

iv

Klaus stood aside as Michael climbed the three creaking steps, grateful to be out of the wind and damp. He stepped into an immaculate but crowded room dominated by a massive iron stove. Curtains partially concealed two beds in alcoves. Unfinished shelves held jars and boxes of staples. In the center of the pegged floor stood a large table that had seen hard use. On the table were a flickering lamp, ledgers, scribbled slips of paper, and an open Bible.

Hannah had been seated with her back toward the porch. She rose as Klaus shut the door from outside. Her joyous smile reached deep into her blue-gray eyes.

"Michael!"

He noticed she was wearing a faded gingham dress. It flattered her figure. "Hello, Hannah. I imagine you're surprised to see me."

"No, I've been expecting you, though I wasn't certain when."

He caught the clean soap fragrance of her skin. "I can't believe that."

Still smiling, she walked to a shelf and drew down a milk glass jar containing something dark. She set the jar on the table.

"See for yourself."

He lifted the lid. Inhaled the aroma of pipe tobacco.

"I'm afraid it's dry, but it's all we had in the store. I've ordered more."

He laughed. "My God. You do have cheek!"

"Faith."

His weariness started to slough away. Gazing into her eyes, he experienced an unfamiliar and wondrous sense of calm.

"Are you hungry?" she asked.

"Ravenous!"

"Before I fix you some food, I must say something. I know you have that other woman to think about. I won't blame you if you do. For a while," she added, teasing just a little. "I plan to keep you too busy, and too happy, to bother with her for very long. Now what would you like to eat?"

"Coffee will be enough—but not yet. I want to say something as well. I have a bit of money I didn't mention before—"

A *bit* of money! God above, that insulted Amanda's memory, and Jephtha's goodness. He'd never be able to overcome a sense of guilt at having taken the inheritance from its rightful possessor. But circumstance and Jephtha Kent had dictated that he have it. He wondered how he'd tell Hannah he'd probably be rich as Croesus before he died.

Conscience-stricken, he realized why he wasn't telling her now.

She was waiting for him to finish. "Um," he said, collecting himself, "the money. I believe I can draw on it. I thought—I thought it might help buy goods. Put the place in order." His smile had grown almost shy.

"That's wonderful, Michael. In Kearney I saw a piece of property ideal for a store. We needn't limit ourselves to just one."

We?

The audacity! He burst out laughing again.

"I don't know why you're so amused," Hannah said in a cheerfully tart way. "You look wretched. Sit down. Rest. We'll discuss the store later."

"Hannah—"

"Coffee will be here in just—"

"Hannah."

She turned.

"I must be fair to you. I must warn you."

"My, that sounds forbidding." She hurried on to the stove.

"Please listen! I've resigned from Casement's crew. I've come back. But the thing is—"

Exhaling, he thumped the bundle on a chair.

"I don't know if—ah, *damn*!"

He faced away from her.

"Are you trying to tell me you're uncertain about whether you'll stay?"

"Yes, that's it."

She walked back from the stove with a soft rustling of underskirts. He peeked over his shoulder. Her hair and eyes glowed in the lamplight, but it was that astonishing smile which truly illuminated her face.

"I just don't know, Hannah."

She picked up the jar of tobacco and set it close to the Bible. Lord, what a lovely sight she was! How peaceful it seemed in this plain room—

"I do," she said, and put her arms around his neck and kissed him.

★ *Book Five* ★

The Scarlet Woman

Chapter I

Meeting with a Mountebank

i

Be careful, Louis Kent thought as he poured brandy for himself and his guest. Forget the man's nautical pretensions and his air of butcher-boy innocence. Remember his reputation. He could be baiting a pretty trap.

Louis stoppered the decanter. His swarthy hand was steady. Only his black eyes betrayed his tension, shifting to the left to see what his visitor was doing.

The man's fat legs straddled the hearth. His stubby pink fingers were locked behind his back, exactly as if he were on the bridge of one of those steamships he fancied. He was studying the objects above the marble fireplace of Kentland's overheated library. A servant had kindled the fire while Louis and his three guests had dined on boned squab.

Slender and erect, Louis lifted the crystal snifters and swirled the brandy. The huge neo-Gothic house he'd built to indulge his unlamented former wife was utterly still this January evening in 1868. All the help had retired to their quarters on his instructions. Just after arriving, Louis' male guest had whispered that sending the servants away might be advisable. Once business was disposed of, the gentlemen could then enjoy themselves in privacy.

Upstairs, one of the women laughed. Louis was startled by his body's sudden and pronounced reaction. The little ballerina brought along for him was equally as vapid as Mr Fisk's inamorata, an actress named Josie Mansfield. Neither woman had uttered an intelligent sentence during dinner.

Intelligence was not a quality Louis Kent demanded or even found desirable in a woman, however. Fortunately most women lacked it. He knew from experience that pretenses in that direction merely led to trouble.

Still, the companions of Mr. James Fisk, Junior, were particularly witless. Fisk didn't seem to mind. During the meal he'd repeatedly tickled Josie Mansfield's chin, which sent the other girl into convulsive laughter. The dark-haired, pale-skinned, and voluptuous Miss Josie saw nothing improper about tickling Fisk right back—in front of a relative stranger. She'd also kissed Fisk's cheek several times, and called him Sardines, which nearly forced Louis to retire and throw up.

Now the ladies had gone upstairs to bathe. Quite against his will, Louis found himself vividly recalling the little blond dancer whose "professional" name—Nedda Chetwynd—was almost as ludicrous as her lack of social graces. Miss Chetwynd had clearly been brought along as a bribe. He had no intention of availing himself of the gift until he spied the trap or, if there was none, struck a bargain.

Yet the trill of feminine laughter had aroused him. Annoyingly, he found himself perspiring. His olive forehead glistened as he continued warming the snifters.

There'd been a January thaw. Fog drifted past the stained-glass windows at the end of the long, rectangular library. No lights showed outside. Kentland stood on the bluffs of the Hudson near Tarrytown, well separated from neighboring estates. The isolation was appropriate for a chat involving polite treachery.

He had to be wary. A mistake, even a wrong inflection, might cost him everything. The stakes which had brought Mr. Fisk to Kentland were immense.

Fisk fingered his yellow curls and smacked his lips as he surveyed the various articles on display. A scabbarded French sword hung above the mantel. Immediately below was a polished Kentucky rifle.

On a bookshelf to the left of the hearth stood a small

green bottle containing a thin layer of tea leaves which would soon be a century old. A stylized version of the bottle still appeared on the masthead of Louis Kent's lucrative newspaper, the New York *Union,* and served as the colophon of the Boston printing house to which he no longer devoted much attention.

In a corresponding nook on the other side, the gaslights glared on the glass front of a display case with wooden ends. Inside the case, a slotted velvet pedestal held a tarnished fob medallion. In front of the pedestal lay a small circle of tarred rope.

The sword, rifle, and bottle had all been accumulated by the founder of the family, Philip Kent. Philip's second son Gilbert—begetter of Louis' mother, Amanda Kent—had struck the medallion, incorporating the tea bottle symbol and adding a pretentious Latin motto, *Cape locum et fac vestigium.* Gilbert had given the medallion to Amanda's cousin Jared, who had also acquired the little bracelet. It dated from the 1812 war. The tarred cordage had come from the frigate popularly known as *Old Ironsides,* on which Jared had served.

With another smack of his lips, the man the press liked to call Jubilee Jim completed his survey. He was a red-cheeked New Englander with a sizable paunch that Louis found reprehensible in one so young. Fisk was thirty-three, two years older than his crony, the melancholy Mr. Gould of the Wall Street brokerage firm of Smith, Gould, and Martin.

At thirty, Louis Kent was trim, handsome, and urbane. His father's Spanish blood showed in his coloring and the Latin cast of his features. Two more dissimilar conspirators could hardly have been found; Mr. Fisk looked deceptively soft and jocular. He enhanced his aura of good-humored innocence with his wardrobe—tonight dark blue trousers and a sea captain's jacket aglow with brass buttons and dripping with gold frogging.

It seemed improbable that this man who had once hawked tinware in the Green Mountains and shoveled up manure in Van Amburgh's Circus was a power in the American financial community. Outwardly, Fisk deserved the opprobrius description uttered by the influential minister, Harry Ward Beecher: "The supreme mountebank of fortune." But Louis Kent wasn't deceived by catchphrases. He knew that behind the clown demeanor there lurke something far more substantial than a mind bemused b ballerinas and braid. Men who allowed themselves to b lulled by Fisk's facade usually paid dearly.

Louis didn't intend to find himself suddenly included i that group—no matter what sort of trap Jubilee Jim wa baiting.

ii

"Fascinating collection of trinkets," Fisk declared. A pudgy hand rose to twist the points of his Napoleon II mustache. "Have some significance in the family, do they?

"They did at one time." Louis handed him the brandy "I should have gotten rid of them long ago. The sword, th rifle, and that tea come from my great-grandfather."

"The mean-looking fellow whose portrait's in the draw ing room?"

Louis nodded. "He collected them before or during th Revolution. Apparently he found some inspiration in ther that I fail to perceive."

To begin convincing Fisk that he was the right sort, h added, "I'll stand with Sam Adams."

Fisk gulped the brandy as if it were water. "What'd h have to say?"

"That there wasn't a democracy in the history of th world that had not eventually committed suicide. I assum he meant common people were uniformly venal and gull ible. I agree. I don't noise it about, though. I prefer to tak advantage of it while stump speakers divert the rabble wit fairy stories about the goodness of democracy an humankind."

Fisk waddled to a chair. "Careful, now. In the Congres sional elections a year ago last fall, you were a pretty hc stump speaker yourself."

Louis flicked a bead of sweat from his lip. The man wa beginning to test him.

"God forbid that you should ever find me standing on stump, Mr. Fisk."

The visitor didn't smile. "You addressed certain dinner parties. Quite a few, Jay reminded me."

A deliberate thrust, Louis decided. *Jay* was a name men feared. It was vital he not seem intimidated.

"Certainly," he snapped. He sat down opposite the fat man. "I waved the bloody shirt just as all good Republicans did. The objective was to pack the Congress, and we achieved it. This fall we'll get that drunken tailor out of the White House and elect someone more amenable to friendship with business. General Grant, I hope."

Fisk meditated. "Andy may be out sooner than the fall. All I hear from Washington is talk of impeaching him. Thad Stevens and his Congressional crowd want his scalp."

"Johnson was a fool to defy the Tenure of Office Act by trying to remove Secretary Stanton from the War Department."

"Still can't see why old Thad's so hell bent on impeachment, though. Andy was whipped last year when the military reconstruction bills put the cork in Lincoln's bottle of sweet forgiveness. The five military districts down South will soon be filled with twenty thousand Federal soldiers. Including some nigger militia, I'm told. I s'pose you're in favor?"

Louis smiled and ignored the obvious bait. "Mr. Fisk, I don't give a goddamn what happens down South unless it helps national elections come out the right way."

"Helps the industrial and financial sector?"

"Exactly."

"You aren't all wild to promote nigger freedom?"

"Only when it serves the purpose I mentioned."

"You aren't thumping to get 'em treated just like white men?"

"Absolutely not. They aren't."

Louis drank too much brandy then. It scalded his throat. He was having a devil of a time convincing Fisk. The inquisition irritated him. He supposed it was the price of gaining the man's confidence.

He hadn't done so yet.

"Don't mean to doubt you, Mr. Kent. Just trying to establish where you stand. You *have* been pretty closely identified with the Radical Republicans. You were quoted all over the East Coast before the sixty-six elections—"

Fisk leaned back and closed his eyes in a drowsy way. " 'Every unregenerate rebel calls himself a Democrat.' "

Louis' hand constricted on the snifter. The foxy bastard knew his speech by heart!

" 'Every man who murdered Union prisoners—who invented dangerous compounds to burn steamboats and trains—who contrived hellish schemes to introduce yellow fever into Northern cities—calls himself a Democrat. In short' "—Fisk's eyes popped open; his lips curved into a cupid's bow smile—" 'the Democratic Party may be described as a common sewer and loathsome receptacle.' " Fisk sipped. "You were quoted, Mr. Kent."

Louis gave it right back. "I arranged it, Mr. Fisk. For public consumption. Hell"—he waggled the snifter—"I stole most of those words from Oliver Morton of Indiana. I think it's intelligent to be on the right side at the right time. But I never permit politics—or what the public perceives as my politics—to interfere with business. I chatted with Mr. Gould at that dinner for major shareholders—"

"Made a good impression, too," Fisk admitted.

Louis concealed his excitement. The offhand remark partially answered a question he'd been pondering for the past five days—ever since he'd received the note from his guest written on the gold-embossed stationery of Fisk & Belden, Stockbrokers. The note had requested a confidential meeting.

Louis had sent a reply via messenger, inviting Fisk to Kentland. But he hadn't been sure whether Fisk had acted independently. Now he suspected he hadn't. That made the visit twice as important. It also meant he was swimming with two sharks instead of one.

He pressed his advantage. "Mr. Gould and I discussed a bit of politics. He said that in a Republican district, he's a Republican. In a Democratic district, he's a Democrat. In a doubtful district, he's doubtful—but he's always for the New York and Erie Railroad Company. That's been my position ever since I started acquiring Erie shares three years ago."

The fat man's eyes grew curiously opaque as he heaved himself up from the chair. "Damn fine brandy."

Louis jumped to take the empty snifter. He prayed Fisk would overlook the perspiration he felt on his forehead.

He sensed a watershed had been reached. He hoped he hadn't said the wrong things.

iii

While Louis poured with a hand less steady than before, another squeal of laughter drifted from the high reaches of the house.

"Your comments are helpful, Mr. Kent. Don't mind saying they've increased my confidence in the outcome of this discussion. With millions up for grabs, confidence is important."

Louis shuddered with relief. Fortunately Fisk didn't notice. He had an eye cocked at the library's arched ceiling. The woman upstairs was still laughing.

"Time we got down to issues," he said abruptly. "The ladies might grow impatient if we dawdle too long. I keep my wife Lucy up in Boston, but I don't do it solely to free my schedule for business transactions!"

He winked and snickered like a boy with a lewd secret. Louis gave him the snifter. "Many thanks."

Fisk walked to the stained-glass window and peered at the fog. Louis used the opportunity to whip out a linen handkerchief and wipe his brow. He had the kerchief hidden when Fisk turned.

"I think you know the situation, Mr. Kent. In the next couple of months, the favors of the dear old Scarlet Woman are going to be fought for like the very devil." The Scarlet Woman was the Street's term for the Erie. "That's why Jay and I decided to approach you now."

There it was. The suspicion confirmed.

Fisk's eyes lost any semblance of cordiality. "Just where are you going to stand when the war's declared?"

Louis didn't want to appear too eager. He shrugged.

"On the winning side, I trust."

"All very well to generalize, but I traveled up here for specifics! The first test is right around the corner. Through the board members he controls, the Commodore wants us to cancel our rate reductions on freight. He'd like us to go back to charging the same as his Central Line." Fisk licked his lower lip. "But to do that would only settle the dispute *his* way. I hope you don't object to candid remarks about the Commodore, sir?"

More bait. Louis decided not take the whole piece. He knew the information Fisk was after, but withheld it.

"Not at all. I'll be even more candid. The Commodore may be seventy-two years old, but he still wants to gobble any competition that confronts him. That's always been his style. We both know he's after absolute control of the passenger and freight business between here and the Great Lakes." Carefully Louis revealed a bit more of his feelings. "Christ knows where the foul-mouthed old vulture found his passion for railroads so late in life."

It was working. Hearing the word vulture, Fisk had almost smiled. He put in softly, "Same place we all did. In our pockets."

"He swallowed up the Harlem and Hudson lines. Then he got hold of the New York Central but he still wasn't satisfied. Now he's bought into the Erie and aims to fix the rates."

Fisk's eyes looked tiny and piercing. "And with the Erie in his pocket, the game's won. Everyone but the Commodore comes out a loser."

"I don't propose to be a loser, Mr. Fisk. He's not going to win."

"You sound as if you're offering guarantees."

"You know I can't do that. I don't have a majority position with the Boston group. I do have large holdings, however. The group listens to me. I can offer a substantial degree of advice. And I'm willing."

A genuine smile then. "Capital!"

Louis tried to contain his excitement. To be allied with the two shrewdest and most powerful men on the Street not only meant unbelievable opportunities for profit; it meant prestige. He'd been jockeying toward this goal for months. Fisk's note had abruptly opened the door. Coming so close was almost dizzying.

He feigned a thoughtful, sober attitude.

"But before I say anything further, I must tell you I do *not* fully understand the current situation. I need a clearer picture."

"You just said you're pals with Elbridge and Jordan!"

"But not privy to every one of their secrets. Or those of the Erie board."

Fisk pondered. "All right. I assume you're aware Mr. Elbridge of your group was Vanderbilt's handpicked president of the Erie?"

"Of course. I was getting at the current relationship of Drew and the Commodore."

"Strictly business," Fisk snapped. "Vanderbilt and Uncle Dan'l used to play cards together, but that's over. So is any pretense of friendship. Ever since the Commodore started acquiring stock, he's been very exercised about Uncle Dan'l's fondness for using Erie money as if it were his own."

Louis nodded. On the Street, Drew was sometimes called the Speculative Director. He'd literally purchased the job of Erie treasurer by means of loans he'd provided when the road was foundering. Fisk went on.

"Dan's tapped as much as sixteen million to operate in the Street. So when Vanderbilt said he wanted Uncle Dan'l off the board last fall, your friend Elbridge jumped through a hoop."

"And you and Mr. Gould were somehow spared."

Fisk had no comment. Louis didn't pursue the matter. He'd be foolish to insist on knowing how that little rescue operation had been arranged.

"But Vanderbilt reneged—" he prompted.

A vigorous nod from Fisk. "On his own. There was no consultation with your group, was there?"

"None."

"Thought so. Vanderbilt didn't consult anyone, just forced his position on us through the board members he owns. The truth is, he got scared. He thought Dan Drew might be more dangerous out of sight with his shares and his money than he would be at our table. The rest of us agreed. So back on the board he came."

"Not everyone agreed," Louis said. "Frankly, those of us in the Boston group considered Vanderbilt's sudden reversal a sellout."

"Even Elbridge?"

"Yes. I'm still puzzled, though. Follow me a moment, if you will."

He felt like a man on a rope that spanned an abyss. A wrong step and he was through.

"Vanderbilt removed Drew from the board, then brought him back. You and Mr. Gould are allied with Drew. It's possible all three of you could still be allied with Vanderbilt."

"Mr. Kent," Fisk purred, "if that were true, would I be here?"

"You could be testing the opposition."

Louis' audacity brought a grudging chuckle from Fisk. "You're shrewd, just like Jay said. But it's tit for tat, sir. Elbridge of *your* group was Vanderbilt's tame dog."

"No longer. Not since the sellout."

"Are you speaking personally, or for the group?"

"Well, Elbridge and Jordan and the others—I suppose it's conceivable the Commodore could placate them somehow." He put the offer in plain sight. "Provided someone in the group isn't actively working to prevent it."

"Such as yourself?"

"Draw your own conclusions."

"No, sir. I want it said plain. Are you ready to sell the Commodore out? Form another alliance? Influence your group to stand fast against him?"

"If the reward is sufficiently generous."

"How generous?"

Louis' fingers curled against his palms, pressing hard. His gaze remained locked with Fisk's.

"I had in mind a seat on the board. A directorship."

Fisk didn't react. Louis was sure he'd asked for too much. Overstepped—

Then Jubilee Jim's laugh boomed.

"That's a coincidence, Mr. Kent. Jay sent me up here to offer you just that."

CHAPTER II

THE TAME DOG

i

"WELL, SIR? DO WE HAVE A BARGAIN?"

Louis wanted to give Fisk an immediate yes. He was more than willing to be bought; he was eager. But he didn't want the man thinking him too compliant.

"We're very close."

Fisk's smile disappeared. "There's something else?"

"I'd like a further clarification of your connection with Vanderbilt."

"There is none!"

"I'm sorry, but there's Drew. You and Mr. Gould are again closely associated with that hymn-singing old robber."

Blandly, Fisk said, "Dan Drew brought Jay and myself onto the board last October. Since then, we have never been disassociated. But as I indicated before, the friendly relationship between Drew and the Commodore has been dissolved."

"Does the Commodore know?"

Fisk's grin was sly. "He will before long. Don't be too concerned with appearances, Mr. Kent. When you've gained a bit more experience in this sort of thing"—tact prompted Louis to let the deliberate slur pass without reply—"you'll learn that only two things matter. How much stock you control, and whether you're in a position to influence the price."

The fat man was right, of course. In the last decade, the Erie line from Jersey City to Buffalo had been a speculator's dream. After insinuating himself as treasurer, Drew had repeatedly used his position to advantage. His biggest and most spectacular killing had been in '66, when he'd played his favorite role—the bear.

Erie stock had been trading at a relative high of ninety-five. Bemused by false hopes of a price rise, the bulls had agreed to buy shares from Drew which they assumed he did not as yet own. They believed the old man was mistakenly gambling that the value of Erie shares would fall.

But Drew hadn't been gambling. He'd known exactly what he was about. He quickly manipulated the price of Erie downward from ninety-five to fifty by dumping twenty-eight thousand units of unissued stock along with other shares resulting from conversion of roughly three million in Erie bonds. Something like fifty-eight thousand shares all told deflated the price just as Drew had planned. It had come out later that he'd amassed the secret hoard of stock and bonds as security for one of his loans.

The bulls were trapped. Because of their prior commitment, they were forced to pay ninety-five for shares worth fifty. There was no regulatory agency to even wag a finger. Those not involved laughed—enviously. Those who'd been caught recalled too late the caustic maxim of the Street: "Dan'l says up, Erie goes up. Dan'l says down, Erie goes down. Dan'l says wiggle-waggle, Erie bobs both ways."

Louis himself would be in a position to participate in such a coup if he gained a seat on the board. It all depended on the outcome of this conversation. Three factions were involved. One was Vanderbilt, who wanted the freight rates fixed.

The second faction consisted of Drew and his newfound friends, Gould and Fisk. They wanted to dominate the line for precisely the reason Louis hoped to ally himself with them—the profit that could be milked from stock manipulation.

The third group, membership in which had brought Louis

to the threshold of this stunning opportunity, was nominally led by the Boston money men John Elbridge and Eben Jordan. They sought control of the Erie not only to jiggle its stock, but also to shore up one of their own projects, a planned but as yet unfinished feeder line called the Boston, Hartford, and Erie. In the spring of the preceding year, the backers of the B. H. & E. had arranged a subsidy from the state of Massachusetts to help complete the line. In order to make the funds flow, an ever larger sum had to be raised from outside sources.

Louis remained on the offensive. "I'll grant what you say is true, Mr. Fisk. There's still one thing I don't understand."

Fisk fiddled with a curl. "I thought I was asking the questions tonight. But go ahead."

"I'm flattered you and Mr. Gould chose to approach me. Still, it would be more logical for you to go straight to one of the Boston board members."

"Jay'd be happy to," Fisk said blithely. "Then we wouldn't need you at all. I'm the fly in the ointment. Old Eben and I don't get along."

"I've heard that. But Jordan's closemouthed on certain subjects. I didn't know whether it was a fact or a rumor."

"Fact. During the war, he and I had a falling-out. I was arranging cotton deals for him. The son of a bitch decided my expenses were running too high. He discharged me. You were into cotton yourself, weren't you?"

That was a sore point. "I intended to be. My second cousin had different ideas."

"Who is he, some government busybody?"

"No, at the time he was a reporter. Today he's a cheapjack Methodist preacher. He lives in the city. He, my mother's Irish clerk, and that Jew banker, Rothman, decided my little venture was immoral. They spilled the whole story to the press."

"Must have missed the item. Probably appeared when I was working the Western Theater for Eben."

"Well, I was out of cotton before I got in."

"The luck of the game, Mr. Kent. I spent my cotton days in Memphis. Dealt with some first-rate gentlemen of the Confederacy through a charming go-between. Little actress. Hot piece, she was."

Fisk's pink lips curled in a smile of pride.

"Never got caught, either. I was giving Eben all the goddamn cotton he could mill. He delivered Jordan Marsh blankets to the Army and cleaned up. But he got scared by some prying from Union headquarters. He used my expenses as an excuse. Know what he handed me in severance pay? A measly sixty-five thousand dollars. I haven't any cause to be friends with Mr. Eben Jordan. Actually, I think Jay and I will ultimately be glad we had to deal with you. You strike me as our sort."

Our sort. Louis couldn't resist a moment of self-congratulation. Both Fisk and Jay Gould were giants on the Street. To be accepted as their confidant was a supreme accolade.

He decided it was time to abandon the pose of reluctance. He helped himself to a perfecto from an inlaid box. He lit up and sniffed the fragrant smoke.

"Thank you for saying so, Mr. Fisk. You've answered my questions."

"Hell!" Fisk cried with a flamboyant gesture. "We're getting on well enough to drop the courtesies. Let's make it Louis and Jim."

Louis smiled through a veil of smoke. "Happy to, Jim."

"Do we have a bargain?"

"We do. I'll exert every effort to see the Boston group sides with you and Mr. Gould."

"Your efforts have got to be discreet until the directors meet and the Commodore's men actually put a motion to fix freight rates on the table."

"No one will ever hear about this meeting. When the motion's made, I feel confident it will go down."

Fisk's chubby lips quivered. He was pleased.

"As soon as that happens, the directorship's yours. 'Course, holding a board seat won't be all roses. When the Commodore's motion *is* defeated, he'll know he has a scrap on his hands. Jay and I reckon he'll try like hell to capture a majority position in the stock so he can merge the line into the Central or let it die altogether."

"I'm prepared to fight," Louis returned quietly. "I'm confident we'll win."

Fisk laughed again. "Jay's going to be fond of you, Louis."

"I'm not in this for compliments. When you spy a money

machine, you don't turn your back. I've done well with my steel interests, the spinning works in Rhode Island, the newspaper, and everything else I own."

"Jay likes the notion of your having that sheet. He's always been a keen student of using publicity to his favor."

"I've only lost one money machine in all my career. That cotton-trading company."

A memory of Julia disturbed him. In her own way, hadn't she been such a machine? Deliberately acquired to improve his social standing and thereby gain him introductions to men like Vanderbilt, who could and did suggest investment opportunities? He'd lost her too.

The loss was even more humiliating than the collapse of Federal Suppliers. He could comprehend how that company had been ruined. The reason for the destruction of his marriage still eluded him. He continually fell back on the easiest explanation. Julia had lost her mind.

"I guarantee we'll use the paper to advantage, Jim. In fact, to get what we want, I'm not averse to using any means available."

Fisk slapped the arm of his chair. "Louis, you're a fighter! I'd heard that. Takes a man with nerve to ride in General Lee's Left Wing. Jay did."

Louis preened. The term referred to gold speculation, which he and others in the North had engaged in profitably during the war, ignoring Washington's pleas that the currency must be kept sound.

The perfecto tasted better by the moment. He'd really done a good evening's work. Aligned with the winning side in what the Street was already calling the Erie War, he could conceivably wind up increasing his net worth five- or tenfold.

Abruptly, the euphoric mood disappeared. Fisk had a mild frown on his face. He scrutinized Louis while he scratched the front of his ostentatious jacket. Then he stunned the other man.

"I surely hope we can trust you."

"My God, we have a bargain! Why would you doubt—?"

The tiny eyes never blinked.

"I believe at one time you were pretty thick with Vanderbilt yourself." Fisk was demanding the information Louis had held back earlier.

"Correction." Face darkening, Louis jumped up. "My former wife's father, Oliver Sedgwick, was thick with Vanderbilt. That's how I became interested in the speculative side of the railroad business. Sedgwick's dead. And I haven't played whist at Vanderbilt's house since I divorced Julia a year ago."

Liar. She divorced you.

"Reassuring," Fisk murmured "Jay will be heartened. Uncle Dan'l will be heartened." The fat man relaxed again. "Hate to say it, but in many ways old Daniel's a simpleton. Robs the road six days a week and sings hymns at St. Paul's on Sunday to salve his conscience. He's wild to build more seminaries and have them named after him. Jay and myself, we have no such ambitions. We're in this and everything else to make money—and by Jesus have a good time doing it!"

Fisk thumped his snifter down. Louis' tension drained away. He could appreciate why the hostile press had little good to say for the proper and happily married Gould, but tinged its columns about the "railroad pirates" with grudging admiration of Fisk. Unless you peered closely into his eyes, or paid strict attention to what he said, the man had a bumptious likability which the yellow curls, plump cheeks, and luxuriant moustachios only enhanced.

Gould, by contrast, struck many people as downright sinister. Even now, Louis could see him vividly. It was not a comforting image.

Fisk's partner was barely five foot six inches, with a tubercular cast to his features. He wore a full beard to conceal what he must have considered a weak face. But Louis had come to judge men by their eyes. Gould's lacked any trace of human emotion. Coupled with a murmurous voice and a habit of rarely speaking above a confidential whisper, he inspired respect and sometimes terror among his adversaries. As should any man who'd earned his first million dollars by age twenty-one. At a recent dinner gathering of holders of substantial blocks of Erie, Gould had differed with one of Drew's opinions, and imperiously overridden his objections.

Afterward, old Drew had whispered to Louis in a shaken voice, "That man, Kent—that man's touch is death."

Remembering, Louis shivered. He didn't intend to get

on the wrong side of Mr. Jay Gould. To do so would not only be unprofitable but downright dangerous.

ii

"Glad we've settled things," Fisk said as he lumbered to his feet. He rubbed his hands together and bounced on his toes. "Disreputable and shabby as she is, there's still gold in the Scarlet Lady's drawers. And you're right, no sensible fellow surrenders a money machine. I was wiped out twice in the Street right after the war. Uncle Dan'l came to me needing cash to tighten his hold on the Erie. I helped the old fool unload his Stonington Steamboat Line—God, I love those boats. Must own a line myself one of these days. I'll make it the fanciest the world's ever seen. Marble and mirrors in the saloons! Caged canaries singing in every—well, never mind that. Let's just say I made a smart move getting next to that pious cow drover. You made the same kind of move tonight. We don't have a thing to worry about."

Louis looked faintly cynical. "Except Commodore Vanderbilt's brains, his thirty millions of capital, and the gentlemen he keeps in his pocket. Judge Barnard of the Supreme Court fifth district, for example. Vanderbilt can spew out injunctions the way the Treasury turns out coins."

But Fisk had clearly tabled such concerns for the remainder of the evening. "Let's fret about that when he starts doing it. Right now I feel good about the whole operation. 'Course"—a shrug—"I always feel good working with Jay. He's got the brains and I've got the brass." He laid a pudgy arm across Louis' back. "You'll see. You're one of us now."

Louis was faintly repelled by the odor of sweat oozing from his guest's collar and cuffs. Fisk bubbled on.

"We should join the ladies, don't you think? Oh, but before we do—"

A soft hand closed on Louis' arm. He was again jolted by a change in Fisk's tone.

"Maybe it's not necessary to say this straight out. Still, we shouldn't have any misunderstandings."

"No, we shouldn't," Louis agreed, disturbed by the glint in Fisk's eyes. "Do we?"

A shrug. "Not so long as you keep one fact in mind. Jay and myself, we call and play the tune. I'm an easygoing fellow—"

Louis doubted that, but said nothing.

"But Jay always wants to be firmly in command. No interference. No arguments. Nothing said or done to muck up his plans, or embarrass him."

"In other words, if I'm a tame dog—"

"That's a pretty harsh way to put it, Louis." Fisk smiled. "But a good one. If you ever cross Jay by choice or by accident, you, not Jay, will come out hurt. That's why I threw in with him. He's been a scrapper since he was a little tad helping his pa tend cows on the family farm up by West Settlement. I don't believe Jay's pa thought very much of him. Too frail. Kind of disappointed the old man, Jay did—one boy among five sisters. From the start, I think Jay wanted to show his pa—maybe the whole damn world—that a thick arm doesn't count for as much as a smart head. People say there's sharp blood in Jay's veins, too. Jew blood. His great-grandfather led militia in the Revolution, only his name was Colonel Abraham Gold. The family started calling itself Gould around 1800. There's a lot of reasons Jay's a fighting cock. No man's ever bested him that I heard about."

The fat man's tongue worked across his lower lip, leaving a gleam of saliva.

"No man," he repeated. "Old Charles Leupp tried."

Louis had never met Leupp, but he was familiar with the story. Leupp had been a respected New York leather merchant who prided himself on personal integrity. He'd bought a sixty-thousand-dollar partnership in a Pennsylvania tannery Jay Gould had acquired before he was of legal age. The original tannery partner, Zadoc Pratt, had seen the enterprise thrive under young Gould's managerial ability. But profits appeared skimpy. When Pratt accused Gould of diverting funds for private speculation and doctoring the books to cover his deceit, Gould's reply was reportedly a sardonic smile and a shrug.

Gould offered to buy Pratt's interest using money obtained from Mr. Leupp. The second partner was mulcted just like the first. Leupp discovered Gould had used his name and his capital to effect a corner on hides. Confronted again, Gould admitted his crooked behavior. Threats of legal action merely made him laugh. And he was unmoved by claims that he'd soiled Leupp's good name. Nothing moved Jay Gould save the prospect of a success achieved by speculating with huge sums of money—preferably other people's. He wished Charles Leupp good luck if the firm were dragged into bankruptcy. Leupp went back to his New York mansion, contemplated his dishonored status, and shot himself to death with a handgun.

The point of the reference wasn't lost on Louis. "I know what happened to Leupp. You can assure Mr. Gould I won't oppose him, or embarrass him in any way."

Still, Fisk's oblique threat was hard to swallow. He disliked hearing the truth when it was couched in a phrase such as *tame dog.* He tried to remember the main chance; the millions to be made milking the Erie.

"Just wanted you to understand." Fisk nodded. "No pussyfooting between partners, eh?"

He slapped Louis' shoulder. "Time to frolic! Did your butler send up the champagne?"

"He had orders. Three bottles to each room."

Louis opened the door, relieved to escape the stuffy library. Gaslights flickering in the entrance hall cast a bloated shadow of Fisk against the wall as the men strolled to the opulent staircase and started for the second floor. Fisk rambled on with other anecdotes complimentary to his partner.

They walked down a long corridor to an intricately carved door. When Fisk opened it, Louis saw the dark-haired young woman standing before the blaze in the hearth. Her body was barely concealed by a thin gown.

Josie Mansfield hurried forward. "Sardines, I thought you were going to leave me by myself all night!"

"Be with you in a moment, Dolly."

The actress remained near the door. Fisk's voice grew a shade heavier.

"I said I'll be with you in a moment."

Josie slipped out of sight. Fisk was unsmiling.

"Anything bothering you, Louis?"

His chin lifted. "Yes." In spite of the dictates of good

sense, he blurted, "I don't care to be called anyone' tame dog."

"That's what you are, though. Bought and paid for."

He chuckled. It had a hard sound.

"Being a tame dog isn't so bad, Louis. When the rest c the world's freezing and starving, tame dogs stay warm an well fed. Keep that in mind. Keep Charles Leupp i mind, too."

He reached up to loosen his black sailor's cravat. He wa still smiling as the door closed.

Chapter III

The Portrait

i

Louis didn't bother to knock before entering his own rooms farther down the hall. He surprised Nedda Chetwynd, who was blond, dumpling-cheeked, twenty-one, and eminently forgettable.

She sat naked in bed, her breasts coyly covered by the silk sheet. She'd already opened one of the champagne bottles in the silver stand. One hand clutching the sheet, she used the other to sip from a goblet. Her smile was hesitant.

He didn't return it. Why should he? The girl meant nothing to him. He was sure Fisk had given her explicit instructions, and promised her a handsome present afterward.

He scowled when his body responded to the girl's nearness. He hated to dignify her that way. He reminded himself he was experiencing a reaction solely because his encounters with women had grown less and less frequent during the past year. The press of his personal affairs kept him too busy and, often, too tired.

He stripped off his coat and cravat, then reached up to trim the recently installed gas jet near the oil portrait of Julia. He spun away and attended to the other ornate fixtures around the room, conscious of the girl watching him as she drank champagne in a revoltingly noisy way.

Ah, well. No point fretting about her manners. She'd serve her purpose and he'd never be forced to see her again.

Although the walls between the upstairs rooms were thick, Josie Mansfield's high-pitched laugh was loud enough to catch his attention. Then came a great bullish bellow from Fisk. Almost at once, the bed in the adjacent room began to creak. The rhythmic noise quickened with astonishing rapidity.

"I'll be with you in a moment, my dear." He didn't glance at the girl as he said it.

He stepped into his dressing room, closed the door partway, and began to remove the rest of his clothing. Even in the smaller chamber, the racket of Fisk's bed was audible.

He had to admit some of the man's crude ways repelled him. On the other hand, Fisk definitely was not stupid. Despite the remarks about tame dogs, Louis vowed not to think badly of his new partner. Fisk had given him exactly what he wanted. A directorship was nothing less than a mandate to steal from the poor old Scarlet Woman.

In the past couple of years, the Erie had become notorious because of its directors and its condition. The press, with a few notable exceptions which included the *Union*, constantly decried the line's lack of service to the public.

The hope of such service was, of course, pathetic. "Twin streaks of rust" was a popular term for the Erie and it was a fitting one. The line's seven-hundred-plus miles of track were ancient and dangerous. Its rolling stock was a disgrace. Collisions and derailments took place almost every week, as did injuries and loss of life. Just after New Year's, another switchman had been permanently crippled in the main yards in Jersey City.

Many journalists and labor radicals persisted in spreading the ludicrous idea that the Erie directorate had a responsibility to its passengers and employees. Such esteemed "thinkers" as Charles Francis Adams the younger, the son of Lincoln's war ambassador to Britain, seemed to believe the burgeoning American rail system was somehow intended to benefit the public. If Adams and men like him had had any appreciation of the realities of life, they'd understand that damned few miles of track would have been laid anywhere in the nation if the entrepreneurs hadn't cared more for their purses than for people. The sole function of a railroad was to make money for the insiders. And the only railroad men admired on the Street—and secretly admired by the dim-witted masses, Louis was convinced—were those who understood a line's purpose and acted accordingly.

Now he was one of those men. Or he soon would be. The more he thought about it, the more he was convinced he'd been foolish to object to Fisk's bluntness. He could and would submerge his pride and self-esteem to make sure he did nothing to embarrass or irk Messrs. Drew, Fisk, and Gould.

The reward would be well worth it.

ii

He donned a silk robe, dimmed the gas, and returned to the bedroom. Nedda Chetwynd wiped champagne from her chin, still smiling her fatuous smile.

"May I call you Louis?"

He shrugged. "If you wish." He was growing impatient. Why had he even bothered with the robe?

He knew. That damned painting. He forced himself to glance at it. As always, the pale blue eyes seemed to mock him.

Fisk's trollop helped herself to more champagne. Louis found himself continuing to stare at the porcelain face on the canvas. The picture generated feelings of humiliation and hatred. Why had he kept it?

In a slurred voice, the blond girl asked, "Is that the lady to whom you were married?"

"That is indeed."

"She's pretty."

"She was until she lost her mind."

Miss Chetwynd almost spilled her drink. "You mean she's locked away?"

"She should be. She got mixed up with that idiotic woman's movement. She began complaining she was being used like a household object. That's a woman's primary function—to be used—"

Louis sat down on the edge of the bed. He pushed the sheet away and fondled the girl's nipple.

"To give pleasure. In the kitchen, or here."

The stupid slut could only giggle.

"The next thing I knew, Julia was equating herself with the niggers."

Astonishment: "With the—?"

"You heard me. Niggers. She's always despised them, but overnight they became her sublime symbol! If the niggers are free, she said, why should women be denied voting and property rights? That's one argument Mrs. Stanton, Mrs. Stone, Susan Anthony, and the rest of that deranged crowd use to justify their bizarre ideas. The moment my wife took up with those harridans, the result was inevitable."

Louis was talking quietly and for his own benefit. There was a certain relief in speaking aloud in an attempt to sort out the incomprehensibilities of the recent past.

Not that he was having any luck. His troubled and vaguely baffled expression was genuine. Although he'd listened to dozens of Julia's tirades before she'd departed in December of 1866, he still could not understand her reasoning—or what had changed her in a period of three or four years from a demanding child to an adult with a frightening degree of independence.

As far as he could recollect, her complaints about being used dated all the way to '61, shortly after the disastrous meeting at Kentland when Boyle, Rothman, and his mother's mulatto mine supervisor from California, Israel Hope, had refused to endorse the formation of Federal Suppliers.

Something had happened to Julia that spring. Exactly what, he couldn't guess. Nor would she speak of it when he questioned her. Whatever it was, it had been the start of their difficulties.

She'd begun mentioning the Irishman, to whom she'd never paid more than the most perfunctory attention before. Sometimes she was warm in her praise of Boyle's stand about Federal Suppliers, or of his character generally. At other times—in a totally contradictory way—she spoke his name with what amounted to barely suppressed anger. Louis had tried to laugh off that particular paradox by telling himself she was being typically feminine. It didn't work. "Typical" femininity was precisely what Julia was shedding in slow, inexplicable, and horrifying stages.

Her complaints about being "used" dated from the spring of 1861 as well. So did her resistance of her husband's intimate advances. She'd moderated her crusade briefly in '62; that was when their only child, Carter, had been conceived. The calm was short-lived. Somehow Julia had heard gossip about Louis' involvement with a salesgirl from a Manhattan shop. The war had resumed.

By the time she left him, taking their four-year-old son—no loss: Carter was a vile brat who constantly wanted Louis' attention—Julia had become a model of calm, rational determination. Terrifying!

He'd commissioned her portrait for one of their earliest anniversaries. Many times since '66, he'd come close to ordering the painting burned. Yet he hadn't done it.

Perhaps the picture served as a cautionary warning. He'd already taken a silent pledge that he'd never become entangled with another woman. A woman was like a bad investment: too many unpredictable and therefore unacceptable risks. He was willing to undertake risks of the kind to which he'd committed himself by sealing the pact with Fisk. At least that type of risk offered a chance of profit. With a woman, the best you could hope for was to maintain the status quo.

No, he was through with anything other than casual relationships with members of the opposite sex. Perhaps he kept the painting to strengthen that resolve.

Nedda Chetwynd was watching him in a puzzled, almost nervous way. He feigned a smile, plucked the goblet from her hand, and tossed it to one side without looking. The glass broke, tinkling.

He stood up and removed his robe. For a moment he wasn't the least self-conscious about standing naked in front of Julia's portrait. He rather enjoyed it.

He peeled the silk sheet away, disappointed in the smallness of the girl's breasts. But her stomach was plump and pink.

She simpered at the reaction in his loins. But she let out a cry when he pulled her out of bed.

Belly to belly with her, Louis gave her a quick kiss. She

was practiced. Her tongue licked languorously while she reached for him with a caressing hand.

He pushed it away. "One more thing about my former wife, Miss Chetwynd—"

"Oh, do call me Nedda!"

He tried to hide his disgust. "Very well. Nedda. I should just like to observe that my wife's, ah, problem was essentially a simple one—"

Liar. To the hour he died, Julia's notions would remain aberrations, and the reason for them a mystery.

"She failed to understand where a woman belongs."

He took hold of Nedda's shoulders. The pressure of his grip made her wince. All round eyes and red round mouth, she gazed at his hugeness, then at his face.

Softly, he said, "Let's find out whether you do, shall we?"

Chapter IV
The Man in the Burned Shawl

i

The February twilight softened the raw look of the cottages along General Wayne Street in Jersey City. Gideon Kent stood by the parlor window, his good eye narrowed as he studied the black clouds billowing in from the northwest.

Snowstorm coming. After nearly two years he could recognize the signs.

Raised in Virginia's temperate Shenandoah Valley, he still wasn't accustomed to the Northern weather. Seldom in his boyhood had Lexington received more than an occasional powdering of winter white. Up here, bitter winds blew for days at a time, and snow piled into loaflike drifts that were slow to melt. Since autumn he'd already endured three such storms. Tonight there was obviously going to be another.

The thought had only a marginal connection with his own safety. He seldom fretted about that any longer, although Margaret worried a good deal. The threatening sky reminded him vividly of Augustus Kolb. It had snowed the night after New Year's, when an accident had destroyed Kolb's life in a few seconds.

The memory called up a second one. He thought of the

man to whom he'd listened a couple of hours ago, down at the Diamond N Lager Palace.

Because of the man's reputation, the Diamond N proprietor forced him to convene his discussion group in the saloon storeroom. Even now Gideon could smell the sawdust and see the visitor's lined, exhausted face. The weary yet somehow spirited eyes. The powerful-looking hands resting on threadbare knees as the Philadelphian leaned forward to exhort the nine switchmen from the Erie yards. They had gathered to see what if anything they could do for Augie Kolb and his family.

"You can do nothing," the man told them, "unless you organize. That's the only way we've made gains in the Iron Molders' International."

"We ain't mechanics, Sylvis," a man named Cassidy complained. "We ain't skilled like your journeymen."

The emaciated man plucked at the shawl he wore over his thin overcoat. The shawl was virtually in tatters, pierced by black-edged holes. Sylvis claimed that for every foundry or cluster of foundries he'd organized into a local, he could count a hole burned by molten iron. There were dozens of holes.

"Makes no difference," Bill Sylvis replied. "The principle's the same. Single-handedly you can accomplish nothing of substance or permanence. United, there's no power or wrong you can't defy. I want you to think about that. And think of Kolb's wife Gerda. She's related to a man in our Philadelphia local. He asked me to take the train up here and talk with you."

Gideon was sitting cross-legged in a corner at the very back of the group. He'd only come because Kolb had been a friend. He had little interest in meeting a radical like Sylvis. So he was surprised when he found the man and his message commanding his attention. He was prompted to speak up.

"I suppose it's the same principle General Stuart taught us."

Sylvis craned his head. "What's that? Who spoke?"

"Reb Kent back there," said one of the others, though not unkindly.

Gideon raised his hand. "During the war I rode with Jeb Stuart's cavalry. He taught us to stick together in the field. The more of us there were, he said, the safer we'd be—and the greater the chance we'd be able to execute our orders."

Bill Sylvis nodded in an emphatic way. "That's it exactly. In Kolb's case, an appeal by a few men will probably accomplish nothing. But if a number of men—all the men in the yards—join forces and strike, they can effect a change. We learned that in the Molders. It's a lesson I travel ten thousand miles a year to promote."

A friend of Daphnis Miller uttered a glum chuckle. Miller had been pessimistic about the value of the conclave. He was out in the saloon proper, swilling beer. There was no question about the value of *that.*

Said Miller's friend, "We raise our heads out of the trench, we'll bring change, all right. We'll bring a flock of damn niggers or greenhorn immigrants to the yard. The bosses will replace us!"

Rather than disagreeing, Sylvis nodded in a grave way. "That is the great weapon the employers hold over us. We must find such a weapon ourselves."

"There isn't any."

"Oh, yes, there is. It's so obvious we overlook it. I did for many years, and even now I hesitate to express the idea publicly. It wouldn't be popular. But it's inescapable. If labor is ever to win a lasting victory, it must include everyone in its ranks. *Everyone.* The skilled will have to combine with the unskilled. I suppose that means women will have to be admitted to labor organizations. Black men too."

The quiet statement brought an uproar of protest. Sylvis raised a hand.

"I didn't come to that conclusion easily. I know laboring men think of unions as the purview of the skilled trades. And I once believed the nigras were a threat to every white fellow who sweated for a living. But I've begun to change my mind. The Negro is no longer a slave, but neither is he free." The intense eyes shone as he scanned the troubled faces. "Neither are *you* free. We're slaves together. We must put off our slavery together."

"It's been tried!" objected a burly switchman named Rory Bannock. "Five years ago, twelve railroaders got together out in Detroit to start the Brotherhood of the Footboard. They wanted postmortem benefits for widows of men killed on the job. They had to meet in secret for fear they'd be fired. Whole business never amounted to anything."

"I expect it would have if they'd stuck with it," Sylvis countered.

"Don't be too sure. Boys on the B & O wanted to approach one of the bosses with some complaint or other. They were discharged just for askin' for an appointment!"

Sylvis' eyes had a melancholy cast. "I never said the struggle would be easy. It hasn't been in the Molders. But when you organize—"

"We organize ourselves out of a job!" Bannock exclaimed.

Most agreed. Loudly.

"I agree solidarity isn't without its risks—" Sylvis began.

Cassidy gestured "Let someone else take 'em. I got six kids."

Sylvis looked disappointed. So did the switchmen. They'd hoped Sylvis would recommend some quick and simple plan for securing financial assistance for Augie Kolb and his brood. Instead, he was speaking of abstract matters. Wage slavery. The union movement. A long-range strategy instead of a short-term panacea.

Gideon sat frowning, barely aware of the racket from the saloon. The objections notwithstanding, he suspected the soft-spoken Philadelphian might be right. At the First Manassas, he'd learned the value of standing together. He'd taken a few men off on his own and damn near gotten shot to death by a dying Yankee.

He wanted to help Augustus Kolb's family. But Bill Sylvis poured bitter medicine. He was realistic about the possibility of firings if demands were made. He'd upset and disappointed the switchmen. His candor about eventual mingling of the races in the labor movement hadn't helped either.

Gideon Kent and every other man in the storeroom needed their jobs. That was the difficulty which brought the meeting to a swift and inconclusive end.

ii

All the way home, Gideon had been unable to get forty-year-old William Sylvis out of his thoughts. Now, at the window, the approaching snowstorm again reminded him of the chief officer of the strongest of the nation's fledgling trade unions.

Sylvis was well known among workingmen. He'd personally built the Molders into a network of over a hundred and thirty-five locals. He'd held sometimes reluctant iron workers off their jobs and won a major settlement with the foundry owners who'd staged the famous Albany Lockout of '66. He constantly promoted the formation of worker-owned cooperative foundries as an alternative to the existing iron and steel establishment. And he was being mentioned as a potential president of the National Labor Union, a relatively new association of workers' assemblies, union locals, reformers, and eight-hour leagues pushing for a shorter workday.

Still, the price Bill Sylvis had paid for his achievements was quite apparent. He'd been shunted into the anonymity of a storeroom because even small businessmen considered him dangerous. His clothes were hardly better than rags. His health looked none too good, either. At the meeting he'd declined all refreshment, saying he had a persistent stomach condition. He'd worn himself out—and, Gideon had read, kept his family in poverty—for the trade union cause.

In fact Sylvis had looked fragile and almost forlorn when he left the meeting and walked into the dark day with only his thin overcoat and that burned shawl to protect him. Gideon could still see the ends of the shawl fluttering like bullet-pierced flags.

The image vanished as he chafed his hands to warm them. The cottage parlor was dingy and frigid. The ancient floral wallpaper had a sooty tinge. Wind whistled through gaps in the siding.

The old walnut clock on a rickety table chimed half-past five. Gideon couldn't wholeheartedly admit Sylvis was right. To do so would compel a man to think of taking the next logical step. Like the others gathered at the Lager Palace, he wasn't prepared to do it. Times were too hard, work too scarce.

From the kitchen came the sound of Margaret starting Eleanor's bath. In the midst of the splashing, she called to him, "Gideon? Your supper's ready."

"I'll be there."

But he remained at the window, his gaze fixed on the

ruts of frozen mud and the shabbily identical houses straggling toward the river. His next-door neighbor, Daphnis Miller, said the only way a man who enjoyed his beer could find his way to the right bed after imbibing was to count cottages starting at the corner.

Miller was a generous man. In less than half a year's time, he'd also become a good friend. Last summer, after being discharged from three successive jobs because of his Southern background, Gideon had recalled meeting the trainman at Relay House. In desperation, he'd ridden the ferry to Jersey City.

He'd expected Miller to be long gone or, if he were still employed, to have forgotten him. Certainly he'd have forgotten his casual invitation for Gideon to look him up if he ever needed employment.

On all counts Gideon had been wrong.

Miller had introduced him to the superintendent who hired switchmen. Gideon's infirmity had produced a gale of disbelieving laughter.

But the superintendent hadn't turned him down flat. Despite depressed economic conditions and a scarcity of jobs in the industrial East, few men were hungry enough to risk themselves working for a line as disreputable as the Erie. Even so, Gideon had found it necessary to plead his case for almost fifteen minutes.

He was strong. His tall frame and wide shoulders attested to it. He'd regained most of the weight he'd lost in prison.

He was agile. He'd been a cavalryman during the war.

He'd had to argue heatedly about his eye, though. He thumped the superintendent's desk and informed him he could march into any Army recruiting office and sign up instantly for one of the new regiments of Plains cavalry. If one-eyed men were acceptable to General Hancock or young General Custer—a soldier Gideon tried not to hate for leading the Wolverine horsemen who'd killed Beauty Stuart—then damn it, they should be acceptable to the Erie Railroad! Coupling cars couldn't be any more perilous than facing a band of rampaging Sioux Indians.

The superintendent remarked wryly that Gideon might be surprised, but agreed to give him a try. The man's expression said he didn't expect Gideon to last long. That only increased Gideon's determination to succeed.

The work *did* prove as dangerous as Miller had suggested on that afternoon at Relay House. A man was killed or injured every few weeks. Gideon constantly had to soothe Margaret's anxiety, reminding her he'd finally found employment that would keep him out in the weather, which he liked. Except, of course, during these blasted Northern winters.

Besides the appalling toll of deaths and injuries, the other discouraging element in the young family's situation was the move across the river in August of '67. It was necessary if Gideon planned to work steadily. During the cold months, ice drifting in the river made ferry service undependable at best.

Moving to Jersey City sharply limited their chances to see Jephtha and Molly. But Gideon and Margaret bore the new isolation without complaint. Finding a cottage for rent adjoining the Miller place helped. Daphnis Miller became not only his friend but his mentor. He willingly showed Gideon the tricks of the switchman's trade, and arranged for the younger man to be assigned to his own shift—dusk to dawn. Tonight, Miller would come along as usual about six-thirty, and the two would set out on their half-hour trudge to the yards.

He decided he mustn't tell Margaret about listening to Bill Sylvis. Luckily he'd made a second stop while he was out of the house. It would explain his absence.

He didn't want his wife to think he was flirting with a cause which might lose them what little security they enjoyed. In truth he wasn't. After the war he'd sworn he would never again fight for any so-called lofty principle such as state's rights. Mere survival was struggle enough. He worked a twelve-hour shift for the magnificent sum of one dollar and a half per day. Mr. Greeley's *Tribune* estimated an average family needed $10.57 per week to meet minimum expenses. Only Margaret's sewing enabled the family to reach that figure.

Nevertheless, Gideon and his wife repeatedly refused the gifts of food and clothing offered by Jephtha and Molly. Occasionally—and this was one of the occasions—he wondered if he'd been a lunatic to tell his father he wanted no financial help. A word to Jephtha, and he, Margaret and Eleanor could enjoy a secure life. Eat decently. Inhabit an adequately furnished home over in Manhattan.

He sighed. Independence surely had its price. Was it fair to ask Margaret to continue to pay it? Pride was fine, but it couldn't fill stomachs, or refurbish worn-out wardrobes.

Stop, he thought, irked with himself. He shoved a hand through his long light-colored hair and blinked his right eye to clear it of a speck. He'd made the decision. He'd stick by it, build a future with his own labor and his own wits—even though he frequently felt the latter were still pitifully inadequate.

He was doing something about that, however. Every night. Every spare moment. His goal wasn't unrealistic. Many men were self-educated, including Sylvis. The Philadelphian had told the saloon gathering that his family had hired him out for farmwork when he was eleven. He'd taught himself to read because he could afford no other teacher. Later in life he'd struggled to master extremely complex material, because a grasp of it was essential for a union organizer. Sylvis had mentioned names that meant nothing to Gideon. Adam Smith. David Ricardo. Karl Marx.

He rubbed the sleeves of his flannel shirt. Lord, it was cold! His bladder felt full. But he had no desire to tramp out to the privy in the howling wind. The threatening sky continued to remind him of Kolb.

During the last blizzard, Augustus Kolb had gone to his switchman's job, had slipped on an ice-covered rail, and been crushed between shunting cars. Before midnight, a sawbones had removed both legs at midthigh. He would never work again.

And all Kolb's pregnant wife and two small children had received by way of compensation was a flowery note of sympathy written by some high-living, faceless Erie nabob.

"You can do nothing unless you organize."

"Gideon? Your food will be cold!"

"Coming."

iii

He trimmed the parlor's one kerosene lamp to conserve the fuel. As always, he kept his head turned slightly to the left while using his hands. The flame spurted once, throwing a quick highlight on the black leather patch covering his left eye socket. Then darkness claimed the room.

The bedroom was cold on the parlor side, warmer near the kitchen. The iron stove radiated welcome heat. As he headed for the lighted rectangle of the doorway between the rooms, another remark made by Sylvis slipped into mind: *"Until you have a union, they'll take advantage of you. There are only two classes in the United States. The skinners and the skinned."*

The statement reminded him of his second cousin once removed. He'd never met Louis Kent. Jephtha detested him and, though related, never saw him. But Gideon often read about Louis in the papers. He was a major stockholder of Erie. On a night like this, he certainly wouldn't be shivering and shaking in his fine new mansion on Fifth Avenue, or his palace up the Hudson.

Again Gideon scored himself for envy. He didn't want wealth handed to him. But he did feel men such as Louis should display some responsibility when an employee was maimed for life.

Ridiculous to expect that, though. Louis was one of the skinners. Even before he'd met Sylvis, Gideon had begun to realize gentlemen such as Mr. Louis Kent lived at the expense of others. While Kolb's wife, heavy with child, tended him and probably cried herself to sleep because of the family's predicament, Louis Kent occupied himself with parties, voyages to Europe, and financial manipulations Gideon didn't begin to understand.

He'd tried, certainly. He read every available newspaper account of the current struggle for control of the Erie. None made much sense. He was still hard put to differentiate between "bulls" and "bears," and utterly failed to comprehend what a "pool" was, or a "combination," or a "corner"—

"Gideon Kent, what are you doing out there?"

"What? Oh—" He hadn't realized he'd stopped four paces from the kitchen.

"Why are you standing in the dark? What are you thinking about?"

"You can do nothing unless you organize."

"Nothing important," he said, submerging a pang of guilt and hurrying to her.

CHAPTER V
THE FAMILY

i

HE STEPPED into the warm kitchen, lifted from his pensive mood by the sight of his wife and daughter.

Five-year-old Eleanor stood fidgeting in a washtub. Kneeling beside the tub, Margaret whipped a piece of nappy toweling called a rubber around the little girl's pink rump.

Eleanor Kent was one of the delights of Gideon's life. She was a happy, sturdy child with her mother's dark hair and eyes. Now, though, she was frowning.

"Papa, she's taking the skin off me!"

Gideon chuckled as he sat down at the old table where a plate of stringy beef and boiled potatoes awaited him. "She knows best, Eleanor. That hairbrush"—he pointed to the bristly object lying beside a lump of homemade soap—"does a lot more than warm you up."

"I'm too hot now, Papa!"

"Stop that. All the doctors say children need a good scratching after a bath. Makes the blood run properly."

"I don't care," Eleanor declared. "The scratch brush hurts like the devil!"

"Please don't use that word, Eleanor," Margaret said.

delivering a light swat through the rubber she was using to dry the child.

Margaret Marble Kent was Gideon's age. Nearly twenty-five. She was a slender but full-bosomed young woman with pretty features marred only by a stubby nose she despised. Gideon had met her in Richmond at the start of the war. He loved her deeply and had never regretted his decision to marry her.

She was a strong-minded person and not timid about letting others know her convictions. An embroidered motto on the kitchen wall typified that characteristic.

A NEAT, CHEERFUL HOME
KEEPS SONS FROM BECOMING FAST AND
DAUGHTERS FROM BECOMING FRIVOLOUS

The sight of Margaret jogged Gideon's memory about the present he'd bought after leaving the meeting. He rose, walked to the cupboard, pulled the parcel down, and hid it behind his back.

"Eleanor, kindly stop wiggling like an eel!" Margaret brushed a loose lock of hair off her forehead. She laid the rubber aside and started to drag a heavy nightgown over her daughter's head.

From within the folds, Eleanor answered in a muffled voice, "I will if Papa sings a song."

"Papa must eat his dinner before it turns to icicles." She lifted the child from the tub. "The weather's abysmal, Gideon. They should close the yard when it storms—why on earth are you looking so smug?"

He bounced on the soles of his cracked boots, the small package concealed behind his back. "Got a surprise for you."

"A surprise?" She jumped up, smoothing her stained skirt. "Is that where you went after you woke up? To buy something we can't afford?"

"Didn't cost me all that much," he fibbed. "You'll have to pay for it, though."

Eleanor scampered to him and tugged the leg of his heavy corduroy trousers. "Papa, will you sing?" He slipped a hand around her head, fondling her hair.

"In a minute. First your mama and I must make a little exchange."

He rattled the paper with his other hand. He leaned forward and kissed Margaret, then revealed the parcel and bellowed a kind of fanfare.

Margaret looked increasingly pained. "Whatever it is, we definitely can't afford it. I'll return it."

"Impossible. I already got my kiss. You have to take it."

He pressed the parcel into her red-knuckled hands and picked up his daughter. She giggled while he pulled out the chair and plumped her on his knee.

"Any favorites, Miss Eleanor?"

Arms around his neck, the little girl continued to wriggle. " 'Yellow Rose.' "

"Fair enough." He began to jog her up and down in rhythm as he sang in a strong baritone.

"Where the Rio Grande is flowing,
And the starry skies are bright—"

Eleanor joined in, her voice clear and sweet:

"She walks along the river
In the quiet summer night."

Eleanor jumped down, planted her fists on her hips and hopped from foot to foot—her version of dancing. Gideon clapped and kept singing.

"She thinks if I remember
When we parted long ago,
I promised to return,
And not to leave her so!"

Booming the last words, he seized Eleanor's waist and hugged her so hard she squealed.

"For heaven's sake don't encourage her!" Margaret said. "Ever since three, she's been the most incurable show-off I've ever seen."

"You told me children always show off at age three."

"It's supposed to stop."

Gideon had to admit his daughter was unusually outgoing. He said wryly, "Perhaps the Lord sent us an actress who'll support us in style when we're old."

"An *actress?* I hope not! I want no child of mine in a scandalous profession like—"

"Margaret, I'm teasing."

"What's an actress?" Eleanor wanted to know. She had no difficulty with the word; she'd learned to handle complex words and sentences long before most children of a comparable age. "Is it something nice?"

"An actress is a disreputable person who displays herself and—never you mind!"

"Go ahead and open the present," Gideon prompted.

Still looking perturbed, Margaret unwrapped the brown paper. She uttered a little gasp of delight when she discovered a small, wrinkled lemon and a large brown egg.

"Gideon, how much did you pay for these?"

"Doesn't matter."

Margaret gazed at the purchases as if trying to decide whether to continue the discussion of cost or just enjoy the unexpected gift. She did the latter, bending down and tapping Eleanor's cheek.

"Stand aside and let me kiss him again, miss."

She put her head between her daughter's and Gideon's and pressed her mouth to his. "You're a foolish spendthrift. But I love you for it."

"Well, God—uh, heaven knows"—he corrected as Eleanor clapped a hand over her mouth and rolled her eyes—"a woman who works as hard as you deserves something nice once in a while. The *Tribune* says all the fancy young ladies whose broughams dash up and down Fifth Avenue beautify themselves with egg and lemon. If it's proper for society girls, it's proper for you, Mrs. Kent."

"I've read it truly does work wonders," Margaret said, carefully placing the egg and lemon between Gideon's plate and a book lying on top of a copy of *Leslie's Illustrated Weekly.* A subscription to the popular periodical had been one of Jephtha's and Molly's Christmas presents.

"Softens the skin," she added. "I could use that. The cold weather makes mine rough as bark."

"Always feels fine to me." Gideon grinned. He stuffed a frayed napkin into his collar and began to eat. "I wanted you to have something for yourself."

"Even though we haven't the money."

"Let me worry about the money. Time in this life is short, Margaret. I've been thinking a lot about Augie Kolb—"

"Is that what kept you standing like a statue in the bedroom?"

He nodded. "I wondered if Augie had ever bought his wife a present. He should have. Now he's crippled, and he'll never earn another half-dime—" He flung his fork on the plate. "It's damned unjust. Augie sweated eight years for the Erie. But now that he can't work, Mr. Louis Kent and the rest of the muckamucks have forgotten him. Something should be done to remind them."

"You sound like one of those trade unionists."

He looked away hastily, fearful his face would reveal his guilt.

"Thinking of Louis just about ruins my appetite. Don't let it ruin the present."

"It couldn't! Oh, Gideon—" Her eyes misted a little. "You *are* utterly foolish sometimes. But I can't get angry with you." She touched the lemon. "I'll try this tonight. You're supposed to scoop the pulp out, then beat the egg white and let the lemon peel sit in it. The oils mix. The lemony white whisks away all the wrinkles."

Quietly: "I'm giving you those a lot faster than you deserve. I've forced you to live like this."

She squeezed his hand. "You know I never quarrel with anything you decide after we talk it over."

"Including the decision not to ask Father for money?"

"Yes, including that. You make me very happy, Gideon." She leaned closer, her breast touching his arm and creating a familiar, comfortable warmth. "Especially when you indulge that Virginia gentleman's temperament and buy presents."

She kissed him again, her lips lingering. Eleanor sighed and let her attention wander elsewhere.

Gideon forked a chunk of boiled potato toward his mouth. "I know I didn't make you happy by taking the yard job."

"I only fret when the weather's bad. You told me most of the other men never show up on a night like this. You could stay home."

"Shades of Richmond! 'Don't ride off with old Jeb, Gideon.' "

She flushed. "I'm sorry."

Soberly, he said, "I didn't mean to tease so hard. Truth is, I'd like to stay home. But I'd have to say I was under the weather, and I've never been much good at lying. Besides, we need the money."

Perched on a stool, Eleanor was rubbing her bare toes together. "What about the book, Papa? I want to hear some of the book."

"Oh, dear!" Margaret exclaimed. "I got so excited over the present, I forgot the child's feet—"

She rushed to the bedroom and returned with coarse woolen stockings. Gideon listened to the whine of the wind. The cottage creaked. A roof shingle tore loose and went rattling away. An arduous twelve hours lay ahead.

But before he left, he still had the pleasure of the evening ritual.

Margaret finished forcing the stockings on Eleanor. The little girl looked eagerly at her father. She didn't understand half the words during a reading, but they fascinated her because they fascinated him.

"All right." Gideon smiled. "We'll have the book in just a minute."

ii

Margaret brought him a hot cup of coffee from the claw-footed stove. Jephtha and Molly had ordered the stove installed as a surprise present when the couple moved to Jersey City.

While Gideon sipped, Eleanor raced to a corner to pick up a wire carpet beater. She pretended to capture imaginary insects in an imaginary net. Margaret emptied the woodbox and fed the kindling into the stove.

When he picked up the book he noticed the *Leslie's* cover engraving for the first time. The engraving was a composite of three oval portraits. One of the men pictured, squint-eyed and narrow-lipped, was considerably older than the others. A decorative ribbon beneath his picture identified him as *Drew*.

The plump, sleepy fellow with the luxuriant mustache was *Fisk.* The third, sporting a fan-shaped beard so large it concealed his cravat, was *Gould.* The cover was captioned:

AT WAR WITH VANDERBILT—
THE ERIE TRIUMVIRS

Gideon had never seen likenesses of the men who were part owners of the line for which he worked. He studied them avidly. He was especially fascinated by Gould. If the portrait was accurate, it created a deceptive impression. The infamous Mr. Gould looked about as dangerous as a poverty-stricken clerk.

Margaret finished at the stove and sat down. Eleanor swatted another invisible insect. She fixed her luminous brown eyes on her mother, who turned to a page marked with a slip of lace.

"Oh," Margaret said abruptly, "you mustn't forget to tell Daphnis what we discovered about his name."

Gideon nodded. "I won't."

She began to read aloud from the collection of President Johnson's public speeches. The book came from Jephtha's parsonage library.

" 'The tendency of the legislation in this country is to build up monopolies—' " She glanced at her husband. "Monopolies?"

The ritual reading had begun two years earlier, prompted by Gideon's desire to familiarize himself with America's history and the flow of political and economic thought to the present day. It was Margaret who'd first suggested that she read aloud in the evening. She'd pointed out that Andrew Johnson had learned the same way. In his tailor shop in Tennessee, he'd paid men fifty cents an hour to read to him while he cut cloth and stitched seams.

She'd begun with the Declaration of Independence and the Constitution. Her patience and good humor had eased him through the first weeks in which many of the concepts made only a dim kind of sense. Now he'd progressed far enough so that he enjoyed the challenge of a question, and the chance to show his mastery of an idea.

"Monopolies are groups—small groups—controlling a type of business."

Margaret nodded encouragement.

"They usually agree privately to fix their pricing."

"What do you call a man who does that?"

Gideon rubbed his forehead. God, there was so much to know. He dredged up the answer.

"Monopolist?"

"Yes." Her smile heartened him. "The practice itself is monopolism."

"Ism," he repeated. He smiled. "As in Vanderbiltism."

She laughed. "I don't think it's in the dictionary, but it's apt." She returned to the book. "Build up monopolies—here we go. 'The tendency of legislation is to build up the power of money. To concentrate it in the hands of the few. The tendency is *for* classes, and *against* the great mass of the people.' "

"Sure is true of the Erie," he observed. "The directors run it for themselves, not the passengers. Workers don't count for a hoot either. The directors should remember what happened to old King George."

"But the law doesn't provide for railroad passengers to have any voice in running a line. Or laboring men, for that matter."

"Maybe the law's wrong. Maybe the Erie directors see to it. Maybe things should be changed."

Margaret was staring at him in a curious way.

"What did I do?" he asked.

"Nothing. You just sound like one of those trade unionists again."

He realized she was right. It disturbed him. "Shoot, I was only thinking out loud."

He started at the sound of a fist hammering on the back door. He opened the door to admit Daphnis Miller and a blast of wintry air.

Eleanor let out a screech as the air hit her. Miller lurched as Gideon slammed the door. Gideon's neighbor was bundled in a patched Union Army overcoat. A woolen cap covered his ears and forehead. A scarf was tied around the lower half of his face.

"You're early, Daphnis," Gideon said. Closing the book, Margaret looked almost as disappointed as her husband.

The scarf muffled Miller's voice. "Gonna be a hard tramp to the yards. Sleet's been comin' down like sixty for the last fifteen minutes."

Miller flicked droplets of water from his gray brows. He weaved to the range, extending hands encased in several pairs of mittens. "Real bitch of a night—oops. Beg your pardon, ladies."

Gideon started into the bedroom. He smelled the beer with which his neighbor had fortified himself.

"Maybe they'll cancel most of the runs, Daphnis," Margaret said.

"Not unless she drifts too bad. Gid, you better fetch an extra pair of mittens if you got 'em."

"I haven't," he called, returning with the ragged Confederate greatcoat he'd brought home from Fort Delaware. He put it on, donned his forage cap, stretched a muffler over the top of his head, and knotted it under his chin. Margaret raised on tiptoe to kiss him.

"Don't take any needless chances."

He patted her arm. "I won't." He was concerned about Miller, who had apparently continued to imbibe after coming home from the Lager Palace. In Miller's household, necessities were often sacrificed to pay for alcohol. Gideon religiously avoided drinking before going to work. Beer or spirits slowed response time. To survive in the yards, you had to be quick.

"Bolt the doors when I leave," he said to Margaret.

"I thought I'd go over and help Flo with her laundry."

"Mighty kind of you," Miller mumbled. "Those four youngsters can sure dirty a bale of clothes."

"Take Eleanor with you," Gideon advised. "And when you come back, lock up again. There are too many men out of work wandering around."

Bristling a bit, Margaret said, "Gideon Kent, I'm perfectly capable of looking after myself!"

He grinned. "I know. I keep forgetting. See you in the morning."

"Either that," Miller wheezed, "or a representative of the Erie will bring condolences."

Margaret flared. "That's a poor joke, Daphnis!"

He looked blearily contrite. Gideon hustled him to the door, then bent down to hug Eleanor. As he straightened, Margaret flung an arm around his neck.

"Be very careful."

"Will be. Promise." To Eleanor, he said, "Whose girl are you?"

"Yours!" She blew him a kiss with both hands.

He tugged the door shut behind him, almost reeling in the blast of wind that howled through the tiny back yard. Miller waved his arms, losing his balance on the steps. Gideon caught him and held him steady..With his toe he tested the exposed edge of the porch. Slippery as glass.

The sleet was freezing wherever it hit. He didn't blame Margaret for worrying. He was worried too.

Chapter VI
The Accident

i

The white world of the storm dimmed lamps in distant cottages and drove stinging sleet against Gideon's exposed upper cheeks. The wind blew with such force, he felt as if a huge man were trying to push him back at every step. Before he and Miller had completed half of the two-mile trek to the yards, he was laboring for breath.

Ruts in the deserted streets were rapidly filling with a treacherous accumulation of frozen snow. It crunched under foot. Gideon knew it would cling to the metal of the cars they'd be coupling. Cling and freeze.

Miller's gait continued to be erratic. But he kept up a nonstop conversation, another indication that he'd drunk too much. Several times Gideon yelled, "Can't hear you!" Miller simply kept talking.

It seemed they'd been trudging for hours. Suddenly Miller yanked his arms, then jammed his face close to the scarf covering Gideon's left ear.

"You promised—more'n two weeks ago!"

Gideon shook his head. He had no idea what Miller meant.

A switch engine whistled in the murk. They were close to the yards. In spite of the weather, service hadn't stopped.

The older man shook his arm doggedly. "Gid, you *promised!* You said you were readin' that fairy story book at supper—"

He understood what his friend wanted. Margaret had urged him to mention it and he'd forgotten. "Myths," he bawled back. "A book by Bulfinch."

"Bull what?" Miller almost took a tumble. Gideon grabbed Miller's overcoat and helped him right himself. They leaned into the wind again.

"Finch. *Finch!*"

Months ago, Miller had begun badgering him about his first name. The railroad man's parents had been illiterate farmers in the Mohawk River Valley. Few people with whom Miller came in contact were conversant with anything but the daily papers. He'd appealed to Gideon to help him discover the origin and meaning of Daphnis.

So on Jephtha's last visit, Gideon had asked him for any book which might contain the answer Miller sought. Jephtha had located a volume on his shelves and posted it to Jersey City. This was no time to discuss it, though.

"Come on, Gid!" Miller sounded peevish. "Tell me what the book says."

They turned a corner and started down a dark street of warehouses next to the yards. At the end of the street, the light box of a slow-moving locomotive glared. The buildings shielded them from the worst of the wind; conversation was easier.

"How much beer have you had today, Daphnis?"

"Plenty. I said, *plenty.* Knew it was gonna be a pistol of a night. Now what'd you find out?"

A gust of wind blurred Gideon's answer.

"You won't tell me," Miller growled. "It's a woman's name. My mama gave me a woman's name. I always knew it."

"She did not. It's a perfectly proper man's name. The original Daphnis was a Greek shepherd."

Miller's grumbling told Gideon he couldn't hear. Cold and irritated, Gideon roared, "Sheep! Daphnis herded *sheep!*"

"That the honest to God truth?"

"Yes."

"My daddy kept some sheep—tell me the rest."

Gideon coughed. His throat was growing raw. "Daphnis played music on some kind of pipe or flute. He fooled around with a"—he could see the word: *Naiad*; he wasn't sure how to pronounce it—"a girl who lived in the water all the time."

"You say they were Greeks?" Miller cried. "Like the Greeks comin' off the boats with the Slovaks and the Dutchmen and the Jews? The kind of Greeks you see at Castle Garden and Wards Island?"

"No. They weren't real people. It's just an old story. A legend. Now keep quiet till we get in where it's warm."

He doubted he'd ever be warm again.

ii

They cleared the line of warehouses. To the left, between switch tracks, haloed lamplight shone from the shack belonging to the yard superintendent. The locomotive he'd glimpsed was chugging in the other direction, already hidden behind eight white-roofed freight cars.

They hurried toward the shack. Miller chuckled.

"Well, by God, I finally found out I wasn't named for any silly female—Gid, I truly thank you. First time we met on that prison train, I knew you were all right."

Gideon laughed, practically pushing his friend toward the shack. As a result he nearly lost his balance. Every exposed surface in the yards was covered with ice.

Miller blundered against the door, yanked it open, and careened inside. Gideon followed. The corner stove created a welcome island of heat.

Water dripped from the coats of both men. Miller slumped on a bench and appeared to study his mittens. "Named for a damn Greek sheep herder. D'you fancy that?"

The night superintendent, a short balding man named Cuthbertson, sat at a desk in front of a board. The board displayed the numbers and departure times of a dozen trains. Chalk lines had been run through all but two.

Cuthbertson jerked a foul-smelling black cigar out of his mouth. "Hallo, Gid. Who's your mush-mouthed friend?"

Miller's watering eyes blinked above the scarf. "Cuthie, kiss my sheep."

Cuthbertson looked dour. "You been puttin' in too much saloon time, Daphnis. Again."

"He's just tired," Gideon lied. The wind rattled grimy windows. The icy crust of a four-inch snow buildup glittered on the outer sills.

Gideon sat on the bench and dragged the muffler away from his mouth. His lips and chin felt numb. So did his fingers and feet. He peeled off his soggy mittens and hung them on the stove's open door.

"What's the situation, Cuthie?"

The superintendent pointed to the board. "All the passenger runs are canceled. We got two freights to make up, starting with the eight-thirty for Albany." Those were probably the uncoupled cars Gideon had seen as he approached.

"Maybe I could work with someone else," he suggested. "Daphnis could rest and handle the second train."

"I ain't got anyone else!" Cuthbertson snapped. Despite his perpetually brusque manner, he wasn't a bad sort. Just overworked, and hampered by inferior equipment. "We been hit by another of those mysterious plagues. Happens every time it snows."

"You mean nobody else reported?"

"Nobody."

Gideon's frown deepened. Four switch crews of two men each usually worked the shift.

"I can't wait to hear all the touching tales," Cuthbertson snorted. "Chilblains. Flux. A sudden call to visit a sick friend. I know who *that* is. The barkeep at the Diamond N. Oh, we'll have a grand session of lying tomorrow!"

Melted snow trickled off Gideon's boots and formed little pools around his toes. The superintendent jerked his head at Miller and raised his eyebrows. Miller didn't notice. He was still contemplating his mittens and mumbling.

"Sure, we'll get it done," Gideon said in reply to Cuthbertson's silent question. His eye drifted to the open stove. In the flames he saw Augustus Kolb. The man had been thirty-one at the time of the accident.

Cuthbertson lit a second cigar from the stub of the first. "You don't exactly seem the soul of cheer tonight."

"Oh—" Gideon untied his scarf, took off his forage cap,

then his mittens. He used his fingers like the teeth of a comb, raking snow out of the hair around his ears. Cuthbertson was waiting for an answer. "For some reason I've been thinking a lot about Augie Kolb today."

Cuthbertson nearly took his head off. "Why?"

Irked by the reaction, Gideon retorted, "I just have." He noticed the superintendent's face. "Cuthie, what's wrong? Something is. Tell me."

Cuthbertson exhaled a cloud of smoke. "They found Gerda early this morning."

"Gerda Kolb?" A nod. "Where?"

Miller's chin had dropped onto the lap of his overcoat. He snored softly.

After more prodding from Gideon, Cuthbertson said, "One of the youngsters found her in the shed behind their cottage. She used strips from a blanket to hang herself."

iii

"My God. She was expecting!"

"Don't you let on I told you! I got orders from the headquarters in Manhattan. Ain't to be no reports of accidents in the papers. The bosses are gettin' whipped plenty hard enough over this stock war. I hear Vanderbilt's after a majority of the shares, and Gould wants all the favorable publicity his side can get. With him and his chums playin' their games, it don't help to have engines derailed and switchmen's wives doing themselves in—"

Cuthbertson stopped, peering at the end of his cigar. He pressed his chest as if his digestion were upset.

"Why would Gerda Kolb kill herself?" Gideon asked. "She had Augie to care for. Two boys to support. A child on the way."

A weary shrug. "I s'pose that's the very reason. Too many mouths and no money. You know the line didn't give Augie one cent after the accident."

"What'll happen to the boys?"

"I guess they'll take to the streets. Steal. It's that or starve."

"Jesus. You'd think someone high up would have the decency to pay them something."

"Why, no," Cuthbertson said. "High up, they got more important matters to think about. Meaning no disrespect to any relative of yours," the superintendent added sarcastically.

Gideon waved. "I don't know a thing about Louis Kent except what my father and the newspapers tell me. I gather Louis is the kind who wouldn't spend a dime to put flowers on his mother's grave—damn it, Cuthie, we ought to *force* the line to do something for men who die or get hurt!"

"Go right ahead. Call on your cousin! You might start lookin' for another job at the same time."

"Job or no job, someone's got to stand up for people like Augie's widow and kids."

"Not me. I like my three squares and a roof over my head." The superintendent rose. "You and Daphnis better start making up the eight-thirty. Provided you can get him on his feet."

"Daphnis—"

Gideon prodded the older man. Miller snorted. He shifted sideways on the bench, slow to rouse.

Cuthbertson lifted the angled lid of a storage box. He pulled out a pair of yard-long clubs of hickory wood.

"You boys want these? The links and pins may be froze pretty bad."

Miller was awake. "Listen, Cuthie. As long as I've been with the Erie, I've never used the staff of ignorance. I don't propose to start now."

"How about you, Gid?"

Gideon shook his head, settling his cap and retying the scarf. The brakeman's clubs were helpful in coupling cars. But experienced men considered using one to be an indication of inferior skill and a lack of confidence. Cuthbertson tossed the clubs back into the box and slammed the lid. Out in the storm, a whistle blew twice.

"The lads are waitin' on you," Cuthbertson said.

Gideon brought two lanterns from the corner. He stuck a twist of straw into the stove and used it to fire the wicks. He handed one lantern to Miller, who almost dropped it before he worked the bail over his arm.

Bundling up, Gideon was still upset by the news of Gerda Kolb's hanging herself, killing her unborn child in the process. It wouldn't have happened if the line compensated men for injuries and provided postmortem benefits for widows. He thought of Jeb Stuart.

Stay together. Press right on toward the objective—together.

He saw the burned shawl of Bill Sylvis.

Organize.

Like Cuthbertson, he didn't really want to lead the way into what would inevitably become a storm of conflict and controversy.

Still, he couldn't escape one truth. Until *someone* led, the problem would never be solved.

Miller lumbered to the door and jerked it open. The storm tearing through the yards drove the imaginary one out of Gideon's mind.

iv

They tramped toward the switch locomotive, the glowing lanterns hanging from their arms. As they negotiated the ice-covered ties on the track beside the eight boxcars, Gideon shouted that he'd take the first, the one to be connected to the switcher's tender.

The wind garbled Miller's reply. He slipped again; almost fell. Gideon realized wearily that he might have to couple the entire train by himself. With the link-and-pin system, switchmen usually handled alternate cars.

Gideon wigwagged his lantern at the engineer leaning from the cab. The sleet slanted through the backwash of the headlight like tiny silver arrows. " 'Bout time, you damn lazy clods!" the engineer shouted. "Let's get her together!"

"Blasted thing"—Miller was struggling with the lid of the link box between the first boxcar and the adjacent track—"she's stuck tight."

Gideon beat on the lid with his fist. Ice cracked. Pieces rattled on the frozen cinders of the roadbed. He wrenched the lid. On the third try he got the link box open.

He checked the iron drawbars on the tender and the boxcar. To his relief he saw the bars were on the same level. He reached into the box for a link—a hoop of iron thirteen inches across—and two iron spikes.

There was about a yard of working space between the cars. The minute he forced the link into the horizontal slot of the tender's drawbar, he knew this would be no simple job. Ice clogged the slot. The link wouldn't seat properly.

He set his lantern down and began chipping at the ice with one of the pins. Then he used both pins to hammer the link home.

He positioned a pin over the opening in the drawbar. More ice kept it from falling. He pounded with the other pin. Finally the first pin dropped, securing the link to the bar.

Gideon stepped from between the cars and waved the lantern. "Back 'er up!"

The engineer retreated into the cab. Gideon averted his face from the wind as the drivers reversed. Slippage on the rails produced a sound like a scream.

The fireman clambered down, swearing loud enough to be heard above the storm. He flung four buckets of cinders and sand on the rails. Abruptly, the wheels found traction. The tender rolled backward. Horizontal wooden beams that served as car bumpers crunched under the impact. Gideon was lucky; the force of the collision drove the link into the boxcar's drawbar. The pin dropped without difficulty.

"I'll take the next one," Miller called. His lantern bobbed as he fished in the link box. The flickering light revealed a gooseneck in his glove. A gooseneck meant the drawbar of the second freight car was not at the same height as that on the first. It was a perennial problem with rolling stock; there were no uniform manufacturing standards.

Gideon followed his friend and waited tensely while Miller wedged the gooseneck into the bar of the first car. Miller stepped back to signal the switch engine. He slipped. The engineer interpreted the sudden jerk of his lantern as a signal. Gideon barely had time to drag the floundering man to safety before the cars crashed together.

"Too damn close, Daphnis. Let me do it—"

He pried the pin out of Miller's mittened hand. The older man snatched it back.

"Listen, Gid. You been treating me like a baby all night. I knew how to do this job 'fore you were a pup!"

Reluctantly Gideon let Miller have his way. It took the older man five minutes to seat the pin in the icy slot. Above the moan of the wind he heard the engineer hectoring them for taking so long.

"Keep your britches on!" Gideon shouted. "We're going as fast as we can!"

His right hand was growing numb again. The wind had intensified, hurling the mingled snow and freezing rain almost horizontally. He managed to couple the third car fairly fast; the drawbars were parallel.

Miller ran past with the link and pins for the next one. Again Gideon followed him, fretting. Miller stepped into the four-foot space between the cars. He had trouble with the link.

"Lord! The slot's solid ice—"

"I've got an extra pin. Let me in. I'll work on it."

He stepped to the edge of the boxcar. His boot skidded. He lost his grip on the pin. Without thinking, he bent to retrieve it as Miller again attacked the slot.

Doubled over, Gideon realized his error. The lantern on his arm had dipped.

The drivers squealed. Sparks shot from the cindered rails. He heard a chuffing, loud as doom.

Standing up, he inadvertently smashed the lens of his lantern on the corner of the car. He reached for Miller's bent back. "Daphnis, get out of there!"

The cry went unheard. But Miller felt Gideon touch him. He swung around, his eyes angry. The train was shunting backward.

Miller saw the end of the forward car moving. He tried to jump to safety. The toe of his boot caught on a tie. Gideon had hold of Miller's overcoat. Trying to regain his balance, Miller jerked too hard and lurched the other way.

The bumper beam of the forward car closed the gap and thudded against the one behind. Daphnis Miller was pinned at the waist between them.

V

Time seemed to stop. Gideon heard bones crack. Miller's lantern went out.

The older man's upper body was twisted toward Gideon and projecting from between the cars. Not twelve inches from Gideon's eyes, Miller's face contorted. His hands scratched Gideon's sleeve as he hung there and screamed.

The scream faded. Miller's eyes bulged. He slumped forward. His head slammed Gideon's chest.

"Daphnis!"

Gideon seized his friend's head, tore off the scarf, and slapped his cheeks in a wild, irrational effort to strike life into the body bent at the waist like a corn-husk doll. Terrified, Gideon went floundering toward the locomotive.

"Go ahead! *Ahead,* damn it! Miller's caught!"

He heard the consternation in the cab. He couldn't tell whether it was the engineer or the fireman who shouted, "You signaled! I saw the lantern—"

"Just go ahead so we can get him free!" Snow mingled with tears in his good eye. *"Just go ahead!"*

vi

When the cars separated, Daphnis Miller was dying.

Gideon caught him as he fell and dragged him to a spot between the tracks. He was nauseated by the wet feel of Miller's overcoat. Not the watery wetness of snow—something sticky, welling from hidden ruptures in Miller's body.

The engineer and fireman bent over the switchman, stricken speechless. Snow whitened Miller's coat. It turned dark as blood soaked it.

Gideon ran like a man pursued.

I didn't think.

I should have put the lantern aside; I saw Daphnis make the same mistake.

I SHOULD HAVE DONE THE WHOLE TRAIN MYSELF!

"Cuthbertson!" He almost fell into the shack. "Cuthbertson, hurry up! Daphnis has been killed."

"Oh Lord almighty—" White-faced, the superintendent ran for the door without stopping for a coat.

vii

Daphnis Miller resembled a fallen snowman by the time Gideon and the superintendent reached him. The fireman had located a lantern, but Gideon wished he hadn't. The diffused rays illuminated Miller's contorted face. Life had gone out of him at a moment of extreme pain. His mouth was open. Unmelted snow lay on his tongue. Sleet spattered his distended eyes.

"My fault," Gideon said, struggling out of his gray overcoat and kneeling beside the body. He flung off his scarf and cap. He was unable to hold back his tears.

He'd seen men perish in wheatfields and forests. He'd seen them sabered, shot, blown apart by artillery fire. Terrible as that was, he'd never been shaken as profoundly as he was now. His hand stretched out to close Miller's hideous eyes, and he wept his rage and shame.

"Oh, Daphnis, goddamn it! This is my fault."

"Quit it, Gid," Cuthbertson said. "He was tipsy when you come to work. Tipsy and half asleep."

"But it was *my* lantern—oh, hell, it's too late."

Full of self-loathing, he covered Miller's body with the Confederate overcoat. He cried into the palms of his mittens.

"Listen, Gid," Cuthbertson said gently. "I take a big share of the blame. I should have ordered him to stay inside the shack till he sobered up."

"His mind wasn't on it." Gideon talked to himself, and the storm. "He had a lot to drink today, but he was happy. He finally found out what his first name meant." The tears dried up but the pain consumed him. "Jesus. *Jesus*!"

Even the engineer seemed moved. "Kent, don't take on so. Accidents happen."

"Happen all the time on this rotten line," Cuthbertson agreed.

Gideon's head jerked up. The leather patch was white. His good eye glared.

"I know. I know what happens afterward, too. Nothing."

The fireman didn't understand. Gideon's finger stabbed toward the body.

"Miller's my neighbor. He has a family, just like Augie Kolb. A wife. Four youngsters—"

Cuthbertson batted snow from his eyes. "Who's going to tell them?"

"I'll tell them. I'll tell them I killed him."

"Gid, you didn't!" Cuthbertson protested.

"They're not the only ones I'm going to tell. I won't see his children starve to death or his wife go to her grave like Gerda Kolb."

Cuthbertson tried to shush him.

"Cuthie, if you'll take him back to the shack, I'll couple the rest of this goddamn train."

"Sure, Gid."

Snow flecked Gideon's light hair. He twisted his scarf in his hands, the wind-raw skin under his right eye wet again. He thought of Louis Kent. His face grew ugly.

He bent his head and whispered a promise to himself, "Once I tell them, they won't forget, either. I swear before God they won't."

Chapter VII
Call to War

i

"Can't you sleep, darling?"

"No," Gideon said.

She shifted her head close to his and tucked her forehead against his chin. Her hair smelled of the harsh homemade soap.

The bed creaked as she changed position and brought her right leg to rest on his thigh. The warmth of her body was comforting. But it couldn't banish the images of Daphnis Miller's corpse, or Flo Miller's worn face changing from disbelief to hysterical sorrow when he stood at the door of the neighboring cottage in the blustery dawn following the accident.

All the heat of the kitchen stove had dissipated. A chilly dampness clung to the rooms; warmer temperatures had arrived twenty-four hours after the storm hurled by and swept out to sea.

Gideon slid his right arm around Margaret while he folded his left under his head. The noise roused Eleanor in the truckle bed. Margaret tensed.

When the child settled down, she said, "You haven't had a decent rest in three days."

Nor had he reported for work at the yards.

"Is it Daphnis?"

He worked his head around and kissed her, but it was done in an absent way. "Don't fret about me. I'll be fine."

"Fine! Gideon Kent, we've been married long enough for me to know when you're fibbing. Tell me what you're thinking."

Silence.

Rain began to patter the roof. In moments it built to a downpour. A familiar dripping started in the parlor.

"I'd better set the pail out."

She tugged him back. "Not until you say what's on your mind."

"I don't want to upset you, Margaret."

"Do you think I can sleep, or keep my mind on the house, or help Flo get ready to go upstate for the funeral when you're in such a state? Refusing to eat? Sitting in the parlor till all hours with the lamp out? Barking at Eleanor?" A forgiving caress of his face. "Say it."

There was a peculiar blend of anxiety and relief in finally doing so. "I have to go after them."

"The owners?"

"Yes. I'm going to get money for Flo, and for Augie Kolb."

She pondered that, said gently, "You know what the outcome will be."

"They'll say no?"

"You won't get close enough for that. No one in a position of authority will even talk to you."

"They might."

"If they did, the answer would still be no."

"Cuthbertson said the owners are dead afraid of any bad publicity right now."

"They'll accept bad publicity rather than meet demands that could set a precedent."

"Goddamn it, Margaret. I know the chances are slim. But I've got to try."

"I didn't mean to anger you. I just want you to be realistic."

"I know. I'm sorry." He hugged her. The drip in the parlor quickened. Eleanor turned again, muttering.

"You'll lose your job, won't you." It wasn't a question.

"Yes. That's why I've been reluctant to say anything."

"Gideon, you know I'm willing to stand by you when I think you're right."

"Do you this time?"

"Your idea may be right. But it's hopeless."

He tried to sound more confident that he was. "Maybe not."

"Your father would be glad to give you enough money to keep Mr. Kolb and Flo secure for the rest of their lives."

"It wouldn't be the same. It'd be charity, not something deserved. The Erie *owes* those two families!"

"You're doing this because you feel guilty about Daphnis—"

"In part. I think I wanted to do it for Augie before Daphnis got killed. I kept trying to deny it to myself. The accident tipped the scale, that's all."

"You realize it's almost like going to war again? You said you never would."

He nodded. "A man changes his mind, Margaret. Circumstances change his mind." The exhausted face of Bill Sylvis drifted past his inner eye. "Daphnis was kind to us. When he died, he was almost as close to me as I am to you. Have you ever been close to someone who died violently?"

"No."

"Well, it's ugly. Ugly and dirty and sad beyond belief. Last month Cuthie was reading one of those Beadle novels. Some tale about Army scouts in the West. I looked at a column or two. Three men were killed in as many paragraphs. The author knocked them down like ninepins. There was no hint of pain. Nothing about the foulness when a dying man's functions fail. The writer made it clean and—and trivial. The deaths shocked no one. Left no one hurt. Undoubtedly the author's never seen men die either. A real human being can't be forgotten so easily."

"It's still a lost cause, Gideon."

A short, sad laugh. "I expect. But I fought for one of those before and survived. The thing is—I have no choice."

"Well," Margaret murmured, "it's decided. We can go to sleep."

"You're not against it?"

"I can't say I like it. But I suspected it was coming."

He rumpled her hair, tried to tease. "Aren't you going

to caution me not to canter off with Beauty Stuart because I'll get hurt?"

"No, Gideon. I've learned something about you and your family. The Kents have a tendency to go wherever they must, and hang the consequences. Just the other night, when everyone else stayed home during the storm, your conscience sent you to work with Daphnis. Even when I think about what might happen this time, I can't help feeling proud of you—"

She kissed his cheek. "Where will you start? The superintendent of the yards? The general manager?"

"They only take orders. I'll start with the people who can make a decision. I don't know any of them. But I have a connection with one."

Astonishment: "You don't mean Louis?"

"Why not? They elected him a director last week. It was in all the papers."

"He'll give you no special treatment. He despises your father. And you've never even seen him."

"Even so, I'm closer to him than to any of the others. I know where Louis lives. Father knows what he looks like. I must fix that damn pail—"

He disentangled himself, climbed out of bed, barked his shin on a post of the truckle bed and almost woke Eleanor. The rain pelted harder as he groped his way into the kitchen.

She's right, he thought as he lugged the pail to the parlor and placed it beneath the leak. *She's too loving to insist you abandon the idea, but she knows you're a damn fool. She knows it as well as you do.*

It had simply come down to a choice between doing nothing or making an effort. He had no great hope of success. But without making an effort, he'd never sleep well again.

ii

His tension and the river's choppiness combined to unsettle his stomach when he rode the ferry to the foot of Courtland Street next morning. Margaret had emptied her jar of kitchen money to provide him with a dollar and a half for boat fare and trips on the horsecar lines. He walked to the parsonage on Orange Street.

The study in the house next to St. Mark's Methodist Episcopal Church reeked of cigar smoke. But there was no cigar in evidence when Jephtha Kent opened the door, just the haze of his secret vice.

"Gideon!"

"Hello, Father."

"I thought I heard the bell."

"Molly let me in."

Gideon entered the cozy, book-lined room. Outside the window, the narrow walkway between the parsonage and the church proper looked dark as twilight.

"I hardly expected to see you in town during the week," Jephtha said.

He looks old, Gideon thought with a touch of astonishment. In not much more than a year, Jephtha would be fifty; his long, straight black hair had a generous streaking of white. Age had softened his gaunt features. But many of his flock said he still resembled a red Indian.

"There's nothing wrong with Margaret or the baby?"

"No, they're fine." Gideon sank into a chair in front of the littered desk. He coughed.

A flush crept into Jephtha's gaunt cheeks. "Stuffy in here," he muttered as he raised the window. The sudden rush of air set the smoke moving and only made it doubly noticeable.

Self-consciously Jephtha sat down. His desk was strewn with sheets of notes for a sermon. He stacked some of them on top of an open Bible and picked up a large, stiff rectangle of paper that Gideon hadn't noticed before.

"Look what the morning post brought. A photograph of the new store. It's their fourth."

Absently Gideon took the photograph, which showed an unfamiliar man and woman posed in front of a frame building with plate-glass windows and a large signboard:

H. & M. K. BOYLE
OF CHEYENNE

An unconscious jealousy crept over him as he stared at the brown-tinted image. He'd never met Amanda Kent's clerk, Michael Boyle, to whom his father had willed Jeremiah's portion of the California wealth. He knew Jephtha loved and respected the Irishman. Yet he'd always felt it somewhat unjust that family money should be given to Boyle, no matter how strong Jephtha's feelings.

Still, he and his father didn't agree on everything. Since he was entitled to no voice in the decision, he'd never mentioned his reservations.

"I tell you, Gideon, that wife of Michael's must be a clever women. They've already trebled the money I advanced them, paid the principal back with interest, and wherever they open an establishment along the railroad, they can't keep up with the volume of business. There's a letter somewhere—" He rummaged among the notes. "They'll be coming east in the spring to buy merchandise."

Suddenly Jephtha's dark hands ceased shuffling the papers. He noticed the look of strain on his son's face.

"I'm sorry," he said. "There is something wrong, and I'm rattling."

Gideon drew a deep breath. "I need some information about Louis."

"*Louis?* What on earth for?"

Gideon explained. Jephtha leaned back in his chair with his fingertips touching beneath his chin. When Gideon finished, Jephtha asked immediately, "Do you know what you're doing?"

"Hell, yes!"

He fell back in the chair, embarrassed by the outburst. "Margaret and I have already discussed the certainty that I'll lose my job. Let's not waste time on that. I'd like to know what Cousin Louis looks like."

"Easy enough," Jephtha said, and described him in a few sentences. Gideon felt uncomfortable. Jephtha's face had grown expressionless, showing neither approval nor disapproval. "Where do you plan to see him, Gideon?"

"I intend to try his home first."

"I'll ask you again—do you know what you're doing?"

"If you mean to say I'm a fool for trying to wring money out of the Erie for those two families, I know it. I must try anyway."

"Even though you're asking for the impossible? Generosity from men who have no concern for the welfare of others? That hypocrite Drew. Fisk—an out and out libertine. And Gould—possibly the worst of the lot. Pious and proper in his personal life—a positive maniac on the subject of keeping it above reproach. I sometimes wonder if his wife deceives herself or is simply ignorant. Propriety at home and piracy everywhere else, that's Gould's style. I know a few pale imitators in my own congregation," he added with a sad chuckle. "As for Louis—what can I tell you that you haven't already heard? Before Amanda died, she feared she'd set him a bad example. She was a wonderful woman, but in that respect she was right. She failed with Louis. He's venal, self-centered—and the last person on God's earth who deserves to possess the family heirlooms. He has as much human kindness as his newfound partners in fortune, which is to say he has exactly none. He doesn't even share Gould's virtue of maintaining a decent home."

"Do you know where he spends his time when he's away from Fifth Avenue?"

"I've no idea. I would imagine he belongs to a club or two. The Erie headquarters downtown would be another possibility. Since this amoral stock war began, the papers say the directors gather there every day or so."

Gideon sighed. "I'd best begin with the Fifth Avenue address. From there I'll trust to luck."

"You'll need plenty," Jephtha said in a sober way. "Despite Mr. Gould's concern for editorial opinion, how the public feels generally doesn't affect those men. Of course if Gould's wife saw a story saying he was chasing another female, you'd see him deny it oftener than Simon Peter denied the Lord. Still—"

A glint of amusement lit Jephtha's dark eyes. "We might be able to singe some trousers in that crowd."

"We?" Gideon shook his head. "You aren't going to be dragged into this in any way."

"Perhaps I'll choose to be! I'm in sympathy with what you're attempting, Gideon. I suspect it's futile but that doesn't make it unworthy. So consider it a family endeavor. I might be able to help you from my pulpit. It's been a long time since I've given my congregation a good teeth-rattling sermon on some public issue. Everyone's agog over the affairs of the Erie. Postmortem benefits for Erie laborers might be an ideal subject—and who knows? Gould might be sensitive just now."

"I'll keep that in mind," Gideon promised. "Meantime, I'd best be going—"

Jephtha leaned forward. "Are you sure Margaret's in full agreement with this course?"

"Yes. She's not enthusiastic. But she'll go along."

"Even if by some miracle you should win a small concession, you realize it wouldn't be the end. Rather, it would be just the beginning."

"What do you mean?"

"You'd be a marked man. Reprisals might be attempted. Certainly no business of substance on the East Coast would give you even a menial position—if that. Any future you hoped to find in commerce would be wiped out. Consciously or otherwise, you're behaving like some of the most hated men in America."

"You mean the trade union people?"

"I do."

Gideon bristled. "Everyone keeps throwing that in my face. I'm no damned unionist!"

"You are when you concern yourself with death benefits for laborers." Jephtha held up his hand. "I'm not objecting. In fact, I'm proud of you. We haven't had a good cause in the Kent family for quite a while. Perhaps it's time we did."

He circled the desk and gave his son's shoulder an affectionate squeeze. "Before you launch off, come along to the kitchen. There's hot tea on the stove, and Molly's baking bread. It should be ready soon. You look as if you could stand a bit of nourishment."

Gideon reached across with his right hand and clasped his father's fingers. "I've already gotten a good portion. Thank you."

"Just remember my offer of a sermon." Jephtha opened the study door. "A trade unionist. Imagine that. Your poor mother's probably whirling in her grave."

"Father, I do not see myself in that role at all."

Jephtha turned, his eyes intense. "I believe you. But you see, I don't count. Anyone who threatens the status quo, no matter how humane and sensible the reason, is usually accused of being a radical of the most extreme sort. Perhaps it doesn't happen without cause. Perhaps any time you *do* threaten the status quo, you *are* a radical. You're in good company, however. When your great-great-grandfather Kent fired his musket at Concord Bridge, he upset the status quo with a vengeance. But he was right. So are you. In the end, nothing else matters."

He clapped Gideon's shoulder and preceded him out of the study, walking with an exuberance Gideon wished he could match.

iii

For five cents, a car on the Sixth Avenue Railroad took him nearly to the end of the line. Shortly past noon he approached the portico of the handsome house Louis Kent had built at upper Fifth Avenue and Fifty-fifth Street.

The city was spreading north, all the way to Central Park. Property owners around Madison Square, a highly fashionable address just a decade ago, bemoaned the growing commercialization of the area. Louis had done more than bemoan.

A stiff-backed manservant informed Gideon that Mr. Louis Kent was out for the remainder of the day. The brief and one-sided conversation ended when the great carved door slammed without Gideon having an opportunity to state his name or his business.

He clacked the knocker again. The servant appeared at one of the window lights beside the door. He motioned Gideon away, then disappeared. He didn't respond to the third knock.

Gideon went down the drive, out the gate and south along the rain-drenched avenue. A farmer from the open country above Fifty-ninth Street was driving a dozen squealing hogs in the center of the street. He gave Gideon's gray overcoat a suspicious examination. Head bowed, Gideon paid no attention.

Where should he go next? The only possibility was the one his father had suggested—the Erie headquarters located on the Lower West Side near the line's Pier 15 ticket office. He turned west to catch the Sixth Avenue horsecar again.

By early afternoon he was loitering in a dim cul-de-sac opposite a handsome, cupolaed building housing the railroad's general offices. Trash bins at the mouth of the cul-de-sac shielded him from direct observation. A second floor overhang provided protection from the weather. But he still felt wretched in his soggy coat.

A half block west, the Duane Street pier jutted into the river. A great steam liner belching smoke from its funnels went churning toward the ocean, the British ensign hanging limp in the rain. Gideon bent his leg and braced the toe of his right boot against the brick wall. He opened the copy of the *Union* he'd purchased. At the end of fifteen minutes he decided he might have gambled correctly. Expensive carriages began to pull up in front of the headquarters, depositing well-dressed gentlemen who hurried inside.

Employees came and went as well. The traffic was observed by a couple of wide-shouldered men lounging on the porch. They had the look of toughs, but they tipped their derbies deferentially to the new arrivals.

A handsome victoria approached along Duane Street. Its calash top was folded down to shield its passenger from the rain. A young man of about thirty climbed out. Gideon only had a glimpse of him, but the man's age and swarthy skin convinced him it was Louis Kent. No one else fitting Jephtha's description had shown up.

That man is my relative, he thought as he stared at the gilt-lettered doors through which Louis had vanished. A curt laugh helped him overcome a curious sense of awe. Gradually, Louis began to assume more human proportions.

Despite his fine clothing, he'd looked perfectly ordinary. The same applied to the rest of the visitors. At long range, their wealth and power lent them an—Olympian, that was the word he wanted—an Olympian aura. But they were men exactly like he was. They could feel pain and fear. If he remembered that, he'd have a useful weapon.

Soon the last of the gentlemen went inside. Gideon had counted eleven in all.

To pass the time, he began to leaf through the paper. He found the usual collection of lurid material—a staple of the *Union*—including an account of a train robbery in the Nebraska Territory:

UNION PACIFIC LOOTED!
Armed Bandits Conduct Daring Raid
Near North Platte!

The dispatch was a week old. It described the theft of a payroll from a supply train by an unidentified white man and his Indian confederate. The robbers had stopped the train by piling three frozen buffalo carcasses on the track. They'd gotten away safely and Dr. Thomas Durant had announced a substantial reward for their capture.

On the next page he came across the editorial drawing. It made him smile. A huge loathsome octopus with a wizened human face imprisoned six anguished maidens in its tentacles. The octopus was captioned *Vanderbilt* while each of the suffering females had the word *Competition* lettered on the hem of her gown.

Eventually the rain slacked off. He finished the paper as the street began to darken. His empty stomach ached. He had no timepiece, but he guessed the conclave had already lasted about three hours.

One of the toughs lit gas lamps beside the office entrance. The other applied a match to kindling in a metal drum at the curb. One by one the carriages returned, including the victoria.

From the direction of the river a poorly dressed boot boy appeared, carrying his homemade shoe stand. He scrutinized the waiting vehicles, the fine horses, and the well-dressed drivers congregated around the blazing barrel. The boy set up shop by squatting on his box. One of the guards made a halfhearted attempt to shoo him away, but he paid no attention. The guards returned to scrutiny of the street and their diamond rings.

In another few minutes the doors opened. The gentlemen who'd been meeting started to emerge. One thwacked his silk hat on his head angrily. Several were arguing. The fire helped Gideon observe faces. Earlier, he'd seen almost nothing but the backs of heads.

If he recalled the *Leslie's* cover correctly, the round-faced chap was Jim Fisk. He looked sleepy and phlegmatic. Gideon searched for Gould but couldn't find him in the crowd.

The doors opened again. Louis emerged, followed by an old fellow with unkempt gray hair and a choleric countenance. The gray-haired man negotiated the steps with arthritic caution, planting his drover's boots carefully. His cranky high-pitched voice carried across the street. "You come here and listen, Fisk!"

The portly Fisk ignored him and escaped into a brougham. Gideon heard him call instructions to his driver as the carriage clattered off.

The old man—Drew, he recognized—was suddenly blocked by the boy, who addressed him in heavily accented English.

"Black your boots, sir? I'll do a fine job."

Louis stepped up, grabbed the boy's shoulder and flung him aside. Old Drew, still seeking someone to listen to his complaints, chose Louis. Above the racket of departing vehicles, Drew exclaimed, "Ain't going to Ludlow Street for you or any of the rest of these sharps!"

Louis turned his back rudely and jumped in the victoria. The door slammed. The vehicle shot away across the rain-slicked cobbles. The opening where it had been standing gave Gideon a clear look at Daniel Drew. Furious, the old man crammed a battered cowman's hat on his head and headed for his own carriage.

In moments the entire curb was deserted. The bootblack picked up his box, heading east. The toughs disappeared inside. Gideon heard the rattle of a bolt on the gilt doors.

"Young fellow!" He stuffed the paper in his overcoat and ran.

The bootblack's pinched face showed suspicion as Gideon approached. The suspicion intensified when a gusting flame in the barrel showed the boy the color of Gideon's overcoat.

"I don't shine no boots for Rebs."

"That man who shoved you"—Gideon slipped two coins into the boy's hand—"did you hear him speak to his driver?"

The boy examined the coins as if they were tainted. But he pocketed them.

"Might have."

"Did he say where he was going?"

"Someplace on East Twenty-seventh."

"Did you catch the number?"

The boy's eyes had an old, weary look. He stuck his hand in his pocket and rattled the coins, almost tauntingly. Gideon found another ten-cent piece and held it up in the firelight. The boy repeated an address.

"Is that someone's home?"

The boy sneezed and wiped mucus from his nose. His smirk said Gideon, not he, was the naive stranger.

"Everybody knows Mrs. Bell's Universal."

"I don't. Is it a saloon?"

"Whorehouse. Too rich for you."

The boy strolled away. In the distance an omnibus bell clanged.

Gideon debated. East Twenty-seventh Street was across town, a long car ride. By the time he arrived, Louis could well be gone. Still, he might have a better chance to see him at a brothel than he did at the Fifth Avenue mansion.

As he started east on Duane, the rain began again. He clenched his teeth to keep them from chattering and put his hands in his pockets. Five cents bought him warm chestnuts from a pushcart vendor. The hunger pains abated a little.

But the food did nothing to warm him as he trudged on. The rain fell harder. It promised to be a long, cold night.

Chapter VIII

At the Universal

i

In a private second-floor parlor of Mrs. Hester Bell's establishment on East Twenty-seventh Street, Jubilee Jim was having a bath. If Louis had ever witnessed such a bizarre scene, he couldn't recall it.

The parlor's walls and ceiling were covered with mirrors. On a dais in the center of the carpet sat an oversized zinc tub topped with imported marble. A mirrored door led to a bedchamber. Mrs. Bell also provided a piano for patrons aesthetically inclined.

The club's blind black musician was working downstairs at the moment. The arpeggios of a classical piece drifted to the parlor, interspersed with restrained feminine merriment. The door to the hall was bolted on the inside. After the formal board meeting had broken up, Fisk had insisted on a private conference. He refused to go anywhere but the club; Miss Mansfield was suffering her monthly indisposition.

Louis sat at a small marble table next to the wall opposite the bedroom. Across the table was the small and sallow Jay Gould. An obligatory glass of lager stood beside his pale hand. He resembled a church deacon transported to hell against his will.

Wherever Louis looked—right, left, or overhead—he saw Jubilee Jim submerged to his chest in perfumed water and surrounded by a constantly changing mosaic of bare buttocks, dark-rippled breasts, and black hair. Fisk had a sea captain's hat cocked on his yellow curls. He was being tended by a pair of Oriental girls. Chinese, Mrs. Bell said. Neither was more than eighteen.

The Universal Club employed girls of eleven nationalities—plus two men, a Portuguese and a West Indian mulatto, who catered to a small segment of the clientele. Mrs. Bell guaranteed none of the employees could speak English, thus assuring their discretion. A cadaverous fellow named Dr. Randolph acted as club manager and translator; he'd been a professor of languages at a New England academy for boys until his dismissal on morals charges.

Fisk, a regular at the Universal, had brought Louis there for the first time three weeks ago. Louis had heard of the place before that, of course. But it took a man of Fisk's status to gain him admittance as a customer.

He wished the meeting had been arranged for another location, though. Somehow the sight of the naked young women bothered him, reminded him of the little dancer, Nedda, whom he thought he'd forgotten.

Giggling, one of the girls refilled Fisk's champagne glass. The other girl, kneeling on the tub's far side, was vigorously bathing the fat man. At least her arm was immersed to the elbow, and her unseen hand appeared quite busy. Fisk's face was a study in simple-minded bliss.

Louis cleared his throat. Gould said, "Jim, you've inconvenienced me by insisting we traipse over to a place like this. Let's get on with the business."

"Jay, my friend"—Fisk tilted his glass, drank, and smacked his lips; some of the liquid dribbled down his chin—"the trouble with you is, you're too starched. Too blasted starched."

He winked at Louis. "I always tell Jay there's one big difference between us. I have more trouble to get my dinner than to digest it. He has more trouble to digest it than to get it. Enjoy yourself for a change, Jay!"

"My idea of a good time is to be home with Helen and the boys."

"All right." Fisk pouted. He jiggled the forearm of the girl bathing him. "You wait in the bedroom."

The girl blushed, unable to understand. Fisk waved the champagne goblet. "In there. Vamoose! Scat!"

The two retired, rumps jiggling. The mirrored door closed. With a pallid hand Gould pushed his beer glass toward Louis.

"You may have this if you want it. I haven't touched it."

"Jesus, what an old stiff neck!" Fisk heaved himself out of the tub, snatched a towel, and began drying his genitals. He wrapped the towel around his paunch, sat on the marble tub rim, and wiggled his pink toes. "We do need to have a talk, though. I think Uncle Dan'l's losing his nerve."

Gould shrugged, unexpectedly tolerant.

"When a fellow passes seventy, he's bound to be less than steady."

"Oh, shit on that, Jay. The Commodore's three years older than Dan and *he* hasn't lost his nerve. He's busy as a flea on a hound. He's out to corner Erie shares, keep us from issuing any more, and use his majority to shovel in a whole new board of directors next month. Unless we prevent it."

Louis knocked back the rest of his champagne and reached for the bottle in its silver stand. "We took action to prevent it this afternoon. Jay's inspiration solved our problem."

He said it with genuine respect. Gould had remembered an antique printing press stored in the basement of the Erie offices.

Louis hoped the press was the answer to the difficulties they'd encountered in the past few weeks. The war was intensifying. After the vote on rate fixing had gone against the Commodore thanks to Louis' efforts, the old man had realized the Boston group was abandoning him. He'd issued a terse order in the Street: "Buy Erie and keep on buying."

While his brokers piled up shares, he took steps to prevent Gould's faction from doing the same. Just two days ago, his captive State Supreme Court judge had issued an injunction preventing the Erie from paying Drew interest or principal on an outstanding loan of three and a half million dollars—money that could have bought shares. Judge Barnard had separately enjoined Drew from speculating with a sizable block of stock still in his possession.

That had been the gloomy picture until the afternoon's gathering of the board—from which the Commodore's men had lately absented themselves. In his most confidential manner, Gould had pointed out that despite the injunctions, the Vanderbilt group had failed to plug up an escape hatch—a complex New York state law permitting issuance of new shares when one railroad acquired another. A few weeks before, the Erie had secretly purchased the moribund Buffalo, Bradford, & Pittsburgh line just in case injunctions were forthcoming.

Now it was necessary to invoke the law to legalize a new float of bonds convertible to stock. Following Mr. Gould's quiet but stunning mention of the old printing press in the basement, a vote had been taken authorizing ten millions of such bonds.

Louis had helped draft the language for the minutes. In outrageously straight-faced sentences, the directors had declared the move was being made because of an *urgent and distressing report* from the line's general manager. He was pleading for funds to repair the Erie trackage, *where,* the minutes now read, *it is wholly unsafe to run a passenger train at the ordinary speed. Broken wheels, rails, engines, and cars off the track have been of daily, almost hourly occurrence for the past two months.*

It looked marvelously official. But the three gentlemen at Mrs. Bell's knew the worried general manager would never see a penny of the income from the new issue.

Louis chuckled. "By God, it *is* a brilliant move—churning out bonds in the basement."

"That's the spirit I like to see!" Fisk exclaimed, jumping up. The towel fell away, but he paid no attention. He capered like an overage cherub. "Just give me enough rag paper and we'll hammer the everlasting tar out of that old mariner from Staten Island!"

"Of course," Gould thought aloud, "the Commodore will soon know we're simply dumping more shares on the market."

"And he'll go after them," Louis agreed. "It's no strain

on his bank account. He still has thirty millions to play with."

Fisk waved that aside. "After we've swallowed eight or nine million of his money, maybe he'll realize he's throwing it down a sewer." Warming to the subject, he practically pranced. "We can print bonds faster than his brokerages can buy 'em! Ink's cheap. White paper's cheap. If we can make Vanderbilt pay us fifty or sixty dollars for little pieces of paper that haven't cost us two cents, it's good night, Commodore!"

"Unless he moves against us in the courts again," Gould warned.

"I'm more worried about Uncle Dan'l," Louis put in. "Jim's right—I think he's going soft."

That sobered Fisk dramatically. "Yes, Drew's the real reason I wanted us to meet. If we lose his vote, we're hulled and sunk. He has enough influence on the board to stop us from running the press. And he's scared. Jay, you saw how he turned white when you proposed the printing scheme. Danny still wants to win, I think. But the question is—how badly?"

Jay Gould didn't answer immediately. He sat like a meditating ascetic, his mournful eyes probing places beyond the ken of his companions. Finally he roused.

"I agree, Dan's a queer case these days. It may be senility. Or perhaps he's just gotten too fond of endowing seminaries and preening in his pew at St. Paul's. Business and religion are oil and water. Whatever the reason, he's forgotten that."

Fisk agreed vehemently. "When he voted for the bond issue this afternoon, his hands were shaking."

"And he tried to hector me about the idea afterward—" Louis began.

"I suppose all he can see is a cell at Ludlow Street," Gould said. "He'd be devastated to have his pious reputation soiled by a term in the clink."

"Well, Christ," Fisk laughed, "I don't want to see the inside of the lockup any more than he does. But as Dan himself used to say, if a cat wants to eat a fish, she's got to be willing to wet her feet. We're going to print the bonds as fast as possible. While we do, it's up to each one of us to keep pounding at Dan. Keep reminding him we can't win any other way, and this way, we're sure to win. Every time we dump shares, the price'll drop. Vanderbilt's hirelings will jump in and spend like Midas. The price'll go up, then we'll crank the press and drive the market down again. We'll have him dizzy and half broke if we stick to it!"

"I'm in agreement," Gould said. "We must all work on Drew. Bolster his nerve."

"I'll take him to lunch at the Union Club tomorrow," Louis promised.

"A good start." Gould's almost colorless lips curved in a tiny smile barely visible between his mustache and beard. "You've already proved your persuasive powers are considerable, Louis. Just don't utter the word injunction to Dan. It terrifies him. However, I do think it's probable Vanderbilt will get another one to prevent us from running the press."

"That's another point on which we have to agree." Fisk nodded. "What if it happens? Do we stop?" He barely paused. "I say no."

Louis pondered. The prospect of lengthy court proceedings—even an arrest—was unappetizing. But he didn't dare offend Fisk; he was in too deeply.

"So do I," he said.

Gould said, "I'm wondering how long we can keep Vanderbilt from realizing what we're up to."

"Mmm." Fisk scratched his jowl. "Today's the nineteenth. I'd guess a week. Maybe two."

"We can take a hell of a lot of his money in that time," Louis said.

"But how do you vote on stopping, Jay?" Fisk prodded. "I'd like it to be unanimous."

Gould's face showed no hint of hesitation. "It is. We go straight ahead until the constables bring an injunction to the doorsill. Then we'll figure out our next move."

"If there *is* an injunction," Fisk said, "Uncle Dan'l will quit."

"*Want* to quit," Gould corrected. "Again it's up to us to prevent him. Remind him that if he buckles, he'll not only be unable to shower endowments on churches; he'll be a ruined man. We must keep cautioning Danny that jail is bad, a tarnished reputation is worse, but being ruined is worst of all. *Ruined* is the key word. It's better to risk

Ludlow Street now—or hell in the hereafter—than be ruined. Deep down, Drew knows it."

The balding financier's eyes were brightly thoughtful. Louis shivered. Gould was an absolute wizard, not only of share manipulation but of the forces that motivated men. In the contemporary vocabulary there was no word more potent than ruined. Men would risk almost anything rather than be labeled with it. So would women—although to the female sex, ruin meant a loss of something other than wealth.

Louis began to feel less anxious. Fisk too seemed relieved. He lifted one flabby leg into the tub and lowered himself. "Knew we'd see eye to eye. We'll go ahead." He belched, adjusted his nautical cap, and used an index finger to dribble perfumed water into his navel. "And, between us, we'll keep Danny's pecker stiff when it droops. Every one of us is responsible."

A glance at Louis. It said he was being tested again. He still didn't enjoy the full measure of confidence Fisk and Gould had in one another. But they'd handed him another chance to prove his worth. He wouldn't neglect it.

Out in the hall, someone knocked.

Gould jerked upright. "Confound it, Jim, we issued explicit orders."

The words carried an edge of concern. Louis strode to the door.

"Who's there?"

"Mrs. Bell," a basso voice replied. "That you, Mr. Kent?"

"Yes. We said we weren't to be interrupted."

"Well, sir, I'm afraid you'll have to be," the woman retorted. "We have a peculiar situation downstairs. Some fellow's asking for you."

Louis' stomach knotted when he heard Gould's sharp intake of breath. Fisk began to burble outraged questions.

"Tell him I'm not here, for God's sake!"

"He knows you are. He's polite but he's insistent."

Louis turned. As he pointed to the bolt, his nervous eyes queried the other two men. He got a curt nod from Gould, unlocked the door, and admitted a massive woman in a brocaded gown.

"Why didn't you have Dr. Randolph get rid of him?" Louis demanded.

"Because," Mrs. Bell shot back, "he says his name's the same as yours. He says his name's Kent."

ii

Jay Gould stormed toward them.

"Louis, what the devil is going on here?"

Stunned, Louis lifted both hands. "Jay, it's a damned mystery to me. How old is this man, Mrs. Bell? Forty-five? Is he wearing shabby clothes, like a parson's?"

Hester Bell shook her head. "He's shabby, all right. But I've never seen a parson in a Confederate overcoat. The boy's in his twenties. Partially blind. That is, I assume so. He wears a patch—"

One of her ringed hands touched the powdered skin below her left eye. She added, "He says he won't go till he speaks with you."

"Blast it, I knew we shouldn't have come here!" Gould cried. "Who is he, Louis?"

"I don't know!"

"You've talked about your cousin, the preacher. I've never heard you mention any other Kents."

Louis began to perspire. Even Fisk no longer looked cordial.

"Reverend Kent has a couple of sons," Louis explained hastily. "I've never met them. I had no idea any of them were in New York. They're Virginians."

"Frankly," Gould murmured, "I don't care who it is. Someone knows you're on the premises—and may know I am too. I have a reputation to protect."

That amused Mrs. Bell.

"About the same kind as a Kansas rattlesnake's."

Gould went livid. "I'm referring to Helen and my sons. I sent my carriage home. You get that blasted Dr. Randolph to whistle up a hack. Send it to the entrance by the back stairs right away."

He snatched up his overcoat, stick, and gloves. Mrs. Bell sighed. "I'll do the best I can. It's still raining. May take a little while."

Gould's eyes reflected the gaslight like chips of burning coal.

"It better not take longer than two or three minutes or

I'll speak to Bill Tweed, and then all the cash on the Street won't help you keep your doors open."

The warning was softly spoken. But Hester Bell looked terrified. Gould turned his wrath on Louis.

"I don't care what personal matters have brought your relative here, but you damned well—" He thrust the gold head of his cane into Louis' chest. Louis turned red but held his temper. Gould was in an absolute fury; that was plain from his use of profanity.

"—*damned* well better get rid of him, and not let on you're here for any reason except pleasure!"

Fisk came flopping out of the tub like a white whale. "It's all damned puzzling. Smacks of one of the Commodore's tricks—sending some fellow around to spy on us. You came in your own rig, didn't you, Louis?"

His voice was unexpectedly weak. "Y-yes. Straight from the headquarters."

"Was there anyone hanging around when you left?"

He tried to recollect. "Just the other board members. Oh, and a boot boy."

"Did you give this address to your driver?"

"Of course."

"Loud enough so the boy could hear?"

"I honestly paid no attention."

He began to feel increasingly threatened. Cornered, Fisk and Gould stuck together. In a space of seconds he'd again become an outsider—and all because of some damned act of carelessness he couldn't remember! His voice trailed off in a lame way. "I suppose it's possible."

"Well," Gould snapped, "you've created a devil of a mess."

"Jay, I'll take care of it!"

The black eyes were those of an enemy. "I know you will."

Gould swept by, turned right in the corridor, and disappeared down the back stairs. Louis shivered again.

"Get out of here, get out, for Christ's sake!" Fisk exclaimed. He shoved Louis into the hall, and Hester Bell after him. The door slammed. The bolt rattled in its socket.

Louis' stomach was hurting fiercely now. If he had needed to be reminded of the stakes for which the Erie War was being fought—or the way an ally could be abandoned at the slightest hint of trouble—the last few minutes had done it.

"Mrs. Bell, are you sure this fellow said his name was Kent?"

"I'm not deaf. He said it."

"Is he armed?"

"Not that I could tell."

He thought quickly. "You have a back parlor downstairs, don't you?"

"Yes."

"Private?"

"Quite."

"Show him in there. I'll be down in three or four minutes." He reached into his pocket, pulled out a clip containing greenbacks and gold certificates. "There's a hundred for your help."

Hester Bell slipped the money down her bodice. But she'd turned on him too. "I don't want any scrapes here, Mr. Kent. I pay off too many policemen—and through them, the Boss himself." She meant the man to whom Gould had referred—William Tweed, who virtually ruled the city through his control of the Tammany Society and the board of supervisors.

"I'm paying you to help me *avoid* a scrape!" Louis countered. "Are your two roughnecks in the house?"

"At night they're never out of the house."

"Have them stand by near the parlor."

"All right." She started away, then swung back. "Mr. Kent, I can be almost as vindictive as little Jay. If you've brought personal quarrels into my club and are trying to pretend you don't know anything about it—"

"I don't!"

"You'd better be telling the truth." She smiled, picking up the train of her dress and hurrying toward the main staircase.

Damn her! Where did the madam of a brothel get the gall to speak to him that way?

He knew very well. She was an intimate of Jubilee Jim—he was tight with Gould—and Louis had only been lately admitted to their confidence. If he bungled again, he would be out.

Tormented by worry, he paced the upper hall until he judged three minutes had passed. Then he wiped his palms on his trousers and started for the front stairs.

Chapter IX

"I'm on Top, Ain't I?"

i

The tinted glass bowls of the hallway gas jets cast a watery aquamarine light. Gideon paced back and forth in the entrance of the parlor to which Mrs. Bell had led him. The room opened off the long, narrow corridor at a point midway between the front foyer and a vestibule leading to a back door with an elaborate stained-glass window.

About ten feet back of the parlor and perhaps six feet from the vestibule, there was a large dark recess in the opposite wall. The well of a rear staircase, he suspected. He kept his eye on it. He had no idea where Louis would appear—or if he would. But for several moments now, he'd had an eerie feeling that someone was lurking in the recess. Hesitating there—perhaps hoping he'd desert the hall.

Could it be his cousin?

The presence of the unseen observer only heightened his fear and uncertainty. He'd brazened his way into the Universal Club by using Louis Kent's name and pretending a familiarity that didn't exist. Now he wasn't sure how to proceed. He was beginning to think he was foolish indeed to believe he could stand up to one of the directors of the line—or even speak his mind in a coherent way.

He was uncomfortably conscious of the fetid stench of his wet overcoat. He must look a sight. Certainly he looked out of place in this quiet, elegant corridor where blue light shimmered.

A faint squeak by the back stairs. He was virtually certain someone was there. He turned and walked into the parlor—but not far.

He heard the footsteps distinctly. Two long strides took him back to the hall. A short man with a walking stick was hurrying toward the vestibule. He darted a look over his shoulder.

Gideon's heart pounded. Recognition was instantaneous. The bearded man averted his head and rushed on toward the stained-glass door. Afterward Gideon never knew where he found the courage—better, the idiotic audacity—to go charging down the hall in pursuit. Perhaps it came from an unconscious realization that he'd never again have such an opportunity.

"Mr. Gould?"

The short man broke stride. Gideon's mouth went dry.

"Mr. Gould, wait. You're one of the men I want to see."

The man hesitated. Then he turned around. Gideon almost winced under the impact of the piercing dark eyes. The cover of *Leslie's* had sprung to life.

He hadn't realized Gould was so small. Five foot six or seven inches. The financier spoke softly, but with more than a hint of strain. "You've mistaken me for someone else, sir."

"No, I don't believe—*wait!*" Gideon lunged for Gould's arm as he started away.

Gould panicked, wrenched out of Gideon's grip. At the front end of the hall, footsteps quickened to a run.

"Let go of him!"

Someone seized Gideon's shoulder, flung him against the wall. Pendants on the gas fixtures tinkled.

"Jesus, Jay, I'm sorry. Are you all right?"

Dots of color appeared above Gould's beard. In the stairwell Gideon glimpsed two heavyset men watching. Where had they come from?

There was confusion on Louis Kent's swarthy face. Gould's anger seemed chiefly directed at him. Gideon forced himself to say, "You'd better listen to me, Mr.

Gould"—the short man ignored that, giving Louis another furious glance before starting for the stained-glass door again—"unless you'd care to have it noised about that you frequent whorehouses."

Jay Gould stood absolutely still, his head tilted back slightly. When he turned, his lips barely moved. "Is this your relative, Louis?"

"Jay, I've never seen him before! I don't know—"

"Will you stop repeating my name like a parrot?"

Gould glowered past Gideon's shoulder. In the front foyer, two round-eyed girls ducked out of sight. Suddenly Gould stalked to Gideon and pushed him toward the parlor.

"In there! I don't discuss *anything* in hallways!"

ii

Gideon tried to walk calmly, straight to the center of the parlor. Louis, distraught and sweating, fumbled at the sliding door. He couldn't seem to locate the handle. Gould thrust him aside and closed the door with a thump.

Two trimmed gas jets cast a blue light much weaker than that in the corridor. Gould seated himself at one of the marble tables, his gloved hands planted on the head of his stick. Louis leaned against the door, breathing noisily.

"Identify yourself," Gould said.

"My name is Gideon Kent."

"You *are* this gentleman's cousin?"

Gideon could barely nod. He tried to remember the financier was as mortal as he. The remark about a whorehouse, a sudden inspiration prompted by Jephtha's comment on Gould's personal life, had given him Gould's attention. He must take advantage of that.

"Mr. Kent and my father are actually second cousins—"

"State your business."

Gideon's voice steadied. "I'm employed in the Erie yards over in Jersey City." Louis inhaled sharply. "I'm a switchman. Since the first of the year, two men—friends of mine—have been in serious accidents while on the job."

He was perspiring. But he dared not stop. "One lost both legs. The other was killed, just this week. Both left dependents. Families that now have no income. They did your work, Mr. Gould. I want"—on an impulse, he doubled the figure he'd had in mind—"I want twenty thousand dollars for each family."

"Twenty thousand?" Louis gasped. He started to snicker. A gesture from Gould cut it off.

"Let me correct one thing you said," the financier murmured to Gideon. "You *were* employed by the Erie line. As of tonight, that connection is severed."

"Of all the lunatic demands!" Louis exclaimed.

Astonishingly, Gould chuckled. His black eyes remained fixed on Gideon.

"You have brass, Mr. Kent. I'll give you that. But in all sincerity, I must tell you that your cousin's word—lunatic—barely covers it. No railroad, including the Erie, pays money to those who are killed or injured while on duty. The risk is a condition of employment. You're very foolish to think otherwise"—he leaned forward—"unless you're some sort of union rabble-rouser. But we have no union that I'm aware of."

"Perhaps it's time you did."

Louis started to slide the door back. "This has gone far enough. Let me whistle up the boys—"

Gould's raised glove checked him. "I want to hear the rest."

"I've said my piece, Mr. Gould. Except for this. You make plenty of money from the Erie. A fortune, I've heard. You can afford something for the families of two men whose lives were wiped out while they were working to fatten your bank balance."

"Of course I could afford it," Gould agreed. "You're not speaking to the issue. You completely misinterpret the purpose of a business—or the purpose of employees." His voice dropped; he became the weary father dealing with a slow child. "Any employee of the Erie line must look after himself as I do for myself. Employees are parts of the machinery of the Erie, nothing more. Sound business policy dictates that when a part is ruined, money be spent for a new one, *not* on trying to salvage a useless one."

Gideon was thunderstruck. "Parts of the machinery? That's how you regard human beings?"

"Exactly."

"In"—Gideon forced himself to speak up—"in this case it's going to be different."

"Merely because you ask?"

"Yes."

"Well," Gould said with another shrug, "you're quite wrong. Your friends mean nothing to me, and I daresay any other astute manager would feel exactly the same." He wagged the ferrule of his stick under Gideon's nose. "I do admire your nerve, Mr. Kent. But your thinking is pitifully naive. Good evening."

Parts of the machinery. That was the sorry truth of it, Gideon had no doubt. Nor would Jay Gould change his position or bend even a little. It was evident in the brisk way Gould started for the sliding door; it was evident from the relieved smile on Louis Kent's face. The momentarily annoying gnat had been killed.

Terrible discouragement swept over Gideon. Louis and Gould would laugh for years over his clumsy demands.

As Gould approached the door, Gideon noted a glint of perspiration on his forehead. *By God, I did unsettle him a little!* It was enough to drive him to one last gamble.

"I thank you for listening to me, anyway. Your decision will be announced Sunday. Along with an account of when and where you made it."

Jay Gould's balding forehead gleamed as if it had been oiled. "What do you mean—announced?"

"Just what I said. I'm not alone in this effort. Your comments will be repeated from the pulpit of St. Mark's Methodist Episcopal Church on Orange Street."

"That must be his father's church." Louis said.

Gould whispered, "Mr. Kent, your father surely would not make reference to a place like this in a sermon."

"On the contrary. He's a very forthright man."

"I am here on *business*!"

Somehow Gideon managed to laugh. "I'm sure you are, sir."

Gideon was conscious of Louis' having moved around behind him, to his left. He was hidden by Gideon's limited field of vision. He heard leather scrape the carpeting, turned his head and saw Louis start for him. "We've had enough from you—"

"Stand where you are and shut your damned mouth!"

Gould's shaken voice stopped Louis like a child's marionette whose string had been jerked taut. Gideon was almost delirious to see the little man so badly out of control. He prayed he could keep his voice steady another five seconds.

"Perhaps you should bring your family to St. Mark's on the Sabbath, Mr. Gould. Perhaps your wife would be interested in learning where you conduct your affairs."

The parlor was still. A classical melody drifted from the front of the club. Gideon caught the creak of a board in the corridor. Undoubtedly the two men from the stairwell. All Gould had to do was summon them and Gideon was done for.

"Jay, it's a damn bluff!" Louis insisted. Gould didn't even glance at him. Gideon couldn't fathom what had happened to his cousin. Louis seemed to sag, lose confidence. He stared at Gould like a worried boy who'd failed to please his parents.

Gould swallowed. Ran his tongue over his upper lip. "Yes, I suspect it is a bluff. But I don't intend to find out. I don't intend to have Helen find out."

Gideon felt dizzy.

"Mr. Kent, you or your representative may call at my brokerage tomorrow. There'll be a draft waiting. In the amount you specified. The draft will be drawn on The Bank of Commerce in Nassau Street. It will bear the name of an account holder who is unfamiliar to you. There will be no way for you to link the money with the New York & Erie, or with me. If you try, you'll be laughed at. Are you willing to accept those terms?"

Gould's voice was quiet. Yet Gideon was still terrified. He managed to nod. The small dark eyes locked with his.

"I'll say it again. You have brass. Jim Fisk has brass. I have a touch of it myself. Always have. When I was a boy, I had one good friend. Twice as tall as I am. We used to wrestle. Most of the time I'd beat him. A fellow my size—that's unlikely, eh? But you see, I wouldn't beat him fair. I'd use every trick I knew. He'd complain, but it didn't bother me. Know what I'd tell him? 'I'm on top, ain't I?' You're on top for the moment, though you're not entirely responsible. This—gentleman"—a scorching look at Louis—"smoothed your path without intending to do so. Nevertheless, I admire any man who comes out on top by using whatever means he finds at his disposal. That's not to say you'll ever be on top of Jay Gould again."

He smiled. Gideon's mouth was bone dry.

"I'll pay you what you demand—once. But I won't forget the way you forced me to do it."

He pointed the stick at Gideon's face.

"I promise you, I won't forget."

He started for the door. Louis hurried to his side, but before he could speak, Gould slashed the stick against Louis' arm.

"Get out of my way!"

Gideon's cousin stumbled aside. Gould poked the ferrule in the handle of the sliding door. The door rolled back, and Jay Gould scurried off in the watery blue light.

iii

Louis gaped at Gideon as if he were some creature on exhibit in a menagerie, beyond his comprehension. The heavyset men glided into sight in the hall. For a moment Gideon was positive he'd never leave the Universal Club on his own feet.

Then Gould called from down the hall, "Let him go, boys. If anyone fixes him, it'll be me."

The rear door closed. The men eyed one another. Gideon took advantage of their hesitation and started to walk.

Speechless with anger, Louis watched him pass. Gideon turned right. Moved with feigned calm toward the foyer of the brothel. He listened for the sound of a rush, but it didn't come. He kept his hands thrust in his pockets so the girls and a couple of male patrons in the front parlor wouldn't see him shaking as he passed.

In the parlor, the blind black musician lifted his fingers from the keys, sniffed, "Old wool coat. Don't belong in this place."

Hester Bell opened the front door and held it, eyeing Gideon with a curiously awed expression. He stepped into the rain and closed his eye briefly as he walked down the steps. Now his legs were shaking.

When he was out of sight of the entrance, he ran.

CHAPTER X

CASUALTY OF WAR

i

UNDER JUBILEE JIM'S none too friendly scrutiny, Louis jammed the last of the greenbacks in the cheap suitcase. He handed the suitcase to the burly guard, who rushed it down the stairs and outside.

Louis looked wan in the March sunlight slanting through the high windows of the Erie office. Fisk and Gould were treating him as if he were hired help, not a partner.

"That's the lot, Jay." He leaned against the side of the great iron safe, empty now.

Gould finished scanning some papers, shoved them into the stove, and asked, "You made an accurate count?"

Louis started to reply, then realized Gould hadn't been speaking to him.

Fisk's brow furrowed at the attempted intrusion; he answered the question. "Twenty-eight suitcases. All but two are already gone in the first hack."

"How much in total?"

"Six millions. For God's sake, will you hurry up with that damned paper shuffling?"

"I'm done," Gould said, reaching for his expensive tweed overcoat.

Jay Gould had sent a messenger to upper Fifth Avenue to summon Louis. By the time Louis had arrived on Duane Street at a quarter to one, all the headquarters employees had been sent home. One guard occupied the porch, admitting no one without permission of Gould or Fisk. The other guard toted the suitcases to a hack as fast as Louis and the fat man could fill them.

Gould had spent the time sorting through documents, retaining a few in a valise, burning others and discarding the rest on the floor. The large office looked as if it had been struck by a paper blizzard.

"How's Daniel holding up?" Gould wanted to know.

"He's out there blubbering like an infant. He don't like the idea of running to Jersey. We won't get the chance if you don't shake a leg. I have boys waiting at the Cortlandt Street Ferry to act as a rear guard, but until we reach the terminal we're fair game."

Gould remained unperturbed. "Have you booked a hotel?"

"I sent Chad to Jersey City right after we got the news from court. He's arranging for suites at Taylor's. I'm also having three cannon sent over so Vanderbilt can't surprise us. We'll be snug by dark—*if* we get out of here."

Louis decided he should take encouragement from having been asked to help with the clean-out. Gould wouldn't have dispatched the messenger if their alliance had been permanently damaged. The thought took the sting from the way they'd ignored him the past hour or so.

The abandonment of Duane Street was the result of the latest in the series of bizarre moves and countermoves in the struggle for dominance of the Erie.

Gould's scheme to use the basement printing press had worked exactly as planned. In fact it had worked so well that the thousands of shares dumped in the Street had depressed not only the price of Erie but those of other issues. The papers had started screaming about an "Erie Panic."

Naturally Vanderbilt had caught on to what was happening. Supreme Court Judge Barnard had enjoined the line from issuing any more stock. Gould had immediately paid for a counterinjunction from another member of the bench. Then Vanderbilt retaliated with still more court orders, placing the line into receivership and ordering the arrest of key directors for stock fraud. The last decree had been handed down late that morning.

Now the six million in the suitcases—the money earned by the basement press—was going out of the jurisdiction of New York law, together with Messrs. Gould and Fisk. Louis had overheard the two discussing reorganization of the line as a New Jersey corporation. In Jersey, Vanderbilt would have difficulty exerting his influence. Of course, the reorganization remained strictly theoretical while the planners were still in Manhattan.

"You go along, Jim," Gould instructed. "I'll be there shortly."

With a baleful glance at his huge pocket watch, Fisk vanished down the stairs.

A tug hooted on the river. Dust motes moved slowly through pale sunbeams. It seemed unthinkable to Louis that a carriage load of deputy sheriffs might be clattering toward Duane Street this very moment. It seemed nearly as unthinkable that weeks had passed since Gould had met Gideon Kent and surrendered what amounted to pocket change to save himself from a potential scandal. In all that time, Louis had not heard a syllable of reproof from the financier.

Of course, Gould had been frantically busy with Erie affairs. On several occasions Louis had tried to invite Gould to his club for a drink, an expensive dinner—and an apology. Each time Gould had brushed him aside. Finally Louis had attempted to apologize after a board meeting, only to have Gould walk away. He was beginning to think Gould might have accepted the defeat and put it behind him in the face of more pressing problems.

Louis started to don his coat. "You needn't do that," Gould remarked quietly. "You're not coming with us."

"*Not coming?* What about the warrant?"

"You're not named. Just Drew, Jim, and myself. I've checked. Even if you were included, my original statement stands. You're not coming with us to Jersey City."

"Then why did you call me down here? Why in hell did you let me help and think I was still part of it—?"

He stopped. Gould smiled at his discomfort. He knew the answers.

"You did it so you could build me up to this. You son of a bitch!"

"I'll overlook that," Gould murmured as he tugged on leather driving gloves. His voice was so muted Louis had to strain to hear. "If there's name-calling to be done, I'd say I deserve first crack. When you were approached to help guarantee a favorable vote on the freight rates, I believe Jim made it clear I'd tolerate no objections to my decisions. Nor would I think well of any man whose actions intentionally or inadvertently subjected me to personal embarrassment. You nearly cost me the love and respect of my wife and children, Louis. You nearly saw to it that an announcement was made from a pulpit, a *public* pulpit, that I frequent houses of ill repute."

Sweating, Louis exclaimed, "For Christ's sake, it was Fisk who insisted we meet there!"

"But it was you who led that cousin of yours to Mrs. Bell's."

"How many times must I tell you, Jay? I had *no idea* he was following me!"

"Carelessness is not a virtue in a businessman, Louis."

The dark eyes bit into him like augers. "Once we're safely in New Jersey, there will be a vote to remove you from the board of directors. Danny, Jim and I are authorized to act as an executive committee and do that, you know. I trust you enjoyed your brief career with the Erie. You'll never have a similar opportunity if my word means anything."

"You just used me for the freight vote, is that it?"

"I use whoever it's expedient to use. That's how I stay on top. Some of the people I use remain my friends. Some don't. You fall in the latter group. You can't be trusted."

"*Jay*—" Louis groped at him.

"Don't touch me," Gould whispered, and walked out.

ii

The hack careened through darkening streets. "I don't like this," Drew complained from his seat beside one of the guards. "I don't like being carted off to Jersey, away from my church."

The guard tactfully ignored the outburst. He continued

to stare out the window, his hand curled around the butt of a pistol.

"You'll find another over there," Gould assured the old man. "Just remember there are no regular services in the Ludlow Street jail."

"Vanderbilt's sure to send bullyboys after us," Fisk said. He actually sounded pleased. "The hotel's near the waterfront, y'know. I think we should have a shore patrol. Three or four lifeboats carrying men we can trust. We'll call it the Erie Navy and Coast Guard. What do you think, Jay?"

Gould pursed his lips in distaste. "Before you start playing admiral, I want you to attend to another piece of business. It pertains to that young man who milked me for forty thousand dollars."

He shifted his eyes quickly to indicate the suffering Dan Drew. "I needn't go into it now, though."

"I'll see to it whenever you're ready," Fisk promised.

Soon the hack rattled up to the Cortlandt Street Ferry Terminal. A dozen slum roughnecks Fisk had recruited and sworn in as Erie detectives were already unloading the suitcases from the first cab. As Fisk hoisted the last two bags, Drew again complained about leaving New York. Fisk hustled him toward the entrance.

"Listen, Danny, I plan to send for Miss Josie soon as I can. Say the word and I'll have her bring a parson to keep you company."

Gould lingered in the windy March twilight. When the last of the suitcases disappeared inside the building, he approached the guard who'd been riding with him.

"Biggs, I want you to do a chore after we've gone."

"Yes, sir?" The taller man smoothed an index finger along his mustache. He had to bend to hear the next.

"I want Louis Kent hurt."

"Badly?"

Gould nodded. His dark eyes looked almost benign. "I leave the means to you. But I don't want to be connected. Ever."

Biggs smiled. "Got you." He touched his derby.

Jay Gould's head lifted in response to the shriek of the ferry whistle. Smiling, he hurried into the terminal.

iii

Barely awake, Gideon scratched his nose. Not only had he forgotten to extinguish the lamp in the kitchen, but Margaret had forgotten to damp the stove and save the wood.

He could have ignored the stove. But the light was a problem. He'd have to get up.

He yawned. He was exhausted. He'd spent the day working for a farmer out in the county west of Hoboken. Helping the farmer tend his hogs. For fifty cents. When he'd come home, he'd been too weary to do what he'd been meaning to do for days: drop down to the Diamond N, see who was there from the yards, speak to them—

No, exhaustion wasn't the only reason he hadn't gone. He was sure they'd reject him, out of fear.

But he'd already recognized that there'd be scores of rejections before he achieved even one success. Why was he letting potential defeat incapacitate him?

He knew that too. The moment he stepped inside the Diamond N and uttered what was on his mind, he could never turn back—

Hell. It was too taxing to think about right now.

The coverlet rustled. He propped himself on his elbows; squinted. Eleanor peeped over the edge of the bed.

"Papa? What's burning?"

He awoke instantly.

Eleanor coughed. She began to whimper as Gideon prodded Margaret's hip.

"Margaret, get up. The place is on fire!"

His lethargy was gone. The glow in the kitchen was brightening to a blaze. The smell he'd mistaken for stove wood grew heavier. Smoke began to drift in the bedroom.

He heard a crackling in the parlor. Margaret was stirring, but slowly. God almighty! There were flames near the front door as well—

"Eleanor, run to the window. Open it!"

He rammed his hands under his wife's body and lifted. Her eyes flew open.

The flames shot around the frame of the kitchen door, eating the thin walls, the old paper. Margaret saw the fire as she hung in his arms.

Gideon was having trouble breathing. *Why was the cot-*

tage going up so quickly? Then he smelled a telltale odor mingled with the smoke.

Eleanor struggled with the sash. "It's stuck, Papa!"

"The blasted snow and ice—let me at it."

He set Margaret on the floor. He could feel heat on his bare soles now. He fisted his hand and drove it through the curtain and the glass. A piece nicked his wrist. Blood sopped the cuff of his nightshirt.

He picked up a chair, battered the most dangerous shards out of the window frame. "Come here, Eleanor. Hurry!" He had to shout above the mounting roar.

Trembling, she let him lift her to the sill. She jerked suddenly, frightened. Glass slashed her instep. She screamed and fell back into Gideon's arms.

That cost them precious seconds. When he'd quieted the child, the fire was covering the wall by the window. It had spread the other way too, along the wall behind the bed. Red reflections glared in Margaret's eyes.

He hooked his bloodied hand around Eleanor's waist and dragged her to his shoulder. "Hold tight to my neck." Margaret clutched his other arm.

"Why is it burning so fast, Gideon?"

"Because it was set! We have to go out the front."

He dragged his wife to the parlor. Fire ran along the baseboard moldings. The smoke was so thick he could barely see the front door. Before they reached it, a barrier of flame confronted them.

His eyes watered. The hem of his nightshirt began to smolder from stray sparks. "Hang on, Eleanor. Margaret, stay close to me. We'll have to go through."

The fire glowed on the leather eye patch. There wasn't even time to tell her he loved her. He lowered his head and ran at the rising wall of heat and flame.

iv

The wine from Delmonico's blurred his sight, aroused him, too. Yet it did nothing to ease the monstrous feeling of loss.

He had come so close, cooperated, played the tame

dog—and he'd been within reach of the very top rung of the ladder. Then, because his second cousin's son had been clever and nervy enough to follow him to Mrs. Bell's, it had all come undone.

Financially, he wouldn't suffer. He'd taken maximum advantage of his tenure as an insider, selling certain issues a day or two before a dump of new Erie stock depressed prices on the Street, and buying others advantageously when the prices bottomed out. He'd more than doubled the paper worth of his investments in only a couple of months.

But the real cost of that profit had been the dismissal from the board. Never again would men at the highest levels of the financial community deal with him as an equal—or as a man worthy of confidence. He had been deemed unworthy by Jay Gould.

He knew it was being talked about on the Street and in the clubs: *Gould got thick with Louis Kent for a few weeks. But he dumped him. Gould's a piratical son of a bitch, but there's no shrewder man. Must be something wrong with that Kent fellow.*

The divorce from Julia had cost him his friendship with Vanderbilt. The Erie fiasco had cost him the friendship of Vanderbilt's foremost peers. He was well aware of how the Street would describe his situation: *Kent may still have his money. But for all practical purposes, he's ruined.*

Clinging to the wrist strap of the victoria, Louis tried to fix his attention on the squalid street. An almost stygian blackness enveloped it. The damp air smelled of garbage and the river. It was a filthy neighborhood, only a block from the Bowery. The victoria was proceeding slowly while Louis' driver searched for an address.

God, he hoped she was there. It was past midnight. It had taken him two days to locate the address through a theatrical agent. He didn't know what he'd do if she were gone. He couldn't stay by himself one more night.

She still meant nothing to him. But it had become impossible to sleep or even think rationally in the mansion on Fifth Avenue. He was sick of going over and over his failure. What if? *What if—*

To come after her this way was an admission of weakness. He didn't care. The solitude of the mansion was unbearable. The solitude contained too many specters. Too many reminders of how close he'd come to absolute preeminence on the Street, in America—the world.

"Believe this is it, sir." The victoria swayed to a halt. "Not a very savory location. Do you wish me to wait?"

"No. Pick me up at eight in the morning."

He stumbled to the curb, stepped across the corpse of a cat and climbed the steep steps as his carriage rattled off. He was peering at the tenant board when the hollow *clop-clop* of another carriage horse caught his attention.

The hack was coming from the direction of the Bowery. His own vehicle was already out of sight. But he was too drunk to give the slowing cab more than a glance.

He struck a match. Among the cluster of dirty cards he found one reading *N. Chetwynd.* He heard a door close softly as he noted the number on the card. The match went out.

All at once he realized a man was coming up the steps. His responses were sluggish from the prolonged evening of drinking; he'd had virtually no food.

"Hallo, Mr. Kent."

The voice was unfamiliar. A tic started in his right cheek. He was still facing the tenant's board, slightly bent. Panic spread through him and he started to turn.

"Wait. I'm not—"

His grunt interrupted the sentence. Then he shrieked from the pain of the knife rammed into the lower quarter of his back.

V

Gideon could still smell the smoke: not the same kind of pungent tobacco smoke lying heavily in the Diamond N—the acrid smoke of charred siding, burned cloth, ruined upholstery.

He spied Rory Bannock leaning on the mahogany bar.

"Evening, Rory."

"Gid! Jesus, boy, we heard you got burned out last night."

Gideon noted the ornamental clock. A quarter past five.

Soon Bannock would be leaving for the night shift. He slid a coin across the bar and signaled for lager.

"Yes," he said, "there's nothing left of the cottage. It's the landlord's responsibility, but what little furniture we owned is gone. I barely got Margaret and Eleanor out soon enough."

"Heard the fire was set."

"That's right."

"Coppers catch anyone?"

He shook his head. "Whoever poured the kerosene ran away the moment it was lighted."

Bannock winced. "You got an idea who done it?"

"No," Gideon lied. He knew very well. A man who had met his demands but who had not forgiven him. A man who was living down at Taylor's Hotel right now, delighting the New York press with his armed guards and his cohort's rowboat navy.

It was impossible to prove, of course. But Jephtha's warning about retaliation had been correct. Oddly, once Gideon's loved ones were safe and the shock of the fire had passed, he was almost pleased that Gould had seen fit to respond as he did. The fire had finally given him the courage to make his commitment.

"Anyone could have done it," he said before he sipped from the stein. Bannock drained his. "There are a lot of hungry men wandering around these days. Hunger and failure can drive a fellow to crazy things."

"You're out of a job, aren't you, Gid? Cuthie said so."

"He's right."

"The Erie giveth and the Erie taketh away," the other man remarked with a sour smile. "Speakin' of giving, has anyone learned who sent all that money to Flo Miller and Mr. Kolb?"

"No. I suppose it was some charitable person in New York."

"Didn't know there was any charitable persons in that town. Guess it doesn't matter who's responsible, though. The families are deserving."

"So are the families of men who are still alive, Rory. Your family. You deserve some things too. Better wages. Shorter hours. Things the Erie'll never grant you unless you demand them."

"Ah, that Sylvis stuff again," Bannock grumbled. "Spare me."

For the moment.

"You're the one I fret about," Bannock went on. "I hate to see you down. I never said this before, but you're a helluva good lad, Gideon."

"That's quite a compliment." He smiled. "Especially from a Yankee."

Bannock waved. "A witless Philadelphia mick, you mean. Let's have no more of this Yankee business, eh? The war's been over for three years."

That war. Another's beginning.

Bannock leaned on his forearms, boozily cordial. "Me and the missus, we talked about you being bounced out of the yards. Now there's this fire—how will you get by?"

"I don't know. But we will."

Sheltered temporarily at the Miller cottage, he and Margaret had already discussed the future and agreed on what Gideon had to do. He planned to keep on working at whatever jobs he could find. But first he had a job here.

"Anyway, Rory, that's not what I came to discuss."

He still had an opportunity to retreat. He was pledging himself to a mission that would make him a—a pariah, that was it. Fine word.

He'd be a pariah to a great many respectable people. Yet the work needed doing. Unless someone took the first step, it would go undone. Responsibility couldn't be shrugged aside. Most of the Kents had believed that for generations. He would not be an exception.

He dug his last coin out of his pocket. "Let me buy you another beer, Rory." He grinned. "That way, maybe you'll listen to what I have to say."

Standing straight and speaking calmly, he added, "I want to talk with you about the necessity of starting a union in the yards."

Epilogue at Kentland

The Lifted Sword

i

THAT SPRING OF 1868 was a season of war. After almost forty-nine years on the planet, the Reverend Jephtha Kent was beginning to suspect there was no season that was not.

The fiercest struggle was being waged in Washington. The Congressional radicals had succeeded in charging President Johnson with violation of the Tenure of Office Act and other deeds of misconduct. Johnson's impeachment trial had begun in mid-March. How it would end, no one could say. A close outcome was predicted.

If the radicals won, they would have won it all. Under bills they'd sponsored, military governors enforced the law at bayonet point throughout the South. Jephtha had watched the steady and deliberate expansion of Republican power, and at the same time, seen his worst fears about manipulation of the black vote confirmed. His ardent Republicanism was waning.

Closer to home, the so-called Erie War had diverted the public's attention for months. For a time, Fort Taylor—Jim Fisk's name for the Jersey City hotel serving as the line's temporary headquarters—had received national attention. Daily press dispatches had provided thrilling accounts of bulls and bears locked in combat. No detail was ignored. Mr. Fisk's mistress was interviewed. Members of his navy of thugs were interviewed as they rowed up and down keeping watch for a Vanderbilt flotilla. Anonymous "confidants" were interviewed, and they described everything from the breakfast served Mr. Gould in his suite to Dan Drew's worsening tantrums; he feared affairs of his church were foundering without him.

No Vanderbilt flotilla had appeared from Manhattan. The Erie directors had escaped the enemy's wrath, but at a cost of exiling themselves from the nation's financial center. Finally Gould had packed some valises, containing close to a million in cash, it was reliably stated. He'd hustled to Albany to end the stalemate by wooing the Black Horse Cavalry. The Cavalry was a group within the New York legislature which made no secret of its willingness to sponsor and support any desired piece of legislation—so long as the price was right.

The Commodore's men had rushed money to Albany to counterattack. But Gould's ante was the highest. An act permanently legalizing conversion of bonds within the state passed both houses. Now Vanderbilt faced a threat of endless issues of Erie stock—and a skillful publicity campaign to which Gould had turned his attention.

The newspapers had started carrying Gould's warnings to the citizenry. A new predatory animal was abroad in the land! Beware the archmonopolist! Jephtha couldn't recall hearing the term before, but Vanderbilt made a vivid prototype.

In the face of Gould's carefully orchestrated campaign, one paper inexplicably reversed itself and began to praise the Commodore. It took Jephtha four days at the end of March to learn, through a member of his congregation active in the Street, the shocking reason the New York *Union* had changed its editorial policy.

While not openly hostile to Vanderbilt, other papers found Mr. Gould and his gratuitous warnings to be good copy. Why, Gould cried, the villainous Commodore would soon swallow so many firms and rail systems that his whim would dictate the very price of a loaf of bread on the commonest table! Blithely disregarding the source of the charges, some molders of opinion were demanding that

Vanderbilt's power be checked. They never specified how it should be done.

Recently there'd been a development to indicate that the peculiar war might be limping to an end. Faced with the law legalizing the Duane Street printing press, and already poorer by close to ten million dollars, the Commodore was said to be sick of the struggle. The member of Jephtha's congregation with Street connections claimed Vanderbilt had invited Dan Drew to call on him, to patch things up. If that was true, the Commodore had run up the white flag for perhaps the first time in his life.

The Erie War had its comic aspects, but the seething struggle in the South had none. That tragic situation was creating hatreds that would last a generation or more.

Northern politicians continued to flood into the region lugging their despised carpetbags. With the cooperation of the so-called scalawags—Southerners who turned their backs on their own people in order to ally themselves with the Northern power bloc—the invaders were capturing control of state and local governments. The military governors encouraged it.

Private citizens of the lately defeated Confederacy had other battles on their hands. They hurled charges of shiftlessness, impudence and outright criminality at the freed black. Some had begun a guerrilla war to cow the Negro.

The war's military organization was an innocently conceived social society founded by a group of bored veterans around Christmas 1865. In a law office in Pulaski, Tennessee, the veterans had created a secret fraternity called the *Kuklos,* after the Greek word for circle. Someone had added *clan* to reflect the area's Scotch-Irish heritage, and the whole thing had been transmuted to a spreading network of night riders whose aim was to discipline and sometimes punish blacks.

The clan was operating in most of the South these days. The pranks of its members had taken on an ugly tone. The illiteracy of most of the blacks was played upon. A favorite trick of the colorfully robed and hooded clansmen was to surround a Negro cottage at night and, in sepulchral voices, beg for drinks. The mounted visitors would claim to be dead men who hadn't tasted water since perishing at, say, Shiloh Church.

When water was offered, almost endless quantities of it appeared to vanish magically through the mouth slits of the hoods. Jephtha had read the trick was performed with a tube and concealed rubber bag, but few of the victims knew that—or were sufficiently calm to think it out. One had died of a heart seizure early in April. Even the former Confederate cavalryman, Bedford Forrest, who at first had vigorously supported the clan's activities, was reportedly disenchanted by growing excesses.

Jephtha refrained from condemnation of all Southerners, however. He felt the North should set its own house in order first.

The scorned greenhorns pouring off the immigrant boats from all sections of the Continent were being crowded into slums and manipulated to the advantage of industrialists, who used the threat of immigrant labor to beat off the demands of trade unionists. Gideon had allied himself with the unionists. He was struggling to start a small organization in the Erie yards. Jephtha respected and admired Gideon's dedication. But he had no illusions about his son's future. Gideon had merely exchanged one war for another.

Blacks remained an even more despised minority in the North. Jephtha needed to go no further than Forty-fourth Street and Fifth Avenue to be reminded of that.

Every time some pastoral chore took him by the spot, he recalled four simmering days in July of '63. Right after Gettysburg, New York had fallen into anarchy as rioters—mostly poor whites—protested the Federal draft.

Blacks had been beaten, hanged from lamp poles, had kerosene poured in their wounds, then lit. Even children had not been spared. The Colored Orphan Asylum at Forty-fourth Street and Fifth had been surrounded by a howling mob of three thousand. Fortunately soldiers had arrived to shepherd two hundred Negro children and the staff to safety. Afterward the mob had rampaged through the orphanage. One frightened black girl was discovered still huddling beneath her bed. Jephtha would never forget reading the account of how she'd been beaten to death. Until such incidents were forever banished, the North had no right to be sanctimonious.

The '63 holocaust had resulted in the burning of more than a hundred buildings and in the deaths of as many as two thousand civilians, soldiers, and police. No one would ever know the exact total. Once Federal troops had quelled the worst of the violence, a pundit had jeered, "This is a nice town to call itself a center of civilization!" Five years later, Jephtha wearily decided the same could be said of the nation. The great war had won freedom for the Negro, but there were few signs it had won equality, or even acceptance.

In view of his calling, Jephtha was always ashamed when he felt so pessimistic. He tried to remember that no era in human history had been free of the passions fed by ignorance and greed. Certainly Christ's had not.

But the nation had been created to offer a shining hope of liberty, justice, *change.* Occasionally Jephtha felt progress in America was unconscionably slow, if not altogether absent. Sometimes he wondered whether Jeremiah had gone to his grave for nothing.

With his faith and his wife Molly to help him, Jephtha had learned to accept the pain of realizing his youngest son was gone. Every six months or so he still dispatched a letter to a friend in Washington and requested another search of the Federal casualty records. No new information had ever been forthcoming. The day and place of Jeremiah Kent's dying were apparently forever hidden. Jephtha only prayed the death had not been meaningless.

In brighter moments, he knew it was not. The slave system was gone forever. The country was expanding at an unprecedented rate, and a much more worthwhile war was being won in the West. The Central Pacific and the Union Pacific were annihilating time and distance. In mid-April the Union Pacific had reached its highest elevation above the sea, Sherman's Summit at 8,248 feet, and had begun laying track on the Wyoming downgrade.

Out there, in land abounding in the free space in which men could build new futures, thousands were doing exactly that. Michael had done that with his mercantile enterprises. His letters said he had found deep satisfaction. He didn't use the word peace, but Jephtha knew that was what he meant.

Perhaps Matt too had found his version of the same thing. His enthusiastic letters, crammed with sketches, said he and his wife Dolly were enjoying their splendid poverty in Paris. Matt's surprising inclination toward drawing was finally receiving some direction through exposure to great museums and the ferment of the city's art colony.

Spring weather usually banished the worst of Jephtha's pessimism, and it was no exception this year, even though he had lately been forced to resort to spectacles for reading, and his knuckles and knees hurt a great deal of the time. When he heard an item of gossip from the Wall Street attorney who belonged to his church, his spirits positively soared.

He had resigned himself about purchasing Kent and Son, Boston. It struck him as an unattainable goal.

But something else he coveted just as shamelessly might not be unattainable. The Monday morning after he heard that, he set out for Tarrytown.

ii

Outside the little office, sunlight glowed through rustling trees. "Yes, sir," the agent said. "We are the authorized representatives." He cast a dubious eye at Jephtha's rumpled black suit. "It's quite expensive."

"But it *is* for sale?"

"Most definitely. The owner has been confined to St. Luke's Hospital in the city, as perhaps you know."

Jephtha nodded.

"A ruffianly attack by street thieves, we've been told."

Jephtha said nothing. He'd heard the same thing in March.

"Mr. Kent is paralyzed," the agent went on. "He may never regain the use of his lower body. He is divesting himself of several properties."

"Does you price include the furnishings?"

"It does."

"Everything? Every last book? Every item of bric-a-brac?"

The agent frowned. "May I ask why that's so important to you, Mr.—?"

"Kent."

He said it quietly and watched for the reaction, which was pronounced. He continued. "I don't want my name mentioned. That's a condition of my offer. If you violate it, you've lost a commission."

"Are you related to the owner?"

"Distantly. I don't wish to be identified with the sale for personal reasons. Attorneys will act in my stead. I'll meet the price, whatever it is."

The agent had a stunned look.

"But only if all furnishings are left intact. Are you willing to proceed on those terms?"

An unctuous smile curled the agent's mouth. "Of course. Buyers in this price category are not numerous. I'm sure everything can be arranged to your satisfaction."

iii

On the seventeenth of May, Mr. Patrick Willet, contractor, sat in his wagon in the driveway of Kentland. It was a brilliant morning, breezy and full of the sweet smells of living earth and foliage. Just the preceding day, the eleventh article of impeachment had failed to gain the needed two-thirds majority in the Senate. The margin of defeat had been one vote.

Mr. Willet wasn't thinking of that sensational news today, though. He was in a state bordering on euphoria. The reason was his prospective client, the estate's new and somewhat unusual owner—a shabby-looking but clearly wealthy minister from the city.

The gray-haired cleric's last name was the same as that of Kentland's former tenant. Willet had mentioned the coincidence but had received no explanation. He didn't press for one. The potential fee was too important.

The Reverend Kent had contacted him a week ago. Willet had eagerly agreed to drive him out from Tarrytown when he took possession of the property. He was inside doing just that. The front doors were open on darkness and a smell of dust.

Mr. Willet cut a piece of tobacco from his plug and slipped it up next to his gum. It might be a while until he was summoned. He'd gladly wait. He'd wait till judgment for an opportunity to earn the huge sum which would accompany a major alteration.

He was startled when the Reverend Kent appeared in less than five minutes.

Kent was carrying the portmanteau he'd taken into the house. It bulged now. And, curiosity of curiosities, the preacher had a scabbarded sword and an old rifle under his arm.

Kent put the carpetbag on the drive, then the rifle. He walked from the shadow of the portico to the sunlight. Almost reverently, he drew the sword a third of the way out of the brass-tipped scabbard.

Willet scrambled down and peered over the other man's shoulder. The sword had a handsome ribbed grip and a pommel shaped like a bird's head.

Kent noted the contractor's interest. He raised the sword a little higher.

"It's a French infantry briquet. Given to the founder of our family by the Marquis de Lafayette, before the Revolution."

"Handsome," Willet murmured. Kent slid the blade back into the scabbard and as he did, the hilt caught the sun and shot off a star of light. The minister's dark eyes gleamed.

Fellow's crying! the astonished contractor said to himself. There was certainly no accounting for the queerness of parsons.

That was demonstrated again as Kent carefully laid the sword, rifle and portmanteau in the back of the wagon, then inserted a key in Kentland's front door.

"Here, Reverend!" Willet exclaimed. "Aren't we going to have a look inside?"

"No, Mr. Willet. I have the things I came for, with the exception of one painting in the drawing room. That will have to be crated and removed later. The other mementos are going to my oldest son. He's in a line of work I doubt you'd approve of," Kent added with a smile. "You being the proprietor of a business, I mean."

"What's your boy do?"

"He's a labor organizer."

"You're right. I don't approve," Willet shot back. "Fellows like that upset the equilibrium of society."

"Society needs upsetting every generation or so, Mr. Willet. Peacefully, of course. Otherwise things that need changing are accepted without question."

Willet sniffed. "If you don't mind my asking, sir, how did your son become involved in such radical work?"

"He's not a radical, I assure you. Perhaps he'll become one. He'll certainly be called one. To answer your question, let's say a passion for causes runs in the family."

Willet was mystified when Kent glanced at the house and added, "Certain branches of the family."

The contractor wanted to enlighten Kent with more of his views about the union movement. But he was beholden to the man, so he changed the subject:

"Well, sir, if we're to examine the place, you oughtn't to lock up."

Kent climbed to the seat. "You can give me your estimate on the way back to Tarrytown."

"Reverend, I can't estimate repairs without seeing—"

"Wait," Kent interrupted. "I'm not hiring you to make repairs."

Willet's brow shot up. "But I thought—"

The minister shook his head. He studied the sun-drenched facade, smiling in a curious way.

"I never said I wanted alterations, or that I was planning to live here. I'm going to pay you to tear Kentland down."

"Tear it down?"

"Yes, Mr. Willet. Every last stone."

PS 3560 .A37 W3 2005
Jakes, John, 1932-
The warriors
AUG 1 9 2010

The Bestselling Kent Family Chronicles

by John Jakes

"John Jakes makes history come alive."
—*Washington Post*

The Bastard
The Rebels
The Seekers
The Furies
The Titans
The Warriors
The Lawless
The Americans

Available wherever books are sold or at
penguin.com

W9-BZF-551

DEWEY CANYON II:
You are there with . . .

GENERAL SID BERRY—A general who always led from the front. Assigned to the Screaming Eagles, he embodied their combat spirit with his four Silver Stars for valor . . . and his old-fashioned guts.

SGT. RAYMOND C. KEEFER—A tough combat veteran in Alpha Troop on his second tour. With four Purple Hearts, he didn't have to go back under fire . . . but his Lieutenant needed Keefer to get his men home alive.

Sp4 HAL SPURGEON—A gung-ho nineteen-year-old kid in the sniper section of Hq&Hq Company. He saw Vietnam as a place to let loose the energies that got him in trouble back home . . . and solve all his problems with an M-16.

CAPT. PHILIP BODENHORN—CO of Alpha Company, awarded four Purple Hearts in seven months as a result of his up-front style of command. He knew Dewey Canyon II could be the most dramatic action of Vietnam.

QUANTITY SALES

Most Dell Books are available at special quantity discounts when purchased in bulk by corporations, organizations, and special-interest groups. Custom imprinting or excerpting can also be done to fit special needs. For details write: Dell Publishing Co., Inc., 666 Fifth Avenue, New York, NY 10103. Attn.: Special Sales Dept.

INDIVIDUAL SALES

Are there any Dell Books you want but cannot find in your local stores? If so, you can order them directly from us. You can get any Dell book in print. Simply include the book's title, author, and ISBN number, if you have it, along with a check or money order (no cash can be accepted) for the full retail price plus $1.50 to cover shipping and handling. Mail to: Dell Readers Service, P.O. Box 5057, Des Plaines, IL 60017.

INTO LAOS

The Story of Dewey Canyon II/ Lam Son 719; Vietnam 1971

Keith William Nolan

A DELL BOOK

Published by
Dell Publishing Co., Inc.
1 Dag Hammarskjold Plaza
New York, New York 10017

Copyright © 1986 by Keith William Nolan

All rights reserved. No part of this book may be reproduced or transmitted in any form or by any means, electronic or mechanical, including photocopying, recording, or by any information storage and retrieval system, without the written permission of the Publisher, except where permitted by law. For information address: Presidio Press, Novato, California.

Dell ® TM 681510, Dell Publishing Co., Inc.

ISBN: 0-440-20044-X

Reprinted by arrangement with Presidio Press

Printed in the United States of America

February 1988

10 9 8 7 6 5 4 3 2 1

WFH

VIETNAM
DS
557.8
.L3
N65
1988

This book is for all those
who soldiered in Vietnam
especially those
who in the demoralized last days
still looked out for
the man to their right
and the man to their left

. . . and for April

What makes people rebel against suffering is not really suffering itself, but the senselessness of suffering. Man, the most courageous animal, and the most inured to trouble, does not deny suffering per se; he wants it, he seeks it out, provided that it can be given meaning.

Friedrich Nietzsche
The Genealogy of Morals

CONTENTS

PART FOUR: A RENEWED EFFORT

Preface

The return of our Vietnam veterans was not greeted with a parade or handshake, but with a magazine article which warned the parents and wives of ex-soldiers, "If you avoid argument because he's been trained to killing and to anger, and you are afraid of his releasing them on you—another common problem—you've got to talk about it. Chances are he has been afraid about this, too."

It was just such glib and abhorrent generalizations about those young Americans who went to Vietnam—all the old tales of psycho killers, human time bombs, and drug addicts—that first prompted my interest in the subject. My main concern is, and has always been, not so much the tactics of the campaigns, but the personalities, motivations, and behavior of the individual American soldier. For this reason I sought out the veterans themselves; men, it turned out, who, despite the ominous warning cited above, were usually willing to talk, encouraging, and well settled back into civilian life. Or they were as well settled as any man who has seen war, especially an unpopular war, can be.

My initial efforts were met by overwhelming support from the Vietnam veterans with whom I had the honor of communicating. The result was a history of the U.S. Marines in the Battle of Hue City. That was the story of young men who were all volunteers and who fought in early 1968, a time when even though the nation was divided, there were at least no major outcries against the warriors themselves. But what about the latter stages of the war when draftees filled the ranks. Incidents like My Lai warped the nation's attitudes towards its fighting men, and dark stories of drug addiction, murder, and mutiny in the U.S. Army made the headlines.

The last major operation the Americans fought in Vietnam was the invasion of Laos in 1971, when the crisis in morale was at its peak. It was a sad, confusing time; a time when American politicians declared, while young Americans were dying on the Vietnam battlefield, that the true heroes of the Vietnam War were those who protested; a time when the media inferred that the American soldier was no match for the North Vietnamese; a time when returning veterans were physically and mentally attacked by their own countrymen.

Just how bad were things on the battlefield of 1971? To attempt an answer, the invasion of Laos seemed a natural focal point as it was the last major campaign that the U.S. Army mounted in Vietnam, involving in combat infantry, aviation, armor, artillery, and support units. There is no denying that morale was bad but not as bad as reported. My main concern is to explore the reasons things had soured. Hopefully this book will illustrate the frustration which drove morale down, and how this change in attitude manifested itself in the day-to-day performance of the U.S. Army in Vietnam.

The veterans of the Laos campaign who helped in preparing this book were: Lt. Gen. Sidney Berry, USA (Ret.); Lt. Gen. Donn Robertson, USMC, (Ret.); Lt. Gen. Donald Rosenblum, USA (Ret.); Lt. Gen. James Sutherland, USA (Ret.); Maj. Gen. Ben Harrison, USA (Ret.); Maj. Gen. Robert Molinelli, USA; Brig. Gen. Phan Hoa Hiep, ARVN, (Ret.); Brig. Gen. Richard Morton, USA (Ret.); Brig. Gen. Charles Pitman, USMC; Col. Ray Battreall, USA (Ret.); Col. George Chase, USA (Ret.); Col. William Dabney, USMC; Col. Edward Davis, USA (Ret.); Col. Joseph Ganahl, USA (Ret.); Col. Gerald Kirklighter, USA (Ret.); Col. John Klose, USA (Ret.); Col. Richard Meyer, USA (Ret.); Col. John Miller, USMC; Lt. Col. Tom Stewart, USA (Ret.); Majors Philip Bodenhorn, John Christian, John Dewing, USAR; Majors David Ferrell, Charles Garwood, John Mercadante, Steve Overstreet, and Euell White, USA (Ret.); ex-Capt. Gerald Downey, USA; Capt. Rich Johnson, USA; ex-Capt. Ken Lord, USA; Capt. Drayton Markle, USAR; Capt. Harold Spurgeon, ARNG; ex-Capt. Bruce Updyke; ex-Lt. Don Malmstrom; Lt. Philip Smith, ARNG; Lt. Harry Walters, ARNG; ex-Lt. Don Stephen; CW4 Chuck Hawk, USA; ex-WO Lyle Borders, USA; ex-WO Harold Smith, USA; Sgt. Maj. Roy Nelson, USA (Ret.); 1st Sgt. Roy Hatfield, USA, (Ret.); M. Sgt. Guy Shelley, USA; T. Sgt. Charles Barnett, USAF, (Ret.); ex-Sergeants James Brock, Frank Burnett, Michael Daugherty, Ray Keefer, John Kucera, Jim McCormack, Charles McKenzie, John Michalak, and Larry White, USA; ex-Sp5s John Carney, Dennis Fujii, Dennis Lundstrom, and Bill Wilder, USA; ex-Cpl. Carson Bartels, USMC; ex-Sp4s Mike Castro, John Coleman, Mike Davis, Mike DeAngelis, Mike Fitzmaurice, Pat Hallman, Jim Keeney, Russ Morse, Steve Rhodes, Ron Smith, and William Warren, USA; and John Saar of Time-Life, Inc.

A special note of thanks also goes to Mr. and Mrs. William Stahl whose son, Roger, was killed during the Laotian operation while with the 101st Airborne Division. They contacted me and provided valuable information. In the same vein, a heartfelt thanks goes to Mr. John Palm whose son was killed while a platoon leader with the 101st Airborne in the Ripcord operation. He was most helpful. And another thank you for the information provided by Mrs. John Cope Pence; her husband participated in Operation Lamson 719 and I wrote to his address, not realizing he'd passed away.

There were numerous other veterans whom I interviewed who were not in the Laotian campaign; their help is much appreciated. Those whose thoughts or commentary were specifically used in this book include: Col. William Hauser, USA (Ret.); Maj. Charles Hawkins, USAR; Dr. Jim Bannon; ex-Lt. John Bayers, USA; ex-Sgt. Larry Moss, USA; ex-Sgt. Kim Rider, USA; ex-Sp5 John Weller, USA; ex-Cpl. Lewis Lawhorn, USMC; and a veteran who requested anonymity and who is described in the prologue.

Numerous official agencies helped in the research, including: Administrative Service, Veterans Administration, Washington, D.C.; Association of Graduates, and the Library, U.S. Military Academy; Chief of Military History and the Center of Military History, Washington, D.C.; Fort Polk Military Museum, Louisiana; Naval Historical Center, Washington Navy Yard; Office of the Adjutant General, Alexandria, Virginia; U.S. Army Enlisted Records and Evaluation Center, Fort Benjamin Harrison, Indiana; U.S. Army Transportation Technical Information and Research Center, Fort Eustis, Virginia; and the U.S. Marine Corps History and Museums Division, Washington Navy Yard.

This then is the story of those Americans fighting the country's last major operation in Vietnam. Few generalizations can be made about them, as in the confusion of the time they responded as individuals, not members of a united effort. Perhaps the only generalization that can be made is that, whatever their beliefs and motives, most of the men depicted in these pages were brave.

For that alone, they deserve America's recognition.

For Jim Al with admiration from a later generation
20.07.21

Prologue

The Green Berets of the 5th Special Forces Group were the best trained American soldiers in Vietnam, and the college professor had been one of them. He spent eighteen months in Nam, coming in-country in 1968 when he was twenty-three and newly married. He was a staff sergeant, tattooed and tough, but he was also an educated man. When his reconnaissance teams crossed the border for operations along the Ho Chi Minh Trail in Laos, he thought of the line from Corneille: "Deeds of great courage were done in the darkness and never seen or recorded." Cross-border ops in Laos were not publicly authorized and therefore did not happen; most of the sergeant's friends would not discuss the matter with outsiders (reporters), and he emphasized that his statements were merely guesses.

What he guessed was detailed and immersed in the incredibly euphemistic language of Vietnam. The Special Forces units that raided Laos were designated SOG (Studies and Observation Group). They were ostensibly in Vietnam to study the tactics of the forces fighting the war. The teams were issued maps without international border lines. After-action reports were couched in a bizarre language: Laos was "denied and enemy-controlled territory," the U.S. recon teams were FGUs or "Friendly Guerrilla Units," casualties were recorded as having been incurred inside South Vietnam. The reconnaissance teams didn't go out with U.S. weapons, carrying instead "sterile" ones, communist-made Ak-47 automatic rifles or Swedish K submachineguns, keeping their ammunition in North Vietnamese pouches slung across their chests. They even wore modified jungle boots, the cleated soles having been replaced with tire rubber so the prints resembled those of the enemy's Ho Chi Minh sandals.

The sergeant and his team of U.S. soldiers and Montagnard mercenaries crossed the border on a variety of missions: recon, prisoner snatch, trail watch, truck counting, bomb-damage assessment from the B52 Arc Lights, and harassment of NVA supply columns coming down the Ho Chi Minh Trail. Whenever they went in big, up to twenty-four men, with the purpose of raising hell, they were met punch for punch by the many North Vietnamese Army units bunkered along the Trail. The NVA probably loved hunting down the small commando teams, the sergeant thought, after having endured numerous U.S. airstrikes where they could only shake a fist skyward in helpless rage. Using air and artillery to cut the Trail usually met with disaster; the NVA, realizing that someone must be in the hills adjusting the fire, would sweep the high ground. They usually flushed out the recon teams and bitter firefights ensued with the woefully outnumbered Americans and Montagnards calling in close air support while they scrambled aboard extraction helicopters under fire. Sometimes entire teams vanished in the Laotian mountains, overrun, the few survivors captured. Nearly everyone, including the young sergeant, ended up with some kind of wound.

The only time they came through unscathed was when they worked small, two Americans and two to four Montagnards (primitive hill tribesmen, suspicious of Saigon but fiercely loyal to the Green Berets). They wore tigerstripe fatigues and went out loaded down with ammunition, gear, medical supplies, and demolitions. They moved silently through the jungles of Laos, gear fastened so it didn't rattle, the pointman not hacking at the brush with a machete but only pushing the bramble aside, the last man in line pushing it back in place. Sometimes they reached a deserted point on the Trail and took intelligence photos, installed electronic listening devices, or pulled dirty tricks like booby trapping ammunition caches with exploding mortar rounds and AK-47 magazines.

The sergeant could only marvel at the Ho Chi Minh Trail. It was not a single road, but a tangle of trails woven and interconnected; and anything but a trail. It was more a high-speed, two-lane highway of laterite clay, with bunkers along the side and living vines and palms thatched overhead to hide it from U.S. planes. All the constructions were well planned, underground, sturdy. Even the individual spider-holes for the NVA soldiers were perfectly dug, all sides squared off and reinforced with lashed bamboo. Hundreds of them dotted the branches of the Trail, all exactly the same. The sergeant had heard that the Communists copied the foxhole dimensions from French manuals and never deviated a millimeter from the textbook examples. Ants, the enemy soldiers were called. Even down under the sweating triple-canopy jungle, amid wreckage from airstrikes, political indoctrination classrooms were found equipped with chalk boards, benches, and stacks of mimeographed communist doctrine.

Fighting the North Vietnamese was like battling an army of robots; an indoctrinated mass, without imagination or individuality, who blindly kept fighting despite horrendous losses. Regardless of motives, they were brave and disciplined and the sergeant had a lot of respect for them.

Written by Al Farrell of
Sydney-Hampton College in
Virginia, who went with
me on my return trip
to VN in January, 1990

The Khe Sanh Area and Lam Son 719 Offensive

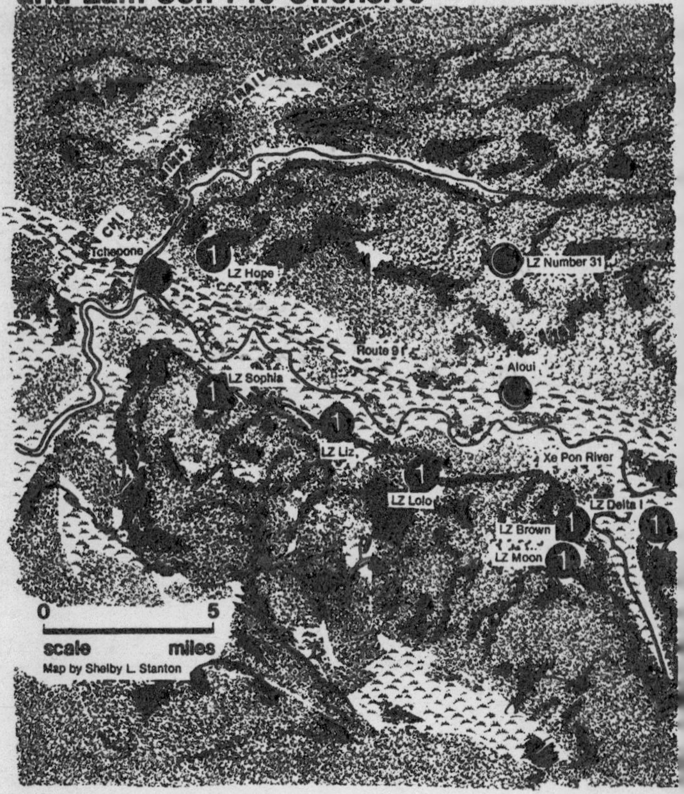

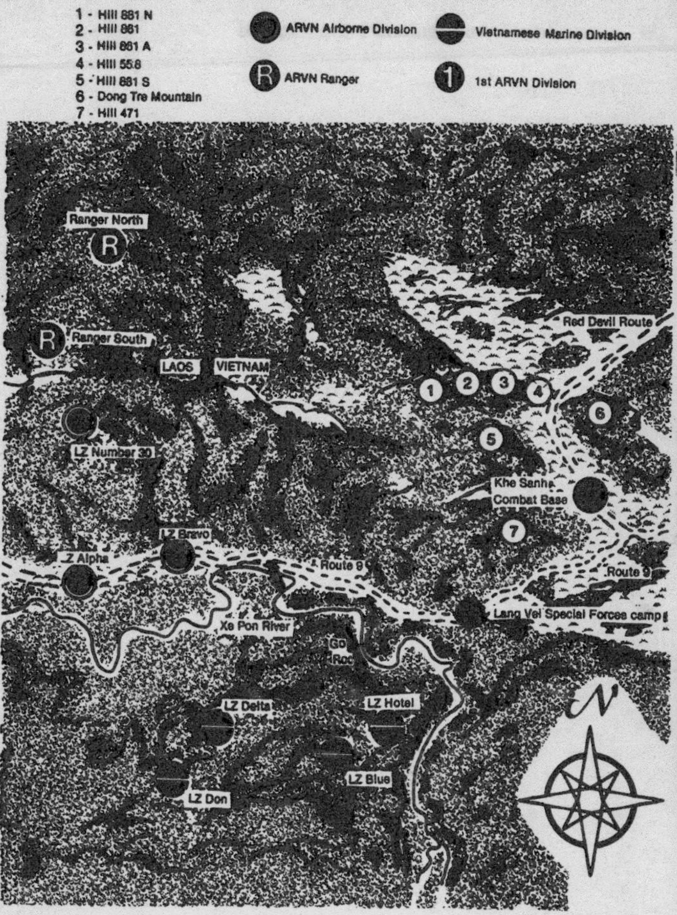
1 - Hill 881 N
2 - Hill 861
3 - Hill 861 A
4 - Hill 558
5 - Hill 881 S
6 - Dong Tre Mountain
7 - Hill 471
ARVN Airborne Division
Vietnamese Marine Division
ARVN Ranger
1st ARVN Division
Ranger North
Ranger South
LAOS
VIETNAM
LZ Number 30
LZ Bravo
Z Alpha
Route 9
Xe Pon River
Red Devil Route
Khe Sanh
Combat Base
Route 9
Lang Vei Special Forces camp
LZ Delta
LZ Hotel
LZ Blue
LZ Don
N

PART ONE:
Operation Dewey Canyon II

CHAPTER ONE:
The Cambodian Prelude

The grunts of D Company, 6th Battalion, 31st Infantry, 9th Division were nervous. Two days before, they'd been airlifted from an operation in the Plain of Reeds in the Mekong Delta and deposited at an abandoned sugar mill in the jungle near the Cambodian border. There was no word on why they were there. One of the officers, Lt. John Bayer, the company's artillery forward observer, was as uneasy as the young infantrymen. He was a thin man with eyeglasses and a toothbrush mustache, cajoled into the service after graduate school. A world apart in age and education from most of the grunts in Delta Company, Bayer shared at least two things with them; he wanted nothing to do with Vietnam and was there because, even though he thought it a nonsensical war, his sense of duty would not allow him to rationalize an excuse by which he could shirk his way out.

On the company's second day of rumor-filled waiting, Bayer and the four platoon leaders joined their company commander in the gutted mill building, sitting casually on their cots as the captain explained that the battalion was going to be part of an offensive into the North-Vietnamese-Army sanctuaries in the Parrot's Beak.

They were invading Cambodia.

The next day, the entire battalion boarded UH1 Hueys, troop-carrying helicopters nicknamed slicks because they had only two door-gunners in the cabins for protection. They crossed the invisible line separating the South Vietnamese and Cambodian jungles and made an airmobile combat assault (CA'd) into an NVA basecamp. It was a cold insertion—free of enemy fire—and, as the infantrymen fanned out, they found no enemy soldiers but did uncover bunkers and caches of food provisions in the sweltering patchwork of bamboo groves and rice paddies. From that jumping-off point, Delta Company was detached from the main body of the battalion and humped (patrolled) a few kilometers deeper into the jungle. The company commander established his command post amid the weeds and began sending platoon patrols out to hunt for the North Vietnamese and their supply caches.

One of the platoons was ordered to patrol near a beautiful Cambodian village called Chantrea and, although Lieutenant Bayer's FO team was not assigned to go, his radio-telephone operator, a blond kid named Lonsdale, asked to go with him. Bayer told him he didn't have to but Lonsdale grinned and said he wanted to; he loved to go out and hump, playing John Wayne with the grunts. The company had not had a serious contact for a long time and this still seemed much like a war game. They moved out, Lonsdale took the point and, on the outskirts of Chantrea, an NVA blew him away with a burst of AK-47 automatic rifle fire. The radio reports crackled back to the CP that the platoon was pinned down in a dry rice paddy. Bayer grabbed his helmet and M-16 rifle with a vengeance, absolutely boiling for revenge: Lonsdale had been a rock-steady kid. He clambered aboard the slicks which had come to whisk the remainder of Delta Company to the firefight, feeling the desire to kill for the first time in his life.

They sailed in over the treetops and CA'd into the parched paddy field, the door-gunners firing madly toward the village, the grunts jumping out and hitting the ground at a run. It was a hot LZ, under enemy fire. Bayer threw himself to the ground scrunched against a one-foot-high paddy dike, GIs on line beside him the length of the berm, pouring fire back at the far treeline. A grunt next to him held up his M-16 to fire blindly over the dike, and a GI crouching nearby broke into snarled obscenities when his weapon jammed in his hands. The North Vietnamese fire relentlessly tore holes in the air around them sounding, Bayer thought like bees, AK rounds zipping over his head and thunking loudly into the paddy behind them. His whole body tensed up in anticipation of a bullet hitting him. Finally he relaxed a bit and got on the radio to the artillery battery which had been airlifted into Cambodia to support them. He requested white phosphorus shells be fired on the bamboo grove between them and the ville, hoping to burn it down and expose the NVA. A half-dozen rounds slammed into the treeline, burning white and smokey against the green before the artilleryman on the other end of the radio said they only had three Willy Peter rounds left. Jesus Christ, Bayer cursed inwardly, typical, fucking typical. He started calling in high explosive shot and the village of Chantrea shuddered under the shrapnel-spewing explosions. But, for all that, the NVA kept up their fire and Delta Company was stuck in the rice field. Finally as the sun went down, the enemy fire slacked off enough for the company commander to order them north to set up for the night behind a network of higher paddy dikes.

That night five mortar rounds exploded in the space they had vacated.

In the morning, Delta Company swept forward on foot. The NVA were gone. The grunts shared their C rations with the Cambodians in the village, then told them to leave. The company commander ordered Chantrea burned. The young grunts loved it, finding it a catharsis for the memory of their buddies who'd been killed or wounded the day before. They dragged torches through the thatch hootches, gunning down pigs and water buffalos, rock'n'rolling from the hip. Bayer thought of William Calley, under investigation at the time for My Lai; before long he and the other officers were shouting to get the worked-up infantrymen back under control.

The next day, they were back on the move, Bayer humping along with the company commander in the broiling sun as they patrolled down a dirt road in the jungle. Coming upon a deserted bamboo village, it was gut-tightening to see food and NVA gear stacked beside the hootches. The company kept moving, everyone a little more tense and alert. The platoon off on the right flank began to get disorganized in the bramble of vines, trees, and bushes—then the NVA hit. AK-47 fire erupted from the front and Bayer jumped flat into a ditch alongside the foot-path. NVA mortar shells began thunking from their tubes and exploding among the trees. Bayer could see a small concrete building tucked in the vegetation up the road and was sure the NVA had a forward observer sitting in there with a radio.

With NVA fire slashing around them, the captain got on the horn to call for air support. AH1G Cobra gunships came on station and began circling and strafing; the jungle shook in the blizzard from 7.62mm miniguns screaming at two thousand rounds a minute and 2.75-inch flechette rockets pumping down with white trails. Bayer could see figures among the trees on the other side of the trail. He got up to run to them but hesitated, and instead, a tall, mustached GI named Macomber ran onto the path—just as one of the Cobras plunged down in a strafing run and fired two more rockets. The pilot pressed the button a moment too soon and the rockets exploded amid Delta Company. Bayer curled up in the dirt, clutching his helmet, shrapnel and dirt clods blowing over him, a piece of U.S. steel stinging in his hip.

In seconds the dust and roar was settling and then he could hear screams from the platoon across the path. AK rounds continued to punch past. There was a moment of hesitation, but then the young grunts ran like hell towards the carnage. It was all chaos and blood. Macomber was sprawled on the road, his chest peppered with shrapnel. Bayer crouched next to him as he gave a long sigh and then was dead. Another grunt ran up, clutching his weapon, blood running down his arms, dripping from his fingers. The kid stumbled about in shock, screaming at people to get up and help the wounded, then he blew off his M-16 magazine into the dirt and collapsed. Bayer started helping with the casualties, then saw the platoon leader sitting dazed in the grass. He was a big friendly man from Georgia who'd been in the company since Bayer had transferred in. The back of his head was ragged with shrapnel and streaming blood. He turned to his platoon sergeant, told him he was in charge, then slumped mortally wounded in the undergrowth.

The NVA fire kept up, most of it coming from a bunker twenty yards away. If if wasn't silenced, the wounded might be pinned down and die. Bayer began crawling towards it, firing his M-16 nonstop until he realized he had only two magazines left from the fourteen he'd been carrying. Two more grunts ran up to fire on the bunker; then a fair-haired kid named Walker stood up in the brush across the road, and as Bayer watched, amazed at his cool, he just walked through the AK bursts, firing his M-16 and lobbing fragmentation grenades. With an M-79 grenade launcher he popped rounds right into the bunker aperture.

The North Vietnamese fire stopped.

They rushed back to carry the dead and wounded down the path, and medevacs—medical evacuation helicopters—came in. The captain got back on the radio to call in F4 Phantom jets splashing napalm canisters. The grunts crouched down while eighty feet ahead, the jungle turned into a black and yellow fireball, flames rolling up in thick streamers, heat shimmering back. The jets banked off, the captain said to saddle up, and Delta Company started forward again. Bayer found a book on the path that had fallen out of the thigh pocket of his jungle fatigues. It was a collection of readings from western philosophy and was burnt from the napalm. He thought it a morbid symbol.

They overran the NVA bunkers, but the enemy had fallen back, disappeared. Delta set up in a tight night position and Bayer sat there, getting more and more spooked as he stared at the lumpy body bag of Macomber lying inside the perimeter with them. The next day, Bayer got his reprieve; he was choppered out of Cambodia to attend the memorial service for his dead radioman at their battalion basecamp. He was still numb from his first and last heavy contact, not caring much when the captain said he was up for the Silver Star. The only things on his mind were guilt and waste; guilt because Lonsdale had been eighteen when he died, a solid young man, and it had been Bayer who had allowed him to accompany the patrol; waste because he could find no good coming out of the deaths he'd just seen.

Lieutenant Bayer and Delta Company had crossed the border into Cambodia on 1 May 1970 as part of Operation Toan Thang (Total Victory) 43. It was a major attack along the border aimed at destroying the NVA basecamps and supply caches which had long been in the area, safe as a sanctuary because of Cambodia's previous neutrality. The invasion force included ground elements of the 1st Air Cavalry Division, the 4th, 9th, and 25th Infantry Divisions, the 101st Airborne Division, the 11th Armored Cavalry Regiment, and a host of ARVN (Army of the Republic of Vietnam) units. President Richard Nixon's decision to launch the incursion into Cambodia was a radical departure from the policies of the Johnson administration, and a dramatic indication of the aggressive methods the new president was willing to pursue in the fight against the North Vietnamese invasion of South Vietnam. It was a politically divisive move, but a military imperative if "Vietnamization" was to be given the breathing room to grow and mature.

Cambodia and its northern neighbor, Laos, had long been thorns in the side of the U.S. war effort in Vietnam. The Communists, taking advantage of the weakness of the leaders and armies of the two nations, moved in force to occupy the sparsely-populated border regions. There they constructed elaborate roadways for infiltration into South Vietnam, supply depots, basecamps for the rest and refitting of units, artillery emplacements to shell across the border, and the like. Cambodia and Laos gave the North Vietnamese sanctuaries from which to launch attacks and for retreat when bloodied in battle.

Before Nixon, President Johnson had followed a policy of essentially ignoring the sanctuaries and instructing the military to do the same. Gen. William Westmoreland, Commander of U.S. forces in Vietnam from 1964 to 1968 (his official title was Commander, U.S. Military Assistance Command—Vietnam) had always suspected the importance of the sanctuaries. As early as 1965, Westmoreland's intelligence chief had compiled evidence of seven major NVA bases in Cambodia (including the Parrot's Beak, a bulge less than thirty miles from Saigon) and of the Cambodian port town of Sihanoukville being used to bring arms and supplies which were then infiltrated into South Vietnam. By 1966 the continued investigations by MACV Intelligence showed that the NVA was using Laos and Cambodia as major infiltration routes, converging into South Vietnam from the north by the Ho Chi Minh Trail and from the south by the Sihanouk Trail.

The evidence was duly reported to the Johnson administration, with the weight of the reports falling on Cambodia. The government's response was to try to court the Cambodian premier, Prince Norodom Sihanouk, and usher him into the allies' circle (". . . which seemed to us in Saigon to be naive," General Westmoreland wrote in his memoirs, "unless we should demonstrate unmistakably that we were going to succeed in South Vietnam, for Sihanouk clearly was out to play the winner."). The administration was timid about responding openly and forcefully to the Communist presence in Laos and Cambodia, afraid that too strong a flexing of muscle would drive Sihanouk into open collusion with Hanoi. Therefore, Westmoreland was forbidden to reveal the presence of sanctuaries to the world press. There came as a result, some embarrassing moments such as a lieutenant general telling reporters his units would engage the NVA on the border and then they "disappeared to the west." Did this mean the enemy was operating within Cambodia? "One can draw no other conclusion." A journalist pursued the point with Secretary of Defense Robert McNamara who answered that there was insufficient evidence to support the general's comment. Asked to clarify this disagreement, the lieutenant general smiled, "I stand corrected."

The Cambodian and Laotian sanctuaries were major assets to the Communist invasion effort, and U.S. commanders chafed with frustration at their inability to do anything; their stated mission was to hunt down the Communists and destroy them, but they were not only denied access to North Vietnam but also to the border regions. General Westmoreland shared that bitterness. Starting in 1965, he requested permission to launch counter-measures in Cambodia which included air and ground reconnaissance across the border, hot pursuit against NVA units retreating into the sanctuary, and B52 bombing missions against confirmed enemy basecamp. The Joint Chiefs of Staff approved most of his ideas; the State Department vetoed them. Westmoreland bitterly wrote, ". . . all we could do to the enemy in Cambodia was drop propaganda leaflets on our side of the border whenever the wind was right to blow them across."

In 1966 President Johnson acquiesced slightly to the general's requests. Permission was granted to conduct air and artillery strikes in Cambodia against NVA units firing from across the border. In rare cases, usually when the survival of an allied unit was at stake, hot pursuit was permitted. Later, permission was granted to conduct limited air reconnaissance over Cambodia, but the pilots were not allowed to return fire. Still later, ground recon patrols were authorized. Most were organized by MACV-SOG and their covert form of war was given a free hand in Laos. However, in Cambodia, they were only allowed to fight in self defense. Such measures were small and did little to upset the Communists' continued use of sanctuaries. It wasn't until late 1967 that Johnson even admitted their presence, and that was forced upon him after reporters visited an NVA camp in Cambodia. Still, no major actions were mounted. Westmoreland's contingency plans of multi-division invasions of Laos and Cambodia only collected dust at MACV Headquarters. Even in 1968, when the North Vietnamese Army and Viet Cong were crippled and on the verge of collapse after their disastrous Tet Offensive, President Johnson would not allow the military to press home a meaningful victory by cleaning out the sanctuaries.

As history would have it, it fell to Gen. Creighton Abrams (Westmoreland's successor as COMUSMACV) to launch the Cambodian and Laotian incursions. The change in policy was instigated by President Nixon who, in 1969, soon after taking office, authorized secret B52 bombing raids on the NVA in Cambodia. In March 1970, Prince Sihanouk was overthrown by Gen. Lon Nol, the anti-Vietnamese prime minister. Lon Nol closed the Sihanoukville port to communist ships and ordered the NVA and VC to remove themselves from Cambodia. The NVA responded by pummeling the Cambodian's "palace-guard" army, Lon Nol requested U.S. support. With this impetus, Secretary of State Henry Kissinger brought up the idea of finally moving into Cambodia to neutralize the sanctuaries. Nixon gave the go-ahead.

When the U.S. and ARVN divisions crossed the border they were limited to a thirty-kilometer penetration. Antiwar protests quickly broke out, the most tragic being at Kent State where panicky National Guardsmen killed four students during a riot.

Yielding to the antiwar outcry, Nixon ordered all U.S. troops out of Cambodia by 30 June 1970. The ARVN stayed behind to continue operations against NVA still holding in the area. The results of the two-month

American intervention were impressive. The Communists put up several bitter fights against the invasion force (over two thousand NVA were reported killed), but most had retreated in disorder, abandoning basecamps and supply caches. To put the number of captured or destroyed NVA gear into understandable terms, one analysis computed that the U.S./ARVN incursion had denied the NVA enough weapons to equip fifty-five battalions, enough crew-served weapons for eighty-five to ninety battalions, and enough small-arms ammunition to provide the basic combat load to fifty-two thousand soldiers. Also captured were ninety-five thousand tons of foodstuffs and twenty-eight tons of medical supplies. The blow had been severe (but not permanent because of the short duration of the invasion) and enemy activity in the South Vietnamese provinces bordering Cambodia dropped dramatically.

Impressive intelligence data was collected in Cambodia, much of it adding detail to what Westmoreland's intelligence officers had been saying since 1965. It was learned that Prince Sihanouk had sided with Hanoi in March 1965 (not so much out of ideological agreement, but because he felt they would be the side to emerge victorious from the long war) and had geared his policies accordingly. For example, the Cambodian army did not interfere with the NVA on their soil and the government itself sold fifty-five thousand tons of rice annually to the Communists (another hundred thousand tons came every year directly from Cambodian farmers).

The Cambodian incursion shut down the Sihanoukville port, Phnom Penh airfield, the Sihanouk Trail, and the North Vietnamese sanctuaries. It was a crippling setback for the Communists. From that point on, the NVA had to depend solely on their Laotian basecamps and the Ho Chi Minh Trail. Following the logic which had set in motion the spoiling attack against Cambodia, the natural corollary would be similarly to disrupt the Laotian sanctuaries. As it turned out, seven months separated the two invasions;* the U.S./ARVN drive into Laos was launched in February 1971.

---

* Invasion was the term used by the media and in popular history. It was not favored by the military, as Col. John Miller, a U.S. Marine advisor during Cambodia and Laos explained: "Those of us who had participated in the earlier cross-border thrust into Cambodia were both amused and irritated by the eagerness of the media—once again—to slap the hyped-up, pejorative label of 'invasion' (with its ponderous and chilling WWII connotations) on these relatively limited operations. Instead of wallowing in self-inflicted guilt, Americans should have been cheering about the long-

The communist response to the Cambodian invasion was typical of their tactics throughout the war—tenacious. With the Cambodian mainland closed to them and the coast actively patrolled by the U.S. Navy, the NVA worked feverishly to improve and expand the Ho Chi Minh Trail in Laos. Their ultimate goal was to use Laos as a springboard for an offensive back into Cambodia and east into the northern regions of South Vietnam. Directly east of the Laotian border were four South Vietnamese provinces (Quang Tri Province, furthest north and facing the DMZ border between the two Vietnams, followed by Thua Thien, Quang Nam, and Quang Ngai). They were what the U.S. called Military Region 1, and the ARVN called I Corps. The American command in the area was XXIV Corps (Lt. Gen. James W. Sutherland) and the ARVN was I Corps Headquarters (Lt. Gen. Hoang Xuan Lam). XXIV Corps controlled three major combat elements in MR1: 1st Brigade, 5th Infantry Division (Mechanized) (Brig. Gen. John G. Hill); 23d Infantry Division (Americal) (Maj. Gen. James L. Baldwin); and the 101st Airborne Division (Airmobile) (Maj. Gen. John J. Hennessey).

The first stage of the North Vietnamese counterattack in the wake of Cambodia was to strike from Laos towards the cities in MR1. One branch of the Ho Chi Minh Trail diverted into South Vietnam through the A Shau Valley of Thua Thien Province; it was a major infiltration route to Hue City and the various military installations in the coastal lowlands. The A Shau/Hue area of operations was under (as supervised by XXIV Corps and I Corps) the U.S. 101st Airborne Division and the ARVN 1st Infantry Division. To meet the build-up in the A Shau Valley in July 1970, the 101st "Screaming Eagles" mounted operations from Fire Support Base Ripcord, and the 1st Division from Fire Support Base O'Reilly. Fighting was so intense that FSB Ripcord was evacuated under fire before July was over, and the ARVN withdrew from O'Reilly in early October before the onset of the rainy season further complicated defense of the firebase. The Ripcord/O'Reilly campaign did not drive the NVA from the A Shau Valley, but it did blunt their aim of an offensive against Hue City.

---

delayed disruption of North Vietnam's sanctuaries along the Ho Chi Minh Trail and along the Cambodian border. We knew that the fight was not with the Laotians; it was with the NVA which had long before seized Laotian turf for its own use. Hysteria about so-called 'invasions' only further muddied the water, which had never been quite clear to begin with." The U.S. military described the operations as limited incursions or preemptive defensive raids.

Despite the initial stalemate, the NVA continued their Laotian buildup and it soon became disturbingly obvious to intelligence officers that serious trouble was brewing across the border.

On 8 December 1970, Gen. Creighton Abrams (COMUSMACV) convened a special meeting of selected MACV staff members and field commanders to discuss countermeasures against the NVA buildup in Laos. The conference was top secret and only six officers were called to attend: Gen. Fred Weyand (DEPCOMUSMACV); Lt. Gen. Welborn Dolvin (Chief of Staff, MACV); Lt. Gen. Michael Davison (CG, II Field Force); Lt. Gen. James Sutherland (CG, XXIV Corps); Maj. Gen. Donald Cowles (G3, MACV), and Maj. Gen. Petts (G2, MACV).

It was General Petts who presented the estimates of the situation in Laos to the group. Following the Cambodian incursion, the enemy had conducted a massive buildup in the A Shau Valley and although their plans had been stunted, the foe was still concentrating on efforts to strike at the vulnerable city of Hue. Intelligence data from August and September indicated the NVA was preparing a full-scale logistical effort on the Ho Chi Minh Trail; logic indicated that the communist effort would begin in earnest when the Laotian dry season began in early October.

The Trail was not a single highway cutting from North Vietnam, but a twisting maze ranging from foot paths to two lane roads; it had started as a small trail during the war against the French and had grown haphazardly to thirty-five hundred miles of roadways contained in a thirty-mile corridor. A Laotian coolie labor force and an estimated thirty thousand NVA of the 559th Transportation Group were assigned to maintain the network. Located along the intermingling branches were military relay stations, Binh Trams, with permanent complements of engineers, transportation soldiers, and antiaircraft crews. Each Binh Tram was independent and responsible for their section of the Trail; this included maintaining land-line telephones, local patrolling against the occasional MACV-SOG raid, and constant engineer work to repair what the weather and the U.S. Air Force did their best to crumble. To avoid the USAF, the NVA truck drivers on the Trail worked almost exclusively at night with headlights dimmed or off; drivers were only assigned a twenty-mile portion of road so they could learn to navigate it in the pitch black night. Material was stored in bunkers and caves at each twenty-mile point, then reloaded to continue the trek. The estimated time for transporting, from North to South Vietnam, each load of weapons, ammunition, and medical gear was two months.

U.S. efforts to interdict the Trail were in full swing with the USAF's Operation Igloo White. Electronic surveillance devices were dropped to monitor vehicle-and-troop movement in Laos, and a constant orbit of manned and drone planes relayed the signals from under the jungle blanket to the Infiltration Surveillance Center in Thailand. There, two computers processed high-speed printouts showing which sensors had been activated, how often, and when. Other computers fed this information to an Airborne Battlefield Command & Control aircraft which then called in appropriate air power. A typical day over Laos saw the Ho Chi Minh Trail hit by thirty B52 bomber strikes and three hundred USAF, USN, and USMC aircraft. C130 transport planes, mounted with Gatling miniguns, flew night and day to strafe convoys and troop marches. Bombs mounted with lasers and televisions were sent against cave entrances. Cluster bombs were sowed over Binh Trams. Mines and booby-traps were airdropped, some designed to demolish trucks, others to mangle a man's foot so he became a burden to his comrades. The destruction was staggering; but the Soviet Union, East Germany, Czechoslovakia, and Red China continued to funnel war material to North Vietnam, the engineers on the Trail kept constructing new branches amid the wreckage, and contingent after contingent of NVA willingly marched down those paths. Firepower alone could not stop the flow.

And, thus, came Abram's meeting to discuss the alternatives.

Turning to the map, General Petts indicated the main areas of communist concentration in Laos, which MACV had labelled Base Areas 604 and 611. Running generally east—west, a French colonial road called Route 9 extended from South Vietnam through the Laotian mountains; sixty kilometers into Laos along this dirt highway was Tchepone, a small village which was now only a deserted and bombed-out section in the jungle. All branches of the Ho Chi Minh Trail passed through the Tchepone area, and BA 604 was the encompassing NVA group. Southeast of this grouping, and closer to the border, was BA 611, another major storage area along the Trail.

As predicted, in the five weeks since the advent of the October dry season, the Communists had greatly increased their activity, particularly around BA 604. NVA efforts had been numerous: repair and rebuilding of the Ho Chi Minh Trail where it had been destroyed by the rainy season and the USAF bombing campaign; construction of new roads to accommodate the increased flow of supplies; improvement of a river channel from the western tip of the DMZ to Tchepone which would permit the floating of supply containers; extension of a POL (Petroleum-

Oil-Lubricants) pipeline from the western DMZ southward; improvement and enlargement of basecamps. Such activities had been spied upon by the electronic sensors and the daily USAF aerial photography flights.

To counter this buildup, Petts explained, the air force had intensified its interdiction effort. Despite the increased use of firepower, though, the sensors in BA 604, BA 611, and the A Shau Valley noted increased truck movement. In BA 604, more trucks were counted entering from the north than were leaving for the south toward BA 611 and the A Shau, indicating a particularly heavy buildup around Tchepone. One intelligence report indicated that 90 percent of the material coming down the Trail was being funnelled into MR1. These factors led MACV to predict a four-part NVA offensive as soon as their efforts in Laos came to a conclusion:

1. A multi-division invasion of various targets in Quang Tri and Thua Thien Provinces with BA 604 as the launching pad into Quang Tri City, and BA 611 using the adjacent A Shau Valley as a channel pointing at Hue City
2. A renewed attack in Cambodia, aimed primarily at the capitol of Phnom Penh to overthrow the pro-American Lon Nol Government
3. A rebuilding operation along the Cambodian-South Vietnamese frontier to reclaim their vanquished sanctuaries
4. A continued buildup in southern Laos throughout the dry season (October to April) with obvious results for MR1

The first phase of this strategy, as MACV understood it, would be the attacks in Quang Tri and Thua Thien. To sit and wait for the Communists to take the initiative was a dangerous prospect, since they grew stronger by the week and the U.S. Army grew weaker with troop withdrawals continuing at a steady pace. To attack into Laos was also a dangerous gambit; the Laotian border and the Ho Chi Minh Trail belonged to the NVA. There had been no allied ground operations there and in the past twenty years, the NVA had built elaborate defensive positions. The jungled mountains and river valleys in Laos contained thousands of mutually-supporting anti-aircraft positions, bunker systems, and machine-gun emplacements. Any foray into Laos would be costly.

General Abrams, however, was a boldly aggressive commander. Hulking, cigar chewing, and gruffly brilliant, he had been a tank hero at the Battle of the Bulge and was in his fourth year in Vietnam.

His commentary revolved around only one concept—attack.

But any offensive planning at that stage had a major stumbling block imposed by the U.S. Congress. The Cooper-Church amendment, born from the antiwar hysteria following Cambodia, prohibited U.S. ground troops from entering Laos. American infantrymen could be employed as support along the border, and aviation units could actually attack Laos, but only the ARVN could mount the necessary search and destroy campaign in Laos. Not even the U.S. advisors could accompany the ARVN. This was a major departure from procedure, for every South Vietnamese unit had Americans with them to help coordinate support fire and logistics from U.S. sources, and to offer guidance on the waging of war. Command of the ARVN invasion force would go to the local commander, General Lam of I Corps, but because of the top-secret nature of General Abrams' conference, Lam had not yet been notified.

With the weather dictating the amount of supplies coming down the Trail, movement would be greatest in February and March (the peak of the dry season); Abrams, accordingly, wanted the invasion to take place in February 1971, when the finds would be the greatest. The offensive, as they conceived it in the airconditioned conference room, would not be a takeover of Laos, but a spoiling attack toward Tchepone to destroy the stockpiling in BA 604 and 611, and thus stunt the coming NVA offensive. U.S. troops were to pave the way to the border along Route 9. U.S. aviation would ferry the ARVN across into Laos where the ARVN were to wreak damage for as long as possible, hopefully up to the advent of the rainy season in April.

Simultaneously, it was hoped, the ARVN could launch a second offensive in Cambodia to halt the stirrings-up there. Two days later, on 10 December, the seven generals met again at MACV Headquarters. The topic this time was detailed analysis of precisely how to carry out the spoiling attack, covering the number of U.S. and ARM troops required, the numbers actually available, the timing of the planned campaign, and the area of operation. On that day, the unnamed Laotian operation was no longer a broad concept but a reality becoming more and more clearly defined.

A frontier of approximately fifty kilometers faced the DMZ at the end of South Vietnam, and the terrain ranged from low sandy areas on the South China Sea, to rolling grasslands, and finally great mountains which stretched into Laos. Militarily, the center of MR1 was the coastal city of Da Nang which housed the headquarters of both XXIV Corps and I Corps, as well as the vital logistical base maintained by U.S. Army Support Command, Da Nang, USARV (Brig. Gen. Arthur Sweeney). The main highway was Route 1, a paved all-weather strip which ran along the coast all the way from Saigon to beyond Da Nang. From there it continued past a succession of military bases and cities, including Hue and Quang Tri, and finally ended its northern trek at a village called Dong Ha below the DMZ. Route 9 began at Dong Ha and extended all the way to Tchepone, running west. It was a paved highway until halfway to the border from Dong Ha at an abandoned U.S. Marine combat base (Vandegrift); here Route 9 turned into a narrow dirt path. It cut through the mountains there, past Khe Sanh and Lang Vei which had been made famous during the 1968 Tet Offensive but which had been abandoned for nearly three years. Since Tet no major operations had been launched west of Vandegrift and the deserted mountains belonged to the North Vietnamese Army.

As commanding general of XXIV Corps, the responsibility of on-scene American command for the Laotian campaign fell to Lieutenant General Sutherland. His duties were divided into three main areas:

1. To provide complete support for the ARVN in Laos, including logistics, helicopters, engineers, artillery and opening and securing a main line of communications (LOC) along Route 9
2. To reopen the Khe Sanh airfield to support the operation
3. To coordinate air support for the invasion as provided by the U.S. Air Force, Navy, and Marine Corps

Roughly speaking, Sutherland's mammoth undertaking had several simultaneous components. Drawing from the ground assets of the 101st Airborne and the 1/5 Mechanized Brigade, Route 9 was to be secured physically and patrolled to ensure the ARVN a bloodless entry into Laos. Engineers were to upgrade the dirt highway and reopen the Khe Sanh airstrip. Artillery units were to establish firebases along the border to lend support fire. Aviation units would then have the mission of transportation, support, medical evacuation, and withdrawal of ARVN troops in Laos.

The operational concepts they were developing were classified top secret. General Sutherland, for example was forbidden to discuss the plan with his XXIV Corps staff or subordinate commanders. He could not even mention it to his Vietnamese counterpart, General Lam, whose I Corps troops would be the ones entering Laos. All messages relating to the plan were to be passed by military courier, none by electronic means.

With such a premium on security, Sutherland discussed a problem with Abrams which had occurred in MR1. The monsoon storms of October and November had wreaked havoc on the river ports at Hue and

Dong Ha (most supplies to these forward bases came via boat from the Da Nang Support Command) and ammunition, food rations, and fuel stockpiles were far below desired levels. When informed of this situation by General Sweeney and the XXIV Corps G4, Sutherland ordered an all-out effort to fill the ammunition and fuel depots to capacity. Then came the call to Saigon. Abrams told Sutherland to continue the resupply effort in MR1 so that the NVA in the area would view the logistics as the natural follow-up to the monsoon, and not as the prelude to an impending invasion.

At the end of the 10 December meeting, the assembled generals agreed on the broad concepts of the operation. General Abrams said he would send the proposals for the joint Laos-Cambodia drives to the JCS in Washington, D.C., whose approval would allow the development of a detailed plan. From that day on, the invasion of Laos and the Ho Chi Minh Trail was merely a matter of time.

Response from Washington over Abrams' secret message did not come immediately. They were still in waiting stage when General Sutherland was told of a situation that may have drastically affected all their hopes. On 22 December 1970, Vice President Nguyen Cao Ky and Bob Hope's troupe were scheduled to arrive at Camp Eagle, the home of the 101st Airborne between Da Nang and Hue on Route 1. Generals Sutherland and Lam flew in from Da Nang to meet Ky at the adjacent Phu Bai airfield. With them was Brig. Gen. Pham Van Phu, newly appointed commander of the ARVN 1st Infantry Division, and a colonel who was his senior U.S. advisor.

As they waited in the VIP lounge of the airport, Lam and Phu began conversing in Vietnamese. Their talk lasted twenty minutes and Sutherland and the colonel could only stare uncomprehendingly, not understanding Vietnamese, their counterparts choosing not to include them in talk. Ky arrived as scheduled, the entourage watched the last half of the Bob Hope show, then they visited various field units and wound up their inspection tour at Da Nang by late afternoon. At nine that night, the colonel telephoned Sutherland and asked if Lam had revealed the subject of the conversation in the VIP lounge. He had not. The colonel insisted that it was imperative that he see Sutherland as soon as possible. Since the XXIV Corps commander was scheduled to visit wounded soldiers the next morning at nine, they arranged to meet at the Phu Bai hospital.

There, the colonel explained to Sutherland that after Ky had departed, he and Phu had returned to their division headquarters in Hue. In the privacy of Phu's office, he had told the American that he and Lam had been discussing the possibility of an operation in Laos. Lam wanted a plan worked up, and Phu wanted his advisors to help develop it. Sutherland feigned ignorance of the subject, but told the colonel he had no authorization to work in any such plans. He also ordered him not to discuss the content of Lam and Phu's conversation with anyone. Back at Da Nang, Sutherland quickly dispatched a military courier to COMUSMACV in Saigon to report the possible breach of security. The VIP lounge, where Lam and Phu had openly discussed the idea of a Laos campaign, could have been easily monitored by communist agents.

Six days later, on 29 December Sutherland met with Lam at I Corps HQ. For the first time, Lam told him that the ARVN were disturbed by the NVA buildup in Laos and were working on invasion plans. Sutherland had no choice but to again feign ignorance, but he was deeply worried and reported this second incident to Abrams. As evidenced by the open discussion in the airport, the South Vietnamese had little patience for secrecy in their military planning. Sutherland knew, for example, that officers at I Corps, including General Lam, often used telephones to discuss tactical matters with Saigon. Such methods of communication were easily tapped by the Communists, but most ARVN refused to shake their naive assumption that speaking English was a sufficient countermeasure against any NVA eavesdropping.

Sutherland's reports caused grave concern among Generals Abrams and Weyand at MACV: it was entirely possible that the North Vietnamese were now aware that an invasion was at least being planned.

CHAPTER TWO:
The Soldiers

The American fighting man who was to face the North Vietnamese along the Laotian front in 1971 was perhaps the least motivated in U.S. history.

It had not always been that way; in fact the decay had been a slow (and predictable) progression from best to poor, brought on not by events on the battlefield but by the politics in the United States. To examine the extent of the problems and what effect they had, it is necessary to look at the evolution of the U.S. Army in Vietnam. General Westmoreland remarked, "Having fought in three wars, I am convinced the United States never fielded a more professional force than in South Vietnam during the years 1966–69." In short, morale and performance were excellent. The average infantryman was nineteen and was generally athletic, intelligent, and patriotic. On the battlefield, every major action ended in an American victory. This is not to imply that the soldiers were spoiling for a fight or that they were not miserable, homesick, and scared like the mud-slogging grunts have always been. But it does mean that the majority were willing to set aside their fear and discomfort to get the job done. It was a time when two-thirds of the troops had enlisted (compared to two-thirds having been drafted in WWII) and when 150,000 men volunteered to extend their one year tour of duty in Vietnam.

Mainly it was a time when they felt they had the backing of the nation and that victory was not far off. Cpl. John Musgrave, wounded four times along the DMZ as a marine rifleman in 1967, graphically described the combat grunt's view of the war, "There was no withdrawal. We were still bombing the living shit out of the North, and we were literally waiting for the orders that would let us cross the Ben Hai

River and get into North Vietnam and start kicking their ass. Take Uncle Ho by his inscrutable balls and lead him down the streets of Hanoi."

But those orders to attack Hanoi—to, in effect, fight aggressively without political restraints—never came and therein lay the first seeds of decay. The nature of the war as decreed by Washington called for search and destroy, for units to patrol repeatedly through the same patch of ground, measuring success not by positions taken—and held—but by the all-important Body Count. Search and destroy could wear down even the most willing. Sgt. Larry Moss had not resisted when he was drafted out of college, and he believed in the war when they sent him to a tank battalion, but, "We were fighting to stay alive. No other reason. You did not accomplish anything in the field. Wasn't any territory taken. Honest to God, when I was going over I left a map with my wife and said, 'Here, I'll let you know all the places I've been and you can follow me on the map.' Well, goddamn, I didn't do anything. It was totally alien to what we were taught. I was still fighting the way Patton used to fight—I wanted to anyway. It was very frustrating mentally. When I joined my platoon, it was in War Zone C. When I left, we were still there trying to do the same goddamned thing."

It produced a cycle of frustration: no matter how much firepower and bravery were thrust into the jungle, no matter how many body counts were racked up, nothing changed because the war was not taken home to North Vietnam, because the land was not developed, because the communist leadership was willing to absorb horrific losses in their patient wait for the U.S. war effort to burn itself out. The gung-ho zeal which had buoyed the American soldier was drastically deflated in 1969 when President Nixon ushered in Vietnamization (turning the ground war back to the ARVN) and the scheduled withdrawal of U.S. troops. Politicians began saying the war was over, protesters screamed for the other side, the president said the ARVN were shouldering the fighting—but, as any grunt would acidly note, those Americans in Vietnam were still out there. The fact that the war was supposed to be over meant nothing to a grunt walking point in the jungle with a hundred pound pack on his back and bands around his trouser legs to keep the leeches out of his crotch. Politicians pointed with reassurance that the U.S. weekly death toll, after the withdrawals began, was only 81 or 49, instead of 460 or 300 as it had been previously. Cold comfort to the man left to trundle a dead buddy into a body bag in a forgotten war.

No military victory was called for, no speedy withdrawal could occur, and it wasn't long before the average draftee in Vietnam thought himself the expendable rear guard at the butt-end of a war no one wanted anymore. Said a medic in the 1st Air Cav in late 1970, "The first time I was here in 1968, we were more aggressive. Then people felt if we really went at it, we could finish the war. Now we know it will go on after we leave, so why get killed?" Such sentiments found an echo up the line; said a 25th Division lieutenant, "The men see very small returns for their accomplishments. . . . They kill a few Viet Cong, but more will be there next time. They know the army will be leaving and that the job is not going to be finished. Six months or a year from now, Vietnam won't be much different from today."

Finally, the U.S. Army in Vietnam was composed of combat units, swollen to 80 percent with draftees, who saw little purpose in the war—and were increasingly unwilling to fight it. In late 1970, British correspondent John Saar spent time with Alpha Company, 1st Battalion, 8th Cavalry Division, conducting ground patrols in the sweltering jungles along the Cambodian border. Saar's portrayal of Alpha Company was representative of most infantry units at the time. The men continued to function not out of any commitment to the war, but because of the able leadership of their young West Point captain, whom they respected for his abilities and common sense. Combat was rare for the company, most of their two-week patrols being hot walks in the sun; most of the GIs were glad about that, as one said in reviewing their last operation. "It was all right. Main thing was we got through without anyone hurt. We didn't get anything done, but I don't care." There were some discipline problems (for example, a young private refusing to go on a night ambush patrol because he thought his comrades were too inexperienced to pull it off correctly), but the company commander handled them mildly, allowing troubles to fade away because "military justice has no answer to the grunt's ironic question: What can they do to me, send me to Vietnam?" There was no drug use in the field for safety's sake, but at their firebase between missions the grunts split into the juicers (beer) and the rollers or heads (marijuana). "We pass the pipe around," said a squad leader, "and ask what the hell are we doing here." It was a baffling army to the veterans. One old first sergeant, wounded with the unit in 1966 then sent back in 1970, had to be transferred out because he couldn't deal with the new crop of draftees. As the sergeant said, "Things have changed. Before, everyone was gung-ho and wanted to mix it with Charlie. Now it seems everyone's trying to avoid him."

The reporter, Saar, concluded about the unit:

> Virtually no draftee wants to be fighting in Vietnam anyway, and in return for his reluctant participation he demands, and gets, personal freedoms that would have driven a MacArthur or a Patton apoplectic. It is an Army in which all questions—including "Why?"—are permissible. Alpha Company seethes with problems, but it has not fallen into chaos . . . the company commander's continuing problem is to find an effective compromise between his own professional dedication and his draftees' frank disinterest in anything that might cost an American life. . . . Grunt logic argues that since the U.S. has decided not to go out and win the war, there's no sense in being the last one to die.

Soldiers were less willing to take risks in an ending war, and such sentiments sometimes resulted in the grunts simply refusing to fight. Usually such instances were without drama and Col. Ben Harrison, a brigade commander in the 101st Airborne in 1970, thought most resulted from poor leadership. By then most of the veteran NCOs he saw had already done one or two combat tours, no longer wanted to hump up and down the mountains with reluctant draftees, and wangled rear area jobs. Consequently the small-unit leadership in his brigade was left to young draftee lieutenants who were fresh from the turmoil of the campuses and unsure about the war, and young draftee sergeants who had been sent to instant "shake'n'bake" NCO academies. Mostly they were inexperienced and shared the bitterness of the grunts they were supposed to lead. "When we can get away with it," a lieutenant said in 1970, "we radio the Old Man that we are moving our platoon forward into the bush to search for the enemy. But if there is any risk of getting shot at, we just stay where we are until the choppers come to pick us up."

The fact that the intensity of the Vietnam ground war was waning by 1970 and 1971 also contributed to poor morale in the field. Too much combat can drain a unit but no action can, contrariwise, turn an infantry unit into a mob. For example, in March of '71, the 1st Battalion, 46th Infantry, Americal Division saw little of the NVA around their basecamp, FSB Mary Ann. The men became bored and sloppy and the officers decided recon patrols weren't even worth the effort anymore—until the night the NVA sappers hit. Fifty North Vietnamese overran Mary Ann in the middle of the night, killed thirty-three Americans and wounded seventy-six out of a two-hundred-man company on the hill, and faded into the black before the company could get organized. The

NVA left behind only twelve bodies. Disciplinary action was taken against the commanding general and five other officers.

And yet, most combat units continued to function. Debacles like Mary Ann were rare. Albeit, the effort was at half-step compared to 1965–69, but the American soldier did fight well when combat was forced on him. The men were not cowards; Sp4 Mark Jury, an Army photographer in 1969–70, described that unique mix of courage and hopelessness in poignant detail, "The fact that they wear love beads and peace medallions doesn't mean they can't fight. The kids learn quickly that the best way to stay alive is to kill the guy trying to kill you. And in combat they're ferocious. But once the firefight is over, it's back to being peace and pot lovers. Often their opposition to the military has nothing to do with the moral aspects of Vietnam. It's just that they pick up a battered copy of *Life* magazine and see everybody else skinny-dipping at Woodstock, and that's a hell of a lot better than *'greasing gooks,'* fighting malaria, and maybe going home in a plastic bag."

In more conventional terms, Col. William Hauser, a battalion commander wrote, "What kept them going, in spite of a pervasive sense that the war served no real purpose and the country didn't care, was a combination of pride, mutual interest, and loyalty to good leadership."

Those three ingredients were missing in the rear-echelon support units of the U.S. Army, Vietnam, and that was where the morale problems exploded. Menial jobs in rear outfits were almost always performed without pride, but with a big dose of boredom, bitterness at the privileges of the officers, and frustration at the petty disciplines of the military. Such lobotomized routines were endured when there seemed a worthwhile goal to be reached; take away the mission, and morale hit rock bottom. Adding to the problem of bored, sullen draftees, was the fact that combat units often transferred their drug abusers and malcontents to the rear. By 1970 the combination had turned the Vietnam rear areas into hotbeds of discontent between the career "lifers" and draftees, and between blacks and whites. Drug use flourished and macabre talk of "fragging" was always in the air.

As Lieutenant Bayer commented after he'd been rotated to a desk job with the 4th Division, "They just cruised around, there was no discipline. When I was with the grunts, they called them REMFs—Rear Echelon Motherfuckers. They had nothing to do and their lives weren't on the line. They didn't do anything except sit around and smoke dope and get in trouble. It was real flaky. I thought, Jesus, what kind of place is this? You drive around the perimeter and look at the defenses, bunkers and wire, and it was not very tight. Wire falling down, a few claymores scattered around. The impression was just a general lax attitude."

Added an Americal grunt, "We had tremendous comradeship in the bush, and didn't really like coming to the rear. The dope and race problems were crazy."

The most widespread problem in the rear was drug abuse. In 1965 the Army arrested or investigated forty-five servicemen in Vietnam for using drugs; in 1970 the number was eleven thousand. Marijuana had always been present; even during the gung-ho days of the war, it was not unknown for a young soldier to smoke grass out of curiosity or to relax between operations. But by '70, the drug problem in the U.S. was rampant, many young draftees arrived in Vietnam already having experienced narcotics, and others turned to them to escape the insanity of their situation. There was some drug use in the field by combat units, but most followed the credo explained by an Americal grunt in 1971, "When we got there the first sergeant said, '90 percent of the company are probably heads, but don't smoke in the field because you might get killed or get someone else hurt.' I never saw anyone smoke in the field." Most combat officers would not tolerate drug use in the field, but ignored it in basecamp.

In the rear, though, there was no danger, only restless boredom and rebellion, and when inexpensive but potent heroin (known as skag or smack) appeared on the Vietnamese black market in mid-1970, the problem spread like wildfire. In short order, horror stories were circulating. Said a first sergeant, "The drug situation is horrible, really horrible. . . . In my unit, some of the medics were on heroin, using needles from their own stores. You could see the punctures right up and down their arms." In one four-month period in 1970, seventy-five GIs died of heroin overdose in Vietnam.

By 1971 it was estimated that 10 to 15 percent of the soldiers in Vietnam used heroin and an additional 40 percent smoked marijuana. The army, displaying a certain practicality, ignored pot as a mild problem and concentrated on heroin addiction. Amnesty houses were opened where an addict could turn himself in for medical and psychological treatment without fear of court-martial. The program was ineffective: veteran sergeants considered it a five-day vacation for the malcontent junkies in their units and let their feelings be known when the trooper returned, and it was hard to shake the habit when the frustrations that had spawned it were still present and when the drug was always close at hand. One draftee, who had a history of drug abuse as a civilian and became a heroin addict while with a supply unit in the Mekong Delta, described it: "I lasted a week out of the amnesty house when a buddy talked me into smoking some smack with him behind the barracks. I thought this time I know what I'm doing, I can handle it. But you don't. I saw so many young kids messed up."

The army found no solution to the drug problem. Nor could it remedy another social ill that was carried to Vietnam—racial conflict. As with drugs, there were only rare problems in the infantry; the stress of combat transcended the color of one's skin and it was common for black and white grunts to be the best of friends. But in the rear, there was no bond of fire and the races tended voluntarily to segregate. The problem was not helped by black soldiers who, displaying the racial pride of the time, took to wearing clenched fist amulets, slave bracelets, and greeting other blacks with an elaborate handshake ritual known as the dap. In rear units, intense peer pressure developed among young blacks to ostracize "brothers" who became too friendly with white soldiers. Racial tension was heated by the widespread but mistaken belief that blacks were dying in a higher proportion in relation to their numbers in society. This was not true, but virtually every black draftee believed it and many arrived in Vietnam already convinced they were objects of discrimination.

The average black GI had been as gung-ho as his white counterpart in the beginning, but by 1969, Black Panther and Mau Mau groups were clandestinely organized in some units, and there was much bitter talk about the White Man's War. Unfortunately, for some blacks the solution to their dissatisfaction and racial pride was to strike blindly at their white comrades. In 1969 the crime rate in the U.S. Army, Vietnam, went up, with half of those in the stockade being black. It is important to note that reviews of court-martial decisions show no prejudice; nevertheless, cases of black attacks on white victims accounted for 19.2 percent of murders, 50 percent of attempted murders, 43 percent of aggravated assaults, and 71 percent of robberies.

The military instituted discussion groups for blacks and whites to talk out their gripes, and most strife simmered down to segregation in the mess halls and barracks, a few sullen looks, and relatively peaceful coexistence. But no viable remedy was found and—like back home—there were occasional outbreaks of violence. In August 1968, black inmates at the Long Binh stockade rioted and beat a white inmate to death. In October 1970, at the Americal Division Headquarters in Chu Lai, a fight broke out between the races at an EM Club, turned into a four-hundred-man melee, and left a white soldier shot to death by a black GI. In March, 1971, a white GI killed a black GI in a brawl at Camp Baxter. At the memorial service, black soldiers turned their backs on the chaplain and the American flag and raised their own banner, a red field with a clenched fist and the legend BLACK POWER.

Then there were fraggings—deliberate attempts to kill officers and NCOs by enlisted men. Every war has had such murders, usually the result of a commander callously endangering the lives of his men and the troops responding in kind. In Vietnam, a near-ritual method developed: first a smoke grenade in the officer's tent to warn him; then a tear gas grenade if no reforms had been made; and then as a last resort, a lethal fragmentation grenade. There is no evidence, however, that the rate of fragging in infantry units in Vietnam was any different from WWII or Korea.

But fraggings did make a dramatic rise in rear units. With the initial breakdown of morale in 1969, there were one hundred and twenty-six cases; in '70 the count was 271; and in '71 it had increased to 333 incidents. Certainly every officer or sergeant was not in fear for his life, but there was an air of distrust between the lifers and draftees which caused men to proceed with caution even if there was no immediate threat. All the loose talk about fragging often intimidated officers to the point where just the rumor of such a threat would cause them to change attitudes. In 1969, when fraggings first made an upsurge, the 126 cases resulted in thirty-seven deaths, but in 1971, when the officers realized the enlisted men were serious, the 333 cases resulted in only 12 deaths.

Some fraggings were committed by soldiers especially bitter against abusive commanders or those who did not see the withdrawals as a signal to be more cautious in sacrificing lives for pieces of ground; some happened because innocent officers became symbols of the situation to heroin addicts, black militants, and malcontents, because the loosening of morale and discipline set the stage for criminals in uniform to settle personal vendettas with a grenade. One theory pointed to age as a key factor; the average soldier in WWII was in his late twenties with a wife and a job, whereas the average GI in Vietnam was nineteen, the type more likely to use violence rather than discussion to solve a problem. As reporter Eugene Linden noted, ". . . it seems as though the commanding officer of every unit leads what in any other war would be singled out as a rare 'trouble' unit. . . . A drug counselor with the 101st Airborne told me that for many GIs fighting a war in Vietnam is so confusing and unassimilable that when they are there they feel as though they are in a dream, that they are not really themselves. Because life there is not real, it becomes acceptable to snort skag and frag the sarge."

On one hand, the officer in the rear was expected to accomplish the mission; on the other hand he had to deal with social problems no expert in America could solve. Unlike WWII, where an officer's veteran sergeants associated man-to-man with the enlisted men and were a buffer and personal link between command and troops, the sergeants in the Vietnam rear usually avoided the junkies and draftees below them. Linden wrote, "The overall futility and senselessness of the war makes hollow all the individual acts that constitute it. The Army is stalled in Vietnam; there is no front on which to advance, no cause to fight for that can be convincingly argued, and not even any real sense of withdrawal as we withdraw. . . . The frustrations that spawn fraggings have to do with the collision of a people who don't accept our mission in Vietnam and those who do. We are still killing people in Vietnam; yet, there are no convincing arguments to continue doing so. If you can kill Vietnamese without convincing arguments, you can kill officers too because to the battle-weary grunt the gung-ho, nit-picking officer is as inhuman and remote as the gook."

There were rare counter-fraggings in which career NCOs, discouraged because no hard evidence could bring a young fragger to justice, took matters into their own hands.

Somehow, the U.S. Army continued on in Vietnam, running combat operations with reluctant warriors, trying to keep the rear functioning despite drug, racial, and fragging incidents. Little could be done because the roots of the problems were in the soldiers' weariness with the war itself. The only redeeming factor was that the individual soldier on the frontlines still exhibited a strong bond of loyalty with his comrades. Cpl. Lewis Lawhorn, a black grunt, described it from the heart, "I know that there was problems in the rear, racial incidents back in the rear. But we didn't have time for stuff like that. We were too busy ducking and dodging and trying to stay alive. The North Vietnamese didn't care what color you was when he shot. My outfit—we had people from down south, deep south, we had people from New York, we had people from Massachusetts, different places, different accents—but we all was together as a team. We had blacks, Puerto Ricans, Indians, whites. We had no problems. The white brothers, the blue-eyed brothers we called them. We got along great because, for one thing, we were Marines; we were all there to do our tour and go home. Another thing, we had to depend on each other. That's one thing about being in the infantry, when you're a grunt. You live with each other, you sleep with each other, you cry with each other, you pray with each other. I was friends with everybody in the platoon. We were all friends."

CHAPTER THREE:
Background, Planning, and Mobilization

On 7 January 1971, Lieutenant General Sutherland was in his office at XXIV Corps Headquarters, Da Nang, when Major General Cowles walked in to deliver a sealed letter from Saigon. It was from COMUS-MACV. The directive instructed Sutherland and Lam to go ahead with detailed planning for an attack against Base Areas 604 and 611 in Laos. Abrams's letter said the Laotian operation should commence in February, just after the Tet Lunar New Year holiday. As soon as possible, but no later than 16 January, Sutherland and Lam were to submit their plans for the approval of Abrams and his ARVN counterpart, Gen. Cao Van Vien, Chief of the RVNAF Joint General Staff. That gave them nine days.

After reading the letter, Sutherland immediately met with Lam, who had been informed by an ARVN colonel from the JGS. They decided to include only two more officers, one U.S. and one ARVN, in the immediate planning circle at corps level. They would use a secure area at XXIV Corps HQ for the planning conferences, and all maps, written scenarios, and similar material would remain in that area. Later that day Sutherland called Major Hennessey and Brigadier General Hill to his headquarters. He described the concept of the operation, gave them authority to assemble small planning groups, and detailed their specific responsibilities.

General Hill's 1st Brigade, 5th Mechanized Infantry Division would be the lead element with four main areas of responsibility:

1. To launch a ground attack from the brigade basecamp at Quang Tri north along Route 1 to Dong Ha, then west along Route 9 to the Laotian border

2. To secure Route 9 as the main line of communications to the operation, and to protect the engineer units assigned to upgrade the highway
3. To physically secure Vandegrift, Khe Sanh, and Lang Vei and conduct intensive patrolling in these areas and along Route 9 to keep an NVA counterattack from disrupting the South Vietnamese side of the campaign
4. To construct a pioneer road to Khe Sanh as an alternate LOC in case the NVA severed Route 9 (as they had done during the Siege of Khe Sanh in 1968 against the 26th Marines)

The 101st Airborne was to have an equally vital role in the operation, although in different areas, as Sutherland dictated five jobs to Hennessey:

1. To provide command and control for all U.S. Army Aviation units in the operation, including maintenance support (this to include not only the helicopter, maintenance, and repair units organic to the 101st, but also attached aviation units from the Americal Division, 1st Aviation Brigade, and 1st Marine Air Wing, which would more than double the number of helicopters available to the division)
2. To take over responsibility for the AO of the ARVN 1st Infantry Division (Thua Thien and Quang Tri Provinces) when they moved into Laos
3. To attach the required units to the 5th Mech ground task force
4. To help secure the stretch of Route 9 from Dong Ha to Vandegrift
5. To provide helicopter support for all U.S. and ARVN units committed to the operation, on both sides of the border

From 7 January on, the activity among the senior American and South Vietnamese commanders in MR1 was furious; "With each passing day," Sutherland wrote, "the tempo of planning increased and with it more personnel were added to the combined planning staff. With more people having knowledge of the plans the risk for leaks and compromises increased. A list was maintained of all persons having knowledge of the plan."

Basic concepts began taking detailed form. It was decided that the supply buildup in northern MR1 (Quang Tri and Dong Ha before commencement of the operation; Vandegrift and Khe Sanh after D day) would be initially handled by U.S. logistics exclusively. They would be responsible for the ARVN's supply needs for the first ten days of the operation, thus delaying the need to bring ARVN supply officers into the planning group and avoiding that security mess. As it was, the efforts of General Sweeney's Da Nang Support Command were sufficient to get the needed material in place (Sweeney was informed of the operation on 13 January and assigned to provide all logistical support on the RVN side of the border).

On 8 January Sutherland brought the engineers into the planning. They were to play a vital role in the first stage of the campaign, reopening Route 9 to wheeled traffic to the border, rebuilding the Khe Sanh airstrip for C130 transport aircraft, and constructing the pioneer road. Except for small engineer units assigned to combat divisions, all engineers in Vietnam were under the centralized control of the U.S. Army Engineer Command, Vietnam, in Saigon. Missions were assigned to various units through the Command. Sutherland thought undue strain would be put on security if all echelons of the Engineer Command were made aware of the impending operation so he requested operational control of the engineers headquartered in Da Nang (the 45th Engineer Group, 18th Engineer Brigade); this was granted (effective 19 January), meaning the headquarters elements of the 18th Brigade and Engineer Command were not to question the activities of the 45th Group or request status reports.

Security again hampered the engineers. An on-the-ground inspection of Route 9 and Khe Sanh by the 45th Group commander would alert the NVA, so the engineer colonel could only study aerial photographs. Every bridge on Route 9 from Vandegrift to Khe Sanh was either destroyed or damaged, and over thirty new bridges and culverts would have to be installed. The highway itself was merely a narrow path, overgrown from disuse in many areas. After an aerial recon and two days of planning, the colonel returned with his report that it would take a week to reopen Route 9. Sutherland rejected that answer. He wanted the highway operational within twenty-four hours of D day and envisioned not repairing bridge-by-bridge as they proceeded down the road, but placing the engineer teams and required material at their work sites as the 5th Mech task force pushed through, then simultaneously airlifting in prefabricated bridges and culverts by CH47 Chinook and CH54 Sky Crane helicopters. The engineers went back to the drawing board and worked up a one-day scheme. On 13 January agreement was reached on placing the main supply base at Quang Tri and of the need for two forward bases—one at Ca Lu (Vietnamese name for Vandegrift) and the other at Khe Sanh.

By then the Laotian campaign was basically described as a four-phase effort. Phase I was the U.S. ground attack to the border and the securing of the LOC and airhead to pave the way for the ARVN border crossing in Phase II. Following this, Phase III called for the ARVN to search and destroy in BA 604 and the simultaneous continuation of the U.S. ground effort to keep the supply lines open. Phase IV was the withdrawal sequence which had two options, one in which they would simply pull back after BA 604 had been razed, and the other, which Abrams favored, a fighting withdrawal through BA 611 to wreak more destruction on the NVA sanctuary. As sketched by ARVN I Corps, the South Vietnamese invasion called for an armor element to strike west on Route 9, while infantry units were airmobiled on the northern and southern flanks of the highway to leapfrog to Tchepone in a series of successive and mutually supporting firebase. The key was mobility as provided by U.S. Army aviation.

There were no delusions among the planners that it would not be a costly campaign. In Cambodia the NVA had been hit by surprise and had retreated; in Laos, however, they had before established elaborate defensive positions and they would be fighting with their backs to the wall—the wall being North Vietnam. To lose Laos would be to lose their last buffer between the allies and their homeland. To prevent the Communists from rushing reinforcements to Laos, several cover-and-deception operations were envisioned to confuse Hanoi as to allied intentions. A fifteen-hundred-man U.S. Marine task force and the 7th Fleet were to go station off the coast of North Vietnam, and ARVN units were to assemble along the eastern DMZ to give a show of preparing for an invasion of the North. At the same time, elements of 101st Airborne were to move into the A Shau Valley as a supposed spearhead for further U.S. attacks against those basecamps (these plans were employed and, according to U.S. intelligence, proved highly successful in keeping NVA forces in the A Shau and DMZ from being repositioned to reinforce their comrades in Laos).

On the following day, 14 January, the campaign was given its official operational titles. Phase I, the exclusively American effort, was dubbed Operation Dewey Canyon II. The original Dewey Canyon had been a 1969 U.S. Marine drive in the Khe Sanh area, directed to the south, not the west; this was hoped to have some deception value. The Marine operation also had a dramatic sense of history because during it a regimental commander, who later became Commandant of the Marine Corps, without authorization from higher command, sent one of his companies on a highly successful ambush raid into Laos. The second half of the Dewey Campaign II was named Operation Lam Son 719;

Lam Son was the birthplace of a famous Vietnamese patriot who defeated an invading Chinese army in 1427 A.D., and the numerical designation came from combining the year, '71, with the main highway to be used, Route 9.

Two days later, Generals Sutherland and Lam flew to Saigon with the plans from U.S. XXIV Corps and ARVN I Corps, and presented them to Generals Abrams and Vien. They were approved. That night, U.S. officers left Saigon for Honolulu and Washington to obtain final authorization for Operation Dewey Canyon II/Lam Son 719. Sutherland and Lam, in the meantime, were directed to continue building up their forces on the assumption they would get the go-ahead.

The submitted plans fit General Abrams' wishes almost exactly. The ARVN, though, were not overly enthused. General Vien had supported an invasion all along, but wanted a short hit-and-run raid. His plan called for an airborne attack to Tchepone and an armor push down Route 9; after link-up, they would exit via BA 611, destroying targets along the way. When he saw the more ambitious plans endorsed by MACV, he feared that his objections would interfere with obtaining necessary U.S. fire support, so he did not discuss them with Abrams. President Nguyen Van Thieu, meanwhile, privately concluded that if three thousand ARVN were killed in Laos, he would cancel the operation at that point. The Americans were not informed of these reservations and restrictions.

While XXIV Corps pieced together the big picture, the subordinate units were also organizing for Laos. In the 101st Airborne Headquarters at Camp Eagle, the initial planning group consisted of Major General Hennessey, Col. Don Siebert (Chief of Staff), and Lt. Col. John Bard (G3). It soon became apparent, though, that further planning would have to include officers adept in aviation and logistics. The next meeting included at least four more key officers: Brig. Gen. Sidney B. Berry (Assistant Division Commander for Operations), Brig. Gen. Olin P. Smith (ADC for Support), Col. Edward Davis (CO, 101st Aviation Group), and Lt. Col. Donald E. Rosenblum (CO, Division Support Command). General Hennessey was not present at this meeting; he had rotated home on 15 January. His replacement (Maj. Gen. Thomas Tarpley) was not due until 1 February, leaving Berry in temporary command.

Following the routine briefing that night, Lieutenant Colonel Rosenblum was walking back to his quarters when Lieutenant Colonel Bard called him aside. Bard looked around to ensure that no one was in listening distance, then whispered that several officers in the division were to be made aware of an operation code-named Lam Son 719. A secret meeting was to be held that night. Rosenblum was to tell no one, but was to start thinking about how to support a large ARVN force.

"What is a 'large' ARVN force?" he asked Bard.

"Think about five divisions."

Rosenblum was worried; the 101st Division Support Command did not have such capabilities.

At the meeting, Rosenblum first heard of the plan to disrupt the Ho Chi Minh Trail in Laos. General Berry and Colonel Davis were assigned the monumental task of providing the aviation support. The only word about Rosenblum's DISCOM was some vague talk about "supporting the operation." He tried to pin it down, but no one was really sure what responsibility DISCOM would have. One officer suggested that they would be called to handle setting up of refuel/rearm stations for the helicopters. With that mission in mind Rosenblum bent security to talk with Lt. Col. Ken Jacobs, commander of DISCOM's 426th Support & Service Battalion. He asked what material would be needed to establish helo points for a multi-division force, swearing Jacobs to secrecy and indicating he thought the division was going to conduct a test operation. The list was astronomical.

Rosenblum travelled to XXIV Corps HQ in Da Nang to talk with someone in the logistical or operational field to find out just what was happening. The Corps G4 said he was not up on DISCOM's capabilities, and suggested he see General Sweeney of the Da Nang SUPCOM. He made an appointment with Sweeney that same day and showed him the list. He also mentioned the name Lam Son 719.

Sweeney's eyes widened and he said, "Are you cleared for all this?"

"Yes, I am."

Sweeney rose from his desk and shut all the windows and doors, saying it was all top secret.

"General, the only way I know of to get this equipment is to come to you direct. I have a handwritten list. I have one other copy in my safe back at Camp Eagle. And you and I and one other are the only ones who know about it, but I need this equipment in order to set up these refuel points and rearm points that I think I'm responsible for setting up."

Sweeney said he would do the best he could, and directed Rosenblum to contact Col. Emil Konopnicki, CO, 26th General Support Group, Da Nang SUPCOM.

And so it went. Responsibilities of commanders and units were slowly pieced together. General Berry and Colonel Davis were to control the aviation aspects of the operation (over six hundred helicopters were involved initially) and these helicopter units organic to the 101st Airborne were to be employed:

101st Aviation Group
101st Aviation Battalion
158th Aviation Battalion
159th Aviation Battalion
2d Squadron, 17th Air Cavalry
4th Battalion, 77th Aerial Field Artillery

A large number of aviation units were to be attached to their command, most of them from the 1st Aviation Brigade unless otherwise noted:

14th Aviation Battalion
212th Combat Aviation Battalion
223d Combat Aviation Battalion
71st Assault Helicopter Company
116th Assault Helicopter Company (opcon from the Americal Division)
174th Assault Helicopter Company (opcon from the Americal Division)
132nd Assault Support Helicopter Company
Troop B, 7th Squadron, 1st Air Cavalry
Troop F, 8th Air Cavalry
Troop C, 7th Squadron, 17th Air Cavalry
HMH-463 (opcon from the 1st Marine Air Wing)
HML-367 (opcon from the 1st Marine Air Wing)

To provide fuel and ammunition to these helicopter units, Lieutenant Colonel Rosenblum was assigned construction of five depots, using DISCOM's organic assets:

426th Supply & Service Battalion
801st Maintenance Battalion
326th Medical Battalion
5th Transportation Battalion

In conjunction with these efforts, the 101st Airborne was taxed to provide a ground force to take up the AO of the ARVN 1st Infantry Division and to move on the feint operation into the A Shau Valley.

Headed by Col. Paul F. Gorman (CO, 1st Brigade, 101st Airborne), this task force included four infantry battalions.

The men of the 101st Airborne who were saddling up for Laos were mostly experienced veterans. Even during the withdrawals, the Screaming Eagles conducted aggressive operations and made sporadic contact regularly with the NVA. Their combat spirit was embodied in Sid Berry, a key player in the new operation. He was lean, athletic, his white hair closely cropped, coolly professional, personally brave, a man of old-fashioned ways and values. A graduate of West Point, class of 1948, he was an infantry officer throughout his career: platoon and company commander with the 25th Division in Korea, 1950–51; a senior advisor to the ARVN 7th Division, 1965–66; brigade commander with the 1st Infantry Division in Vietnam, 1966–67. From lieutenant to general, Berry always led from the front. He had been wounded twice and had received four Silver Stars. He arrived for his third Vietnam tour as Assistant Division Commander on 2 July 1970. He was just in time to take charge of the division's FSB Ripcord operation in the mountains between the A Shau and the coastal plains.

The battle for Firebase Ripcord was the most costly U.S. campaign during the time between the Cambodian and the Laotian incursions. It pitted one infantry battalion of the 101st Airborne against the NVA F4 Division, and evolved from the allied response to the NVA buildup in the A Shau Valley following Cambodia. Recon patrols had discovered fabulous bunker systems under the triple-canopy jungle, including complexes carved several stories underground with hospitals, supply depots, and troop bunkers. At the time, Division Intelligence placed several NVA companies in the area, the forerunners, they thought, of enemy divisions who could attack Hue from the developing basecamps. General Hennessey decided to hit them first.

Perhaps the biggest plus regarding Ripcord was the performance of General Berry. Berry had arrived after Ripcord had already commenced but, as Assistant Division Commander, found himself commanding the entire division (General Hennessey, after two years in Vietnam, had taken three weeks' leave).

As it became obvious that Ripcord was going under, Berry was constantly overhead in his C&C ship. While some commanders were more of a nuisance than an asset during combat, breaking in on radios, asking questions, and generally distracting the lieutenants and captains who were trying to fight the war, Berry was too professional for that. He had the deftness to simply listen and calculate ahead, to understand what was happening on the ground, because he'd been in similar circumstances, and to be ready to bring in whatever support was requested by the ground commander. The men appreciated his efforts, even if they were sometimes surprised by them. Three days before the evacuation, Berry spent an hour on Ripcord. After a few mortar rounds dropped in, he knelt beside a young GI who was sitting on the ground in the artillery berm, cleaning a 155mm breechlock. He stuck out his hand and said, "I'm General Berry. What's your name?" The artilleryman looked up astonished, shook the offered hand with an oily one, and exclaimed, "Jesus, what's a general doing here? I thought you'd be back at headquarters or some shit like that!"

Ripcord was just the first action in which Berry proved himself to the Screaming Eagles. He often accompanied infantry companies in the field and his reputation was almost legendary among senior officers, although precious few chose to copy it. Capt. Charles F. Hawkins was proud that it was Berry who pinned on his Silver Star for Ripcord, and he spoke with admiration: "General Berry is one of the few generals I know with any real guts. Once, after Ripcord, when we were working in the FSB Kathryn AO, General Berry landed his C&C ship in the midst of a CA I was conducting. His aide kicked out a ruck and an M-16 and took off with the ship. Berry told me he would be spending the night and not to worry about him, he would join my CP after the dust had settled. He spent the next four hours talking to and working with the troops. He helped them assign sectors of fire, construct foxholes, fire in defensive targets, debriefed recon patrols, you name it. Then he and my RTO dug his foxhole at the CP and we settled in for an evening of discussion. Our big bitch was radio call signs for forward observers, which remained the same and allowed the NVA to identify the units after listening to the FO for a few minutes. Three days later, Berry had the Signal Security Instructions/Signal Operating Instructions completely revamped."

General Berry's professionalism was complemented in kind by the performance of the entire division. By the time of the Laotian incursion, the 101st Airborne Screaming Eagles was arguably the best combat unit still in Vietnam. This stemmed from the generally high quality of its commanders and because it operated in an area where, despite the withdrawals and the toning down of the war, contact was still made on a regular basis. The grunts had no opportunity to get flaky.

Another reason for the relatively good morale was that the 101st was one of the few units which could see progress in their war effort. When they had moved to MR1 during the 1968 Tet Offensive, the outskirts of

Camp Eagle were hotly contested; by 1971 Eagle was a rear base with spit-shined jungle boots and starched fatigues. As Hawkins explained, "Tet 1968 saw the NVA in the city of Hue. Okay, so they're tough guys who can mount an offensive. Where were they in the spring and summer of '68? Kicked back some five to ten kilometers from the population centers. Where were they in '69? Some fifteen to thirty kilometers back in the A Shau Valley where, incidentally, the 101st conducted a brilliant operation culminating in the successful assault on Dong Ap Bia-Hamburger Hill. By the time Lam Son 719 kicked off, we had to strike into Laos to find them and cut supply lines. The point is that each time the infantry grunt took to the bush he believed he would win—maybe not the war, that was someone else's job, but he could and would win his little part of it."

This positive thinking, however, was not enough to sustain even the Screaming Eagles through the withdrawals. As Hawkins continued, "The war wasn't won. But, in my opinion, it wasn't the rifle squads, platoon, company, or battalion that lost it. I've had guys, draftees, come to me just prior to DEROS back to the world and unequivocally state that if they thought the U.S. wanted to win the war, really win it, that they would be happy to stay and fight. They'd be on the first combat assault into Hanoi if they thought it would be won." The point, of course, is that there would never be any attack on Hanoi and, deep down, even the proudest soldiers came to realize their efforts were futile. Morale could not help but be eroded. Sometimes the men sardonically referred to the division as the One-Oh-Worst, and the 1971 issue of the division's yearbook, *Rendezvous With Destiny,* was an underground classic. The cover was a watercolor of several GIs slingloading artillery rounds to a hovering helicopter; a closer examination shows that the young sergeant who painted it had put peace signs on the artillery fuses and had twisted the tree branches in the background to spell FTA—Fuck The Army—the draftees' celebrated phrase.

Yet, the 101st Airborne was still a fine field unit. The NVA gave them no chance to grow rusty from inactivity and most of the men accepted as fact that the best way to survive was to hunt and kill the enemy before they could do likewise to you.

"How did I lead men like this?" asked Captain Hawkins. "By listening to their ideas, incorporating their thinking into my tactical planning, letting them know what we were doing each day and why. By taking weak platoon leaders and putting them where they could do the least harm until they matured. By walking point on a night move. By showing a rifleman how to throw grenades at an NVA bunker and assaulting it with him. By recognizing performance and knowing that each man performs as an individual part of the whole. By making sure the medevac got there or by holding the man in my arms if I knew he wouldn't make it. And a lot more. I think I fit in well with the men. They called me Charlie Oscar, short for CO, I called them by their nicknames and surnames. There were no titles. When I screwed up, one of the NCOs would tell me. My radio operators and I would share food packages from home. The Kit Carson Scout take me by the hand and show me where positions needed more camouflage or where the likely avenues of enemy approach would be. I recall few discipline problems that weren't handled man-to-man."*

Morale and performance in the 101st Airborne were such that even Pfc Bill Warren, an unenthusiastic draftee destined to fight in the Laotian incursion, couldn't help but be impressed, "I would say morale was high and everyone had pride in the 101st. I don't think the 101st was ever disgraced like other units were. Like disobeying orders, retreating, fraggings, and so forth. The drugs were not widespread and never used in the field. The racial problem that other units had was nonexistent, for everyone knew the next day you would be covering him and he would be covering you. The morale of the men was high because we had USO shows, good food, and what we used to call no Mickey Mouse Bullshit, which means we were not harassed with typical Army waste-your-time nonsense. The leadership was good. We were not asked to do stupid things in or out of the field, or take unnecessary chances. We never stayed in a safe position or faked our coordinates. We never avoided contact and always fought our hardest when we encountered the enemy. As a matter of fact, we had a lot of men who were gung-ho and loved a good fight. I am still proud to this day that I served in this unit and with its gallant men."

The 1st Brigade, 5th Mechanized Infantry Division—the other major American ground unit in the operation—did its planning at its headquarters at the Quang Tri Combat Base (between Hue City and Dong Ha on Route 1). The brigade was equipped with M48A3 main battle tanks, M551 Sheridan armored reconnaissance assault vehicles, and M113 armored personnel carriers.

The brigade commander, Brigadier General Hill, was a fine leader, an infantry officer who had won the Distinguished Service Cross and Silver

* From a letter to author, 1984.

Star in Korea and Vietnam combat. He was respected by men throughout the ranks, including General Sutherland who commented that Hill was "a very effective and low-key commander; he went about his job, didn't cry wolf, and carried out all assigned missions." Hill's brigade was to be the lead element in Operation Lam Son 719, charged with securing the area along the border and then holding it. His task force was tailored primarily around ground-combat elements, both organic and attached:

2d Battalion, 1st Infantry (opcon from the Americal Division)
4th Battalion, 3d Infantry (opcon from the Americal Division)
1st Battalion, 11th Infantry
1st Battalion, 61st Infantry (Mechanized)
P Company, 75th Infantry (Rangers)
3d Battalion, 187th Infantry (opcon from the 101st Airborne)
1st Squadron, 1st Cavalry (opcon from the Americal Division)
E Troop, 1st Cavalry, 11th LIB (opcon from the Americal Division)
3d Squadron, 5th Cavalry (assigned to the 9th Division but permanently opconned to the 1/5 Mech)
A Troop, 4th Squadron, 12th Cavalry
H Troop, 17th Cavalry (opcon from the Americal Division)
C Battery, 6th Battalion, 11th Artillery (opcon from the Americal Division)
5th Battalion, 4th Artillery
C Battery, 1st Battalion, 82d Artillery (opcon from the Americal Division)
A Battery, 3d Battalion, 82d Artillery (opcon from the Americal Division)
A Company, 7th Engineer Battalion
C Company, 26th Engineer Battalion (opcon from the Americal Division)
11th Support Battalion (Provisional)
75th Support Battalion
298th Signal Company
B Company, 23d Medical Battalion (opcon from Americal)

It was an impressive force in numbers, Hill was a good commander—but the troops were mostly combat green. The brigade AO was northern MR1 and the NVA in the area generally had been content to remain elusive. To the grunts of the 5th Mech, the war consisted of endless patrolling where they rarely if ever saw a "gook," but were sometimes made bloody by booby traps, rockets, and quick ambushes. By the time Hill took command in August 1970, he inherited a brigade chafing with frustration, bitter over unavenged casualties, abounding with problems. The rear areas at Dong Ha and Quang Tri had become hotbeds of drug use and racial conflict, many of the blacks organizing into bullying cliques, and fraggings were not unknown. The grunts had pinned a cynical label to the brigade—"The Worst of the Fifth."

The brigade was significantly beefed up with components of the Americal Division, a unit also growing rusty by 1971. The Americal had become the hard-luck outfit of Vietnam, one which had more than its share of incompetent officers and confusing operations, which had the worst fragging and drug-abuse rates, which had been rubbed raw by the booby-trap war. The massacre at My Lai and the case of an Americal general charged with shooting civilians from his helicopter cast a shadow over the entire division.

The men of the 5th Mech and the Americal were not cowards. They were generally unenthusiastic because of the withdrawals, demoralized and bitter because their patrols seemed to produce nothing but amputees. When the shooting war was finally forced upon them during Operation Lam Son 719, it brought out the worst in some, but the best in most.

With the initial planning and confirmation completed in mid-January, the tempo of activity in northern MR1 increased to the point that, despite the emphasis on security, it was obvious something big was coming. Thousands of troops from various commands were alerted: MACV, USARV, XXIV Corps, the 101st Airborne, 5th Mech, Americal, 1st Aviation Brigade, 1st Marine Air Wing, 1st Signal Brigade, the Support Commands, Transportation Command, Engineer Command. Men and materiel from all quarters of Vietnam converged north by road, sea, and air.

Many of the Americans caught up in the operation were support troops who had virtually no combat experience. Their reaction to the confusion and secrecy of the movements around them was a mixture of dread and nervous excitement. The one common trait among most of these support units was that they were, in a word, flaky. One such unit saddling up was the 39th Transportation Battalion, 26th General Support Group, Da Nang Support Command, USARV. And one soldier typical of the flaky attitude was Sp4 John J. Carney, the battalion mail clerk. The first word he had that something big was coming was a remark from his Vietnamese hootch maid; then three truck companies arrived to augment the battalion, they moved from Camp Eagle to Quang Tri, and the rumors started flying.

The general consensus among the enlisted men was that they were getting ready to invade North Vietnam. For the first time, Carney thought, things got tight and a sense of esprit de corps actually gripped the battalion. For the first time there seemed to be a purpose—no carting truckloads of soda anymore but hitting the enemy where it hurt. Carney was amazed at the transformation among the GIs at such a prospect; short-timers, guys who didn't care, dudes whose major concern previously had been to have enough dope to pass the time, all seemed suddenly motivated.

It was the only time Carney saw such high morale in his battalion, for he was not a model soldier and the 39th Transportation was not a model component of the U.S. Army. Carney, who was twenty, came to the Army unwillingly. He'd grown up poor in a Massachusetts housing project, with a laborer father who moved from job to job and a mother who spent her nights playing bingo. His draft notice had come right after high-school graduation but, troubled over the war, his thoughts honed down to one issue: could he think of any reason to die for South Vietnam? He couldn't and when a favorite relative asked him to come live with her in Nova Scotia, he decided he would. He tried to talk to his father about it, but was quickly cut off with, "If you go to Canada, you can't step back in my house." Carney was surprised at such an outburst. His father was not a stern man; he usually just went to work, came home drunk, and didn't talk to him. The only other alternative would have been a college deferment but lack of money and poor grades made that impossible, so he finally did what he hated: he enlisted in the army. Carney was sent to medics school but did not last. The army said it was because he failed an examination; Carney said that he and several others who had signed an antiwar petition were all eventually kicked out on one pretense or another.

The army retrained Carney as a clerk and in July 1970 shipped him to Vietnam. During processing at Tan Son Nhut, the NCO behind the counter rattled off a regulation that clerk-typists were supposed to be cross-trained as drivers, and assigned him as a truck driver with the 666th Truck Company of the 39th Transportation Battalion. Carney was much too sensitive and insecure for Vietnam and it wasn't long before he was devastated. On his first day in the company, the first sergeant tore the strand of beads from around his neck (a gift from his sister), then shouted at him to shine his jungle boots.

That first night with the 666th, he was assigned a cot inside a hootch occupied by several southern NCOs. Carney lay there, thoroughly miserable, as the old sergeants drank whiskey and listened to country and western tapes, until he finally had to get out and talk with someone. He ran into some of the company truckers and fell in with their talking and laughing. They were passing weed; Carney didn't know if it was peer pressure or what, but it just seemed natural, and he got high for the first time in his life. It mellowed out all his fears and anxieties. Before long, he was getting stoned every day. After a few lessons with the trucks, he started with the convoys. He lasted a week. He didn't know how to handle a big truck, was overwhelmed by the whole depressing atmosphere of lifer sergeants and abundant drugs and, when a convoy he was on took sniper fire, he cracked. The company commander sent him back to Camp Eagle to rest. While there, he heard that, if you broke your eyeglasses, it took a month for replacements to arrive, so he smashed his and hung around battalion showing how well he could type and do paperwork. He was finally cut orders to Headquarters & Headquarters Company.

Three days in-country, Carney had been sitting with his company on benches at an outdoor movie. There was a sudden explosion and Carney jerked around to see a hootch blowing up. He dove under the benches, but everyone else just began hooting and laughing, telling him, "Don't worry, it's just the first sergeant's hootch." The sergeant wasn't in it that time; but later some men in the 666th got him with a frag. They heard that the old sergeant went home with one leg.

For Carney, the worst of the lifers was the battalion commander. One incident in particular earned for the colonel hatred of the draftees. The scuttlebutt was this: a convoy was out in a monsoon storm that winter and had stopped on one side of a flooded river near Quang Tri because the convoy commander did not trust the bridge in the weather. Since they were only carrying soda and PX goods, he radioed the CO for permission to turn back. But the colonel gave him a direct order to keep moving. Some of the jeeps made it, but the first truck on the rain-slicked bridge slid off into the swollen river and two soldiers were drowned. The colonel was just trying to play the tough commander again, Carney thought, and the story, true or not, was widely believed by the enlisted men.

Things grew ugly in the battalion. The group Carney smoked dope with decided to frag the colonel. They planned to wire a claymore mine to the commo wires outside the battalion operations hootch so that when he picked up the field phone it would set off the claymore and send seven hundred steel balls exploding through the plywood wall and into him. They stole a claymore. They never used it. Perhaps they were afraid, but Carney said it was because they could never catch the colonel alone and they didn't want to kill an innocent bystander.

Carney was amazed that the colonel survived his tour in Vietnam but, even when the battalion was in formation for his change-of-command ceremony, the draftees stamped one more mark of rebellion on him. During the night, someone painted a peace symbol on the helo pad so it would be the first thing the new commander saw when he choppered in. He boarded the helicopter and left, Carney noted, "looking like a tired, sick old man. He was shaking."

But such disputes were temporarily forgotten when they headed for Quang Tri. They set up in the noisy tent cities that were going up to accommodate the influx of troops, and prepared for what they thought was to be the invasion of North Vietnam. They were rear-echelon troops about to experience their first taste of the shooting war in Vietnam.

In January 1971, the ARVN launched a second offensive in Cambodia. On 19 January the Department of the Army authorized the detailed plans for Operation Dewey Canyon II/Lam Son 719.

On 20 January, XXIV and I Corps completed the draft of the operations order.

On 21 January, XXIV and I Corps received approval of their plan.

On 22 January, XXIV and I Corps revised and finalized the operations order.

On 23 January, rumors began circulating in earnest throughout Da Nang and Hue that a major allied push was coming sometime after the Tet Lunar New Year.

On 25 January, information was received by MACV that the Communists had some knowledge of the impending operation; also that day, a XXIV Corps Forward Staff (twenty officers and fifteen enlisted men) was selected and briefed.

On 26 January, Generals Abrams and Vien, with Ambassador Ellsworth Bunker, presented the plan to President Thieu for his final approval. A former infantry division commander, Thieu gave his consent.

On 28 January, intelligence reported the NVA were reinforcing their units in Laos. At that time, the U.S. had approximately nine thousand, and the ARVN twenty thousand combat and support troops slated for the operation. MACV estimates, at the time, put ten thousand NVA combat troops in BA 604, with the ability to reinforce with thirty thousand more. A five-day news embargo was imposed by Abrams as a security measure.

The campaign was to begin on the next day, 29 January 1971.

CHAPTER FOUR:
The Road to Khe Sanh

Sgt. Raymond C. Keefer had been fighting for a long time. In a sense, his entire life had been a struggle. He was born on a chicken farm in Maryland. His father died when he was three, and Keefer dropped out of school, hitting the streets when he was fifteen. He was on his second tour in Vietnam, all of it with A Troop, 1st Squadron, 1st Cavalry, Americal Division; and now he was twenty-one, a long-haired, mustached, and cynical veteran.

His first tour had been back in '68 and '69, a grotesquely bloody experience when he was still a gung-ho kid. The cav was the division's fire brigade, dispatched from firefight to firefight, sometimes finishing one battle only to be immediately sent to another unit in trouble. In those situations, they would break jungle back to Route 1, block off the highway to civilian traffic with their tanks and APC tracks, and Chinooks would drop cargo nets of ammunition and blivets of diesel fuel. Then they'd hit the throttles, pass a joint, and haul ass down the road toward the sound of shooting. When friends were killed, the grunts wanted revenge and Keefer could remember actually being enthused going on a search-and-destroy mission, the tracks on line, jets shrieking low to tumble napalm canisters on the treeline and village ahead, the colonel buzzing over in his C&C, the adrenaline pumping as they swept forward, firing on line, lighting up anything that moved.

That had all changed by the time Keefer returned to Alpha Troop in 1970. There were no more bloody firefights. The patrols were all routine, lackadaisical meanderings through villes and aimless foot patrols through treelines. They spent the days simply moving from one point on the map to the next, half-heartedly poking around for the enemy, and rarely finding anything. The withdrawals were well under way and procedures were becoming so garrison-like it was almost a joke: they received an order to use their .50-caliber machine guns only on enemy bunkers and concentrations, not to waste the expensive ammunition on lone individuals. Keefer thought, man, I don't even want to hear that. You see a dink, you burn him with anything you have.

He quickly noticed, though, that few of the men had the desire to "kill gooks" anymore. It didn't seem that they minded being in Vietnam, that much (it was, after all, interesting), but with the way things were going, nobody seemed interested in getting shot at for any reason. It wasn't long before Keefer began seeing things the same way; sometimes, on patrol, he'd just halt the column in a brushy grove, radio the captain that they were on the move without finding anything, and sit down to smoke grass and snort smack. Why go looking for a booby trap, was the rationale, when we're all going home soon? He thought the enemy had a corresponding outlook; they knew the Americans were pulling out, and Alpha Troop was not hit constantly as it was on his first tour.

In that environment, Keefer found his own officers to be the biggest threat. One platoon leader was resented because his gung-ho zeal to kill Communists was much greater than his willingness to take personal risks. He couldn't read a map or figure out a compass so the platoon was constantly getting lost in the coastal sand dunes or in the jungle. Even the captain seemed nervous about his abilities. Keefer thought, he's kind of like a colonel in his own right, in his own little world buzzing around. As the most combat-experienced soldier in the platoon, Keefer felt he was running things. It finally evolved to the point where the lieutenant took him aside before each patrol and asked him to come up with the plan. Keefer carried his own set of maps and the lieutenant usually agreed with his recommendations; sometimes when they disagreed, the lieutenant would shout, "Okay, then fuck it, you spoiled brat." Sometimes the platoon leader would come up with something needlessly dangerous and would not budge; then Keefer and the grunts would politely tell him to go to hell. The lieutenant would threaten to court-martial them for it and finally just go away.

The situation finally came to a heated confrontation one blistering day when the platoon was working a dismounted foot patrol through some parched, listless villes outside Da Nang. Keefer was talking with a friend of his, Pfc Ollie from Baltimore, when the lieutenant walked up. He gave Ollie an order—something so idiotic, Keefer thought, that he couldn't even remember what it was—and Ollie said no way. The lieutenant got pissed and, to show who was boss, told Ollie to take the point.

Ollie, a platoon old-timer, a wild man with his front teeth knocked out, said he wouldn't go.

The lieutenant said it was a direct order.

Pfc Ollie looked at him. "Fuck you, I ain't taking point."

The lieutenant turned to Keefer, "You heard him refuse a direct order," then screamed at Ollie that he was going to bring him up on court-martial charges when they returned to basecamp—and Ollie, suddenly levelling his M-16 at the lieutenant's chest, snapped, "You ain't back yet, motherfucker! I wouldn't do too much talking if I was you!"

The lieutenant stepped back, eyes wide, babbling that Keefer would be a witness at the court-martial. Keefer smiled and said he hadn't seen a damn thing.

The next day, as they continued the foot patrols down a stream in a ville, Ollie called Keefer up. He had found an M-79 grenade-launcher round in the dirt. It didn't look booby-trapped, but Keefer prepared to wire it with explosives anyway—destroying it if it was a trap, denying its use to the enemy if it wasn't. Before he had a chance, the lieutenant came up asking what the delay was. Ollie pointed to the grenade and said they were getting ready to blow it in place. The lieutenant glanced at the M-79 round, then at the grunts gathered around, and said, "That's ridiculous. That's not booby-trapped." With that he snatched it up and threw it into the stream. Keefer instantly boiled with anger—if it had been rigged, the lieutenant's impatience would have made casualties of them all—and he swung up his M-16, snarling, "Look. If you ever do something that stupid again, I'll blow your head off. You won't have to worry about having any hassles with Ollie or anybody else in the platoon. There ain't no way in the world I'm going to put up with having some stupid sonuvabitch like you getting me killed over here."

The platoon had barely simmered down from the two hot-headed fragging threats when the captain recalled them to Da Nang. Once there, they were told they would be going up north for an unidentified operation, and to clean out their vehicles, pick up ammunition, and repair weapons and engines. The GIs milled around, talking with friends from other units, but no one knew what was going on. They finally got down to sweating as they loaded their APCs and Sheridan tanks with crates of ammo. They were finally getting ready to move out when Keefer noticed that the lieutenant was nowhere to be found. He asked around and found that the lieutenant had previously been slotted for an R&R leave out of Vietnam. If he gave a damn about his men, Keefer thought, he would have stayed for the operation up north. Bastard weaseled out of it. But then Keefer caught himself: Well, why shouldn't he? We really don't take orders from him and he's afraid of half of us. The platoon was to be led by its platoon sergeant.

Noisy confusion abounded as the 1/1 Cav headed for the U.S. Navy docks where they boarded transport ships. The flotilla, crammed with men and vehicles, steamed into the deep blue glitter of the South China Sea and headed north along the coast. After four hot, cramped days at sea, the transport ships followed the Perfume River to the U.S. Navy boat ramp detachment at Hue City. The cavalry squadron was put ashore, reorganized, and then it hit Route 1. They drove nonstop. The grunts knew of only one target this far north, and their talk was: "We're going to invade North Vietnam."

On 28 January, General Hill held the operational briefing for Dewey Canyon II. His battalion commanders and a few select company commanders gathered in the 1/5 Mech TOC at Quang Tri and, for the first time, received solid information on what the growing tempo in the area meant. The operation was ultrasecret, Hill cautioned, and subordinates were only to be briefed the next day, after the task force had left Quang Tri where the GIs had contact with the locals.

Hill explained that their brigade was to secure Route 9 all the way to the Laotian border so an ARVN force could roll down and invade Laos from that beachhead. They were to depart after midnight, 29 January, leaving Quang Tri on Route 1, obtaining additional units at Dong Ha, then advance west on Route 9. At a mountain nicknamed the Rockpile, where the highway took a southern turn, Vandegrift Combat Base was to be secured, followed by Khe Sanh, Lang Vei, and, finally, the border. Vandegrift and Khe Sanh were abandoned U.S. Marine firebases with nothing left but overgrown bunkers. As a security measure, the halfway point to Vandegrift was to be referred to as Ca Lu, a nearby village. Radio silence was to be maintained until the lead elements passed Mai Loc (between Dong Ha and the Rockpile) or made contact with the enemy, so the NVA would not immediately know the location of the mechanized column. The road march to Vandegrift would resemble, it was hoped, a routine artillery raid (as in the past, when 5th Mech ground units had secured areas near Vandegrift, brought in artillery batteries, shelled suspected NVA supply trails around Khe Sanh, then returned to Quang Tri); after the size of the buildup became obvious, it was hoped the enemy would suspect a thrust into the DMZ, not Laos.

Hill assigned the 1/77 Armor as lead element to Vandegrift, where the tank battalion would reestablish the firebase, while the 1/1 and 3/5

Cav would continue the push to Khe Sanh. Since Route 9 turned into a dirt trail at Vandegrift, engineer units were attached to the cav to widen the road and install bridges. In addition, three infantry battalions were to be airmobiled along Route 9 between Vandegrift and Khe Sanh to secure the road's flanks: 1/11 on the Khe Sanh plateau itself, 4/3 in the middle, and 3/187 furthest east, up to the western edge of the new 1/77 AO. Simultaneously, the 3/5 Cav was to begin constructing the pioneer road from the Rockpile to Khe Sanh.

When General Hill and his staff concluded the briefing, the commanders quickly caught jeeps and helicopters back to their units. They had only a few hours to organize: D day was set for 0400 hours on 29 January, 1971. The weather had turned unexpectedly foul. Heavy fighting was expected.

Under Hill's plan, the point went to an armor-infantry task force organized around the 1st Battalion, 77th Armor, and commanded by Lt. Col. Richard Meyer. Meyer's battalion was the only one in Vietnam still equipped with the heavy and sturdy M48 tanks. He was to proceed north on Route 1 with B and C Companies in the lead, followed by the Scout Platoon, Mortar Platoon, and Hq&Hq. Continuing west on Route 9 from Dong Ha, other units already in the field were to link up under Meyer's command to secure Vandegrift. These units included: A and C Companies 1/61 Mech Infantry; A Troop 4/12 Cav; B Battery 5/4 Artillery; and various Vietnamese Regional Force units to patrol the flanks of the road. Such an organization was in keeping with the artillery raid cover concept, of the type 1/77 Armor had executed a month before.

Meyer prepared his tankers for the move, organizing and coordinating with his Executive Officer, Maj. Dan Wilson, and his Operations Officer, Maj. Bill Murphy. Meyer was an ex-staff sergeant from River Rouge, Michigan, a family man in his forties on his fourth tour of duty in Vietnam. He'd seen action in that time with MACV and the 5th, 9th, and Americal Divisions, but it had all been in staff positions. Except for brief periods as an acting commander, the tank battalion was his first combat command and he was proud that General Hill, whom he greatly respected, had picked him to spearhead the operation.

Mostly, though, he simply wanted to get his men in the field on a viable combat operation. The battalion had been growing restless at Quang Tri; the bitterness of the patrols, the despair brought on by the withdrawals, and the abundance of heroin and marijuana at Quang Tri had presented Meyer with a volatile situation. His XO and S3 were brand new to him because their predecessors had been attacked only two weeks before. It had happened on another depressing, do-nothing night at Quang Tri. Several blacks in the Radar Section of Hq&Hq Company refused to turn down their stereo in the maintenance hootch at two or three in the morning. A disgruntled and sleepy GI fetched Maj. Mike Davis, the XO, and Maj. Bob Degen, the S3. They ordered the soldiers to turn down the stereo, were obeyed, then told two of the blacks from another unit to leave. In defiance, they turned the stereo back up; an angry major yanked the cord out—and suddenly one brother, Sp4 Alfred Flint, drew a .22 pistol and opened fire. He shot them both in the head, killing Degen, a West Pointer, and seriously wounding Davis. In minutes, xenon searchlights were trained on the troop barracks, the soldiers were ordered to fall out in formation while MPs searched for Flint and the murder weapon. The battalion was convulsed with turmoil, and Flint eventually got thirty years hard labor.

The withdrawals had taken away a goal for the GIs of 1/77 Armor and the boredom of Quang Tri was robbing them of whatever discipline they might still have mustered. Meyer was sick of such problems. He wanted his battalion in a major combat operation that would give the men a chance to act like American soldiers. He knew they had the capability to win but, in a place like Quang Tri, all they did was boil with frustration.

In the 1/77 area of Quang Tri, the sniper section of Hq&Hq Company was indulging in late night revelries in their private hootch. The eight volunteers for sniper duty were downing beers and trading war stories when the leader of the battalion Scout Platoon, a Lieutenant Revelak, walked in. He was obviously keyed up and in a hurry. He told the snipers to be prepared to move out by 0300 hours atop the Scout's tracks.

Sp4 Harold Spurgeon pointed to all their gear. "Everything?"

"Just your fighting loads," Revelak answered, "enough to sustain yourselves for awhile."

The snipers were impressed. There had been a number of rumors that the brigade was going to be pulled out of Vietnam and the lieutenant's urgency confirmed their suspicions. They couldn't think of anything else this important so late in the game.

"We're always getting screwed on transportation," Spurgeon continued. "Just exactly which armored personnel carriers do you want us to ride on so we don't have to argue with your Scouts?"

Lieutenant Revelak made a quick head count and said someone would meet them and direct them onto the last three APCs of the Scout Platoon. Then he was gone as quickly as he'd come. The snipers packed their gear into rucksacks with aluminum frames. Then the ones still buzzed from the party slept it off, crashed on their cots, and the rest waited nervously. At around three in the morning, a GI stuck his head into their hootch and told them it was time to go. They hefted their rucks and filed to an adjacent conex box where a supply sergeant, using a flashlight to check serial numbers, issued them their M-14 rifles, sniper scopes, and boxes of match ammunition.

The vehicles were forming up several hundred yards away, the Scout tracks parked in single file; the snipers climbed aboard, Spurgeon sitting on the back of the last APC. He looked around. The whole camp was in motion, vehicles moving, dust flying in the headlights. They slowly clanked forward a hundred yards towards the edge of the perimeter and then sat idling in the dark, the GIs repeating the old joke of hurry-up-and-wait, but not too harshly because it was obvious that something big was on its way. And it did not look like any withdrawal. Most of the men nestled among their packs on the vehicles, trying to snatch a bit of sleep, but Spurgeon could only stare with excitement. He couldn't believe the volume of the engine noise around him. To his front, all he could see was a line of red taillights, and behind him, more vehicles had moved up, forming a line of white headlights. There seemed to be no end to the column, and Spurgeon shook his partners awake in glee.

Hal Spurgeon had come to Vietnam for combat and it looked as if he was going to get his chance. The oldest son born to a career U.S. Navy man and a Japanese mother, he was a handsome mixture of races, thick black hair, strong features, a thin mustache, and cold, flinty eyes. He was a gung-ho, nineteen-year-old kid without any responsibilities back home, and to him the war was an adventure. He had thrived on the television combat footage, had decided to join the army because they had the highest weekly casualty figure in the papers, and three days out of high school, he had signed his enlistment papers. He didn't care about the political or moral questions. Vietnam was simply the place to let loose the energies that got him in trouble back home. He loved it. Us against them in the bush, he thought, us against us in the rear; all problems solved with an M-16.

Yet, even though he'd been in-country for fifteen months and had been in the Cambodian invasion, he wasn't satisfied. By a draftee's definition, Spurgeon had already done enough, winning an Army Commendation Medal for Valor for blowing apart a wounded VC with an M-60 during a five-minute skirmish in the Mekong Delta, and picking up a Purple Heart from a minor booby-trap wound. Mostly, though, he'd just been bored. He'd never been in a heavy firefight or seen a living, fighting enemy soldier. He wanted more out of Vietnam and was willing to take nonsensical risks in the field for a little excitement; some of his comrades found him downright dangerous to be with. Most of all, he wanted to line up a "dink's" head in the crosshairs of his rifle and squeeze the trigger.

That's why he'd extended his tour, why he'd volunteered for the battalion snipers, and that's why he was enthused to see the battalion gearing up for a major combat operation. Spurgeon didn't think it was to be an historical event—even as he sat atop the APC, he couldn't help but reflect that the American public didn't care about them—but it was a moment of personal glory. He stared at the tremendous armor column, thinking it was like the Roman army on the march, or like a scene from Gettysburg; it was the glory part of war, standing and looking invincible, preparing to attack. For all their griping and reluctance, Spurgeon thought most of the soldiers felt as he did: "Men say that they didn't like battles or the war, but at those exact moments you would have had to physically remove many of them from their vehicles if you told them they couldn't go. It appeared, on that particular morning, that others were not immune to adventure either."

By 0400 hours, the tanks and armored personnel carriers of 1/77 Armor were on line at the north gate of the Quang Tri Combat Base. Previously, Lieutenant Colonel Meyer had assembled the men in the mess hall; he had told them they were heading into likely heavy combat and that he saw it as his job to get as many back alive as possible. To do that, he said, they would have to cooperate; to not shed helmets and flak jackets because it gets hot; to follow orders. With the battalion ready to go, he climbed into a jeep and the lead tanks rolled onto the hard surface of Route 1.

It was still dark and a heavy ground fog blanketed the road; Meyer thought it looked like a WWII newsreel. They drove with only their blackout lights on, maintaining radio silence as they reached Dong Ha and rendezvoused with the 3/5 Cavalry. They left the gates, making a left onto Route 9, as the attached units began rolling out of the fog of the Cam Lo River valley to link up with the convoy. Shortly after dawn, as they were travelling in the hill country east of Mai Loc, Meyer left his jeep to take his place in the fifty hatch of the lead tank. They had passed the Rockpile and were on the southern leg of Route 9 when he began receiving calls from General Hill. There had been no encounters with the NVA and Meyer had no intention of breaking radio silence.

By mid-morning, Meyer's tank was crashing through the brush of Vandegrift, nestled in a lush green valley surrounded by jungled ridges. Soon General Hill helicoptered in and shouted at Meyer for ignoring his radio calls; the general had just been naturally nervous, and soon began asking about the tactical situation. Hill and Meyer enjoyed a good rapport.

By noon 1/77 Armor was digging in at Vandegrift.

The armor left Quang Tri at intervals to avoid bunching up on the roads, and it was well after daybreak before the Scout Platoon and the hitchhiking sniper team rolled out of Quang Tri. The sun was up by then, burning away the fog, and Sp4 Spurgeon sat enjoying the ride and listening to the radio inside the track. The talk was not of combat, but of maintaining distance between units on the highways to avoid traffic jams.

By around two in the afternoon, the Scouts clanked down the southern dip of Route 9, and Lieutenant Revelak radioed to pull into a roadside dirt clearing a few yards to their left. They sat idling for about twenty minutes and Spurgeon soaked up the scenery, feeling good in the sun, content with being back in the field. To their right rear, the Rockpile rose like a volcanic island from the brushy flatlands between it and the road. Craters and tread marks scarred the flatlands from operations long past. To their left down the road, Spurgeon was surprised to see literally an anthill of GIs: tanks, tracks, jeeps, vehicles of every description, self-propelled artillery pieces, engineer equipment, tents going up, soldiers hustling back and forth.

They were still paused in the clearing when Spurgeon heard two shrieks begin a high whining descent from the direction of the Rockpile. The rush became louder. They stared over their shoulders into a vacant blue sky and, suddenly, two explosions boomed fifty yards to their front, raising mushroom clouds of dirt and debris. Spurgeon saw the GIs ahead instantly slam shut the hatches of their APCs, but he and the other snipers stayed topside, not catching on yet and feeling curious. Two more rounds exploded, one on each side. Spurgeon, astonished that they hadn't been touched, was grooving on the whole thing. Inside the APC, he could hear Lieutenant Revelak's voice screaming over the radio to the artillery support:

"Check fire, check fire, check fire!"

"All missions have stopped. Are you still taking fire? Over."

"Affirmative."

"Standby. . . . All friendlies have stopped firing. Must be bad guys. Over."

"Roger."

Lieutenant Revelak swung his APC back onto the highway and they hauled ass, one or two more rounds exploding behind them. Once inside the developing Vandegrift perimeter, the snipers dismounted, met up with the commander of Hq&Hq Company, and were shown to a hole in the ground that was to be their new home.

The armor spearhead had paved the way for the influx of troops, including the airmobile insertion of three infantry battalions to secure Route 9 from Vandegrift to Khe Sanh. The grunts were in the rear, at the time, and it was a truism that the U.S. Army infantry units that patrolled the Vietnamese countryside in '71 changed completely when they were pulled out of the field. The rests—standdowns—only lasted two or three days, sandwiched between weeks or months in the bush and, inside the safety of basecamp, even the sharpest field units unwound to the point of ill-discipline.

The 3d Battalion, 187th Infantry, 101st Airborne Division was a good combat outfit, but was no exception to the rebellion of standdown. The dramatic change that came over the men was a shock, at first, for Sp4 Michael E. Daugherty, the senior RTO in the Second Platoon of D Company. Daugherty was twenty-two, bright, a tough kid from Fall River, Massachusetts, who was raised by his grandmother and had gotten out of school with a young bride and a factory job. The draft notice came in February 1970, and he was in Vietnam by August. His first assignment had been with the Triple Deuce, a mech infantry battalion of the 25th Division near Saigon. In October, the battalion stood down and the unit colors went home with the withdrawals, while the remaining men were reassigned to other units. Daugherty drew the Screaming Eagles, and was pinned with a routine Army Commendation Medal and Purple Heart in the mass ceremony prior to the dissolving of the unit. Actually, Daugherty had been wounded twice; the first time had been when the VC had turned around a U.S. claymore mine and he'd caught some light shrapnel in the snafu, and then again in October when his APC had hit a mine which peppered him with shrapnel and cracked several ribs.

The change that took over when they hit the rear, which Daugherty found most noticeable and shocking, was the stratification between black and white soldiers. He'd seen it first with the 25th, when they would come clanking into basecamp atop their dusty tracks. The blacks on the road would throw the clenched fist of Black Power, and their brothers on the APCs would shout and smile and throw power too; some of the white troopers would look with disgust and raise a clenched fist with the other hand curled over it—White Supremacy. Daugherty didn't do that, but was irritated when two brothers meeting each other would go through the elaborate dap ritual; he and a buddy took to mocking it by playing patty-cake when they saw blacks doing it. Daugherty's squad leader in the 25th was a black sergeant who was a great soldier in the field; back at basecamp, he wouldn't even talk to the whites in his squad, stayed with the brothers, and looked ashamed to be seen with whites.

The race problem existed with the 101st Airborne at Camp Evans also. The blacks in the 3d of the 187th were particularly militant, having been organized, by an angry black soldier, into a paramilitary clan, complete with a chain-of-command and identifying arm bands. In the battalion area, each company had a row of ramshackle hootches used as barracks and the blacks seized one of the shacks as their own, a place in which to smoke dope, listen to soul music, and talk about the burden of the "White Man's War." Blacks from the whole battalion gathered there, men from the rifle companies as well as clerks and supply people who would have been dismissed as REMFs if not for the allegiance of brotherhood. The white GIs called it the Ghetto of the Harlem Hootch and some, like Daugherty, thought it was a disgrace. For example, there were seven blacks in his platoon, four of whom were fine field soldiers. The other three were AWOL and hiding in the Harlem Hootch.

The Harlem Hootch did, in fact, become a haven for the malcontents and drug addicts. It was a constant irritant to the career men. On the battalion's Christmas 1970 standdown, the battalion executive officer got drunk in the Officer's Club and, together with the battalion sergeant major, stormed off to the Harlem Hootch. The major stood in the middle of the all-black shack, drunkenly ranting that they were all a bunch of niggers and revolutionaries, until the sergeant major, waking up to all the hostile stares coming back at them, managed to drag him out. The sergeant reported the incident to the battalion commander who had enough street-sense to have the major immediately sent to Division to keep out of harm's way. The next night, there was a fragging against an officer's hootch. It was unoccupied at the time but the message was clear. To defuse the tension, the colonel decided to break up the Harlem Hootch and transfer the men to other units. A black supply sergeant was sent in to mediate, and the young blacks were loaded aboard several trucks. As they were preparing to depart, their leader began shouting against the "conspiracy" and they bolted. MPs surrounded the hootch with V100 gun vehicles and got them to surrender only after many shouted threats.

Friction between the lifers and draftees was another manifestation of the basecamps. The GIs were on standdown to get high, get drunk, parlay with the local prostitutes, sleep without having to worry about guard duty, and generally to say FTA for three days. The lifers wanted haircuts, mustache trims, shined boots, and manpower to fill sandbags and dig new bunkers. The 3/187 sergeant major was a short, fat man. His office hootch overlooked the main battalion area and he would sit inside all day with the door open. When a grunt came by with his shirt unbuttoned, unshaven, his hair too long, his trousers not bloused correctly, or wearing a boonie hat which was unauthorized for basecamp use, the sergeant major would charge out, screaming madly for the trooper to square away. The blacks hated him over the Harlem Hootch incident; the rest resented the fact that he rarely made it to the field and, as Daugherty thought, who needs that kind of shit while fighting a war.

Another major change in basecamp behavior was considered a problem by the career men, but relished by Daugherty and about half the battalion. You could get stoned, get drunk, and no one cared. Daugherty never touched drugs in the field but, in the hootches and bunkers at Camp Evans, he and his buddies would light some candles and pass the grass. They have some damn fine dew in the Nam, he thought. For a certain percent of the battalion, the abuse did not stop with marijuana; some of the GIs were heroin addicts.

Delta Company 3/187 was helicoptered to Camp Evans in mid-January for another two-day standdown. Then they were given three days and the grunts loved it. They were given a fourth day and Daugherty started getting nervous; it seemed like the lifers were always nice to them before they were sent someplace rotten. Then it was five days, then six—and they were confined to the company area and ordered not to write home. Everyone was on edge. On the evening of 29 January, Delta Company was confined to its barracks. The grunts nervously sat around, trying to occupy their time, and Daugherty decided to attend the briefing on the upcoming mission they'd been told about. He walked into the operations hootch, nicknamed the War Room, and found his way through the crowd. All the company and platoon leaders in the battalion were there, along with platoon sergeants, RTOs, and the like. The officers sat in chairs or stood against the walls, while the enlisted men sat cross-legged on the plywood floor.

The battalion command group sat behind a desk in the back of the hootch. They were a professionally competent group, but there were very few similarities between the officers and men in the battalion. The warning order for the operation had been met with general enthusiasm by the commanders; career men or not, most saw the war as a job that had to be done and, if a battle was to be fought, they wanted the Screaming Eagles in the thick of it. Few could have been more willing to go than the battalion commander Lt. Col. Bryan Sutton, a small man, a former Green Beret, who often worked side-by-side with his men in the field. He was a gentleman of the old school, who rarely cursed, and drank only an occasional glass of wine, who had enough respect for his troopers to treat them each as individuals. He was also a good fighter; during a previous Vietnam tour, Sutton had been a Special Forces officer working in an area under the control of then-Colonel Hill. Hill, who had a general dislike for the mavericks in the SF, had nevertheless been impressed by Sutton; when Lam Son 719 was being planned, he specifically asked that it be Sutton's battalion attached to his brigade task force.

Sitting with Sutton at the battalion briefing were his Executive Officer, Maj. Euell T. White, and his Operations Officer, Maj. Ron Scharnberg. All three officers had been professional friends during previous stints with the Special Forces. Major White was a mustang, the eighth child of a poor Alabama family, who had dropped out of high school at fifteen and had joined the army at seventeen, taken in by the allure of the paratroopers. In ten years he'd made it to sergeant first class, then was given a direct commission to second lieutenant. In the years since his commission, he'd spent fifteen months as an ARVN advisor, during which time he'd been twice wounded and twice decorated for bravery. He'd only recently arrived to the 3/187, replacing the previous exec who'd been transferred after the Harlem Hootch incident. The Op. Officer, Major Scharnberg, was young for his rank, a dedicated and enthusiastic officer always ready for a good fight; the grunts thought him a good soldier, but found him almost amusing in his shouted enthusiasm to mix it with Charlie.

The hootch fell silent as Lieutenant Colonel Sutton began the operational briefing. He went into detail about a big operation they were to participate in the next morning, then pulled down a map behind him—the roll-up kind, Daugherty noted, just like in school. He used a pointer to locate Khe Sanh on the map.

Daugherty blanked out the colonel's talk after that. Oh shit, he thought, that's where we're going. Khe Sanh! That's bad, bad, bad bush.

Daugherty didn't know it but his new platoon leader was also at the briefing. Lt. Donald E. Stephen had signed into the battalion only two hours before. He was twenty-four, drafted out of college within a month of divorcing his wife and losing that exemption; they'd sent him to OCS and now he was in Nam, willing to do his bit, but still green. After the briefing, Stephen packed his first combat rucksack and nervously entered the hootch housing Second Platoon. His lieutenant's bars were met by cold stares. He introduced himself, said he would do the best job he knew how, but that they were veterans and he'd be depending on their help. Then Stephen told them to get packed for the CA coming at four in the morning.

Daugherty was tentatively impressed; you couldn't ask for a better attitude from a brand new lieutenant. The man seemed to have common sense.

They spent the rest of the night preparing for combat, packing ammunition and C rations, cleaning weapons, testing the radios. When Daugherty finally rolled into his cot, he could not sleep. The usual uneasiness before any operation was there, that terrible fear of the unknown. Khe Sanh. Jesus. His gut was tight all night and Daugherty just wanted to get moving. Let's go get this over!

The second of the three infantry battalions to be alerted for the Route 9 securing operation was the 4th Battalion, 3rd Infantry, 11th Light Infantry Brigade, Americal Division (Lt. Col. Albert F. Coast). The unit operated from a dot on the map called FSB San Juan Hill, with its rear at LZ Bronco—Viet Cong—booby-trap country down south in Quang Ngai Province. The 4/3 was in the field when the operations order came. In fact, Lt. John Dewing and the First Platoon of Alpha Company were in the middle of a contact.

The platoon was working through some treelines and paddies when they found a hole, and Pvt. Russel "Doc" Morse climbed in to check it out for false walls. There was a sudden eruption of shots. His buddy, Pfc Ary "Chip" Park, hauled him out and they ran to a paddy berm; six-hundred yards away, two VC were sprinting across an open rice field for the far trees. Pfc Tim Barnhart fired his M-16, Pfc Richard "Buddy-Fucker" Wessells his M-79, and Morse went to the prone, popping rounds from his M-14 rifle. Pfc Denny Able opened up with his M-60 pig gun. Morse saw the lead VC disappear in the brush, then watched enthused as the second VC went down in their flurry of tracers. He started to change magazines, when the Viet Cong suddenly jumped back up and made it to cover with tracers dancing all around him. Lieutenant Dewing called in artillery to block and the platoon swept forward on line.

They found nothing; not even a blood trail.

The grunts shot up a thatched hootch they found in the treeline. Then Dewing searched the inside while the men spilled over the U.S. and Chinese ammo cans filled with rice and corn. Denny and Chip found a tunnel and called for the lieutenant. Their shouts of "Chieu hoi!" went unanswered, so Morse handed his M-14 to a buddy and borrowed his lighter sixteen. Denny prepped the tunnel with a long burst from his pig, and Morse climbed in, holding a flashlight in his left hand and the M-16 on rock'n'roll in his right. The tunnel and bunker were empty. The platoon used their Zippo lighters to burn down the hootch. They kept moving, with Morse taking the point, following some footprints through a sandy area to a half-buried dud 155mm artillery round, which they gave a wide berth. After a while, they took five and Morse asked Buddy-Fucker why he hadn't used his M-79 grenade launcher more on the dinks in the paddy; they laughed when he said that they were out of range and the damn gun was only good for sound effects.

Lieutenant Dewing came over then to pass the word: they were going to be pulled out in the morning. He didn't know why their patrol was being cancelled.

A stream was there so the platoon knocked off, half on guard, the rest swimming and washing off. While Morse was in the water, an old Vietnamese woman wandered into their perimeter, and he hustled over to have a look. She seemed to be about seventy, mumbled and pointed to the mountains, and hungrily gulped down the C rations the GIs gave her. The platoon sergeant joined them and commented bitterly that they should shoot her. Morse was taken aback; the sergeant was fearless but scuttlebutt said he'd lost a good friend on his first tour and despised the Vietnamese. He was a lifer, but a good dude if you got to know him—and another Calley, Morse thought, if someone didn't watch him.

He said to tie the old woman up, but no one wanted to, so he said he'd do it himself. Morse was afraid he'd bind her too tight, so he stepped up and loosely tied her arms with some GI shoelaces. A helicopter came in and they lifted the terrified woman aboard. Morse could see the hate in the door-gunner's eyes and, when the pilot pulled up, the helo veered sharply and the old woman almost fell to her death. Morse didn't think twice about the few dead VC he'd seen, but civilians were another matter. The men were pissed at the sergeant. Buddy-Fucker tried to pull the pin on a CS tear-gas grenade hanging on the sergeant's ruck to give him some hell. He fended him off with a shout, everyone laughed, and things were back to normal.

They spent the night in the jungle, then were picked up by Hueys in the sandy area the next morning. At the 4/3 Rear at LZ Bronco, the company received replacements, plus new fatigues, air mattresses, and the like; that night, the grunts partied with steaks, beer, coke—and some marijuana. At eight the next morning, the company commander held a formation to tell them they had an important mission ahead of them. They spent the rest of the day cleaning weapons and packing gear, and welcoming more replacements. Spirits were high. The next day a warm rain swept LZ Bronco, more news arrived, more gear was issued, and an Australian band with the USO played rock music for the GIs in the battalion area. Midway through the concert, loudspeakers blared for the battalion to saddle up. They packed aboard C130 transport planes, everyone starting to get nervous when they learned their destination was Quang Tri on the DMZ. To break the depressed mood, Morse began running through some dirty jokes and things grew more relaxed; he finally stopped when he noticed the battalion chaplain laughing along and got embarrassed.

They landed at Da Nang, then sat on the runway, broiling under a savage noontime sun. They waited for hours, and it was dark by the time they got to Quang Tri. Lieutenant Dewing stared from the window at the runway lights glowing in the fog. It was an eerie sight. They disembarked from the back cargo ramps, carrying only their rifles and rucksacks, and were met by a chilling night mist. They were directed to a swamp field to spend the night. It was miserably wet and cold. People milled around in the dark, tripping over each other. There were no dry places to sleep. Nearby, the runway was a constant roar of departing and landing aircraft. Dewing couldn't understand why they were risking such flights in the fog. He looked around him; in the dark, there was no way to tell where the perimeter was. Things seemed confused, no one knew what was going to happen, and it was an uneasy night.

It was nearly midnight when Lt. Col. Raymond E. Farrar, commander of the 1st Battalion, 11th Infantry, 5th Division circulated the operations order to his subordinate commanders. Most of the battalion spent the night in their barracks at Quang Tri, but Alpha Company under Capt. Philip Bodenhorn was in the field at the time. They'd spent the last two months at Mai Loc, between Dong Ha and Vandegrift; it was near the NVA infiltration routes to Quang Tri and the company was constantly conducting airmobile and infantry sweeps in the flatland country. They had seen a smattering of action. Bodenhorn, himself, had been awarded four Purple Hearts in the last seven months as a result of his up-front style of command; shrapnel from two booby-trap incidents and a night mortar raid, and an RPG fired during a hasty ambush.

Captain Bodenhorn decoded the warning order battalion had sent over the radio; It said they would be combat—assaulting onto the Khe Sanh plateau in several hours. His first emotion was one of simple disbelief. As far as he was concerned, the area west of them belonged to the North Vietnamese. There were occasional air cav or ranger forays, but generally the foe was left undisturbed at Khe Sanh. It was "Indian Country." The name itself brought back vivid recollections to Bodenhorn of the news clippings he'd seen of the bloody Marine siege there when he was still a senior at the University of Arizona.

The captain gathered his company around his bunker that night, one hundred twenty men in four platoons: First under Lt. Blake Clark; Second under Staff Sgt. Terry LeGore; Third under Lt. William McConnell; and the Weapons Platoon under Lt. William Stremky. Bodenhorn gave them a sketchy outline of their upcoming CA to Khe Sanh. Morale was relatively high because of some previous successes, and it did not seem to waver at the bad news; but mumbles of, "Aw, Jesus," and "We're really going to be stepping into some shit," broke out among the young infantrymen.

It wasn't going to be a cakewalk, Bodenhorn told his men; it would probably be the most dramatic action they would see in Vietnam. To convey the danger of what they were getting into, and to try to reinforce the spirit of the infantry, Captain Bodenhorn sent his men to their positions only after having fixed a bayonet to his own M-16 rifle.

Waiting in the bush west of Vandegrift was Capt. Thomas Stewart, commander of Alpha Troop, 3rd Squadron, 5th Cavalry. His troop had been personally selected by General Hill to lead the second phase of the operation, the road march to secure Khe Sanh. Stewart had been one of the few captains at the operational briefing the day before, having helicoptered in from Dong Ha and returned immediately thereafter. Hill had taken him aside after the briefing to reiterate his mission to Khe Sanh and let him know he had broad latitude to carry it out as he saw fit.

When he informed his platoon lieutenants and sergeants, they joked that it was a mixed blessing, an honor to have been chosen over all the other units but still a risky prospect. Captain Stewart did not share such misgivings. He was a family man from Las Vegas who had decided to become a professional soldier after his first tour as an ARVN advisor, during which he'd been wounded twice. He volunteered for a second tour in March 1970, serving with the brigade staff and as S3 of the 3/5 Cav, until being happily "demoted" to command Alpha Troop in November. Stewart took much professional pride in his troop being selected as point, in light of the ill-disciplined state it had been in when he took over. One of the platoons had balked at a combat mission which had resulted in the troop commander being quietly transferred to a new post. Hill knew Stewart well from his staff assignments, so he placed him in command of the reluctant cavalrymen. In short order, he confirmed his suspicions about the platoon leaders: one was indecisive; one burnt out; the third too gung-ho. He transferred them all, and brought in three experienced lieutenants. He also beefed up the number of sergeants first class in the platoons to compensate for some staff sergeants considered to be lazy. After the revamping, Alpha Troop began to perform better (this being measured at a time of little combat, by meeting schedules of movement) and, in the two brief contacts they had before the Laos operation, they came out on top.

Alpha Troop's major problem in getting to Khe Sanh was that Route 9 was merely a narrow dirt trail, overgrown in some spots, all the bridges down. The road had not been travelled—not at least by U.S. troops—since 1968. Twelve major river crossings required bridges and a number of creeks needed culvert crossways. Stewart's primary mission, then, was to place engineers along Route 9 and guard them as the construction began. A platoon of bulldozers from the 59th Land Clearing Company and two companies from the 14th Engineer Battalion, 18th Engineer Brigade were to accompany the troop's road march. Captain Stewart decided to go down the road with the troops dismounted. They organized and checked their equipment outside the Vandegrift wire, only the drivers staying with the ACPs, two men per mortar track so they could fire illumination rounds if needed, two men per Sheridan so the main gun could be employed, the rest walking forward with the engineer teams.

By the time they began their slow march down Route 9 it was pitch black, around one in the morning of 30 January. The point was taken by Alpha Troop's best platoon leader, Lt. Jimmie Johnson of Second Platoon, with a small group of grunts, accompanied by an engineer minesweep team and a mine-dog team. As they walked into the blackness of the road a trio of vehicles followed them: a Sheridan tank using its infrared searchlight to scope out the trail for enemy movement; a mortar track for fast firepower; and a single bulldozer. Captain Stewart walked behind the armor with First Sgt. William Bradley, plus his forward observer and radiomen, the chief engineers of the two engineer companies, and the bulk of his dismounted troopers. The rear was brought up by the loudly rumbling procession of Sheridans and APCs, Armored Vehicle Launched Bridges and bulldozers, under Lt. Dave Boyd of First Platoon.

They were just moving out when the platoon sergeant in Third Platoon reported that one of his men was refusing to go. The man was a chronic complainer and, on the verge of what looked like a dangerous patrol, he claimed to be a drug addict who should be sent to the amnesty house in the rear. Stewart scoffed at such an attempt to avoid combat. The platoon sergeant, taking away the GI's M-16, chewed him out and forced him to go along.

Only a short way down Route 9, the lead Sheridan and APC both threw tracks on the rough road and had to be abandoned until daylight. The dozer driver said he couldn't effectively clear the road of brush without his headlights so Stewart said, "What the hell, turn 'em on." They proceeded then with headlights blazing and engines coughing. To deter NVA attacks, Stewart had his FO place artillery fire north of the road; the noise of their column was so loud and the hills so foggy that they could neither hear nor see the impacting rounds. The first bridge was already repaired, an AVLB having been launched from Vandegrift that afternoon. At the next downed bridge, a half-dozen cavalrymen and engineers were left with a radio and an M-60 machine gun. They radioed for the helicopter to bring in the span bridges which were being assembled and slingloaded at Quang Tri, and for another helicopter to transport the necessary equipment. They worked throughout the night. In all, six M4T6 dry-span bridges and five AVLB bridges were installed.

Trailing behind A/3/5 and the engineers was the 1st Squadron, 1st Cavalry. Sergeant Keefer sat hunkered behind his fifty shield in the cold mist, nervously eyeing the darkness around him. The long column came to a halt, rumbling idle in the mud, and someone came by and shouted to Keefer, "Hey, the Old Man wants to see you!"

At the command track, Capt. James W. Pierson had his map out and Keefer joined the other platoon lieutenants and sergeants gathered around him. In two hours, the captain told them, they would be pushing down Route 9 to the Laotian border for a major operation. Seven to eight thousand NVA were suspected of being in the area, and intelligence said they were fully equipped with artillery, tanks, trucks, heavy weapons, and maybe even jets. Keefer could feel his gut tighten when he heard that.

After the briefing, Captain Pierson called Sergeant Keefer over and told him the acting leader of First Platoon, a staff sergeant, had slipped off his Sheridan turret in the rain. He'd wrenched his back badly and had been sent back down the column for medevac. The captain wanted Keefer to assume command of First Platoon.

No way, Keefer said, there were two other E-5s in the platoon and he didn't want the responsibility.

That may be so, Pierson responded, but, since Keefer had pulled another combat tour, he was the most experienced and the best man for the job. Keefer knew the Old Man was right and finally relented. Like it or not, he figured, I am the best qualified. He didn't want to let Pierson down; the captain had always done right by his troops. Still, as Keefer trudged back to his APC, he almost shook with anger and fear. I'm not even supposed to be here, he cursed inwardly. Four Purple Hearts and they got me back in this shit. The thought of all those NVA in the Laotian border mountains, and the responsibility that was now his, forced him to squat in the roadside brush and defecate in raw terror.

After all he'd been through, he didn't want to die now.

Keefer had first arrived in Vietnam in September 1968, an unruly eighteen-year-old who had the notion that war was an adventure and the army would make a good career. By the time that first year with Alpha Troop was over, he'd been wounded four times, he'd been pinned with an end-of-tour Army Commendation Medal, and his mind had been shut down with an intense loathing of the army, the lifers, and the dinks. He'd joined the National Guard originally at sixteen because his family had always served. It was a proud tradition; his grandfather had been gassed and severely wounded in France during the Great War; his father had contracted a lung ailment aboard a burning ship in WWII which eventually killed him; his brother Frank had been wounded twice as a Marine in Nam. Keefer wanted his piece of the action. The dudes in the neighborhood said Nam was for suckers, but his working-class background upheld the ideals of duty to one's country and made him volunteer for the "Regular Army" and for Vietnam. It wasn't long before the hatred set in. It was as if the army didn't care; you're ready to give your life for your country, Keefer thought, but all you are is another number.

Army don't care, officers are incompetent, grunts die. That's how he saw it.

His first sign that the military was not to be trusted came when he volunteered for Vietnam. Since his basic training had been geared for the National Guard, with obsolete weapons and classes in riot control, he requested to go through infantry training again to catch up on the new weapons and tactics. He was amazed that this permission was denied, that he was sent directly to Vietnam. They don't care what kind of combat soldier you make, Keefer thought. They don't care if you survive the war. They just want warm bodies to fill the ranks.

His hatred for army bureaucracy was crystallized by the fate of a soldier in his platoon back in '69. His name was Robert and he was a tall, gawky bookworm who'd been a mathematical genius in college. Everyone liked him, but he had absolutely no common sense. A good kid, Keefer concluded, but he should have been a clerk-typist somewhere in the rear, not humping around with the infantry, and Keefer hated the Army for sending Robert to a place where it was obvious he wouldn't have the sense to survive. Robert was killed in May. The platoon received a letter from his father; a newspaper article was enclosed in which the father had said, "His death was a complete and tragic waste. His life has gone for nothing in a senseless military adventure." It was a humble letter from parents to the platoon, asking to hear from men who had known their son. It went on to say that they had sent their boy a package of candy and cookies the day he was killed; they hoped his friends had enjoyed them, and they were praying for all of them. The father said the Army had told him that Robert had been killed by an enemy rocket-propelled grenade while driving an APC. Keefer was furious at that. The kid had not been killed by the enemy. They'd been in a firefight when the genius, whom everyone liked but who knew nothing about the bush, had wandered forward, got lost in the tall grass between the two sides, and had been accidentally raked across the back by one of the track-mounted machine guns. You're just a number, Keefer thought over and over. They take a good kid, send him to the wrong job, then lie when he's predictably killed. They don't care who they hurt. He never wrote to the father; he was afraid of being court-martialled on some trumped-up charges.

Keefer despised the Vietnamese with an equal fury. When his brother had come back from Vietnam in '66, he'd told how they'd gone into villages with medical programs and had raised money for orphans. By '68, when Keefer had arrived, the Americal Division was no longer interested in civic action; the name of the game was S&D, free-fire zones, and body count—especially body count. He'd come over ready to help the Vietnamese people and had made good friends with an old woman and her two children who did the GI's laundry. They were nice people and he would write his mother to get tennis shoes and clothes for the little boy. But Keefer learned to hate the rest of them; they seemed so maddeningly indifferent to American deaths.

When they passed through villages, the people seemed to have ample amounts of rice, plus water buffalos, chickens, and gardens. But when a GI tossed a can of C rations from his truck, they would fight like dogs to get it. Men would pummel little children for a measly can of Cs. Greedy bastards, Keefer thought, no better'n animals. The platoon would take their revenge on the Vietnamese. If they'd been cheated buying beer, dope, or whores in the shantytowns around Da Nang and Chu Lai, they would roar through on the next time around, raising dust and pitching smoke and CS grenades. When they went through the hamlets, they had another nasty trick. They would punch a hole in a C ration meal can, then hold it with an asbestos glove over a flame of C4. They'd start tossing C rats, the people would fall into a kicking, screaming mob, then someone would toss in the scorched can. Keefer thought it was funny as hell to watch "the slant-eyed animals" keep grabbing at it and burning their fingers. The can would go through the whole village.

And, when they went through the tiny villes deep in the jungle, they killed the Vietnamese. Once Keefer watched a tank driver in his platoon simply swerve and crush to death three Vietnamese standing beside the road they were on. The ARVN interpreters with the troop were ruthless; at first Keefer couldn't believe what he saw. They threw babies down wells and hung women from trees. Keefer knew the Vietnamese were in a murderous bind; if they helped the Americans, the VC would butcher them and, if they did nothing, an angry GI might open fire. But, after a while, the circumstances meant nothing to him. They would hit a mine and the farmers nearby would act as if they hadn't seen a thing; they never pointed out the booby traps in their fields. Women and children in a paddy would suddenly start walking quickly for the woodline, and then the platoon would be ambushed; the people never warned the Americans of the NVA waiting for them. Keefer felt sick the first time he saw his buddies shoot at civilians in revenge, but soon he fell into the same brutal mindset. After seeing friends dismembered by mines, he found it easy . . . a catharsis. You forget about home, Keefer mused;

you lived with death, could feel it in every hedgerow and villager's stare, and could see it every day they tallied the body count.

"Let's just kill everybody and go home," was the attitude.

It was the lifers' fault, he concluded, with their condoning and encouraging of anything to beef up the kill. They had turned him into something he did not like to ponder. They just wanted the glory and the medals, and didn't care who got killed or warped in the process. Half the time, it seemed as if they had to fight the lifers as much as the enemy. In '69 on Hawk Hill, they had a first sergeant they called Teddy Bear. One night, the platoon was getting stoned in a bunker when one of the guys went out to piss; he ran back in saying he'd seen men in front of the perimeter wire. Flares had popped in the distance, he said, and he'd just made out their shadows in the paddy water. They called Teddy Bear but, unable to see anything, he mocked them by standing at the wire and shouting, "If there's anybody out there, shoot me, I dare ya!" The sergeant laughed at his men and walked away. The grunts hustled back to the bunker, piled up ammo and grenades, and waited; twenty minutes later, a trip flare went off in the wire and they cut loose. The next morning they counted over a dozen dead NVA sappers in the wire. The shooting over, Teddy Bear reappeared and strutted around with a cigar in his mouth. He ordered the platoon to go count the bodies and patrol for the survivors, and Keefer complained that they'd been fighting all night; why not send another platoon. The sergeant laughed, "No, you guys started this battle, you're going to finish it." Keefer felt that they were being spit on for doing their jobs. The platoon left the perimeter, sat down out of sight in the brush, and radioed in a fake patrol report.

Keefer blamed the lifers for his being back in the combat infantry. After that year of heavy fighting, he'd finally rotated out in September 1969, and had ended up in Germany; but he couldn't get along with the spit-and-shine officers there and was shocked by the racial violence he saw. As a sergeant, he was told to put only whites on work details. When he complained, the battalion commander said that, they, at least, wouldn't revolt when given orders. One old first sergeant who didn't see it that way was manhandled into a wall locker by some blacks and heaved out of a second-floor window. After the camaraderie of Vietnam, it was saddening to see black and white GIs not only fist fighting, but pulling knives and chucking grenades into each other's clubs. He didn't want to be beaten to death by a gang of blacks who didn't even know him so he decided to get away by volunteering for a second Vietnam tour. He would get overseas and hazardous-duty pay, a drop in the time left on his enlistment, and (an officer in personnel told him) with four Purple Hearts, he could not be assigned to a combat unit.

When he came in-country again in December 1970, someone saw his combat experience and put him in exactly the same unit he'd survived before: A Troop, 1st Squadron, 1st Cavalry Americal Division. Keefer raised hell, showing a letter an officer had written saying he couldn't be sent back to combat, but the personnel staff said no such letter was in his file and that he must have forged it. Disgruntled, he reported for duty. When he showed the letter to the troop commander, Captain Pierson, and explained why he should be sent back to the rear, Pierson answered, "Boy, we sure need you. We can really use some experience."

Keefer developed an almost immediate rapport with Pierson; the CO seemed to be a good officer so Keefer dropped the whole issue at that point. As the weeks went by, Pierson, virtually alone among the officers, impressed Keefer as a trustworthy combat leader. He didn't like being in Vietnam any more than the grunts liked it; he just did his job, performed the mission with the least risks, and never told his troops to do anything he wouldn't do personally. And that night on Route 9, when Keefer found himself in command of a platoon, he shook away his fright thinking of the leadership he'd seen Pierson exhibit.

After the captain's roadside huddle, the lieutenants and sergeants returned to their vehicles and the column continued its bumpy passage along Route 9. Other vehicles appeared out of the black until no matter which way you looked, there were lines of road lights curving along. Keefer had never seen so much armor together before. At one point, he noticed, the road was carved almost directly into the side of the mountains, a sheer wall and above them a cliff. Keefer found himself cursing the Army again, "Stupid lifers got us on this road. All the dinks have to do is blow up the front and rear vehicles, and we're trapped."

As they rolled slowly on, Sergeant Keefer resolved one thing in his mind: his only duty was to keep his platoon alive. He didn't care about the success of the operation. All that mattered was that his friends should make it home in one piece from this insane war, and if that meant refusing an order or faking a patrol, so be it. He wasn't going to take any more chances. And he intended to keep himself alive too. By 1971 the grunts had a saying: "You owe it to yourself." After all he'd been through, Keefer figured he owed it to himself to survive.

By early morning, the men of 1/11 Infantry were crowded at the Quang Tri airfield. It was cold, wet, and overcast and the young grunts wore field jackets and towels like scarves. An air armada, including forty-five Hueys for the infantry, deposited them at Mai Loc, then picked them up again and sped towards Khe Sanh. Maj. Harlow Stevens, battalion operations officer, rode the lead slick. It was his second trip to Khe Sanh; as a young Green Beret in 1963, he had worked at the original SF outpost there.

The son of one of Stevens's commanders at Khe Sanh in '63 was riding the second Huey in. That was Lt. Charles Garwood, twenty-three, recently married, of the Pathfinder Platoon, 101st Aviation Group, 101st Airborne Division. With him were Cpls. Guy "Evergreen" Fearn and "Blinky" Collins; they had hooked up with 1/11 at Mai Loc to control aircraft into the LZ once the CA was completed. The Hueys flew in line down the river bordering Route 9, skids barely off the surface; Garwood, whose baptism of fire had been the Ripcord retreat, stared uneasily at the brushy banks whizzing behind them.

There was no shooting.

They CA'd onto the shell-pocked airstrip, and the grunts fanned out across the desolate plateau. There was no one in sight, and Major Stevens shouted, "This force will be dug in before dark!" The GIs, who'd been expecting a fight, put aside their rifles for picks and shovels, while Lieutenant Garwood's team set up in the elephant grass beside the strip and directed in the other helicopters.

The last company of the battalion into Khe Sanh was Captain Bodenhorn's Alpha, coming out of Mai Loc and overshooting the armor column on Route 9. Through the overcast Bodenhorn could see the jungled mountains; then the base appeared, helicopters circling above it, some lowering cargo nets of gear. The terrain brought back more vivid flashbacks of the full-color television footage he'd seen as a college student: the bombed hills; the low plateau in fog; the ravines running up to the base. They settled down on the strip and the company sat along the edge, helmets off, taking a cigarette break. Bodenhorn reported to Major Stevens who assigned Alpha the job of securing the east side of the strip, with a warning to beware of uncharted "friendly" minefields.

They moved out through the mud and overgrowth, Bodenhorn surveying the haunting landscape of old Marine trenches, abandoned gear, rusting pieces of a C130, three years destroyed strewn across the perimeter. Beyond the overgrown and dilapidated coils of concertina wire on the edge of what used to be the perimeter, they could see other collapsed trenches zig-zagging forward. They assumed those had been the NVA positions during the '68 siege. Eerie, Bodenhorn thought, eerie and haunting. The grunts began digging bunkers with interconnecting slit trenches, "very mindful," the company commander reported, "of the fighting positions that had been abandoned a few years earlier, their strength, their absolute screaming necessity. We had no problems constructing our positions. The materials were ample and the spirit was more than willing."

Alpha Company 4/3 Infantry was also on the Quang Tri strip. They were issued maps of their new AO and Lieutenant Dewing joined the company command group huddle. Capt. William Spinning, their reasonable and calm CO, was there with Lt. Jerry Cunningham, the artillery forward observer, Lt. Larry Walker of Second Platoon, Lt. John Sheridan of Third Platoon, and the RTOs. As leader of First Platoon of A Company, Dewing was to lead in the battalion CA and report back if the LZ was hot or cold. The landing zone was between Route 9 and the river.

Dewing's platoon broke into groups of seven or eight to board the Hueys, then jogged to them, ducking under the whirling blades. The ships flew high and took direction from the ribbon of road below them while the grunts, letting their legs dangle out the open cabin doors, endured the freezing wind. Below, Dewing could see some convoys on Route 9 and the raw mud splotch of Vandegrift, but he was more intent in the jungled mountains towards which he was being sped. Smoke drifted over the intended LZ and nervous chatter broke out on the headphones. As they slowed down and dipped lower, the door-gunner beside Dewing tapped him and shouted for the grunts to move their heads back. In the next second, he swivelled his M-60 around and opened fire. Dewing recoiled in shock as the muzzle flash exploded three feet from his face.

The slicks came in at a hover and the grunts jumped the six or eight feet from the skids into the brush of the landing zone. Dewing leaped from one side of the cabin, his RTO went out the other door, and they suddenly realized they'd been CA'd into a brush fire. There were artillery craters from the prep barrage in the area, and some of the elephant grass was ablaze. A few grunts laughed and stomped out the fire while Dewing radioed Captain Spinning that the LZ was cold. Before long, more slicks began to appear in the sky, smoke grenades were popped as guides, and the remainder of the battalion began disembarking.

With the LZ expanding, First Platoon moved out on its preassigned mission to find Route 9 and be at a particular point on the map by a particular time. The area was all thick brush, elephant grass, and rolling hills. Dewing told Private Morse to walk point. Morse was a favorite of his; he'd known him in a stateside unit and was surprised to see Morse already a vet in his platoon when Dewing arrived in Vietnam. They were friends, but Morse wasn't a model soldier. He was notorious for drug use back in the rear, and did not adapt well to military discipline. One of his bigger adventures had been during a standdown at LZ Bronco. Bored with the steam'n'cream massage parlors in the adjacent ville, he and three other grunts had gone AWOL to the Americal Division Headquarters at Chu Lai; they'd wanted a crack at the beaches, skivvy joints, and Donut Dollies about whom there were many tantalizing rumors. They hadn't gotten a Donut Dolly, but had found a sandbag with eight pounds of grass, and had hidden in a transit hootch full of new guys, rolling joints, and passing bamboo bowls and ivory pipes. The shack had filled with thick smoke and the few new guys who hadn't joined the pot party had gotten stoned just lying on their cots.

Morse was a different man in the field, though. He had joined the army at seventeen, wanting an escape from his impoverished beginnings and gung-ho over John Wayne movies. He'd earned his jump wings, had volunteered for Vietnam, and had taken a Purple Heart for a VC grenade. He was damned proud to be a grunt and consistently walked point. He moved expertly through the jungle, tight as a drum, ready to blow away anything that moved—which was exactly the attitude Lieutenant Dewing wanted.

Before long, Morse came upon a small trail in the brush. They gathered on it and scraped the surface with their boots, moving aside grass and vines. Underneath was a surface of packed earth and quarter-sized rocks from an engineer rock crusher (probably from the French days, Dewing reckoned). He checked his maps and realized that the little cart trail was Route 9. They organized on the road, then moved out, well spaced for fear of ambush. Morse on point moved along, slow and quiet, especially nervous about tripping a booby trap. He had led them perhaps a kilometer when something rustled to his left front and, throwing himself down in the brush, he emptied his M-14 rifle at it. The rest of the platoon dove into the bushes.

Morse slammed in another magazine to fire again as the platoon sergeant ran up, shouting "What the hell are you firing at?"

Morse suddenly noticed that no one else, U.S. or NVA, was shooting.

The sergeant checked the riddled area and came back shaking his head. By the time Dewing worked his way up, Buddy-Fucker, Chip, and Denny were razzing an embarrassed Morse, calling him a farmer. A scrawny wild boar lay in the brush, shot across the belly.

By late afternoon, the platoon reached its position atop a hill on the northern side of the highway. They hacked away some bushes, laid out air mattresses, strung ponchos, and set out claymore mine booby traps on Route 9—devices the army euphemistically termed Mechanical Ambushes.

The 3/187 Infantry was on the Camp Evans airstrip before sunrise. Lieutenant Colonel Sutton and Majors White and Scharnberg were in a cluster, watching the line companies form up to wait for the lift birds. White could feel the apprehension in the air; everyone expected heavy contact and responded with a tight-lipped, no-nonsense demeanor.

As for Delta Company, they had been picked up by trucks at their barracks, deposited alongside the airstrip, and now stood in an expectant mass. They were to CA onto Route 9 to hold one of the damaged bridges for the mechanized engineer teams. Sp4 Daugherty looked with apprehensive wonder; he'd never seen so many helicopters and men in one place. The company commander conferred with his platoon leaders and Daugherty eyed him uneasily. The CO was new, inexperienced, and never seemed to catch on. A plump, noninfantry type, he was so gunhappy he'd traded his M-16 for a WWII style grease gun. That was really good for hitting the broad side of a barn, Daugherty thought, but not too cool if a dink popped up. The men called him Porky the Pig, and only stuck with him because he was willing to listen to advice. Besides, he reckoned, he'd seen worse officers and, if they let the captain down and he screwed up, he'd take a lot of grunts with him.

Waiting in the predawn darkness, Lieutenant Stephen was having his own worries. He knew only four of his men by sight—the platoon sergeant, the radioman, the medic, and a rifleman. The rest of them were anonymous in the dusk light. Within one day of getting to the battalion, he was heading for a major airmobile assault and it was extremely unsettling to Stephen that some of his men might die in a few hours and he didn't even know their names.

Finally, Delta Company was directed onto their Hueys. The sky was filled with formations of helicopters and, past Quang Tri, Daugherty's radio crackled with a helo pilot reporting ground fire. Daugherty couldn't hear or see a thing. There was no more shooting. By the time they started their descent into the hills astride Route 9, the armada that had taken off from Camp Evans had thinned down to the fifteen or so slicks carrying Delta. They came low into a brushy field that was their LZ, the door gunners blasting precautionary fire from their sixties into the treelines. The skids hit the ground and the grunts piled out the cabin doors, quickly jogging away from the birds.

The LZ was cold.

Lieutenant Colonel Sutton and Major Scharnberg were in their C&C controlling the insertion of the battalion's four rifle companies and one recon platoon, while Major White monitored the action from Camp Evans. The infantrymen had successfully secured their various LZs around Khe Sanh and Route 9, but the expected enemy resistance had not materialized. The only reported casualties were sprains and bruises caused by men jumping out of helicopters that hadn't been low enough.

For Delta Company, the afternoon went methodically. They secured their position, sent out patrols which made no contact, and firmed up back to field discipline standards. Daugherty's nerves had calmed too. Out in the bush, with things to do and people depending on you, you just didn't have time to be scared.

Hours earlier, as dawn was just hazily breaking through the mountain fog, Captain Stewart's force took a break in place along Route 9. Everyone was dragged out from the sleepless night and long march. They got moving again, reached the next bridge by ten, were supposed to have a bridge brought in by chopper at eleven, but finally left the engineer team without the bridge at two in the afternoon. A bit further down the road, Stewart's dismounted grunts and CP linked up with Delta 3/187.

Sp4 Daugherty and his platoon were on patrol at that time, sweeping the high ground above Route 9. It was steep and tough going and, looking back down the forested slope, he couldn't even see the bridge they had come to secure. They scouted the ridgeline, found nothing, and humped back downhill. Daugherty had no idea about a rendezvous and was surprised to see bulldozers, tanks, and tracks on the road inside the company perimeter. Out of sight around a bend further down the road, they heard the shout, "Fire in the hole!" and the grunts dove into the grass as an explosion was followed by a shower of fragmented rocks. One thudded into Daugherty's back.

At the river bank, the engineers were working on the site. It was supposed to have been ready for a bridge to be dropped in place by AVLB, but first they had to blow big boulders which clogged the route. Stewart radioed for an AVLB to be driven up, but it could not make it down the road until all the other bridges had been put in place. There was no telling how long that might be, so the dozers cleared space in the roadside brush in case a night defensive position would have to be set up. The men took another break at around four in the afternoon, and the AVLB finally made it to the position at around six o'clock as dusk was coming.

By dusk Lieutenant Stephen's platoon was ordered back to the high ground overlooking the bridge to establish their NDP and watch for enemy movement. The grunts humped and sweated in the dim light and were still moving into position when night came and blackness enveloped the ridgeline. The men put some claymores around them, divided up the watch time, and tried to get to sleep on the jungle floor. There were no foxholes or wire. Daugherty looked back down the hill and could see APCs and Sheridans on the road. The tank cannons were trained into the brush. He was afraid that, if something went down, the tanks would accidentally hit them with their return fire. "Tankers are taking it easy tonight," he grinned, "with all us grunts up here protecting them."

Sitting atop the ridgeline with tank cannons pointed at them, with only a few claymores between them and the no-man's-land of black jungle, Daugherty was as nervous as common sense dictated. But he wasn't terrified. The men beside him were dependable, the problems of basecamp having disappeared as soon as they'd hit the bush. The blacks and whites again stuck together. The officers exhibited good leadership and even the colonels, Daugherty thought, had learned enough by '71 to have them not do stupid things. And the dope stayed stashed at Camp Evans. The general consensus was that you could get as stoned as you liked at camp but, when you boarded the helicopter in the morning, you'd better be straight: you couldn't trust somebody who was high watching the flank or walking point. Daugherty was sure that, somewhere along the line, somebody from Delta must have broken the rule. If anybody'd been caught, his buddies would have felt no guilt in beating the shit out of the offender. But Daugherty had never caught anyone.

They were tight, Daugherty thought. They stuck together and did their job. It wasn't because they believed in the war; from a grunt's point of view, he reckoned, it was all pretty hopeless. As far as he could see their efforts merely made a small percentage of Vietnamese black marketeers and businessmen rich while doing nothing for the average person. The rice farmers he saw did not care about democracy, capitalism, communism, or nationalism; they just wanted to be left alone to tend their rice and water buffalos, and to scratch a living out of the soil. If there had to be a war here, Daugherty didn't feel right in attacking his own government for it. The worst thing, to him, was that after they went to the trouble of waging a war, they never committed themselves. He could find no sense in coming and going, coming and going.

What kept Daugherty going was that the grunts in the bush had to stick together. There were the high points and the low points, he surmised; the lows were really low and the highs weren't all that great. No one wanted to be the last man to die in Vietnam—Daugherty heard that many times—but he dismissed it; no one wants to get killed—first, middle, or last—and if you were the last, you'd never know it. You were just there, he thought, you were drafted and in the Nam and you did your job with the least number of hassles. Just put one foot in front of the other and keep moving.

The AVLB at the bridge site was just preparing to turn on the road to face the bank when Captain Stewart noticed that four end-connectors were missing on the left side. He wasn't willing to take the chance of the AVLB breaking a track before it turned completely and blocked the road, and he shouted at the driver to stop. It took another couple of hours to repair the track. They finally crossed the river just before midnight, with the minesweeps still up front, and everyone else now back on their vehicles. They left the 3/187 AO and crossed the imaginary line into 4/3's area.

Around midnight, Lieutenant Dewing's platoon could hear all kinds of racket coming down the road, and got a radio call from the combat engineers. Dewing gave his position to them, sent a detail to pull in the MAs, and told the engineers he would meet them on the road. He was hesitant to send one of his grunts for fear, if the man were not careful enough, he might get blown away by a nervous engineer guard. He waved at the column as it approached and stepped into the glare of the lead dozer's headlights. Dismounted sweep teams were in front, the bulldozer using its light to illuminate the road for them and its blade to carve away the roadside tangle for the column following them.

As they passed, Dewing talked with some of the engineers who said they were clearing Route 9 all the way to Khe Sanh. He still didn't know what the whole operation was about, but for the first time his road security job made sense. The rest of the story would fall in place soon and, Dewing would reflect, the operation was the only one he'd been in which was clearly a campaign with specific objectives. The rest had been merely like a nine-to-five job to keep the VC off balance; "waltzing through the woods," he called it, "chasing the commies." It rarely made sense. But the new op was different and Dewing thought the change was for the better. After the tedium of their booby-trap war down south, where casualties were rarely avenged with even the sight of a live VC, the platoon appeared glad to be on the DMZ. They were doing something different and their depression was replaced by a state of nervous alertness and excitement.

Continuing down Route 9, Stewart's sweep teams stayed up front, followed by the line of combat vehicles from A/3/5 and the bulk of 1/1 Cav. Around two in the morning, the lead Sheridan of Alpha Troop—back behind the point, the minesweepers, the mine dog, and the bulldozer—hit a mine in the road. There were no casualties, but it blew off a tread and blocked Route 9. The whole column came to a halt in the mud and Stewart radioed the nearest infantry unit. He explained that he had a tank down and, if they were to continue at their set pace, he needed permission to bulldoze it off the cliff along the roadside. Otherwise, it would require several hours of hard labor to jockey the vehicle enough to the side to allow passage. The infantryman on the other end of the radio had no idea what he was talking about and gave him no answer. Stewart ordered the GIs to push the Sheridan to the side of the road.

It was not until the next morning that they finally moved again. Just then the lieutenant of the bulldozer platoon refused to go any further, claiming he had maintenance problems with his dozers and needed to work on them. Stewart suspected that the lieutenant was balking from fear of encroaching so deeply into NVA territory or from simple exhaustion, but he didn't know enough about dozers to say anything. He left the engineers and walked ahead only to find another problem: troopers from the 326th Engineer Battalion, 101st Airborne—who had airmobiled to Khe Sanh and were supposed to have installed the last bridge to the base—were still at work. The old bridge abutments were not usable so they had had to construct new ones a bit upstream. They said another two or three hours were needed. General Hill was there, his C&C helicopter sitting in the brush, and Stewart got clarification of his command over the engineer lieutenant. Hill told him to use his gun if that's what it took to get the man moving again.

By the time Stewart walked back, the lieutenant said his dozers were ready to go and they moved up to where the 326th Engineers were hard at work. Finally, a chopper hovered a slingloaded span bridge into place. Captain Stewart's task force went across, then churned through the mud and elephant grass to link up with 1/11 Infantry which was securing the Khe Sanh plateau. Mission completed, Route 9 was officially declared open to tracked vehicles that afternoon at 1130 hours, 31 January.

Earlier in the day, the 8th Battalion, 4th Artillery, XXIV Corps was alerted to move from its basecamp at Dong Ha to Vandegrift, to provide additional fire support to the task force. The soldier who took the phone call for the move was Sfc. Roy H. Hatfield, first sergeant of Headquarters and Headquarters Battery. He, for one, was extremely nervous at the prospect of heading into a hot area. In the argot of the draftees, he considered 8/4 Arty a flaky battalion. Hatfield was himself an experienced vet, a thirty-three-year-old family man on his twenty-first month in Vietnam; he'd been in field units the entire time, had been with the Marines during the Khe Sanh siege, was twice decorated for valor. With that experience behind him, he thought the outfit was not ready for action.

The problems started with the battalion commander who, Hatfield thought, was typical of the career officers at that stage in the War. Most of them had their six-month slots in the battalion and seemed only to want to promote their careers with a war record. One captain had told him he would be making major soon and that, if the war lasted long enough, he might get to be a lieutenant colonel.

The leadership problem affected his Hq&Hq battery also; Hatfield thought of their captain as a good-old-boy type, just there to get his ticket punched. He simply floated along, not too concerned about how things got done and not willing to be a bad guy to the troops by enforcing discipline. He thought the young sergeants were trying their best, but most had earned instant stripes in the shake'n'bake NCO schools and lacked the experience and deftness to effectively lead disaffected draftees. They would show up in Hatfield's orderly room, complaining that so-and-so wasn't doing this or that, then threaten to put the man on report. Very few GIs responded well to that type of threatening leadership.

It was the young artillerymen who were Sergeant Hatfield's biggest headache. Since he'd arrived in the battalion in October, things had been quiet in the area and virtually no one had any combat experience. They'd been leading the good life, he thought, and he worried about how they'd hold up under fire. In their boredom, they'd been mostly bitter and frustrated and the battalion had experienced a few fragging incidents. There were some subliminal racial problems, but Hatfield's major concern was drug abuse. He was never able to catch a single user or pusher, but it was obvious that more than one of the artillerymen were heroin addicts. He was convinced that some of the medics bought dope from the locals, hid it among their medical gear, then brought it back to the troopers.

Trying to pack away his apprehensions, Sergeant Hatfield joined the 8/4 Artillery road march. The trucks of Hq&Hq fell in behind another unit on Route 9, and the firing batteries strung out behind them aboard their self-propelled artillery pieces. It was nearly dark by the time they got to Vandegrift, and the base was so crowded with people and machinery, that someone just pointed to a patch of brush and told them to spend the night there. They dismounted from their vehicles but Hatfield told the men only to risk sleeping on the ground if they had cots—so the tanks and trucks rumbling through the grass would see them and not run them over.

The grunts of 1/1 Cav pulled perimeter security around Khe Sanh, while Stewart's A/3/5 immediately departed for their next objective. The bulk of 3/5 Cav, with A Company, 7th Engineers, had started the pioneer road through the mountains, from the Rockpile to Khe Sanh, the day before, and Alpha Troop was to secure the end point of the road north of Khe Sanh. That evening, they set up their NDP in the foothills, Stewart being damned careful to get his Sheridans and APCs in a tight wagon-train circle—command group in the center, RPG screens, claymores, and trips in place—and to having the FO call in protective artillery fire all around them in the dark. Stewart knew how vulnerable they were—the only U.S. unit so far north of Khe Sanh, in only spotty communication with arty, days before 3/5 could open the road and link up with them—but, surprisingly, the North Vietnamese didn't fire a single shot at them. In fact, by the end of the third day of Operation Dewey Canyon II, no fighting had been reported.

It was still early in the morning, 1 February, when 8/4 Artillery prepared to move out again, this time to Khe Sanh. They passed other artillery batteries already dug into the green elephant grass along the road, the troops waving and exchanging peace signs and throwing power. Sergeant Hatfield thought the men already in position looked damned happy to see the war going past them.

Hatfield was sitting in a truck near the front of the convoy, the rocky terrain and dirt road bringing back memories of the bad shellings and ambushes in the area when he'd been with the Marines in '68. It was a peaceful day and it could have been a nice ride in the country, but he couldn't shake his worries about snipers. He kept studying the beautiful terrain, thinking how easy it would be for the NVA to ambush them; all they would have to do was blow two of the newly-installed bridges on either end of the column and it would have been nearly impossible to maneuver effectively from the narrow road. Few of the young artillerymen seemed to share his concerns; they had never been shot at, had no feeling for the possible dangers around them, and looked almost awkward in their helmets and flak jackets.

When they reached Khe Sanh, the plateau was overcast but bustling with activity. Hatfield quickly went about pointing out places for the men to dig their bunkers and foxholes in case of shelling, then watched unhappily as they lazily pretended to dig in. They began finding abandoned gear on the edge of the perimeter, including old Marine grenades and ammunition, and a dud 500-pound bomb half-buried in the dirt. An engineer ordnance disposal team was called up, and the artillerymen took cover as the ammo was blown in place. Hatfield ordered the men back to digging and a kid beside him began breaking earth with a pick. He swung, there was an explosion, and the artilleryman was suddenly on his butt, astonished and cut by shrapnel. He'd hit an old M-79 grenade round.

The first day of the operation, General Sutherland moved his XXIV Corps HQ into the TOC bunker of the displaced 5th Mech at Quang Tri. By the evening of 1 February, the reports coming to him indicated that the initial objectives of Operation Dewey Canyon II had been achieved. At that time, the whole of three infantry battalions, one mechanized infantry battalion, one armor battalion, two cavalry squadrons, three engineer battalions, three artillery battalions, and assets of other units were in position with no enemy-related casualties.

The fact that enemy resistance had been nonexistent in an area where the NVA had held sway for over two years was a surprise. Some sources, primarily the news media, ventured to propose that Dewey Canyon II was a failure because no impressive body count had been tallied, or that the NVA were swarming around Khe Sanh and were suckering the allies into a trap. General Sutherland responded that only the "unknowing and uninformed" would think that the area was teeming with North Vietnamese. With no allied presence in the area, the Communists did not need to maintain a large force at Khe Sanh. Dewey Canyon II was a race of sorts. Sutherland's intelligence officers suspected that the NVA may have been forewarned as early as 25 January and were probably converging on the area to delay opening of the road and airstrip. The 5th Mechanized Infantry Division won the race, and any North Vietnamese in the hills had little choice but to stay concealed and simply watch the enormous American buildup.

Sutherland was most impressed by the combat engineer effort along Route 9 which, in two labor-filled days, had made the whole operation possible. "One of the many parts of Dewey Canyon II and Lam Son 719 which I continue to recall with professional pride and admiration," Sutherland said, "was the performance of the 45th Engineer Group with its two battalions, the 14th and 27th. Other than I, there is probably no person who participated in the operation who can really appreciate the contribution of those engineers. It was the most outstanding performance that I observed in my thirty-four years of service. . . . the sight on D day was magnificent to behold—a steady stream of helicopters moving engineer equipment, culvert and bridge sections from the rear areas to the front."

CHAPTER FIVE:
The Buildup

In the week following the opening of the offensive, the Quang Tri front was a flurry of activity. The ground operations continued along Route 9, while 1/1 Cav and 1/11 Infantry continued the push to the Laotian border. In their wake, elements of the 7th and 14th Engineers performed several tasks: upgrading the highway; carving tank trails in the mountains; installing water points, rock crushers, and basecamp facilities. Meanwhile, Dong Ha filled with thousands of ARVN troops coming by sea and air and long convoys of ARVN trucks hit Route 9 to basecamp around Khe Sanh.

A Company, 14th Engineers began improving Vandegrift (Forward Support Area-I) with ammunition storage areas, fuel blivet berms, vehicle staging areas, and more. The rest of the battalion (with the 326th Engineers and a platoon from the 59th Engineer Company) upgraded Route 9 to Khe Sanh, while the 27th Engineers and the rest of the 59th continued the job to Laos. Khe Sanh (Forward Support Area-II) was simultaneously revamped. DISCOM, 101st Airborne handled the slingloading of heliborne materials and the Da Nang Support Command brought in supplies by convoy.

At Khe Sanh, the 27th and 326th Engineer teams worked on the airfield. Aerial photographs taken before the operation had not revealed the extent of damage to the original strip, thick brush covering the shell holes made in 1968. Much time had to be devoted to minesweeping the area, while EOD teams destroyed dud rounds and abandoned explosives, and the decision was made to begin simultaneous work on a second assault airstrip parallel to the original.

Things were falling behind schedule.

The day the op began, an allocation came down to the 24th Transportation Battalion, 124th Transportation Command, U.S. Army Support Command, Cam Ranh Bay, to detach two convoy officers to travel the four-hundred miles to Quang Tri. The battalion commander assigned the mission to Lieutenants John Doyle and Don Malmstrom of the 442d Truck Company. After the colonel called Malmstrom into his office and gave him his orders, he said apologetically, "We're sending you because you're the only unmarried officer." Malmstrom wasn't bothered by that, and the colonel told him to get his gear and meet up with Doyle.

Lieutenant Doyle had just transferred in from the 1/5 Mech, extending his Vietnam tour in a rear job in exchange for a drop in his Army commitment, and it gave Malmstrom some confidence to be going into an unknown area with an experienced veteran. His confidence faded when he talked with Doyle, who described the area as a quagmire of broken bridges and ambushes, with no secure areas. He was also angry that, after just getting a safe job with the transportation corps at Cam Ranh Bay, he was being sent right back to the Quang Tri bush. He said he was getting the shaft.

Malmstrom was also unhappy with the assignment. He was twenty-three, from Aberdeen, Washington, and had been cajoled into the Army by signing up for ROTC in college to avoid the draft. Reading the newspaper, he had been convinced that the American public would put an end to the war before it became a personal threat to him, but that was not to be. In August, 1970, he had found himself with orders to South Vietnam. Since his parents owned an automotive store, he'd been able to talk his way into the transportation corps and avoided the grunt's war. If it had been WWII, Malmstrom felt, he would have gone willingly, but Vietnam seemed nonsensical to him. He'd been in-country five months, but it had been in the security and lax discipline of Cam Ranh Bay and he felt inexperienced and unwilling to head to the war up north.

Lieutenants Doyle and Malmstrom took a plane to Da Nang, where they met with a Major Butler, a transportation officer from Saigon. He was a capable, friendly man and was to be their commander for the mission. They spent the night at the airbase, then signed out a jeep and started north on Route 1, a relatively secure stretch of road that only became noticeably dangerous in the Hai Van Pass area. They were coming out of the pass, going downhill, when they saw a ROK unit with VC prisoners along the roadside. The Koreans had just been through a firefight and were keyed up as they manhandled their black-pajama-clad prisoners out of the elephant grass and threw them down on the side of the road. The scene only made Malmstrom even more nervous about what they were getting into.

They passed Camps Eagle and Hue, stopped for lunch at Camp Evans, then finally pulled into Quang Tri, only to find hustle, bustle, and confusion. Major Butler immediately left for Vandegrift to coordinate what was becoming the major convoy staging area on the way to Khe Sanh. Malmstrom stayed at Quang Tri, sticking with Doyle, who seemed used to the confusion inherent in any major operation and who was in no rush to leave until their mission had been pinned down. They asked around, but got different stories from everyone, and finally hitched a ride to Dong Ha where they spent the night with some 5th Mech folks. In the morning, they were back at Quang Tri but were only told to go down the road, with no specific mission, so they again retired to Dong Ha. The next day, a colonel collared them and said, "Get your asses down that road!" which is exactly what they did, thumbing a ride in a five-ton troop truck. Before they left Quang Tri, Doyle pointed out something with partisan pride; a hootch with the sign 1/5 MECH INFANTRY DIVISION REAR HEADQUARTERS was next to another shack with the sign 101ST SCREAMING EAGLES FORWARD HEADQUARTERS.

Route 9 from Dong Ha was blacktop, and military vehicles rumbled back and forth at will. The weather was brisk, though, and the terrain a foreboding patchwork of elephant grass, hills, and treelines. Doyle tried to impress upon Malmstrom how easily the NVA could lay in ambush, that other units had had their asses kicked on Route 9, and to always keep alert. Malmstrom was nervous and the five or six GIs sharing the ride in the back of the truck were in helmets and flak jackets and had their M-16s trained towards the underbrush as they rolled along.

The two-way paved highway turned into a one-way dirt trail at Vandegrift. Major Butler met them there on the road and explained that one of them would stay there with him while the other went to Khe Sanh to coordinate the convoys there.

Lieutenant Doyle said he wanted to stay at Vandegrift.

"Well, Malmstrom," Butler said, "that leaves you to go to Khe Sanh."

"Hey, no problem."

He knew Doyle was unhappy to be there to begin with and, besides, a friend of his had been through the '68 siege at Khe Sanh so he was curious about the place. Butler gave him some instructions (which were vague because even he didn't know the whole picture yet) and told him to play it by ear, to do nothing drastic without consulting him. Malmstrom hitched a ride with the 300th MP Company, 18th MP Brigade, sitting in a jeep with a captain, a lieutenant, and several young military policemen. They had come straight out of Saigon and were excited, asking Malmstrom questions about being "up north." They did not seem to have any concept of the dangers of snipers and ambushes. They skirted around a few hills, made a final turn, and rolled into the southern rim of the Khe Sanh perimeter where several dirt roads made a juncture in the elephant grass and brush. The place looked dusty and raw, still in the process of going up, with helicopters and cargo nets overhead, tents being pitched, minesweep teams out. Someone met them and said not to wander off the roads for fear of the old Marine minefields. The main dirt trail went right to the airstrip and the 300th MPs camped alongside it, having had a bulldozer dig a large hole in the ground, putting up a troop tent and breaking out cots and C rations.

Lieutenant Malmstrom was assigned to establish a convoy checkpoint at the juncture to help organize truckers for the return trip to Vandegrift and to aid convoy commanders in finding places. He was assigned two Sp5 MPs and their checkpoint was simply the MP jeep parked on the road. The job was not as easy as it seemed; no helicopter was available for Malmstrom, so he could not recon the area and see what the dots and lines on his map really meant, and the radio line to Major Butler was spotty. Thus, no on-the-spot coordination could be made with the many convoys running on the one-way road between Vandegrift and Khe Sanh.

The situation was still new and confusing when a headquarters detachment wearing 101st shoulder patches pulled up. The major in the lead jeep pointed on his map to a spot along the main road to the runway. A large convoy had already rumbled past and was bottlenecked near the ammo dump so Malmstrom figured this new convoy would just fuel the chaos. He shrugged and laughed, "I have no idea where that is."

"Aren't you controlling the road?"

"Yeah, but I just got here and they won't let me look around."

The major craned his neck, looking around, and Malmstrom thought he looked so anxious that he wouldn't wait his turn around the ammo dump. So he checked the map again and said, "I think that's where you should be going, sir," pointing him in the direction of Lang Vei. By the time the convoy returned, the traffic jam into Khe Sanh had cleared up, but the major was furious. Malmstrom could see that, because of his lack of communication, he was hacking off a lot of convoy commanders (as well as the organizers at Vandegrift, who never knew when he would be sending an unloaded convoy to them).

Hundreds of trucks were coming and going every day but Malmstrom didn't have the acreage to form a convoy staging area—meaning whole convoys would have to pull to the shoulder on the one-way dirt trail while other convoys slowly squeezed past. He wanted an area where the truckers could do maintenance, wait for the road to clear, and organize for the trip back; he also wanted enough land cleared so three hundred trucks could spread out to minimize damage during a possible rocket attack. He headed up the road to the airfield and found a lieutenant colonel. He explained the situation but the colonel seemed unconcerned and Malmstrom blurted out in frustration, "Well if you don't need these trucks in a convoy staging area, then maybe we can put some of the trucks getting ready for the ammo dump, maybe we can put them right alongside your tent out here." The colonel stared at him as if to say he did not need such outbursts from a young lieutenant, then finally said he would try to get some dozers. When? In a couple of days. Malmstrom was worried about rocket attacks on the crowded trucks, but did not know how to press the issue with a colonel.

The next day he went to find help elsewhere. He'd been ordered to stay at the checkpoint but shrugged that off. The Sp5s were responsible for their jeep, but they recognized the problem and he appreciated their lending it to him. He headed down Route 9 and found a small engineer compound along the way to Vandegrift. A number of dozers were on the highway pushing away brush to widen the trail and grading the clay surface. Malmstrom explained the situation to the young lieutenant in charge, saying he needed three dozers to scrape away a three-hundred by two-hundred-foot area that the minesweepers had okayed. The lieutenant, knowing his business, said one cat could do that in an hour, and detailed one of his Sp4s to follow Malmstrom back. The kid cleared the area in the northwest corner of the checkpoint intersection.

The area proved to be too small and the next day Malmstrom called again on the engineers, who dispatched another dozer. Even two staging areas were not enough to accommodate all the convoys, and the trucks usually sat bumper-to-bumper in them—Malmstrom was thankful that no rockets were coming. It was mostly a boring routine of counting trucks. He still hadn't been able to scout the area, so when troops asked for directions he could only say, "Beats me, ask your convoy commander."

The ARVN literally descended like a plague out of the sky on Lieutenant Malmstrom's checkpoint, in the form of an infantry battalion helicoptering into his second convoy staging area. He had been given no notice so he rushed over to their MACV advisor, exchanging a few terse words with the captain. The ARVN were given the area as their camp, but friction soon developed between the allies. The South Vietnamese soldiers were seemingly undisciplined, wandering around outside their perimeter, so gunhappy that they tossed grenades and fired their rifles like toys, getting on everyone's nerves. Malmstrom complained to the MACV captain, who said he would take care of the problem; it seemed to Malmstrom that, the more he complained, the more he understood how little actual control an American officer had over Vietnamese troops.

The ARVN also made the mistake of wandering into the U.S. convoy areas. The GI truckers did not trust them, didn't like "gooks" anyway, and one night, having caught an ARVN snooping around their vehicles, they nonchalantly punched him silly. The man turned out to be a South Vietnamese officer. The next morning, a lieutenant colonel and a major cornered Malmstrom, looking for an MP officer and, finding none, blamed the problem on him. No, Malmstrom defended himself, he took orders from Major Butler at Vandegrift, was there to organize convoys and had no authority over the troops. They discussed it back and forth and, finally, the lieutenant colonel told him that he was in charge of all the transportation personnel who came into the area. Malmstrom balked. He didn't want to ride roughshod over the truckers, and said the individual company commanders should be in charge of their men. The colonel said no and left.

The friction with the ARVN continued unabated. A back-trail east of the checkpoint was cleared of mines and set up as a way station for the ARVN convoys beginning to arrive. The South Vietnamese truckers seemed to have no grasp of the organizational aspects of convoys, felt they could come and go as they pleased, and made no attempt to coordinate their moves with the Americans. Malmstrom had no interpreters, but he tried to work the ARVN into the routine of waiting in the staging areas and leaving on Route 9 only when permission was given. He hoped they would imitate the American truckers; but they didn't. The biggest problem was that they would run the checkpoint. Four or five times a day, an ARVN convoy would come down the road; Malmstrom and the two MPs would shout, "Slow, slow down! Dung lai, dung lai!" and the ARVN would curve around them and keep going.

Since the road was one-way, coordination was essential and the

ARVN often found themselves head-to-head with U.S. convoys. The bush was so thick along the side that convoys could barely pull over or back up, turning the highway into dusty, shouting chaos as the two columns jockeyed for position. Malmstrom knew it wouldn't be long before the angry GIs simply began manhandling the ARVN drivers out and shoving the trucks off the side to make room, so he and the MPs adopted a drastic tactic: when the South Vietnamese tried to run the checkpoint, they shot out the tires of the lead truck and the fed-up young MPs levelled their M-16s to quiet the now screaming ARVN. They had been hesitant to build a barricade, since the U.S. convoys never ran the point and it could cause accidents during the foggy nights, but they finally had to in order to control the ARVN.

Other problems stemmed from the South Vietnamese's more casual outlook in war. Sometimes, when Malmstrom drove the road with the MPs they found ARVN convoys stopped on the road cooking rice in upturned helmets. If they played around too long, the direction of the road would be switched on them and they would come up against some mean GI truckers coming from the opposite direction. Malmstrom and the MPs would hurry the ARVN along and the complaints went back and forth on both sides. It ended up with another visit to Malmstrom from some ARVN officers, an interpreter, and more U.S. brass. The discussion concluded with his being put in charge of not only the GIs, but also any ARVN who came into the staging areas. The two MPs in the checkpoint jeep joked with him about how he'd gone from a glorified truck counter to the commander of a multi-national force.

CW3 Chuck Hawk, second-in-command of the Flight Check Section, 165th Aviation Group, 1st Aviation Brigade, was summoned to a classified briefing at 7th USAF HQ at Tan Son Nhut airbase when the operation began. Most of those at the meeting were air force officers; they discussed the opening of the Khe Sanh runway and said they hoped to establish an almost continuous daisy-chain of C130s from Da Nang to Khe Sanh. Only one pass was to be allowed. If the C130 missed because of ground fire, weather, or damage to the runway, the pilot was to divert to Quang Tri, follow the coast back to Da Nang, and loop back into the daisy-chain. At peak efficiency, they hoped to have a C130 land every three minutes, slide off the supply pallets without even shutting off the engines, and have forklifts clear the taxiway for the next plane.

Hawk's section was to install the air-traffic-control tower at Khe Sanh; he jeeped back to his base at Long Binh, reported to the lieutenant colonel commanding the section, and they organized a crew of six master sergeants. They started off in a U21 turboprop plane with Hawk flying over four hundred miles to Khe Sanh, only to find the field socked in with fog and visibility at zero.

The next day, they departed Long Binh again, this time with a civilian tech rep who was a radar expert. Hawk circled Khe Sanh as engineers moved their equipment off the new dirt strip they were constructing. As soon as he landed and taxied to the side, the vehicles clanked back to work. Hawk was amazed at the scene around them. Rough-terrain forklifts raised dust as they noisily filled in old bunkers and cleared away rusting wire. Men were digging new positions, putting up tents. Minesweep teams moved slowly and methodically. Others worked on the old, shell-pocked strip. A swarm of helicopters came and went with supplies, raising great sheets of red dust. Hawk couldn't believe all the dust; everything and everyone was covered by the fine red clay and you couldn't tell a black man from a white man unless he rolled up his sleeve.

The airstrip ran east-west and the ATC tower was built north of it. A team from the 125th Air Traffic Control Company had arrived from Quang Tri the day before, and the engineers had already dug the support holes for the tower. Forklifts dropped in the thirty-foot-telephone-pole supports, and a Chinook, with a standard army ATC cab slingloaded underneath it, gingerly set the box atop the four poles. The civilian tech rep was an expert in his field and he schooled the young army specialists in getting the radar and radio equipment installed. After four hours, they had the FM, VHF, and UHF radios working, along with a GCA (Ground Control Approach) radar, and a non-directional beacon. Hawk then had to fly repetitive patterns in the area so they could make adjustments and work out the GCA glide path.

Hawk and two of the master sergeants got in the U21 and flew a pattern at fifteen hundred feet, going back and forth between Khe Sanh and Lang Vei. That was the part of the job he disliked; it could take up to twenty patterns over the same piece of ground to align the radar correctly, giving the enemy ample time to track the unarmed, slow, low-flying plane. Sure enough, as they passed by one of the Lang Vei hills, Hawk heard the distinctive crack of three or four AK-47 rounds going past his ship. It happened again on the next orbit and Hawk decided to call for an airstrike. But the two sergeants were nonplussed; they figured it was just some lone NVA popping off with his AK. They were crustier and older than Hawk, and just shrugged, "Aw, Mister Hawk, don't even call it in. If the Air Force blows him away, they'll just bring in someone who knows how to shoot." It took about twelve patterns to get the radar on target, and the sniper blasted away without hitting a thing.

A day or two later, on 4 February, after the engineers had finished grading the dirt strip, Hawk received a call from 7th USAF HQ at Tan Son Nhut. They wanted to know if the new strip would support C130 traffic; he said he doubted it, the ground was too soft. He was surprised when, a bit later, a C130 began its landing approach. It hit the sod strip, used reverse props to slow down, and then the nose tilted forward as the giant plane sunk in several inches. Hawk and his crew muttered, "Well, what did they expect?" Within a couple of hours, they had drained the bulk of the fuel and chained forklifts to the front landing gears; with the props going, they pulled the C130 out and to the end of strip. It turned around, the pilot hit high speed and they hurtled back down the twelve hundred feet of runway. The engineers began laying down pierced-steel matting, and the delays continued. With the airfield completion behind schedule and the terrain of Route 9 hindering the supply convoys, the buildup at Khe Sanh was below par. Fuel shortages were especially a problem.

The old marine minefields also continued to be a problem. One morning at Khe Sanh, Lieutenant Garwood and a Sergeant Crowle of the 101st Pathfinders monitored a radio request for medevacs for two men wounded on a perimeter patrol. They had walked into the mines outside the wire. Garwood radioed to sit tight, help was on the way, but they called back a minute later saying they had another casualty, and shouting, "Are you going to do anything?" Garwood and Crowle attached a couple of cargo slings to the underbelly of a Huey and hung onto them as the pilot sped to the patrol. The pilot hovered over them, and three wounded grunts could be seen—one with his toes blown off, one with his heel missing, another with a chunk blown out of the back of his leg. They'd stepped on U.S. antipersonnel mines; designed to maim, not kill. Garwood shouted to halt another patrol he could see filing towards the minefield, then they ferried the men out, two at a time on the slings. Garwood and Crowle jumped off, helped the wounded aboard, grabbed dropped gear, and came out last. A man in the second patrol elected to come out on the chopper rather than walk back; he lost his grip and fell to his death.

On 5 February, the first official U.S. deaths of the operation were recorded. A Cobra from D/3/5 Cav, lost in a pocket of fog, flew into a mountain northwest of Khe Sanh, and the two pilots were killed. The following evening, the next official casualty report indicated A/1/82

Artillery, Americal, was hit by 122mm rockets on Route 9 near the Rockpile; one American killed, four wounded. Gunships from the 2/17 Air Cav caught ten NVA on the Laotian border that morning and killed six.

While the 1/11 Infantry and 1/1 Cavalry secured the land route into Laos, the South Vietnamese began moving up their units which were to cross the border on Route 9. This task force consisted of two airborne battalions attached to the ARVN 1st Armor Brigade, commanded by Col. Nguyen Trong Luat. For security reasons, Luat had not been included in the planning of the operation and was only made aware of his role in it on 5 February, by a call to his headquarters in Da Nang. His orders were to take his command group and the 17th Cav and road-march to Dong Ha, where he would be joined by the 7th and 11th Cav. He was then to continue to the Laotian border and make camp adjacent to the U.S. 1/1 Cav until further orders.

The operation was Colonel Luat's first major campaign as a brigade commander, but he had already seen much war, earning prominence as a national hero during the '65 Plei Me battle and receiving high accolades from his U.S. advisors. General Sutherland, however, was an old armor officer who had not been impressed by his inspection of the brigade the past winter. He felt it necessary to visit Luat to impress his mission upon him. That evening he helicoptered from Quang Tri to Dong Ha, where the brigade was preparing to camp overnight, and spoke with Luat and his American advisor. Sutherland went into detail on the POL problem, namely that the delays in rebuilding the strip for C130 traffic meant that the only way to get fuel to the forward supply base at Khe Sanh was in rubber bladders slingloaded to CH47 and CH53 helicopters, or by fuel trucks on the highway. Both methods were precarious and allowed only a minimal amount to be stockpiled; Sutherland, therefore, had issued a general order that all U.S. vehicles and helicopters top off with fuel at Vandegrift so the fuel reserves at Khe Sanh could be used exclusively for the machinery in the area and for occasional emergencies. Sutherland emphasized the problem to Luat and his major, stating that they must top off their tanks and APCs at Vandegrift but as a U.S. commander, Sutherland could only suggest such an action to an ARVN officer.

In the morning, the brigade continued west. When they passed Vandegrift, Colonel Luat did not order a halt for refueling, but continued straight for Khe Sanh. Command relations between the Americans and Vietnamese were frequently baffling and usually frustrating for the U.S. officers involved. In this case, as in most, there was no way to know why the ARVN did not respond to a clear-cut and logical directive. Perhaps as Sutherland had detailed the problem, Luat, struggling to keep up with the English and failing that, had fallen back upon the maddening Vietnamese practice of politely smiling and nodding even though he understood nothing he was hearing. Perhaps, like most ARVN officers, Luat lacked sophisticated training in logistics and from that had developed a cavalier attitude towards the subject, always confident that the Americans would solve any problems that arose.

Either way, the 1st Armor was nearly out of fuel by the time they reached Khe Sanh and, as expected, the Americans did come up with the solution; they had to open their fuel reserves to the ARVN. General Sutherland was furious. When the reports reached him that Luat had not refueled at Vandegrift, but instead, at Khe Sanh, he made a point of discussing the problem with General Lam and expressed his doubts about Luat's abilities as a commander. He would have liked to relieve the colonel of command, but was again restrained because he had no operational control over any ARVN units.

By late afternoon, the 1st Armor was past Lang Vei and they simply pulled off Route 9 into the low hills and scrub brush to make camp. Settling in for the night with the lead force, the 11th Cav, were a half-dozen hitchhiking journalists. Among them were two Englishmen, both on assignment for *Life:* Larry Burrows, a frail-looking man with thick eyeglasses, an utterly noble and unassuming character, who had been covering the war since '62; and John Saar, an athletic blond, a paratrooper officer in the British reserves, who had been there since '69.

This was their first day on the new Laotian front.

The reporters sat down for the evening at the command track of the 11th Cav which had a tent rigged like an awning behind it. The regimental commander, Lt. Col. Bui The Dung, knew enough English to greet them with a warm smile, and the entourage of U.S. advisors was relaxed and open as they ate dinner with their Vietnamese friends. It was a quaint scene, men in a grassy field on the way to war; as Saar noted, "Rice savored with onions and vegetables bubbles over dozens of fires, scalding tea in blue-and-white china bowls passes delicately from one hand to the next." The war seemed far away, its only reminder the jets dropping bombs in the distance.

Saar was standing and talking with Burrows about film shipments when the scream of a diving jet sounded too near. The next moment, two explosions erupted close by—and then suddenly, the space around them was all blast, noise, and confusion. His brain lurched at the abrupt impact of the explosions; for a freeze-framed microsecond he could see the horror and incredulity on the faces around him, and then everything was a scramble for cover. Saar jumped into a cooking trench, catching a blur from the corner of his eye of a body diving through mid-air for another slit trench. Two large fires and two boiling pots were inches away as Saar hugged the earth—thinking, Christ, I'm going to roast to death—too paralyzed with fear to move, afraid another salvo of what he thought had been mortars would land. He reached for his helmet, looked up to the din and confusion at ground level, and saw Burrows already up and running for the impact zone.

Without thinking, Saar followed him.

They were the first ones to the craters and Burrows hit the prone to photograph the scene. Saar stood shocked and sickened, his mind unable to accept what he was seeing. ARVN soldiers, dead and wounded, were strewn in the elephant grass and brush, screams of pain and cries for help coming amid the explosions. And things were still exploding, flashing red in the black. Patches of brush were on fire and an APC was ablaze, cooking off ammunition. All around was confusion and shock. One officer, an advisor major, sat hunched up, chin on his chest, momentarily too rattled to move. Others were galvanized with adrenaline; two officers quickly jumped to a radio to call for medevacs; and then the unshakable Burrows was again at Saar's side, shouting, "Come and help me bring that chap in!"

There were no stretchers so Burrows and Saar awkwardly picked up a wounded ARVN by his arms and legs. They stumbled back over the uneven ground, sweating hard, Saar feeling the blood soak into his shirt. The man was torn up by shrapnel, his chest, stomach, and head oozing life, and he suddenly gave a shuddering groan of terrible pain. Burrows answered with a groan of pity. They dragged the soldier into an old crater where ARVN medics were frantically setting up an aid station. Saar could hear the American advisors shouting back and forth and their talk was not of a mortar raid, but of a jet accidentally hitting them with cluster bombs. Three bombs had been dropped, each one splitting open in mid-air to disperse dozens of cluster bomblets over the field. They kept exploding at random points, spewing shrapnel.

Men still kept moving. Saar was crouched in the crater when a young ARVN medic raced in barefoot, wide-eyed but still clutching his aid bag. South Vietnamese soldiers ran amid the explosions to drag wounded comrades back. Two more times, Saar and Burrows ventured out into the chaos to drag men back and lay them at the edge of the crater. It was pandemonium around the aid station, the Americans excitedly calling out on the radios, men running into each other in the dark, the APC going up in a roar of exploding ammunition. The wounded kept piling in, few able to walk alone. Saar recoiled at the individual scenes. One ARVN rolled in the pool of his own blood, rocking to and fro with pain, until three medics tried to hold him down to change dressings and he bucked in anguish, ramming his head into a body sprawled beside him. Another man lifted his head to see his leg, reduced to bone and flayed flesh, with medics crouched above it scissoring away the trousers, and silently let his head fall back. An ARVN lying in the crucifix position inched across the dirt to the man beside him; they clasped hands tightly and talked in murmurs. Saar couldn't imagine what they were saying, couldn't imagine a worse scenario: two medics killed outright in the first explosions, the rest undermanned to handle such carnage. They worked on those who had a chance, abandoning the seriously wounded. Saar watched one man die, wishing to God he would die quickly, die peacefully—not as he did, heaving his chest, laboriously trying to suck air down a blood-filled throat, suddenly dying with his chest still expanded. He saw the first man he and Burrows had brought in, already dead, the other two they'd carried still unattended in the dirt.

Saar and Burrows finally left the wounded and moved about the perimeter, taking photographs, watchful of the cluster bombs nestled unexploded in the brush. Saar was terrified of them, having no idea what might set them off. At the command APC, they found Lieutenant Colonel Dung wearing a long coat and hunched over the radios. He was trying to coordinate the evacuation of the wounded, alerting his outer posts lest the NVA take advantage of the chaos with an attack. Among the advisors, the most assertive was a Major Todd, a Georgian with the ARVN paratroopers. He shouted at the Vietnamese in bastard English and French, getting them ready to evacuate the wounded when the choppers came.

The first helicopter circled over Route 9, came down cautiously through the night fog, then abruptly pulled up when clouds of red road dust whipped up.

"What's the problem?"

"He can't see to land!"

"Throw water to dampen the dust!"

The helicopter landed, still churning up considerable dust, and Major Todd shouted at his paratroopers, "Only the men! No stretchers 'cause so beaucoup many!" The red lights of the helo glowed eerily on the helmets of the ARVN as they ran forward with the most seriously wounded. Saar watched them, "forced to treat their comrades like so many carcasses, the paratroops shove wounded on top of one another until the cabin is a surreal slaughterhouse."

With the wounded gone, Saar could see the ARVN regain their confidence. He heard a man laugh; others began to talk and joke again, and shovels clanked in the dark as soldiers covered the bloodstains and bandages. Although it had been a U.S. jet that had caused the casualties, he detected no animosity among the South Vietnamese. They accepted it as an accident of war. The dead were wrapped in ponchos and tied to stretchers with bandages. One of the advisors suggested the helo pilots be called back to get the bodies without being told they were running risks for the dead, but Major Todd quickly axed that idea.

When the final reckoning was done, it was duly noted that at 1920 hours on 6 February 1971, one aircraft from the U.S.S. Ranger attacked a moving target on Route 9, accidentally hitting friendly forces and causing the deaths of six ARVN, the wounding of fifty-one, and the destruction of one APC. They were the first South Vietnamese casualties of Operation Lam Son 719. Four days later, the reporter who had behaved so courageously during the mishap, Larry Burrows, boarded an ARVN helicopter to cover the war in Laos. The helo was shot down. His body was never recovered.

On 7 February, Lieutenant Malmstrom was at his Khe Sanh checkpoint when a small column of empty five-thousand-gallon tanker trucks pulled up. They had come to field-test the large trucks on Route 9 and, although their captain seemed excited, the truckers were less than enthusiastic. They talked about maintenance problems that were sure to develop and that the turns were too tricky for their wide loads. It was about an hour before dawn the next morning when an MP radioman woke Malmstrom, saying, "You gotta be kidding me!" He couldn't understand why higher would send the vulnerable fuel trucks at night, when in the morning they could have air cover.

He could just think they were hurting for fuel worse than reported.

Sp4 Spurgeon was asleep in an APC of the 1/77 Scouts—he was suddenly startled awake by a big ball of fire illuminating the area. He stood up in the crew hatch to see what was happening. The track sentry was standing astonished on deck with a blanket hanging from his shoulders; to their west, around the Rockpile, there were shots and explosions. They cranked up their APC just as a lone track sped from the direction of the ambush. Lieutenant Revelak sat atop the open driver's hatch beside the fifty mount, yelling to follow him. They sped down the paved highway right up to three burning fuel trucks, one of which had crashed over the road embankment, and Spurgeon could see figures moving in the brush. He held his fire, unable to distinguish friend from foe. Revelak jumped onto his track, there were eight GIs on deck; Spurgeon grabbed an M-60, and they hauled ass further into the ambush area. A GI wearing a steel pot jogged alongside them for a second, screaming something, but they ignored him. Revelak shouted to fire, Spurgeon started to ask, "What about our guys?"—and sides of the road lit up with tracers.

They didn't fire straight ahead; there were more burning trucks there.

They crossed a bridge, passed the burning trucks, then saw a gun truck on fire down the highway. Spurgeon then saw a bareheaded man ten feet from his APC, crawling in a puddle of blood which reflected in the flames. He levelled his M-60 to blow the NVA away—then abruptly noticed the man was too big to be a Vietnamese, and that he looked black. The GI was painfully struggling to get up. Spurgeon pulled his gun away as they sped past. Another soldier appeared from the shadows, running in a crouch beside their APC, shouting something they could not hear. They stopped at the burning gun truck, its weapons hanging down, unmanned; there was only darkness past that point. They did a pivot on the highway and roared back, Revelak screaming to fire up the place again, Spurgeon cradling the M-60 as they bumpily tore on, emptying a hundred-round belt at the gun truck, grooving on the tracers and ricochets.

They stopped and dismounted at the ambush scene. Spurgeon could see a burnt-out truck, four others parked, all of them riddled with AK bullet holes. The truckers were gone, already evacuated. A jeep full of lifers arrived, all in helmets and flak jackets, and they stood in the headlight beam, bullshitting, Spurgeon thought, like cops at a traffic accident. The next morning, he talked with a GI who said the NVA had ambushed the lead of the convoy with AK-47 and RPG fire; they had tried to stop traffic from crossing the bridge, he said, but the gun-truck crew had shouted at them to get out of the way and had barrelled towards the shooting. The North Vietnamese then blew them away. The two GIs who'd been yelling at the APC, it turned out, had been trying to get them to turn back before it was too late. APCs began clearing the wrecks off the highway and Spurgeon thought it looked like some kind of graveyard, the burnt-out shells shoved together down the road embankment. The official word was that one GI was killed, eight wounded, and six tanker trucks destroyed.

Lieutenant Colonel Meyer arrived and directed the tank-infantry teams of 1/77 Armor to conduct a search for the ambushers. An NVA RPG crew tried to hit a tank, but the GIs gunned them down before they could get their round off. They were still cleaning up the mess when a helicopter armada began beating overhead. This was the morning the ARVN had chosen to invade Laos.

PART TWO:
Operation Lam Son 719

CHAPTER SIX:
D Day into Laos

Lieutenant General Lam chose 8 February 1971, as the day the South Vietnamese would invade Laos. It was not a date he preferred but rather one which had been pressed upon him. The rainy weather and the unexploded ordnance on the Khe Sanh plateau had delayed construction of the airstrip and, thus, the fuel and ammunition reserves had not reached their peak. To wait, though, invited disaster as by now the NVA were well aware of the allies' intentions, and were moving to bolster their forces in Laos. Lam had little choice but to attack as soon as possible.

To carry out the spoiling operations, Lam had five major combat units assembled on the border: the 1st Infantry Division, 1st Airborne Division, Vietnamese Marine Corps Division, 1st Ranger Group, and 1st Armor Brigade. With Tchepone as the western objective of the attack and Route 9 the straight line to the target, Lam's plan called for his units to leapfrog to the objective through a series of firebases along the mountainous flanks of the road, while the armor headed straight down the dirt highway. Destroying as they went, they were eventually to reach Tchepone, then begin the withdrawal phase. It was hoped (especially by U.S. planners) that the ARVN could maintain the offensive until the advent of the rainy season in May and then withdraw through BA 611 and the A Shau Valley.

The battlefield from the border to Tchepone was split north/south by Route 9 and a branch of the Tchepone River which ran generally east/west. The terrain was divided into three areas; mountain ranges to the north, flat brushy country in the river valley, and more rolling mountains to the south. The latter region was marked by two overpowering terrain features. A fifteen hundred foot escarpment ran thirty-five kilometers, from the border nearly all the way to Tchepone. There was also the Co Roc, a mountain range four kilometers long, which rose abruptly on the border, just inside Laos. The escarpment and the Co Roc dominated the battlefield. Lam's plan called for the 1st Infantry Division to secure these two vantage points while the main thrust occurred to the north. The 1st Armor was to slice down Route 9, while the 1st Airborne and 1st Rangers were airmobiled into the northern mountains to move on Tchepone. The Vietnamese Marines were to be the reserve force in the Khe Sanh area.

General Lam had never before commanded such a large-scale operation, a fact which did not particularly disturb his counterpart, General Sutherland; he considered Lam "a strong, positive leader who could be very decisive with his commanders in I Corps. I respected and trusted General Lam and I believe that he had the same feelings toward me." Others gave more mixed reviews. To them, Lam was a large, moonfaced man with a pompous air, who had been made the Corps commander because he'd kept his infantry division loyal to Saigon during the '66 Buddhist Rebellion. Like most ARVN corps commanders, he was an administrator who gave broad directives and left the tactical planning to his division and regimental commanders. He had no experience in actually controlling a major campaign, and the Vietnamese Marines gave him the nickname Old Bloody Hands after his manner of grandly sweeping his hands over tactical maps when discussing operational concepts, leaving the impression that the welfare of his men was not an overriding concern.

Lam's command was complicated by a host of petty jealousies and political jostling among his subordinate commanders. Except for the 1st Infantry Division, the other units assigned to the operation had never operated as complete divisions in the field; thus, brigade commanders were used to operating independently and division commanders were accustomed neither to exercising control nor to being controlled. For example, when the 1st Airborne Division set up its command post within three kilometers of the I Corps HQ on the Khe Sanh plateau, its commander, Lt. Gen. Du Quoc Dong, refused to leave his plush villa headquarters in Saigon. As an officer equal in rank to Lam, he was upset at being given a secondary role. He finally joined his CP, but still refused to go to I Corps briefings at FSB Kilo, I Corps HQ south of Khe Sanh, sending a staff major instead. To further complicate the matter, the Airborne Division was considered an elite unit by President Thieu and had previously been afforded special considerations; Dong was the type to flaunt his friendship with the president and to try to use governmental pressures to get what he wanted.

With a commander as weak as Dong, it was no wonder the paratroopers performed as they did. As the Deputy Commander of II Field Force during the Cambodian invasion, General Sutherland had been dismayed to watch an Airborne unit secure an LZ without opposition, then sit out the duration of the campaign. No amount of cajoling could persuade Dong to seek the sound of battle. Dong was placed in operational control of the 1st Armor Brigade for the Laos operation. After the armor set up a CP at FSB Kilo, little liaison was established between them and the Airborne CP; and Dong, an inexperienced commander with no expertise in armor, virtually ignored the brigade, giving them inadequate tactical guidance and logistical support.

Similar problems arose with the VNMC Division. The Commandant of the VNMC, Lt. Gen. Le Nguyen Khang, held a slight seniority edge over Lam but—either because he was miffed at being placed in a subordinate position, or because, realizing his own inexperience, he wanted to save face—Khang stayed in Saigon. His only visits to the Quang Tri front consisted of brief tours in the company of his political ally, Vice President Ky, and were more of a show to bully Lam than for any military value. Khang left the operational command of the marines to the assistant commandant, Col. Bui The Lan, who set up his CP in the general vicinity of Kilo. Fortunately, Lan was an intense, taciturn man, a field soldier who exercised firm control over the independent-minded brigade commanders. The Vietnamese Marines were, likewise, a tough, combat-proven bunch.

Perhaps Lam's best asset was the 1st Infantry Division. Its commander, Brigadier General Phu, was not a brilliant leader but he was a combat veteran, competent, and hard working. His division, alone in the invasion force, had often worked as a single force under his command in major operations. The division had seen much combat in MR1 and its troops were experienced men who had exhibited much bravery and tenacity. As things developed, Phu was the only major commander who followed Lam's orders.

The actual ARVN push across the border was wholly dependent on U.S. Army Aviation; helicopter units had been streaming north before, during, and after the opening of the operation. The largest aviation unit setting up for the invasion was the 223rd Combat Aviation Battalion under Lt. Col. Gerald W. Kirklighter, a gruff, blunt, and experienced pilot on his second Vietnam tour. He had taken command only a week before the operation began, and the 223rd CAB was itself a confusing hodgepodge of various helicopter companies thrown together solely for this campaign.

When the shift north began, Kirklighter had been a deputy group commander at Tuy Hoa in MR2; the deputy commander of the 1st Aviation Brigade flew in, had a private conversation with his group commander, and the two officers, who both knew him well, picked Kirklighter to command the 223rd during Laos. At the time, the battalion was in the process of standing down, its former CO and staff rotating home or being assigned to other units. The battalion command consisted of a mere hundred men in the Hq&Hq Company. Maj. "Banjo" Davis, a former enlisted man with a touch for administration, was assigned as executive officer. Maj. John A. G. Klose, ex-sergeant, an unassuming but dedicated aviator just arrived for his second combat tour, was made the operations officer.

The battalion was still getting back on its feet when Kirklighter was informed that Dong Ha was to be his new CP. He had no information on the upcoming mission when he and Major Klose hopped a U21 from Tuy Hoa to Camp Eagle. There they met with officers of the 101st Aviation Group and took a Huey for a quick recon of Dong Ha. They landed in a desolate area of the base; a lieutenant colonel gestured grandly at the bushy plain and said to Kirklighter and Klose, "This is yours. We have secured permission from the Vietnamese to make this your battalion headquarters."

The only structure in view was a tin-roofed hootch with no walls.

Within a few days, the 223d CAB received a list of its components (the 48th AHC, 173d AHC, 282nd AHC, 235th AWC, D/227th AWC, 179th ASHC, and the 75th Med), and Majors Davis and Klose worked from Tuy Hoa to get the companies up to Dong Ha via air, ship, and convoy. Kirklighter went first with the advance party of Hq&Hq Company. They took a C130 to Quang Tri, then begged, borrowed, and stole some trucks to get to Dong Ha. It was raining when they arrived and the abandoned airstrip was just as cold, wet, and miserable as everyone had feared. There was little left save some old Marine tent frames which the locals hadn't carried away for firewood. In short order, they moved in, throwing canvas over the frames to escape the weather, laying down C ration cardboard and ammo-box wood on the dirt floors, setting up cots and commo gear. They lived in tents, ate C rats, and, by the end of that first day, were swept by freezing winds and rains. If it hadn't been so miserable, Kirklighter could have found it amusingly incongruous to see soldiers, in one of the hottest regions of the world, huddled around campfires, wearing flak jackets for warmth, with blankets wrapped around them.

One at a time, the helicopter companies began arriving at the 223rd CAB HQ. Kirklighter's major problem at Dong Ha was security. For the first time in his experiences in Vietnam, an aviation unit was in the field without infantry support. He was in contact with the 5th Mech but they had no units assigned to the airfield, and the mech units he saw passing through appeared ill-disciplined. There were jeeps full of ARVN roaring through the area, but he had no communications with their commanders and was leery of depending on them to move if anything happened. Kirklighter had no choice but to force his men to pull double duty. Door gunners, clerks, cooks, and mechanics began piling sandbags around the tents, stringing wire, standing night guard duty. The bitching doubled. Aviators don't lead a charmed life, Kirklighter mused, and he was taking no chances. Luckily, even though Dong Ha was in easy range of the NVA artillery in the DMZ, not a round was fired at them.

This made Kirklighter's next biggest headache the lack of information. He had no idea why his battalion had been dispatched to the DMZ. Security was tight.

The briefing for aviation support to Lam Son 719 was held by General Berry and Colonel Davis at Khe Sanh on the evening of 7 February, in the 101st Airborne Forward Headquarters. The CP was emplaced just south of the runway in an ingenious construction of four trailers lowered into giant trenches, in the shape of a Greek cross, with a connecting catwalk between them and sturdy overhead cover. The headquarters was virtually impregnable to enemy shelling. The helicopters of the various aviation commanders were parked on the runway, and the men assembled in one of the underground trailers. They sat in folding chairs, facing Berry and Davis, who stood before the map board under soft fluorescent light.

In his calm, professional tone, Berry announced the invasion of Laos.

"I'll be a son of a bitch," Kirklighter mumbled to himself, "I thought we were going into the A Shau."

Berry and Davis proceeded to detail the ARVN I Corps plan, and noted that no U.S. advisors were allowed in Laos. Therefore, U.S. ground rescue teams which could have been used to recover crews of shot-down helicopters, were also forbidden. Because of security, the LZs in Laos had not been reconned—a very sticky point. The attack was to begin in the morning with the armor brigade crossing the Tchepone

River on Route 9. At 1000 hours, U.S. helicopters were to launch three simultaneous combat assaults; the Rangers and Airborne along the north flank, the Infantry on the escarpment.

The 101st Airborne Division and the 101st Aviation Group were to form the nucleus of command from Khe Sanh, and the duties of the divisional and attached units were detailed at the briefing as follows:

> The 223d Combat Aviation Battalion, 1st Aviation Brigade (Lt. Col. Gerald Kirklighter) to support the 1st Infantry Division.
>
> The 158th Aviation Battalion, 101st Airborne Division (Lt. Col. William Peachy) to support the 1st Airborne Division, 1st Ranger Group, and the 1st Armor Brigade.
>
> The 14th Combat Aviation Battalion, 1st Aviation Brigade (Lt. Col. Joseph Rutkowski) to support the Vietnamese Marine Corps Division.
>
> The 159th Support Aviation Battalion, 101st Airborne Division (Lt. Col. George Newton) to control all medium and heavy lift support to all U.S. and ARVN units on both sides of the border.
>
> The 4th Battalion, 77th Aerial Field Artillery, 101st Airborne Division (Lt. Col. C. L. Nowalk) to provide Cobra gunship support for 101st ABD aviation missions in Laos and U.S. ground missions in South Vietnam.
>
> The 2nd Squadron, 17th Air Cavalry, 101st Airborne Division (Lt. Col. Robert Molinelli) to control all air cav troops and to provide scouting and gunship support to the entire ARVN invasion force as personally dictated by the CG, ARVN I Corps.

When the briefing concluded, Kirklighter received permission from Berry to leave his aircraft at Dong Ha—he did not trust Khe Sanh's vulnerability to rocket attacks—then sent Major Klose and the company commanders back to Dong Ha to organize the battalion. Kirklighter spent the night at Khe Sanh to catch up on last minute details and to establish radio communications with Colonel Harrison—recently appointed as senior advisor, ARVN 1st Infantry Division, after commanding a brigade in the 101st Airborne—to coordinate the pickup and assault. The hectic procedure was being repeated by all the commanders involved; as Major Klose remarked, "It was like twelve football games going on at the same time."

General Sutherland had planned to put three days of airstrikes into Laos to soften up the numerous NVA AA positions, but the unexpectedly foul weather had grounded the jets for one of those days and had hampered them for the other two. The plans had been prepared in a rush and there was no chance for careful analysis. They were already behind schedule. Nevertheless, a spirit of easy victory pervaded the commanders as their units boiled along the border, waiting to be released. As the senior advisor to the Airborne wrote in his after-action report: "It was apparent at this time that United States intelligence felt that the operation would be lightly opposed and that a two-day preparation of the area prior to D day by tactical air would effectively neutralize the enemy antiaircraft capability although the enemy was credited with having one hundred seventy to two hundred antiaircraft weapons of mixed caliber in the operational area. The tank threat was considered minimal and the reinforcement capability was listed as fourteen days for two divisions from north of the DMZ." The ARVN were expected to be in Tchepone in about three days.

The official word put the ARVN 1st Armor Brigade crossing the border at 0700 hours, 8 February, 1971. The helicopter combat assaults followed shortly. The Dong Ha airstrip was alive and in motion as the 223rd Combat Aviation Battalion mounted up. Major Klose and the company commanders had briefed the aircraft commanders the evening before. The briefing reminded Klose of a football huddle, all conversations pared down to the essentials, everyone knowing the routine. It all depended on professionalism and teamwork. The facts were quickly outlined: time of departure, coordinates of the pick-up zones and landing zones, radio frequencies to be used, route of flight, coordination of gunship escort. "Any questions? Okay, go brief your flights." The night had been a nervous one, and busy, with crew chiefs and mechanics going over the helicopters by flashlight.

It was cold and brisk in the morning, steam coming from the breath, men putting on gloves and jungle fatigues over their flight suits for warmth. C ration coffee was sipped, cigarettes chain-smoked, maps rechecked, door guns mounted, rocket pods loaded. Word came to go and crews climbed aboard their machines. In moments the helicopters were vibrating, blades thumping and turbine-engines screaming. They lifted off the strip, circled, then assumed a trail formation. Major Klose piloted the battalion C&C and set the group down at FSB Kilo. There Kirklighter joined them and another quick briefing was held with General Phu and Colonel Harrison. The CA was to be made on the Co Roc ridgeline to secure the vantage point overlooking Route 9; the position was designated LZ Hotel and the ARVN 4/3 Infantry was slotted for the CA. The South Vietnamese infantrymen stood in long lines by the helo pad boarding the waiting choppers one squad to a bird.

They took off again. Kirklighter and Klose flew the C&C, the ARVN battalion commander and staff in the cabin with radio headsets. They crossed the border on schedule and reconned the Co Roc in the C&C. Two small clearings, about fifty feet by fifty feet and relatively flat, were visible in the jungled ridgeline and they pulled up after marking them with smoke. The slicks went in and the ARVN jumped out. There was no shooting. The CA continued with the helicopters shuttling back to Kilo for more troops while the Chinooks began coming in with slingloaded bulldozers, bunker material, and 105mm artillery pieces.

Lt. Philip Smith of the 48th Blue Stars hadn't been able to sleep the night before. The cold LZ made them all feel a lot better. They figured Laos would be no sweat.

The 158th Aviation Battalion took fire from the moment they crossed the border. One of the pilots, WO Harold Smith of A Company, was flying with an ARVN squad aboard his Huey. He would have preferred to have been anyplace else. Twenty-one years old, from South Mountain, Pennsylvania, Smith was on his second Vietnam tour. The first had been as a teenage marine at the siege of Khe Sanh; he'd joined the army, within months of his discharge, for their warrant officer pilot program—he'd always wanted to fly—and thinking his previous combat tour made it illegal to send him back to Vietnam. It didn't. His company, the Alpha Ghostriders, spent the night in the bunkers at Khe Sanh and awoke to the sight of two hundred helicopters on the sod strip. Their battalion, thirty slicks, crossed into Laos with Rangers aboard.

Once across the river, the tracers began floating up at them. A 12.7mm machine-gun position took them under fire from somewhere in the jungle blanket, strafing the whole trail formation. The third ship in formation, piloted by WO Paul Stewart and WO Tom Doody, took a burst in the tailboom. Stewart calmly reported on the radio, "Lead, chalk three has taken some hits. I've lost pedal control. Am returning to Khe Sanh."

A buddy shouted over the radio that he wanted to follow him as cover.

Lieutenant Colonel Peachy screamed to stay in formation.

A few moments later, Stewart was again calmly on the radio, even as panicked shouts could be heard from the ARVN and maybe some of the crewmen on board, "Lead, chalk three is going inverted at this time." In the next moment, the ship crashed upside down in the treetops and exploded. There were no survivors.

There was a helpless, angry silence over the radios.

Smith's crew chief hollered on the intercom that he had a make on the 12.7mm, and requested permission to fire.

"Go ahead!"

The man's M-60 popped ineffectually at the trees far below.

All along the way, NVA fire poured up at them. This is fucking ridiculous, Smith thought, just glad his ship wasn't taking any hits. He made five more trips into Laos that afternoon, to ferry in ARVN infantrymen, taking more and more fire each time as the NVA prepared for them. Each mission was a story unto itself, he thought, but there were so many, his mind began to blur from exhaustion. Around noontime, WO Lyle Borders, a Cobra pilot with B/7/1 Air Cav, was screening west of the 1st Infantry Division insertions. His team of two Cobra gunships, two Loach scout ships, and a C&C Huey slick found nothing and was heading back to refuel at Khe Sanh. Another team from the Bravo Dutchmasters flew west past them to take over the air reconnaissance; and within minutes, the second team was urgently radioing that they were taking fire, that their C&C Huey was hit at four thousand feet and going in. It burned all the way to the ground. WO Borders and his team circled around and as they came in high; he took photographs through the plexiglass windshield. The C&C was crashed upside down in a field of tall elephant grass and bamboo, white smoke pouring from it. The Loaches buzzed low, throwing red smoke grenades at the sound of NVA weapons in the treelines. The smoke slowly filtered over the tops of two-hundred-foot trees, and Borders banked his Cobra down to rake the area with rockets and minigun bursts.

On the ground, the crew chief of the downed Huey, Sgt. John Seaman, had been hurled from the wreck. It was a cold morning and he wore a set of jungle fatigues over his fireproof nomex flight suit; the fatigues were on fire and he burned his hands as he frantically beat out the flames. He ran back to his helicopter. The copilot, Capt. David Fox, and the door-gunner, a young private, were dead. The pilot, Capt. Joseph Beardon, was hanging upside down, strapped in his seat. He was semi-conscious and being burned by the fire, but when Seaman moved to get him, the blistering heat set his clothes afire again. He retreated. Seaman charged again into the flames and managed to drag Beardon out into the grass.

The Cobras continued pumping fire into the trees; Borders could see no bodies but the NVA fire ceased. A Loach landed about forty meters from the Huey and the door gunner ran to the wreck. Because of the thick bamboo and elephant grass, he had to run into the wall of vegetation and mash it down bit by bit before he could reach the badly burned Beardon and Seaman.

The troop's aero rifle platoon (Blue Team) was on alert at Lang Vei with the Hoc Bao Company, ARVN 1st Infantry Division. The Blues were perimeter security, the Hoc for pilot rescue, to conform to the ban on U.S. ground troops in Laos; but when the air mission commander requested the reaction force, the Blues shrugged with the attitude of, "If you didn't intend to use us, why'd you bring us up?" and climbed into their Hueys. They secured the crash site and medevacked Beardon and Seaman. The Blues were still on the ground in Laos—reportedly in contact with the NVA—when Lieutenant Colonel Molinelli, the cav commander, ordered in the Hoc Bao. The ARVN were inserted behind the Dutchmaster Blues and took their place in an orderly transition of lines under fire. Molinelli assembled the Blues back in South Vietnam, told them their CA had been a direct violation of presidential orders, and asked them not to discuss it with reporters. He then reported the incident to General Berry; it followed the chain of command to Nixon. Days later, he publicly changed policy and U.S. troops could now be inserted to evacuate downed airmen. The U.S. aero rifle platoons were, however, never again inserted into Laos.

The initial three-pronged airmobile assault into Laos was underway when the 223rd CAB was taxed to bring in another ARVN battalion. Their first move to LZ Hotel had been the only aviation operation of the day not taken under fire, and their next assignment was to CA the ARVN 1/3 and 2/3 Infantry to LZ Blue, several miles south of Hotel. Lieutenant Colonel Kirklighter and Major Klose again dropped into Kilo, consulting with Colonel Harrison and the ARVN commanders. Several ARVN rode with them, including the battalion staff, an English-speaking radioman, and the deputy division commander, a Colonel Ghai. Kirklighter heard that Ghai had been nicknamed the John Wayne of the DMZ, and he appeared to be a tough customer, complete with a pair of pearl-handled revolvers worn Patton-style at the waist. The South Vietnamese troopers looked tough too, he thought; they appeared well disciplined and effective, each man with a helmet, rucksack, and modern U.S. weapons—a far cry from the ARVN he'd seen on his first tour four years earlier.

With Klose flying, the C&C circled the jungle at the coordinates designated for LZ Blue. It looked good, big and level without too many shrubs or trees in the way, and they made another pass to mark it with smoke for the Hueys following them. They sailed low, the crew chief holding a smoke grenade with the pin pulled and the spoon held tight; Kirklighter said, "Now," and the chief dropped it from the cabin door. It jetted below them, thick and bright. They were pulling up when the crack of small arms fire erupted. They gained altitude unscathed, Kirklighter got on the horn for air cav gunships and recon support, but word came that they were tied up with the airborne and recon insertions. In their place, Kirklighter ordered in the UH1C Huey gunships of the 48th Joker Guns, and they skimmed at treetop level around the intended LZ. The first shots had not been much, the recon did not draw any fire, and no enemy gun positions could be seen through the foliage. The ARVN commanders on board elected to continue the CA.

The slicks of the 48th led the approach into the LZ, Maj. Willis R. Bunting flying the lead Huey as he usually did, gunships shadowing them as security. Lieutenant Smith was piloting a slick five back from the major, when he suddenly saw so many black spots burst around chalk four that he thought his engine was malfunctioning. Then he was abruptly aware of the rattle of fire around him, of Major Bunting shouting into the radio that he was hit. He watched the major's slick trail smoke and make a crash landing on a sandbar in a river.

A rescue Huey quickly darted down to get the crew.

A quarter-mile from the LZ, they dropped low and Smith could see a bush shaking below them, fire coming from it. His door-gunners fired madly at it and Smith watched the stream, every fifth round a tracer, bounce harmlessly off the bush. Jesus, he thought, they must have a concrete or steel bunker in there. He piloted his ship into the LZ, the door-gunners still going hot, the five ARVN aboard scrambled out, and he quickly pulled pitch out of there, enemy fire cracking in all directions the entire time.

Several more Hueys were hit coming out of the LZ and Kirklighter began directing them in from different directions. It did no good; the NVA 12.7mm machine gun emplacements under the trees had the range to track the ships no matter which direction they came in from. The ninth chopper in and out of the LZ was strafed and it crashed in the brush. North Vietnamese soldiers began moving towards the wreck and the crew radioed their position while moving away. Kirklighter figured the best thing to do was simply to go on in and get them. He told Klose to bring them down. The crewmen were in a tangle of elephant grass and scrub brush and as the Huey skimmed low towards them, the door-gunner said over the helmet intercom that he could see NVA moving towards the crew. He opened fire with his M-60. As they came closer, some of the stranded men tried to wave them away because of the fire, but Klose took the ship down. They landed in the field of elephant grass, the rotor blades whacking noisily at it, more NVA fire cracking around them. Two rounds thudded into the Huey, jostling them like a car going over a bump, as the crew emerged from the brush and ran through the prop-blasted grass. They scrambled aboard, and Kirklighter and Klose worked the controls, building up rpm for the overcrowded Huey, then quickly lifted up and away from the NVA fire.

The caution-lights on the console had flashed the moment the two AK rounds had hit the bird, but it was still flyable so they headed for the border, radioing ahead for another C&C helicopter to be prepared for them. Lang Vei was the first safe haven across the border from Laos—if an injured helo managed to cross the border, the pilot could practically autorotate down to it—and they landed there at the refuel/rearm pad manned by the 101st DISCOM. The two bullet holes in the transmission were smoking. Colonel Ghai, who had been educated in the United States, joked to Kirklighter that he felt like Lee changing mounts as they climbed aboard a new ship and headed back into Laos.

When the day was finally over, the men of the 158th Aviation Battalion returned to Camp Evans, as they would every night during the campaign. Theirs was another world where the hell of the day was washed away with clean beds, free-flowing booze, and rock music in the Officer's Club. Young and trying to bolster themselves through the horrors they were enduring, they would get drunk and sing, "Gory, gory, what a helluva way to die. . . ." The enlisted men of the battalion let off steam at night too; sometimes when the pilots walked past the EM barracks, the smell of marijuana was overpowering. The attitude of most of the officers was, "If the enlisted men do their job, don't hassle them about the grass."

The men of C Company were the most wrung out that night. The Huey that'd exploded had been from their Phoenix Birds and four of their comrades, including Stewart and Doody, were dead. They were most saddened about Stewart, who had previously earned the nickname Mr. Invincible for his cool courage and who had just extended his tour. Lt. Bruce Updyke, a twenty-three-year-old slick pilot from Ohio, was getting drunk in the O Club when someone said, "Wasn't that a bitch about Stewart getting wasted?"

"Yeah," Updyke said, "it really was."

"Fuck it," his friend mumbled, "better him than me."

The sad part, Updyke thought, was that they really meant that, even when a good friend was involved. One had to become calloused to carry on and, as the days wore on, he had buddies morbidly joke to him before he took off, "Hey, man, if something happens, can I have your stereo?" In spite of the banter they all knew they could rely on each other.

By the end of 8 February, the ARVN 1st Infantry Division had established two firebases in Laos south of Route 9: LZ Hotel held by 4/3 and LZ Blue held by 1/3 and 2/3. The ARVN 1st Airborne Division had two firebases north of Route 9: Hill 30, held by the 2nd and 7th Airborne Battalions; and Hill 31, held by the 3d Airborne Battalion. The ARVN 1st Ranger Group had established two firebases northeast of the paratroopers: Ranger North, held by the 39th Ranger Battalion; and Ranger South, held by the 21st Ranger Battalion. The ARVN 1st Armor Brigade had advanced nine kilometers into Laos on Route 9. While the air moves had been met with heavy fire (seven helos were recorded shot down on the first day), the ARVN foot patrols met virtually no resistance. There were no delusions that the Communists were not there. The next morning, bad weather cancelled all air moves, knocking the ARVN back another notch in their schedule and giving the NVA additional time to prepare.

CHAPTER SEVEN:
An Uneasy Start

The foul weather, which hampered air moves on 9 February, did not tie down the armor spearhead. The 1st Armor Brigade continued the attack down Route 9 that day and Akihiko Okamura, a Japanese photojournalist who had briefly been a prisoner of the Viet Cong in 1964, smuggled himself aboard a supply truck.

The truck stopped at the head of the 1st Armor column. They were nine kilometers inside Laos, and preparing to push deeper, when Okamura climbed aboard the third APC in line. Morale seemed high among the combat troops; he thought the paratroopers riding atop the vehicles looked sharp and disciplined and the APC crew was friendly. He was a nonsmoker, but carried many cigarettes to give to the troops, and sat talking with them as they lurched forward. The dirt highway was narrow at that point, unused and overgrown, hemmed in by a wall of bamboo and vines. The tracks ground through the foliage corridor, occasionally cutting across narrow footpaths that crossed the highway. The paratroopers would hop from the vehicles each time, pointing and shouting enthusiastically, "Ho Chi Minh Trail!" They camped on Route 9 that night, the soldiers inviting Okamura to their dinner, boiled rice in bowls. The young ARVN loved his cameras and leather boots, and touched them, asking how much they cost. Okamura laughed with them, "If I'm killed, then you can have them. But now I need them." They slept under their APCs for protection, but the only noise that night was the thunder of their own artillery.

The next day, 10 February, they reached their objective, a spot on the map called Aloui, about twenty kilometers inside Laos. Helicopters lifted the 9th Airborne Battalion through heavy AA fire to the target, and they secured it in twenty minutes. Two hours later, at around seven that evening, the lead elements of the 1st Armor linked up with them. When Okamura drove in, the grassy field was still smoking from the Cobra prep strikes. He inspected a main branch of the Ho Chi Minh Trail which intersected Route 9 at Aloui, running south. The surface was crushed stone and it showed numerous tire marks. For two days, patrols worked the enemy trail but found neither NVA nor supplies. The troops seemed mightily disappointed.

The 1st Armor Brigade had already consolidated at Aloui when the senior Armor advisor, Col. Raymond R. Battreall, arrived at Khe Sanh. A crewcut, bespectacled man of forty-four, he was on his second tour with the ARVN, his current assignment a MACV post as senior advisor, RVNAF Armor Command, Saigon. Battreall had originally joined the Army as an eighteen-year-old from Omaha, Nebraska, swept up in the romantic patriotism of WWII. He soon had had the distinction of being selected from the ranks for West Point. Vietnam was his first combat assignment and he exulted in it; it was what being a soldier was all about. He felt a close kinship with the Vietnamese he soldiered beside—one he knew that the average GI could never know. He thought it sad that the young Americans asked to die for the Vietnamese saw only the prostitutes, pushers, and dregs of society; it gave them an unbalanced understanding of why they were sacrificing, made outrages like My Lai possible, and fueled the weariness in the ranks.

As for himself, Battreall developed a great and lasting respect for the ARVN after serving with them on a day-to-day basis. He was a man of old-fashioned patriotism and idealism, and thought of his nation's involvement in Vietnam as the most altruistic act a great nation ever made, sacrificing lives and capital to help a struggling nation against communist tyranny, while asking nothing in return. He applauded the invasion of Laos as a vital step to win the peace in South Vietnam. He wrote to his wife, "It is almost childishly obvious that if one wishes to get an enemy off one's back one must strike that enemy where he is. We did not widen the war, the enemy did years ago. We were stupid not to challenge him at the time. If we had done so the war would long since have been over. And all the strident screams in the world won't change these basic facts."

When the 1st Armor crossed the border, Colonel Battreall was at his post in Saigon. It didn't take long to recognize that the reports filtering back had lost their coherency, so he, his sergeant major, and his ARVN counterpart caught a plane to Hue, then a helo to FSB Kilo. There they found that Colonel Luat had left two M577 command vehicles, an

ARVN sergeant major, and a half-dozen enlisted men in a rear CP. The APCs were parked back to back beside the I Corps command bunker and Battreall's group spent their days monitoring the radios in them, and occasionally ducking in them for cover when the NVA harassed the command bases with rockets and artillery. As an advisor, Battreall could give no orders to the ARVN and, because of politics, he wasn't allowed to see first hand what was going on in Laos. The frustrations could be tremendous at times.

All in all, Colonel Battreall was guarded about the status of the 1st Armor Brigade at Aloui. His concerns, however, had nothing to do with the caliber of the South Vietnamese soldiers. He considered the troops to be first rate and their commanders superb. Colonel Luat impressed him as a brave commander who led from the front. His counterpart at Armor Command, Col. Phan Hoa Hiep, was also an able officer.

No, Battreall thought, the problem lay not with the combatants but with the plan—with the no-advisors-in-Laos policy. He had begged General Berry for permission to at least overfly the armor's area of operations to get a handle on the terrain and physical disposition of the troops; Berry had no choice but to deny the request and Battreall was one step further removed from the reality of the radio messages from Laos. The armor brigade was attached to the airborne division who were, according to MACV and XXIV Corps, to provide them with logistical support. That is how the Americans defined "attached." Not so with the Vietnamese, Battreall knew, who did not consider an attached unit as a logistical dependent. The airborne made no attempts to support their armor brigade.

Another major problem arose in the airborne's assignment to "secure Route 9" for the armor. To an American officer, such an order meant physically patrolling the road to prevent ambushes and having engineer elements upgrade the surface for traffic. That is what the planners at XXIV Corps had intended; but to the Vietnamese securing a road simply meant being able to bring it under fire. Battreall noted that, on the map, the airborne's LZ Alpha and LZ Bravo sat astride the highway giving the 105mm howitzers there overlapping fire along the entire route. In their minds, the airborne sincerely believed they had accomplished their mission—but the NVA were virtually free to attack the road at will because the paratroopers were not aggressively patrolling it. In addition, the dirt road from Bravo to Aloui was so treacherous that only tracked vehicles could make it; no engineer work was started and no supply trucks got through. Aloui was totally dependent on U.S. Army aviation.

Such problems were bound to occur when U.S. and ARVN forces worked together, but the peculiarities imposed on the Laotian campaign fueled the difficulties, as Battreall noted, "Although titular Senior Advisor, I Corps, the XXIV Corps CG in normal times concerned himself exclusively with his own U.S. units, leaving the advisory function to a brigadier general, Jackson at this particular time. When XXIV Corps Headquarters began planning Lam Son 719, therefore, they did not know their counterparts in I Corps. They wrote a perfectly good plan using standard U.S. military terminology, not realizing the Vietnamese would often nod politely even when they disagreed and that, even when they did agree, they sometimes understood terms differently than the American authors intended. The disconnect between XXIV Corps and reality at the point of contact could not have gone undetected and uncorrected had advisors been at the point of contact."

Some of the difficulties, though, rested squarely on the shoulders of the ARVN. The 1st Armor's initial assignment had been to secure Aloui; this they did with little trouble, and there they sat. General Dong, inexperienced in the ways of war, did not know what else to do with the brigade and Colonel Luat did not pursue any other mission (as Battreall noted, "Initiative by a subordinate, unhappily, never became part of the ARVN character and many, many opportunities were lost.") The 1st Armor Brigade had been able to execute a virtually bloodless attack to Aloui but now they sat on a patch of barren high ground. The terrain around them seriously hampered tank movement, the highway was impassable even to a jeep, and the helicopter resupply was coming under more AA fire every day. Before leaving Saigon, Battreall had seen a MACV intelligence estimate which said no NVA tanks were in southern Laos and none could get there without being detected by the electronic sensors and destroyed by the USAF; he doubted this and was worried, because the brigade had fewer than fifty light M41 tanks at Aloui. He trusted Colonel Luat and his troopers to fight bravely if the NVA brought pressure to bear but, as things stood, he thought a major battle would result in needless chaos and casualties.

Chaotic was the word Okamura chose to describe the developments with the 1st Armor Brigade. Things went badly the third day at Aloui when a bulldozer hit a mine. He was photographing the burnt-out hulk of a Soviet tank when there was another thunderous blast; another dozer had run over a mine and two ARVN were killed. As the brigade returned to the Aloui perimeter, the NVA began mortaring them in broad daylight.

Things were getting dark, Okamura thought.

For five days they tried to sweep onward, but each time an APC would go up in a mine explosion. Okamura was walking down the bamboo tunnel of Route 9 when the lead APC of the latest patrol crossed a stream and exploded. Three bareheaded soldiers stumbled stiffly out of the smoke and collapsed in shock as other ARVN ran forward to help. The driver was pinned under the upturned track and grimaced as blood poured from his mouth. Comrades tried to pull him out, but he died. The NVA began probing the perimeter that first week. Each night Okamura could hear the AKs and RPGs raising a racket somewhere on the perimeter. The ARVN would scatter the brush with return volleys from their tanks and tracks. Mortars hit the camp every night.

One morning Okamura joined a group of ARVN who noisily picked over some dead NVA outside the perimeter. They had walked into the claymores and machine guns the night before, and fifteen dead and one wounded man lay there. The ARVN stripped them of souvenirs, but became more thoughtful and quiet when they saw the NVA had only poor uniforms, no helmets, no food, and some had tattoos which read, "Born in the North, die in the South." An officer muttered to Okamura, "Look at us. Boots, jackets, rifles, food—everything supplied by America." Okamura thought the man had an inferiority complex; all the ARVN seemed robbed of their independent spirit, and he felt it gave the Communists an important edge. The wounded North Vietnamese died, but not before saying his unit had been in the North only five days before. The reinforcements were moving in and Okamura imagined that the NVA had let the ARVN proceed so easily into Laos in order to encircle and destroy them. The troops seemed to sense that too, and morale waned as they sat impotent atop Aloui, under daily shelling.

The ground war in Laos may have gotten off to a slow start, but the air war was a hectic, bloody one from the first day to the last. A pilot summed it up when he told a reporter, "I don't write home much. What am I supposed to say? That I took fire eight times today, and that if I had stayed on those LZs five seconds longer each time, I'd have been dead?"

It was the worst concentration of fire U.S. aircrews experienced in the Vietnam War, frail Hueys going through WWII-style flak barrages. The casualties were high in men and materiel, but the NVA never succeeded in halting U.S. Army Aviation support. Still, for those involved, it was a personal nightmare. CW3 Hawk saw glimpses of it back at the Khe Sanh control tower, the helos coming back with holes torn in them, crewmen dead or wounded, an occasional Chinook dropping off cargo nets of dead ARVN. He saw one of the obsolete UH1C gunships try to take off, so overloaded with ammunition that a skid caught in the perimeter wire—and it abruptly flipped upside down and went up in the flames of old mines and exploding rockets. Another helo hovered with a rope for the crew.

What amazed Hawk the most was the density of air traffic. It was a hornet's nest. Every square yard seemed to be occupied with helicopters and milling crewmen, and the skies were always buzzing; lift-platoons on the move, gunships darting with them, lone ships dropping in to refuel or crash-land. C130 transport planes came in all day, and it was a real challenge to avoid mid-air collisions between the large planes and the helos, whose flight patterns took them right below the cargo planes. Once, Lieutenant Smith of the 48th Blue Stars, having hydraulic problems and heading back for Khe Sanh, contacted the ATC tower to make a landing and was slotted to come in seventh. "You don't understand," Smith called, "this is an emergency." The air traffic controller answered that there were six emergencies ahead of him.

On the northern flank, the ARVN were in position and the 158th Aviation Battalion busied itself with resupply and medevac. On the southern flank, the 1st Infantry Division was still installing firebases along the escarpment and the 223rd CAB had to perform not only the resupply and rescue missions, but numerous CAs under heavy fire. The 223rd had been quickly slapped together and it lacked the cohesion of the Screaming Eagle units; the battalion experienced its share of problems. Lieutenant Smith thought the biggest one was simple battle exhaustion. He had come primed with gung-ho patriotism, but soon was just wrung out. The whole company seemed affected by the routine—flying combat all day, doing night maintenance on the birds, then being up before the sun for another day over Laos. When they lifted from Dong Ha, he could see the big red communist flag across the DMZ and, when they refueled at Khe Sanh, one man always stayed in the cockpit so he could lift off if more mortar rounds came in. The thought that kept grinding in the back of Smith's mind was that it was all for nothing, that it was just a big show of Vietnamization being played out at the expense of American pilots.

Lieutenant Smith had another job which served further to demoralize him. He was company scheduling officer and, at night, some of the pilots came to him, crying over wives and children, begging not to be slotted for Laos again. Smith hated making them go, and he began to hate

Kirklighter and Klose for taking them there. He pictured them flying high and dry in their C&C.

The enlisted men were taking it the worst, he thought. They seemed confused about Vietnam to begin with, horrified by their experiences, demoralized with the thought that they were dying for nothing. One night Smith's crew chief came crying to him, saying he had to get off heroin, and he sweated out two nights cold turkey in Smith's tent. Smith was a straight arrow, had never seen anyone light up around him, and was shocked that his chief was a head—the man had always been dependable during the missions into Laos. He told Smith that most of the door-gunners got stoned at night to relieve the pressure. But no one, he said, smoked during combat. What kept them going, Smith figured, was simple comradeship. If Laos and Kirklighter were bad, then the aircrews pulled together that much more. If a man went down, every action was taken to rescue the crew. It didn't matter if you hated the guy's guts, he reckoned, if he crashed, you went through whatever the NVA threw at you to save him. That was the mutual respect they had for each other and if it had been any less, Smith would have refused to fly. He thought of the men in the 48th Blue Stars as heroes, simply that, and he respected hell out of his company commander. Major Bunting always flew the lead ship, "so we automatically wanted to follow."

Sp5 Dennis Lundstrom was also in the 223rd CAB, a twenty-one-year-old South Dakotan flying-crew chief on UH1C of the 173rd Crossbow Guns. He was glad his pilot knew his job expertly, because Lieutenant Colonel Kirklighter made him nervous. Sometimes he could hear on the radio, as Kirklighter ordered them to do something which seemed needlessly dangerous:

"No fucking way," someone would mumble.

"Knock that off," Kirklighter would say hotly.

"Heyyy," someone would cut in, "fuck you," and they'd burst out laughing.

Lundstrom wondered if the colonel baited them along like that to allow them to let off some steam. He couldn't figure Kirklighter out. Sometimes he seemed very brave, but then again it was more as if he were oblivious. Few of the men took the time to analyze it; they just muttered how they wanted to frag his ass. He seemed, to Lundstrom, an absolutely intolerant man who refused to listen to anyone, and who seemed more concerned about the mission than their lives.

Laos changed the war Lundstrom had known. It made him feel like a new guy again. He'd enlisted right out of high school when he'd gotten his draft notice, so he wouldn't have to slog it out as a grunt. He'd gone through high school drinking, driving, and chasing girls, and it had bothered him not a bit when they'd sent him to Nam. He wasn't even very nervous when, after being a supply clerk for two months, an antagonistic first sergeant assigned him as a door-gunner. Then he was shot down, his two pilots badly wounded; he killed four NVA; he saw a dead grunt's brain slide out during a medevac mission, and he was sick for days and wanted to quit. His buddies said you would get used to it. For some sick reason, he thought, you did. In fact, he began to like the action. He made crew chief and, when his tour ended in December 1970, he extended for more combat duty.

But Laos reduced all of the bravado to simply trying to survive day by day. He was shot down once in Laotian territory. Sometimes in the morning, as they cranked up on the Dong Ha pad, a buddy would mutter to Lundstrom, "Hey, I don't think I'm coming back."

"Bullshit, don't even talk that way."

Laos weighed heavily on all of their minds.

During the third week, when they were making a CA to LZ Delta One, a friend who was standby talked Lundstrom into giving him his place on one of the Charlie-model gunships because the friend's good buddy was crew chief on it. When the company came back, two ships were missing, and Lundstrom got the story; the slick his buddy's gunnie had been escorting had hit its skids down into their rotors, and both birds had shattered in mid-air. Eight Americans had died, along with six ARVN passengers. Lundstrom's pilot never volunteered them for resupply missions, but a buddy from Colorado had a pilot who did. When they came back from one his friend had been shot through the face by a 12.7mm—KIA.

Even some of the young pilots turned to drugs and Lundstrom trusted none of them—except for a captain who occasionally smoked smack and was loose and cool in the air. Once a kid WO was assigned to fly his UH1C on perimeter security around Dong Ha and his first comment was, "You got a bucket in here? I'm really getting sick on this smack."

"I ain't got no bucket," Lundstrom shot back, "You better not get sick in my helicopter."

The pilot flew crazily, the skids smacking the surface of the river, and Lundstrom gripped his M-60, terrified, muttering, "Bullshit, bullshit, bullshit." When they landed, he reported the WO to his platoon leader and had the satisfaction of seeing the idiot grounded for the duration of Laos.

Capt. Rich Johnson, operations officer of the 173rd, could understand why morale was so poor during the op. His company commander was shot down at LZ Blue and, in Johnson's mind, it ruined him; he flew only select missions after that. The men began calling him Prettyboy, and Johnson became de facto commander of the 173rd. If the intensity of the air war could affect a professional soldier like that, Johnson recognized what it could do to a draftee door-gunner. It seemed to them worst in the afternoon, when they were preparing to go back into Laos after refueling from the morning trip. Over the radios, they could hear what was happening to those still flying, punctuated by the occasional sight of a Chinook coming over with a slingloaded wreck. Some guys would put on a facade of toughness as they got ready to go back. Others would vomit their lunch of cold C rations before climbing in. Captain Johnson made it a point not to eat lunch because he would be gripped with dry heaves right before he took off; it wasn't until he cranked the engine that he could replace his anxiety with flying skill.

He knew that many of the men took it out on Kirklighter and Klose (claymores blew apart Kirklighter's private latrine and HQ hootch—while unoccupied). They were hated men in the battalion, but were not the monsters the troops thought them to be. As Johnson saw it, they had been assigned a mission and, to carry it out, they had to put some people in precarious situations. And men died. Johnson himself had some shouting matches with Klose at Dong Ha on tactics—but unlike most of the men, he remembered that Kirklighter and Klose were sharing the danger every day over Laos. Big, red haired, and hard drinking, Kirklighter impressed Johnson as one of the toughest and bravest commanders he knew.

And for those qualities, his men—who thought the war over and it was time to go home—hated him.

Despite difficulties, army aviation got the job done in Laos. General Berry was the commander of air operations (with the call sign Big Ben) and his can-do attitude and personal courage influenced the course of the campaign. As Colonel Battreall remembered, "Sid Berry was absolutely superb. He could easily have run the U.S. Army Aviation support of Lam Son 719 from a secure bunker at the Khe Sanh airfield, but he never missed a day commanding it 'eyeball' from his own chopper over the scene of action in Laos. He always made Lieutenant General Lam's afternoon briefings and offered clear and incisive comments on the status of the fighting. I recall vividly one afternoon after he'd been shot at in his helicopter and nearly hit by the 76mm main gun of a PT76 tank.

'Damn it,' he said, 'That's not in my contract!' The point was, of course, that with the exception of Humphrey Bogart in *Sahara* nobody ever tried to use a tank cannon for antiaircraft. We all believed that the Soviets had succeeded in doing what our own ordnance said was impossible: designing a proximity fuse that would withstand the severe setback of a high-velocity tank gun."

There were 90,000 U.S. helicopter sorties into Laos. For four days the South Vietnamese invasion force had a relatively easy time. They cut branches of the Ho Chi Minh Trail, uncovered abandoned bunkers and supply caches, but found only a few North Vietnamese. On 12 February, the first intense firefights broke out around Aloui. On that day the battle for the Ho Chi Minh Trail was joined. President Thieu was unsettled by the casualties (he personally visited ARVN infantrymen on the Co Roc that day) and instructed his commanders to proceed with extreme caution. (Unknown to both Nixon and Abrams, he planned all along to call off the operation if three thousand ARVN were killed.) If Lam Son 719 ever had the momentum to be a daring strike, bad weather was not the only thing which slowed it down.

Each day the tempo and number of firefights between the ARVN and NVA increased. The press gave the impression that the NVA had suckered the ARVN into Laos and were now slamming the door behind them and moving in to annihilate effortlessly. Such a scenario was an exaggeration; the Communists, presumably, had been lying low for the first four days, not to lure the ARVN deeper into Laos but to wait for reinforcements to be shifted from North and South Vietnam. The NVA did not want their foe in Laos for any reason; it put their backs to the wall.

And for that reason, the Communists fought ferociously.

CHAPTER EIGHT:
Defeat

The U.S./ARVN plan underestimated two important aspects: the speed at which North Vietnam could reinforce its units in Laos and the fierceness of their counterattack. When the allies had invaded the communist sanctuaries in Cambodia, the NVA generally chose to melt away and allowed their basecamps to be seized. But Laos was their last sanctuary and they fought like men defending their homeland. It was conventional war along the Ho Chi Minh Trail in Laos which challenged army aviation with the densest wall of antiaircraft fire of the long war, and the ARVN with the bloodiest sustained ground combat since the Tet Offensive of 1968. No one had anticipated the amount of artillery and armor the NVA would muster.

U.S. Army Intelligence estimated that the NVA had deployed forty thousand to sixty thousand troops to meet the invasion augmented with two hundred Soviet-built tanks; taking the conservative estimate, the NVA outnumbered ARVN two to one. A captured NVA sergeant said they'd been preparing for the invasion since October 1970. The ARVN plan of leapfrogging firebases to Tchepone required speed to succeed; suspected security leaks had given the Communists warning and time to mobilize a defense, and unexpectedly bad weather had hampered any quick assault. Critics of the firebase plan said it isolated the ARVN in tiny pockets deep in enemy territory and allowed the NVA, who knew the land and had the multistranded Ho Chi Minh Trail for mobility, to isolate them and attack one by one.

No contingency plans had been prepared by the U.S. or ARVN.

In mid-February, the hammer fell on the ARVN in Laos as six of their firebases came under increasing pressure: Aloui on Route 9; Hills 30, 31 and Rangers North and South on the northern flank; and LZ Hotel Two on the southern flank. In the face of this threat, the XXIV Corps Deputy Senior Advisor, to ARVN I Corps, Brig. Gen. Charles A. Jackson, was kept busy; co-located with General Lam's CP, his team was responsible for the final coordination of the U.S. helicopter, artillery, and tactical air support to the ARVN. There were many problems involving U.S. firepower, not the least of which was an intelligence report stating that the NVA in Laos knew in advance where the B52s were going to bomb (speculation was that Soviet trawlers off Guam, from where the B52s were launched, were intercepting strike-mission information and had broken the code). In addition, the Communists woefully outnumbered the defenders of the bases, and U.S. firepower alone could not decide the contest between ground troops—especially when the other side knew the terrain, was well deployed and motivated, had been preparing for months, and was willing to sacrifice thousands of troops like cannon fodder.

Things turned particularly hot for the 39th Ranger Battalion at Ranger North. Lieutenant Colonel Peachy's 158th Aviation Battalion flew around the clock to keep them resupplied and to get out the casualties. The conditions were horrendous and Lieutenant Updyke of C Company was involved in a resupply mission which described them all. A lone ARVN stood in the dust of Ranger North, directing Updyke's bird in. He put it down in the swirling dust, the nose to the guide's belly. The door-gunners kicked out the supplies, he pulled up at a turn—and three seconds later an artillery round made a direct hit in the LZ. The ARVN disintegrated in the flash, Updyke's ship rocked from the concussion, and the next ship, piloted by a warrant officer named Doan, was pelted with shrapnel. Back at Khe Sanh, Updyke and others ran to check on Doan. He was okay, but laughed that the only thing left of the ARVN was a hunk of meat the size of a ham. The plexiglass of his Huey was riddled with shrapnel, and flecked with bits of flesh, bone, and hair. Guys were nervously laughing, picking off pieces of meat and pretending to flip them on each other. Updyke knew you needed such a morbid sense of humor to steel yourself against the daily horrors, but he felt his buddies wouldn't have acted that way if it'd been an American who'd been killed.

WO Smith of A Company was going in on another resupply mission to Ranger North when he dropped to a hover over a group of troops on the perimeter. His crew chief prepared to kick out the gear, then suddenly screamed, "Pull up! They're gooks!" The NVA were hugging the perimeter, actually crawling through the wire and firing at helicopters while lying on their backs, in an attempt to avoid artillery and airstrikes. That kind of danger accompanied the aircrews all the time. Updyke, for one, had a wife and three children at home, a Distinguished Flying Cross from Ripcord, and only three months left in a war he thought was useless because the politicians were abandoning it. He could feel the acid burn his gut the entire time he was over Laos and he wished to God a caution-light would come on so he could turn around. It was a shared wish. Once a helo from the 1st Aviation Brigade flew with them into Laos and the pilot radioed, "I'm heading back, I've got a caution-light."

"Roger," the flight leader answered, "What's the problem?"

"The APU warning light is on." The Alternate Power Unit was a small compartment in the fuselage which could be used to jumpstart other helos.

"You dumb shit, that just means your little APU door is open."

The timid pilot stayed with the flight, and Updyke took some pride in the fact that that was the only time he saw any shirking. For all the fear and danger, the men clung to their personal and unit loyalties and did the job. Colonel Davis monitored one telling radio conversation: a USAF Phantom pilot bombed the NVA AA positions in preparation for the slicks, then watched them sail through the blizzards of flak and bullets, and commented admiringly, "Those helicopter guys must have steel balls." Because of the numerous shoot-downs, many of the pilots augmented their standard .38 Smith & Wesson revolvers by carrying M-16 rifles and bandoliers of ammunition in the cockpits.

February 18 marked the beginning of the last act for Ranger North.

That morning, the crew of DMZ Dust Off—a Huey medevac from the 237th Medical Detachment, 61st Medical Battalion, 44th Medical Brigade—was waiting on the Khe Sanh pad. An emergency medevac call came in and the crew dropped their C ration breakfast and climbed aboard, two pilots up front; the crew chief; Sp5s Costello, Fujii, and Simpco, in the back. En route to Laos, the aircraft commander came over the intercom, explaining the mission: the 39th Rangers had heavy casualties, the LZ was extremely hot, and two Cobras would escort them in. The Cobras joined the Huey over Laos. Three klicks from Ranger North, they began taking heavy ground fire. The medevac AC decided it was too hot and turned the ship around for Khe Sanh. The Cobras, low on ammo and fuel, turned back, too.

Then the AC changed his mind, banked back towards Ranger North. Sp5 Fujii saw the Cobras disappearing to the east.

The Huey came in low, green tracers from AK-47s and 12.7mms

burning lines all around them. Fujii tensed; looking down he could see NVA in the brush at the base of Ranger North and mortar rounds exploding on the denuded, bunkered hill. They landed on the LZ, screaming at the ARVN litter teams to hurry with the wounded and the AC instantly pulled pitch to get out. A mortar round exploded on the LZ as they lifted off and they came crashing back down into the dust. The AC was slumped in his seat, mortally wounded; the pilot, gravely injured from shrapnel, was temporarily paralyzed below the waist. The wounded ARVN were trying to climb off. Fujii and Simpco had shrapnel in their backs; Costello was the only one unscathed. Yanking their radio helmets off, they jumped out amid the continuing mortar barrage.

Fujii and Simpco crawled off looking for cover and a hundred yards down from the LZ found the opening to a bunker. They tumbled inside. Two ARVN were already in it and Costello rushed in moments later. They bandaged each other's wounds, crouching in the bunker while mortar shells kept walking across the hill.

A rescue Huey landed near their disabled medevac.

Somehow, in all the fire, the wounded pilots were carried aboard. Then Costello dashed from the bunker, followed by Simpco, then Fujii. Costello and Simpco flung themselves aboard, but Fujii had just cleared the bunker entrance when an explosion bowled him over. In a daze, he stumbled to his feet and waved at the pilot to get out, the LZ was too hot. He paused long enough to see the Huey miraculously glide off the LZ amid a torrent of fire, then hustled back into the bunker.

There was a PRC25 there and he radioed for all aviators to stay clear of Ranger North. The AA fire was simply impenetrable.

That night, the mortaring stopped for a while and, under cover of darkness, Fujii left the bunker with an ARVN sergeant and walked to the LZ. Fujii opened the fuel release valve on his crippled Huey, draining the JP4 fuel, then they salvaged whatever usable gear they could find. It was the end of the first day of what for Sp5 Dennis Fujii, a soft-spoken, twenty-one-year-old half-Irish, half-Japanese Hawaiian, would be a five-day ordeal.

The reason for the ferocious NVA counterattack was obvious: the allied invasion was hitting them where it hurt. The Ho Chi Minh Trail was being disrupted and supply caches uncovered. While the ARVN on the northern flank found themselves increasingly besieged in their firebases, it was the U.S. Air Cavalry which continued to reap the most finds. The Air Cav was under the control of General Lam, and personally commanded by Lieutenant Colonel Molinelli of the 2/17 Air Cav,

101st Airborne Division. Molinelli had three units to augment his squadron: B/7/1 Air Cav, C/7/17 Air Cav, and the Hoc Bao Company, ARVN 1st Infantry Division. The Hoc Baos ("Black Panthers") were all experienced volunteers, the elite reaction force of the division (arguably the best of the entire South Vietnamese army); they were used to secure downed aircraft since U.S. aero rifle platoons were barred from Laos.

The air cav maintained perhaps the best morale among the aviation units fighting in Laos; the Cobra pilots were selected from the top of the class in flight school, and the Loach crews were strictly volunteers. Over Laos, they worked what was called a Heavy Pink Team or Hunter-Killer Team, consisting of two Loaches, two Cobras, and a C&C Huey. The Loaches flew low and slow at treetop level, trying to draw enemy fire; if shot at, the door-gunner/observer instantly released a red smoke grenade and opened fire with his M-60 as the pilot pulled up. The Cobras, which flew at a high altitude behind the scouts, would then dive in to neutralize the area around the smoke with rockets, automatic grenades, and minigun fire.

The Loaches flew as bait and the Cobras went through walls of AA fire; it was a highly dangerous job. Most of the air-cav crews were young, nineteen- and twenty-year-olds, with hot-rod cars at home, and they went at their work with a sense of cool skill, cocksure daredeviltry, and raw guts. The men of the air cav liked to set themselves apart, wearing starched jungle fatigues and black stetsons with crossed-sabre insignia pinned to the front. When new guys arrived, they were greeted in the roughhouse way of the air cav; while the new ones grinned weakly and shied like ponies in one corner of the unit bar, the vets swaggered in their stetsons and sprayed beer, singing, "You're going home in a body bag, do dah, you'll get shot between the thighs, oh do da day. . . ."

To Capt. John F. Mercadante, of the Bravo Dutchmasters, it was like the bomber pilots in England during WWII: hell during the day; beer and games of pool in the O Club at night. Before Laos his troop had operated in the Mekong Delta where they rarely suffered casualties and what fire they did receive only heightened their sense of bravado. But Mercadante found from day one that men were dying. No one in the Dutchmasters refused to fly or appeared outwardly frightened, but the swaggering and wild parties disappeared, to be replaced by small groups that spoke in hushed tones. Mercadante, the son of immigrants, kept up his morale because he was proud to be cav, loved the guys he was with, and believed in the war. More than that, all of the heavy fire they took over Laos simply reaffirmed his belief that they were hitting the Communists where it hurt.

The fire was, indeed, incredibly bad. WO Borders and another Dutchmasters Cobra crew were covering a medevac one day, the NVA so close to the ARVN firebase perimeter that the helos couldn't fire for fear of also strafing the South Vietnamese. So the two Cobras nonchalantly did a couple of nonfiring runs down low to draw fire away from the medevac going in. It worked, but Borders was surprised when they all were written up for Air Medals. It was just another day, he thought. You just got numb and kept going.

The cav commander, Lieutenant Colonel Molinelli, was on his second tour and held two Silver Stars, eight Distinguished Flying Crosses, and two Purple Hearts. He was a flamboyant, handsome man whose personal bravery was almost legendary. He often flew lead ship into Laos and, without notifying the command channels, had occasionally gotten on the ground with the ARVN to get a better handle on what was going on. Many of his men considered him the best combat leader they'd ever seen. There were others, however, who resented his the-mission-comes-first attitude; to them Molinelli's own valor was not an excuse to send his men into places made virtually suicidal by heavy antiaircraft fire.

Such occasional disputes did not affect the general performance of the air cav over Laos. In fact on February 18, the same day that the NVA launched their drive against Ranger North, the air cav was knocking another dent in the communist network. At noon, scout and gunship teams reconning west along Route 9 spotted, marked with smoke, and strafed an NVA unit, blowing up one truck and damaging a truck and a tank. In the same area, they discovered three six-inch-wide fuel pipelines and attacked; one pipe was severed and drained fuel on the jungle floor while the other two went up in flames. The NVA poured fire at the diving attackers and a Cobra from A/2/17 caught fire and crashed; the two pilots were wounded but immediately rescued by another helo.

To the south of this action, teams from the Dutchmasters made more finds. A Loach, piloted by a cocky and bold lieutenant named Bruce Cannon, followed vehicle tracks to a solid wall of jungle. He put a burst of minigun fire through the vegetation—and a fuel truck exploded in a ball of fire. Cannon had discovered an NVA truck-park under the triple-canopy jungle. Cannon quickly radioed for tac air but USAF rules-of-engagement prevented them from bombing so close to the main road so he maintained his low-level maneuvering as his door-gunner sprayed with his M-60 and hurled fragmentation grenades. The trucks did not explode so the gunner began putting bursts into the fuel tanks, getting gas on the ground, then tossing white phosphorus grenades. WO Borders came in to provide fire support and could see only the Loach darting below with Cannon shouting excitedly on the radio, then another explosion and a column of black smoke rolling up from the roof of jungle. The Cobras rolled in to finish the job and took some fire, but finally tallied up the destruction of ten fuel trucks, two large fuel blivets, two supply caches, a hootch, and several telephone poles and communication lines which Cannon had spotted down amid the trees.

The day's low overcast deteriorated by late evening, preventing some of the cav teams from returning to Khe Sanh or Quang Tri. Those aircrews were forced to shut down at Lang Vei where elements of the Blues, Delta 2/17, 101st DISCOM, and ARVN Hoc Bao maintained a forward staging area/refuel/rearm point. At dusk, the NVA struck back with mortars, RPGs, and AK-47 fire against the perimeter. Mortar fragments tore a ten-thousand-gallon fuel bladder and JP4 aviation fuel soaked the ground around the airstrip. An RPG sent one parked Huey up in a ball of fire so, while the men on the perimeter returned fire, the pilots ran from their bunkers and revved up their birds before the NVA could destroy any more. Cobras circled Lang Vei, but could not fire on the NVA attack because the U.S. perimeter was not visible in the dark. A quick-thinking young sergeant in the Dutchmaster Blues shouted for his lieutenant and together they dashed almost a hundred yards outside the perimeter; there they ignited a five-gallon can of JP4 which burned fiercely, marking the perimeter. The Cobras dove in on the NVA. Artillery from U.S. firebases pounded in. The NVA attack broke up.

In the morning, Lieutenant Colonel Rosenblum (CO, 101st DISCOM) helicoptered to Lang Vei to supervise the replacing of some equipment burnt up in the night probe. He was informed that a young Sp4 in the 426th S&S Battalion, manning the refuel/rearm point, had performed bravely; when the fuel bladder was punctured by mortar shrapnel, the Sp4 had jumped into the berm under fire and had waded through ankle-deep fuel, successfully patching the holes.

"Did you know," Rosenblum asked the man, "that if there'd been a spark, you'd have gone up?"

"Yes, sir," the short, curly-haired kid answered, "but, hell, those pilots needed that fuel."

Rosenblum wrote him up for a Bronze Star for Valor.

Meanwhile the air cav helicopters were sputtering to life at Lang Vei and heading back into Laos. That afternoon they set another pipeline ablaze, gunned down four NVA, and directed airstrikes on NVA tanks and trucks moving down a jungle trail. Coming back at twenty-seven hundred feet a Cobra from the Dutchmasters was hit by AA fire in the main rotor blade. The ship vibrated fiercely, the strained, wobbly pitch echoing for miles, but the pilot made a successful landing at Khe Sanh. The hole in the blade was big enough to put your head through—and the pilot did just that, grinning for the civilian photographers there.

While the U.S. air cavalry wreaked havoc on the NVA, the NVA in turn, tightened the noose on the ARVN.

The initial NVA attack against Ranger North petered out and, on the morning of 19 February they reverted to mortaring the base. Lieutenant Colonel Peachy took the Ghostriders and Phoenix Birds in to resupply the base, and maintained his C&C orbit at about six thousand feet—so high, Lieutenant Updyke laughed, "that his bird looked like a gnat's ass." Peachy ordered two slicks from the Ghostriders to go on in, and WO Smith watched anxiously as two of his buddies headed down. They hadn't even gotten their supplies out before an NVA mortar team raised havoc on the LZ and they had to back off. The pilots were on the radio, clamoring for ARVN artillery or gunships to knock out the mortar, but Peachy ordered two more slicks to give it a try. The pilots reluctantly obliged him, but barely got out alive as mortar shells burst all around them.

Peachy told two more ships to go in.

A kid WO nicknamed Sandy said it for all of them, "Why don't you go!"

"Who was that!"

Sandy identified himself by his Ghostrider call sign.

Lieutenant Colonel Peachy prudently cancelled the mission until air and arty could knock out the NVA mortars. Sandy was given a letter of reprimand, and everyone kept flying.

That night the North Vietnamese launched another full frontal assault against Ranger North.

Sp5 Fujii had set himself up with a PRC25 radio at the battalion commander's commo bunker. It was on the high ground, offering a panoramic view of the whole hill, and Fujii maintained contact with a USAF FAC pilot throughout the day; Fujii calling in the coordinates where he saw muzzle flashes and smoke, the FAC firing WP into the areas then banking off as jets roared in to strafe and bomb. Fujii was wounded, tired, and scared, but he kept his cool and the NVA paid grievously for the firepower he was able to direct in.

He was becoming a hero to the aviators in the area.

At dusk, the NVA mortaring increased from harassment to bombardment. The slopes suddenly came alive with North Vietnamese infantry men charging uphill into the ARVN bunkers and slit trenches. Fujii frantically called Cobras in to catch NVA in the open. Phantoms shrieked low, dropping bombs and napalm canisters. The whole hill was electrified with fire. The ARVN battalion commander was inside the bunker, calmly directing the defense. But other officers were panicking, removing rank insignia and destroying ID cards: better to be captured as a puppet soldier, than a warmongering officer.

Fujii had no intention of surrendering. He climbed back atop the sandbags outside the bunker. NVA were running towards the command bunker. He grabbed an M-16, sighted quickly on a charging figure, fired once, then again, and again as they kept coming.

Within ten furious minutes, ARVN Rangers throwing grenades managed to retake the fallen bunkers and close the gap. The shooting continued throughout the night, aircraft overhead in relays dropping flares and strafing around the perimeter. Fujii sat with his PRC25 and M-16 all night. We're all going to die on this little hill. His fear must have been in his voice because the Air Force pilot orbiting above spoke reassuringly: take it easy, buddy everything's going to be all right. They were simple words but Fujii clung to them. It felt so good to hear another American, to know they were out there trying to help.

In the morning, February 20, the 39th Rangers still held Ranger North. The ARVN around the commo bunker moved as if in a daze, pulling weapons and ammunition from the bodies of ARVN and NVA alike. They formed a tight perimeter around the bunker, Fujii and the battalion commander in the middle. The sun was already blazing.

The NVA began to pound the hill with mortars.

At Khe Sanh WO Fred Hayden was sipping tea in the heavily sandbagged bunker of the 4/77 AFA TOC, when the call came to mount up. He sprinted across the airstrip and scrambled into the front seat of his Cobra; his co-pilot joined him and in two minutes they were airborne. A series of letters were relayed over the radio. Hayden decoded them on his Whiz Wheel, then banked to the northwest as a second Cobra sailed in alongside. In twenty minutes, they were over Ranger North. Hayden pulled the Cobra up to three thousand feet to get his bearings, watching as other gunships pumped rockets into the disorder below, seeming to hit friendlies and enemies alike. Supply and medevac helicopters circled high, waiting for a chance to get through the ground fire. Hayden pushed his Cobra into a wind-screaming dive and punched off four rockets. He kept strafing until he had expended all his ordnance and was forced to depart for the Khe Sanh to refuel and rearm.

On the ground, the NVA had broken through the perimeter and it was hand-to-hand in some places. Ranger North was going under. Fujii radioed that they could no longer hold out. He was told to hold his ground; rescue birds were coming in as soon as possible.

Meanwhile, the ten helicopters of the Phoenix Birds headed for the base laden with supplies. They had the additional mission of rescuing Fujii and any wounded ARVN they could get aboard before the base was completely overrun. To make Fujii readily identifiable, he was instructed to take off his shirt. Some ARVN saw him and did likewise. The NVA fire was too fierce to penetrate so Maj. Jim Lloyd and Nelson flew through the withering fire and made a quick landing atop the firebase. They kicked out the ammunition resupply and waited for Fujii a few excruciating seconds, blades pumping, fire pouring in.

Fujii had seen the Cobras blaze in, a Huey landing behind them. It was all open ground to the LZ. He ran for it, turning to fire on the run at NVA rushing the commo bunker, AK-47 fire kicking up the dirt around him, ARVN running with him falling in the fire. He threw himself inside the cabin, screaming "go, go, go." They lifted off, the door gunners leaning out, blazing madly, the ship vibrating from hits.

The rescue bird was on fire.

Lloyd and Nelson managed to nurse the Huey four kilometers to Ranger South. They crashed on the LZ, but everyone managed to scramble clear before the ship exploded. Lieutenant Updyke could see thick smoke rising from Ranger South; there was no radio contact from the crash, and he debated with himself if he should risk going in. Before he could decide, he felt guilty and relieved to see his friend, WO Doan, peel off from the circling pack of gunships and head in towards the flaming wreck. Doan took several hits but came out of the LZ with Major Lloyd and the door gunners. Nelson and Fujii were still on the ground, and another slick barrelled in. Nelson jumped aboard, but Fujii hollered that he'd stay to help the ARVN on the firebase. Fujii was already a hero to the aviators, but Nelson's rescue also provided a piece of pilot folklore: he was a quiet man who loved spit and polish and as they sped out of the hot LZ, taking hits, Nelson reportedly merely grimaced and pointed to a scratch across the toe of his boot.

Major Lloyd, Captain Nelson, WO Doan, and the three other Huey pilots involved in the aborted rescue won Silver Stars, while the six crew chiefs and door gunners won Distinguished Flying Crosses. They were the first medals awarded to U.S. troops for the Laotian operation. Captain Nelson reportedly only had three weeks to enjoy his Silver Star; pilots of his company remember hearing that Nelson's bird took fire at three thousand feet and turned into a mid-air fireball.

The evening of February 20 and the morning of February 21 were a nightmare. Hundreds of dead NVA could be seen from the air around Ranger North, but many more had broken through the perimeter and were capturing the base. The 39th Rangers, outnumbered, out of ammunition, and exhausted, retreated down one side of the hill. They left about one hundred thirty dead and sixty wounded, and came out with about two hundred men, half of whom were walking wounded. Dozens of private firefights broke out as the survivors ran through the night, intermingling with NVA in the jungle, trying to reach Ranger South. The NVA began mortaring the base and Sp5 Fujii once again set up a radio vigil, calling in suppressive fire. Hueys from the 158th Aviation Battalion began coming in for the wounded at daybreak. Fujii jumped aboard the first bird. The survivors of the 39th Rangers mobbed the helicopters in a panicked frenzy to get medevacked. The AC of the lead ship began shouting frantically, "Get off, get off, get off!" and Fujii did. He started yanking ARVN out of the cabin, the door gunners kicked at them, and the ship finally got airborne with several men clinging to the skids. Fujii watched them fall to their deaths. Colonel Davis instructed Lieutenant Colonel Peachy to cancel the medevacs and make supply drops from a hover until the ARVN commanders could get their troops under control.

The battalion commander at Ranger South sent NCOs to reorganize the LZ and weed out the real wounded from the fakers. It was dark by then; it was another night of mortar and artillery fire before the helicopters returned in the morning. Tac air, air cav gunships, aerial field artillery, ground artillery, and smoke screens were hammered around Ranger South, suppressing most of the NVA fire long enough for medevacs to land. This time the ARVN did not lose control, and the wounded Fujii, after five days on the ground in Laos, was finally able to board a Huey. Flying out of Ranger South, Fujii couldn't relax; he was convinced he'd be shot down again, he couldn't believe he was actually getting out alive. The reporters photographed Fujii being awarded the Purple Heart and twenty-six days after being rescued, he was pinned with the Distinguished Service Cross. He was the only televised hero of the Laotian operation.

At Aloui, Okamura thought the position of the 1st Armor was fast deteriorating. An ARVN officer told him there was nothing to prevent the NVA from moving behind them to sow Route 9 with mines, and commented, "We came in in only two days, but it will take us a week at least to get out." Every day 122mm rockets pounded the firebase. Tank patrols that advanced more than two hundred meters ran into blistering NVA fire. Antiaircraft fire hampered the medevac and resupply choppers. The ARVN soldiers seemed to be holding up under the pressure, but they were homesick and tired of sitting and being pummelled. It was time to get out, Okamura thought; a reporter always had that option. He gathered his gear and waited at the Aloui helo pad, just in time for another rocket raid. The shells walked through the area and a fuel blivet burst into flames. As American helicopters appeared, the ARVN atop their tanks and APCs on the perimeter laid down suppressive fire. The second helo landed, and Okamura joined the rush for it. Two paratroopers with slight wounds fell on him as they jumped aboard, and three ARVN officers also climbed in. One tried to draw his pistol to keep other ARVN off, as the helicopter lifted away.

Ranger North was the first domino to fall in the NVA counterattack; the Communists had sustained severe casualties for the victory, but they did not pause. They continued to hammer at Aloui, Ranger South, Hill 30, Hill 31, and LZ Hotel Two. On 23 February, the 223rd CAB went in to assist the ARVN Hotel Two, where the NVA were hugging the perimeter and keeping the defenders underground with mortars. The firebase was on the verge of being overrun, so Lieutenant Colonel Kirklighter and Major Klose circled above with the mission of evacuating the base's 155mm artillery pieces lest they fall into enemy hands.

Marine helicopters, CH53 Sea Stallions of HMH-463, arrived on station to lift the artillery out by slingloads. One of them was being piloted by Lt. Col. Charles Pitman and Maj. Mike Wasco; Wasco was the squadron op officer, but Pitman was the CO of Headquarters and Maintenance Squadron 16 at Marble Mountain. He was in the helo because he was in the process of checking out in the CH53 prior to taking command of HMH-463. Pitman and Wasco, on the radio with the C&C, said the mission didn't look good, but they would give it a try. They and their wingman sailed through the fire and stopped at a hover over the artillery parapets.

North Vietnamese fire drove them away.

The pair of Sea Stallions made another try, some ARVN emerging from a bunker to attach the 155mm pieces, but mortars began impacting atop the dirt knob. As Kirklighter and Klose watched from a thousand feet, a lucky round hit the engine of Pitman's chopper. The helicopter settled atop the artillery tube, blades still spinning, looking, Klose thought, like a chicken hatching an egg. The second Sea Stallion banked in. Ground fire cracked from the trees as the pilot brought his ship to a hover and the door-gunners threw a rope ladder out the rear cargo hatch. Men appeared from the wreck, grabbed the dangling ladder, then held tight as the pilot headed east with them hanging far below.

The radio crackled from the downed Sea Stallion: Pitman and Wasco were still pinned down, and a 12.7mm round had shattered the tibia in Pitman's right leg.

Klose piloted the C&C Huey in and started to set down near the crash just as two mortar rounds exploded in front of them. He pulled pitch and they shot out of the LZ. Most of the enemy fire appeared to be coming from a valley west of Hotel Two, so they sailed in again from due north, veering east at the last moment and heading for a small ridgeline on the firebase which would shield them from some of the fire. They flew in, the ridge to their right, and Kirklighter, in the right-hand seat, took over the controls. He set down the right skid, the other dangling in open air, and the slick hovered bumpily on the crest of the hill. Klose nervously repeated, "Steady, keep it steady!" into his mike as he watched the controls, ready to take over in an emergency, too filled with adrenaline to notice the volume of fire directed at their Huey. Bullets punched holes through the ship and the plexiglass windshield exploded in their faces. The noise around them was overwhelming.

Klose saw Wasco momentarily appear near the Sea Stallion, then reappear helping the leg-shot Pitman towards them. One of the door-gunners jumped out to help them aboard and the sudden shift in weight almost sent the blades smacking into the top of the ridgeline. Wasco and several ARVN tried to load Pitman into the Huey but, in the frantic rush, one of the ARVN stepped on the bandage hastily tied to Pitman's leg. It kept tugging him back out. Pitman finally managed to get the man's attention. He stepped clear, they threw Pitman in again, and he ended up hanging out the door on the other side, peering down at the mountain. Someone jumped on his back and Kirklighter quickly pulled them out of the cone of fire just as two mortar rounds exploded behind them.

They flew straight for Khe Sanh where Pitman and Wasco were transferred to one of the CH53s for the flight to the Quang Tri hospital. (Months later, Major Klose was stationed in Washington, D.C., when a man in civilian clothes walked in with a cane. The next thing he knew, the man was hugging him. It was Lieutenant Colonel Pitman. That night, Klose was invited over for dinner, a block party, for which the whole neighborhood turned out; it was something Klose long remembered.)

The evening of the 23rd, Lieutenant Colonel Peachy was directing a resupply mission for the paratroopers at Hill 31 when he spotted movement outside the perimeter. He sent Cobras in on the position—and by the time the screaming on the radio stopped, the paratrooper patrol had sustained twelve ARVN KIA and thirty one ARVN WIA from the gunships. Lieutenant Updyke was at Khe Sanh when he saw Peachy land and get out of his helicopter with his chin hanging. Updyke didn't particularly like the colonel, but he knew that the man was sincerely regretful.

The evacuation of Hotel Two was completed the following afternoon. Lieutenant Smith of the 48th Blue Stars was in the air when word came that twenty-three ARVN were left in the perimeter. They were about to be overrun. He and two other pilots got on the horn and said they'd give it a try. The three slicks broke from the formation and headed towards the coordinates, as two Cobras and two UH1C gunships swooped in to provide cover. They came in, Smith flying the last slick. AK-47 fire popped furiously below them. Rounds slammed through his ship. He abruptly noticed there were North Vietnamese infantrymen, crawling through the wire, ten yards from the ARVN perimeter bunkers.

A firefight was raging below.

The Hueys set down in the landing zone, mortar shells impacting all around them, and they quickly pulled out, a piece of shrapnel smacking into the tailboom of Smith's slick.

They went in again. The mortars drove them away again.

Milling above Hotel Two, Smith spotted the flash of a mortar round leaving its tube on a hillside five hundred yards away. He alerted the gunships, then watched one of the Cobras dodge a wall of bursting flak to pump rockets into the trees. The mortar crew disintegrated in the explosions. Another mortar promptly resumed the shelling. The two UH1Cs had to depart station to refuel and rearm so, while the two Cobras fired up the jungle, the three Hueys went in for another try. The first two made it through the curtain of mortar shrapnel. Smith came in last. The last few ARVN, running like hell, piled aboard, and he pulled up through the mortar bursts. It was a haunting sight for him to look back and see only abandoned, smoking bunkers and the Cobras banking away.

The North Vietnamese overran the rubble. Airstrikes were called in on them and the helicopter and artillery pieces left behind.

Lieutenant Colonel Molinelli's 2/17 Air Cav had several encounters with NVA in Soviet-made tanks. A scout ship spotted their first tank when he noticed what looked like a hootch moving. On closer inspection, the pilot saw a barrel protruding from the thatch and realized that the hut was built on an A-frame over the tank hull as camouflage. In another engagement, the 2/17 overflew fourteen tanks and rolled in on them firing. The tanks responded with their main guns and 12.7mm flexibles, but the Cobras punched holes in three of them with HEAT rockets, blowing up the crews, and immobilized the other eleven. The USAF came in at night, perfunctorily strafed the column, and reported fourteen kills. But in the morning, the cav found only the three burnt wrecks. The NVA had recovered the rest.

On another occasion, Lt. Col. Joseph Ganahl, commander of U.S. artillery on the border, was in his C&C bird when NVA tanks attacked an ARVN position. His S3 got on the radio to say an airborne forward air controller would direct the battalion's fire on the enemy armor, and that the corps commander was monitoring the frequency. Extremely nervous about all of the brass listening in, the FAC reported it was a good shot, but to drop two hundred meters on the gun target line and go right a hundred. The battery commander answered that his next round was on the way; there was a pause, then the FAC cried, "Holy Christ!" Ganahl thought his men must have dropped a short round into the ARVN, but the FAC caught his breath and said just the opposite was true. The artillery round had exploded between two NVA tanks, bowling them both over. They claimed two tank kills with one shell.

Things were falling apart for the 3rd Airborne Battalion on Hill 31. Their patrols around the base met fierce resistance; NVA artillery, rockets, and mortars pummelled the hill every day, and sappers had been killed in the perimeter wire. General Lam sent the 6th Airborne Battalion into a valley southeast of Hill 31 to destroy the NVA gun positions there. An Arc Light was put on the LZ, but intense NVA fire still forced the helicopters away. They dropped the battalion at alternate LZs, but they were under artillery fire and the battalion retreated in the direction of Hill 31, losing twenty-eight KIA, fifty WIA, and twenty-three MIA in a single afternoon. The 6th Airborne Battalion was helicoptered out, having accomplished nothing.

The death knell for Hill 31 came on 25 February.

At eleven in the morning, 130mm artillery began hitting the base. Hours later a company from the 3rd Airborne Battalion on patrol about a kilometer east of the basecamp spotted an NVA tank and infantry column moving in the direction of Hill 31. They estimated over twenty tanks and two thousand infantrymen. There were only four hundred ARVN atop Hill 31. The company commander quickly moved his men back to the base and the battalion operations officer, a Major Hong, radioed the artillery batteries at Aloui and Hill 30. They began firing on the advancing column, felling numerous NVA foot soldiers, but the tanks rolled through unscathed. Major Hong requested airstrikes, but the ARVN aerial observer, in his circling OV10 plane, was convinced that they must be ARVN tanks, and it took much haggling and an hour before tac air arrived.

The ARVN paratroopers fired madly at the oncoming mass of North Vietnamese, moving in the perimeter wire to the south, as a flight of U.S. Marine A4 Skyhawk jets roared in, led by Col. A. C. Pommerenk and Lt. Col. Jerry T. Hagen. They could see five PT76 tanks—one atop a knoll, dueling point blank with the ARVN artillery on Hill 31, four others rolling down a trail behind the knoll. As the four moved around the hill, two to the left, two to the right, Colonel Pommerenk rolled in. His bombs exploded just in front of two of the PT76s, halting them. Lieutenant Colonel Hagen dove in next, the stalled tanks firing at him with their cannons as he released cigar-shaped napalm canisters. The two tanks were consumed in the fiery billows, the crews burning to death inside. The other pair split up, one tank disappearing into the woods. Hagen blew up the one that remained in the open.

The NVA began traversing to make another attack up the northern slope. They still had about fifteen tanks left.

Moments before the attack began, a heavy gun team from C Troop 7/17 Air Cav, consisting of three Cobras, two Loaches, and a command and control Huey, had overflown Hill 31. Lt. David Ferrell and WO David Lancaster were flying one of the Cobras, and all they could see were the tops of bunkers and a burnt-out Huey in the middle of the perimeter. No one was in sight. West of the hill, the scout ships discovered a group of hootches atop a small hill and the gunnies made their runs low and straight, punching off rockets. The hill rocked with fireballs as a fuel cache went up. The team was heading back to Khe Sanh to refuel and rearm, when word came over the radio that Hill 31 was being overrun. Lancaster commented to Ferrell that the NVA had probably hidden in the brush as they flew over, preparing for their assault.

It was Lieutenant Ferrell's first day in Laos.

Ferrell was from St. Albans, West Virginia, twenty-four years old and married for the last two. He came from a poor family, but had worked his way through college, joined ROTC, and excelled in flight school. His brother, a career sergeant in the USAF, had flown C130 gunship missions over the Ho Chi Minh Trail in 1970, and Ferrell was proud to follow him to Vietnam in February 1971. He joined C Troop at their new tents at Khe Sanh, but there was no time to give him a flight check. The troop commander assigned him to fly with WO Lancaster to learn the ropes. An excellent pilot, Lancaster was young, tall, well educated, and friendly, and Ferrell hit it off well with him.

As soon as the rocket pods were refilled with 2.75-inch flechette rockets and the JP4 fuel nozzle unscrewed, Ferrell and Lancaster climbed back into their Cobra and slammed the canopy shut. In minutes the three Cobras and single Huey were close enough to Hill 31 to see the battle. They could make out the lumbering shapes of several NVA tanks going up the barren slope of the firebase, infantrymen running behind them in a frontal assault. Tracers poured from the ARVN bunker line. Shells exploded and smoke hung over the scene. The airborne FAC came on the radio and directed the gun team to take a high orbit southeast of Hill 31 to clear the way for a pair of USAF Phantoms coming in.

The jets streaked low, one behind the other, flashing north to south over the battlefield, releasing bombs. They pulled up and circled low; then Ferrell watched the lead Phantom dive in again. It dropped napalm amid the North Vietnamese on the hillside, then pulled up from its low dive just as a 12.7mm machine gun cut loose from the treeline at the base of the hill, Ferrell watched astonished as the stream of green tracers nailed the Phantom. The jet seemed to hang in the sky a millisecond; then smoke began pouring out and, a second later, the two pilots ejected, their parachutes opening high up. The Phantom burst into flames, began tumbling through the sky, and exploded in a fireball against the side of a mountain.

The two pilots floated down on the opposite side of Hill 31 from the gun position. They were lost from sight in the jungle.

The C Troop command helicopter immediately radioed that they were going in to get the pilots, ignoring calls to wait for the gunships. The three Cobras, Ferrell and Lancaster in the second ship, peeled off and dropped to fifty feet off the deck racing after the C&C. They darted through a lush green valley, about five hundred feet across, and Ferrell abruptly noticed dozens of NVA infantrymen moving in the elephant grass on the slopes. Most of them opened up with their AK-47s, some high enough in the hills to fire down on the Cobras, and it was like being in a popcorn pan as all three pilots reported taking hits. It was Ferrell's first time under fire, and he could hear a dozen rounds stitch through the tailboom—but training took over and he felt detached from the danger, too intent on getting the pilots to really worry.

The lead Cobra disappeared over a hill ahead of them but, when Ferrell and Lancaster crested it, no one was in sight. They took a guess and Lancaster banked to the left. Unable to raise anyone on the radio and seeing no other helicopters, Lancaster turned the ship around and they zigzagged over the treetops to see if their partners had been shot down. In moments they overflew the C&C Huey which had crashed in a field surrounded by trees. The Huey had only been on the ground a minute or two and the crew waved frantically as the Cobra flew past. Other helos arrived and the third Cobra of the team landed beside the Huey. A door-gunner and a captain were wounded in the C&C, so the Cobra copilot, a new warrant officer named David Nelson, volunteered to stay on the ground while the captain took his place in the two-seater gunship.

Other slicks arrived to evacuate the rest so, because they were low on fuel and their radios did not work, Ferrell and Lancaster departed for Khe Sanh. Once on the ground, they counted thirteen bullet holes in their fuselage and noted their radio cables had been severed. They also found out that two of the Cobra pilots had been wounded, and the injured door-gunner had died while being medevacked.

The search for the two Phantom pilots continued.

The F4 had gone down at around four in the afternoon, and the U.S. FAC and OV10 observer who'd been directing in the firepower had instantly left station to coordinate the search-and-rescue. Such was the policy of the USAF. Accustomed to bombing stationary targets deep in enemy territory, it was an excellent morale booster that, if a plane went down, the airstrike was cancelled and full attention was given to extracting the crew. In cases of close air support, this was done without regard to the troops who had requested the tac air. The policy had previously caused few problems because AA fire in South Vietnam rarely bagged a jet. But the fact that hundreds of NVA with tank support were now free to charge up Hill 31 did not prevent USAF doctrine from taking over. The ARVN 3rd Airborne Battalion was abandoned for two downed American pilots.

Back at the ARVN command bunkers in South Vietnam, Lieutenant General Dong and his U.S. advisors monitored the radio conversations. Col. Nguyen Van Tho (CO, 3d Airborne Brigade) and Lieutenant Colonel Phat (CO, 3d Airborne Battalion) kept a running dialogue from their bunkers in the middle of the shooting on Hill 31. To support the besieged garrison, General Dong instructed Colonel Luat to dispatch elements of his armor brigade. Tanks and APCs from the 11th and 17th Cavalry Regiments departed Aloui and began pushing north, driving cross-country through forested hills. At around five in the afternoon, they were ambushed, a dozen ARVN wounded, two of their M41 tanks and one APC blown up.

What happened next is a mystery.

The official version is that a conflict in orders from two headquarters, far removed from the battlefield and each other, forced the armor to halt in place. Lam ordered them on to Hill 31, while Dong, thinking the base was being overrun, ordered them to stop south of it and wait for instructions. The upshot was that the average nonaggressive ARVN officers reacted to this confusion by remaining where they were. Colonel Battreall, monitoring the armor radios, could envision the stress and frustration in General Dong's CP when in the midst of the chaos over Hill 31, a question was posed of what to do about the ambushed armor. A weak commander with no understanding of armor capabilities, he probably just shrugged.

Colonel Harrison, forced, as were all of the advisors, to get his information secondhand, thought that General Dong's incompetence caused the stalling of the armor relief column, whereas it had been merely a contributing factor to the cavalry commander's own timid spirits. He heard that, after the three vehicles had been knocked out in the ambush, the cav commander had radioed Dong for infantry support to clear the hills, then had sat idling in place, waiting. Dong sent neither reinforcement nor confirmation of his order that Hill 31—with NVA tanks in the wire—must be immediately rescued. The tanks, supposedly, just sat waiting, idling, until they ran out of fuel and more had to be helicoptered to them. "The armor's supposed to be able to charge through," Harrison thought disgustedly, "but they just sat there."

Whether because of the weakness of Dong, the cowardice of the cav commander, or both, the 11th and 17th Cav halted its rescue rush to Hill

31. The 3d Airborne Battalion was truly alone in their fight against a well-coordinated tank and infantry assault, the USAF having forsaken them for their own comrades, the ARVN armor having halted in place to wait and see. The only aircraft above Hill 31 was a helicopter with several airborne advisors aboard. It dipped down to fire an M-60 ineffectually at the surging attack.

At the time that the Phantom went down and air support ceased to exist for the defenders of Hill 31, Lieutenant General Sutherland arrived by helicopter to Lieutenant General Dong's command post. With him was General Weyand (DEPCOMUSMACV); he had arrived at XXIV Corps HQ at Quang Tri that afternoon for one of his frequent visits to the Laotian operation. After lunch Weyand and Sutherland first visited Lieutenant General Lam and then Brigadier General Phu, who updated them on the current tactical situation. Lam mentioned that Hill 31 was experiencing a tank/infantry attack but, generally had no complaints (commented General Vien of the RVNAF JGS, ". . . another characteristic about General Lam . . . should be avoided by leaders at every level. He would not report bad news or was very slow to do so.")

At the Airborne CP, their last visit, Dong, overwhelmed by the events crashing down around him, poured out a catalogue of complaints to Weyand and Sutherland. He accused General Lam and I Corps of failing to support him, and Colonel Luat and his 1st Armor of not responding to his orders. He also attacked the U.S. air support that his paratroopers were receiving. One of the air force officers present said that the air support was more than adequate. Col. Arthur Pence, senior advisor to the Airborne Division, spoke up then, saying Dong was correct; yes, officially the USAF FACs were on station for the ARVN, but there were a host of problems involving them—not the least of which was that they were looking for two pilots while a battalion was in the process of being overrun.

To Sutherland, Pence was a constant complainer. To the other advisors, he was a competent officer who saw it as his duty to support the ARVN to the hilt. And by doing so, he got himself in hot water. General Sutherland's job was to provide all of the necessary support to the South Vietnamese in Laos and Pence had said, in effect, that he was not doing his job. Pence was a West Point man, on his second Vietnam tour, one not known for his tact; instead of discussing the issue privately, he had embarrassed the U.S. commanding general in front of his counterparts.

There is evidence that the complaints of Dong and Pence were justified. That same day, Colonel Harrison had typed a long letter to XXIV Corps from his command bunker, (25 February 1971) echoing in detail similar complaints:

> As the Senior Advisor to the 1st Infantry Division (ARVN), I have experienced considerable difficulty in obtaining adequate FAC/ALO Support for the division for Operation Lam Son 719. . . .
>
> I asked for an ALO to go forward with the CP to Khe Sanh, an ALO normally with the division main CP at Hue to move to the Main CP at Dong Ha. This amounted to one additional ALO requirement.
>
> LTC Vallejo, Air Force advisor to I Corps, told me there was no requirement for an ALO at the Forward CP because all the air support was already planned for operations in Laos and there would be nothing for him to do. He finally agreed to let one go to Khe Sanh. After several days of my repeated requests for the Division ALO to move to Dong Ha, I was told that Colonel Howell in MR 1 would not allow the division ALO to move to the Division Main CP at Dong Ha.
>
> Maj Mahoney, ALO to the division forward CP, moved with the CP to Khe Sanh. He was able to use his communications to get some information of the strikes being made in Laos and transmit requests to the Hammer FAC working the Laos area. The concept of the ARVN officer in the TOC calling a Vietnamese riding with the FAC to obtain information on strikes flown, BDA, and transmit immediate requests just does not work well enough for an operation with the tempo and intensity of Lam Son 719. Having an ALO available at the forward CP is a major assist. Notwithstanding, we are still unable to capitalize on the great potential of tactical air support and achieve the maximum responsiveness the US Air Force is capable of and anxious to provide. . . .
>
> When an air move is underway and enemy fire threatens the success of the move, tactical air support is needed immediately. The Army Air Mission Commander (AMC) must control his lift helicopters and direct the fire of his gunships. The ARVN ground force commander flying in the command control (C&C) helicopter must direct the fire of his artillery and infantry troops and have the friendly forces mark their positions. There is an urgent need for an ALO to be on board the C&C to talk with the FAC to request

immediate air as the ALO concurrently coordinates with the ground commander and the AMC. In a dire emergency when a Hammer FAC is not available, the ALO could direct the airstrike himself. On the evening of 23 Feb, I requested the ALO at the forward CP to get another Air Force officer forward so he could be in the C&C helicopter when major air moves were being made. I anticipated no trouble in having another Air Force officer available since in the past 16 days we have had four different officers serve as the ALO at Khe Sanh and the Air Force Officers that remained at Hue have extremely little to do. Unfortunately, I was informed that LTC Vallejo and Col Howell disapproved the use of an ALO in a C&C helicopter in Laos. I simply cannot understand the inertia and lack of "can do" attitude on the part of some middle management Air Force officers when I am certain the Commander, Seventh Air Force, sincerely desires that ARVN troops in Laos receive the most responsive and best possible US Air Force Support.

Colonel Harrison received no static for his complaints about USAF support, merely a formal typed reply from Brigadier General Jackson that, "The contents of your February letter concerning FAC/ALO support is appreciated and has been made known to the appropriate individuals. Every effort is being made to correct and improve the responsiveness of Tac Air support. . . ." Colonel Pence, whose comments were more urgent and made in public, received a different fate. The incident destroyed Sutherland's confidence in Pence's ability to advise effectively; when they helicoptered back to Quang Tri, Sutherland commented to Weyand how lackluster Dong was in comparison to Lam and Phu. He thought the inexperienced and politically-prompted Dong was simply losing his nerve over Laos and was being "supported, abetted, and indeed egged on" by Pence.

At Quang Tri, Weyand caught his plane to report back to General Abrams in Saigon, and Sutherland had to figure out what to do with Colonel Pence who, in reality, had not failed in his professional duties but in his tact. Sutherland ordered his XXIV Corps staff immediately to investigate Pence's charges about U.S. air support, detailing three of them:

1. that there was only one FAC over the ARVN 1st Airborne Division AO when he had been promised two such aircraft
2. that the one FAC Pence said he had was inexperienced with the airborne AO and could not even locate Hill 31

3. that there was only one air cav pink team available to the airborne

Sutherland did not include the story of the Phantom shoot-down. His staff answered that all of Colonel Pence's allegations were false and that, in addition, there had been a rainstorm over Hill 31 which had grounded all air support, making the complaints moot and a probable cover-up of the airborne's failings. Sutherland was furious that neither Dong nor Pence had mentioned this fact (the answer being, of course, that weather conditions had not been a problem when the battle started or the Phantom that had been shot down would not have been over Hill 31 to begin with).

After meeting with his staff, Sutherland radioed his XXIV Corps advisor to I Corps, General Jackson, and detailed his difficulties with Pence. He also noted that the advisor had been a burr under his saddle from the beginning: "Each time that I visited the Airborne Division, Colonel Pence tried to convince me that the Airborne Division should have two FAC's dedicated to the Airborne Division and that they and their aircraft should be based at the Khe Sanh airfield. The Khe Sanh airfield was normally closed by fog until about 1100 hours. It was not prudent for us to station FAC aircraft at Khe Sanh since they had to be able to get airborne at any hour of the day or night. They could only do this from the Quang Tri airfield. Lieutenant General Dong, abetted by Colonel Pence, refused to accept the realities of the situation."

Sutherland asked Jackson to confer with Lam on whether he should relieve Colonel Pence of his duties. Jackson's answer was no surprise.

The slopes of Hill 31 were a killing ground as the third NVA attack took advantage of the disappearance of the jets to charge from three sides—tanks from the northeast, infantry from the northwest and south.

Overhead Lieutenant Colonel Molinelli and Charlie Troop 2/17 Air Cav homed in, diverted by General Lam from an extended recon to the north. The scene below was confusion on the grand scale. The USAF and numerous helos were darting above the trees, looking for the two pilots, while some eighteen hundred meters away, the ARVN armor sat impotent, seemingly frozen in place because they perceived themselves to be outgunned. Molinelli sent his Cobras in on the NVA running up Hill 31, but their antipersonnel rockets ricocheted harmlessly off the tank armor.

On the ground, the ARVN paratroopers fired furiously from their bunkers, killing many of the charging North Vietnamese in their tracks. The tanks tore through the wire and the ARVN fired LAW rockets from twenty yards; they scored numerous hits but did no damage with the small rockets because they had not been properly trained in the vulnerable spots of a tank. The firebase artillery had been mostly disabled by previous shellings, but two 105mm howitzers were wheeled around in their parapets. They fired point-blank, destroying two tanks. The rest of the armor made it to the top of Hill 31, foot soldiers pouring in with them.

The NVA swarmed into bunkers and trenches. Combat was hand to hand.

From above, the American aircrews could only look on helplessly. WO Smith of the Ghostriders, who had been heading with his company to evacuate the survivors, watched the Phantoms lay napalm; the chaos on the radio when the jet went down had resulted in his company's being put in a circling pattern two miles south of Hill 31. From his perch, Smith could see tracers, puffs of explosions, an occasional darting figure—then three Soviet-made tanks crashed into view and began doing pedal-turns atop the ARVN bunkers to cave them in. Someone on the radio told Smith to head back for Khe Sanh.

Their rescue mission was cancelled.

A squall-line and heavy clouds rolled over Hill 31, and Lieutenant Colonel Molinelli saw the last of the NVA tanks rolling uphill into the clouds and out of sight, even as his Cobras fired at them from the valley. Finally the weather forced the USAF out of the area, and Molinelli also departed to refuel.

At fifteen minutes after five, Colonel Tho ordered the firebase evacuated. His executive officer and twelve soldiers immediately managed to escape down the southern slope of Hill 31, followed by Lieutenant Colonel Phat and twenty more ARVN, and then by Major Hong with another twenty men. Colonel Tho remained in his command bunker to go out with the last of his paratroopers.

Moments later, all communication with Hill 31 was lost.

The North Vietnamese charged victoriously across the fog-shrouded firebase and there were some last, isolated bursts of fire. Exhausted ARVN paratroopers raised their hands in surrender. The NVA surrounded the command bunkers and Colonel Tho and some of his staff emerged to be greeted by AK-47 barrels. By seven that night, the NVA were securing Hill 31, while the groups of ARVN survivors who had run away in the chaos hid out the night in the jungled valley.

Ironically the two air force pilots were not located by the search and rescue efforts that had been diverted away from Hill 31. Lieutenant

Ferrell had the opportunity later to speak with some USAF officers who said the pilots had wandered for three days in the jungle before finally being picked up.

In the morning, 26 February, General Jackson walked over to the command bunker of the ARVN 1st Infantry Division to tell Colonel Harrison that he was now temporary senior advisor to the airborne, replacing Pence. He was still responsible as SA to the 1st Division but, since they were doing well and Phu was a competent commander, Harrison felt secure in leaving to catch a jeep for the two-kilometer ride to General Dong's command post. Harrison was not all impressed by his new counterpart; Dong seemed like a politician, a friend of the president, a palace-guard officer who'd probably been made a general to insure his loyalty to the government should another coup occur. He was not well versed on tactics and made little attempt to monitor the day-to-day status of his units.

Meanwhile, that morning, Lieutenant Colonel Molinelli led a recon flight over Hill 31 to determine exactly who still held the position. He could see several tanks, some artillery pieces, and a few people walking around the base; they went down for a closer look and were greeted with heavy NVA fire. In response, General Dong ordered the survivors of the 3d Airborne Battalion, augmented by the now-moving ARVN armor, to counterattack. Two hundred meters from the firebase, they were halted by intense NVA fire and eventually fell back with an additional twenty-seven dead and forty-one wounded.

The ARVN tankers were up front during the engagement, losing four of five M41s to RPGs, but blowing up a number of NVA tanks on Hill 31. Back at his CP, Colonel Battreall and the other advisors were elated at the 17th Cav's reports on the brigade net as they reported twenty-two tank kills. And in this, the 1st Armor Brigade found itself once again embroiled in controversy. General Sutherland completely dismissed the report as a fabrication by Luat; the fact that the NVA tanks had scored not a single kill in such a supposedly fierce battle added fuel to his fire. The truth, most likely, was somewhere in between—the ARVN tankers, in fact, doing their duty and engaging the NVA tanks on Hill 31, but, in the heat of battle, unable to distinguish between live tanks and those knocked out the day before, they probably thus claimed an exaggerated number of kills.

General Lam also did some exaggerating of his own, using the reports to claim that parts of Hill 31 were back in ARVN hands. Perhaps that is what some of his field commanders were claiming, but U.S. aerial recon showed no ARVN on the hill. The NVA also left it, as they had no reason to maintain an open position once they had knocked the South Vietnamese off.

On 27 February, the Bravo Dutchmasters were in the air again over Laos, the pink teams doing low-level scouting in the AO of the ARVN 1st Infantry Division. Lt. Ronald Babcock was flying one of the Loaches and his door-gunner/observer was the scout platoon sergeant. A man in his forties, the sergeant was not required to fly, but he volunteered to show the young draftees that old lifers could be as tough as they were.

Skimming low over the trees, their Loach was nailed by NVA fire. Babcock radioed that they were going down. The C&C Huey, piloted by Capt. "Mother" Waters, commander of the troop's lift platoon, chased after the descending ship. (Waters claimed his nickname came from some virile exploit, but his troops loved him and called him that because he watched after them like a mother hen.) As Waters zipped down in his Huey, the Loach crashed on a dirt road, and Babcock and the platoon sergeant, jumping out, ran like hell across a grassy clearing. North Vietnamese in the treeline cut them down with their AK-47s. Waters brought his bird to a ten foot hover over them and called on the radio that, from their appearance, he had no doubt they were dead. The C&C crew chief, Sergeant Seaman, dueled the NVA in the treeline with his M60—until a burst from a 12.7mm tore through the Huey. Seaman's ankle was shattered, a ten-inch hole was blown through the floor, the fuel tanks ruptured, and aviation fuel sloshed in the helicopter. Captain Waters managed to pull out and get them back to Khe Sanh.

Another helo went into the crash site but was also driven away by intense fire. Lieutenant Babcock and the platoon sergeant were declared missing in action, and the aircrews simply kept flying.

Relations between the U.S. and ARVN were not superb, as General Berry noted in his journal: "0630, 22 Feb 71. General Lam, the ARVN Corps Commander, is the decision-maker for the operation in Laos. General Sutherland commands the US supporting operations and has little real influence on what General Lam does in the Laotian operations, at least on Lam's tactical decisions. . . .

"0515, 26 Feb 71, Quang Tri. General Sutherland has great pressures on him. This Laotian operation must succeed. Sutherland is the senior US field commander working with the senior Vietnamese field commander, LTG Lam. Sutherland had a large role in planning the operation. Now it's Lam who commands the ground forces in Laos while Sutherland commands the supporting US forces. Command of ground forces in Laos is the decisive element. Therefore, Sutherland lacks control of the decisive element in the campaign. Yet, from the US point of view, Sutherland is the responsible field commander. There is no unity of command in this very difficult operation. That's a major weakness and vulnerability. . . .

"0600, 27 Feb 71, Quang Tri. There is a vast potential for bitterness, recrimination, and misunderstanding between the South Vietnamese and the Americans involved in this operation. If the operation were a great success, everyone would be happy and swapping congratulations. But as the operation bogs down and losses mount, Americans tend to blame the Vietnamese for having been too cautious and conservative in their ground maneuver plan and too unaggressive in their tactics. Vietnamese will tend to blame Americans for having failed to provide the air support, helicopter support, logistical support promised at the beginning of the operations."

Ranger North was overrun on 20 February. LZ Hotel Two was evacuated and abandoned on 24 February. Ranger South was evacuated and abandoned, and Hill 31 was overrun on 25 February. The evacuation of the 2d Airborne Battalion from Hill 30 began in earnest on March 2 when the 158th Aviation Battalion flew through murderous fire in a resupply-medevac mission. In the midst of a shelling, ARVN mobbed the Hueys. One of those who deserted on a helicopter was the ARVN battalion commander of Hill 30. The evacuation was called off while airstrikes came in, and the helicopters were diverted to the armor. Chinooks came in to Hill 30 with resupply and artillery-extraction missions, but were driven away by the intense AA fire. The evacuation was finally completed three days later despite fire from the NVA tanks.

The only base among the six hit in the NVA counterattack which did not fall was Aloui, held by Colonel Luat's 1st Armor Brigade. With the airborne and ranger units pulling out on the northern flank, the pressure on the brigade was intense. Those in the most danger were the men of the 17th Cavalry (reinforced with two companies from the 8th Airborne Battalion and survivors of the 3d Airborne Battalion); when Hill 31 fell, they found themselves cut off. They were alone in the hills and, without orders to attack or withdraw, they simply sat and were pummelled.

The situation only served to aggravate General Sutherland's impatience with the 1st Armor. He considered the armor typical of the "elite" ARVN units, more concerned about polished boots, comfortable barracks, and a sparkling motor pool, than about taking to the field to fight the war. He was tired of complaints that Laos was not tank country (aerial photos of what appeared to be ditches were often thirty-foot ravines), and would respond acidly that the NVA tankers seemed able to get around. The answer may have been that they knew where the good trails were. The ARVN complained that their M41 tanks only had 76mm guns, while the NVA T54s had 100mms.

In all quarters, the friction grew.

Sutherland blamed most of the difficulties on Colonel Luat whom he tried without success to convince Lam to replace, and who he, personally, felt was "a martinet, incompetent, and a coward." He thought that the failure of the armor to come to Hill 31's rescue was not the result of a conflict of orders, but of Luat being shocked into inaction by the report of NVA tanks. He thought that the friction between Generals Lam and Dong was heightened by Luat playing one against the other. Following the collapse of Hill 31, Sutherland received a radio call from General Jackson at I Corps; he said that Luat had arrived on a resupply helicopter, uncalled and unexpected, and that Lam had furiously ordered him to get back to his unit in the field.

Colonels Battreall and Hiep saw Luat that day—tired, but cheerful and confident—and understood that Lam had called him for an update of his brigade's situation. Battreall heard nothing about Lam being angry, and was convinced that Jackson's report to Sutherland about Luat skulking out of combat was based on a personal grudge towards Battreall. Jackson and Battreall had long been at odds, and Battreall thought the general's personal dislike for him was prejudicing his reports on the ARVN armor, Battreall advised. Whatever the cause, Luat's brief visit to the I Corps command bunker was the only time he was not with his brigade in Laos. In the midst of all of the attacks on the armor, Battreall thought bitterly, why did no one ask why the 17th Cavalry continued to hold its position after the airborne had withdrawn? If they were cowards, why didn't they bolt the five kilometers south to Aloui?

The 17th Cav's position was indeed grave. Isolated in the hills, the NVA had been able to bombard them and maneuver infantrymen close enough to fill the air above them with lead, keeping the helicopters away. At noon on 27 February, the North Vietnamese tried to overrun the position with a wave of tank and infantry. Jets and gunships came to their aid and, when the smoke cleared, the ARVN were still holding their ground. The skirmishing continued until the night of 1 March, when the NVA launched another major attack.

For the second time, the 17th Cav held.

Colonel Harrison urged General Dong to do something, either reinforce the 17th Cav or order their withdrawal to Aloui. Dong just shrugged, bewildered under the pressure of command. On 3 March, the NVA attacked again and Colonel Battreall listened anxiously to the radio reports. The ARVN were taking fire from three sides and had tank shells exploding to their rear. They had suffered a hundred more dead and wounded; ten more APCs were destroyed and two attempts to resupply them and evacuate casualties by helicopter had been driven away by the hornet's nest of fire. Dong was unresponsive to the situation, Lam was at a XXIV Corps briefing, and Battreall did not know to whom to turn. He feared the 17th Cav would be completely overwhelmed, so he and his counterpart, Colonel Hiep, took matters into their own hands. They collared Lieutenant Colonel Vallejo, USAF advisor to I Corps, and, after five minutes on the radio, he had six B52 bombers diverted to the 17th Cav. The Arc Light came in like close air support, the hills disappearing in explosions several hundred yards from the surrounded ARVN, and the NVA attack was halted in its tracks. Battreall and Hiep radioed them to break contact and the armor-airborne task force withdrew to a better position to allow helicopters to come in for their wounded. Then they continued a rearguard action to rejoin the brigade at Aloui.

At Colonel Hiep's suggestion, Colonel Battreall and his sergeant major joined him on a helicopter for Da Nang. Hiep thought it advisable to be out of the area when General Lam returned, lest he be angered that a mere colonel had stepped in like that. They spent the night in Hiep's private home, then signed out a jeep in the morning to return to FSB Kilo. With the sergeant major driving, Battreall joined a U.S. ammunition convoy on Route 9 and arrived, caked in red dust, hoping Lam had better things to worry about by then. Colonel Hiep, meanwhile, reported to President Thieu in Saigon. His observations and recommendations were that General Dong of the airborne and General Khang of the marines were failing to perform, and that, unless the 1st Armor Brigade were given some viable mission, they should be withdrawn from Aloui before the NVA could make Route 9 completely impassable. Hiep then went to XXIV Corps to organize fifty men from each ARVN armor regiment to go back with him as replacements to Luat's mauled brigade.

PART THREE:
Americans at War

CHAPTER NINE:
The Rockpile

As the ARVN fought in Laos, the U.S. ground forces continued their simultaneous effort to keep Route 9 open and the new firebases secure. To do so, General Hill and the 1st Brigade, 5th Mechanized Infantry Division, were initially concerned with the Rockpile, that incongruous jutting of jungle-covered granite north of Vandegrift. North Vietnamese rocket teams with infantry support had taken advantage of the high perches just west of the Rockpile to bring Vandegrift and Route 9 under almost daily shelling. Casualties had been inflicted on the American units in the area, and it fell initially to Lieutenant Colonel Meyer's 1st Battalion, 77th Armor, to scout the Rockpile area and flush the enemy teams.

In the same time frame as the 8 February crossing into Laos, a patrol under 1/77 control found two recently abandoned NVA basecamps in the hills three kilometers west of the actual Rockpile. They held many antitank mines, and 60mm mortar and RPG rounds. The next day, Meyer helicoptered to join the unit on foot as they continued patrolling, pushing north of the 3/5 Cav pioneer road in the hills, and west of the Rockpile. The captain in charge appeared nervous to have a battalion commander on the ground with him, and his fears for the colonel's safety were soon justified: at noon, NVA opened up from a bunker with AK-47 automatic rifles. The GIs returned the fire, located the bunker, and the forward observer called in artillery support. None came. Meyer grabbed the radio and spoke to the battery commander, "We needed that arty five minutes ago." Still none came. Finally Meyer radioed for a combat-engineer vehicle with a 165mm demolition gun to be dispatched. It clanked up through the thick brush and blasted shells into the NVA bunker.

The patrol moved up, found two dead North Vietnamese, and the captain joked to Meyer that he was welcome along any time. Things were off to an easy start.

To press the NVA, Meyer ordered one of his tank companies to sweep the high ground around the Rockpile. In support, the battalion scout platoon and a detachment from the 1/61 Mech Infantry were attached to the tankers. As they rolled north from the Vandegrift perimeter, Sp4 Spurgeon of the battalion snipers jumped on one of Lieutenant Revelak's scout tracks, hoping to see some action. The patrol halted below one of the smaller hills, and the tanks proceeded to deploy in the heavy underbrush to lob shells uphill.

Lieutenant Revelak said something about a reconnaissance team up the hill being stuck in an NVA bunker complex. He made a head count of the men and said they were going uphill "light" (without rucksacks). Spurgeon noticed uneasily that a disproportionate number of the men had dark-green fatigues and new jungle boots. He noticed a Puerto Rican sergeant beside him, a tall guy with a beard, looking nervous. Spurgeon asked if he really thought there were any NVA up there.

"There're definitely some dinks on that hill. Lots of 'em." Spurgeon was feeling gung-ho. "Good."

But that didn't mean he was crazy. Everyone else was wearing helmets, but he'd turned one down in favor of the bravado of his bush hat. The sergeant's comment got to him and he grinned, "I'll take that steel pot now." A grunt on an APC laughed and tossed him one. The tanks ceased firing and the patrol pushed out. A Kit Carson Scout took the point, the Puerto Rican sergeant following him, the rest of the scouts and 1/61 grunts in trace behind them. The hill was steep and lush with heavy green foliage, but a one-foot-wide trail wove up through the tangle and the grunts snaked up single file. The jungle canopy enveloped them from above. They splashed across a stream, only two feet deep but fifty yards wide, and hauled themselves back into the wall of brush on the other side, continuing uphill. It was a clear day and not a shot was fired. Spurgeon had been through a year of patrols without a single serious contact and he disgustedly thought this was going to be another useless walk in the sun. He bummed a Salem off one of the grunts and continued trudging along.

They stopped amid the brush, forming a hasty perimeter as the Kit Carson and sergeant pushed on. Spurgeon waited with the grunts, the 1/61 lieutenant standing with an o.d. sweat towel around his neck and a helmet over his bush hat. Spurgeon, fed up with the humping, sarcastically asked, "What now?" to the lieutenant and his RTO.

A single shot broke the silence from the point.

Then a long burst of automatic fire followed.

The patrol crouched in place amid the high shrubbery, not sure what was going on or what to do. Then Spurgeon saw something tumbling end over end through the air and the lieutenant was shouting "Chicom!" The grenade exploded thirty feet from Spurgeon, and he looked up terrified to see seven more arching down towards them. The NVA were lobbing them from the high ground. GIs began heaving grenades uphill and Spurgeon watched the stunning sight of a half-dozen U.S. grenades sailing up, spoons popping off in flight, while a dozen NVA stick grenades sailed downhill. They bounced and fizzed and sprayed shrapnel over the patrol. Everyone was firing back from the prone. A North Vietnamese mortar added to the cacophony. Spurgeon, pumped with adrenaline, got up clutching his M-14 rifle, screaming for them to charge. No one moved. No one was giving orders, and he finally jumped back down, afraid he'd accidentally be shot from behind if he actually ran forward.

"Medic! We need a medic!" men were screaming, hidden in the brush.

Spurgeon dropped down in the bushes beside three black GIs who were spraying their M-16s and throwing grenades into a patch of burning elephant grass. Spurgeon fired blindly into the smoking brush and lobbed his last two grenades. To his right, he could see men trying to outflank the NVA. They were halted by the heavy fire. He was kneeling and firing when another grenade bounced in. He grabbed his ears, it boomed, and his right knee suddenly stung. He yanked up his trouser-leg to see a tear in the cloth and a scrape on his skin; a piece of shrapnel had kicked him without drawing any blood. He rolled away towards Lieutenant Revelak who was down flat on the slope, fire raking near him.

Someone was moaning, "I'm hit, I'm hit," and Spurgeon crabwalked towards the sound. A medic was balled up in the grass. He patted over his field jacket, looking for the wound. He finally found a tiny shrapnel hole which barely bled, and it dawned on him that the man wasn't dying, but was just scared. He wrapped the medic's arm around his shoulder and they rolled downhill.

The shooting continued without letup, and soon the patrol was out of grenades and short of ammunition. Men began shouting, "We're leaving, let's get outta here!" and the patrol retreated down the trail. Two or three GIs at the end tried to drag the body of the sergeant with them—the first shots of the ambush had killed him. Spurgeon grabbed his shirt, the others his feet and arms, and they laboriously scurried down the path, sliding on their butts. The NVA opened up with a renewed fury, volleys of AK slashing the leaves and limbs above them. The dead man's shirt ripped off of him as they tugged. Spurgeon grabbed his wrist. His helmet bounced off. A GI ahead of him tumbled, a ricochet swelling his eye. Spurgeon stopped, enraged, and fired his rifle uphill. Someone down the trail yelled to pop smoke to mark them for supporting fire so Spurgeon tugged a yellow smoke grenade off of the M-16 bandolier tied to the dead sergeant's waist.

The AKs kept hurrying them along, sounding like popcorn in a pan.

They reached the stream and made a pell-mell dash across it, running and falling. Lieutenant Revelak tried to hoist the dead sergeant on his back, but the body was too heavy and they tumbled into the water. The AK fire increased, roaring above their heads into the far bank. Spurgeon began crawling, his head and back above the water, his rifle submerged, his mind paralyzed with the thought of a bullet smashing through his forehead. He threw himself behind a small rock in the middle of the creek. Several grunts splashed back across to get the body which had been dropped, and Spurgeon felt like a coward. "Let them do it," he thought, "this kid ain't getting shot." Tears of fear stung his eyes. The NVA fire was too heavy. The men ran back, leaving the dead sergeant.

Spurgeon bolted for the bank, grabbing handfuls of elephant grass to haul himself up. He stopped at the edge of the water, sitting in the mud, turning to fire. Water sprayed from the bolt at each shot. They finally straggled back to the tank site and a helicopter landed. The crew chief hopped out to take a photograph as Spurgeon and another GI helped the medic aboard. Another chopper came in; about seven men had been wounded.

The grunts took a breather on the tanks, wearily smoking and talking. Spurgeon was exhausted. It had been his first real firefight and he'd not seen a single NVA. He felt they'd been beaten because they'd underrated the power of the NVA on that hill. A U.S. Navy Phantom roared in dropping bombs and the grunts cheered inside. The second pass splashed napalm, then rockets, then it made a strafing run. The pilot radioed he was taking ground fire, then reported "dusting a dink" with a rocket.

Firepower was brought to bear against the hill all that night.

In the morning, Lieutenant Colonel Meyer arrived. He reviewed the firefight. The captain in charge had been back with the tanks instead of up with the patrol. He had not aggressively responded to the NVA ambush, but had allowed them to get the upper hand; he had ordered a withdrawal not based on what he saw personally but on the excited reports of a young radioman. And the body of an American soldier had been left behind in the chaotic retreat under fire. Meyer relieved the captain on the spot; the man resigned, saying, "Yes, sir," and disappeared. Meyer directed more fire against the bunkers atop the hill, then took out a foot patrol to retrieve the body. Although they recovered the dead sergeant without any contact, it was obvious that the NVA had more than just a few rocket teams in the Rockpile hills. Reinforcements were needed to clear the high ground.

The reinforcements sent by General Hill were Lieutenant Colonel Coast's 4th Battalion, 3d Infantry, Americal Division, which was airlifted from Khe Sanh to Vandegrift on 10 February. That first day, Alpha Company 4/3 manned some old marine dugouts on the perimeter, and immediately came under 122mm rocket fire. When the shelling stopped, the grunts stood on the bunker line to cheer on a pair of Cobra gunships which pumped rockets into a neighboring ridgeline.

The men spent the night in the flimsy bunkers listening, detached, as an occasional one-two-two exploded somewhere else on Vandegrift. The whole battalion was going to CA into the Rockpile area the next morning; and Pvt Russ Morse knew they'd be stepping into the shit. He was tense, but he wasn't collapsing, and that was because they had a good platoon. Lieutenant Dewing had his shit together, Morse thought; they called him Mad Dog out of respect for the lieutenant's willingness to share the risks. And the guys themselves, Morse reckoned, were just dynamite. They did their best, and it irked him that the war protesters and draft dodgers seemed to be getting the hero's treatment back home. It was something they rarely talked about in the field. Most of them didn't want to be in Nam. But Morse thought it was the only honorable choice, even if it was a lousy choice. You just did your job.

Sitting in a bunker that night, Lieutenant Dewing was having similar thoughts. He was deeply moved by the performance of his grunts, only two of whom were not draftees. They were mostly just kids, nineteen-year-old working-class kids like his friend Morse, who smoked dope and flashed the peace sign, and couldn't give a shit about the army or Vietnam—and who would risk their lives in a moment for another GI. Underneath the veneer of being rough-and-tough killers, he thought, they were caring, dependable men. All you had to do was treat them with dignity; they would refuse orders from a screaming second lieutenant, but go on the hairiest patrol for someone who led them personally. As for Dewing, he was there by choice. He'd grown up a high-school athlete in the Alaskan outback country, and had dropped out of college to join the army in a moment of apathy after his girlfriend had broken up with him. In retrospect, he'd never regretted the move. A stint with an engineer unit in Vietnam had earned him a recommendation to OCS; he'd arrived for his second tour as a lieutenant in October 1970. He'd come in to the Tan Son Nhut airbase aboard a commercial jet filled with captains and lieutenants, many of whom jumped at the chance when the reception clerks asked who wanted to go to the support commands. After a year in the rear and primed with the gung-ho attitude of OCS, Dewing had been adamant about going to the infantry. He'd volunteered for everything he got in Vietnam and, at the age of twenty-three, Lieutenant Dewing felt content leading the First Platoon in combat.

The sun broke through the overcast on the morning of 11 February as the grunts of 4/3 made last-minute preparations on the Vandegrift helicopter pad. Slicks and guns from the 14th CAB took the lead elements into a hilltop LZ west of the Rockpile. C Company went first; it was a hot LZ; a Huey and an OH58 Kiowa Scout were shot down, and a firefight around the crash site killed two Americans. One dead NVA and an AK-47 were found in the brush. The helicopters were destroyed in place, the crews extracted.

While the initial CA was being conducted, Captain Spinning's Alpha Company waited at the helipad. Helicopters came back from the Charlie Company insertion, riddled with bullet holes, and the men began boarding. They knew this was it—a hot LZ and birds down—and some of the men got shakey. Pvt. Morse could feel the hesitation well up in him and he asked Lieutenant Dewing if he could stay at Vandegrift since he was slotted for an R&R the next day. Dewing said no, they needed all the men they could have; and Morse agreed to postpone his leave until after the op. As he hustled towards the birds, he noticed two GIs, one black and one white, refusing to board the helicopters; the black GI muttered, "I'm not going out there to get killed." It was the last Morse ever saw of those two.

They climbed into the cabins, hunkered under their gear, and sat for a long time as the blades churned and the cabins vibrated around them; the engines shut down and still they waited. Finally, word came to go, the blades picked up to a dervish pitch, and Alpha Company watched Vandegrift skim away underneath them and the hills of the Rockpile rise to the north. Morse sat beside Denny in the second slick, M-16s across their laps, legs hanging out the doors; they touched down in the LZ with a few AKs sputtering from the treeline, and Morse bolted out, jumping behind a fallen tree with a Charlie Company grunt. The NVA fire dried up and the rest of Alpha CA'd in without difficulty.

After a brief huddle, they moved out in file down a thin mountain trail. Morse took the point, grinning back at Buddy-Fucker over the dead North Vietnamese sprawled inside the LZ, then stopped at the edge of the perimeter. Dewing gave him general directions and Morse led the patrol, moving slowly down a well-used path. He came to a lesser-used fork, followed that to the top of the ridgeline, then descended the other slope; it was shaky footing straight down. After three exhausting hours of humping, they took a short break, then more patrolling along the slope until dusk when they set up their night defensive position on the trail. The fog and cold rolled in around the mountaintops. Colder than a nun's butt, Dewing thought; the men had no blankets or extra shirts so they lay shivering miserably on the cold ground.

The sun was breaking on the horizon and Morse had just opened a C ration breakfast when three M-16 shots popped from the edge of the perimeter. He grabbed his M-14 and ran over to see the Staff Sergeant and Buddy-Fucker lowering their rifles. They said they'd gone to take a leak and had spotted a dink on the trail. He'd run away before they'd gotten a bead on him.

Things calmed down and Alpha moved out again down the path, First Platoon up front, Morse again on point. He hated the trail for it followed the narrow crest of the ridgeline, the slopes falling away like cliffs on either side making their movement predictable and thus ambushable. He wanted to hack through the brush on the side. Three hours of patrolling yielded nothing and the company halted, strung out along the trail to take five. The company leaders stood talking and, as was routine, Captain Spinning assigned Lieutenant Walker's Second Platoon to take over the point.

Morse sat in the brush, his fatigues soaked with sweat, watching Second Platoon file past, Lieutenant Walker on point and two GIs named English and Moran walking slack. The lone NVA they'd spotted weighed on his mind. It was too quiet out there. Some premonition clicked in his head and he was tempted to fake it—to shout, "Dinks!" and start shooting, halting the move. He let the thought pass, knowing that would simply pinpoint their exact location to the North Vietnamese—as if they didn't already know.

Morse walked over to Denny, sat down, lit up a cigarette—and the whole world suddenly went up. A Chinese claymore slambanged under the canopy of trees, spraying chunks of metal down the path, AK-47s drilled from the brush and, in a millisecond, Lieutenant Walker was blasted with shrapnel and hurled against a tree stump, English and Moran were blown away, Morse and Denny were throwing themselves into the bushes, Chip was down with shrapnel, and five other GIs were screaming in pain. It was all chaos and noise. Behind him Morse could hear Lieutenant Dewing shout, "On line, move out!" and someone started pouring down fire with a pig. He glanced at Denny and they rolled to their knees, firing in the direction of the NVA. Morse emptied two magazines, jammed in a third, rose from his crouch to move towards the casualties, and a sudden stinging explosion rippled through his back and side. He spun, and two more rounds punched through his stomach. He collapsed and the pain exploded through him. He couldn't move his legs.

A stray M-16 burst from behind had hit him; a medic from Second Platoon scrambled over to patch him up.

Dewing jogged forward to the point of contact and saw Lieutenant Walker dropped at the foot of the stump. He was peppered with shrapnel along the right side of his body and was bleeding badly—it looked as if his helmet had saved his life. Dewing hesitated a moment, but Walker shouted, "Go on!" and Dewing ran past. In a few minutes, it was all over—the NVA emptying a few AK mags then disappearing back into the jungle, no one seeing a single one of them. Dewing got on the radio to call in artillery on the slope that the NVA were probably moving down. The company FO, Lieutenant Cunningham, ran up and took over, directing a roar of air and arty into the jungled valley below them. The company formed a hasty perimeter while the medics worked on GIs moaning in the grass. There were two dead and eight wounded. Medevacs circled but the trees and brush were too dense for them to land, so they had to use a jungle penetrator. One at a time, the dead and wounded were strapped in the basket and winched up to the hovering helicopter by a cable.

Morse was the last out, two guys dragging him, as he heard AKs open up on the hovering bird. It remained in place and Morse loved those pilots. As he was winched up, he could see muzzle flashes below him and heard the zing of an AK round go past him, but he was too drowsy on the medic's morphine to realize he was in danger.

12 February had been a bad day for the grunts, but Alpha Company

humped the rest of the afternoon on patrol. After another freezing night, they returned to sweeping the ridgeline, getting further and further away from the battalion command post set up in the original landing zone. Instead of patrolling single file, they put out five point men—one on the crest, two more on each slope—with the rest of the company following in a skirmish line behind again.

It was obvious that the ridges they were patrolling had long been the site of war. Lost in the undergrowth, they found many U.S. gas masks (poison gas was not used in Vietnam so, when infantrymen were issued protective masks, they routinely dropped them in the brush on the next patrol to lighten the load they were humping). They also found that an occasional tree had been sawed down by North Vietnamese soldiers for their bunkers. The stumps would have been like white dots looking skyward as a signal to U.S. reconnaissance planes, so the NVA had rubbed dirt on them for camouflage. Dewing was impressed by such attention to detail; the enemy they were hunting were professionals and all of the grunts had a lot of respect for them. While they saw evidence of bunkers being built, they saw no bunkers.

The terrain was rough going, with sharp inclines and steep hills, and the thick brush and trees slowed progress. Tall clumps of elephant grass had to be pushed through, and Dewing was amazed when the metal blades of a few machetes actually snapped in half as exhausted grunts clubbed at the grass with them. Like all tough humps, it turned into a plodding monotony of aching muscles, sweat-drenched fatigues, and mumbled curses at the lifers, the oppressive packs on their backs, the hills, the sun. Heavy fog shrouded the mountains, disrupting regular resupply to the company, and water became critical. There was little to drink, none to waste on washing or brushing teeth, and the grunts began looking around, as they patrolled, for bamboo stalks which had water inside.

On 14 February, Captain Spinning decided it was becoming too exhausting and passed the word to drop the rucks and travel light. One platoon halted to guard the equipment until helicopters could get in for them, and the other two platoons continued on, the men putting their C ration cans in pockets, and carrying nothing but weapons, ammunition, and half-empty canteens. They were moving up another hill on the ridgeline when Dewing got a call from the Loach scouting ahead of them, "You got some traffic ahead of you. Dink in a bunker." The company came upon a small clearing where they could make out the NVA dugout in the brush, an elaborate construction that looked as if it would withstand artillery. The Loach orbited it, the door-gunner throwing smoke and frag grenades. It banked off and Dewing shouted, "Chieu hoi, chieu hoi!" Surrender! There was no response from the bunker, so he cautiously jogged forward. Seeing a figure move inside, he dropped down, threw in a grenade, and scurried back. Sergeant First Class Rojas, of another platoon, crawled forward and tossed in two more frags. The sergeant waited a bit, then climbed into the bunker and dragged out the body of the North Vietnamese soldier killed by the blast. The grunts curiously gathered around. Someone pulled out his wallet, and they passed around several black-and-white photographs of the dead soldier with his wife and children. That brought the whole war down to a personal level for Dewing; this guy was a draftee like us, he thought, just a rice farmer from Hanoi fighting for his country. It was the first time he'd thought of his enemy as a human being, and he was amazed at the man's courage. Whereas the Americans would send several men to do a job, the Communists had just sent one. And he died fighting, all alone, one man against a whole company.

15 February. The bunker of the dead NVA sat atop a little hill, and the 4/3 jump command post moved into it. Early the next morning, a battalion element reported contact with about two dozen NVA. Three GIs were wounded and the enemy slipped away in the jungle. Two hours later, the GIs ambushed an NVA patrol and reported killing fifteen enemy soldiers. By noon Alpha Company was leaving the battalion area for another hump, but Captain Spinning was concerned about the sightings of the NVA groups. He told Lieutenant Sheridan to take his Third Platoon back down the trail in the direction they'd come and check for any NVA who might be trailing them.

They moved down the path, and were in the valley between the command post and a small hill, when the sudden roar of another Chinese-claymore ambush thunderclapped. AK-47s hit the platoon in the draw from the hill. Lieutenant Sheridan went down with dust and bamboo splinters blown into his eyes. Two grunts behind the point, Benjamin Burgos-Torres and David Comber, were killed instantly by the claymore. The point man, Pfc Julian Marquez, charged towards the NVA ambushers, only to be shot dead in the brushy slope of the hill.

The platoon fell back.

Dewing's First Platoon was still at the CP when the ambush was sprung and, before the lieutenant could say a word, the grunts were up and rushing downhill towards the fire. It was an instantaneous reaction, the company falling on line, firing into the jungle, unable to see any of the NVA. A platoon of NVA were firing from the hill and it was impossible to move forward without heavy casualties. The overcast was too low to bring in the gunships, so Captain Spinning shouted to fall back. The company began pulling back, dragging their wounded with them, but leaving the three dead men who were right under the enemy guns. The NVA fired on the retreat and Pfc Barnhart flopped forward, shot in the foot. The round had hit the sole of his foot, ripped through to the ankle, and he lay clutching his leg in intense pain. Dewing jumped down beside him and could see the copper-jacketed AK-47 bullet protruding from the canvas of Barnhart's jungle boot. He plucked out the bullet, put it in Barnhart's hand, and curled his fist around it, telling him to keep it for a souvenir. Then the medics helped him limp back, with the rest of the grunts, jogging between the trees.

At the command post, medevacs came in for their six wounded. The company spent the night there, everyone nervous about the next morning when they would have to go back to get the bodies of Burgos-Torres, Comber, and Marquez. Dewing was hurt that a young fighter like Marquez had to die like that, but he really felt sorry for Comber. Comber was new to the company and scuttlebutt was that he'd had a rear job until he'd pissed off a sergeant major.

It was still chilly and brisk in the morning and the fog hadn't burned away, when the helicopters came in with a resupply of water and the company's rucksacks. Dewing took a detail down to the only suitable LZ in the jungled area, a crater on the other side of their hill position. The choppers came in at a slow hover, door-gunners kicking out the rucks and "Donkey Dick" water blivets; and then the North Vietnamese opened up with a mortar. The first round fell short and exploded in the valley as they scrambled for cover. The next one whistled over their heads and burst in the opposite valley, and Dewing shouted to get back before the NVA bracketed them.

The grunts scrambled hand-over-hand uphill, dragging the gear.

Dewing ran to the crest of the ridgeline before realizing one of his men was still back in the open area, hunkered down in the crater, afraid to move. He shouted to come on but the kid hesitated another moment, then scurried over the rim of the shell hole, dragging his ruck. The NVA had the range by then. Another shell exploded as the kid popped up, and he flopped back into the crater. Dewing and Sp5 Larry Gann, a super medic, scrambled down the hill. They tore off the GI's shirt. He had only seven minute shrapnel holes on the left side of his chest but he was dying. Gann worked quickly and efficiently, getting a plastic trachea tube down his throat so he could breathe, and starting an IV in his arm. A medevac was requested.

They put the wounded man in the helicopter but he died en route.

In the afternoon, Alpha Company mounted up again and moved slowly towards the three bodies in the jungled draw. They were again met by a torrent of fire. They shot back futilely into the bushes and fell back before they suffered any casualties. This day, though, the grunts had some revenge for their frustration and fear. They were moving back along the ridgeline when NVA were spotted in the valley below them, pulling away from the hill mass. Lieutenant Cunningham quickly got on the radio and called for TOT—Time On Target, several batteries of artillery firing simultaneously into the same kill zone. The air rushed with the freight-train sound of incoming artillery, and the valley floor literally erupted around the dozens of NVA swarming through the trees. The grunts crouched on the hilltop and cheered inside as the FO watched through his binoculars and kept up a running commentary on the massacre. He said he could see groups of NVA trying to run away, a blinding flash, then shredded foliage and pieces of bodies strewn about. To the grunts it was sweet, sweet revenge.

The fighting did not end that night. As the grunts settled in their foxholes for another black night of fog and chill, the NVA sent probing teams creeping through the brush. The company's 4.2-inch mortar team did an expert job dropping shells on the edge of the perimeter, driving the enemy away. By that night, someone in supply had helicoptered more than fifty Arctic Mountain sleeping bags to Alpha. Dewing, with four hours to sleep, climbed in, feeling snug, just thankful for the warmth. He was sleeping when the whole world seemed to come ripping apart and he bolted awake, terrified. Airstrikes were pummelling the valleys on either side of the ridge. No one in higher headquarters had taken the trouble to alert Alpha Company.

On 17 February, the company was again met by a hail of fire when it tried to get to the three bodies, but pulled back unscathed. The grunts began calling the NVA-held knoll Track-meet Hill for all of the times they'd run up and run back. It was grinding the men down—some worse than others. Captain Spinning was using the captured NVA bunker as his CP, and Dewing was inside with him when a grunt stumbled in, crying and shaking. He had cracked up from the stress. A medic grabbed him, Dewing and the others reassuring the sobbing man, "It's all right . . . don't worry about it." He was slated for a medevac. There was a lot of peer pressure among the grunts for each to hold up his end and the man was afraid he'd be laughed at. He wasn't. Sometimes Americans can be such vindictive bastards, Dewing thought. But it made him proud that the grunts had shown only compassion for a fellow soldier who simply couldn't take it anymore.

Another soldier in Alpha Company also quit for less tangible reasons, and with less drama. He had performed well during the unsuccessful attacks to get the bodies and was in for a Bronze Star. The day after he earned the medal, he told his platoon leader that there was no way he was going up again. The story spread like wildfire among the grunts, and Captain Spinning told him he would be court-martialled. He left the shooting war aboard a helicopter, bound for trial, and it amazed Dewing how a subtle, unspoken shift in a man's mood could make him a hero one day and a coward the next.

On the evening of 17 February, Captain Spinning, Lieutenant Cunningham, and Lieutenant Dewing sat down once again to discuss the next attempt to get the bodies. They were frustrated, but there was never a question of abandoning the mission; it left a bad taste in their mouths to leave dead Americans to the Communists, and the officers felt it would be disastrous for morale if anything but a maximum effort was made to recover soldiers, dead or alive. The only thing they hadn't tried was coming in from two angles, so that if the NVA ambushed one column, the other could still move in. They agreed that this time nothing would stop them.

They moved out the next day at noon. Captain Spinning walked point in one column. Out of sight on the other slope of the ridgeline, the First Platoon advanced. Staff Sergeant Kegerreis walked point with Dewing walking slack behind him. The rest of the platoon followed single file, a good distance between them so they wouldn't be bunched up if the NVA let loose with another claymore. They walked to the side of the trail, where the NVA had previously hacked away the underbrush, making it relatively easy going. Keg, on point, was wearing a helmet and flak jacket, and set a cautious, deliberate pace. Dewing followed, a thirty-round magazine in his M-16, twenty-four more mags wrapped around him in bandoliers and an empty claymore bag, and three grenades in each pocket.

It was cold and overcast, the dampened forest a gloomy gray.

Staff Sergeant Kegerreis led them to the bodies without a shot being fired, then spotted an NVA bunker in the brush. Keg moved for it, Dewing behind him. Then as Dewing watched, everything happened too quickly for fear to surface; a bareheaded North Vietnamese popped waist-high from the bunker, his AK-47 pointed at them. The silence was shattered by the metallic burst. Something thudded into Dewing's hip, and Keg spun back, tumbling over him head over heels at the impact of the AK rounds. Dewing dropped down, frantically grabbed a grenade from his pocket, yanked the pin out. The NVA dropped back down to reload and Dewing lobbed the frag into the bunker. There was a muffled boom from within and he waited a second. The North Vietnamese soldier did not reappear. He crawled quickly to Keg, who was lying in the brush, wide awake although the AK had raked him from the waist up. The meat was blown off his right forearm. Dewing tugged off the sergeant's flak jacket and wrapped two compress bandages around the bare bone to stop the bleeding. He talked to Keg, to keep him out of shock, until a medic ran up from the platoon column to take over. The rest of the grunts fanned out around them. There was no shooting. The NVA were gone.

Jesus, Dewing thought, this is eerie.

The silence was the cue to the NVA that their man in the bunker was dead, and they opened up with mortars. The grunts hugged earth. Dewing could still walk and felt no pain, but he noticed a bulge of flesh sticking through a small hole in his trousers. He ripped at the cloth and could see a small bullet hole in his hip; there was an AK-47 round in him.

The bodies of Burgos-Torres, Comber, and Marquez were lying where they'd fallen; the cold nights had prevented them from decomposing. The grunts, used to the VC down south who booby-trapped anything and everything, used grappling hooks and ropes to tug at the bodies, but they were clean. An occasional mortar shell whistled in, hurrying the grunts along as they rolled the dead men onto litters fashioned of ponchos and hardwood branches, and started dragging them back up the hill. The mortar rounds hit the treetops, sending fragments spraying down like rain. Dewing was walking back with the rear of the platoon when he noticed other GIs moving slowly past them, towards the bunker they had blown.

At the hilltop, he saw the battalion operations officer and asked, "Who are the guys in the clean fatigues?" The major said a battalion from the 101st Airborne was moving in and their whole battalion was pulling out.

The ridge was a scene of windy confusion as helicopters came and went, the Americal conducting medevacs and extractions in the midst of the Screaming Eagles combat assault. Dewing climbed aboard a Huey with Keg and two men from the 101st who had shrapnel wounds. He noticed they had clean fatigues and black jungle boots; after eight days in the Rockpile, his grunts looked like bums. He sat cross-legged on the metal floor, his rifle and rucksack gone, and Keg lay flat on his back beside him, still conscious. The helicopter lifted off and Dewing asked the door-gunner if it was okay to smoke. He lit up and Keg rolled over and smacked his lips. The lieutenant placed the cigarette between his lips and the sergeant took a long drag.

They landed at the 18th Surgical in Quang Tri at around four in the afternoon. When they came in, a medic asked, "What's wrong with you?"

"Well, I think I've been shot," Dewing replied.

Since he was still on his feet, hardly bleeding, and in little pain, Dewing was ushered to a bench while Keg was immediately wheeled into surgery. Dewing watched, very impressed with the professionalism of the doctors, nurses, and medics.

There was a CBS-TV News camera crew there and they interviewed Dewing. He felt automatically hostile towards the press. It seemed that every time they came to a firebase, they scrounged around for the biggest malcontent to put on television. He felt the reporters had stained the bravery of his grunts with their constant harping on drugs, fraggings, and refusals. He was angered that My Lai had been made synonymous with all activities of the Americal Division. He saw no atrocities, only tragedies. Once, before Laos, his man Morse had been on point when they were patrolling triple-canopy jungle at dusk. Morse, hearing Vietnamese voices coming down the trail, had waved the platoon down and opened fire. He'd thrown a couple of frags, and moved forward with some grunts, firing from the hip. When they'd parted the brush they'd found two dead little boys, a dead papa-san, and the mama-san, hit in the chest, side, and legs wailing over the bodies. A medic had patched her up, given her morphine, but they'd heard she'd died on the medevac. There had been no weapons, packs, or VC documents on the bodies. It had happened in a free-fire zone, but that hadn't made Morse feel any better. The whole platoon had felt gutted, an attitude rarely reflected in press reporters.

Dewing resented the newsmen and gave them a hawkish line.

The reporter asked why they'd kept going back for the bodies.

"I don't believe in leaving anything American behind."

The interview was aired on the network news before Dewing's parents had even received notification from the army of his WIA status.

The medics eventually got around to Dewing, giving him a tetanus shot and X rays. A doctor returned with the X rays and said he'd been hit by a ricochet AK-47 round. The bullet had hit the ground first, lost its copper jacket, then the lead slug had bounced into his hip. He was lucky; had the round been going full force, it would have shattered his pelvis. He was carted into an operating room and the anesthesiologist strolled in—just back from a Hawaiian R&R and decked out in a beach hat and a brightly colored tourist shirt. He gave Dewing a spinal, joking that it was working when you could scratch between your legs and not feel anything. Then the doctor operated and removed the bullet. There was little pain involved and, after the quick surgery, Dewing said he was starving. They told him to wait for midnight chow, but the last time he looked at his watch before falling into exhausted sleep it was half past eleven.

The next day, he saw Keg for the last time, in bed with two tubes in his nose and an IV going. Then he was air evacked to the 67th Semimobile Evacuation Hospital in Qui Nhon. He arrived there stinking like a grunt would after three weeks in the bush without anything but drinking water, so the nurses finally taped his wound with fourteen layers of plastic and ordered him to the showers. He spent forty-five minutes under the hot nozzle. It was unbelievable. Later he sent a postcard to his grunts, addressing it to Captain "Take-the-hill" Spinning. Alpha Company had gone into the Rockpile with one hundred and twenty-two men; they came out with eighty-eight. The battalion as a whole was credited with one hundred and twenty-two NVA kills.

It was Lieutenant Colonel Sutton's 3d Battalion, 187th Infantry, 101st Airborne Division that combat assaulted into the Rockpile to replace the battered 4/3. The welcome for the Screaming Eagles was an ugly one. Echo Recon went in first, CAing to the bottom of the 4/3 CP hill which was in the process of being evacuated. Charlie Company followed them in, landing atop the hill in the middle of the Americal pullout and a mortar raid, and in half an hour they had two dead and a dozen wounded. The grunts called it Purple Heart Hill. The battalion operations officer, Major Scharnberg, helicoptered in only to be seriously wounded by mortar shrapnel.

The battalion executive officer Major Euell White, monitoring the chaos by radio, heard that dead Americans were found in the LZ from the pell-mell pullout of 4/3. Artillery was directed against the area and Bravo Company went in next to CA atop a knoll west of Purple Heart

Hill. Artillery pasted the jungle, the helicopters circled, arty lifted, and they sailed in.

The LZ was cold.

The next day, 19 February, an Arc Light was directed just northwest of the Rockpile and things began to quiet down in the area. For the battalion's Delta Company, the move to the Rockpile AO was mostly more of the same. They were airmobiled to relieve C Company atop Purple Heart Hill. The sheer hilltop was too small, so the CP set up atop it while the rifle platoons filed onto the fingers on patrol. The routine was set again and there were only a few times when the enemy was close, when the grunts had some excitement and could grasp at some reason for their being there. One night the North Vietnamese dropped mortars on them and Sergeant Silvers, a little red-haired guy who was sharp with the mortars, lobbed a few rounds at suspected locations. The NVA fire stopped for a while, but then more rounds whistled in and it was clear that, somewhere in the jungle, an NVA mortar crew was watching, firing, moving. One day on patrol, Delta overran an NVA basecamp moments after the enemy had hastily retreated. They found abandoned gear, food still cooking.

So, mostly, Delta Company and the others in the battalion did their work diligently, but with few results. There were bad moments such as when Captain Edward's senior RTO rotated home and Daugherty was selected to leave Second Platoon to replace him. He did not want the job; he liked the men in his platoon and had come to trust and respect Lieutenant Stephen. He suspected the captain's abilities and felt that the job was a burden. It made each day in Vietnam go by a little more slowly. For Daugherty that was the whole point; he could see no sense in Lam Son 719. It was just another no-win operation that had to be survived before he could go home.

The enemy was the sun, the terrain, the hundred-pound rucks and the lifers who thought up the patrols. It was immersion foot, jungle rot, snakes, and scorpions. It was Lieutenant Colonel Sutton himself who broke the monotony one day when he helicoptered to the Delta CP to, as Daugherty cynically noted, "check on the morale of the troops and all those wonderful things lieutenant colonels do." As far as he was concerned, visiting lifers were a waste of time; they didn't seem concerned about clean rifles, fields of fire, or registration of artillery—only shaves and haircuts. The hassles from officers and career NCOs to clean up were a pain. The last time the colonel had dropped in, Daugherty had been in the process of growing an oversized Frank Zappa mustache and goatee. The captain bugged everyone to shave, but Daugherty'd been in one of his difficult moods so, when he'd seen the colonel get off the bird, he'd loaded his face with shaving cream and was holding a mirror in front of himself. The colonel had walked by, said hello, moved on, after which Daugherty had wiped his face clean. The captain had been pissed, but the young grunt had figured he'd owed it to himself.

The colonel had been with Delta only a short time when two NVA mortars opened up. Lieutenant Colonel Sutton immediately departed aboard his C&C, while rounds exploded on both sides of the narrow ridge the company occupied. Lieutenant Stephen could see smoke rising from the jungle. It was too close to hit with air or arty so he told two M-60 gunners and three M-16 riflemen to open fire. They poured two thousand rounds onto the spot where the NVA tubes were located and the mortaring abruptly stopped.

They debated whether to dig in or pull out until Lieutenant Colonel Sutton flew back in. He said aerial recon had spotted several North Vietnamese coming up the ridge towards them. While the officers talked, Daugherty sat with a medic from Texas shooting the breeze.

He thought he heard a pop.

He turned to the medic, "Didja hear that?"

"What?"

"Incoming!"

They scrambled for cover as the air filled with a succession of pops and explosions. The NVA finally got their range, so the men grabbed their gear and tried to outrun the shelling. They sprinted down the ridge, Lieutenant Stephen's platoon in the lead. A hundred yards downhill they hit the valley and discovered an NVA trail in the jungle. It was well used, had commo wire, and was foreboding enough for Stephen to leave three men to guard it for the rest of the company. A hundred yards up the opposite slope, they set up a hasty NDP as the rest of the company jogged up, having successfully outrun the mortars. Stephen watched amused as overweight Captain Edwards straggled in and passed out in a sweaty pile.

In the morning, they went out to retrieve their claymore mines. They were gone. The NVA had crept up, cut the wires, and taken them.

From that hillock, Delta Company continued their patrolling. Captain Edwards kept Lieutenant Stephen on point every day. He thought it was because the CO was angry with him for the antics of some of the grunts in his platoon. Sometimes, at night, they would shout, "Heyyyy, Captain!"

"What is it?" would come Edwards' nervous reply.

"Fuck you, fuck you!" the grunts would bellow, mimicking the sound of jungle lizards.

Stephen thought it was funny secretly, but told the captain he couldn't stumble around the NDP in the middle of the night looking for whoever was shouting. Edwards was not amused. So it was Stephen's platoon again on point when they stumbled into an NVA bunker complex in the valley east of Purple Heart Hill. The point man turned the corner of a jungle trail and walked right into several North Vietnamese. He opened fire, putting them to flight. The platoon quickly secured the abandoned complex—and there was shooting off and on, for the rest of the day. Some NVA strolled in at sling arms, and ran away astonished with M-16 rounds zipping past them. Three bunkers were full of dud U.S. bombs of all sizes, and in another Stephen found a crude map with the bunker complex detailed and arrows pointing to D Company's hill. He quickly radioed Lt. Mike Daltan, leading the platoon behind him, and had no sooner gotten off the horn when several NVA walked into Daltan's people.

Back at the company command post, Sp4 Daugherty got a report from Stephen's platoon, of six blood trails, two heavy and probably fatal. Edwards, all excited, told Daugherty to take point and the two of them moved alone into the brush as automatic-rifle fire popped at the base of the ridge. Daugherty walked slowly and quietly through the jungle, thinking, "This is crazy! The gooks're scattering, our guys are firing up anything that moves, and we're just strolling down into this." He came to a small clearing in the jungle, levelled by artillery, and stopped short —he wasn't about to walk across an open area during a firefight. Captain Edwards came up from behind and walked right into the clearing. Daugherty was about to call him back to cover when Edwards spun around and jumped back. He tried to hide his massive body behind a slender tree.

The captain said he'd seen a man dash through the trees on the other side of the clearing, but they held their fire, unsure whether the figure was American or Vietnamese. Daugherty thought Edwards suddenly looked very hesitant. He told Daugherty to radio the trail platoon and have the last man in their file make a noise. They didn't hear anything, confirming that the CO had spotted an NVA. But the platoon RTO said all the North Vietnamese had bugged out. Edwards, nonetheless, seemed unwilling to keep moving, Daugherty was getting disgusted with the whole thing, and he finally snapped, "If it was a gook, he's gone now."

He started back down the hill and the captain trailed behind.

By the time they hooked up with Stephen's platoon the grunts were cleaning out the bunkers. There were almost forty of them, sundecks on top of some, an underground cooking shack, and makeshift showers at a nearby stream. Daugherty was impressed with the NVA bunkers; from ground level, they were hidden amid the brush and almost impossible to see even when you knew where they were. Men began destroying the bunkers and captured gear while others followed the blood trails. A couple led to the stream and a few grunts waded in, but could find nothing. Nonetheless, Daugherty thought that the guys looked happy, content that, after weeks of humping and sweating, they had made a solid contact, come through unscathed, and had done a little good. The grunts just seemed disappointed that they had no tangible evidence of their success in the form of a North Vietnamese body to count, kick, and take pictures of.

It had been a long war for Major White, the battalion executive officer. When he'd been commissioned in '62, after ten years as a sergeant, the advisors were being sent to Vietnam in growing numbers and the career men would joke that they all would be going to Vietnam soon. White believed in the war and the Domino Theory, but to him the tragic mistake was made when the president landed the troops and Americanized the war; the Asian mind, he thought, would always beat the impatient American.

He'd gone over in '65 as an advisor to a Vietnamese Special Forces battalion in Project Delta and lasted three months before he was seriously wounded. He'd come back again as an advisor by Christmas of '67. The ARVN battalion he'd been assigned had held a party in his honor when he'd arrived. In a large tent, an ARVN officer had proposed a toast to White and the United States for coming to help the Vietnamese people in their struggle for freedom against communism; he'd said that America would never let them down. When he'd finished they had called for White to give a speech, the expectation seeming to be that he would reciprocate the assurances. But, he had only felt comfortable saying what he'd felt to be true, that the Americans had come with the best of intentions and that he hoped they would stick it out—but that the U.S. government was very responsive to public opinion which, in turn, was being shaped by adverse media coverage. He had told the ARVN officers that the patience of the American people would probably run thin and the government would be forced to forsake South Vietnam.

By the time he arrived for his third tour in '71, Nixon was finally doing what White thought should have been done all along—turning off the Americanization of the war and building up the ARVN through what was now labelled Vietnamization. But, as he perceived it, the spirit was not that of success but of bucking up Saigon long enough for the U.S. to retreat with some face. It was such an incredibly different war they were fighting this time. Now the mission was to minimize casualties rather than destroy the enemy. There were some exceptions to the rule—Operation Lam Son 719 being the most dramatic example—but the battalion was mostly restricted to defensive action and local patrolling. It chafed professional soldiers to speak of anything less than aggressiveness and total victory, especially in a unit with the proud reputation of the Screaming Eagles, but battalion headquarters often got subtle messages from brigade about not taking any chances.

They were hanging it up, White mused, cutting loose and leaving Vietnam to the Communists. No one seemed to have any illusions that the ARVN had reached the point of being able to go it alone. And with that sense of defeatism, the battalion was a changed entity. White attended a battalion commanders' conference during which the brigade commander gave them a little speech about having to instill in the individual trooper an understanding of the purpose of the conflict so as to raise morale. White interjected that that would be hard to accomplish because, the way they were disposed now, the purpose wasn't even clear to him anymore. The colonels gave him irritated stares; they were good men, he thought, but he had hit a raw nerve within all of them. No one wanted to admit that there was no purpose in what they were doing. They were preparing to leave, and the Communists were going to conquer in their wake.

Despite the doubts, Major White was a professional soldier. To give less than his all, even to a losing cause, would have been a disgrace to the uniform he proudly wore and a disservice to the commanders and men of the battalion. So the war continued for him. This time around, he spent much of his efforts with two new headaches brought on by the winding down of the war: the increased number of malingerers and malcontents ghosting in the rear, and the drug problem. Heroin was epidemic in the battalion, as easy to buy as cigarettes. White was always suspicious of Salem smokers because the mentholated cigarettes were the easiest to load. He saw only one man with track marks; smoking and snorting were the norm, for heroin was easy to hide in vials and, unlike marijuana, it was odorless when smoked. The joke among the draftees was that you could take a toke with one hand and salute a lifer with the other. It was a quagmire in which he and a couple of old hardnosed sergeants did their best to catch GIs for possession and have them court-martialled. Many of those apprehended turned informant on other users and pushers in order to get easier sentences. White suspected collusion between the dopers and some of the young GIs in the criminal investigation division office; too often, records of a man's crime were lost before the trial. The major and the sergeants heard through the grapevine that there were frag threats against them. No one ever actually tried.

The drug problems in the rear spilled over into the problem of shirkers in the field. For every one-hundred-thirty-man rifle company, about ten of the men would be playing an angle to stay at the 3/187 Rear at Camp Evans. It was a constant struggle for White to round up the dope addicts, black militants, demoralized kids, and slackers and helicopter them back out to the field. The shirkers quickly found they had a confederate in the battalion surgeon. He was a young draftee, antimilitary and antiwar, who saw his job not as that of keeping up the field strength but of getting kids out of combat. White suspected that some of the slackers may have threatened him for his cooperation. A favorite trick was to complain about ear problems, whereupon the doctor captain would send the soldier on an air-conditioned vacation as an outpatient at the Phu Bai hospital for audiometer tests. He would then write the soldier a light-duty slip and try to have his commander keep him permanently out of the field. Major White asked the division surgeon to have a talk with the doctor about discriminating more between real patients and loafers, but it did not help.

The company commanders did not appreciate White's efforts; they would rather have a smaller unit they could depend on, than one beefed up with heads and nonhackers, and as soon as the shirkers started complaining, the captains usually allowed them to depart on the next resupply helicopter to pursue whatever excuse they had dreamed up this time. A small percentage of the men in the 3/187 simply did not do their jobs, but most of the problems did not extend to the grunts hunting and being hunted around the Rockpile. Considering the constant problems in the rear, White thought it no small testament that those young grunts actually in the bush, although demoralized, were loyal to each other and to good leadership, and did as much as anyone could expect of infantrymen.

Sp4 Jack Kucera was a twenty-one-year-old in Weapons Platoon of Bravo Company 3/187 Infantry. He was from Milwaukee, Wisconsin, and had grown up with little concern about the war until his third year in college. He'd been majoring in biology, not sure what he'd wanted to do with his life. When he'd sat down to think about it, he'd concluded he was only in school to dodge the draft. That had seemed an ignoble reason, so he had dropped out, allowing himself to be drafted, and had been proud when assigned to the 101st Airborne—his father had served with them in WWII. It was Kucera's service with the Screaming Eagles that shaped his new opinion on the war. During the first week of the operation, his eleven-man platoon was not resupplied. They threw their C rations into a community pile, each man getting two spoonfuls. Then they went four more days without food, until they got dizzy just standing up with their packs on. But they had all hung together during that miniature ordeal, and that kind of comradeship made Kucera think they must be doing some good in Vietnam. And if it weren't for the "candy-ass" protestors back home tying the hands of the government, he reckoned, the war would have been won long ago.

Bravo Company CA'd into the Rockpile area atop a hill west of Firebase Scotch. Scotch was just north of Purple Heart Hill, along the same ridgeline, and the Echo Recon platoon held the foxholes ringing it. The valley between Bravo and Echo was literally crawling with North Vietnamese; the grunts could sit in their foxholes and watch NVA on the move through the jungle. Each time, they pumped 81mm mortar fire at them and called in airstrikes—once cheering the breathtaking sight of an Arc Light bombing on an adjacent valley. At night the NVA in the valley mortared Echo Recon and sent probes against the Bravo hill. The North Vietnamese never fired, but just crept up to observe, and the GIs responded to every noise in the black jungle with a dozen grenades. Once Kucera was trying to get to sleep when he heard movement ten yards outside the perimeter; he grabbed a frag, the pin stuck, and the noise crept away down the hill. Every morning, a helicopter would drop off an emergency resupply of grenades.

On their fourth night in the Rockpile, 21 February, the NVA hit just before dawn. Scotch was blanketed with fog, Kucera watched across the valley on perimeter guard, when suddenly all hell broke loose. Green and red tracers intermingled in the mist as NVA sappers overran the hill, and Echo Recon fought to retake the position. When it was over, there were seven dead North Vietnamese amongst the Echo foxholes and several blood trails leading away in the elephant grass. The medevacs came in at first light and, true to the bravado spirit of reconnaissance units, the three men who'd been wounded hobbled unaided to the helicopter. While the Bravo mortar team stayed in position, the rifle platoons airmobiled to Scotch to sweep the perimeter for bodies and survivors. A diary found on one of the dead enemy soldiers indicated his sapper team planned to hit the Bravo hill next.

The rifle platoons, plus a Screaming Eagle sniper team, helicoptered back to the hill and every man was awake on the perimeter line that night. The snipers, using Starlite scopes, opened fire with single shots at around midnight. The North Vietnamese fell back. In the morning, the Americans swept the slopes and found blood trails. It was funny, Kucera thought, that the press always talked about inflated body counts, but in a situation like this, where NVA had obviously been killed but no bodies were recovered, 101st Airborne Division policy dictated they could claim no kills.

Soon afterwards, helicopter scouts over the valley reported a massive bunker complex and Bravo Company mounted up to go on patrol. Their two Kit Carson Scouts refused to go. Kucera decided that they were basically tough troopers but were spooked at the sight of all those NVA down in the valley; they knew full well what their former compatriots would do to them if captured. When a helicopter landed to drop off food and ammunition and pick up their extra gear, the two Vietnamese tried to jump aboard. The grunts managed to drag them off, but then they simply sat down and refused to move. The GIs then took their M-16s away and said they would leave them behind, so the Kit Carsons finally relented.

They spent three days patrolling the valley before being lifted to Khe Sanh for a rest. On the first day, they found flashlights and bloody bandages, remnants of a few nights before when Bravo had seen lights in the valley and had called in arty. Coming up another small hill, they surprised a few NVA and opened fire, but the NVA escaped into the jungle. On the second day, they happened upon an NVA high-speed trail, a fabulous construction with logs built like steps down the mountainside. They NDP'd right on it, setting up M-60s at either end. Kucera used his E-tool to scrape away a flat spot on the side of the slope so he could sleep without rolling down. Before being airlifted out, they did find the complex. They hauled many NVA packs and 122mm rockets out of the thirty abandoned bunkers. Battalion wanted the 122s extracted so the grunts had to hack an LZ in the jungle and hump the rockets to it; Kucera watched, glad he wasn't one of those fingered to be a pack mule, as the grunts cursed and humped towards the LZ with hundred-pound rucksacks on their backs, and communist rockets in their hands.

In early March, additional units were dispatched to augment the 4/3 and 3/187 scouring the hills around the Rockpile. The 2d Battalion, 1st Infantry, 196th Infantry Brigade, Americal Division operated primarily down south out of Hawk Hill on Route 1, but had been on the eastern DMZ since soon after the operation had commenced. It had been mostly quiet along the North Vietnamese front and, when ARVN units moved in to take their place, the battalion was opconned to the 11th LIB HQ at Dong Ha. The battalion commander was on R&R at the time so the exec, Maj. Hugh Peppers, set up his command post in a small hootch on the base.

The 2/1 was just getting organized for the move into the mountains when Major Peppers called the commander of C Company, Capt. Gerald Downey, into the CP hootch. He described the objectives, then said one company was to be immediately detached to 4/3 for what would probably be the most dangerous segment of the battalion's mission. Captain Downey's company had not performed as well as expected on the DMZ, and he wanted to redeem himself. He also thought that the exec was an outstanding officer who had probably set this whole scenario up to give him the chance; as soon as Downey volunteered his company, Peppers accepted. The grunts in Charlie Company were less than enthused and responded with sullen stares at Downey when he passed the word.

They were helicoptered to Vandegrift, landing precariously among the many choppers crowded on the small landing zone. They were quickly ushered off the LZ into a small depressed patch of raw earth. They were to be CA'd out that day. Downey watched his grunts flake out in the field with the foot soldiers' eternal problem of bored waiting. It was a clear blue day and the sun was savage above them, the heat sticking like paint to their bodies. It was all dust and noise around them, helos coming and going, truck convoys refueling nearby, giant M48 tanks clanking about the perimeter. The grunts sat, fatigued and bored, shed of helmets, idly smoking and talking.

Sometimes Captain Downey could only stare helplessly at the infantrymen of his company. His background certainly hadn't prepared him for the demoralized attitudes and absurdities unique to Vietnam that faced him as a combat commander. He was himself a patriotic small-town kid from California, who'd enlisted a year out of high school in '65, going from private to lieutenant in OCS, and commanding a platoon in the 101st his first tour. Now he commanded a factionalized, dispirited company of draftees and lifers, whites and blacks, heads and juicers, each clan usually grumbling against the other. He knew that, in the rear, a sizeable portion of his men turned on and a few were soldiering while supporting heroin habits. He saw no fraggings, drug use, or open disobedience in the field; the men did their jobs, but most of it was just going through the motions.

Downey could think of few times in American history when it might have been harder to be a company commander. He saw the young captains caught in the middle of the announcement of phased withdrawals, pressed from above by the lieutenant colonels and majors, who saw their career-enhancing war fading away and who were anxious to squeeze whatever combat they could out of it before they all went home, and from below by the troops, who were convinced the war was a farce that was soon to be ended, and that any more deaths were useless and wasted. Captain Downey soon discovered his young lieutenants sided with the disaffected grunts. His three rifle-platoon leaders were all competent and shared a common sense of identity, he thought. "They hated the war, misunderstood their role in it, disliked the Army and career officers, and had important plans for their futures as soon as they were shed of their uniforms. In each case they had been draftees before being commissioned."

In the field, his lieutenants often employed evasive tactics designed to look as if they were carrying out the mission while actually cutting down on the platoon's chances of bumping into the enemy.

All of which left captains like Downey, still trying to fight a war, constantly compromising between gung-ho battalion commanders and fed-up, reluctant draftee grunts. It was an extremely unpopular position. "In truth," he said, "I failed at least as often as I succeeded. On the good days everything went fine, you accomplished the mission, killed the enemy, and lost no men. On the worst of days the battalion CO screamed at you all the time, the troops were sullen and angry, the enemy kicked your behind or deftly managed to avoid your best laid ambushes, and your lieutenants were unresponsive to your orders without being insubordinate."

Downey did not feel loved by his men; he felt tolerated and reluctantly obeyed.

The doubts and hypocrisy of the situation were not only wearing down the troops, but had muddied Downey's thoughts also. He had graduated from OCS with the intention of being a professional soldier, but since then had soured on that career choice. He felt his patriotism drain at the reception his uniform received back home, was angered at the way politicians seemed willing to let American youth die for votes, was frustrated with the no-win attrition tactics of two successive presidents. And, even at the ground level in Vietnam, he'd seen enough politicking to turn him off.

For example, last Christmas Eve his company had set up in a fog-covered field in Antenna Valley, when the battalion operations officer had radioed that the Christmas Truce was in effect. This dictated that his company was to hold its position and avoid contact with the enemy. The Communists, knowing the rules the Americans imposed on themselves, had taken advantage of it. A platoon of NVA, moving to a better position, had filed right past one of Downey's platoons, the last North Vietnamese in line turning to wave mockingly at the grunts. An hour later, a perimeter claymore had exploded and Downey, unwilling to send his men into a foggy night with NVA spotted in the area just to make a possible body count, had decided to wait until morning to check it out. But the operations officer had radioed from the rear, "Check it out. We may need proof that it was a defensive action in case we get charged with violating the truce." Downey's protests had been met by the battalion commander coming on the air to reinforce the order, and a squad finally moved out into the fog, trudging past Downey with hot stares. They bumped into a party of NVA, carrying away one of the North Vietnamese. As the sergeant threw a grenade it short-fused, nearly blowing his hand off at the wrist. The medic, who raced through the no-man's-land to treat the casualty, radioed that the sergeant would lose his hand if a medevac didn't get in immediately. But the local medevac commander had grounded his birds because of the fog, and could not be reached via radio because the pilots were all at their Christmas party. It'd taken a U.S. Marine helicopter crew, defying the weather, foggy mountains, and orders not to fly, to come in and pick up the wounded soldier.

Downey had been disillusioned by such games in combat, by an army which fraudulently awarded medals to officers, by having to push kids through a war he thought they were losing. He found it harder and harder to maintain a disciplined command, when in the back of his mind he'd lost the faith. "What my men did," he said, "was halfheartedly run their missions and fail to search diligently for the enemy. My feelings about the war and its inevitable end were changing by then and I must admit that I tolerated a great deal of mediocrity in the name of caution."

Charlie Company had not been waiting long at Vandegrift when other elements of 2/1 began choppering in, and Downey watched amazed that so many helos could maneuver in such a small LZ. The op officer and two other company commanders joined him on the berm beside the LZ. Before long, a reporter and his Vietnamese cameraman appeared, asking permission to talk with the troops, and Downey pointed to the waiting infantrymen. The reporter came back a bit later and collared the operations officer while his cameraman filmed the interview.

"Major, is there any truth in the rumor that American troops are going to be introduced to the ground combat in Laos?"

"I don't know anything about that."

"Well, what are you going to do with all these troops and helicopters?"

The major shrugged, "I really can't say."

"Is it true that you are going to the rescue of the South Vietnamese who are being slaughtered by the NVA?"

Exasperated, the major locked eyes with the reporter and said, "I don't know." The man irritably motioned his cameraman to stop filming and stomped off. As soon as he was out of earshot, the officers broke into laughter, one of the captains joking, "I can see it in tomorrow's headlines—Major in command knows nothing!"

An officer from 4/3 walked over, asking for Downey, and said, "Your lift birds should be coming in about an hour. Tune into the air channel and monitor it. I'll be back with some maps in a few minutes."

They were still standing on the berm when the terrible sound of metal ripping metal screeched above the landing zone. A Cobra and a Huey had collided in midair over Vandegrift. Downey snapped up to see a torn rotor blade slowly whirling towards them and everyone ducked to the ground, except the major, who had his back to the scene. Another officer grabbed his collar and jerked him down as the broken blade flew directly over their heads, over the huddled soldiers on the low ground, over a fuel truck driving up from the fuel depot, and crashed loudly against the turret of an M48 tank.

Officers were counting heads. No one on the ground had been hurt.

Downey kept waiting, but no choppers called on the radio. It was getting dark. He had no idea where he was going, and he was worried that nightfall would cancel the CA before he had his whole company on the ground. He had just decided that, if the birds were not there in five minutes, he would not allow the lift to start, when a sergeant from 4/3 ran up, panting, and handed him a fistful of maps. "Here's your maps. Your LZ is marked on the first map. The colonel says to tell you he's sorry he couldn't get this thing in better order, but you'd better get going right away."

"Fine, but where are my birds?"

The sergeant pointed to a staggered trail of ten slicks making the approach to the LZ. "Those are yours. They've been trying to talk to you for five minutes!"

"I haven't heard anything on the air channel."

The sergeant squinted, confused, then blurted, "Air channel? Hell, those ships are on the arty channel! The air channel's been compromised."

Down in the shallow area, Downey could see his forward observer standing beside the tank, frantically waving the men toward the landing helicopters. Downey told his RTO to turn to the arty channel and started towards his men, just in time to hear a pilot shout over the radio, "Why the hell have you people been on the wrong channel!" In five minutes, Charlie Company was in the air and Downey sat on the metal floor of one of the birds, trying to orient his maps, the radio tucked against his shoulder, Lieutenant Colonel Coast counselling him, "Move off your LZ about five hundred meters and go into a night perimeter. I'll call you tonight and give you tomorrow's objectives and mission. I'll do my best to get out and visit you in the next day or two."

The LZ was a level spot in the Rockpile foothills; it was a cold landing, but they lost another bird when the pilot, having hovered nervously at eight feet over the top of the elephant grass as the infantrymen leaped out, veered away too sharply and smacked blades into a tree. The rattled crew was evacuated and the grunts stripped off the two M-60s for their use. The company began hacking through the thick brush towards their hill and a FAC plane circled overhead, getting on the radio with Downey. He said he had a couple of very bored jet pilots running low on fuel, and asked if they could expend their ordnance on the ridgeline. Downey said to have at it, and the GIs paused to watch the jets shriek in, pumping rockets at nothing. There were a couple of small secondary explosions but Downey was not impressed, figuring it was probably just grenades or C4 abandoned or lost by other units passing through the area.

By seven that night, they were digging in along the slope of the ridgeline. The next few days, they made several patrols but, much to Downey's surprise, no enemy were found; it was not the dangerous mission he had envisioned. The biggest noise was a spectacular airstrike to destroy the crashed slick. On the fourth day, Lieutenant Colonel Coast helicoptered in with the water resupply and told the company to move closer to Route 9 the next day. They were to continue their daily patrolling in the high ground, and be prepared to move to the highway as a reaction force if needed. From the other slope of the mountain, they had a better view of the road and surrounding terrain. It was mountainous, highly vegetated, easily capable, Downey noted, of hiding entire NVA divisions. Signs of the fighting were all around; burnt-out trucks on Route 9, blown-up enemy bunkers, chunks of equipment and bodies. They found a jungle boot with a rotting foot in it, and a splatter of brain plastered to a bunker support.

But that's all they found.

Perhaps the tough fighting with 4/3 and 3/187 had forced the NVA in the area to retire; perhaps they were simply hiding in the jungle and biding their time; and maybe it was a little of both.

After about three weeks in the hospital, the doctor caught Lieutenant Dewing playing football in the surf and rightly decided he'd recuperated enough to rejoin his unit. At that time, he'd been going through physical therapy at the 6th Convalescent Center at Cam Ranh Bay and he only needed his lieutenant's bars and an ID card to start catching rides up north. At Chu Lai, he hitchhiked a flight out to the 4/3 Rear at LZ Bronco and spent the day swapping lies and war stories with a young GI who'd been a super troop in his platoon but was now in the rear as company clerk because he knew how to type. It was there that Dewing learned that he and Keg had been given impact awards of the Silver Star for John Wayneing the NVA bunker.

At Bronco he got a new rucksack, picked up a half-dozen machetes for the platoon, and caught a USAF flight to Da Nang. He hitched a ride on the back of an ARVN's moped to the nearby U.S. Marine compound and spent the night drinking beer with an old friend who was an engineer lieutenant there. He spent half the next day sweating in the Da Nang airport until he heard that a C130 was leaving for Khe Sanh with a load of 81mm mortar ammunition. The plane having set down on the Khe Sanh airstrip, the air force crew hurriedly shoved the pallets of ammo out and the loadmaster shouted, "Get the hell outta here!" Dewing jumped from the still moving aircraft. On the side of the strip, he accidentally ran into the battalion exec, who had a small CP set up adjacent to the airfield. They had hardly exchanged greetings when NVA shelling began and they hustled for a bunker.

Dewing managed to catch a resupply bird to his platoon that afternoon and found them in the flatlands below the Rockpile. A new staff sergeant was there. The grunts told Dewing of their latest travails: they had been in the mountains, fog had kept away resupply for six days, and they had had to rummage down old trails looking for C rat cans they'd discarded to lighten the load on previous humps. Shortly after getting back, Lieutenant Colonel Coast called him up to the battalion field CP to welcome him back. They sat on the perimeter berm and shot the bull. Coast was a very personable commander and Dewing felt proud when the colonel confirmed that he was to be decorated, saying, "There's a lot of colonels that are flying around at six thousand feet that are getting Silver Stars but, lieutenant, you can be proud of yours. You've earned it."

The infantry operations around the Rockpile had, by early March, severely tempered NVA activity in the area. Yet nothing ever went easily in the debacle-prone Americal Division. Once Dewing was listening to a radio at the 4/3 CP hill, when another unit on an adjacent ridge took fire. He listened to the platoon leader call for artillery and get none; then he saw a Cobra gunship bravely come screaming down from a high altitude, roaring fire, and inadvertently strafe the American position because the smoke grenades they'd pitched at the enemy had blown back over them. Dewing saw the little puffs erupt on the hill at the same time the man on the radio screamed and the line went dead; a moment later, a new man came on the radio saying his lieutenant was hit. In the same period, a 101st Airborne night patrol wandered into the Americal AO and hit a mechanical ambush. The Americal troopers automatically directed fire towards them, and the ambushed Screaming Eagles, thinking they were being hit by NVA in the dark, returned the fire. Both platoon leaders called for artillery support and it took an artillery officer in the Fire Direction Center to realize that the calls for supporting arms were within a few hundred yards of each other. He radioed for both elements to stop firing and the mistaken ambush abruptly ended.

Lieutenant Dewing sat in the elephant grass at daylight, watching the medevacs go in and out.

CHAPTER TEN: Patrol Action in the Hills

To effect some type of blocking operation against the NVA withdrawing from the Rockpile area, General Hill directed Lieutenant Colonel Meyer to step up the patrolling of his 1/77 Armor at the base of the hills. The 1/77 AO encompassed the Rockpile and the stretch of Route 9 from there to Vandegrift; the tank and infantry patrols of the battalion task force made sporadic contact as the Americal and 101st mopped up. Most of the men in the armor battalion had never been in combat before, not counting mines and rockets, but they generally performed well.

The battalion had a set pattern in their AO. To cover the highway, teams of tanks and APCs were posted at intervals, camped on the side of the road. If a supply convoy were ambushed, the nearest team moved towards the firefight. Such tactics resulted in several skirmishes and the destruction of two or three RPG teams. In addition, day and night foot patrols were conducted to keep the main body of NVA at least out of 82mm mortar range of the highway. Each unit commander additionally was taxed to establish twenty-four-hour observation posts on the high ground, using starlite scopes, field radars, and other electronic devices to monitor NVA movement in the hills and to call in fire support accordingly. Fighting was only sporadic for the 1/77, but its area was infiltrated with NVA who maintained constant surveillance of all the units in the area. If a platoon consistently slacked off, didn't wear flak jackets, or man the fifties, they invited attack.

Ironically, the single most insecure place in the 1/77 AO was its basecamp at Vandegrift. Set in a lush valley surrounded by low ridges, it was subjected to almost daily 122mm rocket raids, but the more telling danger came from the North Vietnamese sapper teams that lurked in the area. At least twice they penetrated the perimeter to blow up equipment and raise general hell, and there were numerous other shooting incidents. The perimeter consisted of only some culvert-and-sandbag bunkers and a single roll of concertina wire; what was worse was that the soldiers manning it were generally unenthusiastic rear-echelon support troops from various XXIV Corps and USARV units. One of the sapper raids occurred before dawn on 1 March; the battalion command sergeant major, Roy Nelson, was in the CP bunker when a gigantic roar lit the sky and shots cracked from the perimeter. No one was willing to move for fear nervous sentries might shoot them. In the morning, Sergeant Major Nelson joined Lieutenant Colonel Meyer to inspect the damage and determine where the NVA had infiltrated. Dug-in fuel bladders containing forty-five thousand gallons of JP4 and ten thousand gallons of diesel had been blown up; burnt enemy equipment indicated that one of the NVA had gone up in his own explosion. Meyer and Nelson talked to the perimeter guards; they were young draftees, lackadaisical, not particularly interested in what was going on. Although they weren't flagrant about it, it was obvious to Nelson that they were pot heads. One of the men said he had seen two NVA creep through the wire and dart past his bunker. Nelson asked why he hadn't done anything and could only shake his head when the GI said he hadn't wanted to give his position away. The sergeant major was taken aback; the soldier hadn't even taken the time to alert anyone. He might have been too stoned.

Such problems with inexperience, and lack of motivation and discipline, also intruded, upon occasion, on the field performance of the battalion. Sp4 Spurgeon accompanied one five-man patrol on a ridgeline overlooking Vandegrift. It was a miserable day. The grunts wearily trudged through the mist and cold, using cigarettes to burn away the leeches that dropped on them from the wet leaves. The sergeant leading the patrol was a shake'n'bake who must not have wanted trouble with the men because, when they stopped for the night, he posted no guards and simply sat down to start a big fire and talk the night away. Eventually Meyer overflew the patrol in his C&C, saw the fire, and ordered the whole patrol extracted that night.

Lieutenant Colonel Meyer was a staunch disciplinarian who came down hard on the problems he saw. Once, he and Sergeant Major Nelson drove up to inspect a lone tank outpost outside Vandegrift, and found no one out on the ground to watch for the marauding RPG teams. Meyer shouted for the tank commander, held a Field Grade Article 15 and busted the man from staff sergeant to sergeant. On another field inspection, Meyer was riding a tank to one of his line companies and monitoring the radio. First he heard the GI at a company outpost radio the captain to warn him that the battalion commander was coming, then the captain radio all of his tank crews to get into their helmets and flak jackets. Meyer's standing order was always to wear the body armor in case of ambush or booby-traps, but as it was a hot day, the young captain was letting his grunts flake out. Meyer didn't need a subordinate who, by feeling sorry for the men, would get them killed; as soon as he reached the CP tank, he told the captain, a West Pointer, that he was relieved of command.

On the whole, though, the 1/77 Armor performed the job at hand. A hard line commander, not well liked by his men, Meyer was, nonetheless, a good leader. He often accompanied his troops on their armor and foot patrols, enduring the dangers and field conditions of his grunts. Sergeant Major Nelson, who had been wounded four times on a previous tour with long-range reconnaissance patrols of the 9th Division, thought Meyer a fine officer and that the men, lifers and draftees alike, performed professionally in the field. The drug and race problems which had exploded at Quang Tri were shoved beneath the surface; they were not completely gone, Meyer knew, but, given a viable mission for the first time, the young draftees were doing their jobs. And, Nelson noted, for all their bitching, most of the grunts did not balk at their new hardships. After weeks of finagling with XXIV Corps, Nelson managed to get a shower and laundry sent up to Vandegrift, only to discover that he had to order the grunts to use it. They had a reputation to uphold and they prided themselves in their raunchy, dusty appearance as a sign that they were not REMFs or FNGs.

Sometimes reporters would come to Vandegrift and Meyer would explain what 1/77 Armor was doing. Most did not seem interested, Meyer remembered. "I had reporters seek out other units than mine because my troops were just doing their duty without any of the race and dope problems that made stateside headlines. They went looking for problems elsewhere."

Working simultaneously to hunt for the NVA in the hills around Khe Sanh, Vandegrift, and the Rockpile, was P Company, 75th Infantry (Rangers), 5th Division. A small, elite unit, Papa Ranger worked in six-man teams and conducted seven-day operations. They had to carry enough food, water, and ammunition to last the week because, once inserted into the jungle, their only contact with other Americans was by radio. Their mission was to patrol for the NVA rocket teams and to lay ambush on NVA trails. Their success depended on stealth; therefore, they received no resupply in the bush because a hovering helicopter would pinpoint their location to the enemy. And because they did not have the security of a thirty-man platoon, the six-man teams had to be resourceful and daring if they were to win. Every man was a volunteer and if someone wanted to transfer out, he could do so anytime.

One of the men who embodied the spirit of professionalism in Papa Ranger was Sp4 Harry E. Walters, Jr., an eighteen-year-old from Lebanon, Pennsylvania. His father had made a career in the army because of hard financial times and as soon as the young Walters had turned seventeen he too wanted to sign up. He'd dropped out of high school and gone in three days after his birthday, his father having agreed to sign the enlistment papers only if he took the teletype-repairman option so he would have a trade when discharged. Walters had said sure, had volunteered for the infantry within a week, and then had reenlisted to get to Vietnam. His father had been slotted for a second tour there, but his son's volunteering had automatically disqualified his father for another year in the war. When he'd hit the 5th Mech in December, 1970, he had immediately volunteered for the brigade ranger company. As for the war, Walters had been soured by the cities where it seemed most of the Vietnamese were just out to rip off the GI; but in the bush, where he could see little village children with hardly any clothes and ribs sticking out from hunger, it had made him feel America must be in Vietnam to help. Walters was young, athletic, motivated, and exactly what the rangers wanted.

Walters was in a team which had been dropped into the Khe Sanh mountains on the first day of the operation to guard the advance force. They had seen no NVA, but now, with the increase of activity around the Rockpile, they were going back. Walters and his five partners boarded a Huey; a Cobra and a Kiowa Scout flew escort and, as they lifted from the Quang Tri strip, other rangers threw the thumbs-up sign. The first night, they heard an NVA mortar being fired and, taking a guess at the location, the team leader called in artillery. In the morning, they came upon some fresh tracks on a thin jungle path and the leader decided to follow them. They filed silently down the NVA trail, especially alert, for the enemy couldn't be far ahead. Walters ruck was kicking his butt as they labored up the ridgeline, and he slipped, the barrel of his rifle jamming into the mud. They stopped for a quick breather atop the crest and he tried to scrape the muck away with a stick; the point man joked that if they did catch the dinks, ". . . just say, here's mud in your eye." They kept moving through the thick brush on the spine of the ridge.

A burst of AK-47 fire suddenly startled Walters back into reality.

The three rangers ahead of him disappeared from sight in the bushes, and he immediately hit the prone, levelled his M-16, and fired at the chattering sound of the AK. He didn't know exactly what was going on and it amazed him that his mind was really a million miles away as his trained reflexes had him calmly firing and changing magazines. He wasn't thinking about what he was doing, the situation not yet registering in his mind, the sound of his own rifle strangely seeming far away.

It was Walters's first firefight.

The first sound that clicked in his mind was that of the team leader scrambling back from the point, yelling to throw grenades and fall back. They ran back thirty yards before realizing there were only four of them there—the point man and RTO were missing. Two of the rangers fired blindly through the foliage at the NVA, while Walters and the team leader waded back through the heavy vegetation to find their people. They began calling their names but no one answered. Walters spotted the RTO's ruck and radio sticking from the bush on the side of the hill, and shouted to the team leader that no one answered him. "I think he's dead!" He scrambled down the hill and grabbed the pack, but no one was in it. The team leader followed him down and crouched in the bush calling for air support on the radio. They kept shouting names and, finally, a nervous reply came. It was from the point man. Walters ran towards the sound and found the man lying in the grass, splattered with blood. A graze wound over his eyebrow poured blood, and a dozen AK rounds had stitched across his waist—all of them, miraculously, hitting an ammunition bandolier and doing no more than scaring hell out of the soldier. Walters began helping the point man up the hill, when he heard the RTO yelling from the top. Walters was wildly relieved (he had gone through basic training with the man) and answered with, "Get your ass down here and help me!" It turned out the RTO and the point man had not answered because they had heard each other in the brush and each had thought the other was an NVA.

They were struggling up with the wounded man, when more AK fire splattered nearby. The assistant team leader ran through the brush towards the NVA, and fired a LAW right into them. It must have been an NVA mortar team they'd bumped into, because the rocket explosion set off a chain reaction that made them think the whole top of the hill was going up in smoke. Helicopters were overhead and a pilot directed the team to a bomb crater a couple of hundred yards down the trail. While a Cobra shot in low to lay down cover fire, a slick lowered a jungle penetrator and they hung tight as the bird lifted them up and out. An airstrike followed their departure.

Other rangers met the helicopter when it dropped them off at Quang Tri—they always monitored the radio reports of their comrades—and they made sure to visit the wounded man in the hospital. Said Walters, "We never abandoned anyone in the field. Dead or alive, if six went out, six came back. Always. The leadership in P Company was superb, the morale, camaraderie, courage, and dedication of our people were unequalled. As far as drug abuse, fraggings, racial friction, and combat refusals, they were nonexistent in Papa Company. As far as I'm concerned, my association with the men of P Company Rangers was one of the best experiences of my life."

Two men from Papa Rangers were killed on a mission near the Rockpile. They were in a different team from Walters, but they were friends and he didn't want to talk about it. Sp4 Spurgeon, however, was there. He'd been tagging along with a 3/5 Cav platoon when, one night, a helicopter came in, lights off. It deposited five rangers, in camouflage paint and bush hats, and Spurgeon was surprised to see that a buddy of his, a short guy with glasses and the nickname Recon Smitty, was one of them. Smitty had wanted to join the armor snipers, but Spurgeon had talked him out of it because he was still new; so Smitty had turned around and volunteered for the rangers. He was very excited about his new unit and told Spurgeon it was his first mission.

The next morning, the rangers moved out into the jungle and, almost immediately, there was a burst of automatic weapons fire and shouts on the radio. By the time the cav platoon got there, the shooting was over. Only two rangers were still on their feet. They said they'd walked right into an NVA unit; the lead North Vietnamese had dived for cover as they had, but the second NVA had stepped forward with an RPD machine gun and shot down the three men at the end of the patrol before they could get down. Two Americans were KIA, one WIA, and the enemy had vanished.

Spurgeon helped carry out one of the dead men. It was Recon Smitty.

Back at the 1/77 bunkers at Vandegrift, Spurgeon regaled the snipers with an exciting version of what happened. When he got to the part about Smitty getting shot in the face, one of the men, a Mexican-American named Felix, suddenly snarled to cut the bullshit. Spurgeon took offense. He shot back, "You know and always have known how I've operated and how I talk, Felix! I'm not glad Recon's dead. Just because I'm not crying now, doesn't mean I wasn't crying up in those hills when you or anyone else wasn't there to see me! He was closer to me than anyone else because I met him first; he was my security first. I talked him out of the snipers for the very same reason we're talking about him now. I carried his goddamned body and loaded him onto the bird, for God's sake!"

Felix looked down and muttered that there was more to it. He was just so goddamned sick of Spurgeon's fanatic zeal.

"Felix, you and I and everyone else who's a sniper ought to be prepared for things like this. We're volunteers, goddammit, we're fucking killers. That's our fucking job! Recon volunteered for the Rangers, he's dead, tomorrow one of us will be dead. We volunteered! If you can't take it, Felix, transfer to the mess section or be a truck driver. For God's sake, go back to being a supply clerk. Wilds went back to driving a tank with his old outfit, Bravo Company. We're still friends. No one's going to laugh at you. We're sure as hell not laughing at Wilds."

Felix was crying, but he stared at Spurgeon with hate.

He grabbed Spurgeon's collar, twisted it in his hand, pulled him towards him. Spurgeon grabbed Felix's collar, and they stared into each other's eyes. Spurgeon let go first. Felix walked away. Spurgeon stood there, suddenly aware of his furiously pounding heart.

At the same time that the Rockpile was being fought over, the 3d Squadron, 5th Cavalry, under Lt. Col. Robert B. Osborn, was enduring its own struggles—mostly against the terrain and the weather.

The 3/5 Cav had been tasked to construct the pioneer road from the Rockpile to north of Khe Sanh, as an alternate route to the main logistical base in case Route 9 was blocked. Working in tandem with the brigade's A Company, 7th Engineers, construction began on 30 January. C Troop patrolled the eastern starting point. At what was to be the western anchor of the pioneer road, Captain Stewart's A Troop had previously secured a patch of rolling hills surrounded by thick jungle. Although Alpha was isolated, the NVA did not hit them. (Their most serious problem occurred when they began running perilously low on C rations and ammunition. Stewart reported this to Osborn, who helicoptered ahead with ten cases of C rations. That was not nearly enough, so First Sergeant Bradley took four APCs with trailer hitches to Khe Sanh. Through persuasion or thievery, the gruff old sergeant returned with three hundred cases of C rats and crates of ammunition.) On 8 February, the engineers, with B Troop providing escort, linked up with

A Troop. Lieutenant Colonel Osborn set up the squadron command post in the clearing Alpha had secured; the command vehicles went into wide trenches, the cooks put up a mess tent, and the engineers bulldozed a berm around the camp. Since the CO's nickname was the Wizard of Oz, the basecamp was christened Emerald City and the pioneer road became the Yellow Brick Road.

The official name was the Red Devil Drive, and using it was a shaky venture; one lane and muddy, it was carved right into the sides and tops of mountains, virtually straight up and down at some points. The entire area was forested ridgelines, and the 3/5 Cav took to the hills to conduct patrols to keep the NVA away from the road. The North Vietnamese did not make a show of force against the pioneer road, but they were out there. The first night after the rendezvous, Alpha Troop split into platoon laagers and Captain Stewart was on the radio with his lieutenants, making sure they set up strong NDPs. Squadron and brigade policy dictated that positions were to be constructed at dusk to avoid observation by the enemy; Stewart thought that was bullshit and ordered his men to set up while it was still light. That gave them time and light to set up well and to hell with the NVA seeing them, he thought, because, if the RPG screens, trips, and claymores are well situated, he can't get through. That night the NVA hit the NPD of Lieutenant Boyd's First Platoon; no GIs were hit, and in the morning, they found two or three dead North Vietnamese outside the wire.

Sometimes at night, the cav men could see 122mm rockets flashing from their tubes, and would fire their Sheridan tanks at them and call in artillery. Other times they could look through their nightscopes and, seeing NVA pilfering their old positions, would direct in more arty. The NVA usually stayed shadowy. Sgt. Louis Forrisi was with a platoon of the 3/5 patrolling a valley between Emerald City and the Rockpile nicknamed the Punchbowl. He wrote in his diary: "Our first day in the Punch Bowl was to search for another of these phantom NVA artillery spotters that higher-ups say are calling rounds into Khe Sanh. So someone gets the idea he's in a group of trees in the middle of the place. . . . Khe Sanh is miles away up in the hills and here we are far below it on a valley floor. But we are ordered to assault this treeline. The lieutenant plays the game by lining up the platoon and letting go with everything we have for about five minutes. After this show, we dismount and walk through what is now a burned out bunch of trees and all that's there is two dead snakes. Every night we move to one of the three positions the engineers prepared for us while they were cutting the road at the beginning of the operation. The ground surveillance team is with us constantly now. And then radar picks up movement every night, but at long ranges. So we lob a few mortar shells in that area and find nothing there in the morning. Every day we'd patrol a different area of the Punch Bowl, checking out the woods or under the culverts the engineers put under the road to prevent washouts. The night went by quietly. It was like the war didn't exist."

But the war was always waiting and watching, and men died. One of them was Sp4 Steve Warner; he was killed in action on 14 February 1971, days before he was to rotate home. Two weeks earlier, on the first night of the op, Hq&Hq Troop had stopped at the foot of the Rockpile, the APCs running to recharge their batteries and the night defensive position hastily set up so they could move quickly. Sgt. Charles W. McKenzie, Jr., a twenty-two-year-old draftee from Salem, Ohio, who worked on the TOC track, was more than nervous that night. He could remember as a kid hearing his father and the other WWII veterans sitting on the back porch telling stories, so he'd tried to soldier well in Vietnam, avoiding the drugs and discontent—but he had only two weeks to go in-country and the Rockpile had a bad reputation. Sp4 Warner introduced himself that night—he was a small, bespectacled man with the Information Service Office, USARV. He sat down with McKenzie and a couple of other GIs to ask them questions and shoot the breeze. An Ernie Pyle type, McKenzie thought, an experienced guy with a personable manner that put you right at ease. Warner opened his pack, stuffed with pistachio nuts, Slim Jims, Kool Aid, and such and they sat talking, eating, and drinking Cokes. McKenzie felt his anxiety drain away.

Two weeks later, McKenzie was sitting in the TOC APC with a couple of radiomen as Lieutenant Colonel Osborn bullshitted about a previous tour where his helicopter had been hit and had had to autogyrate down. McKenzie was just waiting for transport back to Dong Ha to process home. Word came over the TOC radio: Alpha Engineers and 3/5 Cav escort hit in an RPG ambush while laying a culvert over a mountain stream. Two Americans killed, three wounded. An APC pulled into camp and it hit McKenzie like a weight when someone dropped Warner's fantastic pack into the dirt and said that the army photographer was dead. All McKenzie could think was: man what a stinking waste. He was glad Warner's body was not in sight. Osborn picked up the broken camera, splattered with blood; he threw it to a GI standing there and told him to clean it up so Warner's next-of-kin wouldn't have to see it like that, then told an officer to make sure an Army Commendation Medal Citation was written up. Then the colonel sat back down and, to McKenzie's disgust, nonchalantly continued with his war story. A bit later, a major landed in the C&C bird and ushered Sergeant McKenzie aboard. McKenzie slumped in the seat with his gear; this was his last day in the Vietnam bush.

The firefight on the night of 28 February was the worst one Sgt. Larry White ever experienced. He'd enlisted in the army a naive seventeen-year-old from Kentucky and had ended up in Germany. Then he'd reenlisted—he was so gung-ho to get to Vietnam. Now he was a nineteen-year-old buck sergeant commanding a Sheridan tank in Alpha Troop 3/5 Cav. The eight weeks he'd been in Nam, so far, had changed him. Whatever sense of glory he'd been looking for was not easily found, but what was obvious was that most of the guys didn't give a shit about blowing grass in the field, the war, or the lifers. Before long the frustration and bitterness had eaten into White also. He was introduced to marijuana, and his new philosophy could be explained in the squadron's favorite piece of helmet graffiti, STAY HIGH AND KEEP LOW.

Sergeant White was in Lieutenant Johnson's platoon but, since Lieutenant Kincer's Third Platoon was undermanned and alone, he was dispatched to them. He hooked up with them at around three in the afternoon and joined their circle of vehicles, three Sheridans and six APCs, on a small elephant grass-covered hillock. At dusk they posted guards and sacked out around the vehicles. Lieutenant Kincer walked around to each vehicle every ninety minutes to check on things.

It was just another night.

White was sleeping in the grass beside his tank—when an explosion jolted him to his feet. He awoke to instant bedlam: men screaming, tripflares shrieking up, fifties and sixties sweeping the wire around them like some sustained Mad Minute. The North Vietnamese were assaulting their little perimeter. White scrambled barefoot to the top of his Sheridan, screaming at the driver to get out of the commander hatch, and jumped behind the fifty. He could see shadows darting in the tall elephant grass and he joined the roar, pounding out rounds. His loader jumped into the turret to slam shells into the breach, as White fired the main 152mm gun with his TC override control. The driver crouched on the back deck, firing an M-79 grenade launcher. White shouted at the gunner to stay topside and the GI knelt behind the turret, breaking open crates of .50-caliber ammunition.

Jesus, it's a nightmare, White thought, firing wildly at shadows and muzzle flashes. Rocket grenades whooshed by, exploding inside the perimeter. Another RPG screamed in from the right and burst through the turret ring. The explosion sent shrapnel burning into White's legs and feet; and the main gun, radio, and electronics on the tank instantly shut off. He glanced down inside the turret. The loader was slumped over, an arm blown off, his head caved in, brains splattered on the metal around him. Another shriek, and another RPG smacked into the Sheridan, this one from the left. The gunner screamed; White saw him jump off the back deck, tumbling as he landed, and then noticed the man's foot lying on the deck, pulsing blood. The driver, a little new guy, dropped his M-79 and bolted, diving headfirst into a mortar pit for the duration. White heard someone running towards his tank and turned to see Lieutenant Kincer coming to help—he suddenly disappeared in an exploding RPG round. When White opened his eyes, Kincer was down with an arm and leg in tatters. A medic jumped on his tank. White was bleeding but in no pain and he shouted, "Go to the lieutenant!"

He didn't know Kincer was dead. He kept shooting.

Forty yards to his right front, the darting shadows suddenly came into focus and he could see three North Vietnamese rising up from the elephant grass. They wore green fatigues and sandals, one was toting an RPG launcher and the other two had extra rounds and satchel charges. A second later, two more NVA popped up on the left and White didn't even have time to think as he pulled a long sweeping burst across them with his fifty. He saw the bodies fall back, the bullets punching them like baseball bats. A sixth NVA emerged from the grass, drawing back to throw a satchel charge, and White blew him away in turn.

For thirty minutes the little hill was a cacophony of weapons, shouts, and flares, until gunships streaked in, strafing the edge of the perimeter. The NVA attack faded away and White noticed the empty ammo boxes and expended brass and links piled around him. He'd fired ten thousand rounds. When the sun came up, the medic bound his superficial shrapnel wounds. Several North Vietnamese lay dead in the brush and wire. White was bitter over his gunner and loader, and when he saw the driver, he exploded.

"You no good sonuvabitch," White screamed, "Get out of my sight or I'll blow your fucking head off!"

"I'm sorry," he said quietly, "I was scared."

"So was I. Keep your fucking distance from me."

A Loach landed in the battered perimeter and Brigadier General Hill and Lieutenant Colonel Osborn stepped out. They walked about, talking to the grunts, saying that the numerous blood trails indicated they'd defeated a numerically superior enemy force, "Outstanding job, men." The whole nine yards, White thought, the lifers are just eating this shit up. He was standing there, filthy, sweaty, his feet bandaged, and Hill stopped to talk with him for a few minutes. "Good job, trooper, we'll see a citation written up, and don't worry about your tank, we'll have it fixed in no time." White simply said, "Yes sir." But he was raging inside: Well, what about my people? Loader's dead, gunner's crippled, they were damn good friends, you gonna fix them? We're expendable, he surmised, like a can of C rations you use once then throw away. It was a shocking new thought to him: Nobody gives a shit about you lifers being out here. His only concern was that their presence might draw fire.

The next day, an M88 dragged White's gutted Sheridan back to Emerald City. He had just dismounted when a sergeant major was shouting in his face to shave, clean up, put on his jungle boots.

"Well, I'll tell you what, sergeant major. We've been out for weeks. Ain't got no soap, ain't got no reason to shave. Gear's fucking blown away by RPGs. Main gun's down, radio and electronics is down. My crew's fucking wasted. And you want to start telling me about shaving?"

The sergeant major patted him on the shoulder, "Young sergeant, don't you worry. I will get you some gear." He got on the radio, a helicopter came in with parts, and the sergeant major hustled the mechanics over. It took three days to piece the tank back together, and White was sent right back to the field, since his wounds weren't serious enough for a medevac.

The skirmishing around the Yellow Brick Road continued at a sporadic pace, and eventually the brigade's Papa Rangers were inserted into the mountains. Sp4 Walters's six-man team was helicoptered to a small knoll carpeted with elephant grass where they set up an observation post and put booby-traps out around them. These consisted of frag grenades, the fuses screwed out and replaced with smoke grenade fuses which went off instantaneously, rigged with trip wires. Their first day went by quietly, and Walters sometimes found himself forgetting where he was, taken in by the sweeping beauty of the mountains.

In the morning, two rangers went out to retrieve the grenades.

Walters was getting his gear ready when a grenade suddenly boomed and AK-47s opened up. The four of them jogged downhill, tree to tree, and found the other two men at the prone, one wounded, firing into the bushes straight ahead. They shouted that they had four dinks. Walters crouched behind a tree, shooting at the muzzle flashes, until they noticed that the NVA fire had stopped. They cautiously walked down at a crouch, still firing. Two North Vietnamese were sprawled dead in the bushes. They set up a hasty perimeter, found a blood trail, but pursued it with no results. The team moved back to their hilltop with their wounded man, who had shrapnel in his leg and back. He'd been hit, it turned out, by their own booby-trap—when he'd seen the four NVA walking towards him, he'd started to run back, but his foot had snagged the trip wire.

A helicopter came in, taking the wounded man and dropping off two boxes of ammunition and a ranger lieutenant. The teams were usually extracted after contact, since the NVA then knew the location of the six men, but the lieutenant said that the area was hot, and higher-ups wanted the contact pursued. They were getting organized for the patrol when one of the rangers spotted three NVA five hundred yards away in the valley below their hill, walking unaware in an open area. The team's M-60 man shouldered his machine gun, took slow aim, and squeezed the trigger. Walters watched the tracers burn into the group, saw two of the NVA collapse and the third sprint for a treeline. The rangers laughed and patted the gunner on the back, calling him a damn good shot, while the lieutenant brought artillery to bear on the grove into which the NVA had disappeared.

The team spent a second night on the hill.

In the morning, they were scheduled to be picked up, and three guys were picking up their M-16s to make a quick walk around the slope to secure the LZ for helicopters; then they all abruptly heard swishing on the hillside. Instantly they dropped side by side in the tall elephant grass, weapons on full auto and trained at the approaching sound. Walters canted his head to get a better view through the thick grass and saw a bare head bob into view ten yards away; he was walking up the hill right to them. It was the NVA point man.

He could see the man's eyes.

The team leader cut loose and, just that fast, Walters was pumping rounds, the North Vietnamese point man in his sights slamming to the ground.

The NVA patrol fled without firing a shot.

The rangers quickly fanned out, finding two bodies and a blood trail. One of the NVA had a Chinese or North Vietnamese pocket manual, complete with photographs of U.S. vehicles, crosses marking the spots most vulnerable to rocket-propelled grenades. At the same time, a platoon from the 3/5 Cav appeared at the base of the hill, and a foot patrol beat the bush to the top. They got geared to follow the blood trail. The cav point man looked gung-ho; the cav lieutenant must have trusted him because he insisted his man walk point. They pushed off down the hill, the grunt on point, followed by his lieutenant, the ranger team leader, Walters, and the rest of the rangers and grunts.

They filed through the high grass, then came to some thick brush a hundred yards out. They started pushing through, uncomfortably crouched over. Walters was coming through the bramble when a sudden grenade blast pulsed his adrenaline; then M-16s and AK-47s dueled in sharp bursts. He scrambled forward. The point man was down with shrapnel. Walters joined the shooting, but the firefight dried up in a minute. The point man said he'd come upon two NVA carrying a wounded man, but one had spun and tossed a grenade. They searched the brush, finding a dead North Vietnamese and a blood trail. They were getting ready to pursue, when an explosion echoed from the hill; the cav lieutenant got a radio call from his vehicles that some NVA had snuck in and cut loose with an RPG. They moved quickly back to the grassy knoll, where medevac and ranger extraction helicopters came in.

The results of those three days were two GIs wounded, against seven North Vietnamese killed and two wounded. These American soldiers were still winning their part of the war.

But not all of the men were rangers; the troop commanders in the 3/5 Cav had their share of difficulties in leading the reluctant draftees. Captain Stewart of Alpha Troop was a case in point. Sergeant White, for one, respected Stewart's leadership, but there were a minority of GIs in the troop who were generally surly and unresponsive to orders. The grunts of the 3/5 rarely made contact but, when there was a firefight, it always seemed to happen to Alpha. The men had developed a salty, don't-tread-on-me attitude so, when their captain was relieved of command, Stewart inherited an already rebellious situation. Some of the grunts did not adapt well to Stewart's all-army attitude.

And the drug problem didn't help.

The GI who had tried to balk, the first day of the operation, fell apart in short order. He began suffering through heroin withdrawal, and had to be kept under guard on the platoon leader's track because he seemed crazy enough to go for a grenade. A helicopter finally ferried him away to the drug amnesty program. He was released in a week and ghosted in the rear, despite Stewart's repeated attempts to have him returned to the field. The GI finally came back—for one day, before he helicoptered back to Dong Ha on a complaint he filed with the inspector general.

Stewart could not court-martial the man for drug use because he had voluntarily surrendered to the amnesty program. Stewart did, however, catch a second addict going through withdrawal and filed charges against him.

About two weeks into the operation, the troop got their first batch of mail. First Sergeant Bradley sorted it out and found a package addressed to a mechanic on the maintenance track who was a suspected drug pusher. Stewart and Bradley called the young GI to their APC, gave him the package, and mockingly requested him to open it right away. Inside were some cans of food—and a test-tube-size vial of white powder.

"Hey," the mechanic blurted, "I don't know what that is, sir!"

Stewart said they could either send it in for chemical analysis to see if it was heroin, or destroy it and forget it. The GI opted for the latter, and Stewart walked over to a small bonfire where men were drying out clothes and poured the powder in. The GI visibly cringed as he watched his heroin go up in smoke.

A night or two later, Stewart was asleep when an explosion woke him. No shooting followed, so he shrugged back to sleep, thinking a sentry had fired an M-79 at the shadows on the perimeter. In the morning, he saw the shrapnel gouges from a grenade in the side of his APC and realized that he'd been fragged. He didn't know whether it was a warning or a serious attempt on his life, nor could he prove who was responsible. He was convinced, though, that the smack freaks had done it for disrupting their heroin supply. He assembled the troop, stared at the GIs on the maintenance track, and snarled, "You guys better get me next time because I'm going to kill you myself if you don't. It won't do you any good, anyway, because the first sergeant's going to look after me."

First Sergeant Bradley stepped forward to say damn right.

Captain Stewart rotated home, unscathed, in March. Scuttlebutt said that someone later tossed a frag at Bradley; it only served to make the gruff sergeant angry, and he also went home in one piece.

Those certainly were not the only fraggings. The 3/5 Cav had a bad reputation for such activities. Every time units rotated to the rear, there were threats and scare frags; searches through tents and bunkers would turn up grenades hidden in milk cartons. One night the sniper squad was put on the roofs of the 3/5 Cav Rear in Dong Ha to deter marauders. It was this atmosphere which helped one bland private first class to attempt to kill Capt. Wayne R. Young, the commander of Bravo Troop. Near the end of the operation, Captain Young rotated into Third Platoon, the poorest in the troop. True or not, the rumor got around that they had been scheduled for a rest break in Emerald City or Khe Sanh, but that Young had volunteered them to stay in the bush.

Three heroin addicts bitched the night away in their APC, about how Young had cancelled several resupply missions so they could keep pushing for the dinks, how he'd volunteered them for more shit, how they should frag a lifer like him. One of them, the bland pfc, took the talk to heart. He was—and it was the word that came first to his mind—irritated. A tough firefight they'd been through, the cold weather, rain, mud, the lack of hot food and baths—it was made all the worse by the perceived callousness of the captain. Conditions had simply reached an unacceptable point for the young soldier. He did not consider trying to talk with Young, for he didn't think the captain would listen; and the fragging talk of his buddies acted as a catalyst in him. The pfc was going with the flow when he took three claymores that night, wired them under what he thought was Young's APC, then unhesitatingly set them off. The floor of the APC blew open. In the ensuing scramble, it was discovered that Young was in a different track; the platoon mortar track had been destroyed, and four GIs sleeping nearby had been wounded. The unspooled detonation wire led directly to the APC of the three junkies. They were put aboard a helicopter for court-martials, the private charged with attempted murder, the other two with conspiracy to commit murder for urging him on.

The would-be fragger ended up in Long Binh stockade, and was interviewed by the reporter Linden, who wrote: "The magnitude of what he attempted still escapes him. At one point before his trial he looked up and asked naively, 'Look, wouldn't it save everybody a lot of trouble if I took a Section Ten {discharge in lieu of a court-martial} and went home?' Later, after he was convicted of attempted murder and sentenced to ten years at hard labor, he was asked how he would have felt had the claymore mines he had rigged actually killed his CO. {He} said, 'I'd have been tickled pink.' {He} is a passive man, easily impressed by the impulses of his peers. He seems to have no strong convictions on any matter, not even his own fate. Murder is generally associated with ruthless people driven by desperation or greed, and not with lackluster men . . . who cannot comprehend that what they attempt is murder. Murder was not in his heart, it was in the air, and what he attempted is more aptly described by the Army term for killing: to neutralize. Bland, affable {he} is a typical fragger."

There were even more. After Sp4 Spurgeon extended his tour he was sent to Charlie Troop 3/5 Cav on the Dong Ha bunker line. He noticed that the draftees in Charlie hated their lifer first sergeant for pushing them too hard on trivial police calls and shining boots when they were in from the bush. One night Spurgeon was sitting atop his Sheridan when someone broke in on the radio. The sound of an exploding claymore blasted through the speaker; then a GI came on the horn laughing, "Did ya hear that? Ha, ha guess who that was? Ha, that's right, baby!" The first sergeant was medevacked with a limb blown off, and the next morning the captain held a troop formation and called the fragger—whoever he was—a cowardly swine.

As Linden put it, murder was in the air. For example, White knew of a sergeant and his new crew who had pulled a short stint of perimeter security at the Khe Sanh airfield. The sergeant was sitting on his tank one afternoon, writing a letter, when an ARVN ran from the other side of the vehicle, a case of U.S. C rations under each arm. He fired a warning shot from his M-16 but did not halt the fleeing ARVN. He put his second round in the thief's back.

The ARVN died instantly.

There was an investigation of sorts. When the sergeant was asked if he'd really done it, he grinned, "No way, Top."

"I don't give a fuck what you tell the MPs, troop," the first sergeant growled, "but don't lie to me. Did you shoot that gook?"

"Yes, sir, I did."

But nothing really came of the investigation.

It was like hide and seek. Weeks went by when platoons in the Punchbowl and along the Yellow Brick Road would never see a single NVA; then out of nowhere ten or fifteen minutes of terror, called contact, would erupt. And even then, they usually never saw their foe. One morning late in the campaign, Sergeant White was in the lead Sheridan, an M88 towing a disabled APC was behind him, and another Sheridan brought up the rear. They were heading east on the Yellow Brick Road towards Emerald City, escorting the downed track out of the Punchbowl. Without warning, a North Vietnamese sprung from the elephant grass thirty yards ahead and, before White could swing the fifty around, let go with an RPG and dropped back down. The round missed his tank by feet and exploded against the driver's hatch of the M88.

The two Sheridans opened up with their fifties and 152mm main guns, aiming at sounds in the thick grass. AK-47s and RPGs cracked back at them. The wounded M88 and attached APC rolled back; then over the embankment. Two mechanics climbed out and ran up to the

Sheridans. It was an eternity of perhaps five minutes before help arrived, a platoon from Alpha Troop crashing in at full throttle. They raked the roadside with fire, and the NVA faded off. The new captain, Stewart's replacement, was with them and it was White's first look at him. The look did not inspire confidence; the captain was prematurely bald—his helmet had been lost in the brush—he had horn-rimmed glasses and looked sweaty and shaken. He looked like an FNG. They made a quick dismounted patrol off the road and found a blood trail. Then a party of GIs climbed down to the M88 to recover the dead driver and salvage gear from it. White unhooked the .50-cal while a couple of grunts lifted the driver out. He was a gory mess, arm and face charred, splattered with blood, his scalp opened in an ugly slice that exposed the skull.

The next morning, White had his tank in a trench on the Emerald City berm line. He was relaxing, sipping a beer, when the new captain came up and snapped, "You stand up and salute when you talk to me—and get rid of that beer."

White followed orders, hating the games.

Lieutenant Boyd took over as troop exec, and later complained that he had had to run Alpha because the new captain would constantly commute to the rear and take extra R&R leaves.

And so it went for the men of the 3/5 Cav in their skirmishing around the Yellow Brick Road. It was the scene of some successes by the U.S. ground troops committed to the operation; also of some disasters. Lieutenant Christian, West Point '69 and executive officer of Bravo Troop, had the sorry experience of eavesdropping on one of the debacles. Early one day in February, he picked up the troop's payroll at Khe Sanh and helicoptered a ride to the First Platoon under Lt. Steve Overstreet. They held the middle position of the Bravo line in the Punchbowl. Night was falling by the time he finished handing out the MPC notes, and Christian had the choice of paying the troops and staying overnight with either Second or Third Platoon. He had commanded Second when he'd first arrived in Vietnam, many of his men were still there, and the new platoon leader, Lt. Bob Allen, was competent. Christian felt safe with them. On the other hand, Third Platoon had a bad reputation for heroin and incompetence (for example, one GI in the platoon, mishandling a case of C4 explosives, had totalled an APC, killing three GIs and wounding four in the process). Their platoon leader had been injured on the first day of the operation when his APC threw a track, rolled on its side, and the fin on a loose mortar round split open his calf. A lieutenant took command. He too had a bad reputation, having been relieved of command earlier and shuffled away to another job. Since Bravo Troop was short of officers, Lieutenant Colonel Osborn had elected to give him another crack at commanding a platoon.

Lieutenant Christian decided to play it safe and hitched a ride to Allen's platoon. After paying the troops, he sacked out on a litter beside a track in the Second Platoon laager. It was around four in the morning, when Allen shook him awake and said to follow him to his command track, so they could monitor the action—all hell had broken loose on the little grassy knoll held by Third Platoon.

They sat in the APC, listening to the chaos on the radio.

North Vietnamese were in the perimeter wire, two Sheridans and two APCs were ablaze, and Lieutenant Overstreet, whose platoon held an adjacent position, was trying to scream sense into the Third Platoon lieutenant over the radio. Overstreet had his 81mm mortar crew pump HE and illumination shells around the embattled platoon, and radioed the troop commander for permission to crank up and haul into the firefight. The NVA would probably be waiting in ambush for such a move, so permission was denied. On the hill, confusion abounded. The lieutenant refused to leave his APC, so the platoon sergeant took command. The sergeant was hit, an RPG round penetrating the turret of his Sheridan, the explosion blowing off the gunner's head and the sergeant's leg. But the sergeant remained calm, tied his belt as a tourniquet around his stump, and stayed on the radios, trying to direct return fire and bring in artillery around the hill. The squad leaders scrambled from hole to hole around the perimeter, trying to get the terrified troopers up to return fire.

On their own accord, the NVA faded back into the night.

In the morning, Lieutenant Christian took an M88 recovery vehicle to Third Platoon to help get their downed vehicles back to Emerald City. He caught up with the platoon along a jungle trail, halted because a Sheridan in the lead had thrown a track and the crew was repairing it. Christian asked among the soldiers what the hell had happened; it turned out just to have been a continuum of foul-ups. Squadron policy was never to stay in one spot longer than two days, but the lieutenant had been lazy, had complained to the captain, and had received permission to stay another day. Even though this meant the NVA probably had his platoon under observation, Jones neglected to register his 81mm mortar around the perimeter. And for some reason, the lieutenant did not trust claymore mines and, despite the advice of the platoon sergeant, did not employ them. The results of this were one GI killed, seven wounded, two tanks and two tracks burned out by rocket-propelled grenades, and the demoralization of the platoon. A heavy blood trail had been found in the elephant grass, and the frustrated officers in squadron headquarters decided no one could have lost that much blood and lived. They reported one NVA confirmed killed.

Christian was so upset that he jumped off the M88 and stomped along the halted column looking for the Third Platoon lieutenant. No one knew where he was. Christian finally found him sitting on a rock in the middle of a jungle stream, dangling his feet in the water. He looked so distraught that Christian turned around and left without saying a word other than to tell a trooper to take his M-16 and cover the lieutenant in case the NVA reappeared. The good news was that the man was relieved of command a second time and sent to a rear job in Dong Ha. The bad news was that the courageous platoon sergeant, who lost his leg during the firefight, died in a hospital ward in Japan.

Sometimes, though, the grunts had their vengeance.

Working off of the Yellow Brick Road on the second day of April, Lieutenant Allen's platoon had its revenge for the casualties Bravo Troop had suffered. At around four in the morning, a GI with a Starlite scope on the perimeter spotted an NVA patrol north of them on a hillside trail. There were about twenty of them, walking single file, noisily griping their way through the brush, seemingly convinced that the night belonged to them. Allen radioed his troopers to hold their fire until the NVA saw them, or until they were close enough to ambush. A grassy field of some five hundred yards separated the platoon's position from the NVA column; and when they walked into an open spot, the night erupted. The 152mm main gun on a Sheridan tank fired a flechette round which sent ten thousand razor-darts scything through the North Vietnamese; in the same instant, the 81mm-mortar crew began dropping illumination shells and the troops opened up with their fifties and sixties, raking the now starkly lit hillside. In the morning, the grunts picked among the corpses, finding enough severed arms and legs and mangled torsos to claim a body count of nineteen. Sergeant White was monitoring the radios at Emerald City when the report came in. A North Vietnamese unit had been massacred; not a single American had even been wounded. It was the best feeling White had ever had in the field. It was just so damn good to win sometimes.

Working in coordination with the 1/77 Armor and 3/5 Cav in keeping the NVA off balance was the 1st Battalion, 61st Mechanized Infantry (Lt. Col. Arnold Stallman). They worked the furthest east during the op, mostly in the grassy hill country around the Cam Lo Bridge, Dong Ha, and the eastern DMZ. Stallman's 1/61 TOC was a concrete bunker at a muddy knob of a firebase called Charlie Two, situated between Dong Ha and the DMZ. A sister firebase called Alpha Four (known as Con Thien in the days of the Marines) was a bump in the rolling hills to the north. The battalion did not work as a single command; A Company was sent to Vandegrift and C Company to the Rockpile, opcon to 1/77 Armor, while B Company was the reserve at C2 patrolling the Z and the muddy roads that connected the firebases. On occasion the companies rotated assignments.

The grunts of the 1/61 Mech were as reluctant and fed up as any soldiers of the time. Their most recent source of bitterness had come from a foot patrol during which a sergeant in Alpha Company had gotten lost leading a night ambush patrol. They'd walked into an old Marine minefield outside A4; four GIs had been blown apart, one seriously wounded, and only the sergeant had come through the night physically unscathed. That had been around Christmas time and the mood of the battalion could be read in a slogan written on a track at Alpha Four: SANTA IS DEAD.

Nevertheless, the battalion continued to perform its mission.

One of those who served was Pfc Michael J. DeAngelis, an assistant machine-gunner in Bravo Company. Age twenty-two, from a middle-class family in Hartford, Connecticut, he had taken his draft notice with a mixture of pride and relief. His father had fought in WWII; and DeAngelis had gone to Vietnam in October 1970 with a belief he never lost: that it was America's role to help people who wanted to be free. He also had gone with a piece of advice stuck in his mind. A buddy of his had been a Marine grunt and, when DeAngelis had been on leave prior to departing for Nam himself, the ex-infantryman had given him three codes to survive by: No one likes a new guy so keep your mouth shut and do what you're told. Don't let your mouth write a check your ass can't cash. And, the key one, pick out the best grunt in the outfit and follow his example. "If you survive the first three months," his buddy had told him, "only bad luck will kill you."

When DeAngelis rotated into Bravo Company, he stuck with Sgt. "Wolf" Garet, his nickname from the fact that after eight Dear Johns in Nam, he still had seven girlfriends left. The young sergeant was a brave, dependable man with plenty of bush sense. What Tarzan was to the jungle, DeAngelis thought. And he reckoned that, if Garet was the best, most of the grunts were at least giving it their all. The problems arose mostly in the rear. The three line companies rotated for standdown at the 1/61 Rear in Quang Tri every two weeks, or whenever the combat situation allowed. They would come in at night, shower, shave, get clean uniforms, and soak up the mess hall beer and steaks. The next day was spent cleaning weapons, repairing APCs, and being inspected; then mounting out back to the field at four the next morning. If the stand-downs were a time to relax, they were also two days of heated friction. The most prevalent was between the grunts and the rear-echelon lifers. The REMFs seemed afraid of them, DeAngelis thought, as if they knew that pissing off a grunt could result in a vengeance grenade. But they hit them with a harsh regimentation of uniform inspections, police details, shaves, saluting, haircuts, and all the rest. DeAngelis thought the process was to make them hate the rear so much they'd want to get back into the bush, and he resented the ploy as chicken-shit.

Even Bravo Company fell upon itself in the rear. DeAngelis was lucky in that he stayed away from the dope and was easy-going enough to get along with almost everybody. He could stand back and watch. He saw four factions in Bravo; two of them were mean as snakes. The Chicanos and American Indians were a friendly bunch, but the blacks stuck together and had a militant core who cruised around purposely looking for trouble. They were the most violent. There were rednecks, rough factory kids and farmboys, who listened to C&W, got blind drunk, and loved to harass "them niggers." And there were the heads, who usually just wanted to avoid all of the fights and indulge in marijuana. The camaraderie was strange, DeAngelis thought; those who were close were brothers, and the rest hated each others' guts. One USO show in the EM Club turned into a race riot among the 1/61 REMFs. He was convinced that if the hatreds had been allowed to boil long enough in the rear, some of the grunts would have killed each other.

But all of the troubles ended the moment they drove past the Quang Tri wire. The common denominator, he surmised, was hating Charlie and taking care of each other. Even the most militant of the blacks packed away their prejudices, took some solace in falling into tight-lipped silence around the whites, and soldiered with the best of them. There were no drugs in the field. One of the company pot heads was on DeAngelis's track. His nickname was Pockets because he kept everything he owned in them, and he was an original Haight-Ashbury hippie who'd been caught up in the draft. He hated the war but, in the bush, he was a man you could count on.

DeAngelis even considered the leadership in Bravo to be good. The captain was known as Jungle Pimp, after his initials, and he worked with a good mixture of careful planning, caution, and assertiveness. The platoon sergeants also used good judgment. None of the leaders needlessly risked their lives, and even the battalion chaplain went on patrol with them. They were all heroes, DeAngelis thought, but they cursed the war and bitched and the word hero was something they would never have chosen for themselves.

Bravo Company and the rest of the battalion adhered to standard mech-infantry procedures. Each day became a repetition of the one before. The company was assigned ten grid squares on the map to search for a week, and they split up into the four corners of the AO. The tracks established platoon laagers, guards were left behind, and the grunts fanned out on dismounted patrols, usually sweeping out less than a mile before returning. When they travelled mounted, the deltas followed in each others' tread marks to avoid mines. If they took fire, the entire column immediately wheeled about, laid down return fire, and charged, chasing off the NVA.

On most days, nothing happened.

Nights were the hairiest, and construction of the NDPs followed a careful routine. They moved just prior to dusk so the NVA couldn't fix their positions and mortar them at night; the GIs quickly broke into preassigned groups to unload the APCs and set up. The tracks formed a circle in the elephant grass, platoon and mortar tracks in the center, RPG screens in front of each vehicle with engineer stakes; rocket grenades would explode against the fence allowing only shrapnel to spray through. In front of that, each track crew wired several claymores, some of them booby-trapped with grenades to deter NVA sappers, who were adept at crawling in and turning the mines around to face U.S. positions. Around the whole setup a spool of concertina wire was staked down and, thirty yards out from that, trip flares were stuck in the ground with wooden stakes, taut wire zigzagging from flare to flare.

Between each track, the grunts dug two foxholes, claymore firing clackers unwound to the holes, one man awake at all times between each APC. They brought the M-60s into the muddy holes with three thousand rounds per gun. Before dark the gunners would study the terrain, then stick branches into the dirt in front of their holes to indicate terrain features, so even in the pitch black they could fire without sight simply by touching the barrel against the stick that indicated the area at which they wanted to fire. Even if the infantrymen were filthy head to toe, the weapons and ammo were cleaned and oiled and laid across C rat cardboard to keep them out of the dirt. They usually didn't have Starlite scopes, so when the wind rushed through the elephant grass they would sit, nervous and tense, the grass above their helmets, unable to see even their hands, the noises playing with their minds. To keep the NVA similarly off-balance at night, Bravo deployed MAs and ambush teams.

On most nights, nothing happened.

Even so it was numbing and exhausting, DeAngelis thought; the men always seemed to be sleepwalking. Yet, for an untested, middle-class kid like him there was some good to be salvaged from the experience. It was his first real test, and in his mind, he had passed.

DeAngelis never considered himself a very lucky person; as far as he was concerned, he used up all of his luck in the war—for instance, the time he was in the showers at C2, but it was the mess hall that took the rockets; or the time the AK-47 round, meant for his back, was deflected by a little tab of metal inches away from him, while he was firing the M-60 on his track. He thought his transfer saved his life. DeAngelis, who had junior-college training in mechanics, was sent to D Company, the battalion service outfit, located at Quang Tri. He spent his time at OJT, learning to maintain the tracks in the motor pool, and to hate lifers. They were pigs, he thought, never satisfied with anything, always hassling someone. "Lifers are like flies," was the draftees' joke, "they eat shit and bother people."

The mechanics were often dispatched to Charlie Two, where the overriding problem was the living conditions. The firebase itself was simply a bare earthen mound, covered with bunkers, surrounded by wire and mines. Bunker life was austere; ramps had to be built in them because the bottoms were swamped from the monsoon and had become home for rats and snakes. They pulled guard duty atop the bunkers to avoid the rats, but even when they lay wrapped up in a poncho they could feel the things scurry over them. Some GIs were bitten and, when a rat crawled into a man's sleeping bag, they declared war. They put C ration crackers on a berm; then, using a red-lensed flashlight to spot the approaching rodents, they nailed them with M-16s. By morning they had thirty-five rats stacked up.

The next biggest problem was the North Vietnamese Army. Almost every day, fifteen or twenty 122mm rockets thudded into C2, sending almost everyone leaping for bunkers. DeAngelis could look from his underground shelter at some of the bravest men he'd seen; the firebase artillerymen who manned their guns during rocket raids to return fire.

On occasion there would be a need for the men to go to the field to tow in destroyed APCs or to walk the morning minesweep patrol between C2 and A4. The problem was not how to scrounge up a volunteer, but which one to pick, since almost every man would step forward—a sign of dedication which DeAngelis thought the lifers were not impressed by. The most lonely feeling he ever had was walking point on the muddy road in the cool, misty morning, with nothing but wet fields of elephant grass and three APCs following several hundred yards behind. Field duty was all a matter of chance. Once DeAngelis's track went to Vandegrift to tow a downed APC back to Charlie Two. He was waiting to cross the Cam Lo Bridge on his way back, when some APCs roared up from the opposite direction, headed towards Vandegrift. They stopped, asked if DeAngelis had just come from the west, and shook their heads in amazement when he said yes. They said that it must have been the tracks right behind him that had been RPG'd; then they continued their dash to the trouble spot.

On 24 February, word came down that the Delta Company mechanics were going to convoy to Vandegrift to handle the damaged vehicles there. They were sitting in their cots in a bunker that night when a young staff sergeant nicknamed J.D., one of the few lifers DeAngelis liked, collected a bunch of C ration apricots and ate them. That was a bit of bravado on his part because a battalion superstition was that apricots led to ambushes and rockets and injuries; but DeAngelis's warning, "Why tempt fate?" was met by J.D.'s cynical response, "That's a crock of shit." In the morning, they were packed up to leave for Vandegrift with Bravo Company when Charlie Company rotated back, weary and filthy and towing several APCs. J.D. left DeAngelis and three other mechanics to handle the new wrecks, then departed with the Bravo tracks.

Three days later, these four took an APC down Route 9 and made it to Vandegrift without a shot being fired. As they pulled inside the wire, DeAngelis shouted to the sentry, "Is this the right road to Hanoi?" The GI laughed. Sappers had been shot in the wire, the night before, and he could see one of the North Vietnamese corpses lying stiffly against an earthen berm. His legs had been blown off. A few GIs were gathered around, laughing as they switched legs around on the dead man so he looked pigeon-toed. Vandegrift was a noisy, dusty place with traffic roaring in and out, but it struck DeAngelis that most of the GIs seemed to be just milling around, trying to look busy.

They shut down in the motor pool and asked for J.D. Instead they got a bad story. The soldiers there said that, a couple of mornings back, they'd been sitting around boiling some sunrise coffee, while J.D. had stood shirtless on the lowered cargo ramp of an APC, shaving out of an upturned helmet. A couple of 122mm rockets had dropped in from across the perimeter. The GIs had scrambled inside the track, but J.D. had stayed put, laughing at their timidness. Then another rocket had exploded near the motor pool and J.D. suddenly had fallen to his knees, doubled up. He'd grabbed a flak jacket and had pressed it against his stomach to hold in his intestines. The men had quickly hauled him all the way inside the track, and he had been medevacked as soon as the shelling had stopped. After the operation was over, DeAngelis returned home briefly on an emergency leave and on his way back to Vietnam, visited J.D. in a Washington state VA hospital. He looked bad, had a cane and a colostomy bag, but was in good spirits. They joked about the apricot jinx, and J.D. said to tell a staff-sergeant friend of his that he still wanted the ten dollars he'd won in a card game the night before he was wounded. DeAngelis didn't have the heart to tell him that the sergeant had been blown away in another rocket attack.

Tragically, the worst shelling the 1/61 Mech Infantry took came after the operation was over and they had rotated to Charlie Two for a breather. They were lining up for chow at dusk when the rockets started whistling in and the men scrambled for cover. Men crammed inside the nearest bunker, one which doubled as a beer hall—then a single 122mm rocket made a direct hit on the sandbagged roof and, in one screaming flash, twenty-nine GIs were dead.

It even made the papers.

CHAPTER ELEVEN:
Convoy Duty on Route 9

The primary goal of the American ground operation was to maintain Route 9 as a viable supply line to the ARVN invasion force in Laos. In this mission, they were successful. The needed materiel got to the front and Lt. Gen. William J. McCaffrey (Deputy Commander, USARV) could rightfully record with pride, "The support of the operation was one of the major logistical feats of the war. The equivalent of more than four divisions received supplies that travelled, for the most part, over a single road and into a single airhead."

The task facing General Sweeney and the Da Nang Support Command was monumental. Most of the materiel was moved by truck and the final tabulation of traffic monitored on Route 9 during the operation came to 1,163 U.S. convoys (20,995 vehicles) and 621 ARVN convoys (22,858 vehicles). A thousand vehicles a day hit Route 9.

But there were many difficulties that surfaced, and the problem-solving began in earnest on 7 February. That morning General Sweeney telephoned Colonel Richard Morton, commander of the 8th Transportation Group at Qui Nhon, informing him that at 1400 hours an L23 would arrive at his base. Morton was West Point '49 and winner of the Silver Star and three Purple Hearts as a lieutenant in Korea. He was disgruntled, having pressing problems in his own area to contend with, and had no idea what could be so important in MR1. He took his sergeant major and a major with him. It was a brisk evening at Quang Tri when they checked with Colonel Konopnicki at HQ, 26th General Support Group, SUPCOM. In the morning, Sweeney arrived by air and the three commanders got down to the business at hand.

"It was from Konopnicki that I discovered the real reason for my presence," Morton said, "it was that the highway for Lam Son was in shambles and getting worse. Our highers in USARV and MACV had been obsessed about leaks concerning the operation and had limited their planning to only the highest staff officers at both headquarters. Accordingly, no one who really worked on the plan had spotted that the weak point was the paucity of surface transportation assigned to the gigantic task."

For the next two days, Sweeney, Konopnicki, and Morton heli-hopped throughout the AO in Sweeney's helicopter—from Camp Eagle, Vandegrift, Khe Sanh, to Lang Vei—talking with commanders and enlisted men. A firmer picture of the problems plaguing the supply line began to emerge. Route 9 from Dong Ha to Vandegrift was a two-lane, all-weather, paved surface where convoys could average twenty-five mph. A few sections had been washed out in the monsoon and had yet to be repaired, but the major problem lay in the thick elephant grass which flanked the difficult leg of the highway. NVA ambush teams could infiltrate through the heavy foliage and open fire on convoys from only a few yards away. Colonel Morton tried to get an engineer Rome-plow company to level the underbrush, and to have combat units assigned sectors along the road to prevent ambushes. He was unsuccessful on both counts, receiving no explanation why engineers were not dispatched, and being told by infantry commanders that the battalion operations pushing the NVA into the countryside were a more viable answer than falling back on the highway itself.

From Vandegrift, the highway turned into a one-lane dirt road which twisted to the Laotian border, and only allowed convoys to crawl along at eight mph. The physical adversities on this leg of Route 9 were many. The road was hemmed in by underbrush and was subject to ambush, particularly at the makeshift bridges. At some points, the roadside fell into hundred-foot ravines and was without guard rails; many trucks and cargo trailers plummeted off the side. The dirt was composed of red laterite clay which quickly pulverised into a fine dust, two feet deep in places, which rose into great clouds and made driving a very real hazard. They called it the "Khe Sanh Red" and it worked its way incessantly into noses, hair, eyes, mouths, food, drink, engines, and weapons.

Perhaps the most frustrating aspect of travelling the dirt path of Route 9 was caused by the ARVN convoys. Because the road was one way, convoys had to be coordinated carefully and when the South Vietnamese were given the choice of when they wanted to run their supply trucks, they chose most of the daylight hours, leaving the nights and the NVA to the Americans. "Conference after conference failed to get ARVN to yield one second of their times," Morton said. "I was most unhappy about how little our own highers knew about this situation and what little pressure they put on ARVN to change."

At that early point, the only U.S. transportation units making the run were the six truck companies of Lieutenant Colonel Alvin Ellis's 39th Transportation Battalion. Morton was most impressed by Ellis's performance: "He was a first-class commander who got the job done under woefully inadequate conditions. Al frequently led the convoys in person from Vandegrift to Khe Sanh and return." The supplies were pushed through, but the battalion has suffered accordingly. Morale among the truckers was low; the 666th Truck Company had a driver refusal, and the company first sergeant was later fragged. Trucks were burned out. The clouds of red dust had done most of it. In interviewing battalion drivers, Morton thought that they hated the dust more than the enemy; it was their only topic of conversation to him. At Quang Tri, SUPCOM sent the 2d and 63d Maintenance Battalions out to work on the problem and, Morton remembered, "Within two weeks of my arrival you could not put another vehicle into their compound. My deadline rate which averaged five percent in Qui Nhon soared to 35 percent in Quang Tri. The curses of the drivers who lost their vehicles to laterite and had to be taken to the maintenance battalion echoed far and wide. Lam Son needed fresh truck assets and needed them yesterday or even last month."

Thievery between units for parts and vehicles became rampant.

On 10 February, Maj. Gen. Walter Woolwine (Deputy Commander for Material, USARV) arrived at Quang Tri and plans for recovery were shaped up. General Sweeney was to return to Da Nang to supervise the convoy movement along Route 1 from there to Quang Tri. Although Colonel Morton was technically senior to Colonel Konopnicki, the latter had been on the scene longer, was more familiar with the problems at hand, and was to be the local logistical commander with his 26th GSG HQ in Quang Tri. In conference, Woolwine, Sweeney, Konopnicki, and Morton agreed on a six-point plan to revamp the flow of supplies to the ARVN:

1. despite the strain it would put on the logistics in MR2, the HQ, 8th Transportation Group would move to Quang Tri to work in tandem with HQ, 26th GSG
2. also bearing in mind the problems it would cause in MR2, two additional truck companies would be shifted north

3. another battalion headquarters would be moved to work with the 39th
4. ten armored gun trucks would be dispatched to escort convoys
5. seventy-five five-ton tractors were needed to compensate for the maintenance shortfalls
6. fifty fifteen-ton semi-trailers would be moved in to replace losses

By 20 February, the situation along Route 9 began to improve. On or about that date, Colonel Morton's headquarters arrived via C130. Also brought to the scene were fresh drivers, new equipment, and gun trucks. The second battalion to join the 39th was the 57th Transportation Battalion of SUPCOM, commanded by a black lieutenant colonel named Frank Francois. The two battalion commanders were well respected by the logistical commanders: Francois working hard to get the supplies from Da Nang to Vandegrift; Ellis working equally hard to continue the chain to Khe Sanh. The convoys went well protected by MP vehicles, some APCs, and most importantly, the gun trucks. They were an example of battlefield improvisation which had developed because simply mounting a machine gun, as per army regulations, did not protect a thin-skinned truck. The solution was to reinforce a five-ton truck with steel planking (some had APC hulls fitted atop the bed); then put three or four soldiers in the cargo bed, arming them with whatever could be scrounged together—.50-calibers, grenade launchers, numerous M-60s, even an occasional minigun. All of the gun-truckers were volunteers. If a convoy was ambushed, it was the gun truck which hauled into the fire, engaged the enemy, and extracted the truck drivers. The sight of gun trucks in a convoy probably deterred many North Vietnamese ambushers along Route 9.

Nevertheless, problems abounded. The truck convoys began meeting the requirements, but could not always unload at their destinations. The problem was with forklifts; as Morton recounted: "Forklifts require a skilled operator, spare parts, good mechanics, etc. If you are missing any one of these ingredients, you are doomed to failure. The entire chain of command endeavored to solve the forklift problem by rushing more and more forklifts to Quang Tri, Vandegrift, and Khe Sanh. Khe Sanh was a case in point. The number of operational forklifts there in mid-February was eleven. We must have hauled in twenty or more over the next two weeks. But, on March 1 or so, the number of operational forklifts was still eleven. As a result, many of my trailers were arriving at the airhead and there they sat for days or even weeks. A loaded trailer just sitting is a tremendous waste; we began taking fifteen-ton semi-trailers from everywhere in Vietnam and even Okinawa."

This problem occurred at Quang Tri also, where trailers full of ammo sat crammed and waiting at the Ammunition Supply Point. One night in February, an NVA sapper team successfully infiltrated the base perimeter and sent several tons of ordnance sky high.

Through it all, the truckers kept hauling the supplies, enduring bad driving conditions every inch of the way, and occasional bouts with rockets, snipers, and ambushes. The official assessment of the casualties of the Da Nang Support Command and 504th MP Battalion along Route 9 was 11 killed, 55 wounded, 14 fatal traffic accidents, and 68 nonfatal accidents.

Once a week, Lieutenant Malmstrom and one of the checkpoint MPs would race their jeep down Route 9, making it within sight of Vandegrift in under twenty minutes. They would be out to look for any stalled trucks, and would time it so they could see Happy Hour, the rocketing of Vandegrift which happened almost every night at around five to seven. Malmstrom had not taken any incoming at Khe Sanh and felt sorry for Major Butler and Lieutenant Doyle, especially Doyle, who'd picked Vandegrift precisely because he'd already seen enough action. Whenever he could, Malmstrom hitched rides on convoys between Khe Sanh and Vandegrift, to keep his map updated on where the road had been widened or where bad turns were, so he could better brief convoy commanders. He also went to advise the officers on any problems that might develop, but usually everything went smoothly and he just sat and sweated out the ride.

Along the route, Malmstrom would usually see a few abandoned trucks, a five-thousand-gallon fuel tanker crashed at the side of the road and burnt out, and the gutted shell of an APC, its rear ramp blown off and junk scattered around it. Communications were poor, so he didn't know if the vehicles had been blown away three days or three years before. Either way, when they drove past, he had the tendency to tighten up on his flak jacket, finger his M-16, and look down the column of trucks to see if everything was okay.

Malmstrom was lucky; none of the convoys he was on drew fire.

As far as he was concerned, the worst enemy was the terrain and the elements. At night fog covered the road, cutting visibility down to zero, and the drivers had to concentrate every inch of the way. When it rained, the mud road literally turned to red ice. On a hot day, Route 9 was a blizzard of red dust, sun glare magnifying the problems of maneuvering the twisting, narrow road. There was no good time to drive. Some trucks missed turns and Malmstrom organized the wrecker crews to drag vehicles up and to medevac truck drivers with concussions, broken bones, and bad cuts. Once, at the checkpoint, a GI was doing maintenance under his truck when another truck bumped his. Malmstrom hefted him into a jeep and they sped to the Khe Sanh medical bunker, where he was immediately taken out by helicopter. Malmstrom didn't think the GI would make it; his head was literally crushed like an egg.

What impressed Lieutenant Malmstrom the most about duty on Route 9 was the good morale and hard work of the soldiers involved. It was just the opposite of what he was accustomed to at Cam Ranh Bay. It was an odd truism of Vietnam 1971 that the farther away from combat, the worse morale became. Cam Ranh Bay was one of the safest places in the country and Malmstrom couldn't imagine spirits going any lower. Drugs were the biggest problem. When the battalion chaplain sent out an anonymous questionnaire, 25 percent of the men said they smoked heroin daily and an additional 20 percent smoked marijuana and opium. The leadership was no help; he saw two lieutenants smoke grass, heard rumors of a captain on smack, and knew most of the older NCOs carried around bottles. Malmstrom thought most of the transportation corps officers were divided into two groups; easy-going managerial types who cared more about efficiency than about troops, and hard-core ex-infantrymen. Out on convoy, the draftees were without much supervision and grew resentful of authority; there were a few scare fraggings on battalion commanders. A lieutenant Malmstrom knew had an M-16 jammed into his stomach by an enlisted man enraged at his attention to discipline. Racial friction was another quagmire. Two sergeants in Malmstrom's company hated blacks and refused to promote them. The blacks grumbled openly, and the battalion commander ordered Malmstrom to promote several qualified blacks over qualified whites. The next night, one of the sergeants appeared at the company orderly room, drunk and complaining. There were unending scuffles between the races which erupted one night in the EM Club; the blacks slowly moved to the back, the whites gathered up front; then a person or persons unknown chucked a WP grenade through the front door. Malmstrom drove to the emergency room to find a doctor pouring water onto a friend's stomach which was burning with white phosphorus.

Disgusted with the war and the army, some of the young officers at Cam Ranh Bay even refused their end-of-tour medals.

Malmstrom saw no such problems at Khe Sanh. He didn't have time to look for dope among the troopers, he thought cynically that the men hadn't set up their dope supply line yet nevertheless, it never disrupted the work at hand. In the convoy staging area, the truckers were always ready to help; if someone needed maintenance. Everyone cooperated to get the job done. When ARVN hung around, asking questions about vehicle repair, the GIs showed them what to do. When it came to the convoys, they drove in all conditions around the clock, fighting sun glare and veils of dust in the day, and fog banks at night. Sometimes the GIs only got a few hours of sleep under their trucks before Malmstrom roused them at three in the morning; they would climb unhesitatingly back into their trucks and head out to get more supplies. He thought they did a great job and, as far as Malmstrom was concerned, the logistics of the operation would have fallen apart if not for the daily endurance of the GI and ARVN truckers, who braved treacherous roads and bad weather day after day to get the goods in. Maj. George H. Chase would have been the first to agree with such an appraisal of morale. He was a New Yorker who had served as a young officer in Korea and was recalled from reserve status in 1967; in Vietnam he was made the information officer of the Da Nang Support Command. With eleven combat correspondents, Chase hopped between the various SUPCOM units at Da Nang, Quang Tri, Dong Ha, Vandegrift, and Khe Sanh, taking photographs and doing stories. There were numerous outfits spread out along the Quang Tri front, from POL fueling pits, ammo supply points, helo slingloading pads, mechanic workshops, convoy units to the main area at Khe Sanh, designated FSA-II under Maj. Charles Lutz.

The men had a job to do, Chase was proud to report, and they were performing superbly. He knew things weren't perfect: he heard one story of a truck going off the road and ARVN pilfering it at gunpoint. He knew that mama-sans were selling dope in plastic baggies, and he had to relieve some men for drug use. But those were not the stories that Major Chase did; his view was that the civilian press was covering the troublemakers, that it was the military's job to report on the majority of dedicated soldiers who did their jobs without recognition. He and his crew wrote the good news stories to show SUPCOM's professionalism—for instance, the time when General Sweeney and his sergeant major helicoptered, starched and polished, into the dust bowl of Khe Sanh to chat with Major Lutz, make an inspection tour, and pin a Bronze Star on a young, mustached, grease-splattered staff sergeant for his hard work as a maintenance man (the sergeant's comment: "I was damn sure surprised. I was just doing my job like everyone else up here.") Chase hitched rides on several Route 9 convoys and a truck driver was quoted, "We have put on beaucoup miles, but no one seems to mind. There's a reason behind it all. We understand that and it makes a lot of difference."

Chase was greatly impressed by the hard work of all involved, and his major disappointment came in trying to get the civilian press corps to take an interest. The reporters he saw ran the spectrum from big television names, to small town newspapermen, to freelancers trying to make a career, to a few old-fashioned muckrakers. He had limited success with them. Once he had ABC-TV News lined up to do a story on the convoy runs, but they cancelled at the last minute; the morale of the GIs seemed to dip for a moment after that, Chase thought, as if they figured no one really cared. Chase knew enough about journalism to understand the problem. Reporters had to follow the dictates of their editors who knew that, by 1971, a headline like GIs GET SUPPLIES THROUGH ON ROUTE 9 didn't sell papers, but GIs FRAG OFFICER did. Many of the reporters seemed to have preconceived notions on the "evil" of American involvement in Vietnam, and their minds were made up as to what type of stories they would pursue. Sometimes Chase became so frustrated he confronted reporters and told them that what they were doing was a disservice to the nation.

Every man had his own version of what was really happening.

Another convoy was forming up at Da Nang for the run to Khe Sanh, and the men waited, exhibiting a variety of emotions—some calm, others excited, a few almost shaking with nervous fear. It was blistering hot and most of the truckers waited in the shade of their vehicles as forklift crews filled the truck beds. Some of the GIs lit up to mellow out for the ride. Sp4 James Brock of the 23d MP Company, Americal Division, was not alarmed by the dope smoking; he was there to provide convoy security, not to chase pot heads. It didn't matter anyway, he thought; a few of the MPs also used grass, most drank, but it never interfered with their job in the field. Besides, if they were to be measured by their outward appearance, he surmised they would not have measured up; the smell of dew was in the air and almost everyone, including Brock and the MPs, had long hair, mustaches, and peace medallions, while the truck drivers had flak jackets emblazoned with logos like "FTA" or "Is this trip really necessary."

But the men got the job done, Brock reckoned, and that's what counted.

They finally pushed out with about forty supply-laden trucks, plus three MP jeeps, two V100 MP gun vehicles, and overhead helo escort.

The MPs rotated duty on Route 9. For Brock, a twenty-year-old Arkansas country boy who believed in the war, it was his third trip to Khe Sanh. The other two trips had been harassed by snipers; no big deal, he thought, just part of the job. Brock rode front seat in one of the jeeps as radioman, the driver beside him and an M-60 gunner in the back seat. Things changed on Route 9. The weather grew cool and misty. The terrain became more primitive. The threat of enemy action became more serious; dotting the road were units from the 5th Mech, a few tanks and APCs deployed to the side with RPG screens around them, some of the grunts sleeping in the shade while others kept a monotonous lookout. If a convoy was hit hard, they were the reaction force.

Brock was a short-timer, so he slumped in the seat as they bounced along, talking about going home. The gunner knew he was Regular Army and joked back, "Well, you're a lifer, you'll be back next year anyway."

"No way, man!"

The NVA ambushed them after the convoy passed Vandegrift. Bursts of AK-47 rattled from somewhere in the roadside brush, snapping Brock out of his doldrums with a painful whack to his leg. The MPs and one gun truck poured suppressive fire into the bushes, and Brock burned off a magazine from his M-16 in the cacophony. In seconds they zipped past the ambush point, losing no one. At first Brock thought his leg had been blown off, it hurt so bad, throbbing from the hip down. An AK round had passed just below his kneecap, punching a hole in one side and leaving a cut on the other that barely bled. He tore open his trouser leg and wrapped a bandage around the wound.

When they pulled into Khe Sanh, they hauled for the med bunker and Brock limped inside. A medic simply rewrapped the wound and, since it was not serious, Brock elected to return to Da Nang via the unloaded convoy rather than call for a medevac. At the Da Nang hospital, he was stitched up, put on light duty for two weeks; then he spent a few more days in the field before rotating home. Before he left, he was pinned with the Purple Heart and an Army Commendation Medal for Valor. The decoration was for "commanding" the MP jeep during the ambush and "refusing" evacuation for his wound. Brock figured the Army was looking to hand out medals for anything.

It was a hot day at Quang Tri as a twenty-truck convoy, with gun trucks between every fifth vehicle or so, was being loaded with food, water, and ammunition. Someone was asking for volunteers to ride shotgun and Sgt. John Michalak, a twenty-one-year-old Chicago kid, decided that he'd go. At the time, he was a USAF technician temporarily assigned to the TOC at Quang Tri; he was tired of working at his desk in the stifling, windowless bunker and wanted to get out and see what was happening in this big operation they'd been called up for. An Air Force buddy also volunteered and they rode in the seventh truck, a gun truck, sharing the back with four GIs. When the convoy rolled out, the men did not diligently man their guns but slumped in the truck bed to light up. Ah, sweet reefer, Michalak thought, as the soldiers shared their joints; it had been hard to score grass at Quang Tri after their USAF team had moved up, and the only ones who seemed to have any smack were the black GIs, who were not easily approachable. The four soldiers spoke bitterly as they drove along, bitching about the convoys, about just wanting to go home, about the damned weather which either turned the road into a muddy trail or, as on this day, covered them with sweat and caked them with red road dust. Michalak felt sorry for them: Man, they got it rough, always in the field, getting shot at and pushed around by the lifers. Route 9 turned into dirt as they sat talking. The lead of the column disappeared around a bend in the road—and the blast of an RPG suddenly sounded. Michalak popped up to look over the armor plating just as a second RPG exploded against a tree and he caught a spray of wood chips across the front of his flak jacket. He shit his pants and jumped back down as AK-47s cracked from hidden spots in the roadside tangle. The convoy kept moving, gun trucks raking the brush, Michalak getting keyed-up and manning the fifty. He pounded out seventy-five rounds. As they rounded the bend, they could see the result of the first RPG, a truck shoved to the side and burning. The crew scrambled aboard another truck and the shooting petered out as they quickly outdistanced the wreckage, and continued for Khe Sanh.

By '71 the U.S. Marine Corps was practically out of Vietnam. Its small contribution to the Route 9 convoys was C Company, 11th Motor Transport Battalion, III Marine Amphibious Force, detailed to work under the 26th GSG. On 14 February, with the revamping of the assets along the road, another small detachment of marines was committed to the Quang Tri front. This was the Communications Platoon, Headquarters Company, 11th MTB. At least one of the marines, Cpl. Carson C. Bartels, was glad of the prospect to see some action. Bartels, a radioman and jeep driver in the platoon, was a square-jawed, bespectacled twenty-one-year-old from Cedar Falls, Iowa. He'd joined the marines in '68, right out of high school, too young and naive to really care about the issues of the war, but he had been raised with a sense of duty to the nation. He'd also wanted to prove himself. The Marine Corps had seemed like the place to satisfy both urges. He'd already done thirteen months in Vietnam, 1969–70, a hard tour with the 7th Marines south of Da Nang.

After five months of spit-and-shine stateside duty, he had volunteered for a second tour in Vietnam.

For Bartels, his new post with the 11th MTB was nothing but listlessness and hassles. He lived comfortably in a Da Nang basecamp and ran routine convoys on Route 1, an area so secure by then that lone vehicles could leave the perimeter without the security of a convoy and not worry about enemy ambushes. It was a boring routine and Bartels was practically the only man in his platoon with any combat experience. The rear was no luxury to him, with its oppressive heat, smell of diesel and burning dung everywhere, sullen stares between black and white Marines, and a dullness so pervasive that some Marines smoked pot every off-duty day. So, when the word came that they were heading north, Bartels was filled with enthusiasm. No one knew the details, but the prospect of being involved in a major operation in the midst of the withdrawals gave the morale of the marines a boost.

They loaded the commo gear always carried on convoys aboard a command jeep, four trucks, four semi-trailers, and a wrecker. Only a small group was going; a captain, a lieutenant, a gunnery sergeant, and fewer than a dozen enlisted men. They departed Da Nang going north on Route 1, Bartels driving the command jeep with the captain beside him. They tied a bright-orange, waterproof tarp on the roof of the jeep, so a Sea Knight flying above them could keep the convoy easily in sight. The helicopter was in radio contact with Bartels and flew ahead of them, skirting from one side of the road to the other, looking for possible enemy ambushes. There was no shooting. Just a Sunday drive, Bartels thought, par for the course. Route 1 was a modern, two-lane, blacktop highway and mopeds, Citroens, and buses with people clinging all over them zoomed by the Marine column. Villages and cultivated rice paddies flanked the route. The highway skirted the east coast of Vietnam and, off to their right, the marines could sometimes make out the inviting blue shimmer of the South China Sea.

Ten miles out of Da Nang, the villes became fewer and the foilage thicker. A few more miles up Route 1, they neared the Hai Van Pass where the road cut through a jungled mountain. The road began to wind uphill, dropping off sharply to one side, and a few junked vehicles sat rusting in the brush over the edge. Infantrymen from the 1st Marine Division were in bunkered and barbed-wired checkpoints every few hundred yards, situated so that they could make visual contact with the ones on either side. Coming downhill from the pass, the convoy hit the flat hedgerow and paddy country around Camp Eagle. North of Eagle, the highway went straight through Hue City, the old imperial capital of Vietnam. Bartels was amazed; it was a beautiful city with concrete buildings, sidewalks, telephone poles, and even a huge white church in a grove of trees. Crossing the Perfume River on an old French span bridge they passed the Hue Citadel with its eighteenth-century walls and towers.

The country continued to change; fewer civilians, more jungle, and the sight of misty mountains ahead. Bartels had never been so far north and the whole area felt different, like a war was still going on.

Quang Tri City looked like a big shantytown of shacks and markets, beggars, trinket sellers, prostitutes, and pushers. Dong Ha had become a logistical center; it was dusty and noisy, helicopters coming and going from several LZs, crisscrossed with roads, motor pools, aid stations, bunkers, and hootches.

The convoy started rolling on Route 9 and, within a few miles the elephant grass, scrub brush, and rolling hills began rising into jungled mountains. After a few more miles, the road curved south in the direction of Vandegrift. Bartels stared in fascination at the Rockpile; it was like taking a trip back in time, he thought, to places the marines had made famous in the years past. The Vandegrift Combat Base was another eerie sight to Bartels. It had been completely overgrown when the army reopened it after two years of abandonment, but the recent clearing and digging had exposed the old trails and bunkers. Rotted sandbags and abandoned gear was littered in the elephant grass. It was like pulling into a ghost town.

Everything was muddy. Trucks and APCs were parked at random, a few helicopters squatted in makeshift LZs; there were sandbagged culvert bunkers, commo wire stretched atop the mud, some concertina wire thrown up around the stacks of supplies. One of the first things Bartels noticed, as they pulled into Vandegrift, was several tanks ringing the perimeter; they were hidden in the tall grass with sandbags piled around them. Behind them the perimeter was encircled by a single coil of concertina wire and foxholes were dug in along it.

Mountains surrounded Vandegrift, deep green with jungle.

The small marine contingent spent the rest of the day running supplies to Khe Sanh and Lang Vei. At Khe Sanh, Bartels could also see where the old Marine positions had been. They all knew what their fellow Marines had gone through during that famous battle and, at least for Bartels, there was a strong feeling of tradition and pride in those mountains.

Before dark, the platoon returned to Vandegrift. They pulled their trucks side by side in a neat row along the main trail in their little area, and put their personal gear in a small van. They slept in ponchos on the ground.

The protection around them consisted only of some flimsy wire and some unimpressive looking GIs sitting in foxholes. The second lieutenant in charge of the perimeter on their side of the compound appeared to be nineteen or twenty, and seemed to have no idea what was going on nor any real control over his troops. The soldiers themselves looked sloppy. When the sun went down the men in the foxholes kept on talking and smoking. Bartels remembered the field discipline of the marine grunts on his first tour and was amazed at what he was seeing; he could only think the soldiers were poorly trained and inexperienced draftees. The Marines decided they would have to perform their own security. The captain made sure that they all knew where everyone was, in case anything happened during the night, and set up sleeping times so that two men were always on guard.

Bartels had finally fallen asleep when a sudden crash startled him awake. Everyone was yelling. He shook his head, thinking for a second that he was dreaming. An Army truck, barrelling down the road, had rammed into their row of trucks, and now the driver was backing up and smashing into the trucks again. Bartels saw his captain jump up and run to the truck. He grabbed the soldier from behind the wheel, and shook him by the collar, screaming in his face. The GI was high as a kite. In a minute or two, an Army major emerged from a nearby tent and took the stoned soldier away.

In the morning, they moved out from Vandegrift towards Khe Sanh. The country was beautiful. It reminded Bartels of Colorado, with high green mountains stretching as far as you could see. It was misty and cool and sometimes you couldn't see the tops for the fog. The only intrusion into the wilderness was Route 9 and Bartels thought it was a joke to call this narrow dirt path, usually too slim for two trucks to pass easily, a highway. The brush and trees grew right up from the sides of the road, giving the drivers an uneasy, hemmed-in feeling.

A sign had been posted along Route 9, with the Vietnamese translation beneath the English:

KHE GIO TO CALU
FRIENDLY PATROLS
both sides of road
DO NOT RECON BY
FIRE!!

Khe Gio was a large bridge near the Rockpile, and Ca Lu was another name for Vandegrift. Bartels saw only one patrol while driving on Route 9, a line of infantrymen sweeping in the Rockpile flatland. As far as he was concerned, no one was in control between Dong Ha and Lang Vei. Three or four times he heard the muffled pops in the hills along the road, and could see a splash of mud or water. Snipers. The drivers would try to push their trucks faster through the mud. Men on the cab-mounted fifties would join the tank in shooting back, and they would try to outrun the fire. They always made it in one piece.

On that second day, word came that one of the platoon drivers had become so exhausted, he'd fallen asleep at the wheel and run off a steep embankment. The marine was medevacked. The deuce-and-a-half truck had not been destroyed, so the lieutenant and Bartels took the jeep and another marine took the wrecker to go retrieve it. They went first to Dong Ha to pick up an M88 recovery vehicle with seven GIs aboard. Heading west again, they found the crash site just outside Khe Sanh. Bartels found it ironic to be out in the middle of nowhere, with no infantry support, to recover one crashed Marine truck, while along the way they had seen at least six Army trucks, abandoned with only smashed radiators and broken axles. Bartels was not surprised: it seemed to him that the Marines always took better care of their equipment and were able to use what the Army would have replaced.

Bartel's worries were justified. As the retriever winched the truck up, an NVA cut loose with an AK-47, sending Bartels and the rest jumping over the edge of the road. The GI on the retriever fired back on his fifty, evidently cowing the sniper, as they got out with no further problems.

That night the platoon again secured inside the wire at Vandegrift. Around midnight, Bartels was jerked awake by mortar rounds exploding around the base. There were no bunkers for the Marines, so they could just flatten in the grass and mud. Everyone kept low for the minute or two the rounds plopped randomly about; then a lucky shell exploded on the small LZ up from the main camp road. A JP4 fuel bladder went up in a roaring burst of fire and the whole area lit up like daylight.

The next morning, 16 February, the platoon drove to Dong Ha to pick up more supplies. There they were informed that the supply problem for which they had been called up was taken care of and they could return to Da Nang. The Marines were back by lunchtime. Corporal Bartels was glad he'd been able to spend at least those three days and two nights in Operation Lam Son 719.

Others were not coping as well. For Sp4 Carney of the 39th Transportation Battalion, the mud, the cold rain, the rockets and mortars, the shot-up convoys on Route 9 were adding up to destroy him. It just kept up day after day with no break; he couldn't have imagined anything this bad. The worst carnage he saw was when a convoy returned to Vandegrift one morning, after having been hit in a night ambush. Carney had watched the convoy form up hours earlier inside the perimeter at Vandegrift; he'd been feeling strange, depressed and suicidal, and had gone over and said, "Hey, I'll go with you as shotgun." But the battalion sergeant major, an older black man whom the men considered a cool head among the lifers, pulled him to the side. He could see what a wretched state Carney was in; the drugs, violence, the absurdity and waste were falling on him, beating him. On his last run, a sniper had put two rounds in the side of Carney's truck and he hadn't calmed down from that yet. So the sergeant major told him to forget it, to get some rest; and Carney watched the convoy roll out. When it came back, a wrecker was towing the remains of a gun truck which had taken a direct hit. A couple of bodies were laid out in the wreckage. Blood and pieces of flesh were splattered on the metal. Carney felt himself getting sick, felt his bitterness at the lifers grow as he watched them bringing out their cameras.

The good morale that Carney had seen when they first moved out had quickly evaporated. They'd been enthused at the rumor of invading North Vietnam, but were turned off when they saw it was to be an ARVN operation in Laos. They saw it as another useless political battle, and the support troops, who'd rarely even heard a sniper down south, were shocked by the ambushing and horrid driving conditions into which they were thrust. It was all confusion, Carney thought, like some deranged, violent carnival. They were running around like headless chickens. That's how he saw it. Ideas of rebelling against the lifers floated in his head.

As the battalion mail clerk, Carney had another duty which further depressed him: he had to collect the personal effects of the KIAs and ghostwrite the letters to the next of kin for the colonel to sign. During the day, he worked in the command hootch, handling the battalion mail.

At night he pulled perimeter foxhole guard. About three times a week he picked up his M-16 and rode shotgun on the convoys. Once a week he would catch a ride to take the mail to Camp Eagle and Da Nang. He was required to be back at Vandegrift by night and thought catching a helicopter back from Da Nang would be quicker and safer; the battalion commander personally cancelled that idea by telling him, "You're in a transportation unit. You'll go in a truck. Everyone in this unit is going to take the same chances." Fucking colonel, Carney fumed, he's just trying to play the macho trucker, with no practical concern about the safety of his men.

The convoys were bad. He would hitch up with them at Vandegrift, the gun trucks running front and rear of the column. The GIs painted big, elaborate slogans on their gun trucks: DAUGHTER OF DARKNESS, KING KONG, CANNED HEAT, EVE OF DESTRUCTION. A few of the men loved to get out on Route 9 and tear up the countryside with their weapons; some thought they had a job to do, some got stoned as much as they could, and Carney went because he was ordered to. He tried to make most of his convoys with a young mustached buddy named Don. Don was a heroin addict. And if it wasn't the convoys, then just being at Vandegrift was bad. The rockets usually hit at dusk, like clockwork, when the trucks were pulling into the maintenance area and the men were lining up for chow. There was the cold gray silence, the sudden shrieks, the scramble for foxholes, then six or seven explosions; then the silence again until the U.S. artillery batteries at Vandegrift boomed out counterfire.

The nights on the perimeter were a mind-boggling terror to Carney. He was too fragile for war, his nerves constantly on edge. He would sit in his muddy foxhole, holding his uncleaned M-16, and stare out into the black. "All that's out there," he told himself a hundred times, "is some stinking wire—and thousands of Communists. Oh God, they can kill us all any time they want to." He talked to some sentries on the perimeter who said that an NVA sapper, wired down with explosives, had tried to creep through the wire. They'd shot him and the man had exploded. One night it all came too terrifyingly close, when Carney was in the command hootch and the rockets began thudding in. He ran for a culvert bunker, the last rocket exploded; then came the rattle of automatic weapons fire and screams of, "Sappers in the wire!" Carney peered from his bunker and could see the lieutenant colonel standing atop a truck, shouting for his men to organize around him. This dude, he thought, is insane. Satchel charges exploded in one area of the camp.

Carney bolted from his bunker, then saw the grass stir beside him. He didn't know if it was a sapper, the wind, or another GI, but he whirled towards it firing his M-16 on automatic. The filthy weapon jammed and Carney freaked out, making a mad scramble for another bunker. Two soldiers were hunkered inside, staring hotly down their rifle sights into the blackness around them. On the perimeter, truck drivers and clerk-typists fired wildly at shadows while the NVA sappers slid away.

Carney succumbed to the situation and sought his escape through drugs. He was smoking joints for breakfast and drinking obestol to wire himself up for the day. Obestol was like cough syrup, but was really narcotic speed. The speed made it easier to do his work, but prevented him from sleeping when he had a few moments off. Some of the truckers told him that heroin would bring you down, so he began mixing skag and methanol cigarettes. The pot, speed, heroin, and booze were ruining Carney. He did not give a fuck. He got trashed every day, sitting around the motor pool with his buddies, keeping an eye out for the lifers. Shit, he thought, everybody's doing it. They used to laugh about the battalion commander whom no one ever saw asleep. "That lifer is so afraid of getting fragged," they joked, "he's jacked up on speed twenty-four hours a day."

The dope was easy to get, even along the Quang Tri front during the operation. There were few civilians in the area, but along the road, at Dong Ha and Quang Tri, they began to appear: beggars, kids with boxes of trinkets, and the cowboys, Vietnamese teenagers on Hondas, selling dope—sandbags filled with marijuana, vials of heroin, opium, and dew joints machine-rolled and packed in cigarette cartons.

Carney was horrified by it all; he didn't want to die and he didn't want to kill anyone. "You get so fucked up you don't care," he said, "You force yourself into another world." And he was in another world, one which shattered his senses and brought him a deep rage at his government, the lifers, even his own father, whom he blamed for his being in this hellhole. The old man never even used to talk to him; then, nonchalantly, he had threatened to bar Carney from his home if he were to go to Canada. "You don't want me in your house!" Carney had screamed at his father on the day he'd gotten home, "Don't worry, I'm leaving!" They didn't speak again for four years.

The worst convoy Carney ever was in didn't even make contact. There had been shooting along Route 9 during the night, and in the morning there was hesitation about opening the road immediately. The sergeant major wanted him to stay in the compound, but Carney argued that he had to get to Da Nang. They had sent word that they had the DEROS orders for several men in the battalion. Carney knew that one extra day on Route 9 could get them blown away and he wanted to get those orders as soon as possible. The minesweep teams hit the road and Carney sat back to wait, sipping Black Label and smoking joints. Word finally came that the road was clear and his truck headed east. Carney was riding shotgun, Don was driving, and two AWOLs, who wanted to score on the prostitutes and get some dope in Da Nang, sat in the back. All four soldiers were stoned. They were making the windy curves near the Rockpile when they turned another corner, and came upon a truck right ahead of them. It was just sitting there in the cold morning air—on fire, two dead GIs hanging out the doors. Don hit the brake and there was a moment of stunned silence. Carney had a camera on his lap. Without thinking, he raised it and took a photo through the windshield. Then the realization hit. They shouted to each other, "Let's get the fuck outta here!" and Don hauled to the side of the road. They jumped out with their M-16s. The road was hemmed in by a tall wall of elephant grass; they couldn't see a thing. If the truck had hit a mine, they were safe, but if it had been hit by an enemy RPG team, they were in trouble—four guys out in the woods without a radio. They fired blindly into the elephant grass and Carney heaved his four grenades. When the rattle and echo died away, there was only more silence. Two Cobras that had been circling dove in and threw a couple of minigun bursts into the field where they'd been shooting. A moment later, some trucks and a wrecker rumbled up from the direction of Vandegrift, shoved the burning truck out of the way, and they continued on for Da Nang.

From his end of the supply line in a sandbagged tent at Khe Sanh, recently promoted Colonel Rosenblum thought that the truckers were heroes. He watched them come in day and night from perilous road runs, crawl under their trucks to sleep while the supplies were being unloaded; then climb back into their cabs to hit Route 9 again, that being the only sleep they got. They were doing a super job.

Rosenblum worked in tandem with General Smith (ADC for Support, 101st Airborne), getting the trucked-in material to the field via choppers. He also ran the refuel/rearm points. Rosenblum, who had less than two months of logistical experience after an infantry career in Korea and Vietnam, felt that, if ARVN failed, DISCOM would be blamed for not providing sufficient support. So he worked himself and his troops hard, and his four battalions performed well.* The 426th Supply & Service (Lt. Col. Ken Jacobs) handled transportation for DISCOM, manned the refuel/rearm stations, and rigged helicopters with external loads. The 5th Transportation (Lt. Col. William Beasley) performed the maintenance, supply, and repair of the division helicopters, while the 801st Maintenance (Lt. Col. Richard Nidever) maintained all divisional equipment. The 326th Medical (Lt. Col. Robert Day, M.D.) ran the division medevac service.

The biggest task of Rosenblum's list was keeping the refuel/rearm points running at Dong Ha, Mai Loc, Vandegrift, Khe Sanh, and Lang Vei. The delay in building the airfield and the two weeks of convoy problems had kept the 300,000-gallon fuel reserve at Khe Sanh from being up to par, and it was only reached because of a great effort by DISCOM and the 26th GSG with tanker trucks and slingloaded bladders. The choppers worked out of the points all day long, and the tankers came in throughout the night to replenish the fuel supply. It consisted of long hard days for all involved, punctuated by rocket raids; and Rosenblum had an added burden: not only was he responsible for supporting U.S./ARVN units committed to Laos, but at the same time DISCOM had to maintain its services in the entire 101st Airborne AO. His twenty-five-hundred-man force was spread thin. Fortunately, when he asked General Berry for reinforcements, the general had a hundred men straight from the replacement centers given two or three days of training, then had them immediately dispatched to the refuel/rearm points.

Additional supplies reached Khe Sanh via the U.S. Air Force airlift. Shutting down C130 operations in much of South Vietnam and shifting these capabilities to MR1, the 7th USAF brought in an average of five hundred tons per day. The army forklift crews at the airfield (augmented by the U.S. Marines of C Company, 1st Shore Party Battalion, III MAF) unloaded the material from the C130s, which landed about every fifteen minutes on peak days. A record of one thousand tons was recorded one day and, throughout the campaign, 2,734 sorties were flown to bring in

* There was, uncharacteristically, a fragging incident in DISCOM during the operation, in a supply company at Camp Eagle. Someone blew the captain's hootch apart with a claymore mine. The captain miraculously escaped with only shrapnel in his arm. No one was brought to justice for the attempted murder although three angry soldiers, who had been transferred to the rear for being troublesome in their infantry units, were suspect.

28,333 tons of cargo. Enemy fire was not a problem to the C130s; during the '68 siege, shellings prevented the large planes from ever fully stopping, but in '71, a half-dozen of these craft could be seen waiting along the strip at nearly any given time. There were difficulties, however. The secondary assault runway was opened to C130 traffic on 15 February, but the main strip was not finished until 1 March. Then, eight days later, a C130 lost its landing gear and tore up seventeen hundred feet of runway. It was not repaired until 21 March, and logistical support suffered accordingly.

Despite the occasional snafus, the logistical lifeline usually flowed unabated. Konopnicki and Rosenblum were a good team, and they joked amongst themselves, "This is either a logistical nightmare, or the greatest logistical effort that the U.S. Army has made in years." They knew the answer to that question. Major Klose of the 223d CAB saw Rosenblum and the 101st DISCOM in action at Khe Sanh; the helicopter pilots had a saying: "Go haul two for Rosie," which meant that whenever you had free time, to bring two slingloaded blivets of fuel to Colonel Rosenblum. The aviators loved him. He kept them flying.

CHAPTER TWELVE:
The First Regiment of Dragoons

For the men of A Troop, 1st Squadron, 1st Cavalry, the month of February 1971 had been hit and miss. When they patrolled Route 9 to secure engineer teams, nothing happened, but when they pulled perimeter security for the artillery, they got shelled. The worst came towards the end of the month when they moved into the bush south of Lang Vei. "It was Bad, Bad, Bad," Sergeant Keefer wrote home. They were to spend five weeks in the area. The troop commander, Captain Pierson, split the unit up, each platoon assigned a different position from which to conduct patrols. First Platoon was dispatched to a grassy knoll called Hill 400, a miserable place, freezing, muddy, and watersoaked when the rain clouds rolled over; a parched and brittle oven when the sun came out. There was no water to spare on washing and before long, the grunts were unshaven and grubby, their fatigues and skin worn to the colors of the earth.

The top of Hill 400 was ground to dust when the Sheridans and APCs moved in, and it became a garbage pile of poncho shelters, dead grass, discarded C rats, and more GI battle junk. The elephant grass was above their heads at the edge of the perimeter; the dozen tanks and tracks of the platoon were parked in a circle amongst the tangle, weapons trained downhill. Hill 400 was only a bump among the rolling hills that made up the whole area around Lang Vei, the hills rising and dipping, branching off in fingers, the mountains of Laos rising to the west and forming the horizon. The tops of most valleys were thick with clutching brambles where nothing could be seen.

Hill 400 was worst when it was dark. "Night time rolling around again," Keefer wrote home. "We got where we hated to see it come. Because with it we knew the sappers with RPG's and satchel charges would come. And the nights got so cold and lonely." When the sun went down behind the Laotian mountains, the fog rolled in so only the crests could be seen, like islands in a moor. Sergeant Keefer assigned four men to be awake at all times, one at each compass point; and they sat atop their tracks in helmets and flak jackets, the fifties' butterfly handles before them, staring into the settled gray mist. The fear of sappers kept the men awake during the first part of their two-hour watches, but then exhaustion set in. You patrol all day, catch RPGs both night and day, the mind clouds, and before long you are so tired you don't give a damn. When Keefer checked the perimeter at night, he was frightened when he found men asleep at their posts. After finding three guards out of four asleep one night, he assembled the platoon and told them he wasn't going to have any more of that. The next night, Keefer was pulling guard when his buddy, Sgt. Robert Greene, was suddenly shaking him awake, muttering, "What kind of example are you setting?" It was two in the morning, and Keefer was shocked; the last thing he remembered was sitting there, staring over the gun shield at the night sky, concentrating on staying awake. Finally, every night, Keefer had the platoon pull a Mad Minute, firing all the weapons and chucking hand frags around outside their circle, as much to deter NVA sappers as to wake guards up. There was no doubt in his mind that on some nights the entire platoon was asleep atop that hill.

During the day, Keefer got his platoon missions from Captain Pierson via the radio from his position in the hills, and the platoon would mount out. Their patrols were aimed at rooting out the NVA harassing Route 9. They rarely found anything. Sometimes they would bust jungle, the vehicles actually rising up in the face of the brush before crashing down and ploughing through. Making dismounted foot patrols through the mashed areas, they found numerous bunkers and tunnels underneath the crushed foliage, and would harass each hole with a couple of M-16 bursts and hand frags. There was no way, with their limited resources, to get at the bunker networks.

On rare occasions, the platoon added a few North Vietnamese soldiers to the operation's body count.

Weather and resupply were among the many problems plaguing Sergeant Keefer's platoon on Hill 400. It rained a lot, a cold northern rain that combined with the cool night air to shock him. He couldn't believe that in Nam he could actually see steam on his breath. The platoon was ill-prepared for the weather; they had few jackets and blankets to begin with, and were forced to wear the same soaking wet fatigues day after day. On some nights, Keefer watched with pity as young GIs curled up miserably against the cold, teeth chattering, crying from the numbing pain. When the rains came, the engineer trails clogged with mud, helicopter support was hampered, and its priority was for the ARVN in Laos. The platoon did without C rations and water, ran short of trip flares, M-79 rounds, tank rounds, mortar rounds, and track blocks. When it rained, they held their plastic canteens under leaves to catch the runoff. When they found NVA rice, they kept it for themselves.

The recruiting posters called it the New Action Army. Keefer jeered; they can't even keep their combat troops supplied. They just don't give a fuck, he thought. What sustained Keefer were his friends; some deep sense of patriotism, which he never lost; and the feeling that he was good. Back home he was just another aimless dropout punk, who had been a constant problem for his widowed mother. In Nam he was a sergeant of infantry who knew enough about the bush to keep his people alive. It was the first positive thing he'd done in his life, and he was proud. In the jungle, he felt like a man.

He turned down his R&R to stay with the platoon.

One day, as usual, the platoon was low on water and C rations, and Keefer got so fed up he took matters into his own hands. He and his friend, a black kid, Pfc Larry Robinson, decided to drive cross-country to Route 9, try to scrounge some supplies off the convoys on the road, then hustle back before Captain Pierson radioed in and discovered they were gone. Keefer, Robinson, and two other GIs left Hill 400 in the mortar track, Keefer driving because his regular delta, Pfc Ester Wolf, was on R&R. Not knowing if the replacement was experienced, Keefer bumped him from the drivers hatch. It didn't matter. Six hundred yards out, as they were busting jungle down a steep hill, they threw a track and the APC ground to a halt. They jumped off; the bush around them was almost suffocating, reaching maybe thirty feet up, even arching down onto the crippled vehicle.

Night was falling and there was no time for help to come before morning. They prepared for a bad night, and counted up their resources: 500 rounds of M-16 ammo, twenty hand frags, and one smoke grenade. They had eighteen hundred rounds for the fifty but, with the APC stuck going downhill, the barrel was aimed at the ground. They also had the 81mm mortar mounted inside the crew hatch of the APC, but it too was now pointed at an odd angle and the overhead foliage prevented its use. It was a stomach-churning night, the four of them sitting silently in the pitch black in the thick jungle, just waiting for the NVA to creep up and slaughter them.

The night passed without incident.

In the morning, the squadron commander, Lt. Col. Sheldon Burnett, flew to Alpha Troop's command post in his C&C Loach. Typical, Keefer thought, we need a dozer to cut us a path out of this tangle and they send us a colonel. The CO departed shortly and a bit later Captain Pierson arrived at the downed track. An engineer dozer began ploughing a zigzag path up the steep slope. Pierson chewed Keefer out for taking such a chance against orders; then a bigger source of irritation, Burnett's visit, welled up and he muttered, "You ain't going to believe this. The colonel told us that you all needed haircuts and baths so bad that he's going to send his own personal barber out to the field when he gets back to battalion headquarters."

Keefer, Robinson, and the other two GIs who'd sweated out the night looked at each other, mumbling, "Great, just what we need to hear."

North Vietnamese artillery was erupting near the platoon, and the tracks vibrated from the rumble. Keefer jumped into an APC and slammed the cargo hatch shut. Only the platoon medic, a tall and thin soldier called Doc Slim, was inside. Keefer flipped on the red lights and was shocked to see Slim sitting like a statue, drained and crying. Slim never held back in the bush, but the shellings were eating at him, and he pleaded with Keefer, "I just can't take it any more. . . . You gotta send me in."

"Nobody could call anybody a better friend," Keefer said, "but I can't send you in. We wouldn't have a medic if I sent you back."

"Look, you've seen more wounded than I have. You can do everything that I can. You can take care of things."

"Yeah, you're right, I can take care of the guys. But that's your job. I hate being platoon sergeant, but I was the best man for the job. I'm going to have to make sure that as many of these guys get home as I can. If I send you back, Slim, and we get in some heavy contact and somebody gets wounded, I can't leave my command track to go help 'em out. They're all counting on you for that. They're your friends. If I sent you back and we hit some heavy shit, and lost some guys that were close to you, could you take that home with you? You'd always wonder if it could have been different if you would've been there, if you could have helped out."

Doc Slim mustered a small grin, "Yeah, you're right. . . . I don't know what I'm thinking of. Thanks, Keef, I appreciate you telling me that."

"You'd have told me the same thing. And this talk did me as much good as it did you, 'cause I've been feeling the same way you have."

On the afternoon of 4 March, a platoon from Alpha Troop was hit by RPG and AK-47 fire; a Sheridan and APC were reported destroyed, eight GIs wounded. There were no reported enemy casualties. You sit in a position long enough, Keefer knew, and the NVA will map you out and kill you with sappers and ambushes. The only way to prevent this was to disrupt them before they started; he decided to take a night ambush patrol down Hill 400 at dusk to see if the North Vietnamese were moving on them.

Five men volunteered to go with him and they pushed out into the dark night at half past eight, filing wordlessly through the elephant grass of Hill 400. They began crawling slowly through the tangled bramble at the base of the hill, taking an hour and a half to move eight hundred yards, then settling into their ambush position on one of the engineer trails in the jungle.

After an endless wait, they saw lights moving through the brush.

Flashlights: Keefer counted five of them. A North Vietnamese patrol was moving on the path, brashly carrying flashlights in the pitch black jungle, confident that no Americans would actually be out this late. Keefer estimated that there were fifteen NVA walking towards them. He got on the radio to Captain Pierson who turned him over to Sgt. Neil Whipple. Whipple handled the troop's 81mm mortar section, and he was good. The night was still, black, and hushed when the thunks of mortar rounds leaving their tubes echoed softly in the calm. Then the rounds arched down from the sky and erupted in a thunderclap of shrapnel. Several flashlights spun wildly in the air. Got 'em! Keefer was elated. Blew away at least five or six of them!

He moved cautiously down the trail towards the impact area to check it out, but an unseen NVA threw a grenade at him. It exploded nearby and he scrambled back to the patrol, pulling them back to Hill 400. Back on the radio, he had Sergeant Whipple put a heavy concentration of 81mm fire on the trail. When the mortar fire lifted, Keefer wanted to scout for bodies and further NVA movement. Robinson, Wolf, and two other grunts volunteered to go with him. They were wading through the elephant grass on the hillside when Keefer got nervous. The farther they went into the black, the more convinced he became that the NVA would be waiting in ambush this time. He only had four men with him. Two hundred yards out, he turned the patrol around, leaving the body count and possible ambushing to the imagination.

At first light, Keefer had the platoon mount up to sweep the ambush site, leaving only a couple of tracks atop Hill 400. It was still cool and foggy in the valley, the sun gray behind clouds. They halted where the jungle grew thick, and fanned out on line. Keefer prepared a squad-sized patrol to move into the brush with the help of Sgt. Randall Hughes, an older family man from Tennessee. Hughes was both a new guy and a lifer, but Keefer thought he was one of the best men in the platoon. When Hughes had first arrived, they'd already been on the Laos border and he'd told Keefer, "Look, it's your platoon and you're running it. You know what the hell's going on. Just ignore the fact that I got an extra stripe. You keep me posted on what's going on, and show me what I'm going to need to know to take care of these men."

The vehicles were still getting organized, when the patrol moved out, Keefer on point, Hughes walking slack. Keefer was impressed; most lifer sergeants he knew wouldn't even accompany the patrol, let alone walk slack. They had only gone a short distance down slope, when Hughes tugged at the back of Keefer's shirt. "Wait a minute, Sergeant Keefer, let me take point." The patrol paused amid the brush and Hughes put a hand on Keefer's shoulder, pulling him back a bit. "You took out the patrol last night. Let me take point, it's only fair." They were side by side, Hughes walking forward; then Keefer saw the flash of movement out of the corner of his eye. To their left, the crack of explosions and the smoke of back-blast was followed in the next second by two RPGs exploding at their feet. Keefer was propelled backwards, the concussion slamming into him like a baseball bat on the bridge of his nose, a burst of lights before his eyes. He could feel himself falling backwards, dazed, then, crashing down hard into the bushes. He landed on his back, the wind knocked out of him. Then he realized everything was quiet and, gasping for breath, screamed out for the patrol to fire. He snapped back from the concussion, could see nothing but bushes and hanging vines around him; then he realized Staff Sergeant Hughes was lying beside him, still in the grass, blood running from his ears, nose, and from a wound in the side of his head. He looked dead and Keefer felt sick. He screamed for the medic.

Robinson was the first to scramble down beside him. Keefer lay quietly, still coming out of shock, suddenly aware of the hot shrapnel in his face, chest, and arm. The left side of his body had been peppered. More men moved forward along with Doc Rose, a red-haired kid who'd come in as a replacement when Doc Slim had rotated home. They helped Keefer and Hughes stumble back; Robinson came out last, covering their retreat.

Cranking up to return to Hill 400, Ollie told Keefer that Doc Rose had tried to hide when the shooting had started and had only gotten moving when Ollie'd prodded him with his M-16. Sorry bastard, Keefer thought; the new medic had been a slacker since he'd arrived, a smartass with a chip on his shoulder.

Pulling to the top of Hill 400, they found that another Alpha platoon had moved in; they'd captured two North Vietnamese and had moved to the hilltop to call in a helicopter for them. The two NVA sat in some lawn chairs, untied, both of them barefoot and wearing fatigues, glancing around uncomfortably. Keefer was surprised to find a third injured GI on the hill. His nickname was Yo-Yo and he'd been run over by an APC. Typical, Keefer thought; his nickname told it all. He was a California hippie who couldn't figure out the first thing about the infantry. When the RPG ambush had been sprung, a driver had backed up his APC to find a better vantage point to give support fire, running over Yo-Yo's legs in the process.

He lay on a stretcher, shot up with morphine, but still in pain. Keefer sat beside him and Yo-Yo asked how the old staff sergeant was doing. Keefer said it looked bad, that Robinson had told him Hughes was bleeding from multiple head wounds and might lose an eye.

Hughes was led over and sat down. Yo-Yo looked over and said, "Oh, man, I'm sorry to hear you're going to lose your eyesight."

Keefer looked at him sharply—you never tell a man he's hit badly, it might send him into shock. "For two cents," he snapped, "I'd knock your teeth out."

Hughes was levelheaded; he ignored them.

Keefer and Hughes shrugged off Doc Rose, so he squatted beside them filling out their WIA tags. The other platoon's medic worked on them, taking off their tattered shirts and tying bandages around their wounds as they stood behind an APC, grunts snapping photographs. Hughes calmly smoked a cigarette as he was being bandaged; Keefer ducked back into his track to retrieve a prized possession that he wasn't going to let out of his sight—the photo album from his first tour, wrapped in plastic. The NVA prisoners sat a few feet away. Cold wind swept the hill. The mountains were shrouded by fog.

Keefer drank from a canteen as he waited for the medevac, and cursed himself for getting wounded. It was stupid; the NVA knew the U.S.

troops always ran body-count patrols after contacts, and he shouldn't have been so confident when he walked into the brush. They hadn't even gotten the tanks and tracks organized to give effective fire support before he took the patrol out. He figured that NVA, wounded in the mortar ambush and unable to limp away, had probably caught them with the RPGs. A single Huey finally flew into Hill 400. Robinson and another grunt rushed forward under the slapping blades with Yo-Yo's stretcher, and slid him into the cabin. Then Robinson darted around the nose of the chopper to help Keefer and Hughes aboard. Finally they were up and gone.

The phantom war continued. The same night that Alpha hit the NVA with mortars from Hill 400, North Vietnamese sappers hit Bravo Troop with RPGs and satchel charges. Bravo reported two dead, thirteen wounded, a Sheridan and an APC destroyed—but no NVA bodies found. Seventeen hours later, at 2000 hours on 5 March, an Alpha ambush team led by a black lieutenant had fifteen NVA walk into the kill zone of their MAs. The jungle resounded with blasts and screams, and the tally was eight North Vietnamese killed, four weapons captured.

The grunts of the 1st Battalion, 11th Infantry had been sharing the travails of the 1/1 Cav along the Laotian border and Route 9, working in tandem with the armor to keep infiltrating teams of NVA sappers and artillery forward observers away from the highway supply line. The only way effectively to accomplish this mission was to get in the jungle with the enemy, to hump, sweat, and search (and often to succumb to frustration because most patrols produced nothing).

The battalion's Alpha Company, under Captain Bodenhorn, shared this jungle experience; their exception, though, was that they had been placed opcon to the 1/1 Cav. It was from Lieutenant Colonel Burnett that Bodenhorn took his orders and received his resupply. Alpha Company first made solid contact at the beginning of March. The first was when the second squad of Second Platoon, patrolling off a trail they'd located, surprised two North Vietnamese soldiers. They killed them both. The next day, a claymore ambush reaped a bloody harvest—seven dead NVA from an artillery observation party. Bodenhorn ordered the mangled corpses searched and the GIs found maps which showed both U.S. artillery firebases on the border and the NVA mountain artillery positions in Laos. They were packed aboard a chopper for Lieutenant Colonel Burnett.

The next few days of patrols went anxiously, but quietly. On 7 March, the Second Platoon and Captain Bodenhorn's command group patrolled all night, then moved out for another NDP and began digging in at around two in the afternoon. Bodenhorn sat in the grass and checked his platoons on the map: he and Second were about four klicks north of Route 9; First, about two klicks west of them; Third, a scant klick from Laos; and Weapons was dug in along the highway. Around him the GIs had dropped their helmets and rucks and were sweating in the hot afternoon, digging foxholes and hacking at the thick underbrush with machetes to clear fields of fire.

That afternoon Lieutenant McConnell and Third Platoon were NDP'd atop a small hill. The platoon RTO, Sp4 Mike Castro, was a Mexican-American from Arizona who had had to leave his pregnant wife when the draft notice had come. He just wanted to do his time and go home, but somehow Castro couldn't extinguish an ember of pride from serving with Alpha Company; he never touched drugs, and was impressed by the leadership of Bodenhorn and McConnell and the camaraderie of the platoon.

Lieutenant McConnell heard noises in the valley below their hill, and told Castro to call in artillery fire. After it lifted, they moved out to search the area, and found abandoned NVA spider holes deep in the brush. They followed the line of dugouts up another small hill, until the footpath branched. A sergeant took a squad down that fork while the rest continued on, McConnell and Castro right behind the point and slack men. The chilling crack of AK-47s erupted from the direction of the sergeant's squad, answered by M-16s.

Then they too were caught in the ambush.

A volley of AKs tore into them. The slack man was hit, and McConnell was flung back into Castro's arms, a bullet through his neck. They tumbled into an NVA dugout, the radio harness painfully wrenching Castro's back. The North Vietnamese began moving around their flanks, and Castro alternated between his PRC25 radio and M-16 rifle. He emptied twenty magazines into the underbrush. Support fire was denied because the NVA were too close; he screamed for a medevac. They began pulling back before the NVA could box them off, crawling away one at a time, shooting continuously. Castro and three grunts grabbed McConnell and, as the fire kept slashing around them, they ran, crawled, fired back, kept dragging the wounded lieutenant. Their frantic tugs and the thorny bramble tore McConnell's clothes off. Cobras finally roared in behind them, covering their retreat, and a medevac beat overhead.

At the company command post, Bodenhorn was still watching his men dig in when his senior RTO got off the radio and said Third Platoon was in heavy contact.

Captain Bodenhorn relayed the information to Lieutenant Colonel Burnett, and requested an immediate helicopter so he could be dropped off at the platoon CP and work his way down to his men in the ambush. Burnett replied that he would be en route in ten minutes. Bodenhorn checked his M-16, and his .45 side arm; he hung more grenades on his web gear, and slung a LAW rocket over his shoulder. Figuring the colonel would arrive in a Huey slick which would accommodate several people, Bodenhorn picked three others to go with him: his senior RTO, the company forward observer, and an infantryman with an M-79 for security. They waited at their makeshift jungle LZ, and the C&C came in for a landing. It was a Kiowa Scout from the 5th Mech which seated four people max and already had three people in it, WO Randolf J. Ard in the left pilot seat, Burnett beside him, and the squadron sergeant major in the back seat. Bodenhorn walked to the front of the helicopter, hunched under the blades, and held up his green memo pad for Ard to see. On it he had written frequencies, call signs, and coordinates of the Third Platoon CP and a guess at where the contact was.

The sergeant major hopped out to allow two passengers in the back seat, and Bodenhorn climbed in behind Burnett, lugging a radio with the company and squadron frequencies. His forward observer, Lt. Jerry Castillo, boarded the seat behind Ard, also carrying a radio but one with the freqs for the fire support channels. As they lifted off, Bodenhorn noticed that, while Burnett and Ard were plugged into helmet radios, there were no headsets for him and Castillo.

They could not communicate with the pilot or the colonel.

The Third Platoon ambush should have been a short, four-kilometer hop to the northwest, and Bodenhorn peered through the Plexiglas window, expecting to see smoke or movement. But there was nothing, and the helicopter seemed to be sailing due west. He could not hear what Burnett or Ard were saying over the radio, had no idea why they were going off course, and before long it was obvious that they'd headed west too long.

They had crossed the Laotian border.

The Kiowa Scout suddenly dropped from two hundred to seventy-five feet, slowing down over the green hills, and Bodenhorn looked out the window over Ard's shoulder to see yellow smoke rising from the ground. He quickly keyed the radio to Third Platoon and asked if they had popped smoke.

The man on the radio said they had no smoke out.

Bodenhorn lunged from his seat, frantically grabbed Ard's shoulder, and shook him, screaming over the turbines that his platoon had not popped smoke—just as the staccato sound of an RPD machine gun and AK-47s cut loose. Bodenhorn glanced out the side door to see a group of North Vietnamese below. They were clear as day, firing from a brushy hill. Rounds came from two sides, tearing through the tailboom and engine. They were going down fast, Bodenhorn losing his balance. They smashed into the brush in a metal-crunching screech, coming down hard on the right side of the bird and tumbling.

Bodenhorn was the first to wake up, slouched in his seat. The helicopter was nestled upright in some thick grass and brush, the foliage high enough to conceal the crash site. Everything had stopped moving; nothing was on fire. He moved slowly—felt pain. His right eye was bruised shut, his left eye gashed and bleeding badly, impairing his vision, his face was cut and his shoulder dislocated. His M-16 was gone. God, he thought, what a screw up. For who knows what reason, they had flown past the platoon ambush, crossed into Laos, and the NVA had suckered them down with a false smoke marking. The correct procedure for marking a ground position with smoke grenades called for the commander in the air to order his ground element to pop smoke, whereupon he would identify the color he saw, get a confirmation and only then come in to land. This was designed precisely to prevent the enemy from listening to the U.S. radio frequencies and luring helicopters with captured smoke grenades. Either Ard or Burnett had violated procedure and now, as a result, they were crashed and cut off. Bodenhorn could understand such a mistake from a young pilot like Ard—he'd heard he'd only been in-country a few weeks—but not from a supposedly experienced cavalry lieutenant colonel.

Bodenhorn struggled out the door, then slowly pushed through the brush to the pilot's door. He pulled Ard from his seat, but both of his legs were pinned under the crushed instrument panel, and he lay awkwardly on the ground, his feet pinched up inside the open door. The young pilot was injured, but still coherent, relatively calm, and when Bodenhorn handed him his mayday radio, he got on it. Bodenhorn then waded back to the colonel's side. Burnett was in a bad way, the force of the crash having collapsed the panel, door, seat, and having crushed metal around him. He was encapsulated and it would take metal-cutting tools and several hours to get him out.

Lieutenant Castillo had been hurled in the crash and lay pinned under the wreck, badly bruised, ribs cracked, an arm broken and a shoulder wrenched. Bodenhorn pressed his one good shoulder to the tailboom, and shoved with his legs, allowing Castillo to roll his legs out from under. He checked on Castillo, who was hurt but hanging tough, then went back to Ard and took the .45 from his holster. He thrashed around in the brush for their M-16s, and finally tossed Castillo's brand-new rifle to him. Then he found his own in the grass, both handgrips knocked off and the pistolgrip broken. He was very nervous about whether it would work or not.

They'd been on the ground for fifteen minutes. Burnett was stuck in the crash, Ard was lying half on the ground and whispering into his radio, Bodenhorn and Castillo were leaning against the bird on Burnett's side, trying to raise anyone on the squadron, battalion, and company radio nets. The NVA who had shot them down from the adjacent hill must be looking for them, Bodenhorn realized, and it was becoming painfully clear that, if they had to run, there was no way to take Burnett or Ard with them. He was thinking it over, when they heard the voices of at least six Vietnamese coming downhill, breaking brush towards them. As they got closer, the machine gun atop the hill and a couple of NVA with AKs reconned by fire, not spraying, but walking lines ahead of them in the brush. It was erratic, but Bodenhorn froze, heart pounding as bullets cracked past fifteen feet away.

Five yards away, there were more voices. He heard two Vietnamese talking back and forth, walking towards them, pushing through the brush with their rifles. He and Castillo grabbed their M-16s, rolled over in the tall grass, and aimed at the sounds. Footsteps crunched twigs; then an AK barrel parted the grass beside the front of the helicopter and two NVA appeared. They peered at the wreckage, freeze-framed for a moment in Bodenhorn's rifle sights: khaki fatigues, khaki pith helmets, AK-47s.

Lieutenant Castillo fired. His rifle jammed.

Captain Bodenhorn opened up with his broken M-16, dropping both North Vietnamese soldiers from nine feet.

With the rifle burst, the NVA moved quickly. More voices and thrashing came down the hill. The volleys of AK fire slashed closer; Bodenhorn thought they were trying to get them to open fire again and give away their positions. He held his fire. It didn't matter. The first Chicom stick grenade sailed from the brush, bounced off of the helo, and dropped in Castillo's lap as he leaned weakly against the wreck. He managed to flip it away with his good arm just before it exploded.

Another frag was lobbed over the helo and boomed in the brush. The third Chicom bounced off of the helicopter, hit Bodenhorn's leg, and rolled six feet from him. He painfully curled into a tight ball to shield himself, and the explosion sent a two-inch chunk of shrapnel ripping into his inner thigh. Bodenhorn threw two grenades into the brush from where the stick grenades had come.

The NVA stopped lobbing grenades.

Overhead a single UH1C gunship appeared, overflew them, then took a heavy barrage from the hillock. The Huey flew on, Bodenhorn figuring that they must have been short of ammunition, or that the NVA fire was too intense, but convinced that the pilot had seen them. Realizing that the NVA machine gun could prevent a ground team from being inserted to rescue them, Bodenhorn armed his LAW rocket. He held it over his head, took a guess at the NVA position, and squeezed the firing button. The 66mm shell flashed from the tube, exploding in the brush over a hundred yards away. The machine gun fell silent. Bodenhorn figured that only by a fluke could he have actually hit the target, but he hoped the NVA might have been fooled into thinking that other troops were in the area so they would break down their weapon and retreat to a safer location.

He searched the sky for rescue helicopters. It was a clear, cloudless afternoon. No one was in sight.

They'd been on the ground for forty minutes, the sun was setting, no support was apparent. More NVA could be heard coming down the hill, then splitting to break bush on both sides of the crash site. Bodenhorn could hear them to the front, to the right, to the left. In a few minutes they would be surrounded, then captured or killed. This was it, he thought, they had to escape and evade. Only he and Castillo could walk, and only then by supporting one another. Burnett and Ard were hopelessly pinned in the wreck. Bodenhorn felt a sudden sense of ease when he made the decision to abandon them. He rationalized that it was logical, trying to maintain his self-control. He limped over to Sheldon Burnett and pulled the radio code book from his pocket; he still could see no major wounds, but the colonel was fading in and out of consciousness, and there was nothing to say to him. Bodenhorn kneeled beside Ard and told him they were taking off for the south and he was sorry, but there was no way to free him from the wreck. Randy Ard nodded, saying nothing.

Bodenhorn glanced guiltily at the two dead North Vietnamese sprawled in the grass a few feet away. He realized that by killing them he had probably signed the death warrant for the two men he was leaving behind.

Captain Bodenhorn and Lieutenant Castillo departed fifty minutes after the crash. They crawled through the brushy tangle, an excruciating struggle in their condition, Bodenhorn practically blind, his one good eye slowly closing. As they were leaving, they heard voices converge on the crash site and then the banging of metal, as if the NVA were rapping the helicopter with their rifles. They were eighty yards away when another UH1C gunship came in on a single gun run, firing flechette rockets. They seemed to explode right on the downed bird. As it got darker, they watched another aircraft come in, an F4 rolling in for a one-bomb airstrike. The Phantom screamed into a low pass, slicing over the crash site and hill, a two-hundred-fifty-pound bomb exploding in its wake.

Bodenhorn and Castillo hobbled through streambeds and down thin trails in the Laotian jungle, moving generally south, figuring they would have to hide out during the night, and hoping they could find Route 9 in the morning. They splashed down one stream, Bodenhorn smearing blood from his face on the leaves and boughs; then they retraced their steps and continued down another creek. Forty-five minutes after retreating, on a dirt trail, they heard people coming down it towards them. Bodenhorn and Castillo wearily looked at each other, too exhausted to run, no place to hide. They got down in the grass, Castillo clutching his .45, Bodenhorn raising his battered M-16. A Vietnamese came down the trail, point man of the patrol, wearing a GI steel pot and carrying an M-16.

Bodenhorn recognized the ARVN airborne patch on his sleeve.

The South Vietnamese escorted them for an hour down the trail to Route 9, then lifted them into a truck. They were driven to LZ Bravo, about six kilometers inside Laos astride the highway, the Laotian home of the 11th Airborne Battalion. It consisted mostly of sandbagged mortar pits. The ARVN medics worked on them and that night, Bodenhorn was put on the radio to the battalion's advisor in Vietnam. He gave his initial report and the advisor said a medevac would come in the next morning.

At seven A.M., 8 March, as a Huey landed at the post's makeshift LZ, the ARVN carried Bodenhorn and Castillo from the medical bunker on stretchers. The helicopter took them to B Medical Company, 75th Support Battalion, 5th Division on the Khe Sanh strip, then to the 18th Surg at Quang Tri. Bodenhorn saw Lieutenant McConnell there, a bandage around his neck, only able to wave due to the damage done to his throat. From there Bodenhorn followed the standard evacuation chain to Da

Nang, then to Camp Zama, in Japan, the William Beaumont Hospital in El Paso, Texas, and finally to outpatient rehabilitation at Letterman Army Hospital in San Francisco. Later some of his grunts visited him in the hospital. They said that, when news of the crash reached the CP and Second Platoon, the platoon leader didn't have a chance to give an order before the men were slinging on their gear, expecting to be CA'd into the crash site. It was the only gratifying note for the most wretched day of Phil Bodenhorn's life.

Lieutenant Colonel Burnett and Warrant Officer Ard were declared missing in action. Command of the 1/1 Cav passed to Lt. Col. Gene L. Breeding, who had been a classmate of Burnett at West Point. Three days after the action, the story was released to reporters at Khe Sanh. The army spokesman accurately described the NVA ambush, but mistakenly told the press that Burnett had had radio contact with the soldiers on the ground and that he and Ard had been seriously wounded and appeared dead to the two officers who had escaped. The names of the survivors were not released, so the press could not follow up on the story.

The presumed death of a squadron commander was met with dispassion by General Sutherland, who was informed of it by General Hill the next day. He said, "For a reason which I don't recall the decision was not made to employ the Air Cavalry and the Hoc Bao to attempt to retrieve either Lieutenant Colonel Burnett alive or his body.* . . . Burnett had no mission nor units in Laos. He had no reason or authority to take his helicopter over the Laotian border."

Most of the grunts in Burnett's squadron were not sorry to see him go. Sergeant Keefer offered a profane eulogy, "The colonel finally got what he was looking for. I think he was looking for the glory of dying in combat. I hate to say that, but to me he got just what the fuck he deserved."

A couple of days after being wounded, Keefer had his wounds cleaned and was on his way back to his platoon aboard a resupply Chinook. A new lieutenant and staff sergeant were also choppered to Hill 400 to take over First Platoon; "Got a new first lieutenant today," Keefer jotted in his diary. "Don't look like he'll be too good." Perhaps the officer didn't like Keefer's hippie appearance or didn't want to take advice from an

* That day they were successfully rescuing, under heavy fire, seven downed crewmen of the 174th AHC from the vicinity of LZ Sophia Two. That was a major ARVN success story, the tough Hoc Bao killing sixty NVA and rescuing all of the Americans.

unschooled kid, but he cut it with Keefer when he told him, "You've been running things your way. Now I'm here and I'm going to run them my way. Now I'm going to show you the right way to run things."

This guy was another lifer, Keefer thought, disgusted, another Regular Army—Regular Asshole. He was bothered most that the lieutenant seemed to be playing a kind of popularity contest with the platoon. Night patrols were scary, but they kept the NVA off balance, and Keefer had run several and wanted them to continue. The new platoon leader called them off, much to the chagrin of Keefer, who thought that this would give the edge to the North Vietnamese; he was also upset that the slackers seemed to step right up and embrace the new lieutenant, making him feel good but eroding the field discipline of the platoon.

The lieutenant lasted a week.

They were sitting atop Hill 400, some of the men lighting C4 to keep warm, dry out clothes, and heat up some C rats and coffee. At dusk Keefer felt the old nervousness creep in; the NVA liked to hit at twilight, firing a couple of RPGs when there was still enough light to see by and knowing they could escape because by the time the Americans got organized and cranked up their tracks to pursue it would be dark. To chase into the jungle at night was to invite ambush and chaos. Keefer shouted at the GIs on his side of the perimeter to put out the fires, lest the NVA use them to sight in on. A few moments passed and he could see the new lieutenant and maybe ten men warming themselves around a fire built beside the command track in the middle of the laager.

Keefer wearily mumbled to Robinson beside him, "C'mon, Larry, I guess we better go over and educate this guy on some of the finer points here."

They ambled across the hill. "Sir, you better have your men put out them fires over there. It's just about time the enemy's going to be hitting us soon. They'll use them fires to zero in on us."

The lieutenant bristled at this challenge to his authority. He locked eyes with Keefer. "I don't need you minding my business. Mind your own business. I know what I'm doing. You and Robinson go on back over to your side of the laager."

The GIs around the fire laughed. Idiots, Keefer thought.

"All right," he said, "but I suggest you put them fires out."

Sp4 Ron Smith, sitting in the back of the command track with Doc Rose, was amused to see his buddy Keefer piss off the lieutenant again. He was relaxed, listening to a Carpenters tape on his cassette player—then an RPG cracked from a neighboring hillock. Smith stared, shocked at the projectile lobbing towards them. Keefer and Robinson were screaming to get down, but the lieutenant stood bewildered. Smith saw the RPG hit. It seemed to explode right on the lieutenant's leg, and he spun around like a top, then collapsed with a shuddering scream. Doc Rose poked his head out the door to look, then started backing up but Smith booted him out with a kick to the ass. Rose fell out and went flat as more RPGs shrieked up the hill. Men on the perimeter were putting down bursts from their fifties, while Keefer and Robinson ran back and dragged the lieutenant to cover in the back of an APC. Ain't been here long enough, Keefer thought as they helped the sobbing man, to know that hit the dirt means hit the dirt.

Doc Rose went to work on him in the track and, in the glow of the red lights, they grimaced at the devastating effect of the explosion. It looked as if the lieutenant would lose his legs and penis. Rose shot him up with morphine and the screams slowly subsided; then the medic looked up from the bloody bandages and muttered, "Man, he ain't going to make it through the night."

They radioed Captain Pierson for a night medevac and the answer came back shortly: none was available. It had been rainy all day, the clouds were low, and no helicopter could get up in that weather. The lieutenant's shit is in the wind, Keefer thought, but I can't tell him. He and Robinson ducked outside the track to hash it over. The squadron command post at Lang Vei had an aid station, but muddy roads and several kilometers of no-man's-land were between them and it. Keefer was tempted to let the lieutenant bleed to death in the track, rather than risk his men by trying to evacuate him cross-country, but he knew he couldn't. They couldn't watch a man die in front of them without at least doing something, wise-ass idiot or not.

Keefer was alone in the APC with the lieutenant for a moment, when he mumbled through his pain and morphine stupor. He said that he should have listened, but he hadn't wanted to send out patrols because he hadn't wanted to get anyone killed.

"Well, it's too late for that shit now," Keefer answered, "We're just going to have to see what we can do for you."

Deep down Keefer was bitter that some of the GIs had been willing to ignore his experience in keeping them alive, and had sided with the lieutenant because he didn't press them as much.

Finally they cranked up to go, a single track making the run. Keefer took the fifty hatch, Wolf drove, and Ollie and Robinson, Keefer's best friends, volunteered to ride shotgun. The four of them were an inseparable team. Doc Rose went too. "Like it or not," Keefer snarled at him, climbing in the back to keep the lieutenant alive as they made their mad dash to Lang Vei. They left the perimeter, lights out in the pitch black, crashing through brush until they found an engineer trail. They churned to one muddy hill and the track refused to climb it, the treads merely spinning mud, digging in deeper. Keefer tensed behind the fifty, his entire body crackling in preparation for the RPG that he knew was going to slam into them at any second. Wolf jammed it into reverse and they lurched out of the mud. He drove a few yards to one side and hauled up the road again from a different angle. The treads finally found passage, and they drove up and over the long, gradual hill.

They continued along the narrow, muddy trail, splashed across a stream, then hit Route 9, the bumpy highway a luxury in comparison to the jungle run. They weren't going to make it, Keefer sweated, this was suicide. Every hundred yards or so, an RPG burned out of the brush in their direction, all of them going wide because the track was moving fast, lights out, and the NVA had only the engine noise to aim at in the darkness. Somehow they made it to Lang Vei. At the command post, they were told to stay overnight rather than risk another run through unfriendly jungle. Keefer, Robinson, Wolf, and Ollie talked it over; they had Doc Rose and the mortar track and if the platoon were to be hit again during the night they would need both. The four decided that their place was with the platoon. They left Lang Vei at around midnight, roaring back the way they had come, ducking another volley of blindly fired RPGs. Keefer had counselled the gunners to fire only if NVA sprang out of the bushes right on them with satchel charges, so muzzle flashes wouldn't give away their exact position. Ollie and Robinson kept their cool, the engine sound wasn't enough of a target for the NVA, and they made it back to Hill 400 unscathed.

It had been an impossible feat as far as Keefer was concerned. He felt that the four of them deserved Bronze Stars at least, for saving the lieutenant's life. They won no medals; they never even heard if the platoon leader made it home okay.

PART FOUR:
A Renewed Effort

CHAPTER THIRTEEN: Victory

By 28 February, it was obvious that the airborne and ranger drive on the northern flank had been ground to a halt. On that date, General Lam flew to Saigon to confer with President Thieu on an alternate plan. The president had previously sent I Corps a directive to have the Vietnamese Marine Division replace the 1st Airborne Division and press on. Such a switch would have been extremely difficult under the combat conditions in Laos, and it was obvious that Thieu's orders were politically motivated; he wanted to spare his "elite" paratroopers further bloodshed.

General Lam presented an alternate plan. Instead of replacing the Airborne, let them remain in place to screen the northern frontier, while the ARVN 1st Infantry Division took on the weight of the drive to Tchepone. General Phu and his troops were making a good showing of themselves and, at that time, they had eight firebases along the escarpment on the southern flank. The last, LZ Brown, was over halfway to Tchepone. Lam called for three more landing zones to be established along the escarpment (LZ Lolo, LZ Liz, and LZ Sophia Two), followed by a fourth (LZ Hope) to be placed near Tchepone and the area searched from there. Thieu agreed.

One of the problems that had been made apparent in the first phase of the campaign was the lack of coordination between the U.S. and ARVN. General Lam was at FSB Kilo, while General Sutherland was at Quang Tri, while most of the I Corps HQ staff officers were at Dong Ha, while the unit commanders were in command posts spread across the Khe Sanh plateau. On-the-spot decisions during the battle were hard to come by. For example, the reserve forces at Khe Sanh were never once committed, not even when firebases were overrun and the defenders outnumbered. On 1 March, the U.S. Joint Coordinating Group was established at FSB Kilo; controlled by the commander of the 108th Artillery Group, XXIV Corps, it was colocated with Lam's field headquarters, and included representatives of XXIV Corps, 7th Air Force, and the 101st Airborne. Its purpose was to provide the second phase of the campaign with quick and responsive U.S. aviation and fire support.

Once again the crucial factor was this support. As General Berry wrote in his after-action report, "Probably no one unit in the history of air mobile operations was presented a more demanding and challenging task than that assigned to the 223d Combat Aviation Battalion to conduct the assaults 3 to 6 March. Four landing zones were selected along the escarpment which had to be sequentially assaulted to successfully execute the 1st ARVN Corps Commander's plan. Indeed, because of the NVA success at Ranger North and South and at Objectives 30 and 31, the fate of the entire operation was to be determined during this critical four day period."

On 2 March, the Dutchmasters of the 7/1 Air Cav were assigned to conduct photo reconnaissance along the escarpment to Tchepone to determine the best landing zone locations. Captain Mercadante flew only irregularly because of his duties with the troop rear, so he volunteered, flying front seat in one of two Cobras. They came into Tchepone at 8,500 feet and immediately began taking 37mm and 57mm fire; flak bursts appeared around the Cobras and Mercadante couldn't help but think, what is this, a rerun of *Twelve O'Clock High?* He began taking photographs from the cockpit as they pulled up to 11,500 feet, the flak following them the whole way. They radioed for USAF tac air, and a pair of Phantoms came on station. Mercadante asked the FAC what altitude the guns topped out at and was told 12,500 feet for the 37mm, and 16,500 for the 57mm. Incredible, Mercadante thought, it was virtually impossible to get above those guns without oxygen. There was no safe airspace over Laos.

The next morning, the ARVN 1st Infantry Division prepared for LZ Lolo. It was a hill mass atop the escarpment. The ARVN 3/1 was to be inserted, with the 223d CAB controlling the CA using additional helicopters from the 14th and 158th Aviation Battalions. This was to be followed by an airlift of a reinforced artillery battalion. Lieutenant Colonel Kirklighter took his helicopters from Dong Ha, rendezvoused at Khe Sanh with Major Klose, and made plans; then once more they crossed the river into Laos. The ARVN infantrymen, waiting in lines at LZ Delta, peeled off, a squad to a Huey, while guns and command ships circled. Up high again, the staggered trail of choppers beat westward.

Down below, it looked like virgin forest. The land was calm. But the sky was filled with noise and motion, metal birds cutting forward, wind slapping the blades, turbine engines screaming, chatter on the headsets.

Major Klose took the C&C ship down over Lolo, while Kirklighter and the ARVN battalion commander on board decided on two LZs atop the ridge. Smoke grenades billowed yellow and the guns went in to prep, Cobras shark-nosing down at a hundred-and-seventy mph, miniguns flashing at two thousand rounds per minute. Trails of expended brass fell from the sky. There was no return fire from the jungle canopy. With the Cobras maintaining a scouting orbit, the first slicks lit atop the bombed hill and the ARVN disembarked. The first few Hueys went in and out, one at a time, without difficulty. Kirklighter sent in two ships at a time to more quickly beef up the ground elements.

The first pair of Hueys settled down. All hell broke loose.

And that set the stage for the day; despite the heavy tac air prep, the NVA hit LZ Lolo with the fiercest concentration of fire seen in the operation. Seven of the first ten slicks into the hot LZ took hits. Almost immediately four Hueys were down. Kirklighter maintained his C&C circle, controlling the guns, directing in more flights. The slicks kept coming, dropping ARVN, returning to Vietnam to refuel and pick up more troops.

It was semi-controlled chaos.

"Roger, Black Cat, go on in there, go on in there and land as close to the smoke on the high ground, where the smoke is crossing, where the Lima Zulu is."

"Taking fire! Taking fire!"

Pandemonium on the radio: "Yes, I seen the red tracers. We got it in the tailboom, I believe."

"Roger, we have guns on the way."

"Okay, let's hurry 'em up."

"And chalk six is taking fire."

"Roger, where from?"

"I don't know. It's just down, ah, straight below us. Just a minute, we'll get you coordinates."

". . . there at the two o'clock position, down on the river."

"Okay, divert south of the river."

"Okay, where we took fire is approximately four-six-three-eight."

Into the LZ, they flew fire streaking up at them, door-gunners going in hot, crew chiefs screaming to move, ARVN jumping out. Up, they circled back to Lang Vei or Khe Sanh to refuel, then to get more troops, then to go back through the fire, radio headsets buzzing with a constant stream of commentary. The NVA gun crews fired furiously. Another flight of Hueys came in with ARVN, Cobras rolling in to suppress fire. Door-gunners on the trail ship popped smoke out on the LZ for the next flight. Kirklighter was on the horn, "Do you have it now? Black Cat, do you have that smoke?"

"Yes, I sure do. . . . Hold off, I'm coming down to the mark."

Slicks came in, taking fire before they were even close to Lolo.

"Aw shit, I was going to tell you, you're not supposed to fire unless you can see the fire."

"Hell no, I didn't even get a round off."

"What was that pop-pop?"

"Hell!" came the door-gunner's high-pitched exasperated reply, "that was somebody shooting at us!"

So much fire tracked the flights that ships went down before they could even disembark the ARVN passengers. One crashed in the Laotian wilderness, and another chopper broke pattern to cover him while rescue ships came in. A commander shouted to keep the insertion going.

". . . that's affirmative, sir."

"Roger, get him back in business. If he's over that downed bird, get him back with his flight and proceed with your SOP for the recovery. Over."

"Roger, sir. Boats-six, Red Dragon Zero-nine. . . ."

"Hi, this is Boats-six. Roger, you got a recovery aircraft on my bird now. I'm coming on out of the LZ."

"Roger, your flight with you?"

"Negative, I let them go ahead. I got chalk two in charge of the flight now."

"Roger, roger, we have recovery in process."

". . . You've got recovery, now stay with the mission! Over."

"Roger, sir."

The last helicopter of the Black Cats came out of Lolo and popped more smoke; the next flight descended, taking fire, losing two Hueys, two-nine and two-six, still short of the hilltop.

"Two-nine's on fire, two-nine's on fire, going down."

"Did you see the fire?"

"Fire from three o'clock, from that ridgeline that they just passed over."

Pandemonium on the radio, a calm voice came on, "Okay, hold it, hold it down,"—then a ball of fire below them brought more shouts.

"Six, we got a fire."

"It just exploded."

"We got two ships down. One just crashed and burned."

More fire: the flight left two-nine and two-six, making the final descent approach to Lolo, Kirklighter watching from his C&C, trying to counsel them in, "They got twenty-three millimeter all the way down this flight path. You've got to remain south of the river, grab some altitude coming in here, start your descending approach into the LZ."

They descended to the unsettling sight of Hueys still in the LZ, unloading troops, which meant that they might have to overfly the LZ—and possibly have a helo, lifting off at that moment, crash into their underside.

"Tell these guys to unass this thing!"

"Get out of the LZ, you got aircraft on short final."

Coming back from the LZ, choppers passed the two crashed ships.

"Jesus Christ, that thing went up."

"Can we go back and see if them guys are okay?"

Long bursts of M-60 reached down to protect the crews.

A Huey went down through the fire to the crash site, the crew of two-six jumping aboard, except for the missing copilot. An excited voice called from the LZ, "Roger, one-seven has gone in and picked up two-six and a full crew off that ship! We're coming out of the LZ at this time. . . . My ship's running a little rough. We took a lot of fire. Don't know if I had any hits or not. I believe I've got it under control now."

The next flight on the long approach to Lolo took fire, took hits.

"Okay, what's your status? Do you have the LZ in sight?"

"Negative. I broke off the LZ on long final and I'm heading back inbound to Kilo Sierra at this time. I got a gunner hit in the head, some of the troops hit, and the aircraft's hit pretty hard, and I was losing fuel, but it stopped losing the fuel now, so I'm just heading back to Kilo Sierra."

"Okay, who have you designated as your. . . ."

Brigadier General Berry and Lieutenant Colonel Kirklighter, maintaining separate C&C orbits around LZ Lolo, stayed on the radio with each other. The NVA were good; they had allowed troops to be inserted before they threw their ring of steel around the landing zone. Once troops were on the ground, a CA had to be continued at all costs because the alternative—trying to extract the troops under heavy fire—meant chaos and additional casualties with no gain. The enemy understood this. All Berry and Kirklighter could do was radio for all available aircraft to divert to Lolo. Artillery pummelled the jungle at their directions. Cobras made screaming dive runs, pumping rockets and minigun fire into NVA positions. Jets flashed in, tumbling bombs and napalm into the triple-canopy ridgelines around Lolo. Tracers continued to float up from the forest, black and white puffs of flak rounds continued to explode. The sky over Lolo filled with smoke and circling machinery.

The 48th Blue Stars came in with cabins full of ARVN, flying behind the eight Hueys of another company. Five miles from Lolo, a flock of Cobras picked them up to escort them, every fifth slick shadowed by a gunship. Lieutenant Smith gave the thumbs up to his gunship pilot. With two miles to go, he heard an explosion and looked back to see only an ashy spot in the sky a hundred feet away where the Cobra had been. A radar-controlled flak gun had erased the ship and two pilots, and more pandemonium broke out on the radio.

"It was a midair collision!"

"It wasn't a midair collision!"

"Roger, get the hell outta there!"

"That looked like radar."

"Sure is, bigger'n shit."

"Sonuvabitch exploded."

"Did you see that. Goddamn."

"Let's cut the talk."

Coming in, Smith could see USAF jets making low gun runs around Lolo, heard them on the guard freq saying they couldn't neutralize all the NVA emplacements. The LZ was hot, the scene terrifying. The hill was pounded to dust, trees four feet in diameter broken like toothpicks. Parts of downed helicopters were strewn in the upturned earth, dead ARVN lay where they had fallen among the shattered trees. The South Vietnamese on his bird clambered out; then Smith was pushing the cyclic back and they were hauling up and out, taking fire, circling around to make the run back to Vietnam.

Sp5 Bill Wilder of the 174th Helicopter Company had already made several gun runs to Lolo, refueling and rearming at Khe Sanh between each trip. He was crew chief on a UH1C gunship. They were going in again, flying cover for his company's two lift platoons, when he saw flak burst all around one of the slicks. It trailed smoke in its descent. Wilder got on the intercom to his pilots, leading them towards the wreck. Their wingman peeled off to cover. Fire cracked around them and Wilder sprayed bursts back into the foliage. They were rushing forward at tree-top level, popping over the trees—and spotted an NVA 12.7mm gun.

The crew must have been moving, because they were in plain view in a field of elephant grass. They were wearing T-shirts and khaki trousers, Wilder noted, one NVA in the gunner's seat, the two loaders wearing sunglasses. Having fired at a different helo, the crew began swivelling around for the UH1C but the gunship sailed by ten yards away. Wilder, braced in the door, fired his M-60 in a long burst and the three North Vietnamese bounced into the grass.

Losing sight of the downed bird, they bounced to five hundred feet, spotted it again, and directed in the rescue slick. They were hit as they circled giving cover with their minigun and sixties, but the ship was still flyable. Another burst hit the rotors and the Huey began vibrating. Another burst, and they lost hydraulics. The pilot made a controlled crash on a thin dirt trail. It ran north-south and Wilder figured that it must be a branch of the Ho Chi Minh Trail. Their wing ship also took hits and crash landed on the path. The door-gunners laid some precautionary bursts into the treeline, but there was no return fire and everyone was okay. They began destroying their gear so the enemy would not get it, Wilder disconnecting the three radios and the voice scrambler, putting them out of commission with his .45. Then he pulled a pin which dropped the minigun into the dirt. Two lift ships flew in under fire, after dropping ARVN on Lolo, and the downed crews hefted the miniguns and climbed aboard.

Over Lolo another ten-ship company went in; then the flight leader was on the radio, "Okay, so we lost one aircraft in the LZ. We did get the crew out, is that correct?"

"Six, this is one-seven. Roger, I've got chalk four's crew with me, but I do not have his copilot. I repeat, I do not have his copilot."

"Does the crew know what happened to the copilot?"

"That's a negative. We've asked them. They. . . ."

"Okay, was his aircraft burning?"

"Roger, his aircraft was definitely on fire. Very hot. The ammo was popping off."

"Okay."

"And six one-seven, we took a lot of fire and we'll be shutting down at the laager pad to check it out. I think we've sustained some hits."

Two Cobras and two Hueys came on station over the burning ship.

"Okay, did you get two-six himself out?"

"Roger, I have two-six himself."

"And the enlisted crew members?"

"Roger, I have the charlie-echo and the gunner."

"Okay, did they ever see the guy get out of the aircraft, the copilot?"

"That's a negative."

"He probably didn't because that thing went over on its right side and then it exploded."

"Boats six, Boats one-seven. The gunner just said that he got the copilot out and the copilot was walking around the LZ."

Another Huey went through the fire and found the copilot, still alive, down the slope from the hilltop LZ. Crew extracted, the air-mission commander said. "Let's all regroup at POL."

To avoid the intense fire, Berry and Kirklighter tried bringing the slicks in one at a time to the escarpment face. They approached through the river valley, then came in to land, one skid against the crest, the other hanging free, the ARVN jumping out the one side and scrambling up the hill. It usually worked, but the NVA fire continued unabated. Twenty helicopters radioed that they were inbound from the east, taking fire; ARVN wounded were on board, two slicks down. A voice on the radio said, "That's a helpless feeling to have to pull off an LZ like that and know that those guys are down there."

There was more firing.

"We got a slick autorotating to the dirt road. We are dropping down to take a look."

Lieutenant Colonel Kirklighter and Major Klose were in their C&C orbit above the battlefield, when 23mm fire began bursting around them at all angles, looking like bright puffs of white cotton. Four exploded in line behind the tailboom, then the fifth burst outside Klose's left-side door. The ship jerked in space, shrapnel tearing through in screams, and blood suddenly splattered the Plexiglas windshield in front of them. The crew chief, a young spec five, was down with a wounded hand. There were holes in the floor and ceiling of the Huey. Kirklighter radioed for the battalion exec, Major Davis, to continue the assault as Klose turned the ship around. They settled down beside the medical bunker at Khe Sanh and the crew chief was taken inside. Klose then flew to the nearby refuel/rearm pits and set down, leaving the engine running and the blades pumping. A nozzle was screwed in and the JP-4 turned on; then they stared in amazement as the fuel began spraying out as if from a garden sprinkler. Dozens of shrapnel holes had punctured the belly of the ship. The fuel was quickly shut off and Klose, jumping back to the controls, lifted away from the fuel blivets. He sat down, shut off, and another helo was readied for them.

Lieutenant Colonel Kirklighter was sweating in his flight suit. Christ, he thought, this a bitch.

In minutes they were airborne again and headed for LZ Lolo.

Over the landing zone, Major Davis was the temporary air mission commander. His normal duties had nothing to do with combat flying, but he was a man of courage and got into Laos any chance he could. By the end of the day, over five hundred ARVN soldiers had been inserted atop Lolo and, despite the murderous fire, had secured the hill. However, the second phase of the insertion, the airlifting of the artillery, had to be cancelled because it would have been impossible for the big Chinooks to hover long enough for the slingloaded pieces to unload without being blown out of the sky. The day had taken a heavy toll in helicopters, the official tally being seven shot down and thirty-five damaged.

On 4 March, the 223d CAB with the 101st and 158th Aviation Battalions cranked up to complete the move to Lolo. The ARVN 4/1 Infantry and the regimental command post were airmobiled to the firebase, enemy fire having lessened considerably from the day before, then the choppers continued west to LZ Liz. ARVN artillery on Lolo pounded the site designated as Liz, five kilometers further along the escarpment: sixty airstrikes and numerous gunship sorties further pummelled the area. The helos came in with the ARVN 2/1 and artillery, through heavy fire, and secured Liz. Heavy smoke blocked vision around the LZ and General Berry, on station in his Huey C&C, later wrote, "What transpired was an alternating stream of assault helicopters and large cargo helicopters in a stream of combat air traffic which would rival that of a large international airport on a foggy day."

Official toll for the day was one Cobra and one Huey downed, twelve helos hit.

The next day, the ARVN hit LZ Sophia Two, about four kilometers west of Liz. The 2d Regiment secured the hill in the face of heavy fire, and artillery and supplies were brought in ("The coordination had become so polished by this time," a 101st ABD report read, "that CH-47s and CH-53s were able to begin resupply of artillery and ammunition almost concurrently with the troop insertion."). Enemy fire was heavy; two Cobras, two UH1Cs, and two Hueys were shot down. Seventeen other choppers were damaged around the three new firebases. Firefights flared as patrols began moving out.

But the door to Tchepone had been opened.

The deserted and bombed village called Tchepone, in reality, had no military value. The NVA supply caches were in the surrounding mountains, not in the town proper, and the supply lines ran to the east and west of it. But the name Tchepone rang with political significance. The South Vietnamese and foreign press had made it an invasion symbol (with no rebuttal from the RVN government) and the military was ordered to go after the propaganda coup. As one ARVN general noted, ". . . the ARVN effort now seemed to be more directed at setting foot in Tchepone than trying to destroy the NVA logistical system which was the real objective of the offensive."

All was not for naught, though. In three days, U.S. Army Aviation had survived the heaviest AA fire of the war and had moved two full ARVN regiments (1st and 2d) thirty-five miles deeper into enemy territory, a major victory in itself. Also, the military objectives were in no way completely abandoned. Time and effort were going to be exerted in Tchepone for propaganda, but the selection of the landing zone was reassuring; LZ Hope was four kilometers northeast of Tchepone—where it belonged militarily, not politically. The ARVN 2d Infantry Regiment was designated the assault force into LZ Hope on 6 March. The aviation support was to come once again from the 223d Combat Aviation Battalion, 1st Aviation Brigade.

On 5 March Colonel Battreall went to the I Corps HQ Bunker for General Lam's daily decision briefing. The subject was Tchepone. The 2/17 Air Cavalry was to escort the troop-carrying helicopters, and their new commander, Lt. Col. Archie Rider, had just returned from a personal reconnaissance of the area. It was Rider's first day in command of the squadron. His helicopter had almost been blown out of the sky, and he was rattled. He frantically tried to convince Lam that the hills around Tchepone were alive with AA positions. He wanted to postpone the CA, and General Jackson seconded the opinion. Battreall had never been enthused with Lam as a decisive commander, but he was impressed when Lam thought for a moment, then said forcefully, "No! We have B52. We will use them, and then we attack."

That ended all further discussion.

The CA to LZ Hope/Tchepone by the ARVN 2d Regiment was coordinated by the 223d CAB. It was the most complicated air move of the operation, an hour and fifteen minutes required for each helo pickup, flight, insertion, and return. It was seventy-seven kilometers from Khe Sanh to Tchepone. On the morning of 6 March, the helicopters began gathering on the Khe Sanh strip. Three hundred choppers sat in the fierce glare of the sun and the swirling red dust, while their crews waited.

It was a stunning sight, but also a worrisome one; before long, the first 122mm artillery shell impacted in the perimeter wire. The NVA walked their bombardment onto the strip, creating massive confusion as the aircrews rushed for their ships and bolted into the sky. Two men were killed on the ground in the shelling but, amazingly, the three hundred helicopters managed to get airborne above the artillery without losing a single ship.

Meanwhile Lieutenant Colonel Kirklighter, Major Klose, and the ARVN regimental commander were in the C&C bird. They had gone in ahead of the main body to recon LZ Hope. They circled the last firebase along the escarpment, Sophia Two, so as not to alert the NVA of their intentions. The area was pocked with craters from the B52 Arc Lights, and the last landing zone was a clear spot carved out of the jungle with a Daisy Cutter (the detonator extended several feet from the nose of the bomb so that it exploded above ground, felling trees with fifteen thousand pounds of explosive). The ARVN commander confirmed that the LZ was suitable for the insertion and they returned to Lang Vei to refuel. They were headed to Khe Sanh to join their armada when General Berry got on the radio to inform Kirklighter that the airstrip was being shelled, the helicopters were already airborne, and everything was to continue ahead of schedule. If the helicopters had left Khe Sanh in succession, as planned, the first company would have been halfway to Tchepone before the last company had even started its engines. Instead they were burning fuel as they waited in circling patterns. Kirklighter and Klose radioed the pilots to play it by ear, dipping into refueling berms when they could, and it worked itself out.

Phantom jets flew continuous airstrikes around Hope and caused numerous secondary explosions. That firepower, combined with the Arc Lights of the previous night, must have devastated the NVA antiaircraft crews in the area because only a minimal amount of fire was directed at the choppers. Six crewmen were wounded, fourteen helos hit, and only a single Huey was shot down, its crew immediately rescued. In ninety minutes, the ARVN 2d Infantry Regiment was on the ground and securing the area against minimal resistance.

Tchepone had been taken.

The next morning, Berry wrote in his journal, ". . . Yesterday was a good day. We seized our objective. We had very few casualties. . . . What a glorious relief!"

CHAPTER FOURTEEN: The Great Withdrawal

How long were the ARVN in Tchepone before they started screaming to come out, Lieutenant Smith thought bitterly. A few days, was it? And then began what the aircrews cynically referred to as the great withdrawal, marked, Smith noted, by a graveyard of American helicopters.

The plans for invading Laos had not envisioned an army of occupation; the ARVN were to strike to Tchepone, destroy Base Area 604, then withdraw. MACV and XXIV Corps (not to mention the White House) hoped they could destroy the NVA logistical systems until the onset of the rainy season in May, and then make their withdrawal through BA 611 and the A Shau Valley, wreaking further destruction along the way. The ARVN high command had never wholeheartedly embraced that option; when Tchepone was taken, the South Vietnamese had the choice of reinforcing and continuing the fight, or of pulling out as soon as possible. They opted for the latter. The ferocity of the North Vietnamese counterattacks was the main factor in this decision. Intelligence had failed accurately to gauge the great rate at which the NVA could reinforce southern Laos, and even the successful drive to Tchepone had been met with fierce resistance in an area that was still hot. Lolo, Liz, and Sophia Two were under daily shellings and the patrols in the area made numerous contacts.

This phase of the operation could be summed up by noting, for example, that the 1st Regiment, working off of Lolo, had killed hundreds of NVA, discovered tons of supplies, and cut important communist communication lines to the southwest. At the same time, the line battalions were taking heavy casualties, and the bombardment of Lolo kept away practically all resupply and medevac helicopters.

The combat in those jungles was conventional warfare.

To make a propaganda coup of the Tchepone victory, no planned withdrawal could begin until the rubbled village was occupied. Two battalions of the 2d Regiment swept through the valley from LZ Hope. Ironically they had the easiest task, since the NVA caches and commo lines were not in Tchepone and the area was not heavily defended. Okamura, the reporter, joined up with the search battalions, and was correct in writing that the mission was "partially propaganda, partially fishing."

The 2d Regiment walked up the slopes of Sophia Two on 9 March.

With that completed, General Lam reported to the Presidential Palace in Saigon. He met with President Thieu and General Vien, and detailed the campaign as he saw it. In one sense, victory had already been achieved: for every ARVN casualty, ten had been inflicted on the NVA, and, although an early withdrawal meant numerous caches would go undisturbed, they had already destroyed enough supplies to halt the planned communist offensive. In his opinion it was time to get out. The terrain beyond Tchepone was mountainous and so deeply thicketed that ARVN armor could make no headway without knowing the concealed trails. In addition, the NVA were still well dug in. Lam's troops were outnumbered and bloodied, and there was no large reserve. Thieu and Vien agreed it was time to withdraw.

When General Abrams was informed of the order to retreat, he met with Thieu and Vien. Aggressive as always, he suggested that the ARVN 2d Infantry Division be sent into Laos to continue the offensive. President Thieu let his feelings be known when he said that would be fine if a U.S. infantry division were also sent in. The matter was dropped at that point.

In Laos the ARVN began destroying the tons of material they had uncovered (numerous underground storage areas had been unearthed by the B52 strikes) and pulling back to their firebases to be airmobiled out. The NVA, who had enjoyed numerical superiority throughout the entire campaign, pressed relentlessly at the withdrawal as, with each day, there were even fewer ARVN to face them. Combat around the firebases was horrific, casualties high on both sides. The first unit out was the 2d Regiment from Sophia Two on March 11–12; there was surprisingly little fire to hamper the move.

No other unit was blessed with such a bloodless exit from Laos. For U.S. Army Aviation, the spirit of the withdrawal was, as General Berry noted, to "Get them out as fast as you can." He further noted in his after-action report, "The objectives of LAMSON 719 had been achieved.

What remained was the very difficult task of disengaging from the enemy and conducting an orderly withdrawal from Laos. The retrograde operation in land warfare is one of the most difficult to conduct successfully. The difficulty of withdrawing the ARVN forces from Laos was compounded by the terrain, weather, and the aggressive enemy who had been severely embarrassed by the ARVN's ability to penetrate deep into what had been their sanctuary. . . . U.S. aircrews used every trick in the book and invented several new ones to get the job done. Fuel loads were lightened to allow more ARVN troops to get on each helicopter. It looked as if there was no control of the withdrawal during the last days; however, the more troops which crowded on each helicopter meant that less helicopters were subjected to the intense hostile fire in and around every pickup zone. An example of the intensity of the fire around the pickup zones was that 75% of the helicopters used sustained bullet damage during that period."

LZ Lolo, held by the ARVN 1st Infantry Regiment, was the deepest base in enemy territory after the evacuation of Liz and Sophia Two. It had been under attack since the initial insertion. Within a week, the NVA had maneuvered to encircle the bunkered knob, while 120mm rockets and 130mm artillery pounded the firebase round the clock. Sappers raised hell inside the wire. It was virtually a siege. The Cobras of the 4/77 AFA flew constantly to strafe the NVA creeping in the wire, directed by an ARVN who spoke English fluently and whose calmness had earned him a good reputation among the American aircrews. They called him Quebec Whiskey. By 14 March, as the North Vietnamese moved to isolate the withdrawing units, Lolo was cut off. The AA fire was so intense that medical evacuation for the South Vietnamese was impossible, resupply extremely hazardous.

On 15 March, the regimental commander issued an emergency request for small-arms ammunition. It went to the 223d CAB at Dong Ha and Major Klose volunteered to fly as air-mission commander. Five slick crews also volunteered to fly in five slingloads of ammunition. Captain Johnson and one of the best pilots in the 173d Robinhoods, Capt. Henry Pomije, flew the lead ship. They picked up their thousand-pound slingloads at FSB Kilo, then departed for Laos in one-minute intervals. Klose circled the boulder outcropping on which Lolo sat, directing in airstrikes and gunships. One of the Cobras was hit and fell from the sky in flames. But the two wounded pilots crawled away from it.

The lead Huey came in towards the face of the escarpment—and Klose suddenly saw a stream of green 12.7 tracers stitch across its tailboom. The Huey shuddered and veered away, Johnson and Pomije valiantly refusing to punch the slingload which slowed them down in the ground fire. Pomije radioed Klose that he had taken hits but that no caution or warning lights had come on. He turned the ship back around, hovered over Lolo, and gently put the slingload of ammunition on the ground. Then Johnson and Pomije banked the Huey and hovered over the bunker line, looking for the Cobra pilots. Rounds ripped through the helicopter.

Klose screamed on the radio, "Get the hell outta there!"

They maintained their orbit over Lolo and radioed the location of enemy guns to chalk two, boring in next. It hurtled in high and fast, not slowing down or dropping low with its slingload. Johnson mumbled to Pomije, "What the hell is he doing?"—just as the slingload of ammunition was released from two hundred feet, hit the middle of the perimeter in a cloud of dust, and splintered in all directions. Klose exploded on the radio, chewing out the pilot. When finished, the pilot cut to the company frequency and said nonchalantly, "They won't have to uncase that shit." The other pilots came in and dropped their slingloads softly. All five Hueys were riddled with fire.

Captains Johnson and Pomije went back for the Cobra pilots. They emerged from a bunker, waving a red NVA flag they had found, then jumped aboard the slick which pulled out with sixty-five bullet holes in it. Quebec Whiskey got back on the radio, directing the Cobras on NVA attacking the perimeter. During the night, tac air pummeled the NVA. Quebec Whiskey was either killed or wounded in the battle, because another Vietnamese took over the radios. In the morning, 16 March, the 1st Regiment pulled out, leaving five damaged howitzers, destroying three more in place, and abandoning their dead and whatever couldn't be carried.

The 4th Battalion was left behind to conduct a rearguard defense.

The ARVN 4/1 Infantry was immediately hit by NVA artillery which wiped out the battalion command group, including the commander. As they moved on foot to the northeast, they were under almost constant fire and, at noon on 17 March, the North Vietnamese launched a heavy assault.

The battle raged for two hours; the ARVN radioed that they had killed five hundred NVA, but had lost fifty men themselves. Helicopters of the 223d CAB went in through heavy fire to medevac their many wounded. Sergeant Keith, Intelligence NCO with the 101st Airborne, was flying as an observer on one of the Hueys that was diverted towards

Lolo. Cobras zipped in ahead of them, and heavy fire cracked from the escarpment. Keith's slick banked off, but then went back in to get a fix on the gun positions. The tracers began streaming at them—then, suddenly, the Huey lurched in space, the floor exploded. Keith didn't even realize he'd been hit until he looked down. His left leg was literally disintegrated, all white and red, the kneecap gone, and Keith muttered into his radio mike, "Oh damn, I'm hit, I'm hit." His radio cord was severed. The copilot turned to look back in the cabin and almost fainted when he saw Keith—he just shook his head and laughed back, "I've done it now!"

The crew chief helped him lay back. He was in shock until the chief straightened out what was left of his leg; then the pain shot through him. There was no morphine on the helicopter so all they could do for Keith was tie a bandage around the stump. Blood kept seeping onto the floor. Keith's glasses were speckled with it. When he looked up in the vibrating helicopter, he could see bits of his bone and flesh embedded in the ceiling. The pilot struggled to control the bird as all the warning lights flashed, and Keith knew that if they had to ditch in Laos he'd bleed to death before a medevac got in. He was a professional soldier and didn't want to go through life crippled; he forced himself to mumble, "If you want to die you can die right now . . . no, I don't want to die." Keith patted himself, finding other wounds, and kept smiling at the shaken copilot who glanced back at him. The pilot kept the Huey together and headed for Khe Sanh, radioing for medevacs in case they went down. Gunships peeled off to cover them.

When they shut down on the strip, medics from Bravo Med rushed up.

Keith was badly in pain, coming out of the Huey. He was taken to the underground medical bunker. Medics cut off his clothes, stopped the bleeding, kept talking to him, asking questions. A medevac came in soon and he was ferried to the 18th Surg at Quang Tri. He babbled in his morphine stupor, passed out when they started the IV, and woke up five hours later, coming out of it with terrible nightmares and with his left leg amputated. Later he told a reporter, "The pilots I had flown with came in that evening and said a lot of good things to me. That set me on the road to recovery. From then on I had no problem about my mental attitude."

By nightfall the survivors of ARVN 4/1 were seeking refuge in some bomb craters at a bend in the river at the foot of the escarpment. The North Vietnamese surrounded them in the dark and shouted with loudspeakers for their "brothers from the South" to surrender. The battalion had not been supplied for six days and was short of ammunition. They did not surrender. They radioed for more bullets.

Lieutenant Smith had shut down from a day of flying when an emergency call came to Dong Ha for immediate resupply to the survivors of 4/1. Smith had no idea what ARVN unit that was but, when volunteers were asked for, he and WO Del McClure stepped forward. They flew out in a single slick, with door-gunners, tracing down Route 9 at thirty knots and fifteen feet because of ground fog, taking several hits before they even reached Khe Sanh. They shut down on the airfield, checked the tiny holes in the skin, then had a thousand-pound cargo net of ammunition slingloaded under their Huey. An air force major briefed Smith and McClure in a command bunker, "The ARVN are surrounded. We've got them on the Fox Mike frequency. They're instructed to pop a strobe light when you come on final. You're to go straight into the strobe light. They're on the neck of a river. Punch your load off right at the strobe. Take an immediate right turn. They're completely, 360 degrees, surrounded by the enemy. No lights, no dash lights, no nothing on the helicopter. Take a turn to the right and the river's on the right. When you get shot down, you can head for the river."

When, Smith noted, not if.

They departed Khe Sanh with volunteers from the 173d in a second Huey also towing a slingload of ammo. A line of napalm burned red and yellow below them, pointing to the ARVN position, and a USAF pilot came on the horn to say he had splashed nape on the NVA but was still taking ground fire. Smith contacted the South Vietnamese on the FM freq and told them to turn on their strobe light.

Several strobes popped in the dark. The NVA were on the radio.

Just then NVA fire began cracking past Smith's Huey and they aborted the mission with eighteen hits at one thousand feet. Back at Khe Sanh, the major said that they had to give it another try, so they cranked up again, Smith and McClure still flying lead. Ground fog had rolled in around the Khe Sanh plateau from the east, and they churned slowly through it at thirty feet, following the dirt road of Route 9 with landing lights on. They figured that if the fog had also blanketed the Laotian side of the border they would abort the mission; if not, they would instantly climb high as they hit the clear. In Laos the road forked and Smith followed the trail which seemed to go west. It actually made a gradual southern run through a small valley. The fog got thicker, a few rounds cracked below them, and Smith radioed the second chopper that they must be lost and to turn around for Khe Sanh.

Then, abruptly, they were in thicker fog. It was a void, pitch black and foggy on the valley floor—and McClure was seized with vertigo; he felt the chopper wildly spinning in different directions when actually it was flying straight and level. He shoved the cyclic all the way forward. Smith flipped on the spotlight to see where they were just in time to see a mountainside looming before them. With blades clipping at the tree-tops, Smith cut off the light, punched the slingload, grabbed the controls, and went to instrument flying. They levelled off, but the sudden shift in weight had jerked the craft and McClure frantically grabbed the controls again, pulling the cyclic all the way back. The black dot on the console attitude indicator showed they were flying almost straight up, Smith screamed, "I've got the controls! You've got vertigo!" as he punched McClure in the face and wrestled back the cyclic. Oh God, his mind screamed, we've bought the farm. Somehow, they levelled off again and made an ascent into the clouds between two peaks. Lieutenant Smith pulled them up to eight thousand feet and finally broke out of the clouds; then he shot a GCA radar approach back to Khe Sanh.

They made it back safely, nerves shot, the ARVN still out of ammunition.

By sunrise on 18 March, the stranded 4/1 had accomplished its mission covering the retreat of the 1st Regiment. By noon, the 223d CAB was almost finished extracting the regimental command post and the 1st, 2d, and 3d Battalions. The reporter Saar was at Kilo and saw the first four slicks, ". . . cross a melancholic expanse of gray sky." The wounded had been evacked first. Saar watched and wrote his notes later, ". . . One man topples out and lies still until rushing colleagues bear him gently to an ambulance. The rest can walk, the stiff-legged stumble of the exhausted wounded, and with their drawn, grimace-set faces, tattered uniforms and filthy dressings, they come painfully toward us like some terrible march of the damned.

"Then, in air-tearing fleets of Hueys, the unwounded survivors arrive. That first step back to the soil of South Vietnam is for each man a moment of pure joy—the dazed grins, the helpless laughter, the jubilation of friends celebrating joint survival, with arms flailing round necks and shoulders. It takes no oracular powers to understand that in the past six weeks these men have seen fighting they never expected to survive. Yet they have come back, and despite their long unwashed griminess and tatterdemalion fatigues, each man has a steel pot and a rifle, and somehow they have the carriage of the tough, dependable soldier."

"They look good," Saar commented to a pilot.

"Yeah, what there are left of them."

Saar spoke with a crewcut U.S. Marine captain, an ARVN advisor, who watched his returning troops with controlled emotions. The politics of the invasion forbade him from accompanying his charges into Laos and his comments betrayed guilt, "I wish we could have gone with them. We trained them, lived with them. It's kind of like cheating."

The 223d CAB immediately took off again to get the last of the regiment, the 4th Battalion, which was cut off four kilometers east of Lolo. They were in an area where the escarpment tapered off to the river flatlands, still in the higher part where thick scrub grew, seeking shelter in the craters produced by their USAF close air support. Of the 420 men of the 4/1 who went into Laos, only eighty-eight were there. All of the officers were dead and sixty-one of the survivors were wounded. Their final position measured only sixty meters in diameter. A sergeant was in command, and his only link to the vital U.S. air power was a single PRC25 radio. The men were exhausted, outnumbered, almost out of ammunition, and surrounded by the NVA.

Another attack would destroy them.

As soon as the main extraction of the regiment was completed, General Berry got into a C&C orbit above 4/1. Lieutenant Colonel Kirklighter and Major Klose joined him, calling in all available helicopters and directing in more airstrikes. The Phantoms tumbled bombs and napalm around the battalion's crater, sixty-eight airstrikes in all, keeping the North Vietnamese at bay. A flight of Cobra gunships, led by Capt. Keith M. Brandt of D Company, 101st Aviation Battalion, came on station in response to Kirklighter's call for assistance. The ARVN on the radio called Brandt, "We're completely surrounded. You expend on my smoke." He hurled his last smoke grenade from the crater and twelve Cobras rolled in right on top of it.

Captain Brandt stayed over the ARVN all afternoon. Three times he expended his ordnance into the NVA, flew back to Khe Sanh to refuel and rearm, and returned to the crater. He stayed in contact with the ARVN sergeant and dodged the NVA fire on low-level flights to pinpoint 4/1's exact location and calculate the best approach route for the rescue birds.

It was almost five in the afternoon before the 173d Robinhoods began trailing from the east, Captain Johnson flying the lead with Lt. John

Trapani. Captain Brandt was still circling the area, out of ammunition but aware that the ARVN had no smoke grenades left to mark their position. He volunteered to lead the slicks in and contacted Johnson, "This is Music One-six. Follow me, Robinhood Three, and I'll lead you to the friendlies."

The Cobra and Huey darted in at treetop level but overshot the crater as NVA fire exploded around them. The Cobra shuddered, trailed smoke and fire, but Brandt was still on the radio, "I've lost my hydraulics and my mast is on fire." He brought his gunship into a slow, 360-degree turn towards the ARVN, with the slick still following him.

Brandt lined Johnson up with the crater and shouted in the radio, "There it is! Twelve o'clock, a hundred meters. I'm going to try to make the river."

"No sweat, buddy," Johnson answered, "I'm right behind you."

Smoke and flames dragged in the wind behind the Cobra. The rotor rpm slowed as he fell towards the riverbank treeline.

Captain Brandt was on the horn, "I've lost my engine and my transmission is breaking up. Good-bye. Send my love to my family. I'm dead." Then, the Cobra became a ball of fire and crashed into the trees. Captain Johnson brought his Huey to a hundred-foot hover over the burning wreck, and thought he could see an outline of the pilot and copilot lying in the flames. Johnson and Trapani looked at each other, knots forming in their throats.

Major Klose's voice screaming over the radio brought them back to reality, "The troops are at your six! Get'em, get 'em!"

Klose was not being heartless. He had watched Brandt die from his C&C; he could feel the lead weight sink in him and thought, My God, that man was a true hero. He'd given his life for others. Klose wanted to put Brandt in for the Medal of Honor.

But the battle was still being fought.

Johnson landed his Huey and it was chaos. Twenty-four ARVN scrambled aboard, filling the cabin, hanging from the M-60 mounts and skids—one even opened Johnson's door trying to get in with him. They lifted off and Johnson looked back at the survivors in the cabin; their fatigues were shredded, many were without weapons, some had bandages, and one had a hole in his head where once he'd had an eye. They'd just come out of hell. Heading back for Kilo the ship began losing rpm because of the weight, and could not return fire with ARVN on the guns. Johnson did not resent the ARVN; they had fought bravely, and had scrambled aboard now as any man would when a rescue bird came in. But they were going down from the weight.

Johnson ordered his crew chief and door-gunner to throw three ARVN off. They were kicked off of the skids at several hundred feet.

The second Huey in the 173d trail popped up with a dozen ARVN, but was hit on takeoff and crash-landed east of the position. Another slick went in to rescue the crew, and the extraction was temporarily halted as more firepower was laid around the crater.

Two hours later, Lieutenant Smith was flying lead ship for the 48th Blue Stars. Three kilometers from the crater, he could see green tracers burning past him, a couple smacking into his Huey. He radioed ahead to the orbiting C&C, "Do you have the flight in sight?"

Klose gave an affirmative, saying gunship support was coming and to go into the LZ.

Smith insisted he had no contact with the guns.

Klose said they were coming, the LZ was cold, get in there!

The North Vietnamese fire tapered off as they made the final approach to the South Vietnamese position, Smith flying low over the brush. He darted towards where he thought the LZ was, then spotted the ARVN a hundred meters away and quickly hopped over to them. He landed in the one-ship LZ, then stared flabbergasted at the ARVN rushing towards his ship as if someone had fired a starter pistol. The first ones shoved their dead battalion commander aboard, and jumped in. Smith pulled pitch as more ARVN clambered on. The blades bent, the rpm light flashed on, and Smith just managed to get into a transitional lift, give it fifty pounds of torque, and glide away at a shallow departure angle with ten ARVN in the cabin and two hanging from the skids. The crater fell into pandemonium. Smith could hear the pilot of chalk two screaming, "Goddamn!" in the radio, as he sat for a few seconds in a five foot hover, then flew off with ARVN swarming on the skids. The third Huey sat on the ground, overloaded, and couldn't get airborne again until the crew chief and door-gunner punched some of the South Vietnamese out of the cabin.

They were flying back at three thousand feet when the crew chief told Smith that one of their skid riders had just fallen off.

The line of Hueys followed Smith back towards Khe Sanh, the last of the South Vietnamese aboard. More ARVN soldiers lost their grips on the skids in the freezing wind and flew tumbling through the sky.

Smith was a hundred feet from the Khe Sanh strip when the engine stopped, the fuel line finally having ruptured from a hit. He made a controlled crash, then sat shaking in the cockpit. He watched the rest of the company coming back, one slick weighted with too many ARVN. It lost control on landing and bounced to a halt on the runway, its skids sheared off, an ARVN skid rider crushed underneath.

By Captain Johnson's count, of the eighty-eight men in the crater at the beginning of the day, they got thirty-six back to Khe Sanh alive.

Reporters crowded around the strip, photographing the South Vietnamese clinging like insects to the helicopters, interviewing frightened and excited pilots who poured out bitter comments about the panicky ARVN. That's how the ordeal of the 4th Battalion was reported back home, with the inference that the ARVN were cowards. The U.S. command thought otherwise; the ARVN battalion had been fighting hard for six weeks, had successfully defended the pullout of their parent regiment, and was surrounded and out of ammunition when the pickup birds finally came. "I don't know what the press was trying to prove," Lieutenant Colonel Kirklighter said, "I didn't see him hanging from the skids. It does not mean that the unit panicked or acted unmilitarily. It only means that some soldier looked around and, hell, he's the last son of a bitch on the ground and he's not going to be left behind. I'd jump on the skid too. And so would you."

On the afternoon of 19 March, Lieutenant Colonel Peachy's 158th Aviation Battalion controlled a pullout in the airborne sector. Under heavy fire, they managed to evacuate the 2d Airborne Brigade Headquarters, many wounded paratroopers, and some artillery pieces.

Next to come were the 2d and 7th Airborne Battalions, scattered and disorganized on the jungled mountains. WO Smith of the Ghostriders had just flown two resupply missions into Laos, and had shut down his machine on the pad at the 1st Airborne Division CP when word came to mount up again. The whole company, eleven slicks, was going in to get the stranded paratroopers. They began taking heavy fire as soon as they crossed the border and one or two of the Hueys had to turn back with serious hits. They made it to the assigned coordinates, a small clearing on a knoll, and Smith could make out ARVN clustered in the brush, firing from their hastily formed perimeter.

He could see mortar rounds exploding around the LZ, as he sailed through a crossfire of 12.7mm and AK-47 tracers. One round punched through the main rotor blade. First one M-60 stopped firing, then the other, and the crew chief screamed, "They're jammed, let's get outta here!"

"Long as we're here," Smith shrugged, "let's see what we can get."

WO Smith brought the Huey to a ten-foot hover. There was a mad scramble and, within seconds, ten ARVN were hanging from the skids. He pulled up through the fire as the crew chief and door-gunner hauled the men into the cabin. They dropped them at the airborne CP, traded their jammed machine guns for a working pair from a wreck, and prepared to go back again. A captain, the new company commander, came over then and told the copilot to get out; he took the seat to Smith's right. They were almost to the paratroopers again when Peachy came on the horn and cancelled the mission. The ARVN advisors wanted more time to organize the troops via radio.

Smith and the captain were headed back when an emergency call came over the radio. A UH1C was down and they were to extract the crew. They were told to fly on the deck while Cobras led them in. Smith was tempted to pop up to several thousand feet to see for himself, but he obeyed the Cobra pilot leading him. "Go left, go right, okay, flare now!" He brought the Huey to a hover over a jungle clearing, as instructed, and looked through the Plexiglas at his feet. The crashed gunship was nowhere in sight, but he could see figures in the brush fifty feet away—and he realized they were shooting at him. His face suddenly recoiled as if a sledgehammer had hit it and the bullet crashed out the windshield in front of the captain.

Reflexively, Smith grabbed the cyclic between his legs with one hand and reached for his face with the other. There was no blood; then he realized where he'd been hit. The round had come through his door, punched through his lower left side and tumbled out just under his right shoulder blade. His spine had been hit and his legs were paralyzed straight over the foot pedals. There was no real pain; it was numb. As he slumped uncontrollably to the right, gripping the cyclic, the Huey veered from its hover, and he shouted at the captain to take the controls. The captain hesitated a stunned moment, then grabbed the controls and pulled them out of firing range. They banked around for Vietnam. Smith occupied his mind by staring at the control panel. The engine oil pressure suddenly dropped to zero, and the temperature gauge spun up. He shook the captain's shoulder and pointed.

The captain made a controlled crash in the dust of Route 9, still in Laos. They sat vulnerable on the road, the door-gunners sweeping the brush with fire, tracers burning back at them. Smith could hear whistles in the treeline, maybe bugles, and thought, God, I'm going to die. Then he noticed he really wasn't scared. The firing was getting heavy but he was going into shock from his wound, floating into a world of detached bliss. Another Huey, piloted by a buddy nicknamed Muddy Waters, landed right behind them to rake the trees with M-60s, while a medevac bird darted in. The crew chief and door-gunner hauled Smith from his seat and ran to the medevac. They laid him in, then joined the captain running to Muddy's slick. The two Hueys lifted up under fire. The fifth member of the medevac crew, a young medic, worked on Smith as they flew towards Khe Sanh. Harold Smith could feel nothing below his waist.

The airborne advisors stood in a tense cluster at the CP as the Hueys of the Ghostriders came back from Laos. The reporter, Saar, stood nearby as the slicks shut down on the strip cabins empty of ARVN. The pilots joined a huddle.

"I don't know who the hell is running that, but there's NVA right alongside the landing zone and .51 is hitting inside. Six ships hit, one went down, and one aircraft commander hit in the spine so he can't move his legs. What are they trying to prove?"

"We started taking fire from a klick out."

"That's two of my birds got shot up today. They can stick this flying up their ass. What are they trying to prove?"

The height of the debacle, Saar thought, that's what this is. He'd been at the airborne CP for several hours, watching the Hueys coming and going, disgorging over a hundred dead and wounded paratroopers. Almost all of the dead were barefoot and wrapped in ponchos tied with cords, or in U.S. body bags. They were stacked like firewood, weapons and gear piled beside them. ". . . And among the helmets, is one drilled front and rear with odd precision by a Kalashnikov bullet. . . ." he wrote. The underground medical bunker, made of sandbags and carved earth, was a hell of moans and screams under hazy flourescent light. The wounded lay in blood and bandages, just off the choppers, still wearing their muddy uniforms. There were a hundred casualties, so many that they filled the bunker and had to be carried to a troop tent.

The ARVN are losing, Saar thought. He did not think the ARVN were collapsing because they were cowards; in fact, he considered them reasonably well trained, equipped, and led. But, in the final analysis, it is the spirit of the troops on the ground, when all things are equal, that will determine the victors and losers, and the ARVN lacked the fervor and conviction of the North Vietnamese. His attitude must have been obvious to the ARVN; when he was standing with fellow journalist Okamura, some airborne officers asked, "Okay, what would you do if you were the general?" Okamura smiled broadly. "Do you mean a Vietnamese general," he said, adding fierce emphasis on the end, "or a Japanese general?"

Saar returned to the Ghostriders on the strip. Word came to try again and they bitched and cursed, but climbed into their Hueys. It seemed to him that they flew not out of charity for the South Vietnamese but because of personal and unit loyalties. He was still there when the slicks returned, fended off by the intense fire before they could get the ARVN aboard. One of the ships settled on the strip, hit so many times that it reminded Saar of a target drogue. An armored seat in the cockpit was laid back and dripped blood on the metal floor. The pilot, a popular young lifer captain, had had his leg shot apart. A young warrant officer ran up, threw his hat to the ground, and shouted in anguish, "The sons'a bitches just ain't worth it!" The door gunner, a handsome kid, blond hair sweaty against his forehead, stared, haunted, at a hole torn in the metal just above his head. Pilots smiled at him. He wandered aimlessly off the strip, shaking his head. "I can see going out there for GIs," someone grumbled, "but it's not worth it for these guys. What are they trying to prove?" Curious ARVN paratroopers edged closer to have a look at the shot-up Huey. The pilots screamed at them to get the hell out. The advisors jogged over to lead the ARVN away.

That night Saar joined the ARVN doctors for supper in their underground mess; it was a fine affair considering the surroundings, with the surgeons' servants putting liquor, tea, and food on the table. Saar thought the lighting was dramatic, with pools of light and shadow playing against the sandbags. The scene was made even more dramatic when an American advisor noisily cleared his throat from the shadowed bunker entrance. Conversations at the table hushed. The advisor spoke awkwardly, "About the two refusals by the medevac birds today . . . wanted to say that we are going to find out what happened." The advisor excused himself and Saar noted, "There is laughter and normality, but another dividing line had been drawn between allies."

On 20 March, the 2d and 7th Airborne Battalions broke contact with the NVA and regrouped on a ridgeline. The paratroopers, about six hundred of them, held the eastern portion of the hill mass and the NVA fired on them from the west. Lieutenant Colonel Peachy controlled the extraction with birds from his battalion and the 223d CAB. North Vietnamese mortar fire plastered the LZ, so Peachy directed in airstrikes and gunships. At the same time, he courageously escorted each slick in through the foggy valley. Some ARVN were pulled out, but several choppers were hit and went down. Peachy himself was seriously wounded when his C&C was hit.

The initial extraction was cancelled.

The helicopters settled back at Khe Sanh to refuel, rearm, and reorganize. Lieutenant Smith was standing beside his Huey when a pilot with a 101st patch ran down from the medical bunker, screaming about his copilot, "What the hell you send us in there for! There's no way to get in there, you're just leading us to a death trap!" Other pilots held him; he seemed upset enough to go for a commander.

The weather got better. More USAF strikes hammered around the ARVN paratroopers, a naval smoke barrage was laid to the west of the LZ, and the aircrews cranked up to give it another try. Smith was flying chalk eight; a hundred yards short of the LZ, green tracers burned by his ship. There were hits and the engine conked out. Smith brought it in for a controlled crash in a field of low brush, everyone jumped out unscathed, and, before the rotors even slowed down, a UH1C gunship was darting low to cover them. It was from the 48th Joker Guns and piloted by Smith's buddy, WO Fred Cristman, nineteen, of North Carolina. Cristman flew past, raking the brush with his minigun, while a Huey bore in. Smith and his crew climbed aboard it and they headed back for Khe Sanh.

The rest of the helicopters continued into the hot LZ. Cristman's gunship was hit, crashed into the ARVN perimeter, and was hit on the roof by a mortar round just as the crew jumped out. Cristman, his copilot, and the crew chief were thrown to the ground. Only the door gunner, Sp4 Paul Lagenour, survived the direct hit, with shrapnel wounds in his left arm. The North Vietnamese tried to overrun the LZ but the paratroopers opened fire as they pushed Lagenour to a radio. He directed airstrikes and gunships on the NVA and their attack petered out.

The second extraction attempt was halted.

The ARVN still in the LZ clustered around Lagenour all night as he stayed on the radio. He was a young kid and he sounded scared to Smith, who listened with the other crewmen at Dong Ha, but he was holding himself together well under the pressure. Support fire was brought to bear throughout the night.

By the evening of 20 March, only a few remnants of the 1st Infantry Division remained in Laos: the 2d Regiment CP, 2/2, 4/2, 1/3, and an artillery unit. They were located near Delta One, the division's last firebase along the escarpment. A pickup that day by the 223d CAB had gotten the ARVN 3/2 back to Vietnam. Those still in place repelled a night attack and, in the morning, the 14th and 223d CABs came in to get the survivors.

Some infantry and artillery units remained at Delta One to provide support if the NVA launched a final assault during the pullout, while most of the ARVN organized in clear spots around the perimeter. Lieutenant Colonel Kirklighter, having been told he had 550 men to evacuate, figured eighty slick loads would do the job; he and Klose circled high, letting the company commanders run a simple daisy chain. The Hueys went in two or three at a time. There was no NVA fire. Kirklighter figured the NVA were just glad to see them get the hell out.

He finally broke in on the radio, "What's it look like down there?"

A company commander said, "We still got a helluva lot of people down here."

Kirklighter advised the next company flying in, which soon departed with ten more cabins full, and with the report that more ARVN were milling around the area. Ten more Hueys came and went, and their trail ship reported still more troops on the ground. With a hundred slicks already having gone in, Kirklighter and Klose finally brought the C&C down. They were astonished to see some 500 ARVN on the ground; they had been told they were to get 550 and had already taken out 500, but were only halfway through. Slicks kept going in. Kirklighter got on the radio to Colonel Harrison at Kilo and said he would keep pulling the men out, but suggested jokingly that he check their identification because he had no idea who they were. Back at Kilo, General Phu and Colonel Harrison were ecstatic; not only were their last battalions being extracted without difficulty but hundreds of missing soldiers who'd been written off as dead were straggling to the last pickup zone.

Kirklighter and Klose returned to thirty-five hundred feet to supervise. They saw some vehicles several kilometers away, coming east on Route 9. They were running a well-disciplined road march with about fifty meters between each vehicle. Kirklighter ignored them until it dawned on him that no ARVN armor was still supposed to be that far west. The pullout from Delta One was progressing smoothly, so Klose took them down for a look. From a bit closer, they could make out the dark spots on the road as tanks but couldn't tell if they were of U.S. or Soviet make. Kirklighter got on the radio to General Berry at Khe Sanh. He confirmed that there were no ARVN units in that area.

Before long a flight of F100s rolled in to strafe. Kirklighter and Klose departed to watch from a safe distance. The jets roared down from four thousand feet straight at the tanks, dropped their bombs at practically ground level, then pulled up and came around for another pass. They hit the lead and rear tanks, blocking the column, then strafed leisurely—a field day, Kirklighter thought, as he watched the fireworks of snake-eye bombs and twenty mike-mikes. One of the jets made its turn so that Kirklighter found himself looking down the tailpipe and, at the same time, able to see the intended target in a direct line below the plane. The pilot unleashed his ordnance at low level; then he simply flew straight into a gently rolling hill. Kirklighter was shocked. The pilot may have been hit, but there had been nothing erratic in the flight; Kirklighter knew pilots could become locked on a target, mesmerized, and lose touch with everything else. That's what he thought had happened, for the jet had simply followed its dive path into the ground, nose first. The jet exploded and burned in the grass, and Klose felt a particular pang of remorse. The bodies of the two pilots would never be recovered, thus they'd be carried as MIA; though he knew they were just ashes, their parents would never know for sure.

A radio call came from the last company commander over Delta One. They had everyone out of the PZs and were heading for Kilo. Klose turned the C&C around and headed back, as the jets continued strafing and smoke rose from several burning tanks. At Kilo they made a head count: 919 soldiers had been pulled out that afternoon. The ARVN 1st Infantry Division was finally out of Laos.

On the afternoon of 21 March, the choppers went back to pick up Sp4 Lagenour and the ARVN paratroopers still on the ground. They walked east, the wounded door-gunner calling in airstrikes along the way, and grouped at a small hill for the extraction. This is reportedly what happened: The first slick filled with ARVN; Lagenour ran towards the second, but mobbing ARVN shoved him aside and he tumbled into a ravine, out of sight, the helicopters departing without him.

Lagenour was not seen again until eleven days later. He walked east the whole time, travelling by night, sleeping by day, eating leaves and rice, evading NVA units in the area. Twice he was almost captured, and once a U.S. gunship almost killed him. Thirty kilometers and eleven days later, Sp4 Lagenour was found by a U.S. armored patrol west of Khe Sanh. Lieutenant Smith was detailed to investigate the incident, but Lagenour was medically evacuated to the United States before anyone could talk with him. The impression among the aircrews, however erroneous, was that the lifers wanted Lagenour out of the way before he could tell anyone what he'd seen with the ARVN.

As the general withdrawal continued, General Berry and Colonel

Ghai, deputy commander of the ARVN 1st Infantry Division, planned a raid into BA 611 in Laos to keep the enemy guessing and off balance. The always tough Hoc Bao Company conducted the successful foray. This completed, Berry bid his friend and comrade, Ghai, goodbye and asked him how he thought the war would finally end.

"It will never end," Colonel Ghai said. "It will go on forever."

CHAPTER FIFTEEN: Ambush Alley

The ARVN 1st Armor Brigade was also pulling out via Route 9. The North Vietnamese were waiting for them. It was a chaotic and bloody episode, made even more dramatic as American armor and cavalry units rushed to the border to hold the road against repeated ambushes. At the same time, they were trying to evacuate the U.S. artillery in the area before their firebases were overrun. For the American ground troops in the operation, it was perhaps the most sustained action they ever saw.

Captain Downey, observing Route 9 from his hilltop perch, remarked, "It was quite exciting to watch our convoys come charging around that bend with all guns blazing and the NVA rockets coming back at them. Although it became much less a charming scene when you reminded yourself that men were dying down there in some very horrible ways. The color of the tracers, rockets, and explosions was awesomely beautiful. In every case the ambush was overcome or silenced and my arty FO helped by directing howitzer fire against the NVA. The guys from the 5th Mech and the other armored cav outfits were a brave and tough bunch of men. They fought their way up that road every day, sometimes several times a day, and each time they went they knew what to expect. They behaved in a way that would have made the original General Patton proud. If it had been World War Two, someone would have written exciting stories about them. Ernie Pyle'd have loved 'em."

The border firebases were held by the 8/4 and 2/94 Artillery, XXIV Corps, who had moved into position on 9 February. Until then they'd been living in the mud at Vandegrift and Khe Sanh; for Pfc James Keeney, a radioman with C/2/94, this had been an eye-opening week of war. He was nineteen, from the small farming community of Chillicothe, Missouri, a country boy who'd answered the draft unhesitatingly when his number had come up. He arrived as a new guy in January, during a standdown in Da Nang, and the first thing he saw was a burnt-out personnel carrier. It had hit a mine, two men had been killed, and the artillerymen talked of revenge on the enemy. That's what Keeney had expected of Vietnam. But the rest of the standdown was a confusing experience, a shock to see that things were not as he'd thought they'd be. The blacks and whites shunned each other: there were fistfights. Night guard on the bunker line consisted of pot parties and prostitutes who were allowed inside the wire. About half of the battery turned on with grass, but there were a half-dozen men hooked on heroin and they frightened Keeney; they seemed paranoid and crazy enough to kill you if they thought you'd turn them in.

It wasn't until the road-march to Vandegrift that the battalion changed into what Keeney expected from the army and Vietnam. The drug use dropped dramatically, and the artillerymen tucked away their differences to work as an effective team. The soldiers of 8/4 and 2/94 set up on the border off Route 9 at a place called Lao Bao. It was simply a ragged circle in the jungle, trees knocked down, the ground pitted and uneven, and quickly pulverized to dust by all of the machinery pulling in.

They were still digging in that first day, when the NVA began shelling from Laos. Keeney and a buddy nicknamed Whitey jumped into a little bunker meant for one and scrunched up, Keeney terrified at the roar around them and the dirt clods bouncing into the entrance. Most hunkered in holes, waiting it out in a cold sweat, but a staff sergeant in 2/94 jumped up amid the explosions, gathered some volunteers, and ran to one of the 175mm pieces. They climbed aboard and managed to fire several rounds towards the NVA before a shell exploded directly behind them, hurling the men dead or wounded from the cannon.

The NVA shelling finally stopped. Men warily got up. Medevacs came in. Keeney and Whitey climbed from their bunker to see the staff sergeant standing nearby, amid some other GIs, holding his helmet which had a big shrapnel hole in it. He was drained white and shaking. The sergeant was a big, bald, well-muscled Southerner, and Keeney considered him a macho, beer-chugging type. He also didn't think much of his dash to the artillery piece. It was stupid, he thought; instead of keeping his men under cover and calling for support fire, the lifer got gung-ho and ran to do it himself. And two of the guys with him got blown away. But Keeney couldn't drag up much anger at the sergeant. He'd exposed himself to the fire, had taken his chances alongside his men. In a way, he thought, I guess he's a hero.

Sp4 Pat Hallman, a draftee in B/8/4, had no problems determining who was a hero and who was not. When the sergeant and volunteers ran out into the flying steel to return fire, he thought they were the greatest. They'd gotten up and tried. He stood there shaking inside after the shelling, exhausted from his first moments of combat, and hurting inside from a terrible thought. He hadn't been able to move when the artillery was pounding in. In the American rite of passage known as war, his greatest accomplishment had been to cringe in a hole. At the age of twenty-one, he felt like a coward.

Sergeant Hatfield struggled with his own doubts that day. By four in the afternoon, 8/4 had repacked and moved back towards Lang Vei, leaving 2/94 on the border alone, and leaving Hatfield to wonder why they had even gone forward. They had gotten people killed for no reason that he could see; the difference of a couple of kilometers made no difference in their fire missions into Laos, and he wondered why higher had sent them within range of the NVA guns to begin with. His anger increased that night as they set up near Lang Vei; some of the GIs told him a friend of his, a young man also from Washington whose parents he knew, had been one of those killed in the shelling. Hatfield could have cried. It was all such a game, Hatfield thought, and that day he could feel himself in sympathy with the bitterness and frustration of his men. He was a professional soldier, saw Vietnam as a necessary evil, but so often it all seemed such a useless waste.

His only consolation was that the draftees in a unit he had considered garrison, learned to fight day-by-day, and some were even decorated for genuine valor.

The batteries were booming out rounds from Lao Bao into Laos, and Pfc Keeney was standing around watching when the captain told him to hustle down to an engineer truck unloading supplies to get a case each of soda and beer. He was walking towards the truck when a distant boom and shriek hit his ears above the sound of their own artillery, and he threw himself down. Fifty yards ahead of him the truck exploded. A few more shells impacted around the perimeter; then there was silence except for the horrible screaming from the gutted truck. Keeney ran over. Three GIs were sprawled dead around the wreck, mangled by shrapnel. Two other men lay there, one in shock with an eye blown out, the other screaming with his leg split up to his crotch.

They were just fish in a barrel, Keeney thought.

Sights were seared into the memories of those down in the gun pits. When Sp4 Hallman crawled from a hole after bombardment, he could only stare, too scared to do anything, at the wounded gunner before him. The kid leaned against the treads of a 175mm SP, drained white, smoking a cigarette and mumbling to the medic working on him, "I'm going home. . . . I'm going home. . . ." His legs were a bloody mess, his flak jacket practically ripped off of him. They heard later, he died on the medevac. Another man in the battalion put an M-16 to his foot to get out. The worst of it for Hallman was when a buddy, a hard-working religious kid from the South, got blown away. He'd been at his post on the guns and couldn't hear the whistle of incoming over the roar of outgoing. He died instantly. A sergeant came back from R&R with a case of booze; they sat in a bunker that night, not celebrating as they had planned, but drowning their sorrows in alcohol. Hallman felt that a little piece of him had died, and self-hate pounded at him as if he thought he could have done something to save his dead friend. The shellings were cracking him up.

Sgt. Drayton Markle was dispatched with four Dusters and one APC of A/1/44 Artillery, as perimeter security to Lao Bao. It sat like a bulge into Laos. They set up on the southern side of the perimeter, down a small grassy slope so they could hear but not see the 2/94 Artillery. The Co Roc was ahead of them across the border river so they buried their vehicles up to the turrets to protect them. It was just plain shitty, Markle thought, the North Vietnamese dropping in a couple of hundred rounds a day on their little perimeter. You could see the puffs of smoke on the Co Roc, hear the boom and whistle and know you had only seconds to scramble into the nearest bunker or hole.

It was tough, but Markle tried to keep his spirits up by concentrating on the funny things. One hot meal a day was flown in by helicopters in thermite cans, and as soon as a dozen men lined up for chow, the NVA observer would start another shelling. Everyone would run for cover. It would let up in about ten minutes; then heads would start popping up like moles. The first man would get brave and go back to get some chow, another line would form, and the shelling would start all over again. During another bombardment, Markle and a buddy, an Sp4 named Jack Wooten, got gung-ho and ran to their Duster to return fire at the Co Roc. Wooten was pumping rounds amid the incoming when he suddenly asked Markle for his helmet. Markle handed it to him with a puzzled look, because no one put much faith in the GI steel pot to stop anything, and Wooten grinned, "Yeah, I know, but it just feels better." Markle thought the funniest thing he saw happened when a chaplain set up a makeshift altar beside a truck in a bulldozed ditch. About fifteen artillerymen sat on a mound listening to the sermon when the chaplain held up his hands in a blessing—and a boom echoed from the Co Roc. Before Markle could even get to his feet, the chaplain turned and, with his hands still up, bent over, he dove between the truck and the trench wall. REMFs always take everything seriously, Markle thought.

But the bad things were all around and even a trooper like Markle who believed in what they were fighting for couldn't help but be worn down. It pissed him off to see ARVN convoys going by on Route 9 with lumber and steel planking, when the GIs had only sandbags and culverts. There was the time that the barrel on one of the 175mm guns broke in half from metal fatigue, then fired and flew across the perimeter to shatter the skull of a GI sitting on a perimeter bunker, his back to the gun. He never knew what hit him. Another morning Markle woke to see a 175mm SP blown up and a path gouged behind the wreck. The story was that the crew had put in the wrong charge; the breach block had blown off like a cannonball and had caught the gunner in the chest, hurling his body so hard he dug the trench. The two artillerymen beside the gun were caught in the powder blast.

The 8/4 Artillery, camped between Lao Bao and Lang Vei, was the first ordered back from the border. The 2/94 Artillery was the next, but unlike the peaceful withdrawal of their sister battalion, theirs became a trial by fire. On the afternoon of 18 March, Bravo Battery at Lao Bao packed up to move. At the same time, a platoon from the 1/11 Infantry was mortared while holding the road open for them. One GI was killed, six wounded. Whatever could not be loaded on trucks, and whatever vehicles would not start, were abandoned. The NVA shelled Bravo Battery as they hit the road, at a toll of sixteen wounded artillerymen, plus the destruction of much of their equipment and vehicles. Of the materiel left behind, all was blown up by the accurate NVA bombardment except for a broken-down 175mm left in its berm.

At around five in the afternoon, after the departure of B Battery, Alpha Battery prepared to follow. To Pfc Steven Rhodes, of Aberdeen, South Dakota, nothing could have been better. The op had started on an ugly note for Rhodes during the convoy north. A friend had been tossed off of their truck when the driver'd swerved around a shell hold. By the time they had run to the man, a medic was doing mouth-to-mouth; the friend's head was smashed. He'd gasped for air, turned blue, and died on the medevac. At Lao Bao, the shellings had been hitting home, and most of the last few days had been spent underground with some buddies, the earth shaking as if a train was rumbling past, shrapnel pelting off of the sandbags, dust clouds rolling in the bunker entrance. A few nights back, Rhodes had crouched in the bunker with his M-16 at the ready while artillery impacted in a treeline behind him and green AK-47 tracers erupted along the perimeter. Sappers were probing the wire; a quad-fifty, with the cynical slogan PARIS PEACE TALKS on the turret, instantly streamed red tracers in return. He heard the gunner shout, "I got one!" and things quieted back down.

It was getting too close for comfort as far as Rhodes was concerned, and he gladly threw his poncho, cot, and footlocker into a commo truck. His buddy took down a peace flag that they had flown over their bunker, torn with shrapnel holes, and packed that too. In a half hour, the battery was ready to go. They abandoned two trucks, four trailers, and an eight-inch gun that would not start. An artilleryman manned an M-60 atop the FDC track; behind that Rhodes climbed into the commo truck and squeezed among the stacked gear, able only to see rewards due to the side boards. When they hit the road, fire snapped at them and the M-60 gunner raked the brush in return. The commo truck veered to one side and Rhodes saw a helmet lying on the road. He thought someone must have dropped it. With another sharp veer, he saw a jeep on the side, smoke rolling from under the hood: then a body came into view—sprawled on the road, the head blown, nothing remaining but a bloody stump and a pool of blood. They stopped, another truck pulled up behind them, and a sergeant quickly hooked up the wrecked jeep. They took off again, headed for Lang Vei.

Charlie Battery had also been scheduled to leave Lao Bao that afternoon, but the NVA artillery and ground ambushes along Route 9 prevented it. That night Pfc Keeney manned a perimeter bunker with two other artillerymen, unaware that they were cut off and alone. The North Vietnamese knew, though, and a sapper squad moved against the semiabandoned perimeter. The brush moved in the darkness, and Keeney choked to see shadows gliding through the elephant grass. He shouldered his M-16. The sappers crept forward through the high grass; the artillerymen sat silently watching from the bunker, the moonlight catching the details—a dozen sappers, stripped to shorts, smeared with charcoal, and carrying satchel charges. They stepped into an open engineer trail and Keeney fired. A body tumbled in his rifle sights. They sprayed on automatic, a tracer hit one of the satchel charges, and it exploded amid the group. The shooting petered off. In the morning, Keeney took a photograph of the dozen North Vietnamese soldiers spread-eagled on the road. It was the first time he'd killed. He was a hard-muscled, broad-faced, country boy with a country boy's sensibilities. He felt no regret. Them or us, he thought, simple as that.

That evening, 18 March, the gears to withdraw the ARVN 1st Armor Brigade from Aloui were set in motion by General Lam at his nightly I Corps briefing. Until then, the brigade had been pummelled by NVA bombardment and attack. They had held their ground, but little good had come of it, as Colonel Battreall noted in his after-action report: "In the period 4–16 March the Bde received a plethora of instructions from both Div and Corps variously directing it to seize objectives deep in enemy territory, block at ALUI, move 'as far as possible' in one or another direction, not to cross this or that grid line, etc. The result was that the Bde blocked a km or two north and west of ALUI. . . . The principles of the Objective, Mass, and Unity of Command were violated."

Lam directed that the 1st Armor begin its eastward road-march the next morning, and allocated two troops from the 2/17 Air Cav to General Dong for use in covering the withdrawal from ambushes. That evening Colonel Battreall received a radio call from General Sutherland, their only personal contact during the operation. Sutherland was concerned about the numerous disabled vehicles the brigade had at Aloui and offered to dispatch a company of ARVN M578 recovery vehicles with which to tow the downed armor.

"What am I going to do with a company of dragon wagons?" Battreall answered, "the road is not passable."

Sutherland sputtered, obviously hearing this for the first time.

Battreall was shocked at how far removed XXIV Corps was from the realities of the battlefield, but he surmised that it was not the fault of Sutherland or his staff. It was the recurring problem of having no advisors in Laos, and the disjunctions that resulted. This one happened because the U.S. had intended the ARVN Airborne to physically secure Route 9 against the NVA and improve the dirt trail, while the ARVN had interpreted the instructions merely to mean they should bring Route 9 under artillery fire. The highway was in wretched condition west of LZ Bravo, usable only by tanks and tracked vehicles. Not even a jeep could make it to Aloui.

Early the next morning, Colonel Luat and the 1st Armor departed Aloui, bringing out their damaged vehicles, towed by like vehicles. An FAC pilot overflying the abandoned basecamp reported four NVA tanks closing towards it. The two air cav troops which were to have screened ahead of the armor to detect ambushes were diverted by Dong to his airborne units. Thus, the 1st Armor was left to travel the narrow, terrain-restricted road with no flank or scouting security.

The first NVA ambush came before eight in the morning at a stream crossing between Aloui and LZ Alpha. The lead tanks were sloshing through the water when the North Vietnamese cut loose from hidden jungle positions. The lead tank was hit and some of the ARVN panicked, abandoning four vehicles in the stream, some of the attached paratroopers continuing alone down the road in chaos. In three hours of fighting, the ARVN managed to subdue the NVA fire long enough to move two of the abandoned tanks to the side so the rest of the column could continue. The brigade kept moving, leaving one disabled tank in the water and cutting loose seventeen of the disabled vehicles they were towing so that the remaining ones could move and fight when more of the inevitable ambushes occurred.

North Vietnamese units followed the withdrawal and moved into the ambush site with PT76 tanks and infantrymen who clambered aboard the ARVN vehicles. The Dutchmasters of the 7/1 Air Cav, overflying the area, glimpsed a bewildering scene of ARVN and NVA tanks in the same area. They had a moment of shock until they comprehended that there were NVA firing from the ARVN tanks. A Cobra pilot, WO Marvin "Doc" Beck, roared in to unleash a 2.75-inch rocket into the engine deck of one of the PT76s on the road. The tank blew up, blocking the path, and USAF jets arrived to demolish the seventeen abandoned ARVN vehicles. Back at Quang Tri, Beck painted a tank silhouette on the nose of his gunship.

In the morning of 19 March, Pfc Keeney climbed wearily from his bunker only to look shocked at the scene around him: the Lao Bao perimeter looked like a ghost town. Where A and B Batteries had been, there were now only abandoned 175mm and eight-inch guns, stalled trucks, empty bunkers, piles of expended shells, stacks of live ammunition, cartons of C rations, and other odds and ends. Groups of ARVN straggling out of Laos walked through the abandoned perimeter; Keeney thought they looked wild-eyed and hungry, only one or two still carrying rifles. The ARVN ducked into the bunkers to stuff their shirts with C rations and the artillerymen shouted at them to clear out. Someone fired his M-16 over their heads, not too concerned about how close he came, and the ARVN scurried into a bunker. Then they crawled away in the brush; like snakes, Keeney thought, damned cowards.

By noontime the gravity of their situation began to hit them. It was hot and dusty, and down the road they could hear shots and explosions. A helicopter weaved bumpily over the perimeter, shaking from hits, and sailed towards the ground. A hundred yards from the wire, it lurched forward and burst into flames on impact. A patrol of artillerymen quickly moved out to rescue the crew, but there were no survivors. Phantoms pummelled the area around them, a couple screaming low over Lao Bao doing victory rolls. Victory rolls, he thought, my God, what do those pilots see out there? How close are the gooks?

The NVA shelling started again and they scrambled underground. The truth suddenly hit Keeney like a dead weight—they were cut off—and he felt scared, forgotten, glad the jets were on his side. Several hundred artillery rounds exploded on Lao Bao as they crouched in the bunkers, some of the men bitching.

"What the shit's going on?"

"Here we are fighting for a bunch of chicken-shit ARVN, and they leave us!"

By nighttime Keeney was back in his bunker trying to sleep. He'd been able to sustain his flagging spirits during the day because all of his buddies were pulling together in the face of crisis. But that night, alone in his dugout, he could feel his morale sink. Oh God, I'm never going to get home, his mind kept repeating. This is it. Boy, Jim, you've really blown it now. You're trying to be the all-American hero, and now you're going to die in this God-forsaken country. For nothing.

On the morning of 20 March, helicopters dropped off three teams from the Long Range Reconnaissance Patrol (LRRP), 1st Brigade, 5th Mech Division into the AO of the 1/11 Infantry. The five-man teams, wearing bush hats and camouflage fatigues, were inserted at various points along Route 9 to pinpoint the location of the NVA who'd hit the road. At nine o'clock, one of the teams found two mines in the road which they blew in place. Then they were ambushed, and the LRRPs called for artillery support. As soon as the arty lifted, they were promptly hit by 82mm mortars. They called in more firepower, and turned up one dead North Vietnamese and an AK-47 rifle.

The NVA fire kept up.

General Hill alerted the commander of the 3/187 Infantry to prepare his C Company as a reaction force, possibly to CA in. Meanwhile he ordered Lieutenant Colonel Breeding of the 1/1 Cavalry to dispatch immediate reinforcements to the LRRPs. The closest cavalry outfit was two platoons of Bravo Troop, under Capt. Carlos A. Poveda, a thin

Puerto Rican. Bravo clipped down Route 9 only to be ambushed themselves. A raking of AK and RPG fire killed one GI, wounded five, and damaged an APC and a Sheridan. Captain Poveda pulled the two platoons back and called in arty and air on the south side of the road where the NVA were dug in. Napalm and five-hundred-pound bombs raised smoke and Bravo swept forward again; they were met by a level of fire undiminished for all the U.S. firepower employed, and another trooper was killed. More air and arty were called in on the NVA. Bravo moved forward a third time and was again forced back in the face of heavy fire.

Captain Poveda was coming in last, covering the retreat, when his APC hit a mine. He and his crew, one of them wounded, were cut off and left behind in the disorganized withdrawal. A Huey went down on the road nearby and its crew joined the pullout. Bravo troop reorganized on Route 9 and two tracks went back to rescue Poveda and his crew. They tore full throttle down Route 9 on a Thunder Run, the fifty and sixty gunners laying down a constant hail of lead into the roadside brush, and the men climbed aboard one of the APCs.

The retreat under fire continued.

Sgt. Jim McCormack, twenty, a draftee from Waterbury, Connecticut, was in one of the LRRP teams which initially did not make contact. He knew it to be a bad area, though; the night before, his five-man team had crouched silently in the jungle as a North Vietnamese unit filed past. This morning was clear and sunny when the choppers deposited them on Route 9 and, in short order, they walked into an abandoned NVA bunker complex. Another chopper dropped off demolition charges to blow the bunkers.

They were doing this when someone on the radio told McCormack to get his team to haul ass back to the highway.

They heard heavy firing as they moved back, and proceeded with caution, not wanting to be mistaken for the enemy. They emerged from the brush into chaos—a 175mm SP was abandoned on the road, Sheridans and APCs were hauling east in clouds of red dust, fire cracking in both directions. Grunts on the tracks shouted to come on, and the LRRPs ran like hell to get behind some armor. One young Lurp hustled towards a truck dragging a water trailer just as an RPG blew the trailer away: he collapsed in shock. McCormack and the others threw him into the truck bed, then climbed to the deck of an APC. The NVA raked them with fire and they returned it, McCormack firing his M-16, amazed to see North Vietnamese in broad daylight ducking from bush to bush.

They acted as if they owned the place.

Bravo Troop kept hauling east, then pulled into a rough circle on Route 9 and laid down fifty and sixty fire in all directions. AKs cracked back at them. McCormack was firing his rifle when an RPG shrieked at the APC beside his. The track commander's head exploded and the driver, suddenly splattered with blood and bits of flesh, went into shock. Something boomed in front of McCormack's APC and shrapnel stung his face and head; a LRRP medic hastily wrapped a bandage around his forehead as he kept his M-16 in action. The firepower of the wagon-train circle did no good, so they hit Route 9 again, firing and taking fire until they were about a mile from the ambush site.

Bravo Troop halted on the roadside and it was pandemonium as the casualties were carried from the vehicles to be treated. McCormack was waiting for the medevac when the grunts around him began speaking incredulously of an order that had just been radioed to Captain Poveda; because the disabled command APC had a radio decipher code in it, Bravo Troop was to proceed back into the ambush zone to secure the wreck and the nearby downed helicopter. As it was not a matter of rescuing Americans, but of salvaging materiel, none of the GIs McCormack saw seemed willing to go back—for the sake of a radio. He himself was taken aback by the stupidity of such an order. If the gear's so important, he thought, why not just have a Cobra blow it apart so the enemy can't get to it. A medevac came in and Sergeant McCormack got on board, glad to get the hell out of the situation; the bird lifted off with three WIAs and two KIAs.

The MPs at a Route 9 checkpoint told Sgt. Frank Burnett that a cav unit was in trouble. The only cav folks he knew in the area was Bravo Troop. He'd helicoptered to them the day before, dispatched from Hq&Hq Troop to check on some complaints about the mail; when he'd left this morning to hitchhike back to the 1/1 Cav Rear in Chu Lai, Bravo had been laagered off the road with some artillery and ARVN units. His first thought now was that the grunts were in a shooting feud with the ARVN, but he decided to hop in the MP jeep going to the scene.

They halted a hundred feet from Bravo Troop, which was strung out along the side of Route 9. It was chaotic, some men milling around, others lying in the grass with medics bent over them. A helicopter arrived, a senior officer and an NCO hopped out, and Burnett watched the curious sight of the old sergeant running up and down the column, waving his arms and yelling at the men to get back on their vehicles and move out. The grunts ignored him.

Burnett was too far away to hear all of the dialogue.

Lieutenant Colonel Breeding, ten days in command of the squadron, had ordered Poveda to retrieve the APC and helicopter, and Bravo Troop had nonchalantly refused.* Now Breeding and the cavalry sergeant major had come on the scene and were arguing with the grunts who only snapped back with a list of complaints—they had only sixty men left, the NVA were obviously dug in deep and would ambush them again, night was coming, and the equipment just wasn't worth getting killed over. Unimpressed, Breeding said to get moving; one of the grunts guffawed in his face, "You must be out of your fucking mind!" With that the colonel had his sergeant major line up the enlisted men and take down the names of those refusing to go. Two men said they would go; fifty-three refused the order.

General Hill, monitoring the situation from Khe Sanh, got on the radio to calmly ask Poveda why his troop wasn't moving. After Poveda explained the situation, Hill informed him that he was no longer in command.

The GIs of Bravo Troop were disgruntled and when reporters arrived at Lang Vei to give the incident page one coverage, they found the grunts weary, filthy, and bitter. Sp4 Randy Thompson of Evansville, Indiana, was quoted in the press. He was one of the men who had volunteered to go back into the ambush to rescue Poveda, but when it came to Breeding's order, he commented, "The reason given wasn't a very good one. It was after a piece of machinery that could have been replaced. I didn't see any sense in risking any more lives."†

Five days later, Sp4 Thompson was killed in action.

The second day for Charlie Battery, cut off at Lao Bao, was a repeat of the first. Pfc Keeney sat hunched against the impact concussions in a bunker. He could hear no return fire and occupied his mind by counting the incoming rounds: 294. When the shelling finally stopped, the artillerymen ducked a few more harassing rounds to carry the wounded to their LZ, and Keeney stood atop his bunker to watch the Hueys come in. He saw an army chaplain, an older officer, waiting for a ride out. The

* The actual refusal was covered by the press, including a *Time* magazine account (April 5, 1971) "Incident on Route 9" and an article in *Armed Forces Journal* (by Robert Heinl, May 3, 1971).

† As a result of this incident involving Bravo Troop, Lieutenant Colonel Ganahl requested a more reliable armor battalion and the 1/77 Armor was sent in.

chaplain had helicoptered in only the day before, saying he would ride out the siege with his boys; perhaps he'd been called back, but Keeney couldn't shake the feeling that he was running out on them. The Huey was lifting off with the chaplain aboard when the battery's ARVN interpreter suddenly bolted, jumping on a skid and hauling himself inside. The shelling started again.

All that Lieutenant Colonel Ganahl had on his mind was clearing the mess that blocked Route 9. He was the commander of the 2d Battalion, 94th Artillery; his men were trapped at Lao Bao. The situation was critical. Ganahl had been overhead in his C&C when they'd started the withdrawal: he'd been alerted that the road was open, had ordered Bravo Battery to move out, then had watched horrified as 122mm artillery had hit the column as soon as it had rolled onto Route 9. Ganahl was constantly helihopping along the road and it became obvious that the NVA were dug in to stay. Once he and a battery commander had the C&C land in a field outside Lao Bao to check it for use as a camp stop when they finally got out. Time was short, so instead of making a ground inspection, they just looked from the bird, then ordered the pilot up. At that point, AK-47 tracers tore at them from two sides of the treeline and they just managed to veer away. Ganahl flew into Lao Bao and the GIs were tense; their ears were tuned to pick up the sound of incoming amid all of the camp noises, and he noticed they always seemed to be positioned two seconds from a foxhole. He was deeply impressed by the courage and tenacity the artillerymen were displaying, but he knew they were not invincible.

The 1/1 Cavalry had initially been responsible for the road, but they were not the most disciplined troops Ganahl had ever seen. More importantly, as he reported to General Hill, the cav did not have the equipment needed to dig out the NVA. Their Sheridans, for example, were not really tanks, but lightly armored reconnaissance vehicles. With this in mind on the evening of 20 March, General Hill radioed Lieutenant Colonel Meyer with orders to displace the 1/77 Armor with its heavily armored M48 main battle tanks, from Vandegrift to Lang Vei.

It was sunny and hot the next morning as Meyer conferred with Majors Wilson and Murphy; they were to organize the Scout Platoon, Mortar Platoon, the tanks in B and C Companies, and an attached mechanized infantry platoon from B/1/61, and dispatch them down Route 9 to establish the new battalion CP at Lang Vei. At the same time, they were to coordinate the arrival of 101st Airborne elements to take up 1/77's former area of operations. While the units were still gearing up,

Meyer boarded a Loach to fly ahead for a briefing at Khe Sanh. He went alone, trusting Wilson and Murphy to get the battalion moving. He liked to lead from the front, unhindered by staff officers, able to shift quickly from unit to unit. As he took off, they were cleaning up the mess of the previous night's sapper probe on Vandegrift; two blivets of aviation fuel had been burned and one North Vietnamese body found.

At Khe Sanh, General Hill briefed Meyer on the current situation along Route 9. Because the heavy M48 tanks of 1/77 would eventually tear up the unpaved stretch of the highway, they had not maneuvered past Vandegrift in the previous fifty-two days of the operation, and Hill had to orient Meyer on the AO behind Khe Sanh. Lang Vei was more or less secure, but the four miles of road from there to the Laotian border had been nicknamed Ambush Alley by the troops. The Tchepone River, which formed the international boundary, looped north at two points where it was close and parallel to Route 9. It was at these two points that NVA fire was the most intense; the enemy units were able to slip back across the river, which U.S. troops were forbidden to cross, at will. From Lang Vei to a point just west of the first loop in the river, where NVA on the Co Roc could bring the road under fire, was the responsibility of 1/1 Cavalry (Lieutenant Colonel Breeding) with their CP at Lang Vei. From there to the border was the AO of the 1/11 Infantry (Lieutenant Colonel Farrar) with their CP at a point on the border called Ta Bat.

Hill explained that two artillery batteries of the 2/94 Artillery (Lieutenant Colonel Ganahl) were located in the 1/11 AO; the easternmost one was on the south side of the road in the Lao Bao pocket, and the other, an attached battery, was about a kilometer away on the north side of Route 9. The 1/11 CP was only short distance from that artillery position. Hill said that the two batteries had been cut off for three days now, under NVA shelling and probes, and noted that the initial moves into the area had ended with the disaster of the Bravo Troop refusal. A helicopter, some APCs, Sheridans, and 175mm SPs were disabled along Route 9, and General Hill taxed Lieutenant Colonel Meyer with five assignments:

1. reopen Route 9 from Lang Vei to Laos
2. establish effective control of the 1/11 Infantry companies and 1/1 Cavalry troops strung out along the road
3. evacuate the two stranded artillery batteries to the Lang Vei area
4. recover the vehicles and equipment in the area
5. hold the road open for the return of the ARVN 1st Armor Brigade

After his briefing with Hill, Meyer had the Loach pilot fly him to the 1/1 Cav CP at Lang Vei, where he was briefed by Col. James Townes (1/5 Mech Deputy Commander), Lieutenant Colonel Breeding, and Lieutenant Colonel Ganahl. Ganahl and he were friends from West Point, where both had been assistant math professors, and Ganahl wished Dick Meyer good luck, saying he was the man for the job.

While Meyer was being oriented on the situation, the 1/77 Armor task force was moving from Vandegrift with the APCs of the Scout Platoon in the lead. By the time Meyer had the Loach drop him at the front of his moving command, they were just west of Lang Vei. The scouts were linking up with the easternmost element of the 1/1 Cav—Bravo Troop. They were in the process of reorganizing and preparing to evacuate damaged vehicles. Meyer was taken aback at the sight of these Americal Division grunts; they were grubby, unshaven, sloppily dressed, many of the men stripped to the waist in the searing heat. He knew some of his troopers disliked him for forcing them to bake in helmets and flak jackets, but his main concern in enforcing such discipline was to get men home alive. You can't get buddy-buddy with the men, he judged, it only gets them killed in the long run. He talked briefly with the commander of Bravo Troop, told him that he was taking control of the highway, instructed him to get on the 1/77 radio net and to continue reorganizing with his Scout Platoon. He also told the commander to hold their position and secure the flanks for the return of his task force with the artillery.

The tanks and tracks of Charlie Company, which had been following the Scouts in the road march, rumbled in from the east. They halted and Meyer climbed onto the deck of the lead tank, told the staff sergeant to climb to the loader's seat, and took his place in the fifty cupola. The colonel slid the CVC helmet on, snapped the radio mike in front of his mouth, and ordered Charlie Company onward. They roared past the party on the road, churning red dust in the dry, torrid air.

Sergeant Major Nelson was at the 1/77 CP track at Lang Vei, getting things organized, when several tracks from Bravo Troop 1/1 Cav drove into the perimeter. They had four or five dead men in body bags laid across one of the APCs. Some of the tracks had battle damage, and the filthy grunts wearily climbed off, passively mumbling that they were through fighting. They sat down beside a bunker, turning their backs to everything. Nelson inspected the vehicles and discovered that the driving rods and bolts from all of the fifties and sixties were missing. When he asked a couple of Bravo sergeants why the weapons were disabled, they said that the men had done it to prove a point. Nelson asked what the hell was going on, but the young sergeants were long-haired, dusty, and in the same disgusted mood as the grunts; they said they didn't want to talk about it. Nelson, with some of his own NCOs, scrounged spare parts, and repaired the weapons. He called to the GIs about the body bags, but they ignored him, so he and his NCOs had to physically tag the bodies—unzip the bags, check dog tags and wallets on the corpses, and fill out casualty slips to tie to the bags.

Out on Route 9, the rest of Bravo Troop had formed on line, facing west, as 1/77 Armor moved past. Sp4 Spurgeon was walking through and stopped, shocked at the scene. About thirty Bravo grunts stood atop their APCs, many shirtless, six or eight of them yelling and flipping the bird at several officers standing before them. One or two officers shouted back, but Spurgeon could only catch bits of what was said through all of the vehicle noise.

"Fuck you! You wanna get it, get it yourself! You wanted to come here!"

"You'll go because you're a soldier in the United States Army, that's why!"

"Oh yeah, stick it up your ass!"

On the road, the tankers of 1/77 Armor hauled past, raising dust and a loud rumble. They ignored the verbal fighters. They were headed for combat.

Both sides of Route 9 were choked with tangled thickets of elephant grass, brush, and trees, much of it higher than the passing tanks. The column clanked noisily around the first curve west of the Scouts and Bravo and immediately were ambushed. The flash of an RPG being fired came from the left, the shell missed the rear of Meyer's helmet. The 90mm main gun rapidly traversed to roar shot into the brush, the driver accelerated, and Meyer gripped the butterfly handles of the fifty, putting out rounds until the barrel grew steamy, hot brass and links bouncing around his feet. The second tank in the column, with the commander of Charlie Company in the turret, roared in their dusty wake, also hosing down the left side of the road.

Meyer shouted into the intercom for the rest of the column not to fire up the countryside—U.S. troops were in the area.

At the next curve in the road, the NVA opened fire again, RPGs exploded in clouds of smoke and dust, AK rounds clanged against the tanks, and the brush shook in return from 90mm canister rounds and raking bursts from the TC hatches. The tanks never slowed down; their job was rescuing the artillerymen, not routing the entrenched NVA until later. Shortly after outrunning the second ambush, Meyer could see another cav unit on the road, Sheridans and APCs in a wagon-train circle as if expecting a ground attack. It was C/1/1 Cav, and Meyer radioed for their captain to get on the 1/77 net, secure the flanks, and hold the road open for their return. More troops appeared in the area. A company from the 1/11 Infantry was manning roadside foxholes and the battalion commander, Lieutenant Colonel Farrar, was riding in a cav track. Meyer quickly conferred with him on the exact location of the artillery and infantry posts.

Meyer and his tanks got moving again, then slowed down to maneuver around the scene of the Bravo Troop ambush. The burnt-out APC squatted on the side, the Huey, nearby, shot full of holes and the doors hanging open. Blackened rubble lay on the ground, smoke still curling from it. Meyer skirted the wrecks, but when the Charlie Company captain attempted to bypass, his tank lurched into a shell crater. The tank was relatively level, but the tread was down deep enough so only a recovery vehicle could winch it out.

The column came to a halt. The NVA opened up again.

The tanks raised a deafening roar as they fired back into the bushes. An RPG penetrated the command track of Charlie Company and it burst into flames, killing two GIs and wounding three. Mortars and rockets began impacting on the road and the staff sergeant in the turret of the third tank was hurled into the air.

Meyer was hesitant to leave the road, not knowing what obstacles of enemy or terrain might block his tanks. He decided they would just have to maneuver under fire past the wrecks. During a slack in the enemy fire, a lone medevac darted into the swirling road dust to take the casualties aboard. At the same time, a second company from the 1/11 Infantry swept in from the side of the road, and Meyer radioed their CO to stay put to secure the area around the ditched tank. He also ordered his Bravo Company tanks, which were bringing up the rear, to stay and disperse in the area while he proceeded towards the artillery with just Charlie Company.

Inside the artillery perimeter, Keeney could hear the shooting to the east, when they weren't ducking into their bunkers from all of the incoming. He was more than nervous. The treelines shimmered in the wilting heat, flies swarmed thickly over abandoned food and the rotting bodies of ARVN and NVA around the perimeter. The stench was terrible. They were short of ammunition and water. At around noon, he heard the blasts getting closer, heard the distinct roar of vehicle engines.

Keeney had a terrible thought about Soviet-made tanks.

The first U.S. M48 main battle tank roared into the center of camp, easily busting through the elephant grass and the flimsy perimeter of culvert bunkers and a single strand of concertina. Two other tanks drove to the opposite end of the perimeter to set up some kind of defense. Keeney stood near the lead tank and could see the man in the TC hatch from the waist up. He was buttoned up in a CVC helmet and flak jacket, a lieutenant colonel insignia on his collar, and had the 5th Mech Red Devil shoulder patch on his dusty sleeve.

Keeney had no idea who Lieutenant Colonel Meyer was.

Meyer surveyed the grimy artillerymen around the tank. "Are you boys ready to get out of here?"

"Hell yes, let's go!"

Meyer was impressed; the artillerymen looked tough and disciplined.

The link-up had been made with Lao Bao, but Meyer still had to get his tanks another kilometer or so further, to the 1/11 CP, and then double back to the other artillery position, both of which were on the north side of the road. They kept moving and found the infantry CP, which was only some foxholes in the low brush covered with culverts and sandbags. Meyer could see no tents, bunkers, or anything permanent. As the armor took up positions around the perimeter, the freight-train sound of incoming rumbled in. Fired from Laos, 122mm artillery accurately impacted inside the CP. The grunts scrambled for their foxholes and the tankers slammed shut the hatches of their big M48s.

The call for mech infantry support for the 1/77 run to the arty was relayed to Bravo Company 1/61. They mounted out of Charlie Two on the DMZ, packing onto their APCs, and hauled down Route 9. Coming around a bend in the road, the TC in the lead track saw a lone NVA down the stretch, his back to them, burying a mine. The TC cut the North Vietnamese in half with a sweeping burst of his fifty. They stopped at Vandegrift, two of the platoons deploying on the perimeter, and the First Platoon continued full throttle down the dirt highway. Near Lang Vei, they took RPG fire, the third track hit from a hedgerow forty yards away. The rocket-propelled grenade shot a couple of feet over the track deck, and caught an M-60 gunner in the trunk, blowing his head off, and spraying the others with shrapnel. The first two tracks wheeled towards the ambush, laying down a wall of fire against the AK. The Delta on the second APC jumped enraged from his hatch, grabbed an M-60, and charged into the hedgerow, firing madly. The NVA fell back, leaving two bodies and blood trails in the brush.

The platoon continued its dusty race.

At the 1/11 CP, Lieutenant Colonel Meyer stayed hunkered in his tank turret as the NVA barrage continued. He monitored the various actions over the radio, then called Colonel Townes to update him on the situation. He and the tanks of C Company were in place with 1/11 at Ta Bat; he had radio communications with two companies of 1/11 and two troops of 1/1 Cav holding flanking positions on Route 9 with his Scout Platoon; B Company tanks were securing the area where the APC was burning and tracks of B/1/61 had linked up there. To add to the confusion, the single 1/11 company at Ta Bat and the battalion command group were scheduled to be helicoptered to Khe Sanh. Colonel Townes directed that the infantry withdrawal should continue when the shelling allowed, and for Meyer to put the 1/11 vehicles into his road force. Meyer requested permission to try to evacuate the artillery batteries at this point, and Townes gave him the go-ahead.

It was now around four in the afternoon.

When a lull came in the shelling, the helicopter Meyer had requested quickly darted into the Ta Bat LZ and he climbed in. The Kiowa Scout dropped him at the second artillery battery, located between Ta Bat and Lao Bao, and he ordered them to assemble their gear and their 175mm SPs in march order. The tanks of Bravo were ordered up to escort the battery. They were to hit Route 9 going east, link up with the battery at Lao Bao, and continue full throttle for Lang Vei.

It took an hour for Bravo 1/77 and Bravo 1/61 to arrive at the position. Meyer took command of a lieutenant's tank and led the mech-infantry tracks back to Ta Bat, where they joined Charlie Company and the assembled 1/11 vehicles, and prepared to run Ambush Alley all over again. Incoming artillery exploded every now and then as the column formed up.

They departed in a clanking, rumbling cacophony and Meyer stood to watch the dust rise as they disappeared down the road. At that point, he was in a hurry to get back to his forward CP at Lang Vei, and called for another helo. He had operational control of elements of five other battalions (1/11 Infantry, 1/61 Mech Infantry, 1/1 Cavalry, 1/44 Artillery, and 2/94 Artillery) and wanted to insure that they were all on the 1/77 radio net and had secured their assigned positions on the road. His task force was strung out along Route 9 from east of Lang Vei to the Laotian border. He knew Bravo 1/1 had been mauled in the area and hoped his one advantage would bring success—he had at least partial flank security on the highway.

The lead of the column was at Lao Bao and Charlie Battery scrambled to march order. Keeney could see the armor crewmen behind their guns and hatches, their body movements transmitting one message; Move! It felt good to see Dusters in the column; their rapid-fire 40mm cannons can tear up a hill in nothing flat, Keeney thought, as he hoisted himself on the back deck of an M48 tank with two other artillerymen. The column moved out and hit Route 9, gear and vehicles left abandoned.

The North Vietnamese response was immediate, and the convoy responded with a fury: fifties and sixties chattered along the line, 90mm cannons boomed, twin-forties shredded the brush with streams of flashing rounds. Keeney hung on tight to the fast moving, bumping tank, astonished to see NVA on the south side of the road. Fifty yards into the brushy tangle, North Vietnamese in green pith helmets popped up to empty AK-47 magazines. The two men sharing the ride with him were shooting back. Keeney dug into his own ammo bandoliers and burned off mag after mag from his M-16. He couldn't tell if he was hitting a thing, but the crack of AKs continued along the whole route and he kept his rifle working, not pausing to look back. Keep firing! Keep moving! An ambushed and riddled jeep was on the side of the road, wrecked, and the driver lay dead in the thick dust of Route 9. Keeney watched in anguished amazement as the tanks and tracks hurtled over him, some of the treads grinding the corpse even deeper into the road. No one was willing to stop for a dead man and, as they rumbled past, Keeney glanced down to see the insignia of a major on the dead man's jacket collar.

The enemy fire kept up, and the column levelled shattering doses of fire into the brush to keep the enemy down so they could keep moving. By the time they pulled off of Ambush Alley into the sanctuary of Lang Vei, Keeney was filled with one simple emotion—absolute joy at being alive. He hadn't thought he was going to make it. He was alive, he thought, only because other GIs had barrelled through all of that fire to pull them out, and he felt unspoken gratitude to those grimy armor troops climbing off of their machines. There was also a deeper feeling of sorrow at the sight of the blasted vehicles on the route. He knew what those burnt-out hulks meant in human terms. He hustled over to the Hq&Hq Battery where a buddy gave him a big grin and an exaggerated story of how the battalion had written them off and had been ready to send letters to their next of kin. He also repeated the rumor among the artillerymen that as soon as Charlie Battery had left, the NVA had swarmed over Lao Bao, waving communist flags. True or not, Keeney wasn't impressed, thinking, the gooks didn't try anything like that when we were still in place. Outside the command bunker, Keeney was amused to see Lieutenant Colonel Ganahl surveying them with a slack-jawed grin, seemingly astonished to see they'd made it back in one piece. The old chaplain was there too, and as Keeney remembered, "He couldn't even look at us, which I thought was pretty bad for a chaplain. We never did see any more of him after that. We were glad of it, and he was probably glad he didn't see us, too."

The tanks of Charlie Company roared into Lang Vei at dusk, putting a dust haze in the air, stopping so quickly that the giant machines rocked back and forth on their suspensions. Sp4 Spurgeon had served with Charlie before volunteering for the snipers and he jogged to them. The crew of one tank was climbing off, dragged out and dusty, and he saw an old buddy emerging from the driver's hatch. He was shirtless, completely covered with dirt and sweat, and was keyed up.

"Spurgeon, you want body count," he challenged, "If you want some body count, you'd better come with us! I swear to God the place is crawling with dinks, real live gooks, tons of 'em! You won't even have to use your scope!"

"Slow down," Spurgeon answered, unbelieving, and asked for details. "Not tons of 'em, dammit. Where'd you see 'em?"

"Both sides of the road."

"What were they wearing, fatigues, helmets, what?"

"They're NVA, goddammit! They're fully-uniformed NVA using us for target practice! They're dug in in bunkers. Some of 'em let us drive right past 'em, then suddenly appeared in our rears with RPGs. Some of the bastards just stood up in the middle of the road and faced us down with RPGs. Goddammit, Spurgeon, I'm telling you this is it! You ain't ever going to see action like this! Ever! They're firing RPGs at us like machine guns!"

"Hold on, I'll be right back."

"Better hurry up, dammit, we're getting ready to go out again!"

Spurgeon jogged over to battalion operations, but an officer there politely told him it would be crazy for a sniper to hang onto the outside of a tank in that fire: he'd just be blown off. Spurgeon was inwardly happy at the answer. Saying he wanted to go had only been a bit of bravado; he knew it was virtual suicide and thought, thank God for that officer. He walked back to the tank where his friend was standing in the driver's hatch putting his CVC back on. "Coming?"

"Can't," Spurgeon grinned weakly, feeling, for a moment, like a coward. "Battalion says we're too valuable."

His buddy smiled, waved goodbye, and drove his tank back towards the shooting on Route 9.

Sergeant Markle, of the Dusters with A/1/44 Artillery, had left Lao Bao for Dong Ha to scrounge spare parts, when he heard about the fighting at the 2/94 base. He hitchhiked back to Lang Vei, catching up with his Duster section after they'd escorted the artillery back from the border. Then they were ordered to go back west to a little column of recovery vehicles. Heading west, they passed the shot-down Huey on Route 9, then came upon three M48 tanks stopped on the road, a lumpy body bag lying in front of one of their tanks. They appeared to be waiting for a medevac. The Dusters swerved on past, then slowed down at a dip in the road, crossed a culvert over a stream at the bottom, and gunned it up the steep opposite bank. Just as they got to the top, NVA ambushed them from the left, and they hauled through a din of AKs and RPGs. As the fire petered out, Markle noticed a cav Sheridan stopped to the right, two GIs standing on the turret. When suddenly the yellow smoke of an RPG streaked from the brush on the right, he watched, astonished as the two grunts on the Sheridan effortlessly disappeared down the hatches as if trap doors had been sprung beneath them. A second later, the RPG exploded above the tank. Markle shouted, "That sucker's behind us!" and the gunner spun the twin-forties to send a stream of shells after the RPG team. They kept moving through the occasional fire. That was Ambush Alley.

While the Americans were fighting and dying to open Route 9 on 21 March, the men for whom they were wrestling to hold it open were experiencing their own difficulties. The ARVN 1st Armor Brigade had made it to LZ Alpha the day before, regrouped and pushed on, still without the air cav to screen for ambushes. They ran through one particularly tough one, giving and taking casualties. On the 21st, they passed LZ Bravo and were three klicks east of it when another ambush erupted. They immediately requested air support.

Lieutenant Ferrell, of C/7/17 Air Cav, was in their troop tent at Khe Sanh at that time. His friend, WO Lancaster, had just received an anniversary card from his wife and was in good spirits. He showed her photo to Ferrell and bragged how pretty she was, and she really was. Word then came to mount up. Ferrell climbed aboard his Cobra with a big pilot whose flying abilities he did not trust, while Lancaster strapped into a second Cobra with a new warrant officer named Jim Manthei. Manthei had been in-country for a month, serving two weeks with another unit before the losses over Laos had prompted his transfer to Khe Sanh. Lancaster had flown with Ferrell for a month, teaching him the ropes, and now he was doing the same for Manthei.

The two gunships sped into Laos and found the ARVN armor stalled at a point where the road curved south like a horseshoe, a jungled hill in the pocket. The front of the column was under heavy fire east of the horseshoe, but the command vehicles were to the west and out of visual contact with the lead because of the hill. Ferrell dipped his Cobra low, as an English-speaking ARVN officer on the radio directed them in, and noticed the lead ARVN vehicles seemed hardly to be returning fire. Then he noticed NVA foot soldiers swarming in the trees on the north shoulder of the road and several RPGs streaked out with smoke trails to hit a tank and APC. The ammunition and fuel must have ignited because they went up in balls of fire, the tank turret spinning into the air.

Jesus, Ferrell thought, it was like watching a war movie.

Lancaster dove first, Ferrell close behind, strafing the hill from south to north. Three 12.7mm positions cut loose from the trees, the first burst slicing so close to Ferrell's ship that it seemed he could reach out and touch the tracers. He radioed Lancaster that he had three muzzle flashes east of the hill. They banked around and made three more passes, pumping rockets, automatic grenades, and minigun fire into the jungle. After Ferrell's third run, emptying his rocket tubes, only one NVA gun was still firing.

Ferrell, out of ammunition and short of fuel, radioed Lancaster that he was heading for Khe Sanh. Lancaster answered that he had a few more rockets in his tubes and was going in after the last gun position. Ferrell called for him not to—it was too risky without a wingman providing cover—but watched as his partner rolled down anyway and screamed in. Rockets exploded all around the NVA emplacement, Lancaster broke his dive veering left, his broadside to the enemy, and was hit by a torrent of tracers. He calmly reported his tail rotor was destroyed and requested Ferrell to cover while he made an emergency landing. He peeled off to the south, then dropped to a hundred feet over a field of elephant grass. Lancaster tried to bring the vibrating Cobra to a hover, but with the tail rotor gone it only began rotating out of control on its axis. Then it suddenly crashed hard to the ground. Their radio went dead. Ferrell had been calling for medevacs the whole time, so within moments a Huey dropped beside the crashed Cobra and other gunships converged on the field to provide cover. Ferrell departed station to refuel when the medevac crew reported they had both downed pilots aboard.

As it turned out, Lancaster and Manthei were dead. The force of the crash had snapped their necks against the "chicken plate" chest armor worn by pilots.

Lancaster had been Ferrell's best friend.

Meanwhile the ARVN armor was still being battered. USAF airstrikes were requested, but they did more harm than good—napalm canisters missed their mark, killing twelve ARVN and wounding almost a hundred more. Colonel Luat pulled his brigade west into the wake of their own retreat in order to regroup. An NVA prisoner said two regiments were waiting further east on Route 9 to demolish the ARVN armor and Luat radioed the information to airborne headquarters. General Dong, in response, airmobiled a paratrooper unit to clear out the NVA ambushers, but then did not alert Luat that the highway had been secured. Without this information, and only five kilometers from the border, Luat ordered his men off the road and they continued southwest, needlessly fighting the jungle and fording streams.

On 22 March, Lieutenant Colonel Meyer organized his command to retrieve the abandoned vehicles and equipment strewn along Route 9. It was the morning when the two Duster sections of Alpha Battery 1/44 Artillery got the word to escort another artillery run back to Lao Bao for some of the abandoned 175mm guns. It was a hairy idea, Sergeant Markle thought. He'd believed in stopping the Communists. But he'd never seen anything like the chaos on Route 9. They prepared to move out from Lang Vei, one Duster on point, the other at the end, an M48 tank and two M88s in the middle. The GIs had a guest with them that morning, a civilian reporter named Holger Jensen, who had showed up with a flak jacket and a note pad.

The Duster leader, Sgt. Kenny Osborne, said to mount up.

"Hell with it, sarge," a GI bitched, "We don't want to go back there."

Osborne ignored him and climbed onto the last Duster. The grunts followed him aboard. One of the GIs climbed in the driver's hatch on the front deck. The Duster had twin-40mm cannons behind a shield which encompassed them like a turret with no top. Sp4 Wooten dropped into the gunner's seat, and Staff Sergeant Osborne crouched beside him with a grenade launcher. Sergeant Markle stood behind the seat, he and Sgt. William Lore manning an extra M-60 they'd brought along. Sgt.

Wayne Coons was behind the other pig. The reporter, Jensen, hung onto the back deck.

The five vehicles took off from Lang Vei and hit the highway, passing the first signs of wreckage, bomb craters on the road, and the wrecks of two APCs and three trucks. As they rounded the first big curve in the road, the 1/61 APC still smoking down the road from them, and all hell broke loose. AK-47s sprayed from the brush on the left, Osborne pumped rounds from his grenade launcher, and puffs of smoke from NVA mortars rose on the Co Roc. Osborne shouted, "Get 'em, dammit!" and Wooten spun the turret, hammering fire from the twin-forties. One GI grabbed shell clips from the turret ammo wells, Wooten worked the pedal firing button, and fifty rounds shrieked across the Tchepone River, each one a tracer flashing from bright green to red in flight and popping sparks at impact against the brushy ridgeline. Markle grabbed M-60 belts and fed Lore's pig, as he and Coons frantically fired up the left side of the road, all of them too keyed up consciously to notice the AK rounds ricocheting off of the Duster armor.

The mortar fire stopped. They roared past the ambush.

Osborne slumped down, mumbling bitterly to Jensen, "I think we got 'em. That makes four this week. Those damned ARVN sitting on top of the ridge have let the North Vietnamese move in right under them." The Duster crunched over some C ration boxes littering the road, and split a sleeping bag which whirled feathers in their wake. A line of APCs edged past them, on the way back to Lang Vei, and the grunts exchanged peace signs. At an infantry strongpoint in the bushes, the column abruptly halted. Markle glanced ahead and saw a roll of concertina which the grunts had thrown across the road. Aw shit, he cursed, we're sitting ducks stopped like this. Some of the GIs ran out to pull the wire away as the column sat idling, and one of the infantry officers came up to ask Osborne if his Duster could stay to give them fire support.

Mortars came in. The armor column quickly rumbled past the grunts.

The convoy dodged around the junked vehicles, artillery pieces, and helicopter. The ride was quick and bumpy and their extra M-60 bounced off of the Duster. Jensen tapped Markle on the shoulder to point it out, and Markle could only think, are you crazy? We're not stopping for some damned machine gun. It was hard enough just keeping up with the others. At best, on the way back they might run over it so that the NVA couldn't recover it.

They pulled into the abandoned 2/94 firebase at Lao Bao. A dirt trail split the perimeter and they stayed in the side where there were a couple of 175mm guns, a few trucks, and some ammunition and powder charges. A downed helicopter squatted in the elephant grass. The GIs dismounted from the five vehicles, hurriedly moving about as an occasional 122mm round or mortar shell exploded nearby. The crew of one of the M88s hooked a 175mm SP to the back of their track. Men began blowing up the ammunition pits while others rooted through the deserted bunkers for important papers. Markle and another grunt dragged two trailers full of 40mm ammunition and latched one behind their Duster. After thirty minutes, Staff Sergeant Osborne shouted that they were leaving and tossed a thermite grenade into the ammunition trailer that they couldn't drag with them. They hauled back to Route 9, not looking back as the rounds cooked off.

Heading east, Markle looked down into the lush ravine on their right; a 175mm SP was resting on its side down the slope, as if it had been hurriedly shoved off the road. They were coming back at a good clip, swerving in dusty curves around the wrecks on the road, when Markle looked up just in time to see an M48 tank stopped dead ahead of them. "You gotta turn the gun!" The guns were not locked forward because the locks sometimes jammed. A GI sitting in the chair, his hands on the crank to turn the twin-forties, began frantically spinning it. But the Duster hauled past the halted tank too soon. Markle watched the barrels crunch into some C rat cartons hanging on the tank turret and, suddenly, the Duster turret began spinning out of control. Their driver kept hauling. At each revolution, the crank smacked into the helmet of the GI now slumped in the seat, and Markle tried to grab the crank. It whipped painfully into his hand and then the GI grabbed the hand to let Markle know he was okay. Markle was in pain and pissed off: gooks are probably sitting in the bushes laughing their asses off at us stupid Americans.

Passing the smoking APC at the curve, it happened all over again—AK tracers and yellow trails of RPG smoke laced past the vehicles. Mortars impacted near the road. Fifties and sixties chattered furiously from the armor, the Dusters poured down forty mike-mike, and they outran the ambush again. No one was hit and they closed on Lang Vei where the treelines melted down to brushy plains. The men felt safer, even though a few departing mortar rounds exploded nearby. Coons fell asleep against his M-60. Lore said, "Man, I'm hungry," and broke out some Cs. Jensen noticed the back of his flak jacket was peppered with shrapnel. Markle fretted that he had forty-three days to go in-country and this was the worst he'd seen in Nam.

On the morning of 23 March, another patrol with 1/77 Armor protection left Lang Vei to retrieve the last eight-inch gun from Lao Bao. Half of a mile west of the basecamp, the tanks, recovery vehicles, and Dusters passed a hundred Montagnards fleeing Laos after their village had been hit. A mile later, two RPGs whooshed from the brush; two men were slightly wounded, but the patrol kept moving. Two miles from Lao Bao, the lead tank hit a mine and two GIs on board were hurled into the dust, their feet blown off. Mortar fire began dropping around them. Soldiers dragged the casualties to the next vehicle in line as they tore on, grunts spraying the road almost nonstop. When they neared Lao Bao, they stopped on a rise overlooking the river and Laos. The first vehicles of the returning ARVN column were fording the river back to South Vietnam. The ARVN paratroopers on deck waved at the Americans. The grunts did not respond. The day before, Colonel Battreall and the other advisors at Kilo had spent a hard day slingloading fifty-five-gallon gasoline drums under Huey helicopters for transport to the 1st Armor Brigade. At that high altitude, the small slicks could only handle two drums a trip so not enough fuel was transported across the border for all of the vehicles. A small airborne bulldozer was also slingloaded to a Chinook, so it could accompany the returning column and cut the sheer banks of the Tchepone River at whatever point Colonel Luat decided to cross.

At midnight a column of NVA tanks following the ARVN armor was stopped by U.S. air and artillery. By early morning, Luat and the 1st Armor Brigade had finally endured the twelve miles from Aloui to the Tchepone River, and were crossing back into South Vietnam. The advisors constantly monitored the radios of their ARVN counterparts, and when they crossed the river, Battreall and the five brigade and squadron advisors boarded an unarmed Huey so they could link up with Luat on the border. They traced along Route 9 and Battreall, who had heard little about the bitter ambushing along the highway, was taken aback to see at least five tanks and APCs abandoned and still smoking on the road. He didn't know the details, but could picture a U.S. column, confident in its firepower and armor, going down the road fat, dumb, and happy, and getting mauled for its lack of attention to flank security. It was such a mess below them, he remarked to the majors in the cabin, "Christ, somebody really fucked up down there!"

The Co Roc ridge was just outside the left side door, and a concentration of 12.7mm machine guns suddenly cut loose from the crest. It was a long, continuous burst and Battreall could see the muzzle smoke. With no door-gunners, they could just hold tight as the pilot sent the ship into a wild evasive action, flying north and west and crossing the river into Laos. To the delight of the advisors, the pilot circled high, then flew back towards South Vietnam above the trail that the ARVN had followed. At a hundred-foot altitude, they had the chance to observe two or three kilometers of the armor's route of march. They could see only abandoned vehicles on the side of the jungle path.

Battreall was impressed with the scene. If the armor troops had panicked, as the media and others claimed, the men would have simply abandoned their vehicles when they ran out of gas and continued their headlong flight on foot. They would not have stood in line to refuel; yet, the refueling must have been carried out calmly because the only vehicles sitting abandoned with empty fuel tanks were noncombat M577 command tracks and M548 tracked cargo carriers. Passing over the border, Battreall could see the tiny engineer dozer still working to cut the east bank as the last tanks and APCs splashed into the river from the west side. A pair of Phantoms could be seen making repeated passes about eight kilometers behind the armor column. Battreall scanned with binoculars from the Huey door and could just make out the burning hulk of a Soviet-made T54 tank.

When Battreall and the advisors caught up with the 1st Armor, they were in an open parade field at the dilapidated Lao Bao Jail near the abandoned artillery base. The men disembarked from the APC decks and Colonel Luat stood in the brush organizing for the Route 9 drive back to Kilo. They were still within small-arms range of Laos, Battreall noted with concern, but fortunately not a shot was fired at the milling crowd. None of the ARVN seemed to notice their vulnerability. The advisors broke up to find their respective counterparts and Battreall approached Luat, taking in the scene as the ARVN paratroopers with the armor began boarding a truck convoy. "Everyone was visibly pleased and relieved to be 'home,' " he said, "and I saw a great deal of grinning, shouting, back slapping, and hugging going on. I was struck by the very warm and cordial leave-taking between the infantry and armor troops. There was nothing hangdog or crestfallen about anyone on the scene; indeed, everyone seemed to anticipate a hero's welcome upon reaching Khe Sanh."

So did Colonel Luat. He stood in dusty fatigues, calm and cheerful, almost cocky, proud about what his brigade had endured in Laos. It took five hours for the tail end of the column to depart Laos. They finally pushed out with 22 M41 tanks, 54 APCs, and 22 other assorted vehicles.

Left behind in Laos, destroyed or abandoned, were 21 tanks, 26 APCs, 13 bulldozers, 2 road graders, 2 trailers, and 51 assorted vehicles. One of the squadrons raised dust on point and Colonel Luat's three command tracks followed them, with Colonel Battreall aboard. The rest of the brigade spaced out behind them. The brush thick, the road rolled, and, before long, the head of the column was out of sight and stopped. The radio crackled back that an American officer had parked his helicopter smack in the middle of the road so he could inspect the blown-up equipment in one of the ambush zones.

A U.S. tank platoon from the 1/77 Armor had fallen in behind the CP APCs and, as soon as they halted, the lieutenant in the lead tank shouted, "Hey, you slopes, get the hell outta the way!" Battreall slid off the back of his APC, climbed up the front of the tank, looked the young lieutenant in the eyes, and said calmly, "You're yelling at the commander of the 1st Armor Brigade. He's been in Laos for six weeks. You haven't. Keep your mouth shut." The lieutenant then looked as if he were in a stranglehold. In a few minutes, after the column got moving, the U.S. tanks peeled off into the roadside brush.

They had only gone a few hundred more yards when shooting broke out from the point. Battreall, Luat, and the rest ducked inside their vehicles as the ARVN responded with standard procedure—accelerated speed and a sheet of machine gun and 76mm canister shot laid into the flanks. The vehicles hauled past, no one visible in the undergrowth, and the shooting evaporated. Luat ordered a cease fire, then pulled his three command tracks to the side of the road so they could watch the column pass. He waved at the troops, shouting, "Well done, I'm proud of you!" The little dozer was in the column, its engineer sergeant still chugging along and waving back. Battreall was surprised—he had expected the driver to abandon the dozer after the river crossing in exchange for a faster and safer tank or track—and Luat was impressed enough to send a staff officer to get the sergeant's name so that he could be decorated.

The rest of the movement to Kilo was without incident, but before long Battreall discovered that their brief firefight had been with Americans. He had been worried such an incident might take place—rearward passage of lines was a tricky maneuver and during NATO exercises he'd been in, with everyone wearing the same uniform and speaking the same language, there had always been cases of friendly fire or bridges blown up in the face of friendly units about to cross. Battreall had helicoptered to Khe Sanh several days before to discuss just this problem with General Hill. He had also assigned one of his advisor majors the job of coordinating routes, communications, and recognition signals between the ARVN and U.S. units.

He heard that a nervous GI had started the fray. Lieutenant Colonel Meyer was at his 1/77 CP at Lang Vei when the shooting broke out and he remembered not a trigger-happy GI, but the lead ARVN raking the brush as a precaution against ambush. One of his officers had shouted into the radio, "These idiots are shooting at me!" For all the advance preparations, Meyer had no communications with the ARVN and could only relay the problem to Hill and radio his unit commanders to keep their men under cover. When the scene of the accidental firefight was checked, GIs found an abandoned ARVN M41 tank and drove it back to Khe Sanh, jeering once again about their South Vietnamese allies.

After reorganizing at Kilo, Colonel Luat prepared to attend General Lam's briefing. Battreall declined to attend, not wanting to edge in on the credit he felt should go to Luat. With the brigade back in South Vietnam, Battreall's job was done. At the airstrip, he found the aide to General Weyand and asked if he could hitch a ride back to Saigon. When the briefing ended, Weyand and Battreall climbed into the USAF twin-engine executive jet and DEPCOMUSMACV remarked, "That armor commander's a real basket case, isn't he?"

"What?" Battreall almost shouted.

Weyand described how, at the briefing, officers from ARVN I Corps and U.S. XXIV Corps severely criticized Luat for the failures of the 1st Armor, going as far as to call him incompetent and a coward. Weyand said Luat had come unglued under the attacks. No wonder, Battreall thought, he'd come back expecting a hero's welcome and instead was made the scapegoat for whatever had gone wrong during the operation. He could have kicked himself for not going to the briefing where he could have spoken in Luat's defense. During the rest of the flight to Saigon, Battreall described his case to Weyand. Most of the problems lay not with Luat, a brave and fine gentleman, he said, but with General Dong who had been in control of the armor brigade. Dong lacked coherence under pressure and the armor had suffered accordingly, receiving little support or guidance. The debacle at Hill 31 occurred, he said, not because of the failure of the armor, but because of a conflict in orders. Once there, the ARVN tankers had performed well. The brigade lost so many vehicles during the withdrawal, he explained, because the road was in bad repair, because Dong withdrew their air cav support, and because he did not keep them posted on the battlefield situation. There were credible witnesses who would have taken fierce argument with Battreall's explanations in defense of Luat. Weyand, though, seemed receptive and, as things turned out, Colonel Luat retained his command.

A few weeks later, Colonel Battreall flew to Quang Tri to present his after-action report to General Sutherland and to offer further defense for Luat. Battreall considered Sutherland, ". . . a cordial and intelligent gentleman. . . . I found him courteous and willing to listen, which is not all that common a trait among senior commanders." On the other hand, Sutherland was not impressed by Battreall's rationale of why the ARVN armor had failed and thought Battreall to be, ". . . one of those colonels who always tried to paint a picture rosier than reality, always had many reasons and excuses for ARVN armor failures to perform, always could present reasons why armor units should not be used, and was trigger quick to criticize higher headquarters." In the official accounts of the Laos operation, the ARVN 1st Armor Brigade has been described as having done a miserable job in Laos.

Four days after turning twenty on 21 March, Sp4 Spurgeon was in the bush on a sniper patrol. Actually the mission had first been detailed to Sgt. John Wondra and his partner, Felix, when an operations NCO dropped into the sniper bunker at Lang Vei and told them they were to hunt for NVA RPG teams hitting the highway.

Wondra liked Spurgeon and asked if he wanted to go.

"I don't want to break the team apart, if Felix wants to go."

Felix shrugged, "I don't give a fuck."

They geared up, Spurgeon feeling gung-ho again, slapping on a camouflage beret and gun gloves; he shouldered a rucksack and the radio, slung an LAW across his back, and stashed a couple of claymores in a pouch. Wondra wore a bush hat and they both carried M-14 sniper rifles, the scopes unhooked and hanging from their web gear. They joined a squad of grunts aboard a couple of APCs which took them about a mile down the road, east of Lang Vei. They walked fifty yards into the thick brush; then the squad leader said, "Here ya go," and began taking his men back towards their vehicles.

Spurgeon called nervously, "Where you going?"

"We're leaving you two in here." That was the plan the squad leader had been given.

Oh shit, Spurgeon thought, just us two alone—do I really want to do this? Spurgeon and Wondra walked off into the bush, feeling peaceful in the warm sunlight, Spurgeon thinking that it might be best to just screw around. A stunted palm tree in the brush contained a beehive high up, and he pulled out a grenade to frag the hive off so he could climb up and look around. Everybody else calls it fucking off, he laughed inside, I call it reconning by fire. But Sergeant Wondra whispered to knock it off and they kept patrolling, dropping their rucks under a tree and crossing a narrow stream about ten feet away.

Wondra found footprints in the mud of the opposite bank, and Spurgeon was interested again. They started down a path towards a treeline, Wondra disappearing into the brush thirty yards to the left.

Spurgeon glanced down for a moment as he crossed the field, but looking back up, his heart nearly stopped. He saw the shock of black hair first; then he focused on a chest, an arm, the wooden stock of a rifle, a faded shirt. A man was walking across his front, partially hidden among the trees forty yards ahead of him, moving east but looking north, away from Spurgeon. It was the first NVA he'd seen who was not dead, wounded, or a prisoner. He couldn't believe it, and thought for a second, what's an ARVN doing out here? Then he panicked, God, no, ARVN always wear helmets and no ARVN would have the balls to be out here alone. Oh shit, it's a dink! He stood exposed in the grass, M-14 to his shoulder, trying to line up the man's head in the peepsight as he walked in a slow crouch behind the trees. Spurgeon's mind was reeling; I'm in the open. What if he turns and sprays me? What if I lose him? Where are his buddies? His heart was pounding, his hands shaking so that he was unable to keep the NVA's head in his sights. From the corner of his eye he could see Wondra pushing through the brush, and he prayed for him not to make any more noise than he already was. He lined up the black hair one more time; then suddenly Spurgeon was firing, jerking the trigger uncontrollably, rapping off five shots so fast that he didn't know if his eyes were open or closed.

The North Vietnamese was nowhere in sight.

Spurgeon dropped in the grass, tugged off his gun gloves, and knocked off his beret as he frantically unslung the LAW. He extended the rocket to its firing position, put it over his shoulder as he kneeled, and plugged his ears with his left shoulder and hand. Just as Wondra ran up from behind, Spurgeon pressed the firing button. Wondra dove to avoid the backblast, and the 66mm projectile screamed to impact in the woodline. Spurgeon turned and suddenly noticed Wondra sprawled in the grass, his face drained, his eyes with a what-the-hell-are-you-doing expression. Spurgeon pointed to the trees and mouthed, "Gook . . . gook . . . gook."

A look of wonderment appeared on his face. "Oh."

Spurgeon and Wondra looked at each other, Spurgeon exulting in the moment—no one chicken, both ready to fight. They heaved grenades at the treeline, then started forward through the grass in an exaggerated crouch to keep low, M-14 rifles at the ready. Spurgeon saw the NVA in the trees and, thinking he was playing dead, walked quickly to him, firing from the shoulder. The man did not move. They stood over the body. The North Vietnamese was sprawled dead on his back, a tiny shrapnel hole in the back of his head, a trickle of blood from his nose drying in his hair. The man was young, wore sandals, had a faded uniform with a unit designation stitched over the left breast pocket. Spurgeon was still afraid that he might have killed an ARVN until he tugged an AK-47 rifle from under the body. He hefted the weapon, a three-sided bayonet folded against the stock. They were worried that more NVA might be in the area, so Spurgeon pointed the rifle in the direction the man had been coming from. It didn't fire. He flipped the safety, squeezed off a couple of rounds, then dropped it to full auto and emptied the AK's thirty-round banana clip. Then they looted the body for souvenirs.

They ran back across the stream, tripping and giggling with nervous excitement. They tossed a grenade and waited. It was a dud. Then, they grabbed their rucks, and scurried for Route 9. They were afraid of more NVA but felt like a million. They had a kill! They stood on the road, calming down and laughing at themselves for being so gleeful. They walked back to Lang Vei, popping a purple smoke grenade and waving at an American chopper that circled down to look them over. At the operations bunker, they were debriefed, an NCO taking notes as Spurgeon lied, saying he'd killed the NVA with a single head shot. They turned in the captured gear, then walked back to the sniper bunker and kicked back in some lawn chairs, breaking out the sodas and beer to celebrate the team's first victory.

For the artillerymen rescued by the armor, things soon shifted back to the lackadaisical style of the old days now that they no longer were in the real war zone. Pfc Rhodes and his buddies in A/2/94 were able to take quick showers at Khe Sanh on 25 March; then they packed up for Vandegrift where ammunition was being blown in place and things were being packed up. It was quiet there so they loaded aboard a truck to go swimming in a river about a mile down the road, while a couple of GIs kept watch aboard a quad-fifty guntruck. It was Rhodes's first thorough scrubbing in two months. At other times on the Vandegrift perimeter, the Dusters and quad-fifties did extended Mad Minutes and the artillerymen joined the noise, Rhodes popping a few mags on his M-16 and pitching several grenades. It was great fun. From Vandegrift they rejoined the rest of the battalion at Mai Loc, south of Cam Lo.

They were put right on the perimeter line with the ARVN, a situation which gave the battalion commander, Lieutenant Colonel Ganahl, nightmares about night attacks. They built culvert-and-sandbag shelters and got down to scrubbing the caked red dust off of the gun tubes and commo gear. The artillerymen kept up their guard because they knew their position was insecure, but it wasn't the same as Lao Bao and it screeched on their nerves when the lifers began howling about police calls, haircuts, and mustache trims. Someone tossed a frag into the battery first sergeant's tent when he wasn't there, to scare him off their backs. It worked. The captain's jeep driver drilled another unpopular sergeant through the leg with his M-16 one night and was hauled away by the MPs. At night the Dusters and quad-fifties lit the sky with torrents of red tracers, while the searchlight teams and artillery illumination rounds turned the black to white. There was never any return fire. During the day, the mama-sans from a local ville swarmed the perimeter wire to sell beads, headbands, clothes, trinkets, and dope. Rhodes and his buddies hadn't done any pot in a long time; they'd gone dry during the border fighting, but now they could get obestol again. Lieutenant Colonel Ganahl had his suspicions about what was going on and they were confirmed one night when a quad-fifty gunner opened up without warning, managing to riddle the tent of the ARVN base commander with bullets. It turned out he'd been shooting for fun. The ARVN commander had not been in the tent at the time and politely accepted Ganahl's apologies. The next night, an explosion rocked the 2/94 line. Inspecting the crater, which was just far enough away from their bunkers not to hurt anyone, Ganahl discovered fragments from a U.S. 105mm shell and noted that the angle of impact was from the ARVN encampment. The South Vietnamese were just providing a friendly payback.

On the morning of 26 March, Lieutenant Colonel Meyer and Sergeant Major Nelson prepared to make an inspection trip to Charlie Company on the Laotian border. As they were boarding their vehicles at Lang Vei, Meyer noticed Nelson taking extra precaution in lacing and snapping his flak jacket tightly. Early in the operation, the sergeant major had been wounded by a 122mm rocket fragment when in a jeep on Route 9 near the Rockpile, and had spent fifteen days in the hospital.

They pushed west on Route 9, Meyer in the lead tank, followed by a

Scout track. Nelson was in the loader's hatch of the second tank, and another track brought up the rear. They were cutting down the road when Nelson saw the flash of an RPG in the roadside brush to the left, then watched the projectile shriek over the back deck of Meyer's tank, barely missing it. They kept hauling, laying down suppressive fire. The TC beside Nelson was simultaneously firing his fifty and traversing the 90mm main gun to the left. Nelson was reaching down to pull the charging handle to cock the coaxial 7.62mm machine gun when a second RPG suddenly shuddered the tank with a terrific clang. The round penetrated the track blocks hanging as extra armor, punched through the side of the turret, and burst on the ammo feed tray of the coaxial gun, shooting a blizzard of shrapnel, ammo, and pieces of the tank into Nelson. A small grease fire started inside the turret, but the gunner quickly put it out. The front of Nelson's flak jacket was shredded, his right leg ripped, bleeding, and broken, both hands painfully lacerated. The flak jacket had absorbed most of the blast and saved his life.

They kept moving until they reached Charlie Company on a ridgeline off the road overlooking Laos. Meyer got there first, remaining behind the fifty mount of his tank as the gunner traversed the long 90mm cannon and carved out sections of the brush around them with roaring canister shot to discourage any more RPG teams. Nelson painfully climbed down from his tank, limped over, and called to Meyer. The colonel turned to see his old friend standing helpless, bloody, flak jacket hanging in rags, his hands too cut up to unfasten the armor jacket. Nelson shouted in jest, "Why me again?" Within ten minutes a Huey picked him up. After the medevac, the tankers buttoned up inside their machines and Meyer directed airstrikes and artillery along the southern side of the dirt road. Charlie Company swept the burnt-out area and found one dead NVA, remarkably intact for all of the firepower poured in at him.

CHAPTER SIXTEEN: Skirmishes for Khe Sanh

The North Vietnamese counterattack also hit the main base at Khe Sanh. The airfield had taken occasional rocket and mortar raids, but in mid-March the shelling became almost constant and included artillery. The main area of bombardment was the section of the perimeter manned by D Troop, 2d Squadron, 17th Air Cavalry, 101st Airborne Division. Dug between the bunkers of 3/187 Infantry and 4/77 Aerial Field Artillery, the Delta bunker line had gone up at the beginning of the operation to watch for NVA infiltrators. They had seen none, but were now taking up to two hundred rounds a day. Pfc Bill Warren, the troop RTO, spent a lot of time crouched in those bunkers, listening to his heart pound as the NVA artillery erupted at ground level. Many were duds—left over from the marine siege, he guessed—and, when they impacted with the hard red clay, the bunker shook and Warren would mutter nervously, "Man, that was close . . . what would have happened if it went off?"

Sometimes Warren could only wonder what he was doing there. In his own mind, he made a conscious effort to remember that he was just a draftee doing his time in this useless war, and not to get too close to his buddies because he didn't think he could take it if one were killed. But that didn't mean he didn't feel a bond with the men beside him and, in the back of his mind, he knew he had to be in Vietnam. He had been twenty and driving a cab in the Bronx when the draft notice had arrived. He was from a traditional family whose members always served, and his only strong impulse was to go with the program. He'd arrived in Nam in January 1971. He'd been almost surprised at how professional Delta Troop was: he saw men smoke grass and opium at Camp Eagle, but never on missions; and not only did the grunts stick together, but they were damned good at their jobs. Warren even liked their CO; a small, wiry captain named Thomas who always looked out for his troopers and got the job done with no petty harassment.

Most of the Delta troopers took the shelling in stride. It started in earnest on 15 March when nearly two hundred 122mm rounds hit the base at a cost of three GIs wounded and five ARVN killed—plus fourteen damaged helicopters and trucks. The following evening, a salvo of sixty mortar rounds wounded four GIs, blew up a helo and a truck, and damaged four more vehicles. The next night, 17 March, the first rounds hit the airstrip and the men of D/27th Engineers left their bunkers to begin repair. And so it went. It was a tense time, but only a few of their comrades were hit and the Delta cavalrymen tried to laugh it off. Warren provided some comic relief the morning he ran naked from his cot to a bunker during a shelling and found himself squatting beside a 101st chaplain in his undershorts. One of the platoon leaders provided most of the laughs; it seemed that every time he went to the latrine they took incoming, and he would scurry for a bunker holding up his trousers. He varied his times but it did no good, and finally the command-bunker radiomen took to kidding him to hold it for their sakes. One of the wilder grunts refused to climb inside a bunker, even when directly ordered to, saying the only thing he wanted from Nam was a Purple Heart. Yeah, it was tough, Warren reckoned, but everyone was making the best of it.

On 19 March, the NVA shelling picked up in tempo, roughly twenty rounds an hour all day, and the Delta grunts spent most of their time underground.

To combat the increased enemy activity around Khe Sanh, Lieutenant Colonel Sutton's 3/187 Infantry was shifted from the Rockpile to the mountains northwest of the base. The CP was relocated to the airfield on 15 March, and the rifle companies continued what they'd been doing since the first day of the campaign—humping the hills for the North Vietnamese Army. For the grunts, the days seemed to merge together until time meant nothing but another day marked off DEROS calendars. At night they lived in the jungle, and at daybreak they started out again. It was always the same—point man up front, gut tight as he silently snaked through the trees, the rest of the company filing behind, sweat towels soaked around necks, moving under hundred-pound rucks. It was like being in an oven-hot green tunnel. Minute by minute, the landscape and sun were more of an enemy than any Vietnamese who might be lurking; wait-a-minute vines coiled around legs and canteen tops, thorns tore at arms and faces, jungle rot spread, clothes rotted in the humidity, mouths burned from thirst and bile, and leeches appeared seemingly from nowhere to attach themselves.

The grunts humping the Laotian border jungle rarely had any idea of what was going on; it seemed to be useless wanderings. But at a time when many units were just going through the motions the 3d of the 187th could take some pride in exhausting, meandering patrols. They were not searching and evading; they were hunting for the enemy. And when sometimes they did bump into the Communists, men on both sides died. The 3/187 Infantry was credited with killing forty-eight NVA, but nineteen of their own were killed during the operation: two from Hq&Hq; seven from Charlie; three from Delta; five from Echo Recon. Also counted on the list of the dead were the battalion commander and his operations officer. They died on 17 March 1971.

In accordance with their usual policy of getting on the ground with the troops, Lieutenant Colonel Sutton and Major Scharnberg called for a helo to transport them that day. Scharnberg had just returned to the battalion the day before. After being wounded on Purple Heart Hill, he was only in the hospital a few days before he returned; Sutton, knowing the young major was gung-ho enough to head back into combat not fully recovered, radioed Major White at the 3/187 Rear to make sure he was sent home on leave. Against Scharnberg's protests, White did just that. Upon his return, Scharnberg spent one night at Camp Evans, then made it to the Khe Sanh CP on 17 March. The chopper that arrived for them was a Kiowa Scout from the 5th Mech. Sutton had drawn the same pilot and bird for several days and commented to White that he trusted neither; the Scout was too small and frail for his tastes, the pilot too young and reckless—he flew low and fast, hopping hills with the skids barely clearing the trees.

They left for the field but never made it. The bodies of Sutton, Scharnberg, and the pilot were later recovered from the wreck. There is a possibility they were shot down, but a distraught White thought it was probably due to pilot error—flying too low and being smacked to earth by a down draft. Bravo Company was NDP'd atop a hill on the border when news of the colonel's death reached them via the radio. Some of Sp4 Kucera's buddies mockingly put up a cross and told jokes until their lieutenant interrupted sharply with, "You better not let the CO see that." They disliked Sutton because he drove them hard and was willing to take chances to get body count. But on many occasions, Sutton had left his C&C to join his grunts in a firefight on the ground. Kucera decided it was a Patton thing: any fiercely aggressive commander was bound to be disliked by his men. Sutton had balls, Kucera thought. But he, too, did not mourn his death.

The day of the crash, General Hill immediately transferred one of his mech officers, Lt. Col. Robert Steverson, to assume command of the 3/187. Maj. Chester Garrett was sent from the battalion's parent brigade (3d Brigade, 101st ABD) to take over as the S3. The two were a mixed blessing. Steverson had been the 1/5 operations officer and was well qualified to take over, his previous position having made him intimately aware of the daily goings on of all of the units in the AO. He was tactically proficient and doggedly determined; he also had an uncanny ability to look at maps and terrain from his C&C and instantly visualize the whole scheme of where and how his battalion should move. His only weakness was being a workaholic, sometimes pushing himself to exhaustion and suffering from lack of sleep. It wasn't long before the battalion officers thought Major Garrett had been transferred to them simply to get him out of the hair of brigade. He was gung-ho to a fault, stubborn, and refused to take advice; it got to the point, for example, that the 3d Brigade S3 had to call Major White to coordinate because Garrett refused to talk to him.

The new commander's test came on 20 March, when Bravo, Delta, and Echo Recon all had contact in the mountains around Khe Sanh.

Bravo Company had been CA'd into the area the day before in response to recon patrols who could hear NVA artillery firing from smack on the border, several miles north of Route 9. The area was semipinpointed in the jungle. Bravo was to locate the arty and, if found on the RVN side of the blue line, knock it out. When they helicoptered in, some 12.7mm fire cracked at the birds and the door-gunner in Kucera's slick shouted, "Hot LZ!" Kucera frantically tried to untie his helmet hanging from his ruck, finally getting it on just as they touched down atop a hill.

Kucera jumped out and dove into a bomb crater. Then he noticed everyone was looking at him as if he were nuts. The grunts in the first couple of lifts had already secured the hill, and only the helos were still taking fire. They patrolled west toward the border through a valley of rolling elephant grass, and NDP'd in a bamboo thicket. They called in artillery and airstrikes on two NVA mortars that they could hear just west of them on the border; there were three secondary explosions. That night two rounds exploded near them, and NVA artillery could be heard firing all night long. On the morning of the 20th, two more rounds exploded close enough to pelt shrapnel over them. They packed up and continued the hump towards Laos, so close to the NVA guns they could feel the ground vibrate from each round being fired and could hear them whistle towards Khe Sanh. The Bravo captain radioed Steverson that he could definitely hear one tube working on the border, firing every fifteen to twenty seconds.

Meanwhile, teams from Echo Recon worked their way to the border. By half past nine, the leader of Recon Team One reported taking AK-47 fire from an NVA squad and called in arty. The leader suspected that more NVA were in the jungle and requested helicopter extraction before his seven-man team was cut off. Lieutenant Colonel Steverson, in his C&C orbit, replied that an emergency resupply of ammo could be made, but that Recon Team One was to remain on the ground and aggressively seek and engage the enemy. Another recon team made contact with a small group of NVA; they too were denied permission to extract, which was standard reconnaissance procedure.

Steverson was intent on ferreting out the NVA.

By noon Bravo Company was almost on the border, moving towards the sound. They were walking single file through thick brush when they suddenly noticed they were in an NVA bunker complex, bunkers stretching all around, commo wire strung between them. Kucera was next to the lieutenant and RTO when shooting broke out along their strung-out file. Everyone dropped in place, Kucera clutching his M-16 and scanning the brush, holding his fire because he couldn't find a target. He felt damned glad that the lieutenant and the captain knew what to do. A staff sergeant down the line sprang up firing his rifle—drilling an NVA with three rounds through the throat. Another burst of AK cracked and was answered by an M-16. Kucera rolled over to look. A kid three days with the company, had been hit in the leg, but had dropped the NVA who'd shot him with his return burst.

The kid started going into shock.

"Hey man," a grunt joked to keep him awake, "You're going back to the World."

The kid snapped out of it and grinned.

The firing kept rippling along the line, Bravo killing eleven NVA.

Kucera could hear the captain over the RTO's hand mike, arguing with Steverson that he needed AFA, not just arty because the target was too close. Before long two Cobras came in and the pilots told them it looked like an anthill with all of the NVA coming out of the bunkers. They said that the company was surrounded, and just to sit tight. Then the gunships began strafing, expertly putting rockets and minigun fire around the grunts. The pilots had a great time picking off NVA. The lieutenant's RTO tried to contact one of the pilots, but he said, "Wait one, I'm inbound on a gook," and flashed over Kucera's head, pumping rockets and laughing "Got 'em!" The Cobras went back to Khe Sanh three times to refuel and rearm. Phantoms dropped nape; Kucera could not see the explosions for all the vegetation; but he could hear the canisters burst and a second later the wind would be sucked from his lungs. The firepower gave Bravo the breather they needed to pull out of the NVA basecamp. U.S. artillery roared in behind them to cover their movement.

Bravo made it to their NDP in the bamboo, and the captain hurriedly organized a defense, passing LAWs along the line. But nothing happened. The NVA artillery for which they'd been searching was confirmed to be on the Laotian side of the border, and thus immune to U.S. ground attack. But Kucera's platoon leader and another lieutenant, both ex-SF, didn't care about the rules and asked for volunteers to conduct a night raid on the guns. Kucera thought it was suicide, but he was impressed to see many others step forward. They were draftees second, he thought, Screaming Eagles first. It was a great feeling. Steverson, of course, denied them permission to go, and turned his attention back to the mountains. The fight was not over yet.

The seven men of Recon Team One were still running, pursued by the North Vietnamese. The recon platoon leader, a lieutenant named Sloan, was on the ground with them. They could only find clearings in the jungle big enough for one Huey, which would only take five men, and Sloan was not willing to separate the team and risk having two men cut off. At dusk they made a tight position atop a jungled hill and called for reinforcements.

At that time, Lieutenant Stephen's platoon of Delta Company was waiting on the Khe Sanh airfield, preparing to return to the field after a night of pulling security at the 101st ABD TOC. Word came that recon was in trouble and that Second Platoon was going in. It was six in the evening when they CA'd into a clearing on the side of recon's hill, Stephen unaware that it was a hot LZ until he saw green AK tracers zipping up from the treetops, silent under the noise of the rotors and the door-gunners' M-60s. The Hueys hovered, the twenty grunts jumped out, and the firing stopped as soon as the choppers banked away.

A few men from recon came down the hillside and led the platoon up to their NDP. The recon team was out of food and water, three men had collapsed from exhaustion, and Lieutenant Sloan asked that they not be required to pull night guard. The infantrymen were still setting up around them when AK-47 fire shattered the dusk, twenty-five yards from where Stephen was sitting. A magazine or two was emptied, then silence; then one of Stephen's men, a GI nicknamed Tex, started crying out for help.

Lieutenant Stephen immediately took point, followed by Lieutenant Sloan, Sp4 Ken Irons, his new RTO, Sp4 Ronny Wilson, his medic, and six other grunts.

Tex nervously shouted at their approach, "You better speak English or you're dead!"

Stephen yelled, "Tex, it's me!"

It was pitch-black in the jungle as they formed another tight perimeter. The story was that Tex, two recon sergeants, and their Kit Carson Scout had left the NDP to place an MA on a jungle trail. Stephen had not ordered them out, and figured the recon men were still nervous. The NVA had ambushed them. One sergeant was killed instantly and the other had four or five AK rounds in him. They called a medevac and organized for the night. They could hear NVA moving around the hill in the dark, so Stephen radioed to his platoon sergeant to sit tight in the original NDP, while his little group similarly stayed in position. No one was to move, make noise, sleep, or give away his location by shooting in the dark.

Doc Wilson, a young Southerner and a fantastic medic, worked to keep the recon sergeant alive on the jungle floor. Fog had rolled in, delaying the medevac for hours. The North Vietnamese were all around, the moon and stars exposed silhouettes in the dark; but, for those long hours, Doc Wilson kept working, drawing attention to himself by holding an IV bottle high over the wounded man. Doc Wilson was absolutely fearless that night, but it was all in vain. A helo was inbound from Quang Tri with a jungle penetrator basket when the sergeant silently succumbed to his wounds. The medevac was cancelled. Wilson crawled over to Stephen and Sloan and passed out from exhaustion.

Stephen put the young medic in for the Silver Star, but higher downgraded it to a Bronze Star for Valor.

In the morning, helicopters came for the bodies and recon survivors, leaving Second Platoon in place. Fifteen minutes later, Stephen was checking his map when M-16s cut loose. He crawled to an old bomb crater and the three grunts inside said they'd fired up three NVA who were walking right toward them. They pointed at a body several yards away. Stephen couldn't see anything through the foliage so he told them to throw some frags and use the M-60. This done, they yelled, "Chieu hoi!" There was no response, so Stephen crawled toward the spot at which his men were pointing, a black sergeant following him.

The wounded NVA sprang up when he had gotten five feet away, his AK-47 chattering.

Stephen emptied his M-16 into the man.

They counted twenty-one bullet holes in the North Vietnamese, and could see another dead NVA lying further out. Battalion wanted evidence before a kill was claimed, usually items of clothing, but Stephen was too wrung out. He didn't want to risk himself or his men for a body count, so he only radioed in one confirmed kill.

On 22 March, the weather had been foul all day. Charlie Company 3/187, under Capt. Thomas A. Rodgers, continued its patrols northwest of Khe Sanh in search of NVA firing positions. They had not had a contact in about a week and, as the platoon slogged through the rainy jungle, this was more of the same. At noon Second Platoon found a deserted complex of twenty NVA bunkers in the undergrowth. They were empty save for some old tennis shoes and U.S. batteries. About ten minutes later, First Platoon found five small bunkers and destroyed them. The platoons regrouped by dusk and NDP'd in a spot of wet elephant grass.

The weather got worse that night, rain and wind slapping through the brush so that speaking voices were drowned out, and a blanket of fog cutting visibility down to zero. It was half an hour before ten that night, and the grunts were shivering miserably under ponchos in their mud holes, when a burst of fire broke out from the Second Platoon side of the line. About a dozen North Vietnamese had crept up through the wind, rain, and fog to assault the platoon's M-60 position.

They must have watched the Americans set up.

Sp4 Steve Wheeler and Pfc Roger Stahl were two of the first to move. Wheeler was a medic from Florida, a brave man in the bush but a rebel in the rear. Stahl was a draftee from Pennsylvania who had turned twenty-one during his five months in Nam; he was a very quiet, blond kid who'd gone off without question because he thought it was his duty. Stahl and Wheeler were close, the medic feeling that, in the free-for-all of contact, he could count on Stahl to watch out for him. The shy, unassuming kid always did his best and was well liked in the platoon.

When the NVA moved on the M-60 foxhole, Stahl and another grunt crawled from their holes towards the shooting, Stahl shouting back,

"Doc, someone is hurt over here!" Wheeler pushed through the elephant grass on his stomach, whispering that he was coming. He was five feet from them when the NVA suddenly flung satchel charges and grenades around the M-60. Everything went off at once. Mud and shrapnel sprayed all around Wheeler, as Stahl and his companion collapsed. Wheeler rolled to them. Stahl had been hit in the chest by shrapnel. Both men had been killed instantly.

Blind firing erupted from the foxholes, as Captain Rodgers got on the radio to battalion at Khe Sanh, requesting a flareship; he was told it would take too long to get the bird on station. The enemy tormented Charlie Company for the rest of the night, moving unseen through the brush. They even snatched the M-60 from the perimeter. At each rustle around them, the grunts threw hand frags and fired LAWs and M-79 grenade launchers. Artillery illumination burst overhead, serving only to reveal company positions to the enemy who stayed hidden in the thick undergrowth. Each time the flares burned out, the NVA tossed more grenades into the lines. Major Garrett at the 3/187 CP monitoring the radios, ordered mortar fire to be placed around C Company's NDP for the rest of the night, and told them to set fire to the grass near their position so aircraft could find them in the fog. The grenade duel continued through the night, even when a plane circled dropping parachute flares.

Five GIs were dead, four wounded.

The one-sided skirmish was still sputtering when the battalion command post began taking mortar fire, then the crack of automatic weapons could be heard. Khe Sanh itself was under attack.

Captain Thomas and the platoon leaders of Delta Troop were all in the CP bunker with a few RTOs and riflemen. At two in the morning, they were hit by artillery and mortars, and a U.S. artillery battery was alerted to fire illum in case of ground attack. After less than an hour, the artillery barrage stopped, but mortars kept dropping in from the vicinity of the Khe Sanh waterfall.

At 3:15 A.M., the bunker guards suddenly started shooting.

North Vietnamese sappers streamed in behind the mortar rounds, avoiding the claymores in the perimeter wire and disappearing behind the bunker line. Pfc Warren was sleeping on a cot in the CP bunker when someone kicked him and screamed, "Sappers!" He quickly laced up his jungle boots, grabbed his M-16 and bandoliers, and jogged to his preassigned position in a ditch that ran from the bunker to the airstrip. Warren had never been in a firefight before and cringed in his open, solitary spot, flat in the dirt. He looked around apprehensively, but could see no one moving, even though red and green tracers burned in all directions. Time seemed to drag by until a lieutenant finally emerged from the bunker and shouted to get to the airstrip. He ran there alone and went prone in the strip of elephant grass bordering the runway. He could see other GIs on either side of him, fifteen yards away, also down in the grass, rifles ready. He did not call to them, afraid of giving his position away. He had been there for five minutes when an RPG exploded in a white flash against the CP bunker, spraying fragments into the ditch he'd just vacated. Oh shit, Warren thought, the shock of what was really happening beginning to sink in.

A sapper sprinted to the strip to the refuel/rearm point manned by DISCOM, 101st Airborne and hurled in a satchel charge. Then the whole world seemed to explode around Warren, as a ten-thousand-gallon fuel blivet and a store of 2.75-inch rockets went up. Everything was sound and flash. He covered his head with his hands, as rockets tore into the night sky like Roman candles. The berm roared with fire, shrapnel whipped loudly overhead. More RPGs began shrieking in and tracers tore a light show among the bunkers. Grunts from the perimeter appeared out of the shadows, dragging dead sappers. They dropped them on the strip, intent on keeping the NVA from dragging them away. Warren stared at the corpses, the first of the enemy he had ever seen. There were four or five of them, skinny little men with short black hair and dirt smeared on them for camouflage.

Five of the sappers slipped between the 2/17 Air Cav and 4/77 AFA bunkers, then dropped into the communications trench between them. They ran down it, screaming and pitching grenades and satchel charges into the Delta Troop bunkers. Sp4 Michael J. Fitzmaurice, a shy enlistee from South Dakota, and three other GIs were in a bunker when three satchel charges were tossed in. Fitzmaurice scrambled, managed to toss two back out, then dove atop the third with his flak jacket outstretched. The explosion threw him back, riddled with shrapnel. A piece had torn his eye and blood poured down his face. Fitzmaurice stumbled into the trench line, firing his M-16, gunning down two of the sappers. He dropped the empty rifle, grabbed a machete, and stormed down the trench. He ran into three other sappers and hacked them all to death in furious, hand-to-hand combat. Fitzmaurice, the quiet kid, was bleeding badly and out of his mind from adrenaline. Some GIs had to physically drag him back to cover.

The firefight was intense until about four in the morning, when only a few sappers survived to fire back. At around five, the NVA reappeared in the fog outside the wire in what appeared to be an effort to recover their dead. More shooting broke out. The refuel/rearm point continued to explode. In the 4/77 AFA area, a captain, checking bunker to bunker, stepped into one damaged dugout just in time to see a wounded sapper bolt from a cot and run out the side port. The captain chased him down the trench and shot him with his .45 pistol.

While a medic bandaged the prisoner, U.S. and ARVN officers conducted a quick field interrogation. The sapper said he was a member of the 15th Sapper Battalion, only recently dispatched down the Ho Chi Minh Trail to destroy the Cobra gunship and command facilities at Khe Sanh. This was their first mission after extensive training. The prisoner said they had thoroughly reconnoitered the perimeter for two weeks, and had even used the night fog as cover to stage rehearsal attacks. Forty sappers had made the actual assault and most of them had gotten through the wire before anyone had spotted them.

With the sun up and the shooting petering out, Warren rose from his position and trudged back to the CP bunker. Men were moving and scrambling, and he got back on the radio as Captain Thomas called in immediate medevacs for his wounded. The wounded were evacked; the grunts were talking. Warren listened, picking up on what happened. One GI said he'd turned a corner in the trench, had seen a sapper bandaging a wounded comrade and had blown them both away. He'd taken a beautiful 9mm pistol from the one doing the bandaging. Others were talking about the man who'd refused to come in a bunker during the shelling; they said an RPG had exploded near him and he'd freaked out, dropping his rifle and screaming nonsense. He was sent out with the wounded. Some of the GIs said that a woman reporter, strolling into the area when they were cleaning out the last of the NVA, had pissed everybody off by shouting that she would bring the captain up on mutilation charges. The bodies of the sappers had not been mutilated; the effects of a magazine of 5.56mm from an M-16 or of a hacking machete on a naked body at close range were just gruesomely effective.

Most of the talk centered around Mike Fitzmaurice, who had been placed aboard one of the first evacuation helicopters. Warren recalled him as a quiet kid who drank beer and listened to C&W; no one could believe what he'd done. But to his fellow grunts he was a hero and the captain collected witnesses' statements to write up a citation for the Medal of Honor. The cost of the melee was counted up—three GIs killed and fourteen wounded, against fourteen dead NVA, one prisoner, and numerous blood trails in the brush outside the bunker line. Warren looked at the fourteen NVA bodies laid shoulder-to-shoulder on the airstrip, clad only in black briefs, ammunition and explosives strapped to them. When you run into a perimeter, he thought, you know you're not coming out. The courage of the NVA amazed him. Later, in a firefight in the A Shau Valley, he saw them stand in their spider holes on a hillside to duel with AKs against strafing Phantoms. Not a smart idea, he figured, but it took a lot of nerve. Warren was struck by the differences between the American and North Vietnamese troops. The good morale in Delta Troop didn't come from any belief in the war, but from camaraderie and good leaders. When it came to a solid firefight, he thought the grunts were equal to or superior to the NVA. But they didn't measure up when it came to motivation and dedication. By that stage of the game, the war seemed useless to them, and he couldn't help but respect these young Vietnamese who died for their country. The enemy seemed like a stubborn boxer; no matter how many times the Americans pummelled him, he kept coming back.

The action around Khe Sanh did not end with the dramatic sapper raid; the shellings continued and the 3/187 Infantry continued beating the bush. The day after the raid, two helicopters were shot down in the hills on the border, and Delta Company went to get them. The birds were ablaze in a small valley, three NVA 12.7mm positions set up like a horseshoe on the ridges above them. Lieutenant Colonel Steverson planned to insert half of Delta on one side of the ridge, the rest on the other side, and have them sweep to the top. From there they could medevac any survivors. If Delta were halted, elements of B and C Companies, with mortar teams, were readied to CA into the area at the colonel's discretion.

Sp4 Daugherty, sitting in a Huey with Captain Edwards, knew none of the details. They'd suddenly been picked up from their hilltop position, and now he sat beside a buddy named Craig, his feet hanging from the cabin door, cradling his M-16 and feeling tense. They came in low over the LZ, a small plateau on the ridgeline, and Daugherty looked down in horror. The fire from the crash site had spread up the hill and flames now shot up around the landing zone. Their slick went in, the prop wash sending smoke, fire, and ash up in a whirlwind around them. The skids hovered six feet off of the ground, the door-gunner screamed to jump. Daugherty tumbled out, and quickly ran uphill with the rest, cursing the lifers for dropping them in the middle of a brush fire. He noticed then that his plastic canteen had started to melt.

Lieutenant Stephen's Second Platoon was CA'd onto the opposite side of the ridge. Stephen was in the lead bird, Steverson telling him on the radio that his LZ was hot. Because he declined to give Stephen coordinates, Stephen was convinced that the crash site must be in Laos. Fire poured at the Hueys as they came in, the lead ship taking hits, Stephen choked with a sense of helplessness as one or two green tracers zipped through the open cabin. The bird hovered at ten feet and they jumped into tall elephant grass. The second bird also dropped off its troops, but the third took hits on the approach, pulled away over the LZ, and—either because they panicked or had guts—two GIs jumped from it at twenty feet. Only ten men were on the ground with Stephen and they crouched in the elephant grass as AKs and the 12.7mms tore holes in the air. The noise was incredible, the NVA seemed to be everywhere. They could even see them darting among the trees.

Lieutenant Colonel Steverson, above in his C&C, radioed that the downed helos were a hundred meters to the southwest. Lieutenant Stephen refused to move until he had map coordinates.

The colonel angrily read off the digits; they were only a hundred yards from Laos. The NVA kept firing; U.S. artillery pounded in. The next thing Stephen knew, M-79 rounds were lobbing from over the crest where the rest of Delta was setting up. North Vietnamese were spotted between the two groups. Stephen insisted over the radio that grenades were exploding within fifty yards, but Steverson said that the NVA must have a launcher. Stephen had no idea that the rest of Delta Company was even in the area.

On the other side of the ridge, Daugherty could also see NVA among the trees. An FAC plane circled overhead, on the radio with him; the pilot said air was on the way, then sailed low and fired a white-phosphorus rocket. It exploded brightly in the jungle down the slope from them, and Daugherty reported that the marking round was right on the NVA. He read the grid coordinates that they were holding, and the FAC answered that he couldn't bring jets in that close to U.S. troops. Daugherty asked the pilot if he could guarantee that they would put their ordnance on the target. When the FAC answered yes, Daugherty said there'd been a mistake; they were really a klick away from the marking round.

The pilot answered conspiratorially, "That's all I wanted to know."

And then the jets came in. The grunts couldn't even see them from where they hugged earth and curled up. They held their ears and helmets as the sky broke with earsplitting shrieks, the valley erupted in geysers of smoke, splintered trees, and hot shrapnel, and the hill under them shook with concussion waves.

The first airstrike hit a quarter-mile to one side of Stephen's platoon. When the second pass hit on the opposite side, he radioed the colonel that he was bracketed by their own firepower.

Under heavy fire, Steverson took his C&C down on a low-level pass over the jungle, marking the exact NVA positions with red smoke grenades.

After the bombing, Stephen took point as his platoon worked its way towards the wrecks. They exchanged fire with some NVA who disappeared back into the jungle, then found the first crash. The helicopter was still smoking, but the fire was burning itself out. They dragged two bodies from the first bird; at the second, they found three dead but two survivors. The platoon humped back up the ridge and Hueys dropped into the LZ, under fire, to get the five burnt bodies. The slicks started to skim away when, on the other side of the mountain, Daugherty heard someone shout. He jerked his head up in time to see a body falling from one of the choppers. It disappeared behind the treeline. Gunships began darting low, trying to get a fix on where the body had landed, but they couldn't and Lieutenant Colonel Steverson decided to abandon it. It would have been too risky a game of finding a needle in a haystack, considering the NVA presence. The grunts were disgusted; all of this work and danger, and they had just let a body get lost; the door-gunner was too chicken, according to the rumor, to grab the roasted body when the chopper banked away. Daugherty, for one, felt sad that a fellow American soldier, dead or alive, had to be left behind in that stinking jungle.

The LZ was too hot to extract Second Platoon, so Stephen was ordered to hump to the top of the ridgeline. He again took point and, coming to the crest, saw a rifle barrel ahead in the foliage. He instantly shouldered his M-16 and dropped the sights to the man's forehead, ten feet away.

He was about to pull the trigger when he noticed the man was wearing a GI pot.

A grunt from one of the other platoons was lying flat, waiting for them, and only then did Stephen realize his was not the only platoon there. He lowered his M-16 but, still keyed-up from the fire, shouted, "You better speak English, motherfucker, or you're dead!"

Mission accomplished, it was time to get out.

They were waiting for the slicks to arrive when a volley of AKs suddenly burst from the brush forty meters ahead of Daugherty. He scrambled for cover with the others, dropping to the prone in the tall grass and shouldering his M-16. There was nothing to see but a wall of elephant grass and scrub brush ten feet in front of his face. More fire cut overhead and his radio crackled; the RTO on the right flank was taking fire from a ridge, while the RTO on his left said they were taking fire from the left. Daugherty and the rest just fired blind bursts back into the vegetation.

The NVA fire slackened off, the grunts popped smoke, and the choppers began coming in. The infantrymen on the fringe fired furiously while others jogged for the birds. Daugherty looked from his bed of elephant grass at the fourth from last helicopter twenty feet up, smoking from a burst of AK. It caught fire, shuddered as the pilot struggled to control it, and careened towards the grunts. Daugherty frantically grabbed Craig, lying beside him, and they dropped their rucks, grabbed their rifles, and bolted into the grass, stumbling and falling in the thick brush. He fell down, Craig leaped over him, and he scrambled back up, plunging into the wall of elephant grass. The Huey hit the ground hard behind them and burst into flames. Another slick sped into the smoky LZ, got the crew and some grunts aboard, and departed amidst the AK-47 fire.

Only two helicopters were still orbiting and Daugherty was worried; with the shoot-down and the crew evack, that much less space went to the infantrymen. They would have to double up on the last two birds. The Hueys came into the LZ, and the last grunts fired a couple of bursts into the brush and made a dash for them. Daugherty stepped on a skid as the helicopter began lifting off. He swung his other leg into the cabin and a grunt inside grabbed his web gear just as a burst of green AK tracers flew through the open cabin. He fell exhausted to the chopper floor as they gained altitude. The last slick came out of the LZ behind them, rounds punching through the aluminum floor, slightly wounding two grunts.

They set down on the Khe Sanh airstrip and began jumping out, TV crew filming them. The rest of the company gathered around. Buddies, who had before been concerned that they might not get out because of the chopper backup, were now slapping arms and laughing. A friend of Daugherty's from Rhode Island met him on the strip. The TV people had their camera on Daugherty and he didn't know why until his buddy laughed and pointed at his helmet. In the helmet band was the insignia of a lieutenant colonel he had found on the floor of a helicopter and jokingly stuck there.

Delta Company had been in contact for seven hours, and Daugherty wandered off the strip, still numb and shaken. He walked aimlessly and took off his helmet; then a captain he'd never seen before stuck his face in his and screamed, "Just where the hell do you think you are! Put your helmet back on!"

Daugherty went blank.

When he came back to his senses, he was sitting in a bomb crater. It seemed like a safe place. He had no idea what had happened to the captain. By dusk more Hueys had come for them and Delta Company was back in the mountain jungles.

The next day, another fierce firefight broke out in the Khe Sanh mountains, this one fought by Lieutenant Johnson's platoon of Alpha 3/5 Cav in the Punchbowl. Following the debacle of Bravo 1/1 Cav, General Hill had detached some of the reluctant cavalrymen to Johnson because of his good reputation. After some in-the-field retraining, he decided to take them on a daylight foot patrol. They organized at Emerald City, Sergeant White watching from his tank as the 1/1 Cav GIs milled around as if they wished they were anyplace else.

The patrol filed through a narrow valley pass, virtually cut off from one another in the thick foliage; then the NVA cut loose from spider holes flanking the pass. The three GIs in the lead disappeared in the sudden blast of AK-47s; a crossfire tore into the main body of the patrol, and the grunts hit the dirt as Lieutenant Johnson crawled forward. He found two men dead, the other mortally wounded, and then he too was hit, an AK round drilling his leg. Terrified and disorganized, the patrol inched away under the crossfire, abandoning Johnson. The lieutenant, seeing an NVA rise from a spider hole, gunned him down with his M-16.

He scurried into the dead man's dugout to hide.

That, at least is the story the Bravo grunts gave as they straggled back. At Emerald City, the platoon sergeant quickly organized a rescue patrol. He told White to send a volunteer from his tank, so the crew drew high card to see who would go. White pulled the Queen of Spades from the deck. He joined a dozen GIs as they hauled ass toward the shooting aboard a couple of tracks. They dismounted and moved into the thick brush. White was the fourth man in line as they walked downhill on a narrow trail—and it happened all over again. From hidden spider holes, a scythe of AK-47 fire cut down the lead three men, and White dove terrified under a large boulder, cropping from the side of the jungled draw. The sergeant, lying prone ahead of him had two LAWs slung over his shoulder, so White grabbed his web gear and hauled him to the boulder. He suddenly realized the man was dead, stitched across the torso by AK rounds. The rest of the patrol had ducked behind the other side of the giant boulder, and were discussing pulling back. White screamed that he was still there. They set up an M-60 to cover his retreat but every time he tried to move from the boulder AKs opened up. He started tossing grenades downhill at the phantoms in the jungle until the firing died down. He put his bush hat on his M-16 and stuck it out. When it drew no fire, he rolled out and ran like hell back to the patrol. They all pulled back then, leaving the bodies.

White had painfully wrenched his ankle scurrying under the boulder, and a medevac deposited him and a grunt from the patrol with a graze wound at the squadron aid station.

Back in the draw, they could still hear Johnson crying out so a platoon from Bravo 3/5 Cav tried to move in from a different direction. They too were halted by the intense fire. Johnson tried to crawl back, but another burst hit his wounded leg and he shouted that he couldn't move. No one could see him or the North Vietnamese for all the foliage and Lieutenant Colonel Osborn, monitoring the action from Emerald City radioed for the platoons to fall back. He sent in F4s to dislodge the NVA. The Phantoms dropped 250-pound bombs, and no one could be sure that they wouldn't blow up Lieutenant Johnson along with the enemy. Lieutenant Christian, with Osborn at the TOC APC, saw tears in the colonel's eyes after he gave the order.

But it worked. The shooting petered out after the airstrike and a Huey was able to go in for Johnson and the dead men. Sergeant White watched as they carried Lieutenant Johnson into the aid station on a litter. He'd been cut off, all alone, under intense fire, for hours; he faded in and out, his face was ashen, his trousers bloody and stinking. As the doctor cut away the frayed trousers, he mumbled, embarrassed, "I messed myself, I messed myself."

"Looks like you're going home," White said.

"Yeah," Johnson grunted, "I'm not going to have to put up with this bullshit anymore."

White was glad that Johnson had made it out okay; he was good in combat and was the kind of officer, he thought with approval, who wouldn't tolerate heroin, but would look the other way if a dude lit up a little grass.

The official assessment of the contact was six U.S. KIA and five WIA, against thirty-six NVA killed. That sounded good on paper, but did not prevent General Hill from sending the Bravo GIs back to the 1/1 Cav, dissatisfied with their reaction to the ambush. Besides the official repercussions, the incident convinced the 3/5 Cav grunts that 1/1 Cav was flaky. When they finally headed back for Dong Ha, White and his crew were intent on the cold beer and good pot in the rear. They shut down in the motor pool, cleaned the expended brass out of their vehicles, refueled, rearmed; then they wandered back to their hootches only to discover that elements of 1/1 Cav had moved in, laid claim to the barracks and hootch maids, and refused to budge. There were shouts, a few punches, and one of White's buddies started a Sheridan in the 1/1 motor pool, aimed it at the hootches, and jumped out. They laughed like hell as GIs chased after it. First Sergeant Bradley finally broke up the fight and returned their hootches to them. That was a good old army story of unit loyalty, but as the stress of combat wore off, the 3/5 Cav even fell upon itself. It was White's first long standdown and it shocked him to see black troopers who'd fought beside him suddenly band together and travel in groups. They picked fights with whites, and the undercurrent of hate disturbed White enormously. It made him want to get back in the bush just to be away from the rear. Sergeant Keefer's platoon withdrew to the main base at Khe Sanh. He thought it would offer some relief from the punishment they had suffered in the bush, but he soon found that Khe Sanh was just one more bad scene tacked to the end of an operation he thought was a mess from start to finish.

The shelling continued as Keefer noted in his diary:

> March 27. We're on our way back down south now. We are stopped at Khe Sanh. We are taking 140 and 122mm rockets and 152 artillery from across the border.
>
> March 28. We've been taking more rockets. There's just no place to hide. One of our APCs was hit right on top. Three guys died.
>
> March 29. Didn't take any rockets today.
>
> March 30–31. Took about 10 rockets yesterday and about 23 today.
>
> April 1. Took 5 rockets this morning and 8 tonite.
>
> April 2. We were told we'd be leaving today. But now they come telling us we'll be here for another 3 to 10 days. Sure will be glad to leave this place.

Ray Keefer was twenty-one years old, but his face no longer looked as boyish as it had when he'd arrived in Vietnam. Gray hair peppered his blond shag and he felt like a tired old man. The very last note in his Vietnam diary read, "Only God knows how much I miss my home and want to be back home with my family. Just 59 more days left in the Army and I'll be out."

CHAPTER SEVENTEEN: Standdown

The South Vietnamese were in Laos for forty-five days, and the last ones out were the Vietnamese Marines. Initially serving as the I Corps reserve force, they had been committed in early March to occupy the firebases that the 1st Division had abandoned for the drive to Tchepone. As the withdrawals continued, the marines came under increasing pressure. By the time they were the last South Vietnamese in Laos, this was their deployment: the 2d, 4th, and 7th Infantry Battalions, 147th VNMC Brigade on LZ delta; the 1st, 3rd and 8th infantry battalions, 258th VNMC Brigade on LZ hotel; the 369th VNMC Brigade in reserve.

Their formidable task was to blunt the NVA counterattack. The U.S. Marine advisors chafed at their own inability to fight alongside their counterparts in Laos. Headed by Colonels Frank Tief and Pat McMillan, the advisors endured numerous artillery attacks at the rear command post; four of them, Majors Pat Carlisle, Bill Dabney, Bob Martin, and Fred Tolleson, were even allowed to overfly the VNMC AO (these flights were made in the face of heavy fire from radar-controlled 37mm flak guns, for which Carlisle, Martin, and Tolleson won Silver Stars, probably the only advisors decorated for heroism during Laos. For unexplained reasons, Dabney was not decorated, perhaps because, of the four, he was not aerial-observer qualified). But even the flights weren't enough. The marine advisors thought of themselves as a breed apart, all second-tour vets who attacked their new responsibilities as fiercely as they did any enemy hill. They spoke Vietnamese, wore the VNMC uniform, ate their food, lived with them in the field, fought beside them. They usually worked alone or in pairs, and often sneered at some of the U.S. Army advisors, at least the ones whose hootches were little replicas of America with real beds, pinups on the wall, refrigerators full of beer, and a stereo playing in the corner.

They wanted to fight with their comrades in Laos. The Vietnamese Marines were brave, sometimes almost suicidal in their acceptance of the never-ending war. Many of their officers had received training in the United States, and they emulated the training and tactics of the U.S. Marine Corps. They had proven their combat worth in the Mekong Delta and Cambodia. But Laos was a new test. The terrain of unfamiliar, rugged mountains was nothing like the tabletop Delta paddies to which they were accustomed; and they were facing a numerically superior, well-equipped, well-motivated NVA force that knew the area.

A lesser unit would have been destroyed doing the job handed the Vietnamese Marines in Laos. As it was, they were seriously bloodied.

With the 1st Infantry and 1st Airborne Divisions airlifted out, and the 1st Armor Brigade racing for the border, the full weight of the NVA counterattack fell upon the single VNMC brigade at LZ Delta. The North Vietnamese soldiers hugged the perimeter and kept the U.S. helicopters away with heavy small-arms fire. Supply drops to the hilltop missed. The marines were almost out of ammunition and on 20 March, the brigade prepared to pull out. But the NVA attacked that day and penetrated the wire. It was a horrific meatgrinder, but the Vietnamese Marines held. The next day, they were directed to spike their artillery pieces in preparation for helicopter extraction; but the helicopters could not get through, and the NVA shelled them without reprisal.

Men shot across the divided perimeter, and shouted across each other's radio frequencies. The NVA calls were always for surrender.

"You realize too well that we are all around you, and can move in at any time, not because you are bad soldiers, but because you are so few, so lonely, and a little frightened. We are Vietnamese, why do you fight for the American imperialists? You should be fighting for your own country, the Vietnamese people."

One South Vietnamese shouted back on the radio, "Sons of bitches, you are working like dogs for the Chinese, for the Russians, you are selling the country to them."

On 22 March, the NVA shelled LZ Delta all day and, in the late afternoon, the assault came. Ten Soviet-made tanks mounted with flamethrowers spearheaded the attack, infantrymen rushing with them. The marines poured fire from their bunkers, halting the attack. They blew up two tanks with LAWs. Another tank hit a mine and exploded. A Phantom strafed the NVA, blowing up a fourth tank. The NVA simply shelled again, then launched another assault. They ran straight at the marine line, screaming, "Assault, assault!" and they died en masse. But there were too many of them. The marines ran low on ammunition, and their casualties were heavy. All three VNMC battalion commanders on the hill had been wounded. The line began to break.

The order came to retreat to LZ Hotel.

The weather had turned misty and rainy, and the helicopters could not get in to evacuate the marine wounded. Over a hundred who could not walk would have to be left behind. They watched, terrified, as their comrades prepared to pull out, afraid of what the Communists would do to them, knowing that, even if they survived, the American B52s would be coming to bomb the victors. Men pleaded with their friends to shoot them. No one could.

A private named Binh in the 2d Battalion was getting ready to leave when a friend called him over. The man was wounded and could not walk.

He whispered for a grenade.

Binh gave one to his friend and ran away.

Seconds later there was an explosion.

The North Vietnamese surged over the abandoned bunkers, with tanks and infantry, and the marines retreated down the eastern slopes of LZ Delta. The wounded tried to hobble after them, but stumbled and were swallowed up. Tank and artillery fire burst among the survivors; NVA charged after them with the blood-curdling cry, "Assault!" and the retreat disintegrated. In the chaos, commanders lost control of their men, with every man for himself fleeing into the valley. There was no relief—the NVA outnumbered them and were everywhere.

Private Binh found himself with a hundred other marines. They moved through the black jungle, terrified of ambush. North Vietnamese running through the area paused a few times to shoot towards them. Confused and frightened marines also opened up on them in the dark. Some of the men were gripped with panic, and threw away their rifles and gear to run faster.

A captain named Tien finally stopped the group and shouted angrily at them to get their heads together and follow him.

The marines hesitated.

The captain drew his pistol, jogged uphill, and frightened men followed him. Private Binh's group made it to safety.

With daylight and better weather, helicopters were able to come in for some of the survivors, while others kept walking towards the border in small groups, evading the NVA. The brigade reported thirty-seven men missing and hundreds more killed or wounded, but two thousand NVA had died in the overrunning of LZ Delta. Nevertheless, on the morning of 24 March, the hammer fell on the last South Vietnamese in Laos—the 258th VNMC Brigade on Hotel. In two hours before noon, U.S. Air Cavalry teams spotted at least five groupings of Soviet-made tanks on the border, and blew up ten of them. Meanwhile, North Vietnamese probes were launched at the wire around LZ Hotel.

Back in Saigon, Lieutenant General Khang, Commandant of the VNMC, received the situation reports. He had never joined the command post on the Laotian front, presumably because he was miffed at having been relegated to being under Lam's command (no clear reason emerged, however, from within the politics of the Vietnamese hierarchy). In order to minimize casualties among his remaining units, Khang ordered Colonel Lan—without consulting with Lam to weigh the consequences—to evacuate LZ Hotel. An orderly helicopter withdrawal of the troops and artillery pieces on the Co Roc was conducted. The next day, an angry General Lam ordered two VNMC reconnaissance teams back to the high ground of the Co Roc to monitor the counterattack. They had little to report; the Communists' fury did not reach across the border. Perhaps they did not want to risk further heavy casualties and were content to hit-and-run and shell along the Quang Tri front. Most likely, they were too busy licking their wounds after having taken tremendous casualties in wreaking havoc on the ARVN withdrawal. No Americans or South Vietnamese could say for sure.

The last South Vietnamese, the recon teams, were out of Laos on 24 March 1971.* Commented a marine corporal from the 147th Brigade, "The papers and the radio kept on saying there was a Laos victory, I have learned now, but what a joke. We ran out like wounded dogs."

The view was not so bleak at the command level. The 147th Brigade had been mauled, but had survived, was regrouping, and was still combat ready; the 258th had been bloodied; the 369th Brigade had not even been touched. No battle is without its moments of tragedy and panic, but the marines had met the challenge of their first division-sized fight. The North Vietnamese had been halted at the border.

---

* At least that is the official version. One marine advisor saw Colonel Lan talk to the team leaders he was supposed to send to the Co Roc; he seemed distressed at ordering them to almost certain death, and the impression was that he instead had quietly ignored the directive.

Major Dabney, USMC, senior advisor to the 3d Battalion, 258th VNMC Brigade, was more cautious about claiming victory. He had no doubt that the individual South Vietnamese had soldiered bravely in Laos; but that wasn't enough to salvage the operation and he considered Laos a disaster. Dabney was an ex-sergeant, a graduate of VMI, a tough, blunt man on his second voluntary tour. His first year had conditioned him to the realities of Vietnam. He'd been a rifle company commander with the 26th Marines then, in exactly the same area that he was in now. The only fond memory he had from that experience was the stunning spirit of his marines.

Khe Sanh had ended in victory and Dabney had never been prouder of the marine team. But numerous problems had cropped up, some of which reappeared during Lam Son 719. The worst was the lack of turnover of information between units. He'd seen time after time when marine companies would walk into the same NVA ambush spots at different times, because no one had warned them. Battalions and regiments often did not pass on information, and Dabney cynically described intelligence in Vietnam as a few filthy grunts watching another outfit patrolling towards a valley where they'd been mauled and muttering, "Geez, I wish they wouldn't do that." That was a major problem as he saw it with Operation Lam Son 719. The U.S. Marines had been fighting in the area for five years and, in 1969, had even made a raid into Laos. They knew the terrain and disposition of NVA artillery; many of the command and staff officers who had successfully defended Khe Sanh in '68 were readily available for advice, but Dabney knew of no time when the U.S. Army turned to them when planning and executing Lam Son 719. It was wearisome to keep reinventing the wheel.

Dabney had been wary of the operation since first he had been briefed two months earlier at 3d Battalion Headquarters at Quang Tri. He had, in fact, been appalled, thinking the plan invited disaster. If Tchepone was a legitimate target, he thought, why not simply take the divisions and brigades allotted to I Corps and march them en masse to the target and back? That way, he surmised, the Communists could never obtain any substantial victories because they couldn't successfully challenge the size of such a force. In addition, the helicopter LZs would not have been covered with AA fire since they would have been deep in allied lines; bloodied units could have been rotated easily within the moving battle group; and communications would have been similarly simplified, instead of strung out among various firebases and HQ elements all the way back to Dong Ha.

As he saw it, the plan for mutually-supporting firebases called for an adeptness and experience at fire coordination, resupply, and communications that the ARVN simply did not yet possess. The firebases, dropped like islands in an enemy sea, did nothing but allow the NVA to encircle and attack at will, one at a time. The ARVN had never been involved in such a complex operation, and the only way he saw that they might be able to hold their ground was with expertly orchestrated air and artillery support, such as that which the marines had been able to achieve at Khe Sanh. Dabney knew very well, though, that the USMC air-ground team had been in the making for thirty years, and the South Vietnamese had always relied upon their advisors to handle such matters. Now the advisors were removed from the field of battle.

The ARVN advantage in Laos was firepower; but the mere presence of might was meaningless, only its application mattered. The case of the awesome B52 bomber illustrates this. As they had done during the siege of Khe Sanh, the North Vietnamese encircled the firebases in Laos. In 1968 the problem had been that the Marines could not use air and arty against targets so close to their own perimeters without observation and control which could not be achieved in the dark. This scenario was even worse for the firebases in Laos; Dabney suspected that the NVA were in close around-the-clock. Arc Lights would have eliminated them, but the USAF was not given accurate reporting on the disposition of friendly patrols around the firebases. This meant that they were forced to place their bomb loads at least four thousand meters away, well beyond likely NVA locations. So for all of the thousands of tons of ordnance dropped in support of the ARVN firebases, it was logical to assume that it had little effect.

The North Vietnamese, on the other hand, were given a great opportunity by the ARVN firebase plan. Although the NVA had relatively poor communications and could never hope to match the allies in raw firepower, the presence of fixed ARVN positions allowed them to use their limited resources to the greatest effect. The NVA sited their artillery and mortars in scattered, single-gun positions, and ranged the tubes individually at the various South Vietnamese posts. Since they never moved, the NVA could fire without observation, night and day, accurately hitting any targets of opportunity (medevac and resupply helos, for example) on the fixed positions, without going through a lengthy fire-registration process.

That was nothing new, Dabney knew; the NVA had used that tactic against his regiment in '68, but the USMC knew how to use firepower. It was difficult to pinpoint and neutralize single-gun positions in the jungled mountains, but with Marine infantrymen directing Marine aircraft (with one overall Marine commander) they had succeeded. The tools were available to the South Vietnamese in Laos, but the experience and cohesion were missing. To begin with, the Vietnamese Marines were operating as a division when before they had rarely even worked in multibattalion campaigns. So the three brigades headquarters had no firesupport-coordination experience, the battalion commanders having usually left such matters to their U.S. Marine advisors. Now, in Laos, the situation involved South Vietnamese without advisors relying on U.S. Army helicopters, Air Force jets, and U.S. and ARVN artillery. This was a tangle; Dabney was not particularly surprised to learn that when the 147th was being overrun on LZ Delta, the 258th on LZ Hotel had 155mm guns in range but was not alerted to fire in support.

He had seen only a rare VNMC unit with the training and experience to, when in contact, coordinate between squad, platoon, and company leaders on the radio, pinpoint the enemy with spotter rounds, then further coordinate with the battalion commander to place U.S. firepower from different services on the enemy. Even his helicopter flights over Laos did little good because the VNMC mortar crews did not have the capability of accurately marking the NVA with white phosphorus shells; and B52s could not be employed in a carpeting manner since, because of the scattered command posts, it was difficult to locate friendly patrols around the firebases.

The result was that the South Vietnamese trump card over the numerically superior NVA—massive firepower—was negated because of inexperience. In fact the NVA could even outgun the firebases.

Most matters seemed similarly bungled. The logistics officer in Dabney's battalion was an uncaring character who responded to the overwhelming logistics of the operation by adhering to a strict schedule: the battalions were resupplied in turn, not when they specifically needed it. Thus, units were overrun because they had practically no ammunition while others had stockpiles of the stuff which was left behind when they retrograded back to South Vietnam.

Dabney's concerns were so great that, before the withdrawal from Tchepone began, he hopped a helo ride to the U.S. 1st Marines CP at Da Nang. He talked with two old acquaintances, Col. P. X. Kelley* the regimental commander, and Col. Al Smith, G2 of the 1st Marine Divi-

* Now the Commandant, U.S. Marine Corps.

sion. He explained the problems that he saw and predicted that Lam Son 719 was a disaster in the making. Kelley and Smith seemed impressed and arranged a meeting with Lt. Gen. Donn Robertson, commander of III MAF.

When the ARVN began pulling out, the NVA began isolating and overrunning positions. It wasn't the fault of the South Vietnamese, Dabney thought, it was MACV's plan. Without the bravery of the marine and army aviators going in to pull out the men, he surmised that Lam Son 719 could have been annihilation, instead of merely a disaster. Dabney could only thank God that the weather hadn't turned foul and trapped the South Vietnamese inside Laos.

The withdrawal of U.S. troops and installations from the Khe Sanh area went at a steady pace, beginning when the ARVN started pulling out of Laos and heading back south themselves, and was marked by a final few casualties in the rocket raids and convoy ambushes. On 25 March, the 27th Engineers began taking up the assault runway matting at Khe Sanh and, by 1 April, the removal of the airstrip was completed. In the sky, Chinooks could be seen headed east with slingloads of materiel, engineer equipment, bridges, and artillery pieces. Along Route 9, long convoys streamed for Dong Ha and then Quang Tri, stacked with salvaged gear. The man detailed to supervise the evacuation of Khe Sanh, Colonel Rosenblum of the 101st DISCOM, watched impressed as the base perimeter quickly shrank; they had been able to go in, set up a giant logistical center, then pull out leaving nothing behind, the NVA responding with only a few departing rocket raids. The North Vietnamese simply couldn't react to fast-moving situations, Rosenblum thought, and if he were the NVA general he imagined he would court-martial the NVA commander of the Khe Sanh AO for incompetence.

FSA-I at the Vandegrift Combat Base was officially closed on 4 April. By 6 April, FSA-II at the Khe Sanh Combat Base was a desolate ghost town; the last convoys left on Route 9 and the Yellow Brick Road, a small detachment staying long enough to fire tear gas canisters into the U.S. bunkers. The gas crystals would make the shelters unlivable for two years. With gunships and M48 tanks guarding the route, Khe Sanh was evacuated without a major hitch. Also on 6 April, the last elements of the 1/11 Infantry (D Company and the battalion command group) were airlifted from Khe Sanh to Quang Tri. On Route 9, the 1/77 Armor began a leapfrogging, retrograde action back east from Lang Vei, attached engineer elements removing all of the AVLB bridges installed west of Vandegrift. The 1/1 and 3/5 Cavalry, and the 1/61 Mech

Infantry also joined the pullout. On the evening of 8 April, Pfc DeAngelis watched as his old friends in Bravo Company rolled back into Quang Tri. He could see them coming a mile away, the dusty, battered caravan of APCs looking like a Fourth of July celebration as the grunts fired flares, pitched smoke grenades, and raised general hell in their joy to be heading back. DeAngelis joined them in the EM Club to down some beers, and later wrote to his parents, "They were out for 75 days and never got mail or clean clothes the whole time. There fatigues were literally rotted on there backs and they were all caked with dirt and very pooped too. (But happy to be back). . . . They lost 15 men 6 from my old platoon and I think everybody got some small kind of wound at one time or other. Anything that could ever happen to a bunch of grunts happened to them. Believe me, there is now no one left from my old squad. Two of the guys got killed. I've got pictures of them at home someplace. What can I say to tell you how I feel right now."

On 8 April, the 14th Engineers removed the last of the bridges placed for the operation and on 9 April, the last pullout was set in action. Trash fires rose at various points in the jungled hills where the grunts of the Americal and 101st Airborne cleaned up their last NDPs. A flight of Hueys dropped into the jungle home of Bravo 3/187 and the men packed their gear and themselves aboard. They were deposited first in another LZ where they boarded a Chinook, and finally touched down at Camp Evans. The Screaming Eagles' brass band was on the runway playing for the filthy grunts as they trudged off the strip. How hokey, Sp4 Kucera thought, who cares? Shortly thereafter, the battalion held a memorial service formation. Nineteen ponchos were laid out before an altar with nineteen pairs of empty jungle boots. A pet dog of Bravo Company named Yo-Yo wandered out during the ceremony and voided on the late Lieutenant Colonel Sutton's poncho. The grunts collapsed with laughter.

On the last morning, Captain Downey of Charlie 2/1 Infantry received a radio call from the 4/3 CP that they were to be extracted from their hilltop. They were ordered to fire a Mad Minute around their perimeter, expend whatever mortar ammunition they still had, bury their garbage, police the area, and be prepared to leave aboard helicopters at 1130 hours.

That was at around half past seven in the morning; by eleven they were packed and ready to go. Downey was called by the battalion operations officer, who was in his C&C helicopter. The major said that there were some delays and the pickup would probably not be until 1300 hours. It was a little after noon when they heard the first popping thunks of 82mm mortar rounds leaving their tube. Explosions began walking across Charlie Company's position and the grunts jumped into foxholes, unable to fire back because they had used up all of their mortar ammunition that morning. One GI was slightly wounded, but the company RTO could raise no one on the medevac channel. Downey got on the radio and finally convinced the major to leave his C&C orbit to get the wounded trooper. The mortaring stopped as soon as the helicopter came into view; as the C&C was lifting off with the injured man, the major radioed, "Your birds are on the way, be ready in five minutes!"

Downey shouted for his men to get organized. They waited. Thirty minutes passed. No helicopters appeared and his RTO could raise no one on the radio. On nearby hills, they watched other choppers going in to pick up other units. After another twenty minutes, Downey noticed with apprehension that everything was perfectly quiet. No helicopters were overhead, no traffic was on the highway below; so still he could hear the jungle birds.

The North Vietnamese mortar crew opened fire again, and the men dropped back in their holes. It was a heavy, accurate shelling, and the young FO lieutenant crouched beside Downey, shouting into the radio, calling the artillery frequencies at Khe Sanh and Vandegrift. No one answered. The lieutenant and the company's ARVN interpreter just managed to make contact with an ARVN 155mm howitzer outfit on a small firebase barely within range; then the NVA began jamming the radio. They must have been close because their voices were loud and clear through the receiver, effectively blocking transmissions with loud screams and laughs. Downey would have laughed too, if he hadn't been so nervous, when the NVA began shouting corn such as, "You die now, GI!" It was like being in some WWII movie, he thought.

The mortaring continued at a steady pace.

Finally, twenty Huey slicks appeared in the sky above Charlie Company, coming from the direction of Dong Ha, and four Cobra gunships darted down, circling the perimeter in search of a flash from the NVA mortar. The enemy's response was to put a second tube into action; the new one was much closer, Downey noted, the time between the thunk and the explosion being shorter than before. Dodging the mortar attack, the Hueys began coming in, three at a time. They landed on the crest of the hill, above the infantrymen's foxholes, and the grunts dashed for them. Captain Downey's five-man command group was the last out. Their Huey settled down, another mortar round exploding next to their hole; Downey yelled, "Run!" and they bolted uphill. Downey flung himself and his rucksack aboard, his RTO clambered on behind him, and the bird bolted out of the jungle landing zone.

At Dong Ha, the operations officer of 4/3 came over to Captain Downey to tell him that his C Company, 2d Battalion, 1st Infantry, 196th Infantry Brigade, Americal Division had the distinction of being the last U.S. infantry unit withdrawn from Operation Lam Son 719.

Coming in last was Lieutenant Colonel Meyer's 1st Battalion, 77th Armor. The day before, they had camped outside Khe Sanh after departing Lang Vei under mortar fire. As they blew up extra equipment and ammunition, a resupply bird dropped in. The battalion sniper squad brusquely greeted an FNG who hopped out; then they climbed aboard to get back to Quang Tri. Only Sp4 Spurgeon decided to stay with the tank column, hopped up about his kill and hoping for more action. The next morning, 9 April, he was sitting atop a tank with a smoke and a cup of C rat coffee, when a APC from the 3/5 Cav roared into their perimeter, coming to a quick dusty stop. A filthy crewman spotted Spurgeon and hustled over.

"You a sniper?"

"Yeah."

"Well, one of your snipers was killed last night, and another wounded pretty bad. We picked 'em up last night after they called for help."

"My snipers are in Quick Town, they were lifted into the PX for some supplies last night!"

Confused and agitated, Spurgeon jumped on the tank of the Bravo Company captain and asked him to check higher about two snipers being hit the night before. The captain nodded from inside the turret, spoke into the radio, then pulled his helmet off and said, "Yes." Before long they hit Route 9 and it was well after dark when this last group rolled past the Quang Tri perimeter gate. Spurgeon rode on the back deck of one of the tanks, surprised to see an Australian floor show grinding away on a plywood stage in the battalion area. The GI audience greeted the last column with enthusiastic cheers and smiles. The tanks had to slow down because of the applauding soldiers crowded around, and Spurgeon noticed Sergeant Wondra smiling up at him from the crowd, in new fatigues, a bandage taped to the top of his partially-shaved head.

He hopped off the tank and Wondra gave him a big bear hug.

In the sniper hootch, the men were clean shaven, in clean clothes, and cheerful as they passed beers and sodas. Spurgeon asked about what the cavalryman had told him—two snipers shot up—and the story started coming out. The helo taking them to Quang Tri had been diverted to a 3/5 Cav hill outpost, where they joined two 101st snipers, and had dug in for the night. Having been forced to set up in broad daylight on an open hill, the men were nervous. At around midnight they saw flash-lights in the hills to the north. Attention focused in that direction when RPGs and AKs suddenly opened up from their rear. The snipers burrowed into their holes, except for the team of Wondra and Felix who returned fire despite shrapnel wounds. The 101st staff sergeant in charge froze, according to the snipers. One of them had to wrestle the radio from him, and he had just contacted the cav at the bottom of the hill, when an NVA sprang into the perimeter. From three feet away he shot Felix through the head with his AK-47, the body bouncing against Wondra who spun to see the North Vietnamese crouched at the rim of the foxhole. They fired at the same time. The M-14 round hit the NVA in the chest, killing him, while the AK round hit Wondra on the top of his head, knocking him down. Blinded by blood, he heaved grenades at the NVA. Flares burst overhead, the cav tracks rumbled quickly up the hill, and the enemy disappeared back into the night.

Felix was probably the last KIA in the 1/77 Armor, and possibly the last in the operation. The armor battalion had been in the field for seventy days for the Laotian campaign, the first out and the last back in.

CHAPTER EIGHTEEN: Where Victory Lies

The time chosen officially to close the log on Operation Dewey Canyon II/Lam Son 719 was 5:08 P.M., 6 April 1971. No ground troops remained in Laos or in the Khe Sanh area, as the effort had been a spoiling attack, not a land seizure operation. As always in the Vietnam War, a tableau of statistics was presented to determine success or failure. The XXIV Corps After-Action Report gives this breakdown of U.S. casualties during the battle:

101st Airborne Division:	68 KIA	261 WIA	17 MIA
1st Brigade, 5th Division:	55 KIA	431 WIA	3 MIA
America Division:	47 KIA	256 WIA	7 MIA
223d Combat Aviation Battalion:	19 KIA	59 WIA	11 MIA
XXIV Corps Artillery:	9 KIA	76 WIA	0 MIA
U.S. Army Support Command:	8 KIA	40 WIA	0 MIA
45th Engineer Group:	6 KIA	11 WIA	0 MIA
7th U.S. Air Force:	4 KIA	N/A WIA	0 MIA
504th MP Battalion:	3 KIA	15 WIA	0 MIA

While according to XXIV Corps, 219 Americans were officially listed as killed in the Laotian campaign, the figure released for publication—to *Newsweek* for example—was 102 KIA (roughly the number killed in aerial combat over Laos). But the rules of the game dictated that even the higher figure be slightly lower than reality. For example, the total did not take into account various support units which served only sporadically and briefly during the operation (MP detachments, small USMC units, 1st Signal Brigade radio outposts on the battlefield, and others). Also, the mortally wounded were counted as WIA instead of KIA since they died in a hospital or aboard a helicopter, not in the field. Similarly, nonhostile deaths were not tabulated (for instance ten aircrewmen were killed and four missing in mishaps; SUPCOM reported fourteen fatal traffic accidents during the campaign; nine U.S. Marines were killed in a CH53 crash in South Vietnam after nursing their ship out of Laos, apparently with battle damage).

The same type of gerrymandering occurred in the listing of U.S. battle damage. For example, 107 helicopters were reported lost during the operation (fifty-three Hueys, twenty-six Cobras, 9 Loaches, 8 UN1C gunships, 6 Kiowa Scouts, 3 Chinooks, and 2 Sea Stallions); this does not include 5 destroyed in accidents. In addition, a helicopter retrieved from the battlefield, even if it were burnt-out junk, was not counted as lost; thus, although an additional 618 helicopters were reported as damaged, it would be impossible to determine how many had been shot down in combat and then slingloaded out by Chinooks after the shooting was over, or how many made controlled crashes in friendly territory.

The South Vietnamese suffered severe losses, up to 50 percent in some units, with the breakdown as follows:

1st Infantry Division:	537 KIA	1,607 WIA	537 MIA
1st Airborne Division:	455 KIA	1,992 WIA	0 MIA*
VNMC Division:	335 KIA	768 WIA	37 MIA
1st Ranger Group:	93 KIA	435 WIA	27 MIA
I Corps units:	55 KIA	314 WIA	24 MIA
1st Armor Brigade:	54 KIA	367 WIA	0 MIA
	1,529 KIA	5,483 WIA	625 MIA

Compared to the recorded deaths of 219 Americans (and 38 MIA), and 1,529 South Vietnamese (and 625 MIA), the North Vietnamese suffered grievously. The official count was 19,360 killed and 57 captured (of this, the U.S. was credited with 4,795 kills and 8 captures, while those killed by U.S. tac air and bomber missions were included in the ARVN total). Thus, according to the allied figures, perhaps one-half of the NVA committed to Laos were killed.

* A false figure; Colonel Tho, CO, 3d Airborne Brigade, was captured on Hill 31 along with numerous other ARVN paratroopers.

The Laotian operation had not been merely a body-count exercise but, more importantly, an attempt to disrupt the NVA buildup to preempt their invasion of MR1. In this endeavor, the statistics of destruction were these: 5,170 individual weapons; 1,963 crew-served weapons; 2,001 vehicles; 11 combat vehicles; 106 tanks (88 confirmed by U.S. aerial recon); 13 artillery pieces; 93 mortars; 98 radios; 1,250 tons of rice; 170,346 tons of ammunition (20,000 tons verified by the U.S.).

The reading of success or failure into these numbers was a tricky and controversial business. The very nature of the plan—calling for a withdrawal from enemy territory under fire—brought about the specter of disaster; coupled with the ferocious NVA resistance to the operation, a surface examination could easily read failure. As it was all in the eye of the beholder, claims of success by the military quickly conflicted with more pessimistic reports from the press. The world press—and, thus, the American people—were generally convinced that the operation had been ill-planned with too much emphasis on U.S. firepower, the invasion halted, the withdrawal a chaotic rout. By 1971 the press corps generally had become an antiwar body and, to the detriment of unemotional analysis, their commentary on Lam Son 719 most often came from keyed-up sources—exhausted ARVN just off the helicopters from heavy combat in Laos, and bitter American pilots just back from the air war over Laos who spoke vindictively of the ARVN "getting their asses kicked."

The prevailing frame of mind can be understood by media reaction to certain events during the campaign. When General Abrams imposed a news embargo during the buildup in MR1 and during the first days of Dewey Canyon II, his reasoning was for security. Accordingly, he also embargoed the news of the embargo to prevent communist speculation. The press ignored this second constraint and informed home offices of the general facts so that stories could be published in the United States; they hinted without restraint that the troop buildup pointed to an invasion of Laos (blow to the allied ruse-operations aimed at worrying Hanoi about an invasion of North Vietnam); and they implied that the embargo was really a sinister cover-up. Suspicious of the ban on U.S. ground troops in Laos, many reporters turned their attention to trying to find some. They could not, but still managed to leave the impression that U.S. advisors and pathfinders were indeed in Laos. They also indicated that U.S. advisors in ARVN command posts were proof that the South Vietnamese were, in fact, puppets to U.S. commands; the advisors were merely doing what they always did, giving advice which was not always taken.

To accuse the press of going out of its way to show Lam Son 719 in the worst possible light does not, however, necessarily mean that the Laotian campaign was a stunning success. On this subject, even the opinions of military men were mixed. General Westmoreland, Army Chief of Staff, wrote of the problems: "Command arrangements at the top were unsound, and the plan had been developed too quickly for adequate provision for close co-ordination between the ARVN troops and their American support. Long accustomed to working with American advisors, subordinate ARVN commanders had difficulty without them in arranging fire support and resupply. The senior American advisor and the over-all ARVN commander were operating from different bases. Several senior ARVN commanders folded, prompting President Thieu to intervene and start issuing orders himself as far down as regiments, in many cases without General Abrams' knowledge."

The catalogue of disasters could continue. Intelligence had underestimated the speed and fury of the NVA counterattack, and this contributed to the loss of several ARVN firebases; the allies had indeed been defeated in some of the Laotian battles. General Dong and his relation (or lack of) with Colonel Luat of the 1st Armor caused needless problems. The response of some soldiers was cowardly: not merely grabbing a skid during a unit pullout, but shoving wounded aside to desert on medevac choppers. Because of the intelligence failure, the ARVN forces in Laos were too small to defend themselves adequately against the massed NVA units; given the option of beefing up their invasion force and staying longer in Laos, the ARVN commanders opted for a withdrawal, before the Communists closed them off and destroyed them piecemeal. The smaller of the two targeted base areas, BA 611, was untouched, except for a few Hoc Bao commando raids during the withdrawal sequence.

Despite these setbacks, the judgement of the command was expressed by General Sutherland, who called Lam Son 719 a victory in that U.S. and ARVN successes outweighed their mistakes. A few facts were evident, the most important being that the assigned mission to reach Tchepone and destroy BA 604 had been accomplished by the ARVN task force. Some units were badly mauled (the 3d Airborne and 39th Ranger Battalions, for example, were withdrawn as combat ineffective due to casualties), but the NVA plans of invading MR1 had been set back a full year, as the planners had hoped. All of this had been accomplished in the face of grave odds. Outnumbered two-to-one on the ground, the ARVN soldiers (with massive, but not always responsive, U.S. firepower) had inflicted ten casualties on the NVA for every one that they suffered. I

Corps had never previously controlled such a large operation and, except for the 1st Infantry Division, none of the ARVN divisions had worked as an entity before; yet, they had successfully disrupted BA 604 and the Ho Chi Minh Trail. Even though the withdrawal was executed under intense counterattack, most ARVN units pulled out in good military fashion ("They had to have damn good small unit leadership," a U.S. general was quoted in *Time,* "or they wouldn't have got out of there.").

The objectives of the operation had been down-scaled once the strength of the NVA became fully known, but it had nonetheless been a stinging blow to the Communists. There was no NVA invasion of MR1 that year. Vietnamization had been tested, had strained but had not cracked, and now had continued room to grow. Many, especially advisors, rejected the theory that ARVN failed so miserably in Laos that the final communist invasion of 1975 was a foregone conclusion. They blamed that capitulation on the total withdrawal of U.S. air support, the cutoff of U.S. supplies to the ARVN, and a botched attempt by the ARVN to fall back and regroup in the face of numerically overwhelming and well-supplied NVA troops. They point instead to March 1972. It took North Vietnam until then (even with massive Soviet aid and the stripping of many villages of every able-bodied man for the army) to recover from Lam Son 719 and to launch their invasion of MR1. They came across the DMZ in a conventional infantry assault supported by hundreds of Russian-made tanks, quickly defeating an inexperienced ARVN division and seizing the border firebases, as well as Dong Ha and Quang Tri. The ARVN finally recovered and in brutal battles involving house-to-house combat, artillery duels, and tank engagements, the ARVN and VNMC—many of whom were veterans of Laos—drove the NVA invaders back to the DMZ.

After Lam Son 719, the media quoted an American commander who said, "The success or failure of the operation will not be apparent until well into the fall. If there is no serious communist military activity in South Vietnam before then, it will have been well worth its cost."

By that measure, Operation Lam Son 719 was a victory.

The average American soldier in Operation Lam Son 719 knew nothing of the big picture. His view was limited to a platoon, and a patch of jungle or a stretch of road. Some in the rear recalled the drugs and the sense of abandonment, while some in the infantry experienced the misery of the elements, occasional stabs of fear, and the sustaining element of comradeship. What they knew about the invasion came from tattered newspapers; they saw the photographs of ARVN clutching skids and read horrid accounts of disaster. Most thought the ARVN had been defeated in Laos.

The U.S. Army, however, accomplished every mission it had been assigned during Lam Son 719. For all of its morale problems, it had been successful in the field. But, by 1971, the glory of victory meant very little to the average GI who saw it as just another operation in an unending war. The fact that they once again pulled out and abandoned Lang Vei, Khe Sanh, and the rest, made hollow the sacrifices put into the campaign. What they had were their buddies, their pride, and even their patriotism, but little sense of accomplishment. In the eyes of the grunts, Nam was just as hopeless after Lam Son 719 as it had been before.

Operation Lam Son 719 turned out to be the last major operation the U.S. Army executed in Vietnam. The withdrawals continued, the long, dirty war ebbed and flowed. Two more statistics explained the foot soldiers' weariness with the situation: even though Laos was the last big campaign, it was seventeen months before the last U.S. infantrymen were pulled out, and another three years after that before the last American was killed-in-action in Vietnam.

Sergeant Keefer rotated home in August 1971, with a routine Bronze Star and a head full of things he'd rather forget. His homecoming was typical of the time. The jet from Tan Son Nhut took him from the war zone to the state of Washington in under twenty-four hours. He signed some papers, then was on the street with his discharge and a ticket back to Maryland. He had a military standby seat on a civilian airliner, but someone else got it. Keefer approached the man, explaining that he was just back from Vietnam, just out of the service, and hadn't seen his family in a year. He was wearing his uniform with the Bronze Star, Army Commendation Medal, and Purple Heart with four oak-leaf clusters. The man looked at the uniform, said he wouldn't give up his seat to trash, and turned his back. And Keefer wondered why he'd spent eighteen months with his life on the line.

Many, too many, veterans of Operation Lam Son 719 have told the same type of stories about their homecomings.

EPILOGUE

General Abrams (COMUSMACV) became Chief of Staff in 1972, and died in office of cancer after thirty-eight years of distinguished service. General Weyand (DEPCOMUSMACV) followed Abrams as commander in Vietnam, 1972–73, then as Chief of Staff from 1974 to his retirement in 1976. Lieutenant General Sutherland (CG, XXIV Corps) was awarded the DSM* for his corps command, having earned two Silver Stars, a Bronze Star, two Army Commendation Medals, and two Purple Hearts in WWII. He retired to Beaufort, South Carolina. Brigadier General Jackson (Deputy SA, XXIV Corps) retired to Hartsville, South Carolina.

General Vien (Chief of JGS) escaped to the United States when South Vietnam fell in 1975. Lieutenant General Lam (CG, I Corps) was relieved of command during the 1972 Easter Invasion; he too escaped the communist takeover and lives in California. Colonel Luat (CO, 1st Armor Bde.) was wounded during the Easter Invasion; as a province chief during the 1975 takeover, his helo was downed over communist lines and he was never heard from again (a former ARVN regimental commander recently released by Hanoi reported seeing Luat and Lieutenant Colonel Dung of the 11th Cav in a communist "reeducation" camp). Colonel Hiep (Armor Cmd.) made brigadier general; he and his family escaped Saigon and, after working as Refugee Coordinator for Catholic Relief in Florida, he took a job with an aerospace corporation. Colonel

* During unpopular wars, medals are given out liberally as a morale booster and Vietnam was no exception. Consequently, medals earned for specific deeds of valor will be indicated here by writing the full name of the award. Medals for service or end-of-tour awards will be indicated by their abbreviations.

Battreall (SA, Armor Cmd.) was shot in the leg by an AK-47 aboard Luat's APC in the Easter Invasion, then returned for a third Vietnam tour. He retired in 1979 with four LMs, three BSMs, three MSMs, AM, ARCOM, and a Purple Heart; he presently lives with his wife at Sierra Vista, Arizona, and teaches writing improvement to officers at a local army base. Colonel Harrison (SA, 1st Inf. Div.) received two Silver Stars, two LMs, two Distinguished Flying Crosses, a Soldiers Medal, two MSMs, thirty-nine AMs, two JSCMs, and two ARCOMs after two tours in Vietnam; he retired as a major general and now is a businessman in Belton, Texas. Colonel Pence (SA, 1st Airborne Div.) retired as a disabled veteran in 1972, and died of cancer two years later. Major Dabney (SA, 3d Bn., 258th VNMC Bde.) is presently a colonel.

Major General Tarpley (CO, 101st ABD) retired to Columbus, Georgia. Brigadier General Berry (ADC) was Superintendent of the Military Academy at West Point, 1974–77; he later commanded a corps in Europe and retired in 1980 with three stars. After four years as Commissioner of Public Safety in his native state of Mississippi, he retired again and lives with his wife in Falls Church, Virginia. Colonel Rosenblum (CO, DISCOM) received the Bronze Star, Air Medal, and Army Commendation Medal for Valor and retired as a lieutenant general in 1984. Colonel Davis (CO, 101st Aviation Grp.) won the Silver Star, two LMs, two Distinguished Flying Crosses, MSM, and twenty-three AMs. He retired to Stratford, Connecticut, where he is with a defense contractor. Lieutenant Garwood (Pathfinders, 101st Aviation Grp.) won the Soldiers Medal for the minefield rescue, two BSMs, two AMs, and an ARCOM; commander of the Golden Knights Parachute Team, he was recently selected for lieutenant colonel. Corporal Fearn (Pathfinders, 101st Aviation Grp.) was KIA in May 1971, during a CA into a hot LZ. Captain Brandt (D/101st Aviation Bn.) was reportedly given only posthumous awards of the BSM, twenty-seven AMs, and the Purple Heart. Lieutenant Updyke (C/158th) was discharged as a captain in 1972 with the Distinguished Flying Cross, several AMs, and a ARCOM. He was divorced within a year. He is now remarried, has two more children, and lives in Evansville, Indiana. WO Smith (A/158th) won the Distinguished Flying Cross for his first day in Laos, a second for his last day, and was medically retired in 1972 with the BSM, thirty-six AMs, ARCOM, and Purple Heart. His wounds left him in a wheel chair and he was married and divorced within a year of getting out of the VA hospital. He remarried in 1975, lives in Fayetteville, Pennsylvania, and continues his flying with a modified airplane. Lieutenant Colonel Steverson (CO, 3/187 Inf.) retained command until the battalion was withdrawn in December 1971; he retired as a colonel in 1979. Major White (XO, 3/187) retired in 1972 with two Bronze Stars for Valor, two BSMs, MSM, ARCOM, and two Purple Hearts. He has since gone to bible college to earn a Master of Theology and lives with his wife in Florence, Alabama, where he is a minister. Lieutenant Daltan (D/3/187) was KIA in June 1971. Lieutenant Stephen (D/3/187) won the Bronze Star for Valor for the body-recovery mission, plus two BSMs and an AM. He has remarried, has two stepsons and a daughter, and is a farmer in Martinsville, Illinois; he also serves on the board of directors of the State Farm Bureau and makes public appearances to speak for Vietnam veterans. Sp4 Daugherty (D/3/187) was wounded again in May 1971, when noises on the perimeter resulted in a buddy squeezing off a poorly-aimed M-79 round. He rotated home in September as a sergeant, and was discharged the same day with the BSM, AM, two ARCOMs, and two Purple Hearts. He was divorced from his wife within a year of getting back from the war; he is now remarried and works as an industrial engineer in Windsor, Connecticut. Sp4 Kucera (B/3/187) made sergeant, left Vietnam in September 1971, and was mustered out in December with the BSM, AM, and two ARCOMs. He is in his second marriage, lives in Cudahy, Wisconsin, and is a troubleshooter for a hydraulics maintenance service.

Brigadier General Hill (CG, 1/5 Mech Div.) served in Vietnam until June 1972, and retired as a major general in 1978. He lives in Austin, Texas, and is a practicing attorney. Lieutenant Colonel Meyer (CO, 1/77 Armor) earned the Silver Star for the artillery rescue and retired in 1979 as colonel with the DSSM, two LMs, MSM, four BSMs, twelve AMs, and an ARCOM. He lives with his wife in Pebble Beach, California, and teaches computer science at a local junior college. Sergeant Major Nelson (CSM, 1/77) retired in 1973 with the Bronze Star for Valor, BSM, MSM, twelve AMs, three ARCOMs, and six Purple Hearts. He finished college, lives with his German-born wife in Severn, Maryland, and is an industrial safety consultant in business for himself. Sergeant Wondra (HHC/1/77) is a police officer and a helicopter pilot in the Minnesota National Guard. Sp4 Spurgeon (HHC/1/77) extended to C/3/5 Cav after the brigade withdrew from Vietnam in August 1971, and was discharged in 1972 with the Army Commendation Medal for Valor, ARCOM, and Purple Heart. He is in his second marriage, and is a federal correctional officer and a captain in the California National Guard. Captain Bodenhorn (CO, A/1/11 Inf.) won the Bronze Star for Valor in Laos, plus two BSMs and six Purple Hearts; he was recently promoted to lieutenant colonel after a stint with the U.S. Military Assistance Group, El Salvador. Lieutenant Clark (A/1/11) is a professional comedian in California. Sp4 Castro (A/1/11) spent three months with the 101st Airborne after the brigade was withdrawn and was discharged in 1972; after a ten-year fight with the VA, he is drawing a 10 percent disability for his back injury. He is still married, has two children, and is a produce grocery clerk. Lieutenant Colonel Stallman (CO, 1/61 Mech. Inf.) retired as a colonel to Cocoa Beach, Florida. Private First Class DeAngelis (D/1/61) was transferred as a line grunt to A/3/5 Cav, and was discharged Christmas Eve 1971 as a Sp4. He is now married, has a daughter, and is a mechanical engineer in Torrington, Connecticut. Lieutenant Colonel Osborn (CO, 3/5 Cav) retired as a colonel. Captain Stewart (CO, A/3/5) won the Bronze Star for Valor, BSM, Army Commendation Medal for Valor, and two Purple Hearts. He retired for health reasons as a lieutenant colonel in 1984, and lives with his wife and children in Puyallup, Washington. Lieutenant Christian (XO, B/3/5) made captain on his second tour, married, has two children, and is now a major. Sergeant McKenzie (HHT/315) was discharged with a BSM, and lives in Salem, Ohio. Sergeant White (A/3/5) was seriously wounded and medevacked in July 1971, earning the Silver Star, BSM, ARCOM, and two Purple Hearts. His first day home, somebody who didn't know him but hated his uniform, beat him up; that capstoned his bitterness about the war and America, and since then his life has been downhill. He was discharged in 1972, busted to private, and has been arrested twenty-seven times for public drunkenness, disorderly conduct, assaulting a police officer, and other antisocial behavior. He now lives in Owensboro, Kentucky, is in his fifth marriage, and has no job; he receives twenty percent disability from the VA for wounds, and 100 percent for Post-traumatic Stress Disorder. Sergeant McCormack (Brigade LRRP) was discharged in December 1971, with a BSM, ten AMs, Army Commendation Medal for Valor, and two Purple Hearts. He has married, finished college, and is an office manager in Bristol, Connecticut. Sp4 Walters (P/75th Rangers) completed his tour with the 1st Air Cav; he was discharged in 1973 with the standard combat infantryman's complement of BSM, AM, and ARCOM. He was married and divorced, has full custody of his son, and is a lieutenant on full-time status with the Alaska National Guard.

Lieutenant Colonel Burnett (CO, 1/1 Cav, Americal) was carried as MIA until 1979 when his status was changed to Presumed Killed In Action and he was posthumously promoted to colonel. Lieutenant Colonel Breeding (CO, 1/1) left Vietnam with a BSM and a Purple Heart; he died at Fort Knox in 1975. Sergeant Burnett (HHT/1/1) lives in Metairie, Louisiana; he is a purchasing agent with an alarm service and he and his wife rent a catering service. Sergeant Keefer (A/1/1) was mustered out in 1971 with the BSM, ARCOM, and five Purple Hearts; he has been in VA counselling since 1973. He was recently divorced and shares custody of his two sons. Since the war, he has bounced from job to job and is now a security guard and a crab fisherman in Ridgely, Maryland. Sp4 Smith (A/1/1) rotated home with an ARCOM and now works for the civil service in Long Beach, California. Private First Class Ollie (A/1/1) lives in Maryland with his wife. Private First Class Robinson (A/1/1) died outside Da Nang. Bathing in a stream, he stumbled into a deep hole and drowned. Private First Class Wolf (A/1/1) was reportedly killed soon after leaving Vietnam while driving on drugs. Lieutenant Colonel Coast (CO, 4/3 Inf.) was killed on 20 April 1971 when the main blade of a Loach hit him in the head; he was sorely missed by his battalion. Lieutenant Dewing (A/4/3) was discharged with the Silver Star, two BSMs, AM, and a Purple Heart; he is now married, a major in the reserves, and is a Department of Defense management analyst for an infantry brigade at Fort Richardson, Alaska. Private Morse (A/4/3) spent eighteen months in the hospital and was discharged an Sp4 in 1972 with two Purple Hearts and a 100 percent disability—plus, bullet shrapnel in his spine, impotency problems, a colostomy bag, a paralyzed right leg, and an addiction to painkilling drugs. He left the hospital a junkie, continued using drugs to forget his physical and mental pain, then began robbing drugstores in Massachusetts for narcotics. One night he was asleep, stoned, when the police broke in: he sat up, saw the guns, hit the floor Nam-style and came up shooting. He was charged with four counts of armed robbery, attempted murder, and ended up getting a divorce from his new wife. He was in prison 1976–1980; after two years on parole, he was arrested for drug use and sent back to jail. Three days before he was to be paroled to a VA hospital, two cons looted his cell. Morse confronted them and it came down to him, small and disabled, against two big men in a heated confrontation; Morse moved first. He stabbed them both, and wound up in solitary confinement for seventeen months. He was released in 1984 and immediately joined former platoon buddies, Dewing and Barnhart, at the Vietnam Veterans Memorial in Washington, D.C., where they laid a wreath and unit insignia below the names of their friends killed in Operation Lam Son 719. He now lives with his sister in Sherman, Texas.

Captain Downey (CO, C/2/1 Inf.) left the army in 1973, dissatisfied with the service and the direction of the war; he is presently married and manager for personnel security at a large defense contractor in Los Angeles, California.

Lieutenant Colonel Kirklighter (CO, 223d CAB, 1st Aviation Bde.) won the Silver Star at LZ Blue and Distinguished Flying Cross at LZ Hotel Two; he retired as a colonel and lives with his family in Ballwin, Maryland. Major Klose (S3, 223d) received his second Silver Star for LZ Hotel Two and retired as a colonel in 1985; he lives with his wife and children in San Francisco, California. Major Bunting (CO, 48th AHC) is now a colonel. Captain Johnson (173d AHC) is still a captain and continues flying. Lieutenant Smith (48th AHC) won the Distinguished Flying Cross for LZ Hotel Two; in combat after Laos, he earned the Silver Star, BSM, twenty-nine AMs, ARCOM, and two Purple Hearts. He is now a country veterinarian in Griffin, Georgia, and is in the National Guard to continue his flying. Sp5 Lundstrom (173d AHC) was discharged in 1972 with the Distinguished Flying Cross and several AMs; he now has a family and works for the post office in Canton, South Dakota. Lieutenant Colonel Pitman (CO, HQ & Maintenance Sqd., 1st MAW) is presently a brigadier general commanding the 3d Marine Air Wing. CW3 Hawk (165th Aviation Grp.) is now a CW4 with two BSMs, three MSMs, thirty-five AMs, and two ARCOMs. Sp5 Fujii (237th Med. Detachment) was awarded DSC for his four days in Laos (reportedly after being recommended for the Medal of Honor); and later he won the Silver Star, several Bronze Stars and Air Medals, and the Purple Heart. He is now a telephone repairman in Hawaii. Sp5 Wilder (174th AHC, Americal) won the Distinguished Flying Cross for LZ Lolo, and was discharged in 1973 with two Air Medals and an Army Commendation Medal for Valor, plus two Purple Hearts; he is with his third wife in Jonesville, Virginia, and is a hairstylist.

Lieutenant Colonel Molinelli (CO, 2/17 Air Cav, 101st ABD) is presently a major general. Lieutenant Colonel Rider (CO, 2/17) is now a colonel. Sp4 Fitzmaurice (D/2/17) was awarded the Medal of Honor and a Purple Heart for the sapper attack, an event he does not like to discuss. He is married, has two sons, and works for a packing company in Yale, South Dakota. Private First Class Warren (D/2/17) was wounded twice in a firefight in the A Shau Valley in April 1971, and was medically discharged with the Purple Heart. He now lives with his wife and five children in the Bronx, and works for the Department of Environmental Protection. Captain Mercadante (B/7/1) won the Distinguished Flying Cross for the photo recon mission, and an Air Medal for Valor in the Mekong Delta; he also has the BSM, thirteen AMs, four ARCOMs, and is on the list for lieutenant colonel. Lieutenant Cannon (B/7/1) was KIA in the Mekong Delta. WO Beck (B/7/1) flies for Continental Airlines. Wo Borders (B/7/1) won the Air Medal for Valor in Laos; in subsequent action in the Mekong Delta, he earned two Distinguished Flying Crosses, fourteen AMs, a Purple Heart, and suffered an amputated leg. He was medically retired in 1972 and now lives in Longmont, Colorado, with his wife and two children; despite his injuries, he works as a commercial helicopter pilot. Lieutenant Ferrell (C/7/17) won the BSM, three Air Medals for Valor, and thirty-one AMs; he and his wife now have two children and he is a major.

Lieutenant Colonel Ganahl (CO, 2/94 Artillery) received the LM and BSM for his nine months as battalion commander, and retired as a colonel to Great Falls, Virginia. He is now a programs manager and systems engineer with IBM. Private First Class Keeney (C/2/94) was discharged in 1972 as an Sp4 with an ARCOM; he lives in his hometown of Chillicothe, Missouri, and runs a restaurant with his wife and five children. Private First Class Rhodes (A/2/94) was mustered out as an Sp4 and lives in Elk River, Minnesota, with his wife and child, where he is a sheet-metal fabricator and welder. Sergeant First Class Hatfield (HHB/8/4) retired with the Bronze Star for Valor, three BSMs, the Army Commendation Medal for Valor, and four ARCOMs; he lives in Babbitt, Nevada, and works for the army as a quality assurance specialist with ammunition surveillance. Sp4 Hallman (B/8/4) lives in Lolo, Montana, and receives a 100 percent disability for Post-traumatic Stress Disorder; "I'm kind of a recluse," he said, "I spend a lot of time getting drunk and wondering why." Sergeant Markle (A/1/44) was awarded a BSM, ARCOM, and an Army Commendation Medal for Valor for the recovery missions. He lives in Orem, Utah, is married and has adopted a son; he is a captain in the Army Reserve and a junior high school teacher.

Brigadier General Sweeney (CG, Da Nang SUPCOM) retired as a major general to Virginia. Colonel Morton (CO, 8th Trans. Grp.) received the LM and BSM for the operation and retired as a brigadier general; he is presently a military consultant for a civilian firm in Pennsylvania. Major Chase (IO, SUPCOM) retired as a colonel with an LM, two BSMs, DMSM, two MSMs, and three ARCOMs; he lives with his wife in Alexandria, Virginia. Lieutenant Malmstrom (Cam Ranh Bay SUPCOM) won a BSM for Khe Sanh, and an end-of-tour ARCOM before being discharged in 1971; he is presently a bachelor in Saratoga, California, where he owns a retail store that specializes in stained-glass windows. Sergeant Michalak (USAF) was discharged in 1972 after two Vietnam tours; he has since married, has children, and works in Chicago as an overhead crane operator. Corporal Bartels (H&S/11th MTB) was mustered out in 1971, is married, has two children, and is an instructor in graphic arts at the University of Northern Iowa. Sp4 Brock (23d MP Co., Americal) volunteered for a second tour, 1971–1972, with the 504th MP Battalion, where he won the Silver Star for dragging two men from a disabled V100 during an ambush, although himself wounded and under fire. He quit the army as a sergeant in 1973, dissatisfied with the erosion of discipline he saw in the all-volunteer army. He is now in his third marriage and is a police sergeant in McCrory, Arkansas. Sp4 Carney (HHC/39th Trans. Bn.) was discharged in 1972 with an ARCOM and now works for the post office in Hull, Massachusetts; he was recently divorced and is in counselling for war-related psychological problems.

END NOTE

During the writing of this book, I received a plaque from one of the veterans whom I had interviewed by telephone. It certainly took me by surprise, but was a much appreciated gesture, and I'd like to publicly thank Frank Burnett. The inscription reads:

Keith William Nolan
is awarded
"Honorary Membership"
in
The 1st Squadron, 1st Cavalry
First Regiment of Dragoons
For his outstanding and caring
work in telling the truth about "Lam Son 719"
Given by
Trooper F. A. Burnett
1st Squadron, 1st Cavalry
Vietnam 70–71 "Blackhawk"

Needless to say, researching and writing a book has its discouraging moments, but such encouragement from the veterans makes it all worthwhile. Virtually every Vietnam veteran whom I had the opportunity of contacting was most helpful and this work would never have gotten off the ground without their great input. Thanks again, friends.

GLOSSARY

AA: Anti-aircraft fire.
AFA: Aerial Field Artillery.
AK-47 or AK: standard communist 7.62 automatic rifle.
ALO: Air Liaison Officer.
AO: Area of Operations.
APC: Armored Personnel Carrier.
Article 15: Nonjudicial punishment for relatively minor offenses.
ARVN: Army of the Republic of Vietnam; individual South Vietnamese soldier.
AVLB: Armored Vehicle Launch Bridge.
BA: Base area.
Brother: Common form of address between black soldiers.
Bush: Anyplace outside a base where combat is a real prospect.
CA: Combat Assault, helicopter insertion of troops to the field.
CAB: Combat Aviation Battalion.
C&C: Command and Control helicopter used by commanders to supervise units.
C4: Plastic explosive compound.
Chalk: Indicator of a helicopter's position in line (chalk two is the second ship).
Charlie: Nickname for the communist soldiers.
Chinook: Nickname for the CH47 transport helicopter.
Claymore: Above ground, antipersonnel mine used by U.S. forces.
CO: Commanding Officer.
Cobra: Nickname for the AH1G gunship helicopter.
COMUSMACV: Commander, U.S. Military Assistance Command Vietnam.

Concertina: Barbed wire used by U.S. forces.
CP: Command Post.
C rations, C rats, or Cs: Combat field meals packed in tin cans.
CVC: Radio helmet worn by armor crews.
Dap: Ritualized handshake greeting performed between black soldiers.
DEPCOMUSMACV: Deputy Commander, U.S. Military Assistance Command Vietnam.
DEROS: Date of Estimated Return Overseas.
Dew: Nickname for marijuana.
Dink: Derogatory nickname for Vietnamese.
DISCOM: Division Support Command.
DMZ: Demilitarized Zone, dividing line of the two Vietnams on the 17th parallel.
Duster: Nickname for the M42 combat vehicle mounted with two 40mm cannons.
E-tool: Entrenching tool, military term for shovel.
FAC: Forward Air Controller.
Field: Anyplace outside a base where combat is a real prospect.
Flak jacket: Sleeveless armored vest designed to stop shrapnel.
FNG: Fucking New Guy.
FO: Forward Observer, an artilleryman attached to the infantry to direct support fire.
.45: Standard U.S. combat pistol.
Frag: A fragmentation grenade; to destroy something with a grenade; to purposely attempt to kill or wound officers or NCOs over personal grievances or for revenge.
FSA: Forward Support Area.
FSB: Fire Support Base.
GI: Government Issue, popular name for the American soldier.
Gook: Derogatory name for Vietnamese.
Grunt: Affectionate nickname for the combat infantryman.
GSG: General Support Group.
Head: Nickname for drug user.
Head smack: To snort heroin through the nose.
Hootch: Any small shelter.
HQ: Headquarters.
Huey: Nickname for the UH1 series of helicopters.
Incoming: Enemy fire, usually meaning mortar, rocket, or artillery attack.
In-country: To be in Vietnam.

Juicer: Nickname for drinkers.
JP4: Aviation fuel.
KIA: Killed In Action.
Kiowa Scout: Nickname for the OH58 helicopter.
Kit Carson Scout: Communist soldiers who defected to the allies and volunteered to serve with U.S. units as scouts and interpreters.
Laager: Nickname for assembly positions held by armor units.
LAW: Light Antitank Weapon, 66mm rocket, usually shoulder-fired against bunkers.
Lifer: Derogatory term for career soldiers.
Loach: Nickname for the OH6 helicopter.
LOC: Line of Communications.
LP: Listening Post.
LRRP: Long Range Reconnaissance Patrol.
LZ: Landing Zone.
M-14: A 7.62mm rifle generally phased out by U.S. forces in 1967.
M-16: Standard U.S. 5.56mm automatic rifle.
M-60: Standard U.S. 7.62mm machine gun.
M-79: Standard U.S. 40mm grenade launcher.
MA: Mechanical Ambush, euphemism for U.S. booby traps.
MACV: Military Assistance Command-Vietnam.
Mad Minute: Practice of placing heavy fire around a defensive position, usually at night, without warning or apparent reason, to dissuade enemy troops in the area.
Medevac: Medical evacuation helicopter; the act of being evacuated.
MIA: Missing In Action.
Minigun: Gatling guns capable of firing six thousand rounds per minute.
MOS: Military Occupational Specialty.
MP: Military Police.
MPC: Military Pay Currency.
MR: Military Region.
NCO: Noncommissioned Officer.
NVA: North Vietnamese Army; individual North Vietnamese soldier.
OJ: Opium Joint.
Phantom: Nickname for the F4 jet.
Pig: Nickname for the M-60 machine gun.
Point: Lead man on a patrol.
POL: Petroleum Oil Lubricants.
Pot: Nickname for marijuana.
PSP: Pierced Steel Planking.

PZ: Pickup Zone.
Quad-fifty: Truck mounted with four .50-caliber machine guns.
R&R: Rest and Relaxation, one-week leave granted to servicemen in Vietnam.
Reefer: Nickname for marijuana.
REMF: Rear Echelon Motherfucker.
RIF: Reconnaissance In Force.
Rock'n'roll: Nickname for firing a weapon on full auto.
ROK: Republic of Korea.
RPG: Rocket Propelled Grenade, standard communist shoulder-fired projectile.
RPG Screen: Chain-link fence placed around vehicles to absorb the blast of an RPG.
RTO: Radio Telephone Operator, a radioman.
Ruck: Nickname for rucksack or backpack.
S&D: Search and Destroy.
S&S: Supply and Service.
Sea Stallion: Nickname for the H53 helicopter used by the U.S. Marine Corps.
Sheridan: The M551 armored reconnaissance assault vehicle.
Short: Nearly to have completed one's 365-day tour of duty in Vietnam.
Skag: Nickname for heroin.
Sky Crane: Nickname for the CH54 equipment-moving helicopter.
Slack: The second man in a patrol file who covered the pointman.
Slick: Nickname for Huey transport helicopters.
Smack: Nickname for heroin.
SP: Self-Propelled artillery piece.
SUPCOM: Support Command.
Tac Air: Tactical Air Support.
TAOR: Tactical Area of Responsibility.
TC: Tank or Track Commander.
TOC: Tactical Operations Center.
Track: Nickname for the tracked armored personnel carrier.
USAF: United States Air Force.
USARV: United States Army, Vietnam.
USMC: United States Marine Corps.
VC: Viet Cong.
Ville: Village.
VNMC: Vietnamese Marine Corps.

V100: Armored vehicle used by the military police, mounted with machine guns.

WIA: Wounded in Action.

Willy Peter: White Phosphorus.

WO: Warrant Officer.

World, the: Anyplace but Vietnam, usually referring to the United States.

BIBLIOGRAPHY

Books

Brown, Corninne. *Body Shop: Recuperating from Vietnam.* Stein and Day, 1973.

Drendel, Loua. *Gunslingers in Action.* Warren, Michigan: Squadron/Signal Publications, 1974.

Emerson, Gloria. *Winners & Losers.* New York: Random House, 1976.

Esper, George. *The Eyewitness History of the Vietnam War, 1961-1975.* New York: Ballantine Books, 1983.

Graves, Ralph, ed. *Larry Burrows: Compassionate Photographer.* New York: Time, Inc., 1972.

Hauser, William, Lt. Col. *America's Army in Crisis.* Baltimore, Maryland: The Johns Hopkins University Press, 1973.

Hinh, Nguyen Duy, Maj. Gen. *Lam Son 719.* Washington, D.C.: U.S. Army Center of Military History, 1979.

Jason, Alexander. *Heroes: The True Accounts of the Medal of Honor Winners Southeast Asia 1964-1975.* Pinole, California: The Anite Press, 1979.

Kirk, Donald. *Tell it to the Dead: Memories of a War.* Chicago: Nelson-Hall Publishers, 1975.

Kissinger, Henry. *White House Years.* Boston: Little, Brown and Company, 1979.

Lewy, Guenter. *America in Vietnam.* New York: Random House, 1978.

Palmer, Dave Richard. *Summons of the Trumpet: A History of the Vietnam War from a Military Man's Viewpoint.* Novato, California: Presidio Press, 1978.

Shore, Moyers S., Capt. *The Battle for Khe Sanh.* Washington D.C.:

Historical Branch. G-3 Division, Headquarters, U.S. Marine Corps, 1969.
Simmons, E. H., Brig. Gen. *The Marines in Vietnam 1954-1973.* Washington, D.C.: History and Museums Division, Headquarters, U.S. Marine Corps, 1974.
Starry, Donn A., Gen. *Mounted Combat in Vietnam.* Washington, D.C.: Department of the Army, 1978.
Tolson, John J., Gen. *Airmobility, 1961-1971.* Washington, D.C.: Department of the Army, 1973.
Vien, Cao Van, Gen. *Leadership.* Washington, D.C.: U.S. Army Center of Military History, 1980.
Westmoreland, William C., Gen. *A Soldier Reports.* Garden City, New York: Doubleday and Company, Inc., 1976.
Willwerth, James. *Eye in the Last Storm: A Reporter's Journal of One Year in South East Asia.* New York: Grossman Publishers, 1972.

Periodicals

"As Common as Chewing Gum," *Time,* March 1, 1971.
Downey, Gerald. "Christmas Truce," *Leatherneck,* December 1983.
"GI's Other Enemy: Heroin," *Newsweek,* May 24, 1971.
"How the Invasion was Planned," *Newsweek,* February 22, 1971.
"Incident on Route 9," *Time,* April 5, 1971.
"Indispensable Lifeline," *Time,* February 15, 1971.
"Invasion Ends," *Time,* April 5, 1971.
"Just say it was the Commancheros," *Newsweek,* March 15, 1971.
"Last Big Push—Or a Wider War," *Newsweek,* February 15, 1971.
Linden, Eugene. "Fragging and Other Withdrawal Symptoms," *Saturday Review,* January 8, 1972.
McCaffery, Barry, Capt. "The American Soldier in Vietnam," *Soldiers,* July 1972.
McCaffery, William, Lt. Gen. "A Fighting Army Heads for Home," *Army,* October 1971.
Meyer, Richard, Lt. Col. "The Road to Laos," *Armor,* March-April 1972.
Morgenstern, Joseph. "Two Soldiers," *Newsweek,* March 15, 1971.
Okamura, Akihiko. "Crossroads at Tchepone," *Life,* March 26, 1971.
——. "The War in Laos," *Life,* March 12, 1971.

Saar, John. "A Frantic Night on the Edge of Laos," *Life,* February 19, 1971.
——. "You Just Can't Hand Out Orders," *Life,* October 23, 1970.
——. "Scramble for Safety." *Life,* April 2, 1971.
"Shootout at Quang Tri." *Newsweek,* January 25, 1971.
"Troubled U.S. Army in Vietnam." *Newsweek,* January 11, 1971.
"War Within the War." *Time,* January 25, 1971.
Warner, Steve, Sp4. "Darkness is Deadly," *Army Digest,* April 1971.
Weiss, George. "Battle for Control of Ho Chi Minh Trail," *Armed Forces Journal,* February 15, 1971.
——. "CO 2/17 AirCav: 'Gunships Took Tanks. Survived Flak,' in Laos," *Armed Forces Journal,* April 19, 1971.
"Withdrawal Pains." *Newsweek,* June 7, 1971.

Documents

Berry, Sidney, Maj. Gen., "Lamson 719—The Assault Into Laos 8 February–6 April 1971."
"Daily Staff Journal or Duty Officer's Log, 3d Bn, 187th Inf, 101st Abn Div, 19–24 Mar 71."
"Department of the Army. Headquarters, 1st Calvary Division (Airmobile). APO San Francisco 96490, Combat Operations After Action Report. 11 July, 1970. Operation Toan Thang."
"101st Airborne Division (Airmobile). Final Report, Airmobile Operations in Support of Operation Lamson 719, 8 February–6 April 1971. Volumes I and II."
"Operational Report—Lessons Learned, Headquarters, 57th Transportation Bn, Period Ending 31 October 1971 (U)."
"Operational Report—Lessons Learned, 1st Inf Bde, 5th Inf Div (Mech). Period Ending 30 April 1971, RCS CSFOR-65 (R3)(U)."
"Operation Lam Son 719, 8 February 1971 to March 1971. A Narrative Description."
"XXIV Corps, Lam Son 719. After Action Report, 30 Jan–6 Apr 1971."
"U.S. Marine Corps Oral History Program/Interviewee: Col. William H. Dabney, 20 May 1982."

INDEX

D

E

F

K

L

M

N

O

P

Q

R

S

T

U

V

W

Y

★ SPECIAL OFFER ★

The CONGRESSIONAL MEDAL OF HONOR

The Names, The Deeds

"For Extraordinary Heroism Above and Beyond The Call of Duty"

Now, the most powerful record of combat bravery ever

published can be yours in this valuable hardbound edition ▪ 3,412 names with official descriptions of the actions that earned this nation's highest award ▪ Arranged alphabetically within each of the 22 wars and campaigns from Vietnam back through the Civil War ▪ Includes index, tables, and history of the Medal ▪ 1,105 pages

A Sharp & Dunnigan publication ~~$27.50~~

★ WITH THIS COUPON $24.95 ★

Dell

At your local bookstore or use this handy coupon for ordering:

DELL READERS SERVICE, DEPT. DCM2,
666 Fifth Avenue, N.Y., N.Y. 10103

Please send me the above title(s). I am enclosing $______. (Please add $2.00 per order to cover shipping and handling.) Send check or money order—no cash or C.O.D.s please.

Ms./Mrs./Mr. ____________________

Address ____________________

City/State ____________________ Zip ________

DCM2 -2/88

Prices and availability subject to change without notice. Please allow four to six weeks for delivery. This offer expires 8/88.

__CENTRIFUGE, J.C. Pollock 11156-0 $3.95
__CROSSFIRE, J.C. Pollock 11602-3 $3.95
__THE DYING PLACE, David Maurer 12183-3 $3.50
__GOING AFTER CACCIATO, Tim O'Brien 32965-3 $4.95
__MISSION M.I.A., J.C. Pollock 15819-2 $3.95

Dell

At your local bookstore or use this handy coupon for ordering:

DELL READERS SERVICE, DEPT. DVT
P.O. Box 5057, Des Plaines, IL. 60017-5057

Please send me the above title(s). I am enclosing $______. (Please add $1.50 per order to cover shipping and handling.) Send check or money order—no cash or C.O.D.s please.

Ms./Mrs./Mr. ____________________

Address ____________________

City/State ____________________ Zip __________

DVT -2/88

Prices and availability subject to change without notice. Please allow four to six weeks for delivery. This offer expires 8/88.

Special Offer Buy a Dell Book For only 50¢.

Now you can have Dell's Readers Service Listing filled with hundreds of titles. Plus, take advantage of our unique and exciting bonus book offer which gives you the opportunity to purchase a Dell book for *only 50¢*. Here's how!

Just order any five books at the regular price. Then choose any other single book listed (up to $5.95 value) for just 50¢. Use the coupon below to send for Dell's Readers Service Listing of titles today!

Dell

DELL READERS SERVICE LISTING
P.O. Box 1045, South Holland, IL. 60473

Ms./Mrs./Mr. ______________________________

Address ______________________________

City/State ______________________________ Zip ____________

DFCA - 2/88